Jerome K Jerome

Collected Works

Contents

THREE MEN IN A BOAT

THREE MEN ON THE BUMMEL

THE IDLE THOUGHTS OF AN IDLE FELLOW.

THE SECOND THOUGHTS OF AN IDLE FELLOW

TOLD AFTER SUPPER

DIARY OF A PILGRIMAGE

My Friend B.—Invitation to the Theatre.—A Most Unpleasant
Regulation.—Yearnings of the Embryo Traveller.—How to Make the
Most of One's Own Country.—Friday, a Lucky Day.—The Pilgrimage
Decided On.

The Question of Luggage.—First Friend's Suggestion.—Second
Friend's Suggestion.—Third Friend's Suggestion.—Mrs. Briggs'
Advice.—Our Vicar's Advice.—His Wife's Advice.—Medical
Advice.—Literary Advice.—George's Recommendation.—My Sister-
in-Law's Help.—Young Smith's Counsel.—My Own Ideas.—B.'s Idea.

Early Rising.—Ballast should be Stowed Away in the Hold before
Putting to Sea.—Annoying Interference of Providence in Matters that it
Does Not Understand.—A Socialistic Society.—B. Misjudges Me.—An
Uninteresting Anecdote.—We Lay in Ballast.—A Moderate Sailor.—A
Playful Boat.

Arrival at Ostend.—Coffee and Rolls.—Difficulty of Making French
Waiters understand German.—Advantages of Possessing a Conscience
That Does Not Get Up Too Early.—Villainy Triumphant.—Virtue
Ordered Outside.—A Homely English Row.

THE PHILOSOPHER'S JOKE

ALL ROADS LEAD TO CALVARY

SKETCHES IN LAVENDER BLUE AND GREEN

THREE MEN IN A BOAT
BOAT
(TO SAY NOTHING OF THE DOG).

Illustrations by A. Frederics.

PREFACE.

The chief beauty of this book lies not so much in its literary style, or in the extent and usefulness of the information it conveys, as in its simple truthfulness. Its pages form the record of events that really happened. All that has been done is to colour them; and, for this, no extra charge has been made. George and Harris and Montmorency are not poetic ideals, but things of flesh and blood—especially George, who weighs about twelve stone. Other works may excel this in dept of thought and knowledge of human nature: other books may rival it in originality and size; but, for hopeless and incurable veracity, nothing yet discovered can surpass it. This, more than all its other charms, will, it is felt, make the volume precious in the eye of the earnest reader; and will lend additional weight to the lesson that the story teaches.

LONDON, *August*, 1889.

CHAPTER I.

Three invalids.—Sufferings of George and Harris.—A victim to one hundred and seven fatal maladies.—Useful prescriptions.—Cure for liver complaint in children.—We agree that we are overworked, and need rest.—A week on the rolling deep?—George suggests the River.—Montmorency lodges an objection.—Original motion carried by majority of three to one.

There were four of us—George, and William Samuel Harris, and myself, and Montmorency. We were sitting in my room, smoking, and talking about how bad we were—bad from a medical point of view I mean, of course.

We were all feeling seedy, and we were getting quite nervous about it. Harris said he felt such extraordinary fits of giddiness come over him at times, that he hardly knew what he was doing; and then George said that *he* had fits of giddiness too, and hardly knew what *he* was doing. With me, it was my liver that was out of order. I knew it was my liver that was out of order, because I had just been reading a patent liver-pill circular, in which were detailed the various symptoms by which a man could tell when his liver was out of order. I had them all.

It is a most extraordinary thing, but I never read a patent medicine advertisement without being impelled to the conclusion that I am suffering from the particular disease therein dealt with in its most virulent form. The diagnosis seems in every case to correspond exactly with all the sensations that I have ever felt.

I remember going to the British Museum one day to read up the treatment for some slight ailment of which I had a touch—hay fever, I fancy it was. I got down the book, and read all I came to read; and then, in an unthinking moment, I idly turned the leaves, and began to indolently study diseases, generally. I forget which was the first distemper I plunged into—some fearful, devastating scourge, I know—and, before I had glanced half down the list of "premonitory symptoms," it was borne in upon me that I had fairly got it.

I sat for awhile, frozen with horror; and then, in the listlessness of despair, I again turned over the pages. I came to typhoid fever—read the symptoms—discovered that I had typhoid fever, must have had it for months without knowing it—wondered what else I had got; turned up St. Vitus's Dance—found, as I expected, that I had that too,—began to get interested in my case, and determined to sift it to the bottom, and so started alphabetically—read up ague, and learnt that I was sickening for it, and that the acute stage would commence in about another fortnight. Bright's disease, I was relieved to find, I had only in a modified form, and, so far as that was concerned, I might live for years. Cholera I had, with severe complications; and diphtheria I seemed to have been born with. I plodded conscientiously through the twenty-six letters, and the only malady I could conclude I had not got was housemaid's knee.

I felt rather hurt about this at first; it seemed somehow to be a sort of slight. Why hadn't I got housemaid's knee? Why this invidious reservation? After a while, however, less grasping feelings prevailed. I reflected that I had every other known malady in the pharmacology, and I grew less selfish, and determined to do without housemaid's knee. Gout, in its most malignant stage, it would appear, had seized me without my being aware of it; and zymosis I had evidently been suffering with from boyhood. There were no more diseases after zymosis, so I concluded there was nothing else the matter with me.

I sat and pondered. I thought what an interesting case I must be from a medical point of view, what an acquisition I should be to a class! Students would have no need to "walk the hospitals," if they had me. I was a hospital in myself. All they need do would be to walk round me, and, after that, take their diploma.

Then I wondered how long I had to live. I tried to examine myself. I felt my pulse. I could not at first feel any pulse at all. Then, all of a sudden, it seemed to start off. I pulled out my watch and timed it. I made it a hundred and forty-seven to the minute. I tried to feel my heart. I could not feel my heart. It had stopped beating. I have since been induced to come to the opinion that it must have been there all the time, and must have been beating, but I cannot account for it. I patted myself all over my front, from what I call my waist up to my head, and I went a bit round each side, and a little way up the back. But I could not feel or hear anything. I tried to look at my tongue. I stuck it out as far as ever it would go, and I shut one eye, and tried to examine it with the other. I could only see the tip, and the only thing that I could gain from that was to feel more certain than before that I had scarlet fever.

I had walked into that reading-room a happy, healthy man. I crawled out a decrepit wreck.

I went to my medical man. He is an old chum of mine, and feels my pulse, and looks at my tongue, and talks about the weather, all for nothing, when I fancy I'm ill; so I thought I would do him a good turn by going to him now. "What a doctor wants," I said, "is practice. He shall have me. He will get more practice out of me than out of seventeen hundred of your ordinary, commonplace patients, with only one or two diseases each." So I went straight up and saw him, and he said:

"Well, what's the matter with you?"

I said:

"I will not take up your time, dear boy, with telling you what is the matter with me. Life is brief, and you might pass away before I had finished. But I will tell you what is *not* the matter with me. I have not got housemaid's knee. Why I have not got housemaid's knee, I cannot tell you; but the fact remains that I have not got it. Everything else, however, I *have* got."

And I told him how I came to discover it all.

Then he opened me and looked down me, and clutched hold of my wrist, and then he hit me over the chest when I wasn't expecting it—a cowardly thing to do, I call it—and immediately afterwards butted me with the side of his head. After that, he sat down and wrote out a prescription, and folded it up and gave it me, and I put it in my pocket and went out.

I did not open it. I took it to the nearest chemist's, and handed it in. The man read it, and then handed it back.

He said he didn't keep it.

I said:

"You are a chemist?"

He said:

"I am a chemist. If I was a co-operative stores and family hotel combined, I might be able to oblige you. Being only a chemist hampers me."

I read the prescription. It ran:

"1 lb. beefsteak, with
1 pt. bitter beer
every 6 hours.
1 ten-mile walk every morning.
1 bed at 11 sharp every night.
And don't stuff up your head with things you don't understand."

I followed the directions, with the happy result—speaking for myself—that my life was preserved, and is still going on.

In the present instance, going back to the liver-pill circular, I had the symptoms, beyond all mistake, the chief among them being "a general disinclination to work of any kind."

What I suffer in that way no tongue can tell. From my earliest infancy I have been a martyr to it. As a boy, the disease hardly ever left me for a day. They did not know, then, that it was my liver. Medical science was in a far less advanced state than now, and they used to put it down to laziness.

"Why, you skulking little devil, you," they would say, "get up and do something for your living, can't you?"—not knowing, of course, that I was ill.

And they didn't give me pills; they gave me clumps on the side of the head. And, strange as it may appear, those clumps on the head often cured me—for the time being. I have known one clump on the head have more effect upon my liver, and make me feel more anxious to go straight away then and there, and do what was wanted to be done, without further loss of time, than a whole box of pills does now.

You know, it often is so—those simple, old-fashioned remedies are sometimes more efficacious than all the dispensary stuff.

We sat there for half-an-hour, describing to each other our maladies. I explained to George and William Harris how I felt when I got up in the morning, and William Harris told us how he felt when he went to bed; and George stood on the hearth-rug, and gave us a clever and powerful piece of acting, illustrative of how he felt in the night.

George *fancies* he is ill; but there's never anything really the matter with him, you know.

CHAPTER I.

At this point, Mrs. Poppets knocked at the door to know if we were ready for supper. We smiled sadly at one another, and said we supposed we had better try to swallow a bit. Harris said a little something in one's stomach often kept the disease in check; and Mrs. Poppets brought the tray in, and we drew up to the table, and toyed with a little steak and onions, and some rhubarb tart.

I must have been very weak at the time; because I know, after the first half-hour or so, I seemed to take no interest whatever in my food—an unusual thing for me—and I didn't want any cheese.

This duty done, we refilled our glasses, lit our pipes, and resumed the discussion upon our state of health. What it was that was actually the matter with us, we none of us could be sure of; but the unanimous opinion was that it—whatever it was—had been brought on by overwork.

"What we want is rest," said Harris.

"Rest and a complete change," said George. "The overstrain upon our brains has produced a general depression throughout the system. Change of scene, and absence of the necessity for thought, will restore the mental equilibrium."

George has a cousin, who is usually described in the charge-sheet as a medical student, so that he naturally has a somewhat family-physicianary way of putting things.

I agreed with George, and suggested that we should seek out some retired and old-world spot, far from the madding crowd, and dream away a sunny week among its drowsy lanes—some half-forgotten nook, hidden away by the fairies, out of reach of the noisy world—some quaint-perched eyrie on the cliffs of Time, from whence the surging waves of the nineteenth century would sound far-off and faint.

Harris said he thought it would be humpy. He said he knew the sort of place I meant; where everybody went to bed at eight o'clock, and you couldn't get a *Referee* for love or money, and had to walk ten miles to get your baccy.

"No," said Harris, "if you want rest and change, you can't beat a sea trip."

I objected to the sea trip strongly. A sea trip does you good when you are going to have a couple of months of it, but, for a week, it is wicked.

You start on Monday with the idea implanted in your bosom that you are going to enjoy yourself. You wave an airy adieu to the boys on shore, light your biggest pipe, and swagger about the deck as if you were Captain Cook, Sir Francis Drake, and Christopher Columbus all rolled into one. On Tuesday, you wish you hadn't come. On Wednesday, Thursday, and Friday, you wish you were dead. On Saturday, you are able to swallow a little beef tea, and to sit up on deck, and answer with a wan, sweet smile when kind-hearted people ask you how you feel now. On Sunday, you begin to walk about again, and take solid food. And on Monday morning, as, with your bag and umbrella in your hand, you stand by the gunwale, waiting to step ashore, you begin to thoroughly like it.

I remember my brother-in-law going for a short sea trip once, for the benefit of his health. He took a return berth from London to Liverpool; and when he got to Liverpool, the only thing he was anxious about was to sell that return ticket.

It was offered round the town at a tremendous reduction, so I am told; and was eventually sold for eighteenpence to a bilious-looking youth who had just been advised by his medical men to go to the sea-side, and take exercise.

"Sea-side!" said my brother-in-law, pressing the ticket affectionately into his hand; "why, you'll have enough to last you a lifetime; and as for exercise! why, you'll get more exercise, sitting down on that ship, than you would turning somersaults on dry land."

He himself—my brother-in-law—came back by train. He said the North-Western Railway was healthy enough for him.

Another fellow I knew went for a week's voyage round the coast, and, before they started, the steward came to him to ask whether he would pay for each meal as he had it, or arrange beforehand for the whole series.

The steward recommended the latter course, as it would come so much cheaper. He said they would do him for the whole week at two pounds five. He said for breakfast there would be fish, followed by a grill. Lunch was at one, and consisted of four courses. Dinner at six—soup, fish, entree, joint, poultry, salad, sweets, cheese, and dessert. And a light meat supper at ten.

My friend thought he would close on the two-pound-five job (he is a hearty eater), and did so.

Lunch came just as they were off Sheerness. He didn't feel so hungry as he thought he should, and so contented himself with a bit of boiled beef, and some strawberries and cream. He pondered a good deal during the afternoon, and at one time it seemed to him that he had been eating nothing but boiled beef for weeks, and at other times it seemed that he must have been living on strawberries and cream for years.

Neither the beef nor the strawberries and cream seemed happy, either—seemed discontented like.

At six, they came and told him dinner was ready. The announcement aroused no enthusiasm within him, but he felt that there was some of that two-pound-five to be worked off, and he held on to ropes and things and went down. A pleasant odour of onions and hot ham, mingled with fried fish and greens, greeted him at the bottom of the ladder; and then the steward came up with an oily smile, and said:

"What can I get you, sir?"

"Get me out of this," was the feeble reply.

And they ran him up quick, and propped him up, over to leeward, and left him.

For the next four days he lived a simple and blameless life on thin captain's biscuits (I mean that the biscuits were thin, not the captain) and soda-water; but, towards Saturday, he got uppish, and went in for weak tea and dry toast, and on Monday he was gorging himself on chicken broth. He left the ship on Tuesday, and as it steamed away from the landing-stage he gazed after it regretfully.

"There she goes," he said, "there she goes, with two pounds' worth of food on board that belongs to me, and that I haven't had."

He said that if they had given him another day he thought he could have put it straight.

So I set my face against the sea trip. Not, as I explained, upon my own account. I was never queer. But I was afraid for George. George said he should be all right, and would rather like it, but he would advise Harris and me not to think of it, as he felt sure we should both be ill. Harris said that, to himself, it was always a mystery how people managed to get sick at sea—said he thought people must do it on purpose, from affectation—said he had often wished to be, but had never been able.

Then he told us anecdotes of how he had gone across the Channel when it was so rough that the passengers had to be tied into their berths, and he and the captain were the only two living souls on board who were not ill. Sometimes it was he and the second mate who were not ill; but it was generally he and one other man. If not he and another man, then it was he by himself.

It is a curious fact, but nobody ever is sea-sick—on land. At sea, you come across plenty of people very bad indeed, whole boat-loads of them; but I never met a man yet, on land, who had ever known at all what it was to be sea-sick. Where the thousands upon thousands of bad sailors that swarm in every ship hide themselves when they are on land is a mystery.

If most men were like a fellow I saw on the Yarmouth boat one day, I could account for the seeming enigma easily enough. It was just off Southend Pier, I recollect, and he was leaning out through one of the port-holes in a very dangerous position. I went up to him to try and save him.

"Hi! come further in," I said, shaking him by the shoulder. "You'll be overboard."

"Oh my! I wish I was," was the only answer I could get; and there I had to leave him.

Three weeks afterwards, I met him in the coffee-room of a Bath hotel, talking about his voyages, and explaining, with enthusiasm, how he loved the sea.

"Good sailor!" he replied in answer to a mild young man's envious query; "well, I did feel a little queer *once*, I confess. It was off Cape Horn. The vessel was wrecked the next morning."

I said:

"Weren't you a little shaky by Southend Pier one day, and wanted to be thrown overboard?"

"Southend Pier!" he replied, with a puzzled expression.

"Yes; going down to Yarmouth, last Friday three weeks."

"Oh, ah—yes," he answered, brightening up; "I remember now. I did have a headache that afternoon. It was the pickles, you know. They were the most disgraceful pickles I ever tasted in a respectable boat. Did *you* have any?"

For myself, I have discovered an excellent preventive against sea-sickness, in balancing myself. You stand in the centre of the deck, and, as the ship heaves and pitches, you move your body about, so as to keep it always straight. When the front of the ship rises, you lean forward, till the deck almost touches your nose; and when its back end gets up, you lean backwards. This is all very well for an hour or two; but you can't balance yourself for a week.

George said:

"Let's go up the river."

He said we should have fresh air, exercise and quiet; the constant change of scene would occupy our minds (including what there was of Harris's); and the hard work would give us a good appetite, and make us sleep well.

Harris said he didn't think George ought to do anything that would have a tendency to make him sleepier than he always was, as it might be dangerous. He said he didn't very well understand how George was going to sleep any more than he did now, seeing that there were only twenty-four hours in each day, summer and winter alike; but thought that if he *did* sleep any more, he might just as well be dead, and so save his board and lodging.

Harris said, however, that the river would suit him to a "T." I don't know what a "T" is (except a sixpenny one, which includes bread-and-butter and cake *ad lib.*, and is cheap at the price, if you haven't had any dinner). It seems to suit everybody, however, which is greatly to its credit.

It suited me to a "T" too, and Harris and I both said it was a good idea of George's; and we said it in a tone that seemed to somehow imply that we were surprised that George should have come out so sensible.

The only one who was not struck with the suggestion was Montmorency. He never did care for the river, did Montmorency.

"It's all very well for you fellows," he says; "you like it, but *I* don't. There's nothing for me to do. Scenery is not in my line, and I don't smoke. If I see a rat, you won't stop; and if I go to sleep, you get fooling about with the boat, and slop me overboard. If you ask me, I call the whole thing bally foolishness."

We were three to one, however, and the motion was carried.

CHAPTER II.

Plans discussed.—Pleasures of "camping-out," on fine nights.—Ditto, wet nights.—Compromise decided on.—Montmorency, first impressions of.—Fears lest he is too good for this world, fears subsequently dismissed as groundless.—Meeting adjourns.

We pulled out the maps, and discussed plans.

We arranged to start on the following Saturday from Kingston. Harris and I would go down in the morning, and take the boat up to Chertsey, and George, who would not be able to get away from the City till the afternoon (George goes to sleep at a bank from ten to four each day, except Saturdays, when they wake him up and put him outside at two), would meet us there.

Should we "camp out" or sleep at inns?

George and I were for camping out. We said it would be so wild and free, so patriarchal like.

Slowly the golden memory of the dead sun fades from the hearts of the cold, sad clouds. Silent, like sorrowing children, the birds have ceased their song, and only the moorhen's plaintive cry and the harsh croak of the corncrake stirs the awed hush around the couch of waters, where the dying day breathes out her last.

From the dim woods on either bank, Night's ghostly army, the grey shadows, creep out with noiseless tread to chase away the lingering rear-guard of the light, and pass, with noiseless, unseen feet, above the waving river-grass, and through the sighing rushes; and Night, upon her sombre throne, folds her black wings above the darkening world, and, from her phantom palace, lit by the pale stars, reigns in stillness.

Then we run our little boat into some quiet nook, and the tent is pitched, and the frugal supper cooked and eaten. Then the big pipes are filled and lighted, and the pleasant chat goes round in musical undertone; while, in the pauses of our talk, the river, playing round the boat, prattles strange old tales and secrets, sings low the old child's song that it has sung so many thousand years—will sing so many thousand years to come, before its voice grows harsh and old—a song that we, who have learnt to love its changing face, who have so often nestled on its yielding bosom, think, somehow, we understand, though we could not tell you in mere words the story that we listen to.

And we sit there, by its margin, while the moon, who loves it too, stoops down to kiss it with a sister's kiss, and throws her silver arms around it clingingly; and we watch it as it flows, ever singing, ever whispering, out to meet its king, the sea—till our voices die away in silence, and the pipes go out—till we, commonplace, everyday young men enough, feel strangely full of thoughts, half sad, half sweet, and do not care or want to speak—till we laugh, and, rising, knock the ashes from our burnt-out pipes, and say "Good-night," and, lulled by the lapping water and the rustling trees, we fall asleep beneath the great, still stars, and dream that the world is young again—young and sweet as she used to be ere the centuries of fret and care had furrowed her fair face, ere her children's sins and follies had made old her loving heart—sweet as she was in those bygone days when, a new-made mother, she nursed us, her children, upon her own deep breast—ere the wiles of painted civilization had lured us away from her fond arms, and the poisoned sneers of artificiality had made us ashamed of the simple life we led with her, and the simple, stately home where mankind was born so many thousands years ago.

Harris said:

"How about when it rained?"

You can never rouse Harris. There is no poetry about Harris—no wild yearning for the unattainable. Harris never "weeps, he knows not why." If Harris's eyes fill with tears, you can bet it is because Harris has been eating raw onions, or has put too much Worcester over his chop.

If you were to stand at night by the sea-shore with Harris, and say:

"Hark! do you not hear? Is it but the mermaids singing deep below the waving waters; or sad spirits, chanting dirges for white corpses, held by seaweed?" Harris would take you by the arm, and say:

"I know what it is, old man; you've got a chill. Now, you come along with me. I know a place round the corner here, where you can get a drop of the finest Scotch whisky you ever tasted—put you right in less than no time."

Harris always does know a place round the corner where you can get something brilliant in the drinking line. I believe that if you met Harris up in Paradise (supposing such a thing likely), he would immediately greet you with:

"So glad you've come, old fellow; I've found a nice place round the corner here, where you can get some really first-class nectar."

In the present instance, however, as regarded the camping out, his practical view of the matter came as a very timely hint. Camping out in rainy weather is not pleasant.

It is evening. You are wet through, and there is a good two inches of water in the boat, and all the things are damp. You find a place on the banks that is not quite so puddly as other places you have seen, and you land and lug out the tent, and two of you proceed to fix it.

It is soaked and heavy, and it flops about, and tumbles down on you, and clings round your head and makes you mad. The rain is pouring steadily down all the time. It is difficult enough to fix a tent in dry weather: in wet, the task becomes herculean. Instead of helping you, it seems to you that the other man is simply playing the fool. Just as you get your side beautifully fixed, he gives it a hoist from his end, and spoils it all.

"Here! what are you up to?" you call out.

"What are *you* up to?" he retorts; "leggo, can't you?"

CHAPTER II.

"Don't pull it; you've got it all wrong, you stupid ass!" you shout.

"No, I haven't," he yells back; "let go your side!"

"I tell you you've got it all wrong!" you roar, wishing that you could get at him; and you give your ropes a lug that pulls all his pegs out.

"Ah, the bally idiot!" you hear him mutter to himself; and then comes a savage haul, and away goes your side. You lay down the mallet and start to go round and tell him what you think about the whole business, and, at the same time, he starts round in the same direction to come and explain his views to you. And you follow each other round and round, swearing at one another, until the tent tumbles down in a heap, and leaves you looking at each other across its ruins, when you both indignantly exclaim, in the same breath:

"There you are! what did I tell you?"

Meanwhile the third man, who has been baling out the boat, and who has spilled the water down his sleeve, and has been cursing away to himself steadily for the last ten minutes, wants to know what the thundering blazes you're playing at, and why the blarmed tent isn't up yet.

At last, somehow or other, it does get up, and you land the things. It is hopeless attempting to make a wood fire, so you light the methylated spirit stove, and crowd round that.

Rainwater is the chief article of diet at supper. The bread is two-thirds rainwater, the beefsteak-pie is exceedingly rich in it, and the jam, and the butter, and the salt, and the coffee have all combined with it to make soup.

After supper, you find your tobacco is damp, and you cannot smoke. Luckily you have a bottle of the stuff that cheers and inebriates, if taken in proper quantity, and this restores to you sufficient interest in life to induce you to go to bed.

There you dream that an elephant has suddenly sat down on your chest, and that the volcano has exploded and thrown you down to the bottom of the sea—the elephant still sleeping peacefully on your bosom. You wake up and grasp the idea that something terrible really has happened. Your first impression is that the end of the world has come; and then you think that this cannot be, and that it is thieves and murderers, or else fire, and this opinion you express in the usual method. No help comes, however, and all you know is that thousands of people are kicking you, and you are being smothered.

Somebody else seems in trouble, too. You can hear his faint cries coming from underneath your bed. Determining, at all events, to sell your life dearly, you struggle frantically, hitting out right and left with arms and legs, and yelling lustily the while, and at last something gives way, and you find your head in the fresh air. Two feet off, you dimly observe a half-dressed ruffian, waiting to kill you, and you are preparing for a life-and-death struggle with him, when it begins to dawn upon you that it's Jim.

"Oh, it's you, is it?" he says, recognising you at the same moment.

"Yes," you answer, rubbing your eyes; "what's happened?"

"Bally tent's blown down, I think," he says. "Where's Bill?"

Then you both raise up your voices and shout for "Bill!" and the ground beneath you heaves and rocks, and the muffled voice that you heard before replies from out the ruin:

"Get off my head, can't you?"

And Bill struggles out, a muddy, trampled wreck, and in an unnecessarily aggressive mood—he being under the evident belief that the whole thing has been done on purpose.

In the morning you are all three speechless, owing to having caught severe colds in the night; you also feel very quarrelsome, and you swear at each other in hoarse whispers during the whole of breakfast time.

We therefore decided that we would sleep out on fine nights; and hotel it, and inn it, and pub. it, like respectable folks, when it was wet, or when we felt inclined for a change.

Montmorency hailed this compromise with much approval. He does not revel in romantic solitude. Give him something noisy; and if a trifle low, so much the jollier. To look at Montmorency you would imagine that he was an angel sent upon the earth, for some reason withheld from mankind, in the shape of a small fox-terrier. There is a sort of Oh-what-a-wicked-world-this-is-and-how-I-wish-I-could-do-something-to-make-it-better-and-nobler expression about Montmorency that has been known to bring the tears into the eyes of pious old ladies and gentlemen.

When first he came to live at my expense, I never thought I should be able to get him to stop long. I used to sit down and look at him, as he sat on the rug and looked up at me, and think: "Oh, that dog will never live. He will be snatched up to the bright skies in a chariot, that is what will happen to him."

But, when I had paid for about a dozen chickens that he had killed; and had dragged him, growling and kicking, by the scruff of his neck, out of a hundred and fourteen street fights; and had had a dead cat brought round for my inspection by an irate female, who called me a murderer; and had been summoned by the man next door but one for having a ferocious dog at large, that had kept him pinned up in his own tool-shed, afraid to venture his nose outside the door for over two hours on a cold night; and had learned that the gardener, unknown to myself, had won thirty shillings by backing him to kill rats against time, then I began to think that maybe they'd let him remain on earth for a bit longer, after all.

To hang about a stable, and collect a gang of the most disreputable dogs to be found in the town, and lead them out to march round the slums to fight other disreputable dogs, is Montmorency's idea of "life;" and so, as I before observed, he gave to the suggestion of inns, and pubs., and hotels his most emphatic approbation.

Having thus settled the sleeping arrangements to the satisfaction of all four of us, the only thing left to discuss was what we should take with us; and this we had begun to argue, when Harris said he'd had enough oratory for one night, and proposed that we should go out and have a smile, saying that he had found a place, round by the square, where you could really get a drop of Irish worth drinking.

George said he felt thirsty (I never knew George when he didn't); and, as I had a presentiment that a little whisky, warm, with a slice of lemon, would do my complaint good, the debate was, by common assent, adjourned to the following night; and the assembly put on its hats and went out.

CHAPTER III.

Arrangements settled.—Harris's method of doing work.— How the elderly, family-man puts up a picture.—George makes a sensible, remark.—Delights of early morning bathing.—Provisions for getting upset.

So, on the following evening, we again assembled, to discuss and arrange our plans. Harris said:

"Now, the first thing to settle is what to take with us. Now, you get a bit of paper and write down, J., and you get the grocery catalogue, George, and somebody give me a bit of pencil, and then I'll make out a list."

That's Harris all over—so ready to take the burden of everything himself, and put it on the backs of other people.

He always reminds me of my poor Uncle Podger. You never saw such a commotion up and down a house, in all your life, as when my Uncle Podger undertook to do a job. A picture would have come home from the frame-maker's, and be standing in the dining-room, waiting to be put up; and Aunt Podger would ask what was to be done with it, and Uncle Podger would say:

"Oh, you leave that to *me*. Don't you, any of you, worry yourselves about that. *I'll* do all that."

And then he would take off his coat, and begin. He would send the girl out for sixpen'orth of nails, and then one of the boys after her to tell her what size to get; and, from that, he would gradually work down, and start the whole house.

"Now you go and get me my hammer, Will," he would shout; "and you bring me the rule, Tom; and I shall want the step-ladder, and I had better have a kitchen-chair, too; and, Jim! you run round to Mr. Goggles, and tell him, 'Pa's kind regards, and hopes his leg's better; and will he lend him his spirit-level?' And don't you go, Maria, because I shall want somebody to hold me the light; and when the girl comes back, she must go out again for a bit of picture-cord; and Tom!—where's Tom?—Tom, you come here; I shall want you to hand me up the picture."

And then he would lift up the picture, and drop it, and it would come out of the frame, and he would try to save the glass, and cut himself; and then he would spring round the room, looking for his handkerchief. He could not find his handkerchief, because it was in the pocket of the coat he had taken off, and he did not know where he had put the coat, and all the house had to leave off looking for his tools, and start looking for his coat; while he would dance round and hinder them.

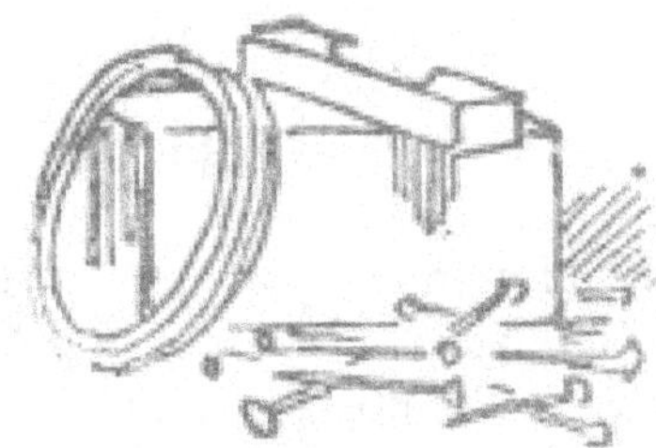

"Doesn't anybody in the whole house know where my coat is? I never came across such a set in all my life—upon my word I didn't. Six of you!—and you can't find a coat that I put down not five minutes ago! Well, of all the—"

Then he'd get up, and find that he had been sitting on it, and would call out:

"Oh, you can give it up! I've found it myself now. Might just as well ask the cat to find anything as expect you people to find it."

And, when half an hour had been spent in tying up his finger, and a new glass had been got, and the tools, and the ladder, and the chair, and the candle had been brought, he would have another go, the whole family, including the girl and the charwoman, standing round in a semi-circle, ready to help. Two people would have to hold the chair, and a third would help him up on it, and hold him there, and a fourth would hand him a nail, and a fifth would pass him up the hammer, and he would take hold of the nail, and drop it.

"There!" he would say, in an injured tone, "now the nail's gone."

And we would all have to go down on our knees and grovel for it, while he would stand on the chair, and grunt, and want to know if he was to be kept there all the evening.

The nail would be found at last, but by that time he would have lost the hammer.

"Where's the hammer? What did I do with the hammer? Great heavens! Seven of you, gaping round there, and you don't know what I did with the hammer!"

We would find the hammer for him, and then he would have lost sight of the mark he had made on the wall, where the nail was to go in, and each of us had to get up on the chair, beside him, and see if we could find it; and we would each discover it in a different place, and he would call us all fools, one after another, and tell us to get down. And he would take the rule, and re-measure, and find that he wanted half thirty-one and three-eighths inches from the corner, and would try to do it in his head, and go mad.

And we would all try to do it in our heads, and all arrive at different results, and sneer at one another. And in the general row, the original number would be forgotten, and Uncle Podger would have to measure it again.

He would use a bit of string this time, and at the critical moment, when the old fool was leaning over the chair at an angle of forty-five, and trying to reach a point three inches beyond what was possible for him to reach, the string would slip, and down he would slide on to the piano, a really fine musical effect being produced by the suddenness with which his head and body struck all the notes at the same time.

And Aunt Maria would say that she would not allow the children to stand round and hear such language.

At last, Uncle Podger would get the spot fixed again, and put the point of the nail on it with his left hand, and take the hammer in his right hand. And, with the first blow, he would smash his thumb, and drop the hammer, with a yell, on somebody's toes.

Aunt Maria would mildly observe that, next time Uncle Podger was going to hammer a nail into the wall, she hoped he'd let her know in time, so that she could make arrangements to go and spend a week with her mother while it was being done.

"Oh! you women, you make such a fuss over everything," Uncle Podger would reply, picking himself up. "Why, I *like* doing a little job of this sort."

And then he would have another try, and, at the second blow, the nail would go clean through the plaster, and half the hammer after it, and Uncle Podger be precipitated against the wall with force nearly sufficient to flatten his nose.

Then we had to find the rule and the string again, and a new hole was made; and, about midnight, the picture would be up—very crooked and insecure, the wall for yards round looking as if it had been smoothed down with a rake, and everybody dead beat and wretched—except Uncle Podger.

"There you are," he would say, stepping heavily off the chair on to the charwoman's corns, and surveying the mess he had made with evident pride. "Why, some people would have had a man in to do a little thing like that!"

Harris will be just that sort of man when he grows up, I know, and I told him so. I said I could not permit him to take so much labour upon himself. I said:

"No; *you* get the paper, and the pencil, and the catalogue, and George write down, and I'll do the work."

The first list we made out had to be discarded. It was clear that the upper reaches of the Thames would not allow of the navigation of a boat sufficiently large to take the things we had set down as indispensable; so we tore the list up, and looked at one another!

George said:

"You know we are on a wrong track altogether. We must not think of the things we could do with, but only of the things that we can't do without."

George comes out really quite sensible at times. You'd be surprised. I call that downright wisdom, not merely as regards the present case, but with reference to our trip up the river of life, generally. How many people, on that voyage, load up the boat till it is ever in danger of swamping with a store of foolish things which they think essential to the pleasure and comfort of the trip, but which are really only useless lumber.

How they pile the poor little craft mast-high with fine clothes and big houses; with useless servants, and a host of swell friends that do not care twopence for them, and that they do not care three ha'pence for; with expensive entertainments that nobody enjoys, with formalities and fashions, with pretence and ostentation, and with—oh, heaviest, maddest lumber of all!—the dread of what will my neighbour think, with luxuries that only cloy, with pleasures that bore, with empty show that, like the criminal's iron crown of yore, makes to bleed and swoon the aching head that wears it!

It is lumber, man—all lumber! Throw it overboard. It makes the boat so heavy to pull, you nearly faint at the oars. It makes it so cumbersome and dangerous to manage, you never know a moment's freedom from anxiety and care, never gain a moment's rest for dreamy laziness—no time to watch the windy shadows skimming lightly o'er the shallows, or the glittering sunbeams flitting in and out among the ripples, or the great trees by the margin looking down at their own image, or the woods all green and golden, or the lilies white and yellow, or the sombre-waving rushes, or the sedges, or the orchis, or the blue forget-me-nots.

Throw the lumber over, man! Let your boat of life be light, packed with only what you need—a homely home and simple pleasures, one or two friends, worth the name, someone to love and someone to love you, a cat, a dog, and a pipe or two, enough to eat and enough to wear, and a little more than enough to drink; for thirst is a dangerous thing.

You will find the boat easier to pull then, and it will not be so liable to upset, and it will not matter so much if it does upset; good, plain merchandise will stand water. You will have time to think as well as to work. Time to drink in life's sunshine—time to listen to the Æolian music that the wind of God draws from the human heart-strings around us—time to—

I beg your pardon, really. I quite forgot.

Well, we left the list to George, and he began it.

"We won't take a tent," suggested George; "we will have a boat with a cover. It is ever so much simpler, and more comfortable."

It seemed a good thought, and we adopted it. I do not know whether you have ever seen the thing I mean. You fix iron hoops up over the boat, and stretch a huge canvas over them, and fasten it down all round, from stem to stern, and it converts the boat into a sort of little house, and it is beautifully cosy, though a trifle stuffy; but there, everything has its drawbacks, as the man said when his mother-in-law died, and they came down upon him for the funeral expenses.

George said that in that case we must take a rug each, a lamp, some soap, a brush and comb (between us), a toothbrush (each), a basin, some tooth-powder, some shaving tackle (sounds like a French exercise, doesn't it?), and a couple of big-towels for bathing. I notice that people always make gigantic arrangements for bathing when they are going anywhere near the water, but that they don't bathe much when they are there.

It is the same when you go to the sea-side. I always determine—when thinking over the matter in London—that I'll get up early every morning, and go and have a dip before breakfast, and I religiously pack up a pair of drawers and a bath towel. I always get red bathing drawers. I rather fancy myself in red drawers. They suit my complexion so. But when I get to the sea I don't feel somehow that I want that early morning bathe nearly so much as I did when I was in town.

On the contrary, I feel more that I want to stop in bed till the last moment, and then come down and have my breakfast. Once or twice virtue has triumphed, and I have got out at six and half-dressed myself, and have taken my drawers and towel, and stumbled dismally off. But I haven't enjoyed it. They seem to keep a specially cutting east wind, waiting for me, when I go to bathe in the early morning; and they pick out all the three-cornered stones, and put them on the top, and they sharpen up the rocks and cover the points over with a bit of sand so that I can't see them, and they take the sea and put it two miles out, so that I have to huddle myself up in my arms and hop, shivering, through six inches of water. And when I do get to the sea, it is rough and quite insulting.

One huge wave catches me up and chucks me in a sitting posture, as hard as ever it can, down on to a rock which has been put there for me. And, before I've said "Oh! Ugh!" and found out what has gone, the wave comes back and carries me out to mid-ocean. I begin to strike out frantically for the shore, and wonder if

I shall ever see home and friends again, and wish I'd been kinder to my little sister when a boy (when I was a boy, I mean). Just when I have given up all hope, a wave retires and leaves me sprawling like a star-fish on the sand, and I get up and look back and find that I've been swimming for my life in two feet of water. I hop back and dress, and crawl home, where I have to pretend I liked it.

In the present instance, we all talked as if we were going to have a long swim every morning.

George said it was so pleasant to wake up in the boat in the fresh morning, and plunge into the limpid river. Harris said there was nothing like a swim before breakfast to give you an appetite. He said it always gave him an appetite. George said that if it was going to make Harris eat more than Harris ordinarily ate, then he should protest against Harris having a bath at all.

He said there would be quite enough hard work in towing sufficient food for Harris up against stream, as it was.

I urged upon George, however, how much pleasanter it would be to have Harris clean and fresh about the boat, even if we did have to take a few more hundredweight of provisions; and he got to see it in my light, and withdrew his opposition to Harris's bath.

Agreed, finally, that we should take *three* bath towels, so as not to keep each other waiting.

For clothes, George said two suits of flannel would be sufficient, as we could wash them ourselves, in the river, when they got dirty. We asked him if he had ever tried washing flannels in the river, and he replied: "No, not exactly himself like; but he knew some fellows who had, and it was easy enough;" and Harris and I were weak enough to fancy he knew what he was talking about, and that three respectable young men, without position or influence, and with no experience in washing, could really clean their own shirts and trousers in the river Thames with a bit of soap.

We were to learn in the days to come, when it was too late, that George was a miserable impostor, who could evidently have known nothing whatever about the matter. If you had seen these clothes after—but, as the shilling shockers say, we anticipate.

George impressed upon us to take a change of under-things and plenty of socks, in case we got upset and wanted a change; also plenty of handkerchiefs, as they would do to wipe things, and a pair of leather boots as well as our boating shoes, as we should want them if we got upset.

CHAPTER IV.

The food question.—Objections to paraffine oil as an atmosphere.—Advantages of cheese as a travelling companion.—A married woman deserts her home.—Further provision for getting upset.—I pack.—Cussedness of tooth-brushes.—George and Harris pack.—Awful behaviour of Montmorency.—We retire to rest.

Then we discussed the food question. George said:

"Begin with breakfast." (George is so practical.) "Now for breakfast we shall want a frying-pan"—(Harris said it was indigestible; but we merely urged him not to be an ass, and George went on)—"a tea-pot and a kettle, and a methylated spirit stove."

"No oil," said George, with a significant look; and Harris and I agreed.

We had taken up an oil-stove once, but "never again." It had been like living in an oil-shop that week. It oozed. I never saw such a thing as paraffine oil is to ooze. We kept it in the nose of the boat, and, from there, it oozed down to the rudder, impregnating the whole boat and everything in it on its way, and it oozed over the river, and saturated the scenery and spoilt the atmosphere. Sometimes a westerly oily wind blew, and at other times an easterly oily wind, and sometimes it blew a northerly oily wind, and maybe a southerly oily wind; but whether it came from the Arctic snows, or was raised in the waste of the desert sands, it came alike to us laden with the fragrance of paraffine oil.

And that oil oozed up and ruined the sunset; and as for the moonbeams, they positively reeked of paraffine.

We tried to get away from it at Marlow. We left the boat by the bridge, and took a walk through the town to escape it, but it followed us. The whole town was full of oil. We passed through the church-yard, and it seemed as if the people had been buried in oil. The High Street stunk of oil; we wondered how people could live in it. And we walked miles upon miles out Birmingham way; but it was no use, the country was steeped in oil.

At the end of that trip we met together at midnight in a lonely field, under a blasted oak, and took an awful oath (we had been swearing for a whole week about the thing in an ordinary, middle-class way, but this was a swell affair)—an awful oath never to take paraffine oil with us in a boat again-except, of course, in case of sickness.

Therefore, in the present instance, we confined ourselves to methylated spirit. Even that is bad enough. You get methylated pie and methylated cake. But methylated spirit is more wholesome when taken into the system in large quantities than paraffine oil.

For other breakfast things, George suggested eggs and bacon, which were easy to cook, cold meat, tea, bread and butter, and jam. For lunch, he said, we could have biscuits, cold meat, bread and butter, and jam—but *no cheese*. Cheese, like oil, makes too much of itself. It wants the whole boat to itself. It goes through the hamper, and gives a cheesy flavour to everything else there. You can't tell whether you are eating apple-pie or German sausage, or strawberries and cream. It all seems cheese. There is too much odour about cheese.

I remember a friend of mine, buying a couple of cheeses at Liverpool. Splendid cheeses they were, ripe and mellow, and with a two hundred horse-power scent about them that might have been warranted to carry three miles, and knock a man over at two hundred yards. I was in Liverpool at the time, and my friend said that if I didn't mind he would get me to take them back with me to London, as he should not be coming up for a day or two himself, and he did not think the cheeses ought to be kept much longer.

"Oh, with pleasure, dear boy," I replied, "with pleasure."

I called for the cheeses, and took them away in a cab. It was a ramshackle affair, dragged along by a knock-kneed, broken-winded somnambulist, which his owner, in a moment of enthusiasm, during conversation, referred to as a horse. I put the cheeses on the top, and we started off at a shamble that would have done credit to the swiftest steam-roller ever built, and all went merry as a funeral bell, until we turned the corner. There, the wind carried a whiff from the cheeses full on to our steed. It woke him up, and, with a snort of terror, he dashed off at three miles an hour. The wind still blew in his direction, and before we reached the end of the street he was laying himself out at the rate of nearly four miles an hour, leaving the cripples and stout old ladies simply nowhere.

It took two porters as well as the driver to hold him in at the station; and I do not think they would have done it, even then, had not one of the men had the presence of mind to put a handkerchief over his nose, and to light a bit of brown paper.

I took my ticket, and marched proudly up the platform, with my cheeses, the people falling back respectfully on either side. The train was crowded, and I had to get into a carriage where there were already seven other people. One crusty old gentleman objected, but I got in, notwithstanding; and, putting my cheeses upon the rack, squeezed down with a pleasant smile, and said it was a warm day.

A few moments passed, and then the old gentleman began to fidget.

"Very close in here," he said.

"Quite oppressive," said the man next him.

And then they both began sniffing, and, at the third sniff, they caught it right on the chest, and rose up without another word and went out. And then a stout lady got up, and said it was disgraceful that a respectable married woman should be harried about in this way, and gathered up a bag and eight parcels and went. The remaining four passengers sat on for a while, until a solemn-looking man in the corner, who, from his dress and general appearance, seemed to belong to the undertaker class, said it put him in mind of dead baby; and the other three passengers tried to get out of the door at the same time, and hurt themselves.

I smiled at the black gentleman, and said I thought we were going to have the carriage to ourselves; and he laughed pleasantly, and said that some people made such a fuss over a little thing. But even he grew strangely depressed after we had started, and so, when we reached Crewe, I asked him to come and have a drink. He accepted, and we forced our way into the buffet, where we yelled, and stamped, and waved our umbrellas for a quarter of an hour; and then a young lady came, and asked us if we wanted anything.

"What's yours?" I said, turning to my friend.

"I'll have half-a-crown's worth of brandy, neat, if you please, miss," he responded.

And he went off quietly after he had drunk it and got into another carriage, which I thought mean.

From Crewe I had the compartment to myself, though the train was crowded. As we drew up at the different stations, the people, seeing my empty carriage, would rush for it. "Here y' are, Maria; come along, plenty of room." "All right, Tom; we'll get in here," they would shout. And they would run along, carrying heavy bags, and fight round the door to get in first. And one would open the door and mount the steps, and stagger back into the arms of the man behind him; and they would all come and have a sniff, and then droop off and squeeze into other carriages, or pay the difference and go first.

From Euston, I took the cheeses down to my friend's house. When his wife came into the room she smelt round for an instant. Then she said:

"What is it? Tell me the worst."

I said:

"It's cheeses. Tom bought them in Liverpool, and asked me to bring them up with me."

And I added that I hoped she understood that it had nothing to do with me; and she said that she was sure of that, but that she would speak to Tom about it when he came back.

My friend was detained in Liverpool longer than he expected; and, three days later, as he hadn't returned home, his wife called on me. She said:

"What did Tom say about those cheeses?"

I replied that he had directed they were to be kept in a moist place, and that nobody was to touch them.

She said:

"Nobody's likely to touch them. Had he smelt them?"

I thought he had, and added that he seemed greatly attached to them.

"You think he would be upset," she queried, "if I gave a man a sovereign to take them away and bury them?"

I answered that I thought he would never smile again.

An idea struck her. She said:

"Do you mind keeping them for him? Let me send them round to you."

"Madam," I replied, "for myself I like the smell of cheese, and the journey the other day with them from Liverpool I shall ever look back upon as a happy ending to a pleasant holiday. But, in this world, we must consider others. The lady under whose roof I have the honour of residing is a widow, and, for all I know, possibly an orphan too. She has a strong, I may say an eloquent, objection to being what she terms 'put upon.' The presence of your husband's cheeses in her house she would, I instinctively feel, regard as a 'put upon'; and it shall never be said that I put upon the widow and the orphan."

"Very well, then," said my friend's wife, rising, "all I have to say is, that I shall take the children and go to an hotel until those cheeses are eaten. I decline to live any longer in the same house with them."

She kept her word, leaving the place in charge of the charwoman, who, when asked if she could stand the smell, replied, "What smell?" and who, when taken close to the cheeses and told to sniff hard, said she could detect a faint odour of melons. It was argued from this that little injury could result to the woman from the atmosphere, and she was left.

The hotel bill came to fifteen guineas; and my friend, after reckoning everything up, found that the cheeses had cost him eight-and-sixpence a pound. He said he dearly loved a bit of cheese, but it was beyond his means; so he determined to get rid of them. He threw them into the canal; but had to fish them out again, as the bargemen complained. They said it made them feel quite faint. And, after that, he took them one dark night and left them in the parish mortuary. But the coroner discovered them, and made a fearful fuss.

He said it was a plot to deprive him of his living by waking up the corpses.

My friend got rid of them, at last, by taking them down to a sea-side town, and burying them on the beach. It gained the place quite a reputation. Visitors said they had never noticed before how strong the air was, and weak-chested and consumptive people used to throng there for years afterwards.

Fond as I am of cheese, therefore, I hold that George was right in declining to take any.

"We shan't want any tea," said George (Harris's face fell at this); "but we'll have a good round, square, slap-up meal at seven—dinner, tea, and supper combined."

Harris grew more cheerful. George suggested meat and fruit pies, cold meat, tomatoes, fruit, and green stuff. For drink, we took some wonderful sticky concoction of Harris's, which you mixed with water and called lemonade, plenty of tea, and a bottle of whisky, in case, as George said, we got upset.

It seemed to me that George harped too much on the getting-upset idea. It seemed to me the wrong spirit to go about the trip in.

But I'm glad we took the whisky.

We didn't take beer or wine. They are a mistake up the river. They make you feel sleepy and heavy. A glass in the evening when you are doing a mouch round the town and looking at the girls is all right enough; but don't drink when the sun is blazing down on your head, and you've got hard work to do.

We made a list of the things to be taken, and a pretty lengthy one it was, before we parted that evening. The next day, which was Friday, we got them all together, and met in the evening to pack. We got a big Gladstone for the clothes, and a couple of hampers for the victuals and the cooking utensils. We moved the table up against the window, piled everything in a heap in the middle of the floor, and sat round and looked at it.

I said I'd pack.

I rather pride myself on my packing. Packing is one of those many things that I feel I know more about than any other person living. (It surprises me myself, sometimes, how many of these subjects there are.) I impressed the fact upon George and Harris, and told them that they had better leave the whole matter entirely to me. They fell into the suggestion with a readiness that had something uncanny about it. George put on a pipe and spread himself over the easy-chair, and Harris cocked his legs on the table and lit a cigar.

This was hardly what I intended. What I had meant, of course, was, that I should boss the job, and that Harris and George should potter about under my directions, I pushing them aside every now and then with, "Oh, you—!" "Here, let me do it." "There you are, simple enough!"—really teaching them, as you might say. Their taking it in the way they did irritated me. There is nothing does irritate me more than seeing other people sitting about doing nothing when I'm working.

I lived with a man once who used to make me mad that way. He would loll on the sofa and watch me doing things by the hour together, following me round the room with his eyes, wherever I went. He said it did him real good to look on at me, messing about. He said it made him feel that life was not an idle dream to be gaped and yawned through, but a noble task, full of duty and stern work. He said he often wondered now how he could have gone on before he met me, never having anybody to look at while they worked.

Now, I'm not like that. I can't sit still and see another man slaving and working. I want to get up and superintend, and walk round with my hands in my pockets, and tell him what to do. It is my energetic nature. I can't help it.

However, I did not say anything, but started the packing. It seemed a longer job than I had thought it was going to be; but I got the bag finished at last, and I sat on it and strapped it.

"Ain't you going to put the boots in?" said Harris.

And I looked round, and found I had forgotten them. That's just like Harris. He couldn't have said a word until I'd got the bag shut and strapped, of course. And George laughed—one of those irritating, senseless, chuckle-headed, crack-jawed laughs of his. They do make me so wild.

I opened the bag and packed the boots in; and then, just as I was going to close it, a horrible idea occurred to me. Had I packed my tooth-brush? I don't know how it is, but I never do know whether I've packed my tooth-brush.

My tooth-brush is a thing that haunts me when I'm travelling, and makes my life a misery. I dream that I haven't packed it, and wake up in a cold perspiration, and get out of bed and hunt for it. And, in the morning, I pack it before I have used it, and have to unpack again to get it, and it is always the last thing I turn out of the bag; and then I repack and forget it, and have to rush upstairs for it at the last moment and carry it to the railway station, wrapped up in my pocket-handkerchief.

CHAPTER IV.

Of course I had to turn every mortal thing out now, and, of course, I could not find it. I rummaged the things up into much the same state that they must have been before the world was created, and when chaos reigned. Of course, I found George's and Harris's eighteen times over, but I couldn't find my own. I put the things back one by one, and held everything up and shook it. Then I found it inside a boot. I repacked once more.

When I had finished, George asked if the soap was in. I said I didn't care a hang whether the soap was in or whether it wasn't; and I slammed the bag to and strapped it, and found that I had packed my tobacco-pouch in it, and had to re-open it. It got shut up finally at 10.5 p.m., and then there remained the hampers to do. Harris said that we should be wanting to start in less than twelve hours' time, and thought that he and George had better do the rest; and I agreed and sat down, and they had a go.

They began in a light-hearted spirit, evidently intending to show me how to do it. I made no comment; I only waited. When George is hanged, Harris will be the worst packer in this world; and I looked at the piles of plates and cups, and kettles, and bottles and jars, and pies, and stoves, and cakes, and tomatoes, &c., and felt that the thing would soon become exciting.

It did. They started with breaking a cup. That was the first thing they did. They did that just to show you what they *could* do, and to get you interested.

Then Harris packed the strawberry jam on top of a tomato and squashed it, and they had to pick out the tomato with a teaspoon.

And then it was George's turn, and he trod on the butter. I didn't say anything, but I came over and sat on the edge of the table and watched them. It irritated them more than anything I could have said. I felt that. It made them nervous and excited, and they stepped on things, and put things behind them, and then couldn't find them when they wanted them; and they packed the pies at the bottom, and put heavy things on top, and smashed the pies in.

They upset salt over everything, and as for the butter! I never saw two men do more with one-and-twopence worth of butter in my whole life than they did. After George had got it off his slipper, they tried to put it in the kettle. It wouldn't go in, and what *was* in wouldn't come out. They did scrape it out at last, and put it down on a chair, and Harris sat on it, and it stuck to him, and they went looking for it all over the room.

"I'll take my oath I put it down on that chair," said George, staring at the empty seat.

"I saw you do it myself, not a minute ago," said Harris.

Then they started round the room again looking for it; and then they met again in the centre, and stared at one another.

"Most extraordinary thing I ever heard of," said George.

"So mysterious!" said Harris.

Then George got round at the back of Harris and saw it.

"Why, here it is all the time," he exclaimed, indignantly.

"Where?" cried Harris, spinning round.

"Stand still, can't you!" roared George, flying after him.

And they got it off, and packed it in the teapot.

Montmorency was in it all, of course. Montmorency's ambition in life, is to get in the way and be sworn at. If he can squirm in anywhere where he particularly is not wanted, and be a perfect nuisance, and make people mad, and have things thrown at his head, then he feels his day has not been wasted.

To get somebody to stumble over him, and curse him steadily for an hour, is his highest aim and object; and, when he has succeeded in accomplishing this, his conceit becomes quite unbearable.

He came and sat down on things, just when they were wanted to be packed; and he laboured under the fixed belief that, whenever Harris or George reached out their hand for anything, it was his cold, damp nose that they wanted. He put his leg into the jam, and he worried the teaspoons, and he pretended that the lemons were rats, and got into the hamper and killed three of them before Harris could land him with the frying-pan.

Harris said I encouraged him. I didn't encourage him. A dog like that don't want any encouragement. It's the natural, original sin that is born in him that makes him do things like that.

The packing was done at 12.50; and Harris sat on the big hamper, and said he hoped nothing would be found broken. George said that if anything was broken it was broken, which reflection seemed to comfort him. He also said he was ready for bed. We were all ready for bed. Harris was to sleep with us that night, and we went upstairs.

We tossed for beds, and Harris had to sleep with me. He said:

"Do you prefer the inside or the outside, J.?"

I said I generally preferred to sleep *inside* a bed.

Harris said it was old.

George said:

"What time shall I wake you fellows?"

Harris said:

"Seven."

I said:

"No—six," because I wanted to write some letters.

Harris and I had a bit of a row over it, but at last split the difference, and said half-past six.

"Wake us at 6.30, George," we said.

George made no answer, and we found, on going over, that he had been asleep for some time; so we placed the bath where he could tumble into it on getting out in the morning, and went to bed ourselves.

CHAPTER IV.

CHAPTER V.

Mrs. P. arouses us.—George, the sluggard.—The "weather forecast" swindle.—Our luggage.—Depravity of the small boy.—The people gather round us.—We drive off in great style, and arrive at Waterloo.—Innocence of South Western Officials concerning such worldly things as trains.—We are afloat, afloat in an open boat.

It was Mrs. Poppets that woke me up next morning.

She said:

"Do you know that it's nearly nine o'clock, sir?"

"Nine o' what?" I cried, starting up.

"Nine o'clock," she replied, through the keyhole. "I thought you was a-oversleeping yourselves."

I woke Harris, and told him. He said:

"I thought you wanted to get up at six?"

"So I did," I answered; "why didn't you wake me?"

"How could I wake you, when you didn't wake me?" he retorted. "Now we shan't get on the water till after twelve. I wonder you take the trouble to get up at all."

"Um," I replied, "lucky for you that I do. If I hadn't woke you, you'd have lain there for the whole fortnight."

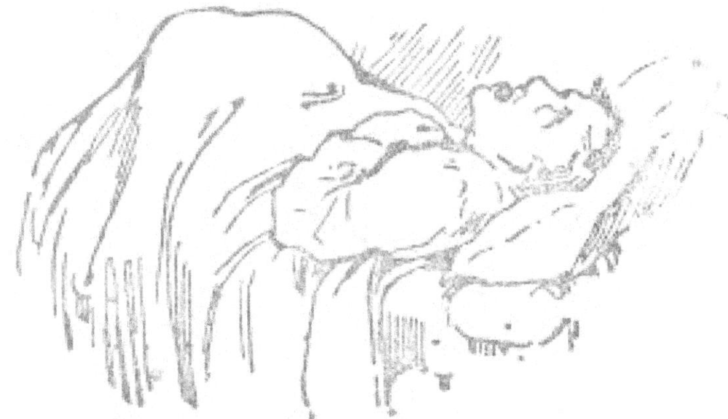

We snarled at one another in this strain for the next few minutes, when we were interrupted by a defiant snore from George. It reminded us, for the first time since our being called, of his existence. There he lay—the man who had wanted to know what time he should wake us—on his back, with his mouth wide open, and his knees stuck up.

I don't know why it should be, I am sure; but the sight of another man asleep in bed when I am up, maddens me. It seems to me so shocking to see the precious hours of a man's life—the priceless moments that will never come back to him again—being wasted in mere brutish sleep.

There was George, throwing away in hideous sloth the inestimable gift of time; his valuable life, every second of which he would have to account for hereafter, passing away from him, unused. He might have been up stuffing himself with eggs and bacon, irritating the dog, or flirting with the slavey, instead of sprawling there, sunk in soul-clogging oblivion.

It was a terrible thought. Harris and I appeared to be struck by it at the same instant. We determined to save him, and, in this noble resolve, our own dispute was forgotten. We flew across and slung the clothes off him, and Harris landed him one with a slipper, and I shouted in his ear, and he awoke.

"Wasermarrer?" he observed, sitting up.

"Get up, you fat-headed chunk!" roared Harris. "It's quarter to ten."

"What!" he shrieked, jumping out of bed into the bath; "Who the thunder put this thing here?"

We told him he must have been a fool not to see the bath.

We finished dressing, and, when it came to the extras, we remembered that we had packed the tooth-brushes and the brush and comb (that tooth-brush of mine will be the death of me, I know), and we had to go downstairs, and fish them out of the bag. And when we had done that George wanted the shaving tackle. We told him that he would have to go without shaving that morning, as we weren't going to unpack that bag again for him, nor for anyone like him.

He said:

"Don't be absurd. How can I go into the City like this?"

It was certainly rather rough on the City, but what cared we for human suffering? As Harris said, in his common, vulgar way, the City would have to lump it.

We went downstairs to breakfast. Montmorency had invited two other dogs to come and see him off, and they were whiling away the time by fighting on the doorstep. We calmed them with an umbrella, and sat down to chops and cold beef.

Harris said:

"The great thing is to make a good breakfast," and he started with a couple of chops, saying that he would take these while they were hot, as the beef could wait.

George got hold of the paper, and read us out the boating fatalities, and the weather forecast, which latter prophesied "rain, cold, wet to fine" (whatever more than usually ghastly thing in weather that may be), "occasional local thunderstorms, east wind, with general depression over the Midland Counties (London and Channel). Bar. falling."

I do think that, of all the silly, irritating tomfoolishness by which we are plagued, this "weather-forecast" fraud is about the most aggravating. It "forecasts" precisely what happened yesterday or a the day before, and precisely the opposite of what is going to happen to-day.

I remember a holiday of mine being completely ruined one late autumn by our paying attention to the weather report of the local newspaper. "Heavy showers, with thunderstorms, may be expected to-day," it would say on Monday, and so we would give up our picnic, and stop indoors all day, waiting for the rain.—And people would pass the house, going off in wagonettes and coaches as jolly and merry as could be, the sun shining out, and not a cloud to be seen.

"Ah!" we said, as we stood looking out at them through the window, "won't they come home soaked!"

And we chuckled to think how wet they were going to get, and came back and stirred the fire, and got our books, and arranged our specimens of seaweed and cockle shells. By twelve o'clock, with the sun pouring into the room, the heat became quite oppressive, and we wondered when those heavy showers and occasional thunderstorms were going to begin.

"Ah! they'll come in the afternoon, you'll find," we said to each other. "Oh, *won't* those people get wet. What a lark!"

At one o'clock, the landlady would come in to ask if we weren't going out, as it seemed such a lovely day.

"No, no," we replied, with a knowing chuckle, "not we. *We* don't mean to get wet—no, no."

And when the afternoon was nearly gone, and still there was no sign of rain, we tried to cheer ourselves up with the idea that it would come down all at once, just as the people had started for home, and were out of the reach of any shelter, and that they would thus get more drenched than ever. But not a drop ever fell, and it finished a grand day, and a lovely night after it.

The next morning we would read that it was going to be a "warm, fine to set-fair day; much heat;" and we would dress ourselves in flimsy things, and go out, and, half-an-hour after we had started, it would commence to rain hard, and a bitterly cold wind would spring up, and both would keep on steadily for the whole day, and we would come home with colds and rheumatism all over us, and go to bed.

The weather is a thing that is beyond me altogether. I never can understand it. The barometer is useless: it is as misleading as the newspaper forecast.

There was one hanging up in a hotel at Oxford at which I was staying last spring, and, when I got there, it was pointing to "set fair." It was simply pouring with rain outside, and had been all day; and I couldn't quite make matters out. I tapped the barometer, and it jumped up and pointed to "very dry." The Boots stopped as he was passing, and said he expected it meant to-morrow. I fancied that maybe it was thinking of the week before last, but Boots said, No, he thought not.

I tapped it again the next morning, and it went up still higher, and the rain came down faster than ever. On Wednesday I went and hit it again, and the pointer went round towards "set fair," "very dry," and "much heat," until it was stopped by the peg, and couldn't go any further. It tried its best, but the instrument was built so that it couldn't prophesy fine weather any harder than it did without breaking itself. It evidently wanted to go on, and prognosticate drought, and water famine, and sunstroke, and simooms, and such things, but the peg prevented it, and it had to be content with pointing to the mere commonplace "very dry."

Meanwhile, the rain came down in a steady torrent, and the lower part of the town was under water, owing to the river having overflowed.

Boots said it was evident that we were going to have a prolonged spell of grand weather *some time*, and read out a poem which was printed over the top of the oracle, about

> "Long foretold, long last;
> Short notice, soon past."

The fine weather never came that summer. I expect that machine must have been referring to the following spring.

Then there are those new style of barometers, the long straight ones. I never can make head or tail of those. There is one side for 10 a.m. yesterday, and one side for 10 a.m. to-day; but you can't always get there as early as ten, you know. It rises or falls for rain and fine, with much or less wind, and one end is "Nly" and the other "Ely" (what's Ely got to do with it?), and if you tap it, it doesn't tell you anything. And you've got to correct it to sea-level, and reduce it to Fahrenheit, and even then I don't know the answer.

But who wants to be foretold the weather? It is bad enough when it comes, without our having the misery of knowing about it beforehand. The prophet we like is the old man who, on the particularly gloomy-looking morning of some day when we particularly want it to be fine, looks round the horizon with a particularly knowing eye, and says:

"Oh no, sir, I think it will clear up all right. It will break all right enough, sir."

"Ah, he knows", we say, as we wish him good-morning, and start off; "wonderful how these old fellows can tell!"

And we feel an affection for that man which is not at all lessened by the circumstances of its *not* clearing up, but continuing to rain steadily all day.

"Ah, well," we feel, "he did his best."

For the man that prophesies us bad weather, on the contrary, we entertain only bitter and revengeful thoughts.

"Going to clear up, d'ye think?" we shout, cheerily, as we pass.

"Well, no, sir; I'm afraid it's settled down for the day," he replies, shaking his head.

"Stupid old fool!" we mutter, "what's *he* know about it?" And, if his portent proves correct, we come back feeling still more angry against him, and with a vague notion that, somehow or other, he has had something to do with it.

It was too bright and sunny on this especial morning for George's blood-curdling readings about "Bar. falling," "atmospheric disturbance, passing in an oblique line over Southern Europe," and "pressure increasing," to very much upset us: and so, finding that he could not make us wretched, and was only wasting his time, he sneaked the cigarette that I had carefully rolled up for myself, and went.

Then Harris and I, having finished up the few things left on the table, carted out our luggage on to the doorstep, and waited for a cab.

There seemed a good deal of luggage, when we put it all together. There was the Gladstone and the small hand-bag, and the two hampers, and a large roll of rugs, and some four or five overcoats and macintoshes, and a few umbrellas, and then there was a melon by itself in a bag, because it was too bulky to go in anywhere, and a couple of pounds of grapes in another bag, and a Japanese paper umbrella, and a frying pan, which, being too long to pack, we had wrapped round with brown paper.

It did look a lot, and Harris and I began to feel rather ashamed of it, though why we should be, I can't see. No cab came by, but the street boys did, and got interested in the show, apparently, and stopped.

Biggs's boy was the first to come round. Biggs is our greengrocer, and his chief talent lies in securing the services of the most abandoned and unprincipled errand-boys that civilisation has as yet produced. If anything more than usually villainous in the boy-line crops up in our neighbourhood, we know that it is Biggs's latest. I was told that, at the time of the Great Coram Street murder, it was promptly concluded by our street that Biggs's boy (for that period) was at the bottom of it, and had he not been able, in reply to the severe cross-examination to which he was subjected by No. 19, when he called there for orders the morning after the crime (assisted by No. 21, who happened to be on the step at the time), to prove a complete *alibi*, it would have gone hard with him. I didn't know Biggs's boy at that time, but, from what I have seen of them since, I should not have attached much importance to that *alibi* myself.

Biggs's boy, as I have said, came round the corner. He was evidently in a great hurry when he first dawned upon the vision, but, on catching sight of Harris and me, and Montmorency, and the things, he eased up and stared. Harris and I frowned at him. This might have wounded a more sensitive nature, but Biggs's boys are not, as a rule, touchy. He came to a dead stop, a yard from our step, and, leaning up against the railings, and selecting a straw to chew, fixed us with his eye. He evidently meant to see this thing out.

In another moment, the grocer's boy passed on the opposite side of the street. Biggs's boy hailed him:

"Hi! ground floor o' 42's a-moving."

The grocer's boy came across, and took up a position on the other side of the step. Then the young gentleman from the boot-shop stopped, and joined Biggs's boy; while the empty-can superintendent from "The Blue Posts" took up an independent position on the curb.

"They ain't a-going to starve, are they?" said the gentleman from the boot-shop.

"Ah! you'd want to take a thing or two with *you*," retorted "The Blue Posts," "if you was a-going to cross the Atlantic in a small boat."

"They ain't a-going to cross the Atlantic," struck in Biggs's boy; "they're a-going to find Stanley."

By this time, quite a small crowd had collected, and people were asking each other what was the matter. One party (the young and giddy portion of the crowd) held that it was a wedding, and pointed out Harris as the bridegroom; while the elder and more thoughtful among the populace inclined to the idea that it was a funeral, and that I was probably the corpse's brother.

At last, an empty cab turned up (it is a street where, as a rule, and when they are not wanted, empty cabs pass at the rate of three a minute, and hang about, and get in your way), and packing ourselves and our belongings into it, and shooting out a couple of Montmorency's friends, who had evidently sworn never to forsake him, we drove away amidst the cheers of the crowd, Biggs's boy shying a carrot after us for luck.

CHAPTER V.

We got to Waterloo at eleven, and asked where the eleven-five started from. Of course nobody knew; nobody at Waterloo ever does know where a train is going to start from, or where a train when it does start is going to, or anything about it. The porter who took our things thought it would go from number two platform, while another porter, with whom he discussed the question, had heard a rumour that it would go from number one. The station-master, on the other hand, was convinced it would start from the local.

To put an end to the matter, we went upstairs, and asked the traffic superintendent, and he told us that he had just met a man, who said he had seen it at number three platform. We went to number three platform, but the authorities there said that they rather thought that train was the Southampton express, or else the Windsor loop. But they were sure it wasn't the Kingston train, though why they were sure it wasn't they couldn't say.

Then our porter said he thought that must be it on the high-level platform; said he thought he knew the train. So we went to the high-level platform, and saw the engine-driver, and asked him if he was going to Kingston. He said he couldn't say for certain of course, but that he rather thought he was. Anyhow, if he wasn't the 11.5 for Kingston, he said he was pretty confident he was the 9.32 for Virginia Water, or the 10 a.m. express for the Isle of Wight, or somewhere in that direction, and we should all know when we got there. We slipped half-a-crown into his hand, and begged him to be the 11.5 for Kingston.

"Nobody will ever know, on this line," we said, "what you are, or where you're going. You know the way, you slip off quietly and go to Kingston."

"Well, I don't know, gents," replied the noble fellow, "but I suppose *some* train's got to go to Kingston; and I'll do it. Gimme the half-crown."

Thus we got to Kingston by the London and South-Western Railway.

We learnt, afterwards, that the train we had come by was really the Exeter mail, and that they had spent hours at Waterloo, looking for it, and nobody knew what had become of it.

Our boat was waiting for us at Kingston just below bridge, and to it we wended our way, and round it we stored our luggage, and into it we stepped.

"Are you all right, sir?" said the man.

"Right it is," we answered; and with Harris at the sculls and I at the tiller-lines, and Montmorency, unhappy and deeply suspicious, in the prow, out we shot on to the waters which, for a fortnight, were to be our home.

CHAPTER VI.

**Kingston.—Instructive remarks on early English history.—
Instructive observations on carved oak and life in general.—
Sad case of Stivvings, junior.—Musings on antiquity.—I
forget that I am steering.—Interesting result.—Hampton
Court Maze.—Harris as a guide.**

It was a glorious morning, late spring or early summer, as you care to take it, when the dainty sheen of grass and leaf is blushing to a deeper green; and the year seems like a fair young maid, trembling with strange, wakening pulses on the brink of womanhood.

The quaint back streets of Kingston, where they came down to the water's edge, looked quite picturesque in the flashing sunlight, the glinting river with its drifting barges, the wooded towpath, the trim-kept villas on the other side, Harris, in a red and orange blazer, grunting away at the sculls, the distant glimpses of the grey old palace of the Tudors, all made a sunny picture, so bright but calm, so full of life, and yet so peaceful, that, early in the day though it was, I felt myself being dreamily lulled off into a musing fit.

I mused on Kingston, or "Kyningestun," as it was once called in the days when Saxon "kinges" were crowned there. Great Cæsar crossed the river there, and the Roman legions camped upon its sloping uplands. Cæsar, like, in later years, Elizabeth, seems to have stopped everywhere: only he was more respectable than good Queen Bess; he didn't put up at the public-houses.

She was nuts on public-houses, was England's Virgin Queen. There's scarcely a pub. of any attractions within ten miles of London that she does not seem to have looked in at, or stopped at, or slept at, some time or other. I wonder now, supposing Harris, say, turned over a new leaf, and became a great and good man, and got to be Prime Minister, and died, if they would put up signs over the public-houses that he had patronised: "Harris had a glass of bitter in this house;" "Harris had two of Scotch cold here in the summer of '88;" "Harris was chucked from here in December, 1886."

No, there would be too many of them! It would be the houses that he had never entered that would become famous. "Only house in South London that Harris never had a drink in!" The people would flock to it to see what could have been the matter with it.

How poor weak-minded King Edwy must have hated Kyningestun! The coronation feast had been too much for him. Maybe boar's head stuffed with sugar-plums did not agree with him (it wouldn't with me, I know), and he had had enough of sack and mead; so he slipped from the noisy revel to steal a quiet moonlight hour with his beloved Elgiva.

Perhaps, from the casement, standing hand-in-hand, they were watching the calm moonlight on the river, while from the distant halls the boisterous revelry floated in broken bursts of faint-heard din and tumult.

Then brutal Odo and St. Dunstan force their rude way into the quiet room, and hurl coarse insults at the sweet-faced Queen, and drag poor Edwy back to the loud clamour of the drunken brawl.

Years later, to the crash of battle-music, Saxon kings and Saxon revelry were buried side by side, and Kingston's greatness passed away for a time, to rise once more when Hampton Court became the palace of the Tudors and the Stuarts, and the royal barges strained at their moorings on the river's bank, and bright-cloaked gallants swaggered down the water-steps to cry: "What Ferry, ho! Gadzooks, gramercy."

Many of the old houses, round about, speak very plainly of those days when Kingston was a royal borough, and nobles and courtiers lived there, near their King, and the long road to the palace gates was gay all day with clanking steel and prancing palfreys, and rustling silks and velvets, and fair faces. The large and spacious houses, with their oriel, latticed windows, their huge fireplaces, and their gabled roofs, breathe of the days of hose and doublet, of pearl-embroidered stomachers, and complicated oaths. They were upraised in the days "when men knew how to build." The hard red bricks have only grown more firmly set with time, and their oak stairs do not creak and grunt when you try to go down them quietly.

Speaking of oak staircases reminds me that there is a magnificent carved oak staircase in one of the houses in Kingston. It is a shop now, in the market-place, but it was evidently once the mansion of some great personage. A friend of mine, who lives at Kingston, went in there to buy a hat one day, and, in a thoughtless moment, put his hand in his pocket and paid for it then and there.

The shopman (he knows my friend) was naturally a little staggered at first; but, quickly recovering himself, and feeling that something ought to be done to encourage this sort of thing, asked our hero if he would like to see some fine old carved oak. My friend said he would, and the shopman, thereupon, took him through the shop, and up the staircase of the house. The balusters were a superb piece of workmanship, and the wall all the way up was oak-panelled, with carving that would have done credit to a palace.

From the stairs, they went into the drawing-room, which was a large, bright room, decorated with a somewhat startling though cheerful paper of a blue ground. There was nothing, however, remarkable about the apartment, and my friend wondered why he had been brought there. The proprietor went up to the paper, and tapped it. It gave forth a wooden sound.

"Oak," he explained. "All carved oak, right up to the ceiling, just the same as you saw on the staircase."

"But, great Cæsar! man," expostulated my friend; "you don't mean to say you have covered over carved oak with blue wall-paper?"

"Yes," was the reply: "it was expensive work. Had to match-board it all over first, of course. But the room looks cheerful now. It was awful gloomy before."

I can't say I altogether blame the man (which is doubtless a great relief to his mind). From his point of view, which would be that of the average householder, desiring to take life as lightly as possible, and not that of the old-curiosity-shop maniac, there is reason on his side. Carved oak is very pleasant to look at, and to have a little of, but it is no doubt somewhat depressing to live in, for those whose fancy does not lie that way. It would be like living in a church.

No, what was sad in his case was that he, who didn't care for carved oak, should have his drawing-room panelled with it, while people who do care for it have to pay enormous prices to get it. It seems to be the rule of this world. Each person has what he doesn't want, and other people have what he does want.

Married men have wives, and don't seem to want them; and young single fellows cry out that they can't get them. Poor people who can hardly keep themselves have eight hearty children. Rich old couples, with no one to leave their money to, die childless.

Then there are girls with lovers. The girls that have lovers never want them. They say they would rather be without them, that they bother them, and why don't they go and make love to Miss Smith and Miss Brown, who are plain and elderly, and haven't got any lovers? They themselves don't want lovers. They never mean to marry.

It does not do to dwell on these things; it makes one so sad.

There was a boy at our school, we used to call him Sandford and Merton. His real name was Stivvings. He was the most extraordinary lad I ever came across. I believe he really liked study. He used to get into awful rows for sitting up in bed and reading Greek; and as for French irregular verbs there was simply no keeping him away from them. He was full of weird and unnatural notions about being a credit to his parents and an honour to the school; and he yearned to win prizes, and grow up and be a clever man, and had all those sorts of weak-minded ideas. I never knew such a strange creature, yet harmless, mind you, as the babe unborn.

Well, that boy used to get ill about twice a week, so that he couldn't go to school. There never was such a boy to get ill as that Sandford and Merton. If there was any known disease going within ten miles of him, he had it, and had it badly. He would take bronchitis in the dog-days, and have hay-fever at Christmas. After a six weeks' period of drought, he would be stricken down with rheumatic fever; and he would go out in a November fog and come home with a sunstroke.

They put him under laughing-gas one year, poor lad, and drew all his teeth, and gave him a false set, because he suffered so terribly with toothache; and then it turned to neuralgia and ear-ache. He was never without a cold, except once for nine weeks while he had scarlet fever; and he always had chilblains. During the great cholera scare of 1871, our neighbourhood was singularly free from it. There was only one reputed case in the whole parish: that case was young Stivvings.

He had to stop in bed when he was ill, and eat chicken and custards and hot-house grapes; and he would lie there and sob, because they wouldn't let him do Latin exercises, and took his German grammar away from him.

And we other boys, who would have sacrificed ten terms of our school-life for the sake of being ill for a day, and had no desire whatever to give our parents any excuse for being stuck-up about us, couldn't catch so much as a stiff neck. We fooled about in draughts, and it did us good, and freshened us up; and we took things to make us sick, and they made us fat, and gave us an appetite. Nothing we could think of seemed to make us ill until the holidays began. Then, on the break-ing-up day, we caught colds, and whooping cough, and all kinds of disorders, which lasted till the term recommenced; when, in spite of everything we could manœuvre to the contrary, we would get suddenly well again, and be better than ever.

Such is life; and we are but as grass that is cut down, and put into the oven and baked.

To go back to the carved-oak question, they must have had very fair notions of the artistic and the beautiful, our great-great-grandfathers. Why, all our art treas-ures of to-day are only the dug-up commonplaces of three or four hundred years ago. I wonder if there is real intrinsic beauty in the old soup-plates, beer-mugs, and candle-snuffers that we prize so now, or if it is only the halo of age glowing around them that gives them their charms in our eyes. The "old blue" that we hang about our walls as ornaments were the common every-day household uten-sils of a few centuries ago; and the pink shepherds and the yellow shepherdesses that we hand round now for all our friends to gush over, and pretend they under-stand, were the unvalued mantel-ornaments that the mother of the eighteenth century would have given the baby to suck when he cried.

Will it be the same in the future? Will the prized treasures of to-day always be the cheap trifles of the day before? Will rows of our willow-pattern dinner-plates be ranged above the chimneypieces of the great in the years 2000 and odd? Will the white cups with the gold rim and the beautiful gold flower inside (species un-known), that our Sarah Janes now break in sheer light-heartedness of spirit, be carefully mended, and stood upon a bracket, and dusted only by the lady of the house?

That china dog that ornaments the bedroom of my furnished lodgings. It is a white dog. Its eyes blue. Its nose is a delicate red, with spots. Its head is painfully erect, its expression is amiability carried to verge of imbecility. I do not admire it myself. Considered as a work of art, I may say it irritates me. Thoughtless friends jeer at it, and even my landlady herself has no admiration for it, and excuses its presence by the circumstance that her aunt gave it to her.

But in 200 years' time it is more than probable that that dog will be dug up from somewhere or other, minus its legs, and with its tail broken, and will be sold for old china, and put in a glass cabinet. And people will pass it round, and admire it. They will be struck by the wonderful depth of the colour on the nose, and speculate as to how beautiful the bit of the tail that is lost no doubt was.

We, in this age, do not see the beauty of that dog. We are too familiar with it. It is like the sunset and the stars: we are not awed by their loveliness because they are common to our eyes. So it is with that china dog. In 2288 people will gush over it. The making of such dogs will have become a lost art. Our descendants will wonder how we did it, and say how clever we were. We shall be referred to lovingly as "those grand old artists that flourished in the nineteenth century, and produced those china dogs."

The "sampler" that the eldest daughter did at school will be spoken of as "tapestry of the Victorian era," and be almost priceless. The blue-and-white mugs of the present-day roadside inn will be hunted up, all cracked and chipped, and sold for their weight in gold, and rich people will use them for claret cups; and travellers from Japan will buy up all the "Presents from Ramsgate," and "Souvenirs of Margate," that may have escaped destruction, and take them back to Jedo as ancient English curios.

At this point Harris threw away the sculls, got up and left his seat, and sat on his back, and stuck his legs in the air. Montmorency howled, and turned a somersault, and the top hamper jumped up, and all the things came out.

I was somewhat surprised, but I did not lose my temper. I said, pleasantly enough:

"Hulloa! what's that for?"

"What's that for? Why—"

No, on second thoughts, I will not repeat what Harris said. I may have been to blame, I admit it; but nothing excuses violence of language and coarseness of expression, especially in a man who has been carefully brought up, as I know Harris has been. I was thinking of other things, and forgot, as any one might easily understand, that I was steering, and the consequence was that we had got mixed up a good deal with the tow-path. It was difficult to say, for the moment, which was us and which was the Middlesex bank of the river; but we found out after a while, and separated ourselves.

Harris, however, said he had done enough for a bit, and proposed that I should take a turn; so, as we were in, I got out and took the tow-line, and ran the boat on past Hampton Court. What a dear old wall that is that runs along by the river there! I never pass it without feeling better for the sight of it. Such a mellow, bright, sweet old wall; what a charming picture it would make, with the lichen creeping here, and the moss growing there, a shy young vine peeping over the top at this spot, to see what is going on upon the busy river, and the sober old ivy clustering a little farther down! There are fifty shades and tints and hues in every ten yards of that old wall. If I could only draw, and knew how to paint, I could make a lovely sketch of that old wall, I'm sure. I've often thought I should like to live at Hampton Court. It looks so peaceful and so quiet, and it is such a dear old place to ramble round in the early morning before many people are about.

But, there, I don't suppose I should really care for it when it came to actual practice. It would be so ghastly dull and depressing in the evening, when your lamp cast uncanny shadows on the panelled walls, and the echo of distant feet rang through the cold stone corridors, and now drew nearer, and now died away, and all was death-like silence, save the beating of one's own heart.

We are creatures of the sun, we men and women. We love light and life. That is why we crowd into the towns and cities, and the country grows more and more deserted every year. In the sunlight—in the daytime, when Nature is alive and busy all around us, we like the open hill-sides and the deep woods well enough: but in the night, when our Mother Earth has gone to sleep, and left us waking, oh! the world seems so lonesome, and we get frightened, like children in a silent house. Then we sit and sob, and long for the gas-lit streets, and the sound of human voices, and the answering throb of human life. We feel so helpless and so little in the great stillness, when the dark trees rustle in the night-wind. There are so many ghosts about, and their silent sighs make us feel so sad. Let us gather together in the great cities, and light huge bonfires of a million gas-jets, and shout and sing together, and feel brave.

Harris asked me if I'd ever been in the maze at Hampton Court. He said he went in once to show somebody else the way. He had studied it up in a map, and it was so simple that it seemed foolish—hardly worth the twopence charged for admission. Harris said he thought that map must have been got up as a practical joke, because it wasn't a bit like the real thing, and only misleading. It was a country cousin that Harris took in. He said:

"We'll just go in here, so that you can say you've been, but it's very simple. It's absurd to call it a maze. You keep on taking the first turning to the right. We'll just walk round for ten minutes, and then go and get some lunch."

They met some people soon after they had got inside, who said they had been there for three-quarters of an hour, and had had about enough of it. Harris told them they could follow him, if they liked; he was just going in, and then should turn round and come out again. They said it was very kind of him, and fell behind, and followed.

They picked up various other people who wanted to get it over, as they went along, until they had absorbed all the persons in the maze. People who had given up all hopes of ever getting either in or out, or of ever seeing their home and friends again, plucked up courage at the sight of Harris and his party, and joined the procession, blessing him. Harris said he should judge there must have been twenty people, following him, in all; and one woman with a baby, who had been there all the morning, insisted on taking his arm, for fear of losing him.

Harris kept on turning to the right, but it seemed a long way, and his cousin said he supposed it was a very big maze.

"Oh, one of the largest in Europe," said Harris.

"Yes, it must be," replied the cousin, "because we've walked a good two miles already."

Harris began to think it rather strange himself, but he held on until, at last, they passed the half of a penny bun on the ground that Harris's cousin swore he had noticed there seven minutes ago. Harris said: "Oh, impossible!" but the woman with the baby said, "Not at all," as she herself had taken it from the child, and thrown it down there, just before she met Harris. She also added that she wished she never had met Harris, and expressed an opinion that he was an impostor. That made Harris mad, and he produced his map, and explained his theory.

"The map may be all right enough," said one of the party, "if you know whereabouts in it we are now."

Harris didn't know, and suggested that the best thing to do would be to go back to the entrance, and begin again. For the beginning again part of it there was not much enthusiasm; but with regard to the advisability of going back to the entrance there was complete unanimity, and so they turned, and trailed after Harris again, in the opposite direction. About ten minutes more passed, and then they found themselves in the centre.

Harris thought at first of pretending that that was what he had been aiming at; but the crowd looked dangerous, and he decided to treat it as an accident.

Anyhow, they had got something to start from then. They did know where they were, and the map was once more consulted, and the thing seemed simpler than ever, and off they started for the third time.

And three minutes later they were back in the centre again.

After that, they simply couldn't get anywhere else. Whatever way they turned brought them back to the middle. It became so regular at length, that some of the people stopped there, and waited for the others to take a walk round, and come back to them. Harris drew out his map again, after a while, but the sight of it only infuriated the mob, and they told him to go and curl his hair with it. Harris said that he couldn't help feeling that, to a certain extent, he had become unpopular.

They all got crazy at last, and sang out for the keeper, and the man came and climbed up the ladder outside, and shouted out directions to them. But all their heads were, by this time, in such a confused whirl that they were incapable of grasping anything, and so the man told them to stop where they were, and he would come to them. They huddled together, and waited; and he climbed down, and came in.

He was a young keeper, as luck would have it, and new to the business; and when he got in, he couldn't find them, and he wandered about, trying to get to them, and then *he* got lost. They caught sight of him, every now and then, rushing about the other side of the hedge, and he would see them, and rush to get to them, and they would wait there for about five minutes, and then he would reappear again in exactly the same spot, and ask them where they had been.

They had to wait till one of the old keepers came back from his dinner before they got out.

Harris said he thought it was a very fine maze, so far as he was a judge; and we agreed that we would try to get George to go into it, on our way back.

CHAPTER VII.

The river in its Sunday garb.—Dress on the river.—A chance for the men.—Absence of taste in Harris.—George's blazer.—A day with the fashion-plate young lady.—Mrs. Thomas's tomb.—The man who loves not graves and coffins and skulls.—Harris mad.—His views on George and Banks and lemonade.—He performs tricks.

It was while passing through Moulsey Lock that Harris told me about his maze experience. It took us some time to pass through, as we were the only boat, and it is a big lock. I don't think I ever remember to have seen Moulsey Lock, before, with only one boat in it. It is, I suppose, Boulter's not even excepted, the busiest lock on the river.

I have stood and watched it, sometimes, when you could not see any water at all, but only a brilliant tangle of bright blazers, and gay caps, and saucy hats, and many-coloured parasols, and silken rugs, and cloaks, and streaming ribbons, and dainty whites; when looking down into the lock from the quay, you might fancy it was a huge box into which flowers of every hue and shade had been thrown pell-mell, and lay piled up in a rainbow heap, that covered every corner.

On a fine Sunday it presents this appearance nearly all day long, while, up the stream, and down the stream, lie, waiting their turn, outside the gates, long lines of still more boats; and boats are drawing near and passing away, so that the sunny river, from the Palace up to Hampton Church, is dotted and decked with yellow, and blue, and orange, and white, and red, and pink. All the inhabitants of Hampton and Moulsey dress themselves up in boating costume, and come and mouch round the lock with their dogs, and flirt, and smoke, and watch the boats; and, altogether, what with the caps and jackets of the men, the pretty coloured dresses of the women, the excited dogs, the moving boats, the white sails, the pleasant landscape, and the sparkling water, it is one of the gayest sights I know of near this dull old London town.

The river affords a good opportunity for dress. For once in a way, we men are able to show *our* taste in colours, and I think we come out very natty, if you ask me. I always like a little red in my things—red and black. You know my hair is a sort of golden brown, rather a pretty shade I've been told, and a dark red matches it beautifully; and then I always think a light-blue necktie goes so well with it, and a pair of those Russian-leather shoes and a red silk handkerchief round the waist—a handkerchief looks so much better than a belt.

Harris always keeps to shades or mixtures of orange or yellow, but I don't think he is at all wise in this. His complexion is too dark for yellows. Yellows don't suit him: there can be no question about it. I want him to take to blue as a background, with white or cream for relief; but, there! the less taste a person has in dress, the more obstinate he always seems to be. It is a great pity, because he will never be a success as it is, while there are one or two colours in which he might not really look so bad, with his hat on.

George has bought some new things for this trip, and I'm rather vexed about them. The blazer is loud. I should not like George to know that I thought so, but there really is no other word for it. He brought it home and showed it to us on Thursday evening. We asked him what colour he called it, and he said he didn't know. He didn't think there was a name for the colour. The man had told him it was an Oriental design. George put it on, and asked us what we thought of it. Harris said that, as an object to hang over a flower-bed in early spring to frighten the birds away, he should respect it; but that, considered as an article of dress for any human being, except a Margate nigger, it made him ill. George got quite huffy; but, as Harris said, if he didn't want his opinion, why did he ask for it?

What troubles Harris and myself, with regard to it, is that we are afraid it will attract attention to the boat.

Girls, also, don't look half bad in a boat, if prettily dressed. Nothing is more fetching, to my thinking, than a tasteful boating costume. But a "boating costume," it would be as well if all ladies would understand, ought to be a costume that can be worn in a boat, and not merely under a glass-case. It utterly spoils an excursion if you have folk in the boat who are thinking all the time a good deal more of their dress than of the trip. It was my misfortune once to go for a water picnic with two ladies of this kind. We did have a lively time!

They were both beautifully got up—all lace and silky stuff, and flowers, and ribbons, and dainty shoes, and light gloves. But they were dressed for a photographic studio, not for a river picnic. They were the "boating costumes" of a French fashion-plate. It was ridiculous, fooling about in them anywhere near real earth, air, and water.

The first thing was that they thought the boat was not clean. We dusted all the seats for them, and then assured them that it was, but they didn't believe us. One of them rubbed the cushion with the forefinger of her glove, and showed the result to the other, and they both sighed, and sat down, with the air of early Christian martyrs trying to make themselves comfortable up against the stake. You are liable to occasionally splash a little when sculling, and it appeared that a drop of water ruined those costumes. The mark never came out, and a stain was left on the dress for ever.

I was stroke. I did my best. I feathered some two feet high, and I paused at the end of each stroke to let the blades drip before returning them, and I picked out a smooth bit of water to drop them into again each time. (Bow said, after a while, that he did not feel himself a sufficiently accomplished oarsman to pull with me, but that he would sit still, if I would allow him, and study my stroke. He said it interested him.) But, notwithstanding all this, and try as I would, I could not help an occasional flicker of water from going over those dresses.

The girls did not complain, but they huddled up close together, and set their lips firm, and every time a drop touched them, they visibly shrank and shuddered. It was a noble sight to see them suffering thus in silence, but it unnerved me altogether. I am too sensitive. I got wild and fitful in my rowing, and splashed more and more, the harder I tried not to.

I gave it up at last; I said I'd row bow. Bow thought the arrangement would be better too, and we changed places. The ladies gave an involuntary sigh of relief when they saw me go, and quite brightened up for a moment. Poor girls! they had better have put up with me. The man they had got now was a jolly, light-hearted, thick-headed sort of a chap, with about as much sensitiveness in him as there might be in a Newfoundland puppy. You might look daggers at him for an hour and he would not notice it, and it would not trouble him if he did. He set a good, rollicking, dashing stroke that sent the spray playing all over the boat like a fountain, and made the whole crowd sit up straight in no time. When he spread more than pint of water over one of those dresses, he would give a pleasant little laugh, and say:

"I beg your pardon, I'm sure;" and offer them his handkerchief to wipe it off with.

"Oh, it's of no consequence," the poor girls would murmur in reply, and covertly draw rugs and coats over themselves, and try and protect themselves with their lace parasols.

At lunch they had a very bad time of it. People wanted them to sit on the grass, and the grass was dusty; and the tree-trunks, against which they were invited to lean, did not appear to have been brushed for weeks; so they spread their handkerchiefs on the ground and sat on those, bolt upright. Somebody, in walking about with a plate of beef-steak pie, tripped up over a root, and sent the pie flying. None of it went over them, fortunately, but the accident suggested a fresh danger to them, and agitated them; and, whenever anybody moved about, after that, with anything in his hand that could fall and make a mess, they watched that person with growing anxiety until he sat down again.

"Now then, you girls," said our friend Bow to them, cheerily, after it was all over, "come along, you've got to wash up!"

They didn't understand him at first. When they grasped the idea, they said they feared they did not know how to wash up.

"Oh, I'll soon show you," he cried; "it's rare fun! You lie down on your—I mean you lean over the bank, you know, and sloush the things about in the water."

The elder sister said that she was afraid that they hadn't got on dresses suited to the work.

"Oh, they'll be all right," said he light-heartedly; "tuck 'em up."

And he made them do it, too. He told them that that sort of thing was half the fun of a picnic. They said it was very interesting.

Now I come to think it over, was that young man as dense-headed as we thought? or was he—no, impossible! there was such a simple, child-like expression about him!

Harris wanted to get out at Hampton Church, to go and see Mrs. Thomas's tomb.

"Who is Mrs. Thomas?" I asked.

"How should I know?" replied Harris. "She's a lady that's got a funny tomb, and I want to see it."

I objected. I don't know whether it is that I am built wrong, but I never did seem to hanker after tombstones myself. I know that the proper thing to do, when you get to a village or town, is to rush off to the churchyard, and enjoy the graves; but it is a recreation that I always deny myself. I take no interest in creeping round dim and chilly churches behind wheezy old men, and reading epitaphs. Not even the sight of a bit of cracked brass let into a stone affords me what I call real happiness.

I shock respectable sextons by the imperturbability I am able to assume before exciting inscriptions, and by my lack of enthusiasm for the local family history, while my ill-concealed anxiety to get outside wounds their feelings.

One golden morning of a sunny day, I leant against the low stone wall that guarded a little village church, and I smoked, and drank in deep, calm gladness from the sweet, restful scene—the grey old church with its clustering ivy and its quaint carved wooden porch, the white lane winding down the hill between tall rows of elms, the thatched-roof cottages peeping above their trim-kept hedges, the silver river in the hollow, the wooded hills beyond!

It was a lovely landscape. It was idyllic, poetical, and it inspired me. I felt good and noble. I felt I didn't want to be sinful and wicked any more. I would come and live here, and never do any more wrong, and lead a blameless, beautiful life, and have silver hair when I got old, and all that sort of thing.

In that moment I forgave all my friends and relations for their wickedness and cussedness, and I blessed them. They did not know that I blessed them. They went their abandoned way all unconscious of what I, far away in that peaceful village, was doing for them; but I did it, and I wished that I could let them know that I had done it, because I wanted to make them happy. I was going on thinking away all these grand, tender thoughts, when my reverie was broken in upon by a shrill piping voice crying out:

"All right, sur, I'm a-coming, I'm a-coming. It's all right, sur; don't you be in a hurry."

I looked up, and saw an old bald-headed man hobbling across the churchyard towards me, carrying a huge bunch of keys in his hand that shook and jingled at every step.

I motioned him away with silent dignity, but he still advanced, screeching out the while:

"I'm a-coming, sur, I'm a-coming. I'm a little lame. I ain't as spry as I used to be. This way, sur."

"Go away, you miserable old man," I said.

"I've come as soon as I could, sur," he replied. "My missis never see you till just this minute. You follow me, sur."

"Go away," I repeated; "leave me before I get over the wall, and slay you."

He seemed surprised.

"Don't you want to see the tombs?" he said.

"No," I answered, "I don't. I want to stop here, leaning up against this gritty old wall. Go away, and don't disturb me. I am chock full of beautiful and noble thoughts, and I want to stop like it, because it feels nice and good. Don't you come fooling about, making me mad, chivying away all my better feelings with this silly tombstone nonsense of yours. Go away, and get somebody to bury you cheap, and I'll pay half the expense."

He was bewildered for a moment. He rubbed his eyes, and looked hard at me. I seemed human enough on the outside: he couldn't make it out.

He said:

"Yuise a stranger in these parts? You don't live here?"

"No," I said, "I don't. *You* wouldn't if *I* did."

"Well then," he said, "you want to see the tombs—graves—folks been buried, you know—coffins!"

"You are an untruther," I replied, getting roused; "I do not want to see tombs—not your tombs. Why should I? We have graves of our own, our family has. Why my uncle Podger has a tomb in Kensal Green Cemetery, that is the pride of all that country-side; and my grandfather's vault at Bow is capable of accommodating eight visitors, while my great-aunt Susan has a brick grave in Finchley Churchyard, with a headstone with a coffee-pot sort of thing in bas-relief upon it, and a six-inch best white stone coping all the way round, that cost pounds. When I want graves, it is to those places that I go and revel. I do not want other folk's. When you yourself are buried, I will come and see yours. That is all I can do for you."

He burst into tears. He said that one of the tombs had a bit of stone upon the top of it that had been said by some to be probably part of the remains of the figure of a man, and that another had some words, carved upon it, that nobody had ever been able to decipher.

I still remained obdurate, and, in broken-hearted tones, he said:

"Well, won't you come and see the memorial window?"

I would not even see that, so he fired his last shot. He drew near, and whispered hoarsely:

"I've got a couple of skulls down in the crypt," he said; "come and see those. Oh, do come and see the skulls! You are a young man out for a holiday, and you want to enjoy yourself. Come and see the skulls!"

Then I turned and fled, and as I sped I heard him calling to me:

"Oh, come and see the skulls; come back and see the skulls!"

Harris, however, revels in tombs, and graves, and epitaphs, and monumental inscriptions, and the thought of not seeing Mrs. Thomas's grave made him crazy. He said he had looked forward to seeing Mrs. Thomas's grave from the first moment that the trip was proposed—said he wouldn't have joined if it hadn't been for the idea of seeing Mrs. Thomas's tomb.

I reminded him of George, and how we had to get the boat up to Shepperton by five o'clock to meet him, and then he went for George. Why was George to fool about all day, and leave us to lug this lumbering old top-heavy barge up and down the river by ourselves to meet him? Why couldn't George come and do some work? Why couldn't he have got the day off, and come down with us? Bank be blowed! What good was he at the bank?

"I never see him doing any work there," continued Harris, "whenever I go in. He sits behind a bit of glass all day, trying to look as if he was doing something. What's the good of a man behind a bit of glass? I have to work for my living. Why can't he work. What use is he there, and what's the good of their banks? They take your money, and then, when you draw a cheque, they send it back smeared all over with 'No effects,' 'Refer to drawer.' What's the good of that?

That's the sort of trick they served me twice last week. I'm not going to stand it much longer. I shall withdraw my account. If he was here, we could go and see that tomb. I don't believe he's at the bank at all. He's larking about somewhere, that's what he's doing, leaving us to do all the work. I'm going to get out, and have a drink."

I pointed out to him that we were miles away from a pub.; and then he went on about the river, and what was the good of the river, and was everyone who came on the river to die of thirst?

It is always best to let Harris have his head when he gets like this. Then he pumps himself out, and is quiet afterwards.

I reminded him that there was concentrated lemonade in the hamper, and a gallon-jar of water in the nose of the boat, and that the two only wanted mixing to make a cool and refreshing beverage.

Then he flew off about lemonade, and "such-like Sunday-school slops," as he termed them, ginger-beer, raspberry syrup, &c., &c. He said they all produced dyspepsia, and ruined body and soul alike, and were the cause of half the crime in England.

He said he must drink something, however, and climbed upon the seat, and leant over to get the bottle. It was right at the bottom of the hamper, and seemed difficult to find, and he had to lean over further and further, and, in trying to steer at the same time, from a topsy-turvy point of view, he pulled the wrong line, and sent the boat into the bank, and the shock upset him, and he dived down right into the hamper, and stood there on his head, holding on to the sides of the boat like grim death, his legs sticking up into the air. He dared not move for fear of going over, and had to stay there till I could get hold of his legs, and haul him back, and that made him madder than ever.

CHAPTER VIII.

Blackmailing.—The proper course to pursue.—Selfish boorishness of river-side landowner.—"Notice" boards.—Unchristianlike feelings of Harris.—How Harris sings a comic song.—A high-class party.—Shameful conduct of two abandoned young men.—Some useless information.—George buys a banjo.

We stopped under the willows by Kempton Park, and lunched. It is a pretty little spot there: a pleasant grass plateau, running along by the water's edge, and overhung by willows. We had just commenced the third course—the bread and jam—when a gentleman in shirt-sleeves and a short pipe came along, and wanted to know if we knew that we were trespassing. We said we hadn't given the matter sufficient consideration as yet to enable us to arrive at a definite conclusion on that point, but that, if he assured us on his word as a gentleman that we *were* trespassing, we would, without further hesitation, believe it.

He gave us the required assurance, and we thanked him, but he still hung about, and seemed to be dissatisfied, so we asked him if there was anything further that we could do for him; and Harris, who is of a chummy disposition, offered him a bit of bread and jam.

I fancy he must have belonged to some society sworn to abstain from bread and jam; for he declined it quite gruffly, as if he were vexed at being tempted with it, and he added that it was his duty to turn us off.

Harris said that if it was a duty it ought to be done, and asked the man what was his idea with regard to the best means for accomplishing it. Harris is what you would call a well-made man of about number one size, and looks hard and bony, and the man measured him up and down, and said he would go and consult his master, and then come back and chuck us both into the river.

Of course, we never saw him any more, and, of course, all he really wanted was a shilling. There are a certain number of riverside roughs who make quite an income, during the summer, by slouching about the banks and blackmailing weak-minded noodles in this way. They represent themselves as sent by the proprietor. The proper course to pursue is to offer your name and address, and leave the owner, if he really has anything to do with the matter, to summon you, and prove what damage you have done to his land by sitting down on a bit of it. But the majority of people are so intensely lazy and timid, that they prefer to encourage the imposition by giving in to it rather than put an end to it by the exertion of a little firmness.

Where it is really the owners that are to blame, they ought to be shown up. The selfishness of the riparian proprietor grows with every year. If these men had their way they would close the river Thames altogether. They actually do this along the minor tributary streams and in the backwaters. They drive posts into the bed of the stream, and draw chains across from bank to bank, and nail huge notice-boards on every tree. The sight of those notice-boards rouses every evil instinct in my nature. I feel I want to tear each one down, and hammer it over the head of the man who put it up, until I have killed him, and then I would bury him, and put the board up over the grave as a tombstone.

I mentioned these feelings of mine to Harris, and he said he had them worse than that. He said he not only felt he wanted to kill the man who caused the board to be put up, but that he should like to slaughter the whole of his family and all his friends and relations, and then burn down his house. This seemed to me to be going too far, and I said so to Harris; but he answered:

"Not a bit of it. Serve 'em all jolly well right, and I'd go and sing comic songs on the ruins."

I was vexed to hear Harris go on in this blood-thirsty strain. We never ought to allow our instincts of justice to degenerate into mere vindictiveness. It was a long while before I could get Harris to take a more Christian view of the subject, but I succeeded at last, and he promised me that he would spare the friends and relations at all events, and would not sing comic songs on the ruins.

You have never heard Harris sing a comic song, or you would understand the service I had rendered to mankind. It is one of Harris's fixed ideas that he *can* sing a comic song; the fixed idea, on the contrary, among those of Harris's friends who have heard him try, is that he *can't* and never will be able to, and that he ought not to be allowed to try.

When Harris is at a party, and is asked to sing, he replies: "Well, I can only sing a *comic* song, you know;" and he says it in a tone that implies that his singing of *that*, however, is a thing that you ought to hear once, and then die.

"Oh, that *is* nice," says the hostess. "Do sing one, Mr. Harris;" and Harris gets up, and makes for the piano, with the beaming cheeriness of a generous-minded man who is just about to give somebody something.

"Now, silence, please, everybody" says the hostess, turning round; "Mr. Harris is going to sing a comic song!"

"Oh, how jolly!" they murmur; and they hurry in from the conservatory, and come up from the stairs, and go and fetch each other from all over the house, and crowd into the drawing-room, and sit round, all smirking in anticipation.

Then Harris begins.

Well, you don't look for much of a voice in a comic song. You don't expect correct phrasing or vocalization. You don't mind if a man does find out, when in the middle of a note, that he is too high, and comes down with a jerk. You don't bother about time. You don't mind a man being two bars in front of the accompaniment, and easing up in the middle of a line to argue it out with the pianist, and then starting the verse afresh. But you do expect the words.

You don't expect a man to never remember more than the first three lines of the first verse, and to keep on repeating these until it is time to begin the chorus. You don't expect a man to break off in the middle of a line, and snigger, and say, it's very funny, but he's blest if he can think of the rest of it, and then try and make it up for himself, and, afterwards, suddenly recollect it, when he has got to an entirely different part of the song, and break off, without a word of warning, to go back and let you have it then and there. You don't—well, I will just give you an idea of Harris's comic singing, and then you can judge of it for yourself.

HARRIS (*standing up in front of piano and addressing the expectant mob*): "I'm afraid it's a very old thing, you know. I expect you all know it, you know. But it's the only thing I know. It's the Judge's song out of *Pinafore*—no, I don't mean *Pinafore*—I mean—you know what I mean—the other thing, you know. You must all join in the chorus, you know."

[*Murmurs of delight and anxiety to join in the chorus. Brilliant performance of prelude to the Judge's song in "Trial by Jury" by nervous Pianist. Moment arrives for Harris to join in. Harris takes no notice of it. Nervous pianist commences prelude over again, and Harris, commencing singing at the same time, dashes off the first two lines of the First Lord's song out of "Pinafore." Nervous pianist tries to push on with prelude, gives it up, and tries to follow Harris with accompaniment to Judge's song out "Trial by Jury," finds that doesn't answer, and tries to recollect what he is doing, and where he is, feels his mind giving way, and stops short.*]

HARRIS (*with kindly encouragement*): "It's all right. You're doing it very well, indeed—go on."

NERVOUS PIANIST: "I'm afraid there's a mistake somewhere. What are you singing?"

HARRIS (*promptly*): "Why the Judge's song out of Trial by Jury. Don't you know it?"

SOME FRIEND OF HARRIS'S (*from the back of the room*): "No, you're not, you chuckle-head, you're singing the Admiral's song from *Pinafore*."

[*Long argument between Harris and Harris's friend as to what Harris is really singing. Friend finally suggests that it doesn't matter what Harris is singing so long as Harris gets on and sings it, and Harris, with an evident sense of injustice rankling inside him, requests pianist to begin again. Pianist, thereupon, starts prelude to the Admiral's song, and Harris, seizing what he considers to be a favourable opening in the music, begins.*]

HARRIS:

"'When I was young and called to the Bar.'"

[*General roar of laughter, taken by Harris as a compliment. Pianist, thinking of his wife and family, gives up the unequal contest and retires; his place being taken by a stronger-nerved man.*]

THE NEW PIANIST (*cheerily*): "Now then, old man, you start off, and I'll follow. We won't bother about any prelude."

HARRIS (*upon whom the explanation of matters has slowly dawned—laughing*): "By Jove! I beg your pardon. Of course—I've been mixing up the two songs. It was Jenkins confused me, you know. Now then.

[*Singing; his voice appearing to come from the cellar, and suggesting the first low warnings of an approaching earthquake.*]

"'When I was young I served a term
As office-boy to an attorney's firm.'

(*Aside to pianist*): "It is too low, old man; we'll have that over again, if you don't mind."

[*Sings first two lines over again, in a high falsetto this time. Great surprise on the part of the audience. Nervous old lady near the fire begins to cry, and has to be led out.*]

HARRIS (*continuing*):

CHAPTER VIII.

> "'I swept the windows and I swept the door,
>   And I—'

No—no, I cleaned the windows of the big front door. And I polished up the floor—no, dash it—I beg your pardon—funny thing, I can't think of that line. And I—and I—Oh, well, we'll get on to the chorus, and chance it (*sings*):

> "'And I diddle-diddle-diddle-diddle-diddle-diddle-de,
>   Till now I am the ruler of the Queen's navee.'

Now then, chorus—it is the last two lines repeated, you know.
GENERAL CHORUS:

> "And he diddle-diddle-diddle-diddle-diddle-diddle-dee'd,
>   Till now he is the ruler of the Queen's navee."

And Harris never sees what an ass he is making of himself, and how he is annoying a lot of people who never did him any harm. He honestly imagines that he has given them a treat, and says he will sing another comic song after supper.

Speaking of comic songs and parties, reminds me of a rather curious incident at which I once assisted; which, as it throws much light upon the inner mental working of human nature in general, ought, I think, to be recorded in these pages.

We were a fashionable and highly cultured party. We had on our best clothes, and we talked pretty, and were very happy—all except two young fellows, students, just returned from Germany, commonplace young men, who seemed restless and uncomfortable, as if they found the proceedings slow. The truth was, we were too clever for them. Our brilliant but polished conversation, and our high-class tastes, were beyond them. They were out of place, among us. They never ought to have been there at all. Everybody agreed upon that, later on.

We played *morceaux* from the old German masters. We discussed philosophy and ethics. We flirted with graceful dignity. We were even humorous—in a high-class way.

Somebody recited a French poem after supper, and we said it was beautiful; and then a lady sang a sentimental ballad in Spanish, and it made one or two of us weep—it was so pathetic.

And then those two young men got up, and asked us if we had ever heard Herr Slossenn Boschen (who had just arrived, and was then down in the supper-room) sing his great German comic song.

None of us had heard it, that we could remember.

The young men said it was the funniest song that had ever been written, and that, if we liked, they would get Herr Slossenn Boschen, whom they knew very well, to sing it. They said it was so funny that, when Herr Slossenn Boschen had sung it once before the German Emperor, he (the German Emperor) had had to be carried off to bed.

They said nobody could sing it like Herr Slossenn Boschen; he was so intensely serious all through it that you might fancy he was reciting a tragedy, and that, of course, made it all the funnier. They said he never once suggested by his tone or manner that he was singing anything funny—that would spoil it. It was his air of seriousness, almost of pathos, that made it so irresistibly amusing.

We said we yearned to hear it, that we wanted a good laugh; and they went downstairs, and fetched Herr Slossenn Boschen.

He appeared to be quite pleased to sing it, for he came up at once, and sat down to the piano without another word.

"Oh, it will amuse you. You will laugh," whispered the two young men, as they passed through the room, and took up an unobtrusive position behind the Professor's back.

Herr Slossenn Boschen accompanied himself. The prelude did not suggest a comic song exactly. It was a weird, soulful air. It quite made one's flesh creep; but we murmured to one another that it was the German method, and prepared to enjoy it.

I don't understand German myself. I learned it at school, but forgot every word of it two years after I had left, and have felt much better ever since. Still, I did not want the people there to guess my ignorance; so I hit upon what I thought to be rather a good idea. I kept my eye on the two young students, and followed them. When they tittered, I tittered; when they roared, I roared; and I also threw in a little snigger all by myself now and then, as if I had seen a bit of humour that had escaped the others. I considered this particularly artful on my part.

I noticed, as the song progressed, that a good many other people seemed to have their eye fixed on the two young men, as well as myself. These other people also tittered when the young men tittered, and roared when the young men roared; and, as the two young men tittered and roared and exploded with laughter pretty continuously all through the song, it went exceedingly well.

And yet that German Professor did not seem happy. At first, when we began to laugh, the expression of his face was one of intense surprise, as if laughter were the very last thing he had expected to be greeted with. We thought this very funny: we said his earnest manner was half the humour. The slightest hint on his part that he knew how funny he was would have completely ruined it all. As we continued to laugh, his surprise gave way to an air of annoyance and indignation, and he scowled fiercely round upon us all (except upon the two young men who, being behind him, he could not see). That sent us into convulsions. We told each other that it would be the death of us, this thing. The words alone, we said, were enough to send us into fits, but added to his mock seriousness—oh, it was too much!

In the last verse, he surpassed himself. He glowered round upon us with a look of such concentrated ferocity that, but for our being forewarned as to the German method of comic singing, we should have been nervous; and he threw such a wailing note of agony into the weird music that, if we had not known it was a funny song, we might have wept.

He finished amid a perfect shriek of laughter. We said it was the funniest thing we had ever heard in all our lives. We said how strange it was that, in the face of things like these, there should be a popular notion that the Germans hadn't any sense of humour. And we asked the Professor why he didn't translate the song into English, so that the common people could understand it, and hear what a real comic song was like.

Then Herr Slossenn Boschen got up, and went on awful. He swore at us in German (which I should judge to be a singularly effective language for that purpose), and he danced, and shook his fists, and called us all the English he knew. He said he had never been so insulted in all his life.

It appeared that the song was not a comic song at all. It was about a young girl who lived in the Hartz Mountains, and who had given up her life to save her lover's soul; and he died, and met her spirit in the air; and then, in the last verse, he jilted her spirit, and went on with another spirit—I'm not quite sure of the details, but it was something very sad, I know. Herr Boschen said he had sung it once before the German Emperor, and he (the German Emperor) had sobbed like a little child. He (Herr Boschen) said it was generally acknowledged to be one of the most tragic and pathetic songs in the German language.

It was a trying situation for us—very trying. There seemed to be no answer. We looked around for the two young men who had done this thing, but they had left the house in an unostentatious manner immediately after the end of the song.

That was the end of that party. I never saw a party break up so quietly, and with so little fuss. We never said good-night even to one another. We came downstairs one at a time, walking softly, and keeping the shady side. We asked the servant for our hats and coats in whispers, and opened the door for ourselves, and slipped out, and got round the corner quickly, avoiding each other as much as possible.

I have never taken much interest in German songs since then.

We reached Sunbury Lock at half-past three. The river is sweetly pretty just there before you come to the gates, and the backwater is charming; but don't attempt to row up it.

I tried to do so once. I was sculling, and asked the fellows who were steering if they thought it could be done, and they said, oh, yes, they thought so, if I pulled hard. We were just under the little foot-bridge that crosses it between the two weirs, when they said this, and I bent down over the sculls, and set myself up, and pulled.

I pulled splendidly. I got well into a steady rhythmical swing. I put my arms, and my legs, and my back into it. I set myself a good, quick, dashing stroke, and worked in really grand style. My two friends said it was a pleasure to watch me. At the end of five minutes, I thought we ought to be pretty near the weir, and I looked up. We were under the bridge, in exactly the same spot that we were when I began, and there were those two idiots, injuring themselves by violent laughing. I had been grinding away like mad to keep that boat stuck still under that bridge. I let other people pull up backwaters against strong streams now.

We sculled up to Walton, a rather large place for a riverside town. As with all riverside places, only the tiniest corner of it comes down to the water, so that from the boat you might fancy it was a village of some half-dozen houses, all told.

Windsor and Abingdon are the only towns between London and Oxford that you can really see anything of from the stream. All the others hide round corners, and merely peep at the river down one street: my thanks to them for being so considerate, and leaving the river-banks to woods and fields and water-works.

Even Reading, though it does its best to spoil and sully and make hideous as much of the river as it can reach, is good-natured enough to keep its ugly face a good deal out of sight.

Cæsar, of course, had a little place at Walton—a camp, or an entrenchment, or something of that sort. Cæsar was a regular up-river man. Also Queen Elizabeth, she was there, too. You can never get away from that woman, go where you will. Cromwell and Bradshaw (not the guide man, but the King Charles's head man) likewise sojourned here. They must have been quite a pleasant little party, altogether.

There is an iron "scold's bridle" in Walton Church. They used these things in ancient days for curbing women's tongues. They have given up the attempt now. I suppose iron was getting scarce, and nothing else would be strong enough.

There are also tombs of note in the church, and I was afraid I should never get Harris past them; but he didn't seem to think of them, and we went on. Above the bridge the river winds tremendously. This makes it look picturesque; but it irritates you from a towing or sculling point of view, and causes argument between the man who is pulling and the man who is steering.

You pass Oatlands Park on the right bank here. It is a famous old place. Henry VIII. stole it from some one or the other, I forget whom now, and lived in it. There is a grotto in the park which you can see for a fee, and which is supposed to be very wonderful; but I cannot see much in it myself. The late Duchess of York, who lived at Oatlands, was very fond of dogs, and kept an immense number. She had a special graveyard made, in which to bury them when they died, and there they lie, about fifty of them, with a tombstone over each, and an epitaph inscribed thereon.

Well, I dare say they deserve it quite as much as the average Christian does.

At "Corway Stakes"—the first bend above Walton Bridge—was fought a battle between Cæsar and Cassivelaunus. Cassivelaunus had prepared the river for Cæsar, by planting it full of stakes (and had, no doubt, put up a notice-board). But Cæsar crossed in spite of this. You couldn't choke Cæsar off that river. He is the sort of man we want round the backwaters now.

Halliford and Shepperton are both pretty little spots where they touch the river; but there is nothing remarkable about either of them. There is a tomb in Shepperton churchyard, however, with a poem on it, and I was nervous lest Harris should want to get out and fool round it. I saw him fix a longing eye on the landing-stage as we drew near it, so I managed, by an adroit movement, to jerk his cap into the water, and in the excitement of recovering that, and his indignation at my clumsiness, he forgot all about his beloved graves.

At Weybridge, the Wey (a pretty little stream, navigable for small boats up to Guildford, and one which I have always been making up my mind to explore, and never have), the Bourne, and the Basingstoke Canal all enter the Thames together. The lock is just opposite the town, and the first thing that we saw, when we came in view of it, was George's blazer on one of the lock gates, closer inspection showing that George was inside it.

Montmorency set up a furious barking, I shrieked, Harris roared; George waved his hat, and yelled back. The lock-keeper rushed out with a drag, under the impression that somebody had fallen into the lock, and appeared annoyed at finding that no one had.

George had rather a curious oilskin-covered parcel in his hand. It was round and flat at one end, with a long straight handle sticking out of it.

"What's that?" said Harris—"a frying-pan?"

"No," said George, with a strange, wild look glittering in his eyes; "they are all the rage this season; everybody has got them up the river. It's a banjo."

"I never knew you played the banjo!" cried Harris and I, in one breath.

"Not exactly," replied George: "but it's very easy, they tell me; and I've got the instruction book!"

CHAPTER IX.

George is introduced to work.—Heathenish instincts of tow-lines.—Ungrateful conduct of a double-sculling skiff.—Towers and towed.—A use discovered for lovers.—Strange disappearance of an elderly lady.—Much haste, less speed.—Being towed by girls: exciting sensation.—The missing lock or the haunted river.—Music.—Saved!

We made George work, now we had got him. He did not want to work, of course; that goes without saying. He had had a hard time in the City, so he explained. Harris, who is callous in his nature, and not prone to pity, said:

"Ah! and now you are going to have a hard time on the river for a change; change is good for everyone. Out you get!"

He could not in conscience—not even George's conscience—object, though he did suggest that, perhaps, it would be better for him to stop in the boat, and get tea ready, while Harris and I towed, because getting tea was such a worrying work, and Harris and I looked tired. The only reply we made to this, however, was to pass him over the tow-line, and he took it, and stepped out.

There is something very strange and unaccountable about a tow-line. You roll it up with as much patience and care as you would take to fold up a new pair of trousers, and five minutes afterwards, when you pick it up, it is one ghastly, soul-revolting tangle.

I do not wish to be insulting, but I firmly believe that if you took an average tow-line, and stretched it out straight across the middle of a field, and then turned your back on it for thirty seconds, that, when you looked round again, you would find that it had got itself altogether in a heap in the middle of the field, and had twisted itself up, and tied itself into knots, and lost its two ends, and become all loops; and it would take you a good half-hour, sitting down there on the grass and swearing all the while, to disentangle it again.

That is my opinion of tow-lines in general. Of course, there may be honourable exceptions; I do not say that there are not. There may be tow-lines that are a credit to their profession—conscientious, respectable tow-lines—tow-lines that do not imagine they are crochet-work, and try to knit themselves up into antimacassars the instant they are left to themselves. I say there *may* be such tow-lines; I sincerely hope there are. But I have not met with them.

This tow-line I had taken in myself just before we had got to the lock. I would not let Harris touch it, because he is careless. I had looped it round slowly and cautiously, and tied it up in the middle, and folded it in two, and laid it down gently at the bottom of the boat. Harris had lifted it up scientifically, and had put it into George's hand. George had taken it firmly, and held it away from him, and had begun to unravel it as if he were taking the swaddling clothes off a new-born infant; and, before he had unwound a dozen yards, the thing was more like a badly-made door-mat than anything else.

It is always the same, and the same sort of thing always goes on in connection with it. The man on the bank, who is trying to disentangle it, thinks all the fault lies with the man who rolled it up; and when a man up the river thinks a thing, he says it.

"What have you been trying to do with it, make a fishing-net of it? You've made a nice mess you have; why couldn't you wind it up properly, you silly dummy?" he grunts from time to time as he struggles wildly with it, and lays it out flat on the tow-path, and runs round and round it, trying to find the end.

On the other hand, the man who wound it up thinks the whole cause of the muddle rests with the man who is trying to unwind it.

"It was all right when you took it!" he exclaims indignantly. "Why don't you think what you are doing? You go about things in such a slap-dash style. You'd get a scaffolding pole entangled *you* would!"

And they feel so angry with one another that they would like to hang each other with the thing. Ten minutes go by, and the first man gives a yell and goes mad, and dances on the rope, and tries to pull it straight by seizing hold of the first piece that comes to his hand and hauling at it. Of course, this only gets it into a tighter tangle than ever. Then the second man climbs out of the boat and comes to help him, and they get in each other's way, and hinder one another. They both get hold of the same bit of line, and pull at it in opposite directions, and wonder where it is caught. In the end, they do get it clear, and then turn round and find that the boat has drifted off, and is making straight for the weir.

This really happened once to my own knowledge. It was up by Boveney, one rather windy morning. We were pulling down stream, and, as we came round the bend, we noticed a couple of men on the bank. They were looking at each other with as bewildered and helplessly miserable expression as I have ever witnessed on any human countenance before or since, and they held a long tow-line between them. It was clear that something had happened, so we eased up and asked them what was the matter.

"Why, our boat's gone off!" they replied in an indignant tone. "We just got out to disentangle the tow-line, and when we looked round, it was gone!"

And they seemed hurt at what they evidently regarded as a mean and ungrateful act on the part of the boat.

We found the truant for them half a mile further down, held by some rushes, and we brought it back to them. I bet they did not give that boat another chance for a week.

I shall never forget the picture of those two men walking up and down the bank with a tow-line, looking for their boat.

One sees a good many funny incidents up the river in connection with towing. One of the most common is the sight of a couple of towers, walking briskly along, deep in an animated discussion, while the man in the boat, a hundred yards behind them, is vainly shrieking to them to stop, and making frantic signs of distress with a scull. Something has gone wrong; the rudder has come off, or the boat-hook has slipped overboard, or his hat has dropped into the water and is floating rapidly down stream.

He calls to them to stop, quite gently and politely at first.

"Hi! stop a minute, will you?" he shouts cheerily. "I've dropped my hat over-board."

Then: "Hi! Tom—Dick! can't you hear?" not quite so affably this time.

Then: "Hi! Confound *you*, you dunder-headed idiots! Hi! stop! Oh you—!"

After that he springs up, and dances about, and roars himself red in the face, and curses everything he knows. And the small boys on the bank stop and jeer at him, and pitch stones at him as he is pulled along past them, at the rate of four miles an hour, and can't get out.

Much of this sort of trouble would be saved if those who are towing would keep remembering that they are towing, and give a pretty frequent look round to see how their man is getting on. It is best to let one person tow. When two are doing it, they get chattering, and forget, and the boat itself, offering, as it does, but little resistance, is of no real service in reminding them of the fact.

As an example of how utterly oblivious a pair of towers can be to their work, George told us, later on in the evening, when we were discussing the subject after supper, of a very curious instance.

He and three other men, so he said, were sculling a very heavily laden boat up from Maidenhead one evening, and a little above Cookham lock they noticed a fellow and a girl, walking along the towpath, both deep in an apparently interesting and absorbing conversation. They were carrying a boat-hook between them, and, attached to the boat-hook was a tow-line, which trailed behind them, its end in the water. No boat was near, no boat was in sight. There must have been a boat attached to that tow-line at some time or other, that was certain; but what had become of it, what ghastly fate had overtaken it, and those who had been left in it, was buried in mystery. Whatever the accident may have been, however, it had in no way disturbed the young lady and gentleman, who were towing. They had the boat-hook and they had the line, and that seemed to be all that they thought necessary to their work.

George was about to call out and wake them up, but, at that moment, a bright idea flashed across him, and he didn't. He got the hitcher instead, and reached over, and drew in the end of the tow-line; and they made a loop in it, and put it over their mast, and then they tidied up the sculls, and went and sat down in the stern, and lit their pipes.

And that young man and young woman towed those four hulking chaps and a heavy boat up to Marlow.

George said he never saw so much thoughtful sadness concentrated into one glance before, as when, at the lock, that young couple grasped the idea that, for the last two miles, they had been towing the wrong boat. George fancied that, if it had not been for the restraining influence of the sweet woman at his side, the young man might have given way to violent language.

The maiden was the first to recover from her surprise, and, when she did, she clasped her hands, and said, wildly:

"Oh, Henry, then *where* is auntie?"

"Did they ever recover the old lady?" asked Harris.

George replied he did not know.

Another example of the dangerous want of sympathy between tower and towed was witnessed by George and myself once up near Walton. It was where the tow-path shelves gently down into the water, and we were camping on the opposite bank, noticing things in general. By-and-by a small boat came in sight, towed through the water at a tremendous pace by a powerful barge horse, on which sat a very small boy. Scattered about the boat, in dreamy and reposeful attitudes, lay five fellows, the man who was steering having a particularly restful appearance.

"I should like to see him pull the wrong line," murmured George, as they passed. And at that precise moment the man did it, and the boat rushed up the bank with a noise like the ripping up of forty thousand linen sheets. Two men, a hamper, and three oars immediately left the boat on the larboard side, and reclined on the bank, and one and a half moments afterwards, two other men disembarked from the starboard, and sat down among boat-hooks and sails and carpet-bags and bottles. The last man went on twenty yards further, and then got out on his head.

This seemed to sort of lighten the boat, and it went on much easier, the small boy shouting at the top of his voice, and urging his steed into a gallop. The fellows sat up and stared at one another. It was some seconds before they realised what had happened to them, but, when they did, they began to shout lustily for the boy to stop. He, however, was too much occupied with the horse to hear them, and we watched them, flying after him, until the distance hid them from view.

I cannot say I was sorry at their mishap. Indeed, I only wish that all the young fools who have their boats towed in this fashion—and plenty do—could meet with similar misfortunes. Besides the risk they run themselves, they become a danger and an annoyance to every other boat they pass. Going at the pace they do, it is impossible for them to get out of anybody else's way, or for anybody else to get out of theirs. Their line gets hitched across your mast, and overturns you, or it catches somebody in the boat, and either throws them into the water, or cuts their face open. The best plan is to stand your ground, and be prepared to keep them off with the butt-end of a mast.

Of all experiences in connection with towing, the most exciting is being towed by girls. It is a sensation that nobody ought to miss. It takes three girls to tow always; two hold the rope, and the other one runs round and round, and giggles. They generally begin by getting themselves tied up. They get the line round their legs, and have to sit down on the path and undo each other, and then they twist it round their necks, and are nearly strangled. They fix it straight, however, at last, and start off at a run, pulling the boat along at quite a dangerous pace. At the end of a hundred yards they are naturally breathless, and suddenly stop, and all sit down on the grass and laugh, and your boat drifts out to mid-stream and turns round, before you know what has happened, or can get hold of a scull. Then they stand up, and are surprised.

"Oh, look!" they say; "he's gone right out into the middle."

They pull on pretty steadily for a bit, after this, and then it all at once occurs to one of them that she will pin up her frock, and they ease up for the purpose, and the boat runs aground.

You jump up, and push it off, and you shout to them not to stop.

"Yes. What's the matter?" they shout back.

"Don't stop," you roar.

"Don't what?"

"Don't stop—go on—go on!"

"Go back, Emily, and see what it is they want," says one; and Emily comes back, and asks what it is.

"What do you want?" she says; "anything happened?"

"No," you reply, "it's all right; only go on, you know—don't stop."

"Why not?"

"Why, we can't steer, if you keep stopping. You must keep some way on the boat."

"Keep some what?"

"Some way—you must keep the boat moving."

"Oh, all right, I'll tell 'em. Are we doing it all right?"

"Oh, yes, very nicely, indeed, only don't stop."

"It doesn't seem difficult at all. I thought it was so hard."

"Oh, no, it's simple enough. You want to keep on steady at it, that's all."

"I see. Give me out my red shawl, it's under the cushion."

You find the shawl, and hand it out, and by this time another one has come back and thinks she will have hers too, and they take Mary's on chance, and Mary does not want it, so they bring it back and have a pocket-comb instead. It is about twenty minutes before they get off again, and, at the next corner, they see a cow, and you have to leave the boat to chivy the cow out of their way.

There is never a dull moment in the boat while girls are towing it.

George got the line right after a while, and towed us steadily on to Penton Hook. There we discussed the important question of camping. We had decided to sleep on board that night, and we had either to lay up just about there, or go on past Staines. It seemed early to think about shutting up then, however, with the sun still in the heavens, and we settled to push straight on for Runnymead, three and a half miles further, a quiet wooded part of the river, and where there is good shelter.

We all wished, however, afterward that we had stopped at Penton Hook. Three or four miles up stream is a trifle, early in the morning, but it is a weary pull at the end of a long day. You take no interest in the scenery during these last few miles. You do not chat and laugh. Every half-mile you cover seems like two. You can hardly believe you are only where you are, and you are convinced that the map must be wrong; and, when you have trudged along for what seems to you at least ten miles, and still the lock is not in sight, you begin to seriously fear that somebody must have sneaked it, and run off with it.

I remember being terribly upset once up the river (in a figurative sense, I mean). I was out with a young lady—cousin on my mother's side—and we were pulling down to Goring. It was rather late, and we were anxious to get in—at least *she* was anxious to get in. It was half-past six when we reached Benson's lock, and dusk was drawing on, and she began to get excited then. She said she must be in to supper. I said it was a thing I felt I wanted to be in at, too; and I drew out a map I had with me to see exactly how far it was. I saw it was just a mile and a half to the next lock—Wallingford—and five on from there to Cleeve.

"Oh, it's all right!" I said. "We'll be through the next lock before seven, and then there is only one more;" and I settled down and pulled steadily away.

We passed the bridge, and soon after that I asked if she saw the lock. She said no, she did not see any lock; and I said, "Oh!" and pulled on. Another five minutes went by, and then I asked her to look again.

"No," she said; "I can't see any signs of a lock."

"You—you are sure you know a lock, when you do see one?" I asked hesitatingly, not wishing to offend her.

The question did offend her, however, and she suggested that I had better look for myself; so I laid down the sculls, and took a view. The river stretched out straight before us in the twilight for about a mile; not a ghost of a lock was to be seen.

"You don't think we have lost our way, do you?" asked my companion.

I did not see how that was possible; though, as I suggested, we might have somehow got into the weir stream, and be making for the falls.

This idea did not comfort her in the least, and she began to cry. She said we should both be drowned, and that it was a judgment on her for coming out with me.

It seemed an excessive punishment, I thought; but my cousin thought not, and hoped it would all soon be over.

I tried to reassure her, and to make light of the whole affair. I said that the fact evidently was that I was not rowing as fast as I fancied I was, but that we should soon reach the lock now; and I pulled on for another mile.

Then I began to get nervous myself. I looked again at the map. There was Wallingford lock, clearly marked, a mile and a half below Benson's. It was a good, reliable map; and, besides, I recollected the lock myself. I had been through it twice. Where were we? What had happened to us? I began to think it must be all a dream, and that I was really asleep in bed, and should wake up in a minute, and be told it was past ten.

I asked my cousin if she thought it could be a dream, and she replied that she was just about to ask me the same question; and then we both wondered if we were both asleep, and if so, who was the real one that was dreaming, and who was the one that was only a dream; it got quite interesting.

I still went on pulling, however, and still no lock came in sight, and the river grew more and more gloomy and mysterious under the gathering shadows of night, and things seemed to be getting weird and uncanny. I thought of hobgoblins and banshees, and will-o'-the-wisps, and those wicked girls who sit up all night on rocks, and lure people into whirl-pools and things; and I wished I had been a better man, and knew more hymns; and in the middle of these reflections I heard the blessed strains of "He's got 'em on," played, badly, on a concertina, and knew that we were saved.

I do not admire the tones of a concertina, as a rule; but, oh! how beautiful the music seemed to us both then—far, far more beautiful than the voice of Orpheus or the lute of Apollo, or anything of that sort could have sounded. Heavenly melody, in our then state of mind, would only have still further harrowed us. A soul-moving harmony, correctly performed, we should have taken as a spirit-warning, and have given up all hope. But about the strains of "He's got 'em on," jerked spasmodically, and with involuntary variations, out of a wheezy accordion, there was something singularly human and reassuring.

The sweet sounds drew nearer, and soon the boat from which they were worked lay alongside us.

It contained a party of provincial 'Arrys and 'Arriets, out for a moonlight sail. (There was not any moon, but that was not their fault.) I never saw more attractive, lovable people in all my life. I hailed them, and asked if they could tell me the way to Wallingford lock; and I explained that I had been looking for it for the last two hours.

"Wallingford lock!" they answered. "Lor' love you, sir, that's been done away with for over a year. There ain't no Wallingford lock now, sir. You're close to Cleeve now. Blow me tight if 'ere ain't a gentleman been looking for Wallingford lock, Bill!"

I had never thought of that. I wanted to fall upon all their necks and bless them; but the stream was running too strong just there to allow of this, so I had to content myself with mere cold-sounding words of gratitude.

We thanked them over and over again, and we said it was a lovely night, and we wished them a pleasant trip, and, I think, I invited them all to come and spend a week with me, and my cousin said her mother would be so pleased to see them. And we sang the soldiers' chorus out of *Faust*, and got home in time for supper, after all.

CHAPTER X.

**Our first night.—Under canvas.—An appeal for help.—
Contrariness of tea-kettles, how to overcome.—Supper.—
How to feel virtuous.—Wanted! a comfortably-appointed,
well-drained desert island, neighbourhood of South Pacific
Ocean preferred.—Funny thing that happened to George's
father.—a restless night.**

Harris and I began to think that Bell Weir lock must have been done away with
after the same manner. George had towed us up to Staines, and we had taken the
boat from there, and it seemed that we were dragging fifty tons after us, and were
walking forty miles. It was half-past seven when we were through, and we all got
in, and sculled up close to the left bank, looking out for a spot to haul up in.

We had originally intended to go on to Magna Charta Island, a sweetly pretty
part of the river, where it winds through a soft, green valley, and to camp in one
of the many picturesque inlets to be found round that tiny shore. But, somehow,
we did not feel that we yearned for the picturesque nearly so much now as we had
earlier in the day. A bit of water between a coal-barge and a gas-works would
have quite satisfied us for that night. We did not want scenery. We wanted to
have our supper and go to bed. However, we did pull up to the point—"Picnic
Point," it is called—and dropped into a very pleasant nook under a great elm-tree,
to the spreading roots of which we fastened the boat.

Then we thought we were going to have supper (we had dispensed with tea, so
as to save time), but George said no; that we had better get the canvas up first,
before it got quite dark, and while we could see what we were doing. Then, he
said, all our work would be done, and we could sit down to eat with an easy mind.

That canvas wanted more putting up than I think any of us had bargained for.
It looked so simple in the abstract. You took five iron arches, like gigantic croquet hoops, and fitted them up over the boat, and then stretched the canvas over
them, and fastened it down: it would take quite ten minutes, we thought.

That was an under-estimate.

We took up the hoops, and began to drop them into the sockets placed for them. You would not imagine this to be dangerous work; but, looking back now, the wonder to me is that any of us are alive to tell the tale. They were not hoops, they were demons. First they would not fit into their sockets at all, and we had to jump on them, and kick them, and hammer at them with the boat-hook; and, when they were in, it turned out that they were the wrong hoops for those particular sockets, and they had to come out again.

But they would not come out, until two of us had gone and struggled with them for five minutes, when they would jump up suddenly, and try and throw us into the water and drown us. They had hinges in the middle, and, when we were not looking, they nipped us with these hinges in delicate parts of the body; and, while we were wrestling with one side of the hoop, and endeavouring to persuade it to do its duty, the other side would come behind us in a cowardly manner, and hit us over the head.

We got them fixed at last, and then all that was to be done was to arrange the covering over them. George unrolled it, and fastened one end over the nose of the boat. Harris stood in the middle to take it from George and roll it on to me, and I kept by the stern to receive it. It was a long time coming down to me. George did his part all right, but it was new work to Harris, and he bungled it.

How he managed it I do not know, he could not explain himself; but by some mysterious process or other he succeeded, after ten minutes of superhuman effort, in getting himself completely rolled up in it. He was so firmly wrapped round and tucked in and folded over, that he could not get out. He, of course, made frantic struggles for freedom—the birthright of every Englishman,—and, in doing so (I learned this afterwards), knocked over George; and then George, swearing at Harris, began to struggle too, and got *himself* entangled and rolled up.

I knew nothing about all this at the time. I did not understand the business at all myself. I had been told to stand where I was, and wait till the canvas came to me, and Montmorency and I stood there and waited, both as good as gold. We could see the canvas being violently jerked and tossed about, pretty considerably; but we supposed this was part of the method, and did not interfere.

We also heard much smothered language coming from underneath it, and we guessed that they were finding the job rather troublesome, and concluded that we would wait until things had got a little simpler before we joined in.

We waited some time, but matters seemed to get only more and more involved, until, at last, George's head came wriggling out over the side of the boat, and spoke up.

It said:

"Give us a hand here, can't you, you cuckoo; standing there like a stuffed mummy, when you see we are both being suffocated, you dummy!"

I never could withstand an appeal for help, so I went and undid them; not before it was time, either, for Harris was nearly black in the face.

It took us half an hour's hard labour, after that, before it was properly up, and then we cleared the decks, and got out supper. We put the kettle on to boil, up in the nose of the boat, and went down to the stern and pretended to take no notice of it, but set to work to get the other things out.

That is the only way to get a kettle to boil up the river. If it sees that you are waiting for it and are anxious, it will never even sing. You have to go away and begin your meal, as if you were not going to have any tea at all. You must not even look round at it. Then you will soon hear it sputtering away, mad to be made into tea.

It is a good plan, too, if you are in a great hurry, to talk very loudly to each other about how you don't need any tea, and are not going to have any. You get near the kettle, so that it can overhear you, and then you shout out, "I don't want any tea; do you, George?" to which George shouts back, "Oh, no, I don't like tea; we'll have lemonade instead—tea's so indigestible." Upon which the kettle boils over, and puts the stove out.

We adopted this harmless bit of trickery, and the result was that, by the time everything else was ready, the tea was waiting. Then we lit the lantern, and squatted down to supper.

We wanted that supper.

For five-and-thirty minutes not a sound was heard throughout the length and breadth of that boat, save the clank of cutlery and crockery, and the steady grinding of four sets of molars. At the end of five-and-thirty minutes, Harris said, "Ah!" and took his left leg out from under him and put his right one there instead.

Five minutes afterwards, George said, "Ah!" too, and threw his plate out on the bank; and, three minutes later than that, Montmorency gave the first sign of contentment he had exhibited since we had started, and rolled over on his side, and spread his legs out; and then I said, "Ah!" and bent my head back, and bumped it against one of the hoops, but I did not mind it. I did not even swear.

How good one feels when one is full—how satisfied with ourselves and with the world! People who have tried it, tell me that a clear conscience makes you very happy and contented; but a full stomach does the business quite as well, and is cheaper, and more easily obtained. One feels so forgiving and generous after a substantial and well-digested meal—so noble-minded, so kindly-hearted.

It is very strange, this domination of our intellect by our digestive organs. We cannot work, we cannot think, unless our stomach wills so. It dictates to us our emotions, our passions. After eggs and bacon, it says, "Work!" After beefsteak and porter, it says, "Sleep!" After a cup of tea (two spoonsful for each cup, and don't let it stand more than three minutes), it says to the brain, "Now, rise, and show your strength. Be eloquent, and deep, and tender; see, with a clear eye, into Nature and into life; spread your white wings of quivering thought, and soar, a god-like spirit, over the whirling world beneath you, up through long lanes of flaming stars to the gates of eternity!"

After hot muffins, it says, "Be dull and soulless, like a beast of the field—a brainless animal, with listless eye, unlit by any ray of fancy, or of hope, or fear, or love, or life." And after brandy, taken in sufficient quantity, it says, "Now, come, fool, grin and tumble, that your fellow-men may laugh—drivel in folly, and splutter in senseless sounds, and show what a helpless ninny is poor man whose wit and will are drowned, like kittens, side by side, in half an inch of alcohol."

We are but the veriest, sorriest slaves of our stomach. Reach not after morality and righteousness, my friends; watch vigilantly your stomach, and diet it with care and judgment. Then virtue and contentment will come and reign within your heart, unsought by any effort of your own; and you will be a good citizen, a loving husband, and a tender father—a noble, pious man.

Before our supper, Harris and George and I were quarrelsome and snappy and ill-tempered; after our supper, we sat and beamed on one another, and we beamed upon the dog, too. We loved each other, we loved everybody. Harris, in moving about, trod on George's corn. Had this happened before supper, George would have expressed wishes and desires concerning Harris's fate in this world and the next that would have made a thoughtful man shudder.

As it was, he said: "Steady, old man; 'ware wheat."

And Harris, instead of merely observing, in his most unpleasant tones, that a fellow could hardly help treading on some bit of George's foot, if he had to move about at all within ten yards of where George was sitting, suggesting that George never ought to come into an ordinary sized boat with feet that length, and advising him to hang them over the side, as he would have done before supper, now said: "Oh, I'm so sorry, old chap; I hope I haven't hurt you."

And George said: "Not at all;" that it was his fault; and Harris said no, it was his.

It was quite pretty to hear them.

We lit our pipes, and sat, looking out on the quiet night, and talked.

George said why could not we be always like this—away from the world, with its sin and temptation, leading sober, peaceful lives, and doing good. I said it was the sort of thing I had often longed for myself; and we discussed the possibility of our going away, we four, to some handy, well-fitted desert island, and living there in the woods.

Harris said that the danger about desert islands, as far as he had heard, was that they were so damp: but George said no, not if properly drained.

And then we got on to drains, and that put George in mind of a very funny thing that happened to his father once. He said his father was travelling with another fellow through Wales, and, one night, they stopped at a little inn, where there were some other fellows, and they joined the other fellows, and spent the evening with them.

They had a very jolly evening, and sat up late, and, by the time they came to go to bed, they (this was when George's father was a very young man) were slightly jolly, too. They (George's father and George's father's friend) were to sleep in the same room, but in different beds. They took the candle, and went up. The candle lurched up against the wall when they got into the room, and went out, and they had to undress and grope into bed in the dark. This they did; but, instead of getting into separate beds, as they thought they were doing, they both climbed into the same one without knowing it—one getting in with his head at the top, and the other crawling in from the opposite side of the compass, and lying with his feet on the pillow.

There was silence for a moment, and then George's father said:

"Joe!"

"What's the matter, Tom?" replied Joe's voice from the other end of the bed.

"Why, there's a man in my bed," said George's father; "here's his feet on my pillow."

"Well, it's an extraordinary thing, Tom," answered the other; "but I'm blest if there isn't a man in my bed, too!"

"What are you going to do?" asked George's father.

"Well, I'm going to chuck him out," replied Joe.

"So am I," said George's father, valiantly.

There was a brief struggle, followed by two heavy bumps on the floor, and then a rather doleful voice said:

"I say, Tom!"

"Yes!"

"How have you got on?"

"Well, to tell you the truth, my man's chucked *me* out."

"So's mine! I say, I don't think much of this inn, do you?"

"What was the name of that inn?" said Harris.

"The Pig and Whistle," said George. "Why?"

"Ah, no, then it isn't the same," replied Harris.

"What do you mean?" queried George.

"Why it's so curious," murmured Harris, "but precisely that very same thing happened to *my* father once at a country inn. I've often heard him tell the tale. I thought it might have been the same inn."

We turned in at ten that night, and I thought I should sleep well, being tired; but I didn't. As a rule, I undress and put my head on the pillow, and then somebody bangs at the door, and says it is half-past eight: but, to-night, everything seemed against me; the novelty of it all, the hardness of the boat, the cramped position (I was lying with my feet under one seat, and my head on another), the sound of the lapping water round the boat, and the wind among the branches, kept me restless and disturbed.

I did get to sleep for a few hours, and then some part of the boat which seemed to have grown up in the night—for it certainly was not there when we started, and it had disappeared by the morning—kept digging into my spine. I slept through it for a while, dreaming that I had swallowed a sovereign, and that they were cutting a hole in my back with a gimlet, so as to try and get it out. I thought it very unkind of them, and I told them I would owe them the money, and they should have it at the end of the month. But they would not hear of that, and said it would be much better if they had it then, because otherwise the interest would accumulate so. I got quite cross with them after a bit, and told them what I thought of them, and then they gave the gimlet such an excruciating wrench that I woke up.

The boat seemed stuffy, and my head ached; so I thought I would step out into the cool night-air. I slipped on what clothes I could find about—some of my own, and some of George's and Harris's—and crept under the canvas on to the bank.

It was a glorious night. The moon had sunk, and left the quiet earth alone with the stars. It seemed as if, in the silence and the hush, while we her children slept, they were talking with her, their sister—conversing of mighty mysteries in voices too vast and deep for childish human ears to catch the sound.

They awe us, these strange stars, so cold, so clear. We are as children whose small feet have strayed into some dim-lit temple of the god they have been taught to worship but know not; and, standing where the echoing dome spans the long vista of the shadowy light, glance up, half hoping, half afraid to see some awful vision hovering there.

And yet it seems so full of comfort and of strength, the night. In its great presence, our small sorrows creep away, ashamed. The day has been so full of fret and care, and our hearts have been so full of evil and of bitter thoughts, and the world has seemed so hard and wrong to us. Then Night, like some great loving mother, gently lays her hand upon our fevered head, and turns our little tear-stained faces up to hers, and smiles; and, though she does not speak, we know what she would say, and lay our hot flushed cheek against her bosom, and the pain is gone.

Sometimes, our pain is very deep and real, and we stand before her very silent, because there is no language for our pain, only a moan. Night's heart is full of pity for us: she cannot ease our aching; she takes our hand in hers, and the little world grows very small and very far away beneath us, and, borne on her dark wings, we pass for a moment into a mightier Presence than her own, and in the wondrous light of that great Presence, all human life lies like a book before us, and we know that Pain and Sorrow are but the angels of God.

Only those who have worn the crown of suffering can look upon that wondrous light; and they, when they return, may not speak of it, or tell the mystery they know.

Once upon a time, through a strange country, there rode some goodly knights, and their path lay by a deep wood, where tangled briars grew very thick and strong, and tore the flesh of them that lost their way therein. And the leaves of the trees that grew in the wood were very dark and thick, so that no ray of light came through the branches to lighten the gloom and sadness.

And, as they passed by that dark wood, one knight of those that rode, missing his comrades, wandered far away, and returned to them no more; and they, sorely grieving, rode on without him, mourning him as one dead.

Now, when they reached the fair castle towards which they had been journeying, they stayed there many days, and made merry; and one night, as they sat in cheerful ease around the logs that burned in the great hall, and drank a loving measure, there came the comrade they had lost, and greeted them. His clothes were ragged, like a beggar's, and many sad wounds were on his sweet flesh, but upon his face there shone a great radiance of deep joy.

And they questioned him, asking him what had befallen him: and he told them how in the dark wood he had lost his way, and had wandered many days and nights, till, torn and bleeding, he had lain him down to die.

Then, when he was nigh unto death, lo! through the savage gloom there came to him a stately maiden, and took him by the hand and led him on through devious paths, unknown to any man, until upon the darkness of the wood there dawned a light such as the light of day was unto but as a little lamp unto the sun; and, in that wondrous light, our way-worn knight saw as in a dream a vision, and so glorious, so fair the vision seemed, that of his bleeding wounds he thought no more, but stood as one entranced, whose joy is deep as is the sea, whereof no man can tell the depth.

And the vision faded, and the knight, kneeling upon the ground, thanked the good saint who into that sad wood had strayed his steps, so he had seen the vision that lay there hid.

And the name of the dark forest was Sorrow; but of the vision that the good knight saw therein we may not speak nor tell.

CHAPTER XI.

How George, once upon a time, got up early in the morning.—George, Harris, and Montmorency do not like the look of the cold water.—Heroism and determination on the part of J.—George and his shirt: story with a moral.—Harris as cook.—Historical retrospect, specially inserted for the use of schools.

I woke at six the next morning; and found George awake too. We both turned round, and tried to go to sleep again, but we could not. Had there been any particular reason why we should not have gone to sleep again, but have got up and dressed then and there, we should have dropped off while we were looking at our watches, and have slept till ten. As there was no earthly necessity for our getting up under another two hours at the very least, and our getting up at that time was an utter absurdity, it was only in keeping with the natural cussedness of things in general that we should both feel that lying down for five minutes more would be death to us.

George said that the same kind of thing, only worse, had happened to him some eighteen months ago, when he was lodging by himself in the house of a certain Mrs. Gippings. He said his watch went wrong one evening, and stopped at a quarter-past eight. He did not know this at the time because, for some reason or other, he forgot to wind it up when he went to bed (an unusual occurrence with him), and hung it up over his pillow without ever looking at the thing.

It was in the winter when this happened, very near the shortest day, and a week of fog into the bargain, so the fact that it was still very dark when George woke in the morning was no guide to him as to the time. He reached up, and hauled down his watch. It was a quarter-past eight.

"Angels and ministers of grace defend us!" exclaimed George; "and here have I got to be in the City by nine. Why didn't somebody call me? Oh, this is a shame!" And he flung the watch down, and sprang out of bed, and had a cold bath, and washed himself, and dressed himself, and shaved himself in cold water because there was not time to wait for the hot, and then rushed and had another look at the watch.

Whether the shaking it had received in being thrown down on the bed had started it, or how it was, George could not say, but certain it was that from a quarter-past eight it had begun to go, and now pointed to twenty minutes to nine.

George snatched it up, and rushed downstairs. In the sitting-room, all was dark and silent: there was no fire, no breakfast. George said it was a wicked shame of Mrs. G., and he made up his mind to tell her what he thought of her when he came home in the evening. Then he dashed on his great-coat and hat, and, seizing his umbrella, made for the front door. The door was not even unbolted. George anathematized Mrs. G. for a lazy old woman, and thought it was very strange that people could not get up at a decent, respectable time, unlocked and unbolted the door, and ran out.

He ran hard for a quarter of a mile, and at the end of that distance it began to be borne in upon him as a strange and curious thing that there were so few people about, and that there were no shops open. It was certainly a very dark and foggy morning, but still it seemed an unusual course to stop all business on that account. *He* had to go to business: why should other people stop in bed merely because it was dark and foggy!

At length he reached Holborn. Not a shutter was down! not a bus was about! There were three men in sight, one of whom was a policeman; a market-cart full of cabbages, and a dilapidated looking cab. George pulled out his watch and looked at it: it was five minutes to nine! He stood still and counted his pulse. He stooped down and felt his legs. Then, with his watch still in his hand, he went up to the policeman, and asked him if he knew what the time was.

"What's the time?" said the man, eyeing George up and down with evident suspicion; "why, if you listen you will hear it strike."

CHAPTER XI.

George listened, and a neighbouring clock immediately obliged.

"But it's only gone three!" said George in an injured tone, when it had finished.

"Well, and how many did you want it to go?" replied the constable.

"Why, nine," said George, showing his watch.

"Do you know where you live?" said the guardian of public order, severely.

George thought, and gave the address.

"Oh! that's where it is, is it?" replied the man; "well, you take my advice and go there quietly, and take that watch of yours with you; and don't let's have any more of it."

And George went home again, musing as he walked along, and let himself in.

At first, when he got in, he determined to undress and go to bed again; but when he thought of the redressing and re-washing, and the having of another bath, he determined he would not, but would sit up and go to sleep in the easy-chair.

But he could not get to sleep: he never felt more wakeful in his life; so he lit the lamp and got out the chess-board, and played himself a game of chess. But even that did not enliven him: it seemed slow somehow; so he gave chess up and tried to read. He did not seem able to take any sort of interest in reading either, so he put on his coat again and went out for a walk.

It was horribly lonesome and dismal, and all the policemen he met regarded him with undisguised suspicion, and turned their lanterns on him and followed him about, and this had such an effect upon him at last that he began to feel as if he really had done something, and he got to slinking down the by-streets and hiding in dark doorways when he heard the regulation flip-flop approaching.

Of course, this conduct made the force only more distrustful of him than ever, and they would come and rout him out and ask him what he was doing there; and when he answered, "Nothing," he had merely come out for a stroll (it was then four o'clock in the morning), they looked as though they did not believe him, and two plain-clothes constables came home with him to see if he really did live where he had said he did. They saw him go in with his key, and then they took up a position opposite and watched the house.

He thought he would light the fire when he got inside, and make himself some breakfast, just to pass away the time; but he did not seem able to handle anything from a scuttleful of coals to a teaspoon without dropping it or falling over it, and making such a noise that he was in mortal fear that it would wake Mrs. G. up, and that she would think it was burglars and open the window and call "Police!" and then these two detectives would rush in and handcuff him, and march him off to the police-court.

He was in a morbidly nervous state by this time, and he pictured the trial, and his trying to explain the circumstances to the jury, and nobody believing him, and his being sentenced to twenty years' penal servitude, and his mother dying of a broken heart. So he gave up trying to get breakfast, and wrapped himself up in his overcoat and sat in the easy-chair till Mrs. G came down at half-past seven.

He said he had never got up too early since that morning: it had been such a warning to him.

We had been sitting huddled up in our rugs while George had been telling me this true story, and on his finishing it I set to work to wake up Harris with a scull. The third prod did it: and he turned over on the other side, and said he would be down in a minute, and that he would have his lace-up boots. We soon let him know where he was, however, by the aid of the hitcher, and he sat up suddenly, sending Montmorency, who had been sleeping the sleep of the just right on the middle of his chest, sprawling across the boat.

Then we pulled up the canvas, and all four of us poked our heads out over the off-side, and looked down at the water and shivered. The idea, overnight, had been that we should get up early in the morning, fling off our rugs and shawls, and, throwing back the canvas, spring into the river with a joyous shout, and revel in a long delicious swim. Somehow, now the morning had come, the notion seemed less tempting. The water looked damp and chilly: the wind felt cold.

"Well, who's going to be first in?" said Harris at last.

There was no rush for precedence. George settled the matter so far as he was concerned by retiring into the boat and pulling on his socks. Montmorency gave vent to an involuntary howl, as if merely thinking of the thing had given him the horrors; and Harris said it would be so difficult to get into the boat again, and went back and sorted out his trousers.

I did not altogether like to give in, though I did not relish the plunge. There might be snags about, or weeds, I thought. I meant to compromise matters by going down to the edge and just throwing the water over myself; so I took a towel and crept out on the bank and wormed my way along on to the branch of a tree that dipped down into the water.

It was bitterly cold. The wind cut like a knife. I thought I would not throw the water over myself after all. I would go back into the boat and dress; and I turned to do so; and, as I turned, the silly branch gave way, and I and the towel went in together with a tremendous splash, and I was out mid-stream with a gallon of Thames water inside me before I knew what had happened.

"By Jove! old J.'s gone in," I heard Harris say, as I came blowing to the surface. "I didn't think he'd have the pluck to do it. Did you?"

"Is it all right?" sung out George.

"Lovely," I spluttered back. "You are duffers not to come in. I wouldn't have missed this for worlds. Why won't you try it? It only wants a little determination."

But I could not persuade them.

Rather an amusing thing happened while dressing that morning. I was very cold when I got back into the boat, and, in my hurry to get my shirt on, I accidentally jerked it into the water. It made me awfully wild, especially as George burst out laughing. I could not see anything to laugh at, and I told George so, and he only laughed the more. I never saw a man laugh so much. I quite lost my temper with him at last, and I pointed out to him what a drivelling maniac of an imbecile idiot he was; but he only roared the louder. And then, just as I was landing the shirt, I noticed that it was not my shirt at all, but George's, which I had mistaken for mine; whereupon the humour of the thing struck me for the first time, and I began to laugh. And the more I looked from George's wet shirt to George, roaring with laughter, the more I was amused, and I laughed so much that I had to let the shirt fall back into the water again.

"Ar'n't you—you—going to get it out?" said George, between his shrieks.

I could not answer him at all for a while, I was laughing so, but, at last, between my peals I managed to jerk out:

"It isn't my shirt—it's *yours*!"

I never saw a man's face change from lively to severe so suddenly in all my life before.

"What!" he yelled, springing up. "You silly cuckoo! Why can't you be more careful what you're doing? Why the deuce don't you go and dress on the bank? You're not fit to be in a boat, you're not. Gimme the hitcher."

I tried to make him see the fun of the thing, but he could not. George is very dense at seeing a joke sometimes.

Harris proposed that we should have scrambled eggs for breakfast. He said he would cook them. It seemed, from his account, that he was very good at doing scrambled eggs. He often did them at picnics and when out on yachts. He was quite famous for them. People who had once tasted his scrambled eggs, so we gathered from his conversation, never cared for any other food afterwards, but pined away and died when they could not get them.

It made our mouths water to hear him talk about the things, and we handed him out the stove and the frying-pan and all the eggs that had not smashed and gone over everything in the hamper, and begged him to begin.

He had some trouble in breaking the eggs—or rather not so much trouble in breaking them exactly as in getting them into the frying-pan when broken, and keeping them off his trousers, and preventing them from running up his sleeve; but he fixed some half-a-dozen into the pan at last, and then squatted down by the side of the stove and chivied them about with a fork.

It seemed harassing work, so far as George and I could judge. Whenever he went near the pan he burned himself, and then he would drop everything and dance round the stove, flicking his fingers about and cursing the things. Indeed, every time George and I looked round at him he was sure to be performing this feat. We thought at first that it was a necessary part of the culinary arrangements.

We did not know what scrambled eggs were, and we fancied that it must be some Red Indian or Sandwich Islands sort of dish that required dances and incantations for its proper cooking. Montmorency went and put his nose over it once, and the fat spluttered up and scalded him, and then *he* began dancing and cursing. Altogether it was one of the most interesting and exciting operations I have ever witnessed. George and I were both quite sorry when it was over.

The result was not altogether the success that Harris had anticipated. There seemed so little to show for the business. Six eggs had gone into the frying-pan, and all that came out was a teaspoonful of burnt and unappetizing looking mess.

Harris said it was the fault of the frying-pan, and thought it would have gone better if we had had a fish-kettle and a gas-stove; and we decided not to attempt the dish again until we had those aids to housekeeping by us.

The sun had got more powerful by the time we had finished breakfast, and the wind had dropped, and it was as lovely a morning as one could desire. Little was in sight to remind us of the nineteenth century; and, as we looked out upon the river in the morning sunlight, we could almost fancy that the centuries between us and that ever-to-be-famous June morning of 1215 had been drawn aside, and that we, English yeomen's sons in homespun cloth, with dirk at belt, were waiting there to witness the writing of that stupendous page of history, the meaning whereof was to be translated to the common people some four hundred and odd years later by one Oliver Cromwell, who had deeply studied it.

It is a fine summer morning—sunny, soft, and still. But through the air there runs a thrill of coming stir. King John has slept at Duncroft Hall, and all the day before the little town of Staines has echoed to the clang of armed men, and the clatter of great horses over its rough stones, and the shouts of captains, and the grim oaths and surly jests of bearded bowmen, billmen, pikemen, and strange-speaking foreign spearmen.

Gay-cloaked companies of knights and squires have ridden in, all travel-stained and dusty. And all the evening long the timid townsmen's doors have had to be quick opened to let in rough groups of soldiers, for whom there must be found both board and lodging, and the best of both, or woe betide the house and all within; for the sword is judge and jury, plaintiff and executioner, in these tempestuous times, and pays for what it takes by sparing those from whom it takes it, if it pleases it to do so.

Round the camp-fire in the market-place gather still more of the Barons' troops, and eat and drink deep, and bellow forth roystering drinking songs, and gamble and quarrel as the evening grows and deepens into night. The firelight sheds quaint shadows on their piled-up arms and on their uncouth forms. The children of the town steal round to watch them, wondering; and brawny country wenches, laughing, draw near to bandy ale-house jest and jibe with the swaggering troopers, so unlike the village swains, who, now despised, stand apart behind, with vacant grins upon their broad, peering faces. And out from the fields around, glitter the faint lights of more distant camps, as here some great lord's followers lie mustered, and there false John's French mercenaries hover like crouching wolves without the town.

And so, with sentinel in each dark street, and twinkling watch-fires on each height around, the night has worn away, and over this fair valley of old Thame has broken the morning of the great day that is to close so big with the fate of ages yet unborn.

Ever since grey dawn, in the lower of the two islands, just above where we are standing, there has been great clamour, and the sound of many workmen. The great pavilion brought there yester eve is being raised, and carpenters are busy nailing tiers of seats, while 'prentices from London town are there with many-coloured stuffs and silks and cloth of gold and silver.

And now, lo! down upon the road that winds along the river's bank from Staines there come towards us, laughing and talking together in deep guttural bass, a half-a-score of stalwart halbert-men—Barons' men, these—and halt at a hundred yards or so above us, on the other bank, and lean upon their arms, and wait.

And so, from hour to hour, march up along the road ever fresh groups and bands of armed men, their casques and breastplates flashing back the long low lines of morning sunlight, until, as far as eye can reach, the way seems thick with glittering steel and prancing steeds. And shouting horsemen are galloping from group to group, and little banners are fluttering lazily in the warm breeze, and every now and then there is a deeper stir as the ranks make way on either side, and some great Baron on his war-horse, with his guard of squires around him, passes along to take his station at the head of his serfs and vassals.

And up the slope of Cooper's Hill, just opposite, are gathered the wondering rustics and curious townsfolk, who have run from Staines, and none are quite sure what the bustle is about, but each one has a different version of the great event that they have come to see; and some say that much good to all the people will come from this day's work; but the old men shake their heads, for they have heard such tales before.

And all the river down to Staines is dotted with small craft and boats and tiny coracles—which last are growing out of favour now, and are used only by the poorer folk. Over the rapids, where in after years trim Bell Weir lock will stand, they have been forced or dragged by their sturdy rowers, and now are crowding up as near as they dare come to the great covered barges, which lie in readiness to bear King John to where the fateful Charter waits his signing.

It is noon, and we and all the people have been waiting patient for many an hour, and the rumour has run round that slippery John has again escaped from the Barons' grasp, and has stolen away from Duncroft Hall with his mercenaries at his heels, and will soon be doing other work than signing charters for his people's liberty.

Not so! This time the grip upon him has been one of iron, and he has slid and wriggled in vain. Far down the road a little cloud of dust has risen, and draws nearer and grows larger, and the pattering of many hoofs grows louder, and in and out between the scattered groups of drawn-up men, there pushes on its way a brilliant cavalcade of gay-dressed lords and knights. And front and rear, and either flank, there ride the yeomen of the Barons, and in the midst King John.

He rides to where the barges lie in readiness, and the great Barons step forth from their ranks to meet him. He greets them with a smile and laugh, and pleasant honeyed words, as though it were some feast in his honour to which he had been invited. But as he rises to dismount, he casts one hurried glance from his own French mercenaries drawn up in the rear to the grim ranks of the Barons' men that hem him in.

Is it too late? One fierce blow at the unsuspecting horseman at his side, one cry to his French troops, one desperate charge upon the unready lines before him, and these rebellious Barons might rue the day they dared to thwart his plans! A bolder hand might have turned the game even at that point. Had it been a Richard there! the cup of liberty might have been dashed from England's lips, and the taste of freedom held back for a hundred years.

But the heart of King John sinks before the stern faces of the English fighting men, and the arm of King John drops back on to his rein, and he dismounts and takes his seat in the foremost barge. And the Barons follow in, with each mailed hand upon the sword-hilt, and the word is given to let go.

Slowly the heavy, bright-decked barges leave the shore of Runningmede. Slowly against the swift current they work their ponderous way, till, with a low grumble, they grate against the bank of the little island that from this day will bear the name of Magna Charta Island. And King John has stepped upon the shore, and we wait in breathless silence till a great shout cleaves the air, and the great cornerstone in England's temple of liberty has, now we know, been firmly laid.

CHAPTER XII.

Henry VIII. and Anne Boleyn.—Disadvantages of living in same house with pair of lovers.—A trying time for the English nation.—A night search for the picturesque.—Homeless and houseless.—Harris prepares to die.—An angel comes along.—Effect of sudden joy on Harris.—A little supper.—Lunch.—High price for mustard.—A fearful battle.—Maidenhead.—Sailing.—Three fishers.—We are cursed.

I was sitting on the bank, conjuring up this scene to myself, when George remarked that when I was quite rested, perhaps I would not mind helping to wash up; and, thus recalled from the days of the glorious past to the prosaic present, with all its misery and sin, I slid down into the boat and cleaned out the frying-pan with a stick of wood and a tuft of grass, polishing it up finally with George's wet shirt.

We went over to Magna Charta Island, and had a look at the stone which stands in the cottage there and on which the great Charter is said to have been signed; though, as to whether it really was signed there, or, as some say, on the other bank at "Runningmede," I decline to commit myself. As far as my own personal opinion goes, however, I am inclined to give weight to the popular island theory. Certainly, had I been one of the Barons, at the time, I should have strongly urged upon my comrades the advisability of our getting such a slippery customer as King John on to the island, where there was less chance of surprises and tricks.

There are the ruins of an old priory in the grounds of Ankerwyke House, which is close to Picnic Point, and it was round about the grounds of this old priory that Henry VIII. is said to have waited for and met Anne Boleyn. He also used to meet her at Hever Castle in Kent, and also somewhere near St. Albans. It must have been difficult for the people of England in those days to have found a spot where these thoughtless young folk were *not* spooning.

Have you ever been in a house where there are a couple courting? It is most trying. You think you will go and sit in the drawing-room, and you march off there. As you open the door, you hear a noise as if somebody had suddenly recollected something, and, when you get in, Emily is over by the window, full of interest in the opposite side of the road, and your friend, John Edward, is at the other end of the room with his whole soul held in thrall by photographs of other people's relatives.

"Oh!" you say, pausing at the door, "I didn't know anybody was here."

"Oh! didn't you?" says Emily, coldly, in a tone which implies that she does not believe you.

You hang about for a bit, then you say:

"It's very dark. Why don't you light the gas?"

John Edward says, "Oh!" he hadn't noticed it; and Emily says that papa does not like the gas lit in the afternoon.

You tell them one or two items of news, and give them your views and opinions on the Irish question; but this does not appear to interest them. All they remark on any subject is, "Oh!" "Is it?" "Did he?" "Yes," and "You don't say so!" And, after ten minutes of such style of conversation, you edge up to the door, and slip out, and are surprised to find that the door immediately closes behind you, and shuts itself, without your having touched it.

Half an hour later, you think you will try a pipe in the conservatory. The only chair in the place is occupied by Emily; and John Edward, if the language of clothes can be relied upon, has evidently been sitting on the floor. They do not speak, but they give you a look that says all that can be said in a civilised community; and you back out promptly and shut the door behind you.

You are afraid to poke your nose into any room in the house now; so, after walking up and down the stairs for a while, you go and sit in your own bedroom. This becomes uninteresting, however, after a time, and so you put on your hat and stroll out into the garden. You walk down the path, and as you pass the summerhouse you glance in, and there are those two young idiots, huddled up into one corner of it; and they see you, and are evidently under the idea that, for some wicked purpose of your own, you are following them about.

"Why don't they have a special room for this sort of thing, and make people keep to it?" you mutter; and you rush back to the hall and get your umbrella and go out.

It must have been much like this when that foolish boy Henry VIII. was courting his little Anne. People in Buckinghamshire would have come upon them unexpectedly when they were mooning round Windsor and Wraysbury, and have exclaimed, "Oh! you here!" and Henry would have blushed and said, "Yes; he'd just come over to see a man;" and Anne would have said, "Oh, I'm so glad to see you! Isn't it funny? I've just met Mr. Henry VIII. in the lane, and he's going the same way I am."

Then those people would have gone away and said to themselves: "Oh! we'd better get out of here while this billing and cooing is on. We'll go down to Kent."

And they would go to Kent, and the first thing they would see in Kent, when they got there, would be Henry and Anne fooling round Hever Castle.

"Oh, drat this!" they would have said. "Here, let's go away. I can't stand any more of it. Let's go to St. Albans—nice quiet place, St. Albans."

And when they reached St. Albans, there would be that wretched couple, kissing under the Abbey walls. Then these folks would go and be pirates until the marriage was over.

From Picnic Point to Old Windsor Lock is a delightful bit of the river. A shady road, dotted here and there with dainty little cottages, runs by the bank up to the "Bells of Ouseley," a picturesque inn, as most up-river inns are, and a place where a very good glass of ale may be drunk—so Harris says; and on a matter of this kind you can take Harris's word. Old Windsor is a famous spot in its way. Edward the Confessor had a palace here, and here the great Earl Godwin was proved guilty by the justice of that age of having encompassed the death of the King's brother. Earl Godwin broke a piece of bread and held it in his hand.

"If I am guilty," said the Earl, "may this bread choke me when I eat it!"

Then he put the bread into his mouth and swallowed it, and it choked him, and he died.

After you pass Old Windsor, the river is somewhat uninteresting, and does not become itself again until you are nearing Boveney. George and I towed up past the Home Park, which stretches along the right bank from Albert to Victoria Bridge; and as we were passing Datchet, George asked me if I remembered our first trip up the river, and when we landed at Datchet at ten o'clock at night, and wanted to go to bed.

I answered that I did remember it. It will be some time before I forget it.

It was the Saturday before the August Bank Holiday. We were tired and hungry, we same three, and when we got to Datchet we took out the hamper, the two bags, and the rugs and coats, and such like things, and started off to look for diggings. We passed a very pretty little hotel, with clematis and creeper over the porch; but there was no honeysuckle about it, and, for some reason or other, I had got my mind fixed on honeysuckle, and I said:

"Oh, don't let's go in there! Let's go on a bit further, and see if there isn't one with honeysuckle over it."

So we went on till we came to another hotel. That was a very nice hotel, too, and it had honey-suckle on it, round at the side; but Harris did not like the look of a man who was leaning against the front door. He said he didn't look a nice man at all, and he wore ugly boots: so we went on further. We went a goodish way without coming across any more hotels, and then we met a man, and asked him to direct us to a few.

He said:

"Why, you are coming away from them. You must turn right round and go back, and then you will come to the Stag."

We said:

"Oh, we had been there, and didn't like it—no honeysuckle over it."

"Well, then," he said, "there's the Manor House, just opposite. Have you tried that?"

Harris replied that we did not want to go there—didn't like the looks of a man who was stopping there—Harris did not like the colour of his hair, didn't like his boots, either.

"Well, I don't know what you'll do, I'm sure," said our informant; "because they are the only two inns in the place."

"No other inns!" exclaimed Harris.

"None," replied the man.

"What on earth are we to do?" cried Harris.

Then George spoke up. He said Harris and I could get an hotel built for us, if we liked, and have some people made to put in. For his part, he was going back to the Stag.

The greatest minds never realise their ideals in any matter; and Harris and I sighed over the hollowness of all earthly desires, and followed George.

We took our traps into the Stag, and laid them down in the hall.

The landlord came up and said:

"Good evening, gentlemen."

"Oh, good evening," said George; "we want three beds, please."

"Very sorry, sir," said the landlord; "but I'm afraid we can't manage it."

"Oh, well, never mind," said George, "two will do. Two of us can sleep in one bed, can't we?" he continued, turning to Harris and me.

Harris said, "Oh, yes;" he thought George and I could sleep in one bed very easily.

"Very sorry, sir," again repeated the landlord: "but we really haven't got a bed vacant in the whole house. In fact, we are putting two, and even three gentlemen in one bed, as it is."

This staggered us for a bit.

But Harris, who is an old traveller, rose to the occasion, and, laughing cheerily, said:

"Oh, well, we can't help it. We must rough it. You must give us a shake-down in the billiard-room."

"Very sorry, sir. Three gentlemen sleeping on the billiard-table already, and two in the coffee-room. Can't possibly take you in to-night."

We picked up our things, and went over to the Manor House. It was a pretty little place. I said I thought I should like it better than the other house; and Harris said, "Oh, yes," it would be all right, and we needn't look at the man with the red hair; besides, the poor fellow couldn't help having red hair.

Harris spoke quite kindly and sensibly about it.

The people at the Manor House did not wait to hear us talk. The landlady met us on the doorstep with the greeting that we were the fourteenth party she had turned away within the last hour and a half. As for our meek suggestions of stables, billiard-room, or coal-cellars, she laughed them all to scorn: all these nooks had been snatched up long ago.

Did she know of any place in the whole village where we could get shelter for the night?

"Well, if we didn't mind roughing it—she did not recommend it, mind—but there was a little beershop half a mile down the Eton road—"

We waited to hear no more; we caught up the hamper and the bags, and the coats and rugs, and parcels, and ran. The distance seemed more like a mile than half a mile, but we reached the place at last, and rushed, panting, into the bar.

The people at the beershop were rude. They merely laughed at us. There were only three beds in the whole house, and they had seven single gentlemen and two married couples sleeping there already. A kind-hearted bargeman, however, who happened to be in the tap-room, thought we might try the grocer's, next door to the Stag, and we went back.

The grocer's was full. An old woman we met in the shop then kindly took us along with her for a quarter of a mile, to a lady friend of hers, who occasionally let rooms to gentlemen.

This old woman walked very slowly, and we were twenty minutes getting to her lady friend's. She enlivened the journey by describing to us, as we trailed along, the various pains she had in her back.

Her lady friend's rooms were let. From there we were recommended to No. 27. No. 27 was full, and sent us to No. 32, and 32 was full.

Then we went back into the high road, and Harris sat down on the hamper and said he would go no further. He said it seemed a quiet spot, and he would like to die there. He requested George and me to kiss his mother for him, and to tell all his relations that he forgave them and died happy.

At that moment an angel came by in the disguise of a small boy (and I cannot think of any more effective disguise an angel could have assumed), with a can of beer in one hand, and in the other something at the end of a string, which he let down on to every flat stone he came across, and then pulled up again, this producing a peculiarly unattractive sound, suggestive of suffering.

We asked this heavenly messenger (as we discovered him afterwards to be) if he knew of any lonely house, whose occupants were few and feeble (old ladies or paralysed gentlemen preferred), who could be easily frightened into giving up their beds for the night to three desperate men; or, if not this, could he recommend us to an empty pigstye, or a disused limekiln, or anything of that sort. He did not know of any such place—at least, not one handy; but he said that, if we liked to come with him, his mother had a room to spare, and could put us up for the night.

We fell upon his neck there in the moonlight and blessed him, and it would have made a very beautiful picture if the boy himself had not been so over-powered by our emotion as to be unable to sustain himself under it, and sunk to the ground, letting us all down on top of him. Harris was so overcome with joy that he fainted, and had to seize the boy's beer-can and half empty it before he could recover consciousness, and then he started off at a run, and left George and me to bring on the luggage.

It was a little four-roomed cottage where the boy lived, and his mother—good soul!—gave us hot bacon for supper, and we ate it all—five pounds—and a jam tart afterwards, and two pots of tea, and then we went to bed. There were two beds in the room; one was a 2ft. 6in. truckle bed, and George and I slept in that, and kept in by tying ourselves together with a sheet; and the other was the little boy's bed, and Harris had that all to himself, and we found him, in the morning, with two feet of bare leg sticking out at the bottom, and George and I used it to hang the towels on while we bathed.

We were not so uppish about what sort of hotel we would have, next time we went to Datchet.

To return to our present trip: nothing exciting happened, and we tugged steadi-ly on to a little below Monkey Island, where we drew up and lunched. We tackled the cold beef for lunch, and then we found that we had forgotten to bring any mustard. I don't think I ever in my life, before or since, felt I wanted mustard as badly as I felt I wanted it then. I don't care for mustard as a rule, and it is very seldom that I take it at all, but I would have given worlds for it then.

I don't know how many worlds there may be in the universe, but anyone who had brought me a spoonful of mustard at that precise moment could have had them all. I grow reckless like that when I want a thing and can't get it.

Harris said he would have given worlds for mustard too. It would have been a good thing for anybody who had come up to that spot with a can of mustard, then: he would have been set up in worlds for the rest of his life.

But there! I daresay both Harris and I would have tried to back out of the bar-gain after we had got the mustard. One makes these extravagant offers in moments of excitement, but, of course, when one comes to think of it, one sees how absurdly out of proportion they are with the value of the required article. I heard a man, going up a mountain in Switzerland, once say he would give worlds for a glass of beer, and, when he came to a little shanty where they kept it, he kicked up a most fearful row because they charged him five francs for a bottle of Bass. He said it was a scandalous imposition, and he wrote to the *Times* about it.

It cast a gloom over the boat, there being no mustard. We ate our beef in si-lence. Existence seemed hollow and uninteresting. We thought of the happy days of childhood, and sighed. We brightened up a bit, however, over the apple-tart, and, when George drew out a tin of pine-apple from the bottom of the hamper, and rolled it into the middle of the boat, we felt that life was worth living after all.

We are very fond of pine-apple, all three of us. We looked at the picture on the tin; we thought of the juice. We smiled at one another, and Harris got a spoon ready.

Then we looked for the knife to open the tin with. We turned out everything in the hamper. We turned out the bags. We pulled up the boards at the bottom of the boat. We took everything out on to the bank and shook it. There was no tin-opener to be found.

Then Harris tried to open the tin with a pocket-knife, and broke the knife and cut himself badly; and George tried a pair of scissors, and the scissors flew up, and nearly put his eye out. While they were dressing their wounds, I tried to make a hole in the thing with the spiky end of the hitcher, and the hitcher slipped and jerked me out between the boat and the bank into two feet of muddy water, and the tin rolled over, uninjured, and broke a teacup.

Then we all got mad. We took that tin out on the bank, and Harris went up into a field and got a big sharp stone, and I went back into the boat and brought out the mast, and George held the tin and Harris held the sharp end of his stone against the top of it, and I took the mast and poised it high up in the air, and gathered up all my strength and brought it down.

It was George's straw hat that saved his life that day. He keeps that hat now (what is left of it), and, of a winter's evening, when the pipes are lit and the boys are telling stretchers about the dangers they have passed through, George brings it down and shows it round, and the stirring tale is told anew, with fresh exaggerations every time.

Harris got off with merely a flesh wound.

After that, I took the tin off myself, and hammered at it with the mast till I was worn out and sick at heart, whereupon Harris took it in hand.

We beat it out flat; we beat it back square; we battered it into every form known to geometry—but we could not make a hole in it. Then George went at it, and knocked it into a shape, so strange, so weird, so unearthly in its wild hideousness, that he got frightened and threw away the mast. Then we all three sat round it on the grass and looked at it.

There was one great dent across the top that had the appearance of a mocking grin, and it drove us furious, so that Harris rushed at the thing, and caught it up, and flung it far into the middle of the river, and as it sank we hurled our curses at it, and we got into the boat and rowed away from the spot, and never paused till we reached Maidenhead.

Maidenhead itself is too snobby to be pleasant. It is the haunt of the river swell and his overdressed female companion. It is the town of showy hotels, patronised chiefly by dudes and ballet girls. It is the witch's kitchen from which go forth those demons of the river—steam-launches. The *London Journal* duke always has his "little place" at Maidenhead; and the heroine of the three-volume novel always dines there when she goes out on the spree with somebody else's husband.

We went through Maidenhead quickly, and then eased up, and took leisurely that grand reach beyond Boulter's and Cookham locks. Clieveden Woods still wore their dainty dress of spring, and rose up, from the water's edge, in one long harmony of blended shades of fairy green. In its unbroken loveliness this is, perhaps, the sweetest stretch of all the river, and lingeringly we slowly drew our little boat away from its deep peace.

We pulled up in the backwater, just below Cookham, and had tea; and, when we were through the lock, it was evening. A stiffish breeze had sprung up—in our favour, for a wonder; for, as a rule on the river, the wind is always dead against you whatever way you go. It is against you in the morning, when you start for a day's trip, and you pull a long distance, thinking how easy it will be to come back with the sail. Then, after tea, the wind veers round, and you have to pull hard in its teeth all the way home.

When you forget to take the sail at all, then the wind is consistently in your favour both ways. But there! this world is only a probation, and man was born to trouble as the sparks fly upward.

This evening, however, they had evidently made a mistake, and had put the wind round at our back instead of in our face. We kept very quiet about it, and got the sail up quickly before they found it out, and then we spread ourselves about the boat in thoughtful attitudes, and the sail bellied out, and strained, and grumbled at the mast, and the boat flew.

I steered.

There is no more thrilling sensation I know of than sailing. It comes as near to flying as man has got to yet—except in dreams. The wings of the rushing wind seem to be bearing you onward, you know not where. You are no longer the slow, plodding, puny thing of clay, creeping tortuously upon the ground; you are a part of Nature! Your heart is throbbing against hers! Her glorious arms are round you, raising you up against her heart! Your spirit is at one with hers; your limbs grow light! The voices of the air are singing to you. The earth seems far away and little; and the clouds, so close above your head, are brothers, and you stretch your arms to them.

We had the river to ourselves, except that, far in the distance, we could see a fishing-punt, moored in mid-stream, on which three fishermen sat; and we skimmed over the water, and passed the wooded banks, and no one spoke.

I was steering.

As we drew nearer, we could see that the three men fishing seemed old and solemn-looking men. They sat on three chairs in the punt, and watched intently their lines. And the red sunset threw a mystic light upon the waters, and tinged with fire the towering woods, and made a golden glory of the piled-up clouds. It was an hour of deep enchantment, of ecstatic hope and longing. The little sail stood out against the purple sky, the gloaming lay around us, wrapping the world in rainbow shadows; and, behind us, crept the night.

We seemed like knights of some old legend, sailing across some mystic lake into the unknown realm of twilight, unto the great land of the sunset.

We did not go into the realm of twilight; we went slap into that punt, where those three old men were fishing. We did not know what had happened at first, because the sail shut out the view, but from the nature of the language that rose up upon the evening air, we gathered that we had come into the neighbourhood of human beings, and that they were vexed and discontented.

Harris let the sail down, and then we saw what had happened. We had knocked those three old gentlemen off their chairs into a general heap at the bottom of the boat, and they were now slowly and painfully sorting themselves out from each other, and picking fish off themselves; and as they worked, they cursed us—not with a common cursory curse, but with long, carefully-thought-out, comprehensive curses, that embraced the whole of our career, and went away into the distant future, and included all our relations, and covered everything connected with us—good, substantial curses.

Harris told them they ought to be grateful for a little excitement, sitting there fishing all day, and he also said that he was shocked and grieved to hear men their age give way to temper so.

But it did not do any good.

George said he would steer, after that. He said a mind like mine ought not to be expected to give itself away in steering boats—better let a mere commonplace human being see after that boat, before we jolly well all got drowned; and he took the lines, and brought us up to Marlow.

And at Marlow we left the boat by the bridge, and went and put up for the night at the "Crown."

CHAPTER XIII.

**Marlow.—Bisham Abbey.—The Medmenham Monks.—
Montmorency thinks he will murder an old Tom cat.—But
eventually decides that he will let it live.—Shameful conduct
of a fox terrier at the Civil Service Stores.—Our departure
from Marlow.—An imposing procession.—The steam
launch, useful receipts for annoying and hindering it.—We
decline to drink the river.—A peaceful dog.—Strange disappearance of Harris and a pie.**

Marlow is one of the pleasantest river centres I know of. It is a bustling, lively little town; not very picturesque on the whole, it is true, but there are many quaint nooks and corners to be found in it, nevertheless—standing arches in the shattered bridge of Time, over which our fancy travels back to the days when Marlow Manor owned Saxon Algar for its lord, ere conquering William seized it to give to Queen Matilda, ere it passed to the Earls of Warwick or to worldly-wise Lord Paget, the councillor of four successive sovereigns.

There is lovely country round about it, too, if, after boating, you are fond of a walk, while the river itself is at its best here. Down to Cookham, past the Quarry Woods and the meadows, is a lovely reach. Dear old Quarry Woods! with your narrow, climbing paths, and little winding glades, how scented to this hour you seem with memories of sunny summer days! How haunted are your shadowy vistas with the ghosts of laughing faces! how from your whispering leaves there softly fall the voices of long ago!

From Marlow up to Sonning is even fairer yet. Grand old Bisham Abbey, whose stone walls have rung to the shouts of the Knights Templars, and which, at one time, was the home of Anne of Cleves and at another of Queen Elizabeth, is passed on the right bank just half a mile above Marlow Bridge. Bisham Abbey is rich in melodramatic properties. It contains a tapestry bed-chamber, and a secret room hid high up in the thick walls. The ghost of the Lady Holy, who beat her little boy to death, still walks there at night, trying to wash its ghostly hands clean in a ghostly basin.

Warwick, the king-maker, rests there, careless now about such trivial things as earthly kings and earthly kingdoms; and Salisbury, who did good service at Poitiers. Just before you come to the abbey, and right on the river's bank, is Bisham Church, and, perhaps, if any tombs are worth inspecting, they are the tombs and monuments in Bisham Church. It was while floating in his boat under the Bisham beeches that Shelley, who was then living at Marlow (you can see his house now, in West street), composed *The Revolt of Islam*.

By Hurley Weir, a little higher up, I have often thought that I could stay a month without having sufficient time to drink in all the beauty of the scene. The village of Hurley, five minutes' walk from the lock, is as old a little spot as there is on the river, dating, as it does, to quote the quaint phraseology of those dim days, "from the times of King Sebert and King Offa." Just past the weir (going up) is Danes' Field, where the invading Danes once encamped, during their march to Gloucestershire; and a little further still, nestling by a sweet corner of the stream, is what is left of Medmenham Abbey.

The famous Medmenham monks, or "Hell Fire Club," as they were commonly called, and of whom the notorious Wilkes was a member, were a fraternity whose motto was "Do as you please," and that invitation still stands over the ruined doorway of the abbey. Many years before this bogus abbey, with its congregation of irreverent jesters, was founded, there stood upon this same spot a monastery of a sterner kind, whose monks were of a somewhat different type to the revellers that were to follow them, five hundred years afterwards.

The Cistercian monks, whose abbey stood there in the thirteenth century, wore no clothes but rough tunics and cowls, and ate no flesh, nor fish, nor eggs. They lay upon straw, and they rose at midnight to mass. They spent the day in labour, reading, and prayer; and over all their lives there fell a silence as of death, for no one spoke.

A grim fraternity, passing grim lives in that sweet spot, that God had made so bright! Strange that Nature's voices all around them—the soft singing of the waters, the whisperings of the river grass, the music of the rushing wind—should not have taught them a truer meaning of life than this. They listened there, through the long days, in silence, waiting for a voice from heaven; and all day long and through the solemn night it spoke to them in myriad tones, and they heard it not.

From Medmenham to sweet Hambledon Lock the river is full of peaceful beauty, but, after it passes Greenlands, the rather uninteresting looking river residence of my newsagent—a quiet unassuming old gentleman, who may often be met with about these regions, during the summer months, sculling himself along in easy vigorous style, or chatting genially to some old lock-keeper, as he passes through—until well the other side of Henley, it is somewhat bare and dull.

We got up tolerably early on the Monday morning at Marlow, and went for a bathe before breakfast; and, coming back, Montmorency made an awful ass of himself. The only subject on which Montmorency and I have any serious difference of opinion is cats. I like cats; Montmorency does not.

When I meet a cat, I say, "Poor Pussy!" and stop down and tickle the side of its head; and the cat sticks up its tail in a rigid, cast-iron manner, arches its back, and wipes its nose up against my trousers; and all is gentleness and peace. When Montmorency meets a cat, the whole street knows about it; and there is enough bad language wasted in ten seconds to last an ordinarily respectable man all his life, with care.

I do not blame the dog (contenting myself, as a rule, with merely clouting his head or throwing stones at him), because I take it that it is his nature. Fox-terriers are born with about four times as much original sin in them as other dogs are, and it will take years and years of patient effort on the part of us Christians to bring about any appreciable reformation in the rowdiness of the fox-terrier nature.

I remember being in the lobby of the Haymarket Stores one day, and all round about me were dogs, waiting for the return of their owners, who were shopping inside. There were a mastiff, and one or two collies, and a St. Bernard, a few retrievers and Newfoundlands, a boar-hound, a French poodle, with plenty of hair round its head, but mangy about the middle; a bull-dog, a few Lowther Arcade sort of animals, about the size of rats, and a couple of Yorkshire tykes.

There they sat, patient, good, and thoughtful. A solemn peacefulness seemed to reign in that lobby. An air of calmness and resignation—of gentle sadness pervaded the room.

Then a sweet young lady entered, leading a meek-looking little fox-terrier, and left him, chained up there, between the bull-dog and the poodle. He sat and looked about him for a minute. Then he cast up his eyes to the ceiling, and seemed, judging from his expression, to be thinking of his mother. Then he yawned. Then he looked round at the other dogs, all silent, grave, and dignified.

He looked at the bull-dog, sleeping dreamlessly on his right. He looked at the poodle, erect and haughty, on his left. Then, without a word of warning, without the shadow of a provocation, he bit that poodle's near fore-leg, and a yelp of agony rang through the quiet shades of that lobby.

The result of his first experiment seemed highly satisfactory to him, and he determined to go on and make things lively all round. He sprang over the poodle and vigorously attacked a collie, and the collie woke up, and immediately commenced a fierce and noisy contest with the poodle. Then Foxey came back to his own place, and caught the bull-dog by the ear, and tried to throw him away; and the bull-dog, a curiously impartial animal, went for everything he could reach, including the hall-porter, which gave that dear little terrier the opportunity to enjoy an uninterrupted fight of his own with an equally willing Yorkshire tyke.

Anyone who knows canine nature need hardly, be told that, by this time, all the other dogs in the place were fighting as if their hearths and homes depended on the fray. The big dogs fought each other indiscriminately; and the little dogs fought among themselves, and filled up their spare time by biting the legs of the big dogs.

The whole lobby was a perfect pandemonium, and the din was terrific. A crowd assembled outside in the Haymarket, and asked if it was a vestry meeting; or, if not, who was being murdered, and why? Men came with poles and ropes, and tried to separate the dogs, and the police were sent for.

And in the midst of the riot that sweet young lady returned, and snatched up that sweet little dog of hers (he had laid the tyke up for a month, and had on the expression, now, of a new-born lamb) into her arms, and kissed him, and asked him if he was killed, and what those great nasty brutes of dogs had been doing to him; and he nestled up against her, and gazed up into her face with a look that seemed to say: "Oh, I'm so glad you've come to take me away from this disgraceful scene!"

She said that the people at the Stores had no right to allow great savage things like those other dogs to be put with respectable people's dogs, and that she had a great mind to summon somebody.

Such is the nature of fox-terriers; and, therefore, I do not blame Montmorency for his tendency to row with cats; but he wished he had not given way to it that morning.

We were, as I have said, returning from a dip, and half-way up the High Street a cat darted out from one of the houses in front of us, and began to trot across the road. Montmorency gave a cry of joy—the cry of a stern warrior who sees his enemy given over to his hands—the sort of cry Cromwell might have uttered when the Scots came down the hill—and flew after his prey.

His victim was a large black Tom. I never saw a larger cat, nor a more disreputable-looking cat. It had lost half its tail, one of its ears, and a fairly appreciable proportion of its nose. It was a long, sinewy-looking animal. It had a calm, contented air about it.

Montmorency went for that poor cat at the rate of twenty miles an hour; but the cat did not hurry up—did not seem to have grasped the idea that its life was in danger. It trotted quietly on until its would-be assassin was within a yard of it, and then it turned round and sat down in the middle of the road, and looked at Montmorency with a gentle, inquiring expression, that said:

"Yes! You want me?"

Montmorency does not lack pluck; but there was something about the look of that cat that might have chilled the heart of the boldest dog. He stopped abruptly, and looked back at Tom.

Neither spoke; but the conversation that one could imagine was clearly as follows:—

THE CAT: "Can I do anything for you?"

MONTMORENCY: "No—no, thanks."

THE CAT: "Don't you mind speaking, if you really want anything, you know."

MONTMORENCY (*backing down the High Street*): "Oh, no—not at all—certainly—don't you trouble. I—I am afraid I've made a mistake. I thought I knew you. Sorry I disturbed you."

THE CAT: "Not at all—quite a pleasure. Sure you don't want anything, now?"

MONTMORENCY (*still backing*): "Not at all, thanks—not at all—very kind of you. Good morning."

THE CAT: "Good-morning."

Then the cat rose, and continued his trot; and Montmorency, fitting what he calls his tail carefully into its groove, came back to us, and took up an unimportant position in the rear.

To this day, if you say the word "Cats!" to Montmorency, he will visibly shrink and look up piteously at you, as if to say:

"Please don't."

We did our marketing after breakfast, and revictualled the boat for three days. George said we ought to take vegetables—that it was unhealthy not to eat vegetables. He said they were easy enough to cook, and that he would see to that; so we got ten pounds of potatoes, a bushel of peas, and a few cabbages. We got a beefsteak pie, a couple of gooseberry tarts, and a leg of mutton from the hotel; and fruit, and cakes, and bread and butter, and jam, and bacon and eggs, and other things we foraged round about the town for.

Our departure from Marlow I regard as one of our greatest successes. It was dignified and impressive, without being ostentatious. We had insisted at all the shops we had been to that the things should be sent with us then and there. None of your "Yes, sir, I will send them off at once: the boy will be down there before you are, sir!" and then fooling about on the landing-stage, and going back to the shop twice to have a row about them, for us. We waited while the basket was packed, and took the boy with us.

We went to a good many shops, adopting this principle at each one; and the consequence was that, by the time we had finished, we had as fine a collection of boys with baskets following us around as heart could desire; and our final march down the middle of the High Street, to the river, must have been as imposing a spectacle as Marlow had seen for many a long day.

The order of the procession was as follows:—

Montmorency, carrying a stick.

Two disreputable-looking curs, friends of Montmorency's.

George, carrying coats and rugs, and smoking a short pipe.

Harris, trying to walk with easy grace,

while carrying a bulged-out Gladstone bag in one hand

and a bottle of lime-juice in the other.

Greengrocer's boy and baker's boy,

with baskets.

Boots from the hotel, carrying hamper.

Confectioner's boy, with basket.

Grocer's boy, with basket.

Long-haired dog.

Cheesemonger's boy, with basket.

Odd man carrying a bag.

Bosom companion of odd man, with his hands in his pockets,

smoking a short clay.

Fruiterer's boy, with basket.

Myself, carrying three hats and a pair of boots,

and trying to look as if I didn't know it.

Six small boys, and four stray dogs.

When we got down to the landing-stage, the boatman said:

"Let me see, sir; was yours a steam-launch or a house-boat?"

On our informing him it was a double-sculling skiff, he seemed surprised.

We had a good deal of trouble with steam launches that morning. It was just before the Henley week, and they were going up in large numbers; some by themselves, some towing houseboats. I do hate steam launches: I suppose every rowing man does. I never see a steam launch but I feel I should like to lure it to a lonely part of the river, and there, in the silence and the solitude, strangle it.

There is a blatant bumptiousness about a steam launch that has the knack of rousing every evil instinct in my nature, and I yearn for the good old days, when you could go about and tell people what you thought of them with a hatchet and a bow and arrows. The expression on the face of the man who, with his hands in his pockets, stands by the stern, smoking a cigar, is sufficient to excuse a breach of the peace by itself; and the lordly whistle for you to get out of the way would, I am confident, ensure a verdict of "justifiable homicide" from any jury of river men.

They used to *have* to whistle for us to get out of their way. If I may do so, without appearing boastful, I think I can honestly say that our one small boat, during that week, caused more annoyance and delay and aggravation to the steam launches that we came across than all the other craft on the river put together.

"Steam launch, coming!" one of us would cry out, on sighting the enemy in the distance; and, in an instant, everything was got ready to receive her. I would take the lines, and Harris and George would sit down beside me, all of us with our backs to the launch, and the boat would drift out quietly into mid-stream.

On would come the launch, whistling, and on we would go, drifting. At about a hundred yards off, she would start whistling like mad, and the people would come and lean over the side, and roar at us; but we never heard them! Harris would be telling us an anecdote about his mother, and George and I would not have missed a word of it for worlds.

Then that launch would give one final shriek of a whistle that would nearly burst the boiler, and she would reverse her engines, and blow off steam, and swing round and get aground; everyone on board of it would rush to the bow and yell at us, and the people on the bank would stand and shout to us, and all the other passing boats would stop and join in, till the whole river for miles up and down was in a state of frantic commotion. And then Harris would break off in the most interesting part of his narrative, and look up with mild surprise, and say to George:

"Why, George, bless me, if here isn't a steam launch!"

And George would answer:

"Well, do you know, I *thought* I heard something!"

Upon which we would get nervous and confused, and not know how to get the boat out of the way, and the people in the launch would crowd round and instruct us:

"Pull your right—you, you idiot! back with your left. No, not *you*—the other one—leave the lines alone, can't you—now, both together. NOT *that* way. Oh, you—!"

Then they would lower a boat and come to our assistance; and, after quarter of an hour's effort, would get us clean out of their way, so that they could go on; and we would thank them so much, and ask them to give us a tow. But they never would.

Another good way we discovered of irritating the aristocratic type of steam launch, was to mistake them for a beanfeast, and ask them if they were Messrs. Cubit's lot or the Bermondsey Good Templars, and could they lend us a saucepan.

Old ladies, not accustomed to the river, are always intensely nervous of steam launches. I remember going up once from Staines to Windsor—a stretch of water peculiarly rich in these mechanical monstrosities—with a party containing three ladies of this description. It was very exciting. At the first glimpse of every steam launch that came in view, they insisted on landing and sitting down on the bank until it was out of sight again. They said they were very sorry, but that they owed it to their families not to be fool-hardy.

We found ourselves short of water at Hambledon Lock; so we took our jar and went up to the lock-keeper's house to beg for some.

George was our spokesman. He put on a winning smile, and said:

"Oh, please could you spare us a little water?"

"Certainly," replied the old gentleman; "take as much as you want, and leave the rest."

"Thank you so much," murmured George, looking about him. "Where—where do you keep it?"

"It's always in the same place my boy," was the stolid reply: "just behind you."

"I don't see it," said George, turning round.

"Why, bless us, where's your eyes?" was the man's comment, as he twisted George round and pointed up and down the stream. "There's enough of it to see, ain't there?"

"Oh!" exclaimed George, grasping the idea; "but we can't drink the river, you know!"

"No; but you can drink *some* of it," replied the old fellow. "It's what *I've* drunk for the last fifteen years."

George told him that his appearance, after the course, did not seem a sufficiently good advertisement for the brand; and that he would prefer it out of a pump.

We got some from a cottage a little higher up. I daresay *that* was only river water, if we had known. But we did not know, so it was all right. What the eye does not see, the stomach does not get upset over.

We tried river water once, later on in the season, but it was not a success. We were coming down stream, and had pulled up to have tea in a backwater near Windsor. Our jar was empty, and it was a case of going without our tea or taking water from the river. Harris was for chancing it. He said it must be all right if we boiled the water. He said that the various germs of poison present in the water would be killed by the boiling. So we filled our kettle with Thames backwater, and boiled it; and very careful we were to see that it did boil.

We had made the tea, and were just settling down comfortably to drink it, when George, with his cup half-way to his lips, paused and exclaimed:

"What's that?"

"What's what?" asked Harris and I.

"Why that!" said George, looking westward.

Harris and I followed his gaze, and saw, coming down towards us on the sluggish current, a dog. It was one of the quietest and peacefullest dogs I have ever seen. I never met a dog who seemed more contented—more easy in its mind. It was floating dreamily on its back, with its four legs stuck up straight into the air. It was what I should call a full-bodied dog, with a well-developed chest. On he came, serene, dignified, and calm, until he was abreast of our boat, and there, among the rushes, he eased up, and settled down cosily for the evening.

George said he didn't want any tea, and emptied his cup into the water. Harris did not feel thirsty, either, and followed suit. I had drunk half mine, but I wished I had not.

I asked George if he thought I was likely to have typhoid.

He said: "Oh, no;" he thought I had a very good chance indeed of escaping it. Anyhow, I should know in about a fortnight, whether I had or had not.

We went up the backwater to Wargrave. It is a short cut, leading out of the right-hand bank about half a mile above Marsh Lock, and is well worth taking, being a pretty, shady little piece of stream, besides saving nearly half a mile of distance.

Of course, its entrance is studded with posts and chains, and surrounded with notice boards, menacing all kinds of torture, imprisonment, and death to everyone who dares set scull upon its waters—I wonder some of these riparian boors don't claim the air of the river and threaten everyone with forty shillings fine who breathes it—but the posts and chains a little skill will easily avoid; and as for the boards, you might, if you have five minutes to spare, and there is nobody about, take one or two of them down and throw them into the river.

Half-way up the backwater, we got out and lunched; and it was during this lunch that George and I received rather a trying shock.

Harris received a shock, too; but I do not think Harris's shock could have been anything like so bad as the shock that George and I had over the business.

You see, it was in this way: we were sitting in a meadow, about ten yards from the water's edge, and we had just settled down comfortably to feed. Harris had the beefsteak pie between his knees, and was carving it, and George and I were waiting with our plates ready.

"Have you got a spoon there?" says Harris; "I want a spoon to help the gravy with."

The hamper was close behind us, and George and I both turned round to reach one out. We were not five seconds getting it. When we looked round again, Harris and the pie were gone!

It was a wide, open field. There was not a tree or a bit of hedge for hundreds of yards. He could not have tumbled into the river, because we were on the water side of him, and he would have had to climb over us to do it.

George and I gazed all about. Then we gazed at each other.

"Has he been snatched up to heaven?" I queried.

"They'd hardly have taken the pie too," said George.

There seemed weight in this objection, and we discarded the heavenly theory.

"I suppose the truth of the matter is," suggested George, descending to the commonplace and practicable, "that there has been an earthquake."

And then he added, with a touch of sadness in his voice: "I wish he hadn't been carving that pie."

With a sigh, we turned our eyes once more towards the spot where Harris and the pie had last been seen on earth; and there, as our blood froze in our veins and our hair stood up on end, we saw Harris's head—and nothing but his head—sticking bolt upright among the tall grass, the face very red, and bearing upon it an expression of great indignation!

George was the first to recover.

"Speak!" he cried, "and tell us whether you are alive or dead—and where is the rest of you?"

"Oh, don't be a stupid ass!" said Harris's head. "I believe you did it on purpose."

"Did what?" exclaimed George and I.

"Why, put me to sit here—darn silly trick! Here, catch hold of the pie."

And out of the middle of the earth, as it seemed to us, rose the pie—very much mixed up and damaged; and, after it, scrambled Harris—tumbled, grubby, and wet.

He had been sitting, without knowing it, on the very verge of a small gully, the long grass hiding it from view; and in leaning a little back he had shot over, pie and all.

He said he had never felt so surprised in all his life, as when he first felt himself going, without being able to conjecture in the slightest what had happened. He thought at first that the end of the world had come.

Harris believes to this day that George and I planned it all beforehand. Thus does unjust suspicion follow even the most blameless for, as the poet says, "Who shall escape calumny?"

Who, indeed!

CHAPTER XIV.

Wargrave.—Waxworks.—Sonning.—Our stew.— Montmorency is sarcastic.—Fight between Montmorency and the tea-kettle.—George's banjo studies.—Meet with discouragement.—Difficulties in the way of the musical amateur.—Learning to play the bagpipes.—Harris feels sad after supper.—George and I go for a walk.—Return hungry and wet.—There is a strangeness about Harris.—Harris and the swans, a remarkable story.—Harris has a troubled night.

We caught a breeze, after lunch, which took us gently up past Wargrave and Shiplake. Mellowed in the drowsy sunlight of a summer's afternoon, Wargrave, nestling where the river bends, makes a sweet old picture as you pass it, and one that lingers long upon the retina of memory.

The "George and Dragon" at Wargrave boasts a sign, painted on the one side by Leslie, R.A., and on the other by Hodgson of that ilk. Leslie has depicted the fight; Hodgson has imagined the scene, "After the Fight"—George, the work done, enjoying his pint of beer.

Day, the author of *Sandford and Merton*, lived and—more credit to the place still—was killed at Wargrave. In the church is a memorial to Mrs. Sarah Hill, who bequeathed 1 pound annually, to be divided at Easter, between two boys and two girls who "have never been undutiful to their parents; who have never been known to swear or to tell untruths, to steal, or to break windows." Fancy giving up all that for five shillings a year! It is not worth it.

It is rumoured in the town that once, many years ago, a boy appeared who really never had done these things—or at all events, which was all that was required or could be expected, had never been known to do them—and thus won the crown of glory. He was exhibited for three weeks afterwards in the Town Hall, under a glass case.

What has become of the money since no one knows. They say it is always handed over to the nearest wax-works show.

Shiplake is a pretty village, but it cannot be seen from the river, being upon the hill. Tennyson was married in Shiplake Church.

The river up to Sonning winds in and out through many islands, and is very placid, hushed, and lonely. Few folk, except at twilight, a pair or two of rustic lovers, walk along its banks. 'Arry and Lord Fitznoodle have been left behind at Henley, and dismal, dirty Reading is not yet reached. It is a part of the river in which to dream of bygone days, and vanished forms and faces, and things that might have been, but are not, confound them.

We got out at Sonning, and went for a walk round the village. It is the most fairy-like little nook on the whole river. It is more like a stage village than one built of bricks and mortar. Every house is smothered in roses, and now, in early June, they were bursting forth in clouds of dainty splendour. If you stop at Sonning, put up at the "Bull," behind the church. It is a veritable picture of an old country inn, with green, square courtyard in front, where, on seats beneath the trees, the old men group of an evening to drink their ale and gossip over village politics; with low, quaint rooms and latticed windows, and awkward stairs and winding passages.

We roamed about sweet Sonning for an hour or so, and then, it being too late to push on past Reading, we decided to go back to one of the Shiplake islands, and put up there for the night. It was still early when we got settled, and George said that, as we had plenty of time, it would be a splendid opportunity to try a good, slap-up supper. He said he would show us what could be done up the river in the way of cooking, and suggested that, with the vegetables and the remains of the cold beef and general odds and ends, we should make an Irish stew.

It seemed a fascinating idea. George gathered wood and made a fire, and Harris and I started to peel the potatoes. I should never have thought that peeling potatoes was such an undertaking. The job turned out to be the biggest thing of its kind that I had ever been in. We began cheerfully, one might almost say skittishly, but our light-heartedness was gone by the time the first potato was finished. The more we peeled, the more peel there seemed to be left on; by the time we had got all the peel off and all the eyes out, there was no potato left—at least none worth speaking of. George came and had a look at it—it was about the size of a pea-nut. He said:

"Oh, that won't do! You're wasting them. You must scrape them."

So we scraped them, and that was harder work than peeling. They are such an extraordinary shape, potatoes—all bumps and warts and hollows. We worked steadily for five-and-twenty minutes, and did four potatoes. Then we struck. We said we should require the rest of the evening for scraping ourselves.

I never saw such a thing as potato-scraping for making a fellow in a mess. It seemed difficult to believe that the potato-scrapings in which Harris and I stood, half smothered, could have come off four potatoes. It shows you what can be done with economy and care.

George said it was absurd to have only four potatoes in an Irish stew, so we washed half-a-dozen or so more, and put them in without peeling. We also put in a cabbage and about half a peck of peas. George stirred it all up, and then he said that there seemed to be a lot of room to spare, so we overhauled both the hampers, and picked out all the odds and ends and the remnants, and added them to the stew. There were half a pork pie and a bit of cold boiled bacon left, and we put them in. Then George found half a tin of potted salmon, and he emptied that into the pot.

He said that was the advantage of Irish stew: you got rid of such a lot of things. I fished out a couple of eggs that had got cracked, and put those in. George said they would thicken the gravy.

I forget the other ingredients, but I know nothing was wasted; and I remember that, towards the end, Montmorency, who had evinced great interest in the proceedings throughout, strolled away with an earnest and thoughtful air, reappearing, a few minutes afterwards, with a dead water-rat in his mouth, which he evidently wished to present as his contribution to the dinner; whether in a sarcastic spirit, or with a genuine desire to assist, I cannot say.

We had a discussion as to whether the rat should go in or not. Harris said that he thought it would be all right, mixed up with the other things, and that every little helped; but George stood up for precedent. He said he had never heard of water-rats in Irish stew, and he would rather be on the safe side, and not try experiments.

Harris said:

"If you never try a new thing, how can you tell what it's like? It's men such as you that hamper the world's progress. Think of the man who first tried German sausage!"

It was a great success, that Irish stew. I don't think I ever enjoyed a meal more. There was something so fresh and piquant about it. One's palate gets so tired of the old hackneyed things: here was a dish with a new flavour, with a taste like nothing else on earth.

And it was nourishing, too. As George said, there was good stuff in it. The peas and potatoes might have been a bit softer, but we all had good teeth, so that did not matter much: and as for the gravy, it was a poem—a little too rich, perhaps, for a weak stomach, but nutritious.

We finished up with tea and cherry tart. Montmorency had a fight with the kettle during tea-time, and came off a poor second.

Throughout the trip, he had manifested great curiosity concerning the kettle. He would sit and watch it, as it boiled, with a puzzled expression, and would try and rouse it every now and then by growling at it. When it began to splutter and steam, he regarded it as a challenge, and would want to fight it, only, at that precise moment, some one would always dash up and bear off his prey before he could get at it.

To-day he determined he would be beforehand. At the first sound the kettle made, he rose, growling, and advanced towards it in a threatening attitude. It was only a little kettle, but it was full of pluck, and it up and spit at him.

"Ah! would ye!" growled Montmorency, showing his teeth; "I'll teach ye to cheek a hard-working, respectable dog; ye miserable, long-nosed, dirty-looking scoundrel, ye. Come on!"

And he rushed at that poor little kettle, and seized it by the spout.

Then, across the evening stillness, broke a blood-curdling yelp, and Montmorency left the boat, and did a constitutional three times round the island at the rate of thirty-five miles an hour, stopping every now and then to bury his nose in a bit of cool mud.

From that day Montmorency regarded the kettle with a mixture of awe, suspicion, and hate. Whenever he saw it he would growl and back at a rapid rate, with his tail shut down, and the moment it was put upon the stove he would promptly climb out of the boat, and sit on the bank, till the whole tea business was over.

George got out his banjo after supper, and wanted to play it, but Harris objected: he said he had got a headache, and did not feel strong enough to stand it. George thought the music might do him good—said music often soothed the nerves and took away a headache; and he twanged two or three notes, just to show Harris what it was like.

Harris said he would rather have the headache.

George has never learned to play the banjo to this day. He has had too much all-round discouragement to meet. He tried on two or three evenings, while we were up the river, to get a little practice, but it was never a success. Harris's language used to be enough to unnerve any man; added to which, Montmorency would sit and howl steadily, right through the performance. It was not giving the man a fair chance.

"What's he want to howl like that for when I'm playing?" George would exclaim indignantly, while taking aim at him with a boot.

"What do you want to play like that for when he is howling?" Harris would retort, catching the boot. "You let him alone. He can't help howling. He's got a musical ear, and your playing *makes* him howl."

So George determined to postpone study of the banjo until he reached home. But he did not get much opportunity even there. Mrs. P. used to come up and say she was very sorry—for herself, she liked to hear him—but the lady upstairs was in a very delicate state, and the doctor was afraid it might injure the child.

Then George tried taking it out with him late at night, and practising round the square. But the inhabitants complained to the police about it, and a watch was set for him one night, and he was captured. The evidence against him was very clear, and he was bound over to keep the peace for six months.

He seemed to lose heart in the business after that. He did make one or two feeble efforts to take up the work again when the six months had elapsed, but there was always the same coldness—the same want of sympathy on the part of the world to fight against; and, after awhile, he despaired altogether, and advertised the instrument for sale at a great sacrifice—"owner having no further use for same"—and took to learning card tricks instead.

It must be disheartening work learning a musical instrument. You would think that Society, for its own sake, would do all it could to assist a man to acquire the art of playing a musical instrument. But it doesn't!

I knew a young fellow once, who was studying to play the bagpipes, and you would be surprised at the amount of opposition he had to contend with. Why, not even from the members of his own family did he receive what you could call active encouragement. His father was dead against the business from the beginning, and spoke quite unfeelingly on the subject.

My friend used to get up early in the morning to practise, but he had to give that plan up, because of his sister. She was somewhat religiously inclined, and she said it seemed such an awful thing to begin the day like that.

So he sat up at night instead, and played after the family had gone to bed, but that did not do, as it got the house such a bad name. People, going home late, would stop outside to listen, and then put it about all over the town, the next morning, that a fearful murder had been committed at Mr. Jefferson's the night before; and would describe how they had heard the victim's shrieks and the brutal oaths and curses of the murderer, followed by the prayer for mercy, and the last dying gurgle of the corpse.

So they let him practise in the day-time, in the back-kitchen with all the doors shut; but his more successful passages could generally be heard in the sitting-room, in spite of these precautions, and would affect his mother almost to tears.

She said it put her in mind of her poor father (he had been swallowed by a shark, poor man, while bathing off the coast of New Guinea—where the connection came in, she could not explain).

Then they knocked up a little place for him at the bottom of the garden, about quarter of a mile from the house, and made him take the machine down there when he wanted to work it; and sometimes a visitor would come to the house who knew nothing of the matter, and they would forget to tell him all about it, and caution him, and he would go out for a stroll round the garden and suddenly get within earshot of those bagpipes, without being prepared for it, or knowing what it was. If he were a man of strong mind, it only gave him fits; but a person of mere average intellect it usually sent mad.

There is, it must be confessed, something very sad about the early efforts of an amateur in bagpipes. I have felt that myself when listening to my young friend. They appear to be a trying instrument to perform upon. You have to get enough breath for the whole tune before you start—at least, so I gathered from watching Jefferson.

He would begin magnificently with a wild, full, come-to-the-battle sort of a note, that quite roused you. But he would get more and more piano as he went on, and the last verse generally collapsed in the middle with a splutter and a hiss.

You want to be in good health to play the bagpipes.

Young Jefferson only learnt to play one tune on those bagpipes; but I never heard any complaints about the insufficiency of his repertoire—none whatever. This tune was "The Campbells are Coming, Hooray—Hooray!" so he said, though his father always held that it was "The Blue Bells of Scotland." Nobody seemed quite sure what it was exactly, but they all agreed that it sounded Scotch.

Strangers were allowed three guesses, and most of them guessed a different tune each time.

Harris was disagreeable after supper,—I think it must have been the stew that had upset him: he is not used to high living,—so George and I left him in the boat, and settled to go for a mouch round Henley. He said he should have a glass of whisky and a pipe, and fix things up for the night. We were to shout when we returned, and he would row over from the island and fetch us.

"Don't go to sleep, old man," we said as we started.

"Not much fear of that while this stew's on," he grunted, as he pulled back to the island.

Henley was getting ready for the regatta, and was full of bustle. We met a goodish number of men we knew about the town, and in their pleasant company the time slipped by somewhat quickly; so that it was nearly eleven o'clock before we set off on our four-mile walk home—as we had learned to call our little craft by this time.

It was a dismal night, coldish, with a thin rain falling; and as we trudged through the dark, silent fields, talking low to each other, and wondering if we were going right or not, we thought of the cosy boat, with the bright light streaming through the tight-drawn canvas; of Harris and Montmorency, and the whisky, and wished that we were there.

We conjured up the picture of ourselves inside, tired and a little hungry; of the gloomy river and the shapeless trees; and, like a giant glow-worm underneath them, our dear old boat, so snug and warm and cheerful. We could see ourselves at supper there, pecking away at cold meat, and passing each other chunks of bread; we could hear the cheery clatter of our knives, the laughing voices, filling all the space, and overflowing through the opening out into the night. And we hurried on to realise the vision.

We struck the tow-path at length, and that made us happy; because prior to this we had not been sure whether we were walking towards the river or away from it, and when you are tired and want to go to bed uncertainties like that worry you. We passed Skiplake as the clock was striking the quarter to twelve; and then George said, thoughtfully:

"You don't happen to remember which of the islands it was, do you?"

"No," I replied, beginning to grow thoughtful too, "I don't. How many are there?"

"Only four," answered George. "It will be all right, if he's awake."

"And if not?" I queried; but we dismissed that train of thought.

We shouted when we came opposite the first island, but there was no response; so we went to the second, and tried there, and obtained the same result.

"Oh! I remember now," said George; "it was the third one."

And we ran on hopefully to the third one, and hallooed.

No answer!

The case was becoming serious. it was now past midnight. The hotels at Skiplake and Henley would be crammed; and we could not go round, knocking up cottagers and householders in the middle of the night, to know if they let apartments! George suggested walking back to Henley and assaulting a policeman, and so getting a night's lodging in the station-house. But then there was the thought, "Suppose he only hits us back and refuses to lock us up!"

We could not pass the whole night fighting policemen. Besides, we did not want to overdo the thing and get six months.

We despairingly tried what seemed in the darkness to be the fourth island, but met with no better success. The rain was coming down fast now, and evidently meant to last. We were wet to the skin, and cold and miserable. We began to wonder whether there were only four islands or more, or whether we were near the islands at all, or whether we were anywhere within a mile of where we ought to be, or in the wrong part of the river altogether; everything looked so strange and different in the darkness. We began to understand the sufferings of the Babes in the Wood.

Just when we had given up all hope—yes, I know that is always the time that things do happen in novels and tales; but I can't help it. I resolved, when I began to write this book, that I would be strictly truthful in all things; and so I will be, even if I have to employ hackneyed phrases for the purpose.

It *was* just when we had given up all hope, and I must therefore say so. Just when we had given up all hope, then, I suddenly caught sight, a little way below us, of a strange, weird sort of glimmer flickering among the trees on the opposite bank. For an instant I thought of ghosts: it was such a shadowy, mysterious light.

The next moment it flashed across me that it was our boat, and I sent up such a yell across the water that made the night seem to shake in its bed.

We waited breathless for a minute, and then—oh! divinest music of the darkness!—we heard the answering bark of Montmorency. We shouted back loud enough to wake the Seven Sleepers—I never could understand myself why it should take more noise to wake seven sleepers than one—and, after what seemed an hour, but what was really, I suppose, about five minutes, we saw the lighted boat creeping slowly over the blackness, and heard Harris's sleepy voice asking where we were.

There was an unaccountable strangeness about Harris. It was something more than mere ordinary tiredness. He pulled the boat against a part of the bank from which it was quite impossible for us to get into it, and immediately went to sleep. It took us an immense amount of screaming and roaring to wake him up again and put some sense into him; but we succeeded at last, and got safely on board.

Harris had a sad expression on him, so we noticed, when we got into the boat. He gave you the idea of a man who had been through trouble. We asked him if anything had happened, and he said—

"Swans!"

It seemed we had moored close to a swan's nest, and, soon after George and I had gone, the female swan came back, and kicked up a row about it. Harris had chivied her off, and she had gone away, and fetched up her old man. Harris said he had had quite a fight with these two swans; but courage and skill had prevailed in the end, and he had defeated them.

Half-an-hour afterwards they returned with eighteen other swans! It must have been a fearful battle, so far as we could understand Harris's account of it. The swans had tried to drag him and Montmorency out of the boat and drown them; and he had defended himself like a hero for four hours, and had killed the lot, and they had all paddled away to die.

"How many swans did you say there were?" asked George.

"Thirty-two," replied Harris, sleepily.

"You said eighteen just now," said George.

"No, I didn't," grunted Harris; "I said twelve. Think I can't count?"

What were the real facts about these swans we never found out. We questioned Harris on the subject in the morning, and he said, "What swans?" and seemed to think that George and I had been dreaming.

Oh, how delightful it was to be safe in the boat, after our trials and fears! We ate a hearty supper, George and I, and we should have had some toddy after it, if we could have found the whisky, but we could not. We examined Harris as to what he had done with it; but he did not seem to know what we meant by "whisky," or what we were talking about at all. Montmorency looked as if he knew something, but said nothing.

I slept well that night, and should have slept better if it had not been for Harris. I have a vague recollection of having been woke up at least a dozen times during the night by Harris wandering about the boat with the lantern, looking for his clothes. He seemed to be worrying about his clothes all night.

Twice he routed up George and myself to see if we were lying on his trousers. George got quite wild the second time.

"What the thunder do you want your trousers for, in the middle of the night?" he asked indignantly. "Why don't you lie down, and go to sleep?"

I found him in trouble, the next time I awoke, because he could not find his socks; and my last hazy remembrance is of being rolled over on my side, and of hearing Harris muttering something about its being an extraordinary thing where his umbrella could have got to.

CHAPTER XV.

Household duties.—Love of work.—The old river hand, what he does and what he tells you he has done.—Scepticism of the new generation.—Early boating recollections.—Rafting.—George does the thing in style.—The old boatman, his method.—So calm, so full of peace.—The beginner.—Punting.—A sad accident.—Pleasures of friendship.—Sailing, my first experience.—Possible reason why we were not drowned.

We woke late the next morning, and, at Harris's earnest desire, partook of a plain breakfast, with "non dainties." Then we cleaned up, and put everything straight (a continual labour, which was beginning to afford me a pretty clear insight into a question that had often posed me—namely, how a woman with the work of only one house on her hands manages to pass away her time), and, at about ten, set out on what we had determined should be a good day's journey.

We agreed that we would pull this morning, as a change from towing; and Harris thought the best arrangement would be that George and I should scull, and he steer. I did not chime in with this idea at all; I said I thought Harris would have been showing a more proper spirit if he had suggested that he and George should work, and let me rest a bit. It seemed to me that I was doing more than my fair share of the work on this trip, and I was beginning to feel strongly on the subject.

It always does seem to me that I am doing more work than I should do. It is not that I object to the work, mind you; I like work: it fascinates me. I can sit and look at it for hours. I love to keep it by me: the idea of getting rid of it nearly breaks my heart.

You cannot give me too much work; to accumulate work has almost become a passion with me: my study is so full of it now, that there is hardly an inch of room for any more. I shall have to throw out a wing soon.

And I am careful of my work, too. Why, some of the work that I have by me now has been in my possession for years and years, and there isn't a finger-mark on it. I take a great pride in my work; I take it down now and then and dust it. No man keeps his work in a better state of preservation than I do.

But, though I crave for work, I still like to be fair. I do not ask for more than my proper share.

But I get it without asking for it—at least, so it appears to me—and this worries me.

George says he does not think I need trouble myself on the subject. He thinks it is only my over-scrupulous nature that makes me fear I am having more than my due; and that, as a matter of fact, I don't have half as much as I ought. But I expect he only says this to comfort me.

In a boat, I have always noticed that it is the fixed idea of each member of the crew that he is doing everything. Harris's notion was, that it was he alone who had been working, and that both George and I had been imposing upon him. George, on the other hand, ridiculed the idea of Harris's having done anything more than eat and sleep, and had a cast-iron opinion that it was he—George himself—who had done all the labour worth speaking of.

He said he had never been out with such a couple of lazily skulks as Harris and I.

That amused Harris.

"Fancy old George talking about work!" he laughed; "why, about half-an-hour of it would kill him. Have you ever seen George work?" he added, turning to me.

I agreed with Harris that I never had—most certainly not since we had started on this trip.

"Well, I don't see how *you* can know much about it, one way or the other," George retorted on Harris; "for I'm blest if you haven't been asleep half the time.

Have you ever seen Harris fully awake, except at meal-time?" asked George, addressing me.

Truth compelled me to support George. Harris had been very little good in the boat, so far as helping was concerned, from the beginning.

"Well, hang it all, I've done more than old J., anyhow," rejoined Harris.

"Well, you couldn't very well have done less," added George.

"I suppose J. thinks he is the passenger," continued Harris.

And that was their gratitude to me for having brought them and their wretched old boat all the way up from Kingston, and for having superintended and managed everything for them, and taken care of them, and slaved for them. It is the way of the world.

We settled the present difficulty by arranging that Harris and George should scull up past Reading, and that I should tow the boat on from there. Pulling a heavy boat against a strong stream has few attractions for me now. There was a time, long ago, when I used to clamour for the hard work: now I like to give the youngsters a chance.

I notice that most of the old river hands are similarly retiring, whenever there is any stiff pulling to be done. You can always tell the old river hand by the way in which he stretches himself out upon the cushions at the bottom of the boat, and encourages the rowers by telling them anecdotes about the marvellous feats he performed last season.

"Call what you're doing hard work!" he drawls, between his contented whiffs, addressing the two perspiring novices, who have been grinding away steadily up stream for the last hour and a half; "why, Jim Biffles and Jack and I, last season, pulled up from Marlow to Goring in one afternoon—never stopped once. Do you remember that, Jack?"

Jack, who has made himself a bed up in the prow of all the rugs and coats he can collect, and who has been lying there asleep for the last two hours, partially wakes up on being thus appealed to, and recollects all about the matter, and also remembers that there was an unusually strong stream against them all the way—likewise a stiff wind.

"About thirty-four miles, I suppose, it must have been," adds the first speaker, reaching down another cushion to put under his head.

"No—no; don't exaggerate, Tom," murmurs Jack, reprovingly; "thirty-three at the outside."

And Jack and Tom, quite exhausted by this conversational effort, drop off to sleep once more. And the two simple-minded youngsters at the sculls feel quite proud of being allowed to row such wonderful oarsmen as Jack and Tom, and strain away harder than ever.

When I was a young man, I used to listen to these tales from my elders, and take them in, and swallow them, and digest every word of them, and then come up for more; but the new generation do not seem to have the simple faith of the old times. We—George, Harris, and myself—took a "raw 'un" up with us once last season, and we plied him with the customary stretchers about the wonderful things we had done all the way up.

We gave him all the regular ones—the time-honoured lies that have done duty up the river with every boating-man for years past—and added seven entirely original ones that we had invented for ourselves, including a really quite likely story, founded, to a certain extent, on an all but true episode, which had actually happened in a modified degree some years ago to friends of ours—a story that a mere child could have believed without injuring itself, much.

And that young man mocked at them all, and wanted us to repeat the feats then and there, and to bet us ten to one that we didn't.

We got to chatting about our rowing experiences this morning, and to recounting stories of our first efforts in the art of oarsmanship. My own earliest boating recollection is of five of us contributing threepence each and taking out a curiously constructed craft on the Regent's Park lake, drying ourselves subsequently, in the park-keeper's lodge.

After that, having acquired a taste for the water, I did a good deal of rafting in various suburban brickfields—an exercise providing more interest and excitement than might be imagined, especially when you are in the middle of the pond and the proprietor of the materials of which the raft is constructed suddenly appears on the bank, with a big stick in his hand.

Your first sensation on seeing this gentleman is that, somehow or other, you don't feel equal to company and conversation, and that, if you could do so without appearing rude, you would rather avoid meeting him; and your object is, therefore, to get off on the opposite side of the pond to which he is, and to go home quietly and quickly, pretending not to see him. He, on the contrary is yearning to take you by the hand, and talk to you.

It appears that he knows your father, and is intimately acquainted with yourself, but this does not draw you towards him. He says he'll teach you to take his boards and make a raft of them; but, seeing that you know how to do this pretty well already, the offer, though doubtless kindly meant, seems a superfluous one on his part, and you are reluctant to put him to any trouble by accepting it.

His anxiety to meet you, however, is proof against all your coolness, and the energetic manner in which he dodges up and down the pond so as to be on the spot to greet you when you land is really quite flattering.

If he be of a stout and short-winded build, you can easily avoid his advances; but, when he is of the youthful and long-legged type, a meeting is inevitable. The interview is, however, extremely brief, most of the conversation being on his part, your remarks being mostly of an exclamatory and mono-syllabic order, and as soon as you can tear yourself away you do so.

I devoted some three months to rafting, and, being then as proficient as there was any need to be at that branch of the art, I determined to go in for rowing proper, and joined one of the Lea boating clubs.

Being out in a boat on the river Lea, especially on Saturday afternoons, soon makes you smart at handling a craft, and spry at escaping being run down by roughs or swamped by barges; and it also affords plenty of opportunity for acquiring the most prompt and graceful method of lying down flat at the bottom of the boat so as to avoid being chucked out into the river by passing tow-lines.

But it does not give you style. It was not till I came to the Thames that I got style. My style of rowing is very much admired now. People say it is so quaint.

George never went near the water until he was sixteen. Then he and eight other gentlemen of about the same age went down in a body to Kew one Saturday, with the idea of hiring a boat there, and pulling to Richmond and back; one of their number, a shock-headed youth, named Joskins, who had once or twice taken out a boat on the Serpentine, told them it was jolly fun, boating!

The tide was running out pretty rapidly when they reached the landing-stage, and there was a stiff breeze blowing across the river, but this did not trouble them at all, and they proceeded to select their boat.

There was an eight-oared racing outrigger drawn up on the stage; that was the one that took their fancy. They said they'd have that one, please. The boatman was away, and only his boy was in charge. The boy tried to damp their ardour for the outrigger, and showed them two or three very comfortable-looking boats of the family-party build, but those would not do at all; the outrigger was the boat they thought they would look best in.

So the boy launched it, and they took off their coats and prepared to take their seats. The boy suggested that George, who, even in those days, was always the heavy man of any party, should be number four. George said he should be happy to be number four, and promptly stepped into bow's place, and sat down with his back to the stern. They got him into his proper position at last, and then the others followed.

A particularly nervous boy was appointed cox, and the steering principle explained to him by Joskins. Joskins himself took stroke. He told the others that it was simple enough; all they had to do was to follow him.

They said they were ready, and the boy on the landing stage took a boat-hook and shoved him off.

What then followed George is unable to describe in detail. He has a confused recollection of having, immediately on starting, received a violent blow in the small of the back from the butt-end of number five's scull, at the same time that his own seat seemed to disappear from under him by magic, and leave him sitting on the boards. He also noticed, as a curious circumstance, that number two was at the same instant lying on his back at the bottom of the boat, with his legs in the air, apparently in a fit.

They passed under Kew Bridge, broadside, at the rate of eight miles an hour. Joskins being the only one who was rowing. George, on recovering his seat, tried to help him, but, on dipping his oar into the water, it immediately, to his intense surprise, disappeared under the boat, and nearly took him with it.

And then "cox" threw both rudder lines over-board, and burst into tears.

How they got back George never knew, but it took them just forty minutes. A dense crowd watched the entertainment from Kew Bridge with much interest, and everybody shouted out to them different directions. Three times they managed to get the boat back through the arch, and three times they were carried under it again, and every time "cox" looked up and saw the bridge above him he broke out into renewed sobs.

George said he little thought that afternoon that he should ever come to really like boating.

Harris is more accustomed to sea rowing than to river work, and says that, as an exercise, he prefers it. I don't. I remember taking a small boat out at Eastbourne last summer: I used to do a good deal of sea rowing years ago, and I thought I should be all right; but I found I had forgotten the art entirely. When one scull was deep down underneath the water, the other would be flourishing wildly about in the air. To get a grip of the water with both at the same time I had to stand up. The parade was crowded with nobility and gentry, and I had to pull past them in this ridiculous fashion. I landed half-way down the beach, and secured the services of an old boatman to take me back.

I like to watch an old boatman rowing, especially one who has been hired by the hour. There is something so beautifully calm and restful about his method. It is so free from that fretful haste, that vehement striving, that is every day becoming more and more the bane of nineteenth-century life. He is not for ever straining himself to pass all the other boats. If another boat overtakes him and passes him it does not annoy him; as a matter of fact, they all do overtake him and pass him—all those that are going his way. This would trouble and irritate some people; the sublime equanimity of the hired boatman under the ordeal affords us a beautiful lesson against ambition and uppishness.

Plain practical rowing of the get-the-boat-along order is not a very difficult art to acquire, but it takes a good deal of practice before a man feels comfortable, when rowing past girls. It is the "time" that worries a youngster. "It's jolly funny," he says, as for the twentieth time within five minutes he disentangles his sculls from yours; "I can get on all right when I'm by myself!"

To see two novices try to keep time with one another is very amusing. Bow finds it impossible to keep pace with stroke, because stroke rows in such an extraordinary fashion. Stroke is intensely indignant at this, and explains that what he has been endeavouring to do for the last ten minutes is to adapt his method to bow's limited capacity. Bow, in turn, then becomes insulted, and requests stroke not to trouble his head about him (bow), but to devote his mind to setting a sensible stroke.

"Or, shall *I* take stroke?" he adds, with the evident idea that that would at once put the whole matter right.

They splash along for another hundred yards with still moderate success, and then the whole secret of their trouble bursts upon stroke like a flash of inspiration.

"I tell you what it is: you've got my sculls," he cries, turning to bow; "pass yours over."

"Well, do you know, I've been wondering how it was I couldn't get on with these," answers bow, quite brightening up, and most willingly assisting in the exchange. "*Now* we shall be all right."

But they are not—not even then. Stroke has to stretch his arms nearly out of their sockets to reach his sculls now; while bow's pair, at each recovery, hit him a violent blow in the chest. So they change back again, and come to the conclusion that the man has given them the wrong set altogether; and over their mutual abuse of this man they become quite friendly and sympathetic.

George said he had often longed to take to punting for a change. Punting is not as easy as it looks. As in rowing, you soon learn how to get along and handle the craft, but it takes long practice before you can do this with dignity and without getting the water all up your sleeve.

One young man I knew had a very sad accident happen to him the first time he went punting. He had been getting on so well that he had grown quite cheeky over the business, and was walking up and down the punt, working his pole with a careless grace that was quite fascinating to watch. Up he would march to the head of the punt, plant his pole, and then run along right to the other end, just like an old punter. Oh! it was grand.

And it would all have gone on being grand if he had not unfortunately, while looking round to enjoy the scenery, taken just one step more than there was any necessity for, and walked off the punt altogether. The pole was firmly fixed in the mud, and he was left clinging to it while the punt drifted away. It was an undignified position for him. A rude boy on the bank immediately yelled out to a lagging chum to "hurry up and see real monkey on a stick."

I could not go to his assistance, because, as ill-luck would have it, we had not taken the proper precaution to bring out a spare pole with us. I could only sit and look at him. His expression as the pole slowly sank with him I shall never forget; there was so much thought in it.

I watched him gently let down into the water, and saw him scramble out, sad and wet. I could not help laughing, he looked such a ridiculous figure. I continued to chuckle to myself about it for some time, and then it was suddenly forced in upon me that really I had got very little to laugh at when I came to think of it. Here was I, alone in a punt, without a pole, drifting helplessly down midstream—possibly towards a weir.

I began to feel very indignant with my friend for having stepped overboard and gone off in that way. He might, at all events, have left me the pole.

I drifted on for about a quarter of a mile, and then I came in sight of a fishingpunt moored in mid-stream, in which sat two old fishermen. They saw me bearing down upon them, and they called out to me to keep out of their way.

"I can't," I shouted back.

"But you don't try," they answered.

I explained the matter to them when I got nearer, and they caught me and lent me a pole. The weir was just fifty yards below. I am glad they happened to be there.

The first time I went punting was in company with three other fellows; they were going to show me how to do it. We could not all start together, so I said I would go down first and get out the punt, and then I could potter about and practice a bit until they came.

I could not get a punt out that afternoon, they were all engaged; so I had nothing else to do but to sit down on the bank, watching the river, and waiting for my friends.

I had not been sitting there long before my attention became attracted to a man in a punt who, I noticed with some surprise, wore a jacket and cap exactly like mine. He was evidently a novice at punting, and his performance was most interesting. You never knew what was going to happen when he put the pole in; he evidently did not know himself. Sometimes he shot up stream and sometimes he shot down stream, and at other times he simply spun round and came up the other side of the pole. And with every result he seemed equally surprised and annoyed.

The people about the river began to get quite absorbed in him after a while, and to make bets with one another as to what would be the outcome of his next push.

In the course of time my friends arrived on the opposite bank, and they stopped and watched him too. His back was towards them, and they only saw his jacket and cap. From this they immediately jumped to the conclusion that it was I, their beloved companion, who was making an exhibition of himself, and their delight knew no bounds. They commenced to chaff him unmercifully.

I did not grasp their mistake at first, and I thought, "How rude of them to go on like that, with a perfect stranger, too!" But before I could call out and reprove them, the explanation of the matter occurred to me, and I withdrew behind a tree.

Oh, how they enjoyed themselves, ridiculing that young man! For five good minutes they stood there, shouting ribaldry at him, deriding him, mocking him, jeering at him. They peppered him with stale jokes, they even made a few new ones and threw at him. They hurled at him all the private family jokes belonging to our set, and which must have been perfectly unintelligible to him. And then, unable to stand their brutal jibes any longer, he turned round on them, and they saw his face!

I was glad to notice that they had sufficient decency left in them to look very foolish. They explained to him that they had thought he was some one they knew. They said they hoped he would not deem them capable of so insulting any one except a personal friend of their own.

Of course their having mistaken him for a friend excused it. I remember Harris telling me once of a bathing experience he had at Boulogne. He was swimming about there near the beach, when he felt himself suddenly seized by the neck from behind, and forcibly plunged under water. He struggled violently, but whoever had got hold of him seemed to be a perfect Hercules in strength, and all his efforts to escape were unavailing. He had given up kicking, and was trying to turn his thoughts upon solemn things, when his captor released him.

He regained his feet, and looked round for his would-be murderer. The assassin was standing close by him, laughing heartily, but the moment he caught sight of Harris's face, as it emerged from the water, he started back and seemed quite concerned.

"I really beg your pardon," he stammered confusedly, "but I took you for a friend of mine!"

Harris thought it was lucky for him the man had not mistaken him for a relation, or he would probably have been drowned outright.

Sailing is a thing that wants knowledge and practice too—though, as a boy, I did not think so. I had an idea it came natural to a body, like rounders and touch. I knew another boy who held this view likewise, and so, one windy day, we thought we would try the sport. We were stopping down at Yarmouth, and we decided we would go for a trip up the Yare. We hired a sailing boat at the yard by the bridge, and started off.

"It's rather a rough day," said the man to us, as we put off: "better take in a reef and luff sharp when you get round the bend."

We said we would make a point of it, and left him with a cheery "Good-morning," wondering to ourselves how you "luffed," and where we were to get a "reef" from, and what we were to do with it when we had got it.

We rowed until we were out of sight of the town, and then, with a wide stretch of water in front of us, and the wind blowing a perfect hurricane across it, we felt that the time had come to commence operations.

Hector—I think that was his name—went on pulling while I unrolled the sail. It seemed a complicated job, but I accomplished it at length, and then came the question, which was the top end?

By a sort of natural instinct, we, of course, eventually decided that the bottom was the top, and set to work to fix it upside-down. But it was a long time before we could get it up, either that way or any other way. The impression on the mind of the sail seemed to be that we were playing at funerals, and that I was the corpse and itself was the winding-sheet.

When it found that this was not the idea, it hit me over the head with the boom, and refused to do anything.

"Wet it," said Hector; "drop it over and get it wet."

He said people in ships always wetted the sails before they put them up. So I wetted it; but that only made matters worse than they were before. A dry sail clinging to your legs and wrapping itself round your head is not pleasant, but, when the sail is sopping wet, it becomes quite vexing.

We did get the thing up at last, the two of us together. We fixed it, not exactly upside down—more sideways like—and we tied it up to the mast with the painter, which we cut off for the purpose.

That the boat did not upset I simply state as a fact. Why it did not upset I am unable to offer any reason. I have often thought about the matter since, but I have never succeeded in arriving at any satisfactory explanation of the phenomenon.

Possibly the result may have been brought about by the natural obstinacy of all things in this world. The boat may possibly have come to the conclusion, judging from a cursory view of our behaviour, that we had come out for a morning's sui-cide, and had thereupon determined to disappoint us. That is the only suggestion I can offer.

By clinging like grim death to the gunwale, we just managed to keep inside the boat, but it was exhausting work. Hector said that pirates and other seafaring people generally lashed the rudder to something or other, and hauled in the main top-jib, during severe squalls, and thought we ought to try to do something of the kind; but I was for letting her have her head to the wind.

As my advice was by far the easiest to follow, we ended by adopting it, and contrived to embrace the gunwale and give her her head.

The boat travelled up stream for about a mile at a pace I have never sailed at since, and don't want to again. Then, at a bend, she heeled over till half her sail was under water. Then she righted herself by a miracle and flew for a long low bank of soft mud.

That mud-bank saved us. The boat ploughed its way into the middle of it and then stuck. Finding that we were once more able to move according to our ideas, instead of being pitched and thrown about like peas in a bladder, we crept forward, and cut down the sail.

We had had enough sailing. We did not want to overdo the thing and get a surfeit of it. We had had a sail—a good all-round exciting, interesting sail—and now we thought we would have a row, just for a change like.

We took the sculls and tried to push the boat off the mud, and, in doing so, we broke one of the sculls. After that we proceeded with great caution, but they were a wretched old pair, and the second one cracked almost easier than the first, and left us helpless.

The mud stretched out for about a hundred yards in front of us, and behind us was the water. The only thing to be done was to sit and wait until someone came by.

It was not the sort of day to attract people out on the river, and it was three hours before a soul came in sight. It was an old fisherman who, with immense difficulty, at last rescued us, and we were towed back in an ignominious fashion to the boat-yard.

What between tipping the man who had brought us home, and paying for the broken sculls, and for having been out four hours and a half, it cost us a pretty considerable number of weeks' pocket-money, that sail. But we learned experience, and they say that is always cheap at any price.

CHAPTER XVI.

Reading.—We are towed by steam launch.—Irritating behaviour of small boats.—How they get in the way of steam launches.—George and Harris again shirk their work.—Rather a hackneyed story.—Streatley and Goring.

We came in sight of Reading about eleven. The river is dirty and dismal here. One does not linger in the neighbourhood of Reading. The town itself is a famous old place, dating from the dim days of King Ethelred, when the Danes anchored their warships in the Kennet, and started from Reading to ravage all the land of Wessex; and here Ethelred and his brother Alfred fought and defeated them, Ethelred doing the praying and Alfred the fighting.

In later years, Reading seems to have been regarded as a handy place to run down to, when matters were becoming unpleasant in London. Parliament generally rushed off to Reading whenever there was a plague on at Westminster; and, in 1625, the Law followed suit, and all the courts were held at Reading. It must have been worth while having a mere ordinary plague now and then in London to get rid of both the lawyers and the Parliament.

During the Parliamentary struggle, Reading was besieged by the Earl of Essex, and, a quarter of a century later, the Prince of Orange routed King James's troops there.

Henry I. lies buried at Reading, in the Benedictine abbey founded by him there, the ruins of which may still be seen; and, in this same abbey, great John of Gaunt was married to the Lady Blanche.

At Reading lock we came up with a steam launch, belonging to some friends of mine, and they towed us up to within about a mile of Streatley. It is very delightful being towed up by a launch. I prefer it myself to rowing. The run would have been more delightful still, if it had not been for a lot of wretched small boats that were continually getting in the way of our launch, and, to avoid running down which, we had to be continually easing and stopping. It is really most annoying, the manner in which these rowing boats get in the way of one's launch up the river; something ought to done to stop it.

And they are so confoundedly impertinent, too, over it. You can whistle till you nearly burst your boiler before they will trouble themselves to hurry. I would have one or two of them run down now and then, if I had my way, just to teach them all a lesson.

The river becomes very lovely from a little above Reading. The railway rather spoils it near Tilehurst, but from Mapledurham up to Streatley it is glorious. A little above Mapledurham lock you pass Hardwick House, where Charles I. played bowls. The neighbourhood of Pangbourne, where the quaint little Swan Inn stands, must be as familiar to the *habitues* of the Art Exhibitions as it is to its own inhabitants.

My friends' launch cast us loose just below the grotto, and then Harris wanted to make out that it was my turn to pull. This seemed to me most unreasonable. It had been arranged in the morning that I should bring the boat up to three miles above Reading. Well, here we were, ten miles above Reading! Surely it was now their turn again.

I could not get either George or Harris to see the matter in its proper light, however; so, to save argument, I took the sculls. I had not been pulling for more than a minute or so, when George noticed something black floating on the water, and we drew up to it. George leant over, as we neared it, and laid hold of it. And then he drew back with a cry, and a blanched face.

It was the dead body of a woman. It lay very lightly on the water, and the face was sweet and calm. It was not a beautiful face; it was too prematurely aged-looking, too thin and drawn, to be that; but it was a gentle, lovable face, in spite of its stamp of pinch and poverty, and upon it was that look of restful peace that comes to the faces of the sick sometimes when at last the pain has left them.

Fortunately for us—we having no desire to be kept hanging about coroners' courts—some men on the bank had seen the body too, and now took charge of it from us.

We found out the woman's story afterwards. Of course it was the old, old vulgar tragedy. She had loved and been deceived—or had deceived herself. Anyhow, she had sinned—some of us do now and then—and her family and friends, naturally shocked and indignant, had closed their doors against her.

Left to fight the world alone, with the millstone of her shame around her neck, she had sunk ever lower and lower. For a while she had kept both herself and the child on the twelve shillings a week that twelve hours' drudgery a day procured her, paying six shillings out of it for the child, and keeping her own body and soul together on the remainder.

Six shillings a week does not keep body and soul together very unitedly. They want to get away from each other when there is only such a very slight bond as that between them; and one day, I suppose, the pain and the dull monotony of it all had stood before her eyes plainer than usual, and the mocking spectre had frightened her. She had made one last appeal to friends, but, against the chill wall of their respectability, the voice of the erring outcast fell unheeded; and then she had gone to see her child—had held it in her arms and kissed it, in a weary, dull sort of way, and without betraying any particular emotion of any kind, and had left it, after putting into its hand a penny box of chocolate she had bought it, and afterwards, with her last few shillings, had taken a ticket and come down to Goring.

It seemed that the bitterest thoughts of her life must have centred about the wooded reaches and the bright green meadows around Goring; but women strangely hug the knife that stabs them, and, perhaps, amidst the gall, there may have mingled also sunny memories of sweetest hours, spent upon those shadowed deeps over which the great trees bend their branches down so low.

She had wandered about the woods by the river's brink all day, and then, when evening fell and the grey twilight spread its dusky robe upon the waters, she stretched her arms out to the silent river that had known her sorrow and her joy. And the old river had taken her into its gentle arms, and had laid her weary head upon its bosom, and had hushed away the pain.

Thus had she sinned in all things—sinned in living and in dying. God help her! and all other sinners, if any more there be.

Goring on the left bank and Streatley on the right are both or either charming places to stay at for a few days. The reaches down to Pangbourne woo one for a sunny sail or for a moonlight row, and the country round about is full of beauty. We had intended to push on to Wallingford that day, but the sweet smiling face of the river here lured us to linger for a while; and so we left our boat at the bridge, and went up into Streatley, and lunched at the "Bull," much to Montmorency's satisfaction.

They say that the hills on each ride of the stream here once joined and formed a barrier across what is now the Thames, and that then the river ended there above Goring in one vast lake. I am not in a position either to contradict or affirm this statement. I simply offer it.

It is an ancient place, Streatley, dating back, like most river-side towns and villages, to British and Saxon times. Goring is not nearly so pretty a little spot to stop at as Streatley, if you have your choice; but it is passing fair enough in its way, and is nearer the railway in case you want to slip off without paying your hotel bill.

CHAPTER XVII.

Washing day.—Fish and fishers.—On the art of angling.—A conscientious fly-fisher.—A fishy story.

We stayed two days at Streatley, and got our clothes washed. We had tried washing them ourselves, in the river, under George's superintendence, and it had been a failure. Indeed, it had been more than a failure, because we were worse off after we had washed our clothes than we were before. Before we had washed them, they had been very, very dirty, it is true; but they were just wearable. *After* we had washed them—well, the river between Reading and Henley was much cleaner, after we had washed our clothes in it, than it was before. All the dirt contained in the river between Reading and Henley, we collected, during that wash, and worked it into our clothes.

The washerwoman at Streatley said she felt she owed it to herself to charge us just three times the usual prices for that wash. She said it had not been like washing, it had been more in the nature of excavating.

We paid the bill without a murmur.

The neighbourhood of Streatley and Goring is a great fishing centre. There is some excellent fishing to be had here. The river abounds in pike, roach, dace, gudgeon, and eels, just here; and you can sit and fish for them all day.

Some people do. They never catch them. I never knew anybody catch anything, up the Thames, except minnows and dead cats, but that has nothing to do, of course, with fishing! The local fisherman's guide doesn't say a word about catching anything. All it says is the place is "a good station for fishing;" and, from what I have seen of the district, I am quite prepared to bear out this statement.

There is no spot in the world where you can get more fishing, or where you can fish for a longer period. Some fishermen come here and fish for a day, and others stop and fish for a month. You can hang on and fish for a year, if you want to: it will be all the same.

The *Angler's Guide to the Thames* says that "jack and perch are also to be had about here," but there the *Angler's Guide* is wrong. Jack and perch may *be* about there. Indeed, I know for a fact that they are. You can *see* them there in shoals, when you are out for a walk along the banks: they come and stand half out of the water with their mouths open for biscuits. And, if you go for a bathe, they crowd round, and get in your way, and irritate you. But they are not to be "had" by a bit of worm on the end of a hook, nor anything like it—not they!

I am not a good fisherman myself. I devoted a considerable amount of attention to the subject at one time, and was getting on, as I thought, fairly well; but the old hands told me that I should never be any real good at it, and advised me to give it up. They said that I was an extremely neat thrower, and that I seemed to have plenty of gumption for the thing, and quite enough constitutional laziness. But they were sure I should never make anything of a fisherman. I had not got sufficient imagination.

They said that as a poet, or a shilling shocker, or a reporter, or anything of that kind, I might be satisfactory, but that, to gain any position as a Thames angler, would require more play of fancy, more power of invention than I appeared to possess.

Some people are under the impression that all that is required to make a good fisherman is the ability to tell lies easily and without blushing; but this is a mistake. Mere bald fabrication is useless; the veriest tyro can manage that. It is in the circumstantial detail, the embellishing touches of probability, the general air of scrupulous—almost of pedantic—veracity, that the experienced angler is seen.

Anybody can come in and say, "Oh, I caught fifteen dozen perch yesterday evening;" or "Last Monday I landed a gudgeon, weighing eighteen pounds, and measuring three feet from the tip to the tail."

There is no art, no skill, required for that sort of thing. It shows pluck, but that is all.

No; your accomplished angler would scorn to tell a lie, that way. His method is a study in itself.

He comes in quietly with his hat on, appropriates the most comfortable chair, lights his pipe, and commences to puff in silence. He lets the youngsters brag away for a while, and then, during a momentary lull, he removes the pipe from his mouth, and remarks, as he knocks the ashes out against the bars:

"Well, I had a haul on Tuesday evening that it's not much good my telling anybody about."

"Oh! why's that?" they ask.

"Because I don't expect anybody would believe me if I did," replies the old fellow calmly, and without even a tinge of bitterness in his tone, as he refills his pipe, and requests the landlord to bring him three of Scotch, cold.

There is a pause after this, nobody feeling sufficiently sure of himself to contradict the old gentleman. So he has to go on by himself without any encouragement.

"No," he continues thoughtfully; "I shouldn't believe it myself if anybody told it to me, but it's a fact, for all that. I had been sitting there all the afternoon and had caught literally nothing—except a few dozen dace and a score of jack; and I was just about giving it up as a bad job when I suddenly felt a rather smart pull at the line. I thought it was another little one, and I went to jerk it up. Hang me, if I could move the rod! It took me half-an-hour—half-an-hour, sir!—to land that fish; and every moment I thought the line was going to snap! I reached him at last, and what do you think it was? A sturgeon! a forty pound sturgeon! taken on a line, sir! Yes, you may well look surprised—I'll have another three of Scotch, landlord, please."

And then he goes on to tell of the astonishment of everybody who saw it; and what his wife said, when he got home, and of what Joe Buggles thought about it.

I asked the landlord of an inn up the river once, if it did not injure him, sometimes, listening to the tales that the fishermen about there told him; and he said:

"Oh, no; not now, sir. It did used to knock me over a bit at first, but, lor love you! me and the missus we listens to 'em all day now. It's what you're used to, you know. It's what you're used to."

I knew a young man once, he was a most conscientious fellow, and, when he took to fly-fishing, he determined never to exaggerate his hauls by more than twenty-five per cent.

"When I have caught forty fish," said he, "then I will tell people that I have caught fifty, and so on. But I will not lie any more than that, because it is sinful to lie."

But the twenty-five per cent. plan did not work well at all. He never was able to use it. The greatest number of fish he ever caught in one day was three, and you can't add twenty-five per cent. to three—at least, not in fish.

So he increased his percentage to thirty-three-and-a-third; but that, again, was awkward, when he had only caught one or two; so, to simplify matters, he made up his mind to just double the quantity.

He stuck to this arrangement for a couple of months, and then he grew dissatisfied with it. Nobody believed him when he told them that he only doubled, and he, therefore, gained no credit that way whatever, while his moderation put him at a disadvantage among the other anglers. When he had really caught three small fish, and said he had caught six, it used to make him quite jealous to hear a man, whom he knew for a fact had only caught one, going about telling people he had landed two dozen.

So, eventually, he made one final arrangement with himself, which he has religiously held to ever since, and that was to count each fish that he caught as ten, and to assume ten to begin with. For example, if he did not catch any fish at all, then he said he had caught ten fish—you could never catch less than ten fish by his system; that was the foundation of it. Then, if by any chance he really did catch one fish, he called it twenty, while two fish would count thirty, three forty, and so on.

It is a simple and easily worked plan, and there has been some talk lately of its being made use of by the angling fraternity in general. Indeed, the Committee of the Thames Angler's Association did recommend its adoption about two years ago, but some of the older members opposed it. They said they would consider the idea if the number were doubled, and each fish counted as twenty.

If ever you have an evening to spare, up the river, I should advise you to drop into one of the little village inns, and take a seat in the tap-room. You will be nearly sure to meet one or two old rod-men, sipping their toddy there, and they will tell you enough fishy stories, in half an hour, to give you indigestion for a month.

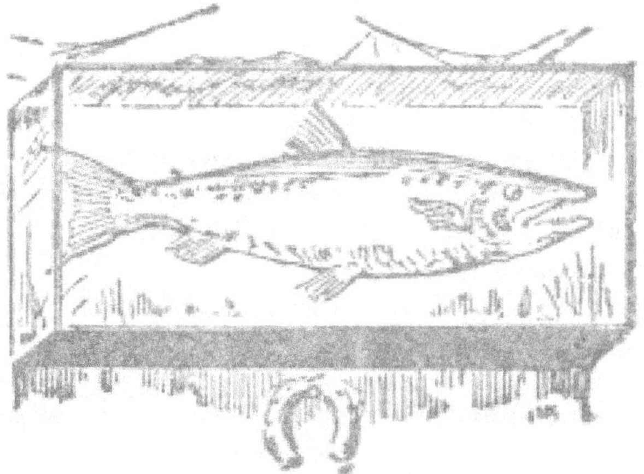

George and I—I don't know what had become of Harris; he had gone out and had a shave, early in the afternoon, and had then come back and spent full forty minutes in pipeclaying his shoes, we had not seen him since—George and I, therefore, and the dog, left to ourselves, went for a walk to Wallingford on the second evening, and, coming home, we called in at a little river-side inn, for a rest, and other things.

We went into the parlour and sat down. There was an old fellow there, smoking a long clay pipe, and we naturally began chatting.

He told us that it had been a fine day to-day, and we told him that it had been a fine day yesterday, and then we all told each other that we thought it would be a fine day to-morrow; and George said the crops seemed to be coming up nicely.

After that it came out, somehow or other, that we were strangers in the neighbourhood, and that we were going away the next morning.

Then a pause ensued in the conversation, during which our eyes wandered round the room. They finally rested upon a dusty old glass-case, fixed very high up above the chimney-piece, and containing a trout. It rather fascinated me, that trout; it was such a monstrous fish. In fact, at first glance, I thought it was a cod.

"Ah!" said the old gentleman, following the direction of my gaze, "fine fellow that, ain't he?"

"Quite uncommon," I murmured; and George asked the old man how much he thought it weighed.

"Eighteen pounds six ounces," said our friend, rising and taking down his coat. "Yes," he continued, "it wur sixteen year ago, come the third o' next month, that I landed him. I caught him just below the bridge with a minnow. They told me he wur in the river, and I said I'd have him, and so I did. You don't see many fish that size about here now, I'm thinking. Good-night, gentlemen, good-night."

And out he went, and left us alone.

We could not take our eyes off the fish after that. It really was a remarkably fine fish. We were still looking at it, when the local carrier, who had just stopped at the inn, came to the door of the room with a pot of beer in his hand, and he also looked at the fish.

"Good-sized trout, that," said George, turning round to him.

"Ah! you may well say that, sir," replied the man; and then, after a pull at his beer, he added, "Maybe you wasn't here, sir, when that fish was caught?"

"No," we told him. We were strangers in the neighbourhood.

"Ah!" said the carrier, "then, of course, how should you? It was nearly five years ago that I caught that trout."

"Oh! was it you who caught it, then?" said I.

"Yes, sir," replied the genial old fellow. "I caught him just below the lock—leastways, what was the lock then—one Friday afternoon; and the remarkable thing about it is that I caught him with a fly. I'd gone out pike fishing, bless you, never thinking of a trout, and when I saw that whopper on the end of my line, blest if it didn't quite take me aback. Well, you see, he weighed twenty-six pound. Good-night, gentlemen, good-night."

Five minutes afterwards, a third man came in, and described how *he* had caught it early one morning, with bleak; and then he left, and a stolid, solemn-looking, middle-aged individual came in, and sat down over by the window.

None of us spoke for a while; but, at length, George turned to the new comer, and said:

"I beg your pardon, I hope you will forgive the liberty that we—perfect strangers in the neighbourhood—are taking, but my friend here and myself would be so much obliged if you would tell us how you caught that trout up there."

"Why, who told you I caught that trout!" was the surprised query.

We said that nobody had told us so, but somehow or other we felt instinctively that it was he who had done it.

"Well, it's a most remarkable thing—most remarkable," answered the stolid stranger, laughing; "because, as a matter of fact, you are quite right. I did catch it. But fancy your guessing it like that. Dear me, it's really a most remarkable thing."

And then he went on, and told us how it had taken him half an hour to land it, and how it had broken his rod. He said he had weighed it carefully when he reached home, and it had turned the scale at thirty-four pounds.

He went in his turn, and when he was gone, the landlord came in to us. We told him the various histories we had heard about his trout, and he was immensely amused, and we all laughed very heartily.

"Fancy Jim Bates and Joe Muggles and Mr. Jones and old Billy Maunders all telling you that they had caught it. Ha! ha! ha! Well, that is good," said the honest old fellow, laughing heartily. "Yes, they are the sort to give it *me*, to put up in *my* parlour, if *they* had caught it, they are! Ha! ha! ha!"

And then he told us the real history of the fish. It seemed that he had caught it himself, years ago, when he was quite a lad; not by any art or skill, but by that unaccountable luck that appears to always wait upon a boy when he plays the wag from school, and goes out fishing on a sunny afternoon, with a bit of string tied on to the end of a tree.

He said that bringing home that trout had saved him from a whacking, and that even his school-master had said it was worth the rule-of-three and practice put together.

He was called out of the room at this point, and George and I again turned our gaze upon the fish.

It really was a most astonishing trout. The more we looked at it, the more we marvelled at it.

It excited George so much that he climbed up on the back of a chair to get a better view of it.

And then the chair slipped, and George clutched wildly at the trout-case to save himself, and down it came with a crash, George and the chair on top of it.

"You haven't injured the fish, have you?" I cried in alarm, rushing up.

"I hope not," said George, rising cautiously and looking about.

But he had. That trout lay shattered into a thousand fragments—I say a thousand, but they may have only been nine hundred. I did not count them.

We thought it strange and unaccountable that a stuffed trout should break up into little pieces like that.

And so it would have been strange and unaccountable, if it had been a stuffed trout, but it was not.

That trout was plaster-of-Paris.

CHAPTER XVIII.

Locks.—George and I are photographed.—Wallingford.— Dorchester.—Abingdon.—A family man.—A good spot for drowning.—A difficult bit of water.—Demoralizing effect of river air.

We left Streatley early the next morning, and pulled up to Culham, and slept under the canvas, in the backwater there.

The river is not extraordinarily interesting between Streatley and Wallingford. From Cleve you get a stretch of six and a half miles without a lock. I believe this is the longest uninterrupted stretch anywhere above Teddington, and the Oxford Club make use of it for their trial eights.

But however satisfactory this absence of locks may be to rowing-men, it is to be regretted by the mere pleasure-seeker.

For myself, I am fond of locks. They pleasantly break the monotony of the pull. I like sitting in the boat and slowly rising out of the cool depths up into new reaches and fresh views; or sinking down, as it were, out of the world, and then waiting, while the gloomy gates creak, and the narrow strip of day-light between them widens till the fair smiling river lies full before you, and you push your little boat out from its brief prison on to the welcoming waters once again.

They are picturesque little spots, these locks. The stout old lock-keeper, or his cheerful-looking wife, or bright-eyed daughter, are pleasant folk to have a passing chat with[1]. You meet other boats there, and river gossip is exchanged. The Thames would not be the fairyland it is without its flower-decked locks.

Talking of locks reminds me of an accident George and I very nearly had one summer's morning at Hampton Court.

---

[1] Or rather *were*. The Conservancy of late seems to have constituted itself into a society for the employment of idiots. A good many of the new lock-keepers, especially in the more crowded portions of the river, are excitable, nervous old men, quite unfitted for their post.

It was a glorious day, and the lock was crowded; and, as is a common practice up the river, a speculative photographer was taking a picture of us all as we lay upon the rising waters.

I did not catch what was going on at first, and was, therefore, extremely surprised at noticing George hurriedly smooth out his trousers, ruffle up his hair, and stick his cap on in a rakish manner at the back of his head, and then, assuming an expression of mingled affability and sadness, sit down in a graceful attitude, and try to hide his feet.

My first idea was that he had suddenly caught sight of some girl he knew, and I looked about to see who it was. Everybody in the lock seemed to have been suddenly struck wooden. They were all standing or sitting about in the most quaint and curious attitudes I have ever seen off a Japanese fan. All the girls were smiling. Oh, they did look so sweet! And all the fellows were frowning, and looking stern and noble.

And then, at last, the truth flashed across me, and I wondered if I should be in time. Ours was the first boat, and it would be unkind of me to spoil the man's picture, I thought.

So I faced round quickly, and took up a position in the prow, where I leant with careless grace upon the hitcher, in an attitude suggestive of agility and strength. I arranged my hair with a curl over the forehead, and threw an air of tender wistfulness into my expression, mingled with a touch of cynicism, which I am told suits me.

As we stood, waiting for the eventful moment, I heard someone behind call out:

"Hi! look at your nose."

I could not turn round to see what was the matter, and whose nose it was that was to be looked at. I stole a side-glance at George's nose! It was all right—at all events, there was nothing wrong with it that could be altered. I squinted down at my own, and that seemed all that could be expected also.

"Look at your nose, you stupid ass!" came the same voice again, louder.

And then another voice cried:

"Push your nose out, can't you, you—you two with the dog!"

Neither George nor I dared to turn round. The man's hand was on the cap, and the picture might be taken any moment. Was it us they were calling to? What was the matter with our noses? Why were they to be pushed out!

But now the whole lock started yelling, and a stentorian voice from the back shouted:

"Look at your boat, sir; you in the red and black caps. It's your two corpses that will get taken in that photo, if you ain't quick."

We looked then, and saw that the nose of our boat had got fixed under the woodwork of the lock, while the in-coming water was rising all around it, and tilting it up. In another moment we should be over. Quick as thought, we each seized an oar, and a vigorous blow against the side of the lock with the butt-ends released the boat, and sent us sprawling on our backs.

We did not come out well in that photograph, George and I. Of course, as was to be expected, our luck ordained it, that the man should set his wretched machine in motion at the precise moment that we were both lying on our backs with a wild expression of "Where am I? and what is it?" on our faces, and our four feet waving madly in the air.

Our feet were undoubtedly the leading article in that photograph. Indeed, very little else was to be seen. They filled up the foreground entirely. Behind them, you caught glimpses of the other boats, and bits of the surrounding scenery; but everything and everybody else in the lock looked so utterly insignificant and paltry compared with our feet, that all the other people felt quite ashamed of themselves, and refused to subscribe to the picture.

The owner of one steam launch, who had bespoke six copies, rescinded the order on seeing the negative. He said he would take them if anybody could show him his launch, but nobody could. It was somewhere behind George's right foot.

There was a good deal of unpleasantness over the business. The photographer thought we ought to take a dozen copies each, seeing that the photo was about nine-tenths us, but we declined. We said we had no objection to being photo'd full-length, but we preferred being taken the right way up.

Wallingford, six miles above Streatley, is a very ancient town, and has been an active centre for the making of English history. It was a rude, mud-built town in the time of the Britons, who squatted there, until the Roman legions evicted them; and replaced their clay-baked walls by mighty fortifications, the trace of which Time has not yet succeeded in sweeping away, so well those old-world masons knew how to build.

But Time, though he halted at Roman walls, soon crumbled Romans to dust; and on the ground, in later years, fought savage Saxons and huge Danes, until the Normans came.

It was a walled and fortified town up to the time of the Parliamentary War, when it suffered a long and bitter siege from Fairfax. It fell at last, and then the walls were razed.

From Wallingford up to Dorchester the neighbourhood of the river grows more hilly, varied, and picturesque. Dorchester stands half a mile from the river. It can be reached by paddling up the Thame, if you have a small boat; but the best way is to leave the river at Day's Lock, and take a walk across the fields. Dorchester is a delightfully peaceful old place, nestling in stillness and silence and drowsiness.

Dorchester, like Wallingford, was a city in ancient British times; it was then called Caer Doren, "the city on the water." In more recent times the Romans formed a great camp here, the fortifications surrounding which now seem like low, even hills. In Saxon days it was the capital of Wessex. It is very old, and it was very strong and great once. Now it sits aside from the stirring world, and nods and dreams.

Round Clifton Hampden, itself a wonderfully pretty village, old-fashioned, peaceful, and dainty with flowers, the river scenery is rich and beautiful. If you stay the night on land at Clifton, you cannot do better than put up at the "Barley Mow." It is, without exception, I should say, the quaintest, most old-world inn up the river. It stands on the right of the bridge, quite away from the village. Its low-pitched gables and thatched roof and latticed windows give it quite a story-book appearance, while inside it is even still more once-upon-a-timeyfied.

It would not be a good place for the heroine of a modern novel to stay at. The heroine of a modern novel is always "divinely tall," and she is ever "drawing herself up to her full height." At the "Barley Mow" she would bump her head against the ceiling each time she did this.

It would also be a bad house for a drunken man to put up at. There are too many surprises in the way of unexpected steps down into this room and up into that; and as for getting upstairs to his bedroom, or ever finding his bed when he got up, either operation would be an utter impossibility to him.

We were up early the next morning, as we wanted to be in Oxford by the afternoon. It is surprising how early one *can* get up, when camping out. One does not yearn for "just another five minutes" nearly so much, lying wrapped up in a rug on the boards of a boat, with a Gladstone bag for a pillow, as one does in a featherbed. We had finished breakfast, and were through Clifton Lock by half-past eight.

From Clifton to Culham the river banks are flat, monotonous, and uninteresting, but, after you get through Culhalm Lock—the coldest and deepest lock on the river—the landscape improves.

At Abingdon, the river passes by the streets. Abingdon is a typical country town of the smaller order—quiet, eminently respectable, clean, and desperately dull. It prides itself on being old, but whether it can compare in this respect with Wallingford and Dorchester seems doubtful. A famous abbey stood here once, and within what is left of its sanctified walls they brew bitter ale nowadays.

In St. Nicholas Church, at Abingdon, there is a monument to John Blackwall and his wife Jane, who both, after leading a happy married life, died on the very same day, August 21, 1625; and in St. Helen's Church, it is recorded that W. Lee, who died in 1637, "had in his lifetime issue from his loins two hundred lacking but three." If you work this out you will find that Mr. W. Lee's family numbered one hundred and ninety-seven. Mr. W. Lee—five times Mayor of Abingdon—was, no doubt, a benefactor to his generation, but I hope there are not many of his kind about in this overcrowded nineteenth century.

From Abingdon to Nuneham Courteney is a lovely stretch. Nuneham Park is well worth a visit. It can be viewed on Tuesdays and Thursdays. The house contains a fine collection of pictures and curiosities, and the grounds are very beautiful.

The pool under Sandford lasher, just behind the lock, is a very good place to drown yourself in. The undercurrent is terribly strong, and if you once get down into it you are all right. An obelisk marks the spot where two men have already been drowned, while bathing there; and the steps of the obelisk are generally used as a diving-board by young men now who wish to see if the place really *is* dangerous.

Iffley Lock and Mill, a mile before you reach Oxford, is a favourite subject with the river-loving brethren of the brush. The real article, however, is rather disappointing, after the pictures. Few things, I have noticed, come quite up to the pictures of them, in this world.

We passed through Iffley Lock at about half-past twelve, and then, having tidied up the boat and made all ready for landing, we set to work on our last mile.

Between Iffley and Oxford is the most difficult bit of the river I know. You want to be born on that bit of water, to understand it. I have been over it a fairish number of times, but I have never been able to get the hang of it. The man who could row a straight course from Oxford to Iffley ought to be able to live comfortably, under one roof, with his wife, his mother-in-law, his elder sister, and the old servant who was in the family when he was a baby.

First the current drives you on to the right bank, and then on to the left, then it takes you out into the middle, turns you round three times, and carries you up stream again, and always ends by trying to smash you up against a college barge.

Of course, as a consequence of this, we got in the way of a good many other boats, during the mile, and they in ours, and, of course, as a consequence of that, a good deal of bad language occurred.

I don't know why it should be, but everybody is always so exceptionally irritable on the river. Little mishaps, that you would hardly notice on dry land, drive you nearly frantic with rage, when they occur on the water. When Harris or George makes an ass of himself on dry land, I smile indulgently; when they behave in a chuckle-head way on the river, I use the most blood-curdling language to them. When another boat gets in my way, I feel I want to take an oar and kill all the people in it.

The mildest tempered people, when on land, become violent and blood-thirsty when in a boat. I did a little boating once with a young lady. She was naturally of the sweetest and gentlest disposition imaginable, but on the river it was quite awful to hear her.

"Oh, drat the man!" she would exclaim, when some unfortunate sculler would get in her way; "why don't he look where he's going?"

And, "Oh, bother the silly old thing!" she would say indignantly, when the sail would not go up properly. And she would catch hold of it, and shake it quite brutally.

Yet, as I have said, when on shore she was kind-hearted and amiable enough.

The air of the river has a demoralising effect upon one's temper, and this it is, I suppose, which causes even barge men to be sometimes rude to one another, and to use language which, no doubt, in their calmer moments they regret.

CHAPTER XIX.

Oxford.—Montmorency's idea of Heaven.—The hired up-river boat, its beauties and advantages.—The "Pride of the Thames."—The weather changes.—The river under different aspects.—Not a cheerful evening.—Yearnings for the unattainable.—The cheery chat goes round.—George performs upon the banjo.—A mournful melody.—Another wet day.—Flight.—A little supper and a toast.

We spent two very pleasant days at Oxford. There are plenty of dogs in the town of Oxford. Montmorency had eleven fights on the first day, and fourteen on the second, and evidently thought he had got to heaven.

Among folk too constitutionally weak, or too constitutionally lazy, whichever it may be, to relish up-stream work, it is a common practice to get a boat at Oxford, and row down. For the energetic, however, the up-stream journey is certainly to be preferred. It does not seem good to be always going with the current. There is more satisfaction in squaring one's back, and fighting against it, and winning one's way forward in spite of it—at least, so I feel, when Harris and George are sculling and I am steering.

To those who do contemplate making Oxford their starting-place, I would say, take your own boat—unless, of course, you can take someone else's without any possible danger of being found out. The boats that, as a rule, are let for hire on the Thames above Marlow, are very good boats. They are fairly water-tight; and so long as they are handled with care, they rarely come to pieces, or sink. There are places in them to sit down on, and they are complete with all the necessary arrangements—or nearly all—to enable you to row them and steer them.

But they are not ornamental. The boat you hire up the river above Marlow is not the sort of boat in which you can flash about and give yourself airs. The hired up-river boat very soon puts a stop to any nonsense of that sort on the part of its occupants. That is its chief—one may say, its only recommendation.

The man in the hired up-river boat is modest and retiring. He likes to keep on the shady side, underneath the trees, and to do most of his travelling early in the morning or late at night, when there are not many people about on the river to look at him.

When the man in the hired up-river boat sees anyone he knows, he gets out on to the bank, and hides behind a tree.

I was one of a party who hired an up-river boat one summer, for a few days' trip. We had none of us ever seen the hired up-river boat before; and we did not know what it was when we did see it.

We had written for a boat—a double sculling skiff; and when we went down with our bags to the yard, and gave our names, the man said:

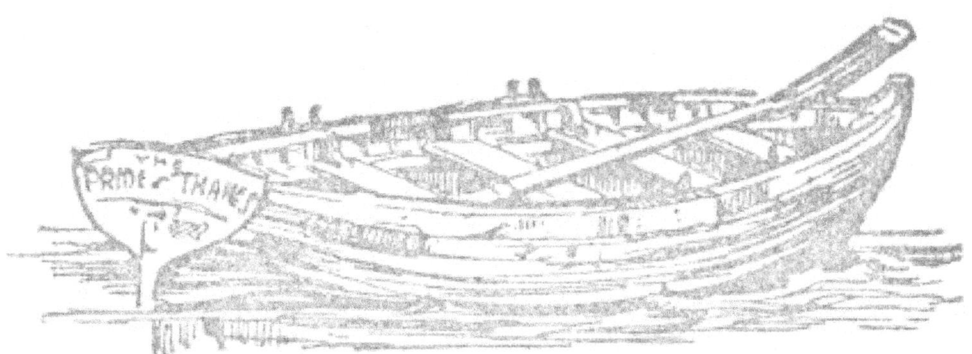

"Oh, yes; you're the party that wrote for a double sculling skiff. It's all right. Jim, fetch round *The Pride of the Thames.*"

The boy went, and re-appeared five minutes afterwards, struggling with an antediluvian chunk of wood, that looked as though it had been recently dug out of somewhere, and dug out carelessly, so as to have been unnecessarily damaged in the process.

My own idea, on first catching sight of the object, was that it was a Roman relic of some sort,—relic of *what* I do not know, possibly of a coffin.

The neighbourhood of the upper Thames is rich in Roman relics, and my surmise seemed to me a very probable one; but our serious young man, who is a bit of a geologist, pooh-poohed my Roman relic theory, and said it was clear to the meanest intellect (in which category he seemed to be grieved that he could not conscientiously include mine) that the thing the boy had found was the fossil of a whale; and he pointed out to us various evidences proving that it must have belonged to the preglacial period.

To settle the dispute, we appealed to the boy. We told him not to be afraid, but to speak the plain truth: Was it the fossil of a pre-Adamite whale, or was it an early Roman coffin?

The boy said it was *The Pride of the Thames.*

We thought this a very humorous answer on the part of the boy at first, and somebody gave him twopence as a reward for his ready wit; but when he persisted in keeping up the joke, as we thought, too long, we got vexed with him.

"Come, come, my lad!" said our captain sharply, "don't let us have any nonsense. You take your mother's washing-tub home again, and bring us a boat."

The boat-builder himself came up then, and assured us, on his word, as a practical man, that the thing really was a boat—was, in fact, *the* boat, the "double sculling skiff" selected to take us on our trip down the river.

We grumbled a good deal. We thought he might, at least, have had it white-washed or tarred—had *something* done to it to distinguish it from a bit of a wreck; but he could not see any fault in it.

He even seemed offended at our remarks. He said he had picked us out the best boat in all his stock, and he thought we might have been more grateful.

He said it, *The Pride of the Thames*, had been in use, just as it now stood (or rather as it now hung together), for the last forty years, to *his* knowledge, and nobody had complained of it before, and he did not see why we should be the first to begin.

We argued no more.

We fastened the so-called boat together with some pieces of string, got a bit of wall-paper and pasted over the shabbier places, said our prayers, and stepped on board.

They charged us thirty-five shillings for the loan of the remnant for six days; and we could have bought the thing out-and-out for four-and-sixpence at any sale of drift-wood round the coast.

The weather changed on the third day,—Oh! I am talking about our present trip now,—and we started from Oxford upon our homeward journey in the midst of a steady drizzle.

The river—with the sunlight flashing from its dancing wavelets, gilding gold the grey-green beech-trunks, glinting through the dark, cool wood paths, chasing shadows o'er the shallows, flinging diamonds from the mill-wheels, throwing kisses to the lilies, wantoning with the weirs' white waters, silvering moss-grown walls and bridges, brightening every tiny townlet, making sweet each lane and meadow, lying tangled in the rushes, peeping, laughing, from each inlet, gleaming gay on many a far sail, making soft the air with glory—is a golden fairy stream.

But the river—chill and weary, with the ceaseless rain-drops falling on its brown and sluggish waters, with a sound as of a woman, weeping low in some dark chamber; while the woods, all dark and silent, shrouded in their mists of vapour, stand like ghosts upon the margin; silent ghosts with eyes reproachful, like the ghosts of evil actions, like the ghosts of friends neglected—is a spirit-haunted water through the land of vain regrets.

Sunlight is the life-blood of Nature. Mother Earth looks at us with such dull, soulless eyes, when the sunlight has died away from out of her. It makes us sad to be with her then; she does not seem to know us or to care for us. She is as a widow who has lost the husband she loved, and her children touch her hand, and look up into her eyes, but gain no smile from her.

We rowed on all that day through the rain, and very melancholy work it was. We pretended, at first, that we enjoyed it. We said it was a change, and that we liked to see the river under all its different aspects. We said we could not expect to have it all sunshine, nor should we wish it. We told each other that Nature was beautiful, even in her tears.

Indeed, Harris and I were quite enthusiastic about the business, for the first few hours. And we sang a song about a gipsy's life, and how delightful a gipsy's existence was!—free to storm and sunshine, and to every wind that blew!—and how he enjoyed the rain, and what a lot of good it did him; and how he laughed at people who didn't like it.

George took the fun more soberly, and stuck to the umbrella.

We hoisted the cover before we had lunch, and kept it up all the afternoon, just leaving a little space in the bow, from which one of us could paddle and keep a look-out. In this way we made nine miles, and pulled up for the night a little below Day's Lock.

I cannot honestly say that we had a merry evening. The rain poured down with quiet persistency. Everything in the boat was damp and clammy. Supper was not a success. Cold veal pie, when you don't feel hungry, is apt to cloy. I felt I wanted whitebait and a cutlet; Harris babbled of soles and white-sauce, and passed the remains of his pie to Montmorency, who declined it, and, apparently insulted by the offer, went and sat over at the other end of the boat by himself.

George requested that we would not talk about these things, at all events until he had finished his cold boiled beef without mustard.

CHAPTER XIX.

We played penny nap after supper. We played for about an hour and a half, by the end of which time George had won fourpence—George always is lucky at cards—and Harris and I had lost exactly twopence each.

We thought we would give up gambling then. As Harris said, it breeds an unhealthy excitement when carried too far. George offered to go on and give us our revenge; but Harris and I decided not to battle any further against Fate.

After that, we mixed ourselves some toddy, and sat round and talked. George told us about a man he had known, who had come up the river two years ago and who had slept out in a damp boat on just such another night as that was, and it had given him rheumatic fever, and nothing was able to save him, and he had died in great agony ten days afterwards. George said he was quite a young man, and was engaged to be married. He said it was one of the saddest things he had ever known.

And that put Harris in mind of a friend of his, who had been in the Volunteers, and who had slept out under canvas one wet night down at Aldershot, "on just such another night as this," said Harris; and he had woke up in the morning a cripple for life. Harris said he would introduce us both to the man when we got back to town; it would make our hearts bleed to see him.

This naturally led to some pleasant chat about sciatica, fevers, chills, lung diseases, and bronchitis; and Harris said how very awkward it would be if one of us were taken seriously ill in the night, seeing how far away we were from a doctor.

There seemed to be a desire for something frolicksome to follow upon this conversation, and in a weak moment I suggested that George should get out his banjo, and see if he could not give us a comic song.

I will say for George that he did not want any pressing. There was no nonsense about having left his music at home, or anything of that sort. He at once fished out his instrument, and commenced to play "Two Lovely Black Eyes."

I had always regarded "Two Lovely Black Eyes" as rather a commonplace tune until that evening. The rich vein of sadness that George extracted from it quite surprised me.

The desire that grew upon Harris and myself, as the mournful strains progressed, was to fall upon each other's necks and weep; but by great effort we kept back the rising tears, and listened to the wild yearnful melody in silence.

When the chorus came we even made a desperate effort to be merry. We refilled our glasses and joined in; Harris, in a voice trembling with emotion, leading, and George and I following a few words behind:

> "Two lovely black eyes;
> Oh! what a surprise!
> Only for telling a man he was wrong,
> Two—"

There we broke down. The unutterable pathos of George's accompaniment to that "two" we were, in our then state of depression, unable to bear. Harris sobbed like a little child, and the dog howled till I thought his heart or his jaw must surely break.

George wanted to go on with another verse. He thought that when he had got a little more into the tune, and could throw more "abandon," as it were, into the rendering, it might not seem so sad. The feeling of the majority, however, was opposed to the experiment.

There being nothing else to do, we went to bed—that is, we undressed ourselves, and tossed about at the bottom of the boat for some three or four hours. After which, we managed to get some fitful slumber until five a.m., when we all got up and had breakfast.

The second day was exactly like the first. The rain continued to pour down, and we sat, wrapped up in our mackintoshes, underneath the canvas, and drifted slowly down.

One of us—I forget which one now, but I rather think it was myself—made a few feeble attempts during the course of the morning to work up the old gipsy foolishness about being children of Nature and enjoying the wet; but it did not go down well at all. That—

"I care not for the rain, not I!"

was so painfully evident, as expressing the sentiments of each of us, that to sing it seemed unnecessary.

On one point we were all agreed, and that was that, come what might, we would go through with this job to the bitter end. We had come out for a fortnight's enjoyment on the river, and a fortnight's enjoyment on the river we meant to have. If it killed us! well, that would be a sad thing for our friends and relations, but it could not be helped. We felt that to give in to the weather in a climate such as ours would be a most disastrous precedent.

"It's only two days more," said Harris, "and we are young and strong. We may get over it all right, after all."

At about four o'clock we began to discuss our arrangements for the evening. We were a little past Goring then, and we decided to paddle on to Pangbourne, and put up there for the night.

"Another jolly evening!" murmured George.

We sat and mused on the prospect. We should be in at Pangbourne by five. We should finish dinner at, say, half-past six. After that we could walk about the village in the pouring rain until bed-time; or we could sit in a dimly-lit bar-parlour and read the almanac.

"Why, the Alhambra would be almost more lively," said Harris, venturing his head outside the cover for a moment and taking a survey of the sky.

"With a little supper at the ---[1] to follow," I added, half unconsciously.

---

[1] A capital little out-of-the-way restaurant, in the neighbourhood of ---, where you can get one of the best-cooked and cheapest little French dinners or suppers that I know of, with an excellent bottle of Beaune, for three-and-six; and which I am not going to be idiot enough to advertise.

"Yes it's almost a pity we've made up our minds to stick to this boat," answered Harris; and then there was silence for a while.

"If we *hadn't* made up our minds to contract our certain deaths in this bally old coffin," observed George, casting a glance of intense malevolence over the boat, "it might be worth while to mention that there's a train leaves Pangbourne, I know, soon after five, which would just land us in town in comfortable time to get a chop, and then go on to the place you mentioned afterwards."

Nobody spoke. We looked at one another, and each one seemed to see his own mean and guilty thoughts reflected in the faces of the others. In silence, we dragged out and overhauled the Gladstone. We looked up the river and down the river; not a soul was in sight!

Twenty minutes later, three figures, followed by a shamed-looking dog, might have been seen creeping stealthily from the boat-house at the "Swan" towards the railway station, dressed in the following neither neat nor gaudy costume:

Black leather shoes, dirty; suit of boating flannels, very dirty; brown felt hat, much battered; mackintosh, very wet; umbrella.

We had deceived the boatman at Pangbourne. We had not had the face to tell him that we were running away from the rain. We had left the boat, and all it contained, in his charge, with instructions that it was to be ready for us at nine the next morning. If, we said—*if* anything unforeseen should happen, preventing our return, we would write to him.

We reached Paddington at seven, and drove direct to the restaurant I have before described, where we partook of a light meal, left Montmorency, together with suggestions for a supper to be ready at half-past ten, and then continued our way to Leicester Square.

We attracted a good deal of attention at the Alhambra. On our presenting our-selves at the paybox we were gruffly directed to go round to Castle Street, and were informed that we were half-an-hour behind our time.

We convinced the man, with some difficulty, that we were *not* "the world-renowned contortionists from the Himalaya Mountains," and he took our money and let us pass.

Inside we were a still greater success. Our fine bronzed countenances and pic-turesque clothes were followed round the place with admiring gaze. We were the cynosure of every eye.

It was a proud moment for us all.

We adjourned soon after the first ballet, and wended our way back to the res-taurant, where supper was already awaiting us.

I must confess to enjoying that supper. For about ten days we seemed to have been living, more or less, on nothing but cold meat, cake, and bread and jam. It had been a simple, a nutritious diet; but there had been nothing exciting about it, and the odour of Burgundy, and the smell of French sauces, and the sight of clean napkins and long loaves, knocked as a very welcome visitor at the door of our inner man.

We pegged and quaffed away in silence for a while, until the time came when, instead of sitting bolt upright, and grasping the knife and fork firmly, we leant back in our chairs and worked slowly and carelessly—when we stretched out our legs beneath the table, let our napkins fall, unheeded, to the floor, and found time to more critically examine the smoky ceiling than we had hitherto been able to do—when we rested our glasses at arm's-length upon the table, and felt good, and thoughtful, and forgiving.

Then Harris, who was sitting next the window, drew aside the curtain and looked out upon the street.

It glistened darkly in the wet, the dim lamps flickered with each gust, the rain splashed steadily into the puddles and trickled down the water-spouts into the running gutters. A few soaked wayfarers hurried past, crouching beneath their dripping umbrellas, the women holding up their skirts.

"Well," said Harris, reaching his hand out for his glass, "we have had a pleasant trip, and my hearty thanks for it to old Father Thames—but I think we did well to chuck it when we did. Here's to Three Men well out of a Boat!"

And Montmorency, standing on his hind legs, before the window, peering out into the night, gave a short bark of decided concurrence with the toast.

THREE MEN ON THE BUMMEL

TO THE GENTLE
GUIDE
WHO LETS ME EVER GO MY OWN WAY, YET BRINGS ME RIGHT—
TO THE LAUGHTER-LOVING
PHILOSOPHER
WHO, IF HE HAS NOT RECONCILED ME TO BEARING THE TOOTHACHE
PATENTLY, AT LEAST HAS TAUGHT ME THE COMFORT THAT
THIS EVEN WILL ALSO PASS—
TO THE GOOD
FRIEND
WHO SMILES WHEN I TELL HIM OF MY TROUBLES, AND WHO
WHEN I ASK FOR HELP, ANSWERS ONLY "WAIT!"—
TO THE GRAVE-FACED
JESTER
TO WHOM ALL LIFE IS BUT A VOLUME OF OLD HUMOUR—
TO GOOD MASTER
Time
THIS LITTLE WORK OF A POOR
PUPIL
IS DEDICATED

CHAPTER I

Three men need change—Anecdote showing evil result of deception—Moral cowardice of George—Harris has ideas—Yarn of the Ancient Mariner and the Inexperienced Yachtsman—A hearty crew—Danger of sailing when the wind is off the land—Impossibility of sailing when the wind is off the sea—The argumentativeness of Ethelbertha—The dampness of the river—Harris suggests a bicycle tour—George thinks of the wind—Harris suggests the Black Forest—George thinks of the hills—Plan adopted by Harris for ascent of hills—Interruption by Mrs. Harris.

"What we want," said Harris, "is a change."

At this moment the door opened, and Mrs. Harris put her head in to say that Ethelbertha had sent her to remind me that we must not be late getting home because of Clarence. Ethelbertha, I am inclined to think, is unnecessarily nervous about the children. As a matter of fact, there was nothing wrong with the child whatever. He had been out with his aunt that morning; and if he looks wistfully at a pastrycook's window she takes him inside and buys him cream buns and "maids-of-honour" until he insists that he has had enough, and politely, but firmly, refuses to eat another anything. Then, of course, he wants only one helping of pudding at lunch, and Ethelbertha thinks he is sickening for something. Mrs. Harris added that it would be as well for us to come upstairs soon, on our own account also, as otherwise we should miss Muriel's rendering of "The Mad Hatter's Tea Party," out of *Alice in Wonderland*. Muriel is Harris's second, age eight: she is a bright, intelligent child; but I prefer her myself in serious pieces. We said we would finish our cigarettes and follow almost immediately; we also begged her not to let Muriel begin until we arrived. She promised to hold the child back as long as possible, and went. Harris, as soon as the door was closed, resumed his interrupted sentence.

"You know what I mean," he said, "a complete change."

The question was how to get it.

George suggested "business." It was the sort of suggestion George would make. A bachelor thinks a married woman doesn't know enough to get out of the way of a steam-roller. I knew a young fellow once, an engineer, who thought he would go to Vienna "on business." His wife wanted to know "what business?" He told her it would be his duty to visit the mines in the neighbourhood of the Austrian capital, and to make reports. She said she would go with him; she was that sort of woman. He tried to dissuade her: he told her that a mine was no place for a beautiful woman. She said she felt that herself, and that therefore she did not intend to accompany him down the shafts; she would see him off in the morning, and then amuse herself until his return, looking round the Vienna shops, and buying a few things she might want. Having started the idea, he did not see very well how to get out of it; and for ten long summer days he did visit the mines in the neighbourhood of Vienna, and in the evening wrote reports about them, which she posted for him to his firm, who didn't want them.

I should be grieved to think that either Ethelbertha or Mrs. Harris belonged to that class of wife, but it is as well not to overdo "business"—it should be kept for cases of real emergency.

"No," I said, "the thing is to be frank and manly. I shall tell Ethelbertha that I have come to the conclusion a man never values happiness that is always with him. I shall tell her that, for the sake of learning to appreciate my own advantages as I know they should be appreciated, I intend to tear myself away from her and the children for at least three weeks. I shall tell her," I continued, turning to Harris, "that it is you who have shown me my duty in this respect; that it is to you we shall owe—"

Harris put down his glass rather hurriedly.

"If you don't mind, old man," he interrupted, "I'd really rather you didn't. She'll talk it over with my wife, and—well, I should not be happy, taking credit that I do not deserve."

"But you do deserve it," I insisted; "it was your suggestion."

"It was you gave me the idea," interrupted Harris again. "You know you said it was a mistake for a man to get into a groove, and that unbroken domesticity cloyed the brain."

"I was speaking generally," I explained.

"It struck me as very apt," said Harris. "I thought of repeating it to Clara; she has a great opinion of your sense, I know. I am sure that if—"

"We won't risk it," I interrupted, in my turn; "it is a delicate matter, and I see a way out of it. We will say George suggested the idea."

There is a lack of genial helpfulness about George that it sometimes vexes me to notice. You would have thought he would have welcomed the chance of assisting two old friends out of a dilemma; instead, he became disagreeable.

"You do," said George, "and I shall tell them both that my original plan was that we should make a party—children and all; that I should bring my aunt, and that we should hire a charming old château I know of in Normandy, on the coast, where the climate is peculiarly adapted to delicate children, and the milk such as you do not get in England. I shall add that you over-rode that suggestion, arguing we should be happier by ourselves."

With a man like George kindness is of no use; you have to be firm.

"You do," said Harris, "and I, for one, will close with the offer. We will just take that château. You will bring your aunt—I will see to that,—and we will have a month of it. The children are all fond of you; J. and I will be nowhere. You've promised to teach Edgar fishing; and it is you who will have to play wild beasts. Since last Sunday Dick and Muriel have talked of nothing else but your hippopotamus. We will picnic in the woods—there will only be eleven of us,—and in the evenings we will have music and recitations. Muriel is master of six pieces already, as perhaps you know; and all the other children are quick studies."

George climbed down—he has no real courage—but he did not do it gracefully. He said that if we were mean and cowardly and false-hearted enough to stoop to such a shabby trick, he supposed he couldn't help it; and that if I didn't intend to finish the whole bottle of claret myself, he would trouble me to spare him a glass. He also added, somewhat illogically, that it really did not matter, seeing both Ethelbertha and Mrs. Harris were women of sense who would judge him better than to believe for a moment that the suggestion emanated from him.

This little point settled, the question was: What sort of a change?

Harris, as usual, was for the sea. He said he knew a yacht, just the very thing—one that we could manage by ourselves; no skulking lot of lubbers loafing about, adding to the expense and taking away from the romance. Give him a handy boy, he would sail it himself. We knew that yacht, and we told him so; we had been on it with Harris before. It smells of bilge-water and greens to the exclusion of all other scents; no ordinary sea air can hope to head against it. So far as sense of smell is concerned, one might be spending a week in Limehouse Hole. There is no place to get out of the rain; the saloon is ten feet by four, and half of that is taken up by a stove, which falls to pieces when you go to light it. You have to take your bath on deck, and the towel blows overboard just as you step out of the tub. Harris and the boy do all the interesting work—the lugging and the reefing, the letting her go and the heeling her over, and all that sort of thing,—leaving George and myself to do the peeling of the potatoes and the washing up.

"Very well, then," said Harris, "let's take a proper yacht, with a skipper, and do the thing in style."

That also I objected to. I know that skipper; his notion of yachting is to lie in what he calls the "offing," where he can be well in touch with his wife and family, to say nothing of his favourite public-house.

Years ago, when I was young and inexperienced, I hired a yacht myself. Three things had combined to lead me into this foolishness: I had had a stroke of unexpected luck; Ethelbertha had expressed a yearning for sea air; and the very next morning, in taking up casually at the club a copy of the *Sportsman*, I had come across the following advertisement:—

TO YACHTSMEN.—Unique Opportunity.—"Rogue," 28-ton Yawl.—Owner, called away suddenly on business, is willing to let this superbly-fitted "greyhound of the sea" for any period short or long. Two cabins and saloon; pianette, by Woffenkoff; new copper. Terms, 10 guineas a week.—Apply Pertwee and Co., 3A Bucklersbury.

It had seemed to me like the answer to a prayer. "The new copper" did not interest me; what little washing we might want could wait, I thought. But the "pianette by Woffenkoff" sounded alluring. I pictured Ethelbertha playing in the evening—something with a chorus, in which, perhaps, the crew, with a little training, might join—while our moving home bounded, "greyhound-like," over the silvery billows.

I took a cab and drove direct to 3A Bucklersbury. Mr. Pertwee was an unpretentious-looking gentleman, who had an unostentatious office on the third floor. He showed me a picture in water-colours of the *Rogue* flying before the wind. The deck was at an angle of 95 to the ocean. In the picture no human beings were represented on the deck; I suppose they had slipped off. Indeed, I do not see how anyone could have kept on, unless nailed. I pointed out this disadvantage to the agent, who, however, explained to me that the picture represented the *Rogue* doubling something or other on the well-known occasion of her winning the Medway Challenge Shield. Mr. Pertwee assumed that I knew all about the event, so that I did not like to ask any questions. Two specks near the frame of the picture, which at first I had taken for moths, represented, it appeared, the second and third winners in this celebrated race. A photograph of the yacht at anchor off Gravesend was less impressive, but suggested more stability. All answers to my inquiries being satisfactory, I took the thing for a fortnight. Mr. Pertwee said it was fortunate I wanted it only for a fortnight—later on I came to agree with him,—the time fitting in exactly with another hiring. Had I required it for three weeks he would have been compelled to refuse me.

The letting being thus arranged, Mr. Pertwee asked me if I had a skipper in my eye. That I had not was also fortunate—things seemed to be turning out luckily for me all round,—because Mr. Pertwee felt sure I could not do better than keep on Mr. Goyles, at present in charge—an excellent skipper, so Mr. Pertwee assured me, a man who knew the sea as a man knows his own wife, and who had never lost a life.

It was still early in the day, and the yacht was lying off Harwich. I caught the ten forty-five from Liverpool Street, and by one o'clock was talking to Mr. Goyles on deck. He was a stout man, and had a fatherly way with him. I told him my idea, which was to take the outlying Dutch islands and then creep up to Norway. He said, "Aye, aye, sir," and appeared quite enthusiastic about the trip; said he should enjoy it himself. We came to the question of victualling, and he grew more enthusiastic. The amount of food suggested by Mr. Goyles, I confess, surprised me. Had we been living in the days of Drake and the Spanish Main, I should have feared he was arranging for something illegal. However, he laughed in his fatherly way, and assured me we were not overdoing it. Anything left the crew would divide and take home with them—it seemed this was the custom. It appeared to me that I was providing for this crew for the winter, but I did not like to appear stingy, and said no more. The amount of drink required also surprised me. I arranged for what I thought we should need for ourselves, and then Mr. Goyles spoke up for the crew. I must say that for him, he did think of his men.

"We don't want anything in the nature of an orgie, Mr. Goyles," I suggested.

"Orgie!" replied Mr. Goyles; "why they'll take that little drop in their tea."

He explained to me that his motto was, Get good men and treat them well.

"They work better for you," said Mr. Goyles; "and they come again."

Personally, I didn't feel I wanted them to come again. I was beginning to take a dislike to them before I had seen them; I regarded them as a greedy and guzzling crew. But Mr. Goyles was so cheerfully emphatic, and I was so inexperienced, that again I let him have his way. He also promised that even in this department he would see to it personally that nothing was wasted.

I also left him to engage the crew. He said he could do the thing, and would, for me, with the help two men and a boy. If he was alluding to the clearing up of the victuals and drink, I think he was making an under-estimate; but possibly he may have been speaking of the sailing of the yacht.

I called at my tailors on the way home and ordered a yachting suit, with a white hat, which they promised to bustle up and have ready in time; and then I went home and told Ethelbertha all I had done. Her delight was clouded by only one reflection—would the dressmaker be able to finish a yachting costume for her in time? That is so like a woman.

Our honeymoon, which had taken place not very long before, had been somewhat curtailed, so we decided we would invite nobody, but have the yacht to ourselves. And thankful I am to Heaven that we did so decide. On Monday we put on all our clothes and started. I forget what Ethelbertha wore, but, whatever it may have been, it looked very fetching. My own costume was a dark blue trimmed with a narrow white braid, which, I think, was rather effective.

Mr. Goyles met us on deck, and told us that lunch was ready. I must admit Goyles had secured the services of a very fair cook. The capabilities of the other members of the crew I had no opportunity of judging. Speaking of them in a state of rest, however, I can say of them they appeared to be a cheerful crew.

My idea had been that so soon as the men had finished their dinner we would weigh anchor, while I, smoking a cigar, with Ethelbertha by my side, would lean over the gunwale and watch the white cliffs of the Fatherland sink imperceptibly into the horizon. Ethelbertha and I carried out our part of the programme, and waited, with the deck to ourselves.

"They seem to be taking their time," said Ethelbertha.

"If, in the course of fourteen days," I said, "they eat half of what is on this yacht, they will want a fairly long time for every meal. We had better not hurry them, or they won't get through a quarter of it."

"They must have gone to sleep," said Ethelbertha, later on. "It will be tea-time soon."

They were certainly very quiet. I went for'ard, and hailed Captain Goyles down the ladder. I hailed him three times; then he came up slowly. He appeared to be a heavier and older man than when I had seen him last. He had a cold cigar in his mouth.

"When you are ready, Captain Goyles," I said, "we'll start."

Captain Goyles removed the cigar from his mouth.

"Not to-day we won't, sir," he replied, "*with* your permission."

"Why, what's the matter with to-day?" I said. I know sailors are a superstitious folk; I thought maybe a Monday might be considered unlucky.

"The day's all right," answered Captain Goyles, "it's the wind I'm a-thinking of. It don't look much like changing."

"But do we want it to change?" I asked. "It seems to me to be just where it should be, dead behind us."

"Aye, aye," said Captain Goyles, "dead's the right word to use, for dead we'd all be, bar Providence, if we was to put out in this. You see, sir," he explained, in answer to my look of surprise, "this is what we call a 'land wind,' that is, it's a-blowing, as one might say, direct off the land."

When I came to think of it the man was right; the wind was blowing off the land.

"It may change in the night," said Captain Goyles, more hopefully "anyhow, it's not violent, and she rides well."

Captain Goyles resumed his cigar, and I returned aft, and explained to Ethelbertha the reason for the delay. Ethelbertha, who appeared to be less high spirited than when we first boarded, wanted to know *why* we couldn't sail when the wind was off the land.

"If it was not blowing off the land," said Ethelbertha, "it would be blowing off the sea, and that would send us back into the shore again. It seems to me this is just the very wind we want."

I said: "That is your inexperience, love; it *seems* to be the very wind we want, but it is not. It's what we call a land wind, and a land wind is always very dangerous."

Ethelbertha wanted to know *why* a land wind was very dangerous.

Her argumentativeness annoyed me somewhat; maybe I was feeling a bit cross; the monotonous rolling heave of a small yacht at anchor depresses an ardent spirit.

"I can't explain it to you," I replied, which was true, "but to set sail in this wind would be the height of foolhardiness, and I care for you too much, dear, to expose you to unnecessary risks."

I thought this rather a neat conclusion, but Ethelbertha merely replied that she wished, under the circumstances, we hadn't come on board till Tuesday, and went below.

In the morning the wind veered round to the north; I was up early, and observed this to Captain Goyles.

"Aye, aye, sir," he remarked; "it's unfortunate, but it can't be helped."

"You don't think it possible for us to start to-day?" I hazarded.

He did not get angry with me, he only laughed.

"Well, sir," said he, "if you was a-wanting to go to Ipswich, I should say as it couldn't be better for us, but our destination being, as you see, the Dutch coast—why there you are!"

I broke the news to Ethelbertha, and we agreed to spend the day on shore. Harwich is not a merry town, towards evening you might call it dull. We had some tea and watercress at Dovercourt, and then returned to the quay to look for Captain Goyles and the boat. We waited an hour for him. When he came he was more cheerful than we were; if he had not told me himself that he never drank anything but one glass of hot grog before turning in for the night, I should have said he was drunk.

The next morning the wind was in the south, which made Captain Goyles rather anxious, it appearing that it was equally unsafe to move or to stop where we were; our only hope was it would change before anything happened. By this time, Ethelbertha had taken a dislike to the yacht; she said that, personally, she would rather be spending a week in a bathing machine, seeing that a bathing machine was at least steady.

We passed another day in Harwich, and that night and the next, the wind still continuing in the south, we slept at the "King's Head." On Friday the wind was blowing direct from the east. I met Captain Goyles on the quay, and suggested that, under these circumstances, we might start. He appeared irritated at my persistence.

"If you knew a bit more, sir," he said, "you'd see for yourself that it's impossible. The wind's a-blowing direct off the sea."

I said: "Captain Goyles, tell me what is this thing I have hired? Is it a yacht or a house-boat?"

He seemed surprised at my question.

He said: "It's a yawl."

"What I mean is," I said, "can it be moved at all, or is it a fixture here? If it is a fixture," I continued, "tell me so frankly, then we will get some ivy in boxes and train over the port-holes, stick some flowers and an awning on deck, and make the thing look pretty. If, on the other hand, it can be moved—"

"Moved!" interrupted Captain Goyles. "You get the right wind behind the *Rogue*—"

I said: "What is the right wind?"

Captain Goyles looked puzzled.

"In the course of this week," I went on, "we have had wind from the north, from the south, from the east, from the west—with variations. If you can think of any other point of the compass from which it can blow, tell me, and I will wait for it. If not, and if that anchor has not grown into the bottom of the ocean, we will have it up to-day and see what happens."

He grasped the fact that I was determined.

"Very well, sir," he said, "you're master and I'm man. I've only got one child as is still dependent on me, thank God, and no doubt your executors will feel it their duty to do the right thing by the old woman."

His solemnity impressed me.

"Mr. Goyles," I said, "be honest with me. Is there any hope, in any weather, of getting away from this damned hole?"

Captain Goyles's kindly geniality returned to him.

"You see, sir," he said, "this is a very peculiar coast. We'd be all right if we were once out, but getting away from it in a cockle-shell like that—well, to be frank, sir, it wants doing."

I left Captain Goyles with the assurance that he would watch the weather as a mother would her sleeping babe; it was his own simile, and it struck me as rather touching. I saw him again at twelve o'clock; he was watching it from the window of the "Chain and Anchor."

At five o'clock that evening a stroke of luck occurred; in the middle of the High Street I met a couple of yachting friends, who had had to put in by reason of a strained rudder. I told them my story, and they appeared less surprised than amused. Captain Goyles and the two men were still watching the weather. I ran into the "King's Head," and prepared Ethelbertha. The four of us crept quietly down to the quay, where we found our boat. Only the boy was on board; my two friends took charge of the yacht, and by six o'clock we were scudding merrily up the coast.

We put in that night at Aldborough, and the next day worked up to Yarmouth, where, as my friends had to leave, I decided to abandon the yacht. We sold the stores by auction on Yarmouth sands early in the morning. I made a loss, but had the satisfaction of "doing" Captain Goyles. I left the *Rogue* in charge of a local mariner, who, for a couple of sovereigns, undertook to see to its return to Harwich; and we came back to London by train. There may be yachts other than the *Rogue*, and skippers other than Mr. Goyles, but that experience has prejudiced me against both.

George also thought a yacht would be a good deal of responsibility, so we dismissed the idea.

"What about the river?" suggested Harris.

"We have had some pleasant times on that."

George pulled in silence at his cigar, and I cracked another nut.

"The river is not what it used to be," said I; "I don't know what, but there's a something—a dampness—about the river air that always starts my lumbago."

"It's the same with me," said George. "I don't know how it is, but I never can sleep now in the neighbourhood of the river. I spent a week at Joe's place in the spring, and every night I woke up at seven o'clock and never got a wink afterwards."

CHAPTER I

"I merely suggested it," observed Harris. "Personally, I don't think it good for me, either; it touches my gout."

"What suits me best," I said, "is mountain air. What say you to a walking tour in Scotland?"

"It's always wet in Scotland," said George. "I was three weeks in Scotland the year before last, and was never dry once all the time—not in that sense."

"It's fine enough in Switzerland," said Harris.

"They would never stand our going to Switzerland by ourselves," I objected. "You know what happened last time. It must be some place where no delicately nurtured woman or child could possibly live; a country of bad hotels and comfortless travelling; where we shall have to rough it, to work hard, to starve perhaps—"

"Easy!" interrupted George, "easy, there! Don't forget I'm coming with you."

"I have it!" exclaimed Harris; "a bicycle tour!"

George looked doubtful.

"There's a lot of uphill about a bicycle tour," said he, "and the wind is against you."

"So there is downhill, and the wind behind you," said Harris.

"I've never noticed it," said George.

"You won't think of anything better than a bicycle tour," persisted Harris.

I was inclined to agree with him.

"And I'll tell you where," continued he; "through the Black Forest."

"Why, that's *all* uphill," said George.

"Not all," retorted Harris; "say two-thirds. And there's one thing you've forgotten."

He looked round cautiously, and sunk his voice to a whisper.

"There are little railways going up those hills, little cogwheel things that—"

The door opened, and Mrs. Harris appeared. She said that Ethelbertha was putting on her bonnet, and that Muriel, after waiting, had given "The Mad Hatter's Tea Party" without us.

"Club, to-morrow, at four," whispered Harris to me, as he rose, and I passed it on to George as we went upstairs

CHAPTER II

**A delicate business—What Ethelbertha might have said—
What she did say—What Mrs. Harris said—What we told
George—We will start on Wednesday—George suggests the
possibility of improving our minds—Harris and I are doubtful—Which man on a tandem does the most work?—The
opinion of the man in front—Views of the man behind—
How Harris lost his wife—The luggage question—The wisdom of my late Uncle Podger—Beginning of story about a
man who had a bag.**

I opened the ball with Ethelbertha that same evening. I commenced by being purposely a little irritable. My idea was that Ethelbertha would remark upon this. I should admit it, and account for it by over brain pressure. This would naturally lead to talk about my health in general, and the evident necessity there was for my taking prompt and vigorous measures. I thought that with a little tact I might even manage so that the suggestion should come from Ethelbertha herself. I imagined her saying: "No, dear, it is change you want; complete change. Now be persuaded by me, and go away for a month. No, do not ask me to come with you. I know you would rather that I did, but I will not. It is the society of other men you need. Try and persuade George and Harris to go with you. Believe me, a highly strung brain such as yours demands occasional relaxation from the strain of domestic surroundings. Forget for a little while that children want music lessons, and boots, and bicycles, with tincture of rhubarb three times a day; forget there are such things in life as cooks, and house decorators, and next-door dogs, and butchers' bills. Go away to some green corner of the earth, where all is new and strange to you, where your over-wrought mind will gather peace and fresh ideas. Go away for a space and give me time to miss you, and to reflect upon your goodness and virtue, which, continually present with me, I may, human-like, be apt to forget, as one, through use, grows indifferent to the blessing of the sun and the beauty of the moon. Go away, and come back refreshed in mind and body, a brighter, better man—if that be possible—than when you went away."

But even when we obtain our desires they never come to us garbed as we would wish. To begin with, Ethelbertha did not seem to remark that I was irritable; I had to draw her attention to it. I said:

"You must forgive me, I'm not feeling quite myself to-night."

She said: "Oh! I have not noticed anything different; what's the matter with you?"

"I can't tell you what it is," I said; "I've felt it coming on for weeks."

"It's that whisky," said Ethelbertha. "You never touch it except when we go to the Harris's. You know you can't stand it; you have not a strong head."

"It isn't the whisky," I replied; "it's deeper than that. I fancy it's more mental than bodily."

"You've been reading those criticisms again," said Ethelbertha, more sympathetically; "why don't you take my advice and put them on the fire?"

"And it isn't the criticisms," I answered; "they've been quite flattering of late—one or two of them."

"Well, what is it?" said Ethelbertha; "there must be something to account for it."

"No, there isn't," I replied; "that's the remarkable thing about it; I can only describe it as a strange feeling of unrest that seems to have taken possession of me."

Ethelbertha glanced across at me with a somewhat curious expression, I thought; but as she said nothing, I continued the argument myself.

"This aching monotony of life, these days of peaceful, uneventful felicity, they appal one."

"I should not grumble at them," said Ethelbertha; "we might get some of the other sort, and like them still less."

"I'm not so sure of that," I replied. "In a life of continuous joy, I can imagine even pain coming as a welcome variation. I wonder sometimes whether the saints in heaven do not occasionally feel the continual serenity a burden. To myself a life of endless bliss, uninterrupted by a single contrasting note, would, I feel, grow maddening. I suppose," I continued, "I am a strange sort of man; I can hardly understand myself at times. There are moments," I added, "when I hate myself."

Often a little speech like this, hinting at hidden depths of indescribable emotion has touched Ethelbertha, but to-night she appeared strangely unsympathetic. With regard to heaven and its possible effect upon me, she suggested my not worrying myself about that, remarking it was always foolish to go half-way to meet trouble that might never come; while as to my being a strange sort of fellow, that, she supposed, I could not help, and if other people were willing to put up with me, there was an end of the matter. The monotony of life, she added, was a common experience; there she could sympathise with me.

"You don't know I long," said Ethelbertha, "to get away occasionally, even from you; but I know it can never be, so I do not brood upon it."

I had never heard Ethelbertha speak like this before; it astonished and grieved me beyond measure.

"That's not a very kind remark to make," I said, "not a wifely remark."

"I know it isn't," she replied; "that is why I have never said it before. You men never can understand," continued Ethelbertha, "that, however fond a woman may be of a man, there are times when he palls upon her. You don't know how I long to be able sometimes to put on my bonnet and go out, with nobody to ask me where I am going, why I am going, how long I am going to be, and when I shall be back. You don't know how I sometimes long to order a dinner that I should like and that the children would like, but at the sight of which you would put on your hat and be off to the Club. You don't know how much I feel inclined sometimes to invite some woman here that I like, and that I know you don't; to go and see the people that I want to see, to go to bed when *I* am tired, and to get up when *I* feel I want to get up. Two people living together are bound both to be continually sacrificing their own desires to the other one. It is sometimes a good thing to slacken the strain a bit."

On thinking over Ethelbertha's words afterwards, have come to see their wisdom; but at the time I admit I was hurt and indignant.

"If your desire," I said, "is to get rid of me—"

"Now, don't be an old goose," said Ethelbertha; "I only want to get rid of you for a little while, just long enough to forget there are one or two corners about you that are not perfect, just long enough to let me remember what a dear fellow you are in other respects, and to look forward to your return, as I used to look forward to your coming in the old days when I did not see you so often as to become, perhaps, a little indifferent to you, as one grows indifferent to the glory of the sun, just because he is there every day."

I did not like the tone that Ethelbertha took. There seemed to be a frivolity about her, unsuited to the theme into which we had drifted. That a woman should contemplate cheerfully an absence of three or four weeks from her husband appeared to me to be not altogether nice, not what I call womanly; it was not like Ethelbertha at all. I was worried, I felt I didn't want to go this trip at all. If it had not been for George and Harris, I would have abandoned it. As it was, I could not see how to change my mind with dignity.

"Very well, Ethelbertha," I replied, "it shall be as you wish. If you desire a holiday from my presence, you shall enjoy it; but if it be not impertinent curiosity on the part of a husband, I should like to know what you propose doing in my absence?"

"We will take that house at Folkestone," answered Ethelbertha, "and I'll go down there with Kate. And if you want to do Clara Harris a good turn," added Ethelbertha, "you'll persuade Harris to go with you, and then Clara can join us. We three used to have some very jolly times together before you men ever came along, and it would be just delightful to renew them. Do you think," continued Ethelbertha, "that you could persuade Mr. Harris to go with you?"

I said I would try.

"There's a dear boy," said Ethelbertha; "try hard. You might get George to join you."

I replied there was not much advantage in George's coming, seeing he was a bachelor, and that therefore nobody would be much benefited by his absence. But a woman never understands satire. Ethelbertha merely remarked it would look unkind leaving him behind. I promised to put it to him.

I met Harris at the Club in the afternoon, and asked him how he had got on.

He said, "Oh, that's all right; there's no difficulty about getting away."

But there was that about his tone that suggested incomplete satisfaction, so I pressed him for further details.

"She was as sweet as milk about it," he continued; "said it was an excellent idea of George's, and that she thought it would do me good."

"That seems all right," I said; "what's wrong about that?"

"There's nothing wrong about that," he answered, "but that wasn't all. She went on to talk of other things."

"I understand," I said.

"There's that bathroom fad of hers," he continued.

"I've heard of it," I said; "she has started Ethelbertha on the same idea."

"Well, I've had to agree to that being put in hand at once; I couldn't argue any more when she was so nice about the other thing. That will cost me a hundred pounds, at the very least."

"As much as that?" I asked.

"Every penny of it," said Harris; "the estimate alone is sixty."

I was sorry to hear him say this.

"Then there's the kitchen stove," continued Harris; "everything that has gone wrong in the house for the last two years has been the fault of that kitchen stove."

"I know," I said. "We have been in seven houses since we were married, and every kitchen stove has been worse than the last. Our present one is not only incompetent; it is spiteful. It knows when we are giving a party, and goes out of its way to do its worst."

"*We* are going to have a new one," said Harris, but he did not say it proudly. "Clara thought it would be such a saving of expense, having the two things done at the same time. I believe," said Harris, "if a woman wanted a diamond tiara, she would explain that it was to save the expense of a bonnet."

"How much do you reckon the stove is going to cost you?" I asked. I felt interested in the subject.

"I don't know," answered Harris; "another twenty, I suppose. Then we talked about the piano. Could you ever notice," said Harris, "any difference between one piano and another?"

"Some of them seem to be a bit louder than others," I answered; "but one gets used to that."

"Ours is all wrong about the treble," said Harris. "By the way, what *is* the treble?"

"It's the shrill end of the thing," I explained; "the part that sounds as if you'd trod on its tail. The brilliant selections always end up with a flourish on it."

"They want more of it," said Harris; "our old one hasn't got enough of it. I'll have to put it in the nursery, and get a new one for the drawing-room."

"Anything else?" I asked.

"No," said Harris; "she didn't seem able to think of anything else."

"You'll find when you get home," I said, "she has thought of one other thing."

"What's that?" said Harris.

"A house at Folkestone for the season."

"What should she want a house at Folkestone for?" said Harris.

"To live in," I suggested, "during the summer months."

"She's going to her people in Wales," said Harris, "for the holidays, with the children; we've had an invitation."

"Possibly," I said, "she'll go to Wales before she goes to Folkestone, or maybe she'll take Wales on her way home; but she'll want a house at Folkestone for the season, notwithstanding. I may be mistaken—I hope for your sake that I am—but I feel a presentiment that I'm not."

"This trip," said Harris, "is going to be expensive."

"It was an idiotic suggestion," I said, "from the beginning."

"It was foolish of us to listen to him," said Harris; "he'll get us into real trouble one of these days."

"He always was a muddler," I agreed.

"So headstrong," added Harris.

We heard his voice at that moment in the hall, asking for letters.

"Better not say anything to him," I suggested; "it's too late to go back now."

"There would be no advantage in doing so," replied Harris. "I should have to get that bathroom and piano in any case now."

He came in looking very cheerful.

"Well," he said, "is it all right? Have you managed it?"

There was that about his tone I did not altogether like; I noticed Harris resented it also.

"Managed what?" I said.

"Why, to get off," said George.

I felt the time was come to explain things to George.

"In married life," I said, "the man proposes, the woman submits. It is her duty; all religion teaches it."

George folded his hands and fixed his eyes on the ceiling.

"We may chaff and joke a little about these things," I continued; "but when it comes to practice, that is what always happens. We have mentioned to our wives that we are going. Naturally, they are grieved; they would prefer to come with us; failing that, they would have us remain with them. But we have explained to them our wishes on the subject, and—there's an end of the matter."

George said, "Forgive me; I did not understand. I am only a bachelor. People tell me this, that, and the other, and I listen."

I said, "That is where you do wrong. When you want information come to Harris or myself; we will tell you the truth about these questions."

George thanked us, and we proceeded with the business in hand.

"When shall we start?" said George.

"So far as I am concerned," replied Harris, "the sooner the better."

His idea, I fancy, was to get away before Mrs. H. thought of other things. We fixed the following Wednesday.

"What about route?" said Harris.

"I have an idea," said George. "I take it you fellows are naturally anxious to improve your minds?"

I said, "We don't want to become monstrosities. To a reasonable degree, yes, if it can be done without much expense and with little personal trouble."

"It can," said George. "We know Holland and the Rhine. Very well, my suggestion is that we take the boat to Hamburg, see Berlin and Dresden, and work our way to the Schwarzwald, through Nuremberg and Stuttgart."

"There are some pretty bits in Mesopotamia, so I've been told," murmured Harris.

George said Mesopotamia was too much out of our way, but that the Berlin-Dresden route was quite practicable. For good or evil, he persuaded us into it.

"The machines, I suppose," said George, "as before. Harris and I on the tandem, J.—"

"I think not," interrupted Harris, firmly. "You and J. on the tandem, I on the single."

"All the same to me," agreed George. "J. and I on the tandem, Harris—"

"I do not mind taking my turn," I interrupted, "but I am not going to carry George *all* the way; the burden should be divided."

"Very well," agreed Harris, "we'll divide it. But it must be on the distinct understanding that he works."

"That he what?" said George.

"That he works," repeated Harris, firmly; "at all events, uphill."

"Great Scott!" said George; "don't you want *any* exercise?"

There is always unpleasantness about this tandem. It is the theory of the man in front that the man behind does nothing; it is equally the theory of the man behind that he alone is the motive power, the man in front merely doing the puffing. The mystery will never be solved. It is annoying when Prudence is whispering to you on the one side not to overdo your strength and bring on heart disease; while Justice into the other ear is remarking, "Why should you do it all? This isn't a cab. He's not your passenger:" to hear him grunt out:

"What's the matter—lost your pedals?"

Harris, in his early married days, made much trouble for himself on one occasion, owing to this impossibility of knowing what the person behind is doing. He was riding with his wife through Holland. The roads were stony, and the machine jumped a good deal.

"Sit tight," said Harris, without turning his head.

What Mrs. Harris thought he said was, "Jump off." Why she should have thought he said "Jump off," when he said "Sit tight," neither of them can explain.

Mrs. Harris puts it in this way, "If you had said, 'Sit tight,' why should I have jumped off?"

Harris puts it, "If I had wanted you to jump off, why should I have said 'Sit tight!'?"

The bitterness is past, but they argue about the matter to this day.

Be the explanation what it may, however, nothing alters the fact that Mrs. Harris did jump off, while Harris pedalled away hard, under the impression she was still behind him. It appears that at first she thought he was riding up the hill merely to show off. They were both young in those days, and he used to do that sort of thing. She expected him to spring to earth on reaching the summit, and lean in a careless and graceful attitude against the machine, waiting for her. When, on the contrary, she saw him pass the summit and proceed rapidly down a long and steep incline, she was seized, first with surprise, secondly with indignation, and lastly with alarm. She ran to the top of the hill and shouted, but he never turned his head. She watched him disappear into a wood a mile and a half distant, and then sat down and cried. They had had a slight difference that morning, and she wondered if he had taken it seriously and intended desertion. She had no money; she knew no Dutch. People passed, and seemed sorry for her; she tried to make them understand what had happened. They gathered that she had lost something, but could not grasp what. They took her to the nearest village, and found a policeman for her. He concluded from her pantomime that some man had stolen her bicycle. They put the telegraph into operation, and discovered in a village four miles off an unfortunate boy riding a lady's machine of an obsolete pattern. They brought him to her in a cart, but as she did not appear to want either him or his bicycle they let him go again, and resigned themselves to bewilderment.

Meanwhile, Harris continued his ride with much enjoyment. It seemed to him that he had suddenly become a stronger, and in every way a more capable cyclist. Said he to what he thought was Mrs. Harris:

"I haven't felt this machine so light for months. It's this air, I think; it's doing me good."

Then he told her not to be afraid, and he would show her how fast he *could* go. He bent down over the handles, and put his heart into his work. The bicycle bounded over the road like a thing of life; farmhouses and churches, dogs and chickens came to him and passed. Old folks stood and gazed at him, the children cheered him.

In this way he sped merrily onward for about five miles. Then, as he explains it, the feeling began to grow upon him that something was wrong. He was not surprised at the silence; the wind was blowing strongly, and the machine was rattling a good deal. It was a sense of void that came upon him. He stretched out his hand behind him, and felt; there was nothing there but space. He jumped, or rather fell off, and looked back up the road; it stretched white and straight through the dark wood, and not a living soul could be seen upon it. He remounted, and rode back up the hill. In ten minutes he came to where the road broke into four; there he dismounted and tried to remember which fork he had come down.

While he was deliberating a man passed, sitting sideways on a horse. Harris stopped him, and explained to him that he had lost his wife. The man appeared to be neither surprised nor sorry for him. While they were talking another farmer came along, to whom the first man explained the matter, not as an accident, but as a good story. What appeared to surprise the second man most was that Harris should be making a fuss about the thing. He could get no sense out of either of them, and cursing them he mounted his machine again, and took the middle road on chance. Half-way up, he came upon a party of two young women with one young man between them. They appeared to be making the most of him. He asked them if they had seen his wife. They asked him what she was like. He did not know enough Dutch to describe her properly; all he could tell them was she was a very beautiful woman, of medium size. Evidently this did not satisfy them, the description was too general; any man could say that, and by this means perhaps get possession of a wife that did not belong to him. They asked him how she was dressed; for the life of him he could not recollect.

I doubt if any man could tell how any woman was dressed ten minutes after he had left her. He recollected a blue skirt, and then there was something that carried the dress on, as it were, up to the neck. Possibly, this may have been a blouse; he retained a dim vision of a belt; but what sort of a blouse? Was it green, or yellow, or blue? Had it a collar, or was it fastened with a bow? Were there feathers in her hat, or flowers? Or was it a hat at all? He dared not say, for fear of making a mistake and being sent miles after the wrong party. The two young women giggled, which in his then state of mind irritated Harris. The young man, who appeared anxious to get rid of him, suggested the police station at the next town. Harris made his way there. The police gave him a piece of paper, and told him to write down a full description of his wife, together with details of when and where he had lost her. He did not know where he had lost her; all he could tell them was the name of the village where he had lunched. He knew he had her with him then, and that they had started from there together.

The police looked suspicious; they were doubtful about three matters: Firstly, was she really his wife? Secondly, had he really lost her? Thirdly, why had he lost her? With the aid of a hotel-keeper, however, who spoke a little English, he overcame their scruples. They promised to act, and in the evening they brought her to him in a covered wagon, together with a bill for expenses. The meeting was not a tender one. Mrs. Harris is not a good actress, and always has great difficulty in disguising her feelings. On this occasion, she frankly admits, she made no attempt to disguise them.

The wheel business settled, there arose the ever-lasting luggage question.

"The usual list, I suppose," said George, preparing to write.

That was wisdom I had taught them; I had learned it myself years ago from my Uncle Podger.

"Always before beginning to pack," my Uncle would say, "make a list."

He was a methodical man.

"Take a piece of paper"—he always began at the beginning—"put down on it everything you can possibly require, then go over it and see that it contains nothing you can possibly do without. Imagine yourself in bed; what have you got on? Very well, put it down—together with a change. You get up; what do you do? Wash yourself. What do you wash yourself with? Soap; put down soap. Go on till you have finished. Then take your clothes. Begin at your feet; what do you wear on your feet? Boots, shoes, socks; put them down. Work up till you get to your head. What else do you want besides clothes? A little brandy; put it down. A corkscrew, put it down. Put down everything, then you don't forget anything."

That is the plan he always pursued himself. The list made, he would go over it carefully, as he always advised, to see that he had forgotten nothing. Then he would go over it again, and strike out everything it was possible to dispense with.

Then he would lose the list.

Said George: "Just sufficient for a day or two we will take with us on our bikes. The bulk of our luggage we must send on from town to town."

"We must be careful," I said; "I knew a man once—"

Harris looked at his watch.

"We'll hear about him on the boat," said Harris; "I have got to meet Clara at Waterloo Station in half an hour."

"It won't take half an hour," I said; "it's a true story, and—"

"Don't waste it," said George: "I am told there are rainy evenings in the Black Forest; we may be glad of it. What we have to do now is to finish this list."

Now I come to think of it, I never did get off that story; something always interrupted it. And it really was true.

CHAPTER III

Harris's one fault—Harris and the Angel—A patent bicycle lamp—The ideal saddle—The "Overhauler"—His eagle eye—His method—His cheery confidence—His simple and inexpensive tastes—His appearance—How to get rid of him—George as prophet—The gentle art of making oneself disagreeable in a foreign tongue—George as a student of human nature—He proposes an experiment—His Prudence—Harris's support secured, upon conditions.

On Monday afternoon Harris came round; he had a cycling paper in his hand.

I said: "If you take my advice, you will leave it alone."

Harris said: "Leave what alone?"

I said: "That brand-new, patent, revolution in cycling, record-breaking, Tomfoolishness, whatever it may be, the advertisement of which you have there in your hand."

He said: "Well, I don't know; there will be some steep hills for us to negotiate; I guess we shall want a good brake."

I said: "We shall want a brake, I agree; what we shall not want is a mechanical surprise that we don't understand, and that never acts when it is wanted."

"This thing," he said, "acts automatically."

"You needn't tell me," I said. "I know exactly what it will do, by instinct. Going uphill it will jamb the wheel so effectively that we shall have to carry the machine bodily. The air at the top of the hill will do it good, and it will suddenly come right again. Going downhill it will start reflecting what a nuisance it has been. This will lead to remorse, and finally to despair. It will say to itself: 'I'm not fit to be a brake. I don't help these fellows; I only hinder them. I'm a curse, that's what I am;' and, without a word of warning, it will 'chuck' the whole business. That is what that brake will do. Leave it alone. You are a good fellow," I continued, "but you have one fault."

"What?" he asked, indignantly.

"You have too much faith," I answered. "If you read an advertisement, you go away and believe it. Every experiment that every fool has thought of in connection with cycling you have tried. Your guardian angel appears to be a capable and conscientious spirit, and hitherto she has seen you through; take my advice and don't try her too far. She must have had a busy time since you started cycling. Don't go on till you make her mad."

He said: "If every man talked like that there would be no advancement made in any department of life. If nobody ever tried a new thing the world would come to a standstill. It is by—"

"I know all that can be said on that side of the argument," I interrupted. "I agree in trying new experiments up to thirty-five; *after* thirty-five I consider a man is entitled to think of himself. You and I have done our duty in this direction, you especially. You have been blown up by a patent gas lamp—"

He said: "I really think, you know, that was my fault; I think I must have screwed it up too tight."

I said: "I am quite willing to believe that if there was a wrong way of handling the thing that is the way you handle it. You should take that tendency of yours into consideration; it bears upon the argument. Myself, I did not notice what you did; I only know we were riding peacefully and pleasantly along the Whitby Road, discussing the Thirty Years' War, when your lamp went off like a pistol-shot. The start sent me into the ditch; and your wife's face, when I told her there was nothing the matter and that she was not to worry, because the two men would carry you upstairs, and the doctor would be round in a minute bringing the nurse with him, still lingers in my memory."

He said: "I wish you had thought to pick up the lamp. I should like to have found out what was the cause of its going off like that."

I said: "There was not time to pick up the lamp. I calculate it would have taken two hours to have collected it. As to its 'going off,' the mere fact of its being advertised as the safest lamp ever invented would of itself, to anyone but you, have suggested accident. Then there was that electric lamp," I continued.

"Well, that really did give a fine light," he replied; "you said so yourself."

I said: "It gave a brilliant light in the King's Road, Brighton, and frightened a horse. The moment we got into the dark beyond Kemp Town it went out, and you were summoned for riding without a light. You may remember that on sunny afternoons you used to ride about with that lamp shining for all it was worth. When lighting-up time came it was naturally tired, and wanted a rest."

"It was a bit irritating, that lamp," he murmured; "I remember it."

I said: "It irritated me; it must have been worse for you. Then there are saddles," I went on—I wished to get this lesson home to him. "Can you think of any saddle ever advertised that you have *not* tried?"

He said: "It has been an idea of mine that the right saddle is to be found."

I said: "You give up that idea; this is an imperfect world of joy and sorrow mingled. There may be a better land where bicycle saddles are made out of rainbow, stuffed with cloud; in this world the simplest thing is to get used to something hard. There was that saddle you bought in Birmingham; it was divided in the middle, and looked like a pair of kidneys.”

He said: “You mean that one constructed on anatomical principles.”

“Very likely,” I replied. “The box you bought it in had a picture on the cover, representing a sitting skeleton—or rather that part of a skeleton which does sit.”

He said: “It was quite correct; it showed you the true position of the—”

I said: “We will not go into details; the picture always seemed to me indelicate.”

He said: “Medically speaking, it was right.”

“Possibly,” I said, “for a man who rode in nothing but his bones. I only know that I tried it myself, and that to a man who wore flesh it was agony. Every time you went over a stone or a rut it nipped you; it was like riding on an irritable lobster. You rode that for a month.”

“I thought it only right to give it a fair trial,” he answered.

I said: “You gave your family a fair trial also; if you will allow me the use of slang. Your wife told me that never in the whole course of your married life had she known you so bad tempered, so un-Christian like, as you were that month. Then you remember that other saddle, the one with the spring under it.”

He said: “You mean ‘the Spiral.’”

I said: “I mean the one that jerked you up and down like a Jack-in-the-box; sometimes you came down again in the right place, and sometimes you didn’t. I am not referring to these matters merely to recall painful memories, but I want to impress you with the folly of trying experiments at your time of life.”

He said. “I wish you wouldn’t harp so much on my age. A man at thirty-four—”

“A man at what?”

He said: “If you don’t want the thing, don’t have it. If your machine runs away with you down a mountain, and you and George get flung through a church roof, don’t blame me.”

“I cannot promise for George,” I said; “a little thing will sometimes irritate him, as you know. If such an accident as you suggest happen, he may be cross, but I will undertake to explain to him that it was not your fault.”

“Is the thing all right?” he asked.

“The tandem,” I replied, “is well.”

He said: “Have you overhauled it?”

I said: “I have not, nor is anyone else going to overhaul it. The thing is now in working order, and it is going to remain in working order till we start.”

I have had experience of this “overhauling.” There was a man at Folkestone; I used to meet him on the Lees. He proposed one evening we should go for a long bicycle ride together on the following day, and I agreed. I got up early, for me; I made an effort, and was pleased with myself. He came half an hour late: I was waiting for him in the garden. It was a lovely day. He said:—

“That’s a good-looking machine of yours. How does it run?”

"Oh, like most of them!" I answered; "easily enough in the morning; goes a little stiffly after lunch."

He caught hold of it by the front wheel and the fork and shook it violently.

I said: "Don't do that; you'll hurt it."

I did not see why he should shake it; it had not done anything to him. Besides, if it wanted shaking, I was the proper person to shake it. I felt much as I should had he started whacking my dog.

He said: "This front wheel wobbles."

I said: "It doesn't if you don't wobble it." It didn't wobble, as a matter of fact—nothing worth calling a wobble.

He said: "This is dangerous; have you got a screw-hammer?"

I ought to have been firm, but I thought that perhaps he really did know something about the business. I went to the tool shed to see what I could find. When I came back he was sitting on the ground with the front wheel between his legs. He was playing with it, twiddling it round between his fingers; the remnant of the machine was lying on the gravel path beside him.

He said: "Something has happened to this front wheel of yours."

"It looks like it, doesn't it?" I answered. But he was the sort of man that never understands satire.

He said: "It looks to me as if the bearings were all wrong."

I said: "Don't you trouble about it any more; you will make yourself tired. Let us put it back and get off."

He said: "We may as well see what is the matter with it, now it is out." He talked as though it had dropped out by accident.

Before I could stop him he had unscrewed something somewhere, and out rolled all over the path some dozen or so little balls.

"Catch 'em!" he shouted; "catch 'em! We mustn't lose any of them." He was quite excited about them.

We grovelled round for half an hour, and found sixteen. He said he hoped we had got them all, because, if not, it would make a serious difference to the machine. He said there was nothing you should be more careful about in taking a bicycle to pieces than seeing you did not lose any of the balls. He explained that you ought to count them as you took them out, and see that exactly the same number went back in each place. I promised, if ever I took a bicycle to pieces I would remember his advice.

I put the balls for safety in my hat, and I put my hat upon the doorstep. It was not a sensible thing to do, I admit. As a matter of fact, it was a silly thing to do. I am not as a rule addle-headed; his influence must have affected me.

He then said that while he was about it he would see to the chain for me, and at once began taking off the gear-case. I did try to persuade him from that. I told him what an experienced friend of mine once said to me solemnly:—

"If anything goes wrong with your gear-case, sell the machine and buy a new one; it comes cheaper."

He said: "People talk like that who understand nothing about machines. Nothing is easier than taking off a gear-case."

I had to confess he was right. In less than five minutes he had the gear-case in two pieces, lying on the path, and was grovelling for screws. He said it was always a mystery to him the way screws disappeared.

We were still looking for the screws when Ethelbertha came out. She seemed surprised to find us there; she said she thought we had started hours ago.

He said: "We shan't be long now. I'm just helping your husband to overhaul this machine of his. It's a good machine; but they all want going over occasionally."

Ethelbertha said: "If you want to wash yourselves when you have done you might go into the back kitchen, if you don't mind; the girls have just finished the bedrooms."

She told me that if she met Kate they would probably go for a sail; but that in any case she would be back to lunch. I would have given a sovereign to be going with her. I was getting heartily sick of standing about watching this fool breaking up my bicycle.

Common sense continued to whisper to me: "Stop him, before he does any more mischief. You have a right to protect your own property from the ravages of a lunatic. Take him by the scruff of the neck, and kick him out of the gate!"

But I am weak when it comes to hurting other people's feelings, and I let him muddle on.

He gave up looking for the rest of the screws. He said screws had a knack of turning up when you least expected them; and that now he would see to the chain. He tightened it till it would not move; next he loosened it until it was twice as loose as it was before. Then he said we had better think about getting the front wheel back into its place again.

I held the fork open, and he worried with the wheel. At the end of ten minutes I suggested he should hold the forks, and that I should handle the wheel; and we changed places. At the end of his first minute he dropped the machine, and took a short walk round the croquet lawn, with his hands pressed together between his thighs. He explained as he walked that the thing to be careful about was to avoid getting your fingers pinched between the forks and the spokes of the wheel. I replied I was convinced, from my own experience, that there was much truth in what he said. He wrapped himself up in a couple of dusters, and we commenced again. At length we did get the thing into position; and the moment it was in position he burst out laughing.

I said: "What's the joke?"

He said: "Well, I am an ass!"

It was the first thing he had said that made me respect him. I asked him what had led him to the discovery.

He said: "We've forgotten the balls!"

I looked for my hat; it was lying topsy-turvy in the middle of the path, and Ethelbertha's favourite hound was swallowing the balls as fast as he could pick them up.

"He will kill himself," said Ebbson—I have never met him since that day, thank the Lord; but I think his name was Ebbson—"they are solid steel."

I said: "I am not troubling about the dog. He has had a bootlace and a packet of needles already this week. Nature's the best guide; puppies seem to require this kind of stimulant. What I am thinking about is my bicycle."

He was of a cheerful disposition. He said: "Well, we must put back all we can find, and trust to Providence."

We found eleven. We fixed six on one side and five on the other, and half an hour later the wheel was in its place again. It need hardly be added that it really did wobble now; a child might have noticed it. Ebbson said it would do for the present. He appeared to be getting a bit tired himself. If I had let him, he would, I believe, at this point have gone home. I was determined now, however, that he should stop and finish; I had abandoned all thoughts of a ride. My pride in the machine he had killed. My only interest lay now in seeing him scratch and bump and pinch himself. I revived his drooping spirits with a glass of beer and some judicious praise. I said:

"Watching you do this is of real use to me. It is not only your skill and dexterity that fascinates me, it is your cheery confidence in yourself, your inexplicable hopefulness, that does me good."

Thus encouraged, he set to work to refix the gear-case. He stood the bicycle against the house, and worked from the off side. Then he stood it against a tree, and worked from the near side. Then I held it for him, while he lay on the ground with his head between the wheels, and worked at it from below, and dropped oil upon himself. Then he took it away from me, and doubled himself across it like a pack-saddle, till he lost his balance and slid over on to his head. Three times he said:

"Thank Heaven, that's right at last!"

And twice he said:

"No, I'm damned if it is after all!"

What he said the third time I try to forget.

Then he lost his temper and tried bullying the thing. The bicycle, I was glad to see, showed spirit; and the subsequent proceedings degenerated into little else than a rough-and-tumble fight between him and the machine. One moment the bicycle would be on the gravel path, and he on top of it; the next, the position would be reversed—he on the gravel path, the bicycle on him. Now he would be standing flushed with victory, the bicycle firmly fixed between his legs. But his triumph would be short-lived. By a sudden, quick movement it would free itself, and, turning upon him, hit him sharply over the head with one of its handles.

At a quarter to one, dirty and dishevelled, cut and breeding, he said: "I think that will do;" and rose and wiped his brow.

CHAPTER III

The bicycle looked as if it also had had enough of it. Which had received most punishment it would have been difficult to say. I took him into the back kitchen, where, so far as was possible without soda and proper tools, he cleaned himself, and sent him home.

The bicycle I put into a cab and took round to the nearest repairing shop. The foreman of the works came up and looked at it.

"What do you want me to do with that?" said he.

"I want you," I said, "so far as is possible, to restore it."

"It's a bit far gone," said he; "but I'll do my best."

He did his best, which came to two pounds ten. But it was never the same machine again; and at the end of the season I left it in an agent's hands to sell. I wished to deceive nobody; I instructed the man to advertise it as a last year's machine. The agent advised me not to mention any date. He said:

"In this business it isn't a question of what is true and what isn't; it's a question of what you can get people to believe. Now, between you and me, it don't look like a last year's machine; so far as looks are concerned, it might be a ten-year old. We'll say nothing about date; we'll just get what we can."

I left the matter to him, and he got me five pounds, which he said was more than he had expected.

There are two ways you can get exercise out of a bicycle: you can "overhaul" it, or you can ride it. On the whole, I am not sure that a man who takes his pleasure overhauling does not have the best of the bargain. He is independent of the weather and the wind; the state of the roads troubles him not. Give him a screw-hammer, a bundle of rags, an oil-can, and something to sit down upon, and he is happy for the day. He has to put up with certain disadvantages, of course; there is no joy without alloy. He himself always looks like a tinker, and his machine always suggests the idea that, having stolen it, he has tried to disguise it; but as he rarely gets beyond the first milestone with it, this, perhaps, does not much matter. The mistake some people make is in thinking they can get both forms of sport out of the same machine. This is impossible; no machine will stand the double strain. You must make up your mind whether you are going to be an "overhauler" or a rider. Personally, I prefer to ride, therefore I take care to have near me nothing that can tempt me to overhaul. When anything happens to my machine I wheel it to the nearest repairing shop. If I am too far from the town or village to walk, I sit by the roadside and wait till a cart comes along. My chief danger, I always find, is from the wandering overhauler. The sight of a broken-down machine is to the overhauler as a wayside corpse to a crow; he swoops down upon it with a friendly yell of triumph. At first I used to try politeness. I would say:

"It is nothing; don't you trouble. You ride on, and enjoy yourself, I beg it of you as a favour; please go away."

Experience has taught me, however, that courtesy is of no use in such an extremity. Now I say:

"You go away and leave the thing alone, or I will knock your silly head off."

And if you look determined, and have a good stout cudgel in your hand, you can generally drive him off.

George came in later in the day. He said:

"Well, do you think everything will be ready?"

I said: "Everything will be ready by Wednesday, except, perhaps, you and Harris."

He said: "Is the tandem all right?"

"The tandem," I said, "is well."

He said: "You don't think it wants overhauling?"

I replied: "Age and experience have taught me that there are few matters concerning which a man does well to be positive. Consequently, there remain to me now but a limited number of questions upon which I feel any degree of certainty. Among such still-unshaken beliefs, however, is the conviction that that tandem does not want overhauling. I also feel a presentiment that, provided my life is spared, no human being between now and Wednesday morning is going to overhaul it."

George said: "I should not show temper over the matter, if I were you. There will come a day, perhaps not far distant, when that bicycle, with a couple of mountains between it and the nearest repairing shop, will, in spite of your chronic desire for rest, *have* to be overhauled. Then you will clamour for people to tell you where you put the oil-can, and what you have done with the screw-hammer. Then, while you exert yourself holding the thing steady against a tree, you will suggest that somebody else should clean the chain and pump the back wheel."

I felt there was justice in George's rebuke—also a certain amount of prophetic wisdom. I said:

"Forgive me if I seemed unresponsive. The truth is, Harris was round here this morning—"

George said: "Say no more; I understand. Besides, what I came to talk to you about was another matter. Look at that."

He handed me a small book bound in red cloth. It was a guide to English conversation for the use of German travellers. It commenced "On a Steam-boat," and terminated "At the Doctor's"; its longest chapter being devoted to conversation in a railway carriage, among, apparently, a compartment load of quarrelsome and ill-mannered lunatics: "Can you not get further away from me, sir?"—"It is impossible, madam; my neighbour, here, is very stout"—"Shall we not endeavour to arrange our legs?"—"Please have the goodness to keep your elbows down"—"Pray do not inconvenience yourself, madam, if my shoulder is of any accommodation to you," whether intended to be said sarcastically or not, there was nothing to indicate—"I really must request you to move a little, madam, I can hardly breathe," the author's idea being, presumably, that by this time the whole party was mixed up together on the floor. The chapter concluded with the phrase, "Here we are at our destination, God be thanked! (*Gott sei dank*!)" a pious exclamation, which under the circumstances must have taken the form of a chorus.

CHAPTER III

At the end of the book was an appendix, giving the German traveller hints concerning the preservation of his health and comfort during his sojourn in English towns, chief among such hints being advice to him to always travel with a supply of disinfectant powder, to always lock his bedroom door at night, and to always carefully count his small change.

"It is not a brilliant publication," I remarked, handing the book back to George; "it is not a book that personally I would recommend to any German about to visit England; I think it would get him disliked. But I have read books published in London for the use of English travellers abroad every whit as foolish. Some educated idiot, misunderstanding seven languages, would appear to go about writing these books for the misinformation and false guidance of modern Europe."

"You cannot deny," said George, "that these books are in large request. They are bought by the thousand, I know. In every town in Europe there must be people going about talking this sort of thing."

"Maybe," I replied; "but fortunately nobody understands them. I have noticed, myself, men standing on railway platforms and at street corners reading aloud from such books. Nobody knows what language they are speaking; nobody has the slightest knowledge of what they are saying. This is, perhaps, as well; were they understood they would probably be assaulted."

George said: "Maybe you are right; my idea is to see what would happen if they were understood. My proposal is to get to London early on Wednesday morning, and spend an hour or two going about and shopping with the aid of this book. There are one or two little things I want—a hat and a pair of bedroom slippers, among other articles. Our boat does not leave Tilbury till twelve, and that just gives us time. I want to try this sort of talk where I can properly judge of its effect. I want to see how the foreigner feels when he is talked to in this way."

It struck me as a sporting idea. In my enthusiasm I offered to accompany him, and wait outside the shop. I said I thought that Harris would like to be in it, too— or rather outside.

George said that was not quite his scheme. His proposal was that Harris and I should accompany him into the shop. With Harris, who looks formidable, to support him, and myself at the door to call the police if necessary, he said he was willing to adventure the thing.

We walked round to Harris's, and put the proposal before him. He examined the book, especially the chapters dealing with the purchase of shoes and hats. He said:

"If George talks to any bootmaker or any hatter the things that are put down here, it is not support he will want; it is carrying to the hospital that he will need."

That made George angry.

"You talk," said George, "as though I were a foolhardy boy without any sense. I shall select from the more polite and less irritating speeches; the grosser insults I shall avoid."

This being clearly understood, Harris gave in his adhesion; and our start was fixed for early Wednesday morning.

CHAPTER IV

Why Harris considers alarm clocks unnecessary in a family—Social instinct of the young—A child's thoughts about the morning—The sleepless watchman—The mystery of him—His over anxiety—Night thoughts—The sort of work one does before breakfast—The good sheep and the bad—Disadvantages of being virtuous—Harris's new stove begins badly—The daily out-going of my Uncle Podger—The elderly city man considered as a racer—We arrive in London—We talk the language of the traveller.

George came down on Tuesday evening, and slept at Harris's place. We thought this a better arrangement than his own suggestion, which was that we should call for him on our way and "pick him up." Picking George up in the morning means picking him out of bed to begin with, and shaking him awake—in itself an exhausting effort with which to commence the day; helping him find his things and finish his packing; and then waiting for him while he eats his breakfast, a tedious entertainment from the spectator's point of view, full of wearisome repetition.

I knew that if he slept at "Beggarbush" he would be up in time; I have slept there myself, and I know what happens. About the middle of the night, as you judge, though in reality it may be somewhat later, you are startled out of your first sleep by what sounds like a rush of cavalry along the passage, just outside your door. Your half-awakened intelligence fluctuates between burglars, the Day of Judgment, and a gas explosion. You sit up in bed and listen intently. You are not kept waiting long; the next moment a door is violently slammed, and somebody, or something, is evidently coming downstairs on a tea-tray.

"I told you so," says a voice outside, and immediately some hard substance, a head one would say from the ring of it, rebounds against the panel of your door.

By this time you are charging madly round the room for your clothes. Nothing is where you put it overnight, the articles most essential have disappeared entirely; and meanwhile the murder, or revolution, or whatever it is, continues unchecked. You pause for a moment, with your head under the wardrobe, where you think you can see your slippers, to listen to a steady, monotonous thumping upon a distant door. The victim, you presume, has taken refuge there; they mean to have him out and finish him. Will you be in time? The knocking ceases, and a voice, sweetly reassuring in its gentle plaintiveness, asks meekly:

"Pa, may I get up?"

You do not hear the other voice, but the responses are:

"No, it was only the bath—no, she ain't really hurt,—only wet, you know. Yes, ma, I'll tell 'em what you say. No, it was a pure accident. Yes; good-night, papa."

Then the same voice, exerting itself so as to be heard in a distant part of the house, remarks:

"You've got to come upstairs again. Pa says it isn't time yet to get up."

You return to bed, and lie listening to somebody being dragged upstairs, evidently against their will. By a thoughtful arrangement the spare rooms at "Beggarbush" are exactly underneath the nurseries. The same somebody, you conclude, still offering the most creditable opposition, is being put back into bed. You can follow the contest with much exactitude, because every time the body is flung down upon the spring mattress, the bedstead, just above your head, makes a sort of jump; while every time the body succeeds in struggling out again, you are aware by the thud upon the floor. After a time the struggle wanes, or maybe the bed collapses; and you drift back into sleep. But the next moment, or what seems to be the next moment, you again open your eyes under the consciousness of a presence. The door is being held ajar, and four solemn faces, piled one on top of the other, are peering at you, as though you were some natural curiosity kept in this particular room. Seeing you awake, the top face, walking calmly over the other three, comes in and sits on the bed in a friendly attitude.

"Oh!" it says, "we didn't know you were awake. I've been awake some time."

"So I gather," you reply, shortly.

"Pa doesn't like us to get up too early," it continues. "He says everybody else in the house is liable to be disturbed if we get up. So, of course, we mustn't."

The tone is that of gentle resignation. It is instinct with the spirit of virtuous pride, arising from the consciousness of self-sacrifice.

"Don't you call this being up?" you suggest.

"Oh, no; we're not really up, you know, because we're not properly dressed." The fact is self-evident. "Pa's always very tired in the morning," the voice continues; "of course, that's because he works hard all day. Are you ever tired in the morning?"

At this point he turns and notices, for the first time, that the three other children have also entered, and are sitting in a semi-circle on the floor. From their attitude it is clear they have mistaken the whole thing for one of the slower forms of entertainment, some comic lecture or conjuring exhibition, and are waiting patiently for you to get out of bed and do something. It shocks him, the idea of their being in the guest's bedchamber. He peremptorily orders them out. They do not answer him, they do not argue; in dead silence, and with one accord they fall upon him. All you can see from the bed is a confused tangle of waving arms and legs, suggestive of an intoxicated octopus trying to find bottom. Not a word is spoken; that seems to be the etiquette of the thing. If you are sleeping in your pyjamas, you spring from the bed, and only add to the confusion; if you are wearing a less showy garment, you stop where you are and shout commands, which are utterly unheeded. The simplest plan is to leave it to the eldest boy. He does get them out after a while, and closes the door upon them. It re-opens immediately, and one, generally Muriel, is shot back into the room. She enters as from a catapult. She is handicapped by having long hair, which can be used as a convenient handle. Evidently aware of this natural disadvantage, she clutches it herself tightly in one hand, and punches with the other. He opens the door again, and cleverly uses her as a battering-ram against the wall of those without. You can hear the dull crash as her head enters among them, and scatters them. When the victory is complete, he comes back and resumes his seat on the bed. There is no bitterness about him; he has forgotten the whole incident.

"I like the morning," he says, "don't you?"

"Some mornings," you agree, "are all right; others are not so peaceful."

He takes no notice of your exception; a far-away look steals over his somewhat ethereal face.

"I should like to die in the morning," he says; "everything is so beautiful then."

"Well," you answer, "perhaps you will, if your father ever invites an irritable man to come and sleep here, and doesn't warn him beforehand."

He descends from his contemplative mood, and becomes himself again.

"It's jolly in the garden," he suggests; "you wouldn't like to get up and have a game of cricket, would you?"

It was not the idea with which you went to bed, but now, as things have turned out, it seems as good a plan as lying there hopelessly awake; and you agree.

You learn, later in the day, that the explanation of the proceeding is that you, unable to sleep, woke up early in the morning, and thought you would like a game of cricket. The children, taught to be ever courteous to guests, felt it their duty to humour you. Mrs. Harris remarks at breakfast that at least you might have seen to it that the children were properly dressed before you took them out; while Harris points out to you, pathetically, how, by your one morning's example and encouragement, you have undone his labour of months.

On this Wednesday morning, George, it seems, clamoured to get up at a quarter-past five, and persuaded them to let him teach them cycling tricks round the cucumber frames on Harris's new wheel. Even Mrs. Harris, however, did not blame George on this occasion; she felt intuitively the idea could not have been entirely his.

It is not that the Harris children have the faintest notion of avoiding blame at the expense of a friend and comrade. One and all they are honesty itself in accepting responsibility for their own misdeeds. It simply is, that is how the thing presents itself to their understanding. When you explain to them that you had no original intention of getting up at five o'clock in the morning to play cricket on the croquet lawn, or to mimic the history of the early Church by shooting with a cross-bow at dolls tied to a tree; that as a matter of fact, left to your own initiative, you would have slept peacefully till roused in Christian fashion with a cup of tea at eight, they are firstly astonished, secondly apologetic, and thirdly sincerely contrite. In the present instance, waiving the purely academic question whether the awakening of George at a little before five was due to natural instinct on his part, or to the accidental passing of a home-made boomerang through his bed-room window, the dear children frankly admitted that the blame for his uprising was their own. As the eldest boy said:

"We ought to have remembered that Uncle George had a long day, before him, and we ought to have dissuaded him from getting up. I blame myself entirely."

But an occasional change of habit does nobody any harm; and besides, as Harris and I agreed, it was good training for George. In the Black Forest we should be up at five every morning; that we had determined on. Indeed, George himself had suggested half-past four, but Harris and I had argued that five would be early enough as an average; that would enable us to be on our machines by six, and to break the back of our journey before the heat of the day set in. Occasionally we might start a little earlier, but not as a habit.

I myself was up that morning at five. This was earlier than I had intended. I had said to myself on going to sleep, "Six o'clock, sharp!"

There are men I know who can wake themselves at any time to the minute. They say to themselves literally, as they lay their heads upon the pillow, "Four-thirty," "Four-forty-five," or "Five-fifteen," as the case may be; and as the clock strikes they open their eyes. It is very wonderful this; the more one dwells upon it, the greater the mystery grows. Some Ego within us, acting quite independently of our conscious self, must be capable of counting the hours while we sleep. Un-aided by clock or sun, or any other medium known to our five senses, it keeps watch through the darkness. At the exact moment it whispers "Time!" and we awake. The work of an old riverside fellow I once talked with called him to be out of bed each morning half an hour before high tide. He told me that never once had he overslept himself by a minute. Latterly, he never even troubled to work out the tide for himself. He would lie down tired, and sleep a dreamless sleep, and each morning at a different hour this ghostly watchman, true as the tide itself, would silently call him. Did the man's spirit haunt through the darkness the muddy river stairs; or had it knowledge of the ways of Nature? Whatever the process, the man himself was unconscious of it.

In my own case my inward watchman is, perhaps, somewhat out of practice. He does his best; but he is over-anxious; he worries himself, and loses count. I say to him, maybe, "Five-thirty, please;" and he wakes me with a start at half-past two. I look at my watch. He suggests that, perhaps, I forgot to wind it up. I put it to my ear; it is still going. He thinks, maybe, something has happened to it; he is confident himself it is half-past five, if not a little later. To satisfy him, I put on a pair of slippers and go downstairs to inspect the dining-room clock. What happens to a man when he wanders about the house in the middle of the night, clad in a dressing-gown and a pair of slippers, there is no need to recount; most men know by experience. Everything—especially everything with a sharp corner—takes a cowardly delight in hitting him. When you are wearing a pair of stout boots, things get out of your way; when you venture among furniture in woolwork slippers and no socks, it comes at you and kicks you. I return to bed bad tempered, and refusing to listen to his further absurd suggestion that all the clocks in the house have entered into a conspiracy against me, take half an hour to get to sleep again. From four to five he wakes me every ten minutes. I wish I had never said a word to him about the thing. At five o'clock he goes to sleep himself, worn out, and leaves it to the girl, who does it half an hour later than usual.

On this particular Wednesday he worried me to such an extent, that I got up at five simply to be rid of him. I did not know what to do with myself. Our train did not leave till eight; all our luggage had been packed and sent on the night before, together with the bicycles, to Fenchurch Street Station. I went into my study; I thought I would put in an hour's writing. The early morning, before one has breakfasted, is not, I take it, a good season for literary effort. I wrote three paragraphs of a story, and then read them over to myself. Some unkind things have been said about my work; but nothing has yet been written which would have done justice to those three paragraphs. I threw them into the waste-paper basket, and sat trying to remember what, if any, charitable institutions provided pensions for decayed authors.

To escape from this train of reflection, I put a golf-ball in my pocket, and selecting a driver, strolled out into the paddock. A couple of sheep were browsing there, and they followed and took a keen interest in my practice. The one was a kindly, sympathetic old party. I do not think she understood the game; I think it was my doing this innocent thing so early in the morning that appealed to her. At every stroke I made she bleated:

"Go-o-o-d, go-o-o-d ind-e-e-d!"

She seemed as pleased as if she had done it herself.

As for the other one, she was a cantankerous, disagreeable old thing, as discouraging to me as her friend was helpful.

"Ba-a-ad, da-a-a-m ba-a-a-d!" was her comment on almost every stroke. As a matter of fact, some were really excellent strokes; but she did it just to be contradictory, and for the sake of irritating. I could see that.

By a most regrettable accident, one of my swiftest balls struck the good sheep on the nose. And at that the bad sheep laughed—laughed distinctly and undoubtedly, a husky, vulgar laugh; and, while her friend stood glued to the ground, too astonished to move, she changed her note for the first time and bleated:

"Go-o-o-d, ve-e-ry go-o-o-d! Be-e-e-est sho-o-o-ot he-e-e's ma-a-a-de!"

I would have given half-a-crown if it had been she I had hit instead of the other one. It is ever the good and amiable who suffer in this world.

I had wasted more time than I had intended in the paddock, and when Ethelbertha came to tell me it was half-past seven, and the breakfast was on the table, I remembered that I had not shaved. It vexes Ethelbertha my shaving quickly. She fears that to outsiders it may suggest a poor-spirited attempt at suicide, and that in consequence it may get about the neighbourhood that we are not happy together. As a further argument, she has also hinted that my appearance is not of the kind that can be trifled with.

On the whole, I was just as glad not to be able to take a long farewell of Ethelbertha; I did not want to risk her breaking down. But I should have liked more opportunity to say a few farewell words of advice to the children, especially as regards my fishing rod, which they will persist in using for cricket stumps; and I hate having to run for a train. Quarter of a mile from the station I overtook George and Harris; they were also running. In their case—so Harris informed me, jerkily, while we trotted side by side—it was the new kitchen stove that was to blame. This was the first morning they had tried it, and from some cause or other it had blown up the kidneys and scalded the cook. He said he hoped that by the time we returned they would have got more used to it.

We caught the train by the skin of our teeth, as the saying is, and reflecting upon the events of the morning, as we sat gasping in the carriage, there passed vividly before my mind the panorama of my Uncle Podger, as on two hundred and fifty days in the year he would start from Ealing Common by the nine-thirteen train to Moorgate Street.

From my Uncle Podger's house to the railway station was eight minutes' walk. What my uncle always said was:

"Allow yourself a quarter of an hour, and take it easily."

What he always did was to start five minutes before the time and run. I do not know why, but this was the custom of the suburb. Many stout City gentlemen lived at Ealing in those days—I believe some live there still—and caught early trains to Town. They all started late; they all carried a black bag and a newspaper in one hand, and an umbrella in the other; and for the last quarter of a mile to the station, wet or fine, they all ran.

Folks with nothing else to do, nursemaids chiefly and errand boys, with now and then a perambulating costermonger added, would gather on the common of a fine morning to watch them pass, and cheer the most deserving. It was not a showy spectacle. They did not run well, they did not even run fast; but they were earnest, and they did their best. The exhibition appealed less to one's sense of art than to one's natural admiration for conscientious effort.

Occasionally a little harmless betting would take place among the crowd.

"Two to one agin the old gent in the white weskit!"

"Ten to one on old Blowpipes, bar he don't roll over hisself 'fore 'e gets there!"

"Heven money on the Purple Hemperor!"—a nickname bestowed by a youth of entomological tastes upon a certain retired military neighbour of my uncle's,—

a gentleman of imposing appearance when stationary, but apt to colour highly under exercise.

My uncle and the others would write to the *Ealing Press* complaining bitterly concerning the supineness of the local police; and the editor would add spirited leaders upon the Decay of Courtesy among the Lower Orders, especially throughout the Western Suburbs. But no good ever resulted.

It was not that my uncle did not rise early enough; it was that troubles came to him at the last moment. The first thing he would do after breakfast would be to lose his newspaper. We always knew when Uncle Podger had lost anything, by the expression of astonished indignation with which, on such occasions, he would regard the world in general. It never occurred to my Uncle Podger to say to himself:

"I am a careless old man. I lose everything: I never know where I have put anything. I am quite incapable of finding it again for myself. In this respect I must be a perfect nuisance to everybody about me. I must set to work and reform myself."

On the contrary, by some peculiar course of reasoning, he had convinced himself that whenever he lost a thing it was everybody else's fault in the house but his own.

"I had it in my hand here not a minute ago!" he would exclaim.

From his tone you would have thought he was living surrounded by conjurers, who spirited away things from him merely to irritate him.

"Could you have left it in the garden?" my aunt would suggest.

"What should I want to leave it in the garden for? I don't want a paper in the garden; I want the paper in the train with me."

"You haven't put it in your pocket?"

"God bless the woman! Do you think I should be standing here at five minutes to nine looking for it if I had it in my pocket all the while? Do you think I'm a fool?"

Here somebody would explain, "What's this?" and hand him from somewhere a paper neatly folded.

"I do wish people would leave my things alone," he would growl, snatching at it savagely.

He would open his bag to put it in, and then glancing at it, he would pause, speechless with sense of injury.

"What's the matter?" aunt would ask.

"The day before yesterday's!" he would answer, too hurt even to shout, throwing the paper down upon the table.

If only sometimes it had been yesterday's it would have been a change. But it was always the day before yesterday's; except on Tuesday; then it would be Saturday's.

We would find it for him eventually; as often as not he was sitting on it. And then he would smile, not genially, but with the weariness that comes to a man who feels that fate has cast his lot among a band of hopeless idiots.

"All the time, right in front of your noses—!" He would not finish the sentence; he prided himself on his self-control.

This settled, he would start for the hall, where it was the custom of my Aunt Maria to have the children gathered, ready to say good-bye to him.

My aunt never left the house herself, if only to make a call next door, without taking a tender farewell of every inmate. One never knew, she would say, what might happen.

One of them, of course, was sure to be missing, and the moment this was noticed all the other six, without an instant's hesitation, would scatter with a whoop to find it. Immediately they were gone it would turn up by itself from somewhere quite near, always with the most reasonable explanation for its absence; and would at once start off after the others to explain to them that it was found. In this way, five minutes at least would be taken up in everybody's looking for everybody else, which was just sufficient time to allow my uncle to find his umbrella and lose his hat. Then, at last, the group reassembled in the hall, the drawing-room clock would commence to strike nine. It possessed a cold, penetrating chime that always had the effect of confusing my uncle. In his excitement he would kiss some of the children twice over, pass by others, forget whom he had kissed and whom he hadn't, and have to begin all over again. He used to say he believed they mixed themselves up on purpose, and I am not prepared to maintain that the charge was altogether false. To add to his troubles, one child always had a sticky face; and that child would always be the most affectionate.

If things were going too smoothly, the eldest boy would come out with some tale about all the clocks in the house being five minutes slow, and of his having been late for school the previous day in consequence. This would send my uncle rushing impetuously down to the gate, where he would recollect that he had with him neither his bag nor his umbrella. All the children that my aunt could not stop would charge after him, two of them struggling for the umbrella, the others surging round the bag. And when they returned we would discover on the hall table the most important thing of all that he had forgotten, and wondered what he would say about it when he came home.

We arrived at Waterloo a little after nine, and at once proceeded to put George's experiment into operation. Opening the book at the chapter entitled "At the Cab Rank," we walked up to a hansom, raised our hats, and wished the driver "Good-morning."

This man was not to be outdone in politeness by any foreigner, real or imitation. Calling to a friend named "Charles" to "hold the steed," he sprang from his box, and returned to us a bow, that would have done credit to Mr. Turveydrop himself. Speaking apparently in the name of the nation, he welcomed us to England, adding a regret that Her Majesty was not at the moment in London.

We could not reply to him in kind. Nothing of this sort had been anticipated by the book. We called him "coachman," at which he again bowed to the pavement, and asked him if he would have the goodness to drive us to the Westminster Bridge road.

He laid his hand upon his heart, and said the pleasure would be his.

Taking the third sentence in the chapter, George asked him what his fare would be.

The question, as introducing a sordid element into the conversation, seemed to hurt his feelings. He said he never took money from distinguished strangers; he suggested a souvenir—a diamond scarf pin, a gold snuffbox, some little trifle of that sort by which he could remember us.

As a small crowd had collected, and as the joke was drifting rather too far in the cabman's direction, we climbed in without further parley, and were driven away amid cheers. We stopped the cab at a boot shop a little past Astley's Theatre that looked the sort of place we wanted. It was one of those overfed shops that the moment their shutters are taken down in the morning disgorge their goods all round them. Boxes of boots stood piled on the pavement or in the gutter opposite. Boots hung in festoons about its doors and windows. Its sun-blind was as some grimy vine, bearing bunches of black and brown boots. Inside, the shop was a bower of boots. The man, when we entered, was busy with a chisel and hammer opening a new crate full of boots.

George raised his hat, and said "Good-morning."

The man did not even turn round. He struck me from the first as a disagreeable man. He grunted something which might have been "Good-morning," or might not, and went on with his work.

George said: "I have been recommended to your shop by my friend, Mr. X."

In response, the man should have said: "Mr. X. is a most worthy gentleman; it will give me the greatest pleasure to serve any friend of his."

What he did say was: "Don't know him; never heard of him."

This was disconcerting. The book gave three or four methods of buying boots; George had carefully selected the one centred round "Mr. X," as being of all the most courtly. You talked a good deal with the shopkeeper about this "Mr. X," and then, when by this means friendship and understanding had been established, you slid naturally and gracefully into the immediate object of your coming, namely, your desire for boots, "cheap and good." This gross, material man cared, apparently, nothing for the niceties of retail dealing. It was necessary with such an one to come to business with brutal directness. George abandoned "Mr. X," and turning back to a previous page, took a sentence at random. It was not a happy selection; it was a speech that would have been superfluous made to any bootmaker. Under the present circumstances, threatened and stifled as we were on every side by boots, it possessed the dignity of positive imbecility. It ran:—

"One has told me that you have here boots for sale."

For the first time the man put down his hammer and chisel, and looked at us. He spoke slowly, in a thick and husky voice. He said:

"What d'ye think I keep boots for—to smell 'em?"

He was one of those men that begin quietly and grow more angry as they proceed, their wrongs apparently working within them like yeast.

"What d'ye think I am," he continued, "a boot collector? What d'ye think I'm running this shop for—my health? D'ye think I love the boots, and can't bear to part with a pair? D'ye think I hang 'em about here to look at 'em? Ain't there enough of 'em? Where d'ye think you are—in an international exhibition of boots? What d'ye think these boots are—a historical collection? Did you ever hear of a man keeping a boot shop and not selling boots? D'ye think I decorate the shop with 'em to make it look pretty? What d'ye take me for—a prize idiot?"

I have always maintained that these conversation books are never of any real use. What we wanted was some English equivalent for the well-known German idiom: "Behalten Sie Ihr Haar auf."

Nothing of the sort was to be found in the book from beginning to end. However, I will do George the credit to admit he chose the very best sentence that was to be found therein and applied it. He said:.

"I will come again, when, perhaps, you will have some more boots to show me. Till then, adieu!"

With that we returned to our cab and drove away, leaving the man standing in the centre of his boot-bedecked doorway addressing remarks to us. What he said, I did not hear, but the passers-by appeared to find it interesting.

George was for stopping at another boot shop and trying the experiment afresh; he said he really did want a pair of bedroom slippers. But we persuaded him to postpone their purchase until our arrival in some foreign city, where the tradespeople are no doubt more inured to this sort of talk, or else more naturally amiable. On the subject of the hat, however, he was adamant. He maintained that without that he could not travel, and, accordingly, we pulled up at a small shop in the Blackfriars Road.

The proprietor of this shop was a cheery, bright-eyed little man, and he helped us rather than hindered us.

When George asked him in the words of the book, "Have you any hats?" he did not get angry; he just stopped and thoughtfully scratched his chin.

"Hats," said he. "Let me think. Yes"—here a smile of positive pleasure broke over his genial countenance—"yes, now I come to think of it, I believe I have a hat. But, tell me, why do you ask me?"

George explained to him that he wished to purchase a cap, a travelling cap, but the essence of the transaction was that it was to be a "good cap."

The man's face fell.

"Ah," he remarked, "there, I am afraid, you have me. Now, if you had wanted a bad cap, not worth the price asked for it; a cap good for nothing but to clean windows with, I could have found you the very thing. But a good cap—no; we don't keep them. But wait a minute," he continued,—on seeing the disappointment that spread over George's expressive countenance, "don't be in a hurry. I have a cap here"—he went to a drawer and opened it—"it is not a good cap, but it is not so bad as most of the caps I sell."

He brought it forward, extended on his palm.

"What do you think of that?" he asked. "Could you put up with that?"

George fitted it on before the glass, and, choosing another remark from the book, said:

"This hat fits me sufficiently well, but, tell me, do you consider that it becomes me?"

The man stepped back and took a bird's-eye view.

"Candidly," he replied, "I can't say that it does."

He turned from George, and addressed himself to Harris and myself.

"Your friend's beauty," said he, "I should describe as elusive. It is there, but you can easily miss it. Now, in that cap, to my mind, you do miss it."

At that point it occurred to George that he had had sufficient fun with this particular man. He said:

"That is all right. We don't want to lose the train. How much?"

Answered the man: "The price of that cap, sir, which, in my opinion, is twice as much as it is worth, is four-and-six. Would you like it wrapped up in brown paper, sir, or in white?"

George said he would take it as it was, paid the man four-and-six in silver, and went out. Harris and I followed.

At Fenchurch Street we compromised with our cabman for five shillings. He made us another courtly bow, and begged us to remember him to the Emperor of Austria.

Comparing views in the train, we agreed that we had lost the game by two points to one; and George, who was evidently disappointed, threw the book out of window.

We found our luggage and the bicycles safe on the boat, and with the tide at twelve dropped down the river.

CHAPTER V

A necessary digression—Introduced by story containing moral—One of the charms of this book—The Journal that did not command success—Its boast: "Instruction combined with Amusement"—Problem: say what should be considered instructive and what amusing—A popular game— Expert opinion on English law—Another of the charms of this book—A hackneyed tune—Yet a third charm of this book—The sort of wood it was where the maiden lived— Description of the Black Forest.

A story is told of a Scotchman who, loving a lassie, desired her for his wife. But he possessed the prudence of his race. He had noticed in his circle many an otherwise promising union result in disappointment and dismay, purely in consequence of the false estimate formed by bride or bridegroom concerning the imagined perfectability of the other. He determined that in his own case no collapsed ideal should be possible. Therefore, it was that his proposal took the following form:

"I'm but a puir lad, Jennie; I hae nae siller to offer ye, and nae land."

"Ah, but ye hae yoursel', Davie!"

"An' I'm wishfu' it wa' onything else, lassie. I'm nae but a puir ill-seasoned loon, Jennie."

"Na, na; there's mony a lad mair ill-looking than yoursel', Davie."

"I hae na seen him, lass, and I'm just a-thinkin' I shouldna' care to."

"Better a plain man, Davie, that ye can depend a' than ane that would be a speirin' at the lassies, a-bringin' trouble into the hame wi' his flouting ways."

"Dinna ye reckon on that, Jennie; it's nae the bonniest Bubbly Jock that mak's the most feathers to fly in the kailyard. I was ever a lad to run after the petticoats, as is weel kent; an' it's a weary handfu' I'll be to ye, I'm thinkin'."

"Ah, but ye hae a kind heart, Davie! an' ye love me weel. I'm sure on't."

"I like ye weel enoo', Jennie, though I canna say how long the feeling may bide wi' me; an' I'm kind enoo' when I hae my ain way, an' naethin' happens to put me oot. But I hae the deevil's ain temper, as my mither call tell ye, an' like my puir fayther, I'm a-thinkin', I'll grow nae better as I grow mair auld."

"Ay, but ye're sair hard upon yersel', Davie. Ye're an honest lad. I ken ye better than ye ken yersel', an' ye'll mak a guid hame for me."

"Maybe, Jennie! But I hae my doots. It's a sair thing for wife an' bairns when the guid man canna keep awa' frae the glass; an' when the scent of the whusky comes to me it's just as though I hae'd the throat o' a Loch Tay salmon; it just gaes doon an' doon, an' there's nae filling o' me."

"Ay, but ye're a guid man when ye're sober, Davie."

"Maybe I'll be that, Jennie, if I'm nae disturbed."

"An' ye'll bide wi' me, Davie, an' work for me?"

"I see nae reason why I shouldna bide wi' yet Jennie; but dinna ye clack aboot work to me, for I just canna bear the thoct o't."

"Anyhow, ye'll do your best, Davie? As the minister says, nae man can do mair than that."

"An' it's a puir best that mine'll be, Jennie, and I'm nae sae sure ye'll hae ower muckle even o' that. We're a' weak, sinfu' creatures, Jennie, an' ye'd hae some deefficulty to find a man weaker or mair sinfu' than mysel'."

"Weel, weel, ye hae a truthfu' tongue, Davie. Mony a lad will mak fine promises to a puir lassie, only to break 'em an' her heart wi' 'em. Ye speak me fair, Davie, and I'm thinkin' I'll just tak ye, an' see what comes o't."

Concerning what did come of it, the story is silent, but one feels that under no circumstances had the lady any right to complain of her bargain. Whether she ever did or did not—for women do not invariably order their tongues according to logic, nor men either for the matter of that—Davie, himself, must have had the satisfaction of reflecting that all reproaches were undeserved.

I wish to be equally frank with the reader of this book. I wish here conscientiously to let forth its shortcomings. I wish no one to read this book under a misapprehension.

There will be no useful information in this book.

Anyone who should think that with the aid of this book he would be able to make a tour through Germany and the Black Forest would probably lose himself before he got to the Nore. That, at all events, would be the best thing that could happen to him. The farther away from home he got, the greater only would be his difficulties.

I do not regard the conveyance of useful information as my *forte*. This belief was not inborn with me; it has been driven home upon me by experience.

In my early journalistic days, I served upon a paper, the forerunner of many very popular periodicals of the present day. Our boast was that we combined instruction with amusement; as to what should be regarded as affording amusement and what instruction, the reader judged for himself. We gave advice to people about to marry—long, earnest advice that would, had they followed it, have made our circle of readers the envy of the whole married world. We told our subscribers how to make fortunes by keeping rabbits, giving facts and figures. The thing that must have surprised them was that we ourselves did not give up journalism and start rabbit-farming. Often and often have I proved conclusively from authoritative sources how a man starting a rabbit farm with twelve selected rabbits and a little judgment must, at the end of three years, be in receipt of an income of two thousand a year, rising rapidly; he simply could not help himself. He might not want the money. He might not know what to do with it when he had it. But there it was for him. I have never met a rabbit farmer myself worth two thousand a year, though I have known many start with the twelve necessary, assorted rabbits. Something has always gone wrong somewhere; maybe the continued atmosphere of a rabbit farm saps the judgment.

We told our readers how many bald-headed men there were in Iceland, and for all we knew our figures may have been correct; how many red herrings placed tail to mouth it would take to reach from London to Rome, which must have been useful to anyone desirous of laying down a line of red herrings from London to Rome, enabling him to order in the right quantity at the beginning; how many words the average woman spoke in a day; and other such like items of information calculated to make them wise and great beyond the readers of other journals.

We told them how to cure fits in cats. Personally I do not believe, and I did not believe then, that you can cure fits in cats. If I had a cat subject to fits I should advertise it for sale, or even give it away. But our duty was to supply information when asked for. Some fool wrote, clamouring to know; and I spent the best part of a morning seeking knowledge on the subject. I found what I wanted at length at the end of an old cookery book. What it was doing there I have never been able to understand. It had nothing to do with the proper subject of the book whatever; there was no suggestion that you could make anything savoury out of a cat, even when you had cured it of its fits. The authoress had just thrown in this paragraph out of pure generosity. I can only say that I wish she had left it out; it was the cause of a deal of angry correspondence and of the loss of four subscribers to the paper, if not more. The man said the result of following our advice had been two pounds worth of damage to his kitchen crockery, to say nothing of a broken window and probable blood poisoning to himself; added to which the cat's fits were worse than before. And yet it was a simple enough recipe. You held the cat between your legs, gently, so as not to hurt it, and with a pair of scissors made a sharp, clean cut in its tail. You did not cut off any part of the tail; you were to be careful not to do that; you only made an incision.

As we explained to the man, the garden or the coal cellar would have been the proper place for the operation; no one but an idiot would have attempted to perform it in a kitchen, and without help.

We gave them hints on etiquette. We told them how to address peers and bishops; also how to eat soup. We instructed shy young men how to acquire easy grace in drawing-rooms. We taught dancing to both sexes by the aid of diagrams. We solved their religious doubts for them, and supplied them with a code of morals that would have done credit to a stained-glass window.

The paper was not a financial success, it was some years before its time, and the consequence was that our staff was limited. My own apartment, I remember, included "Advice to Mothers"—I wrote that with the assistance of my landlady, who, having divorced one husband and buried four children, was, I considered, a reliable authority on all domestic matters; "Hints on Furnishing and Household Decorations—with Designs" a column of "Literary Counsel to Beginners"—I sincerely hope my guidance was of better service to them than it has ever proved to myself; and our weekly article, "Straight Talks to Young Men," signed "Uncle Henry." A kindly, genial old fellow was "Uncle Henry," with wide and varied experience, and a sympathetic attitude towards the rising generation. He had been through trouble himself in his far back youth, and knew most things. Even to this day I read of "Uncle Henry's" advice, and, though I say it who should not, it still seems to me good, sound advice. I often think that had I followed "Uncle Henry's" counsel closer I would have been wiser, made fewer mistakes, felt better satisfied with myself than is now the case.

A quiet, weary little woman, who lived in a bed-sitting room off the Tottenham Court Road, and who had a husband in a lunatic asylum, did our "Cooking Column," "Hints on Education"—we were full of hints,—and a page and a half of "Fashionable Intelligence," written in the pertly personal style which even yet has not altogether disappeared, so I am informed, from modern journalism: "I must tell you about the *divine* frock I wore at 'Glorious Goodwood' last week. Prince C.—but there, I really must not repeat all the things the silly fellow says; he is *too* foolish—and the *dear* Countess, I fancy, was just the *weeish* bit jealous"—and so on.

Poor little woman! I see her now in the shabby grey alpaca, with the inkstains on it. Perhaps a day at "Glorious Goodwood," or anywhere else in the fresh air, might have put some colour into her cheeks.

Our proprietor—one of the most unashamedly ignorant men I ever met—I remember his gravely informing a correspondent once that Ben Jonson had written *Rabelais* to pay for his mother's funeral, and only laughing good-naturedly when his mistakes were pointed out to him—wrote with the aid of a cheap encyclopedia the pages devoted to "General Information," and did them on the whole remarkably well; while our office boy, with an excellent pair of scissors for his assistant, was responsible for our supply of "Wit and Humour."

It was hard work, and the pay was poor, what sustained us was the consciousness that we were instructing and improving our fellow men and women. Of all games in the world, the one most universally and eternally popular is the game of school. You collect six children, and put them on a doorstep, while you walk up and down with the book and cane. We play it when babies, we play it when boys and girls, we play it when men and women, we play it as, lean and slippered, we totter towards the grave. It never palls upon, it never wearies us. Only one thing mars it: the tendency of one and all of the other six children to clamour for their turn with the book and the cane. The reason, I am sure, that journalism is so popular a calling, in spite of its many drawbacks, is this: each journalist feels he is the boy walking up and down with the cane. The Government, the Classes, and the Masses, Society, Art, and Literature, are the other children sitting on the doorstep. He instructs and improves them.

But I digress. It was to excuse my present permanent disinclination to be the vehicle of useful information that I recalled these matters. Let us now return.

Somebody, signing himself "Balloonist," had written to ask concerning the manufacture of hydrogen gas. It is an easy thing to manufacture—at least, so I gathered after reading up the subject at the British Museum; yet I did warn "Balloonist," whoever he might be, to take all necessary precaution against accident. What more could I have done? Ten days afterwards a florid-faced lady called at the office, leading by the hand what, she explained, was her son, aged twelve. The boy's face was unimpressive to a degree positively remarkable. His mother pushed him forward and took off his hat, and then I perceived the reason for this. He had no eyebrows whatever, and of his hair nothing remained but a scrubby dust, giving to his head the appearance of a hard-boiled egg, skinned and sprinkled with black pepper.

"That was a handsome lad this time last week, with naturally curly hair," remarked the lady. She spoke with a rising inflection, suggestive of the beginning of things.

"What has happened to him?" asked our chief.

"This is what's happened to him," retorted the lady. She drew from her muff a copy of our last week's issue, with my article on hydrogen gas scored in pencil, and flung it before his eyes. Our chief took it and read it through.

"He was 'Balloonist'?" queried the chief.

"He was 'Balloonist,'" admitted the lady, "the poor innocent child, and now look at him!"

"Maybe it'll grow again," suggested our chief.

"Maybe it will," retorted the lady, her key continuing to rise, "and maybe it won't. What I want to know is what you are going to do for him."

Our chief suggested a hair wash. I thought at first she was going to fly at him; but for the moment she confined herself to words. It appears she was not thinking of a hair wash, but of compensation. She also made observations on the general character of our paper, its utility, its claim to public support, the sense and wisdom of its contributors.

"I really don't see that it is our fault," urged the chief—he was a mild-mannered man; "he asked for information, and he got it."

"Don't you try to be funny about it," said the lady (he had not meant to be funny, I am sure; levity was not his failing) "or you'll get something that *you* haven't asked for. Why, for two pins," said the lady, with a suddenness that sent us both flying like scuttled chickens behind our respective chairs, "I'd come round and make your head like it!" I take it, she meant like the boy's. She also added observations upon our chief's personal appearance, that were distinctly in bad taste. She was not a nice woman by any means.

Myself, I am of opinion that had she brought the action she threatened, she would have had no case; but our chief was a man who had had experience of the law, and his principle was always to avoid it. I have heard him say:

"If a man stopped me in the street and demanded of me my watch, I should refuse to give it to him. If he threatened to take it by force, I feel I should, though not a fighting man, do my best to protect it. If, on the other hand, he should assert his intention of trying to obtain it by means of an action in any court of law, I should take it out of my pocket and hand it to him, and think I had got off cheaply."

He squared the matter with the florid-faced lady for a five-pound note, which must have represented a month's profits on the paper; and she departed, taking her damaged offspring with her. After she was gone, our chief spoke kindly to me. He said:

"Don't think I am blaming you in the least; it is not your fault, it is Fate. Keep to moral advice and criticism—there you are distinctly good; but don't try your hand any more on 'Useful Information.' As I have said, it is not your fault. Your information is correct enough—there is nothing to be said against that; it simply is that you are not lucky with it."

I would that I had followed his advice always; I would have saved myself and other people much disaster. I see no reason why it should be, but so it is. If I instruct a man as to the best route between London and Rome, he loses his luggage in Switzerland, or is nearly shipwrecked off Dover. If I counsel him in the purchase of a camera, he gets run in by the German police for photographing fortresses. I once took a deal of trouble to explain to a man how to marry his deceased wife's sister at Stockholm. I found out for him the time the boat left Hull and the best hotels to stop at. There was not a single mistake from beginning to end in the information with which I supplied him; no hitch occurred anywhere; yet now he never speaks to me.

Therefore it is that I have come to restrain my passion for the giving of information; therefore it is that nothing in the nature of practical instruction will be found, if I can help it, within these pages.

There will be no description of towns, no historical reminiscences, no architecture, no morals.

I once asked an intelligent foreigner what he thought of London.

He said: "It is a very big town."

I said: "What struck you most about it?"

He replied: "The people."

I said: "Compared with other towns—Paris, Rome, Berlin,—what did you think of it?"

He shrugged his shoulders. "It is bigger," he said; "what more can one say?"

One anthill is very much like another. So many avenues, wide or narrow, where the little creatures swarm in strange confusion; these bustling by, important; these halting to pow-wow with one another. These struggling with big burdens; those but basking in the sun. So many granaries stored with food; so many cells where the little things sleep, and eat, and love; the corner where lie their little white bones. This hive is larger, the next smaller. This nest lies on the sand, and another under the stones. This was built but yesterday, while that was fashioned ages ago, some say even before the swallows came; who knows?

Nor will there be found herein folk-lore or story.

Every valley where lie homesteads has its song. I will tell you the plot; you can turn it into verse and set it to music of your own.

There lived a lass, and there came a lad, who loved and rode away.

It is a monotonous song, written in many languages; for the young man seems to have been a mighty traveller. Here in sentimental Germany they remember him well. So also the dwellers of the Blue Alsatian Mountains remember his coming among them; while, if my memory serves me truly, he likewise visited the Banks of Allan Water. A veritable Wandering Jew is he; for still the foolish girls listen, so they say, to the dying away of his hoof-beats.

In this land of many ruins, that long while ago were voice-filled homes, linger many legends; and here again, giving you the essentials, I leave you to cook the dish for yourself. Take a human heart or two, assorted; a bundle of human passions—there are not many of them, half a dozen at the most; season with a mixture of good and evil; flavour the whole with the sauce of death, and serve up where and when you will. "The Saint's Cell," "The Haunted Keep," "The Dungeon Grave," "The Lover's Leap"—call it what you will, the stew's the same.

Lastly, in this book there will be no scenery. This is not laziness on my part; it is self-control. Nothing is easier to write than scenery; nothing more difficult and unnecessary to read. When Gibbon had to trust to travellers' tales for a description of the Hellespont, and the Rhine was chiefly familiar to English students through the medium of *Caesar's Commentaries*, it behoved every globe-trotter, for whatever distance, to describe to the best of his ability the things that he had seen. Dr. Johnson, familiar with little else than the view down Fleet Street, could read the description of a Yorkshire moor with pleasure and with profit. To a cockney who had never seen higher ground than the Hog's Back in Surrey, an account of Snowdon must have appeared exciting. But we, or rather the steam-engine and the camera for us, have changed all that. The man who plays tennis every year at the foot of the Matterhorn, and billiards on the summit of the Rigi, does not thank you for an elaborate and painstaking description of the Grampian Hills. To the average man, who has seen a dozen oil paintings, a hundred photographs, a thousand pictures in the illustrated journals, and a couple of panoramas of Niagara, the word-painting of a waterfall is tedious.

An American friend of mine, a cultured gentleman, who loved poetry well enough for its own sake, told me that he had obtained a more correct and more satisfying idea of the Lake district from an eighteenpenny book of photographic views than from all the works of Coleridge, Southey, and Wordsworth put together. I also remember his saying concerning this subject of scenery in literature, that he would thank an author as much for writing an eloquent description of what he had just had for dinner. But this was in reference to another argument; namely, the proper province of each art. My friend maintained that just as canvas and colour were the wrong mediums for story telling, so word-painting was, at its best, but a clumsy method of conveying impressions that could much better be received through the eye.

As regards the question, there also lingers in my memory very distinctly a hot school afternoon. The class was for English literature, and the proceedings commenced with the reading of a certain lengthy, but otherwise unobjectionable, poem. The author's name, I am ashamed to say, I have forgotten, together with the title of the poem. The reading finished, we closed our books, and the Professor, a kindly, white-haired old gentleman, suggested our giving in our own words an account of what we had just read.

"Tell me," said the Professor, encouragingly, "what it is all about."

"Please, sir," said the first boy—he spoke with bowed head and evident reluctance, as though the subject were one which, left to himself, he would never have mentioned,—"it is about a maiden."

"Yes," agreed the Professor; "but I want you to tell me in your own words. We do not speak of a maiden, you know; we say a girl. Yes, it is about a girl. Go on."

"A girl," repeated the top boy, the substitution apparently increasing his embarrassment, "who lived in a wood."

"What sort of a wood?" asked the Professor.

The first boy examined his inkpot carefully, and then looked at the ceiling.

"Come," urged the Professor, growing impatient, "you have been reading about this wood for the last ten minutes. Surely you can tell me something concerning it."

"The gnarly trees, their twisted branches"—recommenced the top boy.

"No, no," interrupted the Professor; "I do not want you to repeat the poem. I want you to tell me in your own words what sort of a wood it was where the girl lived."

The Professor tapped his foot impatiently; the top boy made a dash for it.

"Please, sir, it was the usual sort of a wood."

"Tell him what sort of a wood," said he, pointing to the second lad.

The second boy said it was a "green wood." This annoyed the Professor still more; he called the second boy a blockhead, though really I cannot see why, and passed on to the third, who, for the last minute, had been sitting apparently on hot plates, with his right arm waving up and down like a distracted semaphore signal. He would have had to say it the next second, whether the Professor had asked him or not; he was red in the face, holding his knowledge in.

"A dark and gloomy wood," shouted the third boy, with much relief to his feelings.

"A dark and gloomy wood," repeated the Professor, with evident approval. "And why was it dark and gloomy?"

The third boy was still equal to the occasion.

"Because the sun could not get inside it."

The Professor felt he had discovered the poet of the class.

"Because the sun could not get into it, or, better, because the sunbeams could not penetrate. And why could not the sunbeams penetrate there?"

"Please, sir, because the leaves were too thick."

"Very well," said the Professor. "The girl lived in a dark and gloomy wood, through the leafy canopy of which the sunbeams were unable to pierce. Now, what grew in this wood?" He pointed to the fourth boy.

"Please, sir, trees, sir."

"And what else?"

"Toadstools, sir." This after a pause.

The Professor was not quite sure about the toadstools, but on referring to the text he found that the boy was right; toadstools had been mentioned.

"Quite right," admitted the Professor, "toadstools grew there. And what else? What do you find underneath trees in a wood?"

"Please, sir, earth, sir."

"No; no; what grows in a wood besides trees?"

"Oh, please, sir, bushes, sir."

"Bushes; very good. Now we are getting on. In this wood there were trees and bushes. And what else?"

He pointed to a small boy near the bottom, who having decided that the wood was too far off to be of any annoyance to him, individually, was occupying his leisure playing noughts and crosses against himself. Vexed and bewildered, but feeling it necessary to add something to the inventory, he hazarded blackberries. This was a mistake; the poet had not mentioned blackberries.

"Of course, Klobstock would think of something to eat," commented the Professor, who prided himself on his ready wit. This raised a laugh against Klobstock, and pleased the Professor.

"You," continued he, pointing to a boy in the middle; "what else was there in this wood besides trees and bushes?"

"Please, sir, there was a torrent there."

"Quite right; and what did the torrent do?"

"Please, sir, it gurgled."

"No; no. Streams gurgle, torrents——?"

"Roar, sir."

"It roared. And what made it roar?"

This was a poser. One boy—he was not our prize intellect, I admit— suggested the girl. To help us the Professor put his question in another form:

"When did it roar?"

Our third boy, again coming to the rescue, explained that it roared when it fell down among the rocks. I think some of us had a vague idea that it must have been a cowardly torrent to make such a noise about a little thing like this; a pluck- ier torrent, we felt, would have got up and gone on, saying nothing about it. A torrent that roared every time it fell upon a rock we deemed a poor spirited torrent; but the Professor seemed quite content with it.

"And what lived in this wood beside the girl?" was the next question.

"Please, sir, birds, sir."

"Yes, birds lived in this wood. What else?"

Birds seemed to have exhausted our ideas.

"Come," said the Professor, "what are those animals with tails, that run up trees?"

We thought for a while, then one of us suggested cats.

This was an error; the poet had said nothing about cats; squirrels was what the Professor was trying to get.

I do not recall much more about this wood in detail. I only recollect that the sky was introduced into it. In places where there occurred an opening among the trees you could by looking up see the sky above you; very often there were clouds in this sky, and occasionally, if I remember rightly, the girl got wet.

I have dwelt upon this incident, because it seems to me suggestive of the whole question of scenery in literature. I could not at the time, I cannot now, understand why the top boy's summary was not sufficient. With all due deference to the poet, whoever he may have been, one cannot but acknowledge that his wood was, and could not be otherwise than, "the usual sort of a wood."

I could describe the Black Forest to you at great length. I could translate to you Hebel, the poet of the Black Forest. I could write pages concerning its rocky gorges and its smiling valleys, its pine-clad slopes, its rock-crowned summits, its foaming rivulets (where the tidy German has not condemned them to flow respectably through wooden troughs or drainpipes), its white villages, its lonely farmsteads.

But I am haunted by the suspicion you might skip all this. Were you sufficiently conscientious—or weak-minded enough—not to do so, I should, all said and done, succeed in conveying to you only an impression much better summed up in the simple words of the unpretentious guide book:

"A picturesque, mountainous district, bounded on the south and the west by the plain of the Rhine, towards which its spurs descend precipitately. Its geological formation consists chiefly of variegated sandstone and granite; its lower heights being covered with extensive pine forests. It is well watered with numerous streams, while its populous valleys are fertile and well cultivated. The inns are good; but the local wines should be partaken of by the stranger with discretion."

CHAPTER VI

Why we went to Hanover—Something they do better abroad—The art of polite foreign conversation, as taught in English schools—A true history, now told for the first time—The French joke, as provided for the amusement of British youth—Fatherly instincts of Harris—The road-waterer, considered as an artist—Patriotism of George—What Harris ought to have done—What he did—We save Harris's life—A sleepless city—The cab-horse as a critic.

We arrived in Hamburg on Friday after a smooth and uneventful voyage; and from Hamburg we travelled to Berlin by way of Hanover. It is not the most direct route. I can only account for our visit to Hanover as the nigger accounted to the magistrate for his appearance in the Deacon's poultry-yard.

"Well?"

"Yes, sar, what the constable sez is quite true, sar; I was dar, sar."

"Oh, so you admit it? And what were you doing with a sack, pray, in Deacon Abraham's poultry-yard at twelve o'clock at night?"

"I'se gwine ter tell yer, sar; yes, sar. I'd been to Massa Jordan's wid a sack of melons. Yes, sar; an' Massa Jordan he wuz very 'greeable, an' axed me for ter come in."

"Yes, sar, very 'greeable man is Massa Jordan. An' dar we sat a talking an' a talking—"

"Very likely. What we want to know is what you were doing in the Deacon's poultry-yard?"

"Yes, sar, dat's what I'se cumming to. It wuz ver' late 'fore I left Massa Jordan's, an' den I sez ter mysel', sez I, now yer jest step out with yer best leg foremost, Ulysses, case yer gets into trouble wid de ole woman. Ver' talkative woman she is, sar, very—"

"Yes, never mind her; there are other people very talkative in this town besides your wife. Deacon Abraham's house is half a mile out of your way home from Mr. Jordan's. How did you get there?"

"Dat's what I'm a-gwine ter explain, sar."

"I am glad of that. And how do you propose to do it?"

"Well, I'se thinkin', sar, I must ha' digressed."

I take it we digressed a little.

At first, from some reason or other, Hanover strikes you as an uninteresting town, but it grows upon you. It is in reality two towns; a place of broad, modern, handsome streets and tasteful gardens; side by side with a sixteenth-century town, where old timbered houses overhang the narrow lanes; where through low archways one catches glimpses of galleried courtyards, once often thronged, no doubt, with troops of horse, or blocked with lumbering coach and six, waiting its rich merchant owner, and his fat placid Frau, but where now children and chickens scuttle at their will; while over the carved balconies hang dingy clothes a-drying.

A singularly English atmosphere hovers over Hanover, especially on Sundays, when its shuttered shops and clanging bells give to it the suggestion of a sunnier London. Nor was this British Sunday atmosphere apparent only to myself, else I might have attributed it to imagination; even George felt it. Harris and I, returning from a short stroll with our cigars after lunch on the Sunday afternoon, found him peacefully slumbering in the smoke-room's easiest chair.

"After all," said Harris, "there is something about the British Sunday that appeals to the man with English blood in his veins. I should be sorry to see it altogether done away with, let the new generation say what it will."

And taking one each end of the ample settee, we kept George company.

To Hanover one should go, they say, to learn the best German. The disadvantage is that outside Hanover, which is only a small province, nobody understands this best German. Thus you have to decide whether to speak good German and remain in Hanover, or bad German and travel about. Germany being separated so many centuries into a dozen principalities, is unfortunate in possessing a variety of dialects. Germans from Posen wishful to converse with men of Wurtemburg, have to talk as often as not in French or English; and young ladies who have received an expensive education in Westphalia surprise and disappoint their parents by being unable to understand a word said to them in Mechlenberg. An English-speaking foreigner, it is true, would find himself equally nonplussed among the Yorkshire wolds, or in the purlieus of Whitechapel; but the cases are not on all fours. Throughout Germany it is not only in the country districts and among the uneducated that dialects are maintained. Every province has practically its own language, of which it is proud and retentive. An educated Bavarian will admit to you that, academically speaking, the North German is more correct; but he will continue to speak South German and to teach it to his children.

In the course of the century, I am inclined to think that Germany will solve her difficulty in this respect by speaking English. Every boy and girl in Germany, above the peasant class, speaks English. Were English pronunciation less arbitrary, there is not the slightest doubt but that in the course of a very few years, comparatively speaking, it would become the language of the world. All foreigners agree that, grammatically, it is the easiest language of any to learn. A German, comparing it with his own language, where every word in every sentence is governed by at least four distinct and separate rules, tells you that English has no grammar. A good many English people would seem to have come to the same conclusion; but they are wrong. As a matter of fact, there is an English grammar, and one of these days our schools will recognise the fact, and it will be taught to our children, penetrating maybe even into literary and journalistic circles. But at present we appear to agree with the foreigner that it is a quantity neglectable. English pronunciation is the stumbling-block to our progress. English spelling would seem to have been designed chiefly as a disguise to pronunciation. It is a clever idea, calculated to check presumption on the part of the foreigner; but for that he would learn it in a year.

For they have a way of teaching languages in Germany that is not our way, and the consequence is that when the German youth or maiden leaves the gymnasium or high school at fifteen, "it" (as in Germany one conveniently may say) can understand and speak the tongue it has been learning. In England we have a method that for obtaining the least possible result at the greatest possible expenditure of time and money is perhaps unequalled. An English boy who has been through a good middle-class school in England can talk to a Frenchman, slowly and with difficulty, about female gardeners and aunts; conversation which, to a man possessed perhaps of neither, is liable to pall. Possibly, if he be a bright exception, he may be able to tell the time, or make a few guarded observations concerning the weather. No doubt he could repeat a goodly number of irregular verbs by heart; only, as a matter of fact, few foreigners care to listen to their own irregular verbs, recited by young Englishmen. Likewise he might be able to remember a choice selection of grotesquely involved French idioms, such as no modern Frenchman has ever heard or understands when he does hear.

The explanation is that, in nine cases out of ten, he has learnt French from an "Ahn's First-Course." The history of this famous work is remarkable and instructive. The book was originally written for a joke, by a witty Frenchman who had resided for some years in England. He intended it as a satire upon the conversational powers of British society. From this point of view it was distinctly good. He submitted it to a London publishing firm. The manager was a shrewd man. He read the book through. Then he sent for the author.

"This book of yours," said he to the author, "is very clever. I have laughed over it myself till the tears came."

"I am delighted to hear you say so," replied the pleased Frenchman. "I tried to be truthful without being unnecessarily offensive."

"It is most amusing," concurred the manager; "and yet published as a harmless joke, I feel it would fail."

The author's face fell.

"Its humour," proceeded the manager, "would be denounced as forced and extravagant. It would amuse the thoughtful and intelligent, but from a business point of view that portion of the public are never worth considering. But I have an idea," continued the manager. He glanced round the room to be sure they were alone, and leaning forward sunk his voice to a whisper. "My notion is to publish it as a serious work for the use of schools!"

The author stared, speechless.

"I know the English schoolman," said the manager; "this book will appeal to him. It will exactly fit in with his method. Nothing sillier, nothing more useless for the purpose will he ever discover. He will smack his lips over the book, as a puppy licks up blacking."

The author, sacrificing art to greed, consented. They altered the title and added a vocabulary, but left the book otherwise as it was.

The result is known to every schoolboy. "Ahn" became the palladium of English philological education. If it no longer retains its ubiquity, it is because something even less adaptable to the object in view has been since invented.

Lest, in spite of all, the British schoolboy should obtain, even from the like of "Ahn," some glimmering of French, the British educational method further handicaps him by bestowing upon him the assistance of, what is termed in the prospectus, "A native gentleman." This native French gentleman, who, by-the-by, is generally a Belgian, is no doubt a most worthy person, and can, it is true, understand and speak his own language with tolerable fluency. There his qualifications cease. Invariably he is a man with a quite remarkable inability to teach anybody anything. Indeed, he would seem to be chosen not so much as an instructor as an amuser of youth. He is always a comic figure. No Frenchman of a dignified appearance would be engaged for any English school. If he possess by nature a few harmless peculiarities, calculated to cause merriment, so much the more is he esteemed by his employers. The class naturally regards him as an animated joke. The two to four hours a week that are deliberately wasted on this ancient farce, are looked forward to by the boys as a merry interlude in an otherwise monotonous existence. And then, when the proud parent takes his son and heir to Dieppe merely to discover that the lad does not know enough to call a cab, he abuses not the system, but its innocent victim.

I confine my remarks to French, because that is the only language we attempt to teach our youth. An English boy who could speak German would be looked down upon as unpatriotic. Why we waste time in teaching even French according to this method I have never been able to understand. A perfect unacquaintance with a language is respectable. But putting aside comic journalists and lady novelists, for whom it is a business necessity, this smattering of French which we are so proud to possess only serves to render us ridiculous.

In the German school the method is somewhat different. One hour every day is devoted to the same language. The idea is not to give the lad time between each lesson to forget what he learned at the last; the idea is for him to get on. There is no comic foreigner provided for his amusement. The desired language is taught by a German school-master who knows it inside and out as thoroughly as he knows his own. Maybe this system does not provide the German youth with that perfection of foreign accent for which the British tourist is in every land remarkable, but it has other advantages. The boy does not call his master "froggy," or "sausage," nor prepare for the French or English hour any exhibition of homely wit whatever. He just sits there, and for his own sake tries to learn that foreign tongue with as little trouble to everybody concerned as possible. When he has left school he can talk, not about penknives and gardeners and aunts merely, but about European politics, history, Shakespeare, or the musical glasses, according to the turn the conversation may take.

Viewing the German people from an Anglo-Saxon standpoint, it may be that in this book I shall find occasion to criticise them: but on the other hand there is much that we might learn from them; and in the matter of common sense, as applied to education, they can give us ninety-nine in a hundred and beat us with one hand.

The beautiful wood of the Eilenriede bounds Hanover on the south and west, and here occurred a sad drama in which Harris took a prominent part.

We were riding our machines through this wood on the Monday afternoon in the company of many other cyclists, for it is a favourite resort with the Hanoverians on a sunny afternoon, and its shady pathways are then filled with happy, thoughtless folk. Among them rode a young and beautiful girl on a machine that was new. She was evidently a novice on the bicycle. One felt instinctively that there would come a moment when she would require help, and Harris, with his accustomed chivalry, suggested we should keep near her. Harris, as he occasionally explains to George and to myself, has daughters of his own, or, to speak more correctly, a daughter, who as the years progress will no doubt cease practising catherine wheels in the front garden, and will grow up into a beautiful and respectable young lady. This naturally gives Harris an interest in all beautiful girls up to the age of thirty-five or thereabouts; they remind him, so he says, of home.

We had ridden for about two miles, when we noticed, a little ahead of us in a space where five ways met, a man with a hose, watering the roads. The pipe, supported at each joint by a pair of tiny wheels, writhed after him as he moved, suggesting a gigantic-worm, from whose open neck, as the man, gripping it firmly in both hands, pointing it now this way, and now that, now elevating it, now depressing it, poured a strong stream of water at the rate of about a gallon a second.

"What a much better method than ours," observed Harris, enthusiastically. Harris is inclined to be chronically severe on all British institutions. "How much simpler, quicker, and more economical! You see, one man by this method can in five minutes water a stretch of road that would take us with our clumsy lumbering cart half an hour to cover."

George, who was riding behind me on the tandem, said, "Yes, and it is also a method by which with a little carelessness a man could cover a good many people in a good deal less time than they could get out of the way."

George, the opposite to Harris, is British to the core. I remember George quite patriotically indignant with Harris once for suggesting the introduction of the guillotine into England.

"It is so much neater," said Harris.

"I don't care if it is," said George; "I'm an Englishman; hanging is good enough for me."

"Our water-cart may have its disadvantages," continued George, "but it can only make you uncomfortable about the legs, and you can avoid it. This is the sort of machine with which a man can follow you round the corner and upstairs."

"It fascinates me to watch them," said Harris. "They are so skilful. I have seen a man from the corner of a crowded square in Strassburg cover every inch of ground, and not so much as wet an apron string. It is marvellous how they judge their distance. They will send the water up to your toes, and then bring it over your head so that it falls around your heels. They can—"

"Ease up a minute," said George. I said: "Why?"

He said: "I am going to get off and watch the rest of this show from behind a tree. There may be great performers in this line, as Harris says; this particular artist appears to me to lack something. He has just soused a dog, and now he's busy watering a sign-post. I am going to wait till he has finished."

"Nonsense," said Harris; "he won't wet you."

"That is precisely what I am going to make sure of," answered George, saying which he jumped off, and, taking up a position behind a remarkably fine elm, pulled out and commenced filling his pipe.

I did not care to take the tandem on by myself, so I stepped off and joined him, leaving the machine against a tree. Harris shouted something or other about our being a disgrace to the land that gave us birth, and rode on.

The next moment I heard a woman's cry of distress. Glancing round the stem of the tree, I perceived that it proceeded from the young and elegant lady before mentioned, whom, in our interest concerning the road-waterer, we had forgotten. She was riding her machine steadily and straightly through a drenching shower of water from the hose. She appeared to be too paralysed either to get off or turn her wheel aside. Every instant she was becoming wetter, while the man with the hose, who was either drunk or blind, continued to pour water upon her with utter indifference. A dozen voices yelled imprecations upon him, but he took no heed whatever.

Harris, his fatherly nature stirred to its depths, did at this point what, under the circumstances, was quite the right and proper thing to do. Had he acted throughout with the same coolness and judgment he then displayed, he would have emerged from that incident the hero of the hour, instead of, as happened, riding away followed by insult and threat. Without a moment's hesitation he spurted at the man, sprang to the ground, and, seizing the hose by the nozzle, attempted to wrest it away.

What he ought to have done, what any man retaining his common sense would have done the moment he got his hands upon the thing, was to turn off the tap.

Then he might have played foot-ball with the man, or battledore and shuttlecock as he pleased; and the twenty or thirty people who had rushed forward to assist would have only applauded. His idea, however, as he explained to us afterwards, was to take away the hose from the man, and, for punishment, turn it upon the fool himself. The waterman's idea appeared to be the same, namely, to retain the hose as a weapon with which to soak Harris. Of course, the result was that, between them, they soused every dead and living thing within fifty yards, except themselves. One furious man, too drenched to care what more happened to him, leapt into the arena and also took a hand. The three among them proceeded to sweep the compass with that hose. They pointed it to heaven, and the water descended upon the people in the form of an equinoctial storm. They pointed it downwards, and sent the water in rushing streams that took people off their feet, or caught them about the waist line, and doubled them up.

Not one of them would loosen his grip upon the hose, not one of them thought to turn the water off. You might have concluded they were struggling with some primeval force of nature. In forty-five seconds, so George said, who was timing it, they had swept that circus bare of every living thing except one dog, who, dripping like a water nymph, rolled over by the force of water, now on this side, now on that, still gallantly staggered again and again to its feet to bark defiance at what it evidently regarded as the powers of hell let loose.

Men and women left their machines upon the ground, and flew into the woods. From behind every tree of importance peeped out wet, angry heads.

At last, there arrived upon the scene one man of sense. Braving all things, he crept to the hydrant, where still stood the iron key, and screwed it down. And then from forty trees began to creep more or less soaked human beings, each one with something to say.

At first I fell to wondering whether a stretcher or a clothes basket would be the more useful for the conveyance of Harris's remains back to the hotel. I consider that George's promptness on that occasion saved Harris's life. Being dry, and therefore able to run quicker, he was there before the crowd. Harris was for explaining things, but George cut him short.

"You get on that," said George, handing him his bicycle, "and go. They don't know we belong to you, and you may trust us implicitly not to reveal the secret. We'll hang about behind, and get in their way. Ride zig-zag in case they shoot."

I wish this book to be a strict record of fact, unmarred by exaggeration, and therefore I have shown my description of this incident to Harris, lest anything beyond bald narrative may have crept into it. Harris maintains it is exaggerated, but admits that one or two people may have been "sprinkled." I have offered to turn a street hose on him at a distance of five-and-twenty yards, and take his opinion afterwards, as to whether "sprinkled" is the adequate term, but he has declined the test. Again, he insists there could not have been more than half a dozen people, at the outside, involved in the catastrophe, that forty is a ridiculous misstatement. I have offered to return with him to Hanover and make strict inquiry into the matter, and this offer he has likewise declined. Under these circumstances, I maintain that mine is a true and restrained narrative of an event that is, by a certain number of Hanoverians, remembered with bitterness unto this very day.

We left Hanover that same evening, and arrived at Berlin in time for supper and an evening stroll. Berlin is a disappointing town; its centre over-crowded, its outlying parts lifeless; its one famous street, Unter den Linden, an attempt to combine Oxford Street with the Champs Elysée, singularly unimposing, being much too wide for its size; its theatres dainty and charming, where acting is considered of more importance than scenery or dress, where long runs are unknown, successful pieces being played again and again, but never consecutively, so that for a week running you may go to the same Berlin theatre, and see a fresh play every night; its opera house unworthy of it; its two music halls, with an unnecessary suggestion of vulgarity and commonness about them, ill-arranged and much too large for comfort. In the Berlin cafés and restaurants, the busy time is from midnight on till three. Yet most of the people who frequent them are up again at seven. Either the Berliner has solved the great problem of modern life, how to do without sleep, or, with Carlyle, he must be looking forward to eternity.

Personally, I know of no other town where such late hours are the vogue, except St. Petersburg. But your St. Petersburger does not get up early in the morning. At St. Petersburg, the music halls, which it is the fashionable thing to attend *after* the theatre—a drive to them taking half an hour in a swift sleigh—do not practically begin till twelve. Through the Neva at four o'clock in the morning you have to literally push your way; and the favourite trains for travellers are those starting about five o'clock in the morning. These trains save the Russian the trouble of getting up early. He wishes his friends "Good-night," and drives down to the station comfortably after supper, without putting the house to any inconvenience.

Potsdam, the Versailles to Berlin, is a beautiful little town, situate among lakes and woods. Here in the shady ways of its quiet, far-stretching park of Sans Souci, it is easy to imagine lean, snuffy Frederick "bummeling" with shrill Voltaire.

Acting on my advice, George and Harris consented not to stay long in Berlin; but to push on to Dresden. Most that Berlin has to show can be seen better elsewhere, and we decided to be content with a drive through the town. The hotel porter introduced us to a droschke driver, under whose guidance, so he assured us, we should see everything worth seeing in the shortest possible time. The man himself, who called for us at nine o'clock in the morning, was all that could be desired. He was bright, intelligent, and well-informed; his German was easy to understand, and he knew a little English with which to eke it out on occasion. With the man himself there was no fault to be found, but his horse was the most unsympathetic brute I have ever sat behind.

He took a dislike to us the moment he saw us. I was the first to come out of the hotel. He turned his head, and looked me up and down with a cold, glassy eye; and then he looked across at another horse, a friend of his that was standing facing him. I knew what he said. He had an expressive head, and he made no attempt to disguise his thought.

He said:

"Funny things one does come across in the summer time, don't one?"

George followed me out the next moment, and stood behind me. The horse again turned his head and looked. I have never known a horse that could twist himself as this horse did. I have seen a camelopard do trick's with his neck that compelled one's attention, but this animal was more like the thing one dreams of after a dusty days at Ascot, followed by a dinner with six old chums. If I had seen his eyes looking at me from between his own hind legs, I doubt if I should have been surprised. He seemed more amused with George if anything, than with myself. He turned to his friend again.

"Extraordinary, isn't it?" he remarked; "I suppose there must be some place where they grow them"; and then he commenced licking flies off his own left shoulder. I began to wonder whether he had lost his mother when young, and had been brought up by a cat.

George and I climbed in, and sat waiting for Harris. He came a moment later. Myself, I thought he looked rather neat. He wore a white flannel knickerbocker suit, which he had had made specially for bicycling in hot weather; his hat may have been a trifle out of the common, but it did keep the sun off.

The horse gave one look at him, said "Gott in Himmel!" as plainly as ever horse spoke, and started off down Friedrich Strasse at a brisk walk, leaving Harris and the driver standing on the pavement. His owner called to him to stop, but he took no notice. They ran after us, and overtook us at the corner of the Dorotheen Strasse. I could not catch what the man said to the horse, he spoke quickly and excitedly; but I gathered a few phrases, such as:

"Got to earn my living somehow, haven't I? Who asked for your opinion? Aye, little you care so long as you can guzzle."

The horse cut the conversation short by turning up the Dorotheen Strasse on his own account. I think what he said was:

"Come on then; don't talk so much. Let's get the job over, and, where possible, let's keep to the back streets."

Opposite the Brandenburger Thor our driver hitched the reins to the whip, climbed down, and came round to explain things to us. He pointed out the Thiergarten, and then descanted to us of the Reichstag House. He informed us of its exact height, length, and breadth, after the manner of guides. Then he turned his attention to the Gate. He said it was constructed of sandstone, in imitation of the "Properleer" in Athens.

At this point the horse, which had been occupying its leisure licking its own legs, turned round its head. It did not say anything, it just looked.

The man began again nervously. This time he said it was an imitation of the "Propeyedliar."

Here the horse proceeded up the Linden, and nothing would persuade him not to proceed up the Linden. His owner expostulated with him, but he continued to trot on. From the way he hitched his shoulders as he moved, I somehow felt he was saying:

"They've seen the Gate, haven't they? Very well, that's enough. As for the rest, you don't know what you are talking about, and they wouldn't understand you if you did. You talk German."

It was the same throughout the length of the Linden. The horse consented to stand still sufficiently long to enable us to have a good look at each sight, and to hear the name of it. All explanation and description he cut short by the simple process of moving on.

"What these fellows want," he seemed to say to himself, "is to go home and tell people they have seen these things. If I am doing them an injustice, if they are more intelligent than they look, they can get better information than this old fool of mine is giving them from the guide book. Who wants to know how high a steeple is? You don't remember it the next five minutes when you are told, and if you do it is because you have got nothing else in your head. He just tires me with his talk. Why doesn't he hurry up, and let us all get home to lunch?"

Upon reflection, I am not sure that wall-eyed old brute had not sense on its side. Anyhow, I know there have been occasions, with a guide, when I would have been glad of its interference.

But one is apt to "sin one's mercies," as the Scotch say, and at the time we cursed that horse instead of blessing it.

CHAPTER VII

George wonders—German love of order—"The Band of the Schwarzwald Blackbirds will perform at seven"—The china dog—Its superiority over all other dogs—The German and the solar system—A tidy country—The mountain valley as it ought to be, according to the German idea—How the waters come down in Germany—The scandal of Dresden—Harris gives an entertainment—It is unappreciated—George and the aunt of him—George, a cushion, and three damsels.

At a point between Berlin and Dresden, George, who had, for the last quarter of an hour or so, been looking very attentively out of the window, said:

"Why, in Germany, is it the custom to put the letter-box up a tree? Why do they not fix it to the front door as we do? I should hate having to climb up a tree to get my letters. Besides, it is not fair to the postman. In addition to being most exhausting, the delivery of letters must to a heavy man, on windy nights, be positively dangerous work. If they will fix it to a tree, why not fix it lower down, why always among the topmost branches? But, maybe, I am misjudging the country," he continued, a new idea occurring to him. "Possibly the Germans, who are in many matters ahead of us, have perfected a pigeon post. Even so, I cannot help thinking they would have been wiser to train the birds, while they were about it, to deliver the letters nearer the ground. Getting your letters out of those boxes must be tricky work even to the average middle-aged German."

I followed his gaze out of window. I said:

"Those are not letter-boxes, they are birds' nests. You must understand this nation. The German loves birds, but he likes tidy birds. A bird left to himself builds his nest just anywhere. It is not a pretty object, according to the German notion of prettiness. There is not a bit of paint on it anywhere, not a plaster image all round, not even a flag. The nest finished, the bird proceeds to live outside it. He drops things on the grass; twigs, ends of worms, all sorts of things. He is indelicate. He makes love, quarrels with his wife, and feeds the children quite in public. The German householder is shocked. He says to the bird:

"'For many things I like you. I like to look at you. I like to hear you sing. But I don't like your ways. Take this little box, and put your rubbish inside where I can't see it. Come out when you want to sing; but let your domestic arrangements be confined to the interior. Keep to the box, and don't make the garden untidy.'"

In Germany one breathes in love of order with the air, in Germany the babies beat time with their rattles, and the German bird has come to prefer the box, and to regard with contempt the few uncivilised outcasts who continue to build their nests in trees and hedges. In course of time every German bird, one is confident, will have his proper place in a full chorus. This promiscuous and desultory warbling of his must, one feels, be irritating to the precise German mind; there is no method in it. The music-loving German will organise him. Some stout bird with a specially well-developed crop will be trained to conduct him, and, instead of wasting himself in a wood at four o'clock in the morning, he will, at the advertised time, sing in a beer garden, accompanied by a piano. Things are drifting that way.

Your German likes nature, but his idea of nature is a glorified Welsh Harp. He takes great interest in his garden. He plants seven rose trees on the north side and seven on the south, and if they do not grow up all the same size and shape it worries him so that he cannot sleep of nights. Every flower he ties to a stick. This interferes with his view of the flower, but he has the satisfaction of knowing it is there, and that it is behaving itself. The lake is lined with zinc, and once a week he takes it up, carries it into the kitchen, and scours it. In the geometrical centre of the grass plot, which is sometimes as large as a tablecloth and is generally railed round, he places a china dog. The Germans are very fond of dogs, but as a rule they prefer them of china. The china dog never digs holes in the lawn to bury bones, and never scatters a flower-bed to the winds with his hind legs. From the German point of view, he is the ideal dog. He stops where you put him, and he is never where you do not want him. You can have him perfect in all points, according to the latest requirements of the Kennel Club; or you can indulge your own fancy and have something unique. You are not, as with other dogs, limited to breed. In china, you can have a blue dog or a pink dog. For a little extra, you can have a double-headed dog.

On a certain fixed date in the autumn the German stakes his flowers and bushes to the earth, and covers them with Chinese matting; and on a certain fixed date in the spring he uncovers them, and stands them up again. If it happens to be an exceptionally fine autumn, or an exceptionally late spring, so much the worse for the unfortunate vegetable. No true German would allow his arrangements to be interfered with by so unruly a thing as the solar system. Unable to regulate the weather, he ignores it.

Among trees, your German's favourite is the poplar. Other disorderly nations may sing the charms of the rugged oak, the spreading chestnut, or the waving elm. To the German all such, with their wilful, untidy ways, are eyesores. The poplar grows where it is planted, and how it is planted. It has no improper rugged ideas of its own. It does not want to wave or to spread itself. It just grows straight and upright as a German tree should grow; and so gradually the German is rooting out all other trees, and replacing them with poplars.

Your German likes the country, but he prefers it as the lady thought she would the noble savage—more dressed. He likes his walk through the wood—to a restaurant. But the pathway must not be too steep, it must have a brick gutter running down one side of it to drain it, and every twenty yards or so it must have its seat on which he can rest and mop his brow; for your German would no more think of sitting on the grass than would an English bishop dream of rolling down One Tree Hill. He likes his view from the summit of the hill, but he likes to find there a stone tablet telling him what to look at, find a table and bench at which he can sit to partake of the frugal beer and "belegte Semmel" he has been careful to bring with him. If, in addition, he can find a police notice posted on a tree, forbidding him to do something or other, that gives him an extra sense of comfort and security.

Your German is not averse even to wild scenery, provided it be not too wild. But if he consider it too savage, he sets to work to tame it. I remember, in the neighbourhood of Dresden, discovering a picturesque and narrow valley leading down towards the Elbe. The winding roadway ran beside a mountain torrent, which for a mile or so fretted and foamed over rocks and boulders between wood-covered banks. I followed it enchanted until, turning a corner, I suddenly came across a gang of eighty or a hundred workmen. They were busy tidying up that valley, and making that stream respectable. All the stones that were impeding the course of the water they were carefully picking out and carting away. The bank on either side they were bricking up and cementing. The overhanging trees and bushes, the tangled vines and creepers they were rooting up and trimming down. A little further I came upon the finished work—the mountain valley as it ought to be, according to German ideas. The water, now a broad, sluggish stream, flowed over a level, gravelly bed, between two walls crowned with stone coping. At every hundred yards it gently descended down three shallow wooden platforms. For a space on either side the ground had been cleared, and at regular intervals young poplars planted. Each sapling was protected by a shield of wickerwork and bossed by an iron rod. In the course of a couple of years it is the hope of the local council to have "finished" that valley throughout its entire length, and made it fit for a tidy-minded lover of German nature to walk in. There will be a seat every fifty yards, a police notice every hundred, and a restaurant every half-mile.

They are doing the same from the Memel to the Rhine. They are just tidying up the country. I remember well the Wehrthal. It was once the most romantic ravine to be found in the Black Forest. The last time I walked down it some hundreds of Italian workmen were encamped there hard at work, training the wild little Wehr the way it should go, bricking the banks for it here, blasting the rocks for it there, making cement steps for it down which it can travel soberly and without fuss.

For in Germany there is no nonsense talked about untrammelled nature. In Germany nature has got to behave herself, and not set a bad example to the children. A German poet, noticing waters coming down as Southey describes, somewhat inexactly, the waters coming down at Lodore, would be too shocked to stop and write alliterative verse about them. He would hurry away, and at once report them to the police. Then their foaming and their shrieking would be of short duration.

"Now then, now then, what's all this about?" the voice of German authority would say severely to the waters. "We can't have this sort of thing, you know. Come down quietly, can't you? Where do you think you are?"

And the local German council would provide those waters with zinc pipes and wooden troughs, and a corkscrew staircase, and show them how to come down sensibly, in the German manner.

It is a tidy land is Germany.

We reached Dresden on the Wednesday evening, and stayed there over the Sunday.

Taking one consideration with another, Dresden, perhaps, is the most attractive town in Germany; but it is a place to be lived in for a while rather than visited. Its museums and galleries, its palaces and gardens, its beautiful and historically rich environment, provide pleasure for a winter, but bewilder for a week. It has not the gaiety of Paris or Vienna, which quickly palls; its charms are more solidly German, and more lasting. It is the Mecca of the musician. For five shillings, in Dresden, you can purchase a stall at the opera house, together, unfortunately, with a strong disinclination ever again to take the trouble of sitting out a performance in any English, French, or, American opera house.

The chief scandal of Dresden still centres round August the Strong, "the Man of Sin," as Carlyle always called him, who is popularly reputed to have cursed Europe with over a thousand children. Castles where he imprisoned this discarded mistress or that—one of them, who persisted in her claim to a better title, for forty years, it is said, poor lady! The narrow rooms where she ate her heart out and died are still shown. Chateaux, shameful for this deed of infamy or that, lie scattered round the neighbourhood like bones about a battlefield; and most of your guide's stories are such as the "young person" educated in Germany had best not hear. His life-sized portrait hangs in the fine Zwinger, which he built as an arena for his wild beast fights when the people grew tired of them in the market-place; a beetle-browed, frankly animal man, but with the culture and taste that so often wait upon animalism. Modern Dresden undoubtedly owes much to him.

But what the stranger in Dresden stares at most is, perhaps, its electric trams. These huge vehicles flash through the streets at from ten to twenty miles an hour, taking curves and corners after the manner of an Irish car driver. Everybody travels by them, excepting only officers in uniform, who must not. Ladies in evening dress, going to ball or opera, porters with their baskets, sit side by side. They are all-important in the streets, and everything and everybody makes haste to get out of their way. If you do not get out of their way, and you still happen to be alive when picked up, then on your recovery you are fined for having been in their way. This teaches you to be wary of them.

One afternoon Harris took a "bummel" by himself. In the evening, as we sat listening to the band at the Belvedere, Harris said, *à propos* of nothing in particular, "These Germans have no sense of humour."

"What makes you think that?" I asked.

"Why, this afternoon," he answered, "I jumped on one of those electric tramcars. I wanted to see the town, so I stood outside on the little platform—what do you call it?"

"The Stehplatz," I suggested.

"That's it," said Harris. "Well, you know the way they shake you about, and how you have to look out for the corners, and mind yourself when they stop and when they start?"

I nodded.

"There were about half a dozen of us standing there," he continued, "and, of course, I am not experienced. The thing started suddenly, and that jerked me backwards. I fell against a stout gentleman, just behind me. He could not have been standing very firmly himself, and he, in his turn, fell back against a boy who was carrying a trumpet in a green baize case. They never smiled, neither the man nor the boy with the trumpet; they just stood there and looked sulky. I was going to say I was sorry, but before I could get the words out the tram eased up, for some reason or other, and that, of course, shot me forward again, and I butted into a white-haired old chap, who looked to me like a professor. Well, *he* never smiled, never moved a muscle."

"Maybe, he was thinking of something else," I suggested.

"That could not have been the case with them all," replied Harris, "and in the course of that journey, I must have fallen against every one of them at least three times. You see," explained Harris, "they knew when the corners were coming, and in which direction to brace themselves. I, as a stranger, was naturally at a disadvantage. The way I rolled and staggered about that platform, clutching wildly now at this man and now at that, must have been really comic. I don't say it was high-class humour, but it would have amused most people. Those Germans seemed to see no fun in it whatever—just seemed anxious, that was all. There was one man, a little man, who stood with his back against the brake; I fell against him five times, I counted them. You would have expected the fifth time would have dragged a laugh out of him, but it didn't; he merely looked tired. They are a dull lot."

George also had an adventure at Dresden. There was a shop near the Altmarkt, in the window of which were exhibited some cushions for sale. The proper business of the shop was handling of glass and china; the cushions appeared to be in the nature of an experiment. They were very beautiful cushions, hand-embroidered on satin. We often passed the shop, and every time George paused and examined those cushions. He said he thought his aunt would like one.

George has been very attentive to this aunt of his during the journey. He has written her quite a long letter every day, and from every town we stop at he sends her off a present. To my mind, he is overdoing the business, and more than once I have expostulated with him. His aunt will be meeting other aunts, and talking to them; the whole class will become disorganised and unruly. As a nephew, I object to the impossible standard that George is setting up. But he will not listen.

Therefore it was that on the Saturday he left us after lunch, saying he would go round to that shop and get one of those cushions for his aunt. He said he would not be long, and suggested our waiting for him.

We waited for what seemed to me rather a long time. When he rejoined us he was empty handed, and looked worried. We asked him where his cushion was. He said he hadn't got a cushion, said he had changed his mind, said he didn't think his aunt would care for a cushion. Evidently something was amiss. We tried to get at the bottom of it, but he was not communicative. Indeed, his answers after our twentieth question or thereabouts became quite short.

In the evening, however, when he and I happened to be alone, he broached the subject himself. He said:

"They are somewhat peculiar in some things, these Germans."

I said: "What has happened?"

"Well," he answered, "there was that cushion I wanted."

"For your aunt," I remarked.

"Why not?" he returned. He was huffy in a moment; I never knew a man so touchy about an aunt. "Why shouldn't I send a cushion to my aunt?"

"Don't get excited," I replied. "I am not objecting; I respect you for it."

He recovered his temper, and went on:

"There were four in the window, if you remember, all very much alike, and each one labelled in plain figures twenty marks. I don't pretend to speak German fluently, but I can generally make myself understood with a little effort, and gather the sense of what is said to me, provided they don't gabble. I went into the shop. A young girl came up to me; she was a pretty, quiet little soul, one might almost say, demure; not at all the sort of girl from whom you would have expected such a thing. I was never more surprised in all my life."

"Surprised about what?" I said.

George always assumes you know the end of the story while he is telling you the beginning; it is an annoying method.

"At what happened," replied George; "at what I am telling you. She smiled and asked me what I wanted. I understood that all right; there could have been no mistake about that. I put down a twenty mark piece on the counter and said:

"Please give me a cushion."

"She stared at me as if I had asked for a feather bed. I thought, maybe, she had not heard, so I repeated it louder. If I had chucked her under the chin she could not have looked more surprised or indignant.

"She said she thought I must be making a mistake.

"I did not want to begin a long conversation and find myself stranded. I said there was no mistake. I pointed to my twenty mark piece, and repeated for the third time that I wanted a cushion, 'a twenty mark cushion.'

"Another girl came up, an elder girl; and the first girl repeated to her what I had just said: she seemed quite excited about it. The second girl did not believe her—did not think I looked the sort of man who would want a cushion. To make sure, she put the question to me herself.

"'Did you say you wanted a cushion?' she asked.

"'I have said it three times,' I answered. 'I will say it again—I want a cushion.'

"She said: 'Then you can't have one.'

"I was getting angry by this time. If I hadn't really wanted the thing I should have walked out of the shop; but there the cushions were in the window, evidently for sale. I didn't see *why* I couldn't have one.

"I said: 'I will have one!' It is a simple sentence. I said it with determination.

"A third girl came up at this point, the three representing, I fancy, the whole force of the shop. She was a bright-eyed, saucy-looking little wench, this last one. On any other occasion I might have been pleased to see her; now, her coming only irritated me. I didn't see the need of three girls for this business.

"The first two girls started explaining the thing to the third girl, and before they were half-way through the third girl began to giggle—she was the sort of girl who would giggle at anything. That done, they fell to chattering like Jenny Wrens, all three together; and between every half-dozen words they looked across at me; and the more they looked at me the more the third girl giggled; and before they had finished they were all three giggling, the little idiots; you might have thought I was a clown, giving a private performance.

"When she was steady enough to move, the third girl came up to me; she was still giggling. She said:

"'If you get it, will you go?'

"I did not quite understand her at first, and she repeated it.

"'This cushion. When you've got it, will you go—away—at once?'

"I was only too anxious to go. I told her so. But, I added I was not going without it. I had made up my mind to have that cushion now if I stopped in the shop all night for it.

"She rejoined the other two girls. I thought they were going to get me the cushion and have done with the business. Instead of that, the strangest thing possible happened. The two other girls got behind the first girl, all three still giggling, Heaven knows what about, and pushed her towards me. They pushed her close up to me, and then, before I knew what was happening, she put her hands on my shoulders, stood up on tiptoe, and kissed me. After which, burying her face in her apron, she ran off, followed by the second girl. The third girl opened the door for me, and so evidently expected me to go, that in my confusion I went, leaving my twenty marks behind me. I don't say I minded the kiss, though I did not particularly want it, while I did want the cushion. I don't like to go back to the shop. I cannot understand the thing at all."

I said: "What did you ask for?"

He said: "A cushion"

I said: "That is what you wanted, I know. What I mean is, what was the actual German word you said."

He replied: "A kuss."

I said: "You have nothing to complain of. It is somewhat confusing. A 'kuss' sounds as if it ought to be a cushion, but it is not; it is a kiss, while a 'kissen' is a cushion. You muddled up the two words—people have done it before. I don't know much about this sort of thing myself; but you asked for a twenty mark kiss, and from your description of the girl some people might consider the price reasonable. Anyhow, I should not tell Harris. If I remember rightly, he also has an aunt."

George agreed with me it would be better not.

CHAPTER VIII

Mr. and Miss Jones, of Manchester—The benefits of co-coa—A hint to the Peace Society—The window as a mediaeval argument—The favourite Christian recreation—The language of the guide—How to repair the ravages of time—George tries a bottle—The fate of the German beer drinker—Harris and I resolve to do a good action—The usual sort of statue—Harris and his friends—A pepperless Paradise—Women and towns.

We were on our way to Prague, and were waiting in the great hall of the Dresden Station until such time as the powers-that-be should permit us on to the platform. George, who had wandered to the bookstall, returned to us with a wild look in his eyes. He said:

"I've seen it."

I said, "Seen what?"

He was too excited to answer intelligently. He said

"It's here. It's coming this way, both of them. If you wait, you'll see it for yourselves. I'm not joking; it's the real thing."

As is usual about this period, some paragraphs, more or less serious, had been appearing in the papers concerning the sea-serpent, and I thought for the moment he must be referring to this. A moment's reflection, however, told me that here, in the middle of Europe, three hundred miles from the coast, such a thing was impossible. Before I could question him further, he seized me by the arm.

"Look!" he said; "now am I exaggerating?"

I turned my head and saw what, I suppose, few living Englishmen have ever seen before—the travelling Britisher according to the Continental idea, accompanied by his daughter. They were coming towards us in the flesh and blood, unless we were dreaming, alive and concrete—the English "Milor" and the English "Mees," as for generations they have been portrayed in the Continental comic press and upon the Continental stage. They were perfect in every detail. The man was tall and thin, with sandy hair, a huge nose, and long Dundreary whiskers. Over a pepper-and-salt suit he wore a light overcoat, reaching almost to his heels. His white helmet was ornamented with a green veil; a pair of opera-glasses hung at his side, and in his lavender-gloved hand he carried an alpenstock a little taller than himself. His daughter was long and angular. Her dress I cannot describe: my grandfather, poor gentleman, might have been able to do so; it would have been more familiar to him. I can only say that it appeared to me unnecessarily short, exhibiting a pair of ankles—if I may be permitted to refer to such points—that, from an artistic point of view, called rather for concealment. Her hat made me think of Mrs. Hemans; but why I cannot explain. She wore side-spring boots—"prunella," I believe, used to be the trade name—mittens, and pince-nez. She also carried an alpenstock (there is not a mountain within a hundred miles of Dresden) and a black bag strapped to her waist. Her teeth stuck out like a rabbit's, and her figure was that of a bolster on stilts.

Harris rushed for his camera, and of course could not find it; he never can when he wants it. Whenever we see Harris scuttling up and down like a lost dog, shouting, "Where's my camera? What the dickens have I done with my camera? Don't either of you remember where I put my camera?"—then we know that for the first time that day he has come across something worth photographing. Later on, he remembered it was in his bag; that is where it would be on an occasion like this.

They were not content with appearance; they acted the thing to the letter. They walked gaping round them at every step. The gentleman had an open Baedeker in his hand, and the lady carried a phrase book. They talked French that nobody could understand, and German that they could not translate themselves! The man poked at officials with his alpenstock to attract their attention, and the lady, her eye catching sight of an advertisement of somebody's cocoa, said "Shocking!" and turned the other way.

Really, there was some excuse for her. One notices, even in England, the home of the proprieties, that the lady who drinks cocoa appears, according to the poster, to require very little else in this world; a yard or so of art muslin at the most. On the Continent she dispenses, so far as one can judge, with every other necessity of life. Not only is cocoa food and drink to her, it should be clothes also, according to the idea of the cocoa manufacturer. But this by the way.

Of course, they immediately became the centre of attraction. By being able to render them some slight assistance, I gained the advantage of five minutes' conversation with them. They were very affable. The gentleman told me his name was Jones, and that he came from Manchester, but he did not seem to know what part of Manchester, or where Manchester was. I asked him where he was going to, but he evidently did not know. He said it depended. I asked him if he did not find an alpenstock a clumsy thing to walk about with through a crowded town; he admitted that occasionally it did get in the way. I asked him if he did not find a veil interfere with his view of things; he explained that you only wore it when the flies became troublesome. I enquired of the lady if she did not find the wind blow cold; she said she had noticed it, especially at the corners. I did not ask these questions one after another as I have here put them down; I mixed them up with general conversation, and we parted on good terms.

I have pondered much upon the apparition, and have come to a definite opinion. A man I met later at Frankfort, and to whom I described the pair, said he had seen them himself in Paris, three weeks after the termination of the Fashoda incident; while a traveller for some English steel works whom we met in Strassburg remembered having seen them in Berlin during the excitement caused by the Transvaal question. My conclusion is that they were actors out of work, hired to do this thing in the interest of international peace. The French Foreign Office, wishful to allay the anger of the Parisian mob clamouring for war with England, secured this admirable couple and sent them round the town. You cannot be amused at a thing, and at the same time want to kill it. The French nation saw the English citizen and citizeness—no caricature, but the living reality—and their indignation exploded in laughter. The success of the stratagem prompted them later on to offer their services to the German Government, with the beneficial results that we all know.

Our own Government might learn the lesson. It might be as well to keep near Downing Street a few small, fat Frenchmen, to be sent round the country when occasion called for it, shrugging their shoulders and eating frog sandwiches; or a file of untidy, lank-haired Germans might be retained, to walk about, smoking long pipes, saying "So." The public would laugh and exclaim, "War with such? It would be too absurd." Failing the Government, I recommend the scheme to the Peace Society.

Our visit to Prague we were compelled to lengthen somewhat. Prague is one of the most interesting towns in Europe. Its stones are saturated with history and romance; its every suburb must have been a battlefield. It is the town that conceived the Reformation and hatched the Thirty Years' War. But half Prague's troubles, one imagines, might have been saved to it, had it possessed windows less large and temptingly convenient. The first of these mighty catastrophes it set rolling by throwing the seven Catholic councillors from the windows of its Rathhaus on to the pikes of the Hussites below. Later, it gave the signal for the second by again throwing the Imperial councillors from the windows of the old Burg in the Hradschin—Prague's second "Fenstersturz." Since, other fateful questions have been decide in Prague, one assumes from their having been concluded without violence that such must have been discussed in cellars. The window, as an argument, one feels, would always have proved too strong a temptation to any true-born Praguer.

In the Teynkirche stands the worm-eaten pulpit from which preached John Huss. One may hear from the selfsame desk to-day the voice of a Papist priest, while in far-off Constance a rude block of stone, half ivy hidden, marks the spot where Huss and Jerome died burning at the stake. History is fond of her little ironies. In this same Teynkirche lies buried Tycho Brahe, the astronomer, who made the common mistake of thinking the earth, with its eleven hundred creeds and one humanity, the centre of the universe; but who otherwise observed the stars clearly.

Through Prague's dirty, palace-bordered alleys must have pressed often in hot haste blind Ziska and open-minded Wallenstein—they have dubbed him "The Hero" in Prague; and the town is honestly proud of having owned him for citizen. In his gloomy palace in the Waldstein-Platz they show as a sacred spot the cabinet where he prayed, and seem to have persuaded themselves he really had a soul. Its steep, winding ways must have been choked a dozen times, now by Sigismund's flying legions, followed by fierce-killing Tarborites, and now by pale Protestants pursued by the victorious Catholics of Maximilian. Now Saxons, now Bavarians, and now French; now the saints of Gustavus Adolphus, and now the steel fighting machines of Frederick the Great, have thundered at its gates and fought upon its bridges.

The Jews have always been an important feature of Prague. Occasionally they have assisted the Christians in their favourite occupation of slaughtering one another, and the great flag suspended from the vaulting of the Altneuschule testifies to the courage with which they helped Catholic Ferdinand to resist the Protestant Swedes. The Prague Ghetto was one of the first to be established in Europe, and in the tiny synagogue, still standing, the Jew of Prague has worshipped for eight hundred years, his women folk devoutly listening, without, at the ear holes provided for them in the massive walls. A Jewish cemetery adjacent, "Bethchajim, or the House of Life," seems as though it were bursting with its dead. Within its narrow acre it was the law of centuries that here or nowhere must the bones of Israel rest. So the worn and broken tombstones lie piled in close confusion, as though tossed and tumbled by the struggling host beneath.

The Ghetto walls have long been levelled, but the living Jews of Prague still cling to their foetid lanes, though these are being rapidly replaced by fine new streets that promise to eventually transform this quarter into the handsomest part of the town.

At Dresden they advised us not to talk German in Prague. For years racial animosity between the German minority and the Czech majority has raged throughout Bohemia, and to be mistaken for a German in certain streets of Prague is inconvenient to a man whose staying powers in a race are not what once they were. However, we did talk German in certain streets in Prague; it was a case of talking German or nothing. The Czech dialect is said to be of great antiquity and of highly scientific cultivation. Its alphabet contains forty-two letters, suggestive to a stranger of Chinese. It is not a language to be picked up in a hurry. We decided that on the whole there would be less risk to our constitution in keeping to German, and as a matter of fact no harm came to us. The explanation I can only surmise. The Praguer is an exceedingly acute person; some subtle falsity of accent, some slight grammatical inaccuracy, may have crept into our German, revealing to him the fact that, in spite of all appearances to the contrary, we were no true-born Deutscher. I do not assert this; I put it forward as a possibility.

To avoid unnecessary danger, however, we did our sight-seeing with the aid of a guide. No guide I have ever come across is perfect. This one had two distinct failings. His English was decidedly weak. Indeed, it was not English at all. I do not know what you would call it. It was not altogether his fault; he had learnt English from a Scotch lady. I understand Scotch fairly well—to keep abreast of modern English literature this is necessary,—but to understand broad Scotch talked with a Sclavonic accent, occasionally relieved by German modifications, taxes the intelligence. For the first hour it was difficult to rid one's self of the conviction that the man was choking. Every moment we expected him to die on our hands. In the course of the morning we grew accustomed to him, and rid ourselves of the instinct to throw him on his back every time he opened his mouth, and tear his clothes from him. Later, we came to understand a part of what he said, and this led to the discovery of his second failing.

It would seem he had lately invented a hair-restorer, which he had persuaded a local chemist to take up and advertise. Half his time he had been pointing out to us, not the beauties of Prague, but the benefits likely to accrue to the human race from the use of this concoction; and the conventional agreement with which, under the impression he was waxing eloquent concerning views and architecture, we had met his enthusiasm he had attributed to sympathetic interest in this wretched wash of his.

The result was that now there was no keeping him away from the subject. Ruined palaces and crumbling churches he dismissed with curt reference as mere frivolities, encouraging a morbid taste for the decadent. His duty, as he saw it, was not to lead us to dwell upon the ravages of time, but rather to direct our attention to the means of repairing them. What had we to do with broken-headed heroes, or bald-headed saints? Our interest should be surely in the living world; in the maidens with their flowing tresses, or the flowing tresses they might have, by judicious use of "Kophkeo," in the young men with their fierce moustaches— as pictured on the label.

Unconsciously, in his own mind, he had divided the world into two sections. The Past ("Before Use"), a sickly, disagreeable-looking, uninteresting world. The Future ("After Use") a fat, jolly, God-bless-everybody sort of world; and this unfitted him as a guide to scenes of mediaeval history.

He sent us each a bottle of the stuff to our hotel. It appeared that in the early part of our converse with him we had, unwittingly, clamoured for it. Personally, I can neither praise it nor condemn it. A long series of disappointments has disheartened me; added to which a permanent atmosphere of paraffin, however faint, is apt to cause remark, especially in the case of a married man. Now, I never try even the sample.

I gave my bottle to George. He asked for it to send to a man he knew in Leeds. I learnt later that Harris had given him his bottle also, to send to the same man.

A suggestion of onions has clung to this tour since we left Prague. George has noticed it himself. He attributes it to the prevalence of garlic in European cooking.

It was in Prague that Harris and I did a kind and friendly thing to George. We had noticed for some time past that George was getting too fond of Pilsener beer. This German beer is an insidious drink, especially in hot weather; but it does not do to imbibe too freely of it. It does not get into your head, but after a time it spoils your waist. I always say to myself on entering Germany:

"Now, I will drink no German beer. The white wine of the country, with a little soda-water; perhaps occasionally a glass of Ems or potash. But beer, never— or, at all events, hardly ever."

It is a good and useful resolution, which I recommend to all travellers. I only wish I could keep to it myself. George, although I urged him, refused to bind himself by any such hard and fast limit. He said that in moderation German beer was good.

"One glass in the morning," said George, "one in the evening, or even two. That will do no harm to anyone."

Maybe he was right. It was his half-dozen glasses that troubled Harris and myself.

"We ought to do something to stop it," said Harris; "it is becoming serious."

"It's hereditary, so he has explained to me," I answered. "It seems his family have always been thirsty."

"There is Apollinaris water," replied Harris, "which, I believe, with a little lemon squeezed into it, is practically harmless. What I am thinking about is his figure. He will lose all his natural elegance."

We talked the matter over, and, Providence aiding us, we fixed upon a plan. For the ornamentation of the town a new statue had just been cast. I forget of whom it was a statue. I only remember that in the essentials it was the usual sort of street statue, representing the usual sort of gentleman, with the usual stiff neck, riding the usual sort of horse—the horse that always walks on its hind legs, keeping its front paws for beating time. But in detail it possessed individuality. Instead of the usual sword or baton, the man was holding, stretched out in his hand, his own plumed hat; and the horse, instead of the usual waterfall for a tail, possessed a somewhat attenuated appendage that somehow appeared out of keeping with his ostentatious behaviour. One felt that a horse with a tail like that would not have pranced so much.

It stood in a small square not far from the further end of the Karlsbrücke, but it stood there only temporarily. Before deciding finally where to fix it, the town authorities had resolved, very sensibly, to judge by practical test where it would look best. Accordingly, they had made three rough copies of the statue—mere wooden profiles, things that would not bear looking at closely, but which, viewed from a little distance, produced all the effect that was necessary. One of these they had set up at the approach to the Franz-Josefsbrücke, a second stood in the open space behind the theatre, and the third in the centre of the Wenzelsplatz.

"If George is not in the secret of this thing," said Harris—we were walking by ourselves for an hour, he having remained behind in the hotel to write a letter to his aunt,—"if he has not observed these statues, then by their aid we will make a better and a thinner man of him, and that this very evening."

So during dinner we sounded him, judiciously; and finding him ignorant of the matter, we took him out, and led him by side-streets to the place where stood the real statue. George was for looking at it and passing on, as is his way with statues, but we insisted on his pulling up and viewing the thing conscientiously. We walked him round that statue four times, and showed it to him from every possible point of view. I think, on the whole, we rather bored him with the thing, but our object was to impress it upon him. We told him the history of the man who rode upon the horse, the name of the artist who had made the statue, how much it weighed, how much it measured. We worked that statue into his system. By the time we had done with him he knew more about that statue, for the time being, than he knew about anything else. We soaked him in that statue, and only let him go at last on the condition that he would come again with us in the morning, when we could all see it better, and for such purpose we saw to it that he made a note in his pocket-book of the place where the statue stood.

Then we accompanied him to his favourite beer hall, and sat beside him, telling him anecdotes of men who, unaccustomed to German beer, and drinking too much of it, had gone mad and developed homicidal mania; of men who had died young through drinking German beer; of lovers that German beer had been the means of parting for ever from beautiful girls.

At ten o'clock we started to walk back to the hotel. It was a stormy-looking night, with heavy clouds drifting over a light moon. Harris said:

"We won't go back the same way we came; we'll walk back by the river. It is lovely in the moonlight."

Harris told a sad history, as we walked, about a man he once knew, who is now in a home for harmless imbeciles. He said he recalled the story because it was on just such another night as this that he was walking with that man the very last time he ever saw the poor fellow. They were strolling down the Thames Embankment, Harris said, and the man frightened him then by persisting that he saw the statue of the Duke of Wellington at the corner of Westminster Bridge, when, as everybody knows, it stands in Piccadilly.

It was at this exact instant that we came in sight of the first of these wooden copies. It occupied the centre of a small, railed-in square a little above us on the opposite side of the way. George suddenly stood still and leant against the wall of the quay.

"What's the matter?" I said; "feeling giddy?"

He said: "I do, a little. Let's rest here a moment."

He stood there with his eyes glued to the thing.

He said, speaking huskily:

"Talking of statues, what always strikes me is how very much one statue is like another statue."

Harris said: "I cannot agree with you there—pictures, if you like. Some pictures are very like other pictures, but with a statue there is always something distinctive. Take that statue we saw early in the evening," continued Harris, "before we went into the concert hall. It represented a man sitting on a horse. In Prague you will see other statues of men on horses, but nothing at all like that one."

"Yes they are," said George; "they are all alike. It's always the same horse, and it's always the same man. They are all exactly alike. It's idiotic nonsense to say they are not."

He appeared to be angry with Harris.

"What makes you think so?" I asked.

"What makes me think so?" retorted George, now turning upon me. "Why, look at that damned thing over there!"

I said: "What damned thing?"

"Why, that thing," said George; "look at it! There is the same horse with half a tail, standing on its hind legs; the same man without his hat; the same—"

Harris said: "You are talking now about the statue we saw in the Ringplatz."

"No, I'm not," replied George; "I'm talking about the statue over there."

"What statue?" said Harris.

George looked at Harris; but Harris is a man who might, with care, have been a fair amateur actor. His face merely expressed friendly sorrow, mingled with alarm. Next, George turned his gaze on me. I endeavoured, so far as lay with me, to copy Harris's expression, adding to it on my own account a touch of reproof.

"Will you have a cab?" I said as kindly as I could to George. "I'll run and get one."

"What the devil do I want with a cab?" he answered, ungraciously. "Can't you fellows understand a joke? It's like being out with a couple of confounded old women," saying which, he started off across the bridge, leaving us to follow.

"I am so glad that was only a joke of yours," said Harris, on our overtaking him. "I knew a case of softening of the brain that began—"

"Oh, you're a silly ass!" said George, cutting him short; "you know everything."

He was really most unpleasant in his manner.

We took him round by the riverside of the theatre. We told him it was the shortest way, and, as a matter of fact, it was. In the open space behind the theatre stood the second of these wooden apparitions. George looked at it, and again stood still.

"What's the matter?" said Harris, kindly. "You are not ill, are you?"

"I don't believe this is the shortest way," said George.

"I assure you it is," persisted Harris.

"Well, I'm going the other," said George; and he turned and went, we, as before, following him.

Along the Ferdinand Strasse Harris and I talked about private lunatic asylums, which, Harris said, were not well managed in England. He said a friend of his, a patient in a lunatic asylum—

George said, interrupting: "You appear to have a large number of friends in lunatic asylums."

He said it in a most insulting tone, as though to imply that that is where one would look for the majority of Harris's friends. But Harris did not get angry; he merely replied, quite mildly:

"Well, it really is extraordinary, when one comes to think of it, how many of them have gone that way sooner or later. I get quite nervous sometimes, now."

At the corner of the Wenzelsplatz, Harris, who was a few steps ahead of us, paused.

"It's a fine street, isn't it?" he said, sticking his hands in his pockets, and gazing up at it admiringly.

George and I followed suit. Two hundred yards away from us, in its very centre, was the third of these ghostly statues. I think it was the best of the three—the most like, the most deceptive. It stood boldly outlined against the wild sky: the horse on its hind legs, with its curiously attenuated tail; the man bareheaded, pointing with his plumed hat to the now entirely visible moon.

"I think, if you don't mind," said George—he spoke with almost a pathetic ring in his voice, his aggressiveness had completely fallen from him,—"that I will have that cab, if there's one handy."

"I thought you were looking queer," said Harris, kindly. "It's your head, isn't it?"

"Perhaps it is," answered George.

"I have noticed it coining on," said Harris; "but I didn't like to say anything to you. You fancy you see things, don't you?"

"No, no; it isn't that," replied George, rather quickly. "I don't know what it is."

"I do," said Harris, solemnly, "and I'll tell you. It's this German beer that you are drinking. I have known a case where a man—"

"Don't tell me about him just now," said George. "I dare say it's true, but somehow I don't feel I want to hear about him."

"You are not used to it," said Harris.

"I shall give it up from to-night," said George. "I think you must be right; it doesn't seem to agree with me."

We took him home, and saw him to bed. He was very gentle and quite grateful.

One evening later on, after a long day's ride, followed by a most satisfactory dinner, we started him on a big cigar, and, removing things from his reach, told him of this stratagem that for his good we had planned.

"How many copies of that statue did you say we saw?" asked George, after we had finished.

"Three," replied Harris.

"Only three?" said George. "Are you sure?"

"Positive," replied Harris. "Why?"

"Oh, nothing!" answered George.

But I don't think he quite believed Harris.

From Prague we travelled to Nuremberg, through Carlsbad. Good Germans, when they die, go, they say, to Carlsbad, as good Americans to Paris. This I doubt, seeing that it is a small place with no convenience for a crowd. In Carlsbad, you rise at five, the fashionable hour for promenade, when the band plays under the Colonnade, and the Sprudel is filled with a packed throng over a mile long, being from six to eight in the morning. Here you may hear more languages spoken than the Tower of Babel could have echoed. Polish Jews and Russian princes, Chinese mandarins and Turkish pashas, Norwegians looking as if they had stepped out of Ibsen's plays, women from the Boulevards, Spanish grandees and English countesses, mountaineers from Montenegro and millionaires from Chicago, you will find every dozen yards. Every luxury in the world Carlsbad provides for its visitors, with the one exception of pepper. That you cannot get within five miles of the town for money; what you can get there for love is not worth taking away. Pepper, to the liver brigade that forms four-fifths of Carlsbad's customers, is poison; and, prevention being better than cure, it is carefully kept out of the neighbourhood. "Pepper parties" are formed in Carlsbad to journey to some place without the boundary, and there indulge in pepper orgies.

Nuremberg, if one expects a town of mediaeval appearance, disappoints. Quaint corners, picturesque glimpses, there are in plenty; but everywhere they are surrounded and intruded upon by the modern, and even what is ancient is not nearly so ancient as one thought it was. After all, a town, like a woman, is only as old as it looks; and Nuremberg is still a comfortable-looking dame, its age somewhat difficult to conceive under its fresh paint and stucco in the blaze of the gas and the electric light. Still, looking closely, you may see its wrinkled walls and grey towers.

CHAPTER IX

Harris breaks the law—The helpful man: The dangers that beset him—George sets forth upon a career of crime—Those to whom Germany would come as a boon and a blessing—The English Sinner: His disappointments—The German Sinner: His exceptional advantages—What you may not do with your bed—An inexpensive vice—The German dog: His simple goodness—The misbehaviour of the beetle—A people that go the way they ought to go—The German small boy: His love of legality—How to go astray with a perambulator—The German student: His chastened wilfulncss.

All three of us, by some means or another, managed, between Nuremberg and the Black Forest, to get into trouble.

Harris led off at Stuttgart by insulting an official. Stuttgart is a charming town, clean and bright, a smaller Dresden. It has the additional attraction of containing little that one need to go out of one's way to see: a medium-sized picture gallery, a small museum of antiquities, and half a palace, and you are through with the entire thing and can enjoy yourself. Harris did not know it was an official he was insulting. He took it for a fireman (it looked like a fireman), and he called it a "dummer Esel."

In German you are not permitted to call an official a "silly ass," but undoubtedly this particular man was one. What had happened was this: Harris in the Stadgarten, anxious to get out, and seeing a gate open before him, had stepped over a wire into the street. Harris maintains he never saw it, but undoubtedly there was hanging to the wire a notice, "Durchgang Verboten!" The man, who was standing near the gates stopped Harris, and pointed out to him this notice. Harris thanked him, and passed on. The man came after him, and explained that treatment of the matter in such off-hand way could not be allowed; what was necessary to put the business right was that Harris should step back over the wire into the garden. Harris pointed out to the man that the notice said "going through forbidden," and that, therefore, by re-entering the garden that way he would be infringing the law a second time. The man saw this for himself, and suggested that to get over the difficulty Harris should go back into the garden by the proper entrance, which was round the corner, and afterwards immediately come out again by the same gate. Then it was that Harris called the man a silly ass. That delayed us a day, and cost Harris forty marks.

I followed suit at Carlsruhe, by stealing a bicycle. I did not mean to steal the bicycle; I was merely trying to be useful. The train was on the point of starting when I noticed, as I thought, Harris's bicycle still in the goods van. No one was about to help me. I jumped into the van and hauled it out, only just in time. Wheeling it down the platform in triumph, I came across Harris's bicycle, standing against a wall behind some milk-cans. The bicycle I had secured was not Harris's, but some other man's.

It was an awkward situation. In England, I should have gone to the station-master and explained my mistake. But in Germany they are not content with your explaining a little matter of this sort to one man: they take you round and get you to explain it to about half a dozen; and if any one of the half dozen happens not to be handy, or not to have time just then to listen to you, they have a habit of leaving you over for the night to finish your explanation the next morning. I thought I would just put the thing out of sight, and then, without making any fuss or show, take a short walk. I found a wood shed, which seemed just the very place, and was wheeling the bicycle into it when, unfortunately, a red-hatted railway official, with the airs of a retired field-marshal, caught sight of me and came up. He said:

"What are you doing with that bicycle?"

I said: "I am going to put it in this wood shed out of the way." I tried to convey by my tone that I was performing a kind and thoughtful action, for which the railway officials ought to thank me; but he was unresponsive.

"Is it your bicycle?" he said.

"Well, not exactly," I replied.

"Whose is it?" he asked, quite sharply.

"I can't tell you," I answered. "I don't know whose bicycle it is."

"Where did you get it from?" was his next question. There was a suspiciousness about his tone that was almost insulting.

"I got it," I answered, with as much calm dignity as at the moment I could assume, "out of the train."

"The fact is," I continued, frankly, "I have made a mistake."

He did not allow me time to finish. He merely said he thought so too, and blew a whistle.

Recollection of the subsequent proceedings is not, so far as I am concerned, amusing. By a miracle of good luck—they say Providence watches over certain of us—the incident happened in Carlsruhe, where I possess a German friend, an official of some importance. Upon what would have been my fate had the station not been at Carlsruhe, or had my friend been from home, I do not care to dwell; as it was I got off, as the saying is, by the skin of my teeth. I should like to add that I left Carlsruhe without a stain upon my character, but that would not be the truth. My going scot free is regarded in police circles there to this day as a grave mis-carriage of justice.

But all lesser sin sinks into insignificance beside the lawlessness of George. The bicycle incident had thrown us all into confusion, with the result that we lost George altogether. It transpired subsequently that he was waiting for us outside the police court; but this at the time we did not know. We thought, maybe, he had gone on to Baden by himself; and anxious to get away from Carlsruhe, and not, perhaps, thinking out things too clearly, we jumped into the next train that came up and proceeded thither. When George, tired of waiting, returned to the station, he found us gone and he found his luggage gone. Harris had his ticket; I was act-ing as banker to the party, so that he had in his pocket only some small change. Excusing himself upon these grounds, he thereupon commenced deliberately a career of crime that, reading it later, as set forth baldly in the official summons, made the hair of Harris and myself almost to stand on end.

German travelling, it may be explained, is somewhat complicated. You buy a ticket at the station you start from for the place you want to go to. You might think this would enable you to get there, but it does not. When your train comes up, you attempt to swarm into it; but the guard magnificently waves you away. Where are your credentials? You show him your ticket. He explains to you that by itself that is of no service whatever; you have only taken the first step towards travelling; you must go back to the booking-office and get in addition what is called a "schnellzug ticket." With this you return, thinking your troubles over. You are allowed to get in, so far so good. But you must not sit down anywhere, and you must not stand still, and you must not wander about. You must take an-other ticket, this time what is called a "platz ticket," which entitles you to a place for a certain distance.

What a man could do who persisted in taking nothing but the one ticket, I have often wondered. Would he be entitled to run behind the train on the six-foot way? Or could he stick a label on himself and get into the goods van? Again, what could be done with the man who, having taken his schnellzug ticket, obsti-nately refused, or had not the money to take a platz ticket: would they let him lie in the umbrella rack, or allow him to hang himself out of the window?

To return to George, he had just sufficient money to take a third-class slow train ticket to Baden, and that was all. To avoid the inquisitiveness of the guard, he waited till the train was moving, and then jumped in.

That was his first sin:

(a) Entering a train in motion;

(b) After being warned not to do so by an official.

Second sin:

(a) Travelling in train of superior class to that for which ticket was held.

(b) Refusing to pay difference when demanded by an official. (George says he did not "refuse"; he simply told the man he had not got it.)

Third sin:

(a) Travelling in carriage of superior class to that for which ticket was held.

(b) Refusing to pay difference when demanded by an official. (Again George disputes the accuracy of the report. He turned his pockets out, and offered the man all he had, which was about eightpence in German money. He offered to go into a third class, but there was no third class. He offered to go into the goods van, but they would not hear of it.)

Fourth sin:

(a) Occupying seat, and not paying for same.

(b) Loitering about corridor. (As they would not let him sit down without paying, and as he could not pay, it was difficult to see what else he could do.)

But explanations are held as no excuse in Germany; and his journey from Carlsruhe to Baden was one of the most expensive perhaps on record.

Reflecting upon the case and frequency with which one gets into trouble here in Germany, one is led to the conclusion that this country would come as a boon and a blessing to the average young Englishman. To the medical student, to the eater of dinners at the Temple, to the subaltern on leave, life in London is a wearisome proceeding. The healthy Briton takes his pleasure lawlessly, or it is no pleasure to him. Nothing that he may do affords to him any genuine satisfaction. To be in trouble of some sort is his only idea of bliss. Now, England affords him small opportunity in this respect; to get himself into a scrape requires a good deal of persistence on the part of the young Englishman.

I spoke on this subject one day with our senior churchwarden. It was the morning of the 10th of November, and we were both of us glancing, somewhat anxiously, through the police reports. The usual batch of young men had been summoned for creating the usual disturbance the night before at the Criterion. My friend the churchwarden has boys of his own, and a nephew of mine, upon whom I am keeping a fatherly eye, is by a fond mother supposed to be in London for the sole purpose of studying engineering. No names we knew happened, by fortunate chance, to be in the list of those detained in custody, and, relieved, we fell to moralising upon the folly and depravity of youth.

"It is very remarkable," said my friend the churchwarden, "how the Criterion retains its position in this respect. It was just so when I was young; the evening always wound up with a row at the Criterion."

"So meaningless," I remarked.

"So monotonous," he replied. "You have no idea," he continued, a dreamy expression stealing over his furrowed face, "how unutterably tired one can become of the walk from Piccadilly Circus to the Vine Street Police Court. Yet, what else was there for us to do? Simply nothing. Sometimes we would put out a street lamp, and a man would come round and light it again. If one insulted a policeman, he simply took no notice. He did not even know he was being insulted; or, if he did, he seemed not to care. You could fight a Covent Garden porter, if you fancied yourself at that sort of thing. Generally speaking, the porter got the best of it; and when he did it cost you five shillings, and when he did not the price was half a sovereign. I could never see much excitement in that particular sport.

I tried driving a hansom cab once. That has always been regarded as the acme of modern Tom and Jerryism. I stole it late one night from outside a public-house in Dean Street, and the first thing that happened to me was that I was hailed in Golden Square by an old lady surrounded by three children, two of them crying and the third one half asleep. Before I could get away she had shot the brats into the cab, taken my number, paid me, so she said, a shilling over the legal fare, and directed me to an address a little beyond what she called North Kensington. As a matter of fact, the place turned out to be the other side of Willesden. The horse was tired, and the journey took us well over two hours. It was the slowest lark I ever remember being concerned in. I tried once or twice to persuade the children to let me take them back to the old lady: but every time I opened the trap-door to speak to them the youngest one, a boy, started screaming; and when I offered other drivers to transfer the job to them, most of them replied in the words of a song popular about that period: 'Oh, George, don't you think you're going just a bit too far?' One man offered to take home to my wife any last message I might be thinking of, while another promised to organise a party to come and dig me out in the spring. When I mounted the dickey I had imagined myself driving a peppery old colonel to some lonesome and cabless region, half a dozen miles from where he wanted to go, and there leaving him upon the kerbstone to swear. About that there might have been good sport or there might not, according to circumstances and the colonel. The idea of a trip to an outlying suburb in charge of a nursery full of helpless infants had never occurred to me. No, London," concluded my friend the churchwarden with a sigh, "affords but limited opportunity to the lover of the illegal."

Now, in Germany, on the other hand, trouble is to be had for the asking. There are many things in Germany that you must not do that are quite easy to do. To any young Englishman yearning to get himself into a scrape, and finding himself hampered in his own country, I would advise a single ticket to Germany; a return, lasting as it does only a month, might prove a waste.

In the Police Guide of the Fatherland he will find set forth a list of the things the doing of which will bring to him interest and excitement. In Germany you must not hang your bed out of window. He might begin with that. By waving his bed out of window he could get into trouble before he had his breakfast. At home he might hang himself out of window, and nobody would mind much, provided he did not obstruct anybody's ancient lights or break away and injure any passer underneath.

In Germany you must not wear fancy dress in the streets. A Highlander of my acquaintance who came to pass the winter in Dresden spent the first few days of his residence there in arguing this question with the Saxon Government. They asked him what he was doing in those clothes. He was not an amiable man. He answered, he was wearing them. They asked him why he was wearing them. He replied, to keep himself warm. They told him frankly that they did not believe him, and sent him back to his lodgings in a closed landau. The personal testimony of the English Minister was necessary to assure the authorities that the

Highland garb was the customary dress of many respectable, law-abiding British subjects. They accepted the statement, as diplomatically bound, but retain their private opinion to this day. The English tourist they have grown accustomed to; but a Leicestershire gentleman, invited to hunt with some German officers, on appearing outside his hotel, was promptly marched off, horse and all, to explain his frivolity at the police court.

Another thing you must not do in the streets of German towns is to feed horses, mules, or donkeys, whether your own or those belonging to other people. If a passion seizes you to feed somebody else's horse, you must make an appointment with the animal, and the meal must take place in some properly authorised place. You must not break glass or china in the street, nor, in fact, in any public resort whatever; and if you do, you must pick up all the pieces. What you are to do with the pieces when you have gathered them together I cannot say. The only thing I know for certain is that you are not permitted to throw them anywhere, to leave them anywhere, or apparently to part with them in any way whatever. Presumably, you are expected to carry them about with you until you die, and then be buried with them; or, maybe, you are allowed to swallow them.

In German streets you must not shoot with a crossbow. The German lawmaker does not content himself with the misdeeds of the average man—the crime one feels one wants to do, but must not: he worries himself imagining all the things a wandering maniac might do. In Germany there is no law against a man standing on his head in the middle of the road; the idea has not occurred to them. One of these days a German statesman, visiting a circus and seeing acrobats, will reflect upon this omission. Then he will straightway set to work and frame a clause forbidding people from standing on their heads in the middle of the road, and fixing a fine. This is the charm of German law: misdemeanour in Germany has its fixed price. You are not kept awake all night, as in England, wondering whether you will get off with a caution, be fined forty shillings, or, catching the magistrate in an unhappy moment for yourself, get seven days. You know exactly what your fun is going to cost you. You can spread out your money on the table, open your Police Guide, and plan out your holiday to a fifty pfennig piece. For a really cheap evening, I would recommend walking on the wrong side of the pavement after being cautioned not to do so. I calculate that by choosing your district and keeping to the quiet side streets you could walk for a whole evening on the wrong side of the pavement at a cost of little over three marks.

In German towns you must not ramble about after dark "in droves." I am not quite sure how many constitute a "drove," and no official to whom I have spoken on this subject has felt himself competent to fix the exact number. I once put it to a German friend who was starting for the theatre with his wife, his mother-in-law, five children of his own, his sister and her *fiancé*, and two nieces, if he did not think he was running a risk under this by-law. He did not take my suggestion as a joke. He cast an eye over the group.

"Oh, I don't think so," he said; "you see, we are all one family."

"The paragraph says nothing about its being a family drove or not," I replied; "it simply says 'drove.' I do not mean it in any uncomplimentary sense, but, speaking etymologically, I am inclined personally to regard your collection as a 'drove.' Whether the police will take the same view or not remains to be seen. I am merely warning you."

My friend himself was inclined to pooh-pooh my fears; but his wife thinking it better not to run any risk of having the party broken up by the police at the very beginning of the evening, they divided, arranging to come together again in the theatre lobby.

Another passion you must restrain in Germany is that prompting you to throw things out of window. Cats are no excuse. During the first week of my residence in Germany I was awakened incessantly by cats. One night I got mad. I collected a small arsenal—two or three pieces of coal, a few hard pears, a couple of candle ends, an odd egg I found on the kitchen table, an empty soda-water bottle, and a few articles of that sort,—and, opening the window, bombarded the spot from where the noise appeared to come. I do not suppose I hit anything; I never knew a man who did hit a cat, even when he could see it, except, maybe, by accident when aiming at something else. I have known crack shots, winners of Queen's prizes—those sort of men,—shoot with shot-guns at cats fifty yards away, and never hit a hair. I have often thought that, instead of bull's-eyes, running deer, and that rubbish, the really superior marksman would be he who could boast that he had shot the cat.

But, anyhow, they moved off; maybe the egg annoyed them. I had noticed when I picked it up that it did not look a good egg; and I went back to bed again, thinking the incident closed. Ten minutes afterwards there came a violent ringing of the electric bell. I tried to ignore it, but it was too persistent, and, putting on my dressing gown, I went down to the gate. A policeman was standing there. He had all the things I had been throwing out of the window in a little heap in front of him, all except the egg. He had evidently been collecting them. He said:

"Are these things yours?"

I said: "They were mine, but personally I have done with them. Anybody can have them—you can have them."

He ignored my offer. He said:

"You threw these things out of window."

"You are right," I admitted; "I did."

"Why did you throw them out of window?" he asked. A German policeman has his code of questions arranged for him; he never varies them, and he never omits one.

"I threw them out of the window at some cats," I answered.

"What cats?" he asked.

It was the sort of question a German policeman would ask. I replied with as much sarcasm as I could put into my accent that I was ashamed to say I could not tell him what cats. I explained that, personally, they were strangers to me; but I offered, if the police would call all the cats in the district together, to come round and see if I could recognise them by their yaul.

The German policeman does not understand a joke, which is perhaps on the whole just as well, for I believe there is a heavy fine for joking with any German uniform; they call it "treating an official with contumely." He merely replied that it was not the duty of the police to help me recognise the cats; their duty was merely to fine me for throwing things out of window.

I asked what a man was supposed to do in Germany when woke up night after night by cats, and he explained that I could lodge an information against the owner of the cat, when the police would proceed to caution him, and, if necessary, order the cat to be destroyed. Who was going to destroy the cat, and what the cat would be doing during the process, he did not explain.

I asked him how he proposed I should discover the owner of the cat. He thought for a while, and then suggested that I might follow it home. I did not feel inclined to argue with him any more after that; I should only have said things that would have made the matter worse. As it was, that night's sport cost me twelve marks; and not a single one of the four German officials who interviewed me on the subject could see anything ridiculous in the proceedings from beginning to end.

But in Germany most human faults and follies sink into comparative insignificance beside the enormity of walking on the grass. Nowhere, and under no circumstances, may you at any time in Germany walk on the grass. Grass in Germany is quite a fetish. To put your foot on German grass would be as great a sacrilege as to dance a hornpipe on a Mohammedan's praying-mat. The very dogs respect German grass; no German dog would dream of putting a paw on it. If you see a dog scampering across the grass in Germany, you may know for certain that it is the dog of some unholy foreigner. In England, when we want to keep dogs out of places, we put up wire netting, six feet high, supported by buttresses, and defended on the top by spikes. In Germany, they put a notice-board in the middle of the place, "Hunden verboten," and a dog that has German blood in its veins looks at that notice-board and walks away. In a German park I have seen a gardener step gingerly with felt boots on to grass-plot, and removing therefrom a beetle, place it gravely but firmly on the gravel; which done, he stood sternly watching the beetle, to see that it did not try to get back on the grass; and the beetle, looking utterly ashamed of itself, walked hurriedly down the gutter, and turned up the path marked "Ausgang."

In German parks separate roads are devoted to the different orders of the community, and no one person, at peril of liberty and fortune, may go upon another person's road. There are special paths for "wheel-riders" and special paths for "foot-goers," avenues for "horse-riders," roads for people in light vehicles, and roads for people in heavy vehicles; ways for children and for "alone ladies." That no particular route has yet been set aside for bald-headed men or "new women" has always struck me as an omission.

In the Grosse Garten in Dresden I once came across an old lady, standing, helpless and bewildered, in the centre of seven tracks. Each was guarded by a threatening notice, warning everybody off it but the person for whom it was intended.

"I am sorry to trouble you," said the old lady, on learning I could speak English and read German, "but would you mind telling me what I am and where I have to go?"

I inspected her carefully. I came to the conclusion that she was a "grown-up" and a "foot-goer," and pointed out her path. She looked at it, and seemed disappointed.

"But I don't want to go down there," she said; "mayn't I go this way?"

"Great heavens, no, madam!" I replied. "That path is reserved for children."

"But I wouldn't do them any harm," said the old lady, with a smile. She did not look the sort of old lady who would have done them any harm.

"Madam," I replied, "if it rested with me, I would trust you down that path, though my own first-born were at the other end; but I can only inform you of the laws of this country. For you, a full-grown woman, to venture down that path is to go to certain fine, if not imprisonment. There is your path, marked plainly— *Nur für Fussgänger*, and if you will follow my advice, you will hasten down it; you are not allowed to stand here and hesitate."

"It doesn't lead a bit in the direction I want to go," said the old lady.

"It leads in the direction you *ought* to want to go," I replied, and we parted.

In the German parks there are special seats labelled, "Only for grown-ups" (*Nur für Erwachsene*), and the German small boy, anxious to sit down, and reading that notice, passes by, and hunts for a seat on which children are permitted to rest; and there he seats himself, careful not to touch the woodwork with his muddy boots. Imagine a seat in Regent's or St. James's Park labelled "Only for grown-ups!" Every child for five miles round would be trying to get on that seat, and hauling other children off who were on. As for any "grown-up," he would never be able to get within half a mile of that seat for the crowd. The German small boy, who has accidentally sat down on such without noticing, rises with a start when his error is pointed out to him, and goes away with down-cast head, brushing to the roots of his hair with shame and regret.

Not that the German child is neglected by a paternal Government. In German parks and public gardens special places (*Spielplätze*) are provided for him, each one supplied with a heap of sand. There he can play to his heart's content at making mud pies and building sand castles. To the German child a pie made of any other mud than this would appear an immoral pie. It would give to him no satisfaction: his soul would revolt against it.

"That pie," he would say to himself, "was not, as it should have been, made of Government mud specially set apart for the purpose; it was nor manufactured in the place planned and maintained by the Government for the making of mud pies. It can bring no real blessing with it; it is a lawless pie." And until his father had paid the proper fine, and he had received his proper licking, his conscience would continue to trouble him.

Another excellent piece of material for obtaining excitement in Germany is the simple domestic perambulator. What you may do with a "kinder-wagen," as it is called, and what you may not, covers pages of German law; after the reading of which, you conclude that the man who can push a perambulator through a German town without breaking the law was meant for a diplomatist. You must not loiter with a perambulator, and you must not go too fast. You must not get in anybody's way with a perambulator, and if anybody gets in your way you must get out of their way. If you want to stop with a perambulator, you must go to a place specially appointed where perambulators may stop; and when you get there you *must* stop. You must not cross the road with a perambulator; if you and the baby happen to live on the other side, that is your fault. You must not leave your perambulator anywhere, and only in certain places can you take it with you. I should say that in Germany you could go out with a perambulator and get into enough trouble in half an hour to last you for a month. Any young Englishman anxious for a row with the police could not do better than come over to Germany and bring his perambulator with him.

In Germany you must not leave your front door unlocked after ten o'clock at night, and you must not play the piano in your own house after eleven. In England I have never felt I wanted to play the piano myself, or to hear anyone else play it, after eleven o'clock at night; but that is a very different thing to being told that you must not play it. Here, in Germany, I never feel that I really care for the piano until eleven o'clock, then I could sit and listen to the "Maiden's Prayer," or the Overture to "Zampa," with pleasure. To the law-loving German, on the other hand, music after eleven o'clock at night ceases to be music; it becomes sin, and as such gives him no satisfaction.

The only individual throughout Germany who ever dreams of taking liberties with the law is the German student, and he only to a certain well-defined point. By custom, certain privileges are permitted to him, but even these are strictly limited and clearly understood. For instance, the German student may get drunk and fall asleep in the gutter with no other penalty than that of having the next morning to tip the policeman who has found him and brought him home. But for this purpose he must choose the gutters of side-streets. The German student, conscious of the rapid approach of oblivion, uses all his remaining energy to get round the corner, where he may collapse without anxiety. In certain districts he may ring bells. The rent of flats in these localities is lower than in other quarters of the town; while the difficulty is further met by each family preparing for itself a secret code of bell-ringing by means of which it is known whether the summons is genuine or not. When visiting such a household late at night it is well to be acquainted with this code, or you may, if persistent, get a bucket of water thrown over you.

Also the German student is allowed to put out lights at night, but there is a prejudice against his putting out too many. The larky German student generally keeps count, contenting himself with half a dozen lights per night. Likewise, he may shout and sing as he walks home, up till half-past two; and at certain restaurants it is permitted to him to put his arm round the Fraulein's waist. To prevent any suggestion of unseemliness, the waitresses at restaurants frequented by students are always carefully selected from among a staid and elderly classy of women, by reason of which the German student can enjoy the delights of flirtation without fear and without reproach to anyone.

They are a law-abiding people, the Germans.

CHAPTER X

Baden from the visitor's point of view—Beauty of the early morning, as viewed from the preceding afternoon—Distance, as measured by the compass—Ditto, as measured by the leg—George in account with his conscience—A lazy machine—Bicycling, according to the poster: its restfulness—The poster cyclist: its costume; its method—The griffin as a household pet—A dog with proper self-respect—The horse that was abused.

From Baden, about which it need only be said that it is a pleasure resort singularly like other pleasure resorts of the same description, we started bicycling in earnest. We planned a ten days' tour, which, while completing the Black Forest, should include a spin down the Donau-Thal, which for the twenty miles from Tuttlingen to Sigmaringen is, perhaps, the finest valley in Germany; the Danube stream here winding its narrow way past old-world unspoilt villages; past ancient monasteries, nestling in green pastures, where still the bare-footed and bare-headed friar, his rope girdle tight about his loins, shepherds, with crook in hand, his sheep upon the hill sides; through rocky woods; between sheer walls of cliff, whose every towering crag stands crowned with ruined fortress, church, or castle; together with a blick at the Vosges mountains, where half the population is bitterly pained if you speak to them in French, the other half being insulted when you address them in German, and the whole indignantly contemptuous at the first sound of English; a state of things that renders conversation with the stranger somewhat nervous work.

We did not succeed in carrying out our programme in its entirety, for the reason that human performance lags ever behind human intention. It is easy to say and believe at three o'clock in the afternoon that: "We will rise at five, breakfast lightly at half-past, and start away at six."

"Then we shall be well on our way before the heat of the day sets in," remarks one.

"This time of the year, the early morning is really the best part of the day. Don't you think so?" adds another.

"Oh, undoubtedly."

"So cool and fresh."

"And the half-lights are so exquisite."

The first morning one maintains one's vows. The party assembles at half-past five. It is very silent; individually, somewhat snappy; inclined to grumble with its food, also with most other things; the atmosphere charged with compressed irritability seeking its vent. In the evening the Tempter's voice is heard:

"I think if we got off by half-past six, sharp, that would be time enough?"

The voice of Virtue protests, faintly: "It will be breaking our resolution."

The Tempter replies: "Resolutions were made for man, not man for resolutions." The devil can paraphrase Scripture for his own purpose. "Besides, it is disturbing the whole hotel; think of the poor servants."

The voice of Virtue continues, but even feebler: "But everybody gets up early in these parts."

"They would not if they were not obliged to, poor things! Say breakfast at half-past six, punctual; that will be disturbing nobody."

Thus Sin masquerades under the guise of Good, and one sleeps till six, explaining to one's conscience, who, however, doesn't believe it, that one does this because of unselfish consideration for others. I have known such consideration extend until seven of the clock.

Likewise, distance measured with a pair of compasses is not precisely the same as when measured by the leg.

"Ten miles an hour for seven hours, seventy miles. A nice easy day's work."

"There are some stiff hills to climb?"

"The other side to come down. Say, eight miles an hour, and call it sixty miles. Gott in Himmel! if we can't average eight miles an hour, we had better go in bath-chairs." It does seem somewhat impossible to do less, on paper.

But at four o'clock in the afternoon the voice of Duty rings less trumpet-toned:

"Well, I suppose we ought to be getting on."

"Oh, there's no hurry! don't fuss. Lovely view from here, isn't it?"

"Very. Don't forget we are twenty-five miles from St. Blasien."

"How far?"

"Twenty-five miles, a little over if anything."

"Do you mean to say we have only come thirty-five miles?"

"That's all."

"Nonsense. I don't believe that map of yours."

"It is impossible, you know. We have been riding steadily ever since the first thing this morning."

"No, we haven't. We didn't get away till eight, to begin with."

"Quarter to eight."

"Well, quarter to eight; and every half-dozen miles we have stopped."

"We have only stopped to look at the view. It's no good coming to see a country, and then not seeing it."

"And we have had to pull up some stiff hills."

"Besides, it has been an exceptionally hot day to-day."

"Well, don't forget St. Blasien is twenty-five miles off, that's all."

"Any more hills?"

"Yes, two; up and down."

"I thought you said it was downhill into St. Blasien?"

"So it is for the last ten miles. We are twenty-five miles from St. Blasien here."

"Isn't there anywhere between here and St. Blasien? What's that little place there on the lake?"

"It isn't St. Blasien, or anywhere near it. There's a danger in beginning that sort of thing."

"There's a danger in overworking oneself. One should study moderation in all things. Pretty little place, that Titisee, according to the map; looks as if there would be good air there."

"All right, I'm agreeable. It was you fellows who suggested our making for St. Blasien."

"Oh, I'm not so keen on St. Blasien! poky little place, down in a valley. This Titisee, I should say, was ever so much nicer."

"Quite near, isn't it?"

"Five miles."

General chorus: "We'll stop at Titisee."

George made discovery of this difference between theory and practice on the very first day of our ride.

"I thought," said George—he was riding the single, Harris and I being a little ahead on the tandem—"that the idea was to train up the hills and ride down them."

"So it is," answered Harris, "as a general rule. But the trains don't go up *every* hill in the Black Forest."

"Somehow, I felt a suspicion that they wouldn't," growled George; and for awhile silence reigned.

"Besides," remarked Harris, who had evidently been ruminating the subject, "you would not wish to have nothing but downhill, surely. It would not be playing the game. One must take a little rough with one's smooth."

Again there returned silence, broken after awhile by George, this time.

"Don't you two fellows over-exert yourselves merely on my account," said George.

"How do you mean?" asked Harris.

"I mean," answered George, "that where a train does happen to be going up these hills, don't you put aside the idea of taking it for fear of outraging my finer feelings. Personally, I am prepared to go up all these hills in a railway train, even if it's not playing the game. I'll square the thing with my conscience; I've been up at seven every day for a week now, and I calculate it owes me a bit. Don't you consider me in the matter at all."

We promised to bear this in mind, and again the ride continued in dogged dumbness, until it was again broken by George.

"What bicycle did you say this was of yours?" asked George.

Harris told him. I forget of what particular manufacture it happened to be; it is immaterial.

"Are you sure?" persisted George.

"Of course I am sure," answered Harris. "Why, what's the matter with it?"

"Well, it doesn't come up to the poster," said George, "that's all."

"What poster?" asked Harris.

"The poster advertising this particular brand of cycle," explained George. "I was looking at one on a hoarding in Sloane Street only a day or two before we started. A man was riding this make of machine, a man with a banner in his hand: he wasn't doing any work, that was clear as daylight; he was just sitting on the thing and drinking in the air. The cycle was going of its own accord, and going well. This thing of yours leaves all the work to me. It is a lazy brute of a machine; if you don't shove, it simply does nothing: I should complain about it, if I were you."

When one comes to think of it, few bicycles do realise the poster. On only one poster that I can recollect have I seen the rider represented as doing any work. But then this man was being pursued by a bull. In ordinary cases the object of the artist is to convince the hesitating neophyte that the sport of bicycling consists in sitting on a luxurious saddle, and being moved rapidly in the direction you wish to go by unseen heavenly powers.

Generally speaking, the rider is a lady, and then one feels that, for perfect bodily rest combined with entire freedom from mental anxiety, slumber upon a water-bed cannot compare with bicycle-riding upon a hilly road. No fairy travelling on a summer cloud could take things more easily than does the bicycle girl, according to the poster. Her costume for cycling in hot weather is ideal. Old-fashioned landladies might refuse her lunch, it is true; and a narrowminded police force might desire to secure her, and wrap her in a rug preliminary to summonsing her. But such she heeds not. Uphill and downhill, through traffic that might tax the ingenuity of a cat, over road surfaces calculated to break the average steam roller she passes, a vision of idle loveliness; her fair hair streaming to the wind, her sylph-like form poised airily, one foot upon the saddle, the other resting lightly upon the lamp. Sometimes she condescends to sit down on the saddle; then she puts her feet on the rests, lights a cigarette, and waves above her head a Chinese lantern.

Less often, it is a mere male thing that rides the machine. He is not so accomplished an acrobat as is the lady; but simple tricks, such as standing on the saddle and waving flags, drinking beer or beef-tea while riding, he can and does perform. Something, one supposes, he must do to occupy his mind: sitting still hour after hour on this machine, having no work to do, nothing to think about, must pall upon any man of active temperament. Thus it is that we see him rising on his pedals as he nears the top of some high hill to apostrophise the sun, or address poetry to the surrounding scenery.

Occasionally the poster pictures a pair of cyclists; and then one grasps the fact how much superior for purposes of flirtation is the modern bicycle to the old-fashioned parlour or the played-out garden gate. He and she mount their bicycles, being careful, of course, that such are of the right make. After that they have nothing to think about but the old sweet tale. Down shady lanes, through busy towns on market days, merrily roll the wheels of the "Bermondsey Company's Bottom Bracket Britain's Best," or of the "Camberwell Company's Jointless Eureka." They need no pedalling; they require no guiding. Give them their heads, and tell them what time you want to get home, and that is all they ask. While Edwin leans from his saddle to whisper the dear old nothings in Angelina's ear, while Angelina's face, to hide its blushes, is turned towards the horizon at the back, the magic bicycles pursue their even course.

And the sun is always shining and the roads are always dry. No stern parent rides behind, no interfering aunt beside, no demon small boy brother is peeping round the corner, there never comes a skid. Ah me! Why were there no "Britain's Best" nor "Camberwell Eurekas" to be hired when *we* were young?

Or maybe the "Britain's Best" or the "Camberwell Eureka" stands leaning against a gate; maybe it is tired. It has worked hard all the afternoon, carrying these young people. Mercifully minded, they have dismounted, to give the machine a rest. They sit upon the grass beneath the shade of graceful boughs; it is long and dry grass. A stream flows by their feet. All is rest and peace.

That is ever the idea the cycle poster artist sets himself to convey—rest and peace.

But I am wrong in saying that no cyclist, according to the poster, ever works. Now I come to reflect, I have seen posters representing gentlemen on cycles working very hard—over-working themselves, one might almost say. They are thin and haggard with the toil, the perspiration stands upon their brow in beads; you feel that if there is another hill beyond the poster they must either get off or die. But this is the result of their own folly. This happens because they will persist in riding a machine of an inferior make. Were they riding a "Putney Popular" or "Battersea Bounder," such as the sensible young man in the centre of the poster rides, then all this unnecessary labour would be saved to them. Then all required of them would be, as in gratitude bound, to look happy; perhaps, occasionally to back-pedal a little when the machine in its youthful buoyancy loses its head for a moment and dashes on too swiftly.

You tired young men, sitting dejectedly on milestones, too spent to heed the steady rain that soaks you through; you weary maidens, with the straight, damp hair, anxious about the time, longing to swear, not knowing how; you stout bald men, vanishing visibly as you pant and grunt along the endless road; you purple, dejected matrons, plying with pain the slow unwilling wheel; why did you not see to it that you bought a "Britain's Best" or a "Camberwell Eureka"? Why are these bicycles of inferior make so prevalent throughout the land

Or is it with bicycling as with all other things: does Life at no point realise the Poster?

The one thing in Germany that never fails to charm and fascinate me is the German dog. In England one grows tired of the old breeds, one knows them all so well: the mastiff, the plum-pudding dog, the terrier (black, white or rough-haired, as the case may be, but always quarrelsome), the collie, the bulldog; never anything new. Now in Germany you get variety. You come across dogs the like of which you have never seen before: that until you hear them bark you do not know are dogs. It is all so fresh, so interesting. George stopped a dog in Sigmaringen and drew our attention to it. It suggested a cross between a codfish and a poodle. I would not like to be positive it was *not* a cross between a codfish and a poodle. Harris tried to photograph it, but it ran up a fence and disappeared through some bushes.

I do not know what the German breeder's idea is; at present he retains his secret. George suggests he is aiming at a griffin. There is much to bear out this theory, and indeed in one or two cases I have come across success on these lines would seem to have been almost achieved. Yet I cannot bring myself to believe that such are anything more than mere accidents. The German is practical, and I fail to see the object of a griffin. If mere quaintness of design be desired, is there not already the Dachshund! What more is needed? Besides, about a house, a griffin would be so inconvenient: people would be continually treading on its tail. My own idea is that what the Germans are trying for is a mermaid, which they will then train to catch fish.

For your German does not encourage laziness in any living thing. He likes to see his dogs work, and the German dog loves work; of that there can be no doubt. The life of the English dog must be a misery to him. Imagine a strong, active, and intelligent being, of exceptionally energetic temperament, condemned to spend twenty-four hours a day in absolute idleness! How would you like it yourself? No wonder he feels misunderstood, yearns for the unattainable, and gets himself into trouble generally.

Now the German dog, on the other hand, has plenty to occupy his mind. He is busy and important. Watch him as he walks along harnessed to his milk cart. No churchwarden at collection time could feel or look more pleased with himself. He does not do any real work; the human being does the pushing, he does the barking; that is his idea of division of labour. What he says to himself is:

"The old man can't bark, but he can shove. Very well."

The interest and the pride he takes in the business is quite beautiful to see. Another dog passing by makes, maybe, some jeering remark, casting discredit upon the creaminess of the milk. He stops suddenly, quite regardless of the traffic.

"I beg your pardon, what was that you said about our milk?"

"I said nothing about your milk," retorts the other dog, in a tone of gentle innocence. "I merely said it was a fine day, and asked the price of chalk."

"Oh, you asked the price of chalk, did you? Would you like to know?"

"Yes, thanks; somehow I thought you would be able to tell me."

"You are quite right, I can. It's worth—"

"Oh, do come along!" says the old lady, who is tired and hot, and anxious to finish her round.

"Yes, but hang it all; did you hear what he hinted about our milk?"

"Oh, never mind him! There's a tram coming round the corner: we shall all get run over."

"Yes, but I do mind him; one has one's proper pride. He asked the price of chalk, and he's going to know it! It's worth just twenty times as much—"

"You'll have the whole thing over, I know you will," cries the old lady, pathetically, struggling with all her feeble strength to haul him back. "Oh dear, oh dear! I do wish I had left you at home."

The tram is bearing down upon them; a cab-driver is shouting at them; another huge brute, hoping to be in time to take a hand, is dragging a bread cart, followed by a screaming child, across the road from the opposite side; a small crowd is collecting; and a policeman is hastening to the scene.

"It's worth," says the milk dog, "just twenty-times as much as you'll be worth before I've done with you."

"Oh, you think so, do you?"

"Yes, I do, you grandson of a French poodle, you cabbage-eating—"

"There! I knew you'd have it over," says the poor milk-woman. "I told him he'd have it over."

But he is busy, and heeds her not. Five minutes later, when the traffic is renewed, when the bread girl has collected her muddy rolls, and the policeman has gone off with the name and address of everybody in the street, he consents to look behind him.

"It *is* a bit of an upset," he admits. Then shaking himself free of care, he adds, cheerfully, "But I guess I taught him the price of chalk. He won't interfere with us again, I'm thinking."

"I'm sure I hope not," says the old lady, regarding dejectedly the milky road.

But his favourite sport is to wait at the top of the hill for another dog, and then race down. On these occasions the chief occupation of the other fellow is to run about behind, picking up the scattered articles, loaves, cabbages, or shirts, as they are jerked out. At the bottom of the hill, he stops and waits for his friend.

"Good race, wasn't it?" he remarks, panting, as the Human comes up, laden to the chin. "I believe I'd have won it, too, if it hadn't been for that fool of a small boy. He was right in my way just as I turned the corner. *You noticed him?* Wish I had, beastly brat! What's he yelling like that for? *Because I knocked him down and ran over him?* Well, why didn't he get out of the way? It's disgraceful, the way people leave their children about for other people to tumble over. Halloa! did all those things come out? You couldn't have packed them very carefully;

you should see to a thing like that. *You did not dream of my tearing down the hill twenty miles an hour?* Surely, you knew me better than to expect I'd let that old Schneider's dog pass me without an effort. But there, you never think. You're sure you've got them all? *You believe so?* I shouldn't 'believe' if I were you; I should run back up the hill again and make sure. *You feel too tired?* Oh, all right! don't blame me if anything is missing, that's all."

He is so self-willed. He is cock-sure that the correct turning is the second on the right, and nothing will persuade him that it is the third. He is positive he can get across the road in time, and will not be convinced until he sees the cart smashed up. Then he is very apologetic, it is true. But of what use is that? As he is usually of the size and strength of a young bull, and his human companion is generally a weak-kneed old man or woman, or a small child, he has his way. The greatest punishment his proprietor can inflict upon him is to leave him at home, and take the cart out alone. But your German is too kind-hearted to do this often.

That he is harnessed to the cart for anybody's pleasure but his own it is impossible to believe; and I am confident that the German peasant plans the tiny harness and fashions the little cart purely with the hope of gratifying his dog. In other countries—in Belgium, Holland and France—I have seen these draught dogs ill-treated and over-worked; but in Germany, never. Germans abuse animals shockingly. I have seen a German stand in front of his horse and call it every name he could lay his tongue to. But the horse did not mind it. I have seen a German, weary with abusing his horse, call to his wife to come out and assist him. When she came, he told her what the horse had done. The recital roused the woman's temper to almost equal heat with his own; and standing one each side of the poor beast, they both abused it. They abused its dead mother, they insulted its father; they made cutting remarks about its personal appearance, its intelligence, its moral sense, its general ability as a horse. The animal bore the torrent with exemplary patience for awhile; then it did the best thing possible to do under the circumstances. Without losing its own temper, it moved quietly away. The lady returned to her washing, and the man followed it up the street, still abusing it.

A kinder-hearted people than the Germans there is no need for. Cruelty to animal or child is a thing almost unknown in the land. The whip with them is a musical instrument; its crack is heard from morning to night, but an Italian coachman that in the streets of Dresden I once saw use it was very nearly lynched by the indignant crowd. Germany is the only country in Europe where the traveller can settle himself comfortably in his hired carriage, confident that his gentle, willing friend between the shafts will be neither over-worked nor cruelly treated.

CHAPTER XI

Black Forest House: and the sociability therein—Its perfume—George positively declines to remain in bed after four o'clock in the morning—The road one cannot miss—My peculiar extra instinct—An ungrateful party—Harris as a scientist—His cheery confidence—The village: where it was, and where it ought to have been—George: his plan—We promenade à la Français—The German coachman asleep and awake—The man who spreads the English language abroad.

There was one night when, tired out and far from town or village, we slept in a Black Forest farmhouse. The great charm about the Black Forest house is its sociability. The cows are in the next room, the horses are upstairs, the geese and ducks are in the kitchen, while the pigs, the children, and the chickens live all over the place.

You are dressing, when you hear a grunt behind you.

"Good-morning! Don't happen to have any potato peelings in here? No, I see you haven't; good-bye."

Next there is a cackle, and you see the neck of an old hen stretched round the corner.

"Fine morning, isn't it? You don't mind my bringing this worm of mine in here, do you? It is so difficult in this house to find a room where one can enjoy one's food with any quietness. From a chicken I have always been a slow eater, and when a dozen—there, I thought they wouldn't leave me alone. Now they'll all want a bit. You don't mind my getting on the bed, do you? Perhaps here they won't notice me."

While you are dressing various shock heads peer in at the door; they evidently regard the room as a temporary menagerie. You cannot tell whether the heads belong to boys or girls; you can only hope they are all male. It is of no use shutting the door, because there is nothing to fasten it by, and the moment you are gone they push it open again. You breakfast as the Prodigal Son is generally represented feeding: a pig or two drop in to keep you company; a party of elderly geese criticise you from the door; you gather from their whispers, added to their shocked expression, that they are talking scandal about you. Maybe a cow will condescend to give a glance in.

This Noah's Ark arrangement it is, I suppose, that gives to the Black Forest home its distinctive scent. It is not a scent you can liken to any one thing. It is as if you took roses and Limburger cheese and hair oil, some heather and onions, peaches and soapsuds, together with a dash of sea air and a corpse, and mixed them up together. You cannot define any particular odour, but you feel they are all there—all the odours that the world has yet discovered. People who live in these houses are fond of this mixture. They do not open the window and lose any of it; they keep it carefully bottled up. If you want any other scent, you can go outside and smell the wood violets and the pines; inside there is the house; and after a while, I am told, you get used to it, so that you miss it, and are unable to go to sleep in any other atmosphere.

We had a long walk before us the next day, and it was our desire, therefore, to get up early, even so early as six o'clock, if that could be managed without disturbing the whole household. We put it to our hostess whether she thought this could be done. She said she thought it could. She might not be about herself at that time; it was her morning for going into the town, some eight miles off, and she rarely got back much before seven; but, possibly, her husband or one of the boys would be returning home to lunch about that hour. Anyhow, somebody should be sent back to wake us and get our breakfast.

As it turned out, we did not need any waking. We got up at four, all by ourselves. We got up at four in order to get away from the noise and the din that was making our heads ache. What time the Black Forest peasant rises in the summer time I am unable to say; to us they appeared to be getting up all night. And the first thing the Black Forester does when he gets up is to put on a pair of stout boots with wooden soles, and take a constitutional round the house. Until he has been three times up and down the stairs, he does not feel he is up. Once fully awake himself, the next thing he does is to go upstairs to the stables, and wake up a horse. (The Black Forest house being built generally on the side of a steep hill, the ground floor is at the top, and the hay-loft at the bottom.) Then the horse, it would seem, must also have its constitutional round the house; and this seen to, the man goes downstairs into the kitchen and begins to chop wood, and when he has chopped sufficient wood he feels pleased with himself and begins to sing. All things considered, we came to the conclusion we could not do better than follow the excellent example set us. Even George was quite eager to get up that morning.

We had a frugal breakfast at half-past four, and started away at five. Our road lay over a mountain, and from enquiries made in the village it appeared to be one of those roads you cannot possibly miss. I suppose everybody knows this sort of road. Generally, it leads you back to where you started from; and when it doesn't, you wish it did, so that at all events you might know where you were. I foresaw evil from the very first, and before we had accomplished a couple of miles we came up with it. The road divided into three. A worm-eaten sign-post indicated that the path to the left led to a place that we had never heard of—that was on no map. Its other arm, pointing out the direction of the middle road, had disappeared. The road to the right, so we all agreed, clearly led back again to the village.

"The old man said distinctly," so Harris reminded us, "keep straight on round the hill."

"Which hill?" George asked, pertinently.

We were confronted by half a dozen, some of them big, some of them little.

"He told us," continued Harris, "that we should come to a wood."

"I see no reason to doubt him," commented George, "whichever road we take."

As a matter of fact, a dense wood covered every hill.

"And he said," murmured Harris, "that we should reach the top in about an hour and a half."

"There it is," said George, "that I begin to disbelieve him."

"Well, what shall we do?" said Harris.

Now I happen to possess the bump of locality. It is not a virtue; I make no boast of it. It is merely an animal instinct that I cannot help. That things occasionally get in my way—mountains, precipices, rivers, and such like obstructions—is no fault of mine. My instinct is correct enough; it is the earth that is wrong. I led them by the middle road. That the middle road had not character enough to continue for any quarter of a mile in the same direction; that after three miles up and down hill it ended abruptly in a wasps' nest, was not a thing that should have been laid to my door. If the middle road had gone in the direction it ought to have done, it would have taken us to where we wanted to go, of that I am convinced.

Even as it was, I would have continued to use this gift of mine to discover a fresh way had a proper spirit been displayed towards me. But I am not an angel— I admit this frankly,—and I decline to exert myself for the ungrateful and the ribald. Besides, I doubt if George and Harris would have followed me further in any event. Therefore it was that I washed my hands of the whole affair, and that Harris entered upon the vacancy.

"Well," said Harris. "I suppose you are satisfied with what you have done?"

"I am quite satisfied," I replied from the heap of stones where I was sitting. "So far, I have brought you with safety. I would continue to lead you further, but no artist can work without encouragement. You appear dissatisfied with me because you do not know where you are. For all you know, you may be just where you want to be. But I say nothing as to that; I expect no thanks. Go your own way; I have done with you both."

I spoke, perhaps, with bitterness, but I could not help it. Not a word of kindness had I had all the weary way.

"Do not misunderstand us," said Harris; "both George and myself feel that without your assistance we should never be where we now are. For that we give you every credit. But instinct is liable to error. What I propose to do is to substitute for it Science, which is exact. Now, where's the sun?"

"Don't you think," said George, "that if we made our way back to the village, and hired a boy for a mark to guide us, it would save time in the end?"

"It would be wasting hours," said Harris, with decision. "You leave this to me. I have been reading about this thing, and it has interested me." He took out his watch, and began turning himself round and round.

"It's as simple as A B C," he continued. "You point the short hand at the sun, then you bisect the segment between the short hand and the twelve, and thus you get the north."

He worried up and down for a while, then he fixed it.

"Now I've got it," he said; "that's the north, where that wasps' nest is. Now give me the map."

We handed it to him, and seating himself facing the wasps, he examined it.

"Todtmoos from here," he said, "is south by south-west."

"How do you mean, from here?" asked George.

"Why, from here, where we are," returned Harris.

"But where are we?" said George.

This worried Harris for a time, but at length he cheered up.

"It doesn't matter where we are," he said. "Wherever we are, Todtmoos is south by south-west. Come on, we are only wasting time."

"I don't quite see how you make it out," said George, as he rose and shouldered his knapsack; "but I suppose it doesn't matter. We are out for our health, and it's all pretty!"

"We shall be all right," said Harris, with cheery confidence. "We shall be in at Todtmoos before ten, don't you worry. And at Todtmoos we will have something to eat."

He said that he, himself, fancied a beefsteak, followed by an omelette. George said that, personally, he intended to keep his mind off the subject until he saw Todtmoos.

We walked for half an hour, then emerging upon an opening, we saw below us, about two miles away, the village through which we had passed that morning. It had a quaint church with an outside staircase, a somewhat unusual arrangement.

The sight of it made me sad. We had been walking hard for three hours and a half, and had accomplished, apparently, about four miles. But Harris was delighted.

"Now, at last," said Harris, "we know where we are."

"I thought you said it didn't matter," George reminded him.

"No more it does, practically," replied Harris, "but it is just as well to be certain. Now I feel more confidence in myself."

"I'm not so sure about that being an advantage," muttered George. But I do not think Harris heard him.

"We are now," continued Harris, "east of the sun, and Todtmoos is south-west of where we are. So that if—"

He broke off. "By-the-by," he said, "do you remember whether I said the bisecting line of that segment pointed to the north or to the south?"

"You said it pointed to the north," replied George.

"Are you positive?" persisted Harris.

"Positive," answered George "but don't let that influence your calculations. In all probability you were wrong."

Harris thought for a while; then his brow cleared.

"That's all right," he said; "of course, it's the north. It must be the north. How could it be the south? Now we must make for the west. Come on."

"I am quite willing to make for the west," said George; "any point of the compass is the same to me. I only wish to remark that, at the present moment, we are going dead east."

"No we are not," returned Harris; "we are going west."

"We are going east, I tell you," said George.

"I wish you wouldn't keep saying that," said Harris, "you confuse me."

"I don't mind if I do," returned George; "I would rather do that than go wrong. I tell you we are going dead east."

"What nonsense!" retorted Harris; "there's the sun."

"I can see the sun," answered George, "quite distinctly. It may be where it ought to be, according to you and Science, or it may not. All I know is, that when we were down in the village, that particular hill with that particular lump of rock upon it was due north of us. At the present moment we are facing due east."

"You are quite right," said Harris; "I forgot for the moment that we had turned round."

"I should get into the habit of making a note of it, if I were you," grumbled George; "it's a manoeuvre that will probably occur again more than once."

We faced about, and walked in the other direction. At the end of forty minutes' climbing we again emerged upon an opening, and again the village lay just under our feet. On this occasion it was south of us.

"This is very extraordinary," said Harris.

"I see nothing remarkable about it," said George. "If you walk steadily round a village it is only natural that now and then you get a glimpse of it. Myself, I am glad to see it. It proves to me that we are not utterly lost."

"It ought to be the other side of us," said Harris.

"It will be in another hour or so," said George, "if we keep on."

I said little myself; I was vexed with both of them; but I was glad to notice George evidently growing cross with Harris. It was absurd of Harris to fancy he could find the way by the sun.

"I wish I knew," said Harris, thoughtfully, "for certain whether that bisecting line points to the north or to the south."

"I should make up my mind about it," said George; "it's an important point."

"It's impossible it can be the north," said Harris, "and I'll tell you why."

"You needn't trouble," said George; "I am quite prepared to believe it isn't."

"You said just now it was," said Harris, reproachfully.

"I said nothing of the sort," retorted George. "I said you said it was—a very different thing. If you think it isn't, let's go the other way. It'll be a change, at all events."

So Harris worked things out according to the contrary calculation, and again we plunged into the wood; and again after half an hour's stiff climbing we came in view of that same village. True, we were a little higher, and this time it lay between us and the sun.

"I think," said George, as he stood looking down at it, "this is the best view we've had of it, as yet. There is only one other point from which we can see it. After that, I propose we go down into it and get some rest."

"I don't believe it's the same village," said Harris; "it can't be."

"There's no mistaking that church," said George. "But maybe it is a case on all fours with that Prague statue. Possibly, the authorities hereabout have had made some life-sized models of that village, and have stuck them about the Forest to see where the thing would look best. Anyhow, which way do we go now?"

"I don't know," said Harris, "and I don't care. I have done my best; you've done nothing but grumble, and confuse me."

"I may have been critical," admitted George "but look at the thing from my point of view. One of you says he's got an instinct, and leads me to a wasps' nest in the middle of a wood."

"I can't help wasps building in a wood," I replied.

"I don't say you can," answered George. "I am not arguing; I am merely stating incontrovertible facts. The other one, who leads me up and down hill for hours on scientific principles, doesn't know the north from the south, and is never quite sure whether he's turned round or whether he hasn't. Personally, I profess to no instincts beyond the ordinary, nor am I a scientist. But two fields off I can see a man. I am going to offer him the worth of the hay he is cutting, which I estimate at one mark fifty pfennig, to leave his work, and lead me to within sight of Todtmoos. If you two fellows like to follow, you can. If not, you can start another system and work it out by yourselves."

George's plan lacked both originality and aplomb, but at the moment it appealed to us. Fortunately, we had worked round to a very short distance away from the spot where we had originally gone wrong; with the result that, aided by the gentleman of the scythe, we recovered the road, and reached Todtmoos four hours later than we had calculated to reach it, with an appetite that took forty-five minutes' steady work in silence to abate.

From Todtmoos we had intended to walk down to the Rhine; but having regard to our extra exertions of the morning, we decided to promenade in a carriage, as the French would say: and for this purpose hired a picturesque-looking vehicle, drawn by a horse that I should have called barrel-bodied but for contrast with his driver, in comparison with whom he was angular. In Germany every vehicle is arranged for a pair of horses, but drawn generally by one. This gives to the equipage a lop-sided appearance, according to our notions, but it is held here to indicate style. The idea to be conveyed is that you usually drive a pair of horses, but that for the moment you have mislaid the other one. The German driver is not what we should call a first-class whip. He is at his best when he is asleep. Then, at all events, he is harmless; and the horse being, generally speaking, intelligent and experienced, progress under these conditions is comparatively safe. If in Germany they could only train the horse to collect the money at the end of the journey, there would be no need for a coachman at all. This would be a distinct relief to the passenger, for when the German coachman is awake and not cracking his whip he is generally occupied in getting himself into trouble or out of it. He is better at the former. Once I recollect driving down a steep Black Forest hill with a couple of ladies. It was one of those roads winding corkscrew-wise down the slope. The hill rose at an angle of seventy-five on the off-side, and fell away at an angle of seventy-five on the near-side. We were proceeding very comfortably, the driver, we were happy to notice, with his eyes shut, when suddenly something, a bad dream or indigestion, awoke him. He seized the reins, and, by an adroit movement, pulled the near-side horse over the edge, where it clung, half supported by the traces. Our driver did not appear in the least annoyed or surprised; both horses, I also, noticed, seemed equally used to the situation. We got out, and he got down. He took from under the seat a huge clasp-knife, evidently kept there for the purpose, and deftly cut the traces. The horse, thus released, rolled over and over until he struck the road again some fifty feet below. There he regained his feet and stood waiting for us. We re-entered the carriage and descended with the single horse until we came to him. There, with the help of some bits of string, our driver harnessed him again, and we continued on our way. What impressed me was the evident accustomedness of both driver and horses to this method of working down a hill.

Evidently to them it appeared a short and convenient cut. I should not have been surprised had the man suggested our strapping ourselves in, and then rolling over and over, carriage and all, to the bottom.

Another peculiarity of the German coachman is that he never attempts to pull in or to pull up. He regulates his rate of speed, not by the pace of the horse, but by manipulation of the brake. For eight miles an hour he puts it on slightly, so that it only scrapes the wheel, producing a continuous sound as of the sharpening of a saw; for four miles an hour he screws it down harder, and you travel to an accompaniment of groans and shrieks, suggestive of a symphony of dying pigs. When he desires to come to a full stop, he puts it on to its full. If his brake be a good one, he calculates he can stop his carriage, unless the horse be an extra powerful animal, in less than twice its own length. Neither the German driver nor the German horse knows, apparently, that you can stop a carriage by any other method. The German horse continues to pull with his full strength until he finds it impossible to move the vehicle another inch; then he rests. Horses of other countries are quite willing to stop when the idea is suggested to them. I have known horses content to go even quite slowly. But your German horse, seemingly, is built for one particular speed, and is unable to depart from it. I am stating nothing but the literal, unadorned truth, when I say I have seen a German coachman, with the reins lying loose over the splash-board, working his brake with both hands, in terror lest he would not be in time to avoid a collision.

At Waldshut, one of those little sixteenth-century towns through which the Rhine flows during its earlier course, we came across that exceedingly common object of the Continent: the travelling Briton grieved and surprised at the unacquaintance of the foreigner with the subtleties of the English language. When we entered the station he was, in very fair English, though with a slight Somersetshire accent, explaining to a porter for the tenth time, as he informed us, the simple fact that though he himself had a ticket for Donaueschingen, and wanted to go to Donaueschingen, to see the source of the Danube, which is not there, though they tell you it is, he wished his bicycle to be sent on to Engen and his bag to Constance, there to await his arrival. He was hot and angry with the effort of the thing. The porter was a young man in years, but at the moment looked old and miserable. I offered my services. I wish now I had not—though not so fervently, I expect, as he, the speechless one, came subsequently to wish this. All three routes, so the porter explained to us, were complicated, necessitating changing and rechanging. There was not much time for calm elucidation, as our own train was starting in a few minutes. The man himself was voluble—always a mistake when anything entangled has to be made clear; while the porter was only too eager to get the job done with and so breathe again. It dawned upon me ten minutes later, when thinking the matter over in the train, that though I had agreed with the porter that it would be best for the bicycle to go by way of Immendingen, and had agreed to his booking it to Immendingen, I had neglected to give instructions for its departure from Immendingen. Were I of a despondent temperament I should be worrying myself at the present moment with the reflection that in all probability that bicycle is still at Immendingen to this day. But I regard it as good philosophy to endeavour always to see the brighter side of things. Possibly the porter corrected my omission on his own account, or some simple miracle may have happened to restore that bicycle to its owner some time before the end of his tour. The bag we sent to Radolfzell: but here I console myself with the recollection that it was labelled Constance; and no doubt after a while the railway authorities, finding it unclaimed at Radolfzell, forwarded it on to Constance.

But all this is apart from the moral I wished to draw from the incident. The true inwardness of the situation lay in the indignation of this Britisher at finding a German railway porter unable to comprehend English. The moment we spoke to him he expressed this indignation in no measured terms.

"Thank you very much indeed," he said; "it's simple enough. I want to go to Donaueschingen myself by train; from Donaueschingen I am going to walk to Geisengen; from Geisengen I am going to take the train to Engen, and from Engen I am going to bicycle to Constance. But I don't want to take my bag with me; I want to find it at Constance when I get there. I have been trying to explain the thing to this fool for the last ten minutes; but I can't get it into him."

"It is very disgraceful," I agreed. "Some of these German workmen know hardly any other language than their own."

"I have gone over it with him," continued the man, "on the time table, and explained it by pantomime. Even then I could not knock it into him."

"I can hardly believe you," I again remarked; "you would think the thing explained itself."

Harris was angry with the man; he wished to reprove him for his folly in journeying through the outlying portions of a foreign clime, and seeking in such to accomplish complicated railway tricks without knowing a word of the language of the country. But I checked the impulsiveness of Harris, and pointed out to him the great and good work at which the man was unconsciously assisting.

Shakespeare and Milton may have done their little best to spread acquaintance with the English tongue among the less favoured inhabitants of Europe. Newton and Darwin may have rendered their language a necessity among educated and thoughtful foreigners. Dickens and Ouida (for your folk who imagine that the literary world is bounded by the prejudices of New Grub Street, would be surprised and grieved at the position occupied abroad by this at-home-sneered-at lady) may have helped still further to popularise it. But the man who has spread the knowledge of English from Cape St. Vincent to the Ural Mountains is the Englishman who, unable or unwilling to learn a single word of any language but his own, travels purse in hand into every corner of the Continent. One may be shocked at his ignorance, annoyed at his stupidity, angry at his presumption. But the practical fact remains; he it is that is anglicising Europe. For him the Swiss peasant tramps through the snow on winter evenings to attend the English class open in every village. For him the coachman and the guard, the chambermaid and the laundress, pore over their English grammars and colloquial phrase books. For him the foreign shopkeeper and merchant send their sons and daughters in their thousands to study in every English town. For him it is that every foreign hotel- and restaurant-keeper adds to his advertisement: "Only those with fair knowledge of English need apply."

Did the English-speaking races make it their rule to speak anything else than English, the marvellous progress of the English tongue throughout the world would stop. The English-speaking man stands amid the strangers and jingles his gold.

"Here," cries, "is payment for all such as can speak English."

He it is who is the great educator. Theoretically we may scold him; practically we should take our hats off to him. He is the missionary of the English tongue.

CHAPTER XII

We are grieved at the earthly instincts of the German—A superb view, but no restaurant—Continental opinion of the Englishman—That he does not know enough to come in out of the rain—There comes a weary traveller with a brick— The hurting of the dog—An undesirable family residence— A fruitful region—A merry old soul comes up the hill— George, alarmed at the lateness of the hour, hastens down the other side—Harris follows him, to show him the way—I hate being alone, and follow Harris—Pronunciation special- ly designed for use of foreigners.

A thing that vexes much the high-class Anglo-Saxon soul is the earthly instinct prompting the German to fix a restaurant at the goal of every excursion. On mountain summit, in fairy glen, on lonely pass, by waterfall or winding stream, stands ever the busy Wirtschaft. How can one rhapsodise over a view when surrounded by beer-stained tables? How lose one's self in historical reverie amid the odour of roast veal and spinach?

One day, on elevating thoughts intent, we climbed through tangled woods.

"And at the top," said Harris, bitterly, as we paused to breathe a space and pull our belts a hole tighter, "there will be a gaudy restaurant, where people will be guzzling beefsteaks and plum tarts and drinking white wine."

"Do you think so?" said George.

"Sure to be," answered Harris; "you know their way. Not one grove will they consent to dedicate to solitude and contemplation; not one height will they leave to the lover of nature unpolluted by the gross and the material."

"I calculate," I remarked, "that we shall be there a little before one o'clock, provided we don't dawdle."

"The 'mittagstisch' will be just ready," groaned Harris, "with possibly some of those little blue trout they catch about here. In Germany one never seems able to get away from food and drink. It is maddening!"

We pushed on, and in the beauty of the walk forgot our indignation. My estimate proved to be correct.

At a quarter to one, said Harris, who was leading:

"Here we are; I can see the summit."

"Any sign of that restaurant?" said George.

"I don't notice it," replied Harris; "but it's there, you may be sure; confound it!"

Five minutes later we stood upon the top. We looked north, south, east and west; then we looked at one another.

"Grand view, isn't it?" said Harris.

"Magnificent," I agreed.

"Superb," remarked George.

"They have had the good sense for once," said Harris, "to put that restaurant out of sight."

"They do seem to have hidden it," said George. "One doesn't mind the thing so much when it is not forced under one's nose," said Harris.

"Of course, in its place," I observed, "a restaurant is right enough."

"I should like to know where they have put it," said George.

"Suppose we look for it?" said Harris, with inspiration.

It seemed a good idea. I felt curious myself. We agreed to explore in different directions, returning to the summit to report progress. In half an hour we stood together once again. There was no need for words. The face of one and all of us announced plainly that at last we had discovered a recess of German nature untarnished by the sordid suggestion of food or drink.

"I should never have believed it possible," said Harris: "would you?"

"I should say," I replied, "that this is the only square quarter of a mile in the entire Fatherland unprovided with one."

"And we three strangers have struck it," said George, "without an effort."

"True," I observed. "By pure good fortune we are now enabled to feast our finer senses undisturbed by appeal to our lower nature. Observe the light upon those distant peaks; is it not ravishing?"

"Talking of nature," said George, "which should you say was the nearest way down?"

"The road to the left," I replied, after consulting the guide book, "takes us to Sonnensteig—where, by-the-by, I observe the 'Goldener Adler' is well spoken of—in about two hours. The road to the right, though somewhat longer, commands more extensive prospects."

"One prospect," said Harris, "is very much like another prospect; don't you think so?"

"Personally," said George, "I am going by the left-hand road." And Harris and I went after him.

But we were not to get down so soon as we had anticipated. Storms come quickly in these regions, and before we had walked for quarter of an hour it became a question of seeking shelter or living for the rest of the day in soaked clothes. We decided on the former alternative, and selected a tree that, under ordinary circumstances, should have been ample protection. But a Black Forest thunderstorm is not an ordinary circumstance. We consoled ourselves at first by telling each other that at such a rate it could not last long. Next, we endeavoured to comfort ourselves with the reflection that if it did we should soon be too wet to fear getting wetter.

"As it turned out," said Harris, "I should have been almost glad if there had been a restaurant up here."

"I see no advantage in being both wet *and* hungry," said George. "I shall give it another five minutes, then I am going on."

"These mountain solitudes," I remarked, "are very attractive in fine weather. On a rainy day, especially if you happen to be past the age when—"

At this point there hailed us a voice, proceeding from a stout gentleman, who stood some fifty feet away from us under a big umbrella.

"Won't you come inside?" asked the stout gentleman.

"Inside where?" I called back. I thought at first he was one of those fools that will try to be funny when there is nothing to be funny about.

"Inside the restaurant," he answered.

We left our shelter and made for him. We wished for further information about this thing.

"I did call to you from the window," said the stout gentleman, as we drew near to him, "but I suppose you did not hear me. This storm may last for another hour; you will get *so* wet."

He was a kindly old gentleman; he seemed quite anxious about us.

I said: "It is very kind of you to have come out. We are not lunatics. We have not been standing under that tree for the last half-hour knowing all the time there was a restaurant, hidden by the trees, within twenty yards of us. We had no idea we were anywhere near a restaurant."

"I thought maybe you hadn't," said the old gentleman; "that is why I came."

It appeared that all the people in the inn had been watching us from the windows also, wondering why we stood there looking miserable. If it had not been for this nice old gentleman the fools would have remained watching us, I suppose, for the rest of the afternoon. The landlord excused himself by saying he thought we looked like English. It is no figure of speech. On the Continent they do sincerely believe that every Englishman is mad. They are as convinced of it as is every English peasant that Frenchmen live on frogs. Even when one makes a direct personal effort to disabuse them of the impression one is not always successful.

It was a comfortable little restaurant, where they cooked well, while the Tischwein was really most passable. We stopped there for a couple of hours, and dried ourselves and fed ourselves, and talked about the view; and just before we left an incident occurred that shows how much more stirring in this world are the influences of evil compared with those of good.

A traveller entered. He seemed a careworn man. He carried a brick in his hand, tied to a piece of rope. He entered nervously and hurriedly, closed the door carefully behind him, saw to it that it was fastened, peered out of the window long and earnestly, and then, with a sigh of relief, laid his brick upon the bench beside him and called for food and drink.

There was something mysterious about the whole affair. One wondered what he was going to do with the brick, why he had closed the door so carefully, why he had looked so anxiously from the window; but his aspect was too wretched to invite conversation, and we forbore, therefore, to ask him questions. As he ate and drank he grew more cheerful, sighed less often. Later he stretched his legs, lit an evil-smelling cigar, and puffed in calm contentment.

Then it happened. It happened too suddenly for any detailed explanation of the thing to be possible. I recollect a Fräulein entering the room from the kitchen with a pan in her hand. I saw her cross to the outer door. The next moment the whole room was in an uproar. One was reminded of those pantomime transformation scenes where, from among floating clouds, slow music, waving flowers, and reclining fairies, one is suddenly transported into the midst of shouting policemen tumbling yelling babies, swells fighting pantaloons, sausages and harlequins, buttered slides and clowns. As the Fräulein of the pan touched the door it flew open, as though all the spirits of sin had been pressed against it, waiting. Two pigs and a chicken rushed into the room; a cat that had been sleeping on a beer-barrel spluttered into fiery life. The Fräulein threw her pan into the air and lay down on the floor. The gentleman with the brick sprang to his feet, upsetting the table before him with everything upon it.

One looked to see the cause of this disaster: one discovered it at once in the person of a mongrel terrier with pointed ears and a squirrel's tail. The landlord rushed out from another door, and attempted to kick him out of the room. Instead, he kicked one of the pigs, the fatter of the two. It was a vigorous, well-planted kick, and the pig got the whole of it; none of it was wasted. One felt sorry for the poor animal; but no amount of sorrow anyone else might feel for him could compare with the sorrow he felt for himself. He stopped running about; he sat down in the middle of the room, and appealed to the solar system generally to observe this unjust thing that had come upon him. They must have heard his complaint in the valleys round about, and have wondered what upheaval of nature was taking place among the hills.

As for the hen it scuttled, screaming, every way at once. It was a marvellous bird: it seemed to be able to run up a straight wall quite easily; and it and the cat between them fetched down mostly everything that was not already on the floor. In less than forty seconds there were nine people in that room, all trying to kick one dog. Possibly, now and again, one or another may have succeeded, for occasionally the dog would stop barking in order to howl. But it did not discourage him. Everything has to be paid for, he evidently argued, even a pig and chicken hunt; and, on the whole, the game was worth it.

Besides, he had the satisfaction of observing that, for every kick he received, most other living things in the room got two. As for the unfortunate pig—the stationary one, the one that still sat lamenting in the centre of the room—he must have averaged a steady four. Trying to kick this dog was like playing football with a ball that was never there—not when you went to kick it, but after you had started to kick it, and had gone too far to stop yourself, so that the kick had to go on in any case, your only hope being that your foot would find something or another solid to stop it, and so save you from sitting down on the floor noisily and completely. When anybody did kick the dog it was by pure accident, when they were not expecting to kick him; and, generally speaking, this took them so unawares that, after kicking him, they fell over him. And everybody, every half-minute, would be certain to fall over the pig the sitting pig, the one incapable of getting out of anybody's way.

How long the scrimmage might have lasted it is impossible to say. It was ended by the judgment of George. For a while he had been seeking to catch, not the dog but the remaining pig, the one still capable of activity. Cornering it at last, he persuaded it to cease running round and round the room, and instead to take a spin outside. It shot through the door with one long wail.

We always desire the thing we have not. One pig, a chicken, nine people, and a cat, were as nothing in that dog's opinion compared with the quarry that was disappearing. Unwisely, he darted after it, and George closed the door upon him and shot the bolt.

Then the landlord stood up, and surveyed all the things that were lying on the floor.

"That's a playful dog of yours," said he to the man who had come in with the brick.

"He is not my dog," replied the man sullenly.

"Whose dog is it then?" said the landlord.

"I don't know whose dog it is," answered the man.

"That won't do for me, you know," said the landlord, picking up a picture of the German Emperor, and wiping beer from it with his sleeve.

"I know it won't," replied the man; "I never expected it would. I'm tired of telling people it isn't my dog. They none of them believe me."

"What do you want to go about with him for, if he's not your dog?" said the landlord. "What's the attraction about him?"

"I don't go about with him," replied the man; "he goes about with me. He picked me up this morning at ten o'clock, and he won't leave me. I thought I had got rid of him when I came in here. I left him busy killing a duck more than a quarter of an hour away. I'll have to pay for that, I expect, on my way back."

"Have you tried throwing stones at him?" asked Harris.

"Have I tried throwing stones at him!" replied the man, contemptuously. "I've been throwing stones at him till my arm aches with throwing stones; and he thinks it's a game, and brings them back to me. I've been carrying this beastly brick about with me for over an hour, in the hope of being able to drown him, but he never comes near enough for me to get hold of him. He just sits six inches out of reach with his mouth open, and looks at me."

"It's the funniest story I've heard for a long while," said the landlord.

"Glad it amuses somebody," said the man.

We left him helping the landlord to pick up the broken things, and went our way. A dozen yards outside the door the faithful animal was waiting for his friend. He looked tired, but contented. He was evidently a dog of strange and sudden fancies, and we feared for the moment lest he might take a liking to us. But he let us pass with indifference. His loyalty to this unresponsive man was touching; and we made no attempt to undermine it.

Having completed to our satisfaction the Black Forest, we journeyed on our wheels through Alt Breisach and Colmar to Münster; whence we started a short exploration of the Vosges range, where, according to the present German Emperor, humanity stops. Of old, Alt Breisach, a rocky fortress with the river now on one side of it and now on the other—for in its inexperienced youth the Rhine never seems to have been quite sure of its way,—must, as a place of residence, have appealed exclusively to the lover of change and excitement. Whoever the war was between, and whatever it was about, Alt Breisach was bound to be in it. Everybody besieged it, most people captured it; the majority of them lost it again; nobody seemed able to keep it. Whom he belonged to, and what he was, the dweller in Alt Breisach could never have been quite sure. One day he would be a Frenchman, and then before he could learn enough French to pay his taxes he would be an Austrian. While trying to discover what you did in order to be a good Austrian, he would find he was no longer an Austrian, but a German, though what particular German out of the dozen must always have been doubtful to him. One day he would discover that he was a Catholic, the next an ardent Protestant. The only thing that could have given any stability to his existence must have been the monotonous necessity of paying heavily for the privilege of being whatever for the moment he was. But when one begins to think of these things one finds oneself wondering why anybody in the Middle Ages, except kings and tax collectors, ever took the trouble to live at all.

For variety and beauty, the Vosges will not compare with the hills of the Schwarzwald. The advantage about them from the tourist's point of view is their superior poverty. The Vosges peasant has not the unromantic air of contented prosperity that spoils his *vis-a-vis* across the Rhine. The villages and farms possess more the charm of decay. Another point wherein the Vosges district excels is its ruins. Many of its numerous castles are perched where you might think only eagles would care to build. In others, commenced by the Romans and finished by the Troubadours, covering acres with the maze of their still standing walls, one may wander for hours.

The fruiterer and greengrocer is a person unknown in the Vosges. Most things of that kind grow wild, and are to be had for the picking. It is difficult to keep to any programme when walking through the Vosges, the temptation on a hot day to stop and eat fruit generally being too strong for resistance. Raspberries, the most delicious I have ever tasted, wild strawberries, currants, and gooseberries, grow upon the hill-sides as black-berries by English lanes. The Vosges small boy is not called upon to rob an orchard; he can make himself ill without sin. Orchards exist in the Vosges mountains in plenty; but to trespass into one for the purpose of stealing fruit would be as foolish as for a fish to try and get into a swimming bath without paying. Still, of course, mistakes do occur.

One afternoon in the course of a climb we emerged upon a plateau, where we lingered perhaps too long, eating more fruit than may have been good for us; it was so plentiful around us, so varied. We commenced with a few late strawberries, and from those we passed to raspberries. Then Harris found a greengage-tree with some early fruit upon it, just perfect.

"This is about the best thing we have struck," said George; "we had better make the most of this." Which was good advice, on the face of it.

"It is a pity," said Harris, "that the pears are still so hard."

He grieved about this for a while, but later on came across some remarkably fine yellow plums and these consoled him somewhat.

"I suppose we are still a bit too far north for pineapples," said George. "I feel I could just enjoy a fresh pineapple. This commonplace fruit palls upon one after a while."

"Too much bush fruit and not enough tree, is the fault I find," said Harris. "Myself, I should have liked a few more greengages."

"Here is a man coming up the hill," I observed, "who looks like a native. Maybe, he will know where we can find some more greengages."

"He walks well for an old chap," remarked Harris.

He certainly was climbing the hill at a remarkable pace. Also, so far as we were able to judge at that distance, he appeared to be in a remarkably cheerful mood, singing and shouting at the top of his voice, gesticulating, and waving his arms.

"What a merry old soul it is," said Harris; "it does one good to watch him. But why does he carry his stick over his shoulder? Why doesn't he use it to help him up the hill?"

"Do you know, I don't think it is a stick," said George.

"What can it be, then?" asked Harris.

"Well, it looks to me," said George, "more like a gun."

"You don't think we can have made a mistake?" suggested Harris. "You don't think this can be anything in the nature of a private orchard?"

I said: "Do you remember the sad thing that happened in the South of France some two years ago? A soldier picked some cherries as he passed a house, and the French peasant to whom the cherries belonged came out, and without a word of warning shot him dead."

"But surely you are not allowed to shoot a man dead for picking fruit, even in France?" said George.

"Of course not," I answered. "It was quite illegal. The only excuse offered by his counsel was that he was of a highly excitable disposition, and especially keen about these particular cherries."

"I recollect something about the case," said Harris, "now you mention it. I believe the district in which it happened—the 'Commune,' as I think it is called—had to pay heavy compensation to the relatives of the deceased soldier; which was only fair."

George said: "I am tired of this place. Besides, it's getting late."

Harris said: "If he goes at that rate he will fall and hurt himself. Besides, I don't believe he knows the way."

I felt lonesome up there all by myself, with nobody to speak to. Besides, not since I was a boy, I reflected, had I enjoyed a run down a really steep hill. I thought I would see if I could revive the sensation. It is a jerky exercise, but good, I should say, for the liver.

We slept that night at Barr, a pleasant little town on the way to St. Ottilienberg, an interesting old convent among the mountains, where you are waited upon by real nuns, and your bill made out by a priest. At Barr, just before supper a tourist entered. He looked English, but spoke a language the like of which I have never heard before. Yet it was an elegant and fine-sounding language. The landlord stared at him blankly; the landlady shook her head. He sighed, and tried another, which somehow recalled to me forgotten memories, though, at the time, I could not fix it. But again nobody understood him.

"This is damnable," he said aloud to himself.

"Ah, you are English!" exclaimed the landlord, brightening up.

"And Monsieur looks tired," added the bright little landlady. "Monsieur will have supper."

They both spoke English excellently, nearly as well as they spoke French and German; and they bustled about and made him comfortable. At supper he sat next to me, and I talked to him.

"Tell me," I said—I was curious on the subject—"what language was it you spoke when you first came in?"

"German," he explained.

"Oh," I replied, "I beg your pardon."

"You did not understand it?" he continued.

"It must have been my fault," I answered; "my knowledge is extremely limited. One picks up a little here and there as one goes about, but of course that is a different thing."

"But *they* did not understand it," he replied, "the landlord and his wife; and it is their own language."

"I do not think so," I said. "The children hereabout speak German, it is true, and our landlord and landlady know German to a certain point. But throughout Alsace and Lorraine the old people still talk French."

"And I spoke to them in French also," he added, "and they understood that no better."

"It is certainly very curious," I agreed.

"It is more than curious," he replied; "in my case it is incomprehensible. I possess a diploma for modern languages. I won my scholarship purely on the strength of my French and German. The correctness of my construction, the purity of my pronunciation, was considered at my college to be quite remarkable. Yet, when I come abroad hardly anybody understands a word I say. Can you explain it?"

"I think I can," I replied. "Your pronunciation is too faultless. You remember what the Scotsman said when for the first time in his life he tasted real whisky: 'It may be puir, but I canna drink it'; so it is with your German. It strikes one less as a language than as an exhibition. If I might offer advice, I should say: Mispronounce as much as possible, and throw in as many mistakes as you can think of."

It is the same everywhere. Each country keeps a special pronunciation exclusively for the use of foreigners—a pronunciation they never dream of using themselves, that they cannot understand when it is used. I once heard an English lady explaining to a Frenchman how to pronounce the word Have.

"You will pronounce it," said the lady reproachfully, "as if it were spelt H-a-v. It isn't. There is an 'e' at the end."

"But I thought," said the pupil, "that you did not sound the 'e' at the end of h-a-v-e."

"No more you do," explained his teacher. "It is what we call a mute 'e'; but it exercises a modifying influence on the preceding vowel."

Before that, he used to say "have" quite intelligently. Afterwards, when he came to the word he would stop dead, collect his thoughts, and give expression to a sound that only the context could explain.

Putting aside the sufferings of the early martyrs, few men, I suppose, have gone through more than I myself went through in trying to I attain the correct pronunciation of the German word for church—"Kirche." Long before I had done with it I had determined never to go to church in Germany, rather than be bothered with it.

"No, no," my teacher would explain—he was a painstaking gentleman; "you say it as if it were spelt K-i-r-c-h-k-e. There is no k. It is——." And he would illustrate to me again, for the twentieth time that morning, how it should be pronounced; the sad thing being that I could never for the life of me detect any difference between the way he said it and the way I said it. So he would try a new method.

"You say it from your throat," he would explain. He was quite right; I did. "I want you to say it from down here," and with a fat forefinger he would indicate the region from where I was to start. After painful efforts, resulting in sounds suggestive of anything rather than a place of worship, I would excuse myself.

"I really fear it is impossible," I would say. "You see, for years I have always talked with my mouth, as it were; I never knew a man could talk with his stomach. I doubt if it is not too late now for me to learn."

By spending hours in dark corners, and practising in silent streets, to the terror of chance passers-by, I came at last to pronounce this word correctly. My teacher was delighted with me, and until I came to Germany I was pleased with myself. In Germany I found that nobody understood what I meant by it. I never got near a church with it. I had to drop the correct pronunciation, and painstakingly go back to my first wrong pronunciation. Then they would brighten up, and tell me it was round the corner, or down the next street, as the case might be.

I also think pronunciation of a foreign tongue could be better taught than by demanding from the pupil those internal acrobatic feats that are generally impossible and always useless. This is the sort of instruction one receives:

"Press your tonsils against the underside of your larynx. Then with the convex part of the septum curved upwards so as almost—but not quite—to touch the uvula, try with the tip of your tongue to reach your thyroid. Take a deep breath, and compress your glottis. Now, without opening your lips, say 'Garoo.'"

And when you have done it they are not satisfied.

CHAPTER XIII

An examination into the character and behaviour of the German student—The German Mensur—Uses and abuses of use—Views of an impressionist—The humour of the thing—Recipe for making savages—The Jungfrau: her peculiar taste in laces—The Kneipe—How to rub a Salamander—Advice to the stranger—A story that might have ended sadly—Of two men and two wives—Together with a bachelor.

On our way home we included a German University town, being wishful to obtain an insight into the ways of student life, a curiosity that the courtesy of German friends enabled us to gratify.

The English boy plays till he is fifteen, and works thence till twenty. In Germany it is the child that works; the young man that plays. The German boy goes to school at seven o'clock in the summer, at eight in the winter, and at school he studies. The result is that at sixteen he has a thorough knowledge of the classics and mathematics, knows as much history as any man compelled to belong to a political party is wise in knowing, together with a thorough grounding in modern languages. Therefore his eight College Semesters, extending over four years, are, except for the young man aiming at a professorship, unnecessarily ample. He is not a sportsman, which is a pity, for he should make good one. He plays football a little, bicycles still less; plays French billiards in stuffy cafés more. But generally speaking he, or the majority of him, lays out his time bummeling, beer drinking, and fighting. If he be the son of a wealthy father he joins a Korps—to belong to a crack Korps costs about four hundred pounds a year. If he be a middle-class young man, he enrols himself in a Burschenschaft, or a Landsmannschaft, which is a little cheaper. These companies are again broken up into smaller circles, in which attempt is made to keep to nationality. There are the Swabians, from Swabia; the Frankonians, descendants of the Franks; the Thuringians, and so forth. In practice, of course, this results as all such attempts do result—I believe half our Gordon Highlanders are Cockneys—but the picturesque object is obtained of dividing each University into some dozen or so separate companies of students, each one with its distinctive cap and colours, and, quite as important, its own particular beer hall, into which no other student wearing his colours may come.

The chief work of these student companies is to fight among themselves, or with some rival Korps or Schaft, the celebrated German Mensur.

The Mensur has been described so often and so thoroughly that I do not intend to bore my readers with any detailed account of it. I merely come forward as an impressionist, and I write purposely the impression of my first Mensur, because I believe that first impressions are more true and useful than opinions blunted by intercourse, or shaped by influence.

A Frenchman or a Spaniard will seek to persuade you that the bull-ring is an institution got up chiefly for the benefit of the bull. The horse which you imagined to be screaming with pain was only laughing at the comical appearance presented by its own inside. Your French or Spanish friend contrasts its glorious and exciting death in the ring with the cold-blooded brutality of the knacker's yard. If you do not keep a tight hold of your head, you come away with the desire to start an agitation for the inception of the bull-ring in England as an aid to chivalry. No doubt Torquemada was convinced of the humanity of the Inquisition. To a stout gentleman, suffering, perhaps, from cramp or rheumatism, an hour or so on the rack was really a physical benefit. He would rise feeling more free in his joints—more elastic, as one might say, than he had felt for years. English huntsmen regard the fox as an animal to be envied. A day's excellent sport is provided for him free of charge, during which he is the centre of attraction.

Use blinds one to everything one does not wish to see. Every third German gentleman you meet in the street still bears, and will bear to his grave, marks of the twenty to a hundred duels he has fought in his student days. The German children play at the Mensur in the nursery, rehearse it in the gymnasium. The Germans have come to persuade themselves there is no brutality in it—nothing offensive, nothing degrading. Their argument is that it schools the German youth to coolness and courage. If this could be proved, the argument, particularly in a country where every man is a soldier, would be sufficiently one-sided. But is the virtue of the prize-fighter the virtue of the soldier? One doubts it. Nerve and dash are surely of more service in the field than a temperament of unreasoning indifference as to what is happening to one. As a matter of fact, the German student would have to be possessed of much more courage not to fight. He fights not to please himself, but to satisfy a public opinion that is two hundred years behind the times.

All the Mensur does is to brutalise him. There may be skill displayed—I am told there is,—but it is not apparent. The mere fighting is like nothing so much as a broadsword combat at a Richardson's show; the display as a whole a successful attempt to combine the ludicrous with the unpleasant. In aristocratic Bonn, where style is considered, and in Heidelberg, where visitors from other nations are more common, the affair is perhaps more formal. I am told that there the contests take place in handsome rooms; that grey-haired doctors wait upon the wounded, and liveried servants upon the hungry, and that the affair is conducted throughout with a certain amount of picturesque ceremony. In the more essentially German Universities, where strangers are rare and not much encouraged, the simple essentials are the only things kept in view, and these are not of an inviting nature.

Indeed, so distinctly uninviting are they, that I strongly advise the sensitive reader to avoid even this description of them. The subject cannot be made pretty, and I do not intend to try.

The room is bare and sordid; its walls splashed with mixed stains of beer, blood, and candle-grease; its ceiling, smoky; its floor, sawdust covered. A crowd of students, laughing, smoking, talking, some sitting on the floor, others perched upon chairs and benches form the framework.

In the centre, facing one another, stand the combatants, resembling Japanese warriors, as made familiar to us by the Japanese tea-tray. Quaint and rigid, with their goggle-covered eyes, their necks tied up in comforters, their bodies smothered in what looks like dirty bed quilts, their padded arms stretched straight above their heads, they might be a pair of ungainly clockwork figures. The seconds, also more or less padded—their heads and faces protected by huge leather-peaked caps,—drag them out into their proper position. One almost listens to hear the sound of the castors. The umpire takes his place, the word is given, and immediately there follow five rapid clashes of the long straight swords. There is no interest in watching the fight: there is no movement, no skill, no grace (I am speaking of my own impressions.) The strongest man wins; the man who, with his heavily-padded arm, always in an unnatural position, can hold his huge clumsy sword longest without growing too weak to be able either to guard or to strike.

The whole interest is centred in watching the wounds. They come always in one of two places—on the top of the head or the left side of the face. Sometimes a portion of hairy scalp or section of cheek flies up into the air, to be carefully preserved in an envelope by its proud possessor, or, strictly speaking, its proud former possessor, and shown round on convivial evenings; and from every wound, of course, flows a plentiful stream of blood. It splashes doctors, seconds, and spectators; it sprinkles ceiling and walls; it saturates the fighters, and makes pools for itself in the sawdust. At the end of each round the doctors rush up, and with hands already dripping with blood press together the gaping wounds, dabbing them with little balls of wet cotton wool, which an attendant carries ready on a plate. Naturally, the moment the men stand up again and commence work, the blood gushes out again, half blinding them, and rendering the ground beneath them slippery. Now and then you see a man's teeth laid bare almost to the ear, so that for the rest of the duel he appears to be grinning at one half of the spectators, his other side, remaining serious; and sometimes a man's nose gets slit, which gives to him as he fights a singularly supercilious air.

As the object of each student is to go away from the University bearing as many scars as possible, I doubt if any particular pains are taken to guard, even to the small extent such method of fighting can allow. The real victor is he who comes out with the greatest number of wounds; he who then, stitched and patched almost to unrecognition as a human being, can promenade for the next month, the envy of the German youth, the admiration of the German maiden. He who obtains only a few unimportant wounds retires sulky and disappointed.

But the actual fighting is only the beginning of the fun. The second act of the spectacle takes place in the dressing-room. The doctors are generally mere medical students—young fellows who, having taken their degree, are anxious for practice. Truth compels me to say that those with whom I came in contact were coarse-looking men who seemed rather to relish their work. Perhaps they are not to be blamed for this. It is part of the system that as much further punishment as possible must be inflicted by the doctor, and the ideal medical man might hardly care for such job. How the student bears the dressing of his wounds is as important as how he receives them. Every operation has to be performed as brutally as may be, and his companions carefully watch him during the process to see that he goes through it with an appearance of peace and enjoyment. A clean-cut wound that gapes wide is most desired by all parties. On purpose it is sewn up clumsily, with the hope that by this means the scar will last a lifetime. Such a wound, judiciously mauled and interfered with during the week afterwards, can generally be reckoned on to secure its fortunate possessor a wife with a dowry of five figures at the least.

These are the general bi-weekly Mensurs, of which the average student fights some dozen a year. There are others to which visitors are not admitted. When a student is considered to have disgraced himself by some slight involuntary movement of the head or body while fighting, then he can only regain his position by standing up to the best swordsman in his Korps. He demands and is accorded, not a contest, but a punishment. His opponent then proceeds to inflict as many and as bloody wounds as can be taken. The object of the victim is to show his comrades that he can stand still while his head is half sliced from his skull.

Whether anything can properly be said in favour of the German Mensur I am doubtful; but if so it concerns only the two combatants. Upon the spectators it can and does, I am convinced, exercise nothing but evil. I know myself sufficiently well to be sure I am not of an unusually bloodthirsty disposition. The effect it had upon me can only be the usual effect. At first, before the actual work commenced, my sensation was curiosity mingled with anxiety as to how the sight would trouble me, though some slight acquaintance with dissecting-rooms and operating tables left me less doubt on that point than I might otherwise have felt. As the blood began to flow, and nerves and muscles to be laid bare, I experienced a mingling of disgust and pity. But with the second duel, I must confess, my finer feelings began to disappear; and by the time the third was well upon its way, and the room heavy with the curious hot odour of blood, I began, as the American expression is, to see things red.

I wanted more. I looked from face to face surrounding me, and in most of them I found reflected undoubtedly my own sensations. If it be a good thing to excite this blood thirst in the modern man, then the Mensur is a useful institution. But is it a good thing? We prate about our civilisation and humanity, but those of us who do not carry hypocrisy to the length of self-deception know that underneath our starched shirts there lurks the savage, with all his savage instincts untouched. Occasionally he may be wanted, but we never need fear his dying out. On the other hand, it seems unwise to over-nourish him.

In favour of the duel, seriously considered, there are many points to be urged. But the Mensur serves no good purpose whatever. It is childishness, and the fact of its being a cruel and brutal game makes it none the less childish. Wounds have no intrinsic value of their own; it is the cause that dignifies them, not their size. William Tell is rightly one of the heroes of the world; but what should we think of the members of a club of fathers, formed with the object of meeting twice a week to shoot apples from their sons' heads with cross-bows? These young German gentlemen could obtain all the results of which they are so proud by teasing a wild cat! To join a society for the mere purpose of getting yourself hacked about reduces a man to the intellectual level of a dancing Dervish. Travellers tell us of savages in Central Africa who express their feelings on festive occasions by jumping about and slashing themselves. But there is no need for Europe to imitate them. The Mensur is, in fact, the *reductio ad absurdum* of the duel; and if the Germans themselves cannot see that it is funny, one can only regret their lack of humour.

But though one may be unable to agree with the public opinion that supports and commands the Mensur, it at least is possible to understand. The University code that, if it does not encourage it, at least condones drunkenness, is more difficult to treat argumentatively. All German students do not get drunk; in fact, the majority are sober, if not industrious. But the minority, whose claim to be representative is freely admitted, are only saved from perpetual inebriety by ability, acquired at some cost, to swill half the day and all the night, while retaining to some extent their five senses. It does not affect all alike, but it is common in any University town to see a young man not yet twenty with the figure of a Falstaff and the complexion of a Rubens Bacchus. That the German maiden can be fascinated with a face, cut and gashed till it suggests having been made out of odd materials that never could have fitted, is a proved fact. But surely there can be no attraction about a blotched and bloated skin and a "bay window" thrown out to an extent threatening to overbalance the whole structure. Yet what else can be expected, when the youngster starts his beer-drinking with a "Fruhschoppen" at 10 a.m., and closes it with a "Kneipe" at four in the morning?

The Kneipe is what we should call a stag party, and can be very harmless or very rowdy, according to its composition. One man invites his fellow-students, a dozen or a hundred, to a café, and provides them with as much beer and as many cheap cigars as their own sense of health and comfort may dictate, or the host may be the Korps itself. Here, as everywhere, you observe the German sense of discipline and order. As each new comer enters all those sitting round the table rise, and with heels close together salute. When the table is complete, a chairman is chosen, whose duty it is to give out the number of the songs. Printed books of these songs, one to each two men, lie round the table. The chairman gives out number twenty-nine. "First verse," he cries, and away all go, each two men holding a book between them exactly as two people might hold a hymn-book in church. There is a pause at the end of each verse until the chairman starts the company on the next. As every German is a trained singer, and as most of them have fair voices, the general effect is striking.

Although the manner may be suggestive of the singing of hymns in church, the words of the songs are occasionally such as to correct this impression. But whether it be a patriotic song, a sentimental ballad, or a ditty of a nature that would shock the average young Englishman, all are sung through with stern earnestness, without a laugh, without a false note. At the end, the chairman calls "Prosit!" Everyone answers "Prosit!" and the next moment every glass is empty. The pianist rises and bows, and is bowed to in return; and then the Fräulein enters to refill the glasses.

Between the songs, toasts are proposed and responded to; but there is little cheering, and less laughter. Smiles and grave nods of approval are considered as more seeming among German students.

A particular toast, called a Salamander, accorded to some guest as a special distinction, is drunk with exceptional solemnity.

"We will now," says the chairman, "a Salamander rub" ("Einen Salamander reiben"). We all rise, and stand like a regiment at attention.

"Is the stuff prepared?" ("Sind die stoffe parat?") demands the chairman.

"Sunt," we answer, with one voice.

"Ad exercitium Salamandri," says the chairman, and we are ready.

"Eins!" We rub our glasses with a circular motion on the table.

"Zwei!" Again the glasses growl; also at "Drei!"

"Drink!" ("Bibite!")

And with mechanical unison every glass is emptied and held on high.

"Eins!" says the chairman. The foot of every empty glass twirls upon the table, producing a sound as of the dragging back of a stony beach by a receding wave.

"Zwei!" The roll swells and sinks again.

"Drei!" The glasses strike the table with a single crash, and we are in our seats again.

The sport at the Kneipe is for two students to insult each other (in play, of course), and to then challenge each other to a drinking duel. An umpire is appointed, two huge glasses are filled, and the men sit opposite each other with their hands upon the handles, all eyes fixed upon them. The umpire gives the word to go, and in an instant the beer is gurgling down their throats. The man who bangs his perfectly finished glass upon the table first is victor.

Strangers who are going through a Kneipe, and who wish to do the thing in German style, will do well, before commencing proceedings, to pin their name and address upon their coats. The German student is courtesy itself, and whatever his own state may be, he will see to it that, by some means or another, his guest gets safely home before the morning. But, of course, he cannot be expected to remember addresses.

A story was told me of three guests to a Berlin Kneipe which might have had tragic results. The strangers determined to do the thing thoroughly. They explained their intention, and were applauded, and each proceeded to write his address upon his card, and pin it to the tablecloth in front of him. That was the mistake they made. They should, as I have advised, have pinned it carefully to their coats. A man may change his place at a table, quite unconsciously he may come out the other side of it; but wherever he goes he takes his coat with him.

Some time in the small hours, the chairman suggested that to make things more comfortable for those still upright, all the gentlemen unable to keep their heads off the table should be sent home. Among those to whom the proceedings had become uninteresting were the three Englishmen. It was decided to put them into a cab in charge of a comparatively speaking sober student, and return them. Had they retained their original seats throughout the evening all would have been well; but, unfortunately, they had gone walking about, and which gentleman belonged to which card nobody knew—least of all the guests themselves. In the then state of general cheerfulness, this did not to anybody appear to much matter. There were three gentlemen and three addresses. I suppose the idea was that even if a mistake were made, the parties could be sorted out in the morning. Anyhow, the three gentlemen were put into a cab, the comparatively speaking sober student took the three cards in his hand, and the party started amid the cheers and good wishes of the company.

There is this advantage about German beer: it does not make a man drunk as the word drunk is understood in England. There is nothing objectionable about him; he is simply tired. He does not want to talk; he wants to be let alone, to go to sleep; it does not matter where—anywhere.

The conductor of the party stopped his cab at the nearest address. He took out his worst case; it was a natural instinct to get rid of that first. He and the cabman carried it upstairs, and rang the bell of the Pension. A sleepy porter answered it. They carried their burden in, and looked for a place to drop it. A bedroom door happened to be open; the room was empty; could anything be better?—they took it in there. They relieved it of such things as came off easily, and laid it in the bed. This done, both men, pleased with themselves, returned to the cab.

At the next address they stopped again. This time, in answer to their summons, a lady appeared, dressed in a tea gown, with a book in her hand. The German student looked at the top one of two cards remaining in his hand, and enquired if he had the pleasure of addressing Frau Y. It happened that he had, though so far as any pleasure was concerned that appeared to be entirely on his side. He explained to Frau Y. that the gentleman at that moment asleep against the wall was her husband. The reunion moved her to no enthusiasm; she simply opened the bedroom door, and then walked away. The cabman and the student took him in, and laid him on the bed. They did not trouble to undress him, they were feeling tired! They did not see the lady of the house again, and retired therefore without adieus.

The last card was that of a bachelor stopping at an hotel. They took their last man, therefore, to that hotel, passed him over to the night porter, and left him.

To return to the address at which the first delivery was made, what had happened there was this. Some eight hours previously had said Mr. X. to Mrs. X.: "I think I told you, my dear, that I had an invitation for this evening to what, I believe, is called a Kneipe?"

"You did mention something of the sort," replied Mrs. X. "What is a Kneipe?"

"Well, it's a sort of bachelor party, my dear, where the students meet to sing and talk and—and smoke, and all that sort of thing, you know."

"Oh, well, I hope you will enjoy yourself!" said Mrs. X., who was a nice woman and sensible.

"It will be interesting," observed Mr. X. "I have often had a curiosity to see one. I may," continued Mr. X.,—"I mean it is possible, that I may be home a little late."

"What do you call late?" asked Mrs. X.

"It is somewhat difficult to say," returned Mr. X. "You see these students, they are a wild lot, and when they get together—And then, I believe, a good many toasts are drunk. I don't know how it will affect me. If I can see an opportunity I shall come away early, that is if I can do so without giving offence; but if not—"

Said Mrs. X., who, as I remarked before, was a sensible woman: "You had better get the people here to lend you a latchkey. I shall sleep with Dolly, and then you won't disturb me whatever time it may be."

"I think that an excellent idea of yours," agreed Mr. X. "I should hate disturbing you. I shall just come in quietly, and slip into bed."

Some time in the middle of the night, or maybe towards the early morning, Dolly, who was Mrs. X.'s sister, sat up in bed and listened.

"Jenny," said Dolly, "are you awake?"

"Yes, dear," answered Mrs. X. "It's all right. You go to sleep again."

"But whatever is it?" asked Dolly. "Do you think it's fire?"

"I expect," replied Mrs. X., "that it's Percy. Very possibly he has stumbled over something in the dark. Don't you worry, dear; you go to sleep."

But so soon as Dolly had dozed off again, Mrs. X., who was a good wife, thought she would steal off softly and see to it that Percy was all right. So, putting on a dressing-gown and slippers, she crept along the passage and into her own room. To awake the gentleman on the bed would have required an earthquake. She lit a candle and stole over to the bedside.

It was not Percy; it was not anyone like Percy. She felt it was not the man that ever could have been her husband, under any circumstances. In his present condition her sentiment towards him was that of positive dislike. Her only desire was to get rid of him.

But something there was about him which seemed familiar to her. She went nearer, and took a closer view. Then she remembered. Surely it was Mr. Y., a gentleman at whose flat she and Percy had dined the day they first arrived in Berlin.

But what was he doing here? She put the candle on the table, and taking her head between her hands sat down to think. The explanation of the thing came to her with a rush. It was with this Mr. Y. that Percy had gone to the Kneipe. A mistake had been made. Mr. Y. had been brought back to Percy's address. Percy at this very moment—

The terrible possibilities of the situation swam before her. Returning to Dolly's room, she dressed herself hastily, and silently crept downstairs. Finding, fortunately, a passing night-cab, she drove to the address of Mrs. Y. Telling the man to wait, she flew upstairs and rang persistently at the bell. It was opened as before by Mrs. Y., still in her tea-gown, and with her book still in her hand.

"Mrs. X.!" exclaimed Mrs. Y. "Whatever brings you here?"

"My husband!" was all poor Mrs. X. could think to say at the moment, "is he here?"

"Mrs. X.," returned Mrs. Y., drawing herself up to her full height, "how dare you?"

"Oh, please don't misunderstand me!" pleaded Mrs. X. "It's all a terrible mistake. They must have brought poor Percy here instead of to our place, I'm sure they must. Do please look and see."

"My dear," said Mrs. Y., who was a much older woman, and more motherly, "don't excite yourself. They brought him here about half an hour ago, and, to tell you the truth, I never looked at him. He is in here. I don't think they troubled to take off even his boots. If you keep cool, we will get him downstairs and home without a soul beyond ourselves being any the wiser.

Indeed, Mrs. Y. seemed quite eager to help Mrs. X.

She pushed open the door, and Mrs. X, went in. The next moment she came out with a white, scared face.

"It isn't Percy," she said. "Whatever am I to do?"

"I wish you wouldn't make these mistakes," said Mrs. Y., moving to enter the room herself.

Mrs. X. stopped her. "And it isn't your husband either."

"Nonsense," said Mrs. Y.

"It isn't really," persisted Mrs. X. "I know, because I have just left him, asleep on Percy's bed."

"What's he doing there?" thundered Mrs. Y.

"They brought him there, and put him there," explained Mrs. X., beginning to cry. "That's what made me think Percy must be here."

The two women stood and looked at one another; and there was silence for awhile, broken only by the snoring of the gentleman the other side of the half-open door.

"Then who is that, in there?" demanded Mrs. Y., who was the first to recover herself.

"I don't know," answered Mrs. X., "I have never seen him before. Do you think it is anybody you know?"

But Mrs. Y. only banged to the door.

"What are we to do?" said Mrs. X.

"I know what *I* am going to do," said Mrs. Y. "I'm coming back with you to fetch my husband."

"He's very sleepy," explained Mrs. X.

"I've known him to be that before," replied Mrs. Y., as she fastened on her cloak.

"But where's Percy?" sobbed poor little Mrs. X., as they descended the stairs together.

"That my dear," said Mrs. Y., "will be a question for you to ask *him*."

"If they go about making mistakes like this," said Mrs. X., "it is impossible to say what they may not have done with him."

"We will make enquiries in the morning, my dear," said Mrs. Y., consolingly.

"I think these Kneipes are disgraceful affairs," said Mrs. X. "I shall never let Percy go to another, never—so long as I live."

"My dear," remarked Mrs. Y., "if you know your duty, he will never want to." And rumour has it that he never did.

But, as I have said, the mistake was in pinning the card to the tablecloth instead of to the coat. And error in this world is always severely punished.

CHAPTER XIV

Which is serious: as becomes a parting chapter—The German from the Anglo-Saxon's point of view—Providence in buttons and a helmet—Paradise of the helpless idiot—German conscience: its aggressiveness—How they hang in Germany, very possibly—What happens to good Germans when they die?—The military instinct: is it all-sufficient?—The German as a shopkeeper—How he supports life—The New Woman, here as everywhere—What can be said against the Germans, as a people—The Bummel is over and done.

"Anybody could rule this country," said George; "*I* could rule it."

We were seated in the garden of the Kaiser Hof at Bonn, looking down upon the Rhine. It was the last evening of our Bummel; the early morning train would be the beginning of the end.

"I should write down all I wanted the people to do on a piece of paper," continued George; "get a good firm to print off so many copies, have them posted about the towns and villages; and the thing would be done."

In the placid, docile German of to-day, whose only ambition appears to be to pay his taxes, and do what he is told to do by those whom it has pleased Providence to place in authority over him, it is difficult, one must confess, to detect any trace of his wild ancestor, to whom individual liberty was as the breath of his nostrils; who appointed his magistrates to advise, but retained the right of execution for the tribe; who followed his chief, but would have scorned to obey him. In Germany to-day one hears a good deal concerning Socialism, but it is a Socialism that would only be despotism under another name. Individualism makes no appeal to the German voter. He is willing, nay, anxious, to be controlled and regulated in all things. He disputes, not government, but the form of it. The policeman is to him a religion, and, one feels, will always remain so. In England we regard our man in blue as a harmless necessity. By the average citizen he is employed chiefly as a signpost, though in busy quarters of the town he is considered useful for taking old ladies across the road. Beyond feeling thankful to him for these services, I doubt if we take much thought of him. In Germany, on the other hand, he is worshipped as a little god and loved as a guardian angel. To the German child he is a combination of Santa Claus and the Bogie Man. All good things come from him: Spielplätze to play in, furnished with swings and giant-strides, sand heaps to fight around, swimming baths, and fairs. All misbehaviour is punished by him. It is the hope of every well-meaning German boy and girl to please the police. To be smiled at by a policeman makes it conceited. A German child that has been patted on the head by a policeman is not fit to live with; its self-importance is unbearable.

The German citizen is a soldier, and the policeman is his officer. The policeman directs him where in the street to walk, and how fast to walk. At the end of each bridge stands a policeman to tell the German how to cross it. Were there no policeman there, he would probably sit down and wait till the river had passed by. At the railway station the policeman locks him up in the waiting-room, where he can do no harm to himself. When the proper time arrives, he fetches him out and hands him over to the guard of the train, who is only a policeman in another uniform. The guard tells him where to sit in the train, and when to get out, and sees that he does get out. In Germany you take no responsibility upon yourself whatever. Everything is done for you, and done well. You are not supposed to look after yourself; you are not blamed for being incapable of looking after yourself; it is the duty of the German policeman to look after you. That you may be a helpless idiot does not excuse him should anything happen to you. Wherever you are and whatever you are doing you are in his charge, and he takes care of you—good care of you; there is no denying this.

If you lose yourself, he finds you; and if you lose anything belonging to you, he recovers it for you. If you don't know what you want, he tells you. If you want anything that is good for you to have, he gets it for you. Private lawyers are not needed in Germany. If you want to buy or sell a house or field, the State makes out the conveyance. If you have been swindled, the State takes up the case for you. The State marries you, insures you, will even gamble with you for a trifle.

"You get yourself born," says the German Government to the German citizen, "we do the rest. Indoors and out of doors, in sickness and in health, in pleasure and in work, we will tell you what to do, and we will see to it that you do it. Don't you worry yourself about anything."

And the German doesn't. Where there is no policeman to be found, he wanders about till he comes to a police notice posted on a wall. This he reads; then he goes and does what it says.

I remember in one German town—I forget which; it is immaterial; the incident could have happened in any—noticing an open gate leading to a garden in which a concert was being given. There was nothing to prevent anyone who chose from walking through that gate, and thus gaining admittance to the concert without paying. In fact, of the two gates quarter of a mile apart it was the more convenient. Yet of the crowds that passed, not one attempted to enter by that gate. They plodded steadily on under a blazing sun to the other gate, at which a man stood to collect the entrance money. I have seen German youngsters stand longingly by the margin of a lonely sheet of ice. They could have skated on that ice for hours, and nobody have been the wiser. The crowd and the police were at the other end, more than half a mile away, and round the corner. Nothing stopped their going on but the knowledge that they ought not. Things such as these make one pause to seriously wonder whether the Teuton be a member of the sinful human family or not. Is it not possible that these placid, gentle folk may in reality be angels, come down to earth for the sake of a glass of beer, which, as they must know, can only in Germany be obtained worth the drinking?

In Germany the country roads are lined with fruit trees. There is no voice to stay man or boy from picking and eating the fruit, except conscience. In England such a state of things would cause public indignation. Children would die of cholera by the hundred. The medical profession would be worked off its legs trying to cope with the natural results of over-indulgence in sour apples and unripe walnuts. Public opinion would demand that these fruit trees should be fenced about, and thus rendered harmless. Fruit growers, to save themselves the expense of walls and palings, would not be allowed in this manner to spread sickness and death throughout the community.

But in Germany a boy will walk for miles down a lonely road, hedged with fruit trees, to buy a pennyworth of pears in the village at the other end. To pass these unprotected fruit trees, drooping under their burden of ripe fruit, strikes the Anglo-Saxon mind as a wicked waste of opportunity, a flouting of the blessed gifts of Providence.

I do not know if it be so, but from what I have observed of the German character I should not be surprised to hear that when a man in Germany is condemned to death he is given a piece of rope, and told to go and hang himself. It would save the State much trouble and expense, and I can see that German criminal taking that piece of rope home with him, reading up carefully the police instructions, and proceeding to carry them out in his own back kitchen.

The Germans are a good people. On the whole, the best people perhaps in the world; an amiable, unselfish, kindly people. I am positive that the vast majority of them go to Heaven. Indeed, comparing them with the other Christian nations of the earth, one is forced to the conclusion that Heaven will be chiefly of German manufacture. But I cannot understand how they get there. That the soul of any single individual German has sufficient initiative to fly up by itself and knock at St. Peter's door, I cannot believe. My own opinion is that they are taken there in small companies, and passed in under the charge of a dead policeman.

Carlyle said of the Prussians, and it is true of the whole German nation, that one of their chief virtues was their power of being drilled. Of the Germans you might say they are a people who will go anywhere, and do anything, they are told. Drill him for the work and send him out to Africa or Asia under charge of somebody in uniform, and he is bound to make an excellent colonist, facing difficulties as he would face the devil himself, if ordered. But it is not easy to conceive of him as a pioneer. Left to run himself, one feels he would soon fade away and die, not from any lack of intelligence, but from sheer want of presumption.

The German has so long been the soldier of Europe, that the military instinct has entered into his blood. The military virtues he possesses in abundance; but he also suffers from the drawbacks of the military training. It was told me of a German servant, lately released from the barracks, that he was instructed by his master to deliver a letter to a certain house, and to wait there for the answer. The hours passed by, and the man did not return. His master, anxious and surprised, followed. He found the man where he had been sent, the answer in his hand. He was waiting for further orders. The story sounds exaggerated, but personally I can credit it.

The curious thing is that the same man, who as an individual is as helpless as a child, becomes, the moment he puts on the uniform, an intelligent being, capable of responsibility and initiative. The German can rule others, and be ruled by others, but he cannot rule himself. The cure would appear to be to train every German for an officer, and then put him under himself. It is certain he would order himself about with discretion and judgment, and see to it that he himself obeyed himself with smartness and precision.

For the direction of German character into these channels, the schools, of course, are chiefly responsible. Their everlasting teaching is duty. It is a fine ideal for any people; but before buckling to it, one would wish to have a clear understanding as to what this "duty" is. The German idea of it would appear to be: "blind obedience to everything in buttons." It is the antithesis of the Anglo-Saxon scheme; but as both the Anglo-Saxon and the Teuton are prospering, there must be good in both methods. Hitherto, the German has had the blessed fortune to be exceptionally well governed; if this continue, it will go well with him. When his troubles will begin will be when by any chance something goes wrong with the governing machine. But maybe his method has the advantage of producing a continuous supply of good governors; it would certainly seem so.

As a trader, I am inclined to think the German will, unless his temperament considerably change, remain always a long way behind his Anglo-Saxon competitor; and this by reason of his virtues. To him life is something more important than a mere race for wealth. A country that closes its banks and post-offices for two hours in the middle of the day, while it goes home and enjoys a comfortable meal in the bosom of its family, with, perhaps, forty winks by way of dessert, cannot hope, and possibly has no wish, to compete with a people that takes its meals standing, and sleeps with a telephone over its bed. In Germany there is not, at all events as yet, sufficient distinction between the classes to make the struggle for position the life and death affair it is in England. Beyond the landed aristocracy, whose boundaries are impregnable, grade hardly counts. Frau Professor and Frau Candlestickmaker meet at the Weekly Kaffee-Klatsch and exchange scandal on terms of mutual equality. The livery-stable keeper and the doctor hobnob together at their favourite beer hall. The wealthy master builder, when he prepares his roomy waggon for an excursion into the country, invites his foreman and his tailor to join him with their families. Each brings his share of drink and provisions, and returning home they sing in chorus the same songs. So long as this state of things endures, a man is not induced to sacrifice the best years of his life to win a fortune for his dotage. His tastes, and, more to the point still, his wife's, remain inexpensive. He likes to see his flat or villa furnished with much red plush upholstery and a profusion of gilt and lacquer. But that is his idea; and maybe it is in no worse taste than is a mixture of bastard Elizabethan with imitation Louis XV, the whole lit by electric light, and smothered with photographs. Possibly, he will have his outer walls painted by the local artist: a sanguinary battle, a good deal interfered with by the front door, taking place below, while Bismarck, as an angel, flutters vaguely about the bedroom windows. But for his Old Masters he is quite content to go to the public galleries; and "the Celebrity at Home" not having as yet taken its place amongst the institutions of the Fatherland, he is not impelled to waste his, money turning his house into an old curiosity shop.

The German is a gourmand. There are still English farmers who, while telling you that farming spells starvation, enjoy their seven solid meals a day. Once a year there comes a week's feast throughout Russia, during which many deaths occur from the over-eating of pancakes; but this is a religious festival, and an exception. Taking him all round, the German as a trencherman stands pre-eminent among the nations of the earth. He rises early, and while dressing tosses off a few cups of coffee, together with half a dozen hot buttered rolls. But it is not until ten o'clock that he sits down to anything that can properly be called a meal. At one or half-past takes place his chief dinner. Of this he makes a business, sitting at it for a couple of hours. At four o'clock he goes to the café, and eats cakes and drinks chocolate. The evening he devotes to eating generally—not a set meal, or rarely, but a series of snacks,—a bottle of beer and a Belegete-semmel or two at seven, say; another bottle of beer and an Aufschnitt at the theatre between the acts; a small bottle of white wine and a Spiegeleier before going home; then a piece of cheese or sausage, washed down by more beer, previous to turning in for the night.

But he is no gourmet. French cooks and French prices are not the rule at his restaurant. His beer or his inexpensive native white wine he prefers to the most costly clarets or champagnes. And, indeed, it is well for him he does; for one is inclined to think that every time a French grower sells a bottle of wine to a German hotel- or shop-keeper, Sedan is rankling in his mind. It is a foolish revenge, seeing that it is not the German who as a rule drinks it; the punishment falls upon some innocent travelling Englishman. Maybe, however, the French dealer remembers also Waterloo, and feels that in any event he scores.

In Germany expensive entertainments are neither offered nor expected. Everything throughout the Fatherland is homely and friendly. The German has no costly sports to pay for, no showy establishment to maintain, no purse-proud circle to dress for. His chief pleasure, a seat at the opera or concert, can be had for a few marks; and his wife and daughters walk there in home-made dresses, with shawls over their heads. Indeed, throughout the country the absence of all ostentation is to English eyes quite refreshing. Private carriages are few and far be-between, and even the droschke is made use of only when the quicker and cleaner electric car is not available.

By such means the German retains his independence. The shopkeeper in Germany does not fawn upon his customers. I accompanied an English lady once on a shopping excursion in Munich. She had been accustomed to shopping in London and New York, and she grumbled at everything the man showed her. It was not that she was really dissatisfied; this was her method. She explained that she could get most things cheaper and better elsewhere; not that she really thought she could, merely she held it good for the shopkeeper to say this. She told him that his stock lacked taste—she did not mean to be offensive; as I have explained, it was her method;—that there was no variety about it; that it was not up to date; that it was commonplace; that it looked as if it would not wear. He did not argue with her; he did not contradict her. He put the things back into their respective boxes, replaced the boxes on their respective shelves, walked into the little parlour behind the shop, and closed the door.

"Isn't he ever coming back?" asked the lady, after a couple of minutes had elapsed.

Her tone did not imply a question, so much as an exclamation of mere impatience.

"I doubt it," I replied.

"Why not?" she asked, much astonished.

"I expect," I answered, "you have bored him. In all probability he is at this moment behind that door smoking a pipe and reading the paper."

"What an extraordinary shopkeeper!" said my friend, as she gathered her parcels together and indignantly walked out.

"It is their way," I explained. "There are the goods; if you want them, you can have them. If you do not want them, they would almost rather that you did not come and talk about them."

On another occasion I listened in the smoke-room of a German hotel to a small Englishman telling a tale which, had I been in his place, I should have kept to myself.

"It doesn't do," said the little Englishman, "to try and beat a German down. They don't seem to understand it. I saw a first edition of *The Robbers* in a shop in the Georg Platz. I went in and asked the price. It was a rum old chap behind the counter. He said: 'Twenty-five marks,' and went on reading. I told him I had seen a better copy only a few days before for twenty—one talks like that when one is bargaining; it is understood. He asked me 'Where?' I told him in a shop at Leipsig. He suggested my returning there and getting it; he did not seem to care whether I bought the book or whether I didn't. I said:

"'What's the least you will take for it?'

"'I have told you once,' he answered; 'twenty-five marks.' He was an irritable old chap.

"I said: 'It's not worth it.'

"'I never said it was, did I?' he snapped.

"I said: 'I'll give you ten marks for it.' I thought, maybe, he would end by taking twenty.

"He rose. I took it he was coming round the counter to get the book out. Instead, he came straight up to me. He was a biggish sort of man. He took me by the two shoulders, walked me out into the street, and closed the door behind me with a bang. I was never more surprised in all my life.

"Maybe the book was worth twenty-five marks," I suggested.

"Of course it was," he replied; "well worth it. But what a notion of business!"

If anything change the German character, it will be the German woman. She herself is changing rapidly—advancing, as we call it. Ten years ago no German woman caring for her reputation, hoping for a husband, would have dared to ride a bicycle: to-day they spin about the country in their thousands. The old folks shake their heads at them; but the young men, I notice, overtake them and ride beside them. Not long ago it was considered unwomanly in Germany for a lady to be able to do the outside edge. Her proper skating attitude was thought to be that of clinging limpness to some male relative. Now she practises eights in a corner by herself, until some young man comes along to help her. She plays tennis, and, from a point of safety, I have even noticed her driving a dog-cart.

Brilliantly educated she always has been. At eighteen she speaks two or three languages, and has forgotten more than the average Englishwoman has ever read. Hitherto, this education has been utterly useless to her. On marriage she has retired into the kitchen, and made haste to clear her brain of everything else, in order to leave room for bad cooking. But suppose it begins to dawn upon her that a woman need not sacrifice her whole existence to household drudgery any more than a man need make himself nothing else than a business machine. Suppose she develop an ambition to take part in the social and national life. Then the influence of such a partner, healthy in body and therefore vigorous in mind, is bound to be both lasting and far-reaching.

For it must be borne in mind that the German man is exceptionally sentimental, and most easily influenced by his women folk. It is said of him, he is the best of lovers, the worst of husbands. This has been the woman's fault. Once married, the German woman has done more than put romance behind her; she has taken a carpet-beater and driven it out of the house. As a girl, she never understood dressing; as a wife, she takes off such clothes even as she had, and proceeds to wrap herself up in any odd articles she may happen to find about the house; at all events, this is the impression she produces. The figure that might often be that of a Juno, the complexion that would sometimes do credit to a healthy angel, she proceeds of malice and intent to spoil. She sells her birth-right of admiration and devotion for a mess of sweets. Every afternoon you may see her at the café, loading herself with rich cream-covered cakes, washed down by copious draughts of chocolate. In a short time she becomes fat, pasty, placid, and utterly uninteresting.

When the German woman gives up her afternoon coffee and her evening beer, takes sufficient exercise to retain her shape, and continues to read after marriage something else than the cookery-book, the German Government will find it has a new and unknown force to deal with. And everywhere throughout Germany one is confronted by unmistakable signs that the old German Frauen are giving place to the newer Damen.

Concerning what will then happen one feels curious. For the German nation is still young, and its maturity is of importance to the world. They are a good people, a lovable people, who should help much to make the world better.

The worst that can be said against them is that they have their failings. They themselves do not know this; they consider themselves perfect, which is foolish of them. They even go so far as to think themselves superior to the Anglo-Saxon: this is incomprehensible. One feels they must be pretending.

"They have their points," said George; "but their tobacco is a national sin. I'm going to bed."

We rose, and leaning over the low stone parapet, watched the dancing lights upon the soft, dark river.

"It has been a pleasant Bummel, on the whole," said Harris; "I shall be glad to get back, and yet I am sorry it is over, if you understand me."

"What is a 'Bummel'?" said George. "How would you translate it?"

"A 'Bummel'," I explained, "I should describe as a journey, long or short, without an end; the only thing regulating it being the necessity of getting back within a given time to the point from which one started. Sometimes it is through busy streets, and sometimes through the fields and lanes; sometimes we can be spared for a few hours, and sometimes for a few days. But long or short, but here or there, our thoughts are ever on the running of the sand. We nod and smile to many as we pass; with some we stop and talk awhile; and with a few we walk a little way. We have been much interested, and often a little tired. But on the whole we have had a pleasant time, and are sorry when 'tis over."

THE IDLE THOUGHTS OF AN IDLE FELLOW.

TO
THE VERY DEAR AND WELL-BELOVED
FRIEND
OF MY PROSPEROUS AND EVIL DAYS—
TO THE FRIEND
WHO, THOUGH IN THE EARLY STAGES OF OUR ACQUAINTANCESHIP
DID OFTTIMES DISAGREE WITH ME, HAS SINCE
BECOME TO BE MY VERY WARMEST COMRADE—
TO THE FRIEND
WHO, HOWEVER OFTEN I MAY PUT HIM OUT, NEVER (NOW)
UPSETS ME IN REVENGE—
TO THE FRIEND
WHO, TREATED WITH MARKED COOLNESS BY ALL THE FEMALE
MEMBERS OF MY HOUSEHOLD, AND REGARDED WITH SUSPICION
BY MY VERY DOG, NEVERTHELESS SEEMS DAY BY
DAY TO BE MORE DRAWN BY ME, AND IN RETURN
TO MORE AND MORE IMPREGNATE ME WITH
THE ODOR OF HIS FRIENDSHIP—
TO THE FRIEND
WHO NEVER TELLS ME OF MY FAULTS, NEVER WANTS TO
BORROW MONEY, AND NEVER TALKS ABOUT HIMSELF—
TO THE COMPANION
OF MY IDLE HOURS, THE SOOTHER OF MY SORROWS,
THE CONFIDANT OF MY JOYS AND HOPES—
MY OLDEST AND STRONGEST
PIPE,
THIS LITTLE VOLUME
IS
GRATEFULLY AND AFFECTIONATELY
DEDICATED.

PREFACE

One or two friends to whom I showed these papers in MS. having observed that they were not half bad, and some of my relations having promised to buy the book if it ever came out, I feel I have no right to longer delay its issue. But for this, as one may say, public demand, I perhaps should not have ventured to offer these mere "idle thoughts" of mine as mental food for the English-speaking peoples of the earth. What readers ask nowadays in a book is that it should improve, instruct, and elevate. This book wouldn't elevate a cow. I cannot conscientiously recommend it for any useful purposes whatever. All I can suggest is that when you get tired of reading "the best hundred books," you may take this up for half an hour. It will be a change.

ON BEING IDLE.

Now, this is a subject on which I flatter myself I really am *au fait*. The gentleman who, when I was young, bathed me at wisdom's font for nine guineas a term—no extras—used to say he never knew a boy who could do less work in more time; and I remember my poor grandmother once incidentally observing, in the course of an instruction upon the use of the Prayer-book, that it was highly improbable that I should ever do much that I ought not to do, but that she felt convinced beyond a doubt that I should leave undone pretty well everything that I ought to do.

I am afraid I have somewhat belied half the dear old lady's prophecy. Heaven help me! I have done a good many things that I ought not to have done, in spite of my laziness. But I have fully confirmed the accuracy of her judgment so far as neglecting much that I ought not to have neglected is concerned. Idling always has been my strong point. I take no credit to myself in the matter—it is a gift. Few possess it. There are plenty of lazy people and plenty of slow-coaches, but a genuine idler is a rarity. He is not a man who slouches about with his hands in his pockets. On the contrary, his most startling characteristic is that he is always intensely busy.

It is impossible to enjoy idling thoroughly unless one has plenty of work to do. There is no fun in doing nothing when you have nothing to do. Wasting time is merely an occupation then, and a most exhausting one. Idleness, like kisses, to be sweet must be stolen.

Many years ago, when I was a young man, I was taken very ill—I never could see myself that much was the matter with me, except that I had a beastly cold. But I suppose it was something very serious, for the doctor said that I ought to have come to him a month before, and that if it (whatever it was) had gone on for another week he would not have answered for the consequences. It is an extraordinary thing, but I never knew a doctor called into any case yet but what it transpired that another day's delay would have rendered cure hopeless. Our medical guide, philosopher, and friend is like the hero in a melodrama—he always comes upon the scene just, and only just, in the nick of time. It is Providence, that is what it is.

Well, as I was saying, I was very ill and was ordered to Buxton for a month, with strict injunctions to do nothing whatever all the while that I was there. "Rest is what you require," said the doctor, "perfect rest."

It seemed a delightful prospect. "This man evidently understands my complaint," said I, and I pictured to myself a glorious time—a four weeks' *dolce far niente* with a dash of illness in it. Not too much illness, but just illness enough—just sufficient to give it the flavor of suffering and make it poetical. I should get up late, sip chocolate, and have my breakfast in slippers and a dressing-gown. I should lie out in the garden in a hammock and read sentimental novels with a melancholy ending, until the books should fall from my listless hand, and I should recline there, dreamily gazing into the deep blue of the firmament, watching the fleecy clouds floating like white-sailed ships across its depths, and listening to the joyous song of the birds and the low rustling of the trees. Or, on becoming too weak to go out of doors, I should sit propped up with pillows at the open window of the ground-floor front, and look wasted and interesting, so that all the pretty girls would sigh as they passed by.

And twice a day I should go down in a Bath chair to the Colonnade to drink the waters. Oh, those waters! I knew nothing about them then, and was rather taken with the idea. "Drinking the waters" sounded fashionable and Queen Anne-fied, and I thought I should like them. But, ugh! after the first three or four mornings! Sam Weller's description of them as "having a taste of warm flat-irons" conveys only a faint idea of their hideous nauseousness. If anything could make a sick man get well quickly, it would be the knowledge that he must drink a glassful of them every day until he was recovered. I drank them neat for six consecutive days, and they nearly killed me; but after then I adopted the plan of taking a stiff glass of brandy-and-water immediately on the top of them, and found much relief thereby. I have been informed since, by various eminent medical gentlemen, that the alcohol must have entirely counteracted the effects of the chalybeate properties contained in the water. I am glad I was lucky enough to hit upon the right thing.

But "drinking the waters" was only a small portion of the torture I experienced during that memorable month—a month which was, without exception, the most miserable I have ever spent. During the best part of it I religiously followed the doctor's mandate and did nothing whatever, except moon about the house and garden and go out for two hours a day in a Bath chair. That did break the monotony to a certain extent. There is more excitement about Bath-chairing—especially if you are not used to the exhilarating exercise—than might appear to the casual observer. A sense of danger, such as a mere outsider might not understand, is ever present to the mind of the occupant. He feels convinced every minute that the whole concern is going over, a conviction which becomes especially lively whenever a ditch or a stretch of newly macadamized road comes in sight. Every vehicle that passes he expects is going to run into him; and he never finds himself ascending or descending a hill without immediately beginning to speculate upon his chances, supposing—as seems extremely probable—that the weak-kneed controller of his destiny should let go.

But even this diversion failed to enliven after awhile, and the *ennui* became perfectly unbearable. I felt my mind giving way under it. It is not a strong mind, and I thought it would be unwise to tax it too far. So somewhere about the twentieth morning I got up early, had a good breakfast, and walked straight off to Hayfield, at the foot of the Kinder Scout—a pleasant, busy little town, reached through a lovely valley, and with two sweetly pretty women in it. At least they were sweetly pretty then; one passed me on the bridge and, I think, smiled; and the other was standing at an open door, making an unremunerative investment of kisses upon a red-faced baby. But it is years ago, and I dare say they have both grown stout and snappish since that time. Coming back, I saw an old man breaking stones, and it roused such strong longing in me to use my arms that I offered him a drink to let me take his place. He was a kindly old man and he humored me. I went for those stones with the accumulated energy of three weeks, and did more work in half an hour than he had done all day. But it did not make him jealous.

Having taken the plunge, I went further and further into dissipation, going out for a long walk every morning and listening to the band in the pavilion every evening. But the days still passed slowly notwithstanding, and I was heartily glad when the last one came and I was being whirled away from gouty, consumptive Buxton to London with its stern work and life. I looked out of the carriage as we rushed through Hendon in the evening. The lurid glare overhanging the mighty city seemed to warm my heart, and when, later on, my cab rattled out of St. Pancras' station, the old familiar roar that came swelling up around me sounded the sweetest music I had heard for many a long day.

I certainly did not enjoy that month's idling. I like idling when I ought not to be idling; not when it is the only thing I have to do. That is my pig-headed nature. The time when I like best to stand with my back to the fire, calculating how much I owe, is when my desk is heaped highest with letters that must be answered by the next post. When I like to dawdle longest over my dinner is when I have a heavy evening's work before me. And if, for some urgent reason, I ought to be up particularly early in the morning, it is then, more than at any other time, that I love to lie an extra half-hour in bed.

Ah! how delicious it is to turn over and go to sleep again: "just for five minutes." Is there any human being, I wonder, besides the hero of a Sunday-school "tale for boys," who ever gets up willingly? There are some men to whom getting up at the proper time is an utter impossibility. If eight o'clock happens to be the time that they should turn out, then they lie till half-past. If circumstances change and half-past eight becomes early enough for them, then it is nine before they can rise. They are like the statesman of whom it was said that he was always punctually half an hour late. They try all manner of schemes. They buy alarm-clocks (artful contrivances that go off at the wrong time and alarm the wrong people). They tell Sarah Jane to knock at the door and call them, and Sarah Jane does knock at the door and does call them, and they grunt back "awri" and then go comfortably to sleep again. I knew one man who would actually get out and have a cold bath; and even that was of no use, for afterward he would jump into bed again to warm himself.

I think myself that I could keep out of bed all right if I once got out. It is the wrenching away of the head from the pillow that I find so hard, and no amount of over-night determination makes it easier. I say to myself, after having wasted the whole evening, "Well, I won't do any more work to-night; I'll get up early to-morrow morning;" and I am thoroughly resolved to do so—then. In the morning, however, I feel less enthusiastic about the idea, and reflect that it would have been much better if I had stopped up last night. And then there is the trouble of dressing, and the more one thinks about that the more one wants to put it off.

It is a strange thing this bed, this mimic grave, where we stretch our tired limbs and sink away so quietly into the silence and rest. "O bed, O bed, delicious bed, that heaven on earth to the weary head," as sang poor Hood, you are a kind old nurse to us fretful boys and girls. Clever and foolish, naughty and good, you take us all in your motherly lap and hush our wayward crying. The strong man full of care—the sick man full of pain—the little maiden sobbing for her faithless lov-er—like children we lay our aching heads on your white bosom, and you gently soothe us off to by-by.

Our trouble is sore indeed when you turn away and will not comfort us. How long the dawn seems coming when we cannot sleep! Oh! those hideous nights when we toss and turn in fever and pain, when we lie, like living men among the dead, staring out into the dark hours that drift so slowly between us and the light. And oh! those still more hideous nights when we sit by another in pain, when the low fire startles us every now and then with a falling cinder, and the tick of the clock seems a hammer beating out the life that we are watching.

But enough of beds and bedrooms. I have kept to them too long, even for an idle fellow. Let us come out and have a smoke. That wastes time just as well and does not look so bad. Tobacco has been a blessing to us idlers. What the civil-service clerk before Sir Walter's time found to occupy their minds with it is hard to imagine. I attribute the quarrelsome nature of the Middle Ages young men en-tirely to the want of the soothing weed. They had no work to do and could not smoke, and the consequence was they were forever fighting and rowing. If, by any extraordinary chance, there was no war going, then they got up a deadly fami-ly feud with the next-door neighbor, and if, in spite of this, they still had a few spare moments on their hands, they occupied them with discussions as to whose sweetheart was the best looking, the arguments employed on both sides being bat-tle-axes, clubs, etc. Questions of taste were soon decided in those days. When a twelfth-century youth fell in love he did not take three paces backward, gaze into her eyes, and tell her she was too beautiful to live. He said he would step outside and see about it. And if, when he got out, he met a man and broke his head—the other man's head, I mean—then that proved that his—the first fellow's—girl was a pretty girl. But if the other fellow broke *his* head—not his own, you know, but the other fellow's—the other fellow to the second fellow, that is, because of course the other fellow would only be the other fellow to him, not the first fellow who—well, if he broke his head, then *his* girl—not the other fellow's, but the fellow who *was* the—Look here, if A broke B's head, then A's girl was a pretty girl; but if B broke A's head, then A's girl wasn't a pretty girl, but B's girl was. That was their method of conducting art criticism.

Nowadays we light a pipe and let the girls fight it out among themselves.

They do it very well. They are getting to do all our work. They are doctors, and barristers, and artists. They manage theaters, and promote swindles, and edit newspapers. I am looking forward to the time when we men shall have nothing to do but lie in bed till twelve, read two novels a day, have nice little five-o'clock teas all to ourselves, and tax our brains with nothing more trying than discussions upon the latest patterns in trousers and arguments as to what Mr. Jones' coat was made of and whether it fitted him. It is a glorious prospect—for idle fellows.

ON BEING IN LOVE.

You've been in love, of course! If not you've got it to come. Love is like the measles; we all have to go through it. Also like the measles, we take it only once. One never need be afraid of catching it a second time. The man who has had it can go into the most dangerous places and play the most foolhardy tricks with perfect safety. He can picnic in shady woods, ramble through leafy aisles, and linger on mossy seats to watch the sunset. He fears a quiet country-house no more than he would his own club. He can join a family party to go down the Rhine. He can, to see the last of a friend, venture into the very jaws of the marriage ceremony itself. He can keep his head through the whirl of a ravishing waltz, and rest afterward in a dark conservatory, catching nothing more lasting than a cold. He can brave a moonlight walk adown sweet-scented lanes or a twilight pull among the somber rushes. He can get over a stile without danger, scramble through a tangled hedge without being caught, come down a slippery path without falling. He can look into sunny eyes and not be dazzled. He listens to the siren voices, yet sails on with unveered helm. He clasps white hands in his, but no electric "Lulu"-like force holds him bound in their dainty pressure.

No, we never sicken with love twice. Cupid spends no second arrow on the same heart. Love's handmaids are our life-long friends. Respect, and admiration, and affection, our doors may always be left open for, but their great celestial master, in his royal progress, pays but one visit and departs. We like, we cherish, we are very, very fond of—but we never love again. A man's heart is a firework that once in its time flashes heavenward. Meteor-like, it blazes for a moment and lights with its glory the whole world beneath. Then the night of our sordid commonplace life closes in around it, and the burned-out case, falling back to earth, lies useless and uncared for, slowly smoldering into ashes. Once, breaking loose from our prison bonds, we dare, as mighty old Prometheus dared, to scale the Olympian mount and snatch from Phoebus' chariot the fire of the gods. Happy those who, hastening down again ere it dies out, can kindle their earthly altars at its flame. Love is too pure a light to burn long among the noisome gases that we breathe, but before it is choked out we may use it as a torch to ignite the cozy fire of affection.

And, after all, that warming glow is more suited to our cold little back parlor of a world than is the burning spirit love. Love should be the vestal fire of some mighty temple—some vast dim fane whose organ music is the rolling of the spheres. Affection will burn cheerily when the white flame of love is flickered out. Affection is a fire that can be fed from day to day and be piled up ever higher as the wintry years draw nigh. Old men and women can sit by it with their thin hands clasped, the little children can nestle down in front, the friend and neighbor has his welcome corner by its side, and even shaggy Fido and sleek Titty can toast their noses at the bars.

Let us heap the coals of kindness upon that fire. Throw on your pleasant words, your gentle pressures of the hand, your thoughtful and unselfish deeds. Fan it with good-humor, patience, and forbearance. You can let the wind blow and the rain fall unheeded then, for your hearth will be warm and bright, and the faces round it will make sunshine in spite of the clouds without.

I am afraid, dear Edwin and Angelina, you expect too much from love. You think there is enough of your little hearts to feed this fierce, devouring passion for all your long lives. Ah, young folk! don't rely too much upon that unsteady flicker. It will dwindle and dwindle as the months roll on, and there is no replenishing the fuel. You will watch it die out in anger and disappointment. To each it will seem that it is the other who is growing colder. Edwin sees with bitterness that Angelina no longer runs to the gate to meet him, all smiles and blushes; and when he has a cough now she doesn't begin to cry and, putting her arms round his neck, say that she cannot live without him. The most she will probably do is to suggest a lozenge, and even that in a tone implying that it is the noise more than anything else she is anxious to get rid of.

Poor little Angelina, too, sheds silent tears, for Edwin has given up carrying her old handkerchief in the inside pocket of his waistcoat.

Both are astonished at the falling off in the other one, but neither sees their own change. If they did they would not suffer as they do. They would look for the cause in the right quarter—in the littleness of poor human nature—join hands over their common failing, and start building their house anew on a more earthly and enduring foundation. But we are so blind to our own shortcomings, so wide awake to those of others. Everything that happens to us is always the other person's fault. Angelina would have gone on loving Edwin forever and ever and ever if only Edwin had not grown so strange and different. Edwin would have adored Angelina through eternity if Angelina had only remained the same as when he first adored her.

It is a cheerless hour for you both when the lamp of love has gone out and the fire of affection is not yet lit, and you have to grope about in the cold, raw dawn of life to kindle it. God grant it catches light before the day is too far spent. Many sit shivering by the dead coals till night come.

But, there, of what use is it to preach? Who that feels the rush of young love through his veins can think it will ever flow feeble and slow! To the boy of twenty it seems impossible that he will not love as wildly at sixty as he does then. He cannot call to mind any middle-aged or elderly gentleman of his acquaintance who is known to exhibit symptoms of frantic attachment, but that does not interfere in his belief in himself. His love will never fall, whoever else's may. Nobody ever loved as he loves, and so, of course, the rest of the world's experience can be no guide in his case. Alas! alas! ere thirty he has joined the ranks of the sneerers. It is not his fault. Our passions, both the good and bad, cease with our blushes. We do not hate, nor grieve, nor joy, nor despair in our thirties like we did in our teens. Disappointment does not suggest suicide, and we quaff success without intoxication.

We take all things in a minor key as we grow older. There are few majestic passages in the later acts of life's opera. Ambition takes a less ambitious aim. Honor becomes more reasonable and conveniently adapts itself to circumstances. And love—love dies. "Irreverence for the dreams of youth" soon creeps like a killing frost upon our hearts. The tender shoots and the expanding flowers are nipped and withered, and of a vine that yearned to stretch its tendrils round the world there is left but a sapless stump.

My fair friends will deem all this rank heresy, I know. So far from a man's not loving after he has passed boyhood, it is not till there is a good deal of gray in his hair that they think his protestations at all worthy of attention. Young ladies take their notions of our sex from the novels written by their own, and compared with the monstrosities that masquerade for men in the pages of that nightmare literature, Pythagoras' plucked bird and Frankenstein's demon were fair average specimens of humanity.

In these so-called books, the chief lover, or Greek god, as he is admiringly referred to—by the way, they do not say which "Greek god" it is that the gentleman bears such a striking likeness to; it might be hump-backed Vulcan, or double-faced Janus, or even driveling Silenus, the god of abstruse mysteries. He resembles the whole family of them, however, in being a blackguard, and perhaps this is what is meant. To even the little manliness his classical prototypes possessed, though, he can lay no claim whatever, being a listless effeminate noodle, on the shady side of forty. But oh! the depth and strength of this elderly party's emotion for some bread-and-butter school-girl! Hide your heads, ye young Romeos and Leanders! this *blase* old beau loves with an hysterical fervor that requires four adjectives to every noun to properly describe.

It is well, dear ladies, for us old sinners that you study only books. Did you read mankind, you would know that the lad's shy stammering tells a truer tale than our bold eloquence. A boy's love comes from a full heart; a man's is more often the result of a full stomach. Indeed, a man's sluggish current may not be called love, compared with the rushing fountain that wells up when a boy's heart is struck with the heavenly rod. If you would taste love, drink of the pure stream that youth pours out at your feet. Do not wait till it has become a muddy river before you stoop to catch its waves.

Or is it that you like its bitter flavor—that the clear, limpid water is insipid to your palate and that the pollution of its after-course gives it a relish to your lips? Must we believe those who tell us that a hand foul with the filth of a shameful life is the only one a young girl cares to be caressed by?

That is the teaching that is bawled out day by day from between those yellow covers. Do they ever pause to think, I wonder, those devil's ladyhelps, what mischief they are doing crawling about God's garden, and telling childish Eves and silly Adams that sin is sweet and that decency is ridiculous and vulgar? How many an innocent girl do they not degrade into an evil-minded woman? To how many a weak lad do they not point out the dirty by-path as the shortest cut to a maiden's heart? It is not as if they wrote of life as it really is. Speak truth, and right will take care of itself. But their pictures are coarse daubs painted from the sickly fancies of their own diseased imagination.

We want to think of women not—as their own sex would show them—as Lorleis luring us to destruction, but as good angels beckoning us upward. They have more power for good or evil than they dream of. It is just at the very age when a man's character is forming that he tumbles into love, and then the lass he loves has the making or marring of him. Unconsciously he molds himself to what she would have him, good or bad. I am sorry to have to be ungallant enough to say that I do not think they always use their influence for the best. Too often the female world is bounded hard and fast within the limits of the commonplace. Their ideal hero is a prince of littleness, and to become that many a powerful mind, enchanted by love, is "lost to life and use and name and fame."

And yet, women, you could make us so much better if you only would. It rests with you, more than with all the preachers, to roll this world a little nearer heaven. Chivalry is not dead: it only sleeps for want of work to do. It is you who must wake it to noble deeds. You must be worthy of knightly worship.

You must be higher than ourselves. It was for Una that the Red Cross Knight did war. For no painted, mincing court dame could the dragon have been slain. Oh, ladies fair, be fair in mind and soul as well as face, so that brave knights may win glory in your service! Oh, woman, throw off your disguising cloaks of selfishness, effrontery, and affectation! Stand forth once more a queen in your royal robe of simple purity. A thousand swords, now rusting in ignoble sloth, shall leap from their scabbards to do battle for your honor against wrong. A thousand Sir Rolands shall lay lance in rest, and Fear, Avarice, Pleasure, and Ambition shall go down in the dust before your colors.

What noble deeds were we not ripe for in the days when we loved? What noble lives could we not have lived for her sake? Our love was a religion we could have died for. It was no mere human creature like ourselves that we adored. It was a queen that we paid homage to, a goddess that we worshiped.

And how madly we did worship! And how sweet it was to worship! Ah, lad, cherish love's young dream while it lasts! You will know too soon how truly little Tom Moore sang when he said that there was nothing half so sweet in life. Even when it brings misery it is a wild, romantic misery, all unlike the dull, worldly pain of after-sorrows. When you have lost her—when the light is gone out from your life and the world stretches before you a long, dark horror, even then a half-enchantment mingles with your despair.

And who would not risk its terrors to gain its raptures? Ah, what raptures they were! The mere recollection thrills you. How delicious it was to tell her that you loved her, that you lived for her, that you would die for her! How you did rave, to be sure, what floods of extravagant nonsense you poured forth, and oh, how cruel it was of her to pretend not to believe you! In what awe you stood of her! How miserable you were when you had offended her! And yet, how pleasant to be bullied by her and to sue for pardon without having the slightest notion of what your fault was! How dark the world was when she snubbed you, as she often did, the little rogue, just to see you look wretched; how sunny when she smiled! How jealous you were of every one about her! How you hated every man she shook hands with, every woman she kissed—the maid that did her hair, the boy that cleaned her shoes, the dog she nursed—though you had to be respectful to the last-named! How you looked forward to seeing her, how stupid you were when you did see her, staring at her without saying a word! How impossible it was for you to go out at any time of the day or night without finding yourself eventually opposite her windows! You hadn't pluck enough to go in, but you hung about the corner and gazed at the outside. Oh, if the house had only caught fire—it was insured, so it wouldn't have mattered—and you could have rushed in and saved her at the risk of your life, and have been terribly burned and injured! Anything to serve her. Even in little things that was so sweet. How you would watch her, spaniel-like, to anticipate her slightest wish! How proud you were to do her bidding! How delightful it was to be ordered about by her! To devote your whole life to her and to never think of yourself seemed such a simple thing. You would go without a holiday to lay a humble offering at her shrine, and felt more than repaid if she only deigned to accept it. How precious to you was everything that she had hallowed by her touch—her little glove, the ribbon she had worn, the rose that had nestled in her hair and whose withered leaves still mark the poems you never care to look at now.

And oh, how beautiful she was, how wondrous beautiful! It was as some angel entering the room, and all else became plain and earthly. She was too sacred to be touched. It seemed almost presumption to gaze at her. You would as soon have thought of kissing her as of singing comic songs in a cathedral. It was desecration enough to kneel and timidly raise the gracious little hand to your lips.

Ah, those foolish days, those foolish days when we were unselfish and pure-minded; those foolish days when our simple hearts were full of truth, and faith, and reverence! Ah, those foolish days of noble longings and of noble strivings! And oh, these wise, clever days when we know that money is the only prize worth striving for, when we believe in nothing else but meanness and lies, when we care for no living creature but ourselves!

ON BEING IN THE BLUES.

I can enjoy feeling melancholy, and there is a good deal of satisfaction about being thoroughly miserable; but nobody likes a fit of the blues. Nevertheless, everybody has them; notwithstanding which, nobody can tell why. There is no accounting for them. You are just as likely to have one on the day after you have come into a large fortune as on the day after you have left your new silk umbrella in the train. Its effect upon you is somewhat similar to what would probably be produced by a combined attack of toothache, indigestion, and cold in the head. You become stupid, restless, and irritable; rude to strangers and dangerous toward your friends; clumsy, maudlin, and quarrelsome; a nuisance to yourself and everybody about you.

While it is on you can do nothing and think of nothing, though feeling at the time bound to do something. You can't sit still so put on your hat and go for a walk; but before you get to the corner of the street you wish you hadn't come out and you turn back. You open a book and try to read, but you find Shakespeare trite and commonplace, Dickens is dull and prosy, Thackeray a bore, and Carlyle too sentimental. You throw the book aside and call the author names. Then you "shoo" the cat out of the room and kick the door to after her. You think you will write your letters, but after sticking at "Dearest Auntie: I find I have five minutes to spare, and so hasten to write to you," for a quarter of an hour, without being able to think of another sentence, you tumble the paper into the desk, fling the wet pen down upon the table-cloth, and start up with the resolution of going to see the Thompsons. While pulling on your gloves, however, it occurs to you that the Thompsons are idiots; that they never have supper; and that you will be expected to jump the baby. You curse the Thompsons and decide not to go.

By this time you feel completely crushed. You bury your face in your hands and think you would like to die and go to heaven. You picture to yourself your own sick-bed, with all your friends and relations standing round you weeping. You bless them all, especially the young and pretty ones. They will value you when you are gone, so you say to yourself, and learn too late what they have lost; and you bitterly contrast their presumed regard for you then with their decided want of veneration now.

These reflections make you feel a little more cheerful, but only for a brief period; for the next moment you think what a fool you must be to imagine for an instant that anybody would be sorry at anything that might happen to you. Who would care two straws (whatever precise amount of care two straws may represent) whether you are blown up, or hung up, or married, or drowned? Nobody cares for you. You never have been properly appreciated, never met with your due deserts in any one particular. You review the whole of your past life, and it is painfully apparent that you have been ill-used from your cradle.

Half an hour's indulgence in these considerations works you up into a state of savage fury against everybody and everything, especially yourself, whom anatomical reasons alone prevent your kicking. Bed-time at last comes, to save you from doing something rash, and you spring upstairs, throw off your clothes, leaving them strewn all over the room, blow out the candle, and jump into bed as if you had backed yourself for a heavy wager to do the whole thing against time. There you toss and tumble about for a couple of hours or so, varying the monotony by occasionally jerking the clothes off and getting out and putting them on again. At length you drop into an uneasy and fitful slumber, have bad dreams, and wake up late the next morning.

At least, this is all we poor single men can do under the circumstances. Married men bully their wives, grumble at the dinner, and insist on the children's going to bed. All of which, creating, as it does, a good deal of disturbance in the house, must be a great relief to the feelings of a man in the blues, rows being the only form of amusement in which he can take any interest.

The symptoms of the infirmity are much the same in every case, but the affliction itself is variously termed. The poet says that "a feeling of sadness comes o'er him." 'Arry refers to the heavings of his wayward heart by confiding to Jimee that he has "got the blooming hump." Your sister doesn't know what is the matter with her to-night. She feels out of sorts altogether and hopes nothing is going to happen. The every-day young man is "so awful glad to meet you, old fellow," for he does "feel so jolly miserable this evening." As for myself, I generally say that "I have a strange, unsettled feeling to-night" and "think I'll go out."

By the way, it never does come except in the evening. In the sun-time, when the world is bounding forward full of life, we cannot stay to sigh and sulk. The roar of the working day drowns the voices of the elfin sprites that are ever singing their low-toned *miserere* in our ears. In the day we are angry, disappointed, or indignant, but never "in the blues" and never melancholy. When things go wrong at ten o'clock in the morning we—or rather you—swear and knock the furniture about; but if the misfortune comes at ten P.M., we read poetry or sit in the dark and think what a hollow world this is.

But, as a rule, it is not trouble that makes us melancholy. The actuality is too stern a thing for sentiment. We linger to weep over a picture, but from the original we should quickly turn our eyes away. There is no pathos in real misery: no luxury in real grief. We do not toy with sharp swords nor hug a gnawing fox to our breast for choice. When a man or woman loves to brood over a sorrow and takes care to keep it green in their memory, you may be sure it is no longer a pain to them. However they may have suffered from it at first, the recollection has become by then a pleasure. Many dear old ladies who daily look at tiny shoes lying in lavender-scented drawers, and weep as they think of the tiny feet whose toddling march is done, and sweet-faced young ones who place each night beneath their pillow some lock that once curled on a boyish head that the salt waves have kissed to death, will call me a nasty cynical brute and say I'm talking nonsense; but I believe, nevertheless, that if they will ask themselves truthfully whether they find it unpleasant to dwell thus on their sorrow, they will be compelled to answer "No." Tears are as sweet as laughter to some natures. The proverbial Englishman, we know from old chronicler Froissart, takes his pleasures sadly, and the Englishwoman goes a step further and takes her pleasures in sadness itself.

I am not sneering. I would not for a moment sneer at anything that helps to keep hearts tender in this hard old world. We men are cold and common-sensed enough for all; we would not have women the same. No, no, ladies dear, be always sentimental and soft-hearted, as you are—be the soothing butter to our coarse dry bread. Besides, sentiment is to women what fun is to us. They do not care for our humor, surely it would be unfair to deny them their grief. And who shall say that their mode of enjoyment is not as sensible as ours? Why assume that a doubled-up body, a contorted, purple face, and a gaping mouth emitting a series of ear-splitting shrieks point to a state of more intelligent happiness than a pensive face reposing upon a little white hand, and a pair of gentle tear-dimmed eyes looking back through Time's dark avenue upon a fading past?

I am glad when I see Regret walked with as a friend—glad because I know the saltness has been washed from out the tears, and that the sting must have been plucked from the beautiful face of Sorrow ere we dare press her pale lips to ours. Time has laid his healing hand upon the wound when we can look back upon the pain we once fainted under and no bitterness or despair rises in our hearts. The burden is no longer heavy when we have for our past troubles only the same sweet mingling of pleasure and pity that we feel when old knight-hearted Colonel Newcome answers "*adsum*" to the great roll-call, or when Tom and Maggie Tulliver, clasping hands through the mists that have divided them, go down, locked in each other's arms, beneath the swollen waters of the Floss.

Talking of poor Tom and Maggie Tulliver brings to my mind a saying of George Eliot's in connection with this subject of melancholy. She speaks somewhere of the "sadness of a summer's evening." How wonderfully true—like everything that came from that wonderful pen—the observation is! Who has not felt the sorrowful enchantment of those lingering sunsets? The world belongs to Melancholy then, a thoughtful deep-eyed maiden who loves not the glare of day. It is not till "light thickens and the crow wings to the rocky wood" that she steals forth from her groves. Her palace is in twilight land. It is there she meets us. At her shadowy gate she takes our hand in hers and walks beside us through her mystic realm. We see no form, but seem to hear the rustling of her wings.

Even in the toiling hum-drum city her spirit comes to us. There is a somber presence in each long, dull street; and the dark river creeps ghostlike under the black arches, as if bearing some hidden secret beneath its muddy waves.

In the silent country, when the trees and hedges loom dim and blurred against the rising night, and the bat's wing flutters in our face, and the land-rail's cry sounds drearily across the fields, the spell sinks deeper still into our hearts. We seem in that hour to be standing by some unseen death-bed, and in the swaying of the elms we hear the sigh of the dying day.

A solemn sadness reigns. A great peace is around us. In its light our cares of the working day grow small and trivial, and bread and cheese—ay, and even kisses—do not seem the only things worth striving for. Thoughts we cannot speak but only listen to flood in upon us, and standing in the stillness under earth's darkening dome, we feel that we are greater than our petty lives. Hung round with those dusky curtains, the world is no longer a mere dingy workshop, but a stately temple wherein man may worship, and where at times in the dimness his groping hands touch God's.

ON BEING HARD UP.

It is a most remarkable thing. I sat down with the full intention of writing something clever and original; but for the life of me I can't think of anything clever and original—at least, not at this moment. The only thing I can think about now is being hard up. I suppose having my hands in my pockets has made me think about this. I always do sit with my hands in my pockets except when I am in the company of my sisters, my cousins, or my aunts; and they kick up such a shindy—I should say expostulate so eloquently upon the subject—that I have to give in and take them out—my hands I mean. The chorus to their objections is that it is not gentlemanly. I am hanged if I can see why. I could understand its not being considered gentlemanly to put your hands in other people's pockets (especially by the other people), but how, O ye sticklers for what looks this and what looks that, can putting his hands in his own pockets make a man less gentle? Perhaps you are right, though. Now I come to think of it, I have heard some people grumble most savagely when doing it. But they were mostly old gentlemen. We young fellows, as a rule, are never quite at ease unless we have our hands in our pockets. We are awkward and shifty. We are like what a music-hall Lion Comique would be without his opera-hat, if such a thing can be imagined. But let us put our hands in our trousers pockets, and let there be some small change in the right-hand one and a bunch of keys in the left, and we will face a female post-office clerk.

It is a little difficult to know what to do with your hands, even in your pockets, when there is nothing else there. Years ago, when my whole capital would occasionally come down to "what in town the people call a bob," I would recklessly spend a penny of it, merely for the sake of having the change, all in coppers, to jingle. You don't feel nearly so hard up with eleven pence in your pocket as you do with a shilling. Had I been "La-di-da," that impecunious youth about whom we superior folk are so sarcastic, I would have changed my penny for two ha'pennies.

I can speak with authority on the subject of being hard up. I have been a provincial actor. If further evidence be required, which I do not think likely, I can add that I have been a "gentleman connected with the press." I have lived on 15 shilling a week. I have lived a week on 10, owing the other 5; and I have lived for a fortnight on a great-coat.

It is wonderful what an insight into domestic economy being really hard up gives one. If you want to find out the value of money, live on 15 shillings a week and see how much you can put by for clothes and recreation. You will find out that it is worth while to wait for the farthing change, that it is worth while to walk a mile to save a penny, that a glass of beer is a luxury to be indulged in only at rare intervals, and that a collar can be worn for four days.

Try it just before you get married. It will be excellent practice. Let your son and heir try it before sending him to college. He won't grumble at a hundred a year pocket-money then. There are some people to whom it would do a world of good. There is that delicate blossom who can't drink any claret under ninety-four, and who would as soon think of dining off cat's meat as off plain roast mutton. You do come across these poor wretches now and then, though, to the credit of humanity, they are principally confined to that fearful and wonderful society known only to lady novelists. I never hear of one of these creatures discussing a *menu* card but I feel a mad desire to drag him off to the bar of some common east-end public-house and cram a sixpenny dinner down his throat—beefsteak pudding, fourpence; potatoes, a penny; half a pint of porter, a penny. The recollection of it (and the mingled fragrance of beer, tobacco, and roast pork generally leaves a vivid impression) might induce him to turn up his nose a little less frequently in the future at everything that is put before him. Then there is that generous party, the cadger's delight, who is so free with his small change, but who never thinks of paying his debts. It might teach even him a little common sense. "I always give the waiter a shilling. One can't give the fellow less, you know," explained a young government clerk with whom I was lunching the other day in Regent Street. I agreed with him as to the utter impossibility of making it elevenpence ha'penny; but at the same time I resolved to one day decoy him to an eating-house I remembered near Covent Garden, where the waiter, for the better discharge of his duties, goes about in his shirt-sleeves—and very dirty sleeves they are, too, when it gets near the end of the month. I know that waiter. If my friend gives him anything beyond a penny, the man will insist on shaking hands with him then and there as a mark of his esteem; of that I feel sure.

There have been a good many funny things said and written about hardupishness, but the reality is not funny, for all that. It is not funny to have to haggle over pennies. It isn't funny to be thought mean and stingy. It isn't funny to be shabby and to be ashamed of your address. No, there is nothing at all funny in poverty—to the poor. It is hell upon earth to a sensitive man; and many a brave gentleman who would have faced the labors of Hercules has had his heart broken by its petty miseries.

It is not the actual discomforts themselves that are hard to bear. Who would mind roughing it a bit if that were all it meant? What cared Robinson Crusoe for a patch on his trousers? Did he wear trousers? I forget; or did he go about as he does in the pantomimes? What did it matter to him if his toes did stick out of his boots? and what if his umbrella was a cotton one, so long as it kept the rain off? His shabbiness did not trouble him; there was none of his friends round about to sneer him.

Being poor is a mere trifle. It is being known to be poor that is the sting. It is not cold that makes a man without a great-coat hurry along so quickly. It is not all shame at telling lies—which he knows will not be believed—that makes him turn so red when he informs you that he considers great-coats unhealthy and never carries an umbrella on principle. It is easy enough to say that poverty is no crime. No; if it were men wouldn't be ashamed of it. It's a blunder, though, and is punished as such. A poor man is despised the whole world over; despised as much by a Christian as by a lord, as much by a demagogue as by a footman, and not all the copy-book maxims ever set for ink stained youth will make him respected. Appearances are everything, so far as human opinion goes, and the man who will walk down Piccadilly arm in arm with the most notorious scamp in London, provided he is a well-dressed one, will slink up a back street to say a couple of words to a seedy-looking gentleman. And the seedy-looking gentleman knows this—no one better—and will go a mile round to avoid meeting an acquaintance. Those that knew him in his prosperity need never trouble themselves to look the other way. He is a thousand times more anxious that they should not see him than they can be; and as to their assistance, there is nothing he dreads more than the offer of it. All he wants is to be forgotten; and in this respect he is generally fortunate enough to get what he wants.

One becomes used to being hard up, as one becomes used to everything else, by the help of that wonderful old homeopathic doctor, Time. You can tell at a glance the difference between the old hand and the novice; between the case-hardened man who has been used to shift and struggle for years and the poor devil of a beginner striving to hide his misery, and in a constant agony of fear lest he should be found out. Nothing shows this difference more clearly than the way in which each will pawn his watch. As the poet says somewhere: "True ease in pawning comes from art, not chance." The one goes into his "uncle's" with as much composure as he would into his tailor's—very likely with more. The assistant is even civil and attends to him at once, to the great indignation of the lady in the next box, who, however, sarcastically observes that she don't mind being kept waiting "if it is a regular customer." Why, from the pleasant and businesslike manner in which the transaction is carried out, it might be a large purchase in the three per cents. Yet what a piece of work a man makes of his first "pop." A boy popping his first question is confidence itself compared with him. He hangs about outside the shop until he has succeeded in attracting the attention of all the loafers in the neighborhood and has aroused strong suspicions in the mind of the policeman on the beat. At last, after a careful examination of the contents of the windows, made for the purpose of impressing the bystanders with the notion that he is going in to purchase a diamond bracelet or some such trifle, he enters, trying to do so with a careless swagger, and giving himself really the air of a member of the swell mob. When inside he speaks in so low a voice as to be perfectly inaudible, and has to say it all over again. When, in the course of his rambling conversation about a "friend" of his, the word "lend" is reached, he is promptly told to go up the court on the right and take the first door round the corner. He comes out of the shop with a face that you could easily light a cigarette at, and firmly under the impression that the whole population of the district is watching him. When he does get to the right place he has forgotten his name and address and is in a general condition of hopeless imbecility. Asked in a severe tone how he came by "this," he stammers and contradicts himself, and it is only a miracle if he does not confess to having stolen it that very day. He is thereupon informed that they don't want anything to do with his sort, and that he had better get out of this as quickly as possible, which he does, recollecting nothing more until he finds himself three miles off, without the slightest knowledge how he got there.

By the way, how awkward it is, though, having to depend on public-houses and churches for the time. The former are generally too fast and the latter too slow. Besides which, your efforts to get a glimpse of the public house clock from the outside are attended with great difficulties. If you gently push the swing-door ajar and peer in you draw upon yourself the contemptuous looks of the barmaid, who at once puts you down in the same category with area sneaks and cadgers. You also create a certain amount of agitation among the married portion of the customers. You don't see the clock because it is behind the door; and in trying to withdraw quietly you jam your head. The only other method is to jump up and down outside the window. After this latter proceeding, however, if you do not bring out a banjo and commence to sing, the youthful inhabitants of the neighborhood, who have gathered round in expectation, become disappointed.

I should like to know, too, by what mysterious law of nature it is that before you have left your watch "to be repaired" half an hour, some one is sure to stop you in the street and conspicuously ask you the time. Nobody even feels the slightest curiosity on the subject when you've got it on.

Dear old ladies and gentlemen who know nothing about being hard up—and may they never, bless their gray old heads—look upon the pawn-shop as the last stage of degradation; but those who know it better (and my readers have no doubt, noticed this themselves) are often surprised, like the little boy who dreamed he went to heaven, at meeting so many people there that they never expected to see. For my part, I think it a much more independent course than borrowing from friends, and I always try to impress this upon those of my acquaintance who incline toward "wanting a couple of pounds till the day after to-morrow." But they won't all see it. One of them once remarked that he objected to the principle of the thing. I fancy if he had said it was the interest that he objected to he would have been nearer the truth: twenty-five per cent. certainly does come heavy.

There are degrees in being hard up. We are all hard up, more or less—most of us more. Some are hard up for a thousand pounds; some for a shilling. Just at this moment I am hard up myself for a fiver. I only want it for a day or two. I should be certain of paying it back within a week at the outside, and if any lady or gentleman among my readers would kindly lend it me, I should be very much obliged indeed. They could send it to me under cover to Messrs. Field & Tuer, only, in such case, please let the envelope be carefully sealed. I would give you my I.O.U. as security.

ON VANITY AND VANITIES.

All is vanity and everybody's vain. Women are terribly vain. So are men—more so, if possible. So are children, particularly children. One of them at this very moment is hammering upon my legs. She wants to know what I think of her new shoes. Candidly I don't think much of them. They lack symmetry and curve and possess an indescribable appearance of lumpiness (I believe, too, they've put them on the wrong feet). But I don't say this. It is not criticism, but flattery that she wants; and I gush over them with what I feel to myself to be degrading effusiveness. Nothing else would satisfy this self-opinionated cherub. I tried the conscientious-friend dodge with her on one occasion, but it was not a success. She had requested my judgment upon her general conduct and behavior, the exact case submitted being, "Wot oo tink of me? Oo peased wi' me?" and I had thought it a good opportunity to make a few salutary remarks upon her late moral career, and said: "No, I am not pleased with you." I recalled to her mind the events of that very morning, and I put it to her how she, as a Christian child, could expect a wise and good uncle to be satisfied with the carryings on of an infant who that very day had roused the whole house at five AM.; had upset a water-jug and tumbled downstairs after it at seven; had endeavored to put the cat in the bath at eight; and sat on her own father's hat at nine thirty-five.

What did she do? Was she grateful to me for my plain speaking? Did she ponder upon my words and determine to profit by them and to lead from that hour a better and nobler life?

No! she howled.

That done, she became abusive. She said:

"Oo naughty—oo naughty, bad unkie—oo bad man—me tell MAR."

And she did, too.

Since then, when my views have been called for I have kept my real sentiments more to myself like, preferring to express unbounded admiration of this young person's actions, irrespective of their actual merits. And she nods her head approvingly and trots off to advertise my opinion to the rest of the household. She appears to employ it as a sort of testimonial for mercenary purposes, for I subsequently hear distant sounds of "Unkie says me dood dirl—me dot to have two bikkies [biscuits]."

There she goes, now, gazing rapturously at her own toes and murmuring "pittie"—two-foot-ten of conceit and vanity, to say nothing of other wickednesses.

They are all alike. I remember sitting in a garden one sunny afternoon in the suburbs of London. Suddenly I heard a shrill treble voice calling from a top-story window to some unseen being, presumably in one of the other gardens, "Gamma, me dood boy, me wery good boy, gamma; me dot on Bob's knickiebockies."

Why, even animals are vain. I saw a great Newfoundland dog the other day sitting in front of a mirror at the entrance to a shop in Regent's Circus, and examining himself with an amount of smug satisfaction that I have never seen equaled elsewhere outside a vestry meeting.

I was at a farm-house once when some high holiday was being celebrated. I don't remember what the occasion was, but it was something festive, a May Day or Quarter Day, or something of that sort, and they put a garland of flowers round the head of one of the cows. Well, that absurd quadruped went about all day as perky as a schoolgirl in a new frock; and when they took the wreath off she became quite sulky, and they had to put it on again before she would stand still to be milked. This is not a Percy anecdote. It is plain, sober truth.

As for cats, they nearly equal human beings for vanity. I have known a cat get up and walk out of the room on a remark derogatory to her species being made by a visitor, while a neatly turned compliment will set them purring for an hour.

I do like cats. They are so unconsciously amusing. There is such a comic dignity about them, such a "How dare you!" "Go away, don't touch me" sort of air. Now, there is nothing haughty about a dog. They are "Hail, fellow, well met" with every Tom, Dick, or Harry that they come across. When I meet a dog of my acquaintance I slap his head, call him opprobrious epithets, and roll him over on his back; and there he lies, gaping at me, and doesn't mind it a bit.

Fancy carrying on like that with a cat! Why, she would never speak to you again as long as you lived. No, when you want to win the approbation of a cat you must mind what you are about and work your way carefully. If you don't know the cat, you had best begin by saying, "Poor pussy." After which add "did 'ums" in a tone of soothing sympathy. You don't know what you mean any more than the cat does, but the sentiment seems to imply a proper spirit on your part, and generally touches her feelings to such an extent that if you are of good manners and passable appearance she will stick her back up and rub her nose against you. Matters having reached this stage, you may venture to chuck her under the chin and tickle the side of her head, and the intelligent creature will then stick her claws into your legs; and all is friendship and affection, as so sweetly expressed in the beautiful lines—

> "I love little pussy, her coat is so warm,
> And if I don't tease her she'll do me no harm;
> So I'll stroke her, and pat her, and feed her with food,
> And pussy will love me because I am good."

The last two lines of the stanza give us a pretty true insight into pussy's notions of human goodness. It is evident that in her opinion goodness consists of stroking her, and patting her, and feeding her with food. I fear this narrow-minded view of virtue, though, is not confined to pussies. We are all inclined to adopt a similar standard of merit in our estimate of other people. A good man is a man who is good to us, and a bad man is a man who doesn't do what we want him to. The truth is, we each of us have an inborn conviction that the whole world, with everybody and everything in it, was created as a sort of necessary appendage to ourselves. Our fellow men and women were made to admire us and to minister to our various requirements. You and I, dear reader, are each the center of the universe in our respective opinions. You, as I understand it, were brought into being by a considerate Providence in order that you might read and pay me for what I write; while I, in your opinion, am an article sent into the world to write something for you to read. The stars—as we term the myriad other worlds that are rushing down beside us through the eternal silence—were put into the heavens to make the sky look interesting for us at night; and the moon with its dark mysteries and ever-hidden face is an arrangement for us to flirt under.

I fear we are most of us like Mrs. Poyser's bantam cock, who fancied the sun got up every morning to hear him crow. "'Tis vanity that makes the world go round." I don't believe any man ever existed without vanity, and if he did he would be an extremely uncomfortable person to have anything to do with. He would, of course, be a very good man, and we should respect him very much. He would be a very admirable man—a man to be put under a glass case and shown round as a specimen—a man to be stuck upon a pedestal and copied, like a school exercise—a man to be reverenced, but not a man to be loved, not a human brother whose hand we should care to grip. Angels may be very excellent sort of folk in their way, but we, poor mortals, in our present state, would probably find them precious slow company. Even mere good people are rather depressing. It is in our faults and failings, not in our virtues, that we touch one another and find sympathy. We differ widely enough in our nobler qualities. It is in our follies that we are at one. Some of us are pious, some of us are generous. Some few of us are honest, comparatively speaking; and some, fewer still, may possibly be truthful. But in vanity and kindred weaknesses we can all join hands. Vanity is one of those touches of nature that make the whole world kin. From the Indian hunter, proud of his belt of scalps, to the European general, swelling beneath his row of stars and medals; from the Chinese, gleeful at the length of his pigtail, to the "professional beauty," suffering tortures in order that her waist may resemble a peg-top; from draggle-tailed little Polly Stiggins, strutting through Seven Dials with a tattered parasol over her head, to the princess sweeping through a drawing-room with a train of four yards long; from 'Arry, winning by vulgar chaff the loud laughter of his pals, to the statesman whose ears are tickled by the cheers that greet his high-sounding periods; from the dark-skinned African, bartering his rare oils and ivory for a few glass beads to hang about his neck, to the Christian maiden selling her white body for a score of tiny stones and an empty title to tack before her name—all march, and fight, and bleed, and die beneath its tawdry flag.

Ay, ay, vanity is truly the motive-power that moves humanity, and it is flattery that greases the wheels. If you want to win affection and respect in this world, you must flatter people. Flatter high and low, and rich and poor, and silly and wise. You will get on famously. Praise this man's virtues and that man's vices. Compliment everybody upon everything, and especially upon what they haven't got. Admire guys for their beauty, fools for their wit, and boors for their breeding. Your discernment and intelligence will be extolled to the skies.

Every one can be got over by flattery. The belted earl—"belted earl" is the correct phrase, I believe. I don't know what it means, unless it be an earl that wears a belt instead of braces. Some men do. I don't like it myself. You have to keep the thing so tight for it to be of any use, and that is uncomfortable. Anyhow, whatever particular kind of an earl a belted earl may be, he is, I assert, get-overable by flattery; just as every other human being is, from a duchess to a cat's-meat man, from a plow boy to a poet—and the poet far easier than the plowboy, for butter sinks better into wheaten bread than into oaten cakes.

As for love, flattery is its very life-blood. Fill a person with love for themselves, and what runs over will be your share, says a certain witty and truthful Frenchman whose name I can't for the life of me remember. (Confound it! I never can remember names when I want to.) Tell a girl she is an angel, only more angelic than an angel; that she is a goddess, only more graceful, queenly, and heavenly than the average goddess; that she is more fairy-like than Titania, more beautiful than Venus, more enchanting than Parthenope; more adorable, lovely, and radiant, in short, than any other woman that ever did live, does live, or could live, and you will make a very favorable impression upon her trusting little heart. Sweet innocent! she will believe every word you say. It is so easy to deceive a woman—in this way.

Dear little souls, they hate flattery, so they tell you; and when you say, "Ah, darling, it isn't flattery in your case, it's plain, sober truth; you really are, without exaggeration, the most beautiful, the most good, the most charming, the most divine, the most perfect human creature that ever trod this earth," they will smile a quiet, approving smile, and, leaning against your manly shoulder, murmur that you are a dear good fellow after all.

By Jove! fancy a man trying to make love on strictly truthful principles, determining never to utter a word of mere compliment or hyperbole, but to scrupulously confine himself to exact fact! Fancy his gazing rapturously into his mistress' eyes and whispering softly to her that she wasn't, on the whole, bad-looking, as girls went! Fancy his holding up her little hand and assuring her that it was of a light drab color shot with red; and telling her as he pressed her to his heart that her nose, for a turned-up one, seemed rather pretty; and that her eyes appeared to him, as far as he could judge, to be quite up to the average standard of such things!

A nice chance he would stand against the man who would tell her that her face was like a fresh blush rose, that her hair was a wandering sunbeam imprisoned by her smiles, and her eyes like two evening stars.

ON VANITY AND VANITIES.

There are various ways of flattering, and, of course, you must adapt your style to your subject. Some people like it laid on with a trowel, and this requires very little art. With sensible persons, however, it needs to be done very delicately, and more by suggestion than actual words. A good many like it wrapped up in the form of an insult, as—"Oh, you are a perfect fool, you are. You would give your last sixpence to the first hungry-looking beggar you met;" while others will swallow it only when administered through the medium of a third person, so that if C wishes to get at an A of this sort, he must confide to A's particular friend B that he thinks A a splendid fellow, and beg him, B, not to mention it, especially to A. Be careful that B is a reliable man, though, otherwise he won't.

Those fine, sturdy John Bulls who "hate flattery, sir," "Never let anybody get over me by flattery," etc., etc., are very simply managed. Flatter them enough upon their absence of vanity, and you can do what you like with them.

After all, vanity is as much a virtue as a vice. It is easy to recite copy-book maxims against its sinfulness, but it is a passion that can move us to good as well as to evil. Ambition is only vanity ennobled. We want to win praise and admiration—or fame as we prefer to name it—and so we write great books, and paint grand pictures, and sing sweet songs; and toil with willing hands in study, loom, and laboratory.

We wish to become rich men, not in order to enjoy ease and comfort—all that any one man can taste of those may be purchased anywhere for 200 pounds per annum—but that our houses may be bigger and more gaudily furnished than our neighbors'; that our horses and servants may be more numerous; that we may dress our wives and daughters in absurd but expensive clothes; and that we may give costly dinners of which we ourselves individually do not eat a shilling's worth. And to do this we aid the world's work with clear and busy brain, spreading commerce among its peoples, carrying civilization to its remotest corners.

Do not let us abuse vanity, therefore. Rather let us use it. Honor itself is but the highest form of vanity. The instinct is not confined solely to Beau Brummels and Dolly Vardens. There is the vanity of the peacock and the vanity of the eagle. Snobs are vain. But so, too, are heroes. Come, oh! my young brother bucks, let us be vain together. Let us join hands and help each other to increase our vanity. Let us be vain, not of our trousers and hair, but of brave hearts and working hands, of truth, of purity, of nobility. Let us be too vain to stoop to aught that is mean or base, too vain for petty selfishness and little-minded envy, too vain to say an unkind word or do an unkind act. Let us be vain of being single-hearted, upright gentlemen in the midst of a world of knaves. Let us pride ourselves upon thinking high thoughts, achieving great deeds, living good lives.

ON GETTING ON IN THE WORLD.

Not exactly the sort of thing for an idle fellow to think about, is it? But outsiders, you know, often see most of the game; and sitting in my arbor by the wayside, smoking my hookah of contentment and eating the sweet lotus-leaves of indolence, I can look out musingly upon the whirling throng that rolls and tumbles past me on the great high-road of life.

Never-ending is the wild procession. Day and night you can hear the quick tramp of the myriad feet—some running, some walking, some halting and lame; but all hastening, all eager in the feverish race, all straining life and limb and heart and soul to reach the ever-receding horizon of success.

Mark them as they surge along—men and women, old and young, gentle and simple, fair and foul, rich and poor, merry and sad—all hurrying, bustling, scrambling. The strong pushing aside the weak, the cunning creeping past the foolish; those behind elbowing those before; those in front kicking, as they run, at those behind. Look close and see the flitting show. Here is an old man panting for breath, and there a timid maiden driven by a hard and sharp-faced matron; here is a studious youth, reading "How to Get On in the World" and letting everybody pass him as he stumbles along with his eyes on his book; here is a bored-looking man, with a fashionably dressed woman jogging his elbow; here a boy gazing wistfully back at the sunny village that he never again will see; here, with a firm and easy step, strides a broad-shouldered man; and here, with stealthy tread, a thin-faced, stooping fellow dodges and shuffles upon his way; here, with gaze fixed always on the ground, an artful rogue carefully works his way from side to side of the road and thinks he is going forward; and here a youth with a noble face stands, hesitating as he looks from the distant goal to the mud beneath his feet.

And now into sight comes a fair girl, with her dainty face growing more wrinkled at every step, and now a care-worn man, and now a hopeful lad.

A motley throng—a motley throng! Prince and beggar, sinner and saint, butcher and baker and candlestick maker, tinkers and tailors, and plowboys and sailors—all jostling along together. Here the counsel in his wig and gown, and here the old Jew clothes-man under his dingy tiara; here the soldier in his scarlet, and here the undertaker's mute in streaming hat-band and worn cotton gloves; here the musty scholar fumbling his faded leaves, and here the scented actor dangling his showy seals. Here the glib politician crying his legislative panaceas, and here the peripatetic Cheap-Jack holding aloft his quack cures for human ills. Here the sleek capitalist and there the sinewy laborer; here the man of science and here the shoe-back; here the poet and here the water-rate collector; here the cabinet minister and there the ballet-dancer. Here a red-nosed publican shouting the praises of his vats and there a temperance lecturer at 50 pounds a night; here a judge and there a swindler; here a priest and there a gambler. Here a jeweled duchess, smiling and gracious; here a thin lodging-house keeper, irritable with cooking; and here a wabbling, strutting thing, tawdry in paint and finery.

Cheek by cheek they struggle onward. Screaming, cursing, and praying, laughing, singing, and moaning, they rush past side by side. Their speed never slackens, the race never ends. There is no wayside rest for them, no halt by cooling fountains, no pause beneath green shades. On, on, on—on through the heat and the crowd and the dust—on, or they will be trampled down and lost—on, with throbbing brain and tottering limbs—on, till the heart grows sick, and the eyes grow blurred, and a gurgling groan tells those behind they may close up another space.

And yet, in spite of the killing pace and the stony track, who but the sluggard or the dolt can hold aloof from the course? Who—like the belated traveler that stands watching fairy revels till he snatches and drains the goblin cup and springs into the whirling circle—can view the mad tumult and not be drawn into its midst? Not I, for one. I confess to the wayside arbor, the pipe of contentment, and the lotus-leaves being altogether unsuitable metaphors. They sounded very nice and philosophical, but I'm afraid I am not the sort of person to sit in arbors smoking pipes when there is any fun going on outside. I think I more resemble the Irishman who, seeing a crowd collecting, sent his little girl out to ask if there was going to be a row—"'Cos, if so, father would like to be in it."

I love the fierce strife. I like to watch it. I like to hear of people getting on in it—battling their way bravely and fairly—that is, not slipping through by luck or trickery. It stirs one's old Saxon fighting blood like the tales of "knights who fought 'gainst fearful odds" that thrilled us in our school-boy days.

And fighting the battle of life is fighting against fearful odds, too. There are giants and dragons in this nineteenth century, and the golden casket that they guard is not so easy to win as it appears in the story-books. There, Algernon takes one long, last look at the ancestral hall, dashes the tear-drop from his eye, and goes off—to return in three years' time, rolling in riches. The authors do not tell us "how it's done," which is a pity, for it would surely prove exciting.

But then not one novelist in a thousand ever does tell us the real story of their hero. They linger for a dozen pages over a tea-party, but sum up a life's history with "he had become one of our merchant princes," or "he was now a great artist, with the world at his feet." Why, there is more real life in one of Gilbert's patter-songs than in half the biographical novels ever written. He relates to us all the various steps by which his office-boy rose to be the "ruler of the queen's navee," and explains to us how the briefless barrister managed to become a great and good judge, "ready to try this breach of promise of marriage." It is in the petty details, not in the great results, that the interest of existence lies.

What we really want is a novel showing us all the hidden under-current of an ambitious man's career—his struggles, and failures, and hopes, his disappointments and victories. It would be an immense success. I am sure the wooing of Fortune would prove quite as interesting a tale as the wooing of any flesh-and-blood maiden, though, by the way, it would read extremely similar; for Fortune is, indeed, as the ancients painted her, very like a woman—not quite so unreasonable and inconsistent, but nearly so—and the pursuit is much the same in one case as in the other. Ben Jonson's couplet—

> "Court a mistress, she denies you;
> Let her alone, she will court you"—

puts them both in a nutshell. A woman never thoroughly cares for her lover until he has ceased to care for her; and it is not until you have snapped your fingers in Fortune's face and turned on your heel that she begins to smile upon you.

But by that time you do not much care whether she smiles or frowns. Why could she not have smiled when her smiles would have filled you with ecstasy? Everything comes too late in this world.

Good people say that it is quite right and proper that it should be so, and that it proves ambition is wicked.

Bosh! Good people are altogether wrong. (They always are, in my opinion. We never agree on any single point.) What would the world do without ambitious people, I should like to know? Why, it would be as flabby as a Norfolk dumpling. Ambitious people are the leaven which raises it into wholesome bread. Without ambitious people the world would never get up. They are busybodies who are about early in the morning, hammering, shouting, and rattling the fire-irons, and rendering it generally impossible for the rest of the house to remain in bed.

Wrong to be ambitious, forsooth! The men wrong who, with bent back and sweating brow, cut the smooth road over which humanity marches forward from generation to generation! Men wrong for using the talents that their Master has intrusted to them—for toiling while others play!

Of course they are seeking their reward. Man is not given that godlike unselfishness that thinks only of others' good. But in working for themselves they are working for us all. We are so bound together that no man can labor for himself alone. Each blow he strikes in his own behalf helps to mold the universe. The stream in struggling onward turns the mill-wheel; the coral insect, fashioning its tiny cell, joins continents to one another; and the ambitious man, building a pedestal for himself, leaves a monument to posterity. Alexander and Caesar fought for their own ends, but in doing so they put a belt of civilization half round the earth. Stephenson, to win a fortune, invented the steam-engine; and Shakespeare wrote his plays in order to keep a comfortable home for Mrs. Shakespeare and the little Shakespeares.

Contented, unambitious people are all very well in their way. They form a neat, useful background for great portraits to be painted against, and they make a respectable, if not particularly intelligent, audience for the active spirits of the age to play before. I have not a word to say against contented people so long as they keep quiet. But do not, for goodness' sake, let them go strutting about, as they are so fond of doing, crying out that they are the true models for the whole species. Why, they are the deadheads, the drones in the great hive, the street crowds that lounge about, gaping at those who are working.

And let them not imagine, either—as they are also fond of doing—that they are very wise and philosophical and that it is a very artful thing to be contented. It may be true that "a contented mind is happy anywhere," but so is a Jerusalem pony, and the consequence is that both are put anywhere and are treated anyhow. "Oh, you need not bother about him," is what is said; "he is very contented as he is, and it would be a pity to disturb him." And so your contented party is passed over and the discontented man gets his place.

If you are foolish enough to be contented, don't show it, but grumble with the rest; and if you can do with a little, ask for a great deal. Because if you don't you won't get any. In this world it is necessary to adopt the principle pursued by the plaintiff in an action for damages, and to demand ten times more than you are ready to accept. If you can feel satisfied with a hundred, begin by insisting on a thousand; if you start by suggesting a hundred you will only get ten.

It was by not following this simple plan that poor Jean Jacques Rousseau came to such grief. He fixed the summit of his earthly bliss at living in an orchard with an amiable woman and a cow, and he never attained even that. He did get as far as the orchard, but the woman was not amiable, and she brought her mother with her, and there was no cow. Now, if he had made up his mind for a large country estate, a houseful of angels, and a cattle-show, he might have lived to possess his kitchen garden and one head of live-stock, and even possibly have come across that *rara-avis*—a really amiable woman.

What a terribly dull affair, too, life must be for contented people! How heavy the time must hang upon their hands, and what on earth do they occupy their thoughts with, supposing that they have any? Reading the paper and smoking seems to be the intellectual food of the majority of them, to which the more energetic add playing the flute and talking about the affairs of the next-door neighbor.

They never knew the excitement of expectation nor the stern delight of accomplished effort, such as stir the pulse of the man who has objects, and hopes, and plans. To the ambitious man life is a brilliant game—a game that calls forth all his tact and energy and nerve—a game to be won, in the long run, by the quick eye and the steady hand, and yet having sufficient chance about its working out to give it all the glorious zest of uncertainty. He exults in it as the strong swimmer in the heaving billows, as the athlete in the wrestle, the soldier in the battle.

And if he be defeated he wins the grim joy of fighting; if he lose the race, he, at least, has had a run. Better to work and fail than to sleep one's life away.

So, walk up, walk up, walk up. Walk up, ladies and gentlemen! walk up, boys and girls! Show your skill and try your strength; brave your luck and prove your pluck. Walk up! The show is never closed and the game is always going. The only genuine sport in all the fair, gentlemen—highly respectable and strictly moral—patronized by the nobility, clergy, and gentry. Established in the year one, gentlemen, and been flourishing ever since—walk up! Walk up, ladies and gentle-gentlemen, and take a hand. There are prizes for all and all can play. There is gold for the man and fame for the boy; rank for the maiden and pleasure for the fool. So walk up, ladies and gentlemen, walk up!—all prizes and no blanks; for some few win, and as to the rest, why—

> "The rapture of pursuing
>   Is the prize the vanquished gain."

ON THE WEATHER.

Things do go so contrary-like with me. I wanted to hit upon an especially novel, out-of-the-way subject for one of these articles. "I will write one paper about something altogether new," I said to myself; "something that nobody else has ever written or talked about before; and then I can have it all my own way." And I went about for days, trying to think of something of this kind; and I couldn't. And Mrs. Cutting, our charwoman, came yesterday—I don't mind mentioning her name, because I know she will not see this book. She would not look at such a frivolous publication. She never reads anything but the Bible and *Lloyd's Weekly News*. All other literature she considers unnecessary and sinful.

She said: "Lor', sir, you do look worried."

I said: "Mrs. Cutting, I am trying to think of a subject the discussion of which will come upon the world in the nature of a startler—some subject upon which no previous human being has ever said a word—some subject that will attract by its novelty, invigorate by its surprising freshness."

She laughed and said I was a funny gentleman.

That's my luck again. When I make serious observations people chuckle; when I attempt a joke nobody sees it. I had a beautiful one last week. I thought it so good, and I worked it up and brought it in artfully at a dinner-party. I forget how exactly, but we had been talking about the attitude of Shakespeare toward the Reformation, and I said something and immediately added, "Ah, that reminds me; such a funny thing happened the other day in Whitechapel." "Oh," said they, "what was that?" "Oh, 'twas awfully funny," I replied, beginning to giggle myself; "it will make you roar;" and I told it them.

There was dead silence when I finished—it was one of those long jokes, too—and then, at last, somebody said: "And that was the joke?"

I assured them that it was, and they were very polite and took my word for it. All but one old gentleman at the other end of the table, who wanted to know which was the joke—what he said to her or what she said to him; and we argued it out.

Some people are too much the other way. I knew a fellow once whose natural tendency to laugh at everything was so strong that if you wanted to talk seriously to him, you had to explain beforehand that what you were going to say would not be amusing. Unless you got him to clearly understand this, he would go off into fits of merriment over every word you uttered. I have known him on being asked the time stop short in the middle of the road, slap his leg, and burst into a roar of laughter. One never dared say anything really funny to that man. A good joke would have killed him on the spot.

In the present instance I vehemently repudiated the accusation of frivolity, and pressed Mrs. Cutting for practical ideas. She then became thoughtful and hazarded "samplers;" saying that she never heard them spoken much of now, but that they used to be all the rage when she was a girl.

I declined samplers and begged her to think again. She pondered a long while, with a tea-tray in her hands, and at last suggested the weather, which she was sure had been most trying of late.

And ever since that idiotic suggestion I have been unable to get the weather out of my thoughts or anything else in.

It certainly is most wretched weather. At all events it is so now at the time I am writing, and if it isn't particularly unpleasant when I come to be read it soon will be.

It always is wretched weather according to us. The weather is like the government—always in the wrong. In summer-time we say it is stifling; in winter that it is killing; in spring and autumn we find fault with it for being neither one thing nor the other and wish it would make up its mind. If it is fine we say the country is being ruined for want of rain; if it does rain we pray for fine weather. If December passes without snow, we indignantly demand to know what has become of our good old-fashioned winters, and talk as if we had been cheated out of something we had bought and paid for; and when it does snow, our language is a disgrace to a Christian nation. We shall never be content until each man makes his own weather and keeps it to himself.

If that cannot be arranged, we would rather do without it altogether.

Yet I think it is only to us in cities that all weather is so unwelcome. In her own home, the country, Nature is sweet in all her moods. What can be more beautiful than the snow, falling big with mystery in silent softness, decking the fields and trees with white as if for a fairy wedding! And how delightful is a walk when the frozen ground rings beneath our swinging tread—when our blood tingles in the rare keen air, and the sheep-dogs' distant bark and children's laughter peals faintly clear like Alpine bells across the open hills! And then skating! scudding with wings of steel across the swaying ice, making whirring music as we fly. And oh, how dainty is spring—Nature at sweet eighteen!

When the little hopeful leaves peep out so fresh and green, so pure and bright, like young lives pushing shyly out into the bustling world; when the fruit-tree blossoms, pink and white, like village maidens in their Sunday frocks, hide each whitewashed cottage in a cloud of fragile splendor; and the cuckoo's note upon the breeze is wafted through the woods! And summer, with its deep dark green and drowsy hum—when the rain-drops whisper solemn secrets to the listening leaves and the twilight lingers in the lanes! And autumn! ah, how sadly fair, with its golden glow and the dying grandeur of its tinted woods—its blood-red sunsets and its ghostly evening mists, with its busy murmur of reapers, and its laden orchards, and the calling of the gleaners, and the festivals of praise!

The very rain, and sleet, and hail seem only Nature's useful servants when found doing their simple duties in the country; and the East Wind himself is nothing worse than a boisterous friend when we meet him between the hedge-rows.

But in the city where the painted stucco blisters under the smoky sun, and the sooty rain brings slush and mud, and the snow lies piled in dirty heaps, and the chill blasts whistle down dingy streets and shriek round flaring gas lit corners, no face of Nature charms us. Weather in towns is like a skylark in a counting-house—out of place and in the way. Towns ought to be covered in, warmed by hot-water pipes, and lighted by electricity. The weather is a country lass and does not appear to advantage in town. We liked well enough to flirt with her in the hay-field, but she does not seem so fascinating when we meet her in Pall Mall. There is too much of her there. The frank, free laugh and hearty voice that sounded so pleasant in the dairy jars against the artificiality of town-bred life, and her ways become exceedingly trying.

Just lately she has been favoring us with almost incessant rain for about three weeks; and I am a demned damp, moist, unpleasant body, as Mr. Mantalini puts it.

Our next-door neighbor comes out in the back garden every now and then and says it's doing the country a world of good—not his coming out into the back garden, but the weather. He doesn't understand anything about it, but ever since he started a cucumber-frame last summer he has regarded himself in the light of an agriculturist, and talks in this absurd way with the idea of impressing the rest of the terrace with the notion that he is a retired farmer. I can only hope that for this once he is correct, and that the weather really is doing good to something, because it is doing me a considerable amount of damage. It is spoiling both my clothes and my temper. The latter I can afford, as I have a good supply of it, but it wounds me to the quick to see my dear old hats and trousers sinking, prematurely worn and aged, beneath the cold world's blasts and snows.

There is my new spring suit, too. A beautiful suit it was, and now it is hanging up so bespattered with mud I can't bear to look at it.

That was Jim's fault, that was. I should never have gone out in it that night if it had not been for him. I was just trying it on when he came in. He threw up his arms with a wild yell the moment he caught sight of it, and exclaimed that he had "got 'em again!"

I said: "Does it fit all right behind?"

"Spiffin, old man," he replied. And then he wanted to know if I was coming out.

I said "no" at first, but he overruled me. He said that a man with a suit like that had no right to stop indoors. "Every citizen," said he, "owes a duty to the public. Each one should contribute to the general happiness as far as lies in his power. Come out and give the girls a treat."

Jim is slangy. I don't know where he picks it up. It certainly is not from me.

I said: "Do you think it will really please 'em?" He said it would be like a day in the country to them.

That decided me. It was a lovely evening and I went.

When I got home I undressed and rubbed myself down with whisky, put my feet in hot water and a mustard-plaster on my chest, had a basin of gruel and a glass of hot brandy-and-water, tallowed my nose, and went to bed.

These prompt and vigorous measures, aided by a naturally strong constitution, were the means of preserving my life; but as for the suit! Well, there, it isn't a suit; it's a splash-board.

And I did fancy that suit, too. But that's just the way. I never do get particularly fond of anything in this world but what something dreadful happens to it. I had a tame rat when I was a boy, and I loved that animal as only a boy would love an old water-rat; and one day it fell into a large dish of gooseberry-fool that was standing to cool in the kitchen, and nobody knew what had become of the poor creature until the second helping.

I do hate wet weather in town. At least, it is not so much the wet as the mud that I object to. Somehow or other I seem to possess an irresistible alluring power over mud. I have only to show myself in the street on a muddy day to be half-smothered by it. It all comes of being so attractive, as the old lady said when she was struck by lightning. Other people can go out on dirty days and walk about for hours without getting a speck upon themselves; while if I go across the road I come back a perfect disgrace to be seen (as in my boyish days my poor dear mother tried often to tell me). If there were only one dab of mud to be found in the whole of London, I am convinced I should carry it off from all competitors.

I wish I could return the affection, but I fear I never shall be able to. I have a horror of what they call the "London particular." I feel miserable and muggy all through a dirty day, and it is quite a relief to pull one's clothes off and get into bed, out of the way of it all. Everything goes wrong in wet weather. I don't know how it is, but there always seem to me to be more people, and dogs, and perambulators, and cabs, and carts about in wet weather than at any other time, and they all get in your way more, and everybody is so disagreeable—except myself—and it does make me so wild. And then, too, somehow I always find myself carrying more things in wet weather than in dry; and when you have a bag, and three parcels, and a newspaper, and it suddenly comes on to rain, you can't open your umbrella.

Which reminds me of another phase of the weather that I can't bear, and that is April weather (so called because it always comes in May). Poets think it very nice. As it does not know its own mind five minutes together, they liken it to a woman; and it is supposed to be very charming on that account. I don't appreciate it, myself. Such lightning-change business may be all very agreeable in a girl. It is no doubt highly delightful to have to do with a person who grins one moment about nothing at all, and snivels the next for precisely the same cause, and who then giggles, and then sulks, and who is rude, and affectionate, and bad-tempered, and jolly, and boisterous, and silent, and passionate, and cold, and stand-offish, and flopping, all in one minute (mind, I don't say this. It is those poets. And they are supposed to be connoisseurs of this sort of thing); but in the weather the disadvantages of the system are more apparent. A woman's tears do not make one wet, but the rain does; and her coldness does not lay the foundations of asthma and rheumatism, as the east wind is apt to. I can prepare for and put up with a regularly bad day, but these ha'porth-of-all-sorts kind of days do not suit me. It aggravates me to see a bright blue sky above me when I am walking along wet through, and there is something so exasperating about the way the sun comes out smiling after a drenching shower, and seems to say: "Lord love you, you don't mean to say you're wet? Well, I am surprised. Why, it was only my fun."

They don't give you time to open or shut your umbrella in an English April, especially if it is an "automaton" one—the umbrella, I mean, not the April.

I bought an "automaton" once in April, and I did have a time with it! I wanted an umbrella, and I went into a shop in the Strand and told them so, and they said:

"Yes, sir. What sort of an umbrella would you like?"

I said I should like one that would keep the rain off, and that would not allow itself to be left behind in a railway carriage.

"Try an 'automaton,'" said the shopman.

"What's an 'automaton'?" said I.

"Oh, it's a beautiful arrangement," replied the man, with a touch of enthusiasm. "It opens and shuts itself."

I bought one and found that he was quite correct. It did open and shut itself. I had no control over it whatever. When it began to rain, which it did that season every alternate five minutes, I used to try and get the machine to open, but it would not budge; and then I used to stand and struggle with the wretched thing, and shake it, and swear at it, while the rain poured down in torrents. Then the moment the rain ceased the absurd thing would go up suddenly with a jerk and would not come down again; and I had to walk about under a bright blue sky, with an umbrella over my head, wishing that it would come on to rain again, so that it might not seem that I was insane.

When it did shut it did so unexpectedly and knocked one's hat off.

I don't know why it should be so, but it is an undeniable fact that there is nothing makes a man look so supremely ridiculous as losing his hat. The feeling of helpless misery that shoots down one's back on suddenly becoming aware that one's head is bare is among the most bitter ills that flesh is heir to. And then there is the wild chase after it, accompanied by an excitable small dog, who thinks it is a game, and in the course of which you are certain to upset three or four innocent children—to say nothing of their mothers—butt a fat old gentleman on to the top of a perambulator, and carom off a ladies' seminary into the arms of a wet sweep.

After this, the idiotic hilarity of the spectators and the disreputable appearance of the hat when recovered appear but of minor importance.

Altogether, what between March winds, April showers, and the entire absence of May flowers, spring is not a success in cities. It is all very well in the country, as I have said, but in towns whose population is anything over ten thousand it most certainly ought to be abolished. In the world's grim workshops it is like the children—out of place. Neither shows to advantage amid the dust and din. It seems so sad to see the little dirt-grimed brats try to play in the noisy courts and muddy streets. Poor little uncared-for, unwanted human atoms, they are not children. Children are bright-eyed, chubby, and shy. These are dingy, screeching elves, their tiny faces seared and withered, their baby laughter cracked and hoarse.

The spring of life and the spring of the year were alike meant to be cradled in the green lap of nature. To us in the town spring brings but its cold winds and drizzling rains. We must seek it among the leafless woods and the brambly lanes, on the heathy moors and the great still hills, if we want to feel its joyous breath and hear its silent voices. There is a glorious freshness in the spring there. The scurrying clouds, the open bleakness, the rushing wind, and the clear bright air thrill one with vague energies and hopes. Life, like the landscape around us, seems bigger, and wider, and freer—a rainbow road leading to unknown ends. Through the silvery rents that bar the sky we seem to catch a glimpse of the great hope and grandeur that lies around this little throbbing world, and a breath of its scent is wafted us on the wings of the wild March wind.

Strange thoughts we do not understand are stirring in our hearts. Voices are calling us to some great effort, to some mighty work. But we do not comprehend their meaning yet, and the hidden echoes within us that would reply are struggling, inarticulate and dumb.

We stretch our hands like children to the light, seeking to grasp we know not what. Our thoughts, like the boys' thoughts in the Danish song, are very long, long thoughts, and very vague; we cannot see their end.

It must be so. All thoughts that peer outside this narrow world cannot be else than dim and shapeless. The thoughts that we can clearly grasp are very little thoughts—that two and two make four-that when we are hungry it is pleasant to eat—that honesty is the best policy; all greater thoughts are undefined and vast to our poor childish brains. We see but dimly through the mists that roll around our time-girt isle of life, and only hear the distant surging of the great sea beyond.

ON CATS AND DOGS.

What I've suffered from them this morning no tongue can tell. It began with Gustavus Adolphus. Gustavus Adolphus (they call him "Gusty" down-stairs for short) is a very good sort of dog when he is in the middle of a large field or on a fairly extensive common, but I won't have him indoors. He means well, but this house is not his size. He stretches himself, and over go two chairs and a what-not. He wags his tail, and the room looks as if a devastating army had marched through it. He breathes, and it puts the fire out.

At dinner-time he creeps in under the table, lies there for awhile, and then gets up suddenly; the first intimation we have of his movements being given by the table, which appears animated by a desire to turn somersaults. We all clutch at it frantically and endeavor to maintain it in a horizontal position; whereupon his struggles, he being under the impression that some wicked conspiracy is being hatched against him, become fearful, and the final picture presented is generally that of an overturned table and a smashed-up dinner sandwiched between two sprawling layers of infuriated men and women.

He came in this morning in his usual style, which he appears to have founded on that of an American cyclone, and the first thing he did was to sweep my coffee-cup off the table with his tail, sending the contents full into the middle of my waistcoat.

I rose from my chair hurriedly and remarking "——," approached him at a rapid rate. He preceded me in the direction of the door. At the door he met Eliza coming in with eggs. Eliza observed "Ugh!" and sat down on the floor, the eggs took up different positions about the carpet, where they spread themselves out, and Gustavus Adolphus left the room. I called after him, strongly advising him to go straight downstairs and not let me see him again for the next hour or so; and he seeming to agree with me, dodged the coal-scoop and went, while I returned, dried myself and finished breakfast. I made sure that he had gone in to the yard, but when I looked into the passage ten minutes later he was sitting at the top of the stairs. I ordered him down at once, but he only barked and jumped about, so I went to see what was the matter.

It was Tittums. She was sitting on the top stair but one and wouldn't let him pass.

Tittums is our kitten. She is about the size of a penny roll. Her back was up and she was swearing like a medical student.

She does swear fearfully. I do a little that way myself sometimes, but I am a mere amateur compared with her. To tell you the truth—mind, this is strictly between ourselves, please; I shouldn't like your wife to know I said it—the women folk don't understand these things; but between you and me, you know, I think it does a man good to swear. Swearing is the safety-valve through which the bad temper that might otherwise do serious internal injury to his mental mechanism escapes in harmless vaporing. When a man has said: "Bless you, my dear, sweet sir. What the sun, moon, and stars made you so careless (if I may be permitted the expression) as to allow your light and delicate foot to descend upon my corn with so much force? Is it that you are physically incapable of comprehending the direction in which you are proceeding? you nice, clever young man—you!" or words to that effect, he feels better. Swearing has the same soothing effect upon our angry passions that smashing the furniture or slamming the doors is so well known to exercise; added to which it is much cheaper. Swearing clears a man out like a pen'orth of gunpowder does the wash-house chimney. An occasional explosion is good for both. I rather distrust a man who never swears, or savagely kicks the foot-stool, or pokes the fire with unnecessary violence. Without some outlet, the anger caused by the ever-occurring troubles of life is apt to rankle and fester within. The petty annoyance, instead of being thrown from us, sits down beside us and becomes a sorrow, and the little offense is brooded over till, in the hot-bed of rumination, it grows into a great injury, under whose poisonous shadow springs up hatred and revenge.

Swearing relieves the feelings—that is what swearing does. I explained this to my aunt on one occasion, but it didn't answer with her. She said I had no business to have such feelings.

That is what I told Tittums. I told her she ought to be ashamed of herself, brought up in at Christian family as she was, too. I don't so much mind hearing an old cat swear, but I can't bear to see a mere kitten give way to it. It seems sad in one so young.

I put Tittums in my pocket and returned to my desk. I forgot her for the moment, and when I looked I found that she had squirmed out of my pocket on to the table and was trying to swallow the pen; then she put her leg into the ink-pot and upset it; then she licked her leg; then she swore again—at me this time.

I put her down on the floor, and there Tim began rowing with her. I do wish Tim would mind his own business. It was no concern of his what she had been doing. Besides, he is not a saint himself. He is only a two-year-old fox-terrier, and he interferes with everything and gives himself the airs of a gray-headed Scotch collie.

Tittums' mother has come in and Tim has got his nose scratched, for which I am remarkably glad. I have put them all three out in the passage, where they are fighting at the present moment. I'm in a mess with the ink and in a thundering bad temper; and if anything more in the cat or dog line comes fooling about me this morning, it had better bring its own funeral contractor with it.

Yet, in general, I like cats and dogs very much indeed. What jolly chaps they are! They are much superior to human beings as companions. They do not quarrel or argue with you. They never talk about themselves but listen to you while you talk about yourself, and keep up an appearance of being interested in the conversation. They never make stupid remarks. They never observe to Miss Brown across a dinner-table that they always understood she was very sweet on Mr. Jones (who has just married Miss Robinson). They never mistake your wife's cousin for her husband and fancy that you are the father-in-law. And they never ask a young author with fourteen tragedies, sixteen comedies, seven farces, and a couple of burlesques in his desk why he doesn't write a play.

They never say unkind things. They never tell us of our faults, "merely for our own good." They do not at inconvenient moments mildly remind us of our past follies and mistakes. They do not say, "Oh, yes, a lot of use you are if you are ever really wanted"—sarcastic like. They never inform us, like our *inamoratas* sometimes do, that we are not nearly so nice as we used to be. We are always the same to them.

They are always glad to see us. They are with us in all our humors. They are merry when we are glad, sober when we feel solemn, and sad when we are sorrowful.

"Halloo! happy and want a lark? Right you are; I'm your man. Here I am, frisking round you, leaping, barking, pirouetting, ready for any amount of fun and mischief. Look at my eyes if you doubt me. What shall it be? A romp in the drawing-room and never mind the furniture, or a scamper in the fresh, cool air, a scud across the fields and down the hill, and won't we let old Gaffer Goggles' geese know what time o' day it is, neither! Whoop! come along."

Or you'd like to be quiet and think. Very well. Pussy can sit on the arm of the chair and purr, and Montmorency will curl himself up on the rug and blink at the fire, yet keeping one eye on you the while, in case you are seized with any sudden desire in the direction of rats.

And when we bury our face in our hands and wish we had never been born, they don't sit up very straight and observe that we have brought it all upon ourselves. They don't even hope it will be a warning to us. But they come up softly and shove their heads against us. If it is a cat she stands on your shoulder, rumples your hair, and says, "Lor,' I am sorry for you, old man," as plain as words can speak; and if it is a dog he looks up at you with his big, true eyes and says with them, "Well you've always got me, you know. We'll go through the world together and always stand by each other, won't we?"

He is very imprudent, a dog is. He never makes it his business to inquire whether you are in the right or in the wrong, never bothers as to whether you are going up or down upon life's ladder, never asks whether you are rich or poor, silly or wise, sinner or saint. You are his pal. That is enough for him, and come luck or misfortune, good repute or bad, honor or shame, he is going to stick to you, to comfort you, guard you, and give his life for you if need be—foolish, brainless, soulless dog!

Ah! old stanch friend, with your deep, clear eyes and bright, quick glances, that take in all one has to say before one has time to speak it, do you know you are only an animal and have no mind? Do you know that that dull-eyed, gin-sodden lout leaning against the post out there is immeasurably your intellectual superior? Do you know that every little-minded, selfish scoundrel who lives by cheating and tricking, who never did a gentle deed or said a kind word, who never had a thought that was not mean and low or a desire that was not base, whose every action is a fraud, whose every utterance is a lie—do you know that these crawling skulks (and there are millions of them in the world), do you know they are all as much superior to you as the sun is superior to rushlight you honorable, brave-hearted, unselfish brute? They are MEN, you know, and MEN are the greatest, and noblest, and wisest, and best beings in the whole vast eternal universe. Any man will tell you that.

Yes, poor doggie, you are very stupid, very stupid indeed, compared with us clever men, who understand all about politics and philosophy, and who know everything, in short, except what we are and where we came from and whither we are going, and what everything outside this tiny world and most things in it are.

Never mind, though, pussy and doggie, we like you both all the better for your being stupid. We all like stupid things. Men can't bear clever women, and a woman's ideal man is some one she can call a "dear old stupid." It is so pleasant to come across people more stupid than ourselves. We love them at once for being so. The world must be rather a rough place for clever people. Ordinary folk dislike them, and as for themselves, they hate each other most cordially.

But there, the clever people are such a very insignificant minority that it really doesn't much matter if they are unhappy. So long as the foolish people can be made comfortable the world, as a whole, will get on tolerably well.

Cats have the credit of being more worldly wise than dogs—of looking more after their own interests and being less blindly devoted to those of their friends. And we men and women are naturally shocked at such selfishness. Cats certainly do love a family that has a carpet in the kitchen more than a family that has not; and if there are many children about, they prefer to spend their leisure time next door. But, taken altogether, cats are libeled. Make a friend of one, and she will stick to you through thick and thin. All the cats that I have had have been most firm comrades. I had a cat once that used to follow me about everywhere, until it even got quite embarrassing, and I had to beg her, as a personal favor, not to accompany me any further down the High Street. She used to sit up for me when I was late home and meet me in the passage. It made me feel quite like a married man, except that she never asked where I had been and then didn't believe me when I told her.

Another cat I had used to get drunk regularly every day. She would hang about for hours outside the cellar door for the purpose of sneaking in on the first opportunity and lapping up the drippings from the beer-cask. I do not mention this habit of hers in praise of the species, but merely to show how almost human some of them are. If the transmigration of souls is a fact, this animal was certainly qualifying most rapidly for a Christian, for her vanity was only second to her love of drink. Whenever she caught a particularly big rat, she would bring it up into the room where we were all sitting, lay the corpse down in the midst of us, and wait to be praised. Lord! how the girls used to scream.

Poor rats! They seem only to exist so that cats and dogs may gain credit for killing them and chemists make a fortune by inventing specialties in poison for their destruction. And yet there is something fascinating about them. There is a weirdness and uncanniness attaching to them. They are so cunning and strong, so terrible in their numbers, so cruel, so secret. They swarm in deserted houses, where the broken casements hang rotting to the crumbling walls and the doors swing creaking on their rusty hinges. They know the sinking ship and leave her, no one knows how or whither. They whisper to each other in their hiding-places how a doom will fall upon the hall and the great name die forgotten. They do fearful deeds in ghastly charnel-houses.

No tale of horror is complete without the rats. In stories of ghosts and murderers they scamper through the echoing rooms, and the gnawing of their teeth is heard behind the wainscot, and their gleaming eyes peer through the holes in the worm-eaten tapestry, and they scream in shrill, unearthly notes in the dead of night, while the moaning wind sweeps, sobbing, round the ruined turret towers, and passes wailing like a woman through the chambers bare and tenantless.

And dying prisoners, in their loathsome dungeons, see through the horrid gloom their small red eyes, like glittering coals, hear in the death-like silence the rush of their claw-like feet, and start up shrieking in the darkness and watch through the awful night.

I love to read tales about rats. They make my flesh creep so. I like that tale of Bishop Hatto and the rats. The wicked bishop, you know, had ever so much corn stored in his granaries and would not let the starving people touch it, but when they prayed to him for food gathered them together in his barn, and then shutting the doors on them, set fire to the place and burned them all to death. But next day there came thousands upon thousands of rats, sent to do judgment on him. Then Bishop Hatto fled to his strong tower that stood in the middle of the Rhine, and barred himself in and fancied he was safe. But the rats! they swam the river, they gnawed their way through the thick stone walls, and ate him alive where he sat.

> "They have whetted their teeth against the stones,
> And now they pick the bishop's bones;
> They gnawed the flesh from every limb,
> For they were sent to do judgment on him."

Oh, it's a lovely tale.

Then there is the story of the Pied Piper of Hamelin, how first he piped the rats away, and afterward, when the mayor broke faith with him, drew all the children along with him and went into the mountain. What a curious old legend that is! I wonder what it means, or has it any meaning at all? There seems something strange and deep lying hid beneath the rippling rhyme. It haunts me, that picture of the quaint, mysterious old piper piping through Hamelin's narrow streets, and the children following with dancing feet and thoughtful, eager faces. The old folks try to stay them, but the children pay no heed. They hear the weird, witched music and must follow. The games are left unfinished and the playthings drop from their careless hands. They know not whither they are hastening. The mystic music calls to them, and they follow, heedless and unasking where. It stirs and vibrates in their hearts and other sounds grow faint. So they wander through Pied Piper Street away from Hamelin town.

I get thinking sometimes if the Pied Piper is really dead, or if he may not still be roaming up and down our streets and lanes, but playing now so softly that only the children hear him. Why do the little faces look so grave and solemn when they pause awhile from romping, and stand, deep wrapt, with straining eyes? They only shake their curly heads and dart back laughing to their playmates when we question them. But I fancy myself they have been listening to the magic music of the old Pied Piper, and perhaps with those bright eyes of theirs have even seen his odd, fantastic figure gliding unnoticed through the whirl and throng.

Even we grown-up children hear his piping now and then. But the yearning notes are very far away, and the noisy, blustering world is always bellowing so loud it drowns the dreamlike melody. One day the sweet, sad strains will sound out full and clear, and then we too shall, like the little children, throw our playthings all aside and follow. The loving hands will be stretched out to stay us, and the voices we have learned to listen for will cry to us to stop. But we shall push the fond arms gently back and pass out through the sorrowing house and through the open door. For the wild, strange music will be ringing in our hearts, and we shall know the meaning of its song by then.

I wish people could love animals without getting maudlin over them, as so many do. Women are the most hardened offenders in such respects, but even our intellectual sex often degrade pets into nuisances by absurd idolatry. There are the gushing young ladies who, having read "David Copperfield," have thereupon sought out a small, longhaired dog of nondescript breed, possessed of an irritating habit of criticising a man's trousers, and of finally commenting upon the same by a sniff indicative of contempt and disgust. They talk sweet girlish prattle to this animal (when there is any one near enough to overhear them), and they kiss its nose, and put its unwashed head up against their cheek in a most touching manner; though I have noticed that these caresses are principally performed when there are young men hanging about.

Then there are the old ladies who worship a fat poodle, scant of breath and full of fleas. I knew a couple of elderly spinsters once who had a sort of German sausage on legs which they called a dog between them. They used to wash its face with warm water every morning. It had a mutton cutlet regularly for breakfast; and on Sundays, when one of the ladies went to church, the other always stopped at home to keep the dog company.

There are many families where the whole interest of life is centered upon the dog. Cats, by the way, rarely suffer from excess of adulation. A cat possesses a very fair sense of the ridiculous, and will put her paw down kindly but firmly upon any nonsense of this kind. Dogs, however, seem to like it. They encourage their owners in the tomfoolery, and the consequence is that in the circles I am speaking of what "dear Fido" has done, does do, will do, won't do, can do, can't do, was doing, is doing, is going to do, shall do, shan't do, and is about to be going to have done is the continual theme of discussion from morning till night.

All the conversation, consisting, as it does, of the very dregs of imbecility, is addressed to this confounded animal. The family sit in a row all day long, watching him, commenting upon his actions, telling each other anecdotes about him, recalling his virtues, and remembering with tears how one day they lost him for two whole hours, on which occasion he was brought home in a most brutal manner by the butcher-boy, who had been met carrying him by the scruff of his neck with one hand, while soundly cuffing his head with the other.

After recovering from these bitter recollections, they vie with each other in bursts of admiration for the brute, until some more than usually enthusiastic member, unable any longer to control his feelings, swoops down upon the unhappy quadruped in a frenzy of affection, clutches it to his heart, and slobbers over it. Whereupon the others, mad with envy, rise up, and seizing as much of the dog as the greed of the first one has left to them, murmur praise and devotion.

Among these people everything is done through the dog. If you want to make love to the eldest daughter, or get the old man to lend you the garden roller, or the mother to subscribe to the Society for the Suppression of Solo-Cornet Players in Theatrical Orchestras (it's a pity there isn't one, anyhow), you have to begin with the dog. You must gain its approbation before they will even listen to you, and if, as is highly probable, the animal, whose frank, doggy nature has been warped by the unnatural treatment he has received, responds to your overtures of friendship by viciously snapping at you, your cause is lost forever.

"If Fido won't take to any one," the father has thoughtfully remarked beforehand, "I say that man is not to be trusted. You know, Maria, how often I have said that. Ah! he knows, bless him."

Drat him!

And to think that the surly brute was once an innocent puppy, all legs and head, full of fun and play, and burning with ambition to become a big, good dog and bark like mother.

Ah me! life sadly changes us all. The world seems a vast horrible grinding machine, into which what is fresh and bright and pure is pushed at one end, to come out old and crabbed and wrinkled at the other.

Look even at Pussy Sobersides, with her dull, sleepy glance, her grave, slow walk, and dignified, prudish airs; who could ever think that once she was the blue-eyed, whirling, scampering, head-over-heels, mad little firework that we call a kitten?

What marvelous vitality a kitten has. It is really something very beautiful the way life bubbles over in the little creatures. They rush about, and mew, and spring; dance on their hind legs, embrace everything with their front ones, roll over and over, lie on their backs and kick. They don't know what to do with themselves, they are so full of life.

Can you remember, reader, when you and I felt something of the same sort of thing? Can you remember those glorious days of fresh young manhood—how, when coming home along the moonlit road, we felt too full of life for sober walking, and had to spring and skip, and wave our arms, and shout till belated farmers' wives thought—and with good reason, too—that we were mad, and kept close to the hedge, while we stood and laughed aloud to see them scuttle off so fast and made their blood run cold with a wild parting whoop, and the tears came, we knew not why? Oh, that magnificent young LIFE! that crowned us kings of the earth; that rushed through every tingling vein till we seemed to walk on air; that thrilled through our throbbing brains and told us to go forth and conquer the whole world; that welled up in our young hearts till we longed to stretch out our arms and gather all the toiling men and women and the little children to our breast and love them all—all. Ah! they were grand days, those deep, full days, when our coming life, like an unseen organ, pealed strange, yearnful music in our ears, and our young blood cried out like a war-horse for the battle. Ah, our pulse beats slow and steady now, and our old joints are rheumatic, and we love our easy-chair and pipe and sneer at boys' enthusiasm. But oh for one brief moment of that god-like life again!

ON BEING SHY.

All great literary men are shy. I am myself, though I am told it is hardly noticeable.

I am glad it is not. It used to be extremely prominent at one time, and was the cause of much misery to myself and discomfort to every one about me—my lady friends especially complained most bitterly about it.

A shy man's lot is not a happy one. The men dislike him, the women despise him, and he dislikes and despises himself. Use brings him no relief, and there is no cure for him except time; though I once came across a delicious recipe for overcoming the misfortune. It appeared among the "answers to correspondents" in a small weekly journal and ran as follows—I have never forgotten it: "Adopt an easy and pleasing manner, especially toward ladies."

Poor wretch! I can imagine the grin with which he must have read that advice. "Adopt an easy and pleasing manner, especially toward ladies," forsooth! Don't you adopt anything of the kind, my dear young shy friend. Your attempt to put on any other disposition than your own will infallibly result in your becoming ridiculously gushing and offensively familiar. Be your own natural self, and then you will only be thought to be surly and stupid.

The shy man does have some slight revenge upon society for the torture it inflicts upon him. He is able, to a certain extent, to communicate his misery. He frightens other people as much as they frighten him. He acts like a damper upon the whole room, and the most jovial spirits become in his presence depressed and nervous.

This is a good deal brought about by misunderstanding. Many people mistake the shy man's timidity for overbearing arrogance and are awed and insulted by it. His awkwardness is resented as insolent carelessness, and when, terror-stricken at the first word addressed to him, the blood rushes to his head and the power of speech completely fails him, he is regarded as an awful example of the evil effects of giving way to passion.

But, indeed, to be misunderstood is the shy man's fate on every occasion; and whatever impression he endeavors to create, he is sure to convey its opposite. When he makes a joke, it is looked upon as a pretended relation of fact and his want of veracity much condemned. His sarcasm is accepted as his literal opinion and gains for him the reputation of being an ass, while if, on the other hand, wishing to ingratiate himself, he ventures upon a little bit of flattery, it is taken for satire and he is hated ever afterward.

These and the rest of a shy man's troubles are always very amusing to other people, and have afforded material for comic writing from time immemorial. But if we look a little deeper we shall find there is a pathetic, one might almost say a tragic, side to the picture. A shy man means a lonely man—a man cut off from all companionship, all sociability. He moves about the world, but does not mix with it. Between him and his fellow-men there runs ever an impassable barrier—a strong, invisible wall that, trying in vain to scale, he but bruises himself against. He sees the pleasant faces and hears the pleasant voices on the other side, but he cannot stretch his hand across to grasp another hand. He stands watching the merry groups, and he longs to speak and to claim kindred with them. But they pass him by, chatting gayly to one another, and he cannot stay them. He tries to reach them, but his prison walls move with him and hem him in on every side. In the busy street, in the crowded room, in the grind of work, in the whirl of pleasure, amid the many or amid the few—wherever men congregate together, wherever the music of human speech is heard and human thought is flashed from human eyes, there, shunned and solitary, the shy man, like a leper, stands apart. His soul is full of love and longing, but the world knows it not. The iron mask of shyness is riveted before his face, and the man beneath is never seen. Genial words and hearty greetings are ever rising to his lips, but they die away in unheard whispers behind the steel clamps. His heart aches for the weary brother, but his sympathy is dumb. Contempt and indignation against wrong choke up his throat, and finding no safety-valve whence in passionate utterance they may burst forth, they only turn in again and harm him. All the hate and scorn and love of a deep nature such as the shy man is ever cursed by fester and corrupt within, instead of spending themselves abroad, and sour him into a misanthrope and cynic.

Yes, shy men, like ugly women, have a bad time of it in this world, to go through which with any comfort needs the hide of a rhinoceros. Thick skin is, indeed, our moral clothes, and without it we are not fit to be seen about in civilized society. A poor gasping, blushing creature, with trembling knees and twitching hands, is a painful sight to every one, and if it cannot cure itself, the sooner it goes and hangs itself the better.

The disease can be cured. For the comfort of the shy, I can assure them of that from personal experience. I do not like speaking about myself, as may have been noticed, but in the cause of humanity I on this occasion will do so, and will confess that at one time I was, as the young man in the Bab Ballad says, "the shyest of the shy," and "whenever I was introduced to any pretty maid, my knees they knocked together just as if I was afraid." Now, I would—nay, have—on this very day before yesterday I did the deed. Alone and entirely by myself (as the schoolboy said in translating the "Bellum Gallicum") did I beard a railway refreshment-room young lady in her own lair. I rebuked her in terms of mingled bitterness and sorrow for her callousness and want of condescension. I insisted, courteously but firmly, on being accorded that deference and attention that was the right of the traveling Briton, and at the end I looked her full in the face. Need I say more?

True, immediately after doing so I left the room with what may possibly have appeared to be precipitation and without waiting for any refreshment. But that was because I had changed my mind, not because I was frightened, you understand.

One consolation that shy folk can take unto themselves is that shyness is certainly no sign of stupidity. It is easy enough for bull-headed clowns to sneer at nerves, but the highest natures are not necessarily those containing the greatest amount of moral brass. The horse is not an inferior animal to the cock-sparrow, nor the deer of the forest to the pig. Shyness simply means extreme sensibility, and has nothing whatever to do with self-consciousness or with conceit, though its relationship to both is continually insisted upon by the poll-parrot school of philosophy.

Conceit, indeed, is the quickest cure for it. When it once begins to dawn upon you that you are a good deal cleverer than any one else in this world, bashfulness becomes shocked and leaves you. When you can look round a roomful of people and think that each one is a mere child in intellect compared with yourself you feel no more shy of them than you would of a select company of magpies or orang-outangs.

Conceit is the finest armor that a man can wear. Upon its smooth, impenetrable surface the puny dagger-thrusts of spite and envy glance harmlessly aside. Without that breast-plate the sword of talent cannot force its way through the battle of life, for blows have to be borne as well as dealt. I do not, of course, speak of the conceit that displays itself in an elevated nose and a falsetto voice. That is not real conceit—that is only playing at being conceited; like children play at being kings and queens and go strutting about with feathers and long trains. Genuine conceit does not make a man objectionable. On the contrary, it tends to make him genial, kind-hearted, and simple. He has no need of affectation—he is far too well satisfied with his own character; and his pride is too deep-seated to appear at all on the outside. Careless alike of praise or blame, he can afford to be truthful. Too far, in fancy, above the rest of mankind to trouble about their petty distinctions, he is equally at home with duke or costermonger. And valuing no one's standard but his own, he is never tempted to practice that miserable pretense that less self-reliant people offer up as an hourly sacrifice to the god of their neighbor's opinion.

The shy man, on the other hand, is humble—modest of his own judgment and over-anxious concerning that of others. But this in the case of a young man is surely right enough. His character is unformed. It is slowly evolving itself out of a chaos of doubt and disbelief. Before the growing insight and experience the diffidence recedes. A man rarely carries his shyness past the hobbledehoy period. Even if his own inward strength does not throw it off, the rubbings of the world generally smooth it down. You scarcely ever meet a really shy man—except in novels or on the stage, where, by the bye, he is much admired, especially by the women.

There, in that supernatural land, he appears as a fair-haired and saintlike young man—fair hair and goodness always go together on the stage. No respectable audience would believe in one without the other. I knew an actor who mislaid his wig once and had to rush on to play the hero in his own hair, which was jet-black, and the gallery howled at all his noble sentiments under the impression that he was the villain. He—the shy young man—loves the heroine, oh so devotedly (but only in asides, for he dare not tell her of it), and he is so noble and unselfish, and speaks in such a low voice, and is so good to his mother; and the bad people in the play, they laugh at him and jeer at him, but he takes it all so gently, and in the end it transpires that he is such a clever man, though nobody knew it, and then the heroine tells him she loves him, and he is so surprised, and oh, so happy! and everybody loves him and asks him to forgive them, which he does in a few well-chosen and sarcastic words, and blesses them; and he seems to have generally such a good time of it that all the young fellows who are not shy long to be shy. But the really shy man knows better. He knows that it is not quite so pleasant in reality. He is not quite so interesting there as in the fiction. He is a little more clumsy and stupid and a little less devoted and gentle, and his hair is much darker, which, taken altogether, considerably alters the aspect of the case.

The point where he does resemble his ideal is in his faithfulness. I am fully prepared to allow the shy young man that virtue: he is constant in his love. But the reason is not far to seek. The fact is it exhausts all his stock of courage to look one woman in the face, and it would be simply impossible for him to go through the ordeal with a second. He stands in far too much dread of the whole female sex to want to go gadding about with many of them. One is quite enough for him.

Now, it is different with the young man who is not shy. He has temptations which his bashful brother never encounters. He looks around and everywhere sees roguish eyes and laughing lips. What more natural than that amid so many roguish eyes and laughing lips he should become confused and, forgetting for the moment which particular pair of roguish ayes and laughing lips it is that he belongs to, go off making love to the wrong set. The shy man, who never looks at anything but his own boots, sees not and is not tempted. Happy shy man!

Not but what the shy man himself would much rather not be happy in that way. He longs to "go it" with the others, and curses himself every day for not being able to. He will now and again, screwing up his courage by a tremendous effort, plunge into roguishness. But it is always a terrible *fiasco*, and after one or two feeble flounders he crawls out again, limp and pitiable.

I say "pitiable," though I am afraid he never is pitied. There are certain misfortunes which, while inflicting a vast amount of suffering upon their victims, gain for them no sympathy. Losing an umbrella, falling in love, toothache, black eyes, and having your hat sat upon may be mentioned as a few examples, but the chief of them all is shyness. The shy man is regarded as an animate joke. His tortures are the sport of the drawing-room arena and are pointed out and discussed with much gusto.

"Look," cry his tittering audience to each other; "he's blushing!"

"Just watch his legs," says one.

"Do you notice how he is sitting?" adds another: "right on the edge of the chair."

"Seems to have plenty of color," sneers a military-looking gentleman.

"Pity he's got so many hands," murmurs an elderly lady, with her own calmly folded on her lap. "They quite confuse him."

"A yard or two off his feet wouldn't be a disadvantage," chimes in the comic man, "especially as he seems so anxious to hide them."

And then another suggests that with such a voice he ought to have been a sea-captain. Some draw attention to the desperate way in which he is grasping his hat. Some comment upon his limited powers of conversation. Others remark upon the troublesome nature of his cough. And so on, until his peculiarities and the company are both thoroughly exhausted.

His friends and relations make matters still more unpleasant for the poor boy (friends and relations are privileged to be more disagreeable than other people). Not content with making fun of him among themselves, they insist on his seeing the joke. They mimic and caricature him for his own edification. One, pretending to imitate him, goes outside and comes in again in a ludicrously nervous manner, explaining to him afterward that that is the way he—meaning the shy fellow— walks into a room; or, turning to him with "This is the way you shake hands," proceeds to go through a comic pantomime with the rest of the room, taking hold of every one's hand as if it were a hot plate and flabbily dropping it again. And then they ask him why he blushes, and why he stammers, and why he always speaks in an almost inaudible tone, as if they thought he did it on purpose. Then one of them, sticking out his chest and strutting about the room like a pouter-pigeon, suggests quite seriously that that is the style he should adopt. The old man slaps him on the back and says: "Be bold, my boy. Don't be afraid of any one." The mother says, "Never do anything that you need be ashamed of, Algernon, and then you never need be ashamed of anything you do," and, beaming mildly at him, seems surprised at the clearness of her own logic. The boys tell him that he's "worse than a girl," and the girls repudiate the implied slur upon their sex by indignantly exclaiming that they are sure no girl would be half as bad.

They are quite right; no girl would be. There is no such thing as a shy woman, or, at all events, I have never come across one, and until I do I shall not believe in them. I know that the generally accepted belief is quite the reverse. All women are supposed to be like timid, startled fawns, blushing and casting down their gentle eyes when looked at and running away when spoken to; while we men are supposed to be a bold and rollicky lot, and the poor dear little women admire us for it, but are terribly afraid of us. It is a pretty theory, but, like most generally accepted theories, mere nonsense. The girl of twelve is self-contained and as cool as the proverbial cucumber, while her brother of twenty stammers and stutters by her side. A woman will enter a concert-room late, interrupt the performance, and disturb the whole audience without moving a hair, while her husband follows her, a crushed heap of apologizing misery.

The superior nerve of women in all matters connected with love, from the casting of the first sheep's-eye down to the end of the honeymoon, is too well acknowledged to need comment. Nor is the example a fair one to cite in the present instance, the positions not being equally balanced. Love is woman's business, and in "business" we all lay aside our natural weaknesses—the shyest man I ever knew was a photographic tout.

ON BABIES.

Oh, yes, I do—I know a lot about 'em. I was one myself once, though not long—not so long as my clothes. They were very long, I recollect, and always in my way when I wanted to kick. Why do babies have such yards of unnecessary clothing? It is not a riddle. I really want to know. I never could understand it. Is it that the parents are ashamed of the size of the child and wish to make believe that it is longer than it actually is? I asked a nurse once why it was. She said:

"Lor', sir, they always have long clothes, bless their little hearts."

And when I explained that her answer, although doing credit to her feelings, hardly disposed of my difficulty, she replied:

"Lor', sir, you wouldn't have 'em in short clothes, poor little dears?" And she said it in a tone that seemed to imply I had suggested some unmanly outrage.

Since than I have felt shy at making inquiries on the subject, and the reason—if reason there be—is still a mystery to me. But indeed, putting them in any clothes at all seems absurd to my mind. Goodness knows there is enough of dressing and undressing to be gone through in life without beginning it before we need; and one would think that people who live in bed might at all events be spared the torture. Why wake the poor little wretches up in the morning to take one lot of clothes off, fix another lot on, and put them to bed again, and then at night haul them out once more, merely to change everything back? And when all is done, what difference is there, I should like to know, between a baby's night-shirt and the thing it wears in the day-time?

Very likely, however, I am only making myself ridiculous—I often do, so I am informed—and I will therefore say no more upon this matter of clothes, except only that it would be of great convenience if some fashion were adopted enabling you to tell a boy from a girl.

At present it is most awkward. Neither hair, dress, nor conversation affords the slightest clew, and you are left to guess. By some mysterious law of nature you invariably guess wrong, and are thereupon regarded by all the relatives and friends as a mixture of fool and knave, the enormity of alluding to a male babe as "she" being only equaled by the atrocity of referring to a female infant as "he". Whichever sex the particular child in question happens not to belong to is considered as beneath contempt, and any mention of it is taken as a personal insult to the family.

And as you value your fair name do not attempt to get out of the difficulty by talking of "it."

There are various methods by which you may achieve ignominy and shame. By murdering a large and respected family in cold blood and afterward depositing their bodies in the water companies' reservoir, you will gain much unpopularity in the neighborhood of your crime, and even robbing a church will get you cordially disliked, especially by the vicar. But if you desire to drain to the dregs the fullest cup of scorn and hatred that a fellow human creature can pour out for you, let a young mother hear you call dear baby "it."

Your best plan is to address the article as "little angel." The noun "angel" being of common gender suits the case admirably, and the epithet is sure of being favorably received. "Pet" or "beauty" are useful for variety's sake, but "angel" is the term that brings you the greatest credit for sense and good-feeling. The word should be preceded by a short giggle and accompanied by as much smile as possible. And whatever you do, don't forget to say that the child has got its father's nose. This "fetches" the parents (if I may be allowed a vulgarism) more than anything. They will pretend to laugh at the idea at first and will say, "Oh, nonsense!" You must then get excited and insist that it is a fact. You need have no conscientious scruples on the subject, because the thing's nose really does resemble its father's—at all events quite as much as it does anything else in nature—being, as it is, a mere smudge.

Do not despise these hints, my friends. There may come a time when, with mamma on one side and grand mamma on the other, a group of admiring young ladies (not admiring you, though) behind, and a bald-headed dab of humanity in front, you will be extremely thankful for some idea of what to say. A man—an unmarried man, that is—is never seen to such disadvantage as when undergoing the ordeal of "seeing baby." A cold shudder runs down his back at the bare proposal, and the sickly smile with which he says how delighted he shall be ought surely to move even a mother's heart, unless, as I am inclined to believe, the whole proceeding is a mere device adopted by wives to discourage the visits of bachelor friends.

It is a cruel trick, though, whatever its excuse may be. The bell is rung and somebody sent to tell nurse to bring baby down. This is the signal for all the females present to commence talking "baby," during which time you are left to your own sad thoughts and the speculations upon the practicability of suddenly recollecting an important engagement, and the likelihood of your being believed if you do. Just when you have concocted an absurdly implausible tale about a man outside, the door opens, and a tall, severe-looking woman enters, carrying what at first sight appears to be a particularly skinny bolster, with the feathers all at one end. Instinct, however, tells you that this is the baby, and you rise with a miserable attempt at appearing eager. When the first gush of feminine enthusiasm with which the object in question is received has died out, and the number of ladies talking at once has been reduced to the ordinary four or five, the circle of fluttering petticoats divides, and room is made for you to step forward. This you do with much the same air that you would walk into the dock at Bow Street, and then, feeling unutterably miserable, you stand solemnly staring at the child. There is dead silence, and you know that every one is waiting for you to speak. You try to think of something to say, but find, to your horror, that your reasoning faculties have left you. It is a moment of despair, and your evil genius, seizing the opportunity, suggests to you some of the most idiotic remarks that it is possible for a human being to perpetrate. Glancing round with an imbecile smile, you sniggeringly observe that "it hasn't got much hair has it?" Nobody answers you for a minute, but at last the stately nurse says with much gravity:

"It is not customary for children five weeks old to have long hair." Another silence follows this, and you feel you are being given a second chance, which you avail yourself of by inquiring if it can walk yet, or what they feed it on.

By this time you have got to be regarded as not quite right in your head, and pity is the only thing felt for you. The nurse, however, is determined that, insane or not, there shall be no shirking and that you shall go through your task to the end. In the tones of a high priestess directing some religious mystery she says, holding the bundle toward you:

"Take her in your arms, sir." You are too crushed to offer any resistance and so meekly accept the burden. "Put your arm more down her middle, sir," says the high-priestess, and then all step back and watch you intently as though you were going to do a trick with it.

What to do you know no more than you did what to say. It is certain something must be done, and the only thing that occurs to you is to heave the unhappy infant up and down to the accompaniment of "oopsee-daisy," or some remark of equal intelligence. "I wouldn't jig her, sir, if I were you," says the nurse; "a very little upsets her." You promptly decide not to jig her and sincerely hope that you have not gone too far already.

At this point the child itself, who has hitherto been regarding you with an expression of mingled horror and disgust, puts an end to the nonsense by beginning to yell at the top of its voice, at which the priestess rushes forward and snatches it from you with "There! there! there! What did ums do to ums?" "How very extraordinary!" you say pleasantly. "Whatever made it go off like that?" "Oh, why, you must have done something to her!" says the mother indignantly; "the child wouldn't scream like that for nothing." It is evident they think you have been running pins into it.

The brat is calmed at last, and would no doubt remain quiet enough, only some mischievous busybody points you out again with "Who's this, baby?" and the intelligent child, recognizing you, howls louder than ever.

Whereupon some fat old lady remarks that "it's strange how children take a dislike to any one." "Oh, they know," replies another mysteriously. "It's a wonderful thing," adds a third; and then everybody looks sideways at you, convinced you are a scoundrel of the blackest dye; and they glory in the beautiful idea that your true character, unguessed by your fellow-men, has been discovered by the untaught instinct of a little child.

Babies, though, with all their crimes and errors, are not without their use—not without use, surely, when they fill an empty heart; not without use when, at their call, sunbeams of love break through care-clouded faces; not without use when their little fingers press wrinkles into smiles.

Odd little people! They are the unconscious comedians of the world's great stage. They supply the humor in life's all-too-heavy drama. Each one, a small but determined opposition to the order of things in general, is forever doing the wrong thing at the wrong time, in the wrong place and in the wrong way. The nurse-girl who sent Jenny to see what Tommy and Totty were doing and "tell 'em they mustn't" knew infantile nature. Give an average baby a fair chance, and if it doesn't do something it oughtn't to a doctor should be called in at once.

They have a genius for doing the most ridiculous things, and they do them in a grave, stoical manner that is irresistible. The business-like air with which two of them will join hands and proceed due east at a break-neck toddle, while an excitable big sister is roaring for them to follow her in a westerly direction, is most amusing—except, perhaps, for the big sister. They walk round a soldier, staring at his legs with the greatest curiosity, and poke him to see if he is real. They stoutly maintain, against all argument and much to the discomfort of the victim, that the bashful young man at the end of the 'bus is "dadda." A crowded street-corner suggests itself to their minds as a favorable spot for the discussion of family affairs at a shrill treble. When in the middle of crossing the road they are seized with a sudden impulse to dance, and the doorstep of a busy shop is the place they always select for sitting down and taking off their shoes.

When at home they find the biggest walking-stick in the house or an umbrella—open preferred-of much assistance in getting upstairs. They discover that they love Mary Ann at the precise moment when that faithful domestic is blackleading the stove, and nothing will relieve their feelings but to embrace her then and there. With regard to food, their favorite dishes are coke and cat's meat. They nurse pussy upside down, and they show their affection for the dog by pulling his tail.

They are a deal of trouble, and they make a place untidy and they cost a lot of money to keep; but still you would not have the house without them. It would not be home without their noisy tongues and their mischief-making hands. Would not the rooms seem silent without their pattering feet, and might not you stray apart if no prattling voices called you together?

It should be so, and yet I have sometimes thought the tiny hand seemed as a wedge, dividing. It is a bearish task to quarrel with that purest of all human affections—that perfecting touch to a woman's life—a mother's love. It is a holy love, that we coarser-fibered men can hardly understand, and I would not be deemed to lack reverence for it when I say that surely it need not swallow up all other affection. The baby need not take your whole heart, like the rich man who walled up the desert well. Is there not another thirsty traveler standing by?

In your desire to be a good mother, do not forget to be a good wife. No need for all the thought and care to be only for one. Do not, whenever poor Edwin wants you to come out, answer indignantly, "What, and leave baby!" Do not spend all your evenings upstairs, and do not confine your conversation exclusively to whooping-cough and measles. My dear little woman, the child is not going to die every time it sneezes, the house is not bound to get burned down and the nurse run away with a soldier every time you go outside the front door; nor the cat sure to come and sit on the precious child's chest the moment you leave the bedside. You worry yourself a good deal too much about that solitary chick, and you worry everybody else too. Try and think of your other duties, and your pretty face will not be always puckered into wrinkles, and there will be cheerfulness in the parlor as well as in the nursery. Think of your big baby a little. Dance him about a bit; call him pretty names; laugh at him now and then. It is only the first baby that takes up the whole of a woman's time. Five or six do not require nearly so much attention as one. But before then the mischief has been done. A house where there seems no room for him and a wife too busy to think of him have lost their hold on that so unreasonable husband of yours, and he has learned to look elsewhere for comfort and companionship.

But there, there, there! I shall get myself the character of a baby-hater if I talk any more in this strain. And Heaven knows I am not one. Who could be, to look into the little innocent faces clustered in timid helplessness round those great gates that open down into the world?

The world—the small round world! what a vast mysterious place it must seem to baby eyes! What a trackless continent the back garden appears! What marvelous explorations they make in the cellar under the stairs! With what awe they gaze down the long street, wondering, like us bigger babies when we gaze up at the stars, where it all ends!

And down that longest street of all—that long, dim street of life that stretches out before them—what grave, old-fashioned looks they seem to cast! What pitiful, frightened looks sometimes! I saw a little mite sitting on a doorstep in a Soho slum one night, and I shall never forget the look that the gas-lamp showed me on its wizen face—a look of dull despair, as if from the squalid court the vista of its own squalid life had risen, ghostlike, and struck its heart dead with horror.

Poor little feet, just commencing the stony journey! We old travelers, far down the road, can only pause to wave a hand to you. You come out of the dark mist, and we, looking back, see you, so tiny in the distance, standing on the brow of the hill, your arms stretched out toward us. God speed you! We would stay and take your little hands in ours, but the murmur of the great sea is in our ears and we may not linger. We must hasten down, for the shadowy ships are waiting to spread their sable sails.

ON EATING AND DRINKING.

I always was fond of eating and drinking, even as a child—especially eating, in those early days. I had an appetite then, also a digestion. I remember a dull-eyed, livid-complexioned gentleman coming to dine at our house once. He watched me eating for about five minutes, quite fascinated seemingly, and then he turned to my father with—

"Does your boy ever suffer from dyspepsia?"

"I never heard him complain of anything of that kind," replied my father. "Do you ever suffer from dyspepsia, Colly wobbles?" (They called me Colly wobbles, but it was not my real name.)

"No, pa," I answered. After which I added:

"What is dyspepsia, pa?"

My livid-complexioned friend regarded me with a look of mingled amazement and envy. Then in a tone of infinite pity he slowly said:

"You will know—some day."

My poor, dear mother used to say she liked to see me eat, and it has always been a pleasant reflection to me since that I must have given her much gratification in that direction. A growing, healthy lad, taking plenty of exercise and careful to restrain himself from indulging in too much study, can generally satisfy the most exacting expectations as regards his feeding powers.

It is amusing to see boys eat when you have not got to pay for it. Their idea of a square meal is a pound and a half of roast beef with five or six good-sized potatoes (soapy ones preferred as being more substantial), plenty of greens, and four thick slices of Yorkshire pudding, followed by a couple of currant dumplings, a few green apples, a pen'orth of nuts, half a dozen jumbles, and a bottle of ginger-beer. After that they play at horses.

How they must despise us men, who require to sit quiet for a couple of hours after dining off a spoonful of clear soup and the wing of a chicken!

But the boys have not all the advantages on their side. A boy never enjoys the luxury of being satisfied. A boy never feels full. He can never stretch out his legs, put his hands behind his head, and, closing his eyes, sink into the ethereal bliss-fulness that encompasses the well-dined man. A dinner makes no difference whatever to a boy. To a man it is as a good fairy's potion, and after it the world appears a brighter and a better place. A man who has dined satisfactorily experiences a yearning love toward all his fellow-creatures. He strokes the cat quite gently and calls it "poor pussy," in tones full of the tenderest emotion. He sympathizes with the members of the German band outside and wonders if they are cold; and for the moment he does not even hate his wife's relations.

A good dinner brings out all the softer side of a man. Under its genial influence the gloomy and morose become jovial and chatty. Sour, starchy individuals, who all the rest of the day go about looking as if they lived on vinegar and Epsom salts, break out into wreathed smiles after dinner, and exhibit a tendency to pat small children on the head and to talk to them—vaguely—about sixpences. Serious men thaw and become mildly cheerful, and snobbish young men of the heavy-mustache type forget to make themselves objectionable.

I always feel sentimental myself after dinner. It is the only time when I can properly appreciate love-stories. Then, when the hero clasps "her" to his heart in one last wild embrace and stifles a sob, I feel as sad as though I had dealt at whist and turned up only a deuce; and when the heroine dies in the end I weep. If I read the same tale early in the morning I should sneer at it. Digestion, or rather indigestion, has a marvelous effect upon the heart. If I want to write any thing very pathetic—I mean, if I want to try to write anything very pathetic—I eat a large plateful of hot buttered muffins about an hour beforehand, and then by the time I sit down to my work a feeling of unutterable melancholy has come over me. I picture heartbroken lovers parting forever at lonely wayside stiles, while the sad twilight deepens around them, and only the tinkling of a distant sheep-bell breaks the sorrow-laden silence. Old men sit and gaze at withered flowers till their sight is dimmed by the mist of tears. Little dainty maidens wait and watch at open casements; but "he cometh not," and the heavy years roll by and the sunny gold tresses wear white and thin. The babies that they dandled have become grown men and women with podgy torments of their own, and the playmates that they laughed with are lying very silent under the waving grass. But still they wait and watch, till the dark shadows of the unknown night steal up and gather round them and the world with its childish troubles fades from their aching eyes.

I see pale corpses tossed on white-foamed waves, and death-beds stained with bitter tears, and graves in trackless deserts. I hear the wild wailing of women, the low moaning of little children, the dry sobbing of strong men. It's all the muffins. I could not conjure up one melancholy fancy upon a mutton chop and a glass of champagne.

A full stomach is a great aid to poetry, and indeed no sentiment of any kind can stand upon an empty one. We have not time or inclination to indulge in fanciful troubles until we have got rid of our real misfortunes. We do not sigh over dead dicky-birds with the bailiff in the house, and when we do not know where on earth to get our next shilling from, we do not worry as to whether our mistress' smiles are cold, or hot, or lukewarm, or anything else about them.

Foolish people—when I say "foolish people" in this contemptuous way I mean people who entertain different opinions to mine. If there is one person I do despise more than another, it is the man who does not think exactly the same on all topics as I do—foolish people, I say, then, who have never experienced much of either, will tell you that mental distress is far more agonizing than bodily. Romantic and touching theory! so comforting to the love-sick young sprig who looks down patronizingly at some poor devil with a white starved face and thinks to himself, "Ah, how happy you are compared with me!"—so soothing to fat old gentlemen who cackle about the superiority of poverty over riches. But it is all nonsense—all cant. An aching head soon makes one forget an aching heart. A broken finger will drive away all recollections of an empty chair. And when a man feels really hungry he does not feel anything else.

We sleek, well-fed folk can hardly realize what feeling hungry is like. We know what it is to have no appetite and not to care for the dainty victuals placed before us, but we do not understand what it means to sicken for food—to die for bread while others waste it—to gaze with famished eyes upon coarse fare steaming behind dingy windows, longing for a pen'orth of pea pudding and not having the penny to buy it—to feel that a crust would be delicious and that a bone would be a banquet.

Hunger is a luxury to us, a piquant, flavor-giving sauce. It is well worth while to get hungry and thirsty merely to discover how much gratification can be obtained from eating and drinking. If you wish to thoroughly enjoy your dinner, take a thirty-mile country walk after breakfast and don't touch anything till you get back. How your eyes will glisten at sight of the white table-cloth and steaming dishes then! With what a sigh of content you will put down the empty beer tankard and take up your knife and fork! And how comfortable you feel afterward as you push back your chair, light a cigar, and beam round upon everybody.

Make sure, however, when adopting this plan, that the good dinner is really to be had at the end, or the disappointment is trying. I remember once a friend and I—dear old Joe, it was. Ah! how we lose one another in life's mist. It must be eight years since I last saw Joseph Taboys. How pleasant it would be to meet his jovial face again, to clasp his strong hand, and to hear his cheery laugh once more! He owes me 14 shillings, too. Well, we were on a holiday together, and one morning we had breakfast early and started for a tremendous long walk. We had ordered a duck for dinner over night. We said, "Get a big one, because we shall come home awfully hungry;" and as we were going out our landlady came up in great spirits. She said, "I have got you gentlemen a duck, if you like. If you get through that you'll do well;" and she held up a bird about the size of a door-mat. We chuckled at the sight and said we would try. We said it with self-conscious pride, like men who know their own power. Then we started.

We lost our way, of course. I always do in the country, and it does make me so wild, because it is no use asking direction of any of the people you meet. One might as well inquire of a lodging-house slavey the way to make beds as expect a country bumpkin to know the road to the next village. You have to shout the question about three times before the sound of your voice penetrates his skull. At the third time he slowly raises his head and stares blankly at you. You yell it at him then for a fourth time, and he repeats it after you. He ponders while you count a couple of hundred, after which, speaking at the rate of three words a minute, he fancies you "couldn't do better than—" Here he catches sight of another idiot coming down the road and bawls out to him the particulars, requesting his advice. The two then argue the case for a quarter of an hour or so, and finally agree that you had better go straight down the lane, round to the right and cross by the third stile, and keep to the left by old Jimmy Milcher's cow-shed, and across the seven-acre field, and through the gate by Squire Grubbin's hay-stack, keeping the bridle-path for awhile till you come opposite the hill where the windmill used to be—but it's gone now—and round to the right, leaving Stiggin's plantation behind you; and you say "Thank you" and go away with a splitting headache, but without the faintest notion of your way, the only clear idea you have on the subject being that somewhere or other there is a stile which has to be got over; and at the next turn you come upon four stiles, all leading in different directions!

We had undergone this ordeal two or three times. We had tramped over fields. We had waded through brooks and scrambled over hedges and walls. We had had a row as to whose fault it was that we had first lost our way. We had got thoroughly disagreeable, footsore, and weary. But throughout it all the hope of that duck kept us up. A fairy-like vision, it floated before our tired eyes and drew us onward. The thought of it was as a trumpet-call to the fainting. We talked of it and cheered each other with our recollections of it. "Come along," we said; "the duck will be spoiled."

We felt a strong temptation, at one point, to turn into a village inn as we passed and have a cheese and a few loaves between us, but we heroically restrained ourselves: we should enjoy the duck all the better for being famished.

We fancied we smelled it when we go into the town and did the last quarter of a mile in three minutes. We rushed upstairs, and washed ourselves, and changed our clothes, and came down, and pulled our chairs up to the table, and sat and rubbed our hands while the landlady removed the covers, when I seized the knife and fork and started to carve.

It seemed to want a lot of carving. I struggled with it for about five minutes without making the slightest impression, and then Joe, who had been eating potatoes, wanted to know if it wouldn't be better for some one to do the job that understood carving. I took no notice of his foolish remark, but attacked the bird again; and so vigorously this time that the animal left the dish and took refuge in the fender.

We soon had it out of that, though, and I was prepared to make another effort. But Joe was getting unpleasant. He said that if he had thought we were to have a game of blind hockey with the dinner he would have got a bit of bread and cheese outside.

I was too exhausted to argue. I laid down the knife and fork with dignity and took a side seat and Joe went for the wretched creature. He worked away in silence for awhile, and then he muttered "Damn the duck" and took his coat off.

We did break the thing up at length with the aid of a chisel, but it was perfectly impossible to eat it, and we had to make a dinner off the vegetables and an apple tart. We tried a mouthful of the duck, but it was like eating India-rubber.

It was a wicked sin to kill that drake. But there! there's no respect for old institutions in this country.

I started this paper with the idea of writing about eating and drinking, but I seem to have confined my remarks entirely to eating as yet. Well, you see, drinking is one of those subjects with which it is inadvisable to appear too well acquainted. The days are gone by when it was considered manly to go to bed intoxicated every night, and a clear head and a firm hand no longer draw down upon their owner the reproach of effeminacy. On the contrary, in these sadly degenerate days an evil-smelling breath, a blotchy face, a reeling gait, and a husky voice are regarded as the hall marks of the cad rather than or the gentleman.

Even nowadays, though, the thirstiness of mankind is something supernatural. We are forever drinking on one excuse or another. A man never feels comfortable unless he has a glass before him. We drink before meals, and with meals, and after meals. We drink when we meet a friend, also when we part from a friend. We drink when we are talking, when we are reading, and when we are thinking. We drink one another's healths and spoil our own. We drink the queen, and the army, and the ladies, and everybody else that is drinkable; and I believe if the supply ran short we should drink our mothers-in-law.

By the way, we never eat anybody's health, always drink it. Why should we not stand up now and then and eat a tart to somebody's success?

To me, I confess the constant necessity of drinking under which the majority of men labor is quite unaccountable. I can understand people drinking to drown care or to drive away maddening thoughts well enough. I can understand the ignorant masses loving to soak themselves in drink—oh, yes, it's very shocking that they should, of course—very shocking to us who live in cozy homes, with all the graces and pleasures of life around us, that the dwellers in damp cellars and windy attics should creep from their dens of misery into the warmth and glare of the public-house bar, and seek to float for a brief space away from their dull world upon a Lethe stream of gin.

But think, before you hold up your hands in horror at their ill-living, what "life" for these wretched creatures really means. Picture the squalid misery of their brutish existence, dragged on from year to year in the narrow, noisome room where, huddled like vermin in sewers, they welter, and sicken, and sleep; where dirt-grimed children scream and fight and sluttish, shrill-voiced women cuff, and curse, and nag; where the street outside teems with roaring filth and the house around is a bedlam of riot and stench.

Think what a sapless stick this fair flower of life must be to them, devoid of mind and soul. The horse in his stall scents the sweet hay and munches the ripe corn contentedly. The watch-dog in his kennel blinks at the grateful sun, dreams of a glorious chase over the dewy fields, and wakes with a yelp of gladness to greet a caressing hand. But the clod-like life of these human logs never knows one ray of light. From the hour when they crawl from their comfortless bed to the hour when they lounge back into it again they never live one moment of real life. Recreation, amusement, companionship, they know not the meaning of. Joy, sorrow, laughter, tears, love, friendship, longing, despair, are idle words to them. From the day when their baby eyes first look out upon their sordid world to the day when, with an oath, they close them forever and their bones are shoveled out of sight, they never warm to one touch of human sympathy, never thrill to a single thought, never start to a single hope. In the name of the God of mercy; let them pour the maddening liquor down their throats and feel for one brief moment that they live!

Ah! we may talk sentiment as much as we like, but the stomach is the real seat of happiness in this world. The kitchen is the chief temple wherein we worship, its roaring fire is our vestal flame, and the cook is our great high-priest. He is a mighty magician and a kindly one. He soothes away all sorrow and care. He drives forth all enmity, gladdens all love. Our God is great and the cook is his prophet. Let us eat, drink, and be merry.

ON FURNISHED APARTMENTS.

"Oh, you have some rooms to let."

"Mother!"

"Well, what is it?"

"'Ere's a gentleman about the rooms."

"Ask 'im in. I'll be up in a minute."

"Will yer step inside, sir? Mother'll be up in a minute."

So you step inside and after a minute "mother" comes slowly up the kitchen stairs, untying her apron as she comes and calling down instructions to some one below about the potatoes.

"Good-morning, sir," says "mother," with a washed-out smile. "Will you step this way, please?"

"Oh, it's hardly worth while my coming up," you say. "What sort of rooms are they, and how much?"

"Well," says the landlady, "if you'll step upstairs I'll show them to you."

So with a protesting murmur, meant to imply that any waste of time complained of hereafter must not be laid to your charge, you follow "mother" upstairs.

At the first landing you run up against a pail and a broom, whereupon "mother" expatiates upon the unreliability of servant-girls, and bawls over the balusters for Sarah to come and take them away at once. When you get outside the rooms she pauses, with her hand upon the door, to explain to you that they are rather untidy just at present, as the last lodger left only yesterday; and she also adds that this is their cleaning-day—it always is. With this understanding you enter, and both stand solemnly feasting your eyes upon the scene before you. The rooms cannot be said to appear inviting. Even "mother's" face betrays no admiration. Untenanted "furnished apartments" viewed in the morning sunlight do not inspire cheery sensations. There is a lifeless air about them. It is a very different thing when you have settled down and are living in them. With your old familiar household gods to greet your gaze whenever you glance up, and all your little knick-knacks spread around you—with the photos of all the girls that you have loved and lost ranged upon the mantel-piece, and half a dozen disreputable-looking pipes scattered about in painfully prominent positions—with one carpet slipper peeping from beneath the coal-box and the other perched on the top of the piano—with the well-known pictures to hide the dingy walls, and these dear old friends, your books, higgledy-piggledy all over the place—with the bits of old blue china that your mother prized, and the screen she worked in those far by-gone days, when the sweet old face was laughing and young, and the white soft hair tumbled in gold-brown curls from under the coal-scuttle bonnet—

Ah, old screen, what a gorgeous personage you must have been in your young days, when the tulips and roses and lilies (all growing from one stem) were fresh in their glistening sheen! Many a summer and winter have come and gone since then, my friend, and you have played with the dancing firelight until you have grown sad and gray. Your brilliant colors are fast fading now, and the envious moths have gnawed your silken threads. You are withering away like the dead hands that wove you. Do you ever think of those dead hands? You seem so grave and thoughtful sometimes that I almost think you do. Come, you and I and the deep-glowing embers, let us talk together. Tell me in your silent language what you remember of those young days, when you lay on my little mother's lap and her girlish fingers played with your rainbow tresses. Was there never a lad near sometimes—never a lad who would seize one of those little hands to smother it with kisses, and who would persist in holding it, thereby sadly interfering with the progress of your making? Was not your frail existence often put in jeopardy by this same clumsy, headstrong lad, who would toss you disrespectfully aside that he—not satisfied with one—might hold both hands and gaze up into the loved eyes? I can see that lad now through the haze of the flickering twilight. He is an eager bright-eyed boy, with pinching, dandy shoes and tight-fitting smalls, snowy shirt frill and stock, and—oh! such curly hair. A wild, light-hearted boy! Can he be the great, grave gentleman upon whose stick I used to ride crosslegged, the care-worn man into whose thoughtful face I used to gaze with childish reverence and whom I used to call "father?" You say "yes," old screen; but are you quite sure? It is a serious charge you are bringing. Can it be possible? Did he have to kneel down in those wonderful smalls and pick you up and rearrange you before he was forgiven and his curly head smoothed by my mother's little hand? Ah! old screen, and did the lads and the lassies go making love fifty years ago just as they do now? Are men and women so unchanged? Did little maidens' hearts beat the same under pearl-embroidered bodices as they do under Mother Hubbard cloaks? Have steel casques and chimney-pot hats made no difference to the brains that work beneath them? Oh, Time! great Chronos! and is this your power? Have you dried up seas and leveled mountains and left the tiny human heart-strings to defy you? Ah, yes! they were spun by a Mightier than thou, and they stretch beyond your narrow ken, for their ends are made fast in eternity. Ay, you may mow down the leaves and the blossoms, but the roots of life lie too deep for your sickle to sever. You refashion Nature's garments, but you cannot vary by a jot the throb-bings of her pulse. The world rolls round obedient to your laws, but the heart of man is not of your kingdom, for in its birthplace "a thousand years are but as yes-terday."

I am getting away, though, I fear, from my "furnished apartments," and I hard-ly know how to get back. But I have some excuse for my meanderings this time.

It is a piece of old furniture that has led me astray, and fancies gather, somehow, round old furniture, like moss around old stones. One's chairs and tables get to be almost part of one's life and to seem like quiet friends. What strange tales the wooden-headed old fellows could tell did they but choose to speak! At what unsuspected comedies and tragedies have they not assisted! What bitter tears have been sobbed into that old sofa cushion! What passionate whisperings the settee must have overheard!

New furniture has no charms for me compared with old. It is the old things that we love—the old faces, the old books, the old jokes. New furniture can make a palace, but it takes old furniture to make a home. Not merely old in itself—lodging-house furniture generally is that—but it must be old to us, old in associations and recollections. The furniture of furnished apartments, however ancient it may be in reality, is new to our eyes, and we feel as though we could never get on with it. As, too, in the case of all fresh acquaintances, whether wooden or human (and there is very little difference between the two species sometimes), everything impresses you with its worst aspect. The knobby wood-work and shiny horse-hair covering of the easy-chair suggest anything but ease. The mirror is smoky. The curtains want washing. The carpet is frayed. The table looks as if it would go over the instant anything was rested on it. The grate is cheerless, the wall-paper hideous. The ceiling appears to have had coffee spilt all over it, and the ornaments—well, they are worse than the wallpaper.

There must surely be some special and secret manufactory for the production of lodging-house ornaments. Precisely the same articles are to be found at every lodging-house all over the kingdom, and they are never seen anywhere else. There are the two—what do you call them? they stand one at each end of the mantel-piece, where they are never safe, and they are hung round with long triangular slips of glass that clank against one another and make you nervous. In the commoner class of rooms these works of art are supplemented by a couple of pieces of china which might each be meant to represent a cow sitting upon its hind legs, or a model of the temple of Diana at Ephesus, or a dog, or anything else you like to fancy. Somewhere about the room you come across a bilious-looking object, which at first you take to be a lump of dough left about by one of the children, but which on scrutiny seems to resemble an underdone cupid. This thing the landlady calls a statue. Then there is a "sampler" worked by some idiot related to the family, a picture of the "Huguenots," two or three Scripture texts, and a highly framed and glazed certificate to the effect that the father has been vaccinated, or is an Odd Fellow, or something of that sort.

You examine these various attractions and then dismally ask what the rent is.

"That's rather a good deal," you say on hearing the figure.

"Well, to tell you the truth," answers the landlady with a sudden burst of candor, "I've always had" (mentioning a sum a good deal in excess of the first-named amount), "and before that I used to have" (a still higher figure).

What the rent of apartments must have been twenty years ago makes one shudder to think of. Every landlady makes you feel thoroughly ashamed of yourself by informing you, whenever the subject crops up, that she used to get twice as much for her rooms as you are paying. Young men lodgers of the last generation must have been of a wealthier class than they are now, or they must have ruined themselves. I should have had to live in an attic.

Curious, that in lodgings the rule of life is reversed. The higher you get up in the world the lower you come down in your lodgings. On the lodging-house ladder the poor man is at the top, the rich man underneath. You start in the attic and work your way down to the first floor.

A good many great men have lived in attics and some have died there. Attics, says the dictionary, are "places where lumber is stored," and the world has used them to store a good deal of its lumber in at one time or another. Its preachers and painters and poets, its deep-browed men who will find out things, its fire-eyed men who will tell truths that no one wants to hear—these are the lumber that the world hides away in its attics. Haydn grew up in an attic and Chatterton starved in one. Addison and Goldsmith wrote in garrets. Faraday and De Quincey knew them well. Dr. Johnson camped cheerfully in them, sleeping soundly—too soundly sometimes—upon their trundle-beds, like the sturdy old soldier of fortune that he was, inured to hardship and all careless of himself. Dickens spent his youth among them, Morland his old age—alas! a drunken, premature old age. Hans Andersen, the fairy king, dreamed his sweet fancies beneath their sloping roofs. Poor, wayward-hearted Collins leaned his head upon their crazy tables; priggish Benjamin Franklin; Savage, the wrong-headed, much troubled when he could afford any softer bed than a doorstep; young Bloomfield, "Bobby" Burns, Hogarth, Watts the engineer—the roll is endless. Ever since the habitations of men were reared two stories high has the garret been the nursery of genius.

No one who honors the aristocracy of mind can feel ashamed of acquaintance-ship with them. Their damp-stained walls are sacred to the memory of noble names. If all the wisdom of the world and all its art—all the spoils that it has won from nature, all the fire that it has snatched from heaven—were gathered together and divided into heaps, and we could point and say, for instance, these mighty truths were flashed forth in the brilliant *salon* amid the ripple of light laughter and the sparkle of bright eyes; and this deep knowledge was dug up in the quiet study, where the bust of Pallas looks serenely down on the leather-scented shelves; and this heap belongs to the crowded street; and that to the daisied field—the heap that would tower up high above the rest as a mountain above hills would be the one at which we should look up and say: this noblest pile of all—these glorious paintings and this wondrous music, these trumpet words, these solemn thoughts, these daring deeds, they were forged and fashioned amid misery and pain in the sordid squalor of the city garret. There, from their eyries, while the world heaved and throbbed below, the kings of men sent forth their eagle thoughts to wing their flight through the ages. There, where the sunlight streaming through the broken panes fell on rotting boards and crumbling walls; there, from their lofty thrones, those rag-clothed Joves have hurled their thunderbolts and shaken, before now, the earth to its foundations.

Huddle them up in your lumber-rooms, oh, world! Shut them fast in and turn the key of poverty upon them. Weld close the bars, and let them fret their hero lives away within the narrow cage. Leave them there to starve, and rot, and die. Laugh at the frenzied beatings of their hands against the door. Roll onward in your dust and noise and pass them by, forgotten.

But take care lest they turn and sting you. All do not, like the fabled phoenix, warble sweet melodies in their agony; sometimes they spit venom—venom you must breathe whether you will or no, for you cannot seal their mouths, though you may fetter their limbs. You can lock the door upon them, but they burst open their shaky lattices and call out over the house-tops so that men cannot but hear. You hounded wild Rousseau into the meanest garret of the Rue St. Jacques and jeered at his angry shrieks. But the thin, piping tones swelled a hundred years later into the sullen roar of the French Revolution, and civilization to this day is quivering to the reverberations of his voice.

As for myself, however, I like an attic. Not to live in: as residences they are inconvenient. There is too much getting up and down stairs connected with them to please me. It puts one unpleasantly in mind of the tread-mill. The form of the ceiling offers too many facilities for bumping your head and too few for shaving. And the note of the tomcat as he sings to his love in the stilly night outside on the tiles becomes positively distasteful when heard so near.

No, for living in give me a suit of rooms on the first floor of a Piccadilly mansion (I wish somebody would!); but for thinking in let me have an attic up ten flights of stairs in the densest quarter of the city. I have all Herr Teufelsdrockh's affection for attics. There is a sublimity about their loftiness. I love to "sit at ease and look down upon the wasps' nest beneath;" to listen to the dull murmur of the human tide ebbing and flowing ceaselessly through the narrow streets and lanes below. How small men seem, how like a swarm of ants sweltering in endless confusion on their tiny hill! How petty seems the work on which they are hurrying and skurrying! How childishly they jostle against one another and turn to snarl and scratch! They jabber and screech and curse, but their puny voices do not reach up here. They fret, and fume, and rage, and pant, and die; "but I, mein Werther, sit above it all; I am alone with the stars."

The most extraordinary attic I ever came across was one a friend and I once shared many years ago. Of all eccentrically planned things, from Bradshaw to the maze at Hampton Court, that room was the most eccentric. The architect who designed it must have been a genius, though I cannot help thinking that his talents would have been better employed in contriving puzzles than in shaping human habitations. No figure in Euclid could give any idea of that apartment. It contained seven corners, two of the walls sloped to a point, and the window was just over the fireplace. The only possible position for the bedstead was between the door and the cupboard. To get anything out of the cupboard we had to scramble over the bed, and a large percentage of the various commodities thus obtained was absorbed by the bedclothes. Indeed, so many things were spilled and dropped upon the bed that toward night-time it had become a sort of small cooperative store. Coal was what it always had most in stock. We used to keep our coal in the bottom part of the cupboard, and when any was wanted we had to climb over the bed, fill a shovelful, and then crawl back. It was an exciting moment when we reached the middle of the bed. We would hold our breath, fix our eyes upon the shovel, and poise ourselves for the last move. The next instant we, and the coals, and the shovel, and the bed would be all mixed up together.

I've heard of the people going into raptures over beds of coal. We slept in one every night and were not in the least stuck up about it.

But our attic, unique though it was, had by no means exhausted the architect's sense of humor. The arrangement of the whole house was a marvel of originality. All the doors opened outward, so that if any one wanted to leave a room at the same moment that you were coming downstairs it was unpleasant for you. There was no ground-floor—its ground-floor belonged to a house in the next court, and the front door opened direct upon a flight of stairs leading down to the cellar. Visitors on entering the house would suddenly shoot past the person who had answered the door to them and disappear down these stairs. Those of a nervous temperament used to imagine that it was a trap laid for them, and would shout murder as they lay on their backs at the bottom till somebody came and picked them up.

It is a long time ago now that I last saw the inside of an attic. I have tried various floors since but I have not found that they have made much difference to me. Life tastes much the same, whether we quaff it from a golden goblet or drink it out of a stone mug. The hours come laden with the same mixture of joy and sorrow, no matter where we wait for them. A waistcoat of broadcloth or of fustian is alike to an aching heart, and we laugh no merrier on velvet cushions than we did on wooden chairs. Often have I sighed in those low-ceilinged rooms, yet disappointments have come neither less nor lighter since I quitted them. Life works upon a compensating balance, and the happiness we gain in one direction we lose in another. As our means increase, so do our desires; and we ever stand midway between the two. When we reside in an attic we enjoy a supper of fried fish and stout. When we occupy the first floor it takes an elaborate dinner at the Continental to give us the same amount of satisfaction.

ON DRESS AND DEPORTMENT.

They say—people who ought to be ashamed of themselves do—that the consciousness of being well dressed imparts a blissfulness to the human heart that religion is powerless to bestow. I am afraid these cynical persons are sometimes correct. I know that when I was a very young man (many, many years ago, as the story-books say) and wanted cheering up, I used to go and dress myself in all my best clothes. If I had been annoyed in any manner—if my washerwoman had discharged me, for instance; or my blank-verse poem had been returned for the tenth time, with the editor's compliments "and regrets that owing to want of space he is unable to avail himself of kind offer;" or I had been snubbed by the woman I loved as man never loved before—by the way, it's really extraordinary what a variety of ways of loving there must be. We all do it as it was never done before. I don't know how our great-grandchildren will manage. They will have to do it on their heads by their time if they persist in not clashing with any previous method.

Well, as I was saying, when these unpleasant sort of things happened and I felt crushed, I put on all my best clothes and went out. It brought back my vanishing self-esteem. In a glossy new hat and a pair of trousers with a fold down the front (carefully preserved by keeping them under the bed—I don't mean on the floor, you know, but between the bed and the mattress), I felt I was somebody and that there were other washerwomen: ay, and even other girls to love, and who would perhaps appreciate a clever, good-looking young fellow. I didn't care; that was my reckless way. I would make love to other maidens. I felt that in those clothes I could do it.

They have a wonderful deal to do with courting, clothes have. It is half the battle. At all events, the young man thinks so, and it generally takes him a couple of hours to get himself up for the occasion. His first half-hour is occupied in trying to decide whether to wear his light suit with a cane and drab billycock, or his black tails with a chimney-pot hat and his new umbrella. He is sure to be unfortunate in either decision. If he wears his light suit and takes the stick it comes on to rain, and he reaches the house in a damp and muddy condition and spends the evening trying to hide his boots. If, on the other hand, he decides in favor of the top hat and umbrella—nobody would ever dream of going out in a top hat without an umbrella; it would be like letting baby (bless it!) toddle out without its nurse. How I do hate a top hat! One lasts me a very long while, I can tell you. I only wear it when—well, never mind when I wear it. It lasts me a very long while. I've had my present one five years. It was rather old-fashioned last summer, but the shape has come round again now and I look quite stylish.

But to return to our young man and his courting. If he starts off with the top hat and umbrella the afternoon turns out fearfully hot, and the perspiration takes all the soap out of his mustache and converts the beautifully arranged curl over his forehead into a limp wisp resembling a lump of seaweed. The Fates are never favorable to the poor wretch. If he does by any chance reach the door in proper condition, she has gone out with her cousin and won't be back till late.

How a young lover made ridiculous by the gawkiness of modern costume must envy the picturesque gallants of seventy years ago! Look at them (on the Christmas cards), with their curly hair and natty hats, their well-shaped legs incased in smalls, their dainty Hessian boots, their ruffling frills, their canes and dangling seals. No wonder the little maiden in the big poke-bonnet and the light-blue sash casts down her eyes and is completely won. Men could win hearts in clothes like that. But what can you expect from baggy trousers and a monkeyjacket?

Clothes have more effect upon us than we imagine. Our deportment depends upon our dress. Make a man get into seedy, worn-out rags, and he will skulk along with his head hanging down, like a man going out to fetch his own supper beer. But deck out the same article in gorgeous raiment and fine linen, and he will strut down the main thoroughfare, swinging his cane and looking at the girls as perky as a bantam cock.

Clothes alter our very nature. A man could not help being fierce and daring with a plume in his bonnet, a dagger in his belt, and a lot of puffy white things all down his sleeves. But in an ulster he wants to get behind a lamp-post and call police.

I am quite ready to admit that you can find sterling merit, honest worth, deep affection, and all such like virtues of the roast-beef-and-plum-pudding school as much, and perhaps more, under broadcloth and tweed as ever existed beneath silk and velvet; but the spirit of that knightly chivalry that "rode a tilt for lady's love" and "fought for lady's smiles" needs the clatter of steel and the rustle of plumes to summon it from its grave between the dusty folds of tapestry and underneath the musty leaves of moldering chronicles.

The world must be getting old, I think; it dresses so very soberly now. We have been through the infant period of humanity, when we used to run about with nothing on but a long, loose robe, and liked to have our feet bare. And then came the rough, barbaric age, the boyhood of our race. We didn't care what we wore then, but thought it nice to tattoo ourselves all over, and we never did our hair. And after that the world grew into a young man and became foppish. It decked itself in flowing curls and scarlet doublets, and went courting, and bragging, and bouncing—making a brave show.

But all those merry, foolish days of youth are gone, and we are very sober, very solemn—and very stupid, some say—now. The world is a grave, middle-aged gentleman in this nineteenth century, and would be shocked to see itself with a bit of finery on. So it dresses in black coats and trousers, and black hats, and black boots, and, dear me, it is such a very respectable gentleman—to think it could ever have gone gadding about as a troubadour or a knight-errant, dressed in all those fancy colors! Ah, well! we are more sensible in this age.

Or at least we think ourselves so. It is a general theory nowadays that sense and dullness go together.

Goodness is another quality that always goes with blackness. Very good people indeed, you will notice, dress altogether in black, even to gloves and neckties, and they will probably take to black shirts before long. Medium goods indulge in light trousers on week-days, and some of them even go so far as to wear fancy waistcoats. On the other hand, people who care nothing for a future state go about in light suits; and there have been known wretches so abandoned as to wear a white hat. Such people, however, are never spoken of in genteel society, and perhaps I ought not to have referred to them here.

By the way, talking of light suits, have you ever noticed how people stare at you the first time you go out in a new light suit They do not notice it so much afterward. The population of London have got accustomed to it by the third time you wear it. I say "you," because I am not speaking from my own experience. I do not wear such things at all myself. As I said, only sinful people do so.

I wish, though, it were not so, and that one could be good, and respectable, and sensible without making one's self a guy. I look in the glass sometimes at my two long, cylindrical bags (so picturesquely rugged about the knees), my stand-up collar and billycock hat, and wonder what right I have to go about making God's world hideous. Then wild and wicked thoughts come into my heart. I don't want to be good and respectable. (I never can be sensible, I'm told; so that don't matter.) I want to put on lavender-colored tights, with red velvet breeches and a green doublet slashed with yellow; to have a light-blue silk cloak on my shoulder, and a black eagle's plume waving from my hat, and a big sword, and a falcon, and a lance, and a prancing horse, so that I might go about and gladden the eyes of the people. Why should we all try to look like ants crawling over a dust-heap? Why shouldn't we dress a little gayly? I am sure if we did we should be happier. True, it is a little thing, but we are a little race, and what is the use of our pretending otherwise and spoiling fun? Let philosophers get themselves up like old crows if they like. But let me be a butterfly.

Women, at all events, ought to dress prettily. It is their duty. They are the flowers of the earth and were meant to show it up. We abuse them a good deal, we men; but, goodness knows, the old world would be dull enough without their dresses and fair faces. How they brighten up every place they come into! What a sunny commotion they—relations, of course—-make in our dingy bachelor chambers! and what a delightful litter their ribbons and laces, and gloves and hats, and parasols and 'kerchiefs make! It is as if a wandering rainbow had dropped in to pay us a visit.

It is one of the chief charms of the summer, to my mind, the way our little maids come out in pretty colors. I like to see the pink and blue and white glancing between the trees, dotting the green fields, and flashing back the sunlight. You can see the bright colors such a long way off. There are four white dresses climbing a hill in front of my window now. I can see them distinctly, though it is three miles away. I thought at first they were mile-stones out for a lark. It's so nice to be able to see the darlings a long way off. Especially if they happen to be your wife and your mother-in-law.

Talking of fields and mile-stones reminds me that I want to say, in all seriousness, a few words about women's boots. The women of these islands all wear boots too big for them. They can never get a boot to fit. The bootmakers do not keep sizes small enough.

Over and over again have I known women sit down on the top rail of a stile and declare they could not go a step further because their boots hurt them so; and it has always been the same complaint—too big.

It is time this state of things was altered. In the name of the husbands and fathers of England, I call upon the bootmakers to reform. Our wives, our daughters, and our cousins are not to be lamed and tortured with impunity. Why cannot "narrow twos" be kept more in stock? That is the size I find most women take.

The waist-band is another item of feminine apparel that is always too big. The dressmakers make these things so loose that the hooks and eyes by which they are fastened burst off, every now and then, with a report like thunder.

Why women suffer these wrongs—why they do not insist in having their clothes made small enough for them I cannot conceive. It can hardly be that they are disinclined to trouble themselves about matters of mere dress, for dress is the one subject that they really do think about. It is the only topic they ever get thoroughly interested in, and they talk about it all day long. If you see two women together, you may bet your bottom dollar they are discussing their own or their friends' clothes. You notice a couple of child-like beings conversing by a window, and you wonder what sweet, helpful words are falling from their sainted lips. So you move nearer and then you hear one say:

"So I took in the waist-band and let out a seam, and it fits beautifully now."

"Well," says the other, "I shall wear my plum-colored body to the Jones', with a yellow plastron; and they've got some lovely gloves at Puttick's, only one and eleven pence."

I went for a drive through a part of Derbyshire once with a couple of ladies. It was a beautiful bit of country, and they enjoyed themselves immensely. They talked dressmaking the whole time.

"Pretty view, that," I would say, waving my umbrella round. "Look at those blue distant hills! That little white speck, nestling in the woods, is Chatsworth, and over there—"

"Yes, very pretty indeed," one would reply. "Well, why not get a yard of sarsenet?"

"What, and leave the skirt exactly as it is?"

"Certainly. What place d'ye call this?"

Then I would draw their attention to the fresh beauties that kept sweeping into view, and they would glance round and say "charming," "sweetly pretty," and immediately go off into raptures over each other's pocket-handkerchiefs, and mourn with one another over the decadence of cambric frilling.

I believe if two women were cast together upon a desert island, they would spend each day arguing the respective merits of sea-shells and birds' eggs considered as trimmings, and would have a new fashion in fig-leaves every month.

Very young men think a good deal about clothes, but they don't talk about them to each other. They would not find much encouragement. A fop is not a favorite with his own sex. Indeed, he gets a good deal more abuse from them than is necessary. His is a harmless failing and it soon wears out. Besides, a man who has no foppery at twenty will be a slatternly, dirty-collar, unbrushed-coat man at forty. A little foppishness in a young man is good; it is human. I like to see a young cock ruffle his feathers, stretch his neck, and crow as if the whole world belonged to him. I don't like a modest, retiring man. Nobody does—not really, however much they may prate about modest worth and other things they do not understand.

A meek deportment is a great mistake in the world. Uriah Heap's father was a very poor judge of human nature, or he would not have told his son, as he did, that people liked humbleness. There is nothing annoys them more, as a rule. Rows are half the fun of life, and you can't have rows with humble, meek-answering individuals. They turn away our wrath, and that is just what we do not want. We want to let it out. We have worked ourselves up into a state of exhilarating fury, and then just as we are anticipating the enjoyment of a vigorous set-to, they spoil all our plans with their exasperating humility.

Xantippe's life must have been one long misery, tied to that calmly irritating man, Socrates. Fancy a married woman doomed to live on from day to day without one single quarrel with her husband! A man ought to humor his wife in these things.

Heaven knows their lives are dull enough, poor girls. They have none of the enjoyments we have. They go to no political meetings; they may not even belong to the local amateur parliament; they are excluded from smoking-carriages on the Metropolitan Railway, and they never see a comic paper—or if they do, they do not know it is comic: nobody tells them.

Surely, with existence such a dreary blank for them as this, we might provide a little row for their amusement now and then, even if we do not feel inclined for it ourselves. A really sensible man does so and is loved accordingly, for it is little acts of kindness such as this that go straight to a woman's heart. It is such like proofs of loving self-sacrifice that make her tell her female friends what a good husband he was—after he is dead.

Yes, poor Xantippe must have had a hard time of it. The bucket episode was particularly sad for her. Poor woman! she did think she would rouse him up a bit with that. She had taken the trouble to fill the bucket, perhaps been a long way to get specially dirty water. And she waited for him. And then to be met in such a way, after all! Most likely she sat down and had a good cry afterward. It must have seemed all so hopeless to the poor child; and for all we know she had no mother to whom she could go and abuse him.

What was it to her that her husband was a great philosopher? Great philosophy don't count in married life.

There was a very good little boy once who wanted to go to sea. And the captain asked him what he could do. He said he could do the multiplication-table backward and paste sea-weed in a book; that he knew how many times the word "begat" occurred in the Old Testament; and could recite "The Boy Stood on the Burning Deck" and Wordsworth's "We Are Seven."

"Werry good—werry good, indeed," said the man of the sea, "and ken ye kerry coals?"

It is just the same when you want to marry. Great ability is not required so much as little usefulness. Brains are at a discount in the married state. There is no demand for them, no appreciation even. Our wives sum us up according to a standard of their own, in which brilliancy of intellect obtains no marks. Your lady and mistress is not at all impressed by your cleverness and talent, my dear reader—not in the slightest. Give her a man who can do an errand neatly, without attempting to use his own judgment over it or any nonsense of that kind; and who can be trusted to hold a child the right way up, and not make himself objectionable whenever there is lukewarm mutton for dinner. That is the sort of a husband a sensible woman likes; not one of your scientific or literary nuisances, who go upsetting the whole house and putting everybody out with their foolishness.

ON MEMORY.

"I remember, I remember,

> In the days of chill November,
> How the blackbird on the—"

I forget the rest. It is the beginning of the first piece of poetry I ever learned; for

> "Hey, diddle diddle,
> The cat and the fiddle,"

I take no note of, it being of a frivolous character and lacking in the qualities of true poetry. I collected fourpence by the recital of "I remember, I remember." I knew it was fourpence, because they told me that if I kept it until I got twopence more I should have sixpence, which argument, albeit undeniable, moved me not, and the money was squandered, to the best of my recollection, on the very next morning, although upon what memory is a blank.

That is just the way with Memory; nothing that she brings to us is complete. She is a willful child; all her toys are broken. I remember tumbling into a huge dust-hole when a very small boy, but I have not the faintest recollection of ever getting out again; and if memory were all we had to trust to, I should be compelled to believe I was there still.

At another time—some years later—I was assisting at an exceedingly interesting love scene; but the only thing about it I can call to mind distinctly is that at the most critical moment somebody suddenly opened the door and said, "Emily, you're wanted," in a sepulchral tone that gave one the idea the police had come for her. All the tender words she said to me and all the beautiful things I said to her are utterly forgotten.

Life altogether is but a crumbling ruin when we turn to look behind: a shattered column here, where a massive portal stood; the broken shaft of a window to mark my lady's bower; and a moldering heap of blackened stones where the glowing flames once leaped, and over all the tinted lichen and the ivy clinging green.

For everything looms pleasant through the softening haze of time. Even the sadness that is past seems sweet. Our boyish days look very merry to us now, all nutting, hoop, and gingerbread. The snubbings and toothaches and the Latin verbs are all forgotten—the Latin verbs especially. And we fancy we were very happy when we were hobbledehoys and loved; and we wish that we could love again. We never think of the heartaches, or the sleepless nights, or the hot dryness of our throats, when she said she could never be anything to us but a sister—as if any man wanted more sisters!

Yes, it is the brightness, not the darkness, that we see when we look back. The sunshine casts no shadows on the past. The road that we have traversed stretches very fair behind us. We see not the sharp stones. We dwell but on the roses by the wayside, and the strong briers that stung us are, to our distant eyes, but gentle tendrils waving in the wind. God be thanked that it is so—that the ever-lengthening chain of memory has only pleasant links, and that the bitterness and sorrow of to-day are smiled at on the morrow.

It seems as though the brightest side of everything were also its highest and best, so that as our little lives sink back behind us into the dark sea of forgetfulness, all that which is the lightest and the most gladsome is the last to sink, and stands above the waters, long in sight, when the angry thoughts and smarting pain are buried deep below the waves and trouble us no more.

It is this glamour of the past, I suppose, that makes old folk talk so much nonsense about the days when they were young. The world appears to have been a very superior sort of place then, and things were more like what they ought to be. Boys were boys then, and girls were very different. Also winters were something like winters, and summers not at all the wretched-things we get put off with nowadays. As for the wonderful deeds people did in those times and the extraordinary events that happened, it takes three strong men to believe half of them.

I like to hear one of the old boys telling all about it to a party of youngsters who he knows cannot contradict him. It is odd if, after awhile, he doesn't swear that the moon shone every night when he was a boy, and that tossing mad bulls in a blanket was the favorite sport at his school.

It always has been and always will be the same. The old folk of our grandfathers' young days sang a song bearing exactly the same burden; and the young folk of to-day will drone out precisely similar nonsense for the aggravation of the next generation. "Oh, give me back the good old days of fifty years ago," has been the cry ever since Adam's fifty-first birthday. Take up the literature of 1835, and you will find the poets and novelists asking for the same impossible gift as did the German Minnesingers long before them and the old Norse Saga writers long before that. And for the same thing sighed the early prophets and the philosophers of ancient Greece. From all accounts, the world has been getting worse and worse ever since it was created. All I can say is that it must have been a remarkably delightful place when it was first opened to the public, for it is very pleasant even now if you only keep as much as possible in the sunshine and take the rain good-temperedly.

Yet there is no gainsaying but that it must have been somewhat sweeter in that dewy morning of creation, when it was young and fresh, when the feet of the tramping millions had not trodden its grass to dust, nor the din of the myriad cities chased the silence forever away. Life must have been noble and solemn to those free-footed, loose-robed fathers of the human race, walking hand in hand with God under the great sky. They lived in sunkissed tents amid the lowing herds. They took their simple wants from the loving hand of Nature. They toiled and talked and thought; and the great earth rolled around in stillness, not yet laden with trouble and wrong.

Those days are past now. The quiet childhood of Humanity, spent in the far-off forest glades and by the murmuring rivers, is gone forever; and human life is deepening down to manhood amid tumult, doubt, and hope. Its age of restful peace is past. It has its work to finish and must hasten on. What that work may be—what this world's share is in the great design—we know not, though our un-conscious hands are helping to accomplish it. Like the tiny coral insect working deep under the dark waters, we strive and struggle each for our own little ends, nor dream of the vast fabric we are building up for God.

Let us have done with vain regrets and longings for the days that never will be ours again. Our work lies in front, not behind us; and "Forward!" is our motto. Let us not sit with folded hands, gazing upon the past as if it were the building; it is but the foundation. Let us not waste heart and life thinking of what might have been and forgetting the may be that lies before us. Opportunities flit by while we sit regretting the chances we have lost, and the happiness that comes to us we heed not, because of the happiness that is gone.

Years ago, when I used to wander of an evening from the fireside to the pleas-ant land of fairy-tales, I met a doughty knight and true. Many dangers had he overcome, in many lands had been; and all men knew him for a brave and well-tried knight, and one that knew not fear; except, maybe, upon such seasons when even a brave man might feel afraid and yet not be ashamed. Now, as this knight one day was pricking wearily along a toilsome road, his heart misgave him and was sore within him because of the trouble of the way. Rocks, dark and of a mon-strous size, hung high above his head, and like enough it seemed unto the knight that they should fall and he lie low beneath them. Chasms there were on either side, and darksome caves wherein fierce robbers lived, and dragons, very terrible, whose jaws dripped blood. And upon the road there hung a darkness as of night. So it came over that good knight that he would no more press forward, but seek another road, less grievously beset with difficulty unto his gentle steed. But when in haste he turned and looked behind, much marveled our brave knight, for lo! of all the way that he had ridden there was naught for eye to see; but at his horse's heels there yawned a mighty gulf, whereof no man might ever spy the bottom, so deep was that same gulf. Then when Sir Ghelent saw that of going back there was none, he prayed to good Saint Cuthbert, and setting spurs into his steed rode for-ward bravely and most joyously. And naught harmed him.

There is no returning on the road of life. The frail bridge of time on which we tread sinks back into eternity at every step we take. The past is gone from us for-ever. It is gathered in and garnered. It belongs to us no more. No single word can ever be unspoken; no single step retraced. Therefore it beseems us as true knights to prick on bravely, not idly weep because we cannot now recall.

A new life begins for us with every second. Let us go forward joyously to meet it. We must press on whether we will or no, and we shall walk better with our eyes before us than with them ever cast behind.

A friend came to me the other day and urged me very eloquently to learn some wonderful system by which you never forgot anything. I don't know why he was so eager on the subject, unless it be that I occasionally borrow an umbrella and have a knack of coming out, in the middle of a game of whist, with a mild "Lor! I've been thinking all along that clubs were trumps." I declined the suggestion, however, in spite of the advantages he so attractively set forth. I have no wish to remember everything. There are many things in most men's lives that had better be forgotten. There is that time, many years ago, when we did not act quite as honorably, quite as uprightly, as we perhaps should have done—that unfortunate deviation from the path of strict probity we once committed, and in which, more unfortunate still, we were found out—that act of folly, of meanness, of wrong. Ah, well! we paid the penalty, suffered the maddening hours of vain remorse, the hot agony of shame, the scorn, perhaps, of those we loved. Let us forget. Oh, Father Time, lift with your kindly hands those bitter memories from off our overburdened hearts, for griefs are ever coming to us with the coming hours, and our little strength is only as the day.

Not that the past should be buried. The music of life would be mute if the chords of memory were snapped asunder. It is but the poisonous weeds, not the flowers, that we should root out from the garden of Mnemosyne. Do you remember Dickens' "Haunted Man"—how he prayed for forgetfulness, and how, when his prayer was answered, he prayed for memory once more? We do not want all the ghosts laid. It is only the haggard, cruel-eyed specters that we flee from. Let the gentle, kindly phantoms haunt us as they will; we are not afraid of them.

Ah me! the world grows very full of ghosts as we grow older. We need not seek in dismal church-yards nor sleep in moated granges to see the shadowy faces and hear the rustling of their garments in the night. Every house, every room, every creaking chair has its own particular ghost. They haunt the empty chambers of our lives, they throng around us like dead leaves whirled in the autumn wind. Some are living, some are dead. We know not. We clasped their hands once, loved them, quarreled with them, laughed with them, told them our thoughts and hopes and aims, as they told us theirs, till it seemed our very hearts had joined in a grip that would defy the puny power of Death. They are gone now; lost to us forever. Their eyes will never look into ours again and their voices we shall never hear. Only their ghosts come to us and talk with us. We see them, dim and shadowy, through our tears. We stretch our yearning hands to them, but they are air.

Ghosts! They are with us night and day. They walk beside us in the busy street under the glare of the sun. They sit by us in the twilight at home. We see their little faces looking from the windows of the old school-house. We meet them in the woods and lanes where we shouted and played as boys. Hark! cannot you hear their low laughter from behind the blackberry-bushes and their distant whoops along the grassy glades? Down here, through the quiet fields and by the wood, where the evening shadows are lurking, winds the path where we used to watch for her at sunset. Look, she is there now, in the dainty white frock we knew so well, with the big bonnet dangling from her little hands and the sunny brown hair all tangled. Five thousand miles away! Dead for all we know! What of that? She is beside us now, and we can look into her laughing eyes and hear her voice. She will vanish at the stile by the wood and we shall be alone; and the shadows will creep out across the fields and the night wind will sweep past moaning. Ghosts! they are always with us and always will be while the sad old world keeps echoing to the sob of long good-bys, while the cruel ships sail away across the great seas, and the cold green earth lies heavy on the hearts of those we loved.

But, oh, ghosts, the world would be sadder still without you. Come to us and speak to us, oh you ghosts of our old loves! Ghosts of playmates, and of sweethearts, and old friends, of all you laughing boys and girls, oh, come to us and be with us, for the world is very lonely, and new friends and faces are not like the old, and we cannot love them, nay, nor laugh with them as we have loved and laughed with you. And when we walked together, oh, ghosts of our youth, the world was very gay and bright; but now it has grown old and we are growing weary, and only you can bring the brightness and the freshness back to us.

Memory is a rare ghost-raiser. Like a haunted house, its walls are ever echoing to unseen feet. Through the broken casements we watch the flitting shadows of the dead, and the saddest shadows of them all are the shadows of our own dead selves.

Oh, those young bright faces, so full of truth and honor, of pure, good thoughts, of noble longings, how reproachfully they look upon us with their deep, clear eyes!

I fear they have good cause for their sorrow, poor lads. Lies and cunning and disbelief have crept into our hearts since those preshaving days—and we meant to be so great and good.

It is well we cannot see into the future. There are few boys of fourteen who would not feel ashamed of themselves at forty.

I like to sit and have a talk sometimes with that odd little chap that was myself long ago. I think he likes it too, for he comes so often of an evening when I am alone with my pipe, listening to the whispering of the flames. I see his solemn little face looking at me through the scented smoke as it floats upward, and I smile at him; and he smiles back at me, but his is such a grave, old-fashioned smile. We chat about old times; and now and then he takes me by the hand, and then we slip through the black bars of the grate and down the dusky glowing caves to the land that lies behind the firelight. There we find the days that used to be, and we wander along them together. He tells me as we walk all he thinks and feels. I laugh at him now and then, but the next moment I wish I had not, for he looks so grave I am ashamed of being frivolous. Besides, it is not showing proper respect to one so much older than myself—to one who was myself so very long before I became myself.

We don't talk much at first, but look at one another; I down at his curly hair and little blue bow, he up sideways at me as he trots. And some-how I fancy the shy, round eyes do not altogether approve of me, and he heaves a little sigh, as though he were disappointed. But after awhile his bashfulness wears off and he begins to chat. He tells me his favorite fairy-tales, he can do up to six times, and he has a guinea-pig, and pa says fairy-tales ain't true; and isn't it a pity? 'cos he would so like to be a knight and fight a dragon and marry a beautiful princess. But he takes a more practical view of life when he reaches seven, and would prefer to grow up be a bargee, and earn a lot of money. Maybe this is the consequence of falling in love, which he does about this time with the young lady at the milk shop aet. six. (God bless her little ever-dancing feet, whatever size they may be now!) He must be very fond of her, for he gives her one day his chiefest treasure, to wit, a huge pocket-knife with four rusty blades and a corkscrew, which latter has a knack of working itself out in some mysterious manner and sticking into its owner's leg. She is an affectionate little thing, and she throws her arms round his neck and kisses him for it, then and there, outside the shop. But the stupid world (in the person of the boy at the cigar emporium next door) jeers at such tokens of love. Whereupon my young friend very properly prepares to punch the head of the boy at the cigar emporium next door; but fails in the attempt, the boy at the cigar emporium next door punching his instead.

And then comes school life, with its bitter little sorrows and its joyous shoutings, its jolly larks, and its hot tears falling on beastly Latin grammars and silly old copy-books. It is at school that he injures himself for life—as I firmly believe—trying to pronounce German; and it is there, too, that he learns of the importance attached by the French nation to pens, ink, and paper. "Have you pens, ink, and paper?" is the first question asked by one Frenchman of another on their meeting. The other fellow has not any of them, as a rule, but says that the uncle of his brother has got them all three. The first fellow doesn't appear to care a hang about the uncle of the other fellow's brother; what he wants to know now is, has the neighbor of the other fellow's mother got 'em? "The neighbor of my mother has no pens, no ink, and no paper," replies the other man, beginning to get wild. "Has the child of thy female gardener some pens, some ink, or some paper?" He has him there. After worrying enough about these wretched inks, pens, and paper to make everybody miserable, it turns out that the child of his own female gardener hasn't any. Such a discovery would shut up any one but a French exercise man. It has no effect at all, though, on this shameless creature. He never thinks of apologizing, but says his aunt has some mustard.

So in the acquisition of more or less useless knowledge, soon happily to be forgotten, boyhood passes away. The red-brick school-house fades from view, and we turn down into the world's high-road. My little friend is no longer little now. The short jacket has sprouted tails. The battered cap, so useful as a combination of pocket-handkerchief, drinking-cup, and weapon of attack, has grown high and glossy; and instead of a slate-pencil in his mouth there is a cigarette, the smoke of which troubles him, for it will get up his nose. He tries a cigar a little later on as being more stylish—a big black Havanna. It doesn't seem altogether to agree with him, for I find him sitting over a bucket in the back kitchen afterward, solemnly swearing never to smoke again.

And now his mustache begins to be almost visible to the naked eye, where-upon he immediately takes to brandy-and-sodas and fancies himself a man. He talks about "two to one against the favorite," refers to actresses as "Little Emmy" and "Kate" and "Baby," and murmurs about his "losses at cards the other night" in a style implying that thousands have been squandered, though, to do him justice, the actual amount is most probably one-and-twopence. Also, if I see aright—for it is always twilight in this land of memories—he sticks an eyeglass in his eye and stumbles over everything.

His female relations, much troubled at these things, pray for him (bless their gentle hearts!) and see visions of Old Bailey trials and halters as the only possible outcome of such reckless dissipation; and the prediction of his first school-master, that he would come to a bad end, assumes the proportions of inspired prophecy.

He has a lordly contempt at this age for the other sex, a blatantly good opinion of himself, and a sociably patronizing manner toward all the elderly male friends of the family. Altogether, it must be confessed, he is somewhat of a nuisance about this time.

It does not last long, though. He falls in love in a little while, and that soon takes the bounce out of him. I notice his boots are much too small for him now, and his hair is fearfully and wonderfully arranged. He reads poetry more than he used, and he keeps a rhyming dictionary in his bedroom. Every morning Emily Jane finds scraps of torn-up paper on the floor and reads thereon of "cruel hearts and love's deep darts," of "beauteous eyes and lovers' sighs," and much more of the old, old song that lads so love to sing and lassies love to listen to while giving their dainty heads a toss and pretending never to hear.

The course of love, however, seems not to have run smoothly, for later on he takes more walking exercise and less sleep, poor boy, than is good for him; and his face is suggestive of anything but wedding-bells and happiness ever after.

And here he seems to vanish. The little, boyish self that has grown up beside me as we walked is gone.

I am alone and the road is very dark. I stumble on, I know not how nor care, for the way seems leading nowhere, and there is no light to guide.

But at last the morning comes, and I find that I have grown into myself.

THE END.

THE SECOND THOUGHTS OF AN IDLE FELLOW

ON THE ART OF MAKING UP ONE'S MIND

"Now, which would you advise, dear? You see, with the red I shan't be able to wear my magenta hat."

"Well then, why not have the grey?"

"Yes—yes, I think the grey will be MORE useful."

"It's a good material."

"Yes, and it's a PRETTY grey. You know what I mean, dear; not a COMMON grey. Of course grey is always an UNINTERESTING colour."

"Its quiet."

"And then again, what I feel about the red is that it is so warm-looking. Red makes you FEEL warm even when you're NOT warm. You know what I mean, dear!"

"Well then, why not have the red? It suits you—red."

"No; do you really think so?"

"Well, when you've got a colour, I mean, of course!"

"Yes, that is the drawback to red. No, I think, on the whole, the grey is SAFER."

"Then you will take the grey, madam?"

"Yes, I think I'd better; don't you, dear?"

"I like it myself very much."

"And it is good wearing stuff. I shall have it trimmed with—Oh! you haven't cut it off, have you?"

"I was just about to, madam."

"Well, don't for a moment. Just let me have another look at the red. You see, dear, it has just occurred to me—that chinchilla would look so well on the red!"

"So it would, dear!"

"And, you see, I've got the chinchilla."

"Then have the red. Why not?"

"Well, there is the hat I'm thinking of."

"You haven't anything else you could wear with that?"

"Nothing at all, and it would go so BEAUTIFULLY with the grey.—Yes, I think I'll have the grey. It's always a safe colour—grey."

"Fourteen yards I think you said, madam?"

"Yes, fourteen yards will be enough; because I shall mix it with—One minute. You see, dear, if I take the grey I shall have nothing to wear with my black jacket."

"Won't it go with grey?"

"Not well—not so well as with red."

"I should have the red then. You evidently fancy it yourself."

"No, personally I prefer the grey. But then one must think of EVERYTHING, and—Good gracious! that's surely not the right time?"

"No, madam, it's ten minutes slow. We always keep our clocks a little slow!"

"And we were too have been at Madame Jannaway's at a quarter past twelve. How long shopping does take I—Why, whatever time did we start?"

"About eleven, wasn't it?"

"Half-past ten. I remember now; because, you know, we said we'd start at half-past nine. We've been two hours already!"

"And we don't seem to have done much, do we?"

"Done literally nothing, and I meant to have done so much. I must go to Madame Jannaway's. Have you got my purse, dear? Oh, it's all right, I've got it."

"Well, now you haven't decided whether you're going to have the grey or the red."

"I'm sure I don't know what I do want now. I had made up my mind a minute ago, and now it's all gone again—oh yes, I remember, the red. Yes, I'll have the red. No, I don't mean the red, I mean the grey."

"You were talking about the red last time, if you remember, dear."

"Oh, so I was, you're quite right. That's the worst of shopping. Do you know I get quite confused sometimes."

"Then you will decide on the red, madam?"

"Yes—yes, I shan't do any better, shall I, dear? What do you think? You haven't got any other shades of red, have you? This is such an ugly red."

The shopman reminds her that she has seen all the other reds, and that this is the particular shade she selected and admired.

"Oh, very well," she replies, with the air of one from whom all earthly cares are falling, "I must take that then, I suppose. I can't be worried about it any longer. I've wasted half the morning already."

Outside she recollects three insuperable objections to the red, and four unanswerable arguments why she should have selected the grey. She wonders would they change it, if she went back and asked to see the shopwalker? Her friend, who wants her lunch, thinks not.

"That is what I hate about shopping," she says. "One never has time to really THINK."

She says she shan't go to that shop again.

We laugh at her, but are we so very much better? Come, my superior male friend, have you never stood, amid your wardrobe, undecided whether, in her eyes, you would appear more imposing, clad in the rough tweed suit that so admirably displays your broad shoulders; or in the orthodox black frock, that, after all, is perhaps more suitable to the figure of a man approaching—let us say, the nine-and-twenties? Or, better still, why not riding costume? Did we not hear her say how well Jones looked in his top-boots and breeches, and, "hang it all," we have a better leg than Jones. What a pity riding-breeches are made so baggy nowadays. Why is it that male fashions tend more and more to hide the male leg? As women have become less and less ashamed of theirs, we have become more and more reticent of ours. Why are the silken hose, the tight-fitting pantaloons, the neat kneebreeches of our forefathers impossible to-day? Are we grown more modest—or has there come about a falling off, rendering concealment advisable?

I can never understand, myself, why women love us. It must be our honest worth, our sterling merit, that attracts them—certainly not our appearance, in a pair of tweed "dittos," black angora coat and vest, stand-up collar, and chimney-pot hat! No, it must be our sheer force of character that compels their admiration.

What a good time our ancestors must have had was borne in upon me when, on one occasion, I appeared in character at a fancy dress ball. What I represented I am unable to say, and I don't particularly care. I only know it was something military. I also remember that the costume was two sizes too small for me in the chest, and thereabouts; and three sizes too large for me in the hat. I padded the hat, and dined in the middle of the day off a chop and half a glass of soda-water. I have gained prizes as a boy for mathematics, also for scripture history—not often, but I have done it. A literary critic, now dead, once praised a book of mine. I know there have been occasions when my conduct has won the approbation of good men; but never—never in my whole life, have I felt more proud, more satis-fied with myself than on that evening when, the last hook fastened, I gazed at my full-length Self in the cheval glass. I was a dream. I say it who should not; but I am not the only one who said it. I was a glittering dream. The groundwork was red, trimmed with gold braid wherever there was room for gold braid; and where there was no more possible room for gold braid there hung gold cords, and tas-sels, and straps. Gold buttons and buckles fastened me, gold embroidered belts and sashes caressed me, white horse-hair plumes waved o'er me. I am not sure that everything was in its proper place, but I managed to get everything on some-how, and I looked well. It suited me. My success was a revelation to me of female human nature. Girls who had hitherto been cold and distant gathered round me, timidly solicitous of notice. Girls on whom I smiled lost their heads and gave themselves airs. Girls who were not introduced to me sulked and were rude to girls that had been. For one poor child, with whom I sat out two dances (at least she sat, while I stood gracefully beside her—I had been advised, by the costumier, NOT to sit), I was sorry. He was a worthy young fellow, the son of a cotton bro-ker, and he would have made her a good husband, I feel sure. But he was foolish to come as a beer-bottle.

Perhaps, after all, it is as well those old fashions have gone out. A week in that suit might have impaired my natural modesty.

One wonders that fancy dress balls are not more popular in this grey age of ours. The childish instinct to "dress up," to "make believe," is with us all. We grow so tired of being always ourselves. A tea-table discussion, at which I once assisted, fell into this:—Would any one of us, when it came to the point, change with anybody else, the poor man with the millionaire, the governess with the princess—change not only outward circumstances and surroundings, but health and temperament, heart, brain, and soul; so that not one mental or physical particle of one's original self one would retain, save only memory? The general opinion was that we would not, but one lady maintained the affirmative.

"Oh no, you wouldn't really, dear," argued a friend; "you THINK you would."

"Yes, I would," persisted the first lady; "I am tired of myself. I'd even be you, for a change."

In my youth, the question chiefly important to me was—What sort of man shall I decide to be? At nineteen one asks oneself this question; at thirty-nine we say, "I wish Fate hadn't made me this sort of man."

In those days I was a reader of much well-meant advice to young men, and I gathered that, whether I should become a Sir Lancelot, a Herr Teufelsdrockh, or an Iago was a matter for my own individual choice. Whether I should go through life gaily or gravely was a question the pros and cons of which I carefully considered. For patterns I turned to books. Byron was then still popular, and many of us made up our minds to be gloomy, saturnine young men, weary with the world, and prone to soliloquy. I determined to join them.

For a month I rarely smiled, or, when I did, it was with a weary, bitter smile, concealing a broken heart—at least that was the intention. Shallow-minded observers misunderstood.

"I know exactly how it feels," they would say, looking at me sympathetically, "I often have it myself. It's the sudden change in the weather, I think;" and they would press neat brandy upon me, and suggest ginger.

Again, it is distressing to the young man, busy burying his secret sorrow under a mound of silence, to be slapped on the back by commonplace people and asked—"Well, how's 'the hump' this morning?" and to hear his mood of dignified melancholy referred to, by those who should know better, as "the sulks."

There are practical difficulties also in the way of him who would play the Byronic young gentleman. He must be supernaturally wicked—or rather must have been; only, alas! in the unliterary grammar of life, where the future tense stands first, and the past is formed, not from the indefinite, but from the present indicative, "to have been" is "to be"; and to be wicked on a small income is impossible. The ruin of even the simplest of maidens costs money. In the Courts of Love one cannot sue in forma pauperis; nor would it be the Byronic method.

"To drown remembrance in the cup" sounds well, but then the "cup," to be fitting, should be of some expensive brand. To drink deep of old Tokay or Asti is poetical; but when one's purse necessitates that the draught, if it is to be deep enough to drown anything, should be of thin beer at five-and-nine the four and a half gallon cask, or something similar in price, sin is robbed of its flavour.

Possibly also—let me think it—the conviction may have been within me that Vice, even at its daintiest, is but an ugly, sordid thing, repulsive in the sunlight;

that though—as rags and dirt to art—it may afford picturesque material to Literature, it is an evil-smelling garment to the wearer; one that a good man, by reason of poverty of will, may come down to, but one to be avoided with all one's effort, discarded with returning mental prosperity.

Be this as it may, I grew weary of training for a saturnine young man; and, in the midst of my doubt, I chanced upon a book the hero of which was a debonnaire young buck, own cousin to Tom and Jerry. He attended fights, both of cocks and men, flirted with actresses, wrenched off door-knockers, extinguished street lamps, played many a merry jest upon many an unappreciative night watch-man. For all the which he was much beloved by the women of the book. Why should not I flirt with actresses, put out street lamps, play pranks on policemen, and be beloved? London life was changed since the days of my hero, but much remained, and the heart of woman is eternal. If no longer prizefighting was to be had, at least there were boxing competitions, so called, in dingy back parlours out Whitechapel way. Though cockfighting was a lost sport, were there not damp cellars near the river where for twopence a gentleman might back mongrel terriers to kill rats against time, and feel himself indeed a sportsman? True, the atmosphere of reckless gaiety, always surrounding my hero, I missed myself from these scenes, finding in its place an atmosphere more suggestive of gin, stale tobacco, and nervous apprehension of the police; but the essentials must have been the same, and the next morning I could exclaim in the very words of my prototype—"Odds crickets, but I feel as though the devil himself were in my head. Peste take me for a fool."

But in this direction likewise my fatal lack of means opposed me. (It affords much food to the philosophic mind, this influence of income upon character.) Even fifth-rate "boxing competitions," organized by "friendly leads," and ratting contests in Rotherhithe slums, become expensive, when you happen to be the only gentleman present possessed of a collar, and are expected to do the honours of your class in dog's-nose. True, climbing lamp-posts and putting out the gas is fairly cheap, providing always you are not caught in the act, but as a recreation it lacks variety. Nor is the modern London lamp-post adapted to sport. Anything more difficult to grip—anything with less "give" in it—I have rarely clasped. The disgraceful amount of dirt allowed to accumulate upon it is another drawback from the climber's point of view. By the time you have swarmed up your third post a positive distaste for "gaiety" steals over you. Your desire is towards arnica and a bath.

Nor in jokes at the expense of policemen is the fun entirely on your side. Maybe I did not proceed with judgment. It occurs to me now, looking back, that the neighbourhoods of Covent Garden and Great Marlborough Street were ill-chosen for sport of this nature. To bonnet a fat policeman is excellent fooling. While he is struggling with his helmet you can ask him comic questions, and by the time he has got his head free you are out of sight. But the game should be played in a district where there is not an average of three constables to every dozen square yards. When two other policemen, who have had their eye on you for the past ten minutes, are watching the proceedings from just round the next corner, you have little or no leisure for due enjoyment of the situation. By the time you have run the whole length of Great Titchfield Street and twice round Oxford Market, you are of opinion that a joke should never be prolonged beyond the point at which there is danger of its becoming wearisome; and that the time has now arrived for home and friends. The "Law," on the other hand, now raised by reinforcements to a strength of six or seven men, is just beginning to enjoy the chase. You picture to yourself, while doing Hanover Square, the scene in Court the next morning. You will be accused of being drunk and disorderly. It will be idle for you to explain to the magistrate (or to your relations afterwards) that you were only trying to live up to a man who did this sort of thing in a book and was admired for it. You will be fined the usual forty shillings; and on the next occasion of your calling at the Mayfields' the girls will be out, and Mrs. Mayfield, an excellent lady, who has always taken a motherly interest in you, will talk seriously to you and urge you to sign the pledge.

Thanks to your youth and constitution you shake off the pursuit at Notting Hill; and, to avoid any chance of unpleasant contretemps on the return journey, walk home to Bloomsbury by way of Camden Town and Islington.

I abandoned sportive tendencies as the result of a vow made by myself to Providence, during the early hours of a certain Sunday morning, while clinging to the waterspout of an unpretentious house situate in a side street off Soho. I put it to Providence as man to man. "Let me only get out of this," I think were the muttered words I used, "and no more 'sport' for me." Providence closed on the offer, and did let me get out of it. True, it was a complicated "get out," involving a broken skylight and three gas globes, two hours in a coal cellar, and a sovereign to a potman for the loan of an ulster; and when at last, secure in my chamber, I took stock of myself—what was left of me,—I could not but reflect that Providence might have done the job neater. Yet I experienced no desire to escape the terms of the covenant; my inclining for the future was towards a life of simplicity.

Accordingly, I cast about for a new character, and found one to suit me. The German professor was becoming popular as a hero about this period. He wore his hair long and was otherwise untidy, but he had "a heart of steel," occasionally of gold. The majority of folks in the book, judging him from his exterior together with his conversation—in broken English, dealing chiefly with his dead mother and his little sister Lisa,—dubbed him uninteresting, but then they did not know about the heart. His chief possession was a lame dog which he had rescued from a brutal mob; and when he was not talking broken English he was nursing this dog.

But his speciality was stopping runaway horses, thereby saving the heroine's life. This, combined with the broken English and the dog, rendered him irresistible.

He seemed a peaceful, amiable sort of creature, and I decided to try him. I could not of course be a German professor, but I could, and did, wear my hair long in spite of much public advice to the contrary, voiced chiefly by small boys. I endeavoured to obtain possession of a lame dog, but failed. A one-eyed dealer in

Seven Dials, to whom, as a last resource, I applied, offered to lame one for me for an extra five shillings, but this suggestion I declined. I came across an uncanny-looking mongrel late one night. He was not lame, but he seemed pretty sick; and, feeling I was not robbing anybody of anything very valuable, I lured him home and nursed him. I fancy I must have over-nursed him. He got so healthy in the end, there was no doing anything with him. He was an ill-conditioned cur, and he was too old to be taught. He became the curse of the neighbourhood. His idea of sport was killing chickens and sneaking rabbits from outside poulterers' shops. For recreation he killed cats and frightened small children by yelping round their legs. There were times when I could have lamed him myself, if only I could have got hold of him. I made nothing by running that dog—nothing whatever. People, instead of admiring me for nursing him back to life, called me a fool, and said that if I didn't drown the brute they would. He spoilt my character utterly—I mean my character at this period. It is difficult to pose as a young man with a heart of gold, when discovered in the middle of the road throwing stones at your own dog. And stones were the only things that would reach and influence him.

I was also hampered by a scarcity in runaway horses. The horse of our suburb was not that type of horse. Once and only once did an opportunity offer itself for practice. It was a good opportunity, inasmuch as he was not running away very greatly. Indeed, I doubt if he knew himself that he was running away. It transpired afterwards that it was a habit of his, after waiting for his driver outside the Rose and Crown for what he considered to be a reasonable period, to trot home on his own account. He passed me going about seven miles an hour, with the reins dragging conveniently beside him. He was the very thing for a beginner, and I prepared myself. At the critical moment, however, a couple of officious policemen pushed me aside and did it themselves.

There was nothing for me to regret, as the matter turned out. I should only have rescued a bald-headed commercial traveller, very drunk, who swore horribly, and pelted the crowd with empty collar-boxes.

From the window of a very high flat I once watched three men, resolved to stop a runaway horse. Each man marched deliberately into the middle of the road and took up his stand. My window was too far away for me to see their faces, but their attitude suggested heroism unto death. The first man, as the horse came charging towards him, faced it with his arms spread out. He never flinched until the horse was within about twenty yards of him. Then, as the animal was evidently determined to continue its wild career, there was nothing left for him to do but to retire again to the kerb, where he stood looking after it with evident sorrow, as though saying to himself—"Oh, well, if you are going to be headstrong I have done with you."

The second man, on the catastrophe being thus left clear for him, without a moment's hesitation, walked up a bye street and disappeared. The third man stood his ground, and, as the horse passed him, yelled at it. I could not hear what he said. I have not the slightest doubt it was excellent advice, but the animal was apparently too excited even to listen. The first and the third man met afterwards, and discussed the matter sympathetically. I judged they were regretting the pig-headedness of runaway horses in general, and hoping that nobody had been hurt.

I forget the other characters I assumed about this period. One, I know, that got me into a good deal of trouble was that of a downright, honest, hearty, outspoken young man who always said what he meant.

I never knew but one man who made a real success of speaking his mind. I have heard him slap the table with his open hand and exclaim—

"You want me to flatter you—to stuff you up with a pack of lies. That's not me, that's not Jim Compton. But if you care for my honest opinion, all I can say is, that child is the most marvellous performer on the piano I've ever heard. I don't say she is a genius, but I have heard Liszt and Metzler and all the crack players, and I prefer HER. That's my opinion. I speak my mind, and I can't help it if you're offended."

"How refreshing," the parents would say, "to come across a man who is not afraid to say what he really thinks. Why are we not all outspoken?"

The last character I attempted I thought would be easy to assume. It was that of a much admired and beloved young man, whose great charm lay in the fact that he was always just—himself. Other people posed and acted. He never made any effort to be anything but his own natural, simple self.

I thought I also would be my own natural, simple self. But then the question arose—What was my own natural, simple self?

That was the preliminary problem I had to solve; I have not solved it to this day. What am I? I am a great gentleman, walking through the world with dauntless heart and head erect, scornful of all meanness, impatient of all littleness. I am a mean-thinking, little-daring man—the type of man that I of the dauntless heart and the erect head despise greatly—crawling to a poor end by devious ways, cringing to the strong, timid of all pain. I—but, dear reader, I will not sadden your sensitive ears with details I could give you, showing how contemptible a creature this wretched I happens to be. Nor would you understand me. You would only be astonished, discovering that such disreputable specimens of humanity contrive to exist in this age. It is best, my dear sir, or madam, you should remain ignorant of these evil persons. Let me not trouble you with knowledge.

I am a philosopher, greeting alike the thunder and the sunshine with frolic welcome. Only now and then, when all things do not fall exactly as I wish them, when foolish, wicked people will persist in doing foolish, wicked acts, affecting my comfort and happiness, I rage and fret a goodish deal.

As Heine said of himself, I am knight, too, of the Holy Grail, valiant for the Truth, reverent of all women, honouring all men, eager to yield life to the service of my great Captain.

And next moment, I find myself in the enemy's lines, fighting under the black banner. (It must be confusing to these opposing Generals, all their soldiers being deserters from both armies.) What are women but men's playthings! Shall there be no more cakes and ale for me because thou art virtuous! What are men but hungry dogs, contending each against each for a limited supply of bones! Do others lest thou be done. What is the Truth but an unexploded lie!

I am a lover of all living things. You, my poor sister, struggling with your heavy burden on your lonely way, I would kiss the tears from your worn cheeks, lighten with my love the darkness around your feet. You, my patient brother, breathing hard as round and round you tramp the trodden path, like some poor half-blind gin-horse, stripes your only encouragement, scanty store of dry chaff in your manger! I would jog beside you, taking the strain a little from your aching shoulders; and we would walk nodding, our heads side by side, and you, remembering, should tell me of the fields where long ago you played, of the gallant races that you ran and won. And you, little pinched brats, with wondering eyes, looking from dirt-encrusted faces, I would take you in my arms and tell you fairy stories. Into the sweet land of make-believe we would wander, leaving the sad old world behind us for a time, and you should be Princes and Princesses, and know Love.

But again, a selfish, greedy man comes often, and sits in my clothes. A man who frets away his life, planning how to get more money—more food, more clothes, more pleasures for himself; a man so busy thinking of the many things he needs he has no time to dwell upon the needs of others. He deems himself the centre of the universe. You would imagine, hearing him grumbling, that the world had been created and got ready against the time when he should come to take his pleasure in it. He would push and trample, heedless, reaching towards these many desires of his; and when, grabbing, he misses, he curses Heaven for its injustice, and men and women for getting in his path. He is not a nice man, in any way. I wish, as I say, he would not come so often and sit in my clothes. He persists that he is I, and that I am only a sentimental fool, spoiling his chances. Sometimes, for a while, I get rid of him, but he always comes back; and then he gets rid of me and I become him. It is very confusing. Sometimes I wonder if I really am myself.

ON THE DISADVANTAGE OF NOT GETTING WHAT ONE WANTS

Long, long ago, when you and I, dear Reader, were young, when the fairies dwelt in the hearts of the roses, when the moonbeams bent each night beneath the weight of angels' feet, there lived a good, wise man. Or rather, I should say, there had lived, for at the time of which I speak the poor old gentleman lay dying. Waiting each moment the dread summons, he fell a-musing on the life that stretched far back behind him. How full it seemed to him at that moment of follies and mistakes, bringing bitter tears not to himself alone but to others also. How much brighter a road might it have been, had he been wiser, had he known!

"Ah, me!" said the good old gentleman, "if only I could live my life again in the light of experience."

Now as he spoke these words he felt the drawing near to him of a Presence, and thinking it was the One whom he expected, raising himself a little from his bed, he feebly cried,

"I am ready."

But a hand forced him gently back, a voice saying, "Not yet; I bring life, not death. Your wish shall be granted. You shall live your life again, and the knowledge of the past shall be with you to guide you. See you use it. I will come again."

Then a sleep fell upon the good man, and when he awoke, he was again a little child, lying in his mother's arms; but, locked within his brain was the knowledge of the life that he had lived already.

So once more he lived and loved and laboured. So a second time he lay an old, worn man with life behind him. And the angel stood again beside his bed; and the voice said,

"Well, are you content now?"

"I am well content," said the old gentleman. "Let Death come."

"And have you understood?" asked the angel.

"I think so," was the answer; "that experience is but as of the memory of the pathways he has trod to a traveller journeying ever onward into an unknown land. I have been wise only to reap the reward of folly. Knowledge has ofttimes kept me from my good. I have avoided my old mistakes only to fall into others that I knew not of. I have reached the old errors by new roads. Where I have escaped sorrow I have lost joy. Where I have grasped happiness I have plucked pain also. Now let me go with Death that I may learn.."

Which was so like the angel of that period, the giving of a gift, bringing to a man only more trouble. Maybe I am overrating my coolness of judgment under somewhat startling circumstances, but I am inclined to think that, had I lived in those days, and had a fairy or an angel come to me, wanting to give me something—my soul's desire, or the sum of my ambition, or any trifle of that kind I should have been short with him.

"You pack up that precious bag of tricks of yours," I should have said to him (it would have been rude, but that is how I should have felt), "and get outside with it. I'm not taking anything in your line to-day. I don't require any supernatural aid to get me into trouble. All the worry I want I can get down here, so it's no good your calling. You take that little joke of yours,—I don't know what it is, but I know enough not to want to know,—and run it off on some other idiot. I'm not priggish. I have no objection to an innocent game of 'catch-questions' in the ordinary way, and when I get a turn myself. But if I've got to pay every time, and the stakes are to be my earthly happiness plus my future existence—why, I don't play. There was the case of Midas; a nice, shabby trick you fellows played off upon him! making pretence you did not understand him, twisting round the poor old fellow's words, just for all the world as though you were a pack of Old Bailey lawyers, trying to trip up a witness; I'm ashamed of the lot of you, and I tell you so—coming down here, fooling poor unsuspecting mortals with your nonsense, as though we had not enough to harry us as it was. Then there was that other case of the poor old peasant couple to whom you promised three wishes, the whole thing ending in a black pudding. And they never got even that. You thought that funny, I suppose. That was your fairy humour! A pity, I say, you have not, all of you, something better to do with your time. As I said before, you take that celestial 'Joe Miller' of yours and work it off on somebody else. I have read my fairy lore, and I have read my mythology, and I don't want any of your blessings. And what's more, I'm not going to have them. When I want blessings I will put up with the usual sort we are accustomed to down here. You know the ones I mean, the disguised brand—the blessings that no human being would think were blessings, if he were not told; the blessings that don't look like blessings, that don't feel like blessings; that, as a matter of fact, are not blessings, practically speaking; the blessings that other people think are blessings for us and that we don't. They've got their drawbacks, but they are better than yours, at any rate, and they are sooner over. I don't want your blessings at any price. If you leave one here I shall simply throw it out after you."

I feel confident I should have answered in that strain, and I feel it would have done good. Somebody ought to have spoken plainly, because with fairies and angels of that sort fooling about, no one was ever safe for a moment. Children could hardly have been allowed outside the door. One never could have told what silly trick some would-be funny fairy might be waiting to play off on them. The poor child would not know, and would think it was getting something worth having. The wonder to me is that some of those angels didn't get tarred and feathered.

I am doubtful whether even Cinderella's luck was quite as satisfying as we are led to believe. After the carpetless kitchen and the black beetles, how beautiful the palace must have seemed—for the first year, perhaps for the first two. And the Prince! how loving, how gallant, how tender—for the first year, perhaps for the first two. And after? You see he was a Prince, brought up in a Court, the atmosphere of which is not conducive to the development of the domestic virtues; and she—was Cinderella. And then the marriage altogether was rather a hurried affair. Oh yes, she is a good, loving little woman; but perhaps our Royal Highness-ship did act too much on the impulse of the moment. It was her dear, dainty feet that danced their way into our heart. How they flashed and twinkled, eased in those fairy slippers. How like a lily among tulips she moved that night amid the over-gorgeous Court dames. She was so sweet, so fresh, so different to all the others whom we knew so well. How happy she looked as she put her trembling little hand in ours. What possibilities might lie behind those drooping lashes. And we were in amorous mood that night, the music in our feet, the flash and glitter in our eyes. And then, to pique us further, she disappeared as suddenly and strangely as she had come. Who was she? Whence came she? What was the mystery surrounding her? Was she only a delicious dream, a haunting phantasy that we should never look upon again, never clasp again within our longing arms? Was our heart to be for ever hungry, haunted by the memory of—No, by heavens, she is real, and a woman. Here is her dear slipper, made surely to be kissed. Of a size too that a man may well wear within the breast of his doublet. Had any woman—nay, fairy, angel, such dear feet! Search the whole kingdom through, but find her, find her. The gods have heard our prayers, and given us this clue. "Suppose she be not all she seemed. Suppose she be not of birth fit to mate with our noble house!" Out upon thee, for an earth-bound, blind curmudgeon of a Lord High Chancellor. How could a woman, whom such slipper fitted, be but of the noblest and the best, as far above us, mere Princelet that we are, as the stars in heaven are brighter than thy dull old eyes! Go, search the kingdom, we tell thee, from east to west, from north to south, and see to it that thou findest her, or it shall go hard with thee. By Venus, be she a swineherd's daughter, she shall be our Queen—an she deign to accept of us, and of our kingdom.

Ah well, of course, it was not a wise piece of business, that goes without saying; but we were young, and Princes are only human. Poor child, she could not help her education, or rather her lack of it. Dear little thing, the wonder is that she has contrived to be no more ignorant than she is, dragged up as she was, neglected and overworked. Nor does life in a kitchen, amid the companionship of peasants and menials, tend to foster the intellect. Who can blame her for being shy and somewhat dull of thought? not we, generous-minded, kind-hearted Prince that we are. And she is very affectionate. The family are trying, certainly; father-in-law not a bad sort, though a little prosy when upon the subject of his domestic troubles, and a little too fond of his glass; mamma-in-law, and those two ugly, ill-mannered sisters, decidedly a nuisance about the palace. Yet what can we do? they are our relations now, and they do not forget to let us know it. Well, well, we had to expect that, and things might have been worse. Anyhow she is not jealous—thank goodness.

So the day comes when poor little Cinderella sits alone of a night in the beautiful palace. The courtiers have gone home in their carriages. The Lord High Chancellor has bowed himself out backwards. The Gold-Stick-in-Waiting and the Grooms of the Chamber have gone to their beds. The Maids of Honour have said "Good-night," and drifted out of the door, laughing and whispering among themselves. The clock strikes twelve—one—two, and still no footstep creaks upon the stair. Once it followed swiftly upon the "good-night" of the maids, who did not laugh or whisper then.

At last the door opens, and the Prince enters, none too pleased at finding Cinderella still awake. "So sorry I'm late, my love—detained on affairs of state. Foreign policy very complicated, dear. Have only just this moment left the Council Chamber."

And little Cinderella, while the Prince sleeps, lies sobbing out her poor sad heart into the beautiful royal pillow, embroidered with the royal arms and edged with the royal monogram in lace. "Why did he ever marry me? I should have been happier in the old kitchen. The black beetles did frighten me a little, but there was always the dear old cat; and sometimes, when mother and the girls were out, papa would call softly down the kitchen stairs for me to come up, and we would have such a merry evening together, and sup off sausages: dear old dad, I hardly ever see him now. And then, when my work was done, how pleasant it was to sit in front of the fire, and dream of the wonderful things that would come to me some day. I was always going to be a Princess, even in my dreams, and live in a palace, but it was so different to this. Oh, how I hate it, this beastly palace where everybody sneers at me—I know they do, though they bow and scrape, and pretend to be so polite. And I'm not clever and smart as they are. I hate them. I hate these bold-faced women who are always here. That is the worst of a palace, everybody can come in. Oh, I hate everybody and everything. Oh, god-mamma, god-mamma, come and take me away. Take me back to my old kitchen. Give me back my old poor frock. Let me dance again with the fire-tongs for a partner, and be happy, dreaming."

Poor little Cinderella, perhaps it would have been better had god-mamma been less ambitious for you, dear; had you married some good, honest yeoman, who would never have known that you were not brilliant, who would have loved you because you were just amiable and pretty; had your kingdom been only a farmhouse, where your knowledge of domestic economy, gained so hardly, would have been useful; where you would have shone instead of being overshadowed; where Papa would have dropped in of an evening to smoke his pipe and escape from his domestic wrangles; where you would have been REAL Queen.

But then you know, dear, you would not have been content. Ah yes, with your present experience—now you know that Queens as well as little drudges have their troubles; but WITHOUT that experience? You would have looked in the glass when you were alone; you would have looked at your shapely hands and feet, and the shadows would have crossed your pretty face. "Yes," you would have said to yourself—"John is a dear, kind fellow, and I love him very much, and all that, but—" and the old dreams, dreamt in the old low-ceilinged kitchen before the dying fire, would have come back to you, and you would have been discontented then as now, only in a different way. Oh yes, you would, Cinderella, though you gravely shake your gold-crowned head. And let me tell you why. It is because you are a woman, and the fate of all us, men and women alike, is to be for ever wanting what we have not, and to be finding, when we have it, that it is not what we wanted. That is the law of life, dear. Do you think as you lie upon the floor with your head upon your arms, that you are the only woman whose tears are soaking into the hearthrug at that moment? My dear Princess, if you could creep unseen about your City, peeping at will through the curtain-shielded windows, you would come to think that all the world was little else than a big nursery full of crying children with none to comfort them. The doll is broken: no longer it sweetly squeaks in answer to our pressure, "I love you, kiss me." The drum lies silent with the drumstick inside; no longer do we make a brave noise in the nursery. The box of tea-things we have clumsily put our foot upon; there will be no more merry parties around the three-legged stool. The tin trumpet will not play the note we want to sound; the wooden bricks keep falling down; the toy cannon has exploded and burnt our fingers. Never mind, little man, little woman, we will try and mend things tomorrow.

And after all, Cinderella dear, you do live in a fine palace, and you have jewels and grand dresses and—No, no, do not be indignant with ME. Did not you dream of these things AS WELL AS of love? Come now, be honest. It was always a prince, was it not, or, at the least, an exceedingly well-to-do party, that handsome young gentleman who bowed to you so gallantly from the red embers? He was never a virtuous young commercial traveller, or cultured clerk, earning a salary of three pounds a week, was he, Cinderella? Yet there are many charming commercial travellers, many delightful clerks with limited incomes, quite sufficient, however, to a sensible man and woman desiring but each other's love. Why was it always a prince, Cinderella? Had the palace and the liveried servants, and the carriages and horses, and the jewels and the dresses, NOTHING to do with the dream?

No, Cinderella, you were human, that is all. The artist, shivering in his conventional attic, dreaming of Fame!-do you think he is not hoping she will come to his loving arms in the form Jove came to Danae? Do you think he is not reckoning also upon the good dinners and the big cigars, the fur coat and the diamond studs, that her visits will enable him to purchase?

There is a certain picture very popular just now. You may see it, Cinderella, in many of the shop-windows of the town. It is called "The Dream of Love," and it represents a beautiful young girl, sleeping in a very beautiful but somewhat disarranged bed. Indeed, one hopes, for the sleeper's sake, that the night is warm, and that the room is fairly free from draughts. A ladder of light streams down from the sky into the room, and upon this ladder crowd and jostle one another a small army of plump Cupids, each one laden with some pledge of love. Two of the Imps are emptying a sack of jewels upon the floor. Four others are bearing, well displayed, a magnificent dress (a "confection," I believe, is the proper term) cut somewhat low, but making up in train what is lacking elsewhere. Others bear bonnet boxes from which peep stylish toques and bewitching hoods. Some, representing evidently wholesale houses, stagger under silks and satins in the piece. Cupids are there from the shoemakers with the daintiest of bottines. Stockings, garters, and even less mentionable articles, are not forgotten. Caskets, mirrors, twelve-buttoned gloves, scent-bottles and handkerchiefs, hair-pins, and the gayest of parasols, has the God of Love piled into the arms of his messengers. Really a most practical, up-to-date God of Love, moving with the times! One feels that the modern Temple of Love must be a sort of Swan and Edgar's; the god himself a kind of celestial shop-walker; while his mother, Venus, no doubt superintends the costume department. Quite an Olympian Whiteley, this latter-day Eros; he has forgotten nothing, for, at the back of the picture, I notice one Cupid carrying a rather fat heart at the end of a string.

You, Cinderella, could give good counsel to that sleeping child. You would say to her—"Awake from such dreams. The contents of a pawnbroker's store-room will not bring you happiness. Dream of love if you will; that is a wise dream, even if it remain ever a dream. But these coloured beads, these Manchester goods! are you then—you, heiress of all the ages—still at heart only as some poor savage maiden but little removed above the monkeys that share the primeval forest with her? Will you sell your gold to the first trader that brings you THIS barter? These things, child, will only dazzle your eyes for a few days. Do you think the Burlington Arcade is the gate of Heaven?"

Ah, yes, I too could talk like that—I, writer of books, to the young lad, sick of his office stool, dreaming of a literary career leading to fame and fortune. "And do you think, lad, that by that road you will reach Happiness sooner than by another? Do you think interviews with yourself in penny weeklies will bring you any satisfaction after the first halfdozen? Do you think the gushing female who has read all your books, and who wonders what it must feel like to be so clever, will be welcome to you the tenth time you meet her? Do you think press cuttings will always consist of wondering admiration of your genius, of paragraphs about your charming personal appearance under the heading, 'Our Celebrities'? Have you thought of the Uncomplimentary criticisms, of the spiteful paragraphs, of the everlasting fear of slipping a few inches down the greasy pole called 'popular taste,' to which you are condemned to cling for life, as some lesser criminal to his weary tread-mill, struggling with no hope but not to fall! Make a home, lad, for the woman who loves you; gather one or two friends about you; work, think, and play, that will bring you happiness. Shun this roaring gingerbread fair that calls itself, forsooth, the 'World of art and letters.' Let its clowns and its contortionists fight among themselves for the plaudits and the halfpence of the mob. Let it be with its shouting and its surging, its blare and its cheap flare. Come away, the summer's night is just the other side of the hedge, with its silence and its stars."

You and I, Cinderella, are experienced people, and can therefore offer good advice, but do you think we should be listened to?

"Ah, no, my Prince is not as yours. Mine will love me always, and I am peculiarly fitted for the life of a palace. I have the instinct and the ability for it. I am sure I was made for a princess. Thank you, Cinderella, for your well-meant counsel, but there is much difference between you and me."

That is the answer you would receive, Cinderella; and my young friend would say to me, "Yes, I can understand YOUR finding disappointment in the literary career; but then, you see, our cases are not quite similar. *I* am not likely to find much trouble in keeping my position. *I* shall not fear reading what the critics say of ME. No doubt there are disadvantages, when you are among the ruck, but there is always plenty of room at the top. So thank you, and goodbye."

Besides, Cinderella dear, we should not quite mean it—this excellent advice. We have grown accustomed to these gew-gaws, and we should miss them in spite of our knowledge of their trashiness: you, your palace and your little gold crown; I, my mountebank's cap, and the answering laugh that goes up from the crowd when I shake my bells. We want everything. All the happiness that earth and heaven are capable of bestowing. Creature comforts, and heart and soul comforts also; and, proud-spirited beings that we are, we will not be put off with a part. Give us only everything, and we will be content. And, after all, Cinderella, you have had your day. Some little dogs never get theirs. You must not be greedy. You have KNOWN happiness. The palace was Paradise for those few months, and the Prince's arms were about you, Cinderella, the Prince's kisses on your lips; the gods themselves cannot take THAT from you.

The cake cannot last for ever if we will eat of it so greedily. There must come the day when we have picked hungrily the last crumb—when we sit staring at the empty board, nothing left of the feast, Cinderella, but the pain that comes of feasting.

It is a naive confession, poor Human Nature has made to itself, in choosing, as it has, this story of Cinderella for its leading moral:—Be good, little girl. Be meek under your many trials. Be gentle and kind, in spite of your hard lot, and one day—you shall marry a prince and ride in your own carriage. Be brave and true, little boy. Work hard and wait with patience, and in the end, with God's blessing, you shall earn riches enough to come back to London town and marry your master's daughter.

You and I, gentle Reader, could teach these young folks a truer lesson, an we would. We know, alas! that the road of all the virtues does not lead to wealth, rather the contrary; else how explain our limited incomes? But would it be well, think you, to tell them bluntly the truth—that honesty is the most expensive luxury a man can indulge in; that virtue, if persisted in, leads, generally speaking, to a six-roomed house in an outlying suburb? Maybe the world is wise: the fiction has its uses.

ON THE DISADVANTAGE OF NOT GETTING WHAT ONE WANTS

I am acquainted with a fairly intelligent young lady. She can read and write, knows her tables up to six times, and can argue. I regard her as representative of average Humanity in its attitude towards Fate; and this is a dialogue I lately overheard between her and an older lady who is good enough to occasionally impart to her the wisdom of the world—

"I've been good this morning, haven't I?"

"Yes—oh yes, fairly good, for you."

"You think Papa WILL take me to the circus to-night?"

"Yes, if you keep good. If you don't get naughty this afternoon."

A pause.

"I was good on Monday, you may remember, nurse."

"Tolerably good."

"VERY good, you said, nurse."

"Well, yes, you weren't bad."

"And I was to have gone to the pantomime, and I didn't."

"Well, that was because your aunt came up suddenly, and your Papa couldn't get another seat. Poor auntie wouldn't have gone at all if she hadn't gone then."

"Oh, wouldn't she?"

"No."

Another pause.

"Do you think she'll come up suddenly to-day?"

"Oh no, I don't think so."

"No, I hope she doesn't. I want to go to the circus to-night. Because, you see, nurse, if I don't it will discourage me."

So, perhaps the world is wise in promising us the circus. We believe her at first. But after a while, I fear, we grow discouraged.

ON THE EXCEPTIONAL MERIT ATTACHING TO THE THINGS WE MEANT TO DO

I can remember—but then I can remember a long time ago. You, gentle Reader, just entering upon the prime of life, that age by thoughtless youth called middle, I cannot, of course, expect to follow me—when there was in great demand a certain periodical ycleped The Amateur. Its aim was noble. It sought to teach the beautiful lesson of independence, to inculcate the fine doctrine of self-help. One chapter explained to a man how he might make flower-pots out of Australian meat cans; another how he might turn butter-tubs into music-stools; a third how he might utilize old bonnet boxes for Venetian blinds: that was the principle of the whole scheme, you made everything from something not intended for it, and as ill-suited to the purpose as possible.

Two pages, I distinctly recollect, were devoted to the encouragement of the manufacture of umbrella stands out of old gaspiping. Anything less adapted to the receipt of hats and umbrellas than gas-piping I cannot myself conceive: had there been, I feel sure the author would have thought of it, and would have recommended it.

Picture-frames you fashioned out of gingerbeer corks. You saved your gingerbeer corks, you found a picture—and the thing was complete. How much gingerbeer it would be necessary to drink, preparatory to the making of each frame; and the effect of it upon the frame-maker's physical, mental and moral well-being, did not concern The Amateur. I calculate that for a fair-sized picture sixteen dozen bottles might suffice. Whether, after sixteen dozen of ginger-beer, a man would take any interest in framing a picture—whether he would retain any pride in the picture itself, is doubtful. But this, of course, was not the point.

One young gentleman of my acquaintance—the son of the gardener of my sister, as friend Ollendorff would have described him—did succeed in getting through sufficient ginger-beer to frame his grandfather, but the result was not encouraging. Indeed, the gardener's wife herself was but ill satisfied.

"What's all them corks round father?" was her first question.

"Can't you see," was the somewhat indignant reply, "that's the frame."

"Oh! but why corks?"

"Well, the book said corks."

Still the old lady remained unimpressed.

"Somehow it don't look like father now," she sighed.

Her eldest born grew irritable: none of us appreciate criticism!

"What does it look like, then?" he growled.

"Well, I dunno. Seems to me to look like nothing but corks."

The old lady's view was correct. Certain schools of art possibly lend themselves to this method of framing. I myself have seen a funeral card improved by it; but, generally speaking, the consequence was a predominance of frame at the expense of the thing framed. The more honest and tasteful of the framemakers would admit as much themselves.

"Yes, it is ugly when you look at it," said one to me, as we stood surveying it from the centre of the room. "But what one feels about it is that one has done it oneself."

Which reflection, I have noticed, reconciles us to many other things beside cork frames.

Another young gentleman friend of mine—for I am bound to admit it was youth that profited most by the advice and counsel of The Amateur: I suppose as one grows older one grows less daring, less industrious—made a rocking-chair, according to the instructions of this book, out of a couple of beer barrels. From every practical point of view it was a bad rocking-chair. It rocked too much, and it rocked in too many directions at one and the same time. I take it, a man sitting on a rocking-chair does not want to be continually rocking. There comes a time when he says to himself—"Now I have rocked sufficiently for the present; now I will sit still for a while, lest a worse thing befall me." But this was one of those headstrong rocking-chairs that are a danger to humanity, and a nuisance to themselves. Its notion was that it was made to rock, and that when it was not rocking, it was wasting its time. Once started nothing could stop it—nothing ever did stop it, until it found itself topsy turvy on its own occupant. That was the only thing that ever sobered it.

I had called, and had been shown into the empty drawing-room. The rocking-chair nodded invitingly at me. I never guessed it was an amateur rocking-chair. I was young in those days, with faith in human nature, and I imagined that, whatever else a man might attempt without knowledge or experience, no one would be fool enough to experiment upon a rocking-chair.

I threw myself into it lightly and carelessly. I immediately noticed the ceiling. I made an instinctive movement forward. The window and a momentary glimpse of the wooded hills beyond shot upwards and disappeared. The carpet flashed across my eyes, and I caught sight of my own boots vanishing beneath me at the rate of about two hundred miles an hour. I made a convulsive effort to recover them. I suppose I over-did it. I saw the whole of the room at once, the four walls, the ceiling, and the floor at the same moment. It was a sort of vision. I saw the cottage piano upside down, and I again saw my own boots flash past me, this time over my head, soles uppermost. Never before had I been in a position where my own boots had seemed so all-pervading. The next moment I lost my boots, and stopped the carpet with my head just as it was rushing past me. At the same instant something hit me violently in the small of the back. Reason, when recovered, suggested that my assailant must be the rocking-chair.

Investigation proved the surmise correct. Fortunately I was still alone, and in consequence was able, a few minutes later, to meet my hostess with calm and dignity. I said nothing about the rocking-chair. As a matter of fact, I was hoping to have the pleasure, before I went, of seeing some other guest arrive and sample it: I had purposely replaced it in the most prominent and convenient position. But though I felt capable of schooling myself to silence, I found myself unable to agree with my hostess when she called for my admiration of the thing. My recent experiences had too deeply embittered me.

"Willie made it himself," explained the fond mother. "Don't you think it was very clever of him?"

"Oh yes, it was clever," I replied, "I am willing to admit that."

"He made it out of some old beer barrels," she continued; she seemed proud of it.

My resentment, though I tried to keep it under control, was mounting higher.

"Oh! did he?" I said; "I should have thought he might have found something better to do with them."

"What?" she asked.

"Oh! well, many things," I retorted. "He might have filled them again with beer."

My hostess looked at me astonished. I felt some reason for my tone was expected.

"You see," I explained, "it is not a well-made chair. These rockers are too short, and they are too curved, and one of them, if you notice, is higher than the other and of a smaller radius; the back is at too obtuse an angle. When it is occupied the centre of gravity becomes—"

My hostess interrupted me.

"You have been sitting on it," she said.

"Not for long," I assured her.

Her tone changed. She became apologetic.

"I am so sorry," she said. "It looks all right."

"It does," I agreed; "that is where the dear lad's cleverness displays itself. Its appearance disarms suspicion. With judgment that chair might be made to serve a really useful purpose. There are mutual acquaintances of ours—I mention no names, you will know them—pompous, self-satisfied, superior persons who would be improved by that chair. If I were Willie I should disguise the mechanism with some artistic drapery, bait the thing with a couple of exceptionally inviting cushions, and employ it to inculcate modesty and diffidence. I defy any human being to get out of that chair, feeling as important as when he got into it. What the dear boy has done has been to construct an automatic exponent of the transitory nature of human greatness. As a moral agency that chair should prove a blessing in disguise."

My hostess smiled feebly; more, I fear, from politeness than genuine enjoyment.

"I think you are too severe," she said. "When you remember that the boy has never tried his hand at anything of the kind before, that he has no knowledge and no experience, it really is not so bad."

Considering the matter from that point of view I was bound to concur. I did not like to suggest to her that before entering upon a difficult task it would be better for young men to ACQUIRE knowledge and experience: that is so unpopular a theory.

But the thing that The Amateur put in the front and foremost of its propaganda was the manufacture of household furniture out of egg-boxes. Why egg-boxes I have never been able to understand, but egg-boxes, according to the prescription of The Amateur, formed the foundation of household existence. With a sufficient supply of egg-boxes, and what The Amateur termed a "natural deftness," no young couple need hesitate to face the furnishing problem. Three egg-boxes made a writing-table; on another egg-box you sat to write; your books were ranged in egg-boxes around you—and there was your study, complete.

For the dining-room two egg-boxes made an overmantel; four egg-boxes and a piece of looking-glass a sideboard; while six egg-boxes, with some wadding and a yard or so of cretonne, constituted a so-called "cosy corner." About the "corner" there could be no possible doubt. You sat on a corner, you leant against a corner; whichever way you moved you struck a fresh corner. The "cosiness," however, I deny. Egg-boxes I admit can be made useful; I am even prepared to imagine them ornamental; but "cosy," no. I have sampled egg-boxes in many shapes. I speak of years ago, when the world and we were younger, when our fortune was the Future; secure in which, we hesitated not to set up house upon incomes folks with lesser expectations might have deemed insufficient. Under such circumstances, the sole alternative to the egg-box, or similar school of furniture, would have been the strictly classical, consisting of a doorway joined to architectural proportions.

I have from Saturday to Monday, as honoured guest, hung my clothes in egg-boxes.

I have sat on an egg-box at an egg-box to take my dish of tea. I have made love on egg-boxes.—Aye, and to feel again the blood running through my veins as then it ran, I would be content to sit only on egg-boxes till the time should come when I could be buried in an egg-box, with an egg-box reared above me as tombstone.—I have spent many an evening on an egg-box; I have gone to bed in egg-boxes. They have their points—I am intending no pun—but to claim for them cosiness would be but to deceive.

How quaint they were, those home-made rooms! They rise out of the shadows and shape themselves again before my eyes. I see the knobbly sofa; the easy-chairs that might have been designed by the Grand Inquisitor himself; the dented settle that was a bed by night; the few blue plates, purchased in the slums off Wardour Street; the enamelled stool to which one always stuck; the mirror framed in silk; the two Japanese fans crossed beneath each cheap engraving; the piano cloth embroidered in peacock's feathers by Annie's sister; the tea-cloth worked by Cousin Jenny. We dreamt, sitting on those egg-boxes—for we were young ladies and gentlemen with artistic taste—of the days when we would eat in Chippendale dining-rooms; sip our coffee in Louis Quatorze drawing-rooms; and be happy. Well, we have got on, some of us, since then, as Mr. Bumpus used to say; and I notice, when on visits, that some of us have contrived so that we do sit on Chippendale chairs, at Sheraton dining-tables, and are warmed from Adam's fireplaces; but, ah me, where are the dreams, the hopes, the enthusiasms that clung like the scent of a March morning about those gim-crack second floors? In the dustbin, I fear, with the cretonne-covered egg-boxes and the penny fans. Fate is so terribly even-handed. As she gives she ever takes away. She flung us a few shillings and hope, where now she doles us out pounds and fears. Why did not we know how happy we were, sitting crowned with sweet conceit upon our egg-box thrones?

Yes, Dick, you have climbed well. You edit a great newspaper. You spread abroad the message—well, the message that Sir Joseph Goldbug, your proprietor, instructs you to spread abroad. You teach mankind the lessons that Sir Joseph Goldbug wishes them to learn. They say he is to have a peerage next year. I am sure he has earned it; and perhaps there may be a knighthood for you, Dick.

Tom, you are getting on now. You have abandoned those unsaleable allegories. What rich art patron cares to be told continually by his own walls that Midas had ass's ears; that Lazarus sits ever at the gate? You paint portraits now, and everybody tells me you are the coming man. That "Impression" of old Lady Jezebel was really wonderful. The woman looks quite handsome, and yet it is her ladyship. Your touch is truly marvellous.

But into your success, Tom—Dick, old friend, do not there creep moments when you would that we could fish up those old egg-boxes from the past, refurnish with them the dingy rooms in Camden Town, and find there our youth, our loves, and our beliefs?

An incident brought back to my mind, the other day, the thought of all these things. I called for the first time upon a man, an actor, who had asked me to come and see him in the little home where he lives with his old father. To my astonishment—for the craze, I believe, has long since died out—I found the house half furnished out of packing cases, butter tubs, and egg-boxes. My friend earns his twenty pounds a week, but it was the old father's hobby, so he explained to me, the making of these monstrosities; and of them he was as proud as though they were specimen furniture out of the South Kensington Museum.

He took me into the dining-room to show me the latest outrage—a new bookcase. A greater disfigurement to the room, which was otherwise prettily furnished, could hardly be imagined. There was no need for him to assure me, as he did, that it had been made out of nothing but egg-boxes. One could see at a glance that it was made out of egg-boxes, and badly constructed egg-boxes at that—egg-boxes that were a disgrace to the firm that had turned them out; egg-boxes not worthy the storage of "shop 'uns" at eighteen the shilling.

We went upstairs to my friend's bedroom. He opened the door as a man might open the door of a museum of gems.

"The old boy," he said, as he stood with his hand upon the door-knob, "made everything you see here, everything," and we entered. He drew my attention to the wardrobe. "Now I will hold it up," he said, "while you pull the door open; I think the floor must be a bit uneven, it wobbles if you are not careful." It wobbled notwithstanding, but by coaxing and humouring we succeeded without mishap. I was surprised to notice a very small supply of clothes within, although my friend is a dressy man.

"You see," he explained, "I dare not use it more than I can help. I am a clumsy chap, and as likely as not, if I happened to be in a hurry, I'd have the whole thing over:" which seemed probable.

I asked him how he contrived. "I dress in the bath-room as a rule," he replied; "I keep most of my things there. Of course the old boy doesn't know."

He showed me a chest of drawers. One drawer stood half open.

"I'm bound to leave that drawer open," he said; "I keep the things I use in that. They don't shut quite easily, these drawers; or rather, they shut all right, but then they won't open. It is the weather, I think. They will open and shut all right in the summer, I dare say." He is of a hopeful disposition.

But the pride of the room was the washstand.

"What do you think of this?" cried he enthusiastically, "real marble top—"

He did not expatiate further. In his excitement he had laid his hand upon the thing, with the natural result that it collapsed. More by accident than design I caught the jug in my arms. I also caught the water it contained. The basin rolled on its edge and little damage was done, except to me and the soap-box.

I could not pump up much admiration for this washstand; I was feeling too wet.

"What do you do when you want to wash?" I asked, as together we reset the trap.

There fell upon him the manner of a conspirator revealing secrets. He glanced guiltily round the room; then, creeping on tip-toe, he opened a cupboard behind the bed. Within was a tin basin and a small can.

"Don't tell the old boy," he said. "I keep these things here, and wash on the floor."

That was the best thing I myself ever got out of egg-boxes—that picture of a deceitful son stealthily washing himself upon the floor behind the bed, trembling at every footstep lest it might be the "old boy" coming to the door.

One wonders whether the Ten Commandments are so all-sufficient as we good folk deem them—whether the eleventh is not worth the whole pack of them: "that ye love one another" with just a common-place, human, practical love. Could not the other ten be comfortably stowed away into a corner of that! One is inclined, in one's anarchic moments, to agree with Louis Stevenson, that to be amiable and cheerful is a good religion for a work-a-day world. We are so busy NOT killing, NOT stealing, NOT coveting our neighbour's wife, we have not time to be even just to one another for the little while we are together here. Need we be so cock-sure that our present list of virtues and vices is the only possibly correct and complete one? Is the kind, unselfish man necessarily a villain because he does not always succeed in suppressing his natural instincts? Is the narrow-hearted, sour-souled man, incapable of a generous thought or act, necessarily a saint because he has none? Have we not—we unco guid—arrived at a wrong method of estimating our frailer brothers and sisters? We judge them, as critics judge books, not by the good that is in them, but by their faults. Poor King David! What would the local Vigilance Society have had to say to him?

Noah, according to our plan, would be denounced from every teetotal platform in the country, and Ham would head the Local Vestry poll as a reward for having exposed him. And St. Peter! weak, frail St. Peter, how lucky for him that his fellow-disciples and their Master were not as strict in their notions of virtue as are we to-day.

Have we not forgotten the meaning of the word "virtue"? Once it stood for the good that was in a man, irrespective of the evil that might lie there also, as tares among the wheat. We have abolished virtue, and for it substituted virtues. Not the hero—he was too full of faults—but the blameless valet; not the man who does any good, but the man who has not been found out in any evil, is our modern ideal. The most virtuous thing in nature, according to this new theory, should be the oyster. He is always at home, and always sober. He is not noisy. He gives no trouble to the police. I cannot think of a single one of the Ten Commandments that he ever breaks. He never enjoys himself, and he never, so long as he lives, gives a moment's pleasure to any other living thing.

I can imagine the oyster lecturing a lion on the subject of morality.

"You never hear me," the oyster might say, "howling round camps and villages, making night hideous, frightening quiet folk out of their lives. Why don't you go to bed early, as I do? I never prowl round the oyster-bed, fighting other gentlemen oysters, making love to lady oysters already married. I never kill antelopes or missionaries. Why can't you live as I do on salt water and germs, or whatever it is that I do live on? Why don't you try to be more like me?"

An oyster has no evil passions, therefore we say he is a virtuous fish. We never ask ourselves—"Has he any good passions?" A lion's behaviour is often such as no just man could condone. Has he not his good points also?

Will the fat, sleek, "virtuous" man be as Welcome at the gate of heaven as he supposes?

"Well," St. Peter may say to him, opening the door a little way and looking him up and down, "what is it now?"

"It's me," the virtuous man will reply, with an oily, self-satisfied smile; "I should say, I—I've come."

"Yes, I see you have come; but what is your claim to admittance? What have you done with your three score years and ten?"

"Done!" the virtuous man will answer, "I have done nothing, I assure you."
"Nothing!"

"Nothing; that is my strong point; that is why I am here. I have never done any wrong."

"And what good have you done?"

"What good!"

"Aye, what good? Do not you even know the meaning of the word? What human creature is the better for your having eaten and drunk and slept these years? You have done no harm—no harm to yourself. Perhaps, if you had you might have done some good with it; the two are generally to be found together down below, I remember. What good have you done that you should enter here? This is no mummy chamber; this is the place of men and women who have lived, who have wrought good—and evil also, alas!—for the sinners who fight for the right, not the righteous who run with their souls from the fight."

It was not, however, to speak of these things that I remembered The Amateur and its lessons. My intention was but to lead up to the story of a certain small boy, who in the doing of tasks not required of him was exceedingly clever. I wish to tell you his story, because, as do most true tales, it possesses a moral, and stories without a moral I deem to be but foolish literature, resembling roads that lead to nowhere, such as sick folk tramp for exercise.

I have known this little boy to take an expensive eight-day clock to pieces, and make of it a toy steamboat. True, it was not, when made, very much of a steamboat; but taking into consideration all the difficulties—the inadaptability of eight-day clock machinery to steamboat requirements, the necessity of getting the work accomplished quickly, before conservatively-minded people with no enthusiasm for science could interfere—a good enough steamboat. With merely an ironing-board and a few dozen meat-skewers, he would—provided the ironing-board was not missed in time—turn out quite a practicable rabbit-hutch. He could make a gun out of an umbrella and a gas-bracket, which, if not so accurate as a Martini-Henry, was, at all events, more deadly. With half the garden-hose, a copper scalding-pan out of the dairy, and a few Dresden china ornaments off the drawing-room mantelpiece, he would build a fountain for the garden. He could make bookshelves out of kitchen tables, and crossbows out of crinolines. He could dam you a stream so that all the water would flow over the croquet lawn. He knew how to make red paint and oxygen gas, together with many other suchlike commodities handy to have about a house. Among other things he learned how to make fireworks, and after a few explosions of an unimportant character, came to make them very well indeed. The boy who can play a good game of cricket is liked. The boy who can fight well is respected. The boy who can cheek a master is loved. But the boy who can make fireworks is revered above all others as a boy belonging to a superior order of beings. The fifth of November was at hand, and with the consent of an indulgent mother, he determined to give to the world a proof of his powers. A large party of friends, relatives, and school-mates was invited, and for a fortnight beforehand the scullery was converted into a manufactory for fireworks. The female servants went about in hourly terror of their lives, and the villa, did we judge exclusively by smell, one might have imagined had been taken over by Satan, his main premises being inconveniently crowded, as an annex. By the evening of the fourth all was in readiness, and samples were tested to make sure that no contretemps should occur the following night. All was found to be perfect.

The rockets rushed heavenward and descended in stars, the Roman candles tossed their fiery balls into the darkness, the Catherine wheels sparkled and whirled, the crackers cracked, and the squibs banged. That night he went to bed a proud and happy boy, and dreamed of fame. He stood surrounded by blazing fireworks, and the vast crowd cheered him. His relations, most of whom, he knew, regarded him as the coming idiot of the family, were there to witness his triumph; so too was Dickey Bowles, who laughed at him because he could not throw straight. The girl at the bun-shop, she also was there, and saw that he was clever.

The night of the festival arrived, and with it the guests. They sat, wrapped up in shawls and cloaks, outside the hall door—uncles, cousins, aunts, little boys and big boys, little girls and big girls, with, as the theatre posters say, villagers and retainers, some forty of them in all, and waited.

But the fireworks did not go off. Why they did not go off I cannot explain; nobody ever COULD explain. The laws of nature seemed to be suspended for that night only. The rockets fell down and died where they stood. No human agency seemed able to ignite the squibs. The crackers gave one bang and collapsed. The Roman candles might have been English rushlights. The Catherine wheels became mere revolving glow-worms. The fiery serpents could not collect among them the spirit of a tortoise. The set piece, a ship at sea, showed one mast and the captain, and then went out. One or two items did their duty, but this only served to render the foolishness of the whole more striking. The little girls giggled, the little boys chaffed, the aunts and cousins said it was beautiful, the uncles inquired if it was all over, and talked about supper and trains, the "villagers and retainers" dispersed laughing, the indulgent mother said "never mind," and explained how well everything had gone off yesterday; the clever little boy crept upstairs to his room, and blubbered his heart out in the dark.

Hours later, when the crowd had forgotten him, he stole out again into the garden. He sat down amid the ruins of his hope, and wondered what could have caused the fiasco. Still puzzled, he drew from his pocket a box of matches, and, lighting one, he held it to the seared end of a rocket he had tried in vain to light four hours ago. It smouldered for an instant, then shot with a swish into the air and broke into a hundred points of fire. He tried another and another with the same result. He made a fresh attempt to fire the set piece. Point by point the whole picture—minus the captain and one mast—came out of the night, and stood revealed in all the majesty of flame. Its sparks fell upon the piled-up heap of candles, wheels, and rockets that a little while before had obstinately refused to burn, and that, one after another, had been thrown aside as useless. Now with the night frost upon them, they leaped to light in one grand volcanic eruption. And in front of the gorgeous spectacle he stood with only one consolation—his mother's hand in his.

The whole thing was a mystery to him at the time, but, as he learned to know life better, he came to understand that it was only one example of a solid but inexplicable fact, ruling all human affairs—YOUR FIREWORKS WON'T GO OFF WHILE THE CROWD IS AROUND.

Our brilliant repartees do not occur to us till the door is closed upon us and we are alone in the street, or, as the French would say, are coming down the stairs. Our after-dinner oratory, that sounded so telling as we delivered it before the looking-glass, falls strangely flat amidst the clinking of the glasses. The passionate torrent of words we meant to pour into her ear becomes a halting rigmarole, at which—small blame to her—she only laughs.

I would, gentle Reader, you could hear the stories that I meant to tell you. You judge me, of course, by the stories of mine that you have read—by this sort of thing, perhaps; but that is not just to me. The stories I have not told you, that I am going to tell you one day, I would that you judge me by those.

They are so beautiful; you will say so; over them, you will laugh and cry with me.

They come into my brain unbidden, they clamour to be written, yet when I take my pen in hand they are gone. It is as though they were shy of publicity, as though they would say to me—"You alone, you shall read us, but you must not write us; we are too real, too true. We are like the thoughts you cannot speak. Perhaps a little later, when you know more of life, then you shall tell us."

Next to these in merit I would place, were I writing a critical essay on myself, the stories I have begun to write and that remain unfinished, why I cannot explain to myself. They are good stories, most of them; better far than the stories I have accomplished. Another time, perhaps, if you care to listen, I will tell you the beginning of one or two and you shall judge. Strangely enough, for I have always regarded myself as a practical, commonsensed man, so many of these still-born children of my mind I find, on looking through the cupboard where their thin bodies lie, are ghost stories. I suppose the hope of ghosts is with us all. The world grows somewhat interesting to us heirs of all the ages. Year by year, Science with broom and duster tears down the moth-worn tapestry, forces the doors of the locked chambers, lets light into the secret stairways, cleans out the dungeons, explores the hidden passages—finding everywhere only dust. This echoing old castle, the world, so full of mystery in the days when we were children, is losing somewhat its charm for us as we grow older. The king sleeps no longer in the hollow of the hills. We have tunnelled through his mountain chamber. We have shivered his beard with our pick. We have driven the gods from Olympus. No wanderer through the moonlit groves now fears or hopes the sweet, death-giving gleam of Aphrodite's face. Thor's hammer echoes not among the peaks—'tis but the thunder of the excursion train. We have swept the woods of the fairies. We have filtered the sea of its nymphs. Even the ghosts are leaving us, chased by the Psychical Research Society.

Perhaps of all, they are the least, however, to be regretted. They were dull old fellows, clanking their rusty chains and groaning and sighing. Let them go.

And yet how interesting they might be, if only they would. The old gentleman in the coat of mail, who lived in King John's reign, who was murdered, so they say, on the outskirts of the very wood I can see from my window as I write—stabbed in the back, poor gentleman, as he was riding home, his body flung into the moat that to this day is called Tor's tomb. Dry enough it is now, and the primroses love its steep banks; but a gloomy enough place in those days, no doubt, with its twenty feet of stagnant water. Why does he haunt the forest paths at night, as they tell me he does, frightening the children out of their wits, blanching the faces and stilling the laughter of the peasant lads and lasses, slouching home from the village dance? Instead, why does he not come up here and talk to me? He should have my easy-chair and welcome, would he only be cheerful and companionable.

What brave tales could he not tell me. He fought in the first Crusade, heard the clarion voice of Peter, met the great Godfrey face to face, stood, hand on sword-hilt, at Runny-mede, perhaps. Better than a whole library of historical novels would an evening's chat be with such a ghost. What has he done with his eight hundred years of death? where has he been? what has he seen? Maybe he has visited Mars; has spoken to the strange spirits who can live in the liquid fires of Jupiter. What has he learned of the great secret? Has he found the truth? or is he, even as I, a wanderer still seeking the unknown?

You, poor, pale, grey nun—they tell me that of midnights one may see your white face peering from the ruined belfry window, hear the clash of sword and shield among the cedar-trees beneath.

It was very sad, I quite understand, my dear lady. Your lovers both were killed, and you retired to a convent. Believe me, I am sincerely sorry for you, but why waste every night renewing the whole painful experience? Would it not be better forgotten? Good Heavens, madam, suppose we living folk were to spend our lives wailing and wringing our hands because of the wrongs done to us when we were children? It is all over now. Had he lived, and had you married him, you might not have been happy. I do not wish to say anything unkind, but marriages founded upon the sincerest mutual love have sometimes turned out unfortunately, as you must surely know.

Do take my advice. Talk the matter over with the young men themselves. Persuade them to shake hands and be friends. Come in, all of you, out of the cold, and let us have some reasonable talk.

Why seek you to trouble us, you poor pale ghosts? Are we not your children? Be our wise friends. Tell me, how loved the young men in your young days? how answered the maidens? Has the world changed much, do you think? Had you not new women even then? girls who hated the everlasting tapestry frame and spinning-wheel? Your father's servants, were they so much worse off than the freemen who live in our East-end slums and sew slippers for fourteen hours a day at a wage of nine shillings a week? Do you think Society much improved during the last thousand years? Is it worse? is it better? or is it, on the whole, about the same, save that we call things by other names? Tell me, what have YOU learned?

Yet might not familiarity breed contempt, even for ghosts.

One has had a tiring day's shooting. One is looking forward to one's bed. As one opens the door, however, a ghostly laugh comes from behind the bed-curtains, and one groans inwardly, knowing what is in store for one: a two or three hours' talk with rowdy old Sir Lanval—he of the lance. We know all his tales by heart, and he will shout them. Suppose our aunt, from whom we have expectations, and who sleeps in the next room, should wake and overhear! They were fit and proper enough stories, no doubt, for the Round Table, but we feel sure our aunt would not appreciate them:—that story about Sir Agravain and the cooper's wife! and he always will tell that story.

Or imagine the maid entering after dinner to say—

"Oh, if you please, sir, here is the veiled lady."

"What, again!" says your wife, looking up from her work.

"Yes, ma'am; shall I show her up into the bedroom?"

"You had better ask your master," is the reply. The tone is suggestive of an unpleasant five minutes so soon as the girl shall have withdrawn, but what are you to do?

"Yes, yes, show her up," you say, and the girl goes out, closing the door.

Your wife gathers her work together, and rises.

"Where are you going?" you ask.

"To sleep with the children," is the frigid answer.

"It will look so rude," you urge. "We must be civil to the poor thing; and you see it really is her room, as one might say. She has always haunted it."

"It is very curious," returns the wife of your bosom, still more icily, "that she never haunts it except when you are down here. Where she goes when you are in town I'm sure I don't know."

This is unjust. You cannot restrain your indignation.

"What nonsense you talk, Elizabeth," you reply; "I am only barely polite to her."

"Some men have such curious notions of politeness," returns Elizabeth. "But pray do not let us quarrel. I am only anxious not to disturb you. Two are company, you know. I don't choose to be the third, that's all." With which she goes out.

And the veiled lady is still waiting for you up-stairs. You wonder how long she will stop, also what will happen after she is gone.

I fear there is no room for you, ghosts, in this our world. You remember how they came to Hiawatha—the ghosts of the departed loved ones. He had prayed to them that they would come back to him to comfort him, so one day they crept into his wigwam, sat in silence round his fireside, chilled the air for Hiawatha, froze the smiles of Laughing Water.

There is no room for you, oh you poor pale ghosts, in this our world. Do not trouble us. Let us forget. You, stout elderly matron, your thin locks turning grey, your eyes grown weak, your chin more ample, your voice harsh with much scolding and complaining, needful, alas! to household management, I pray you leave me. I loved you while you lived. How sweet, how beautiful you were. I see you now in your white frock among the apple-blossom. But you are dead, and your ghost disturbs my dreams. I would it haunted me not.

You, dull old fellow, looking out at me from the glass at which I shave, why do you haunt me? You are the ghost of a bright lad I once knew well. He might have done much, had he lived. I always had faith in him. Why do you haunt me? I would rather think of him as I remember him. I never imagined he would make such a poor ghost.

ON THE PREPARATION AND EMPLOYMENT OF LOVE PHILTRES

Occasionally a friend will ask me some such question as this, Do you prefer dark women or fair? Another will say, Do you like tall women or short? A third, Do you think light-hearted women, or serious, the more agreeable company? I find myself in the position that, once upon a time, overtook a certain charming young lady of taste who was asked by an anxious parent, the years mounting, and the family expenditure not decreasing, which of the numerous and eligible young men, then paying court to her, she liked the best. She replied, that was her difficulty. She could not make up her mind which she liked the best. They were all so nice. She could not possibly select one to the exclusion of all the others. What she would have liked would have been to marry the lot, but that, she presumed, was impracticable.

I feel I resemble that young lady, not so much, perhaps, in charm and beauty as indecision of mind, when questions such as the above are put to me. It is as if one were asked one's favourite food. There are times when one fancies an egg with one's tea. On other occasions one dreams of a kipper. Today one clamours for lobsters. To-morrow one feels one never wishes to see a lobster again; one determines to settle down, for a time, to a diet of bread and milk and rice-pudding. Asked suddenly to say whether I preferred ices to soup, or beefsteaks to caviare, I should be nonplussed.

I like tall women and short, dark women and fair, merry women and grave.

Do not blame me, Ladies, the fault lies with you. Every right-thinking man is an universal lover; how could it be otherwise? You are so diverse, yet each so charming of your kind; and a man's heart is large. You have no idea, fair Reader, how large a man's heart is: that is his trouble—sometimes yours.

May I not admire the daring tulip, because I love also the modest lily? May I not press a kiss upon the sweet violet, because the scent of the queenly rose is precious to me?

"Certainly not," I hear the Rose reply. "If you can see anything in her, you shall have nothing to do with me."

"If you care for that bold creature," says the Lily, trembling, "you are not the man I took you for. Good-bye."

"Go to your baby-faced Violet," cries the Tulip, with a toss of her haughty head. "You are just fitted for each other."

And when I return to the Lily, she tells me that she cannot trust me. She has watched me with those others. She knows me for a gad-about. Her gentle face is full of pain.

So I must live unloved merely because I love too much.

My wonder is that young men ever marry. The difficulty of selection must be appalling. I walked the other evening in Hyde Park. The band of the Life Guards played heart-lifting music, and the vast crowd were basking in a sweet enjoyment such as rarely woos the English toiler. I strolled among them, and my attention was chiefly drawn towards the women. The great majority of them were, I suppose, shop-girls, milliners, and others belonging to the lower middle-class. They had put on their best frocks, their bonniest hats, their newest gloves. They sat or walked in twos and threes, chattering and preening, as happy as young sparrows on a clothes line. And what a handsome crowd they made! I have seen German crowds, I have seen French crowds, I have seen Italian crowds; but nowhere do you find such a proportion of pretty women as among the English middle-class. Three women out of every four were worth looking at, every other woman was pretty, while every fourth, one might say without exaggeration, was beautiful. As I passed to and fro the idea occurred to me: suppose I were an unprejudiced young bachelor, free from predilection, looking for a wife; and let me suppose—it is only a fancy—that all these girls were ready and willing to accept me. I have only to choose! I grew bewildered. There were fair girls, to look at whom was fatal; dark girls that set one's heart aflame; girls with red gold hair and grave grey eyes, whom one would follow to the confines of the universe; baby-faced girls that one longed to love and cherish; girls with noble faces, whom a man might worship; laughing girls, with whom one could dance through life gaily; serious girls, with whom life would be sweet and good, domestic-looking girls—one felt such would make delightful wives; they would cook, and sew, and make of home a pleasant, peaceful place. Then wicked-looking girls came by, at the stab of whose bold eyes all orthodox thoughts were put to a flight, whose laughter turned the world into a mad carnival; girls one could mould; girls from whom one could learn; sad girls one wanted to comfort; merry girls who would cheer one; little girls, big girls, queenly girls, fairy-like girls.

Suppose a young man had to select his wife in this fashion from some twenty or thirty thousand; or that a girl were suddenly confronted with eighteen thousand eligible young bachelors, and told to take the one she wanted and be quick about it? Neither boy nor girl would ever marry. Fate is kinder to us. She understands, and assists us. In the hall of a Paris hotel I once overheard one lady asking another to recommend her a milliner's shop.

"Go to the Maison Nouvelle," advised the questioned lady, with enthusiasm. "They have the largest selection there of any place in Paris."

"I know they have," replied the first lady, "that is just why I don't mean to go there. It confuses me. If I see six bonnets I can tell the one I want in five minutes.

If I see six hundred I come away without any bonnet at all. Don't you know a little shop?"

Fate takes the young man or the young woman aside.

"Come into this village, my dear," says Fate; "into this by-street of this salubrious suburb, into this social circle, into this church, into this chapel. Now, my dear boy, out of these seventeen young ladies, which will you have?—out of these thirteen young men, which would you like for your very own, my dear?"

"No, miss, I am sorry, but I am not able to show you our up-stairs department to-day, the lift is not working. But I am sure we shall be able to find something in this room to suit you. Just look round, my dear, perhaps you will see something."

"No, sir, I cannot show you the stock in the next room, we never take that out except for our very special customers. We keep our most expensive goods in that room. (Draw that curtain, Miss Circumstance, please. I have told you of that before.) Now, sir, wouldn't you like this one? This colour is quite the rage this season; we are getting rid of quite a lot of these."

"NO, sir! Well, of course, it would not do for every one's taste to be the same. Perhaps something dark would suit you better. Bring out those two brunettes, Miss Circumstance. Charming girls both of them, don't you think so, sir? I should say the taller one for you, sir. Just one moment, sir, allow me. Now, what do you think of that, sir? might have been made to fit you, I'm sure. You prefer the shorter one. Certainly, sir, no difference to us at all. Both are the same price. There's nothing like having one's own fancy, I always say. NO, sir, I cannot put her aside for you, we never do that. Indeed, there's rather a run on brunettes just at present. I had a gentleman in only this morning, looking at this particular one, and he is going to call again to-night. Indeed, I am not at all sure—Oh, of course, sir, if you like to settle on this one now, that ends the matter. (Put those others away, Miss Circumstance, please, and mark this one sold.) I feel sure you'll like her, sir, when you get her home. Thank YOU, sir. Good-morning!"

"Now, miss, have YOU seen anything you fancy? YES, miss, this is all we have at anything near your price. (Shut those other cupboards, Miss Circumstance; never show more stock than you are obliged to, it only confuses customers. How often am I to tell you that?) YES, miss, you are quite right, there IS a slight blemish. They all have some slight flaw. The makers say they can't help it—it's in the material. It's not once in a season we get a perfect specimen; and when we do ladies don't seem to care for it. Most of our customers prefer a little faultiness. They say it gives character. Now, look at this, miss. This sort of thing wears very well, warm and quiet. You'd like one with more colour in it? Certainly. Miss Circumstance, reach me down the art patterns. NO, miss, we don't guarantee any of them over the year, so much depends on how you use them. OH YES, miss, they'll stand a fair amount of wear. People do tell you the quieter patterns last longer; but my experience is that one is much the same as another. There's really no telling any of them until you come to try them. We never recommend one more than another. There's a lot of chance about these goods, it's in the nature of them. What I always say to ladies is—'Please yourself, it's you who have got to wear it; and it's no good having an article you start by not liking.' YES, miss, it IS pretty and it looks well against you: it does indeed. Thank you, miss. Put that one aside, Miss Circumstance, please. See that it doesn't get mixed up with the unsold stock."

It is a useful philtre, the juice of that small western flower, that Oberon drops upon our eyelids as we sleep. It solves all difficulties in a trice. Why of course Helena is the fairer. Compare her with Hermia! Compare the raven with the dove! How could we ever have doubted for a moment? Bottom is an angel, Bottom is as wise as he is handsome. Oh, Oberon, we thank you for that drug. Matilda Jane is a goddess; Matilda Jane is a queen; no woman ever born of Eve was like Matilda Jane. The little pimple on her nose—her little, sweet, tip-tilted nose—how beautiful it is. Her bright eyes flash with temper now and then; how piquant is a temper in a woman. William is a dear old stupid, how lovable stupid men can be—especially when wise enough to love us. William does not shine in conversation; how we hate a magpie of a man. William's chin is what is called receding, just the sort of chin a beard looks well on. Bless you, Oberon darling, for that drug; rub it on our eyelids once again. Better let us have a bottle, Oberon, to keep by us.

Oberon, Oberon, what are you thinking of? You have given the bottle to Puck. Take it away from him, quick. Lord help us all if that Imp has the bottle. Lord save us from Puck while we sleep.

Or may we, fairy Oberon, regard your lotion as an eye-opener, rather than as an eye-closer? You remember the story the storks told the children, of the little girl who was a toad by day, only her sweet dark eyes being left to her. But at night, when the Prince clasped her close to his breast, lo! again she became the king's daughter, fairest and fondest of women. There be many royal ladies in Marshland, with bad complexion and thin straight hair, and the silly princes sneer and ride away to woo some kitchen wench decked out in queen's apparel. Lucky the prince upon whose eyelids Oberon has dropped the magic philtre.

In the gallery of a minor Continental town I have forgotten, hangs a picture that lives with me. The painting I cannot recall, whether good or bad; artists must forgive me for remembering only the subject. It shows a man, crucified by the roadside. No martyr he. If ever a man deserved hanging it was this one. So much the artist has made clear. The face, even under its mask of agony, is an evil, treacherous face. A peasant girl clings to the cross; she stands tip-toe upon a patient donkey, straining her face upward for the half-dead man to stoop and kiss her lips.

Thief, coward, blackguard, they are stamped upon his face, but UNDER the face, under the evil outside? Is there no remnant of manhood—nothing tender, nothing, true? A woman has crept to the cross to kiss him: no evidence in his favour, my Lord? Love is blind-aye, to our faults. Heaven help us all; Love's eyes would be sore indeed if it were not so. But for the good that is in us her eyes are keen. You, crucified blackguard, stand forth. A hundred witnesses have given their evidence against you. Are there none to give evidence for him? A woman, great Judge, who loved him. Let her speak.

But I am wandering far from Hyde Park and its show of girls.

They passed and re-passed me, laughing, smiling, talking. Their eyes were bright with merry thoughts; their voices soft and musical. They were pleased, and they wanted to please. Some were married, some had evidently reasonable expectations of being married; the rest hoped to be. And we, myself, and some ten thousand other young men. I repeat it—myself and some ten thousand other young men; for who among us ever thinks of himself but as a young man? It is the world that ages, not we. The children cease their playing and grow grave, the lasses' eyes are dimmer. The hills are a little steeper, the milestones, surely, further apart. The songs the young men sing are less merry than the songs we used to sing. The days have grown a little colder, the wind a little keener. The wine has lost its flavour somewhat; the new humour is not like the old. The other boys are becoming dull and prosy; but we are not changed. It is the world that is growing old. Therefore, I brave your thoughtless laughter, youthful Reader, and repeat that we, myself and some ten thousand other young men, walked among these sweet girls; and, using our boyish eyes, were fascinated, charmed, and captivated. How delightful to spend our lives with them, to do little services for them that would call up these bright smiles. How pleasant to jest with them, and hear their flute-like laughter, to console them and read their grateful eyes. Really life is a pleasant thing, and the idea of marriage undoubtedly originated in the brain of a kindly Providence.

We smiled back at them, and we made way for them; we rose from our chairs with a polite, "Allow me, miss," "Don't mention it, I prefer standing." "It is a delightful evening, is it not?" And perhaps—for what harm was there?—we dropped into conversation with these chance fellow-passengers upon the stream of life. There were those among us—bold daring spirits—who even went to the length of mild flirtation. Some of us knew some of them, and in such happy case there followed interchange of pretty pleasantries. Your English middle-class young man and woman are not adepts at the game of flirtation. I will confess that our methods were, perhaps, elephantine, that we may have grown a trifle noisy as the evening wore on. But we meant no evil; we did but our best to enjoy ourselves, to give enjoyment, to make the too brief time, pass gaily.

And then my thoughts travelled to small homes in distant suburbs, and these bright lads and lasses round me came to look older and more careworn. But what of that? Are not old faces sweet when looked at by old eyes a little dimmed by love, and are not care and toil but the parents of peace and joy?

But as I drew nearer, I saw that many of the faces were seared with sour and angry looks, and the voices that rose round me sounded surly and captious. The pretty compliment and praise had changed to sneers and scoldings. The dimpled smile had wrinkled to a frown. There seemed so little desire to please, so great a determination not to be pleased.

And the flirtations! Ah me, they had forgotten how to flirt! Oh, the pity of it! All the jests were bitter, all the little services were given grudgingly. The air seemed to have grown chilly. A darkness had come over all things.

And then I awoke to reality, and found I had been sitting in my chair longer than I had intended. The band-stand was empty, the sun had set; I rose and made my way home through the scattered crowd.

Nature is so callous. The Dame irritates one at times by her devotion to her one idea, the propagation of the species.

"Multiply and be fruitful; let my world be ever more and more peopled."

For this she trains and fashions her young girls, models them with cunning hand, paints them with her wonderful red and white, crowns them with her glorious hair, teaches them to smile and laugh, trains their voices into music, sends them out into the world to captivate, to enslave us.

"See how beautiful she is, my lad," says the cunning old woman. "Take her; build your little nest with her in your pretty suburb; work for her and live for her; enable her to keep the little ones that I will send."

And to her, old hundred-breasted Artemis whispers, "Is he not a bonny lad? See how he loves you, how devoted he is to you! He will work for you and make you happy; he will build your home for you. You will be the mother of his children."

So we take each other by the hand, full of hope and love, and from that hour Mother Nature has done with us. Let the wrinkles come; let our voices grow harsh; let the fire she lighted in our hearts die out; let the foolish selfishness we both thought we had put behind us for ever creep back to us, bringing unkindness and indifference, angry thoughts and cruel words into our lives. What cares she? She has caught us, and chained us to her work. She is our universal mother-in-law. She has done the match-making; for the rest, she leaves it to ourselves. We can love or we can fight; it is all one to her, confound her.

I wonder sometimes if good temper might not be taught. In business we use no harsh language, say no unkind things to one another. The shopkeeper, leaning across the counter, is all smiles and affability, he might put up his shutters were he otherwise. The commercial gent, no doubt, thinks the ponderous shopwalker an ass, but refrains from telling him so. Hasty tempers are banished from the City. Can we not see that it is just as much to our interest to banish them from Tooting and Hampstead?

The young man who sat in the chair next to me, how carefully he wrapped the cloak round the shoulders of the little milliner beside him. And when she said she was tired of sitting still, how readily he sprang from his chair to walk with her, though it was evident he was very comfortable where he was. And she! She had laughed at his jokes; they were not very clever jokes, they were not very new. She had probably read them herself months before in her own particular weekly journal. Yet the harmless humbug made him happy. I wonder if ten years hence she will laugh at such old humour, if ten years hence he will take such clumsy pains to put her cape about her. Experience shakes her head, and is amused at my question.

I would have evening classes for the teaching of temper to married couples, only I fear the institution would languish for lack of pupils. The husbands would recommend their wives to attend, generously offering to pay the fee as a birthday present. The wife would be indignant at the suggestion of good money being thus wasted. "No, John, dear," she would unselfishly reply, "you need the lessons more than I do. It would be a shame for me to take them away from you," and they would wrangle upon the subject for the rest of the day.

Oh! the folly of it. We pack our hamper for life's picnic with such pains. We spend so much, we work so hard. We make choice pies, we cook prime joints, we prepare so carefully the mayonnaise, we mix with loving hands the salad, we cram the basket to the lid with every delicacy we can think of. Everything to make the picnic a success is there except the salt. Ah! woe is me, we forget the salt. We slave at our desks, in our workshops, to make a home for those we love; we give up our pleasures, we give up our rest. We toil in our kitchen from morning till night, and we render the whole feast tasteless for want of a ha'porth of salt—for want of a soupcon of amiability, for want of a handful of kindly words, a touch of caress, a pinch of courtesy.

Who does not know that estimable housewife, working from eight till twelve to keep the house in what she calls order? She is so good a woman, so untiring, so unselfish, so conscientious, so irritating. Her rooms are so clean, her servants so well managed, her children so well dressed, her dinners so well cooked; the whole house so uninviting. Everything about her is in apple-pie order, and everybody wretched.

My good Madam, you polish your tables, you scour your kettles, but the most valuable piece of furniture in the whole house you are letting to rack and ruin for want of a little pains. You will find it in your own room, my dear Lady, in front of your own mirror. It is getting shabby and dingy, old-looking before its time; the polish is rubbed off it, Madam, it is losing its brightness and charm. Do you remember when he first brought it home, how proud he was of it? Do you think you have used it well, knowing how he valued it? A little less care of your pots and your pans, Madam, a little more of yourself were wiser. Polish yourself up, Madam; you had a pretty wit once, a pleasant laugh, a conversation that was not confined exclusively to the short-comings of servants, the wrong-doings of tradesmen. My dear Madam, we do not live on spotless linen, and crumbless carpets. Hunt out that bundle of old letters you keep tied up in faded ribbon at the back of your bureau drawer—a pity you don't read them oftener. He did not enthuse about your cuffs and collars, gush over the neatness of your darning. It was your tangled hair he raved about, your sunny smile (we have not seen it for some years, Madam—the fault of the Cook and the Butcher, I presume), your little hands, your rosebud mouth—it has lost its shape, Madam, of late. Try a little less scolding of Mary Ann, and practise a laugh once a day: you might get back the dainty curves. It would be worth trying. It was a pretty mouth once.

Who invented that mischievous falsehood that the way to a man's heart was through his stomach? How many a silly woman, taking it for truth, has let love slip out of the parlour, while she was busy in the kitchen. Of course, if you were foolish enough to marry a pig, I suppose you must be content to devote your life to the preparation of hog's-wash. But are you sure that he IS a pig? If by any chance he be not?—then, Madam, you are making a grievous mistake. My dear Lady, you are too modest. If I may say so without making you unduly conceited, even at the dinner-table itself, you are of much more importance than the mutton. Courage, Madam, be not afraid to tilt a lance even with your own cook. You can be more piquant than the sauce a la Tartare, more soothing surely than the melted butter. There was a time when he would not have known whether he was eating beef or pork with you the other side of the table. Whose fault is it? Don't think so poorly of us. We are not ascetics, neither are we all gourmets: most of us plain men, fond of our dinner, as a healthy man should be, but fonder still of our sweethearts and wives, let us hope. Try us. A moderately-cooked dinner—let us even say a not-too-well-cooked dinner, with you looking your best, laughing and talking gaily and cleverly—as you can, you know—makes a pleasanter meal for us, after the day's work is done, than that same dinner, cooked to perfection, with you silent, jaded, and anxious, your pretty hair untidy, your pretty face wrinkled with care concerning the sole, with anxiety regarding the omelette.

My poor Martha, be not troubled about so many things. YOU are the one thing needful—if the bricks and mortar are to be a home. See to it that YOU are well served up, that YOU are done to perfection, that YOU are tender and satisfying, that YOU are worth sitting down to. We wanted a wife, a comrade, a friend; not a cook and a nurse on the cheap.

But of what use is it to talk? the world will ever follow its own folly. When I think of all the good advice that I have given it, and of the small result achieved, I confess I grow discouraged. I was giving good advice to a lady only the other day. I was instructing her as to the proper treatment of aunts. She was sucking a lead-pencil, a thing I am always telling her not to do. She took it out of her mouth to speak.

"I suppose you know how everybody ought to do everything," she said.

There are times when it is necessary to sacrifice one's modesty to one's duty.

"Of course I do," I replied.

"And does Mama know how everybody ought to do everything?" was the second question.

My conviction on this point was by no means so strong, but for domestic reasons I again sacrificed myself to expediency.

"Certainly," I answered; "and take that pencil out of your mouth. I've told you of that before. You'll swallow it one day, and then you'll get perichondritis and die."

She appeared to be solving a problem.

"All grown-up people seem to know everything," she summarized.

There are times when I doubt if children are as simple as they look. If it be sheer stupidity that prompts them to make remarks of this character, one should pity them, and seek to improve them. But if it be not stupidity? well then, one should still seek to improve them, but by a different method.

The other morning I overheard the nurse talking to this particular specimen. The woman is a most worthy creature, and she was imparting to the child some really sound advice. She was in the middle of an unexceptional exhortation concerning the virtue of silence, when Dorothea interrupted her with—

"Oh, do be quiet, Nurse. I never get a moment's peace from your chatter."

Such an interruption discourages a woman who is trying to do her duty.

Last Tuesday evening she was unhappy. Myself, I think that rhubarb should never be eaten before April, and then never with lemonade. Her mother read her a homily upon the subject of pain. It was impressed upon her that we must be patient, that we must put up with the trouble that God sends us. Dorothea would descend to details, as children will.

"Must we put up with the cod-liver oil that God sends us?"

"Yes, decidedly."

"And with the nurses that God sends us?"

"Certainly; and be thankful that you've got them, some little girls haven't any nurse. And don't talk so much."

On Friday I found the mother in tears.

"What's the matter?" I asked.

"Oh, nothing," was the answer; "only Baby. She's such a strange child. I can't make her out at all."

"What has she been up to now?"

"Oh, she will argue, you know."

She has that failing. I don't know where she gets it from, but she's got it.

"Well?"

"Well, she made me cross; and, to punish her, I told her she shouldn't take her doll's perambulator out with her."

"Yes?"

"Well, she didn't say anything then, but so soon as I was outside the door, I heard her talking to herself—you know her way?"

"Yes?"

"She said—"

"Yes, she said?"

"She said, 'I must be patient. I must put up with the mother God has sent me.'"

She lunches down-stairs on Sundays. We have her with us once a week to give her the opportunity of studying manners and behaviour. Milson had dropped in, and we were discussing politics. I was interested, and, pushing my plate aside, leant forward with my elbows on the table. Dorothea has a habit of talking to herself in a high-pitched whisper capable of being heard above an Adelphi love scene. I heard her say—

"I must sit up straight. I mustn't sprawl with my elbows on the table. It is only common, vulgar people behave that way."

I looked across at her; she was sitting most correctly, and appeared to be contemplating something a thousand miles away. We had all of us been lounging! We sat up stiffly, and conversation flagged.

Of course we made a joke of it after the child was gone. But somehow it didn't seem to be OUR joke.

I wish I could recollect my childhood. I should so like to know if children are as simple as they can look.

ON THE DELIGHTS AND BENEFITS OF SLAVERY

My study window looks down upon Hyde Park, and often, to quote the familiar promise of each new magazine, it amuses and instructs me to watch from my tower the epitome of human life that passes to and fro beneath. At the opening of the gates, creeps in the woman of the streets. Her pitiful work for the time being is over. Shivering in the chill dawn, she passes to her brief rest. Poor Slave! Lured to the galley's lowest deck, then chained there. Civilization, tricked fool, they say has need of such. You serve as the dogs of Eastern towns. But at least, it seems to me, we need not spit on you. Home to your kennel! Perchance, if the Gods be kind, they may send you dreams of a cleanly hearth, where you lie with a silver collar round your neck.

Next comes the labourer—the hewer of wood, the drawer of water—slouching wearily to his toil; sleep clinging still about his leaden eyes, his pittance of food carried tied up in a dish-clout. The first stroke of the hour clangs from Big Ben. Haste thee, fellow-slave, lest the overseer's whip, "Out, we will have no lie-a-beds here," descend upon thy patient back.

Later, the artisan, with his bag of tools across his shoulder. He, too, listens fearfully to the chiming of the bells. For him also there hangs ready the whip.

After him, the shop boy and the shop girl, making love as they walk, not to waste time. And after these the slaves of the desk and of the warehouse, employers and employed, clerks and tradesmen, office boys and merchants. To your places, slaves of all ranks. Get you unto your burdens.

Now, laughing and shouting as they run, the children, the sons and daughters of the slaves. Be industrious, little children, and learn your lessons, that when the time comes you may be ready to take from our hands the creaking oar, to slip into our seat at the roaring loom. For we shall not be slaves for ever, little children. It is the good law of the land. So many years in the galleys, so many years in the fields; then we can claim our freedom. Then we shall go, little children, back to the land of our birth. And you we must leave behind us to take up the tale of our work. So, off to your schools, little children, and learn to be good little slaves.

Next, pompous and sleek, come the educated slaves—journalists, doctors, judges, and poets; the attorney, the artist, the player, the priest. They likewise scurry across the Park, looking anxiously from time to time at their watches, lest they be late for their appointments; thinking of the rates and taxes to be earned, of the bonnets to be paid for, the bills to be met. The best scourged, perhaps, of all, these slaves. The cat reserved for them has fifty tails in place of merely two or three. Work, you higher middle-class slave, or you shall come down to the smoking of twopenny cigars; harder yet, or you shall drink shilling claret; harder, or you shall lose your carriage and ride in a penny bus; your wife's frocks shall be of last year's fashion; your trousers shall bag at the knees; from Kensington you shall be banished to Kilburn, if the tale of your bricks run short. Oh, a many-thonged whip is yours, my genteel brother.

The slaves of fashion are the next to pass beneath me in review. They are dressed and curled with infinite pains. The liveried, pampered footman these, kept more for show than use; but their senseless tasks none the less labour to them. Here must they come every day, merry or sad. By this gravel path and no other must they walk; these phrases shall they use when they speak to one another. For an hour they must go slowly up and down upon a bicycle from Hyde Park Corner to the Magazine and back. And these clothes must they wear; their gloves of this colour, their neck-ties of this pattern. In the afternoon they must return again, this time in a carriage, dressed in another livery, and for an hour they must pass slowly to and fro in foolish procession. For dinner they must don yet another livery, and after dinner they must stand about at dreary social functions till with weariness and boredom their heads feel dropping from their shoulders.

With the evening come the slaves back from their work: barristers, thinking out their eloquent appeals; school-boys, conning their dog-eared grammars; City men, planning their schemes; the wearers of motley, cudgelling their poor brains for fresh wit with which to please their master; shop boys and shop girls, silent now as, together, they plod homeward; the artisan; the labourer. Two or three hours you shall have to yourselves, slaves, to think and love and play, if you be not too tired to think, or love, or play. Then to your litter, that you may be ready for the morrow's task.

The twilight deepens into dark; there comes back the woman of the streets. As the shadows, she rounds the City's day. Work strikes its tent. Evil creeps from its peering place.

So we labour, driven by the whip of necessity, an army of slaves. If we do not our work, the whip descends upon us; only the pain we feel in our stomach instead of on our back. And because of that, we call ourselves free men.

Some few among us bravely struggle to be really free: they are our tramps and outcasts. We well-behaved slaves shrink from them, for the wages of freedom in this world are vermin and starvation. We can live lives worth living only by placing the collar round our neck.

There are times when one asks oneself: Why this endless labour? Why this building of houses, this cooking of food, this making of clothes? Is the ant so much more to be envied than the grasshopper, because she spends her life in grubbing and storing, and can spare no time for singing? Why this complex instinct, driving us to a thousand labours to satisfy a thousand desires? We have turned the world into a workshop to provide ourselves with toys. To purchase luxury we have sold our ease.

Oh, Children of Israel! why were ye not content in your wilderness? It seems to have been a pattern wilderness. For you, a simple wholesome food, ready cooked, was provided. You took no thought for rent and taxes; you had no poor among you—no poor-rate collectors. You suffered not from indigestion, nor the hundred ills that follow over-feeding; an omer for every man was your portion, neither more nor less. You knew not you had a liver. Doctors wearied you not with their theories, their physics, and their bills. You were neither landowners nor leaseholders, neither shareholders nor debenture holders. The weather and the market reports troubled you not. The lawyer was unknown to you; you wanted no advice; you had nought to quarrel about with your neighbour. No riches were yours for the moth and rust to damage. Your yearly income and expenditure you knew would balance to a fraction. Your wife and children were provided for. Your old age caused you no anxiety; you knew you would always have enough to live upon in comfort. Your funeral, a simple and tasteful affair, would be furnished by the tribe. And yet, poor, foolish child, fresh from the Egyptian brickfield, you could not rest satisfied. You hungered for the fleshpots, knowing well what flesh-pots entail: the cleaning of the flesh-pots, the forging of the flesh-pots, the hewing of wood to make the fires for the boiling of the flesh-pots, the breeding of beasts to fill the pots, the growing of fodder to feed the beasts to fill the pots.

All the labour of our life is centred round our flesh-pots. On the altar of the flesh-pot we sacrifice our leisure, our peace of mind. For a mess of pottage we sell our birthright.

Oh! Children of Israel, saw you not the long punishment you were preparing for yourselves, when in your wilderness you set up the image of the Calf, and fell before it, crying—"This shall be our God."

You would have veal. Thought you never of the price man pays for Veal? The servants of the Golden Calf! I see them, stretched before my eyes, a weary, endless throng. I see them toiling in the mines, the black sweat on their faces. I see them in sunless cities, silent, and grimy, and bent. I see them, ague-twisted, in the rain-soaked fields. I see them, panting by the furnace doors. I see them, in loin-cloth and necklace, the load upon their head. I see them in blue coats and red coats, marching to pour their blood as an offering on the altar of the Calf. I see them in homespun and broadcloth, I see them in smock and gaiters, I see them in cap and apron, the servants of the Calf. They swarm on the land and they dot the sea. They are chained to the anvil and counter; they are chained to the bench and the desk. They make ready the soil, they till the fields where the Golden Calf is born. They build the ship, and they sail the ship that carries the Golden Calf. They fashion the pots, they mould the pans, they carve the tables, they turn the chairs, they dream of the sauces, they dig for the salt, they weave the damask, they mould the dish to serve the Golden Calf.

The work of the world is to this end, that we eat of the Calf. War and Commerce, Science and Law! what are they but the four pillars supporting the Golden Calf? He is our God. It is on his back that we have journeyed from the primeval forest, where our ancestors ate nuts and fruit. He is our God. His temple is in every street. His blue-robed priest stands ever at the door, calling to the people to worship. Hark! his voice rises on the gas-tainted air—"Now's your time! Now's your time! Buy! Buy! ye people. Bring hither the sweat of your brow, the sweat of your brain, the ache of your heart, buy Veal with it. Bring me the best years of your life. Bring me your thoughts, your hopes, your loves; ye shall have Veal for them. Now's your time! Now's your time! Buy! Buy!"

Oh! Children of Israel, was Veal, even with all its trimmings, quite worth the price?

And we! what wisdom have we learned, during the centuries? I talked with a rich man only the other evening. He calls himself a Financier, whatever that may mean. He leaves his beautiful house, some twenty miles out of London, at a quarter to eight, summer and winter, after a hurried breakfast by himself, while his guests still sleep, and he gets back just in time to dress for an elaborate dinner he himself is too weary or too preoccupied to more than touch. If ever he is persuaded to give himself a holiday it is for a fortnight in Ostend, when it is most crowded and uncomfortable. He takes his secretary with him, receives and despatches a hundred telegrams a day, and has a private telephone, through which he can speak direct to London, brought up into his bedroom.

I suppose the telephone is really a useful invention. Business men tell me they wonder how they contrived to conduct their affairs without it. My own wonder always is, how any human being with the ordinary passions of his race can conduct his business, or even himself, creditably, within a hundred yards of the invention. I can imagine Job, or Griselda, or Socrates liking to have a telephone about them as exercise. Socrates, in particular, would have made quite a reputation for himself out of a three months' subscription to a telephone. Myself, I am, perhaps, too sensitive. I once lived for a month in an office with a telephone, if one could call it life. I was told that if I had stuck to the thing for two or three months longer, I should have got used to it. I know friends of mine, men once fearless and high-spirited, who now stand in front of their own telephone for a quarter of an hour at a time, and never so much as answer it back. They tell me that at first they used to swear and shout at it as I did; but now their spirit seems crushed. That is what happens: you either break the telephone, or the telephone breaks you. You want to see a man two streets off. You might put on your hat, and be round at his office in five minutes. You are on the point of starting when the telephone catches your eye. You think you will ring him up to make sure he is in. You commence by ringing up some half-dozen times before anybody takes any notice of you whatever. You are burning with indignation at this neglect, and have left the instrument to sit down and pen a stinging letter of complaint to the Company when the ring-back re-calls you. You seize the ear trumpets, and shout—

"How is it that I can never get an answer when I ring? Here have I been ringing for the last half-hour. I have rung twenty times." (This is a falsehood. You have rung only six times, and the "half-hour" is an absurd exaggeration; but you feel the mere truth would not be adequate to the occasion.) "I think it disgraceful," you continue, "and I shall complain to the Company. What is the use of my having a telephone if I can't get any answer when I ring? Here I pay a large sum for having this thing, and I can't get any notice taken. I've been ringing all the morning. Why is it?"

Then you wait for the answer.

"What—what do you say? I can't hear what you say."

"I say I've been ringing here for over an hour, and I can't get any reply," you call back. "I shall complain to the Company."

"You want what? Don't stand so near the tube. I can't hear what you say. What number?"

"Bother the number; I say why is it I don't get an answer when I ring?"

"Eight hundred and what?"

You can't argue any more, after that. The machine would give way under the language you want to make use of. Half of what you feel would probably cause an explosion at some point where the wire was weak. Indeed, mere language of any kind would fall short of the requirements of the case. A hatchet and a gun are the only intermediaries through which you could convey your meaning by this time. So you give up all attempt to answer back, and meekly mention that you want to be put in communication with four-five-seven-six.

"Four-nine-seven-six?" says the girl.

"No; four-five-seven-six."

"Did you say seven-six or six-seven?"

"Six-seven—no! I mean seven-six: no—wait a minute. I don't know what I do mean now."

"Well, I wish you'd find out," says the young lady severely. "You are keeping me here all the morning."

So you look up the number in the book again, and at last she tells you that you are in connection; and then, ramming the trumpet tight against your ear, you stand waiting.

And if there is one thing more than another likely to make a man feel ridiculous it is standing on tip-toe in a corner, holding a machine to his head, and listening intently to nothing. Your back aches and your head aches, your very hair aches. You hear the door open behind you and somebody enter the room. You can't turn your head. You swear at them, and hear the door close with a bang. It immediately occurs to you that in all probability it was Henrietta. She promised to call for you at half-past twelve: you were to take her to lunch. It was twelve o'clock when you were fool enough to mix yourself up with this infernal machine, and it probably is half-past twelve by now. Your past life rises before you, accompanied by dim memories of your grandmother. You are wondering how much longer you can bear the strain of this attitude, and whether after all you do really want to see the man in the next street but two, when the girl in the exchange-room calls up to know if you're done.

"Done!" you retort bitterly; "why, I haven't begun yet."

"Well, be quick," she says, "because you're wasting time."

Thus admonished, you attack the thing again. "ARE you there?" you cry in tones that ought to move the heart of a Charity Commissioner; and then, oh joy! oh rapture! you hear a faint human voice replying—"Yes, what is it?"

"Oh! Are you four-five-seven-six?"

"What?"

"Are you four-five-seven-six, Williamson?"

"What! who are you?"

"Eight-one-nine, Jones."

"Bones?"

"No, JONES. Are you four-five-seven-six?"

"Yes; what is it?"

"Is Mr. Williamson in?"

"Will I what—who are you?"

"Jones! Is Mr. Williamson in?"

"Who?"

"Williamson. Will-i-am-son!"

"You're the son of what? I can't hear what you say."

Then you gather yourself for one final effort, and succeed, by superhuman patience, in getting the fool to understand that you wish to know if Mr. Williamson is in, and he says, so it sounds to you, "Be in all the morning."

So you snatch up your hat and run round.

"Oh, I've come to see Mr. Williamson," you say.

"Very sorry, sir," is the polite reply, "but he's out."

"Out? Why, you just now told me through the telephone that he'd be in all the morning."

"No, I said, he 'WON'T be in all the morning.'"

You go back to the office, and sit down in front of that telephone and look at it. There it hangs, calm and imperturbable. Were it an ordinary instrument, that would be its last hour. You would go straight down-stairs, get the coal-hammer and the kitchen-poker, and divide it into sufficient pieces to give a bit to every man in London. But you feel nervous of these electrical affairs, and there is a something about that telephone, with its black hole and curly wires, that cows you. You have a notion that if you don't handle it properly something may come and shock you, and then there will be an inquest, and bother of that sort, so you only curse it.

That is what happens when you want to use the telephone from your end. But that is not the worst that the telephone can do. A sensible man, after a little experience, can learn to leave the thing alone. Your worst troubles are not of your own making. You are working against time; you have given instructions not to be disturbed. Perhaps it is after lunch, and you are thinking with your eyes closed, so that your thoughts shall not be distracted by the objects about the room. In either case you are anxious not to leave your chair, when off goes that telephone bell and you spring from your chair, uncertain, for the moment, whether you have been shot, or blown up with dynamite. It occurs to you in your weakness that if you persist in taking no notice, they will get tired, and leave you alone. But that is not their method. The bell rings violently at ten-second intervals. You have nothing to wrap your head up in. You think it will be better to get this business over and done with. You go to your fate and call back savagely—

"What is it? What do you want?"

No answer, only a confused murmur, prominent out of which come the voices of two men swearing at one another. The language they are making use of is disgraceful. The telephone seems peculiarly adapted for the conveyance of blasphemy. Ordinary language sounds indistinct through it; but every word those two men are saying can be heard by all the telephone subscribers in London.

It is useless attempting to listen till they have done. When they are exhausted, you apply to the tube again. No answer is obtainable. You get mad, and become sarcastic; only being sarcastic when you are not sure that anybody is at the other end to hear you is unsatisfying.

At last, after a quarter of an hour or so of saying, "Are you there?" "Yes, I'm here," "Well?" the young lady at the Exchange asks what you want.

"I don't want anything," you reply.

"Then why do you keep talking?" she retorts; "you mustn't play with the thing."

This renders you speechless with indignation for a while, upon recovering from which you explain that somebody rang you up.

"WHO rang you up?" she asks.

"I don't know."

"I wish you did," she observes.

Generally disgusted, you slam the trumpet up and return to your chair. The instant you are seated the bell clangs again; and you fly up and demand to know what the thunder they want, and who the thunder they are.

"Don't speak so loud, we can't hear you. What do you want?" is the answer.

"I don't want anything. What do you want? Why do you ring me up, and then not answer me? Do leave me alone, if you can!"

"We can't get Hong Kongs at seventy-four."

"Well, I don't care if you can't."

"Would you like Zulus?"

"What are you talking about?" you reply; "I don't know what you mean."

"Would you like Zulus—Zulus at seventy-three and a half?"

"I wouldn't have 'em at six a penny. What are you talking about?"

"Hong Kongs—we can't get them at seventy-four. Oh, half-a-minute" (the half-a-minute passes). "Are you there?"

"Yes, but you are talking to the wrong man."

"We can get you Hong Kongs at seventy-four and seven-eights."

"Bother Hong Kongs, and you too. I tell you, you are talking to the wrong man. I've told you once."

"Once what?"

"Why, that I am the wrong man—I mean that you are talking to the wrong man."

"Who are you?"

"Eight-one-nine, Jones."

"Oh, aren't you one-nine-eight?"

"No."

"Oh, good-bye."

"Good-bye."

How can a man after that sit down and write pleasantly of the European crisis? And, if it were needed, herein lies another indictment against the telephone. I was engaged in an argument, which, if not in itself serious, was at least concerned with a serious enough subject, the unsatisfactory nature of human riches; and from that highly moral discussion have I been lured, by the accidental sight of the word "telephone," into the writing of matter which can have the effect only of exciting to frenzy all critics of the New Humour into whose hands, for their sins, this book may come. Let me forget my transgression and return to my sermon, or rather to the sermon of my millionaire acquaintance.

It was one day after dinner, we sat together in his magnificently furnished dining-room. We had lighted our cigars at the silver lamp. The butler had withdrawn.

"These cigars we are smoking," my friend suddenly remarked, a propos apparently of nothing, "they cost me five shillings apiece, taking them by the thousand."

"I can quite believe it," I answered; "they are worth it."

"Yes, to you," he replied, almost savagely. "What do you usually pay for your cigars?"

We had known each other years ago. When I first met him his offices consisted of a back room up three flights of stairs in a dingy by-street off the Strand, which has since disappeared. We occasionally dined together, in those days, at a restaurant in Great Portland Street, for one and nine. Our acquaintanceship was of sufficient standing to allow of such a question.

"Threepence," I answered. "They work out at about twopence three-farthings by the box."

"Just so," he growled; "and your twopenny-three-farthing weed gives you precisely the same amount of satisfaction that this five shilling cigar affords me. That means four and ninepence farthing wasted every time I smoke. I pay my cook two hundred a year. I don't enjoy my dinner as much as when it cost me four shillings, including a quarter flask of Chianti. What is the difference, personally, to me whether I drive to my office in a carriage and pair, or in an omnibus? I often do ride in a bus: it saves trouble. It is absurd wasting time looking for one's coachman, when the conductor of an omnibus that passes one's door is hailing one a few yards off. Before I could afford even buses—when I used to walk every morning to the office from Hammersmith—I was healthier. It irritates me to think how hard I work for no earthly benefit to myself. My money pleases a lot of people I don't care two straws about, and who are only my friends in the hope of making something out of me. If I could eat a hundred-guinea dinner myself every night, and enjoy it four hundred times as much as I used to enjoy a five-shilling dinner, there would be some sense in it. Why do I do it?"

I had never heard him talk like this before. In his excitement he rose from the table, and commenced pacing the room.

"Why don't I invest my money in the two and a half per cents?" he continued. "At the very worst I should be safe for five thousand a year. What, in the name of common sense, does a man want with more? I am always saying to myself, I'll do it; why don't I?

"Well, why not?" I echoed.

"That's what I want you to tell me," he returned. "You set up for understanding human nature, it's a mystery to me. In my place, you would do as I do; you know that. If somebody left you a hundred thousand pounds to-morrow, you would start a newspaper, or build a theatre—some damn-fool trick for getting rid of the money and giving yourself seventeen hours' anxiety a day; you know you would."

I hung my head in shame. I felt the justice of the accusation. It has always been my dream to run a newspaper and own a theatre.

"If we worked only for what we could spend," he went on, "the City might put up its shutters to-morrow morning. What I want to get at the bottom of is this instinct that drives us to work apparently for work's own sake. What is this strange thing that gets upon our back and spurs us?"

A servant entered at that moment with a cablegram from the manager of one of his Austrian mines, and he had to leave me for his study. But, walking home, I fell to pondering on his words. WHY this endless work? Why each morning do we get up and wash and dress ourselves, to undress ourselves at night and go to bed again? Why do we work merely to earn money to buy food; and eat food so as to gain strength that we may work? Why do we live, merely in the end to say good-bye to one another? Why do we labour to bring children into the world that they may die and be buried?

Of what use our mad striving, our passionate desire? Will it matter to the ages whether, once upon a time, the Union Jack or the Tricolour floated over the battlements of Badajoz? Yet we poured our blood into its ditches to decide the question. Will it matter, in the days when the glacial period shall have come again, to clothe the earth with silence, whose foot first trod the Pole? Yet, generation after generation, we mile its roadway with our whitening bones. So very soon the worms come to us; does it matter whether we love, or hate? Yet the hot blood rushes through our veins, we wear out heart and brain for shadowy hopes that ever fade as we press forward.

The flower struggles up from seed-pod, draws the sweet sap from the ground, folds its petals each night, and sleeps. Then love comes to it in a strange form, and it longs to mingle its pollen with the pollen of some other flower. So it puts forth its gay blossoms, and the wandering insect bears the message from seed-pod to seed-pod. And the seasons pass, bringing with them the sunshine and the rain, till the flower withers, never having known the real purpose for which it lived, thinking the garden was made for it, not it for the garden. The coral insect dreams in its small soul, which is possibly its small stomach, of home and food. So it works and strives deep down in the dark waters, never knowing of the continents it is fashioning.

But the question still remains: for what purpose is it all? Science explains it to us. By ages of strife and effort we improve the race; from ether, through the monkey, man is born. So, through the labour of the coming ages, he will free himself still further from the brute. Through sorrow and through struggle, by the sweat of brain and brow, he will lift himself towards the angels. He will come into his kingdom.

But why the building? Why the passing of the countless ages? Why should he not have been born the god he is to be, imbued at birth with all the capabilities his ancestors have died acquiring? Why the Pict and Hun that *I* may be? Why *I*, that a descendant of my own, to whom I shall seem a savage, shall come after me? Why, if the universe be ordered by a Creator to whom all things are possible, the protoplasmic cell? Why not the man that is to be? Shall all the generations be so much human waste that he may live? Am I but another layer of the soil preparing for him?

Or, if our future be in other spheres, then why the need of this planet? Are we labouring at some Work too vast for us to perceive? Are our passions and desires mere whips and traces by the help of which we are driven? Any theory seems more hopeful than the thought that all our eager, fretful lives are but the turning of a useless prison crank. Looking back the little distance that our dim eyes can penetrate the past, what do we find? Civilizations, built up with infinite care, swept aside and lost. Beliefs for which men lived and died, proved to be mockeries. Greek Art crushed to the dust by Gothic bludgeons. Dreams of fraternity, drowned in blood by a Napoleon. What is left to us, but the hope that the work itself, not the result, is the real monument? Maybe, we are as children, asking, "Of what use are these lessons? What good will they ever be to us?" But there comes a day when the lad understands why he learnt grammar and geography, when even dates have a meaning for him. But this is not until he has left school, and gone out into the wider world. So, perhaps, when we are a little more grown up, we too may begin to understand the reason for our living.

ON THE CARE AND MANAGEMENT OF WOMEN

I talked to a woman once on the subject of honeymoons. I said, "Would you recommend a long honeymoon, or a Saturday to Monday somewhere?" A silence fell upon her. I gathered she was looking back rather than forward to her answer.

"I would advise a long honeymoon," she replied at length, "the old-fashioned month."

"Why," I persisted, "I thought the tendency of the age was to cut these things shorter and shorter."

"It is the tendency of the age," she answered, "to seek escape from many things it would be wiser to face. I think myself that, for good or evil, the sooner it is over—the sooner both the man and the woman know—the better."

"The sooner what is over?" I asked.

If she had a fault, this woman, about which I am not sure, it was an inclination towards enigma.

She crossed to the window and stood there, looking out.

"Was there not a custom," she said, still gazing down into the wet, glistening street, "among one of the ancient peoples, I forget which, ordaining that when a man and woman, loving one another, or thinking that they loved, had been joined together, they should go down upon their wedding night to the temple? And into the dark recesses of the temple, through many winding passages, the priest led them until they came to the great chamber where dwelt the voice of their god. There the priest left them, clanging-to the massive door behind him, and there, alone in silence, they made their sacrifice; and in the night the Voice spoke to them, showing them their future life—whether they had chosen well; whether their love would live or die. And in the morning the priest returned and led them back into the day; and they dwelt among their fellows. But no one was permitted to question them, nor they to answer should any do so. Well, do you know, our nineteenth-century honeymoon at Brighton, Switzerland, or Ramsgate, as the choice or necessity may be, always seems to me merely another form of that night spent alone in the temple before the altar of that forgotten god. Our young men and women marry, and we kiss them and congratulate them; and, standing on the doorstep, throw rice and old slippers, and shout good wishes after them; and he waves his gloved hand to us, and she flutters her little handkerchief from the carriage window; and we watch their smiling faces and hear their laughter until the corner hides them from our view. Then we go about our own business, and a short time passes by; and one day we meet them again, and their faces have grown older and graver; and I always wonder what the Voice has told them during that little while that they have been absent from our sight. But of course it would not do to ask them. Nor would they answer truly if we did."

My friend laughed, and, leaving the window, took her place beside the tea-things, and other callers dropping in, we fell to talk of pictures, plays, and people.

But I felt it would be unwise to act on her sole advice, much as I have always valued her opinion.

A woman takes life too seriously. It is a serious affair to most of us, the Lord knows. That is why it is well not to take it more seriously than need be.

Little Jack and little Jill fall down the hill, hurting their little knees, and their little noses, spilling the hard-earned water. We are very philosophical.

"Oh, don't cry!" we tell them, "that is babyish. Little boys and little girls must learn to bear pain. Up you get, fill the pail again, and try once more."

Little Jack and little Jill rub their dirty knuckles into their little eyes, looking ruefully at their bloody little knees, and trot back with the pail. We laugh at them, but not ill-naturedly.

"Poor little souls," we say; "how they did hullabaloo. One might have thought they were half-killed. And it was only a broken crown, after all. What a fuss children make!" We bear with much stoicism the fall of little Jack and little Jill.

But when WE—grown-up Jack with moustache turning grey; grown-up Jill with the first faint "crow's feet" showing—when WE tumble down the hill, and OUR pail is spilt. Ye Heavens! what a tragedy has happened. Put out the stars, turn off the sun, suspend the laws of nature. Mr. Jack and Mrs. Jill, coming down the hill—what they were doing on the hill we will not inquire—have slipped over a stone, placed there surely by the evil powers of the universe. Mr. Jack and Mrs. Jill have bumped their silly heads. Mr. Jack and Mrs. Jill have hurt their little hearts, and stand marvelling that the world can go about its business in the face of such disaster.

Don't take the matter quite so seriously, Jack and Jill. You have spilled your happiness, you must toil up the hill again and refill the pail. Carry it more carefully next time. What were you doing? Playing some fool's trick, I'll be bound.

A laugh and a sigh, a kiss and good-bye, is our life. Is it worth so much fretting? It is a merry life on the whole. Courage, comrade. A campaign cannot be all drum and fife and stirrup-cup. The marching and the fighting must come into it somewhere. There are pleasant bivouacs among the vineyards, merry nights around the camp fires. White hands wave a welcome to us; bright eyes dim at our going. Would you run from the battle-music? What have you to complain of? Forward: the medal to some, the surgeon's knife to others; to all of us, sooner or later, six feet of mother earth. What are you afraid of? Courage, comrade.

There is a mean between basking through life with the smiling contentment of the alligator, and shivering through it with the aggressive sensibility of the Lama determined to die at every cross word. To bear it as a man we must also feel it as a man. My philosophic friend, seek not to comfort a brother standing by the coffin of his child with the cheery suggestion that it will be all the same a hundred years hence, because, for one thing, the observation is not true: the man is changed for all eternity—possibly for the better, but don't add that. A soldier with a bullet in his neck is never quite the man he was. But he can laugh and he can talk, drink his wine and ride his horse. Now and again, towards evening, when the weather is trying, the sickness will come upon him. You will find him on a couch in a dark corner.

"Hallo! old fellow, anything up?"

"Oh, just a twinge, the old wound, you know. I will be better in a little while."

Shut the door of the dark room quietly. I should not stay even to sympathize with him if I were you. The men will be coming to screw the coffin down soon. I think he would like to be alone with it till then. Let us leave him. He will come back to the club later on in the season. For a while we may have to give him another ten points or so, but he will soon get back his old form. Now and again, when he meets the other fellows' boys shouting on the towing-path; when Brown rushes up the drive, paper in hand, to tell him how that young scapegrace Jim has won his Cross; when he is congratulating Jones's eldest on having passed with honours, the old wound may give him a nasty twinge. But the pain will pass away. He will laugh at our stories and tell us his own; eat his dinner, play his rubber. It is only a wound.

Tommy can never be ours, Jenny does not love us. We cannot afford claret, so we will have to drink beer. Well, what would you have us do? Yes, let us curse Fate by all means—some one to curse is always useful. Let us cry and wring our hands—for how long? The dinner-bell will ring soon, and the Smiths are coming. We shall have to talk about the opera and the picture-galleries. Quick, where is the eau-de-Cologne? where are the curling-tongs? Or would you we committed suicide? Is it worth while? Only a few more years—perhaps to-morrow, by aid of a piece of orange peel or a broken chimney-pot—and Fate will save us all that trouble.

Or shall we, as sulky children, mope day after day? We are a broken-hearted little Jack—little Jill. We will never smile again; we will pine away and die, and be buried in the spring. The world is sad, and life so cruel, and heaven so cold. Oh dear! oh dear! we have hurt ourselves.

We whimper and whine at every pain. In old strong days men faced real dangers, real troubles every hour; they had no time to cry. Death and disaster stood ever at the door. Men were contemptuous of them. Now in each snug protected villa we set to work to make wounds out of scratches. Every head-ache becomes an agony, every heart-ache a tragedy. It took a murdered father, a drowned sweetheart, a dishonoured mother, a ghost, and a slaughtered Prime Minister to produce the emotions in Hamlet that a modern minor poet obtains from a chorus girl's frown, or a temporary slump on the Stock Exchange. Like Mrs. Gummidge, we feel it more. The lighter and easier life gets the more seriously we go out to meet it. The boatmen of Ulysses faced the thunder and the sunshine alike with frolic welcome. We modern sailors have grown more sensitive. The sunshine scorches us, the rain chills us. We meet both with loud self-pity.

Thinking these thoughts, I sought a second friend—a man whose breezy common-sense has often helped me, and him likewise I questioned on this subject of honeymoons.

"My dear boy," he replied; "take my advice, if ever you get married, arrange it so that the honeymoon shall only last a week, and let it be a bustling week into the bargain. Take a Cook's circular tour. Get married on the Saturday morning, cut the breakfast and all that foolishness, and catch the eleven-ten from Charing Cross to Paris. Take her up the Eiffel Tower on Sunday. Lunch at Fontainebleau. Dine at the Maison Doree, and show her the Moulin Rouge in the evening. Take the night train for Lucerne. Devote Monday and Tuesday to doing Switzerland, and get into Rome by Thursday morning, taking the Italian lakes en route. On Friday cross to Marseilles, and from there push along to Monte Carlo. Let her have a flutter at the tables. Start early Saturday morning for Spain, cross the Pyrenees on mules, and rest at Bordeaux on Sunday. Get back to Paris on Monday (Monday is always a good day for the opera), and on Tuesday evening you will be at home, and glad to get there. Don't give her time to criticize you until she has got used to you. No man will bear unprotected exposure to a young girl's eyes. The honeymoon is the matrimonial microscope. Wobble it. Confuse it with many objects. Cloud it with other interests. Don't sit still to be examined. Besides, remember that a man always appears at his best when active, and a woman at her worst. Bustle her, my dear boy, bustle her: I don't care who she may be. Give her plenty of luggage to look after; make her catch trains. Let her see the average husband sprawling comfortably over the railway cushions, while his wife has to sit bolt upright in the corner left to her. Let her hear how other men swear. Let her smell other men's tobacco. Hurry up, and get her accustomed quickly to the sight of mankind. Then she will be less surprised and shocked as she grows to know you. One of the best fellows I ever knew spoilt his married life beyond repair by a long quiet honeymoon. They went off for a month to a lonely cottage in some heaven-forsaken spot, where never a soul came near them, and never a thing happened but morning, afternoon, and night. There for thirty days she overhauled him. When he yawned—and he yawned pretty often, I guess, during that month—she thought of the size of his mouth, and when he put his heels upon the fender she sat and brooded upon the shape of his feet. At meal-time, not feeling hungry herself, having nothing to do to make her hungry, she would occupy herself with watching him eat; and at night, not feeling sleepy for the same reason, she would lie awake and listen to his snoring. After the first day or two he grew tired of talking nonsense, and she of listening to it (it sounded nonsense now they could speak it aloud; they had fancied it poetry when they had had to whisper it); and having no other subject, as yet, of common interest, they would sit and stare in front of them in silence. One day some trifle irritated him and he swore. On a busy railway platform, or in a crowded hotel, she would have said, 'Oh!' and they would both have laughed. From that echoing desert the silly words rose up in widening circles towards the sky, and that night she cried herself to sleep. Bustle them, my dear boy, bustle them. We all like each other better the less we think about one another, and the honeymoon is an exceptionally critical time. Bustle her, my dear boy, bustle her."

My very worst honeymoon experience took place in the South of England in eighteen hundred and—well, never mind the exact date, let us say a few years ago. I was a shy young man at that time. Many complain of my reserve to this day, but then some girls expect too much from a man. We all have our shortcomings. Even then, however, I was not so shy as she. We had to travel from Lyndhurst in the New Forest to Ventnor, an awkward bit of cross-country work in those days.

"It's so fortunate you are going too," said her aunt to me on the Tuesday; "Minnie is always nervous travelling alone. You will be able to look after her, and I shan't be anxious."

I said it would be a pleasure, and at the time I honestly thought it. On the Wednesday I went down to the coach office, and booked two places for Lymington, from where we took the steamer. I had not a suspicion of trouble.

The booking-clerk was an elderly man. He said—

"I've got the box seat, and the end place on the back bench."

I said—

"Oh, can't I have two together?"

He was a kindly-looking old fellow. He winked at me. I wondered all the way home why he had winked at me. He said—

"I'll manage it somehow."

I said—

"It's very kind of you, I'm sure."

He laid his hand on my shoulder. He struck me as familiar, but well-intentioned. He said—

"We have all of us been there."

I thought he was alluding to the Isle of Wight. I said—

"And this is the best time of the year for it, so I'm told." It was early summer time.

He said—"It's all right in summer, and it's good enough in winter—WHILE IT LASTS. You make the most of it, young 'un;" and he slapped me on the back and laughed.

He would have irritated me in another minute. I paid for the seats and left him.

At half-past eight the next morning Minnie and I started for the coach-office. I call her Minnie, not with any wish to be impertinent, but because I have forgotten her surname. It must be ten years since I last saw her. She was a pretty girl, too, with those brown eyes that always cloud before they laugh. Her aunt did not drive down with us as she had intended, in consequence of a headache. She was good enough to say she felt every confidence in me.

The old booking-clerk caught sight of us when we were about a quarter of a mile away, and drew to us the attention of the coachman, who communicated the fact of our approach to the gathered passengers. Everybody left off talking, and waited for us. The boots seized his horn, and blew—one could hardly call it a blast; it would be difficult to say what he blew. He put his heart into it, but not sufficient wind. I think his intention was to welcome us, but it suggested rather a feeble curse. We learnt subsequently that he was a beginner on the instrument.

In some mysterious way the whole affair appeared to be our party. The booking-clerk bustled up and helped Minnie from the cart. I feared, for a moment, he was going to kiss her. The coachman grinned when I said good-morning to him. The passengers grinned, the boots grinned. Two chamber-maids and a waiter came out from the hotel, and they grinned. I drew Minnie aside, and whispered to her. I said—

"There's something funny about us. All these people are grinning."

She walked round me, and I walked round her, but we could neither of us discover anything amusing about the other. The booking-clerk said—

"It's all right. I've got you young people two places just behind the box-seat. We'll have to put five of you on that seat. You won't mind sitting a bit close, will you?"

The booking-clerk winked at the coachman, the coachman winked at the passengers, the passengers winked at one another—those of them who could wink—and everybody laughed. The two chamber-maids became hysterical, and had to cling to each other for support. With the exception of Minnie and myself, it seemed to be the merriest coach party ever assembled at Lyndhurst.

We had taken our places, and I was still busy trying to fathom the joke, when a stout lady appeared on the scene, and demanded to know her place.

The clerk explained to her that it was in the middle behind the driver.

"We've had to put five of you on that seat," added the clerk.

The stout lady looked at the seat.

"Five of us can't squeeze into that," she said.

Five of her certainly could not. Four ordinary sized people with her would find it tight.

"Very well then," said the clerk, "you can have the end place on the back seat."

"Nothing of the sort," said the stout lady. "I booked my seat on Monday, and you told me any of the front places were vacant.

"I'LL take the back place," I said, "I don't mind it.

"You stop where you are, young 'un," said the clerk, firmly, "and don't be a fool. I'll fix HER."

I objected to his language, but his tone was kindness itself.

"Oh, let ME have the back seat," said Minnie, rising, "I'd so like it."

For answer the coachman put both his hands on her shoulders. He was a heavy man, and she sat down again.

"Now then, mum," said the clerk, addressing the stout lady, "are you going up there in the middle, or are you coming up here at the back?"

"But why not let one of them take the back seat?" demanded the stout lady, pointing her reticule at Minnie and myself; "they say they'd like it. Let them have it."

The coachman rose, and addressed his remarks generally.

"Put her up at the back, or leave her behind," he directed. "Man and wife have never been separated on this coach since I started running it fifteen year ago, and they ain't going to be now."

A general cheer greeted this sentiment. The stout lady, now regarded as a would-be blighter of love's young dream, was hustled into the back seat, the whip cracked, and away we rolled.

So here was the explanation. We were in a honeymoon district, in June—the most popular month in the whole year for marriage. Every two out of three couples found wandering about the New Forest in June are honeymoon couples; the third are going to be. When they travel anywhere it is to the Isle of Wight. We both had on new clothes. Our bags happened to be new. By some evil chance our very umbrellas were new. Our united ages were thirty-seven. The wonder would have been had we NOT been mistaken for a young married couple.

A day of greater misery I have rarely passed. To Minnie, so her aunt informed me afterwards, the journey was the most terrible experience of her life, but then her experience, up to that time, had been limited. She was engaged, and devotedly attached, to a young clergyman; I was madly in love with a somewhat plump girl named Cecilia who lived with her mother at Hampstead. I am positive as to her living at Hampstead. I remember so distinctly my weekly walk down the hill from Church Row to the Swiss Cottage station. When walking down a steep hill all the weight of the body is forced into the toe of the boot, and when the boot is two sizes too small for you, and you have been living in it since the early afternoon, you remember a thing like that. But all my recollects of Cecilia are painful, and it is needless to pursue them.

Our coach-load was a homely party, and some of the jokes were broad— harmless enough in themselves, had Minnie and I really been the married couple we were supposed to be, but even in that case unnecessary. I can only hope that Minnie did not understand them. Anyhow, she looked as if she didn't.

I forget where we stopped for lunch, but I remember that lamb and mint sauce was on the table, and that the circumstance afforded the greatest delight to all the party, with the exception of the stout lady, who was still indignant, Minnie and myself. About my behaviour as a bridegroom opinion appeared to be divided. "He's a bit standoffish with her," I overheard one lady remark to her husband; "I like to see 'em a bit kittenish myself." A young waitress, on the other hand, I am happy to say, showed more sense of natural reserve. "Well, I respect him for it," she was saying to the barmaid, as we passed through the hall; "I'd just hate to be fuzzled over with everybody looking on." Nobody took the trouble to drop their voices for our benefit. We might have been a pair of prize love birds on exhibition, the way we were openly discussed. By the majority we were clearly regarded as a sulky young couple who would not go through their tricks.

I have often wondered since how a real married couple would have faced the situation. Possibly, had we consented to give a short display of marital affection, "by desire," we might have been left in peace for the remainder of the journey.

Our reputation preceded us on to the steamboat. Minnie begged and prayed me to let it be known we were not married. How I was to let it be known, except by requesting the captain to summon the whole ship's company on deck, and then making them a short speech, I could not think. Minnie said she could not bear it any longer, and retired to the ladies' cabin. She went off crying. Her trouble was attributed by crew and passengers to my coldness. One fool planted himself opposite me with his legs apart, and shook his head at me.

"Go down and comfort her," he began. "Take an old man's advice. Put your arms around her." (He was one of those sentimental idiots.) "Tell her that you love her."

I told him to go and hang himself, with so much vigour that he all but fell overboard. He was saved by a poultry crate: I had no luck that day.

At Ryde the guard, by superhuman effort, contrived to keep us a carriage to ourselves. I gave him a shilling, because I did not know what else to do. I would have made it half-a-sovereign if he had put eight other passengers in with us. At every station people came to the window to look in at us.

I handed Minnie over to her father on Ventnor platform; and I took the first train the next morning, to London. I felt I did not want to see her again for a little while; and I felt convinced she could do without a visit from me. Our next meeting took place the week before her marriage.

"Where are you going to spend your honeymoon?" I asked her; "in the New Forest?"

"No," she replied; "nor in the Isle of Wight."

To enjoy the humour of an incident one must be at some distance from it either in time or relationship. I remember watching an amusing scene in Whitefield Street, just off Tottenham Court Road, one winter's Saturday night. A woman—a rather respectable looking woman, had her hat only been on straight—had just been shot out of a public-house. She was very dignified, and very drunk. A policeman requested her to move on. She called him "Fellow," and demanded to know of him if he considered that was the proper tone in which to address a lady. She threatened to report him to her cousin, the Lord Chancellor.

"Yes; this way to the Lord Chancellor," retorted the policeman. "You come along with me;" and he caught hold of her by the arm.

She gave a lurch, and nearly fell. To save her the man put his arm round her waist. She clasped him round the neck, and together they spun round two or three times; while at the very moment a piano-organ at the opposite corner struck up a waltz.

"Choose your partners, gentlemen, for the next dance," shouted a wag, and the crowd roared.

I was laughing myself, for the situation was undeniably comical, the constable's expression of disgust being quite Hogarthian, when the sight of a child's face beneath the gas-lamp stayed me. Her look was so full of terror that I tried to comfort her.

"It's only a drunken woman," I said; "he's not going to hurt her."

"Please, sir," was the answer, "it's my mother."

Our joke is generally another's pain. The man who sits down on the tin-tack rarely joins in the laugh.

ON THE MINDING OF OTHER PEOPLE'S BUSINESS

I walked one bright September morning in the Strand. I love London best in the autumn. Then only can one see the gleam of its white pavements, the bold, unbroken outline of its streets. I love the cool vistas one comes across of mornings in the parks, the soft twilights that linger in the empty bye-streets. In June the restaurant manager is off-hand with me; I feel I am but in his way. In August he spreads for me the table by the window, pours out for me my wine with his own fat hands. I cannot doubt his regard for me: my foolish jealousies are stilled. Do I care for a drive after dinner through the caressing night air, I can climb the omnibus stair without a preliminary fight upon the curb, can sit with easy conscience and unsquashed body, not feeling I have deprived some hot, tired woman of a seat. Do I desire the play, no harsh, forbidding "House full" board repels me from the door. During her season, London, a harassed hostess, has no time for us, her intimates. Her rooms are overcrowded, her servants overworked, her dinners hurriedly cooked, her tone insincere. In the spring, to be truthful, the great lady condescends to be somewhat vulgar—noisy and ostentatious. Not till the guests are departed is she herself again, the London that we, her children, love.

Have you, gentle Reader, ever seen London—not the London of the waking day, coated with crawling life, as a blossom with blight, but the London of the morning, freed from her rags, the patient city, clad in mists? Get you up with the dawn one Sunday in summer time. Wake none else, but creep down stealthily into the kitchen, and make your own tea and toast.

Be careful you stumble not over the cat. She will worm herself insidiously between your legs. It is her way; she means it in friendship. Neither bark your shins against the coal-box. Why the kitchen coal-box has its fixed place in the direct line between the kitchen door and the gas-bracket I cannot say. I merely know it as an universal law; and I would that you escaped that coal-box, lest the frame of mind I desire for you on this Sabbath morning be dissipated.

A spoon to stir your tea, I fear you must dispense with. Knives and forks you will discover in plenty; blacking brushes you will put your hand upon in every drawer; of emery paper, did one require it, there are reams; but it is a point with every housekeeper that the spoons be hidden in a different place each night. If anybody excepting herself can find them in the morning, it is a slur upon her. No matter, a stick of firewood, sharpened at one end, makes an excellent substitute.

Your breakfast done, turn out the gas, remount the stairs quietly, open gently the front door and slip out. You will find yourself in an unknown land. A strange city grown round you in the night.

The sweet long streets lie silent in sunlight. Not a living thing is to be seen save some lean Tom that slinks from his gutter feast as you approach. From some tree there will sound perhaps a fretful chirp: but the London sparrow is no early riser; he is but talking in his sleep. The slow tramp of unseen policeman draws near or dies away. The clatter of your own footsteps goes with you, troubling you. You find yourself trying to walk softly, as one does in echoing cathedrals. A voice is everywhere about you whispering to you "Hush." Is this million-breasted City then some tender Artemis, seeking to keep her babes asleep? "Hush, you careless wayfarer; do not waken them. Walk lighter; they are so tired, these myriad children of mine, sleeping in my thousand arms. They are over-worked and over-worried; so many of them are sick, so many fretful, many of them, alas, so full of naughtiness. But all of them so tired. Hush! they worry me with their noise and riot when they are awake. They are so good now they are asleep. Walk lightly, let them rest."

Where the ebbing tide flows softly through worn arches to the sea, you may hear the stone-faced City talking to the restless waters: "Why will you never stay with me? Why come but to go?"

"I cannot say, I do not understand. From the deep sea I come, but only as a bird loosed from a child's hand with a cord. When she calls I must return."

"It is so with these children of mine. They come to me, I know not whence. I nurse them for a little while, till a hand I do not see plucks them back. And others take their place."

Through the still air there passes a ripple of sound. The sleeping City stirs with a faint sigh. A distant milk-cart rattling by raises a thousand echoes; it is the vanguard of a yoked army. Soon from every street there rises the soothing cry, "Mee'hilk—mee'hilk."

London like some Gargantuan babe, is awake, crying for its milk. These be the white-smocked nurses hastening with its morning nourishment. The early church bells ring. "You have had your milk, little London. Now come and say your prayers. Another week has just begun, baby London. God knows what will happen, say your prayers."

One by one the little creatures creep from behind the blinds into the streets. The brooding tenderness is vanished from the City's face. The fretful noises of the day have come again. Silence, her lover of the night, kisses her stone lips, and steals away. And you, gentle Reader, return home, garlanded with the self-sufficiency of the early riser.

But it was of a certain week-day morning, in the Strand that I was thinking. I was standing outside Gatti's Restaurant, where I had just breakfasted, listening leisurely to an argument between an indignant lady passenger, presumably of Irish extraction, and an omnibus conductor.

"For what d'ye want thin to paint Putney on ye'r bus, if ye don't GO to Putney?" said the lady.

"We DO go to Putney," said the conductor.

"Thin why did ye put me out here?"

"I didn't put you out, yer got out."

"Shure, didn't the gintleman in the corner tell me I was comin' further away from Putney ivery minit?"

"Wal, and so yer was."

"Thin whoy didn't you tell me?"

"How was I to know yer wanted to go to Putney? Yer sings out Putney, and I stops and in yer jumps."

"And for what d'ye think I called out Putney thin?"

"'Cause it's my name, or rayther the bus's name. This 'ere IS a Putney."

"How can it be a Putney whin it isn't goin' to Putney, ye gomerhawk?"

"Ain't you an Hirishwoman?" retorted the conductor. "Course yer are. But yer aren't always goin' to Ireland. We're goin' to Putney in time, only we're a-going to Liverpool Street fust. 'Igher up, Jim."

The bus moved on, and I was about cross the road, when a man, muttering savagely to himself, walked into me. He would have swept past me had I not, recognizing him, arrested him. It was my friend B———-, a busy editor of magazines and journals. It was some seconds before he appeared able to struggle out of his abstraction, and remember himself. "Halloo," he then said, "who would have thought of seeing YOU here?"

"To judge by the way you were walking," I replied, "one would imagine the Strand the last place in which you expected to see any human being. Do you ever walk into a short-tempered, muscular man?"

"Did I walk into you?" he asked surprised.

"Well, not right in," I answered, "I if we are to be literal. You walked on to me; if I had not stopped you, I suppose you would have walked over me."

"It is this confounded Christmas business," he explained. "It drives me off my head."

"I have heard Christmas advanced as an excuse for many things," I replied, "but not early in September."

"Oh, you know what I mean," he answered, "we are in the middle of our Christmas number. I am working day and night upon it. By the bye," he added, "that puts me in mind. I am arranging a symposium, and I want you to join. 'Should Christmas,'"—I interrupted him.

"My dear fellow," I said, "I commenced my journalistic career when I was eighteen, and I have continued it at intervals ever since. I have written about Christmas from the sentimental point of view; I have analyzed it from the philosophical point of view; and I have scarified it from the sarcastic standpoint. I have treated Christmas humorously for the Comics, and sympathetically for the Provincial Weeklies. I have said all that is worth saying on the subject of Christmas—maybe a trifle more. I have told the new-fashioned Christmas story—you know the sort of thing: your heroine tries to understand herself, and, failing, runs off with the man who began as the hero; your good woman turns out to be really bad when one comes to know her; while the villain, the only decent person in the story, dies with an enigmatic sentence on his lips that looks as if it meant something, but which you yourself would be sorry to have to explain. I have also written the old-fashioned Christmas story—you know that also: you begin with a good old-fashioned snowstorm; you have a good old-fashioned squire, and he lives in a good old-fashioned Hall; you work in a good old-fashioned murder; and end up with a good old-fashioned Christmas dinner. I have gathered Christmas guests together round the crackling logs to tell ghost stories to each other on Christmas Eve, while without the wind howled, as it always does on these occasions, at its proper cue. I have sent children to Heaven on Christmas Eve—it must be quite a busy time for St. Peter, Christmas morning, so many good children die on Christmas Eve. It has always been a popular night with them.—I have revivified dead lovers and brought them back well and jolly, just in time to sit down to the Christmas dinner. I am not ashamed of having done these things. At the time I thought them good. I once loved currant wine and girls with towzley hair. One's views change as one grows older. I have discussed Christmas as a religious festival. I have arraigned it as a social incubus. If there be any joke connected with Christmas that I have not already made I should be glad to hear it. I have trotted out the indigestion jokes till the sight of one of them gives me indigestion myself. I have ridiculed the family gathering. I have scoffed at the Christmas present. I have made witty use of paterfamilias and his bills. I have—"

"Did I ever show you," I broke off to ask as we were crossing the Haymarket, "that little parody of mine on Poe's poem of 'The Bells'? It begins—" He interrupted me in his turn—

"Bills, bills, bills," he repeated.

"You are quite right," I admitted. "I forgot I ever showed it to you."

"You never did," he replied.

"Then how do you know how it begins?" I asked.

"I don't know for certain," he admitted, "but I get, on an average, sixty-five a year submitted to me, and they all begin that way. I thought, perhaps, yours did also."

"I don't see how else it could begin," I retorted. He had rather annoyed me. "Besides, it doesn't matter how a poem begins, it is how it goes on that is the important thing and anyhow, I'm not going to write you anything about Christmas. Ask me to make you a new joke about a plumber; suggest my inventing something original and not too shocking for a child to say about heaven; propose my running you off a dog story that can be believed by a man of average determination and we may come to terms. But on the subject of Christmas I am taking a rest."

By this time we had reached Piccadilly Circus.

"I don't blame you," he said, "if you are as sick of the subject as I am. So soon as these Christmas numbers are off my mind, and Christmas is over till next June at the office, I shall begin it at home. The housekeeping is gone up a pound a week already. I know what that means. The dear little woman is saving up to give me an expensive present that I don't want. I think the presents are the worst part of Christmas. Emma will give me a water-colour that she has painted herself. She always does. There would be no harm in that if she did not expect me to hang it in the drawing room. Have you ever seen my cousin Emma's water-colours?" he asked.

"I think I have," I replied.

"There's no thinking about it," he retorted angrily. "They're not the sort of water-colours you forget."

He apostrophized the Circus generally.

"Why do people do these things?" he demanded. "Even an amateur artist must have SOME sense. Can't they see what is happening? There's that thing of hers hanging in the passage. I put it in the passage because there's not much light in the passage. She's labelled it Reverie. If she had called it Influenza I could have understood it. I asked her where she got the idea from, and she said she saw the sky like that one evening in Norfolk. Great Heavens! then why didn't she shut her eyes or go home and hide behind the bed-curtains? If I had seen a sky like that in Norfolk I should have taken the first train back to London. I suppose the poor girl can't help seeing these things, but why paint them?"

I said, "I suppose painting is a necessity to some natures."

"But why give the things to me?" he pleaded.

I could offer him no adequate reason.

"The idiotic presents that people give you!" he continued. "I said I'd like Tennyson's poems one year. They had worried me to know what I did want. I didn't want anything really; that was the only thing I could think of that I wasn't dead sure I didn't want. Well, they clubbed together, four of them, and gave me Tennyson in twelve volumes, illustrated with coloured photographs. They meant kindly, of course. If you suggest a tobacco-pouch they give you a blue velvet bag capable of holding about a pound, embroidered with flowers, life-size. The only way one could use it would be to put a strap to it and wear it as a satchel. Would you believe it, I have got a velvet smoking-jacket, ornamented with forget-me-nots and butterflies in coloured silk; I'm not joking. And they ask me why I never wear it. I'll bring it down to the Club one of these nights and wake the place up a bit: it needs it."

We had arrived by this at the steps of the 'Devonshire.'

"And I'm just as bad," he went on, "when I give presents. I never give them what they want. I never hit upon anything that is of any use to anybody. If I give Jane a chinchilla tippet, you may be certain chinchilla is the most out-of-date fur that any woman could wear. 'Oh! that is nice of you,' she says; 'now that is just the very thing I wanted. I will keep it by me till chinchilla comes in again.' I give the girls watch-chains when nobody is wearing watch-chains. When watch-chains are all the rage I give them ear-rings, and they thank me, and suggest my taking them to a fancy-dress ball, that being their only chance to wear the confounded things. I waste money on white gloves with black backs, to find that white gloves with black backs stamp a woman as suburban. I believe all the shop-keepers in London save their old stock to palm it off on me at Christmas time. And why does it always take half-a-dozen people to serve you with a pair of gloves, I'd like to know? Only last week Jane asked me to get her some gloves for that last Mansion House affair. I was feeling amiable, and I thought I would do the thing handsomely. I hate going into a draper's shop; everybody stares at a man as if he were forcing his way into the ladies' department of a Turkish bath. One of those marionette sort of men came up to me and said it was a fine morning. What the devil did I want to talk about the morning to him for? I said I wanted some gloves. I described them to the best of my recollection. I said, 'I want them four buttons, but they are not to be button-gloves; the buttons are in the middle and they reach up to the elbow, if you know what I mean.' He bowed, and said he understood exactly what I meant, which was a damned sight more than I did. I told him I wanted three pair cream and three pair fawn-coloured, and the fawn-coloured were to be swedes. He corrected me. He said I meant 'Suede.' I dare say he was right, but the interruption put me off, and I had to begin over again. He listened attentively until I had finished. I guess I was about five minutes standing with him there close to the door. He said, 'Is that all you require, sir, this morning?' I said it was.

"' Thank you, sir,' he replied. 'This way, please, sir.'

"He took me into another room, and there we met a man named Jansen, to whom he briefly introduced me as a gentleman who 'desired gloves.' 'Yes, sir,' said Mr. Jansen; and what sort of gloves do you desire?'

"I told him I wanted six pairs altogether—three suede, fawn-coloured, and three cream-coloured—kids.

"He said, 'Do you mean kid gloves, sir, or gloves for children?'

"He made me angry by that. I told him I was not in the habit of using slang. Nor am I when buying gloves. He said he was sorry. I explained to him about the buttons, so far as I could understand it myself, and about the length. I asked him to see to it that the buttons were sewn on firmly, and that the stitching everywhere was perfect, adding that the last gloves my wife had had of his firm had been most unsatisfactory. Jane had impressed upon me to add that. She said it would make them more careful.

"He listened to me in rapt ecstacy. I might have been music.

"'And what size, sir?' he asked.

"I had forgotten that. 'Oh, sixes,' I answered, 'unless they are very stretchy indeed, in which case they had better be five and three-quarter.'

"'Oh, and the stitching on the cream is to be black,' I added. That was another thing I had forgotten.

"'Thank you very much,' said Mr. Jansen; 'is there anything else that you require this morning?'

"'No, thank you,' I replied, 'not this morning.' I was beginning to like the man.

"He took me for quite a walk, and wherever we went everybody left off what they were doing to stare at me. I was getting tired when we reached the glove department. He marched me up to a young man who was sticking pins into himself. He said 'Gloves,' and disappeared through a curtain. The young man left off sticking pins into himself, and leant across the counter.

"'Ladies' gloves or gentlemen's gloves?' he said.

"Well, I was pretty mad by this time, as you can guess. It is funny when you come to think of it afterwards, but the wonder then was that I didn't punch his head.

"I said, 'Are you ever busy in this shop? Does there ever come a time when you feel you would like to get your work done, instead of lingering over it and spinning it out for pure love of the thing?'

"He did not appear to understand me. I said, 'I met a man at your door a quarter of an hour ago, and we talked about these gloves that I want, and I told him all my ideas on the subject. He took me to your Mr. Jansen, and Mr. Jansen and I went over the whole business again. Now Mr. Jansen leaves it with you—you who do not even know whether I want ladies' or gentlemen's gloves. Before I go over this story for the third time, I want to know whether you are the man who is going to serve me, or whether you are merely a listener, because personally I am tired of the subject?'

"Well, this was the right man at last, and I got my gloves from him. But what is the explanation—what is the idea? I was in that shop from first to last five-and-thirty minutes. And then a fool took me out the wrong way to show me a special line in sleeping-socks. I told him I was not requiring any. He said he didn't want me to buy, he only wanted me to see them. No wonder the drapers have had to start luncheon and tea-rooms. They'll fix up small furnished flats soon, where a woman can live for a week."

I said it was very trying, shopping. I also said, as he invited me, and as he appeared determined to go on talking, that I would have a brandy-and-soda. We were in the smoke-room by this time.

"There ought to be an association," he continued, "a kind of clearing-house for the collection and distribution of Christmas presents. One would give them a list of the people from whom to collect presents, and of the people to whom to send. Suppose they collected on my account twenty Christmas presents, value, say, ten pounds, while on the other hand they sent out for me thirty presents at a cost of fifteen pounds. They would debit me with the balance of five pounds, together with a small commission. I should pay it cheerfully, and there would be no further trouble. Perhaps one might even make a profit. The idea might include birthdays and weddings. A firm would do the business thoroughly. They would see that all your friends paid up—I mean sent presents; and they would not forget to send to your most important relative. There is only one member of our family capable of leaving a shilling; and of course if I forget to send to any one it is to him. When I remember him I generally make a muddle of the business. Two years ago I gave him a bath—I don't mean I washed him—an india-rubber thing, that he could pack in his portmanteau. I thought he would find it useful for travelling. Would you believe it, he took it as a personal affront, and wouldn't speak to me for a month, the snuffy old idiot."

"I suppose the children enjoy it," I said.

"Enjoy what?" he asked.

"Why, Christmas," I explained.

"I don't believe they do," he snapped; "nobody enjoys it. We excite them for three weeks beforehand, telling them what a good time they are going to have, over-feed them for two or three days, take them to something they do not want to see, but which we do, and then bully them for a fortnight to get them back into their normal condition. I was always taken to the Crystal Palace and Madame Tussaud's when I was a child, I remember. How I did hate that Crystal Palace! Aunt used to superintend. It was always a bitterly cold day, and we always got into the wrong train, and travelled half the day before we got there. We never had any dinner. It never occurs to a woman that anybody can want their meals while away from home. She seems to think that nature is in suspense from the time you leave the house till the time you get back to it. A bun and a glass of milk was her idea of lunch for a school-boy. Half her time was taken up in losing us, and the other half in slapping us when she had found us. The only thing we really enjoyed was the row with the cabman coming home."

I rose to go.

"Then you won't join that symposium?" said B———. "It would be an easy enough thing to knock off—'Why Christmas should be abolished.'"

"It sounds simple," I answered. "But how do you propose to abolish it?" The lady editor of an "advanced" American magazine once set the discussion—"Should sex be abolished?" and eleven ladies and gentlemen seriously argued the question.

"Leave it to die of inanition," said B———; "the first step is to arouse public opinion. Convince the public that it should be abolished."

"But why should it be abolished?" I asked.

"Great Scott! man," he exclaimed; "don't you want it abolished?"

"I'm not sure that I do," I replied.

"Not sure," he retorted; "you call yourself a journalist, and admit there is a subject under Heaven of which you are not sure!"

"It has come over me of late years," I replied. "It used not to be my failing, as you know."

He glanced round to make sure we were out of earshot, then sunk his voice to a whisper.

"Between ourselves," he said, "I'm not so sure of everything myself as I used to be. Why is it?"

"Perhaps we are getting older," I suggested.

He said—"I started golf last year, and the first time I took the club in my hand I sent the ball a furlong. 'It seems an easy game,' I said to the man who was teaching me. 'Yes, most people find it easy at the beginning,' he replied dryly. He was an old golfer himself; I thought he was jealous. I stuck well to the game, and for about three weeks I was immensely pleased with myself. Then, gradually, I began to find out the difficulties. I feel I shall never make a good player. Have you ever gone through that experience?"

"Yes," I replied; "I suppose that is the explanation. The game seems so easy at the beginning."

I left him to his lunch, and strolled westward, musing on the time when I should have answered that question of his about Christmas, or any other question, off-hand. That good youth time when I knew everything, when life presented no problems, dangled no doubts before me!

In those days, wishful to give the world the benefit of my wisdom, and seeking for a candle-stick wherefrom my brilliancy might be visible and helpful unto men, I arrived before a dingy portal in Chequers Street, St. Luke's, behind which a con-clave of young men, together with a few old enough to have known better, met every Friday evening for the purpose of discussing and arranging the affairs of the universe. "Speaking members" were charged ten-and-sixpence per annum, which must have worked out at an extremely moderate rate per word; and "gentlemen whose subscriptions were more than three months in arrear," became, by Rule seven, powerless for good or evil. We called ourselves "The Stormy Petrels," and, under the sympathetic shadow of those wings, I laboured two seasons towards the reformation of the human race; until, indeed, our treasurer, an earnest young man, and a tireless foe of all that was conventional, departed for the East, leaving be-hind him a balance sheet, showing that the club owed forty-two pounds fifteen and fourpence, and that the subscriptions for the current year, amounting to a little over thirty-eight pounds, had been "carried forward," but as to where, the report afforded no indication. Whereupon our landlord, a man utterly without ideals, seized our furniture, offering to sell it back to us for fifteen pounds. We pointed out to him that this was an extravagant price, and tendered him five.

The negotiations terminated with ungentlemanly language on his part, and "The Stormy Petrels" scattered, never to be foregathered together again above the troubled waters of humanity. Now-a-days, listening to the feeble plans of modern reformers, I cannot help but smile, remembering what was done in Chequers Street, St. Luke's, in an age when Mrs. Grundy still gave the law to literature, while yet the British matron was the guide to British art. I am informed that there is abroad the question of abolishing the House of Lords! Why, "The Stormy Pet-rels" abolished the aristocracy and the Crown in one evening, and then only adjourned for the purpose of appointing a committee to draw up and have ready a Republican Constitution by the following Friday evening. They talk of Empire lounges! We closed the doors of every music-hall in London eighteen years ago by twenty-nine votes to seventeen. They had a patient hearing, and were ably de-fended; but we found that the tendency of such amusements was anti-progressive, and against the best interests of an intellectually advancing democracy. I met the mover of the condemnatory resolution at the old "Pav" the following evening, and we continued the discussion over a bottle of Bass. He strengthened his argument by persuading me to sit out the whole of the three songs sung by the "Lion Comique"; but I subsequently retorted successfully, by bringing under his notice the dancing of a lady in blue tights and flaxen hair. I forget her name but never shall I cease to remember her exquisite charm and beauty. Ah, me! how charming and how beautiful "artistes" were in those golden days! Whence have they vanished? Ladies in blue tights and flaxen hair dance before my eyes to-day, but move me not, unless it be towards boredom. Where be the tripping witches of twenty years ago, whom to see once was to dream of for a week, to touch whose white hand would have been joy, to kiss whose red lips would have been to foretaste Heaven. I heard only the other day that the son of an old friend of mine had secretly married a lady from the front row of the ballet, and involuntarily I exclaimed, "Poor devil!" There was a time when my first thought would have been, "Lucky beggar! is he worthy of her?" For then the ladies of the ballet were angels. How could one gaze at them—from the shilling pit—and doubt it? They danced to keep a widowed mother in comfort, or to send a younger brother to school. Then they were glorious creatures a young man did well to worship; but now-a-days—

It is an old jest. The eyes of youth see through rose-tinted glasses. The eyes of age are dim behind smoke-clouded spectacles. My flaxen friend, you are not the angel I dreamed you, nor the exceptional sinner some would paint you; but under your feathers, just a woman—a bundle of follies and failings, tied up with some sweetness and strength. You keep a brougham I am sure you cannot afford on your thirty shillings a week. There are ladies I know, in Mayfair, who have paid an extravagant price for theirs. You paint and you dye, I am told: it is even hinted you pad. Don't we all of us deck ourselves out in virtues that are not our own? When the paint and the powder, my sister, is stripped both from you and from me, we shall know which of us is entitled to look down on the other in scorn.

Forgive me, gentle Reader, for digressing. The lady led me astray. I was speaking of "The Stormy Petrels," and of the reforms they accomplished, which were many. We abolished, I remember, capital punishment and war; we were excellent young men at heart. Christmas we reformed altogether, along with Bank Holidays, by a majority of twelve. I never recollect any proposal to abolish anything ever being lost when put to the vote. There were few things that we "Stormy Petrels" did not abolish. We attacked Christmas on grounds of expediency, and killed it by ridicule. We exposed the hollow mockery of Christmas sentiment; we abused the indigestible Christmas dinner, the tiresome Christmas party, the silly Christmas pantomime. Our funny member was side-splitting on the subject of Christmas Waits; our social reformer bitter upon Christmas drunkenness; our economist indignant upon Christmas charities. Only one argument of any weight with us was advanced in favour of the festival, and that was our leading cynic's suggestion that it was worth enduring the miseries of Christmas, to enjoy the soul-satisfying comfort of the after reflection that it was all over, and could not occur again for another year.

But since those days when I was prepared to put this old world of ours to rights upon all matters, I have seen many sights and heard many sounds, and I am not quite so sure as I once was that my particular views are the only possibly correct ones. Christmas seems to me somewhat meaningless; but I have looked through windows in poverty-stricken streets, and have seen dingy parlours gay with many chains of coloured paper. They stretched from corner to corner of the smoke-grimed ceiling, they fell in clumsy festoons from the cheap gasalier, they framed the fly-blown mirror and the tawdry pictures; and I know tired hands and eyes worked many hours to fashion and fix those foolish chains, saying, "It will please him—she will like to see the room look pretty;" and as I have looked at them they have grown, in some mysterious manner, beautiful to me. The gaudy-coloured child and dog irritates me, I confess; but I have watched a grimy, inartistic personage, smoothing it affectionately with toil-stained hand, while eager faces crowded round to admire and wonder at its blatant crudity. It hangs to this day in its cheap frame above the chimney-piece, the one bright spot relieving those damp-stained walls; dull eyes stare and stare again at it, catching a vista, through its flashy tints, of the far-off land of art. Christmas Waits annoy me, and I yearn to throw open the window and fling coal at them—as once from the window of a high flat in Chelsea I did. I doubted their being genuine Waits. I was inclined to the opinion they were young men seeking excuse for making a noise. One of them appeared to know a hymn with a chorus, another played the concertina, while a third accompanied with a step dance. Instinctively I felt no respect for them; they disturbed me in my work, and the desire grew upon me to injure them. It occurred to me it would be good sport if I turned out the light, softly opened the window, and threw coal at them. It would be impossible for them to tell from which window in the block the coal came, and thus subsequent unpleasantness would be avoided. They were a compact little group, and with average luck I was bound to hit one of them.

I adopted the plan. I could not see them very clearly. I aimed rather at the noise; and I had thrown about twenty choice lumps without effect, and was feeling somewhat discouraged, when a yell, followed by language singularly inappropriate to the season, told me that Providence had aided my arm. The music ceased suddenly, and the party dispersed, apparently in high glee—which struck me as curious.

One man I noticed remained behind. He stood under the lamp-post, and shook his fist at the block generally.

"Who threw that lump of coal?" he demanded in stentorian tones.

To my horror, it was the voice of the man at Eighty-eight, an Irish gentleman, a journalist like myself. I saw it all, as the unfortunate hero always exclaims, too late, in the play. He—number Eighty-eight—also disturbed by the noise, had evidently gone out to expostulate with the rioters. Of course my lump of coal had hit him—him the innocent, the peaceful (up till then), the virtuous. That is the justice Fate deals out to us mortals here below. There were ten to fourteen young men in that crowd, each one of whom fully deserved that lump of coal; he, the one guiltless, got it—seemingly, so far as the dim light from the gas lamp enabled me to judge, full in the eye.

As the block remained silent in answer to his demand, he crossed the road and mounted the stairs. On each landing he stopped and shouted—

"Who threw that lump of coal? I want the man who threw that lump of coal. Out you come."

Now a good man in my place would have waited till number Eighty-eight arrived on his landing, and then, throwing open the door would have said with manly candour—

"*I* threw that lump of coal. I was-," He would not have got further, because at that point, I feel confident, number Eighty—eight would have punched his head. There would have been an unseemly fracas on the staircase, to the annoyance of all the other tenants and later, there would have issued a summons and a cross-summons. Angry passions would have been roused, bitter feeling engendered which might have lasted for years.

I do not pretend to be a good man. I doubt if the pretence would be of any use were I to try: I am not a sufficiently good actor. I said to myself, as I took off my boots in the study, preparatory to retiring to my bedroom—"Number Eighty-eight is evidently not in a frame of mind to listen to my story. It will be better to let him shout himself cool; after which he will return to his own flat, bathe his eye, and obtain some refreshing sleep. In the morning, when we shall probably meet as usual on our way to Fleet Street, I will refer to the incident casually, and sympathize with him. I will suggest to him the truth—that in all probability some fellow-tenant, irritated also by the noise, had aimed coal at the Waits, hitting him instead by a regrettable but pure accident. With tact I may even be able to make him see the humour of the incident. Later on, in March or April, choosing my moment with judgment, I will, perhaps, confess that I was that fellow-tenant, and over a friendly brandy-and-soda we will laugh the whole trouble away."

As a matter of fact, that is what happened. Said number Eighty-eight—he was a big man, as good a fellow at heart as ever lived, but impulsive—"Damned lucky for you, old man, you did not tell me at the time."

"I felt," I replied, "instinctively that it was a case for delay."

There are times when one should control one's passion for candour; and as I was saying, Christmas waits excite no emotion in my breast save that of irritation. But I have known "Hark, the herald angels sing," wheezily chanted by fog-filled throats, and accompanied, hopelessly out of tune, by a cornet and a flute, bring a great look of gladness to a work-worn face. To her it was a message of hope and love, making the hard life taste sweet. The mere thought of family gatherings, so customary at Christmas time, bores us superior people; but I think of an incident told me by a certain man, a friend of mine. One Christmas, my friend, visiting in the country, came face to face with a woman whom in town he had often met amid very different surroundings. The door of the little farmhouse was open; she and an older woman were ironing at a table, and as her soft white hands passed to and fro, folding and smoothing the rumpled heap, she laughed and talked, concerning simple homely things. My friend's shadow fell across her work, and she looking up, their eyes met; but her face said plainly, "I do not know you here, and here you do not know me. Here I am a woman loved and respected." My friend passed in and spoke to the older woman, the wife of one of his host's tenants, and she turned towards, and introduced the younger—"My daughter, sir. We do not see her very often. She is in a place in London, and cannot get away. But she always spends a few days with us at Christmas."

"It is the season for family re-unions," answered my friend with just the suggestion of a sneer, for which he hated himself.

"Yes, sir," said the woman, not noticing; "she has never missed her Christmas with us, have you, Bess?"

"No, mother," replied the girl simply, and bent her head again over her work.

So for these few days every year this woman left her furs and jewels, her fine clothes and dainty foods, behind her, and lived for a little space with what was clean and wholesome. It was the one anchor holding her to womanhood; and one likes to think that it was, perhaps, in the end strong enough to save her from the drifting waters. All which arguments in favour of Christmas and of Christmas customs are, I admit, purely sentimental ones, but I have lived long enough to doubt whether sentiment has not its legitimate place in the economy of life.

ON THE TIME WASTED IN LOOKING BEFORE ONE LEAPS

Have you ever noticed the going out of a woman?

When a man goes out, he says—"I'm going out, shan't be long."

"Oh, George," cries his wife from the other end of the house, "don't go for a moment. I want you to—" She hears a falling of hats, followed by the slamming of the front door.

"Oh, George, you're not gone!" she wails. It is but the voice of despair. As a matter of fact, she knows he is gone. She reaches the hall, breathless.

"He might have waited a minute," she mutters to herself, as she picks up the hats, "there were so many things I wanted him to do."

She does not open the door and attempt to stop him, she knows he is already half-way down the street. It is a mean, paltry way of going out, she thinks; so like a man.

When a woman, on the other hand, goes out, people know about it. She does not sneak out. She says she is going out. She says it, generally, on the afternoon of the day before; and she repeats it, at intervals, until tea-time. At tea, she suddenly decides that she won't, that she will leave it till the day after to-morrow instead. An hour later she thinks she will go to-morrow, after all, and makes arrangements to wash her hair overnight. For the next hour or so she alternates between fits of exaltation, during which she looks forward to going out, and moments of despondency, when a sense of foreboding falls upon her. At dinner she persuades some other woman to go with her; the other woman, once persuaded, is enthusiastic about going, until she recollects that she cannot. The first woman, however, convinces her that she can.

"Yes," replies the second woman, "but then, how about you, dear? You are forgetting the Joneses."

"So I was," answers the first woman, completely non-plussed. "How very awkward, and I can't go on Wednesday. I shall have to leave it till Thursday, now."

"But *I* can't go Thursday," says the second woman.

"Well, you go without me, dear," says the first woman, in the tone of one who is sacrificing a life's ambition.

"Oh no, dear, I should not think of it," nobly exclaims the second woman. "We will wait and go together, Friday!"

"I'll tell you what we'll do," says the first woman. "We will start early" (this is an inspiration), "and be back before the Joneses arrive."

They agree to sleep together; there is a lurking suspicion in both their minds that this may be their last sleep on earth. They retire early with a can of hot water. At intervals, during the night, one overhears them splashing water, and talking.

They come down very late for breakfast, and both very cross. Each seems to have argued herself into the belief that she has been lured into this piece of nonsense, against her better judgment, by the persistent folly of the other one. During the meal each one asks the other, every five minutes, if she is quite ready. Each one, it appears, has only her hat to put on. They talk about the weather, and wonder what it is going to do. They wish it would make up its mind, one way or the other. They are very bitter on weather that cannot make up its mind. After breakfast it still looks cloudy, and they decide to abandon the scheme altogether. The first woman then remembers that it is absolutely necessary for her, at all events, to go.

"But there is no need for you to come, dear," she says.

Up to that point the second woman was evidently not sure whether she wished to go or whether she didn't. Now she knows.

"Oh yes, I'll come," she says, "then it will be over!"

"I am sure you don't want to go," urges the first woman, "and I shall be quicker by myself. I am ready to start now."

The second woman bridles.

"*I* shan't be a couple of minutes," she retorts. "You know, dear, it's generally I who have to wait for you."

"But you've not got your boots on," the first woman reminds her.

"Well, they won't take ANY time," is the answer. "But of course, dear, if you'd really rather I did not come, say so." By this time she is on the verge of tears.

"Of course, I would like you to come, dear," explains the first in a resigned tone. "I thought perhaps you were only coming to please me."

"Oh no, I'd LIKE to come," says the second woman.

"Well, we must hurry up," says the first; "I shan't be more than a minute myself, I've merely got to change my skirt."

Half-an-hour later you hear them calling to each other, from different parts of the house, to know if the other one is ready. It appears they have both been ready for quite a long while, waiting only for the other one.

"I'm afraid," calls out the one whose turn it is to be down-stairs, "it's going to rain."

"Oh, don't say that," calls back the other one.

"Well, it looks very like it."

"What a nuisance," answers the up-stairs woman; "shall we put it off?"

"Well, what do YOU think, dear?" replies the down-stairs.

They decide they will go, only now they will have to change their boots, and put on different hats.

For the next ten minutes they are still shouting and running about. Then it seems as if they really were ready, nothing remaining but for them to say "Good-bye," and go.

They begin by kissing the children. A woman never leaves her house without secret misgivings that she will never return to it alive. One child cannot be found. When it is found it wishes it hadn't been. It has to be washed, preparatory to being kissed. After that, the dog has to be found and kissed, and final instructions given to the cook.

Then they open the front door.

"Oh, George," calls out the first woman, turning round again. "Are you there?"

"Hullo," answers a voice from the distance. "Do you want me?"

"No, dear, only to say good-bye. I'm going."

"Oh, good-bye."

"Good-bye, dear. Do you think it's going to rain?"

"Oh no, I should not say so."

"George."

"Yes."

"Have you got any money?"

Five minutes later they come running back; the one has forgotten her parasol, the other her purse.

And speaking of purses, reminds one of another essential difference between the male and female human animal. A man carries his money in his pocket. When he wants to use it, he takes it out and lays it down. This is a crude way of doing things, a woman displays more subtlety. Say she is standing in the street, and wants fourpence to pay for a bunch of violets she has purchased from a flower-girl. She has two parcels in one hand, and a parasol in the other. With the remaining two fingers of the left hand she secures the violets. The question then arises, how to pay the girl? She flutters for a few minutes, evidently not quite understanding why it is she cannot do it. The reason then occurs to her: she has only two hands and both these are occupied. First she thinks she will put the parcels and the flowers into her right hand, then she thinks she will put the parasol into her left. Then she looks round for a table or even a chair, but there is not such a thing in the whole street. Her difficulty is solved by her dropping the parcels and the flowers. The girl picks them up for her and holds them. This enables her to feel for her pocket with her right hand, while waving her open parasol about with her left. She knocks an old gentleman's hat off into the gutter, and nearly blinds the flower-girl before it occurs to her to close it. This done, she leans it up against the flower-girl's basket, and sets to work in earnest with both hands. She seizes herself firmly by the back, and turns the upper part of her body round till her hair is in front and her eyes behind. Still holding herself firmly with her left hand—did she let herself go, goodness knows where she would spin to;—with her right she prospects herself. The purse is there, she can feel it, the problem is how to get at it. The quickest way would, of course, be to take off the skirt, sit down on the kerb, turn it inside out, and work from the bottom of the pocket upwards. But this simple idea never seems to occur to her. There are some thirty folds at the back of the dress, between two of these folds commences the secret passage. At last, purely by chance, she suddenly discovers it, nearly upsetting herself in the process, and the purse is brought up to the surface. The difficulty of opening it still remains. She knows it opens with a spring, but the secret of that spring she has never mastered, and she never will. Her plan is to worry it generally until it does open. Five minutes will always do it, provided she is not flustered.

At last it does open. It would be incorrect to say that she opens it. It opens because it is sick of being mauled about; and, as likely as not, it opens at the moment when she is holding it upside down. If you happen to be near enough to look over her shoulder, you will notice that the gold and silver lies loose within it. In an inner sanctuary, carefully secured with a second secret spring, she keeps her coppers, together with a postage-stamp and a draper's receipt, nine months old, for elevenpence three-farthings.

I remember the indignation of an old Bus-conductor, once. Inside we were nine women and two men. I sat next the door, and his remarks therefore he addressed to me. It was certainly taking him some time to collect the fares, but I think he would have got on better had he been less bustling; he worried them, and made them nervous.

"Look at that," he said, drawing my attention to a poor lady opposite, who was diving in the customary manner for her purse, "they sit on their money, women do. Blest if you wouldn't think they was trying to 'atch it."

At length the lady drew from underneath herself an exceedingly fat purse.

"Fancy riding in a bumpby bus, perched up on that thing," he continued. "Think what a stamina they must have." He grew confidential. "I've seen one woman," he said, "pull out from underneath 'er a street doorkey, a tin box of lozengers, a pencil-case, a whopping big purse, a packet of hair-pins, and a smelling-bottle. Why, you or me would be wretched, sitting on a plain door-knob, and them women goes about like that all day. I suppose they gets used to it. Drop 'em on an eider-down pillow, and they'd scream. The time it takes me to get tuppence out of them, why, it's 'eart-breaking. First they tries one side, then they tries the other. Then they gets up and shakes theirselves till the bus jerks them back again, and there they are, a more 'opeless 'eap than ever. If I 'ad my way I'd make every bus carry a female searcher as could over'aul 'em one at a time, and take the money from 'em. Talk about the poor pickpocket. What I say is, that a man as finds his way into a woman's pocket—well, he deserves what he gets."

But it was the thought of more serious matters that lured me into reflections concerning the over-carefulness of women. It is a theory of mine—wrong possibly; indeed I have so been informed—that we pick our way through life with too much care. We are for ever looking down upon the ground. Maybe, we do avoid a stumble or two over a stone or a brier, but also we miss the blue of the sky, the glory of the hills. These books that good men write, telling us that what they call "success" in life depends on our flinging aside our youth and wasting our manhood in order that we may have the means when we are eighty of spending a rollicking old age, annoy me. We save all our lives to invest in a South Sea Bubble; and in skimping and scheming, we have grown mean, and narrow, and hard. We will put off the gathering of the roses till tomorrow, to-day it shall be all work, all bargain-driving, all plotting. Lo, when to-morrow comes, the roses are blown; nor do we care for roses, idle things of small marketable value; cabbages are more to our fancy by the time to-morrow comes.

Life is a thing to be lived, not spent, to be faced, not ordered. Life is not a game of chess, the victory to the most knowing; it is a game of cards, one's hand by skill to be made the best of. Is it the wisest who is always the most successful? I think not. The luckiest whist-player I ever came across was a man who was never QUITE certain what were trumps, and whose most frequent observation during the game was "I really beg your pardon," addressed to his partner; a remark which generally elicited the reply, "Oh, don't apologize. All's well that ends well." The man I knew who made the most rapid fortune was a builder in the outskirts of Birmingham, who could not write his name, and who, for thirty years of his life, never went to bed sober. I do not say that forgetfulness of trumps should be cultivated by whist-players. I think my builder friend might have been even more successful had he learned to write his name, and had he occasionally—not overdoing it—enjoyed a sober evening. All I wish to impress is, that virtue is not the road to success—of the kind we are dealing with. We must find other reasons for being virtuous; maybe, there are some. The truth is, life is a gamble pure and simple, and the rules we lay down for success are akin to the infallible systems with which a certain class of idiot goes armed each season to Monte Carlo. We can play the game with coolness and judgment, decide when to plunge and when to stake small; but to think that wisdom will decide it, is to imagine that we have discovered the law of chance. Let us play the game of life as sportsmen, pocketing our winnings with a smile, leaving our losings with a shrug. Perhaps that is why we have been summoned to the board and the cards dealt round: that we may learn some of the virtues of the good gambler; his self-control, his courage under misfortune, his modesty under the strain of success, his firmness, his alertness, his general indifference to fate. Good lessons these, all of them. If by the game we learn some of them our time on the green earth has not been wasted. If we rise from the table having learned only fretfulness and self-pity I fear it has been.

The grim Hall Porter taps at the door: "Number Five hundred billion and twenty-eight, your boatman is waiting, sir."

So! is it time already? We pick up our counters. Of what use are they? In the country the other side of the river they are no tender. The blood-red for gold, and the pale-green for love, to whom shall we fling them? Here is some poor beggar longing to play, let us give them to him as we pass out. Poor devil! the game will amuse him—for a while.

Keep your powder dry, and trust in Providence, is the motto of the wise. Wet powder could never be of any possible use to you. Dry, it may be, WITH the help of Providence. We will call it Providence, it is a prettier name than Chance—perhaps also a truer.

Another mistake we make when we reason out our lives is this: we reason as though we were planning for reasonable creatures. It is a big mistake. Well-meaning ladies and gentlemen make it when they picture their ideal worlds. When marriage is reformed, and the social problem solved, when poverty and war have been abolished by acclamation, and sin and sorrow rescinded by an overwhelming parliamentary majority! Ah, then the world will be worthy of our living in it. You need not wait, ladies and gentlemen, so long as you think for that time. No social revolution is needed, no slow education of the people is necessary. It would all come about to-morrow, IF ONLY WE WERE REASONABLE CREATURES.

Imagine a world of reasonable beings! The Ten Commandments would be unnecessary: no reasoning being sins, no reasoning creature makes mistakes. There would be no rich men, for what reasonable man cares for luxury and ostentation? There would be no poor: that I should eat enough for two while my brother in the next street, as good a man as I, starves, is not reasonable. There would be no difference of opinion on any two points: there is only one reason. You, dear Reader, would find, that on all subjects you were of the same opinion as I. No novels would be written, no plays performed; the lives of reasonable creatures do not afford drama. No mad loves, no mad laughter, no scalding tears, no fierce unreasoning, brief-lived joys, no sorrows, no wild dreams—only reason, reason everywhere.

But for the present we remain unreasonable. If I eat this mayonnaise, drink this champagne, I shall suffer in my liver. Then, why do I eat it? Julia is a charming girl, amiable, wise, and witty; also she has a share in a brewery. Then, why does John marry Ann? who is short-tempered, to say the least of it, who, he feels, will not make him so good a house-wife, who has extravagant notions, who has no little fortune. There is something about Ann's chin that fascinates him—he could not explain to you what. On the whole, Julia is the better-looking of the two. But the more he thinks of Julia, the more he is drawn towards Ann. So Tom marries Julia and the brewery fails, and Julia, on a holiday, contracts rheumatic fever, and is a helpless invalid for life; while Ann comes in for ten thousand pounds left to her by an Australian uncle no one had ever heard of.

I have been told of a young man, who chose his wife with excellent care. Said he to himself, very wisely, "In the selection of a wife a man cannot be too circumspect." He convinced himself that the girl was everything a helpmate should be. She had every virtue that could be expected in a woman, no faults, but such as are inseparable from a woman. Speaking practically, she was perfection. He married her, and found she was all he had thought her. Only one thing could he urge against her—that he did not like her. And that, of course, was not her fault.

How easy life would be did we know ourselves. Could we always be sure that tomorrow we should think as we do today. We fall in love during a summer holiday; she is fresh, delightful, altogether charming; the blood rushes to our head every time we think of her. Our ideal career is one of perpetual service at her feet.

It seems impossible that Fate could bestow upon us any greater happiness than the privilege of cleaning her boots, and kissing the hem of her garment—if the hem be a little muddy that will please us the more. We tell her our ambition, and at that moment every word we utter is sincere. But the summer holiday passes, and with it the holiday mood, and winter finds us wondering how we are going to get out of the difficulty into which we have landed ourselves. Or worse still, perhaps, the mood lasts longer than is usual. We become formally engaged. We marry—I wonder how many marriages are the result of a passion that is burnt out before the altar-rails are reached?—and three months afterwards the little lass is broken-hearted to find that we consider the lacing of her boots a bore. Her feet seem to have grown bigger. There is no excuse for us, save that we are silly children, never sure of what we are crying for, hurting one another in our play, crying very loudly when hurt ourselves.

I knew an American lady once who used to bore me with long accounts of the brutalities exercised upon her by her husband. She had instituted divorce proceedings against him. The trial came on, and she was highly successful. We all congratulated her, and then for some months she dropped out of my life. But there came a day when we again found ourselves together. One of the problems of social life is to know what to say to one another when we meet; every man and woman's desire is to appear sympathetic and clever, and this makes conversation difficult, because, taking us all round, we are neither sympathetic nor clever—but this by the way.

Of course, I began to talk to her about her former husband. I asked her how he was getting on. She replied that she thought he was very comfortable.

"Married again?" I suggested.

"Yes," she answered.

"Serve him right," I exclaimed, "and his wife too." She was a pretty, bright-eyed little woman, my American friend, and I wished to ingratiate myself. "A woman who would marry such a man, knowing what she must have known of him, is sure to make him wretched, and we may trust him to be a curse to her."

My friend seemed inclined to defend him.

"I think he is greatly improved," she argued.

"Nonsense!" I returned, "a man never improves. Once a villain, always a villain."

"Oh, hush!" she pleaded, "you mustn't call him that."

"Why not?" I answered. "I have heard you call him a villain yourself."

"It was wrong of me," she said, flushing. "I'm afraid he was not the only one to be blamed; we were both foolish in those days, but I think we have both learned a lesson."

I remained silent, waiting for the necessary explanation.

"You had better come and see him for yourself," she added, with a little laugh; "to tell the truth, I am the woman who has married him. Tuesday is my day, Number 2, K—— Mansions," and she ran off, leaving me staring after her.

I believe an enterprising clergyman who would set up a little church in the Strand, just outside the Law Courts, might do quite a trade, re-marrying couples who had just been divorced. A friend of mine, a respondent, told me he had never loved his wife more than on two occasions—the first when she refused him, the second when she came into the witness-box to give evidence against him.

"You are curious creatures, you men," remarked a lady once to another man in my presence. "You never seem to know your own mind."

She was feeling annoyed with men generally. I do not blame her, I feel annoyed with them myself sometimes. There is one man in particular I am always feeling intensely irritated against. He says one thing, and acts another. He will talk like a saint and behave like a fool, knows what is right and does what is wrong. But we will not speak further of him. He will be all he should be one day, and then we will pack him into a nice, comfortably-lined box, and screw the lid down tight upon him, and put him away in a quiet little spot near a church I know of, lest he should get up and misbehave himself again.

The other man, who is a wise man as men go, looked at his fair critic with a smile.

"My dear madam," he replied, "you are blaming the wrong person. I confess I do not know my mind, and what little I do know of it I do not like. I did not make it, I did not select it. I am more dissatisfied with it than you can possibly be. It is a greater mystery to me than it is to you, and I have to live with it. You should pity not blame me."

There are moods in which I fall to envying those old hermits who frankly, and with courageous cowardice, shirked the problem of life. There are days when I dream of an existence unfettered by the thousand petty strings with which our souls lie bound to Lilliputia land. I picture myself living in some Norwegian sater, high above the black waters of a rockbound fiord. No other human creature disputes with me my kingdom. I am alone with the whispering fir forests and the stars. How I live I am not quite sure. Once a month I could journey down into the villages and return laden. I should not need much. For the rest, my gun and fishing-rod would supply me. I would have with me a couple of big dogs, who would talk to me with their eyes, so full of dumb thought, and together we would wander over the uplands, seeking our dinner, after the old primitive fashion of the men who dreamt not of ten-course dinners and Savoy suppers. I would cook the food myself, and sit down to the meal with a bottle of good wine, such as starts a man's thoughts (for I am inconsistent, as I acknowledge, and that gift of civilization I would bear with me into my hermitage). Then in the evening, with pipe in mouth, beside my log-wood fire, I would sit and think, until new knowledge came to me. Strengthened by those silent voices that are drowned in the roar of Streetland, I might, perhaps, grow into something nearer to what it was intended that a man should be—might catch a glimpse, perhaps, of the meaning of life.

No, no, my dear lady, into this life of renunciation I would not take a companion, certainly not of the sex you are thinking of, even would she care to come, which I doubt. There are times when a man is better without the woman, when a woman is better without the man. Love drags us from the depths, makes men and women of us, but if we would climb a little nearer to the stars we must say good-bye to it. We men and women do not show ourselves to each other at our best; too often, I fear, at our worst. The woman's highest ideal of man is the lover; to a man the woman is always the possible beloved. We see each other's hearts, but not each other's souls. In each other's presence we never shake ourselves free from the earth. Match-making mother Nature is always at hand to prompt us. A woman lifts us up into manhood, but there she would have us stay. "Climb up to me," she cries to the lad, walking with soiled feet in muddy ways; "be a true man that you may be worthy to walk by my side; be brave to protect me, kind and tender, and true; but climb no higher, stay here by my side." The martyr, the prophet, the leader of the world's forlorn hopes, she would wake from his dream. Her arms she would fling about his neck holding him down.

To the woman the man says, "You are my wife. Here is your America, within these walls, here is your work, your duty." True, in nine hundred and ninety-nine cases out of every thousand, but men and women are not made in moulds, and the world's work is various. Sometimes to her sorrow, a woman's work lies beyond the home. The duty of Mary was not to Joseph.

The hero in the popular novel is the young man who says, "I love you better than my soul." Our favourite heroine in fiction is the woman who cries to her lover, "I would go down into Hell to be with you." There are men and women who cannot answer thus—the men who dream dreams, the women who see visions—impracticable people from the Bayswater point of view. But Bayswater would not be the abode of peace it is had it not been for such.

Have we not placed sexual love on a pedestal higher than it deserves? It is a noble passion, but it is not the noblest. There is a wider love by the side of which it is but as the lamp illumining the cottage, to the moonlight bathing the hills and valleys. There were two women once. This is a play I saw acted in the daylight. They had been friends from girlhood, till there came between them the usual trouble—a man. A weak, pretty creature not worth a thought from either of them; but women love the unworthy; there would be no over-population problem did they not; and this poor specimen, ill-luck had ordained they should contend for.

Their rivalry brought out all that was worst in both of them. It is a mistake to suppose love only elevates; it can debase. It was a mean struggle for what to an onlooker must have appeared a remarkably unsatisfying prize. The loser might well have left the conqueror to her poor triumph, even granting it had been gained unfairly. But the old, ugly, primeval passions had been stirred in these women, and the wedding-bells closed only the first act.

The second is not difficult to guess. It would have ended in the Divorce Court had not the deserted wife felt that a finer revenge would be secured to her by silence.

In the third, after an interval of only eighteen months, the man died—the first piece of good fortune that seems to have occurred to him personally throughout the play. His position must have been an exceedingly anxious one from the beginning. Notwithstanding his flabbiness, one cannot but regard him with a certain amount of pity—not unmixed with amusement. Most of life's dramas can be viewed as either farce or tragedy according to the whim of the spectator. The actors invariably play them as tragedy; but then that is the essence of good farce acting.

Thus was secured the triumph of legal virtue and the punishment of irregularity, and the play might be dismissed as uninterestingly orthodox were it not for the fourth act, showing how the wronged wife came to the woman she had once wronged to ask and grant forgiveness. Strangely as it may sound, they found their love for one another unchanged. They had been long parted: it was sweet to hold each other's hands again. Two lonely women, they agreed to live together. Those who knew them well in this later time say that their life was very beautiful, filled with graciousness and nobility.

I do not say that such a story could ever be common, but it is more probable than the world might credit. Sometimes the man is better without the woman, the woman without the man.

ON THE NOBILITY OF OURSELVES

AN old Anglicized Frenchman, I used to meet often in my earlier journalistic days, held a theory, concerning man's future state, that has since come to afford me more food for reflection than, at the time, I should have deemed possible. He was a bright-eyed, eager little man. One felt no Lotus land could be Paradise to him. We build our heaven of the stones of our desires: to the old, red-bearded Norseman, a foe to fight and a cup to drain; to the artistic Greek, a grove of animated statuary; to the Red Indian, his happy hunting ground; to the Turk, his harem; to the Jew, his New Jerusalem, paved with gold; to others, according to their taste, limited by the range of their imagination.

Few things had more terrors for me, when a child, than Heaven—as pictured for me by certain of the good folks round about me. I was told that if I were a good lad, kept my hair tidy, and did not tease the cat, I would probably, when I died, go to a place where all day long I would sit still and sing hymns. (Think of it! as reward to a healthy boy for being good.) There would be no breakfast and no dinner, no tea and no supper. One old lady cheered me a little with a hint that the monotony might be broken by a little manna; but the idea of everlasting manna palled upon me, and my suggestions, concerning the possibilities of sherbet or jumbles, were scouted as irreverent. There would be no school, but also there would be no cricket and no rounders. I should feel no desire, so I was assured, to do another angel's "dags" by sliding down the heavenly banisters. My only joy would be to sing.

"Shall we start singing the moment we get up in the morning?" I asked.

"There won't be any morning," was the answer. "There will be no day and no night. It will all be one long day without end."

"And shall we always be singing?" I persisted.

"Yes, you will be so happy, you will always want to sing."

"Shan't I ever get tired?"

"No, you will never get tired, and you will never get sleepy or hungry or thirsty."

"And does it go on like that for ever?"

"Yes, for ever and ever."

"Will it go on for a million years?"

"Yes, a million years, and then another million years, and then another million years after that. There will never be any end to it."

I can remember to this day the agony of those nights, when I would lie awake, thinking of this endless heaven, from which there seemed to be no possible escape. For the other place was equally eternal, or I might have been tempted to seek refuge there.

We grown-up folk, our brains dulled by the slowly acquired habit of not thinking, do wrong to torture children with these awful themes. Eternity, Heaven, Hell are meaningless words to us. We repeat them, as we gabble our prayers, telling our smug, self-satisfied selves that we are miserable sinners. But to the child, the "intelligent stranger" in the land, seeking to know, they are fearful realities. If you doubt me, Reader, stand by yourself, beneath the stars, one night, and SOLVE this thought, Eternity. Your next address shall be the County Lunatic Asylum.

My actively inclined French friend held cheerier views than are common of man's life beyond the grave. His belief was that we were destined to constant change, to everlasting work. We were to pass through the older planets, to labour in the greater suns.

But for such advanced career a more capable being was needed. No one of us was sufficient, he argued, to be granted a future existence all to himself. His idea was that two or three or four of us, according to our intrinsic value, would be combined to make a new and more important individuality, fitted for a higher existence. Man, he pointed out, was already a collection of the beasts. "You and I," he would say, tapping first my chest and then his own, "we have them all here—the ape, the tiger, the pig, the motherly hen, the gamecock, the good ant; we are all, rolled into one. So the man of the future, he will be made up of many men—the courage of one, the wisdom of another, the kindliness of a third."

"Take a City man," he would continue, "say the Lord Mayor; add to him a poet, say Swinburne; mix them with a religious enthusiast, say General Booth. There you will have the man fit for the higher life."

Garibaldi and Bismarck, he held, should make a very fine mixture, correcting one another; if needful, extract of Ibsen might be added, as seasoning. He thought that Irish politicians would mix admirably with Scotch divines; that Oxford Dons would go well with lady novelists. He was convinced that Count Tolstoi, a few Gaiety Johnnies (we called them "mashers" in those days), together with a humourist—he was kind enough to suggest myself—would produce something very choice. Queen Elizabeth, he fancied, was probably being reserved to go—let us hope in the long distant future—with Ouida. It sounds a whimsical theory, set down here in my words, not his; but the old fellow was so much in earnest that few of us ever thought to laugh as he talked. Indeed, there were moments on starry nights, as walking home from the office, we would pause on Waterloo Bridge to enjoy the witchery of the long line of the Embankment lights, when I could almost believe, as I listened to him, in the not impossibility of his dreams.

Even as regards this world, it would often be a gain, one thinks, and no loss, if some half-dozen of us were rolled together, or boiled down, or whatever the process necessary might be, and something made out of us in that way.

Have not you, my fair Reader, sometimes thought to yourself what a delightful husband Tom this, plus Harry that, plus Dick the other, would make? Tom is always so cheerful and good-tempered, yet you feel that in the serious moments of life he would be lacking. A delightful hubby when you felt merry, yes; but you would not go to him for comfort and strength in your troubles, now would you? No, in your hour of sorrow, how good it would be to have near you grave, earnest Harry. He is a "good sort," Harry. Perhaps, after all, he is the best of the three—solid, staunch, and true. What a pity he is just a trifle commonplace and unambitious. Your friends, not knowing his sterling hidden qualities, would hardly envy you; and a husband that no other girl envies you—well, that would hardly be satisfactory, would it? Dick, on the other hand, is clever and brilliant. He will make his way; there will come a day, you are convinced, when a woman will be proud to bear his name. If only he were not so self-centred, if only he were more sympathetic.

But a combination of the three, or rather of the best qualities of the three—Tom's good temper, Harry's tender strength, Dick's brilliant masterfulness: that is the man who would be worthy of you.

The woman David Copperfield wanted was Agnes and Dora rolled into one. He had to take them one after the other, which was not so nice. And did he really love Agnes, Mr. Dickens; or merely feel he ought to? Forgive me, but I am doubtful concerning that second marriage of Copperfield's. Come, strictly between ourselves, Mr. Dickens, was not David, good human soul! now and again a wee bit bored by the immaculate Agnes? She made him an excellent wife, I am sure. SHE never ordered oysters by the barrel, unopened. It would, on any day, have been safe to ask Traddles home to dinner; in fact, Sophie and the whole rose-garden might have accompanied him, Agnes would have been equal to the occasion. The dinner would have been perfectly cooked and served, and Agnes' sweet smile would have pervaded the meal. But AFTER the dinner, when David and Traddles sat smoking alone, while from the drawing-room drifted down the notes of high-class, elevating music, played by the saintly Agnes, did they never, glancing covertly towards the empty chair between them, see the laughing, curl-framed face of a very foolish little woman—one of those foolish little women that a wise man thanks God for making—and wish, in spite of all, that it were flesh and blood, not shadow?

Oh, you foolish wise folk, who would remodel human nature! Cannot you see how great is the work given unto childish hands? Think you that in well-ordered housekeeping and high-class conversation lies the whole making of a man? Foolish Dora, fashioned by clever old magician Nature, who knows that weakness and helplessness are as a talisman calling forth strength and tenderness in man, trouble yourself not unduly about those oysters nor the underdone mutton, little woman. Good plain cooks at twenty pounds a year will see to these things for us; and, now and then, when a windfall comes our way, we will dine together at a moderate-priced restaurant where these things are managed even better. Your work, Dear, is to teach us gentleness and kindliness. Lay your curls here, child. It is from such as you that we learn wisdom. Foolish wise folk sneer at you; foolish wise folk would pull up the useless lilies, the needless roses, from the garden, would plant in their places only serviceable wholesome cabbage. But the Gardener knowing better, plants the silly short-lived flowers; foolish wise folk, asking for what purpose.

As for Agnes, Mr. Dickens, do you know what she always makes me think of? You will not mind my saying?—the woman one reads about. Frankly, I don't believe in her. I do not refer to Agnes in particular, but the woman of whom she is a type, the faultless woman we read of. Women have many faults, but, thank God, they have one redeeming virtue—they are none of them faultless.

But the heroine of fiction! oh, a terrible dragon of virtue is she. May heaven preserve us poor men, undeserving though we be, from a life with the heroine of fiction. She is all soul, and heart, and intellect, with never a bit of human nature to catch hold of her by. Her beauty, it appals one, it is so painfully indescribable. Whence comes she, whither goes she, why do we never meet her like? Of women I know a goodish few, and I look among them for her prototype; but I find it not. They are charming, they are beautiful, all these women that I know. It would not be right for me to tell you, Ladies, the esteem and veneration with which I regard you all. You yourselves, blushing, would be the first to cheek my ardour. But yet, dear Ladies, seen even through my eyes, you come not near the ladies that I read about. You are not—if I may be permitted an expressive vulgarism—in the same street with them. Your beauty I can look upon, and retain my reason—for whatever value that may be to me. Your conversation, I admit, is clever and brilliant in the extreme; your knowledge vast and various; your culture quite Bostonian; yet you do not—I hardly know how to express it—you do not shine with the sixteen full-moon-power of the heroine of fiction. You do not—and I thank you for it—impress me with the idea that you are the only women on earth. You, even you, possess tempers of your own. I am inclined to think you take an interest in your clothes. I would not be sure, even, that you do not mingle a little of "your own hair" (you know what I mean) with the hair of your head. There is in your temperament a vein of vanity, a suggestion of selfishness, a spice of laziness. I have known you a trifle unreasonable, a little inconsiderate, slightly exacting. Unlike the heroine of fiction, you have a certain number of human appetites and instincts; a few human follies, perhaps, a human fault, or shall we say two? In short, dear Ladies, you also, even as we men, are the children of Adam and Eve. Tell me, if you know, where I may meet with this supernatural sister of yours, this woman that one reads about. She never keeps any one waiting while she does her back hair, she is never indignant with everybody else in the house because she cannot find her own boots, she never scolds the servants, she is never cross with the children, she never slams the door, she is never jealous of her younger sister, she never lingers at the gate with any cousin but the right one.

Dear me, where DO they keep them, these women that one reads about? I suppose where they keep the pretty girl of Art. You have seen her, have you not, Reader, the pretty girl in the picture? She leaps the six-barred gate with a yard and a half to spare, turning round in her saddle the while to make some smiling remark to the comic man behind, who, of course, is standing on his head in the ditch. She floats gracefully off Dieppe on stormy mornings. Her baigneuse—generally of chiffon and old point lace—has not lost a curve. The older ladies, bathing round her, look wet. Their dress clings damply to their limbs. But the pretty girl of Art dives, and never a curl of her hair is disarranged. The pretty girl of Art stands lightly on tip-toe and volleys a tennis-ball six feet above her head. The pretty girl of Art keeps the head of the punt straight against a stiff current and a strong wind. SHE never gets the water up her sleeve, and down her back, and all over the cushions. HER pole never sticks in the mud, with the steam launch ten yards off and the man looking the other way. The pretty girl of Art skates in high-heeled French shoes at an angle of forty-five to the surface of the ice, both hands in her muff. SHE never sits down plump, with her feet a yard apart, and says "Ough." The pretty girl of Art drives tandem down Piccadilly, during the height of the season, at eighteen miles an hour. It never occurs to HER leader that the time has now arrived for him to turn round and get into the cart. The pretty girl of Art rides her bicycle through the town on market day, carrying a basket of eggs, and smiling right and left. SHE never throws away both her handles and runs into a cow. The pretty girl of Art goes trout fishing in open-work stockings, under a blazing sun, with a bunch of dew-bespangled primroses in her hair; and every time she gracefully flicks her rod she hauls out a salmon. SHE never ties herself up to a tree, or hooks the dog. SHE never comes home, soaked and disagreeable, to tell you that she caught six, but put them all back again, because they were merely two or three-pounders, and not worth the trouble of carrying. The pretty girl of Art plays croquet with one hand, and looks as if she enjoyed the game. SHE never tries to accidentally kick her ball into position when nobody is noticing, or stands it out that she is through a hoop that she knows she isn't.

She is a good, all-round sportswoman, is the pretty girl in the picture. The only thing I have to say against her is that she makes one dissatisfied with the girl out of the picture—the girl who mistakes a punt for a teetotum, so that you land feeling as if you had had a day in the Bay of Biscay; and who, every now and again, stuns you with the thick end of the pole: the girl who does not skate with her hands in her muff; but who, throwing them up to heaven, says, "I'm going," and who goes, taking care that you go with her: the girl who, as you brush her down, and try to comfort her, explains to you indignantly that the horse took the corner too sharply and never noticed the mile-stone; the girl whose hair sea water does NOT improve.

There can be no doubt about it: that is where they keep the good woman of Fiction, where they keep the pretty girl of Art.

Does it not occur to you, Messieurs les Auteurs, that you are sadly disturbing us? These women that are a combination of Venus, St. Cecilia, and Elizabeth Fry!

you paint them for us in your glowing pages: it is not kind of you, knowing, as you must, the women we have to put up with.

Would we not be happier, we men and women, were we to idealize one another less? My dear young lady, you have nothing whatever to complain to Fate about, I assure you. Unclasp those pretty hands of yours, and come away from the darkening window. Jack is as good a fellow as you deserve; don't yearn so much. Sir Galahad, my dear—Sir Galahad rides and fights in the land that lies beyond the sunset, far enough away from this noisy little earth where you and I spend much of our time tittle-tattling, flirting, wearing fine clothes, and going to shows. And besides, you must remember, Sir Galahad was a bachelor: as an idealist he was wise. Your Jack is by no means a bad sort of knight, as knights go nowadays in this un-idyllic world. There is much solid honesty about him, and he does not pose. He is not exceptional, I grant you; but, my dear, have you ever tried the exceptional man? Yes, he is very nice in a drawing-room, and it is interesting to read about him in the Society papers: you will find most of his good qualities there: take my advice, don't look into him too closely. You be content with Jack, and thank heaven he is no worse. We are not saints, we men—none of us, and our beautiful thoughts, I fear, we write in poetry not action. The White Knight, my dear young lady, with his pure soul, his heroic heart, his life's devotion to a noble endeavour, does not live down here to any great extent. They have tried it, one or two of them, and the world—you and I: the world is made up of you and I—has generally starved, and hooted them. There are not many of them left now: do you think you would care to be the wife of one, supposing one were to be found for you? Would you care to live with him in two furnished rooms in Clerkenwell, die with him on a chair bedstead? A century hence they will put up a statue to him, and you may be honoured as the wife who shared with him his sufferings. Do you think you are woman enough for that? If not, thank your stars you have secured, for your own exclusive use, one of us UNexceptional men, who knows no better than to admire you. YOU are not exceptional.

And in us ordinary men there is some good. It wants finding, that is all. We are not so commonplace as you think us. Even your Jack, fond of his dinner, his conversation four-cornered by the Sporting Press—yes, I agree he is not interesting, as he sits snoring in the easy-chair; but, believe it or not, there are the makings of a great hero in Jack, if Fate would but be kinder to him, and shake him out of his ease.

Dr. Jekyll contained beneath his ample waist-coat not two egos, but three—not only Hyde but another, a greater than Jekyll—a man as near to the angels as Hyde was to the demons. These well-fed City men, these Gaiety Johnnies, these plough-boys, apothecaries, thieves! within each one lies hidden the hero, did Fate, the sculptor, choose to use his chisel. That little drab we have noticed now and then, our way taking us often past the end of the court, there was nothing by which to distinguish her. She was not over-clean, could use coarse language on occasion— just the spawn of the streets: take care lest the cloak of our child should brush her.

One morning the district Coroner, not, generally speaking, a poet himself, but an adept at discovering poetry buried under unlikely rubbish-heaps, tells us more about her. She earned six shillings a week, and upon it supported a bed-ridden mother and three younger children. She was housewife, nurse, mother, breadwinner, rolled into one. Yes, there are heroines OUT of fiction.

So loutish Tom has won the Victoria Cross—dashed out under a storm of bullets and rescued the riddled flag. Who would have thought it of loutish Tom? The village alehouse one always deemed the goal of his endeavours. Chance comes to Tom and we find him out. To Harry the Fates were less kind. A ne'er-do-well was Harry—drank, knocked his wife about, they say. Bury him, we are well rid of him, he was good for nothing. Are we sure?

Let us acknowledge we are sinners. We know, those of us who dare to examine ourselves, that we are capable of every meanness, of every wrong under the sun. It is by the accident of circumstance, aided by the helpful watchfulness of the policeman, that our possibilities of crime are known only to ourselves. But having acknowledged our evil, let us also acknowledge that we are capable of greatness. The martyrs who faced death and torture unflinchingly for conscience' sake, were men and women like ourselves. They had their wrong side. Before the small trials of daily life they no doubt fell as we fall. By no means were they the pick of humanity. Thieves many of them had been, and murderers, evil-livers, and evil-doers. But the nobility was there also, lying dormant, and their day came. Among them must have been men who had cheated their neighbours over the counter; men who had been cruel to their wives and children; selfish, scandal-mongering women. In easier times their virtue might never have been known to any but their Maker.

In every age and in every period, when and where Fate has called upon men and women to play the man, human nature has not been found wanting. They were a poor lot, those French aristocrats that the Terror seized: cowardly, selfish, greedy had been their lives. Yet there must have been good, even in them. When the little things that in their little lives they had thought so great were swept away from them, when they found themselves face to face with the realities; then even they played the man. Poor shuffling Charles the First, crusted over with weakness and folly, deep down in him at last we find the great gentleman.

I like to hear stories of the littleness of great men. I like to think that Shakespeare was fond of his glass. I even cling to the tale of that disgraceful final orgie with friend Ben Jonson. Possibly the story may not be true, but I hope it was. I like to think of him as poacher, as village ne'er-do-well, denounced by the local grammar-school master, preached at by the local J. P. of the period. I like to reflect that Cromwell had a wart on his nose; the thought makes me more contented with my own features. I like to think that he put sweets upon the chairs, to see finely-dressed ladies spoil their frocks; to tell myself that he roared with laughter at the silly jest, like any East End 'Arry with his Bank Holiday squirt of dirty water. I like to read that Carlyle threw bacon at his wife and occasionally made himself highly ridiculous over small annoyances, that would have been smiled at by a man of well-balanced mind. I think of the fifty foolish things a week *I* do, and say to myself, "I, too, am a literary man."

I like to think that even Judas had his moments of nobility, his good hours when he would willingly have laid down his life for his Master. Perhaps even to him there came, before the journey's end, the memory of a voice saying—"Thy sins be forgiven thee." There must have been good, even in Judas.

Virtue lies like the gold in quartz, there is not very much of it, and much pains has to be spent on the extracting of it. But Nature seems to think it worth her while to fashion these huge useless stones, if in them she may hide away her precious metals. Perhaps, also, in human nature, she cares little for the mass of dross, provided that by crushing and cleansing she can extract from it a little gold, sufficient to repay her for the labour of the world. We wonder why she troubles to make the stone. Why cannot the gold lie in nuggets on the surface? But her methods are secrets to us. Perchance there is a reason for the quartz. Perchance there is a reason for the evil and folly, through which run, unseen to the careless eye, the tiny veins of virtue.

Aye, the stone predominates, but the gold is there. We claim to have it valued. The evil that there is in man no tongue can tell. We are vile among the vile, a little evil people. But we are great. Pile up the bricks of our sins till the tower knocks at Heaven's gate, calling for vengeance, yet we are great—with a greatness and a virtue that the untempted angels may not reach to. The written history of the human race, it is one long record of cruelty, of falsehood, of oppression. Think you the world would be spinning round the sun unto this day, if that written record were all? Sodom, God would have spared had there been found ten righteous men within its walls. The world is saved by its just men. History sees them not; she is but the newspaper, a report of accidents. Judge you life by that? Then you shall believe that the true Temple of Hymen is the Divorce Court; that men are of two classes only, the thief and the policeman; that all noble thought is but a politician's catchword. History sees only the destroying conflagrations, she takes no thought of the sweet fire-sides. History notes the wrong; but the patient suffering, the heroic endeavour, that, slowly and silently, as the soft processes of Nature reclothing with verdure the passion-wasted land, obliterate that wrong, she has no eyes for. In the days of cruelty and oppression—not altogether yet of the past, one fears—must have lived gentle-hearted men and women, healing with their help and sympathy the wounds that else the world had died of. After the thief, riding with jingle of sword and spur, comes, mounted on his ass, the good Samaritan. The pyramid of the world's evil—God help us! it rises high, shutting out almost the sun. But the record of man's good deeds, it lies written in the laughter of the children, in the light of lovers' eyes, in the dreams of the young men; it shall not be forgotten. The fires of persecution served as torches to show Heaven the heroism that was in man. From the soil of tyranny sprang self-sacrifice, and daring for the Right. Cruelty! what is it but the vile manure, making the ground ready for the flowers of tenderness and pity? Hate and Anger shriek to one another across the ages, but the voices of Love and Comfort are none the less existent that they speak in whispers, lips to ear.

We have done wrong, oh, ye witnessing Heavens, but we have done good. We claim justice. We have laid down our lives for our friends: greater love hath no man than this. We have fought for the Right. We have died for the Truth—as the Truth seemed to us. We have done noble deeds; we have lived noble lives; we have comforted the sorrowful; we have succoured the weak. Failing, falling, making in our blindness many a false step, yet we have striven. For the sake of the army of just men and true, for the sake of the myriads of patient, loving women, for the sake of the pitiful and helpful, for the sake of the good that lies hidden within us,—spare us, O Lord.

ON THE MOTHERLINESS OF MAN

It was only a piece of broken glass. From its shape and colour, I should say it had, in its happier days, formed portion of a cheap scent-bottle. Lying isolated on the grass, shone upon by the early morning sun, it certainly appeared at its best. It attracted him.

He cocked his head, and looked at it with his right eye. Then he hopped round to the other side, and looked at it with his left eye. With either optic it seemed equally desirable.

That he was an inexperienced young rook goes without saying. An older bird would not have given a second glance to the thing. Indeed, one would have thought his own instinct might have told him that broken glass would be a mistake in a bird's nest. But its glitter drew him too strongly for resistance. I am inclined to suspect that at some time, during the growth of his family tree, there must have occurred a mesalliance, perhaps worse. Possibly a strain of magpie blood?—one knows the character of magpies, or rather their lack of character— and such things have happened. But I will not pursue further so painful a train: I throw out the suggestion as a possible explanation, that is all.

He hopped nearer. Was it a sweet illusion, this flashing fragment of rainbow; a beautiful vision to fade upon approach, typical of so much that is understandable in rook life? He made a dart forward and tapped it with his beak. No, it was real—as fine a lump of jagged green glass as any newly-married rook could desire, and to be had for the taking. SHE would be pleased with it. He was a well-meaning bird; the mere upward inclination of his tail suggested earnest though possibly ill-directed endeavour.

He turned it over. It was an awkward thing to carry; it had so very many corners. But he succeeded at last in getting it firmly between his beak, and in haste, lest some other bird should seek to dispute with him its possession, at once flew off with it.

A second rook who had been watching the proceedings from the lime tree, called to a third who was passing. Even with my limited knowledge of the language I found it easy to follow the conversation: it was so obvious.

"Issachar!"

"Hallo!"

"What do you think? Zebulan's found a piece of broken bottle. He's going to line his nest with it."

"No!"

"God's truth. Look at him. There he goes, he's got it in his beak."

"Well, I'm ——!"

And they both burst into a laugh.

But Zebulan heeded them not. If he overheard, he probably put down the whole dialogue to jealousy. He made straight for his tree. By standing with my left cheek pressed close against the window-pane, I was able to follow him. He is building in what we call the Paddock elms—a suburb commenced only last season, but rapidly growing. I wanted to see what his wife would say.

At first she said nothing. He laid it carefully down on the branch near the half-finished nest, and she stretched up her head and looked at it.

Then she looked at him. For about a minute neither spoke. I could see that the situation was becoming strained. When she did open her beak, it was with a subdued tone, that had a vein of weariness running through it.

"What is it?" she asked.

He was evidently chilled by her manner. As I have explained, he is an inexperienced young rook. This is clearly his first wife, and he stands somewhat in awe of her.

"Well, I don't exactly know what it's CALLED," he answered.

"Oh."

"No. But it's pretty, isn't it?" he added. He moved it, trying to get it where the sun might reach it. It was evident he was admitting to himself that, seen in the shade, it lost much of its charm.

"Oh, yes; very pretty," was the rejoinder; "perhaps you'll tell me what you're going to do with it."

The question further discomforted him. It was growing upon him that this thing was not going to be the success he had anticipated. It would be necessary to proceed warily.

"Of course, it's not a twig," he began.

"I see it isn't."

"No. You see, the nest is nearly all twigs as it is, and I thought—"

"Oh, you did think."

"Yes, my dear. I thought—unless you are of opinion that it's too showy—I thought we might work it in somewhere."

Then she flared out.

"Oh, did you? You thought that a good idea. An A1 prize idiot I seem to have married, I do. You've been gone twenty minutes, and you bring me back an eight-cornered piece of broken glass, which you think we might 'work into' the nest. You'd like to see me sitting on it for a month, you would. You think it would make a nice bed for the children to lie on. You don't think you could manage to find a packet of mixed pins if you went down again, I suppose. They'd look pretty 'worked in' somewhere, don't you think?—Here, get out of my way. I'll finish this nest by myself." She always had been short with him.

She caught up the offending object—it was a fairly heavy lump of glass—and flung it out of the tree with all her force. I heard it crash through the cucumber frame. That makes the seventh pane of glass broken in that cucumber frame this week. The couple in the branch above are the worst. Their plan of building is the most extravagant, the most absurd I ever heard of. They hoist up ten times as much material as they can possibly use; you might think they were going to build a block, and let it out in flats to the other rooks. Then what they don't want they fling down again. Suppose we built on such a principle? Suppose a human husband and wife were to start erecting their house in Piccadilly Circus, let us say; and suppose the man spent all the day steadily carrying bricks up the ladder while his wife laid them, never asking her how many she wanted, whether she didn't think he had brought up sufficient, but just accumulating bricks in a senseless fashion, bringing up every brick he could find. And then suppose, when evening came, and looking round, they found they had some twenty cart-loads of bricks lying unused upon the scaffold, they were to commence flinging them down into Waterloo Place. They would get themselves into trouble; somebody would be sure to speak to them about it. Yet that is precisely what those birds do, and nobody says a word to them. They are supposed to have a President. He lives by himself in the yew tree outside the morning-room window. What I want to know is what he is supposed to be good for. This is the sort of thing I want him to look into. I would like him to be worming underneath one evening when those two birds are tidying up: perhaps he would do something then. I have done all I can. I have thrown stones at them, that, in the course of nature, have returned to earth again, breaking more glass. I have blazed at them with a revolver; but they have come to regard this proceeding as a mere expression of light-heartedness on my part, possibly confusing me with the Arab of the Desert, who, I am given to understand, expresses himself thus in moments of deep emotion. They merely retire to a safe distance to watch me; no doubt regarding me as a poor performer, inasmuch as I do not also dance and shout between each shot. I have no objection to their building there, if they only would build sensibly. I want somebody to speak to them to whom they will pay attention.

You can hear them in the evening, discussing the matter of this surplus stock.

"Don't you work any more," he says, as he comes up with the last load, "you'll tire yourself."

"Well, I am feeling a bit done up," she answers, as she hops out of the nest and straightens her back.

"You're a bit peckish, too, I expect," he adds sympathetically. "I know I am. We will have a scratch down, and be off."

"What about all this stuff?" she asks, while titivating herself; "we'd better not leave it about, it looks so untidy."

"Oh, we'll soon get rid of that," he answers. "I'll have that down in a jiffy."

To help him, she seizes a stick and is about to drop it. He darts forward and snatches it from her.

"Don't you waste that one," he cries, "that's a rare one, that is. You see me hit the old man with it."

And he does. What the gardener says, I will leave you to imagine.

Judged from its structure, the rook family is supposed to come next in intelligence to man himself. Judging from the intelligence displayed by members of certain human families with whom I have come in contact, I can quite believe it. That rooks talk I am positive. No one can spend half-an-hour watching a rookery without being convinced of this. Whether the talk be always wise and witty, I am not prepared to maintain; but that there is a good deal of it is certain. A young French gentleman of my acquaintance, who visited England to study the language, told me that the impression made upon him by his first social evening in London was that of a parrot-house. Later on, when he came to comprehend, he, of course, recognized the brilliancy and depth of the average London drawing-room talk; but that is how, not comprehending, it impressed him at first. Listening to the riot of a rookery is much the same experience. The conversation to us sounds meaningless; the rooks themselves would probably describe it as sparkling.

There is a Misanthrope I know who hardly ever goes into Society. I argued the question with him one day. "Why should I?" he replied; "I know, say, a dozen men and women with whom intercourse is a pleasure; they have ideas of their own which they are not afraid to voice. To rub brains with such is a rare and goodly thing, and I thank Heaven for their friendship; but they are sufficient for my leisure. What more do I require? What is this 'Society' of which you all make so much ado? I have sampled it, and I find it unsatisfying. Analyze it into its elements, what is it? Some person I know very slightly, who knows me very slightly, asks me to what you call an 'At Home.' The evening comes, I have done my day's work and I have dined. I have been to a theatre or concert, or I have spent a pleasant hour or so with a friend. I am more inclined for bed than anything else, but I pull myself together, dress, and drive to the house. While I am taking off my hat and coat in the hall, a man enters I met a few hours ago at the Club. He is a man I have very little opinion of, and he, probably, takes a similar view of me. Our minds have no thought in common, but as it is necessary to talk, I tell him it is a warm evening. Perhaps it is a warm evening, perhaps it isn't; in either case he agrees with me. I ask him if he is going to Ascot. I do not care a straw whether he is going to Ascot or not. He says he is not quite sure, but asks me what chance Passion Flower has for the Thousand Guineas. I know he doesn't value my opinion on the subject at a brass farthing—he would be a fool if he did, but I cudgel my brains to reply to him, as though he were going to stake his shirt on my advice. We reach the first floor, and are mutually glad to get rid of one another. I catch my hostess' eye. She looks tired and worried; she would be happier in bed, only she doesn't know it. She smiles sweetly, but it is clear she has not the slightest idea who I am, and is waiting to catch my name from the butler. I whisper it to him. Perhaps he will get it right, perhaps he won't; it is quite immaterial. They have asked two hundred and forty guests, some seventy-five of whom they know by sight, for the rest, any chance passer-by, able, as the theatrical advertisements say, 'to dress and behave as a gentleman,' would do every bit as well. Indeed, I sometimes wonder why people go to the trouble and expense of invitation cards at all. A sandwich-man outside the door would answer the purpose. 'Lady Tompkins, At Home, this afternoon from three to seven; Tea and Music. Ladies and Gentlemen admitted on presentation of visiting card. Afternoon dress indispensable.' The crowd is the thing wanted; as for the items, well, tell me, what is the difference, from the Society point of view, between one man in a black frock-coat and another?

"I remember being once invited to a party at a house in Lancaster Gate. I had met the woman at a picnic. In the same green frock and parasol I might have recognized her the next time I saw her. In any other clothes I did not expect to. My cabman took me to the house opposite, where they were also giving a party. It made no difference to any of us. The hostess—I never learnt her name—said it was very good of me to come, and then shunted me off on to a Colonial Premier (I did not catch his name, and he did not catch mine, which was not extraordinary, seeing that my hostess did not know it) who, she whispered to me, had come over, from wherever it was (she did not seem to be very sure) principally to make my acquaintance. Half through the evening, and by accident, I discovered my mistake, but judged it too late to say anything then. I met a couple of people I knew, had a little supper with them, and came away. The next afternoon I met my right hostess—the lady who should have been my hostess. She thanked me effusively for having sacrificed the previous evening to her and her friends; she said she knew how seldom I went out: that made her feel my kindness all the more. She told me that the Brazilian Minister's wife had told her that I was the cleverest man she had ever met. I often think I should like to meet that man, whoever he may be, and thank him.

"But perhaps the butler does pronounce my name rightly, and perhaps my hostess actually does recognize me. She smiles, and says she was so afraid I was not coming. She implies that all the other guests are but as a feather in her scales of joy compared with myself. I smile in return, wondering to myself how I look when I do smile. I have never had the courage to face my own smile in the looking-glass. I notice the Society smile of other men, and it is not reassuring. I murmur something about my not having been likely to forget this evening; in my turn, seeking to imply that I have been looking forward to it for weeks. A few men shine at this sort of thing, but they are a small percentage, and without conceit I regard myself as no bigger a fool than the average male. Not knowing what else to say, I tell her also that it is a warm evening. She smiles archly as though there were some hidden witticism in the remark, and I drift away, feeling ashamed of myself. To talk as an idiot when you ARE an idiot brings no discomfort; to behave as an idiot when you have sufficient sense to know it, is painful. I hide myself in the crowd, and perhaps I'll meet a woman I was introduced to three weeks ago at a picture gallery. We don't know each other's names, but, both of us feeling lonesome, we converse, as it is called. If she be the ordinary type of woman, she asks me if I am going on to the Johnsons'. I tell her no. We stand silent for a moment, both thinking what next to say. She asks me if I was at the Thompsons' the day before yesterday. I again tell her no. I begin to feel dissatisfied with myself that I was not at the Thompsons'. Trying to get even with her, I ask her if she is going to the Browns' next Monday. (There are no Browns, she will have to say, No.) She is not, and her tone suggests that a social stigma rests upon the Browns. I ask her if she has been to Barnum's Circus; she hasn't, but is going. I give her my impressions of Barnum's Circus, which are precisely the impressions of everybody else who has seen the show.

"Or if luck be against me, she is possibly a smart woman, that is to say, her conversation is a running fire of spiteful remarks at the expense of every one she knows, and of sneers at the expense of every one she doesn't. I always feel I could make a better woman myself, out of a bottle of vinegar and a penn'orth of mixed pins. Yet it usually takes one about ten minutes to get away from her.

"Even when, by chance, one meets a flesh-and-blood man or woman at such gatherings, it is not the time or place for real conversation; and as for the shadows, what person in their senses would exhaust a single brain cell upon such? I remember a discussion once concerning Tennyson, considered as a social item. The dullest and most densely-stupid bore I ever came across was telling how he had sat next to Tennyson at dinner. 'I found him a most uninteresting man,' so he confided to us; 'he had nothing to say for himself—absolutely nothing.' I should like to resuscitate Dr. Samuel Johnson for an evening, and throw him into one of these 'At Homes' of yours."

My friend is an admitted misanthrope, as I have explained; but one cannot dismiss him as altogether unjust. That there is a certain mystery about Society's craving for Society must be admitted. I stood one evening trying to force my way into the supper room of a house in Berkeley Square. A lady, hot and weary, a few yards in front of me was struggling to the same goal.

"Why," remarked she to her companion, "why do we come to these places, and fight like a Bank Holiday crowd for eighteenpenny-worth of food?"

"We come here," replied the man, whom I judged to be a philosopher, "to say we've been here."

I met A——- the other evening, and asked him to dine with me on Monday. I don't know why I ask A——- to dine with me, but about once a month I do. He is an uninteresting man.

"I can't," he said, "I've got to go to the B——-s'; confounded nuisance, it will be infernally dull."

"Why go?" I asked.

"I really don't know," he replied.

A little later B——- met me, and asked me to dine with him on Monday.

"I can't," I answered, "some friends are coming to us that evening. It's a duty dinner, you know the sort of thing."

"I wish you could have managed it," he said, "I shall have no one to talk to. The A——-s are coming, and they bore me to death."

"Why do you ask him?" I suggested.

"Upon my word, I really don't know," he replied.

But to return to our rooks. We were speaking of their social instincts. Some dozen of them—the "scallywags" and bachelors of the community, I judge them to be—have started a Club. For a month past I have been trying to understand what the affair was. Now I know: it is a Club.

And for their Club House they have chosen, of course, the tree nearest my bed-room window. I can guess how that came about; it was my own fault, I never thought of it. About two months ago, a single rook—suffering from indigestion or an unhappy marriage, I know not—chose this tree one night for purposes of reflection. He woke me up: I felt angry. I opened the window, and threw an empty soda-water bottle at him. Of course it did not hit him, and finding nothing else to throw, I shouted at him, thinking to frighten him away. He took no notice, but went on talking to himself. I shouted louder, and woke up my own dog. The dog barked furiously, and woke up most things within a quarter of a mile. I had to go down with a boot-jack—the only thing I could find handy—to soothe the dog. Two hours later I fell asleep from exhaustion. I left the rook still cawing.

The next night he came again. I should say he was a bird with a sense of humour. Thinking this might happen, I had, however, taken the precaution to have a few stones ready. I opened the window wide, and fired them one after another into the tree. After I had closed the window, he hopped down nearer, and cawed louder than ever. I think he wanted me to throw more stones at him: he appeared to regard the whole proceeding as a game. On the third night, as I heard nothing of him, I flattered myself that, in spite of his bravado, I had discouraged him. I might have known rooks better.

What happened when the Club was being formed, I take it, was this:

"Where shall we fix upon for our Club House?" said the secretary, all other points having been disposed of. One suggested this tree, another suggested that. Then up spoke this particular rook:

"I'll tell you where," said he, "in the yew tree opposite the porch. And I'll tell you for why. Just about an hour before dawn a man comes to the window over the porch, dressed in the most comical costume you ever set eyes upon. I'll tell you what he reminds me of—those little statues that men use for decorating fields. He opens the window, and throws a lot of things out upon the lawn, and then he dances and sings. It's awfully interesting, and you can see it all from the yew tree."

That, I am convinced, is how the Club came to fix upon the tree next my window. I have had the satisfaction of denying them the exhibition they anticipated, and I cheer myself with the hope that they have visited their disappointment upon their misleader.

There is a difference between Rook Clubs and ours. In our clubs the respectable members arrive early, and leave at a reasonable hour; in Rook Clubs, it would appear, this principle is reversed. The Mad Hatter would have liked this Club—it would have been a club after his own heart. It opens at half-past two in the morning, and the first to arrive are the most disreputable members. In Rook-land the rowdy-dowdy, randy-dandy, rollicky-ranky boys get up very early in the morning and go to bed in the afternoon. Towards dawn, the older, more orderly members drop in for reasonable talk, and the Club becomes more respectable. The tree closes about six. For the first two hours, however, the goings-on are disgraceful. The proceedings, as often as not, open with a fight. If no two gentlemen can be found to oblige with a fight, the next noisiest thing to fall back upon is held to be a song. It is no satisfaction to me to be told that rooks cannot sing. *I* know that, without the trouble of referring to the natural history book. It is the rook who does not know it; HE thinks he can; and as a matter of fact, he does. You can criticize his singing, you can call it what you like, but you can't stop it—at least, that is my experience. The song selected is sure to be one with a chorus. Towards the end it becomes mainly chorus, unless the soloist be an extra powerful bird, determined to insist upon his rights.

The President knows nothing of this Club. He gets up himself about seven—three hours after all the others have finished breakfast—and then fusses round under the impression that he is waking up the colony, the fat-headed old fool. He is the poorest thing in Presidents I have ever heard of. A South American Republic would supply a better article. The rooks themselves, the married majority, fathers of families, respectable nestholders, are as indignant as I am. I hear complaints from all quarters.

Reflection comes to one as, towards the close of these chill afternoons in early spring, one leans upon the paddock gate watching the noisy bustling in the bare elms.

So the earth is growing green again, and love is come again unto the hearts of us old sober-coated fellows. Oh, Madam, your feathers gleam wondrous black, and your bonnie bright eye stabs deep. Come, sit by our side, and we'll tell you a tale such as rook never told before. It's the tale of a nest in a topmost bough, that sways in the good west wind. It's strong without, but it's soft within, where the little green eggs lie safe. And there sits in that nest a lady sweet, and she caws with joy, for, afar, she sees the rook she loves the best. Oh, he has been east, and he has been west, and his crop it is full of worms and slugs, and they are all for her.

We are old, old rooks, so many of us. The white is mingling with the purple black upon our breasts. We have seen these tall elms grow from saplings; we have seen the old trees fall and die. Yet each season come to us again the young thoughts. So we mate and build and gather that again our old, old hearts may quiver to the thin cry of our newborn.

Mother Nature has but one care, the children. We talk of Love as the Lord of Life: it is but the Minister. Our novels end where Nature's tale begins. The drama that our curtain falls upon, is but the prologue to her play. How the ancient Dame must laugh as she listens to the prattle of her children. "Is Marriage a Failure?" "Is

Life worth Living?" "The New Woman versus the Old." So, perhaps, the waves of the Atlantic discuss vehemently whether they shall flow east or west.

Motherhood is the law of the Universe. The whole duty of man is to be a mother. We labour: to what end? the children—the woman in the home, the man in the community. The nation takes thought for its future: why? In a few years its statesmen, its soldiers, its merchants, its toilers, will be gathered unto their fathers. Why trouble we ourselves about the future? The country pours its blood and treasure into the earth that the children may reap. Foolish Jacques Bonhomie, his addled brain full of dreams, rushes with bloody hands to give his blood for Liberty, Equality, Fraternity. He will not live to see, except in vision, the new world he gives his bones to build—even his spinning word-whipped head knows that. But the children! they shall live sweeter lives. The peasant leaves his fireside to die upon the battle-field. What is it to him, a grain in the human sand, that Russia should conquer the East, that Germany should be united, that the English flag should wave above new lands? the heritage his fathers left him shall be greater for his sons. Patriotism! what is it but the mother instinct of a people?

Take it that the decree has gone forth from Heaven: There shall be no more generations, with this life the world shall die. Think you we should move another hand? The ships would rot in the harbours, the grain would rot in the ground. Should we paint pictures, write books, make music? hemmed in by that onward creeping sea of silence. Think you with what eyes husband and wife would look on one another. Think you of the wooing—the spring of Love dried up; love only a pool of stagnant water.

How little we seem to realize this foundation of our life. Herein, if nowhere else, lies our eternity. This Ego shall never die—unless the human race from beginning to end be but a passing jest of the Gods, to be swept aside when wearied of, leaving room for new experiments. These features of mine—we will not discuss their aesthetic value—shall never disappear; modified, varied, but in essential the same, they shall continue in ever increasing circles to the end of Time. This temperament of mine—this good and evil that is in me, it shall grow with every age, spreading ever wider, combining, amalgamating. I go into my children and my children's children, I am eternal. I am they, they are I. The tree withers and you clear the ground, thankful if out of its dead limbs you can make good firewood; but its spirit, its life, is in fifty saplings. The tree dies not, it changes.

These men and women that pass me in the street, this one hurrying to his office, this one to his club, another to his love, they are the mothers of the world to come.

This greedy trickster in stocks and shares, he cheats, he lies, he wrongs all men—for what? Follow him to his luxurious home in the suburbs: what do you find? A man with children on his knee, telling them stories, promising them toys. His anxious, sordid life, for what object is it lived? That these children may possess the things that he thinks good for them. Our very vices, side by side with our virtues, spring from this one root, Motherhood. It is the one seed of the Universe.

The planets are but children of the sun, the moon but an offspring of the earth, stone of her stone, iron of her iron. What is the Great Centre of us all, life animate and inanimate—if any life be inanimate? Is the eternal universe one dim figure, Motherhood, filling all space?

This scheming Mother of Mayfair, angling for a rich son-in-law! Not a pleasing portrait to look upon, from one point of view. Let us look at it, for a moment, from another. How weary she must be! This is her third "function" to-night; the paint is running off her poor face. She has been snubbed a dozen times by her social superiors, openly insulted by a Duchess; yet she bears it with a patient smile. It is a pitiful ambition, hers: it is that her child shall marry money, shall have carriages and many servants, live in Park Lane, wear diamonds, see her name in the Society Papers. At whatever cost to herself, her daughter shall, if possible, enjoy these things. She could so much more comfortably go to bed, and leave the child to marry some well-to-do commercial traveller. Justice, Reader, even for such. Her sordid scheming is but the deformed child of Motherhood.

Motherhood! it is the gamut of God's orchestra, savageness and cruelty at the one end, tenderness and self-sacrifice at the other.

The sparrow-hawk fights the hen: he seeking food for his brood, she defending hers with her life. The spider sucks the fly to feed its myriad young; the cat tortures the mouse to give its still throbbing carcase to her kittens, and man wrongs man for children's sake. Perhaps when the riot of the world reaches us whole, not broken, we shall learn it is a harmony, each jangling discord fallen into its place around the central theme, Motherhood.

ON THE INADVISABILITY OF FOLLOWING ADVICE

I was pacing the Euston platform late one winter's night, waiting for the last train to Watford, when I noticed a man cursing an automatic machine. Twice he shook his fist at it. I expected every moment to see him strike it. Naturally curious, I drew near softly. I wanted to catch what he was saying. However, he heard my approaching footsteps, and turned on me. "Are you the man," said he, "who was here just now?"

"Just where?" I replied. I had been pacing up and down the platform for about five minutes.

"Why here, where we are standing," he snapped out. "Where do you think 'here' is—over there?" He seemed irritable.

"I may have passed this spot in the course of my peregrinations, if that is what you mean," I replied. I spoke with studied politeness; my idea was to rebuke his rudeness.

"I mean," he answered, "are you the man that spoke to me, just a minute ago?"

"I am not that man," I said; "good-night."

"Are you sure?" he persisted.

"One is not likely to forget talking to you," I retorted.

His tone had been most offensive. "I beg your pardon," he replied grudgingly. "I thought you looked like the man who spoke to me a minute or so ago."

I felt mollified; he was the only other man on the platform, and I had a quarter of an hour to wait. "No, it certainly wasn't me," I returned genially, but ungrammatically. "Why, did you want him?"

"Yes, I did," he answered. "I put a penny in the slot here," he continued, feeling apparently the need of unburdening himself: "wanted a box of matches. I couldn't get anything put, and I was shaking the machine, and swearing at it, as one does, when there came along a man, about your size, and—you're SURE it wasn't you?"

"Positive," I again ungrammatically replied; "I would tell you if it had been. What did he do?"

"Well, he saw what had happened, or guessed it. He said, 'They are trouble-some things, those machines; they want understanding.' I said, 'They want taking up and flinging into the sea, that's what they want!' I was feeling mad because I hadn't a match about me, and I use a lot. He said, 'They stick sometimes; the thing to do is to put another penny in; the weight of the first penny is not always sufficient. The second penny loosens the drawer and tumbles out itself; so that you get your purchase together with your first penny back again. I have often succeeded that way.' Well, it seemed a silly explanation, but he talked as if he had been weaned by an automatic machine, and I was sawney enough to listen to him. I dropped in what I thought was another penny. I have just discovered it was a two-shilling piece. The fool was right to a certain extent; I have got something out. I have got this."

He held it towards me; I looked at it. It was a packet of Everton toffee.

"Two and a penny," he remarked, bitterly. "I'll sell it for a third of what it cost me."

"You have put your money into the wrong machine," I suggested.

"Well, I know that!" he answered, a little crossly, as it seemed to me—he was not a nice man: had there been any one else to talk to I should have left him. "It isn't losing the money I mind so much; it's getting this damn thing, that annoys me. If I could find that idiot Id ram it down his throat."

We walked to the end of the platform, side by side, in silence.

"There are people like that," he broke out, as we turned, "people who will go about, giving advice. I'll be getting six months over one of them, I'm always afraid. I remember a pony I had once." (I judged the man to be a small farmer; he talked in a wurzelly tone. I don't know if you understand what I mean, but an atmosphere of wurzels was the thing that somehow he suggested.) "It was a thoroughbred Welsh pony, as sound a little beast as ever stepped. I'd had him out to grass all the winter, and one day in the early spring I thought I'd take him for a run. I had to go to Amersham on business. I put him into the cart, and drove him across; it is just ten miles from my place. He was a bit uppish, and had lathered himself pretty freely by the time we reached the town.

"A man was at the door of the hotel. He says, 'That's a good pony of yours.'

"'Pretty middling,' I says.

"'It doesn't do to over-drive 'em, when they're young,' he says.

"I says, 'He's done ten miles, and I've done most of the pulling. I reckon I'm a jolly sight more exhausted than he is.

"I went inside and did my business, and when I came out the man was still there. 'Going back up the hill?' he says to me.

"Somehow, I didn't cotton to him from the beginning. 'Well, I've got to get the other side of it,' I says, 'and unless you know any patent way of getting over a hill without going up it, I reckon I am.'

"He says, 'You take my advice: give him a pint of old ale before you start.'

"'Old ale,' I says; 'why he's a teetotaler.'

"'Never you mind that,' he answers; 'you give him a pint of old ale. I know these ponies; he's a good 'un, but he ain't set. A pint of old ale, and he'll take you up that hill like a cable tramway, and not hurt himself.'

"I don't know what it is about this class of man. One asks oneself afterwards why one didn't knock his hat over his eyes and run his head into the nearest horse-trough. But at the time one listens to them. I got a pint of old ale in a hand-bowl, and brought it out. About half-a-dozen chaps were standing round, and of course there was a good deal of chaff.

"'You're starting him on the downward course, Jim,' says one of them. 'He'll take to gambling, rob a bank, and murder his mother. That's always the result of a glass of ale, 'cording to the tracts.'

"'He won't drink it like that,' says another; 'it's as flat as ditch water. Put a head on it for him.'

"'Ain't you got a cigar for him?' says a third.

"'A cup of coffee and a round of buttered toast would do him a sight more good, a cold day like this,' says a fourth.

"I'd half a mind then to throw the stuff away, or drink it myself; it seemed a piece of bally nonsense, giving good ale to a four-year-old pony; but the moment the beggar smelt the bowl he reached out his head, and lapped it up as though he'd been a Christian; and I jumped into the cart and started off, amid cheers. We got up the hill pretty steady. Then the liquor began to work into his head. I've taken home a drunken man more than once and there's pleasanter jobs than that. I've seen a drunken woman, and they're worse. But a drunken Welsh pony I never want to have anything more to do with so long as I live. Having four legs he managed to hold himself up; but as to guiding himself, he couldn't; and as for letting me do it, he wouldn't. First we were one side of the road, and then we were the other. When we were not either side, we were crossways in the middle. I heard a bicycle bell behind me, but I dared not turn my head. All I could do was to shout to the fellow to keep where he was.

"'I want to pass you,' he sang out, so soon as he was near enough.

"'Well, you can't do it,' I called back.

"'Why can't I?' he answered. 'How much of the road do YOU want?'

"'All of it and a bit over,' I answered him, 'for this job, and nothing in the way.'

"He followed me for half-a-mile, abusing me; and every time he thought he saw a chance he tried to pass me. But the pony was always a bit too smart for him. You might have thought the brute was doing it on purpose.

"'You're not fit to be driving,' he shouted. He was quite right; I wasn't. I was feeling just about dead beat.

"'What do you think you are?' he continued, 'the charge of the Light Brigade?' (He was a common sort of fellow.) 'Who sent YOU home with the washing?'

"Well, he was making me wild by this time. 'What's the good of talking to me?' I shouted back. 'Come and blackguard the pony if you want to blackguard anybody. I've got all I can do without the help of that alarm clock of yours. Go away, you're only making him worse.'

"'What's the matter with the pony?' he called out.

"'Can't you see?' I answered. 'He's drunk.'

"Well, of course it sounded foolish; the truth often does.

"'One of you's drunk,' he retorted; 'for two pins I'd come and haul you out of the cart.'

"I wish to goodness he had; I'd have given something to be out of that cart. But he didn't have the chance. At that moment the pony gave a sudden swerve; and I take it he must have been a bit too close. I heard a yell and a curse, and at the same instant I was splashed from head to foot with ditch water. Then the brute bolted. A man was coming along, asleep on the top of a cart-load of windsor chairs. It's disgraceful the way those wagoners go to sleep; I wonder there are not more accidents. I don't think he ever knew what had happened to him. I couldn't look round to see what became of him; I only saw him start. Half-way down the hill a policeman holla'd to me to stop. I heard him shouting out something about furious driving. Half-a-mile this side of Chesham we came upon a girls' school walking two and two—a 'crocodile' they call it, I think. I bet you those girls are still talking about it. It must have taken the old woman a good hour to collect them together again.

"It was market-day in Chesham; and I guess there has not been a busier market-day in Chesham before or since. We went through the town at about thirty miles an hour. I've never seen Chesham so lively—it's a sleepy hole as a rule. A mile outside the town I sighted the High Wycombe coach. I didn't feel I minded much; I had got to that pass when it didn't seem to matter to me what happened; I only felt curious. A dozen yards off the coach the pony stopped dead; that jerked me off the seat to the bottom of the cart. I couldn't get up, because the seat was on top of me. I could see nothing but the sky, and occasionally the head of the pony, when he stood upon his hind legs. But I could hear what the driver of the coach said, and I judged he was having trouble also.

"'Take that damn circus out of the road,' he shouted. If he'd had any sense he'd have seen how helpless I was. I could hear his cattle plunging about; they are like that, horses—if they see one fool, then they all want to be fools.

"'Take it home, and tie it up to its organ,' shouted the guard.

"Then an old woman went into hysterics, and began laughing like an hyena. That started the pony off again, and, as far as I could calculate by watching the clouds, we did about another four miles at the gallop. Then he thought he'd try to jump a gate, and finding, I suppose, that the cart hampered him, he started kicking it to pieces. I'd never have thought a cart could have been separated into so many pieces, if I hadn't seen it done. When he had got rid of everything but half a wheel and the splashboard he bolted again. I remained behind with the other ruins, and glad I was to get a little rest. He came back later in the afternoon, and I was pleased to sell him the next week for a five-pound-note: it cost me about another ten to repair myself.

"To this day I am chaffed about that pony, and the local temperance society made a lecture out of me. That's what comes of following advice."

I sympathized with him. I have suffered from advice myself. I have a friend, a City man, whom I meet occasionally. One of his most ardent passions in life is to make my fortune. He button-holes me in Threadneedle Street. "The very man I wanted to see," he says; "I'm going to let you in for a good thing. We are getting up a little syndicate." He is for ever "getting up" a little syndicate, and for every hundred pounds you put into it you take a thousand out. Had I gone into all his little syndicates, I could have been worth at the present moment, I reckon, two million five hundred thousand pounds. But I have not gone into all his little syndicates. I went into one, years ago, when I was younger. I am still in it; my friend is confident that my holding, later on, will yield me thousands. Being, however, hard-up for ready money, I am willing to part with my share to any deserving person at a genuine reduction, upon a cash basis. Another friend of mine knows another man who is "in the know" as regards racing matters. I suppose most people possess a friend of this type. He is generally very popular just before a race, and extremely unpopular immediately afterwards. A third benefactor of mine is an enthusiast upon the subject of diet. One day he brought me something in a packet, and pressed it into my hand with the air of a man who is relieving you of all your troubles.

"What is it?" I asked.

"Open it and see," he answered, in the tone of a pantomime fairy.

I opened it and looked, but I was no wiser.

"It's tea," he explained.

"Oh!" I replied; "I was wondering if it could be snuff."

"Well, it's not exactly tea," he continued, "it's a sort of tea. You take one cup of that—one cup, and you will never care for any other kind of tea again."

He was quite right, I took one cup. After drinking it I felt I didn't care for any other tea. I felt I didn't care for anything, except to die quietly and inoffensively. He called on me a week later.

"You remember that tea I gave you?" he said.

"Distinctly," I answered; "I've got the taste of it in my mouth now."

"Did it upset you?" he asked.

"It annoyed me at the time," I answered; "but that's all over now."

He seemed thoughtful. "You were quite correct," he answered; "it WAS snuff, a very special snuff, sent me all the way from India."

"I can't say I liked it," I replied.

"A stupid mistake of mine," he went on—"I must have mixed up the packets!"

"Oh, accidents will happen," I said, "and you won't make another mistake, I feel sure; so far as I am concerned."

We can all give advice. I had the honour once of serving an old gentleman whose profession it was to give legal advice, and excellent legal advice he always gave. In common with most men who know the law, he had little respect for it. I have heard him say to a would-be litigant—

"My dear sir, if a villain stopped me in the street and demanded of me my watch and chain, I should refuse to give it to him. If he thereupon said, 'Then I shall take it from you by brute force,' I should, old as I am, I feel convinced, reply to him, 'Come on.' But if, on the other hand, he were to say to me, 'Very well, then I shall take proceedings against you in the Court of Queen's Bench to compel you to give it up to me,' I should at once take it from my pocket, press it into his hand, and beg of him to say no more about the matter. And I should consider I was getting off cheaply."

Yet that same old gentleman went to law himself with his next-door neighbour over a dead poll parrot that wasn't worth sixpence to anybody, and spent from first to last a hundred pounds, if he spent a penny.

"I know I'm a fool," he confessed. "I have no positive proof that it WAS his cat; but I'll make him pay for calling me an Old Bailey Attorney, hanged if I don't!"

We all know how the pudding OUGHT to be made. We do not profess to be able to make it: that is not our business. Our business is to criticize the cook. It seems our business to criticize so many things that it is not our business to do. We are all critics nowadays. I have my opinion of you, Reader, and you possibly have your own opinion of me. I do not seek to know it; personally, I prefer the man who says what he has to say of me behind my back. I remember, when on a lecturing tour, the ground-plan of the hall often necessitated my mingling with the audience as they streamed out. This never happened but I would overhear somebody in front of me whisper to his or her companion—"Take care, he's just behind you." I always felt so grateful to that whisperer.

At a Bohemian Club, I was once drinking coffee with a Novelist, who happened to be a broad-shouldered, athletic man. A fellow-member, joining us, said to the Novelist, "I have just finished that last book of yours; I'll tell you my candid opinion of it." Promptly replied the Novelist, "I give you fair warning—if you do, I shall punch your head." We never heard that candid opinion.

Most of our leisure time we spend sneering at one another. It is a wonder, going about as we do with our noses so high in the air, we do not walk off this little round world into space, all of us. The Masses sneer at the Classes. The morals of the Classes are shocking. If only the Classes would consent as a body to be taught behaviour by a Committee of the Masses, how very much better it would be for them. If only the Classes would neglect their own interests and devote themselves to the welfare of the Masses, the Masses would be more pleased with them.

The Classes sneer at the Masses. If only the Masses would follow the advice given them by the Classes; if only they would be thrifty on their ten shillings a week; if only they would all be teetotalers, or drink old claret, which is not intoxicating; if only all the girls would be domestic servants on five pounds a year, and not waste their money on feathers; if only the men would be content to work for fourteen hours a day, and to sing in tune, "God bless the Squire and his relations," and would consent to be kept in their proper stations, all things would go swimmingly—for the Classes.

The New Woman pooh-poohs the Old; the Old Woman is indignant with the New. The Chapel denounces the Stage; the Stage ridicules Little Bethel; the Minor Poet sneers at the world; the world laughs at the Minor Poet.

Man criticizes Woman. We are not altogether pleased with woman. We discuss her shortcomings, we advise her for her good. If only English wives would dress as French wives, talk as American wives, cook as German wives! if only women would be precisely what we want them to be—patient and hard-working, brilliantly witty and exhaustively domestic, bewitching, amenable, and less suspicious; how very much better it would be for them—also for us. We work so hard to teach them, but they will not listen. Instead of paying attention to our wise counsel, the tiresome creatures are wasting their time criticizing us. It is a popular game, this game of school. All that is needful is a doorstep, a cane, and six other children. The difficulty is the six other children. Every child wants to be the schoolmaster; they will keep jumping up, saying it is their turn.

Woman wants to take the stick now, and put man on the doorstep. There are one or two things she has got to say to him. He is not at all the man she approves of. He must begin by getting rid of all his natural desires and propensities; that done, she will take him in hand and make of him—not a man, but something very much superior.

It would be the best of all possible worlds if everybody would only follow our advice. I wonder, would Jerusalem have been the cleanly city it is reported, if, instead of troubling himself concerning his own twopenny-halfpenny doorstep, each citizen had gone out into the road and given eloquent lectures to all the other inhabitants on the subject of sanitation?

We have taken to criticizing the Creator Himself of late. The world is wrong, we are wrong. If only He had taken our advice, during those first six days!

Why do I seem to have been scooped out and filled up with lead? Why do I hate the smell of bacon, and feel that nobody cares for me? It is because champagne and lobsters have been made wrong.

Why do Edwin and Angelina quarrel? It is because Edwin has been given a fine, high-spirited nature that will not brook contradiction; while Angelina, poor girl, has been cursed with contradictory instincts.

Why is excellent Mr. Jones brought down next door to beggary? Mr. Jones had an income of a thousand a year, secured by the Funds. But there came along a wicked Company promoter (why are wicked Company promoters permitted?) with a prospectus, telling good Mr. Jones how to obtain a hundred per cent. for his money by investing it in some scheme for the swindling of Mr. Jones's fellow-citizens.

The scheme does not succeed; the people swindled turn out, contrary to the promise of the prospectus, to be Mr. Jones and his fellow-investors. Why does Heaven allow these wrongs?

Why does Mrs. Brown leave her husband and children, to run off with the New Doctor? It is because an ill-advised Creator has given Mrs. Brown and the New Doctor unduly strong emotions. Neither Mrs. Brown nor the New Doctor are to be blamed. If any human being be answerable it is, probably, Mrs. Brown's grandfather, or some early ancestor of the New Doctor's.

We shall criticize Heaven when we get there. I doubt if any of us will be pleased with the arrangements; we have grown so exceedingly critical.

It was once said of a very superior young man that he seemed to be under the impression that God Almighty had made the universe chiefly to hear what he would say about it. Consciously or unconsciously, most of us are of this way of thinking. It is an age of mutual improvement societies—a delightful idea, everybody's business being to improve everybody else; of amateur parliaments, of literary councils, of playgoers' clubs.

First Night criticism seems to have died out of late, the Student of the Drama having come to the conclusion, possibly, that plays are not worth criticizing. But in my young days we were very earnest at this work. We went to the play, less with the selfish desire of enjoying our evening, than with the noble aim of elevating the Stage. Maybe we did good, maybe we were needed—let us think so. Certain it is, many of the old absurdities have disappeared from the Theatre, and our rough-and-ready criticism may have helped the happy dispatch. A folly is often served by an unwise remedy.

The dramatist in those days had to reckon with his audience. Gallery and Pit took an interest in his work such as Galleries and Pits no longer take. I recollect witnessing the production of a very blood-curdling melodrama at, I think, the old Queen's Theatre. The heroine had been given by the author a quite unnecessary amount of conversation, so we considered. The woman, whenever she appeared on the stage, talked by the yard; she could not do a simple little thing like cursing the Villain under about twenty lines. When the hero asked her if she loved him she stood up and made a speech about it that lasted three minutes by the watch. One dreaded to see her open her mouth. In the Third Act, somebody got hold of her and shut her up in a dungeon. He was not a nice man, speaking generally, but we felt he was the man for the situation, and the house cheered him to the echo. We flattered ourselves we had got rid of her for the rest of the evening. Then some fool of a turnkey came along, and she appealed to him, through the grating, to let her out for a few minutes. The turnkey, a good but soft-hearted man, hesitated.

"Don't you do it," shouted one earnest Student of the Drama, from the Gallery; "she's all right. Keep her there!"

The old idiot paid no attention to our advice; he argued the matter to himself. "'Tis but a trifling request," he remarked; "and it will make her happy."

"Yes, but what about us?" replied the same voice from the Gallery. "You don't know her. You've only just come on; we've been listening to her all the evening. She's quiet now, you let her be."

"Oh, let me out, if only for one moment!" shrieked the poor woman. "I have something that I must say to my child."

"Write it on a bit of paper, and pass it out," suggested a voice from the Pit. "We'll see that he gets it."

"Shall I keep a mother from her dying child?" mused the turnkey. "No, it would be inhuman."

"No, it wouldn't," persisted the voice of the Pit; "not in this instance. It's too much talk that has made the poor child ill."

The turnkey would not be guided by us. He opened the cell door amidst the execrations of the whole house. She talked to her child for about five minutes, at the end of which time it died.

"Ah, he is dead!" shrieked the distressed parent.

"Lucky beggar!" was the unsympathetic rejoinder of the house.

Sometimes the criticism of the audience would take the form of remarks, addressed by one gentleman to another. We had been listening one night to a play in which action seemed to be unnecessarily subordinated to dialogue, and somewhat poor dialogue at that. Suddenly, across the wearying talk from the stage, came the stentorian whisper—

"Jim!"

"Hallo!"

"Wake me up when the play begins."

This was followed by an ostentatious sound as of snoring. Then the voice of the second speaker was heard—

"Sammy!"

His friend appeared to awake.

"Eh? Yes? What's up? Has anything happened?"

"Wake you up at half-past eleven in any event, I suppose?"

"Thanks, do, sonny." And the critic slept again.

Yes, we took an interest in our plays then. I wonder shall I ever enjoy the British Drama again as I enjoyed it in those days? Shall I ever enjoy a supper again as I enjoyed the tripe and onions washed down with bitter beer at the bar of the old Albion? I have tried many suppers after the theatre since then, and some, when friends have been in generous mood, have been expensive and elaborate. The cook may have come from Paris, his portrait may be in the illustrated papers, his salary may be reckoned by hundreds; but there is something wrong with his art, for all that, I miss a flavour in his meats. There is a sauce lacking.

Nature has her coinage, and demands payment in her own currency. At Nature's shop it is you yourself must pay. Your unearned increment, your inherited fortune, your luck, are not legal tenders across her counter.

You want a good appetite. Nature is quite willing to supply you. "Certainly, sir," she replies, "I can do you a very excellent article indeed. I have here a real genuine hunger and thirst that will make your meal a delight to you. You shall eat heartily and with zest, and you shall rise from the table refreshed, invigorated, and cheerful."

"Just the very thing I want," exclaims the gourmet delightedly. "Tell me the price."

"The price," answers Mrs. Nature, "is one long day's hard work."

The customer's face falls; he handles nervously his heavy purse.

"Cannot I pay for it in money?" he asks. "I don't like work, but I am a rich man, I can afford to keep French cooks, to purchase old wines."

Nature shakes her head.

"I cannot take your cheques, tissue and nerve are my charges. For these I can give you an appetite that will make a rump-steak and a tankard of ale more delicious to you than any dinner that the greatest chef in Europe could put before you. I can even promise you that a hunk of bread and cheese shall be a banquet to you; but you must pay my price in my money; I do not deal in yours."

And next the Dilettante enters, demanding a taste for Art and Literature, and this also Nature is quite prepared to supply.

"I can give you true delight in all these things," she answers. "Music shall be as wings to you, lifting you above the turmoil of the world. Through Art you shall catch a glimpse of Truth. Along the pleasant paths of Literature you shall walk as beside still waters."

"And your charge?" cries the delighted customer.

"These things are somewhat expensive," replies Nature. "I want from you a life lived simply, free from all desire of worldly success, a life from which passion has been lived out; a life to which appetite has been subdued."

"But you mistake, my dear lady," replies the Dilettante; "I have many friends, possessed of taste, and they are men who do not pay this price for it. Their houses are full of beautiful pictures, they rave about 'nocturnes' and 'symphonies,' their shelves are packed with first editions. Yet they are men of luxury and wealth and fashion. They trouble much concerning the making of money, and Society is their heaven. Cannot I be as one of these?"

"I do not deal in the tricks of apes," answers Nature coldly; "the culture of these friends of yours is a mere pose, a fashion of the hour, their talk mere parrot chatter. Yes, you can purchase such culture as this, and pretty cheaply, but a passion for skittles would be of more service to you, and bring you more genuine enjoyment. My goods are of a different class. I fear we waste each other's time."

And next comes the boy, asking with a blush for love, and Nature's motherly old heart goes out to him, for it is an article she loves to sell, and she loves those who come to purchase it of her. So she leans across the counter, smiling, and tells him that she has the very thing he wants, and he, trembling with excitement, likewise asks the figure.

"It costs a good deal," explains Nature, but in no discouraging tone; "it is the most expensive thing in all my shop."

"I am rich," replies the lad. "My father worked hard and saved, and he has left me all his wealth. I have stocks and shares, and lands and factories; and will pay any price in reason for this thing."

But Nature, looking graver, lays her hand upon his arm.

"Put by your purse, boy," she says, "my price is not a price in reason, nor is gold the metal that I deal in. There are many shops in various streets where your bank-notes will be accepted. But if you will take an old woman's advice, you will not go to them. The thing they will sell you will bring sorrow and do evil to you. It is cheap enough, but, like all things cheap, it is not worth the buying. No man purchases it, only the fool."

"And what is the cost of the thing YOU sell then?" asks the lad.

"Self-forgetfulness, tenderness, strength," answers the old Dame; "the love of all things that are of good repute, the hate of all things evil—courage, sympathy, self-respect, these things purchase love. Put by your purse, lad, it will serve you in other ways, but it will not buy for you the goods upon my shelves."

"Then am I no better off than the poor man?" demands the lad.

"I know not wealth or poverty as you understand it," answers Nature. "Here I exchange realities only for realities. You ask for my treasures, I ask for your brain and heart in exchange—yours, boy, not your father's, not another's."

"And this price," he argues, "how shall I obtain it?"

"Go about the world," replies the great Lady. "Labour, suffer, help. Come back to me when you have earned your wages, and according to how much you bring me so we will do business."

Is real wealth so unevenly distributed as we think? Is not Fate the true Socialist? Who is the rich man, who the poor? Do we know? Does even the man himself know? Are we not striving for the shadow, missing the substance? Take life at its highest; which was the happier man, rich Solomon or poor Socrates? Solomon seems to have had most things that most men most desire—maybe too much of some for his own comfort. Socrates had little beyond what he carried about with him, but that was a good deal. According to our scales, Solomon should have been one of the happiest men that ever lived, Socrates one of the most wretched. But was it so?

Or taking life at its lowest, with pleasure its only goal. Is my lord Tom Noddy, in the stalls, so very much jollier than 'Arry in the gallery? Were beer ten shillings the bottle, and champagne fourpence a quart, which, think you, we should clamour for? If every West End Club had its skittle alley, and billiards could only be played in East End pubs, which game, my lord, would you select? Is the air of Berkeley Square so much more joy-giving than the atmosphere of Seven Dials? I find myself a piquancy in the air of Seven Dials, missing from Berkeley Square. Is there so vast a difference between horse-hair and straw, when you are tired? Is happiness multiplied by the number of rooms in one's house? Are Lady Ermintrude's lips so very much sweeter than Sally's of the Alley? What IS success in life?

ON THE PLAYING OF MARCHES AT THE FUNERALS OF MARIONETTES

He began the day badly. He took me out and lost me. It would be so much better, would he consent to the usual arrangement, and allow me to take him out. I am far the abler leader: I say it without conceit. I am older than he is, and I am less excitable. I do not stop and talk with every person I meet, and then forget where I am. I do less to distract myself: I rarely fight, I never feel I want to run after cats, I take but little pleasure in frightening children. I have nothing to think about but the walk, and the getting home again. If, as I say, he would give up taking me out, and let me take him out, there would be less trouble all round. But into this I have never been able to persuade him.

He had mislaid me once or twice, but in Sloane Square he lost me entirely. When he loses me, he stands and barks for me. If only he would remain where he first barked, I might find my way to him; but, before I can cross the road, he is barking half-way down the next street. I am not so young as I was and I sometimes think he exercises me more than is good for me. I could see him from where I was standing in the King's Road. Evidently he was most indignant. I was too far off to distinguish the barks, but I could guess what he was saying—

"Damn that man, he's off again."

He made inquiries of a passing dog—

"You haven't smelt my man about anywhere, have you?"

(A dog, of course, would never speak of SEEING anybody or anything, smell being his leading sense. Reaching the top of a hill, he would say to his companion—"Lovely smell from here, I always think; I could sit and sniff here all the afternoon." Or, proposing a walk, he would say—"I like the road by the canal, don't you? There's something interesting to catch your nose at every turn.")

"No, I haven't smelt any man in particular," answered the other dog. "What sort of a smelling man is yours?"

"Oh, an egg-and-bacony sort of a man, with a dash of soap about him."

"That's nothing to go by," retorted the other; "most men would answer to that description, this time of the morning. Where were you when you last noticed him?"

At this moment he caught sight of me, and came up, pleased to find me, but vexed with me for having got lost.

"Oh, here you are," he barked; "didn't you see me go round the corner? Do keep closer. Bothered if half my time isn't taken up, finding you and losing you again."

The incident appeared to have made him bad-tempered; he was just in the humour for a row of any sort. At the top of Sloane Street a stout military-looking gentleman started running after the Chelsea bus. With a "Hooroo" William Smith was after him. Had the old gentleman taken no notice, all would have been well. A butcher boy, driving just behind, would—I could read it in his eye—have caught Smith a flick as he darted into the road, which would have served him right; the old gentleman would have captured his bus; and the affair would have been ended. Unfortunately, he was that type of retired military man all gout and curry and no sense. He stopped to swear at the dog. That, of course, was what Smith wanted. It is not often he gets a scrimmage with a full-grown man. "They're a poor-spirited lot, most of them," he thinks; "they won't even answer you back. I like a man who shows a bit of pluck." He was frenzied with delight at his success. He flew round his victim, weaving whooping circles and curves that paralyzed the old gentleman as though they had been the mystic figures of a Merlin. The colonel clubbed his umbrella, and attempted to defend himself. I called to the dog, I gave good advice to the colonel (I judged him to be a colonel; the louder he spoke, the less one could understand him), but both were too excited to listen to me. A sympathetic bus driver leaned over, and whispered hoarse counsel.

"Ketch 'im by the tail, sir," he advised the old gentleman; "don't you be afraid of him; you ketch 'im firmly by the tail."

A milkman, on the other hand, sought rather to encourage Smith, shouting as he passed—

"Good dog, kill him!"

A child, brained within an inch by the old gentleman's umbrella, began to cry. The nurse told the old gentleman he was a fool—a remark which struck me as singularly apt The old gentleman gasped back that perambulators were illegal on the pavement; and, between his exercises, inquired after myself. A crowd began to collect; and a policeman strolled up.

It was not the right thing: I do not defend myself; but, at this point, the temptation came to me to desert William Smith. He likes a street row, I don't. These things are matters of temperament. I have also noticed that he has the happy instinct of knowing when to disappear from a crisis, and the ability to do so; mysteriously turning up, quarter of a mile off, clad in a peaceful and pre-occupied air, and to all appearances another and a better dog.

Consoling myself with the reflection that I could be of no practical assistance to him and remembering with some satisfaction that, by a fortunate accident, he was without his collar, which bears my name and address, I slipped round the off side of a Vauxhall bus, making no attempt at ostentation, and worked my way home through Lowndes Square and the Park.

Five minutes after I had sat down to lunch, he flung open the dining-room door, and marched in. It is his customary "entrance." In a previous state of existence, his soul was probably that of an Actor-Manager.

From his exuberant self-satisfaction, I was inclined to think he must have succeeded in following the milkman's advice; at all events, I have not seen the colonel since. His bad temper had disappeared, but his "uppishness" had, if possible, increased. Previous to his return, I had given The O'Shannon a biscuit. The O'Shannon had been insulted; he did not want a dog biscuit; if he could not have a grilled kidney he did not want anything. He had thrown the biscuit on the floor. Smith saw it and made for it. Now Smith never eats biscuits. I give him one occasionally, and he at once proceeds to hide it. He is a thrifty dog; he thinks of the future. "You never know what may happen," he says; "suppose the Guv'nor dies, or goes mad, or bankrupt, I may be glad even of this biscuit; I'll put it under the door-mat—no, I won't, somebody will find it there. I'll scratch a hole in the tennis lawn, and bury it there. That's a good idea; perhaps it'll grow!" Once I caught him hiding it in my study, behind the shelf devoted to my own books. It offended me, his doing that; the argument was so palpable. Generally, wherever he hides it somebody finds it. We find it under our pillows—inside our boots; no place seems safe. This time he had said to himself—"By Jove! a whole row of the Guv'nor's books. Nobody will ever want to take these out; I'll hide it here." One feels a thing like that from one's own dog.

But The O'Shannon's biscuit was another matter. Honesty is the best policy; but dishonesty is the better fun. He made a dash for it, and commenced to devour it greedily; you might have thought he had not tasted food for a week.

The indignation of The O'Shannon was a sight for the gods. He has the good-nature of his race: had Smith asked him for the biscuit he would probably have given it to him; it was the insult—the immorality of the proceeding, that maddened The O'Shannon.

For a moment he was paralyzed.

"Well, of all the—Did ye see that now?" he said to me with his eyes. Then he made a rush and snatched the biscuit out of Smith's very jaws. "Ye onprincipled black Saxon thief," growled The O'Shannon; "how dare ye take my biscuit?"

"You miserable Irish cur," growled Smith; "how was I to know it was your biscuit? Does everything on the floor belong to you? Perhaps you think I belong to you, I'm on the floor. I don't believe it is your biscuit, you long-eared, snubbed-nosed bog-trotter; give it me back."

"I don't require any of your argument, you flop-eared son of a tramp with half a tail," replied The O'Shannon. "You come and take it, if you think you are dog enough."

He did think he was dog enough. He is half the size of The O'Shannon, but such considerations weigh not with him. His argument is, if a dog is too big for you to fight the whole of him, take a bit of him and fight that. He generally gets licked, but what is left of him invariably swaggers about afterwards under the impression it is the victor. When he is dead, he will say to himself, as he settles himself in his grave—"Well, I flatter myself I've laid out that old world at last. It won't trouble ME any more, I'm thinking."

On this occasion, *I* took a hand in the fight. It becomes necessary at intervals to remind Master Smith that the man, as the useful and faithful friend of dog, has his rights. I deemed such interval had arrived. He flung himself on to the sofa, muttering. It sounded like—"Wish I'd never got up this morning. Nobody understands me."

Nothing, however, sobers him for long. Half-an-hour later, he was killing the next-door cat. He will never learn sense; he has been killing that cat for the last three months. Why the next morning his nose is invariably twice its natural size, while for the next week he can see objects on one side of his head only, he never seems to grasp; I suppose he attributes it to change in the weather.

He ended up the afternoon with what he no doubt regarded as a complete and satisfying success. Dorothea had invited a lady to take tea with her that day. I heard the sound of laughter, and, being near the nursery, I looked in to see what was the joke. Smith was worrying a doll. I have rarely seen a more worried-looking doll. Its head was off, and its sawdust strewed the floor. Both the children were crowing with delight; Dorothea, in particular, was in an ecstasy of amusement.

"Whose doll is it?" I asked.

"Eva's," answered Dorothea, between her peals of laughter.

"Oh no, it isn't," explained Eva, in a tone of sweet content; "here's my doll." She had been sitting on it, and now drew it forth, warm but whole. "That's Dorry's doll."

The change from joy to grief on the part of Dorothea was distinctly dramatic. Even Smith, accustomed to storm, was nonplussed at the suddenness of the attack upon him.

Dorothea's sorrow lasted longer than I had expected. I promised her another doll. But it seemed she did not want another; that was the only doll she would ever care for so long as life lasted; no other doll could ever take its place; no other doll would be to her what that doll had been. These little people are so absurd: as if it could matter whether you loved one doll or another, when all are so much alike! They have curly hair, and pink-and-white complexions, big eyes that open and shut, a little red mouth, two little hands. Yet these foolish little people! they will love one, while another they will not look upon. I find the best plan is not to reason with them, but to sympathize. Later on—but not too soon—introduce to them another doll. They will not care for it at first, but in time they will come to take an interest in it. Of course, it cannot make them forget the first doll; no doll ever born in Lowther Arcadia could be as that, but still—— It is many weeks before they forget entirely the first love.

We buried Dolly in the country under the yew tree. A friend of mine who plays the fiddle came down on purpose to assist. We buried her in the hot spring sunshine, while the birds from shady nooks sang joyously of life and love. And our chief mourner cried real tears, just for all the world as though it were not the fate of dolls, sooner or later, to get broken—the little fragile things, made for an hour, to be dressed and kissed; then, paintless and stript, to be thrown aside on the nursery floor. Poor little dolls! I wonder do they take themselves seriously, not knowing the springs that stir their sawdust bosoms are but clockwork, not seeing the wires to which they dance? Poor little marionettes! do they talk together, I wonder, when the lights of the booth are out?

You, little sister doll, were the heroine. You lived in the white-washed cottage, all honeysuckle and clematis without—earwiggy and damp within, maybe. How pretty you always looked in your simple, neatly-fitting print dress. How good you were! How nobly you bore your poverty. How patient you were under your many wrongs. You never harboured an evil thought, a revengeful wish—never, little doll? Were there never moments when you longed to play the wicked woman's part, live in a room with many doors, be-clad in furs and jewels, with lovers galore at your feet? In those long winter evenings? the household work is done—the greasy dishes washed, the floor scrubbed; the excellent child is asleep in the corner; the one-and-elevenpenny lamp sheds its dismal light on the darned tablecloth; you sit, busy at your coarse sewing, waiting for Hero Dick, knowing—guessing, at least, where he is—! Yes, dear, I remember your fine speeches, when you told her, in stirring language the gallery cheered to the echo, what you thought of her and of such women as she; when, lifting your hand to heaven, you declared you were happier in your attic, working your fingers to the bone, than she in her gilded salon—I think "gilded salon" was the term, was it not?—furnished by sin. But speaking of yourself, weak little sister doll, not of your fine speeches, the gallery listening, did you not, in your secret heart, envy her? Did you never, before blowing out the one candle, stand for a minute in front of the cracked glass, and think to yourself that you, too, would look well in low-cut dresses from Paris, the diamonds flashing on your white smooth skin? Did you never, toiling home through the mud, bearing your bundle of needlework, feel bitter with the wages of virtue, as she splashed you, passing by in her carriage? Alone, over your cup of weak tea, did you never feel tempted to pay the price for champagne suppers, and gaiety, and admiration? Ah, yes, it is easy for folks who have had their good time, to prepare copybooks for weary little inkstained fingers, longing for play. The fine maxims sound such cant when we are in that mood, do they not? You, too, were young and handsome: did the author of the play think you were never hungry for the good things of life? Did he think that reading tracts to crotchety old women was joy to a full-blooded girl in her twenties? Why should SHE have all the love, and all the laughter? How fortunate that the villain, the Wicked Baronet, never opened the cottage door at that moment, eh, dear! He always came when you were strong, when you felt that you could denounce him, and scorn his temptations. Would that the villain came to all of us at such time; then we would all, perhaps, be heroes and heroines.

Ah well, it was only a play: it is over now. You and I, little tired dolls, lying here side by side, waiting to know our next part, we can look back and laugh. Where is she, this wicked dolly, that made such a stir on our tiny stage? Ah, here you are, Madam; I thought you could not be far; they have thrown us all into this corner together. But how changed you are, Dolly: your paint rubbed off, your golden hair worn to a wisp. No wonder; it was a trying part you had to play. How tired you must have grown of the glare and the glitter! And even hope was denied you. The peace you so longed for you knew you had lost the power to enjoy. Like the girl bewitched in the fairy tale, you knew you must dance ever faster and faster, with limbs growing palsied, with face growing ashen, and hair growing grey, till Death should come to release you; and your only prayer was he might come ere your dancing grew comic.

Like the smell of the roses to Nancy, hawking them through the hot streets, must the stifling atmosphere of love have been to you. The song of passion, how monotonous in your ears, sung now by the young and now by the old; now shouted, now whined, now shrieked; but ever the one strident tune. Do you remember when first you heard it? You dreamt it the morning hymn of Heaven. You came to think it the dance music of Hell, ground from a cracked hurdy-gurdy, lent out by the Devil on hire.

An evil race we must have seemed to you, Dolly Faustine, as to some Old Bailey lawyer. You saw but one side of us. You lived in a world upside down, where the leaves and the blossoms were hidden, and only the roots saw your day. You imagined the worm-beslimed fibres the plant, and all things beautiful you deemed cant. Chivalry, love, honour! how you laughed at the lying words. You knew the truth—as you thought: aye, half the truth. We were swine while your spell was upon us, Daughter of Circe, and you, not knowing your island secret, deemed it our natural shape.

No wonder, Dolly, your battered waxen face is stamped with an angry sneer. The Hero, who eventually came into his estates amid the plaudits of the Pit, while you were left to die in the streets! you remembered, but the house had forgotten those earlier scenes in always wicked Paris. The good friend of the family, the breezy man of the world, the Deus ex Machina of the play, who was so good to everybody, whom everybody loved! aye, YOU loved him once—but that was in the Prologue. In the Play proper, he was respectable. (How you loathed that word, that meant to you all you vainly longed for!) To him the Prologue was a period past and dead; a memory, giving flavour to his life. To you, it was the First Act of the Play, shaping all the others. His sins the house had forgotten: at yours, they held up their hands in horror. No wonder the sneer lies on your waxen lips.

Never mind, Dolly; it was a stupid house. Next time, perhaps, you will play a better part; and then they will cheer, instead of hissing you. You were wasted, I am inclined to think, on modern comedy. You should have been cast for the heroine of some old-world tragedy. The strength of character, the courage, the power of self-forgetfulness, the enthusiasm were yours: it was the part that was lacking. You might have worn the mantle of a Judith, a Boadicea, or a Jeanne d'Arc, had such plays been popular in your time. Perhaps they, had they played in your day, might have had to be content with such a part as yours. They could not have played the meek heroine, and what else would there have been for them in modern drama? Catherine of Russia! had she been a waiter's daughter in the days of the Second Empire, should we have called her Great? The Magdalene! had her lodging in those days been in some bye-street of Rome instead of in Jerusalem, should we mention her name in our churches?

You were necessary, you see, Dolly, to the piece. We cannot all play heroes and heroines. There must be wicked people in the play, or it would not interest. Think of it, Dolly, a play where all the women were virtuous, all the men honest! We might close the booth; the world would be as dull as an oyster-bed. Without you wicked folk there would be no good. How should we have known and honoured the heroine's worth, but by contrast with your worthlessness? Where would have been her fine speeches, but for you to listen to them? Where lay the hero's strength, but in resisting temptation of you? Had not you and the Wicked Baronet between you robbed him of his estates, falsely accused him of crime, he would have lived to the end of the play an idle, unheroic, incomplete existence. You brought him down to poverty; you made him earn his own bread—a most excellent thing for him; gave him the opportunity to play the man. But for your conduct in the Prologue, of what value would have been that fine scene at the end of the Third Act, that stirred the house to tears and laughter? You and your accomplice, the Wicked Baronet, made the play possible. How would Pit and Gallery have known they were virtuous, but for the indignation that came to them, watching your misdeeds? Pity, sympathy, excitement, all that goes to the making of a play, you were necessary for. It was ungrateful of the house to hiss you.

And you, Mr. Merryman, the painted grin worn from your pale lips, you too were dissatisfied, if I remember rightly, with your part. You wanted to make the people cry, not laugh. Was it a higher ambition? The poor tired people! so much happens in their life to make them weep, is it not good sport to make them merry for awhile? Do you remember that old soul in the front row of the Pit? How she laughed when you sat down on the pie! I thought she would have to be carried out. I heard her talking to her companion as they passed the stage-door on their way home. "I have not laughed, my dear, till to-night," she was saying, the good, gay tears still in her eyes, "since the day poor Sally died." Was not that alone worth the old stale tricks you so hated? Aye, they were commonplace and conventional, those antics of yours that made us laugh; are not the antics that make us weep commonplace and conventional also? Are not all the plays, played since the booth was opened, but of one pattern, the plot old-fashioned now, the scenes now commonplace? Hero, villain, cynic—are their parts so much the fresher? The love duets, are they so very new? The death-bed scenes, would you call them UN-commonplace? Hate, and Evil, and Wrong—are THEIR voices new to the booth? What are you waiting for, people? a play with a plot that is novel, with characters that have never strutted before? It will be ready for you, perhaps, when you are ready for it, with new tears and new laughter.

You, Mr. Merryman, were the true philosopher. You saved us from forgetting the reality when the fiction grew somewhat strenuous. How we all applauded your gag in answer to the hero, when, bewailing his sad fate, he demanded of Heaven how much longer he was to suffer evil fortune. "Well, there cannot be much more of it in store for you," you answered him; "it's nearly nine o'clock already, and the show closes at ten." And true to your prophecy the curtain fell at the time appointed, and his troubles were of the past. You showed us the truth behind the mask. When pompous Lord Shallow, in ermine and wig, went to take his seat amid the fawning crowd, you pulled the chair from under him, and down he sat plump on the floor. His robe flew open, his wig flew off. No longer he awed us. His aped dignity fell from him; we saw him a stupid-eyed, bald little man; he imposed no longer upon us. It is your fool who is the only true wise man.

Yours was the best part in the play, Brother Merryman, had you and the audience but known it. But you dreamt of a showier part, where you loved and fought. I have heard you now and again, when you did not know I was near, shouting with sword in hand before your looking-glass. You had thrown your motley aside to don a dingy red coat; you were the hero of the play, you performed the gallant deeds, you made the noble speeches. I wonder what the play would be like, were we all to write our own parts. There would be no clowns, no singing chambermaids. We would all be playing lead in the centre of the stage, with the lime-light exclusively devoted to ourselves. Would it not be so?

What grand acting parts they are, these characters we write for ourselves alone in our dressing-rooms. We are always brave and noble—wicked sometimes, but if so, in a great, high-minded way; never in a mean or little way. What wondrous deeds we do, while the house looks on and marvels. Now we are soldiers, leading armies to victory. What if we die: it is in the hour of triumph, and a nation is left to mourn. Not in some forgotten skirmish do we ever fall; not for some "affair of outposts" do we give our blood, our very name unmentioned in the dispatches home. Now we are passionate lovers, well losing a world for love—a very different thing to being a laughter-provoking co-respondent in a sordid divorce case.

And the house is always crowded when we play. Our fine speeches always fall on sympathetic ears, our brave deeds are noted and applauded. It is so different in the real performance. So often we play our parts to empty benches, or if a thin house be present, they misunderstand, and laugh at the pathetic passages. And when our finest opportunity comes, the royal box, in which HE or SHE should be present to watch us, is vacant.

Poor little dolls, how seriously we take ourselves, not knowing the springs that stir our bosoms are but clockwork, not seeing the wires to which we dance. Poor little marionettes, shall we talk together, I wonder, when the lights of the booth are out?

We are little wax dollies with hearts. We are little tin soldiers with souls. Oh, King of many toys, are you merely playing with us? IS it only clockwork within us, this thing that throbs and aches? Have you wound us up but to let us run down? Will you wind us again to-morrow, or leave us here to rust? IS it only clockwork to which we respond and quiver? Now we laugh, now we cry, now we dance; our little arms go out to clasp one another, our little lips kiss, then say good-bye. We strive, and we strain, and we struggle. We reach now for gold, now for laurel. We call it desire and ambition: are they only wires that you play? Will you throw the clockwork aside, or use it again, O Master?

The lights of the booth grow dim. The springs are broken that kept our eyes awake. The wire that held us erect is snapped, and helpless we fall in a heap on the stage. Oh, brother and sister dollies we played beside, where are you? Why is it so dark and silent? Why are we being put into this black box? And hark! the little doll orchestra—how far away the music sounds! what is it they are playing:—

[Start of Gounod's Funeral March of a Marionette]

TOLD AFTER SUPPER

INTRODUCTORY

It was Christmas Eve.

I begin this way because it is the proper, orthodox, respectable way to begin, and I have been brought up in a proper, orthodox, respectable way, and taught to always do the proper, orthodox, respectable thing; and the habit clings to me.

Of course, as a mere matter of information it is quite unnecessary to mention the date at all. The experienced reader knows it was Christmas Eve, without my telling him. It always is Christmas Eve, in a ghost story,

Christmas Eve is the ghosts' great gala night. On Christmas Eve they hold their annual fete. On Christmas Eve everybody in Ghostland who IS anybody— or rather, speaking of ghosts, one should say, I suppose, every nobody who IS any nobody—comes out to show himself or herself, to see and to be seen, to promenade about and display their winding-sheets and grave-clothes to each other, to criticise one another's style, and sneer at one another's complexion.

"Christmas Eve parade," as I expect they themselves term it, is a function, doubtless, eagerly prepared for and looked forward to throughout Ghostland, especially the swagger set, such as the murdered Barons, the crime-stained Countesses, and the Earls who came over with the Conqueror, and assassinated their relatives, and died raving mad.

Hollow moans and fiendish grins are, one may be sure, energetically practised up. Blood-curdling shrieks and marrow-freezing gestures are probably rehearsed for weeks beforehand. Rusty chains and gory daggers are over-hauled, and put into good working order; and sheets and shrouds, laid carefully by from the previous year's show, are taken down and shaken out, and mended, and aired.

Oh, it is a stirring night in Ghostland, the night of December the twenty-fourth!

Ghosts never come out on Christmas night itself, you may have noticed. Christmas Eve, we suspect, has been too much for them; they are not used to excitement. For about a week after Christmas Eve, the gentlemen ghosts, no doubt, feel as if they were all head, and go about making solemn resolutions to themselves that they will stop in next Christmas Eve; while lady spectres are contradictory and snappish, and liable to burst into tears and leave the room hurriedly on being spoken to, for no perceptible cause whatever.

Ghosts with no position to maintain—mere middle-class ghosts— occasionally, I believe, do a little haunting on off-nights: on All-hallows Eve, and at Midsummer; and some will even run up for a mere local event—to celebrate, for instance, the anniversary of the hanging of somebody's grandfather, or to prophesy a misfortune.

He does love prophesying a misfortune, does the average British ghost. Send him out to prognosticate trouble to somebody, and he is happy. Let him force his way into a peaceful home, and turn the whole house upside down by foretelling a funeral, or predicting a bankruptcy, or hinting at a coming disgrace, or some other terrible disaster, about which nobody in their senses want to know sooner they could possibly help, and the prior knowledge of which can serve no useful purpose whatsoever, and he feels that he is combining duty with pleasure. He would never forgive himself if anybody in his family had a trouble and he had not been there for a couple of months beforehand, doing silly tricks on the lawn, or balancing himself on somebody's bed-rail.

Then there are, besides, the very young, or very conscientious ghosts with a lost will or an undiscovered number weighing heavy on their minds, who will haunt steadily all the year round; and also the fussy ghost, who is indignant at having been buried in the dust-bin or in the village pond, and who never gives the parish a single night's quiet until somebody has paid for a first-class funeral for him.

But these are the exceptions. As I have said, the average orthodox ghost does his one turn a year, on Christmas Eve, and is satisfied.

Why on Christmas Eve, of all nights in the year, I never could myself understand. It is invariably one of the most dismal of nights to be out in—cold, muddy, and wet. And besides, at Christmas time, everybody has quite enough to put up with in the way of a houseful of living relations, without wanting the ghosts of any dead ones mooning about the place, I am sure.

There must be something ghostly in the air of Christmas—something about the close, muggy atmosphere that draws up the ghosts, like the dampness of the summer rains brings out the frogs and snails.

And not only do the ghosts themselves always walk on Christmas Eve, but live people always sit and talk about them on Christmas Eve. Whenever five or six English-speaking people meet round a fire on Christmas Eve, they start telling each other ghost stories. Nothing satisfies us on Christmas Eve but to hear each other tell authentic anecdotes about spectres. It is a genial, festive season, and we love to muse upon graves, and dead bodies, and murders, and blood.

There is a good deal of similarity about our ghostly experiences; but this of course is not our fault but the fault ghosts, who never will try any new performances, but always will keep steadily to old, safe business. The consequence is that, when you have been at one Christmas Eve party, and heard six people relate their adventures with spirits, you do not require to hear any more ghost stories. To listen to any further ghost stories after that would be like sitting out two farcical comedies, or taking in two comic journals; the repetition would become wearisome.

There is always the young man who was, one year, spending the Christmas at a country house, and, on Christmas Eve, they put him to sleep in the west wing. Then in the middle of the night, the room door quietly opens and somebody—generally a lady in her night-dress—walks slowly in, and comes and sits on the bed. The young man thinks it must be one of the visitors, or some relative of the family, though he does not remember having previously seen her, who, unable to go to sleep, and feeling lonesome, all by herself, has come into his room for a chat. He has no idea it is a ghost: he is so unsuspicious. She does not speak, however; and, when he looks again, she is gone!

The young man relates the circumstance at the breakfast-table next morning, and asks each of the ladies present if it were she who was his visitor. But they all assure him that it was not, and the host, who has grown deadly pale, begs him to say no more about the matter, which strikes the young man as a singularly strange request.

After breakfast the host takes the young man into a corner, and explains to him that what he saw was the ghost of a lady who had been murdered in that very bed, or who had murdered somebody else there—it does not really matter which: you can be a ghost by murdering somebody else or by being murdered yourself, whichever you prefer. The murdered ghost is, perhaps, the more popular; but, on the other hand, you can frighten people better if you are the murdered one, because then you can show your wounds and do groans.

Then there is the sceptical guest—it is always 'the guest' who gets let in for this sort of thing, by-the-bye. A ghost never thinks much of his own family: it is 'the guest' he likes to haunt who after listening to the host's ghost story, on Christmas Eve, laughs at it, and says that he does not believe there are such things as ghosts at all; and that he will sleep in the haunted chamber that very night, if they will let him.

Everybody urges him not to be reckless, but he persists in his foolhardiness, and goes up to the Yellow Chamber (or whatever colour the haunted room may be) with a light heart and a candle, and wishes them all good-night, and shuts the door.

Next morning he has got snow-white hair.

He does not tell anybody what he has seen: it is too awful.

There is also the plucky guest, who sees a ghost, and knows it is a ghost, and watches it, as it comes into the room and disappears through the wainscot, after which, as the ghost does not seem to be coming back, and there is nothing, consequently, to be gained by stopping awake, he goes to sleep.

He does not mention having seen the ghost to anybody, for fear of frightening them—some people are so nervous about ghosts,—but determines to wait for the next night, and see if the apparition appears again.

It does appear again, and, this time, he gets out of bed, dresses himself and does his hair, and follows it; and then discovers a secret passage leading from the bedroom down into the beer-cellar,- -a passage which, no doubt, was not unfrequently made use of in the bad old days of yore.

After him comes the young man who woke up with a strange sensation in the middle of the night, and found his rich bachelor uncle standing by his bedside. The rich uncle smiled a weird sort of smile and vanished. The young man immediately got up and looked at his watch. It had stopped at half-past four, he having forgotten to wind it.

He made inquiries the next day, and found that, strangely enough, his rich uncle, whose only nephew he was, had married a widow with eleven children at exactly a quarter to twelve, only two days ago,

The young man does not attempt to explain the circumstance. All he does is to vouch for the truth of his narrative.

And, to mention another case, there is the gentleman who is returning home late at night, from a Freemasons' dinner, and who, noticing a light issuing from a ruined abbey, creeps up, and looks through the keyhole. He sees the ghost of a 'grey sister' kissing the ghost of a brown monk, and is so inexpressibly shocked and frightened that he faints on the spot, and is discovered there the next morning, lying in a heap against the door, still speechless, and with his faithful latch-key clasped tightly in his hand.

All these things happen on Christmas Eve, they are all told of on Christmas Eve. For ghost stories to be told on any other evening than the evening of the twenty-fourth of December would be impossible in English society as at present regulated. Therefore, in introducing the sad but authentic ghost stories that follow hereafter, I feel that it is unnecessary to inform the student of Anglo-Saxon literature that the date on which they were told and on which the incidents took place was—Christmas Eve.

Nevertheless, I do so.

NOW THE STORIES CAME TO BE TOLD

It was Christmas Eve! Christmas Eve at my Uncle John's; Christmas Eve (There is too much 'Christmas Eve' about this book. I can see that myself. It is beginning to get monotonous even to me. But I don't see how to avoid it now.) at No. 47 Laburnham Grove, Tooting! Christmas Eve in the dimly-lighted (there was a gas-strike on) front parlour, where the flickering fire-light threw strange shadows on the highly coloured wall-paper, while without, in the wild street, the storm raged pitilessly, and the wind, like some unquiet spirit, flew, moaning, across the square, and passed, wailing with a troubled cry, round by the milk-shop.

We had had supper, and were sitting round, talking and smoking.

We had had a very good supper—a very good supper, indeed. Unpleasantness has occurred since, in our family, in connection with this party. Rumours have been put about in our family, concerning the matter generally, but more particularly concerning my own share in it, and remarks have been passed which have not so much surprised me, because I know what our family are, but which have pained me very much. As for my Aunt Maria, I do not know when I shall care to see her again. I should have thought Aunt Maria might have known me better.

But although injustice—gross injustice, as I shall explain later on—has been done to myself, that shall not deter me from doing justice to others; even to those who have made unfeeling insinuations. I will do justice to Aunt Maria's hot veal pasties, and toasted lobsters, followed by her own special make of cheesecakes, warm (there is no sense, to my thinking, in cold cheesecakes; you lose half the flavour), and washed down by Uncle John's own particular old ale, and acknowledge that they were most tasty. I did justice to them then; Aunt Maria herself could not but admit that.

After supper, Uncle brewed some whisky-punch. I did justice to that also; Uncle John himself said so. He said he was glad to notice that I liked it.

Aunt went to bed soon after supper, leaving the local curate, old Dr. Scrubbles, Mr. Samuel Coombes, our member of the County Council, Teddy Biffles, and myself to keep Uncle company. We agreed that it was too early to give in for some time yet, so Uncle brewed another bowl of punch; and I think we all did justice to that—at least I know I did. It is a passion with me, is the desire to do justice.

We sat up for a long while, and the Doctor brewed some gin-punch later on, for a change, though I could not taste much difference myself. But it was all good, and we were very happy—everybody was so kind.

Uncle John told us a very funny story in the course of the evening. Oh, it WAS a funny story! I forget what it was about now, but I know it amused me very much at the time; I do not think I ever laughed so much in all my life. It is strange that I cannot recollect that story too, because he told it us four times. And it was entirely our own fault that he did not tell it us a fifth. After that, the Doctor sang a very clever song, in the course of which he imitated all the different animals in a farmyard. He did mix them a bit. He brayed for the bantam cock, and crowed for the pig; but we knew what he meant all right.

I started relating a most interesting anecdote, but was somewhat surprised to observe, as I went on, that nobody was paying the slightest attention to me whatever. I thought this rather rude of them at first, until it dawned upon me that I was talking to myself all the time, instead of out aloud, so that, of course, they did not know that I was telling them a tale at all, and were probably puzzled to understand the meaning of my animated expression and eloquent gestures. It was a most curious mistake for any one to make. I never knew such a thing happen to me before.

Later on, our curate did tricks with cards. He asked us if we had ever seen a game called the "Three Card Trick." He said it was an artifice by means of which low, unscrupulous men, frequenters of race-meetings and such like haunts, swindled foolish young fellows out of their money. He said it was a very simple trick to do: it all depended on the quickness of the hand. It was the quickness of the hand deceived the eye.

He said he would show us the imposture so that we might be warned against it, and not be taken in by it; and he fetched Uncle's pack of cards from the tea-caddy, and, selecting three cards from the pack, two plain cards and one picture card, sat down on the hearthrug, and explained to us what he was going to do.

He said: "Now I shall take these three cards in my hand—so—and let you all see them. And then I shall quietly lay them down on the rug, with the backs uppermost, and ask you to pick out the picture card. And you'll think you know which one it is." And he did it.

Old Mr. Coombes, who is also one of our churchwardens, said it was the middle card.

"You fancy you saw it," said our curate, smiling.

"I don't 'fancy' anything at all about it," replied Mr. Coombes, "I tell you it's the middle card. I'll bet you half a dollar it's the middle card."

"There you are, that's just what I was explaining to you," said our curate, turning to the rest of us; "that's the way these foolish young fellows that I was speaking of are lured on to lose their money. They make sure they know the card, they fancy they saw it. They don't grasp the idea that it is the quickness of the hand that has deceived their eye."

He said he had known young men go off to a boat race, or a cricket match, with pounds in their pocket, and come home, early in the afternoon, stone broke; having lost all their money at this demoralising game.

He said he should take Mr. Coombes's half-crown, because it would teach Mr. Coombes a very useful lesson, and probably be the means of saving Mr. Coombes's money in the future; and he should give the two-and-sixpence to the blanket fund.

"Don't you worry about that," retorted old Mr. Coombes. "Don't you take the half-crown OUT of the blanket fund: that's all."

And he put his money on the middle card, and turned it up.

Sure enough, it really was the queen!

We were all very much surprised, especially the curate.

He said that it did sometimes happen that way, though—that a man did sometimes lay on the right card, by accident.

Our curate said it was, however, the most unfortunate thing a man could do for himself, if he only knew it, because, when a man tried and won, it gave him a taste for the so-called sport, and it lured him on into risking again and again; until he had to retire from the contest, a broken and ruined man.

Then he did the trick again. Mr. Coombes said it was the card next the coal-scuttle this time, and wanted to put five shillings on it.

We laughed at him, and tried to persuade him against it. He would listen to no advice, however, but insisted on plunging.

Our curate said very well then: he had warned him, and that was all that he could do. If he (Mr. Coombes) was determined to make a fool of himself, he (Mr. Coombes) must do so.

Our curate said he should take the five shillings and that would put things right again with the blanket fund.

So Mr. Coombes put two half-crowns on the card next the coal- scuttle and turned it up.

Sure enough, it was the queen again!

After that, Uncle John had a florin on, and HE won.

And then we all played at it; and we all won. All except the curate, that is. He had a very bad quarter of an hour. I never knew a man have such hard luck at cards. He lost every time.

We had some more punch after that; and Uncle made such a funny mistake in brewing it: he left out the whisky. Oh, we did laugh at him, and we made him put in double quantity afterwards, as a forfeit.

Oh, we did have such fun that evening!

And then, somehow or other, we must have got on to ghosts; because the next recollection I have is that we were telling ghost stories to each other.

TEDDY BIFFLES' STORY

Teddy Biffles told the first story, I will let him repeat it here in his own words.

(Do not ask me how it is that I recollect his own exact words— whether I took them down in shorthand at the time, or whether he had the story written out, and handed me the MS. afterwards for publication in this book, because I should not tell you if you did. It is a trade secret.)

Biffles called his story -

JOHNSON AND EMILY

OR

THE FAITHFUL GHOST

(Teddy Biffles' Story)

I was little more than a lad when I first met with Johnson. I was home for the Christmas holidays, and, it being Christmas Eve, I had been allowed to sit up very late. On opening the door of my little bedroom, to go in, I found myself face to face with Johnson, who was coming out. It passed through me, and uttering a long low wail of misery, disappeared out of the staircase window.

I was startled for the moment—I was only a schoolboy at the time, and had never seen a ghost before,—and felt a little nervous about going to bed. But, on reflection, I remembered that it was only sinful people that spirits could do any harm to, and so tucked myself up, and went to sleep.

In the morning I told the Pater what I had seen.

"Oh yes, that was old Johnson," he answered. "Don't you be frightened of that; he lives here." And then he told me the poor thing's history.

It seemed that Johnson, when it was alive, had loved, in early life, the daughter of a former lessee of our house, a very beautiful girl, whose Christian name had been Emily. Father did not know her other name.

Johnson was too poor to marry the girl, so he kissed her good-bye, told her he would soon be back, and went off to Australia to make his fortune.

But Australia was not then what it became later on. Travellers through the bush were few and far between in those early days; and, even when one was caught, the portable property found upon the body was often of hardly sufficiently negotiable value to pay the simple funeral expenses rendered necessary. So that it took Johnson nearly twenty years to make his fortune.

The self-imposed task was accomplished at last, however, and then, having successfully eluded the police, and got clear out of the Colony, he returned to England, full of hope and joy, to claim his bride.

He reached the house to find it silent and deserted. All that the neighbours could tell him was that, soon after his own departure, the family had, on one foggy night, unostentatiously disappeared, and that nobody had ever seen or heard anything of them since, although the landlord and most of the local tradesmen had made searching inquiries.

Poor Johnson, frenzied with grief, sought his lost love all over the world. But he never found her, and, after years of fruitless effort, he returned to end his lonely life in the very house where, in the happy bygone days, he and his beloved Emily had passed so many blissful hours.

He had lived there quite alone, wandering about the empty rooms, weeping and calling to his Emily to come back to him; and when the poor old fellow died, his ghost still kept the business on.

It was there, the Pater said, when he took the house, and the agent had knocked ten pounds a year off the rent in consequence.

After that, I was continually meeting Johnson about the place at all times of the night, and so, indeed, were we all. We used to walk round it and stand aside to let it pass, at first; but, when we grew at home with it, and there seemed no necessity for so much ceremony, we used to walk straight through it. You could not say it was ever much in the way.

It was a gentle, harmless, old ghost, too, and we all felt very sorry for it, and pitied it. The women folk, indeed, made quite a pet of it, for a while. Its faithfulness touched them so.

But as time went on, it grew to be a bit a bore. You see it was full of sadness. There was nothing cheerful or genial about it. You felt sorry for it, but it irritated you. It would sit on the stairs and cry for hours at a stretch; and, whenever we woke up in the night, one was sure to hear it pottering about the passages and in and out of the different rooms, moaning and sighing, so that we could not get to sleep again very easily. And when we had a party on, it would come and sit outside the drawing-room door, and sob all the time. It did not do anybody any harm exactly, but it cast a gloom over the whole affair.

"Oh, I'm getting sick of this old fool," said the Pater, one evening (the Dad can be very blunt, when he is put out, as you know), after Johnson had been more of a nuisance than usual, and had spoiled a good game of whist, by sitting up the chimney and groaning, till nobody knew what were trumps or what suit had been led, even. "We shall have to get rid of him, somehow or other. I wish I knew how to do it."

"Well," said the Mater, "depend upon it, you'll never see the last of him until he's found Emily's grave. That's what he is after. You find Emily's grave, and put him on to that, and he'll stop there. That's the only thing to do. You mark my words."

The idea seemed reasonable, but the difficulty in the way was that we none of us knew where Emily's grave was any more than the ghost of Johnson himself did. The Governor suggested palming off some other Emily's grave upon the poor thing, but, as luck would have it, there did not seem to have been an Emily of any sort buried anywhere for miles round. I never came across a neighbourhood so utterly destitute of dead Emilies.

I thought for a bit, and then I hazarded a suggestion myself.

"Couldn't we fake up something for the old chap?" I queried. "He seems a simple-minded old sort. He might take it in. Anyhow, we could but try."

"By Jove, so we will," exclaimed my father; and the very next morning we had the workmen in, and fixed up a little mound at the bottom of the orchard with a tombstone over it, bearing the following inscription:-

SACRED TO THE MEMORY OF EMILY HER LAST WORDS WERE - "TELL JOHNSON I LOVE HIM"

"That ought to fetch him," mused the Dad as he surveyed the work when finished. "I am sure I hope it does."

It did!

We lured him down there that very night; and—well, there, it was one of the most pathetic things I have ever seen, the way Johnson sprang upon that tombstone and wept. Dad and old Squibbins, the gardener, cried like children when they saw it.

Johnson has never troubled us any more in the house since then. It spends every night now, sobbing on the grave, and seems quite happy.

"There still?" Oh yes. I'll take you fellows down and show you it, next time you come to our place: 10 p.m. to 4 a.m. are its general hours, 10 to 2 on Saturdays.

INTERLUDE—THE DOCTOR'S STORY

It made me cry very much, that story, young Biffles told it with so much feeling. We were all a little thoughtful after it, and I noticed even the old Doctor covertly wipe away a tear. Uncle John brewed another bowl of punch, however, and we gradually grew more resigned.

The Doctor, indeed, after a while became almost cheerful, and told us about the ghost of one of his patients.

I cannot give you his story. I wish I could. They all said afterwards that it was the best of the lot—the most ghastly and terrible—but I could not make any sense of it myself. It seemed so incomplete.

He began all right and then something seemed to happen, and then he was finishing it. I cannot make out what he did with the middle of the story.

It ended up, I know, however, with somebody finding something; and that put Mr. Coombes in mind of a very curious affair that took place at an old Mill, once kept by his brother-in-law.

Mr. Coombes said he would tell us his story, and before anybody could stop him, he had begun.

Mr Coombes said the story was called -

THE HAUNTED MILL

OR

THE RUINED HOME

(Mr. Coombes's Story)

Well, you all know my brother-in-law, Mr. Parkins (began Mr. Coombes, taking the long clay pipe from his mouth, and putting it behind his ear: we did not know his brother-in-law, but we said we did, so as to save time), and you know of course that he once took a lease of an old Mill in Surrey, and went to live there.

Now you must know that, years ago, this very mill had been occupied by a wicked old miser, who died there, leaving—so it was rumoured- -all his money hidden somewhere about the place. Naturally enough, every one who had since come to live at the mill had tried to find the treasure; but none had ever succeeded, and the local wiseacres said that nobody ever would, unless the ghost of the miserly miller should, one day, take a fancy to one of the tenants, and disclose to him the secret of the hiding-place.

My brother-in-law did not attach much importance to the story, regarding it as an old woman's tale, and, unlike his predecessors, made no attempt whatever to discover the hidden gold.

"Unless business was very different then from what it is now," said my brother-in-law, "I don't see how a miller could very well have saved anything, however much of a miser he might have been: at all events, not enough to make it worth the trouble of looking for it."

Still, he could not altogether get rid of the idea of that treasure.

One night he went to bed. There was nothing very extraordinary about that, I admit. He often did go to bed of a night. What WAS remarkable, however, was that exactly as the clock of the village church chimed the last stroke of twelve, my brother-in-law woke up with a start, and felt himself quite unable to go to sleep again.

Joe (his Christian name was Joe) sat up in bed, and looked around.

At the foot of the bed something stood very still, wrapped in shadow.

It moved into the moonlight, and then my brother-in-law saw that it was the figure of a wizened little old man, in knee-breeches and a pig-tail.

In an instant the story of the hidden treasure and the old miser flashed across his mind.

"He's come to show me where it's hid," thought my brother-in-law; and he resolved that he would not spend all this money on himself, but would devote a small percentage of it towards doing good to others.

The apparition moved towards the door: my brother-in-law put on his trousers and followed it. The ghost went downstairs into the kitchen, glided over and stood in front of the hearth, sighed and disappeared.

Next morning, Joe had a couple of bricklayers in, and made them haul out the stove and pull down the chimney, while he stood behind with a potato-sack in which to put the gold.

They knocked down half the wall, and never found so much as a four- penny bit. My brother-in-law did not know what to think.

The next night the old man appeared again, and again led the way into the kitchen. This time, however, instead of going to the fireplace, it stood more in the middle of the room, and sighed there.

"Oh, I see what he means now," said my brother-in-law to himself; "it's under the floor. Why did the old idiot go and stand up against the stove, so as to make me think it was up the chimney?"

They spent the next day in taking up the kitchen floor; but the only thing they found was a three-pronged fork, and the handle of that was broken.

On the third night, the ghost reappeared, quite unabashed, and for a third time made for the kitchen. Arrived there, it looked up at the ceiling and vanished.

"Umph! he don't seem to have learned much sense where he's been to," muttered Joe, as he trotted back to bed; "I should have thought he might have done that at first."

Still, there seemed no doubt now where the treasure lay, and the first thing after breakfast they started pulling down the ceiling. They got every inch of the ceiling down, and they took up the boards of the room above.

They discovered about as much treasure as you would expect to find in an empty quart-pot.

On the fourth night, when the ghost appeared, as usual, my brother- in-law was so wild that he threw his boots at it; and the boots passed through the body, and broke a looking-glass.

On the fifth night, when Joe awoke, as he always did now at twelve, the ghost was standing in a dejected attitude, looking very miserable. There was an appealing look in its large sad eyes that quite touched my brother-in-law.

"After all," he thought, "perhaps the silly chap's doing his best. Maybe he has forgotten where he really did put it, and is trying to remember. I'll give him another chance."

The ghost appeared grateful and delighted at seeing Joe prepare to follow him, and led the way into the attic, pointed to the ceiling, and vanished.

"Well, he's hit it this time, I do hope," said my brother-in-law; and next day they set to work to take the roof off the place.

It took them three days to get the roof thoroughly off, and all they found was a bird's nest; after securing which they covered up the house with tarpaulins, to keep it dry.

You might have thought that would have cured the poor fellow of looking for treasure. But it didn't.

He said there must be something in it all, or the ghost would never keep on coming as it did; and that, having gone so far, he would go on to the end, and solve the mystery, cost what it might.

Night after night, he would get out of his bed and follow that spectral old fraud about the house. Each night, the old man would indicate a different place; and, on each following day, my brother- in-law would proceed to break up the mill at the point indicated, and look for the treasure. At the end of three weeks, there was not a room in the mill fit to live in. Every wall had been pulled down, every floor had been taken up, every ceiling had had a hole knocked in it. And then, as suddenly as they had begun, the ghost's visits ceased; and my brother-in-law was left in peace, to rebuild the place at his leisure.

"What induced the old image to play such a silly trick upon a family man and a ratepayer?" Ah! that's just what I cannot tell you.

Some said that the ghost of the wicked old man had done it to punish my brother-in-law for not believing in him at first; while others held that the apparition was probably that of some deceased local plumber and glazier, who would naturally take an interest in seeing a house knocked about and spoilt. But nobody knew anything for certain.

INTERLUDE

We had some more punch, and then the curate told us a story.

I could not make head or tail of the curate's story, so I cannot retail it to you. We none of us could make head or tail of that story. It was a good story enough, so far as material went. There seemed to be an enormous amount of plot, and enough incident to have made a dozen novels. I never before heard a story containing so much incident, nor one dealing with so many varied characters.

I should say that every human being our curate had ever known or met, or heard of, was brought into that story. There were simply hundreds of them. Every five seconds he would introduce into the tale a completely fresh collection of characters accompanied by a brand new set of incidents.

This was the sort of story it was:-

"Well, then, my uncle went into the garden, and got his gun, but, of course, it wasn't there, and Scroggins said he didn't believe it."

"Didn't believe what? Who's Scroggins?"

"Scroggins! Oh, why he was the other man, you know—it was wife."

"WHAT was his wife—what's SHE got to do with it?"

"Why, that's what I'm telling you. It was she that found the hat. She'd come up with her cousin to London—her cousin was my sister- in-law, and the other niece had married a man named Evans, and Evans, after it was all over, had taken the box round to Mr. Jacobs', because Jacobs' father had seen the man, when he was alive, and when he was dead, Joseph—"

"Now look here, never you mind Evans and the box; what's become of your uncle and the gun?"

"The gun! What gun?"

"Why, the gun that your uncle used to keep in the garden, and that wasn't there. What did he do with it? Did he kill any of these people with it—these Jacobses and Evanses and Scrogginses and Josephses? Because, if so, it was a good and useful work, and we should enjoy hearing about it."

"No—oh no—how could he?—he had been built up alive in the wall, you know, and when Edward IV spoke to the abbot about it, my sister said that in her then state of health she could not and would not, as it was endangering the child's life. So they christened it Horatio, after her own son, who had been killed at Waterloo before he was born, and Lord Napier himself said—"

"Look here, do you know what you are talking about?" we asked him at this point.

He said "No," but he knew it was every word of it true, because his aunt had seen it herself. Whereupon we covered him over with the tablecloth, and he went to sleep.

And then Uncle told us a story.

Uncle said his was a real story.

THE GHOST OF THE BLUE CHAMBER

(My Uncle's Story)

"I don't want to make you fellows nervous," began my uncle in a peculiarly impressive, not to say blood-curdling, tone of voice, "and if you would rather that I did not mention it, I won't; but, as a matter of fact, this very house, in which we are now sitting, is haunted."

"You don't say that!" exclaimed Mr. Coombes.

"What's the use of your saying I don't say it when I have just said it?" retorted my uncle somewhat pettishly. "You do talk so foolishly. I tell you the house is haunted. Regularly on Christmas Eve the Blue Chamber [they called the room next to the nursery the 'blue chamber,' at my uncle's, most of the toilet service being of that shade] is haunted by the ghost of a sinful man—a man who once killed a Christmas wait with a lump of coal."

"How did he do it?" asked Mr. Coombes, with eager anxiousness.

"Was it difficult?"

"I do not know how he did it," replied my uncle; "he did not explain the process. The wait had taken up a position just inside the front gate, and was singing a ballad. It is presumed that, when he opened his mouth for B flat, the lump of coal was thrown by the sinful man from one of the windows, and that it went down the wait's throat and choked him."

"You want to be a good shot, but it is certainly worth trying," murmured Mr. Coombes thoughtfully.

"But that was not his only crime, alas!" added my uncle. "Prior to that he had killed a solo cornet-player."

"No! Is that really a fact?" exclaimed Mr. Coombes.

"Of course it's a fact," answered my uncle testily; "at all events, as much a fact as you can expect to get in a case of this sort.

"How very captious you are this evening. The circumstantial evidence was overwhelming. The poor fellow, the cornet-player, had been in the neighbourhood barely a month. Old Mr. Bishop, who kept the 'Jolly Sand Boys' at the time, and from whom I had the story, said he had never known a more hard-working and energetic solo cornet-player. He, the cornet-player, only knew two tunes, but Mr. Bishop said that the man could not have played with more vigour, or for more hours in a day, if he had known forty. The two tunes he did play were "Annie Laurie" and "Home, Sweet Home"; and as regarded his performance of the former melody, Mr. Bishop said that a mere child could have told what it was meant for.

"This musician—this poor, friendless artist used to come regularly and play in this street just opposite for two hours every evening. One evening he was seen, evidently in response to an invitation, going into this very house, BUT WAS NEVER SEEN COMING OUT OF IT!"

"Did the townsfolk try offering any reward for his recovery?" asked
Mr. Coombes.

"Not a ha'penny," replied my uncle.

"Another summer," continued my uncle, "a German band visited here, intending—so they announced on their arrival—to stay till the autumn.

"On the second day from their arrival, the whole company, as fine and healthy a body of men as one could wish to see, were invited to dinner by this sinful man, and, after spending the whole of the next twenty-four hours in bed, left the town a broken and dyspeptic crew; the parish doctor, who had attended them, giving it as his opinion that it was doubtful if they would, any of them, be fit to play an air again."

"You—you don't know the recipe, do you?" asked Mr. Coombes.

"Unfortunately I do not," replied my uncle; "but the chief ingredient was said to have been railway refreshment-room pork-pie.

"I forget the man's other crimes," my uncle went on; "I used to know them all at one time, but my memory is not what it was. I do not, however, believe I am doing his memory an injustice in believing that he was not entirely unconnected with the death, and subsequent burial, of a gentleman who used to play the harp with his toes; and that neither was he altogether unresponsible for the lonely grave of an unknown stranger who had once visited the neighbourhood, an Italian peasant lad, a performer upon the barrel- organ.

"Every Christmas Eve," said my uncle, cleaving with low impressive tones the strange awed silence that, like a shadow, seemed to have slowly stolen into and settled down upon the room, "the ghost of this sinful man haunts the Blue Chamber, in this very house. There, from midnight until cock-crow, amid wild muffled shrieks and groans and mocking laughter and the ghostly sound of horrid blows, it does fierce phantom fight with the spirits of the solo cornet- player and the murdered wait, assisted at intervals, by the shades of the German band; while the ghost of the strangled harpist plays mad ghostly melodies with ghostly toes on the ghost of a broken harp.

Uncle said the Blue Chamber was comparatively useless as a sleeping-apartment on Christmas Eve.

"Hark!" said uncle, raising a warning hand towards the ceiling, while we held our breath, and listened; "Hark! I believe they are at it now—in the BLUE CHAMBER!"

THE BLUE CHAMBER

I rose up, and said that I would sleep in the Blue Chamber.

Before I tell you my own story, however—the story of what happened in the Blue Chamber—I would wish to preface it with -

A PERSONAL EXPLANATION

I feel a good deal of hesitation about telling you this story of my own. You see it is not a story like the other stories that I have been telling you, or rather that Teddy Biffles, Mr. Coombes, and my uncle have been telling you: it is a true story. It is not a story told by a person sitting round a fire on Christmas Eve, drinking whisky punch: it is a record of events that actually happened.

Indeed, it is not a 'story' at all, in the commonly accepted meaning of the word: it is a report. It is, I feel, almost out of place in a book of this kind. It is more suitable to a biography, or an English history.

There is another thing that makes it difficult for me to tell you this story, and that is, that it is all about myself. In telling you this story, I shall have to keep on talking about myself; and talking about ourselves is what we modern-day authors have a strong objection to doing. If we literary men of the new school have one praiseworthy yearning more ever present to our minds than another it is the yearning never to appear in the slightest degree egotistical.

I myself, so I am told, carry this coyness—this shrinking reticence concerning anything connected with my own personality, almost too far; and people grumble at me because of it. People come to me and say -

"Well, now, why don't you talk about yourself a bit? That's what we want to read about. Tell us something about yourself."

But I have always replied, "No." It is not that I do not think the subject an interesting one. I cannot myself conceive of any topic more likely to prove fascinating to the world as a whole, or at all events to the cultured portion of it. But I will not do it, on principle. It is inartistic, and it sets a bad example to the younger men. Other writers (a few of them) do it, I know; but I will not—not as a rule.

Under ordinary circumstances, therefore, I should not tell you this story at all. I should say to myself, "No! It is a good story, it is a moral story, it is a strange, weird, enthralling sort of a story; and the public, I know, would like to hear it; and

I should like to tell it to them; but it is all about myself—about what I said, and what I saw, and what I did, and I cannot do it. My retiring, anti-egotistical nature will not permit me to talk in this way about myself."

But the circumstances surrounding this story are not ordinary, and there are reasons prompting me, in spite of my modesty, to rather welcome the opportunity of relating it.

As I stated at the beginning, there has been unpleasantness in our family over this party of ours, and, as regards myself in particular, and my share in the events I am now about to set forth, gross injustice has been done me.

As a means of replacing my character in its proper light—of dispelling the clouds of calumny and misconception with which it has been darkened, I feel that my best course is to give a simple, dignified narration of the plain facts, and allow the unprejudiced to judge for themselves. My chief object, I candidly confess, is to clear myself from unjust aspersion. Spurred by this motive—and I think it is an honourable and a right motive—I find I am enabled to overcome my usual repugnance to talking about myself, and can thus tell -

MY OWN STORY

As soon as my uncle had finished his story, I, as I have already told you, rose up and said that *I* would sleep in the Blue Chamber that very night.

"Never!" cried my uncle, springing up. "You shall not put yourself in this deadly peril. Besides, the bed is not made."

"Never mind the bed," I replied. "I have lived in furnished apartments for gentlemen, and have been accustomed to sleep on beds that have never been made from one year's end to the other. Do not thwart me in my resolve. I am young, and have had a clear conscience now for over a month. The spirits will not harm me. I may even do them some little good, and induce them to be quiet and go away. Besides, I should like to see the show."

Saying which, I sat down again. (How Mr. Coombes came to be in my chair, instead of at the other side of the room, where he had been all the evening; and why he never offered to apologise when I sat right down on top of him; and why young Biffles should have tried to palm himself off upon me as my Uncle John, and induced me, under that erroneous impression, to shake him by the hand for nearly three minutes, and tell him that I had always regarded him as father,—are matters that, to this day, I have never been able to fully understand.)

They tried to dissuade me from what they termed my foolhardy enterprise, but I remained firm, and claimed my privilege. I was 'the guest.' 'The guest' always sleeps in the haunted chamber on Christmas Eve; it is his perquisite.

They said that if I put it on that footing, they had, of course, no answer; and they lighted a candle for me, and accompanied me upstairs in a body.

Whether elevated by the feeling that I was doing a noble action, or animated by a mere general consciousness of rectitude, is not for me to say, but I went upstairs that night with remarkable buoyancy. It was as much as I could do to stop at the landing when I came to it; I felt I wanted to go on up to the roof. But, with the help of the banisters, I restrained my ambition, wished them all good- night, and went in and shut the door.

Things began to go wrong with me from the very first. The candle tumbled out of the candlestick before my hand was off the lock. It kept on tumbling out of the candlestick, and every time I picked put it up and put it in, it tumbled out again: I never saw such a slippery candle. I gave up attempting to use the candlestick at last, and carried the candle about in my hand; and, even then, it would not keep upright. So I got wild and threw it out of window, and undressed and went to bed in the dark.

I did not go to sleep,—I did not feel sleepy at all,—I lay on my back, looking up at the ceiling, and thinking of things. I wish I could remember some of the ideas that came to me as I lay there, because they were so amusing. I laughed at them myself till the bed shook.

I had been lying like this for half an hour or so, and had forgotten all about the ghost, when, on casually casting my eyes round the room, I noticed for the first time a singularly contented-looking phantom, sitting in the easy-chair by the fire, smoking the ghost of a long clay pipe.

I fancied for the moment, as most people would under similar circumstances, that I must be dreaming. I sat up, and rubbed my eyes.

No! It was a ghost, clear enough. I could see the back of the chair through his body. He looked over towards me, took the shadowy pipe from his lips, and nodded.

The most surprising part of the whole thing to me was that I did not feel in the least alarmed. If anything, I was rather pleased to see him. It was company.

I said, "Good evening. It's been a cold day!"

He said he had not noticed it himself, but dared say I was right.

We remained silent for a few seconds, and then, wishing to put it pleasantly, I said, "I believe I have the honour of addressing the ghost of the gentleman who had the accident with the wait?"

He smiled, and said it was very good of me to remember it. One wait was not much to boast of, but still, every little helped.

I was somewhat staggered at his answer. I had expected a groan of remorse. The ghost appeared, on the contrary, to be rather conceited over the business. I thought that, as he had taken my reference to the wait so quietly, perhaps he would not be offended if I questioned him about the organ-grinder. I felt curious about that poor boy.

"Is it true," I asked, "that you had a hand in the death of that Italian peasant lad who came to the town once with a barrel-organ that played nothing but Scotch airs?"

He quite fired up. "Had a hand in it!" he exclaimed indignantly. "Who has dared to pretend that he assisted me? I murdered the youth myself. Nobody helped me. Alone I did it. Show me the man who says I didn't."

I calmed him. I assured him that I had never, in my own mind, doubted that he was the real and only assassin, and I went on and asked him what he had done with the body of the cornet-player he had killed.

He said, "To which one may you be alluding?"

"Oh, were there any more then?" I inquired.

He smiled, and gave a little cough. He said he did not like to appear to be boasting, but that, counting trombones, there were seven.

"Dear me!" I replied, "you must have had quite a busy time of it, one way and another."

He said that perhaps he ought not to be the one to say so, but that really, speaking of ordinary middle-society, he thought there were few ghosts who could look back upon a life of more sustained usefulness.

He puffed away in silence for a few seconds, while I sat watching him. I had never seen a ghost smoking a pipe before, that I could remember, and it interested me.

I asked him what tobacco he used, and he replied, "The ghost of cut cavendish, as a rule."

He explained that the ghost of all the tobacco that a man smoked in life belonged to him when he became dead. He said he himself had smoked a good deal of cut cavendish when he was alive, so that he was well supplied with the ghost of it now.

I observed that it was a useful thing to know that, and I made up my mind to smoke as much tobacco as ever I could before I died.

I thought I might as well start at once, so I said I would join him in a pipe, and he said, "Do, old man"; and I reached over and got out the necessary paraphernalia from my coat pocket and lit up.

We grew quite chummy after that, and he told me all his crimes. He said he had lived next door once to a young lady who was learning to play the guitar, while a gentleman who practised on the bass- viol lived opposite. And he, with fiendish cunning, had introduced these two unsuspecting young people to one another, and had persuaded them to elope with each other against their parents' wishes, and take their musical instruments with them; and they had done so, and, before the honeymoon was over, SHE had broken his head with the bass-viol, and HE had tried to cram the guitar down her throat, and had injured her for life.

My friend said he used to lure muffin-men into the passage and then stuff them with their own wares till they burst and died. He said he had quieted eighteen that way.

Young men and women who recited long and dreary poems at evening parties, and callow youths who walked about the streets late at night, playing concertinas, he used to get together and poison in batches of ten, so as to save expense; and park orators and temperance lecturers he used to shut up six in a small room with a glass of water and a collection-box apiece, and let them talk each other to death.

It did one good to listen to him.

I asked him when he expected the other ghosts—the ghosts of the wait and the cornet-player, and the German band that Uncle John had mentioned. He smiled, and said they would never come again, any of them.

I said, "Why; isn't it true, then, that they meet you here every
Christmas Eve for a row?"

He replied that it WAS true. Every Christmas Eve, for twenty-five years, had he and they fought in that room; but they would never trouble him nor anybody else again. One by one, had he laid them out, spoilt, and utterly useless for all haunting purposes. He had finished off the last German-band ghost that very evening, just before I came upstairs, and had thrown what was left of it out through the slit between the window-sashes. He said it would never be worth calling a ghost again.

"I suppose you will still come yourself, as usual?" I said. "They would be sorry to miss you, I know."

"Oh, I don't know," he replied; "there's nothing much to come for now. Unless," he added kindly, "YOU are going to be here. I'll come if you will sleep here next Christmas Eve."

"I have taken a liking to you," he continued; "you don't fly off, screeching, when you see a party, and your hair doesn't stand on end. You've no idea," he said, "how sick I am of seeing people's hair standing on end."

He said it irritated him.

Just then a slight noise reached us from the yard below, and he started and turned deathly black.

"You are ill," I cried, springing towards him; "tell me the best thing to do for you. Shall I drink some brandy, and give you the ghost of it?"

He remained silent, listening intently for a moment, and then he gave a sigh of relief, and the shade came back to his cheek.

"It's all right," he murmured; "I was afraid it was the cock."

"Oh, it's too early for that," I said. "Why, it's only the middle of the night."

"Oh, that doesn't make any difference to those cursed chickens," he replied bitterly. "They would just as soon crow in the middle of the night as at any other time—sooner, if they thought it would spoil a chap's evening out. I believe they do it on purpose."

He said a friend of his, the ghost of a man who had killed a water- rate collector, used to haunt a house in Long Acre, where they kept fowls in the cellar, and every time a policeman went by and flashed his bull's-eye down the grating, the old cock there would fancy it was the sun, and start crowing like mad; when, of course, the poor ghost had to dissolve, and it would, in consequence, get back home sometimes as early as one o'clock in the morning, swearing fearfully because it had only been out for an hour.

I agreed that it seemed very unfair.

"Oh, it's an absurd arrangement altogether," he continued, quite angrily. "I can't imagine what our old man could have been thinking of when he made it. As I have said to him, over and over again, 'Have a fixed time, and let everybody stick to it—say four o'clock in summer, and six in winter. Then one would know what one was about.'"

"How do you manage when there isn't any cock handy?" I inquired.

He was on the point of replying, when again he started and listened. This time I distinctly heard Mr. Bowles's cock, next door, crow twice.

"There you are," he said, rising and reaching for his hat; "that's the sort of thing we have to put up with. What IS the time?"

I looked at my watch, and found it was half-past three.

"I thought as much," he muttered. "I'll wring that blessed bird's neck if I get hold of it." And he prepared to go.

"If you can wait half a minute," I said, getting out of bed, "I'll go a bit of the way with you."

"It's very good of you," he rejoined, pausing, "but it seems unkind to drag you out."

"Not at all," I replied; "I shall like a walk." And I partially dressed myself, and took my umbrella; and he put his arm through mine, and we went out together.

Just by the gate we met Jones, one of the local constables.

"Good-night, Jones," I said (I always feel affable at Christmas- time).

"Good-night, sir," answered the man a little gruffly, I thought.

"May I ask what you're a-doing of?"

"Oh, it's all right," I responded, with a wave of my umbrella; "I'm just seeing my friend part of the way home."

He said, "What friend?"

"Oh, ah, of course," I laughed; "I forgot. He's invisible to you. He is the ghost of the gentleman that killed the wait. I'm just going to the corner with him."

"Ah, I don't think I would, if I was you, sir," said Jones severely. "If you take my advice, you'll say good-bye to your friend here, and go back indoors. Perhaps you are not aware that you are walking about with nothing on but a night-shirt and a pair of boots and an opera-hat. Where's your trousers?"

I did not like the man's manner at all. I said, "Jones! I don't wish to have to report you, but it seems to me you've been drinking. My trousers are where a man's trousers ought to be—on his legs. I distinctly remember putting them on."

"Well, you haven't got them on now," he retorted.

"I beg your pardon," I replied. "I tell you I have; I think I ought to know."

"I think so, too," he answered, "but you evidently don't. Now you come along indoors with me, and don't let's have any more of it."

Uncle John came to the door at this point, having been awaked, I suppose, by the altercation; and, at the same moment, Aunt Maria appeared at the window in her nightcap.

I explained the constable's mistake to them, treating the matter as lightly as I could, so as not to get the man into trouble, and I turned for confirmation to the ghost.

He was gone! He had left me without a word—without even saying good-bye!

It struck me as so unkind, his having gone off in that way, that I burst into tears; and Uncle John came out, and led me back into the house.

On reaching my room, I discovered that Jones was right. I had not put on my trousers, after all. They were still hanging over the bed-rail. I suppose, in my anxiety not to keep the ghost waiting, I must have forgotten them.

Such are the plain facts of the case, out of which it must, doubtless, to the healthy, charitable mind appear impossible that calumny could spring.

But it has.

Persons—I say 'persons'—have professed themselves unable to understand the simple circumstances herein narrated, except in the light of explanations at once misleading and insulting. Slurs have been cast and aspersions made on me by those of my own flesh and blood.

But I bear no ill-feeling. I merely, as I have said, set forth this statement for the purpose of clearing my character from injurious suspicion.

DIARY OF A
PILGRIMAGE

PREFACE

Said a friend of mine to me some months ago: "Well now, why don't you write a *sensible* book? I should like to see you make people think."

"Do you believe it can be done, then?" I asked.

"Well, try," he replied.

Accordingly, I have tried. This is a sensible book. I want you to understand that. This is a book to improve your mind. In this book I tell you all about Germany—at all events, all I know about Germany—and the Ober-Ammergau Passion Play. I also tell you about other things. I do not tell you all I know about all these other things, because I do not want to swamp you with knowledge. I wish to lead you gradually. When you have learnt this book, you can come again, and I will tell you some more. I should only be defeating my own object did I, by making you think too much at first, give you a perhaps, lasting dislike to the exercise. I have purposely put the matter in a light and attractive form, so that I may secure the attention of the young and the frivolous. I do not want them to notice, as they go on, that they are being instructed; and I have, therefore, endeavoured to disguise from them, so far as is practicable, that this is either an exceptionally clever or an exceptionally useful work. I want to do them good without their knowing it. I want to do you all good—to improve your minds and to make you think, if I can.

What you will think after you have read the book, I do not want to know; indeed, I would rather not know. It will be sufficient reward for me to feel that I have done my duty, and to receive a percentage on the gross sales.

LONDON, *March*, 1891.

MONDAY, 19TH

My Friend B.—Invitation to the Theatre.—A Most Unpleasant Regulation.—Yearnings of the Embryo Traveller.—How to Make the Most of One's Own Country.—Friday, a Lucky Day.—The Pilgrimage Decided On.

My friend B. called on me this morning and asked me if I would go to a theatre with him on Monday next.

"Oh, yes! certainly, old man," I replied. "Have you got an order, then?"

He said:

"No; they don't give orders. We shall have to pay."

"Pay! Pay to go into a theatre!" I answered, in astonishment. "Oh, nonsense! You are joking."

"My dear fellow," he rejoined, "do you think I should suggest paying if it were possible to get in by any other means? But the people who run this theatre would not even understand what was meant by a 'free list,' the uncivilised barbarians! It is of no use pretending to them that you are on the Press, because they don't want the Press; they don't think anything of the Press. It is no good writing to the acting manager, because there is no acting manager. It would be a waste of time offering to exhibit bills, because they don't have any bills—not of that sort. If you want to go in to see the show, you've got to pay. If you don't pay, you stop outside; that's their brutal rule."

"Dear me," I said, "what a very unpleasant arrangement! And whereabouts is this extraordinary theatre? I don't think I can ever have been inside it."

"I don't think you have," he replied; "it is at Ober-Ammergau—first turning on the left after you leave Ober railway-station, fifty miles from Munich."

"Um! rather out of the way for a theatre," I said. "I should not have thought an outlying house like that could have afforded to give itself airs."

"The house holds seven thousand people," answered my friend B., "and money is turned away at each performance. The first production is on Monday next. Will you come?"

I pondered for a moment, looked at my diary, and saw that Aunt Emma was coming to spend Saturday to Wednesday next with us, calculated that if I went I should miss her, and might not see her again for years, and decided that I would go.

To tell the truth, it was the journey more than the play that tempted me. To be a great traveller has always been one of my cherished ambitions. I yearn to be able to write in this sort of strain:—

"I have smoked my fragrant Havana in the sunny streets of old Madrid, and I have puffed the rude and not sweet-smelling calumet of peace in the draughty wigwam of the Wild West; I have sipped my evening coffee in the silent tent, while the tethered camel browsed without upon the desert grass, and I have quaffed the fiery brandy of the North while the reindeer munched his fodder beside me in the hut, and the pale light of the midnight sun threw the shadows of the pines across the snow; I have felt the stab of lustrous eyes that, ghostlike, looked at me from out veil-covered faces in Byzantium's narrow ways, and I have laughed back (though it was wrong of me to do so) at the saucy, wanton glances of the black-eyed girls of Jedo; I have wandered where 'good'—but not too good—Haroun Alraschid crept disguised at nightfall, with his faithful Mesrour by his side; I have stood upon the bridge where Dante watched the sainted Beatrice pass by; I have floated on the waters that once bore the barge of Cleopatra; I have stood where Cæsar fell; I have heard the soft rustle of rich, rare robes in the drawing-rooms of Mayfair, and I have heard the teeth-necklaces rattle around the ebony throats of the belles of Tongataboo; I have panted beneath the sun's fierce rays in India, and frozen under the icy blasts of Greenland; I have mingled with the teeming hordes of old Cathay, and, deep in the great pine forests of the Western World, I have lain, wrapped in my blanket, a thousand miles beyond the shores of human life."

B., to whom I explained my leaning towards this style of diction, said that exactly the same effect could be produced by writing about places quite handy. He said:—

"I could go on like that without having been outside England at all. I should say:

"I have smoked my fourpenny shag in the sanded bars of Fleet Street, and I have puffed my twopenny Manilla in the gilded balls of the Criterion; I have quaffed my foaming beer of Burton where Islington's famed Angel gathers the little thirsty ones beneath her shadowing wings, and I have sipped my tenpenny *ordinaire* in many a garlic-scented salon of Soho. On the back of the strangely-moving ass I have urged—or, to speak more correctly, the proprietor of the ass, or his agent, from behind has urged—my wild career across the sandy heaths of Hampstead, and my canoe has startled the screaming wild-fowl from their lonely haunts amid the sub-tropical regions of Battersea. Adown the long, steep slope of One Tree Hill have I rolled from top to foot, while laughing maidens of the East stood round and clapped their hands and yelled; and, in the old-world garden of that pleasant Court, where played the fair-haired children of the ill-starred Stuarts, have I wandered long through many paths, my arm entwined about the waist of one of Eve's sweet daughters, while her mother raged around indignantly on the other side of the hedge, and never seemed to get any nearer to us. I have chased the lodging-house Norfolk Howard to his watery death by the pale lamp's light; I have, shivering, followed the leaping flea o'er many a mile of pillow and sheet, by the great Atlantic's margin. Round and round, till the heart—and not only the heart—grows sick, and the mad brain whirls and reels, have I ridden the small, but extremely hard, horse, that may, for a penny, be mounted amid the plains of Peckham Rye; and high above the heads of the giddy throngs of Barnet (though it is doubtful if anyone among them was half so giddy as was I) have I swung in highly-coloured car, worked by a man with a rope. I have trod in stately measure the floor of Kensington's Town Hall (the tickets were a guinea each, and included refreshments—when you could get to them through the crowd), and on the green sward of the forest that borders eastern Anglia by the oft-sung town of Epping I have performed quaint ceremonies in a ring; I have mingled with the teeming hordes of Drury Lane on Boxing Night, and, during the run of a high-class piece, I have sat in lonely grandeur in the front row of the gallery, and wished that I had spent my shilling instead in the Oriental halls of the Alhambra."

"There you are," said B., "that is just as good as yours; and you can write like that without going more than a few hours' journey from London."

"We will discuss the matter no further," I replied. "You cannot, I see, enter into my feelings. The wild heart of the traveller does not throb within your breast; you cannot understand his longings. No matter! Suffice it that I will come this journey with you. I will buy a German conversation book, and a check-suit, and a blue veil, and a white umbrella, and suchlike necessities of the English tourist in Germany, this very afternoon. When do you start?"

"Well," he said, "it is a good two days' journey. I propose to start on Friday."

"Is not Friday rather an unlucky day to start on?" I suggested.

"Oh, good gracious!" he retorted quite sharply, "what rubbish next? As if the affairs of Europe were going to be arranged by Providence according to whether you and I start for an excursion on a Thursday or a Friday!"

He said he was surprised that a man who could be so sensible, occasionally, as myself, could have patience to even think of such old-womanish nonsense. He said that years ago, when he was a silly boy, he used to pay attention to this foolish superstition himself, and would never upon any consideration start for a trip upon a Friday.

But, one year, he was compelled to do so. It was a case of either starting on a Friday or not going at all, and he determined to chance it.

He went, prepared for and expecting a series of accidents and misfortunes. To return home alive was the only bit of pleasure he hoped for from that trip.

As it turned out, however, he had never had a more enjoyable holiday in his life before. The whole event was a tremendous success.

And after that, he had made up his mind to *always* start on a Friday; and he always did, and always had a good time.

He said that he would never, upon any consideration, start for a trip upon any other day but a Friday now. It was so absurd, this superstition about Friday.

So we agreed to start on the Friday, and I am to meet him at Victoria Station at a quarter to eight in the evening.

THURSDAY, 22ND

**The Question of Luggage.—First Friend's Suggestion.—
Second Friend's Suggestion.—Third Friend's Suggestion.—
Mrs. Briggs' Advice.—Our Vicar's Advice.—His Wife's Ad-
vice.—Medical Advice.—Literary Advice.—George's
Recommendation.—My Sister-in-Law's Help.—Young
Smith's Counsel.—My Own Ideas.—B.'s Idea.**

I have been a good deal worried to-day about the question of what luggage to take with me. I met a man this morning, and he said:

"Oh, if you are going to Ober-Ammergau, mind you take plenty of warm clothing with you. You'll need all your winter things up there."

He said that a friend of his had gone up there some years ago, and had not taken enough warm things with him, and had caught a chill there, and had come home and died. He said:

"You be guided by me, and take plenty of warm things with you."

I met another man later on, and he said:

"I hear you are going abroad. Now, tell me, what part of Europe are you going to?"

I replied that I thought it was somewhere about the middle. He said:

"Well, now, you take my advice, and get a calico suit and a sunshade. Never mind the look of the thing. You be comfortable. You've no idea of the heat on the Continent at this time of the year. English people will persist in travelling about the Continent in the same stuffy clothes that they wear at home. That's how so many of them get sunstrokes, and are ruined for life."

I went into the club, and there I met a friend of mine—a newspaper correspondent—who has travelled a good deal, and knows Europe pretty well. I told him what my two other friends had said, and asked him which I was to believe. He said:

"Well, as a matter of fact, they are both right. You see, up in those hilly districts, the weather changes very quickly. In the morning it may be blazing hot, and you will be melting, and in the evening you may be very glad of a flannel shirt and a fur coat."

"Why, that is exactly the sort of weather we have in England!" I exclaimed. "If that's all these foreigners can manage in their own country, what right have they to come over here, as they do, and grumble about our weather?"

"Well, as a matter of fact," he replied, "they haven't any right; but you can't stop them—they will do it. No, you take my advice, and be prepared for everything. Take a cool suit and some thin things, for if it's hot, and plenty of warm things in case it is cold."

When I got home I found Mrs. Briggs there, she having looked in to see how the baby was. She said:—

"Oh! if you're going anywhere near Germany, you take a bit of soap with you."

She said that Mr. Briggs had been called over to Germany once in a hurry, on business, and had forgotten to take a piece of soap with him, and didn't know enough German to ask for any when he got over there, and didn't see any to ask for even if he had known, and was away for three weeks, and wasn't able to wash himself all the time, and came home so dirty that they didn't know him, and mistook him for the man that was to come to see what was the matter with the kitchen boiler.

Mrs. Briggs also advised me to take some towels with me, as they give you such small towels to wipe on.

I went out after lunch, and met our Vicar. He said:

"Take a blanket with you."

He said that not only did the German hotel-keepers never give you sufficient bedclothes to keep you warm of a night, but they never properly aired their sheets. He said that a young friend of his had gone for a tour through Germany once, and had slept in a damp bed, and had caught rheumatic fever, and had come home and died.

His wife joined us at this point. (He was waiting for her outside a draper's shop when I met him.) He explained to her that I was going to Germany, and she said:

"Oh! take a pillow with you. They don't give you any pillows—not like our pillows—and it's *so* wretched, you'll never get a decent night's rest if you don't take a pillow." She said: "You can have a little bag made for it, and it doesn't look anything."

I met our doctor a few yards further on. He said:

"Don't forget to take a bottle of brandy with you. It doesn't take up much room, and, if you're not used to German cooking, you'll find it handy in the night."

He added that the brandy you get at foreign hotels was mere poison, and that it was really unsafe to travel abroad without a bottle of brandy. He said that a simple thing like a bottle of brandy in your bag might often save your life.

Coming home, I ran against a literary friend of mine. He said:

"You'll have a goodish time in the train old fellow. Are you used to long railway journeys?"

I said:

"Well, I've travelled down from London into the very heart of Surrey by a South Eastern express."

"Oh! that's a mere nothing, compared with what you've got before you now," he answered. "Look here, I'll tell you a very good idea of how to pass the time. You take a chessboard with you and a set of men. You'll thank me for telling you that!"

George dropped in during the evening. He said:

"I'll tell you one thing you'll have to take with you, old man, and that's a box of cigars and some tobacco."

He said that the German cigar—the better class of German cigar—was of the brand that is technically known over here as the "Penny Pickwick—Spring Crop;" and he thought that I should not have time, during the short stay I contemplated making in the country, to acquire a taste for its flavour.

My sister-in-law came in later on in the evening (she is a thoughtful girl), and brought a box with her about the size of a tea-chest. She said:

"Now, you slip that in your bag; you'll be glad of that. There's everything there for making yourself a cup of tea."

She said that they did not understand tea in Germany, but that with that I should be independent of them.

She opened the case, and explained its contents to me. It certainly was a wonderfully complete arrangement. It contained a little caddy full of tea, a little bottle of milk, a box of sugar, a bottle of methylated spirit, a box of butter, and a tin of biscuits: also, a stove, a kettle, a teapot, two cups, two saucers, two plates, two knives, and two spoons. If there had only been a bed in it, one need not have bothered about hotels at all.

Young Smith, the Secretary of our Photographic Club, called at nine to ask me to take him a negative of the statue of the dying Gladiator in the Munich Sculpture Gallery. I told him that I should be delighted to oblige him, but that I did not intend to take my camera with me.

"Not take your camera!" he said. "You are going to Germany—to Rhineland! You are going to pass through some of the most picturesque scenery, and stay at some of the most ancient and famous towns of Europe, and are going to leave your photographic apparatus behind you, and you call yourself an artist!"

He said I should never regret a thing more in my life than going without that camera.

I think it is always right to take other people's advice in matters where they know more than you do. It is the experience of those who have gone before that makes the way smooth for those who follow. So, after supper, I got together the things I had been advised to take with me, and arranged them on the bed, adding a few articles I had thought of all by myself.

I put up plenty of writing paper and a bottle of ink, along with a dictionary and a few other books of reference, in case I should feel inclined to do any work while I was away. I always like to be prepared for work; one never knows when one may feel inclined for it. Sometimes, when I have been away, and have forgotten to bring any paper and pens and ink with me, I have felt so inclined for writing; and it has quite upset me that, in consequence of not having brought any paper and pens and ink with me, I have been unable to sit down and do a lot of work, but have been compelled, instead, to lounge about all day with my hands in my pockets.

Accordingly, I always take plenty of paper and pens and ink with me now, wherever I go, so that when the desire for work comes to me I need not check it.

That this craving for work should have troubled me so often, when I had no paper, pens, and ink by me, and that it never, by any chance, visits me now, when I am careful to be in a position to gratify it, is a matter over which I have often puzzled.

But when it does come I shall be ready for it.

I also put on the bed a few volumes of Goethe, because I thought it would be so pleasant to read him in his own country. And I decided to take a sponge, together with a small portable bath, because a cold bath is so refreshing the first thing in the morning.

B. came in just as I had got everything into a pile. He stared at the bed, and asked me what I was doing. I told him I was packing.

"Great Heavens!" he exclaimed. "I thought you were moving! What do you think we are going to do—camp out?"

"No!" I replied. "But these are the things I have been advised to take with me. What is the use of people giving you advice if you don't take it?"

He said:

"Oh! take as much advice as you like; that always comes in useful to give away. But, for goodness sake, don't get carrying all that stuff about with you. People will take us for Gipsies."

I said:

"Now, it's no use your talking nonsense. Half the things on this bed are life-preserving things. If people go into Germany without these things, they come home and die."

And I related to him what the doctor and the vicar and the other people had told me, and explained to him how my life depended upon my taking brandy and blankets and sunshades and plenty of warm clothing with me.

He is a man utterly indifferent to danger and risk—incurred by other people—is B. He said:

"Oh, rubbish! You're not the sort that catches a cold and dies young. You leave that co-operative stores of yours at home, and pack up a tooth-brush, a comb, a pair of socks, and a shirt. That's all you'll want."

* * * * *

I have packed more than that, but not much. At all events, I have got everything into one small bag. I should like to have taken that tea arrangement—it would have done so nicely to play at shop with in the train!—but B. would not hear of it.

I hope the weather does not change.

FRIDAY, 23RD

Early Rising.—Ballast should be Stowed Away in the Hold before Putting to Sea.—Annoying Interference of Providence in Matters that it Does Not Understand.—A Socialistic Society.—B. Misjudges Me.—An Uninteresting Anecdote.—We Lay in Ballast.—A Moderate Sailor.—A Playful Boat.

I got up very early this morning. I do not know why I got up early. We do not start till eight o'clock this evening. But I don't regret it—the getting up early I mean. It is a change. I got everybody else up too, and we all had breakfast at seven.

I made a very good lunch. One of those seafaring men said to me once:

"Now, if ever you are going a short passage, and are at all nervous, you lay in a good load. It's a good load in the hold what steadies the ship. It's them half-empty cruisers as goes a-rollin' and a-pitchin' and a-heavin' all over the place, with their stern up'ards half the time. You lay in ballast."

It seemed very reasonable advice.

Aunt Emma came in the afternoon. She said she was so glad she had caught me. Something told her to change her mind and come on Friday instead of Saturday. It was Providence, she said.

I wish Providence would mind its own business, and not interfere in my affairs: it does not understand them.

She says she shall stop till I come back, as she wants to see me again before she goes. I told her I might not be back for a month. She said it didn't matter; she had plenty of time, and would wait for me.

The family entreat me to hurry home.

I ate a very fair dinner—"laid in a good stock of ballast," as my seafaring friend would have said; wished "Good-bye!" to everybody, and kissed Aunt Emma; promised to take care of myself—a promise which, please Heaven, I will faithfully keep, cost me what it may—hailed a cab and started.

I reached Victoria some time before B. I secured two corner seats in a smoking-carriage, and then paced up and down the platform waiting for him.

When men have nothing else to occupy their minds, they take to thinking. Having nothing better to do until B. arrived, I fell to musing.

What a wonderful piece of Socialism modern civilisation has become!—not the Socialism of the so-called Socialists—a system modelled apparently upon the methods of the convict prison—a system under which each miserable sinner is to be compelled to labour, like a beast of burden, for no personal benefit to himself, but only for the good of the community—a world where there are to be no men, but only numbers—where there is to be no ambition and no hope and no fear,—but the Socialism of free men, working side by side in the common workshop, each one for the wage to which his skill and energy entitle him; the Socialism of responsible, thinking individuals, not of State-directed automata.

Here was I, in exchange for the result of some of my labour, going to be taken by Society for a treat, to the middle of Europe and back. Railway lines had been laid over the whole 700 or 800 miles to facilitate my progress; bridges had been built, and tunnels made; an army of engineers, and guards, and signal-men, and porters, and clerks were waiting to take charge of me, and to see to my comfort and safety. All I had to do was to tell Society (here represented by a railway booking-clerk) where I wanted to go, and to step into a carriage; all the rest would be done for me. Books and papers had been written and printed; so that if I wished to beguile the journey by reading, I could do so. At various places on the route, thoughtful Society had taken care to be ready for me with all kinds of re-freshment (her sandwiches might be a little fresher, but maybe she thinks new bread injurious for me). When I am tired of travelling and want to rest, I find So-ciety waiting for me with dinner and a comfortable bed, with hot and cold water to wash in and towels to wipe upon. Wherever I go, whatever I need, Society, like the enslaved genii of some Eastern tale, is ready and anxious to help me, to serve me, to do my bidding, to give me enjoyment and pleasure. Society will take me to Ober-Ammergau, will provide for all my wants on the way, and, when I am there, will show me the Passion Play, which she has arranged and rehearsed and will play for my instruction; will bring me back any way I like to come, explain-ing, by means of her guide-books and histories, everything upon the way that she thinks can interest me; will, while I am absent, carry my messages to those I have left behind me in England, and will bring me theirs in return; will look after me and take care of me and protect me like a mother—as no mother ever could.

All that she asks in return is, that I shall do the work she has given me to do. As a man works, so Society deals by him.

To me Society says: "You sit at your desk and write, that is all I want you to do. You are not good for much, but you can spin out yards of what you and your friends, I suppose, call literature; and some people seem to enjoy reading it. Very well: you sit there and write this literature, or whatever it is, and keep your mind fixed on that. I will see to everything else for you. I will provide you with writ-ing materials, and books of wit and humour, and paste and scissors, and everything else that may be necessary to you in your trade; and I will feed you and clothe you and lodge you, and I will take you about to places that you wish to go to; and I will see that you have plenty of tobacco and all other things practicable that you may desire—provided that you work well. The more work you do, and the better work you do, the better I shall look after you. You write—that is all I want you to do."

"But," I say to Society, "I don't like work; I don't want to work. Why should I be a slave and work?"

"All right," answers Society, "don't work. I'm not forcing you. All I say is, that if you don't work for me, I shall not work for you. No work from you, no dinner from me—no holidays, no tobacco."

And I decide to be a slave, and work.

Society has no notion of paying all men equally. Her great object is to encourage brain. The man who merely works by his muscles she regards as very little superior to the horse or the ox, and provides for him just a little better. But the moment he begins to use his head, and from the labourer rises to the artisan, she begins to raise his wages.

Of course hers is a very imperfect method of encouraging thought. She is of the world, and takes a worldly standard of cleverness. To the shallow, showy writer, I fear, she generally pays far more than to the deep and brilliant thinker; and clever roguery seems often more to her liking than honest worth. But her scheme is a right and sound one; her aims and intentions are clear; her methods, on the whole, work fairly well; and every year she grows in judgment.

One day she will arrive at perfect wisdom, and will pay each man according to his deserts.

But do not be alarmed. This will not happen in our time.

Turning round, while still musing about Society, I ran against B. (literally). He thought I was a clumsy ass at first, and said so; but, on recognising me, apologised for his mistake. He had been there for some time also, waiting for me. I told him that I had secured two corner seats in a smoking-carriage, and he replied that he had done so too. By a curious coincidence, we had both fixed upon the same carriage. I had taken the corner seats near the platform, and he had booked the two opposite corners. Four other passengers sat huddled up in the middle. We kept the seats near the door, and gave the other two away. One should always practise generosity.

There was a very talkative man in our carriage. I never came across a man with such a fund of utterly uninteresting anecdotes. He had a friend with him—at all events, the man was his friend when they started—and he talked to this friend incessantly, from the moment the train left Victoria until it arrived at Dover. First of all he told him a long story about a dog. There was no point in the story whatever. It was simply a bald narrative of the dog's daily doings. The dog got up in the morning and barked at the door, and when they came down and opened the door there he was, and he stopped all day in the garden; and when his wife (not the dog's wife, the wife of the man who was telling the story) went out in the afternoon, he was asleep on the grass, and they brought him into the house, and he played with the children, and in the evening he slept in the coal-shed, and next morning there he was again. And so on, for about forty minutes.

A very dear chum or near relative of the dog's might doubtless have found the account enthralling; but what possible interest a stranger—a man who evidently didn't even know the dog—could be expected to take in the report, it was difficult to conceive.

The friend at first tried to feel excited, and murmured: "Wonderful!" "Very strange, indeed!" "How curious!" and helped the tale along by such ejaculations as, "No, did he though?" "And what did you do then?" or, "Was that on the Monday or the Tuesday, then?" But as the story progressed, he appeared to take a positive dislike to the dog, and only yawned each time that it was mentioned.

Indeed, towards the end, I think, though I trust I am mistaken, I heard him mutter, "Oh, damn the dog!"

After the dog story, we thought we were going to have a little quiet. But we were mistaken; for, with the same breath with which he finished the dog rigmarole, our talkative companion added:

"But I can tell you a funnier thing than that—"

We all felt we could believe that assertion. If he had boasted that he could tell a duller, more uninteresting story, we should have doubted him; but the possibility of his being able to relate something funnier, we could readily grasp.

But it was not a bit funnier, after all. It was only longer and more involved. It was the history of a man who grew his own celery; and then, later on, it turned out that his wife was the niece, by the mother's side, of a man who had made an ottoman out of an old packing-case.

The friend glanced round the carriage apologetically about the middle of this story, with an expression that said:

"I'm awfully sorry, gentlemen; but it really is not my fault. You see the position I'm in. Don't blame me. Don't make it worse for me to bear than it is."

And we each replied with pitying, sympathetic looks that implied:

"That's all right, my dear sir; don't you fret about that. We see how it is. We only wish we could do something to help you."

The poor fellow seemed happier and more resigned after that.

B. and I hurried on board at Dover, and were just in time to secure the last two berths in the boat; and we were glad that we had managed to do this because our idea was that we should, after a good supper, turn in and go comfortably to sleep.

B. said:

"What I like to do, during a sea passage, is to go to sleep, and then wake up and find that I am there."

We made a very creditable supper. I explained to B. the ballast principle held by my seafaring friend, and he agreed with me that the idea seemed reasonable; and, as there was a fixed price for supper, and you had as much as you liked, we determined to give the plan a fair trial.

B. left me after supper somewhat abruptly, as it appeared to me, and I took a stroll on deck by myself. I did not feel very comfortable. I am what I call a moderate sailor. I do not go to excess in either direction. On ordinary occasions, I can swagger about and smoke my pipe, and lie about my Channel experiences with the best of them. But when there is what the captain calls "a bit of a sea on," I feel sad, and try to get away from the smell of the engines and the proximity of people who smoke green cigars.

There was a man smoking a peculiarly mellow and unctuous cigar on deck when I got there. I don't believe he smoked it because he enjoyed it. He did not look as if he enjoyed it. I believe he smoked it merely to show how well he was feeling, and to irritate people who were not feeling very well.

There is something very blatantly offensive about the man who feels well on board a boat.

I am very objectionable myself, I know, when I am feeling all right. It is not enough for me that I am not ill. I want everybody to see that I am not ill. It seems to me that I am wasting myself if I don't let every human being in the vessel know that I am not ill. I cannot sit still and be thankful, like you'd imagine a sensible man would. I walk about the ship—smoking, of course—and look at people who are not well with mild but pitying surprise, as if I wondered what it was like and how they did it. It is very foolish of me, I know, but I cannot help it. I suppose it is the human nature that exists in even the best of us that makes us act like this.

I could not get away from this man's cigar; or when I did, I came within range of the perfume from the engine-room, and felt I wanted to go back to the cigar. There seemed to be no neutral ground between the two.

If it had not been that I had paid for saloon, I should have gone fore. It was much fresher there, and I should have been much happier there altogether. But I was not going to pay for first-class and then ride third—that was not business. No, I would stick to the swagger part of the ship, and feel aristocratic and sick.

A mate, or a boatswain, or an admiral, or one of those sort of people—I could not be sure, in the darkness, which it was—came up to me as I was leaning with my head against the paddle-box, and asked me what I thought of the ship. He said she was a new boat, and that this was her first voyage.

I said I hoped she would get a bit steadier as she grew older.

He replied: "Yes, she is a bit skittish to-night."

What it seemed to me was, that the ship would try to lie down and go to sleep on her right side; and then, before she had given that position a fair trial, would suddenly change her mind, and think she could do it better on her left. At the moment the man came up to me she was trying to stand on her head; and before he had finished speaking she had given up this attempt, in which, however, she had very nearly succeeded, and had, apparently, decided to now play at getting out of the water altogether.

And this is what he called being a "bit skittish!"

Seafaring people talk like this, because they are silly, and do not know any better. It is no use being angry with them.

I got a little sleep at last. Not in the bunk I had been at such pains to secure: I would not have stopped down in that stuffy saloon, if anybody had offered me a hundred pounds for doing so. Not that anybody did; nor that anybody seemed to want me there at all. I gathered this from the fact that the first thing that met my eye, after I had succeeded in clawing my way down, was a boot. The air was full of boots. There were sixty men sleeping there—or, as regards the majority, I should say *trying* to sleep there—some in bunks, some on tables, and some under tables. One man *was* asleep, and was snoring like a hippopotamus—like a hippopotamus that had caught a cold, and was hoarse; and the other fifty-nine were sitting up, throwing their boots at him. It was a snore, very difficult to locate. From which particular berth, in that dimly-lighted, evil-smelling place, it proceeded nobody was quite sure. At one moment, it appeared to come, wailing and sobbing, from the larboard, and the next instant it thundered forth, seemingly from the starboard. So every man who could reach a boot picked it up, and threw it promiscuously, silently praying to Providence, as he did so, to guide it aright and bring it safe to its desired haven.

I watched the weird scene for a minute or two, and then I hauled myself on deck again, and sat down—and went to sleep on a coil of rope; and was awakened, in the course of time, by a sailor who wanted that coil of rope to throw at the head of a man who was standing, doing no harm to anybody, on the quay at Ostend.

SATURDAY, 24TH

**Arrival at Ostend.—Coffee and Rolls.—Difficulty of Making
French Waiters understand German.—Advantages of Possessing a Conscience That Does Not Get Up Too Early.—
Villainy Triumphant.—Virtue Ordered Outside.—A Homely English Row.**

When I say I was "awakened" at Ostend, I do not speak the strict truth. I was not awakened—not properly. I was only half-awakened. I never did get fairly awake until the afternoon. During the journey from Ostend to Cologne I was three-parts asleep and one-part partially awake.

At Ostend, however, I was sufficiently aroused to grasp the idea that we had got somewhere, and that I must find my luggage and B., and do something or other; in addition to which, a strange, vague instinct, but one which I have never yet known deceive me, hovering about my mind, and telling me that I was in the neighbourhood of something to eat and drink, spurred me to vigour and action.

I hurried down into the saloon and there found B. He excused himself for having left me alone all night—he need not have troubled himself. I had not pined for him in the least. If the only woman I had ever loved had been on board, I should have sat silent, and let any other fellow talk to her that wanted to, and that felt equal to it—by explaining that he had met a friend and that they had been talking. It appeared to have been a trying conversation.

I also ran against the talkative man and his companion. Such a complete wreck of a once strong man as the latter looked I have never before seen. Mere sea-sickness, however severe, could never have accounted for the change in his appearance since, happy and hopeful, he entered the railway-carriage at Victoria six short hours ago. His friend, on the other hand, appeared fresh and cheerful, and was relating an anecdote about a cow.

We took our bags into the Custom House and opened them, and I sat down on mine, and immediately went to sleep.

When I awoke, somebody whom I mistook at first for a Field-Marshal, and from force of habit—I was once a volunteer—saluted, was standing over me, pointing melodramatically at my bag. I assured him in picturesque German that I had nothing to declare. He did not appear to comprehend me, which struck me as curious, and took the bag away from me, which left me nothing to sit upon but the floor. But I felt too sleepy to be indignant.

After our luggage had been examined, we went into the buffet. My instinct had not misled me: there I found hot coffee, and rolls and butter. I ordered two coffees with milk, some bread, and some butter. I ordered them in the best German I knew. As nobody understood me, I went and got the things for myself. It saves a deal of argument, that method. People seem to know what you mean in a moment then.

B. suggested that while we were in Belgium, where everybody spoke French, while very few indeed knew German, I should stand a better chance of being understood if I talked less German and more French.

He said:

"It will be easier for you, and less of a strain upon the natives. You stick to French," he continued, "as long as ever you can. You will get along much better with French. You will come across people now and then—smart, intelligent people—who will partially understand your French, but no human being, except a thought-reader, will ever obtain any glimmering of what you mean from your German."

"Oh, are we in Belgium," I replied sleepily; "I thought we were in Germany. I didn't know." And then, in a burst of confidence, I added, feeling that further deceit was useless, "I don't know where I am, you know."

"No, I thought you didn't," he replied. "That is exactly the idea you give anybody. I wish you'd wake up a bit."

We waited about an hour at Ostend, while our train was made up. There was only one carriage labelled for Cologne, and four more passengers wanted to go there than the compartment would hold.

Not being aware of this, B. and I made no haste to secure places, and, in consequence, when, having finished our coffee, we leisurely strolled up and opened the carriage door we saw that every seat was already booked. A bag was in one space and a rug in another, an umbrella booked a third, and so on. Nobody was there, but the seats were gone!

It is the unwritten law among travellers that a man's luggage deposited upon a seat, shall secure that seat to him until he comes to sit upon it himself. This is a good law and a just law, and one that, in my normal state, I myself would die to uphold and maintain.

But at three o'clock on a chilly morning one's moral sensibilities are not properly developed. The average man's conscience does not begin work till eight or nine o'clock—not till after breakfast, in fact. At three a.m. he will do things that at three in the afternoon his soul would revolt at.

Under ordinary circumstances I should as soon have thought of shifting a man's bag and appropriating his seat as an ancient Hebrew squatter would have thought of removing his neighbour's landmark; but at this time in the morning my better nature was asleep.

I have often read of a man's better nature being suddenly awakened. The business is generally accomplished by an organ-grinder or a little child (I would back the latter, at all events—give it a fair chance—to awaken anything in this world that was not stone deaf, or that had not been dead for more than twenty-four hours); and if an organ-grinder or a little child had been around Ostend station that morning, things might have been different.

B. and I might have been saved from crime. Just as we were in the middle of our villainy, the organ-grinder or the child would have struck up, and we should have burst into tears, and have rushed from the carriage, and have fallen upon each other's necks outside on the platform, and have wept, and waited for the next train.

As it was, after looking carefully round to see that nobody was watching us, we slipped quickly into the carriage, and, making room for ourselves among the luggage there, sat down and tried to look innocent and easy.

B. said that the best thing we could do, when the other people came, would be to pretend to be dead asleep, and too stupid to understand anything.

I replied that as far as I was concerned, I thought I could convey the desired impression without stooping to deceit at all, and prepared to make myself comfortable.

A few seconds later another man got into the carriage. He also made room for himself among the luggage and sat down.

"I am afraid that seat's taken, sir," said B. when he had recovered his surprise at the man's coolness. "In fact, all the seats in this carriage are taken."

"I can't help that," replied the ruffian, cynically. "I've got to get to Cologne some time to-day, and there seems no other way of doing it that I can see."

"Yes, but so has the gentleman whose seat you have taken got to get there," I remonstrated; "what about him? You are thinking only of yourself!"

My sense of right and justice was beginning to assert itself, and I felt quite indignant with the fellow. Two minutes ago, as I have explained, I could contemplate the taking of another man's seat with equanimity. Now, such an act seemed to me shameful. The truth is that my better nature never sleeps for long. Leave it alone and it wakens of its own accord. Heaven help me! I am a sinful, worldly man, I know; but there is good at the bottom of me. It wants hauling up, but it's there.

This man had aroused it. I now saw the sinfulness of taking another passenger's place in a railway-carriage.

But I could not make the other man see it. I felt that some service was due from me to Justice, in compensation of the wrong I had done her a few moments ago, and I argued most eloquently.

My rhetoric was, however, quite thrown away. "Oh! it's only a vice-consul," he said; "here's his name on the bag. There's plenty of room for him in with the guard."

It was no use my defending the sacred cause of Right before a man who held sentiments like that; so, having lodged a protest against his behaviour, and thus eased my conscience, I leant back and dozed the doze of the just.

Five minutes before the train started, the rightful owners of the carriage came up and crowded in. They seemed surprised at finding only five vacant seats available between seven of them, and commenced to quarrel vigorously among themselves.

B. and I and the unjust man in the corner tried to calm them, but passion ran too high at first for the voice of Reason to be heard. Each combination of five, possible among them, accused each remaining two of endeavouring to obtain seats by fraud, and each one more than hinted that the other six were liars.

What annoyed me was that they quarrelled in English. They all had languages of their own,—there were four Belgians, two Frenchmen, and a German,—but no language was good enough for them to insult each other in but English.

Finding that there seemed to be no chance of their ever agreeing among themselves, they appealed to us. We unhesitatingly decided in favour of the five thinnest, who, thereupon, evidently regarding the matter as finally settled, sat down, and told the other two to get out.

These two stout ones, however—the German and one of the Belgians— seemed inclined to dispute the award, and called up the station-master.

The station-master did not wait to listen to what they had to say, but at once began abusing them for being in the carriage at all. He told them they ought to be ashamed of themselves for forcing their way into a compartment that was already more than full, and inconveniencing the people already there.

He also used English to explain this to them, and they got out on the platform and answered him back in English.

English seems to be the popular language for quarrelling in, among foreigners. I suppose they find it more expressive.

We all watched the group from the window. We were amused and interested. In the middle of the argument an early gendarme arrived on the scene. The gendarme naturally supported the station-master. One man in uniform always supports another man in uniform, no matter what the row is about, or who may be in the right—that does not trouble him. It is a fixed tenet of belief among uniform circles that a uniform can do no wrong. If burglars wore uniform, the police would be instructed to render them every assistance in their power, and to take into custody any householder attempting to interfere with them in the execution of their business. The gendarme assisted the station-master to abuse the two stout passengers, and he also abused them in English. It was not good English in any sense of the word. The man would probably have been able to give his feelings much greater variety and play in French or Flemish, but that was not his object. His ambition, like every other foreigner's, was to become an accomplished English quarreller, and this was practice for him.

A Customs House clerk came out and joined in the babel. He took the part of the passengers, and abused the station-master and the gendarme, and *he* abused *them* in English.

B. said he thought it very pleasant here, far from our native shores, in the land of the stranger, to come across a little homely English row like this.

SATURDAY, 24TH—CONTINUED

A Man of Family.—An Eccentric Train.—Outrage on an Englishman.—Alone in Europe.—Difficulty of Making German Waiters Understand Scandinavian.—Danger of Knowing Too Many Languages.—A Wearisome Journey.— Cologne, Ahoy!

There was a very well-informed Belgian in the carriage, and he told us something interesting about nearly every town through which we passed. I felt that if I could have kept awake, and have listened to that man, and remembered what he said, and not mixed things up, I should have learnt a good deal about the country between Ostend and Cologne.

He had relations in nearly every town, had this man. I suppose there have been, and are, families as large and as extensive as his; but I never heard of any other family that made such a show. They seemed to have been planted out with great judgment, and were now all over the country. Every time I awoke, I caught some such scattered remark as:

"Bruges—you can see the belfry from this side—plays a polka by Haydn every hour. My aunt lives here." "Ghent—Hôtel de Ville, some say finest specimen of Gothic architecture in Europe—where my mother lives. You could see the house if that church wasn't there." "Just passed Alost—great hop centre. My grandfather used to live there; he's dead now." "There's the Royal chateau—here, just on this side. My sister is married to a man who lives there—not in the palace, I don't mean, but in Laeken." "That's the dome of the Palais de Justice—they call Brussels 'Paris in little'—I like it better than Paris, myself—not so crowded. I live in Brussels." "Louvain—there's Van de Weyer's statue, the 1830 revolutionist. My wife's mother lives in Louvain. She wants us to come and live there. She says we are too far away from her at Brussels, but I don't think so." "Leige—see the citadel? Got some cousins at Leige—only second ones. Most of my first ones live at Maestricht"; and so on all the way to Cologne.

I do not believe we passed a single town or village that did not possess one or more specimens of this man's relatives. Our journey seemed, not so much like a tour through Belgium and part of Northern Germany, as a visit to the neighbour-hood where this man's family resided.

I was careful to take a seat facing the engine at Ostend. I prefer to travel that way. But when I awoke a little later on, I found myself going backwards.

I naturally felt indignant. I said:

"Who's put me over here? I was over there, you know. You've no right to do that!"

They assured me, however, that nobody had shifted me, but that the train had turned round at Ghent.

I was annoyed at this. It seemed to me a mean trick for a train to start off in one direction, and thus lure you into taking your seat (or somebody else's seat, as the case might be) under the impression that you were going to travel that way, and then, afterwards, turn round and go the other way. I felt very doubtful, in my own mind, as to whether the train knew where it was going at all.

At Brussels we got out and had some more coffee and rolls. I forget what language I talked at Brussels, but nobody understood me. When I next awoke, after leaving Brussels, I found myself going forwards again. The engine had apparent-ly changed its mind for the second time, and was pulling the carriages the other way now. I began to get thoroughly alarmed. This train was simply doing what it liked. There was no reliance to be placed upon it whatever. The next thing it would do would be to go sideways. It seemed to me that I ought to get up and see into this matter; but, while pondering the business, I fell asleep again.

I was very sleepy indeed when they routed us out at Herbesthal, to examine our luggage for Germany. I had a vague idea that we were travelling in Turkey, and had been stopped by brigands. When they told me to open my bag, I said, "Never!" and remarked that I was an Englishman, and that they had better be careful. I also told them that they could dismiss any idea of ransom from their minds at once, unless they were prepared to take I.O.U.'s, as it was against the principles of our family to pay cash for anything—certainly not for relatives.

They took no notice of my warning, and caught hold of my Gladstone. I re-sisted feebly, but was over-powered, and went to sleep again.

On awakening, I discovered myself in the buffet. I have no recollection of go-ing there. My instinct must have guided me there during my sleep.

I ordered my usual repast of coffee and rolls. (I must have been full of coffee and rolls by this time.) I had got the idea into my head now that I was in Norway, and so I ordered them in broken Scandinavian, a few words of which I had picked up during a trip through the fiords last summer.

Of course, the man did not understand; but I am accustomed to witnessing the confusion of foreigners when addressed in their native tongue, and so forgave him—especially as, the victuals being well within reach, language was a matter of secondary importance.

I took two cups of coffee, as usual—one for B., and one for myself—and, bringing them to the table, looked round for B. I could not see him anywhere. What had become of him? I had not seen him, that I could recollect, for hours. I did not know where I was, or what I was doing. I had a hazy knowledge that B. and I had started off together—whether yesterday or six months ago, I could not have said to save my life—with the intention, if I was not mistaken, of going somewhere and seeing something. We were now somewhere abroad—somewhere in Norway was my idea; though why I had fixed on Norway is a mystery to me to this day—and I had lost him!

How on earth were we ever to find each other again? A horrible picture presented itself to my mind of our both wandering distractedly up and down Europe, perhaps for years, vainly seeking each other. The touching story of Evangeline recurred to me with terrible vividness.

Something must be done, and that immediately. Somehow or another I must find B. I roused myself, and summoned to my aid every word of Scandinavian that I knew.

It was no good these people pretending that they did not understand their own language, and putting me off that way. They had got to understand it this time. This was no mere question of coffee and rolls; this was a serious business. I would make that waiter understand my Scandinavian, if I had to hammer it into his head with his own coffee-pot!

I seized him by the arm, and, in Scandinavian that must have been quite pathetic in its tragic fervour, I asked him if he had seen my friend—my friend B.

The man only stared.

I grew desperate. I shook him. I said:

"My friend—big, great, tall, large—is he where? Have you him to see where? Here?"

(I had to put it that way because Scandinavian grammar is not a strong point with me, and my knowledge of the verbs is as yet limited to the present tense of the infinitive mood. Besides, this was no time to worry about grace of style.)

A crowd gathered round us, attracted by the man's terrified expression. I appealed to them generally. I said:

"My friend B.—head, red—boots, yellow, brown, gold—coat, little squares—nose, much, large! Is he where? Him to see—anybody—where?"

Not a soul moved a hand to help me. There they stood and gaped!

I repeated it all over again louder, in case anybody on the outskirts of the mob had not heard it; and I repeated it in an entirely new accent. I gave them every chance I could.

They chatted excitedly among themselves, and, then a bright idea seemed to strike one of them, a little more intelligent-looking than the rest, and he rushed outside and began running up and down, calling out something very loudly, in which the word "Norwegian" kept on occurring.

He returned in a few seconds, evidently exceedingly pleased with himself, accompanied by a kindly-looking old gentleman in a white hat.

Way was made in the crowd, and the old gentleman pressed forward. When he got near, he smiled at me, and then proceeded to address to me a lengthy, but no doubt kindly meant, speech in Scandinavian.

Of course, it was all utterly unintelligible to me from beginning to end, and my face clearly showed this. I can grasp a word or two of Scandinavian here and there, if pronounced slowly and distinctly; but that is all.

The old gentleman regarded me with great surprise. He said (in Scandinavian, of course):

"You speak Norwegian?"

I replied, in the same tongue:

"A little, a very little—*very*."

He seemed not only disappointed, but indignant. He explained the matter to the crowd, and they all seemed indignant.

Why everybody should be indignant with me I could not comprehend. There are plenty of people who do not understand Scandinavian. It was absurd to be vexed with me because *I* did not. I do know a little, and that is more than some people do.

I inquired of the old gentleman about B. He did understand me. I must give him credit for that. But beyond understanding me, he was of no more use than the others; and why they had taken so much trouble to fetch him, I could not imagine.

What would have happened if the difficulty had continued much longer (for I was getting thoroughly wild with the lot of them) I cannot say. Fortunately, at this moment I caught sight of B. himself, who had just entered the room.

I could not have greeted him more heartily if I had wanted to borrow money of him.

"Well, I *am* glad to see you again!" I cried. "Well, this *is* pleasant! I thought I had lost you!"

"Why, you are English!" cried out the old gentleman in the white hat, in very good Saxon, on hearing me speak to B.

"Well, I know that," I replied, "and I'm proud of it. Have you any objection to my being English?"

"Not in the least," he answered, "if you'd only talk English instead of Norwegian. I'm English myself;" and he walked away, evidently much puzzled.

B. said to me as we sat down:

"I'll tell you what's the matter with you, J.—you know too many languages for this continent. Your linguistic powers will be the ruin of us if you don't hold them in a bit. You don't know any Sanscrit or Chaldean, do you?"

I replied that I did not.

"Any Hebrew or Chinese?"

"Not a word."

"Sure?"

"Not so much as a full stop in any of them."

"That's a blessing," said B., much relieved. "You would be trying to palm off one or other of them on some simple-minded peasant for German, if you did!"

It is a wearisome journey, through the long, hot hours of the morning, to Cologne. The carriage is stifling. Railway travellers, I have always noticed, regard fresh air as poison. They like to live on the refuse of each other's breath, and close up every window and ventilator tight. The sun pours down through glass and blind and scorches our limbs. Our heads and our bodies ache. The dust and soot drift in and settle on our clothes, and grime our hands and face. We all doze and wake up with a start, and fall to sleep again upon each other. I wake, and find my neighbour with his head upon my shoulder. It seems a shame to cast him off; he looks so trustful. But he is heavy. I push him on to the man the other side. He is just as happy there. We roll about; and when the train jerks, we butt each other with our heads. Things fall from the rack upon us. We look up surprised, and go to sleep again. My bag tumbles down upon the head of the unjust man in the corner. (Is it retribution?) He starts up, begs my pardon, and sinks back into oblivion. I am too sleepy to pick up the bag. It lies there on the floor. The unjust man uses it for a footstool.

We look out, through half-closed eyes, upon the parched, level, treeless land; upon the little patchwork farms of corn and beetroot, oats and fruit, growing undivided, side by side, each looking like a little garden dropped down into the plain; upon the little dull stone houses.

A steeple appears far away upon the horizon. (The first thing that we ask of men is their faith: "What do you believe?" The first thing that they show us is their church: "*This* we believe.") Then a tall chimney ranges itself alongside. (First faith, then works.) Then a confused jumble of roofs, out of which, at last, stand forth individual houses, factories, streets, and we draw up in a sleeping town.

People open the carriage door, and look in upon us. They do not appear to think much of us, and close the door again quickly, with a bang, and we sleep once more.

As we rumble on, the country slowly wakes. Rude V-shaped carts, drawn by yoked oxen, and even sometimes by cows, wait patiently while we cross the long, straight roads stretching bare for many a mile across the plain. Peasants trudge along the fields to work. Smoke rises from the villages and farm-houses. Passengers are waiting at the wayside stations.

Towards mid-day, on looking out, we see two tiny spires standing side by side against the sky. They seem to be twins, and grow taller as we approach. I describe them to B., and he says they are the steeples of Cologne Cathedral; and we all begin to yawn and stretch, and to collect our bags and coats and umbrellas.

HALF OF SATURDAY 24TH, AND SOME OF SUNDAY, 25TH

Difficulty of Keeping this Diary.—A Big Wash.—The German Bed.—Its Goings On.—Manners and Customs of the German Army.—B.'s Besetting Sin.—Cologne Cathedral.— Thoughts Without Words.—A Curious Custom.

This diary is getting mixed. The truth is, I am not living as a man who keeps a diary should live. I ought, of course, to sit down in front of this diary at eleven o'clock at night, and write down all that has occurred to me during the day. But at eleven o'clock at night, I am in the middle of a long railway journey, or have just got up, or am just going to bed for a couple of hours. We go to bed at odd moments, when we happen to come across a bed, and have a few minutes to spare. We have been to bed this afternoon, and are now having another breakfast; and I am not quite sure whether it is yesterday or to-morrow, or what day it is.

I shall not attempt to write up this diary in the orthodox manner, therefore; but shall fix in a few lines whenever I have half-an-hour with nothing better to do.

We washed ourselves in the Rhine at Cologne (we had not had a wash since we had left our happy home in England). We started with the idea of washing ourselves at the hotel; but on seeing the basin and water and towel provided, I decided not to waste my time playing with them. As well might Hercules have attempted to tidy up the Augean stables with a squirt.

We appealed to the chambermaid. We explained to her that we wanted to wash—to clean ourselves—not to blow bubbles. Could we not have bigger basins and more water and more extensive towels? The chambermaid (a staid old lady of about fifty) did not think that anything better could be done for us by the hotel fraternity of Cologne, and seemed to think that the river was more what we wanted.

I fancied that the old soul was speaking sarcastically, but B. said "No;" she was thinking of the baths alongside the river, and suggested that we should go there. I agreed. It seemed to me that the river—the Rhine—would, if anything could, meet the case. There ought to be plenty of water in it now, after the heavy spring rains.

When I saw it, I felt satisfied. I said to B.:

"That's all right, old man; that's the sort of thing we need. That is just the sized river I feel I can get myself clean in this afternoon."

I have heard a good deal in praise of the Rhine, and I am glad to be able to speak well of it myself. I found it most refreshing.

I was, however, sorry that we had washed in it afterwards. I have heard from friends who have travelled since in Germany that we completely spoiled that river for the rest of the season. Not for business purposes, I do not mean. The barge traffic has been, comparatively speaking, uninterfered with. But the tourist trade has suffered terribly. Parties who usually go up the Rhine by steamer have, after looking at the river, gone by train this year. The boat agents have tried to persuade them that the Rhine is always that colour: that it gets like that owing to the dirt and refuse washed down into it during its course among the mountains.

But the tourists have refused to accept this explanation. They have said:

"No. Mountains will account for a good deal, we admit, but not for all *that*. We are acquainted with the ordinary condition of the Rhine, and although muddy, and at times unpleasant, it is passable. As it is this summer, however, we would prefer not to travel upon it. We will wait until after next year's spring-floods."

We went to bed after our wash. To the *blasé* English bed-goer, accustomed all his life to the same old hackneyed style of bed night after night, there is something very pleasantly piquant about the experience of trying to sleep in a German bed. He does not know it is a bed at first. He thinks that someone has been going round the room, collecting all the sacks and cushions and antimacassars and such articles that he has happened to find about, and has piled them up on a wooden tray ready for moving. He rings for the chambermaid, and explains to her that she has shown him into the wrong room. He wanted a bedroom.

She says: "This *is* a bedroom."

He says: "Where's the bed?"

"There!" she says, pointing to the box on which the sacks and antimacassars and cushions lie piled.

"That!" he cries. "How am I going to sleep in that?"

The chambermaid does not know how he is going to sleep there, never having seen a gentleman go to sleep anywhere, and not knowing how they set about it; but suggests that he might try lying down flat, and shutting his eyes.

"But it is not long enough," he says.

The chambermaid thinks he will be able to manage, if he tucks his legs up.

He sees that he will not get anything better, and that he must put up with it.

"Oh, very well!" he says. "Look sharp and get it made, then."

She says: "It is made."

He turns and regards the girl sternly. Is she taking advantage of his being a lonely stranger, far from home and friends, to mock him? He goes over to what she calls the bed, and snatching off the top-most sack from the pile and holding it up, says:

"Perhaps you'll tell me what this is, then?"

"That," says the girl, "that's the bed!"

He is somewhat nonplussed at the unexpected reply.

"Oh!" he says. "Oh! the bed, is it? I thought it was a pincushion! Well, if it is the bed, then what is it doing out here, on the top of everything else? You think that because I'm only a man, I don't understand a bed!"

"That's the proper place for it," responds the chambermaid.

"What! on top?"

"Yes, sir."

"Well, then where are the clothes?"

"Underneath, sir."

"Look here, my good girl," he says; "you don't understand me, or I don't understand you, one or the other. When I go to sleep, I lie on a bed and pull the clothes over me. I don't want to lie on the clothes, and cover myself with the bed. This isn't a comic ballet, you know!"

The girl assures him that there is no mistake about the matter at all. There is the bed, made according to German notions of how a bed should be made. He can make the best of it and try to go to sleep upon it, or he can be sulky and go to sleep on the floor.

He is very much surprised. It looks to him the sort of bed that a man would make for himself on coming home late from a party. But it is no use arguing the matter with the girl.

"All right," he says; "bring me a pillow, and I'll risk it!"

The chambermaid explains that there are two pillows on the bed already, indicating, as she does so, two flat cushions, each one a yard square, placed one on top of the other at one end of the mixture.

"These!" exclaims the weary traveller, beginning to feel that he does not want to go to bed at all. "These are not pillows! I want something to put my head on; not a thing that comes down to the middle of my back! Don't tell me that I've got to sleep on these things!"

But the girl does tell him so, and also implies that she has something else to do than to stand there all day talking bed-gossip with him.

"Well, just show me how to start," he says, "which way you get into it, and then I won't keep you any longer; I'll puzzle out the rest for myself."

She explains the trick to him and leaves, and he undresses and crawls in.

The pillows give him a good deal of worry. He does not know whether he is meant to sit on them or merely to lean up against them. In experimenting upon this point, he bumps his head against the top board of the bedstead. At this, he says, "Oh!" and shoots himself down to the bottom of the bed. Here all his ten toes simultaneously come into sharp contact with the board at the bottom.

Nothing irritates a man more than being rapped over the toes, especially if he feels that he has done nothing to deserve it. He says, "Oh, damn!" this time, and spasmodically doubles up his legs, thus giving his knees a violent blow against the board at the side of the bed. (The German bedstead, be it remembered, is built in the form of a shallow, open box, and the victim is thus completely surrounded by solid pieces of wood with sharp edges. I do not know what species of wood it is that is employed. It is extremely hard, and gives forth a curious musical sound when struck sharply with a bone.)

After this he lies perfectly still for a while, wondering where he is going to be hit next. Finding that nothing happens, he begins to regain confidence, and ventures to gently feel around with his left leg and take stock of his position.

For clothes, he has only a very thin blanket and sheet, and beneath these he feels decidedly chilly. The bed is warm enough, so far as it goes, but there is not enough of it. He draws it up round his chin, and then his feet begin to freeze. He pushes it down over his feet, and then all the top part of him shivers.

He tries to roll up into a ball, so as to get the whole of himself underneath it, but does not succeed; there is always some of him left outside in the cold.

He reflects that a "boneless wonder" or a "man serpent" would be comfortable enough in this bed, and wishes that he had been brought up as a contortionist. If he could only tie his legs round his neck, and tuck his head in under his arm, all would yet be well.

Never having been taught to do any really useful tricks such as these, however, he has to be content to remain spread out, warming a bit of himself at a time.

It is, perhaps, foolish of him, amid so many real troubles, to allow a mere æsthetical consideration to worry him, but as he lies there on his back, looking down at himself, the sight that he presents to himself considerably annoys him. The puffed-up bed, resting on the middle of him, gives him the appearance of a man suffering from some monstrous swelling, or else of some exceptionally well-developed frog that has been turned up the wrong way and does not know how to get on to its legs again.

Another vexation that he has to contend with is, that every time he moves a limb or breathes extra hard, the bed (which is only of down) tumbles off on to the floor.

You cannot lean out of a German bed to pick up anything off the floor, owing to its box-like formation; so he has to scramble out after it, and of course every time he does this he barks both his shins twice against the sides of the bed.

When he has performed this feat for about the tenth time, he concludes that it was madness for him, a mere raw amateur at the business, to think that he could manage a complicated, tricky bed of this sort, that must take even an experienced man all he knows to sleep in it; and gets out and camps on the floor.

At least, that is what I did. B. is accustomed to German beds, and doubled himself up and went off to sleep without the slightest difficulty.

We slept for two hours, and then got up and went back to the railway-station, where we dined. The railway refreshment-room in German towns appears to be as much patronised by the inhabitants of the town as by the travellers passing through. It is regarded as an ordinary restaurant, and used as such by the citizens. We found the dining-room at Cologne station crowded with Cologneists.

All classes of citizens were there, but especially soldiers. There were all sorts of soldiers—soldiers of rank, and soldiers of rank and file; attached soldiers (very much attached, apparently) and soldiers unattached; stout soldiers, thin soldiers; old soldiers, young soldiers. Four very young soldiers sat opposite us, drinking beer. I never saw such young soldiers out by themselves before. They each looked about twelve years old, but may have been thirteen; and they each looked, also, ready and willing to storm a battery, if the order were given to them to do it. There they sat, raising and lowering their huge mugs of beer, discussing military matters, and rising every now and again to gravely salute some officer as he passed, and to receive as gravely his grave salute in return.

There seemed to be a deal of saluting to be gone through. Officers kept entering and passing through the room in an almost continual stream, and every time one came in sight all the military drinkers and eaters rose and saluted, and remained at the salute until the officer had passed.

One young soldier, who was trying to eat a plate of soup near us, I felt quite sorry for. Every time he got the spoon near his mouth an officer invariably hove in view, and down would have to go the spoon, soup and all, and up he would have to rise. It never seemed to occur to the silly fellow to get under the table and finish his dinner there.

We had half-an-hour to spare between dinner and the starting of our train, and B. suggested that we should go into the cathedral. That is B.'s one weakness, churches. I have the greatest difficulty in getting him past a church-door. We are walking along a street, arm in arm, talking as rationally and even as virtuously as need be, when all at once I find that B. has become silent and abstracted.

I know what it is; he has caught sight of a church. I pretend not to notice any change in him, and endeavour to hurry him on. He lags more and more behind, however, and at last stops altogether.

"Come, come," I say to him, encouragingly, "pull yourself together, and be a man. Don't think about it. Put it behind you, and determine that you *won't* be conquered. Come, we shall be round the corner in another minute, where you won't be able to see it. Take my hand, and let's run!"

He makes a few feeble steps forward with me, and then stops again.

"It's no good, old man," he says, with a sickly smile, so full of pathos that it is impossible to find it in one's heart to feel anything but pity for him. "I can't help it. I have given way to this sort of thing too long. It is too late to reform now. You go on and get a drink somewhere; I'll join you again in a few minutes. Don't worry about me; it's no good."

And back he goes with tottering steps, while I sadly pass on into the nearest café, and, over a glass of absinthe or cognac, thank Providence that I learnt to control my craving for churches in early youth, and so am not now like this poor B.

In a little while he comes in, and sits down beside me. There is a wild, unhealthy excitement in his eye, and, under a defiant air of unnatural gaiety, he attempts to hide his consciousness of guilt.

"It was a lovely altar-cloth," he whispers to me, with an enthusiasm that only makes one sorrow for him the more, so utterly impossible does it cause all hope of cure to seem. "And they've got a coffin in the north crypt that is simply a poem. I never enjoyed a sarcophagus more in all my life."

I do not say much at the time; it would be useless. But after the day is done, and we are standing beside our little beds, and all around is as silent as one can expect it to be in an hotel where people seem to be arriving all night long with heavy luggage, and to be all, more or less, in trouble, I argue with him, and gently reprove him. To avoid the appearance of sermonising as much as possible, I put it on mere grounds of expediency.

"How are we to find time," I say, "to go to all the places that we really ought to go to—to all the cafés and theatres and music-halls and beer-gardens and dancing-saloons that we want to visit—if you waste half the precious day loafing about churches and cathedrals?"

He is deeply moved, and promises to swear off. He vows, with tears in his voice, that he will never enter a church-door again. But next morning, when the temptation comes, all his good resolutions are swept away, and again he yields. It is no good being angry with him, because he evidently does really try; but there is something about the mere odour of a church that he simply cannot withstand.

Not knowing, then, that this weakness of his for churches was so strong, I made no objection to the proposed visit to Cologne Cathedral, and, accordingly, towards it we wended our way. B. has seen it before, and knows all about it. He tells me it was begun about the middle of the thirteenth century, and was only completed ten years ago. It seems to me that there must have been gross delay on the part of the builder. Why, a plumber would be ashamed to take as long as that over a job!

B. also asserts that the two towers are the highest church towers in the world. I dispute this, and deprecate the towers generally. B. warmly defends them. He says they are higher than any building in Europe, except the Eiffel Tower.

"Oh, dear no!" I say, "there are many buildings higher than they in Europe—to say nothing of Asia and America."

I have no authority for making this assertion. As a matter of fact, I know nothing whatever about the matter. I merely say it to irritate B. He appears to take a sort of personal interest in the building, and enlarges upon its beauties and advantages with as much fervour as if he were an auctioneer trying to sell the place.

He retorts that the towers are 512 feet high.

I say:

"Nonsense! Somebody has imposed upon you, because they see you are a foreigner."

He becomes quite angry at this, and says he can show me the figures in the guide-book.

"The guide-book!" I reply, scornfully. "You'll believe a newspaper next!"

B. asks me, indignantly, what height I should say they are, then. I examine them critically for a few minutes, and then give it as my opinion that they do not exceed 510 feet at the very outside. B. seems annoyed with me, and we enter the church in silence.

There is little to be said about a cathedral. Except to the professional sight-seer, one is very much like another. Their beauty to me lies, not in the paintings and sculpture they give houseroom to, nor in the bones and bric-à-brac piled up in their cellars, but in themselves—their echoing vastness, their deep silence.

Above the little homes of men, above the noisy teeming streets, they rise like some soft strain of perfect music, cleaving its way amid the jangle of discordant notes. Here, where the voices of the world sound faint; here, where the city's glamour comes not in, it is good to rest for a while—if only the pestering guides would leave one alone—and think.

There is much help in Silence. From its touch we gain renewed life. Silence is to the Soul what his Mother Earth was to Briareus. From contact with it we rise healed of our hurts and strengthened for the fight.

Amid the babel of the schools we stand bewildered and affrighted. Silence gives us peace and hope. Silence teaches us no creed, only that God's arms are around the universe.

How small and unimportant seem all our fretful troubles and ambitions when we stand with them in our hand before the great calm face of Silence! We smile at them ourselves, and are ashamed.

Silence teaches us how little we are—how great we are. In the world's market-places we are tinkers, tailors, apothecaries, thieves—respectable or otherwise, as the case may be—mere atoms of a mighty machine—mere insects in a vast hive.

It is only in Silence that it comes home to us that we are something much greater than this—that we are *men*, with all the universe and all eternity before us.

It is in Silence we hear the voice of Truth. The temples and the marts of men echo all night and day to the clamour of lies and shams and quackeries. But in Silence falsehood cannot live. You cannot float a lie on Silence. A lie has to be puffed aloft, and kept from falling by men's breath. Leave a lie on the bosom of Silence, and it sinks. A truth floats there fair and stately, like some stout ship upon a deep ocean. Silence buoys her up lovingly for all men to see. Not until she has grown worn-out and rotten, and is no longer a truth, will the waters of Silence close over her.

Silence is the only real thing we can lay hold of in this world of passing dreams. Time is a shadow that will vanish with the twilight of humanity; but Silence is a part of the eternal. All things that are true and lasting have been taught to men's hearts by Silence.

Among all nations, there should be vast temples raised where the people might worship Silence and listen to it, for it is the voice of God.

These fair churches and cathedrals that men have reared around them throughout the world, have been built as homes for mere creeds—this one for Protestantism, that one for Romanism, another for Mahomedanism. But God's Silence dwells in all alike, only driven forth at times by the tinkling of bells and the mumbling of prayers; and, in them, it is good to sit awhile and have communion with her.

We strolled round, before we came out. Just by the entrance to the choir an official stopped me, and asked me if I wanted to go and see a lot of fal-lal things he had got on show—relics and bones, and old masters, and such-like Wardour-street rubbish.

I told him, "No"; and attempted to pass on, but he said:

"No, no! You don't pay, you don't go in there," and shut the gate.

He said this sentence in English; and the precision and fluency with which he delivered it rather suggested the idea that it was a phrase much in request, and one that he had had a good deal of practice in.

It is very prevalent throughout Germany, this custom of not allowing you to go in to see a thing unless you pay.

END OF SATURDAY, 24TH, AND BEGINNING OF SUNDAY, 25TH—CONTINUED

The Rhine!—How History is Written.—Complicated Villages.—How a Peaceful Community Was Very Much Upset.— The German Railway Guard.—His Passion for Tickets.— We Diffuse Comfort and Joy Wherever We Go, Gladdening the Weary, and Bringing Smiles to Them that Weep.— "Tickets, Please."—Hunting Experiences.—A Natural Mistake.—Free Acrobatic Performance by the Guard.—The Railway Authorities' Little Joke.—Why We Should Think of the Sorrows of Others.

We returned to the station just in time to secure comfortable seats, and at 5.10 steamed out upon our fifteen hours' run to Munich. From Bonn to Mayence the line keeps by the side of the Rhine nearly the whole of the way, and we had a splendid view of the river, with the old-world towns and villages that cluster round its bank, the misty mountains that make early twilight upon its swiftly rolling waves, the castled crags and precipices that rise up sheer and majestic from its margin, the wooded rocks that hang with threatening frown above its sombre depths, the ruined towers and turrets that cap each point along its shores, the pleasant isles that stud like gems its broad expanse of waters.

Few things in this world come up to expectation, especially those things of which one has been led to expect much, and about which one has heard a good deal. With this philosophy running in my head, I was prepared to find the Rhine a much over-rated river.

I was pleasantly disappointed. The panorama which unfolded itself before our eyes, as we sped along through the quiet twilight that was deepening into starry night, was wonderfully beautiful, entrancing and expressive.

I do not intend to describe it to you. To do justice to the theme, I should have to be even a more brilliant and powerful writer than I am. To attempt the subject, without doing it justice, would be a waste of your time, sweet reader, and of mine—a still more important matter.

I confess it was not my original intention to let you off so easily. I started with the idea of giving you a rapid but glowing and eloquent word-picture of the valley of the Rhine from Cologne to Mayence. For background, I thought I would sketch in the historical and legendary events connected with the district, and against this, for a foreground, I would draw, in vivid colours, the modern aspect of the scene, with remarks and observations thereon.

Here are my rough notes, made for the purpose:—

Mems. for Chapter on Rhine: "Constantine the Great used to come here—so did Agrippa. (N.B.—Try and find out something about Agrippa.) Cæsar had a good deal to do with the Rhine—also Nero's mother."

(To the reader.—The brevity of these memoranda renders their import, at times, confusing. For instance, this means that Cæsar and Nero's mother both had a good deal to do with the Rhine; not that Cæsar had a good deal to do with Nero's mother. I explain this because I should be sorry to convey any false impression concerning either the lady or Cæsar. Scandal is a thing abhorrent to my nature.)

Notes continued: "The Ubii did something on the right bank of the Rhine at an early period, and afterwards were found on the other side. (Expect the Ubii were a tribe; but make sure of this, as they might be something in the fossil line.) Cologne was the cradle of German art. Talk about art and the old masters. Treat them in a kindly and gentle spirit. They are dead now. Saint Ursula was murdered at Cologne, with eleven thousand virgin attendants. There must have been quite a party of them. Draw powerful and pathetic imaginary picture of the slaughter. (N.B.—Find out who murdered them all.) Say something about the Emperor Maximilian. Call him 'the mighty Maximilian.' Mention Charlemagne (a good deal should be made out of Charlemagne) and the Franks. (Find out all about the Franks, and where they lived, and what has become of them.) Sketch the various contests between the Romans and the Goths. (Read up 'Gibbon' for this, unless you can get enough out of *Mangnall's Questions*.) Give picturesque account—with comments—of the battles between the citizens of Cologne and their haughty archbishops. (N.B.—Let them fight on a bridge over the Rhine, unless it is distinctly stated somewhere that they didn't.) Bring in the Minnesingers, especially Walter von Vogelweid; make him sing under a castle-wall somewhere, and let the girl die. Talk about Albert Dürer. Criticise his style. Say it's flat. (If possible, find out if it *is* flat.) "The rat tower on the Rhine," near Bingen. Describe the place and tell the whole story. Don't spin it out too long, because everybody knows it. "The Brothers of Bornhofen," story connected with the twin castles of Sterrenberg and Liebenstein, Conrad and Heinrich—brothers— both love Hildegarde. She was very beautiful. Heinrich generously refuses to marry the beautiful Hildegarde, and goes away to the Crusades, leaving her to his brother Conrad. Conrad considers over the matter for a year or two, and then *he* decides that he won't marry her either, but will leave her for his brother Heinrich, and *he* goes off to the Crusades, from whence he returns, a few years later on, with a Grecian bride. The beautiful H., muddled up between the pair of them, and the victim of too much generosity, gets sulky (don't blame her), and shuts herself up in a lonely part of the castle, and won't see anybody for years. Chivalrous Heinrich returns, and is wild that his brother C. has not married the beautiful H. It does not occur to him to marry the girl even then. The feverish yearning displayed by each of these two brothers, that the other one should marry the beloved Hildegarde, is very touching. Heinrich draws his sword, and throws himself upon his brother C. to kill him. The beautiful Hildegarde, however, throws herself between them and reconciliates them, and then, convinced that neither of them means business, and naturally disgusted with the whole affair, retires into a nunnery. Conrad's Grecian bride subsequently throws herself away on another man, upon which Conrad throws himself on his brother H.'s breast, and they swear eternal friendship. (Make it pathetic. Pretend you have sat amid the ruins in the moonlight, and give the scene—with ghosts.) "Rolandseck," near Bonn. Tell the story of Roland and Hildegunde (see *Baedeker*, p. 66). Don't make it too long, because it is so much like the other. Describe the funeral? The "Watch Tower on the Rhine" below Audernach. Query, isn't there a song about this? If so, put it in. Coblentz and Ehrenbreitstein. Great fortresses. Call them "the Frowning Sentinels of the State." Make reflections on the German army, also on war generally. Chat about Frederick the Great. (Read Carlyle's history of him, and pick out the interesting bits.) The Drachenfels. Quote Byron. Moralise about ruined castles generally, and describe the middle ages, with your views and opinions on same."

There is much more of it, but that is sufficient to let you see the scheme I had in my head. I have not carried out my scheme, because, when I came to reflect upon the matter, it seemed to me that the idea would develop into something that would be more in the nature of a history of Europe than a chapter in a tourist's diary, and I determined not to waste my time upon it, until there arose a greater public demand for a new History of Europe than there appears to exist at present.

"Besides," I argued to myself, "such a work would be just the very thing with which to beguile the tedium of a long imprisonment. At some future time I may be glad of a labour of this magnitude to occupy a period of involuntary inaction."

"This is the sort of thing," I said to myself, "to save up for Holloway or Pentonville."

It would have been a very enjoyable ride altogether, that evening's spin along the banks of the Rhine, if I had not been haunted at the time by the idea that I should have to write an account of it next day in my diary. As it was, I enjoyed it as a man enjoys a dinner when he has got to make a speech after it, or as a critic enjoys a play.

We passed such odd little villages every here and there. Little places so crowded up between the railway and the river that there was no room in them for any streets. All the houses were jumbled up together just anyhow, and how any man who lived in the middle could get home without climbing over half the other houses in the place I could not make out. They were the sort of villages where a man's mother-in-law, coming to pay him a visit, might wander around all day, hearing him, and even now and then seeing him, yet never being able to get at him in consequence of not knowing the way in.

A drunken man, living in one of these villages, could never hope to get home. He would have to sit down outside, and wait till his head was clear.

We witnessed the opening scenes of a very amusing little comedy at one of the towns where the train drew up. The chief characters were played by an active young goat, a small boy, an elderly man and a woman, parents of the small boy and owners of the goat, and a dog.

First we heard a yell, and then, from out a cottage opposite the station, bounded an innocent and happy goat, and gambolled around. A long rope, one end of which was fastened to his neck, trailed behind him. After the goat (in the double sense of the phrase) came a child. The child tried to catch the goat by means of the rope, caught itself in the rope instead, and went down with a bump and a screech. Whereupon a stout woman, the boy's mother apparently, ran out from the cottage, and also made for the goat. The goat flew down the road, and the woman flew after it. At the first corner, the woman trod on the rope, and then *she* went down with a bump and a screech. Then the goat turned and ran up the street, and, as it passed the cottage, the father ran out and tried to stop it. He was an old man, but still seemed to have plenty of vigour in him. He evidently guessed how his wife and child had gone down, and he endeavoured to avoid the rope and to skip over it when it came near him. But the goat's movements were too erratic for him. His turn came, and he trod on the rope, and went down in the middle of the road, opposite his own door, with a thud that shook us all up against each other as we stood looking out of the carriage-window, and sat there and cursed the goat. Then out ran a dog, barking furiously, and he went for the goat, and got the end of the rope in his teeth and held on to it like grim death. Away went the goat, at his end of the rope, and, with him, the dog at the other end. Between them, they kept the rope about six inches above the ground, and with it they remorselessly mowed down every living thing they came across in that once peaceful village. In the course of less than half a minute we counted fourteen persons sitting down in the middle of the road. Eight of them were cursing the goat, four were cursing the dog, and two of them were cursing the old man for keeping the goat, one of these two, and the more violent one, being the man's own wife.

The train left at this juncture. We entreated the railway officials to let us stop and see the show out. The play was becoming quite interesting. It was so full of movement. But they said that we were half-an-hour late as it was, and that they dared not.

We leaned out of the window, and watched for as long as we could; and after the village was lost to view in the distance, we could still, by listening carefully, hear the thuds, as one after another of the inhabitants sat down and began to swear.

At about eleven o'clock we had some beer—you can generally obtain such light refreshment as bottled beer and coffee and rolls from the guard on a through long-distance train in Germany—took off our boots, and saying "Good-night" to each other, made a great show of going to sleep. But we never succeeded in getting there. They wanted to see one's ticket too often for one to get fairly off.

Every few minutes, so it seemed to me, though in reality the intervals may perhaps have been longer, a ghostly face would appear at the carriage-window, and ask to see our tickets.

Whenever a German railway-guard feels lonesome, and does not know what else to do with himself, he takes a walk round the train, and gets the passengers to show him their tickets, after which he returns to his box cheered and refreshed. Some people rave about sunsets and mountains and old masters; but to the German railway-guard the world can show nothing more satisfying, more inspiring, than the sight of a railway-ticket.

Nearly all the German railway officials have this same craving for tickets. If only they get somebody to show them a railway-ticket, they are happy. It seemed a harmless weakness of theirs, and B. and I decided that it would be only kind to humour them in it during our stay.

Accordingly, whenever we saw a German railway official standing about, looking sad and weary, we went up to him and showed him our tickets. The sight was like a ray of sunshine to him; and all his care was immediately forgotten. If we had not a ticket with us at the time, we went and bought one. A mere single third to the next station would gladden him sufficiently in most cases; but if the poor fellow appeared very woe-begone, and as if he wanted more than ordinary cheering up, we got him a second-class return.

For the purpose of our journey to Ober-Ammergau and back, we each carried with us a folio containing some ten or twelve first-class tickets between different towns, covering in all a distance of some thousand miles; and one afternoon, at Munich, seeing a railway official, a cloak-room keeper, who they told us had lately lost his aunt, and who looked exceptionally dejected, I proposed to B. that we should take this man into a quiet corner, and both of us show him all our tickets at once—the whole twenty or twenty-four of them—and let him take them in his hand and look at them for as long as he liked. I wanted to comfort him.

B., however, advised against the suggestion. He said that even if it did not turn the man's head (and it was more than probable that it would), so much jealousy would be created against him among the other railway people throughout Germany, that his life would be made a misery to him.

So we bought and showed him a first-class return to the next station but one; and it was quite pathetic to watch the poor fellow's face brighten up at the sight, and to see the faint smile creep back to the lips from which it had so long been absent.

But at times, one wishes that the German railway official would control his passion for tickets—or, at least, keep it within due bounds.

Even the most kindly-hearted man grows tired of showing his ticket all day and night long, and the middle of a wearisome journey is not the proper time for a man to come to the carriage-window and clamour to see your "billet."

You are weary and sleepy. You do not know where your ticket is. You are not quite sure that you have got a ticket; or if you ever had one, somebody has taken it away from you. You have put it by very carefully, thinking that it would not be wanted for hours, and have forgotten where.

There are eleven pockets in the suit you have on, and five more in the overcoat on the rack. Maybe, it is in one of those pockets. If not, it is possibly in one of the bags—somewhere, or in your pocket-book, if you only knew where that was, or your purse.

You begin a search. You stand up and shake yourself. Then you have another feel all over. You look round in the course of the proceedings; and the sight of the crowd of curious faces watching you, and of the man in uniform waiting with his eye fixed severely upon you, convey to you, in your then state of confusion, the momentary idea that this is a police-court scene, and that if the ticket is found upon you, you will probably get five years.

Upon this you vehemently protest your innocence.

"I tell you I haven't got it!" you exclaim;—"never seen the gentleman's ticket. You let me go! I—"

Here the surprise of your fellow-passengers recalls you to yourself, and you proceed on your exploration. You overhaul the bags, turning everything out on to the floor, muttering curses on the whole railway system of Germany as you do so. Then you feel in your boots. You make everybody near you stand up to see if they are sitting upon it, and you go down on your knees and grovel for it under the seat.

"You didn't throw it out of the window with your sandwiches, did you?" asks your friend.

"No! Do you think I'm a fool?" you answer, irritably. "What should I want to do that for?"

On going systematically over yourself for about the twentieth time, you discover it in your waistcoat pocket, and for the next half-hour you sit and wonder how you came to miss it on the previous nineteen occasions.

Meanwhile, during this trying scene, the conduct of the guard has certainly not tended to allay your anxiety and nervousness. All the time that you have been looking for your ticket, he has been doing silly tricks on the step outside, imperilling his life by every means that experience and ingenuity can suggest.

The train is going at the rate of thirty miles an hour, the express speed in Germany, and a bridge comes in sight crossing over the line. On seeing this bridge, the guard, holding on by the window, leans his body as far back as ever it will go. You look at him, and then at the rapidly-nearing bridge, and calculate that the arch will just take his head off without injuring any other part of him whatever, and you wonder whether the head will be jerked into the carriage or will fall outside.

When he is three inches off the bridge, he pulls himself up straight, and the brickwork, as the train dashes through, kills a fly that was trespassing on the upper part of his right ear.

Then, when the bridge is passed, and the train is skirting the very edge of a precipice, so that a stone dropped just outside the window would tumble straight down 300 feet, he suddenly lets go, and, balancing himself on the foot-board without holding on to anything, commences to dance a sort of Teutonic cellar-flap, and to warm his body by flinging his arms about in the manner of cabmen on a cold day.

The first essential to comfortable railway travelling in Germany is to make up your mind not to care a rap whether the guard gets killed in the course of the journey or not. Any tender feeling towards the guard makes railway travelling in the Fatherland a simple torture.

At five a.m. (how fair and sweet and fresh the earth looks in the early morning! Those lazy people who lie in bed till eight or nine miss half the beauty of the day, if they but knew it. It is only we who rise early that really enjoy Nature properly) I gave up trying to get to sleep, and made my way to the dressing-room at the end of the car, and had a wash.

It is difficult to wash in these little places, because the cars shake so; and when you have got both your hands and half your head in the basin, and are unable to protect yourself, the sides of the room, and the water-tap and the soap-dish, and other cowardly things, take a mean advantage of your helplessness to punch you as hard as ever they can; and when you back away from these, the door swings open and slaps you from behind.

I succeeded, however, in getting myself fairly wet all over, even if I did nothing else, and then I looked about for a towel. Of course, there was no towel. That is the trick. The idea of the railway authorities is to lure the passenger, by providing him with soap and water and a basin, into getting himself thoroughly soaked, and then to let it dawn upon him that there is no towel. That is their notion of fun!

I thought of the handkerchiefs in my bag, but to get to them I should have to pass compartments containing ladies, and I was only in early morning dress.

So I had to wipe myself with a newspaper which I happened to have in my pocket, and a more unsatisfactory thing to dry oneself upon I cannot conceive.

I woke up B. when I got back to the carriage, and persuaded him to go and have a wash; and in listening to the distant sound of his remarks when he likewise discovered that there was no towel, the recollection of my own discomfiture passed gently away.

Ah! how true it is, as good people tell us, that in thinking of the sorrows of others, we learn to forget our own!

For fifty miles before one reaches Munich, the land is flat, stale, and apparently very unprofitable, and there is little to interest the looker-out. He sits straining his eyes towards the horizon, eagerly longing for some sign of the city to come in sight.

It lies very low, however, and does all it can to escape observation; and it is not until he is almost within its streets that he discovers it.

575

THE REST OF SUNDAY, THE 25TH

**We Seek Breakfast.—I Air My German.—The Art of Ges-
ture.—The Intelligence of the Première Danseuse.—
Performance of English Pantomime in the Pyrenees.—Sad
Result Therefrom.—The "German Conversation" Book.—
Its Narrow-minded View of Human Wants and Aspira-
tions.—Sunday in Munich.—Hans and Gretchen.—High
Life v. Low Life.—"A Beer-Cellar."**

At Munich we left our luggage at the station, and went in search of breakfast. Of course, at eight o'clock in the morning none of the big cafés were open; but at length, beside some gardens, we found an old-fashioned looking restaurant, from which came a pleasant odour of coffee and hot onions; and walking through and seating ourselves at one of the little tables, placed out under the trees, we took the bill of fare in our hands, and summoned the waiter to our side.

I ordered the breakfast. I thought it would be a good opportunity for me to try my German. I ordered coffee and rolls as a groundwork. I got over that part of my task very easily. With the practice I had had during the last two days, I could have ordered coffee and rolls for forty. Then I foraged round for luxuries, and ordered a green salad. I had some difficulty at first in convincing the man that it was not a boiled cabbage that I wanted, but succeeded eventually in getting that silly notion out of his head.

I still had a little German left, even after that. So I ordered an omelette also.

"Tell him a savoury one," said B., "or he will be bringing us something full of hot jam and chocolate-creams. You know their style."

"Oh, yes," I answered. "Of course. Yes. Let me see. What is the German for savoury?"

"Savoury?" mused B. "Oh! ah! hum! Bothered if I know! Confound the thing—I can't think of it!"

I could not think of it either. As a matter of fact, I never knew it. We tried the man with French. We said:

"Une omelette aux fines herbes."

As he did not appear to understand that, we gave it him in bad English. We twisted and turned the unfortunate word "savoury" into sounds so quaint, so sad, so unearthly, that you would have thought they might have touched the heart of a savage. This stoical Teuton, however, remained unmoved. Then we tried pantomime.

Pantomime is to language what marmalade, according to the label on the pot, is to butter, "an excellent (occasional) substitute." But its powers as an interpreter of thought are limited. At least, in real life they are so. As regards a ballet, it is difficult to say what is not explainable by pantomime. I have seen the bad man in a ballet convey to the *première danseuse* by a subtle movement of the left leg, together with some slight assistance from the drum, the heartrending intelligence that the lady she had been brought up to believe was her mother was in reality only her aunt by marriage. But then it must be borne in mind that the *première danseuse* is a lady whose quickness of perception is altogether unique. The *première danseuse* knows precisely what a gentleman means when he twirls round forty-seven times on one leg, and then stands on his head. The average foreigner would, in all probability, completely misunderstand the man.

A friend of mine once, during a tour in the Pyrenees, tried to express gratitude by means of pantomime. He arrived late one evening at a little mountain inn, where the people made him very welcome, and set before him their best; and he, being hungry, appreciated their kindness, and ate a most excellent supper.

Indeed, so excellent a meal did he make, and so kind and attentive were his hosts to him, that, after supper, he felt he wanted to thank them, and to convey to them some idea of how pleased and satisfied he was.

He could not explain himself in language. He only knew enough Spanish to just ask for what he wanted—and even to do that he had to be careful not to want much. He had not got as far as sentiment and emotion at that time. Accordingly he started to express himself in action. He stood up and pointed to the empty table where the supper had been, then opened his mouth and pointed down his throat. Then he patted that region of his anatomy where, so scientific people tell us, supper goes to, and smiled.

He has a rather curious smile, has my friend. He himself is under the impression that there is something very winning in it, though, also, as he admits, a touch of sadness. They use it in his family for keeping the children in order.

The people of the inn seemed rather astonished at his behaviour. They regarded him, with troubled looks, and then gathered together among themselves and consulted in whispers.

"I evidently have not made myself sufficiently clear to these simple peasants," said my friend to himself. "I must put more vigour into this show."

Accordingly he rubbed and patted that part of himself to which I have previously alluded—and which, being a modest and properly brought-up young man, nothing on earth shall induce me to mention more explicitly—with greater energy than ever, and added another inch or two of smile; and he also made various graceful movements indicative, as he thought, of friendly feeling and content-ment.

At length a ray of intelligence burst upon the faces of his hosts, and they rushed to a cupboard and brought out a small black bottle.

"Ah! that's done it," thought my friend. "Now they have grasped my mean-ing. And they are pleased that I am pleased, and are going to insist on my drinking a final friendly bumper of wine with them, the good old souls!"

They brought the bottle over, and poured out a wineglassful, and handed it to him, making signs that he should drink it off quickly.

"Ah!" said my friend to himself, as he took the glass and raised it to the light, and winked at it wickedly, "this is some rare old spirit peculiar to the district—some old heirloom kept specially for the favoured guest."

And he held the glass aloft and made a speech, in which he wished long life and many grand-children to the old couple, and a handsome husband to the daughter, and prosperity to the whole village. They could not understand him, he knew; but he thought there might be that in his tones and gestures from which they would gather the sense of what he was saying, and understand how kindly he felt towards them all. When he had finished, he put his hand upon his heart and smiled some more, and then tossed the liquor off at a gulp.

Three seconds later he discovered that it was a stringent and trustworthy emet-ic that he had swallowed. His audience had mistaken his signs of gratitude for efforts on his part to explain to them that he was poisoned, or, at all events, was suffering from acute and agonising indigestion, and had done what they could to comfort him.

The drug that they had given him was not one of those common, cheap medi-cines that lose their effect before they have been in the system half-an-hour. He felt that it would be useless to begin another supper then, even if he could get one, and so he went to bed a good deal hungrier and a good deal less refreshed than when he arrived at the inn.

Gratitude is undoubtedly a thing that should not be attempted by the amateur pantomimist.

"Savoury" is another. B. and I very nearly did ourselves a serious internal in-jury, trying to express it. We slaved like cab-horses at it—for about five minutes, and succeeded in conveying to the mind of the waiter that we wanted to have a game at dominoes.

Then, like a beam of sunlight to a man lost in some dark, winding cave, came to me the reflection that I had in my pocket a German conversation book.

How stupid of me not to have thought of it before. Here had we been racking our brains and our bodies, trying to explain our wants to an uneducated German, while, all the time, there lay to our hands a book specially written and prepared to assist people out of the very difficulty into which we had fallen—a book carefully compiled with the express object of enabling English travellers who, like our-selves, only spoke German in a dilettante fashion, to make their modest requirements known throughout the Fatherland, and to get out of the country alive and uninjured.

I hastily snatched the book from my pocket, and commenced to search for dialogues dealing with the great food question. There were none!

There were lengthy and passionate "Conversations with a laundress" about articles that I blush to remember. Some twenty pages of the volume were devoted to silly dialogues between an extraordinarily patient shoemaker and one of the most irritating and constitutionally dissatisfied customers that an unfortunate shop-keeper could possibly be cursed with; a customer who, after twaddling for about forty minutes, and trying on, apparently, every pair of boots in the place, calmly walks out with:

"Ah! well, I shall not purchase anything to-day. Good-morning!"

The shopkeeper's reply, by-the-by, is not given. It probably took the form of a boot-jack, accompanied by phrases deemed useless for the purposes of the Christian tourist.

There was really something remarkable about the exhaustiveness of this "conversation at the shoemaker's." I should think the book must have been written by someone who suffered from corns. I could have gone to a German shoemaker with this book and have talked the man's head off.

Then there were two pages of watery chatter "on meeting a friend in the street"—"Good-morning, sir (or madam)." "I wish you a merry Christmas." "How is your mother?" As if a man who hardly knew enough German to keep body and soul together, would want to go about asking after the health of a foreign person's mother.

There were also "conversations in the railway carriage," conversations between travelling lunatics, apparently, and dialogues "during the passage." "How do you feel now?" "Pretty well as yet; but I cannot say how long it will last." "Oh, what waves! I now feel very unwell and shall go below. Ask for a basin for me." Imagine a person who felt like that wanting to know the German for it.

At the end of the book were German proverbs and "Idiomatic Phrases," by which latter would appear to be meant in all languages, "phrases for the use of idiots":—"A sparrow in the hand is better than a pigeon on the roof."—"Time brings roses."—"The eagle does not catch flies."—"One should not buy a cat in a sack,"—as if there were a large class of consumers who habitually did purchase their cats in that way, thus enabling unscrupulous dealers to palm off upon them an inferior cat, and whom it was accordingly necessary to advise against the custom.

I skimmed through all this nonsense, but not a word could I discover anywhere about a savoury omelette. Under the head of "Eating and Drinking," I found a short vocabulary; but it was mainly concerned with "raspberries" and "figs" and "medlars" (whatever they may be; I never heard of them myself), and "chestnuts," and such like things that a man hardly ever wants, even when he is in his own country. There was plenty of oil and vinegar, and pepper and salt and mustard in the list, but nothing to put them on. I could have had a hard-boiled egg, or a slice of ham; but I did not want a hard-boiled egg, or a slice of ham. I wanted a savoury omelette; and that was an article of diet that the authors of this "Handy Little Guide," as they termed it in their preface, had evidently never heard of.

Since my return home, I have, out of curiosity, obtained three or four "English-German Dialogues" and "Conversation Books," intended to assist the English traveller in his efforts to make himself understood by the German people, and I have come to the conclusion that the work I took out with me was the most sensible and practical of the lot.

Finding it utterly hopeless to explain ourselves to the waiter, we let the thing go, and trusted to Providence; and in about ten minutes the man brought us a steaming omelette, with about a pound of strawberry jam inside, and powdered sugar all over the outside. We put a deal of pepper and salt on it to try and counteract the flavour of the sweets, but we did not really enjoy it even then.

After breakfast we got a time-table, and looked out for a train to Ober-Ammergau. I found one which started at 3.10. It seemed a very nice train indeed; it did not stop anywhere. The railway authorities themselves were evidently very proud of it, and had printed particulars of it in extra thick type. We decided to patronise it.

To pass away the time, we strolled about the city. Munich is a fine, handsome, open town, full of noble streets and splendid buildings; but in spite of this and of its hundred and seventy thousand inhabitants, an atmosphere of quiet and provincialism hovers over it. There is but little traffic on ordinary occasions along its broad ways, and customers in its well-stocked shops are few and far between. This day being Sunday, it was busier than usual, and its promenades were thronged with citizens and country folk in holiday attire, among whom the Southern peasants, wearing their quaint, centuries-old costume, stood out in picturesque relief. Fashion, in its world-wide crusade against variety and its bitter contest with form and colour, has recoiled, defeated for the present from the mountain fastnesses of Bavaria. Still, as Sunday or gala-day comes round, the broad-shouldered, sunburnt shepherd of the Oberland dons his gay green-embroidered jacket over his snowy shirt, fastens his short knee-breeches with a girdle round his waist, claps his high, feather-crowned hat upon his waving curls, and with bare legs, shod in mighty boots, strides over the hill-sides to his Gretchen's door.

She is waiting for him, you may be sure, ready dressed; and a very sweet, old-world picture she makes, standing beneath the great overhanging gables of the wooden châlet. She, too, favours the national green; but, as relief, there is no lack of bonny red ribbons, to flutter in the wind, and, underneath the ornamented skirt, peeps out a bright-hued petticoat. Around her ample breast she wears a dark tight-fitting bodice, laced down the front. (I think this garment is called a stomacher, but I am not sure, as I have never liked to ask.) Her square shoulders are covered with the whitest of white linen. Her sleeves are also white; and being very full, and of some soft lawnlike material, suggest the idea of folded wings. Upon her flaxen hair is perched a saucy round green hat. The buckles of her dainty shoes, the big eyes in her pretty face, are all four very bright. One feels one would like much to change places for the day with Hans.

Arm-in-arm, looking like some china, but exceedingly substantial china, shepherd and shepherdess, they descend upon the town. One rubs one's eyes and stares after them as they pass. They seem to have stepped from the pictured pages of one of those old story-books that we learnt to love, sitting beside the high brass guard that kept ourselves and the nursery-fire from doing each other any serious injury, in the days when the world was much bigger than it is now, and much more real and interesting.

Munich and the country round about it make a great exchange of peoples every Sunday. In the morning, trainload after trainload of villagers and mountaineers pour into the town, and trainload after trainload of good and other citizens steam out to spend the day in wood and valley, and upon lake and mountain-side.

We went into one or two of the beer-halls—not into the swell cafés, crowded with tourists and Munich masherdom, but into the low-ceilinged, smoke-grimed cellars where the life of the people is to be seen.

The ungenteel people in a country are so much more interesting than the gentlefolks. One lady or gentleman is painfully like every other lady or gentleman. There is so little individuality, so little character, among the upper circles of the world. They talk like each other, they think and act like each other, they dress like each other, and look very much like each other. We gentlefolks only play at living. We have our rules and regulations for the game, which must not be infringed. Our unwritten guide-books direct us what to do and what to say at each turn of the meaningless sport.

To those at the bottom of the social pyramid, however, who stand with their feet upon the earth, Nature is not a curious phenomenon to be looked down at and studied, but a living force to be obeyed. They front grim, naked Life, face to face, and wrestle with it through the darkness; and, as did the angel that strove with Jacob, it leaves its stamp upon them.

There is only one type of a gentleman. There are five hundred types of men and women. That is why I always seek out and frequent the places where the common people congregate, in preference to the haunts of respectability. I have to be continually explaining all this to my friends, to account to them for what they call my love of low life.

With a mug of beer before me, and a pipe in my mouth, I could sit for hours contentedly, and watch the life that ebbs and flows into and out of these old ale-kitchens.

The brawny peasant lads bring in their lasses to treat them to the beloved nectar of Munich, together with a huge onion. How they enjoy themselves! What splendid jokes they have! How they laugh and roar and sing! At one table sit four old fellows, playing cards. How full of character is each gnarled face. One is eager, quick, vehement. How his eyes dance! You can read his every thought upon his face. You know when he is going to dash down the king with a shout of triumph on the queen. His neighbour looks calm, slow, and dogged, but wears a confident expression. The game proceeds, and you watch and wait for him to play the winning cards that you feel sure he holds. He must intend to win. Victory is written in his face. No! he loses. A seven was the highest card in his hand. Everyone turns to him, surprised. He laughs—A difficult man to deal with, that, in other matters besides cards. A man whose thoughts lie a good deal below his skin.

Opposite, a cross-looking old woman clamours for sausages, gets them, and seems crosser than ever. She scowls round on everyone, with a malignant expression that is quite terrifying. A small dog comes and sits down in front of her, and grins at her. Still, with the same savage expression of hatred towards all living things, she feeds him with sausage at the end of a fork, regarding him all the while with an aspect of such concentrated dislike, that one wonders it does not interfere with his digestion. In a corner, a stout old woman talks incessantly to a solemn-looking man, who sits silent and drinks steadily. It is evident that he can stand her conversation just so long as he has a mug of beer in front of him. He has brought her in here to give her a treat. He will let her have her talk out while he drinks. Heavens! how she does talk! She talks without movement, without expression; her voice never varies, it flows on, and on, and on, like a great resistless river. Four young artisans come clamping along in their hob-nailed boots, and seating themselves at one of the rude wooden tables, call for beer. With their arms round the waist of the utterly indifferent Fraulein, they shout and laugh and sing. Nearly all the young folks here are laughing—looking forward to life. All the old folks are talking, remembering it.

What grand pictures some of these old, seared faces round us would make, if a man could only paint them—paint all that is in them, all the tragedy—and comedy that the great playwright, Life, has written upon the withered skins! Joys and sorrows, sordid hopes and fears, child-like strivings to be good, mean selfishness and grand unselfishness, have helped to fashion these old wrinkled faces. The curves of cunning and kindliness lurk round these fading eyes. The lines of greed hover about these bloodless lips, that have so often been tight-pressed in patient heroism.

SUNDAY, 25TH—CONTINUED

We Dine.—A Curious Dish.—"A Feeling of Sadness Comes O'er Me."—The German Cigar.—The Handsomest Match in Europe.—"How Easy 'tis for Friends to Drift Apart," especially in a place like Munich Railway Station.—The Victim of Fate.—A Faithful Bradshaw.—Among the Mountains.—Prince and Pauper.—A Modern Romance.—Arrival at Oberau.—Wise and Foolish Pilgrims.—An Interesting Drive.—Ettal and its Monastery.—We Reach the Goal of our Pilgrimage.

At one o'clock we turned into a restaurant for dinner. The Germans themselves always dine in the middle of the day, and a very substantial meal they make of it. At the hotels frequented by tourists *table d'hôte* is, during the season, fixed for about six or seven, but this is only done to meet the views of foreign customers.

I mention that we had dinner, not because I think that the information will prove exciting to the reader, but because I wish to warn my countrymen, travelling in Germany, against undue indulgence in Liptauer cheese.

I am fond of cheese, and of trying new varieties of cheese; so that when I looked down the cheese department of the bill of fare, and came across "liptauer garnit," an article of diet I had never before heard of, I determined to sample it.

It was not a tempting-looking cheese. It was an unhealthy, sad-looking cheese. It looked like a cheese that had seen trouble. In appearance it resembled putty more than anything else. It even tasted like putty—at least, like I should imagine putty would taste. To this hour I am not positive that it was not putty. The garnishing was even more remarkable than the cheese. All the way round the plate were piled articles that I had never before seen at a dinner, and that I do not ever want to see there again. There was a little heap of split-peas, three or four remarkably small potatoes—at least, I suppose they were potatoes; if not, they were pea-nuts boiled soft,—some caraway-seeds, a very young-looking fish, apparently of the stickleback breed, and some red paint. It was quite a little dinner all to itself.

What the red paint was for, I could not understand. B. thought that it was put there for suicidal purposes. His idea was that the customer, after eating all the other things in the plate, would wish he were dead, and that the restaurant people, knowing this, had thoughtfully provided him with red paint for one, so that he could poison himself off and get out of his misery.

I thought, after swallowing the first mouthful, that I would not eat any more of this cheese. Then it occurred to me that it was a pity to waste it after having ordered it, and, besides, I might get to like it before I had finished. The taste for most of the good things of this world has to be acquired. *I* can remember the time when I did not like beer.

So I mixed up everything on the plate all together—made a sort of salad of it, in fact—and ate it with a spoon. A more disagreeable dish I have never tasted since the days when I used to do Willie Evans's "dags," by walking twice through a sewer, and was subsequently, on returning home, promptly put to bed, and made to eat brimstone and treacle.

I felt very sad after dinner. All the things I have done in my life that I should not have done recurred to me with painful vividness. (There seemed to be a goodish number of them, too.) I thought of all the disappointments and reverses I had experienced during my career; of all the injustice that I had suffered, and of all the unkind things that had been said and done to me. I thought of all the people I had known who were now dead, and whom I should never see again, of all the girls that I had loved, who were now married to other fellows, while I did not even know their present addresses. I pondered upon our earthly existence, upon how hollow, false, and transient it is, and how full of sorrow. I mused upon the wickedness of the world and of everybody in it, and the general cussedness of all things.

I thought how foolish it was for B. and myself to be wasting our time, gadding about Europe in this silly way. What earthly enjoyment was there in travelling— being jolted about in stuffy trains, and overcharged at uncomfortable hotels?

B. was cheerful and frivolously inclined at the beginning of our walk (we were strolling down the Maximilian Strasse, after dinner); but as I talked to him, I was glad to notice that he gradually grew more serious and subdued. He is not really bad, you know, only thoughtless.

B. bought some cigars and offered me one. I did not want to smoke. Smoking seemed to me, just then, a foolish waste of time and money. As I said to B.:

"In a few more years, perhaps before this very month is gone, we shall be lying in the silent tomb, with the worms feeding on us. Of what advantage will it be to us then that we smoked these cigars to-day?"

B. said:

"Well, the advantage it will be to me now is, that if you have a cigar in your mouth I shan't get quite so much of your chatty conversation. Take one, for my sake."

To humour him, I lit up.

I do not admire the German cigar. B. says that when you consider they only cost a penny, you cannot grumble. But what I say is, that when you consider they are dear at six a half-penny, you can grumble. Well boiled, they might serve for greens; but as smoking material they are not worth the match with which you light them, especially not if the match be a German one. The German match is quite a high art work. It has a yellow head and a magenta or green stem, and can certainly lay claim to being the handsomest match in Europe.

We smoked a good many penny cigars during our stay in Germany, and that we were none the worse for doing so I consider as proof of our splendid physique and constitution. I think the German cigar test might, with reason, be adopted by life insurance offices.—Question: "Are you at present, and have you always been, of robust health?" Answer: "I have smoked a German cigar, and still live." Life accepted.

Towards three o'clock we worked our way round to the station, and began looking for our train. We hunted all over the place, but could not find it anywhere. The central station at Munich is an enormous building, and a perfect maze of passages and halls and corridors. It is much easier to lose oneself in it, than to find anything in it one may happen to want. Together and separately B. and I lost ourselves and each other some twenty-four times. For about half an hour we seemed to be doing nothing else but rushing up and down the station looking for each other, suddenly finding each other, and saying, "Why, where the dickens have you been? I have been hunting for you everywhere. Don't go away like that," and then immediately losing each other again.

And what was so extraordinary about the matter was that every time, after losing each other, we invariably met again—when we did meet—outside the door of the third-class refreshment room.

We came at length to regard the door of the third-class refreshment room as "home," and to feel a thrill of joy when, in the course of our weary wanderings through far-off waiting-rooms and lost-luggage bureaus and lamp depots, we saw its old familiar handle shining in the distance, and knew that there, beside it, we should find our loved and lost one.

When any very long time elapsed without our coming across it, we would go up to one of the officials, and ask to be directed to it.

"Please can you tell me," we would say, "the nearest way to the door of the third-class refreshment room?"

When three o'clock came, and still we had not found the 3.10 train, we became quite anxious about the poor thing, and made inquiries concerning it.

"The 3.10 train to Ober-Ammergau," they said. "Oh, we've not thought about that yet."

"Haven't thought about it!" we exclaimed indignantly. "Well, do for heaven's sake wake up a bit. It is 3.5 now!"

"Yes," they answered, "3.5 in the afternoon; the 3.10 is a night train. Don't you see it's printed in thick type? All the trains between six in the evening and six in the morning are printed in fat figures, and the day trains in thin. You have got plenty of time. Look around after supper."

I do believe I am the most unfortunate man at a time-table that ever was born. I do not think it can be stupidity; for if it were mere stupidity, I should occasionally, now and then when I was feeling well, not make a mistake. It must be fate.

If there is one train out of forty that goes on "Saturdays only" to some place I want to get to, that is the train I select to travel by on a Friday. On Saturday morning I get up at six, swallow a hasty breakfast, and rush off to catch a return train that goes on every day in the week "except Saturdays."

I go to London, Brighton and South Coast Railway-stations and clamour for South-Eastern trains. On Bank Holidays I forget it is Bank Holiday, and go and sit on draughty platforms for hours, waiting for trains that do not run on Bank Holidays.

To add to my misfortunes, I am the miserable possessor of a demon time-table that I cannot get rid of, a Bradshaw for August, 1887. Regularly, on the first of each month, I buy and bring home with me a new Bradshaw and a new A.B.C. What becomes of them after the second of the month, I do not know. After the second of the month, I never see either of them again. What their fate is, I can only guess. In their place is left, to mislead me, this wretched old 1887 corpse.

For three years I have been trying to escape from it, but it will not leave me.

I have thrown it out of the window, and it has fallen on people's heads, and those people have picked it up and smoothed it out, and brought it back to the house, and members of my family—"friends" they call themselves—people of my own flesh and blood—have thanked them and taken it in again!

I have kicked it into a dozen pieces, and kicked the pieces all the way downstairs and out into the garden, and persons—persons, mind you, who will not sew a button on the back of my shirt to save me from madness—have collected the pieces and stitched them carefully together, and made the book look as good as new, and put it back in my study!

It has acquired the secret of perpetual youth, has this time-table. Other time-tables that I buy become dissipated-looking wrecks in about a week. This book looks as fresh and new and clean as it did on the day when it first lured me into purchasing it. There is nothing about its appearance to suggest to the casual observer that it is not this month's Bradshaw. Its evident aim and object in life is to deceive people into the idea that it is this month's Bradshaw.

It is undermining my moral character, this book is. It is responsible for at least ten per cent. of the bad language that I use every year. It leads me into drink and gambling. I am continually finding myself with some three or four hours to wait at dismal provincial railway stations. I read all the advertisements on both platforms, and then I get wild and reckless, and plunge into the railway hotel and play billiards with the landlord for threes of Scotch.

I intend to have that Bradshaw put into my coffin with me when I am buried, so that I can show it to the recording angel and explain matters. I expect to obtain a discount of at least five-and-twenty per cent. off my bill of crimes for that Bradshaw.

The 3.10 train in the morning was, of course, too late for us. It would not get us to Ober-Ammergau until about 9 a.m. There was a train leaving at 7.30 (I let B. find out this) by which we might reach the village some time during the night, if only we could get a conveyance from Oberau, the nearest railway-station. Accordingly, we telegraphed to Cook's agent, who was at Ober-Ammergau (we all of us sneer at Mr. Cook and Mr. Gaze, and such-like gentlemen, who kindly conduct travellers that cannot conduct themselves properly, when we are at home; but I notice most of us appeal, on the quiet, to one or the other of them the moment we want to move abroad), to try and send a carriage to meet us by that train; and then went to an hotel, and turned into bed until it was time to start.

We had another grand railway-ride from Munich to Oberau. We passed by the beautiful lake of Starnberg just as the sun was setting and gilding with gold the little villages and pleasant villas that lie around its shores. It was in the lake of Starnberg, near the lordly pleasure-house that he had built for himself in that fair vale, that poor mad Ludwig, the late King of Bavaria, drowned himself. Poor King! Fate gave him everything calculated to make a man happy, excepting one thing, and that was the power of being happy. Fate has a mania for striking balances. I knew a little shoeblack once who used to follow his profession at the corner of Westminster Bridge. Fate gave him an average of sixpence a day to live upon and provide himself with luxuries; but she also gave him a power of enjoying that kept him jolly all day long. He could buy as much enjoyment for a penny as the average man could for a ten-pound note—more, I almost think. He did not know he was badly off, any more than King Ludwig knew he was well off; and all day long he laughed and played, and worked a little—not more than he could help—and ate and drank, and gambled. The last time I saw him was in St. Thomas's Hospital, into which he had got himself owing to his fatal passion for walking along outside the stone coping of Westminster Bridge. He thought it was "prime," being in the hospital, and told me that he was living like a fighting-cock, and that he did not mean to go out sooner than he could help. I asked him if he were not in pain, and he said "Yes," when he "thought about it."

Poor little chap! he only managed to live like a "fighting-cock" for three days more. Then he died, cheerful up to the last, so they told me, like the plucky little English game-cock he was. He could not have been more than twelve years old when he crowed his last. It had been a short life for him, but a very merry one.

Now, if only this little beggar and poor old Ludwig could have gone into partnership, and so have shared between them the shoeblack's power of enjoying and the king's stock of enjoyments, what a good thing it would have been for both of them—especially for King Ludwig. He would never have thought of drowning himself then—life would have been too delightful.

But that would not have suited Fate. She loves to laugh at men, and to make of life a paradox. To the one, she played ravishing strains, having first taken the precaution to make him stone-deaf. To the other, she piped a few poor notes on a cracked tin-whistle, and he thought it was music, and danced!

A few years later on, at the very same spot where King Ludwig threw back to the gods their gift of life, a pair of somewhat foolish young lovers ended their disappointments, and, finding they could not be wedded together in life, wedded themselves together in death. The story, duly reported in the newspapers as an item of foreign intelligence, read more like some old Rhine-legend than the record of a real occurrence in this prosaic nineteenth century.

He was a German Count, if I remember rightly, and, like most German Counts, had not much money; and her father, as fathers will when proposed to by impecunious would-be sons-in-law, refused his consent. The Count then went abroad to try and make, or at all events improve, his fortune. He went to America, and there he prospered. In a year or two he came back, tolerably rich—to find, however, that he was too late. His lady, persuaded of his death, had been urged into a marriage with a rich somebody else. In ordinary life, of course, the man would have contented himself with continuing to make love to the lady, leaving the rich somebody else to pay for her keep. This young couple, however, a little lighter headed, or a little deeper hearted than the most of us, whichever it may have been, and angry at the mocking laughter with which the air around them seemed filled, went down one stormy night together to the lake, and sobered droll Fate for an instant by turning her grim comedy into a somewhat grimmer tragedy.

Soon after losing sight of Starnberg's placid waters, we plunged into the gloom of the mountains, and began a long, winding climb among their hidden recesses. At times, shrieking as if in terror, we passed some ghostly hamlet, standing out white and silent in the moonlight against the shadowy hills; and, now and then, a dark, still lake, or mountain torrent whose foaming waters fell in a long white streak across the blackness of the night.

We passed by Murnau in the valley of the Dragon, a little town which possessed a Passion Play of its own in the olden times, and which, until a few years ago, when the railway-line was pushed forward to Partenkirchen, was the nearest station to Ober-Ammergau. It was a tolerably steep climb up the road from Murnau, over Mount Ettal, to Ammergau—so steep, indeed, that one stout pilgrim not many years ago, died from the exertion while walking up. Sturdy-legged mountaineer and pulpy citizen both had to clamber up side by side, for no horses could do more than drag behind them the empty vehicle.

Every season, however, sees the European tourist more and more pampered, and the difficulties and consequent pleasure and interest of his journey more and more curtailed and spoilt. In a few years' time, he will be packed in cotton-wool in his own back-parlour, labelled for the place he wants to go to, and unpacked and taken out when he gets there. The railway now carries him round Mount Ettal to Oberau, from which little village a tolerably easy road, as mountain roadways go, of about four or five English miles takes him up to the valley of the Ammer.

It was midnight when our train landed us at Oberau station; but the place was far more busy and stirring than on ordinary occasions it is at mid-day. Crowds of tourists and pilgrims thronged the little hotel, wondering, as also did the landlord, where they were all going to sleep; and wondering still more, though this latter consideration evidently did not trouble their host, how they were going to get up to Ober-Ammergau in the morning in time for the play, which always begins at 8 a.m.

Some were engaging carriages at fabulous prices to call for them at five; and others, who could not secure carriages, and who had determined to walk, were instructing worried waiters to wake them at 2.30, and ordering breakfast for a quarter-past three sharp. (I had no idea there were such times in the morning!)

We were fortunate enough to find our land-lord, a worthy farmer, waiting for us with a tumble-down conveyance, in appearance something between a circus-chariot and a bath-chair, drawn by a couple of powerful-looking horses; and in this, after a spirited skirmish between our driver and a mob of twenty or so tourists, who pretended to mistake the affair for an omnibus, and who would have clambered into it and swamped it, we drove away.

Higher and higher we climbed, and grander and grander towered the frowning moon-bathed mountains round us, and chillier and chillier grew the air. For most of the way we crawled along, the horses tugging us from side to side of the steep road; but, wherever our coachman could vary the monotony of the pace by a stretch-gallop—as, for instance, down the precipitous descents that occasionally followed upon some extra long and toilsome ascent—he thoughtfully did so. At such times the drive became really quite exciting, and all our weariness was forgotten.

The steeper the descent, the faster, of course, we could go. The rougher the road, the more anxious the horses seemed to be to get over it quickly. During the gallop, B. and I enjoyed, in a condensed form, all the advantages usually derived from crossing the Channel on a stormy day, riding on a switchback railway, and being tossed in a blanket—a hard, nobbly blanket, full of nasty corners and sharp edges. I should never have thought that so many different sensations could have been obtained from one machine!

About half-way up we passed Ettal, at the entrance to the Valley of the Ammer. The great white temple, standing, surrounded by its little village, high up amid the mountain solitudes, is a famous place of pilgrimage among devout Catholics. Many hundreds of years ago, one of the early Bavarian kings built here a monastery as a shrine for a miraculous image of the Virgin that had been sent down to him from Heaven to help him when, in a foreign land, he had stood sore in need, encompassed by his enemies. Maybe the stout arms and hearts of his Bavarian friends were of some service in the crisis also; but the living helpers were forgotten. The old church and monastery, which latter was a sort of ancient Chelsea Hospital for decayed knights, was destroyed one terrible night some hundred and fifty years ago by a flash of lightning; but the wonder-working image was rescued unhurt, and may still be seen and worshipped beneath the dome of the present much less imposing church which has been reared upon the ruins of its ancestor.

The monastery, which was also rebuilt at the same time, now serves the more useful purpose of a brewery.

From Ettal the road is comparatively level, and, jolting swiftly over it, we soon reached Ober-Ammergau. Lights were passing to and fro behind the many windows of the square stone houses, and dark, strange-looking figures were moving about the streets, busy with preparations for the great business that would commence with the dawn.

We rattled noisily through the village, our driver roaring out "Good Night!" to everyone he passed in a voice sufficient to wake up everybody who might be sleeping within a mile, charged light-heartedly round half-a-dozen corners, trotted down the centre path of somebody's front garden, squeezed our way through a gate, and drew up at an open door, through which the streaming light poured out upon two tall, comely lasses, our host's daughters, who were standing waiting for us in the porch. They led us into a large, comfortably furnished room, where a tempting supper of hot veal-chops (they seem to live on veal in Germany) and white wine was standing ready. Under ordinary circumstances I should have been afraid that such a supper would cause me to be more eager for change and movement during the ensuing six hours than for sleep; but I felt that to-night it would take a dozen half-baked firebricks to keep me awake five seconds after I had got my head on the pillow—or what they call a pillow in Germany; and so, without hesitation, I made a very satisfactory meal.

After supper our host escorted us to our bedroom, an airy apartment adorned with various highly-coloured wood-carvings of a pious but somewhat ghastly character, calculated, I should say, to exercise a disturbing influence upon the night's rest of a nervous or sensitive person.

"Mind that we are called at proper time in the morning," said B. to the man. "We don't want to wake up at four o'clock in the afternoon and find that we have missed the play, after coming all this way to see it."

"Oh! that will be all right," answered the old fellow. "You won't get much chance of oversleeping yourself. We shall all be up and about, and the whole village stirring, before five; and besides, the band will be playing at six just beneath the window here, and the cannon on the Kofel goes off at—"

"Look here," I interrupted, "that won't do for me, you know. Don't you think that I am going to be woke up by mere riots outside the window, and brass-band contests, and earthquakes, and explosions, and those sort of things, because it can't be done that way. Somebody's got to come into this room and haul me out of bed, and sit down on the bed and see that I don't get into it again, and that I don't go to sleep on the floor. That will be the way to get me up to-morrow morning. Don't let's have any nonsense about stirring villages and guns and German bands. I know what all that will end in, my going back to England without seeing the show. I want to be roused in the morning, not lulled off to sleep again."

B. translated the essential portions of this speech to the man, and he laughed and promised upon his sacred word of honour that he would come up himself and have us both out; and as he was a stalwart and determined-looking man, I felt satisfied, and wished him "Good-night," and made haste to get off my boots before I fell asleep.

TUESDAY, THE 27TH

A Pleasant Morning.—What can one Say about the Passion Play?—B. Lectures.—Unreliable Description of Ober-Ammergau.—Exaggerated Description of its Weather.—Possibly Untruthful Account of how the Passion Play came to be Played.—A Good Face.—The Cultured Schoolboy and his Ignorant Relations.

I am lying in bed, or, to speak more truthfully, I am sitting up on a green satin, lace-covered pillow, writing these notes. A green satin, lace-covered bed is on the floor beside me. It is about eleven o'clock in the morning. B. is sitting up in his bed a few feet off, smoking a pipe. We have just finished a light repast of—what do you think? you will never guess—coffee and rolls. We intend to put the week straight by stopping in bed all day, at all events until the evening. Two English ladies occupy the bedroom next to ours. They seem to have made up their minds to also stay upstairs all day. We can hear them walking about their room, muttering. They have been doing this for the last three-quarters of an hour. They seem troubled about something.

It is very pleasant here. An overflow performance is being given in the theatre to-day for the benefit of those people who could not gain admittance yesterday, and, through the open windows, we can hear the rhythmic chant of the chorus. Mellowed by the distance, the wailing cadence of the plaintive songs, mingled with the shrill Haydnistic strains of the orchestra, falls with a mournful sweetness on our ears.

We ourselves saw the play yesterday, and we are now discussing it. I am explaining to B. the difficulty I experience in writing an account of it for my diary. I tell him that I really do not know what to say about it.

He smokes for a while in silence, and then, taking the pipe from his lips, he says:

"Does it matter very much what you say about it?"

I find much relief in that thought. It at once lifts from my shoulders the oppressive feeling of responsibility that was weighing me down. After all, what does it matter what I say? What does it matter what any of us says about any-thing? Nobody takes much notice of it, luckily for everybody. This reflection must be of great comfort to editors and critics. A conscientious man who really felt that his words would carry weight and influence with them would be almost afraid to speak at all. It is the man who knows that it will not make an ounce of difference to anyone what he says, that can grow eloquent and vehement and positive. It will not make any difference to anybody or anything what I say about the Ober-Ammergau Passion Play. So I shall just say what I want to.

But what do I want to say? What can I say that has not been said, and said much better, already? (An author must always pretend to think that every other author writes better than he himself does. He does not really think so, you know, but it looks well to talk as though he did.) What can I say that the reader does not know, or that, not knowing, he cares to know? It is easy enough to talk about nothing, like I have been doing in this diary hitherto. It is when one is confronted with the task of writing about *some*thing, that one wishes one were a respectable well-to-do sweep—a sweep with a comfortable business of his own, and a pony—instead of an author.

B. says:

"Well, why not begin by describing Ober-Ammergau."

I say it has been described so often.

He says:

"So has the Oxford and Cambridge Boat Race and the Derby Day, but people go on describing them all the same, and apparently find other people to read their descriptions. Say that the little village, clustered round its mosque-domed church, nestles in the centre of a valley, surrounded by great fir-robed hills, which stand, with the cross-crowned Kofel for their chief, like stern, strong sentinels guarding its old-world peace from the din and clamour of the outer world. Describe how the square, whitewashed houses are sheltered beneath great overhanging gables, and are encircled by carved wooden balconies and verandahs, where, in the cool of the evening, peasant wood-carver and peasant farmer sit to smoke the long Ba-varian pipe, and chat about the cattle and the Passion Play and village politics; and how, in gaudy colours above the porch, are painted glowing figures of saints and virgins and such-like good folk, which the rains have sadly mutilated, so that a legless angel on one side of the road looks dejectedly across at a headless Ma-donna on the other, while at an exposed corner some unfortunate saint, more cruelly dealt with by the weather than he ever was even by the heathen, has been deprived of everything that he could call his own, with the exception of half a head and a pair of extra-sized feet.

"Explain how all the houses are numbered according to the date they were built, so that number sixteen comes next to number forty-seven, and there is no number one because it has been pulled down. Tell how unsophisticated visitors, informed that their lodgings are at number fifty-three, go wandering for days and days round fifty-two, under the not unreasonable impression that their house must be next door, though, as a matter of fact, it is half a mile off at the other end of the village, and are discovered one sunny morning, sitting on the doorstep of number eighteen, singing pathetic snatches of nursery rhymes, and trying to plat their toes into door-mats, and are taken up and carried away screaming, to end their lives in the madhouse at Munich.

"Talk about the weather. People who have stayed here for any length of time tell me that it rains at Ober-Ammergau three days out of every four, the reason that it does not rain on the fourth day being that every fourth day is set apart for a deluge. They tell me, also, that while it will be pouring with rain just in the village the sun will be shining brightly all round about, and that the villagers, when the water begins to come in through their roofs, snatch up their children and hurry off to the nearest field, where they sit and wait until the storm is over."

"Do you believe them—the persons that you say tell you these tales?" I ask.

"Personally I do not," he replies. "I think people exaggerate to me because I look young and innocent, but no doubt there is a ground-work of truth in their statements. I have myself left Ober-Ammergau under a steady drenching rain, and found a cloudless sky the other side of the Kofel.

"Then," he continues, "you can comment upon the hardihood of the Bavarian peasant. How he or she walks about bare-headed and bare-footed through the fiercest showers, and seems to find the rain only pleasantly cooling. How, during the performance of the Passion Play, they act and sing and stand about upon the uncovered stage without taking the slightest notice of the downpour of water that is soaking their robes and running from their streaming hair, to make great pools upon the boards; and how the audience, in the cheaper, unroofed portion of the theatre, sit with equal stoicism, watching them, no one ever dreaming even of putting up an umbrella—or, if he does dream of doing so, experiencing a very rude awakening from the sticks of those behind."

B. stops to relight his pipe at this point, and I hear the two ladies in the next room fidgeting about and muttering worse than ever. It seems to me they are listening at the door (our room and theirs are connected by a door); I do wish that they would either get into bed again or else go downstairs. They worry me.

"And what shall I say after I have said all that?" I ask B. when at last he has started his pipe again.

"Oh! well, after that," he replies, "you can give the history of the Passion Play; how it came to be played."

"Oh, but so many people have done that already," I say again.

"So much the better for you," is his reply. Having previously heard precisely the same story from half a dozen other sources, the public will be tempted to believe you when you repeat the account. Tell them that during the thirty year's war a terrible plague (as if half a dozen different armies, marching up and down their country, fighting each other about the Lord only knows what, and living on them while doing it, was not plague enough) swept over Bavaria, devastating each town and hamlet. Of all the highland villages, Ober-Ammergau by means of a strictly enforced quarantine alone kept, for a while, the black foe at bay. No soul was allowed to leave the village; no living thing to enter it.

"But one dark night Caspar Schuchler, an inhabitant of Ober-Ammergau, who had been working in the plague-stricken neighbouring village of Eschenlohe, creeping low on his belly, passed the drowsy sentinels, and gained his home, and saw what for many a day he had been hungering for—a sight of his wife and bairns. It was a selfish act to do, and he and his fellow-villagers paid dearly for it. Three days after he had entered his house he and all his family lay dead, and the plague was raging through the valley, and nothing seemed able to stay its course.

"When human means fail, we feel it is only fair to give Heaven a chance. The good people who dwelt by the side of the Ammer vowed that, if the plague left them, they would, every ten years, perform a Passion Play. The celestial powers seem to have at once closed with this offer. The plague disappeared as if by magic, and every recurring tenth year since, the Ober-Ammergauites have kept their promise and played their Passion Play. They act it to this day as a pious observance. Before each performance all the characters gather together on the stage around their pastor, and, kneeling, pray for a blessing upon the work then about to commence. The profits that are made, after paying the performers a wage that just compensates them for their loss of time—wood-carver Maier, who plays the Christ, only receives about fifty pounds for the whole of the thirty or so performances given during the season, to say nothing of the winter's rehearsals—is put aside, part for the temporal benefit of the community, and the rest for the benefit of the Church. From burgomaster down to shepherd lad, from the Mary and the Jesus down to the meanest super, all work for the love of their religion, not for money. Each one feels that he is helping forward the cause of Christianity."

"And I could also speak," I add, "of grand old Daisenberger, the gentle, simple old priest, 'the father of the valley,' who now lies in silence among his children that he loved so well. It was he, you know, that shaped the rude burlesque of a coarser age into the impressive reverential drama that we saw yesterday. That is a portrait of him over the bed. What a plain, homely, good face it is! How pleasant, how helpful it is to come across a good face now and then! I do not mean a sainted face, suggestive of stained glass and marble tombs, but a rugged human face that has had the grit, and rain, and sunshine of life rubbed into it, and that has gained its expression, not by looking up with longing at the stars, but by looking down with eyes full of laughter and love at the human things around it."

"Yes," assented B. "You can put in that if you like. There is no harm in it. And then you can go on to speak of the play itself, and give your impressions concerning it. Never mind their being silly. They will be all the better for that. Silly remarks are generally more interesting than sensible ones."

"But what is the use of saying anything about it at all?" I urge. "The merest school-boy must know all about the Ober-Ammergau Passion Play by this time."

"What has that to do with you?" answers B. "You are not writing for cultured school-boys. You are writing for mere simple men and women. They will be glad of a little information on the subject, and then when the schoolboy comes home for his holiday they will be able, so far as this topic, at all events, is concerned, to converse with him on his own level and not appear stupid.

"Come," he says, kindly, trying to lead me on, "what did you think about it?"

"Well," I reply, after musing for a while, "I think that a play of eighteen acts and some forty scenes, which commences at eight o'clock in the morning, and continues, with an interval of an hour and a half for dinner, until six o'clock in the evening, is too long. I think the piece wants cutting. About a third of it is impressive and moving, and what the earnest student of the drama at home is for ever demanding that a play should be—namely, elevating; but I consider that the other two-thirds are tiresome."

"Quite so," answers B. "But then we must remember that the performance is not intended as an entertainment, but as a religious service. To criticise any part of it as uninteresting, is like saying that half the Bible might very well have been omitted, and that the whole story could have been told in a third of the space."

TUESDAY, THE 27TH—CONTINUED

We talk on.—An Argument.—The Story that Transformed the World.

"And now, as to the right or wrong of the performance as a whole. Do you see any objection to the play from a religious point of view?"

"No," I reply, "I do not; nor do I understand how anybody else, and least of all a really believing Christian, can either. To argue as some do, that Christianity should be treated as a sacred mystery, is to argue against the whole scheme of Christianity. It was Christ himself that rent the veil of the Temple, and brought religion down into the streets and market-places of the world. Christ was a common man. He lived a common life, among common men and women. He died a common death. His own methods of teaching were what a Saturday reviewer, had he to deal with the case, would undoubtedly term vulgar. The roots of Christianity are planted deep down in the very soil of life, amid all that is commonplace, and mean, and petty, and everyday. Its strength lies in its simplicity, its homely humanness. It has spread itself through the world by speaking to the hearts, rather than to the heads of men. If it is still to live and grow, it must be helped along by such methods as these peasant players of Ober-Ammergau employ, not by high-class essays and the learned discussions of the cultured.

"The crowded audience that sat beside us in the theatre yesterday saw Christ of Nazareth nearer than any book, however inspired, could bring him to them; clearer than any words, however eloquent, could show him. They saw the sorrow of his patient face. They heard his deep tones calling to them. They saw him in the hour of his so-called triumph, wending his way through the narrow streets of Jerusalem, the multitude that thronged round him waving their branches of green palms and shouting loud hosannas.

"What a poor scene of triumph!—a poor-clad, pale-faced man, mounted upon the back of a shuffling, unwilling little grey donkey, passing slowly through the byways of a city, busy upon other things. Beside him, a little band of worn, anxious men, clad in thread-bare garments—fishermen, petty clerks, and the like; and, following, a noisy rabble, shouting, as crowds in all lands and in all times shout, and as dogs bark, they know not why—because others are shouting, or barking. And that scene marks the highest triumph won while he lived on earth by the village carpenter of Galilee, about whom the world has been fighting and thinking and talking so hard for the last eighteen hundred years.

"They saw him, angry and indignant, driving out the desecrators from the temple. They saw the rabble, who a few brief moments before had followed him, shouting 'Hosanna,' slinking away from him to shout with his foes.

"They saw the high priests in their robes of white, with the rabbis and doctors, all the great and learned in the land, sitting late into the night beneath the vaulted roof of the Sanhedrin's council-hall, plotting his death.

"They saw him supping with his disciples in the house of Simon. They saw poor, loving Mary Magdalen wash his feet with costly ointment, that might have been sold for three hundred pence, and the money given to the poor—'and us.' Judas was so thoughtful for the poor, so eager that other people should sell all they had, and give the money to the poor—'and us.' Methinks that, even in this nineteenth century, one can still hear from many a tub and platform the voice of Judas, complaining of all waste, and pleading for the poor—'and us.'

"They were present at the parting of Mary and Jesus by Bethany, and it will be many a day before the memory of that scene ceases to vibrate in their hearts. It is the scene that brings the humanness of the great tragedy most closely home to us. Jesus is going to face sorrow and death at Jerusalem. Mary's instinct tells her that this is so, and she pleads to him to stay.

"Poor Mary! To others he is the Christ, the Saviour of mankind, setting forth upon his mighty mission to redeem the world. To loving Mary Mother, he is her son: the baby she has suckled at her breast, the little one she has crooned to sleep upon her lap, whose little cheek has lain against her heart, whose little feet have made sweet music through the poor home at Bethany: he is her boy, her child; she would wrap her mother's arms around him and hold him safe against all the world, against even heaven itself.

"Never, in any human drama, have I witnessed a more moving scene than this. Never has the voice of any actress (and I have seen some of the greatest, if any great ones are living) stirred my heart as did the voice of Rosa Lang, the Burgomaster's daughter. It was not the voice of one woman, it was the voice of Motherdom, gathered together from all the world over.

"Oliver Wendell Holmes, in *The Autocrat of the Breakfast Table*, I think, confesses to having been bewitched at different times by two women's voices, and adds that both these voices belonged to German women. I am not surprised at either statement of the good doctor's. I am sure if a man did fall in love with a voice, he would find, on tracing it to its source, that it was the voice of some homely-looking German woman. I have never heard such exquisite soul-drawing music in my life, as I have more than once heard float from the lips of some sweet-faced German Fraulein when she opened her mouth to speak. The voice has been so pure, so clear, so deep, so full of soft caressing tenderness, so strong to comfort, so gentle to soothe, it has seemed like one of those harmonies musicians tell us that they dream of, but can never chain to earth.

"As I sat in the theatre, listening to the wondrous tones of this mountain peasant-woman, rising and falling like the murmur of a sea, filling the vast sky-covered building with their yearning notes, stirring like a great wind stirs Æolian strings, the thousands of trembling hearts around her, it seemed to me that I was indeed listening to the voice of the 'mother of the world,' of mother Nature herself.

"They saw him, as they had often seen him in pictures, sitting for the last time with his disciples at supper. But yesterday they saw him, not a mute, moveless figure, posed in conventional, meaningless attitude, but a living, loving man, sitting in fellowship with the dear friends that against all the world had believed in him, and had followed his poor fortunes, talking with them for the last sweet time, comforting them.

"They heard him bless the bread and wine that they themselves to this day take in remembrance of him.

"They saw his agony in the Garden of Gethsemane, the human shrinking from the cup of pain. They saw the false friend, Judas, betray him with a kiss. (Alas! poor Judas! He loved Jesus, in a way, like the rest did. It was only his fear of poverty that made him betray his Master. He was so poor—he wanted the money so badly! We cry out in horror against Judas. Let us pray rather that we are never tempted to do a shameful action for a few pieces of silver. The fear of poverty ever did, and ever will, make scamps of men. We would like to be faithful, and noble, and just, only really times are so bad that we cannot afford it! As Becky Sharp says, it is so easy to be good and noble on five thousand a year, so very hard to be it on the mere five. If Judas had only been a well-to-do man, he might have been Saint Judas this day, instead of cursed Judas. He was not bad. He had only one failing—the failing that makes the difference between a saint and a villain, all the world over—he was a coward; he was afraid of being poor.)

"They saw him, pale and silent, dragged now before the priests of his own countrymen, and now before the Roman Governor, while the voice of the people—the people who had cried 'Hosanna' to him—shouted 'Crucify him! crucify him!' They saw him bleeding from the crown of thorns. They saw him, still followed by the barking mob, sink beneath the burden of his cross. They saw the woman wipe the bloody sweat from off his face. They saw the last, long, silent look between the mother and the son, as, journeying upward to his death, he passed her in the narrow way through which he once had ridden in brief-lived triumph. They heard her low sob as she turned away, leaning on Mary Magdalen. They saw him nailed upon the cross between the thieves. They saw the blood start from his side. They heard his last cry to his God. They saw him rise victorious over death.

"Few believing Christians among the vast audience but must have passed out from that strange playhouse with their belief and love strengthened. The God of the Christian, for his sake, became a man, and lived and suffered and died as a man; and, as a man, living, suffering, dying among other men, he had that day seen him.

"The man of powerful imagination needs no aid from mimicry, however excellent, however reverent, to unroll before him in its simple grandeur the great tragedy on which the curtain fell at Calvary some eighteen and a half centuries ago.

"A cultivated mind needs no story of human suffering to win or hold it to a faith.

"But the imaginative and cultured are few and far between, and the peasants of Ober-Ammergau can plead, as their Master himself once pleaded, that they seek not to help the learned but the lowly.

"The unbeliever, also, passes out into the village street full of food for thought. The rude sermon preached in this hillside temple has shown to him, clearer than he could have seen before, the secret wherein lies the strength of Christianity; the reason why, of all the faiths that Nature has taught to her children to help them in their need, to satisfy the hunger of their souls, this faith, born by the Sea of Galilee, has spread the farthest over the world, and struck its note the deepest into human life. Not by his doctrines, not even by his promises, has Christ laid hold upon the hearts of men, but by the story of his life."

TUESDAY, THE 27TH—CONTINUED

We Discuss the Performance.—A Marvellous Piece of Workmanship.—The Adam Family.—Some Living Groups.—The Chief Performers.—A Good Man, but a Bad Judas.—Where the Histrionic Artist Grows Wild.—An Alarm!

"And what do you think of the performance *as* a performance?" asks B.

"Oh, as to that," I reply, "I think what everyone who has seen the play must think, that it is a marvellous piece of workmanship.

"Experienced professional stage-managers, with all the tricks and methods of the theatre at their fingers' ends, find it impossible, out of a body of men and women born and bred in the atmosphere of the playhouse, to construct a crowd that looks like anything else except a nervous group of broken-down paupers waiting for soup.

"At Ober-Ammergau a few village priests and representative householders, who have probably never, any one of them, been inside the walls of a theatre in their lives, dealing with peasants who have walked straight upon the stage from their carving benches and milking-stools, produce swaying multitudes and clamouring mobs and dignified assemblages, so natural and truthful, so realistic of the originals they represent, that you feel you want to leap upon the stage and strangle them.

"It shows that earnestness and effort can very easily overtake and pass mere training and technical skill. The object of the Ober-Ammergau 'super' is, not to get outside and have a drink, but to help forward the success of the drama.

"The groupings, both in the scenes of the play itself and in the various tableaux that precede each act, are such as I doubt if any artist could improve upon. The tableau showing the life of Adam and Eve after their expulsion from Eden makes a beautiful picture. Father Adam, stalwart and sunbrowned, clad in sheepskins, rests for a moment from his delving, to wipe the sweat from his brow. Eve, still looking fair and happy—though I suppose she ought not to,—sits spinning and watching the children playing at 'helping father.' The chorus from each side of the stage explained to us that this represented a scene of woe, the result of sin; but it seemed to me that the Adam family were very contented, and I found myself wondering, in my common, earthly way, whether, with a little trouble to draw them closer together, and some honest work to keep them from getting into mischief, Adam and Eve were not almost better off than they would have been mooning about Paradise with nothing to do but talk.

"In the tableau representing the return of the spies from Canaan, some four or five hundred men, women and children are most effectively massed. The feature of the foreground is the sample bunch of grapes, borne on the shoulders of two men, which the spies have brought back with them from the promised land. The sight of this bunch of grapes, we are told, astonished the children of Israel. I can quite understand its doing so. The picture of it used to astonish me, too, when *I* was a child.

"The scene of Christ's entry into Jerusalem surrounded by the welcoming multitude, is a wonderful reproduction of life and movement, and so also is the scene, towards the end, showing his last journey up to Calvary. All Jerusalem seems to have turned out to see him pass and to follow him, the many laughing, the few sad. The people fill the narrow streets to overflowing, and press round the spears of the Roman Guard.

"They throng the steps and balconies of every house, they strain to catch a sight of Christ above each other's heads. They leap up on each other's backs to gain a better vantage-ground from which to hurl their jeers at him. They jostle irreverently against their priests. Each individual man, woman, and child on the stage acts, and acts in perfect harmony with all the rest.

"Of the chief members of the cast—Maier, the gentle and yet kingly Christ; Burgomaster Lang, the stern, revengeful High Priest; his daughter Rosa, the sweet-faced, sweet-voiced Virgin; Rendl, the dignified, statesman-like Pilate; Peter Rendl, the beloved John, with the purest and most beautiful face I have ever seen upon a man; old Peter Hett, the rugged, loving, weak friend, Peter; Rutz, the leader of the chorus (no sinecure, his post); and Amalie Deschler, the Magdalen— it would be difficult to speak in terms of too high praise. Themselves mere peasants—There are those two women again, spying round our door; I am sure of it!" I exclaim, breaking off, and listening to the sounds that come from the next room. "I wish they would go downstairs; I am beginning to get quite nervous."

"Oh, I don't think we need worry," answers B. "They are quite old ladies, both of them. I met them on the stairs yesterday. I am sure they look harmless enough."

"Well, I don't know," I reply. "We are all by ourselves, you know. Nearly everyone in the village is at the theatre, I wish we had got a dog."

B. reassures me, however, and I continue:

"Themselves mere peasants," I repeat, "they represent some of the greatest figures in the world's history with as simple a dignity and as grand a bearing as could ever have been expected from the originals themselves. There must be a natural inborn nobility in the character of these highlanders. They could never assume or act that manner *au grand seigneur* with which they imbue their parts.

"The only character poorly played was that of Judas. The part of Judas is really *the* part of the piece, so far as acting is concerned; but the exemplary householder who essayed it seemed to have no knowledge or experience of the ways and methods of bad men. There seemed to be no side of his character sufficiently in sympathy with wickedness to enable him to understand and portray it. His amateur attempts at scoundrelism quite irritated me. It sounds conceited to say so, but I am convinced I could have given a much more truthful picture of the blackguard myself.

"'Dear, dear me,' I kept on saying under my breath, 'he is doing it all wrong. A downright unmitigated villain would never go on like that; he would do so and so, he would look like this, and speak like that, and act like the other. I know he would. My instinct tells me so.'

"This actor was evidently not acquainted with even the rudiments of knavery. I wanted to get up and instruct him in them. I felt that there were little subtleties of rascaldom, little touches of criminality, that I could have put that man up to, which would have transformed his Judas from woodenness into breathing life. As it was, with no one in the village apparently who was worth his salt as a felon to teach him, his performance was unconvincing, and Judas became a figure to laugh rather than to shudder at.

"With that exception, the whole company, from Maier down to the donkey, seemed to be fitted to their places like notes into a master's melody. It would appear as though, on the banks of the Ammer, the histrionic artist grew wild."

"They are real actors, all of them," murmurs B. enthusiastically, "the whole village full; and they all live happily together in one small valley, and never try to kill each other. It is marvellous!"

At this point, we hear a sharp knock at the door that separates the before-mentioned ladies' room from our own. We both start and turn pale, and then look at each other. B. is the first to recover his presence of mind. Eliminating, by a strong effort, all traces of nervousness from his voice, he calls out in a tone of wonderful coolness:

"Yes, what is it?"

"Are you in bed?" comes a voice from the other side of the door.

"Yes," answers B. "Why?"

"Oh! Sorry to disturb you, but we shall be so glad when you get up. We can't go downstairs without coming through your room. This is the only door. We have been waiting here for two hours, and our train goes at three."

Great Scott! So that is why the poor old souls have been hanging round the door, terrifying us out of our lives.

"All right, we'll be out in five minutes. So sorry. Why didn't you call out before?"

FRIDAY, 30TH, OR SATURDAY, I AM NOT SURE WHICH

Troubles of a Tourist Agent.—His Views on Tourists.—The English Woman Abroad.—And at Home.—The Ugliest Cathedral in Europe.—Old Masters and New.—Victual-and-Drink-Scapes.—The German Band.—A "Beer Garden."—Not the Women to Turn a Man's Head.—Difficulty of Dining to Music.—Why one should Keep one's Mug Shut.

I think myself it is Saturday. B. says it is only Friday; but I am positive I have had three cold baths since we left Ober-Ammergau, which we did on Wednesday morning. If it is only Friday, then I have had two morning baths in one day. Anyhow, we shall know to-morrow by the shops being open or shut.

We travelled from Oberau with a tourist agent, and he told us all his troubles. It seems that a tourist agent is an ordinary human man, and has feelings just like we have. This had never occurred to me before. I told him so.

"No," he replied, "it never does occur to you tourists. You treat us as if we were mere Providence, or even the Government itself. If all goes well, you say, what is the good of us, contemptuously; and if things go wrong, you say, what is the good of us, indignantly. I work sixteen hours a day to fix things comfortably for you, and you cannot even look satisfied; while if a train is late, or a hotel proprietor overcharges, you come and bully *me* about it. If I see after you, you mutter that I am officious; and if I leave you alone, you grumble that I am neglectful. You swoop down in your hundreds upon a tiny village like Ober-Ammergau without ever letting us know even that you are coming, and then threaten to write to the *Times* because there is not a suite of apartments and a hot dinner waiting ready for each of you.

"You want the best lodgings in the place, and then, when at a tremendous cost of trouble, they have been obtained for you, you object to pay the price asked for them. You all try and palm yourselves off for dukes and duchesses, travelling in disguise. You have none of you ever heard of a second-class railway carriage—didn't know that such things were made. You want a first-class Pullman car reserved for each two of you. Some of you have seen an omnibus in the distance, and have wondered what it was used for. To suggest that you should travel in such a plebeian conveyance, is to give you a shock that takes you two days to recover from. You expect a private carriage, with a footman in livery, to take you through the mountains. You, all of you, must have the most expensive places in the theatre. The eight-mark and six-mark places are every bit as good as the ten-mark seats, of which there are only a very limited number; but you are grossly insulted if it is hinted that you should sit in anything but the dearest chairs. If the villagers would only be sensible and charge you ten marks for the eight-mark places you would be happy; but they won't."

I must candidly confess that the English-speaking people one meets with on the Continent are, taken as a whole, a most disagreeable contingent. One hardly ever hears the English language spoken on the Continent, without hearing grumbling and sneering.

The women are the most objectionable. Foreigners undoubtedly see the very poorest specimens of the female kind we Anglo-Saxons have to show. The average female English or American tourist is rude and self-assertive, while, at the same time, ridiculously helpless and awkward. She is intensely selfish, and utterly inconsiderate of others; everlastingly complaining, and, in herself, drearily uninteresting. We travelled down in the omnibus from Ober-Ammergau with three perfect specimens of the species, accompanied by the usual miserable-looking man, who has had all the life talked out of him. They were grumbling the whole of the way at having been put to ride in an omnibus. It seemed that they had never been so insulted in their lives before, and they took care to let everybody in the vehicle know that they had paid for first-class, and that at home they kept their own carriage. They were also very indignant because the people at the house where they had lodged had offered to shake hands with them at parting. They did not come to Ober-Ammergau to be treated on terms of familiarity by German peasants, they said.

There are many women in the world who are in every way much better than angels. They are gentle and gracious, and generous and kind, and unselfish and good, in spite of temptations and trials to which mere angels are never subjected. And there are also many women in the world who, under the clothes, and not unfrequently under the title of a lady, wear the heart of an underbred snob. Having no natural dignity, they think to supply its place with arrogance. They mistake noisy bounce for self-possession, and supercilious rudeness as the sign of superiority. They encourage themselves in sleepy stupidity under the impression that they are acquiring aristocratic "repose." They would appear to have studied "attitude" from the pages of the *London Journal*, coquetry from barmaids—the commoner class of barmaids, I mean—wit from three-act farces, and manners from the servants'-hall. To be gushingly fawning to those above them, and vulgarly insolent to everyone they consider below them, is their idea of the way to hold and improve their position, whatever it may be, in society; and to be brutally indifferent to the rights and feelings of everybody else in the world is, in their opinion, the hall-mark of gentle birth.

They are the women you see at private views, pushing themselves in front of everybody else, standing before the picture so that no one can get near it, and shouting out their silly opinions, which they evidently imagine to be brilliantly satirical remarks, in strident tones: the women who, in the stalls of the theatre, talk loudly all through the performance; and who, having arrived in the middle of the first act, and made as much disturbance as they know how, before settling down in their seats, ostentatiously get up and walk out before the piece is finished: the women who, at dinner-party and "At Home"—that cheapest and most deadly uninteresting of all deadly uninteresting social functions—(You know the receipt for a fashionable "At Home," don't you? Take five hundred people, two-thirds of whom do not know each other, and the other third of whom cordially dislike each other, pack them, on a hot day, into a room capable of accommodating forty, leave them there to bore one another to death for a couple of hours with drawing-room philosophy and second-hand scandal; then give them a cup of weak tea, and a piece of crumbly cake, without any plate to eat it on; or, if it is an evening affair, a glass of champagne of the you-don't-forget-you've-had-it-for-a-week brand, and a ham-sandwich, and put them out into the street again)—can do nothing but make spiteful remarks about everybody whose name and address they happen to know: the women who, in the penny 'bus (for, in her own country, the lady of the new school is wonderfully economical and business-like), spreads herself out over the seat, and, looking indignant when a tired little milliner gets in, would leave the poor girl standing with her bundle for an hour, rather than make room for her—the women who write to the papers to complain that chivalry is dead!

B., who has been looking over my shoulder while I have been writing the foregoing, after the manner of a *Family Herald* story-teller's wife in the last chapter (fancy a man having to write the story of his early life and adventures with his wife looking over his shoulder all the time! no wonder the tales lack incident), says that I have been living too much on sauerkraut and white wine; but I reply that if anything has tended to interfere for a space with the deep-seated love and admiration that, as a rule, I entertain for all man and woman-kind, it is his churches and picture-galleries.

We have seen enough churches and pictures since our return to Munich to last me for a very long while. I shall not go to church, when I get home again, more than twice a Sunday, for months to come.

The inhabitants of Munich boast that their Cathedral is the ugliest in Europe; and, judging from appearances, I am inclined to think that the claim must be admitted. Anyhow, if there be an uglier one, I hope I am feeling well and strong when I first catch sight of it.

As for pictures and sculptures, I am thoroughly tired of them. The greatest art critic living could not dislike pictures and sculptures more than I do at this moment. We began by spending a whole morning in each gallery. We examined each picture critically, and argued with each other about its "form" and "colour" and "treatment" and "perspective" and "texture" and "atmosphere." I generally said it was flat, and B. that it was out of drawing. A stranger overhearing our discussions would have imagined that we knew something about painting. We would stand in front of a canvas for ten minutes, drinking it in. We would walk round it, so as to get the proper light upon it and to better realise the artist's aim. We would back away from it on to the toes of the people behind, until we reached the correct "distance," and then sit down and shade our eyes, and criticise it from there; and then we would go up and put our noses against it, and examine the workmanship in detail.

This is how we used to look at pictures in the early stages of our Munich art studies. Now we use picture galleries to practise spurts in.

I did a hundred yards this morning through the old Pantechnicon in twenty-two and a half seconds, which, for fair heel-and-toe walking, I consider very creditable. B. took five-eighths of a second longer for the same distance; but then he dawdled to look at a Raphael.

The "Pantechnicon," I should explain, is the name we have, for our own purposes, given to what the Munichers prefer to call the Pinakothek. We could never pronounce Pinakothek properly. We called it "Pynniosec," "Pintactec," and the "Happy Tack." B. one day after dinner called it the "Penny Cock," and then we both got frightened, and agreed to fix up some sensible, practical name for it before any mischief was done. We finally decided on "Pantechnicon," which begins with a "P," and is a dignified, old-established name, and one that we can both pronounce. It is quite as long, and nearly as difficult to spell, before you know how, as the other, added to which it has a homely sound. It seemed to be the very word.

The old Pantechnicon is devoted to the works of the old masters; I shall not say anything about these, as I do not wish to disturb in any way the critical opinion that Europe has already formed concerning them. I prefer that the art schools of the world should judge for themselves in the matter. I will merely remark here, for purposes of reference, that I thought some of the pictures very beautiful, and that others I did not care for.

What struck me as most curious about the exhibition was the number of canvases dealing with food stuffs. Twenty-five per cent. of the pictures in the place seem to have been painted as advertisements for somebody's home-grown seeds, or as coloured supplements to be given away with the summer number of the leading gardening journal of the period.

"What could have induced these old fellows," I said to B., "to choose such very uninteresting subjects? Who on earth cares to look at the life-sized portrait of a cabbage and a peck of peas, or at these no doubt masterly representations of a cut from the joint with bread and vegetables? Look at that 'View in a ham-and-beef shop,' No. 7063, size sixty feet by forty. It must have taken the artist a couple of years to paint. Who did he expect was going to buy it? And that Christmas-hamper scene over in the corner; was it painted, do you think, by some poor, half-starved devil, who thought he would have something to eat in the house, if it were only a picture of it?"

B. said he thought that the explanation was that the ancient patrons of art were gentry with a very strong idea of the fitness of things. For "their churches and cathedrals," said B., "they had painted all those virgins and martyrs and over-fed angels that you see everywhere about Europe. For their bedrooms, they ordered those—well, those bedroom sort of pictures, that you may have noticed here and there; and then I expect they used these victual-and-drink-scapes for their banqueting halls. It must have been like a gin-and-bitters to them, the sight of all that food."

In the new Pantechnicon is exhibited the modern art of Germany. This appeared to me to be exceedingly poor stuff. It seemed to belong to the illustrated Christmas number school of art. It was good, sound, respectable work enough. There was plenty of colour about it, and you could tell what everything was meant for. But there seemed no imagination, no individuality, no thought, anywhere. Each picture looked as though it could have been produced by anyone who had studied and practised art for the requisite number of years, and who was not a born fool. At all events, this is my opinion; and, as I know nothing whatever about art, I speak without prejudice.

One thing I have enjoyed at Munich very much, and that has been the music. The German band that you hear in the square in London while you are trying to compose an essay on the civilising influence of music, is not the sort of band that you hear in Germany. The German bands that come to London are bands that have fled from Germany, in order to save their lives. In Germany, these bands would be slaughtered at the public expense and their bodies given to the poor for sausages. The bands that the Germans keep for themselves are magnificent bands.

Munich of all places in the now united Fatherland, has, I suppose, the greatest reputation for its military bands, and the citizens are allowed, not only to pay for them, but to hear them. Two or three times a day in different parts of the city one or another of them will be playing *pro bono publico*, and, in the evening, they are loaned out by the authorities to the proprietors of the big beer-gardens.

"Go" and dash are the chief characteristics of their method; but, when needed, they can produce from the battered, time-worn trumpets, which have been handed down from player to player since the regiment was first formed, notes as soft and full and clear as any that could start from the strings of some old violin.

The German band in Germany has to know its business to be listened to by a German audience. The Bavarian artisan or shopkeeper understands and appreciates good music, as he understands and appreciates good beer. You cannot impose upon him with an inferior article. A music-hall audience in Munich are very particular as to how their beloved Wagner is rendered, and the trifles from Mozart and Haydn that they love to take in with their sausages and salad, and which, when performed to their satisfaction, they will thunderously applaud, must not be taken liberties with, or they will know the reason why.

The German beer-garden should be visited by everyone who would see the German people as well as their churches and castles. It is here that the workers of all kinds congregate in the evening. Here, after the labours of the day, come the tradesman with his wife and family, the young clerk with his betrothed and—also her mother, alack and well-a-day!—the soldier with his sweetheart, the students in twos and threes, the little grisette with her cousin, the shop-boy and the workman.

Here come grey-haired Darby and Joan, and, over the mug of beer they share between them, they sit thinking of the children—of little Lisa, married to clever Karl, who is pushing his way in the far-off land that lies across the great sea; of laughing Elsie, settled in Hamburg, who has grandchildren of her own now; of fair-haired Franz, his mother's pet, who fell in sunny France, fighting for the fatherland. At the next table sits a blushing, happy little maid, full of haughty airs and graces, such as may be excused to a little maid who has just saved a no doubt promising, but at present somewhat awkward-looking, youth from lifelong misery, if not madness and suicide (depend upon it, that is the alternative he put before her), by at last condescending to give him the plump little hand, that he, thinking nobody sees him, holds so tightly beneath the table-cloth. Opposite, a family group sit discussing omelettes and a bottle of white wine. The father contented, good-humoured, and laughing; the small child grave and solemn, eating and drinking in business-like fashion; the mother smiling at both, yet not forgetting to eat.

I think one would learn to love these German women if one lived among them for long. There is something so sweet, so womanly, so genuine about them. They seem to shed around them, from their bright, good-tempered faces, a healthy atmosphere of all that is homely, and simple, and good. Looking into their quiet, steadfast eyes, one dreams of white household linen, folded in great presses; of sweet-smelling herbs; of savoury, appetising things being cooked for supper; of bright-polished furniture; of the patter of tiny feet; of little high-pitched voices, asking silly questions; of quiet talks in the lamp-lit parlour after the children are in bed, upon important questions of house management and home politics, while long stockings are being darned.

They are not the sort of women to turn a man's head, but they are the sort of women to lay hold of a man's heart—very gently at first, so that he hardly knows that they have touched it, and then, with soft, clinging tendrils that wrap themselves tighter and tighter year by year around it, and draw him closer and closer— till, as, one by one, the false visions and hot passions of his youth fade away, the plain homely figure fills more and more his days—till it grows to mean for him all the better, more lasting, true part of life—till he feels that the strong, gentle mother-nature that has stood so long beside him has been welded firmly into his own, and that they twain are now at last one finished whole.

We had our dinner at a beer-garden the day before yesterday. We thought it would be pleasant to eat and drink to the accompaniment of music, but we found that in practice this was not so. To dine successfully to music needs a very strong digestion—especially in Bavaria.

The band that performs at a Munich beer-garden is not the sort of band that can be ignored. The members of a Munich military band are big, broad-chested fellows, and they are not afraid of work. They do not talk much, and they never whistle. They keep all their breath to do their duty with. They do not blow their very hardest, for fear of bursting their instruments; but whatever pressure to the square inch the trumpet, cornet, or trombone, as the case may be, is calculated to be capable of sustaining without permanent injury (and they are tolerably sound and well-seasoned utensils), that pressure the conscientious German bandsman puts upon each square inch of the trumpet, cornet, or trombone, as the case may be.

If you are within a mile of a Munich military band, and are not stone deaf, you listen to it, and do not think of much else. It compels your attention by its mere noise; it dominates your whole being by its sheer strength. Your mind has to follow it as the feet of the little children followed the playing of the Pied Piper. Whatever you do, you have to do in unison with the band. All through our meal we had to keep time with the music.

We ate our soup to slow waltz time, with the result that every spoonful was cold before we got it up to our mouth. Just as the fish came, the band started a quick polka, and the consequence of that was that we had not time to pick out the bones. We gulped down white wine to the "Blacksmith's Galop," and if the tune had lasted much longer we should both have been blind drunk. With the advent of our steaks, the band struck up a selection from Wagner.

I know of no modern European composer so difficult to eat beefsteak to as Wagner. That we did not choke ourselves is a miracle. Wagner's orchestration is most trying to follow. We had to give up all idea of mustard. B. tried to eat a bit of bread with his steak, and got most hopelessly out of tune. I am afraid I was a little flat myself during the "Valkyries' Ride." My steak was rather underdone, and I could not work it quickly enough.

After getting outside hard beefsteak to Wagner, putting away potato salad to the garden music out of *Faust* was comparatively simple. Once or twice a slice of potato stuck in our throat during a very high note, but, on the whole, our rendering was fairly artistic.

We rattled off a sweet omelette to a symphony in G—or F, or else K; I won't be positive as to the precise letter; but it was something in the alphabet, I know—and bolted our cheese to the ballet music from *Carmen*. After which we rolled about in agonies to all the national airs of Europe.

If ever you visit a German beer-hall or garden—to study character or anything of that kind—be careful, when you have finished drinking your beer, to shut the cover of the mug down tight. If you leave it with the cover standing open, that is taken as a sign that you want more beer, and the girl snatches it away and brings it back refilled.

B. and I very nearly had an accident one warm night, owing to our ignorance of this custom. Each time after we had swallowed the quart, we left the pot, standing before us with the cover up, and each time it was, in consequence, taken away, and brought back to us, brimming full again. After about the sixth time, we gently remonstrated.

"This is very kind of you, my good girl," B. said, "but really I don't think we *can*. I don't think we ought to. You must not go on doing this sort of thing. We will drink this one now that you have brought it, but we really must insist on its being the last."

After about the tenth time we expostulated still more strongly.

"Now, you know what I told you four quarts ago!" remarked B., severely. "This can't go on for ever. Something serious will be happening. We are not used to your German school of drinking. We are only foreigners. In our own country we are considered rather swagger at this elbow-raising business, and for the credit of old England we have done our best. But now there must be an end to it. I simply decline to drink any more. No, do not press me. Not even another gallon!"

"But you both sit there with both your mugs open," replies the girl in an injured tone.

"What do you mean, 'we sit with our mugs open'?" asks B. "Can't we have our mugs open if we like?"

"Ah, yes," she explains pathetically; "but then I think you want more beer. Gentlemen always open their mugs when they want them filled with beer."

We kept our mugs shut after that.

MONDAY, JUNE 9TH

A Long Chapter, but happily the Last.—The Pilgrims' Return.—A Deserted Town.—Heidelberg.—The Common, or Bed, Sheet, Considered as a Towel.—B. Grapples with a Continental Time Table.—An Untractable Train.—A Quick Run.—Trains that Start from Nowhere.—Trains that Arrive at Nowhere.—Trains that Don't Do Anything.—B. Goes Mad.—Railway Travelling in Germany.—B. is Taken Prisoner.—His Fortitude.—Advantages of Ignorance.—First Impressions of Germany and of the Germans.

We are at Ostend. Our pilgrimage has ended. We sail for Dover in three hours' time. The wind seems rather fresh, but they say that it will drop towards the evening. I hope they are not deceiving us.

We are disappointed with Ostend. We thought that Ostend would be gay and crowded. We thought that there would be bands and theatres and concerts, and busy table-d'hôtes, and lively sands, and thronged parades, and pretty girls at Ostend.

I bought a stick and a new pair of boots at Brussels on purpose for Ostend.

There does not seem to be a living visitor in the place besides ourselves—nor a dead one either, that we can find. The shops are shut up, the houses are deserted, the casino is closed. Notice-boards are exhibited outside the hotels to the effect that the police have strict orders to take into custody anybody found trespassing upon or damaging the premises.

We found one restaurant which looked a little less like a morgue than did the other restaurants in the town, and rang the bell. After we had waited for about a quarter of an hour, an old woman answered the door, and asked us what we wanted. We said a steak and chipped potatoes for two, and a couple of lagers. She said would we call again in about a fortnight's time, when the family would be at home? She did not herself know where the things were kept.

We went down on to the sands this morning. We had not been walking up and down for more than half an hour before we came across the distinct imprint of a human foot. Someone must have been there this very day! We were a good deal alarmed. We could not imagine how he came there. The weather is too fine for shipwrecks, and it was not a part of the coast where any passing trader would be likely to land. Besides, if anyone has landed, where is he? We have been able to find no trace of him whatever. To this hour, we have never discovered who our strange visitant was.

It is a very mysterious affair, and I am glad we are going away.

We have been travelling about a good deal since we left Munich. We went first to Heidelberg. We arrived early in the morning at Heidelberg, after an all-night journey, and the first thing that the proprietor of the Royal suggested, on seeing us, was that we should have a bath. We consented to the operation, and were each shown into a little marble bath-room, in which I felt like a bit out of a picture by Alma Tadema.

The bath was very refreshing; but I should have enjoyed the whole thing much better if they had provided me with something more suitable to wipe upon than a thin linen sheet. The Germans hold very curious notions as to the needs and requirements of a wet man. I wish they would occasionally wash and bath themselves, and then they would, perhaps, obtain more practical ideas upon the subject. I have wiped upon a sheet in cases of emergency, and so I have upon a pair of socks; but there is no doubt that the proper thing is a towel. To dry oneself upon a sheet needs special training and unusual agility. A Nautch Girl or a Dancing Dervish would, no doubt, get through the performance with credit. They would twirl the sheet gracefully round their head, draw it lightly across their back, twist it in waving folds round their legs, wrap themselves for a moment in its whirling maze, and then lightly skip away from it, dry and smiling.

But that is not the manner in which the dripping, untaught Briton attempts to wipe himself upon a sheet. The method he adopts is, to clutch the sheet with both hands, lean up against the wall, and rub himself with it. In trying to get the thing round to the back of him, he drops half of it into the water, and from that moment the bathroom is not big enough to enable him to get away for an instant from that wet half. When he is wiping the front of himself with the dry half, the wet half climbs round behind, and, in a spirit of offensive familiarity, slaps him on the back. While he is stooping down rubbing his feet, it throws itself with delirious joy around his head, and he is black in the face before he can struggle away from its embrace. When he is least expecting anything of the kind, it flies round and gives him a playful flick upon some particularly tender part of his body that sends him springing with a yell ten feet up into the air. The great delight of the sheet, as a whole, is to trip him up whenever he attempts to move, so as to hear what he says when he sits down suddenly on the stone floor; and if it can throw him into the bath again just as he has finished wiping himself, it feels that life is worth living after all.

We spent two days at Heidelberg, climbing the wooded mountains that surround that pleasant little town, and that afford, from their restaurant or ruin-crowned summits, enchanting, far-stretching views, through which, with many a turn and twist, the distant Rhine and nearer Neckar wind; or strolling among the crumbling walls and arches of the grand, history-logged wreck that was once the noblest castle in all Germany.

We stood in awed admiration before the "Great Tun," which is the chief object of interest in Heidelberg. What there is of interest in the sight of a big beer-barrel it is difficult, in one's calmer moments, to understand; but the guide book says that it is a thing to be seen, and so all we tourists go and stand in a row and gape at it. We are a sheep-headed lot. If, by a printer's error, no mention were made in the guide book of the Colosseum, we should spend a month in Rome, and not think it worth going across the road to look at. If the guide book says we must by no means omit to pay a visit to some famous pincushion that contains eleven million pins, we travel five hundred miles on purpose to see it!

From Heidelberg we went to Darmstadt. We spent half-an-hour at Darmstadt. Why we ever thought of stopping longer there, I do not know. It is a pleasant enough town to live in, I should say; but utterly uninteresting to the stranger. After one walk round it, we made inquiries as to the next train out of it, and being informed that one was then on the point of starting, we tumbled into it and went to Bonn.

From Bonn (whence we made one or two Rhine excursions, and where we ascended twenty-eight "blessed steps" on our knees—the chapel people called them "blessed steps;" *we* didn't, after the first fourteen) we returned to Cologne. From Cologne we went to Brussels; from Brussels to Ghent (where we saw more famous pictures, and heard the mighty "Roland" ring "o'er lagoon and lake of sand"). From Ghent we went to Bruges (where I had the satisfaction of throwing a stone at the statue of Simon Stevin, who added to the miseries of my school-days, by inventing decimals), and from Bruges we came on here.

Finding out and arranging our trains has been a fearful work. I have left the whole business with B., and he has lost two stone over it. I used to think at one time that my own dear native Bradshaw was a sufficiently hard nut for the human intellect to crack; or, to transpose the simile, that Bradshaw was sufficient to crack an ordinary human nut. But dear old Bradshaw is an axiom in Euclid for stone-wall obviousness, compared with a through Continental time-table. Every morning B. has sat down with the book before him, and, grasping his head between his hands, has tried to understand it without going mad.

"Here we are," he has said. "This is the train that will do for us. Leaves Munich at 1.45; gets to Heidelberg at 4—just in time for a cup of tea."

"Gets to Heidelberg at 4?" I exclaim. "Does the whole distance in two and a quarter hours? Why, we were all night coming down!"

"Well, there you are," he says, pointing to the time-table. "Munich, depart 1.45; Heidelberg, arrive 4."

"Yes," I say, looking over his shoulder; "but don't you see the 4 is in thick type? That means 4 in the morning."

"Oh, ah, yes," he replies. "I never noticed that. Yes, of course. No! it can't be that either. Why, that would make the journey fourteen hours. It can't take fourteen hours. No, of course not. That's not meant for thick type, that 4. That's thin type got a little thick, that's all."

"Well, it can't be 4 this afternoon," I argue. "It must be 4 to-morrow after-noon! That's just what a German express train would like to do—take a whole day over a six hours' job!"

He puzzles for a while, and then breaks out with:

"Oh! I see it now. How stupid of me! That train that gets to Heidelberg at 4 comes from Berlin."

He seemed quite delighted with this discovery.

"What's the good of it to us, then?" I ask.

That depresses him.

"No, it is not much good, I'm afraid," he agrees. "It seems to go straight from Berlin to Heidelberg without stopping at Munich at all. Well then, where does the 1.45 go to? It must go somewhere."

Five minutes more elapse, and then he exclaims:

"Drat this 1.45! It doesn't seem to go anywhere. Munich depart 1.45, and that's all. It must go somewhere!"

Apparently, however, it does not. It seems to be a train that starts out from Munich at 1.45, and goes off on the loose. Possibly, it is a young, romantic train, fond of mystery. It won't say where it's going to. It probably does not even know itself. It goes off in search of adventure.

"I shall start off," it says to itself, "at 1.45 punctually, and just go on anyhow, without thinking about it, and see where I get to."

Or maybe it is a conceited, headstrong young train. It will not be guided or advised. The traffic superintendent wants it to go to St. Petersburg or to Paris. The old grey-headed station-master argues with it, and tries to persuade it to go to Constantinople, or even to Jerusalem if it likes that better—urges it to, at all events, make up its mind where it *is* going—warns it of the danger to young trains of having no fixed aim or object in life. Other people, asked to use their influence with it, have talked to it like a father, and have begged it, for their sakes, to go to Kamskatka, or Timbuctoo, or Jericho, according as they have thought best for it; and then, finding that it takes no notice of them, have got wild with it, and have told it to go to still more distant places.

But to all counsel and entreaty it has turned a deaf ear.

"You leave me alone," it has replied; "I know where I'm going to. Don't you worry yourself about me. You mind your own business, all of you. I don't want a lot of old fools telling me what to do. I know what I'm about."

What can be expected from such a train? The chances are that it comes to a bad end. I expect it is recognised afterwards, a broken-down, unloved, friendless, old train, wandering aimless and despised in some far-off country, musing with bitter regret upon the day when, full of foolish pride and ambition, it started from Munich, with its boiler nicely oiled, at 1.45.

B. abandons this 1.45 as hopeless and incorrigible, and continues his search.

"Hulloa! what's this?" he exclaims. "How will this do us? Leaves Munich at 4, gets to Heidelberg 4.15. That's quick work. Something wrong there. That won't do. You can't get from Munich to Heidelberg in a quarter of an hour. Oh! I see it. That 4 o'clock goes to Brussels, and then on to Heidelberg afterwards. Gets in there at 4.15 to-morrow, I suppose. I wonder why it goes round by Brussels, though? Then it seems to stop at Prague for ever so long. Oh, damn this timetable!"

Then he finds another train that starts at 2.15, and seems to be an ideal train. He gets quite enthusiastic over this train.

"This is the train for us, old man," he says. "This is a splendid train, really. It doesn't stop anywhere."

"Does it *get* anywhere?" I ask.

"Of course it gets somewhere," he replies indignantly. "It's an express! Munich," he murmurs, tracing its course through the timetable, "depart 2.15. First and second class only. Nuremberg? No; it doesn't stop at Nuremberg. Wurtzburg? No. Frankfort for Strasburg? No. Cologne, Antwerp, Calais? Well, where does it stop? Confound it! it must stop somewhere. Berlin, Paris, Brussels, Copenhagen? No. Upon my soul, this is another train that does not go anywhere! It starts from Munich at 2.15, and that's all. It doesn't do anything else."

It seems to be a habit of Munich trains to start off in this purposeless way. Apparently, their sole object is to get away from the town. They don't care where they go to; they don't care what becomes of them, so long as they escape from Munich.

"For heaven's sake," they say to themselves, "let us get away from this place. Don't let us bother about where we shall go; we can decide that when we are once fairly outside. Let's get out of Munich; that's the great thing."

B. begins to grow quite frightened. He says:

"We shall never be able to leave this city. There are no trains out of Munich at all. It's a plot to keep us here, that's what it is. We shall never be able to get away. We shall never see dear old England again!"

I try to cheer him up by suggesting that perhaps it is the custom in Bavaria to leave the destination of the train to the taste and fancy of the passengers. The railway authorities provide a train, and start it off at 2.15. It is immaterial to them where it goes to. That is a question for the passengers to decide among themselves. The passengers hire the train and take it away, and there is an end of the matter, so far as the railway people are concerned. If there is any difference of opinion between the passengers, owing to some of them wishing to go to Spain, while others want to get home to Russia, they, no doubt, settle the matter by tossing up.

B., however, refuses to entertain this theory, and says he wishes I would not talk so much when I see how harassed he is. That's all the thanks I get for trying to help him.

He worries along for another five minutes, and then he discovers a train that gets to Heidelberg all right, and appears to be in most respects a model train, the only thing that can be urged against it being that it does not start from anywhere.

It seems to drop into Heidelberg casually and then to stop there. One expects its sudden advent alarms the people at Heidelberg station. They do not know what to make of it. The porter goes up to the station-master, and says:

"Beg pardon, sir, but there's a strange train in the station."

"Oh!" answers the station-master, surprised, "where did it come from?"

"Don't know," replies the man; "it doesn't seem to know itself."

"Dear me," says the station-master, "how very extraordinary! What does it want?"

"Doesn't seem to want anything particular," replies the other. "It's a curious sort of train. Seems to be a bit dotty, if you ask me."

"Um," muses the station-master, "it's a rum go. Well, I suppose we must let it stop here a bit now. We can hardly turn it out a night like this. Oh, let it make itself comfortable in the wood-shed till the morning, and then we will see if we can find its friends."

At last B. makes the discovery that to get to Heidelberg we must go to Darmstadt and take another train from there. This knowledge gives him renewed hope and strength, and he sets to work afresh—this time, to find trains from Munich to Darmstadt, and from Darmstadt to Heidelberg.

"Here we are," he cries, after a few minutes' hunting. "I've got it!" (He is of a buoyant disposition.) "This will be it. Leaves Munich 10, gets to Darmstadt 5.25. Leaves Darmstadt for Heidelberg 5.20, gets to—"

"That doesn't allow us much time for changing, does it?" I remark.

"No," he replies, growing thoughtful again. "No, that's awkward. If it were only the other way round, it would be all right, or it would do if our train got there five minutes before its time, and the other one was a little late in starting."

"Hardly safe to reckon on that," I suggest; and he agrees with me, and proceeds to look for some more fitable trains.

It would appear, however, that all the trains from Darmstadt to Heidelberg start just a few minutes before the trains from Munich arrive. It looks quite pointed, as though they tried to avoid us.

B.'s intellect generally gives way about this point, and he becomes simply drivelling. He discovers trains that run from Munich to Heidelberg in fourteen minutes, by way of Venice and Geneva, with half-an-hour's interval for breakfast at Rome. He rushes up and down the book in pursuit of demon expresses that arrive at their destinations forty-seven minutes before they start, and leave again before they get there. He finds out, all by himself, that the only way to get from South Germany to Paris is to go to Calais, and then take the boat to Moscow. Before he has done with the timetable, he doesn't know whether he is in Europe,

Asia, Africa, or America, nor where he wants to get to, nor why he wants to go there.

Then I quietly, but firmly, take the book away from him, and dress him for going out; and we take our bags and walk to the station, and tell a porter that, "Please, we want to go to Heidelberg." And the porter takes us one by each hand, and leads us to a seat and tells us to sit there and be good, and that, when it is time, he will come and fetch us and put us in the train; and this he does.

That is my method of finding out how to get from one place to another. It is not as dignified, perhaps, as B.'s, but it is simpler and more efficacious.

It is slow work travelling in Germany. The German train does not hurry or excite itself over its work, and when it stops it likes to take a rest. When a German train draws up at a station, everybody gets out and has a walk. The engine-driver and the stoker cross over and knock at the station-master's door. The station-master comes out and greets them effusively, and then runs back into the house to tell his wife that they have come, and she bustles out and also welcomes them effusively, and the four stand chatting about old times and friends and the state of the crops. After a while, the engine-driver, during a pause in the conversation, looks at his watch, and says he is afraid he must be going, but the station-master's wife won't hear of it.

"Oh, you must stop and see the children," she says. "They will be home from school soon, and they'll be so disappointed if they hear you have been here and gone away again. Lizzie will never forgive you."

The engine-driver and the stoker laugh, and say that under those circumstances they suppose they must stop; and they do so.

Meanwhile the booking-clerk has introduced the guard to his sister, and such a very promising flirtation has been taking place behind the ticket-office door that it would not be surprising if wedding-bells were heard in the neighbourhood before long.

The second guard has gone down into the town to try and sell a dog, and the passengers stroll about the platform and smoke, or partake of a light meal in the refreshment-room—the poorer classes regaling themselves upon hot sausage, and the more dainty upon soup. When everybody appears to be sufficiently rested, a move onward is suggested by the engine-driver or the guard, and if all are agreeable to the proposal the train starts.

Tremendous excitement was caused during our journey between Heidelberg and Darmstadt by the discovery that we were travelling in an express train (they called it an "express:" it jogged along at the rate of twenty miles an hour when it could be got to move at all; most of its time it seemed to be half asleep) with slow-train tickets. The train was stopped at the next station and B. was marched off between two stern-looking gold-laced officials to explain the matter to a stern-looking gold-laced station-master, surrounded by three stern-looking gold-laced followers. The scene suggested a drum-head court-martial, and I could see that B. was nervous, though outwardly calm and brave. He shouted back a light-hearted adieu to me as he passed down the platform, and asked me, if the worst happened, to break it gently to his mother.

However, no harm came of it, and he returned to the carriage without a stain upon his character, he having made it clear to the satisfaction of the court—firstly, That he did not know that our tickets were only slow-train tickets; secondly, That he was not aware that we were not travelling by a slow train; and thirdly, That he was ready to pay the difference in the fares.

He blamed himself for having done this last, however, afterwards. He seemed to think that he could have avoided this expense by assuming ignorance of the German language. He said that two years ago, when he was travelling in Germany with three other men, the authorities came down upon them in much the same way for travelling first-class with second-class tickets.

Why they were doing this B. did not seem able to explain very clearly. He said that, if he recollected rightly, the guard had told them to get into a first-class, or else they had not had time to get into a second-class, or else they did not know they were not in a second-class. I must confess his explanation appeared to me to be somewhat lame.

Anyhow, there they were in a first-class carriage; and there was the collector at the door, looking indignantly at their second-class tickets, and waiting to hear what they had to say for themselves.

One of their party did not know much German, but what little he did know he was very proud of and liked to air; and this one argued the matter with the collector, and expressed himself in German so well that the collector understood and disbelieved every word he said.

He was also, on his part, able, with a little trouble, to understand what the collector said, which was that he must pay eighteen marks. And he had to.

As for the other three, two at all events of whom were excellent German scholars, they did not understand anything, and nobody could make them understand anything. The collector roared at them for about ten minutes, and they smiled pleasantly and said they wanted to go to Hanover. He went and fetched the station-master, and the station-master explained to them for another ten minutes that, if they did not pay eighteen shillings each, he should do the German equivalent for summonsing them; and they smiled and nodded, and told him that they wanted to go to Hanover. Then a very important-looking personage in a cocked-hat came up, and was very angry; and he and the station-master and the collector took it in turns to explain to B. and his two friends the state of the law on the matter.

They stormed and raged, and threatened and pleaded for a quarter of an hour or so, and then they got sick, and slammed the door, and went off, leaving the Government to lose the fifty-four marks.

We passed the German frontier on Wednesday, and have been in Belgium since.

I like the Germans. B. says I ought not to let them know this, because it will make them conceited; but I have no fear of such a result. I am sure they possess too much common-sense for their heads to be turned by praise, no matter from whom.

B. also says that I am displaying more energy than prudence in forming an opinion of a people merely from a few weeks' travel amongst them. But my experience is that first impressions are the most reliable.

At all events, in my case they are. I often arrive at quite sensible ideas and judgments, on the spur of the moment. It is when I stop to think that I become foolish.

Our first thoughts are the thoughts that are given to us; our second thoughts are the thoughts that we make for ourselves. I prefer to trust to the former.

The Germans are a big, square-shouldered, deep-chested race. They do not talk much, but look as though they thought. Like all big things, they are easy-going and good-tempered.

Anti-tobacconists, teetotallers, and such-like faddists, would fare badly in Germany. A German has no anti-nature notions as to its being wicked for him to enjoy his life, and still more criminal for him to let anybody else enjoy theirs. He likes his huge pipe, and he likes his mug of beer, and as these become empty he likes to have them filled again; and he likes to see other people like *their* pipe and *their* mug of beer. If you were to go dancing round a German, shrieking out entreaties to him to sign a pledge that he would never drink another drop of beer again as long as he lived, he would ask you to remember that you were talking to a man, not to a child or an imbecile, and he would probably impress the request upon you by boxing your ears for your impertinence. He can conduct himself sensibly without making an ass of himself. He can be "temperate" without tying bits of coloured ribbon all about himself to advertise the fact, and without rushing up and down the street waving a banner and yelling about it.

The German women are not beautiful, but they are lovable and sweet; and they are broad-breasted and broad-hipped, like the mothers of big sons should be. They do not seem to trouble themselves about their "rights," but appear to be very contented and happy even without votes. The men treat them with courtesy and tenderness, but with none of that exaggerated deference that one sees among more petticoat-ridden nations. The Germans are women lovers, not women worshippers; and they are not worried by any doubts as to which sex shall rule the State, and which stop at home and mind the children. The German women are not politicians and mayors and county councillors; they are housewives.

All classes of Germans are scrupulously polite to one another; but this is the result of mutual respect, not of snobbery. The tramcar conductor expects to be treated with precisely the same courtesy that he tenders. The Count raises his hat to the shopkeeper, and expects the shopkeeper to raise his hat to him.

The Germans are hearty eaters; but they are not, like the French, fussy and finicky over their food. Their stomach is not their God; and the cook, with his sauces and *pâtés* and *ragoûts*, is not their High Priest. So long as the dish is wholesome, and there is sufficient of it, they are satisfied.

In the mere sensuous arts of painting and sculpture the Germans are poor, in the ennobling arts of literature and music they are great; and this fact provides a key to their character.

They are a simple, earnest, homely, genuine people. They do not laugh much; but when they do, they laugh deep down. They are slow, but so is a deep river. A placid look generally rests upon their heavy features; but sometimes they frown, and then they look somewhat grim.

A visit to Germany is a tonic to an Englishman. We English are always sneering at ourselves, and patriotism in England is regarded as a stamp of vulgarity. The Germans, on the other hand, believe in themselves, and respect themselves. The world for them is not played out. Their country to them is still the "Fatherland." They look straight before them like a people who see a great future in front of them, and are not afraid to go forward to fulfil it.

GOOD-BYE, SIR (OR MADAM).

THE
PHILOSOPHER'S
JOKE

THE PHILOSOPHER'S JOKE

Myself, I do not believe this story. Six persons are persuaded of its truth; and the hope of these six is to convince themselves it was an hallucination. Their difficulty is there are six of them. Each one alone perceives clearly that it never could have been. Unfortunately, they are close friends, and cannot get away from one another; and when they meet and look into each other's eyes the thing takes shape again.

The one who told it to me, and who immediately wished he had not, was Armitage. He told it to me one night when he and I were the only occupants of the Club smoking-room. His telling me—as he explained afterwards—was an impulse of the moment. Sense of the thing had been pressing upon him all that day with unusual persistence; and the idea had occurred to him, on my entering the room, that the flippant scepticism with which an essentially commonplace mind like my own—he used the words in no offensive sense—would be sure to regard the affair might help to direct his own attention to its more absurd aspect. I am inclined to think it did. He thanked me for dismissing his entire narrative as the delusion of a disordered brain, and begged me not to mention the matter to another living soul. I promised; and I may as well here observe that I do not call this mentioning the matter. Armitage is not the man's real name; it does not even begin with an A. You might read this story and dine next to him the same evening: you would know nothing.

Also, of course, I did not consider myself debarred from speaking about it, discreetly, to Mrs. Armitage, a charming woman. She burst into tears at the first mention of the thing. It took me all I knew to tranquillize her. She said that when she did not think about the thing she could be happy. She and Armitage never spoke of it to one another; and left to themselves her opinion was that eventually they might put remembrance behind them. She wished they were not quite so friendly with the Everetts. Mr. and Mrs. Everett had both dreamt precisely the same dream; that is, assuming it was a dream. Mr. Everett was not the sort of person that a clergyman ought, perhaps, to know; but as Armitage would always argue: for a teacher of Christianity to withdraw his friendship from a man because that man was somewhat of a sinner would be inconsistent. Rather should he remain his friend and seek to influence him. They dined with the Everetts regularly on Tuesdays, and sitting opposite the Everetts, it seemed impossible to accept as a fact that all four of them at the same time and in the same manner had fallen victims to the same illusion. I think I succeeded in leaving her more hopeful. She acknowledged that the story, looked at from the point of common sense, did sound ridiculous; and threatened me that if I ever breathed a word of it to anyone, she never would speak to me again. She is a charming woman, as I have already mentioned.

By a curious coincidence I happened at the time to be one of Everett's directors on a Company he had just promoted for taking over and developing the Red Sea Coasting trade. I lunched with him the following Sunday. He is an interesting talker, and curiosity to discover how so shrewd a man would account for his connection with so insane—so impossible a fancy, prompted me to hint my knowledge of the story. The manner both of him and of his wife changed suddenly. They wanted to know who it was had told me. I refused the information, because it was evident they would have been angry with him. Everett's theory was that one of them had dreamt it—probably Camelford—and by hypnotic suggestion had conveyed to the rest of them the impression that they had dreamt it also. He added that but for one slight incident he should have ridiculed from the very beginning the argument that it could have been anything else than a dream. But what that incident was he would not tell me. His object, as he explained, was not to dwell upon the business, but to try and forget it. Speaking as a friend, he advised me, likewise, not to cackle about the matter any more than I could help, lest trouble should arise with regard to my director's fees. His way of putting things is occasionally blunt.

It was at the Everetts', later on, that I met Mrs. Camelford, one of the handsomest women I have ever set eyes upon. It was foolish of me, but my memory for names is weak. I forgot that Mr. and Mrs. Camelford were the other two concerned, and mentioned the story as a curious tale I had read years ago in an old Miscellany. I had reckoned on it to lead me into a discussion with her on platonic friendship. She jumped up from her chair and gave me a look. I remembered then, and could have bitten out my tongue. It took me a long while to make my peace, but she came round in the end, consenting to attribute my blunder to mere stupidity. She was quite convinced herself, she told me, that the thing was pure imagination. It was only when in company with the others that any doubt as to this crossed her mind. Her own idea was that, if everybody would agree never to mention the matter again, it would end in their forgetting it. She supposed it was her husband who had been my informant: he was just that sort of ass. She did not say it unkindly. She said when she was first married, ten years ago, few people had a more irritating effect upon her than had Camelford; but that since she had seen more of other men she had come to respect him. I like to hear a woman speak well of her husband. It is a departure which, in my opinion, should be more encouraged than it is. I assured her Camelford was not the culprit; and on the understanding that I might come to see her—not too often—on her Thursdays, I agreed with her that the best thing I could do would be to dismiss the subject from my mind and occupy myself instead with questions that concerned myself.

I had never talked much with Camelford before that time, though I had often seen him at the Club. He is a strange man, of whom many stories are told. He writes journalism for a living, and poetry, which he publishes at his own expense, apparently for recreation. It occurred to me that his theory would at all events be interesting; but at first he would not talk at all, pretending to ignore the whole affair, as idle nonsense. I had almost despaired of drawing him out, when one evening, of his own accord, he asked me if I thought Mrs. Armitage, with whom he knew I was on terms of friendship, still attached importance to the thing. On my expressing the opinion that Mrs. Armitage was the most troubled of the group, he was irritated; and urged me to leave the rest of them alone and devote whatever sense I might possess to persuading her in particular that the entire thing was and could be nothing but pure myth. He confessed frankly that to him it was still a mystery. He could easily regard it as chimera, but for one slight incident. He would not for a long while say what that was, but there is such a thing as perseverance, and in the end I dragged it out of him. This is what he told me.

"We happened by chance to find ourselves alone in the conservatory, that night of the ball—we six. Most of the crowd had already left. The last 'extra' was being played: the music came to us faintly. Stooping to pick up Jessica's fan, which she had let fall to the ground, something shining on the tesselated pavement underneath a group of palms suddenly caught my eye. We had not said a word to one another; indeed, it was the first evening we had any of us met one another—that is, unless the thing was not a dream. I picked it up. The others gathered round me, and when we looked into one another's eyes we understood: it was a broken wine-cup, a curious goblet of Bavarian glass. It was the goblet out of which we had all dreamt that we had drunk."

I have put the story together as it seems to me it must have happened. The incidents, at all events, are facts. Things have since occurred to those concerned affording me hope that they will never read it. I should not have troubled to tell it at all, but that it has a moral.

Six persons sat round the great oak table in the wainscoted *Speise Saal* of that cosy hostelry, the Kneiper Hof at Konigsberg. It was late into the night. Under ordinary circumstances they would have been in bed, but having arrived by the last train from Dantzic, and having supped on German fare, it had seemed to them discreeter to remain awhile in talk. The house was strangely silent. The rotund landlord, leaving their candles ranged upon the sideboard, had wished them "Gute Nacht" an hour before. The spirit of the ancient house enfolded them within its wings.

Here in this very chamber, if rumour is to be believed, Emmanuel Kant himself had sat discoursing many a time and oft. The walls, behind which for more than forty years the little peak-faced man had thought and worked, rose silvered by the moonlight just across the narrow way; the three high windows of the *Speise Saal* give out upon the old Cathedral tower beneath which now he rests. Philosophy, curious concerning human phenomena, eager for experience, unhampered by the limitation Convention would impose upon all speculation, was in the smoky air.

"Not into future events," remarked the Rev. Nathaniel Armitage, "it is better they should be hidden from us. But into the future of ourselves—our temperament, our character—I think we ought to be allowed to see. At twenty we are one individual; at forty, another person entirely, with other views, with other interests, a different outlook upon life, attracted by quite other attributes, repelled by the very qualities that once attracted us. It is extremely awkward, for all of us."

"I am glad to hear somebody else say that," observed Mrs. Everett, in her gentle, sympathetic voice. "I have thought it all myself so often. Sometimes I have blamed myself, yet how can one help it: the things that appeared of importance to us, they become indifferent; new voices call to us; the idols we once worshipped, we see their feet of clay."

"If under the head of idols you include me," laughed the jovial Mr. Everett, "don't hesitate to say so." He was a large red-faced gentleman, with small twinkling eyes, and a mouth both strong and sensuous. "I didn't make my feet myself. I never asked anybody to take me for a stained-glass saint. It is not I who have changed."

"I know, dear, it is I," his thin wife answered with a meek smile. "I was beautiful, there was no doubt about it, when you married me."

"You were, my dear," agreed her husband: "As a girl few could hold a candle to you."

"It was the only thing about me that you valued, my beauty," continued his wife; "and it went so quickly. I feel sometimes as if I had swindled you."

"But there is a beauty of the mind, of the soul," remarked the Rev. Nathaniel Armitage, "that to some men is more attractive than mere physical perfection."

The soft eyes of the faded lady shone for a moment with the light of pleasure. "I am afraid Dick is not of that number," she sighed.

"Well, as I said just now about my feet," answered her husband genially, "I didn't make myself. I always have been a slave to beauty and always shall be. There would be no sense in pretending among chums that you haven't lost your looks, old girl." He laid his fine hand with kindly intent upon her bony shoulder. "But there is no call for you to fret yourself as if you had done it on purpose. No one but a lover imagines a woman growing more beautiful as she grows older."

"Some women would seem to," answered his wife.

Involuntarily she glanced to where Mrs. Camelford sat with elbows resting on the table; and involuntarily also the small twinkling eyes of her husband followed in the same direction. There is a type that reaches its prime in middle age. Mrs. Camelford, *nee* Jessica Dearwood, at twenty had been an uncanny-looking creature, the only thing about her appealing to general masculine taste having been her magnificent eyes, and even these had frightened more than they had allured. At forty, Mrs. Camelford might have posed for the entire Juno.

"Yes, he's a cunning old joker is Time," murmured Mr. Everett, almost inaudibly.

"What ought to have happened," said Mrs. Armitage, while with deft fingers rolling herself a cigarette, "was for you and Nellie to have married."

Mrs. Everett's pale face flushed scarlet.

"My dear," exclaimed the shocked Nathaniel Armitage, flushing likewise.

"Oh, why may one not sometimes speak the truth?" answered his wife petulantly. "You and I are utterly unsuited to one another—everybody sees it. At nineteen it seemed to me beautiful, holy, the idea of being a clergyman's wife, fighting by his side against evil. Besides, you have changed since then. You were human, my dear Nat, in those days, and the best dancer I had ever met. It was your dancing was your chief attraction for me as likely as not, if I had only known myself. At nineteen how can one know oneself?"

"We loved each other," the Rev. Armitage reminded her.

"I know we did, passionately—then; but we don't now." She laughed a little bitterly. "Poor Nat! I am only another trial added to your long list. Your beliefs, your ideals are meaningless to me—mere narrow-minded dogmas, stifling thought. Nellie was the wife Nature had intended for you, so soon as she had lost her beauty and with it all her worldly ideas. Fate was maturing her for you, if only we had known. As for me, I ought to have been the wife of an artist, of a poet." Unconsciously a glance from her ever restless eyes flashed across the table to where Horatio Camelford sat, puffing clouds of smoke into the air from a huge black meerschaum pipe. "Bohemia is my country. Its poverty, its struggle would have been a joy to me. Breathing its free air, life would have been worth living."

Horatio Camelford leant back with eyes fixed on the oaken ceiling. "It is a mistake," said Horatio Camelford, "for the artist ever to marry."

The handsome Mrs. Camelford laughed good-naturedly. "The artist," remarked Mrs. Camelford, "from what I have seen of him would never know the inside of his shirt from the outside if his wife was not there to take it out of the drawer and put it over his head."

"His wearing it inside out would not make much difference to the world," argued her husband. "The sacrifice of his art to the necessity of keeping his wife and family does."

"Well, you at all events do not appear to have sacrificed much, my boy," came the breezy voice of Dick Everett. "Why, all the world is ringing with your name."

"When I am forty-one, with all the best years of my life behind me," answered the Poet. "Speaking as a man, I have nothing to regret. No one could have had a better wife; my children are charming. I have lived the peaceful existence of the successful citizen. Had I been true to my trust I should have gone out into the wilderness, the only possible home of the teacher, the prophet. The artist is the bridegroom of Art. Marriage for him is an immorality. Had I my time again I should remain a bachelor."

"Time brings its revenges, you see," laughed Mrs. Camelford. "At twenty that fellow threatened to commit suicide if I would not marry him, and cordially disliking him I consented. Now twenty years later, when I am just getting used to him, he calmly turns round and says he would have been better without me."

"I heard something about it at the time," said Mrs. Armitage. "You were very much in love with somebody else, were you not?"

"Is not the conversation assuming a rather dangerous direction?" laughed Mrs. Camelford.

"I was thinking the same thing," agreed Mrs. Everett. "One would imagine some strange influence had seized upon us, forcing us to speak our thoughts aloud."

"I am afraid I was the original culprit," admitted the Reverend Nathaniel. "This room is becoming quite oppressive. Had we not better go to bed?"

The ancient lamp suspended from its smoke-grimed beam uttered a faint, gurgling sob, and spluttered out. The shadow of the old Cathedral tower crept in and stretched across the room, now illuminated only by occasional beams from the cloud-curtained moon. At the other end of the table sat a peak-faced little gentleman, clean-shaven, in full-bottomed wig.

"Forgive me," said the little gentleman. He spoke in English, with a strong accent. "But it seems to me here is a case where two parties might be of service to one another."

The six fellow-travellers round the table looked at one another, but none spoke. The idea that came to each of them, as they explained to one another later, was that without remembering it they had taken their candles and had gone to bed. This was surely a dream.

"It would greatly assist me," continued the little peak-faced gentleman, "in experiments I am conducting into the phenomena of human tendencies, if you would allow me to put your lives back twenty years."

Still no one of the six replied. It seemed to them that the little old gentleman must have been sitting there among them all the time, unnoticed by them.

"Judging from your talk this evening," continued the peak-faced little gentleman, "you should welcome my offer. You appear to me to be one and all of exceptional intelligence. You perceive the mistakes that you have made: you understand the causes. The future veiled, you could not help yourselves. What I propose to do is to put you back twenty years. You will be boys and girls again, but with this difference: that the knowledge of the future, so far as it relates to yourselves, will remain with you.

"Come," urged the old gentleman, "the thing is quite simple of accomplishment. As—as a certain philosopher has clearly proved: the universe is only the result of our own perceptions. By what may appear to you to be magic—by what in reality will be simply a chemical operation—I remove from your memory the events of the last twenty years, with the exception of what immediately concerns your own personalities. You will retain all knowledge of the changes, physical and mental, that will be in store for you; all else will pass from your perception."

The little old gentleman took a small phial from his waistcoat pocket, and, filling one of the massive wine-glasses from a decanter, measured into it some half-a-dozen drops. Then he placed the glass in the centre of the table.

"Youth is a good time to go back to," said the peak-faced little gentleman, with a smile. "Twenty years ago, it was the night of the Hunt Ball. You remember it?"

It was Everett who drank first. He drank it with his little twinkling eyes fixed hungrily on the proud handsome face of Mrs. Camelford; and then handed the glass to his wife. It was she perhaps who drank from it most eagerly. Her life with Everett, from the day when she had risen from a bed of sickness stripped of all her beauty, had been one bitter wrong. She drank with the wild hope that the thing might possibly be not a dream; and thrilled to the touch of the man she loved, as reaching across the table he took the glass from her hand. Mrs. Armitage was the fourth to drink. She took the cup from her husband, drank with a quiet smile, and passed it on to Camelford. And Camelford drank, looking at nobody, and replaced the glass upon the table.

"Come," said the little old gentleman to Mrs. Camelford, "you are the only one left. The whole thing will be incomplete without you."

"I have no wish to drink," said Mrs. Camelford, and her eyes sought those of her husband, but he would not look at her.

"Come," again urged the Figure. And then Camelford looked at her and laughed drily.

"You had better drink," he said. "It's only a dream."

"If you wish it," she answered. And it was from his hands she took the glass.

It is from the narrative as Armitage told it to me that night in the Club smoking-room that I am taking most of my material. It seemed to him that all things began slowly to rise upward, leaving him stationary, but with a great pain as though the inside of him were being torn away—the same sensation greatly exaggerated, so he likened it, as descending in a lift. But around him all the time was silence and darkness unrelieved. After a period that might have been minutes, that might have been years, a faint light crept towards him. It grew stronger, and into the air which now fanned his cheek there stole the sound of far-off music. The light and the music both increased, and one by one his senses came back to him. He was seated on a low cushioned bench beneath a group of palms. A young girl was sitting beside him, but her face was turned away from him.

"I did not catch your name," he was saying. "Would you mind telling it to me?"

She turned her face towards him. It was the most spiritually beautiful face he had ever seen. "I am in the same predicament," she laughed. "You had better write yours on my programme, and I will write mine on yours."

So they wrote upon each other's programme and exchanged again. The name she had written was Alice Blatchley.

He had never seen her before, that he could remember. Yet at the back of his mind there dwelt the haunting knowledge of her. Somewhere long ago they had met, talked together. Slowly, as one recalls a dream, it came back to him. In some other life, vague, shadowy, he had married this woman. For the first few years they had loved each other; then the gulf had opened between them, widened. Stern, strong voices had called to him to lay aside his selfish dreams, his boyish ambitions, to take upon his shoulders the yoke of a great duty. When more than ever he had demanded sympathy and help, this woman had fallen away from him. His ideals but irritated her. Only at the cost of daily bitterness had he been able to resist her endeavours to draw him from his path. A face—that of a woman with soft eyes, full of helpfulness, shone through the mist of his dream—the face of a woman who would one day come to him out of the Future with outstretched hands that he would yearn to clasp.

"Shall we not dance?" said the voice beside him. "I really won't sit out a waltz."

They hurried into the ball-room. With his arm about her form, her wondrous eyes shyly, at rare moments, seeking his, then vanishing again behind their drooping lashes, the brain, the mind, the very soul of the young man passed out of his own keeping. She complimented him in her bewitching manner, a delightful blending of condescension and timidity.

"You dance extremely well," she told him. "You may ask me for another, later on."

The words flashed out from that dim haunting future. "Your dancing was your chief attraction for me, as likely as not, had I but known?"

All that evening and for many months to come the Present and the Future fought within him. And the experience of Nathaniel Armitage, divinity student, was the experience likewise of Alice Blatchley, who had fallen in love with him at first sight, having found him the divinest dancer she had ever whirled with to the sensuous music of the waltz; of Horatio Camelford, journalist and minor poet, whose journalism earned him a bare income, but at whose minor poetry critics smiled; of Jessica Dearwood, with her glorious eyes, and muddy complexion, and her wild hopeless passion for the big, handsome, ruddy-bearded Dick Everett, who, knowing it, only laughed at her in his kindly, lordly way, telling her with frank brutalness that the woman who was not beautiful had missed her vocation in life; of that scheming, conquering young gentleman himself, who at twenty-five had already made his mark in the City, shrewd, clever, cool-headed as a fox, except where a pretty face and shapely hand or ankle were concerned; of Nellie Fanshawe, then in the pride of her ravishing beauty, who loved none but herself, whose clay-made gods were jewels, and fine dresses and rich feasts, the envy of other women and the courtship of all mankind.

That evening of the ball each clung to the hope that this memory of the future was but a dream. They had been introduced to one another; had heard each other's names for the first time with a start of recognition; had avoided one another's eyes; had hastened to plunge into meaningless talk; till that moment when young Camelford, stooping to pick up Jessica's fan, had found that broken fragment of the Rhenish wine-glass. Then it was that conviction refused to be shaken off, that knowledge of the future had to be sadly accepted.

What they had not foreseen was that knowledge of the future in no way affected their emotions of the present. Nathaniel Armitage grew day by day more hopelessly in love with bewitching Alice Blatchley. The thought of her marrying anyone else—the long-haired, priggish Camelford in particular—sent the blood boiling through his veins; added to which sweet Alice, with her arms about his neck, would confess to him that life without him would be a misery hardly to be endured, that the thought of him as the husband of another woman—of Nellie Fanshawe in particular—was madness to her. It was right perhaps, knowing what they did, that they should say good-bye to one another. She would bring sorrow into his life. Better far that he should put her away from him, that she should die of a broken heart, as she felt sure she would. How could he, a fond lover, inflict this suffering upon her? He ought of course to marry Nellie Fanshawe, but he could not bear the girl. Would it not be the height of absurdity to marry a girl he strongly disliked because twenty years hence she might be more suitable to him than the woman he now loved and who loved him?

Nor could Nellie Fanshawe bring herself to discuss without laughter the suggestion of marrying on a hundred-and-fifty a year a curate that she positively hated. There would come a time when wealth would be indifferent to her, when her exalted spirit would ask but for the satisfaction of self-sacrifice. But that time had not arrived. The emotions it would bring with it she could not in her present state even imagine. Her whole present being craved for the things of this world, the things that were within her grasp. To ask her to forego them now because later on she would not care for them! it was like telling a schoolboy to avoid the tuck-shop because, when a man, the thought of stick-jaw would be nauseous to him. If her capacity for enjoyment was to be short-lived, all the more reason for grasping joy quickly.

Alice Blatchley, when her lover was not by, gave herself many a headache trying to think the thing out logically. Was it not foolish of her to rush into this marriage with dear Nat? At forty she would wish she had married somebody else. But most women at forty—she judged from conversation round about her—wished they had married somebody else. If every girl at twenty listened to herself at forty there would be no more marriage. At forty she would be a different person altogether. That other elderly person did not interest her. To ask a young girl to spoil her life purely in the interests of this middle-aged party—it did not seem right. Besides, whom else was she to marry? Camelford would not have her; he did not want her then; he was not going to want her at forty. For practical purposes Camelford was out of the question. She might marry somebody else altogether—and fare worse. She might remain a spinster: she hated the mere name of spinster. The inky-fingered woman journalist that, if all went well, she might become: it was not her idea. Was she acting selfishly? Ought she, in his own interests, to refuse to marry dear Nat? Nellie—the little cat—who would suit him at forty, would not have him. If he was going to marry anyone but Nellie he might as well marry her, Alice. A bachelor clergyman! it sounded almost improper. Nor was dear Nat the type. If she threw him over it would be into the arms of some designing minx. What was she to do?

Camelford at forty, under the influence of favourable criticism, would have persuaded himself he was a heaven-sent prophet, his whole life to be beautifully spent in the saving of mankind. At twenty he felt he wanted to live. Weird-looking Jessica, with her magnificent eyes veiling mysteries, was of more importance to him than the rest of the species combined. Knowledge of the future in his ease only spurred desire. The muddy complexion would grow pink and white, the thin limbs round and shapely; the now scornful eyes would one day light with love at his coming. It was what he had once hoped: it was what he now knew. At forty the artist is stronger than the man; at twenty the man is stronger than the artist.

An uncanny creature, so most folks would have described Jessica Dearwood. Few would have imagined her developing into the good-natured, easy-going Mrs. Camelford of middle age. The animal, so strong within her at twenty, at thirty had burnt itself out. At eighteen, madly, blindly in love with red-bearded, deep-voiced Dick Everett she would, had he whistled to her, have flung herself gratefully at his feet, and this in spite of the knowledge forewarning her of the miserable life he would certainly lead her, at all events until her slowly developing beauty should give her the whip hand of him—by which time she would have come to despise him. Fortunately, as she told herself, there was no fear of his doing so, the future notwithstanding. Nellie Fanshawe's beauty held him as with chains of steel, and Nellie had no intention of allowing her rich prize to escape her. Her own lover, it was true, irritated her more than any man she had ever met, but at least he would afford her refuge from the bread of charity. Jessica Dearwood, an orphan, had been brought up by a distant relative. She had not been the child to win affection. Of silent, brooding nature, every thoughtless incivility had been to her an insult, a wrong. Acceptance of young Camelford seemed her only escape from a life that had become to her a martyrdom. At forty-one he would wish he had remained a bachelor; but at thirty-eight that would not trouble her. She would know herself he was much better off as he was. Meanwhile, she would have come to like him, to respect him. He would be famous, she would be proud of him. Crying into her pillow—she could not help it—for love of handsome Dick, it was still a comfort to reflect that Nellie Fanshawe, as it were, was watching over her, protecting her from herself.

Dick, as he muttered to himself a dozen times a day, ought to marry Jessica. At thirty-eight she would be his ideal. He looked at her as she was at eighteen, and shuddered. Nellie at thirty would be plain and uninteresting. But when did consideration of the future ever cry halt to passion: when did a lover ever pause thinking of the morrow? If her beauty was to quickly pass, was not that one reason the more urging him to possess it while it lasted?

Nellie Fanshawe at forty would be a saint. The prospect did not please her: she hated saints. She would love the tiresome, solemn Nathaniel: of what use was that to her now? He did not desire her; he was in love with Alice, and Alice was in love with him. What would be the sense—even if they all agreed—in the three of them making themselves miserable for all their youth that they might be contented in their old age? Let age fend for itself and leave youth to its own instincts. Let elderly saints suffer—it was their *metier*—and youth drink the cup of life. It was a pity Dick was the only "catch" available, but he was young and handsome. Other girls had to put up with sixty and the gout.

Another point, a very serious point, had been overlooked. All that had arrived to them in that dim future of the past had happened to them as the results of their making the marriages they had made. To what fate other roads would lead their knowledge could not tell them. Nellie Fanshawe had become at forty a lovely character. Might not the hard life she had led with her husband—a life calling for continual sacrifice, for daily self-control—have helped towards this end? As the wife of a poor curate of high moral principles, would the same result have been secured? The fever that had robbed her of her beauty and turned her thoughts inward had been the result of sitting out on the balcony of the Paris Opera House with an Italian Count on the occasion of a fancy dress ball. As the wife of an East End clergyman the chances are she would have escaped that fever and its purifying effects. Was there not danger in the position: a supremely beautiful young woman, worldly-minded, hungry for pleasure, condemned to a life of poverty with a man she did not care for? The influence of Alice upon Nathaniel Armitage, during those first years when his character was forming, had been all for good. Could he be sure that, married to Nellie, he might not have deteriorated?

Were Alice Blatchley to marry an artist could she be sure that at forty she would still be in sympathy with artistic ideals? Even as a child had not her desire ever been in the opposite direction to that favoured by her nurse? Did not the reading of Conservative journals invariably incline her towards Radicalism, and the steady stream of Radical talk round her husband's table invariably set her seeking arguments in favour of the feudal system? Might it not have been her husband's growing Puritanism that had driven her to crave for Bohemianism? Suppose that towards middle age, the wife of a wild artist, she suddenly "took religion," as the saying is. Her last state would be worse than the first.

Camelford was of delicate physique. As an absent-minded bachelor with no one to give him his meals, no one to see that his things were aired, could he have lived till forty? Could he be sure that home life had not given more to his art than it had taken from it?

Jessica Dearwood, of a nervous, passionate nature, married to a bad husband, might at forty have posed for one of the Furies. Not until her life had become restful had her good looks shown themselves. Hers was the type of beauty that for its development demands tranquillity.

Dick Everett had no delusions concerning himself. That, had he married Jessica, he could for ten years have remained the faithful husband of a singularly plain wife he knew to be impossible. But Jessica would have been no patient Griselda. The extreme probability was that having married her at twenty for the sake of her beauty at thirty, at twenty-nine at latest she would have divorced him.

Everett was a man of practical ideas. It was he who took the matter in hand. The refreshment contractor admitted that curious goblets of German glass occasionally crept into their stock. One of the waiters, on the understanding that in no case should he be called upon to pay for them, admitted having broken more than one wine-glass on that particular evening: thought it not unlikely he might have attempted to hide the fragments under a convenient palm. The whole thing evidently was a dream. So youth decided at the time, and the three marriages took place within three months of one another.

It was some ten years later that Armitage told me the story that night in the Club smoking-room. Mrs. Everett had just recovered from a severe attack of rheumatic fever, contracted the spring before in Paris. Mrs. Camelford, whom previously I had not met, certainly seemed to me one of the handsomest women I have ever seen. Mrs. Armitage—I knew her when she was Alice Blatchley—I found more charming as a woman than she had been as a girl. What she could have seen in Armitage I never could understand. Camelford made his mark some ten years later: poor fellow, he did not live long to enjoy his fame. Dick Everett has still another six years to work off; but he is well behaved, and there is talk of a petition.

It is a curious story altogether, I admit. As I said at the beginning, I do not myself believe it.

ALL ROADS LEAD TO CALVARY

CHAPTER I

She had not meant to stay for the service. The door had stood invitingly open, and a glimpse of the interior had suggested to her the idea that it would make good copy. "Old London Churches: Their Social and Historical Associations." It would be easy to collect anecdotes of the famous people who had attended them. She might fix up a series for one of the religious papers. It promised quite exceptional material, this particular specimen, rich in tombs and monuments. There was character about it, a scent of bygone days. She pictured the vanished congregations in their powdered wigs and stiff brocades. How picturesque must have been the marriages that had taken place there, say in the reign of Queen Anne or of the early Georges. The church would have been ancient even then. With its air of faded grandeur, its sculptured recesses and dark niches, the tattered banners hanging from its roof, it must have made an admirable background. Perhaps an historical novel in the Thackeray vein? She could see her heroine walking up the aisle on the arm of her proud old soldier father. Later on, when her journalistic position was more established, she might think of it. It was still quite early. There would be nearly half an hour before the first worshippers would be likely to arrive: just time enough to jot down a few notes. If she did ever take to literature it would be the realistic school, she felt, that would appeal to her. The rest, too, would be pleasant after her long walk from Westminster. She would find a secluded seat in one of the high, stiff pews, and let the atmosphere of the place sink into her.

And then the pew-opener had stolen up unobserved, and had taken it so for granted that she would like to be shown round, and had seemed so pleased and eager, that she had not the heart to repel her. A curious little old party with a smooth, peach-like complexion and white soft hair that the fading twilight, stealing through the yellow glass, turned to gold. So that at first sight Joan took her for a child. The voice, too, was so absurdly childish—appealing, and yet confident. Not until they were crossing the aisle, where the clearer light streamed in through the open doors, did Joan see that she was very old and feeble, with about her figure that curious patient droop that comes to the work-worn. She proved to be most interesting and full of helpful information. Mary Stopperton was her name. She had lived in the neighbourhood all her life; had as a girl worked for the Leigh Hunts and had "assisted" Mrs. Carlyle. She had been very frightened of the great man himself, and had always hidden herself behind doors or squeezed herself into corners and stopped breathing whenever there had been any fear of meeting him upon the stairs. Until one day having darted into a cupboard to escape from him and drawn the door to after her, it turned out to be the cupboard in which Carlyle was used to keep his boots. So that there was quite a struggle between them; she holding grimly on to the door inside and Carlyle equally determined to open it and get his boots. It had ended in her exposure, with trembling knees and scarlet face, and Carlyle had addressed her as "woman," and had insisted on knowing what she was doing there. And after that she had lost all terror of him. And he had even allowed her with a grim smile to enter occasionally the sacred study with her broom and pan. It had evidently made a lasting impression upon her, that privilege.

"They didn't get on very well together, Mr. and Mrs. Carlyle?" Joan queried, scenting the opportunity of obtaining first-class evidence.

"There wasn't much difference, so far as I could see, between them and most of us," answered the little old lady. "You're not married, dear," she continued, glancing at Joan's ungloved hand, "but people must have a deal of patience when they have to live with us for twenty-four hours a day. You see, little things we do and say without thinking, and little ways we have that we do not notice ourselves, may all the time be irritating to other people."

"What about the other people irritating us?" suggested Joan.

"Yes, dear, and of course that can happen too," agreed the little old lady.

"Did he, Carlyle, ever come to this church?" asked Joan.

Mary Stopperton was afraid he never had, in spite of its being so near. "And yet he was a dear good Christian—in his way," Mary Stopperton felt sure.

"How do you mean 'in his way'?" demanded Joan. It certainly, if Froude was to be trusted, could not have been the orthodox way.

"Well, you see, dear," explained the little old lady, "he gave up things. He could have ridden in his carriage"—she was quoting, it seemed, the words of the Carlyles' old servant—"if he'd written the sort of lies that people pay for being told, instead of throwing the truth at their head."

"But even that would not make him a Christian," argued Joan.

"It is part of it, dear, isn't it?" insisted Mary Stopperton. "To suffer for one's faith. I think Jesus must have liked him for that."

They had commenced with the narrow strip of burial ground lying between the south side of the church and Cheyne Walk. And there the little pew-opener had showed her the grave of Anna, afterwards Mrs. Spragg. "Who long declining wedlock and aspiring above her sex fought under her brother with arms and manly attire in a flagship against the French." As also of Mary Astell, her contemporary, who had written a spirited "Essay in Defence of the Fair Sex." So there had been a Suffrage Movement as far back as in the days of Pope and Swift.

Returning to the interior, Joan had duly admired the Cheyne monument, but had been unable to disguise her amusement before the tomb of Mrs. Colvile, whom the sculptor had represented as a somewhat impatient lady, refusing to await the day of resurrection, but pushing through her coffin and starting for Heaven in her grave-clothes. Pausing in front of the Dacre monument, Joan wondered if the actor of that name, who had committed suicide in Australia, and whose London address she remembered had been Dacre House just round the corner, was descended from the family; thinking that, if so, it would give an up-to-date touch to the article. She had fully decided now to write it. But Mary Stopperton could not inform her. They had ended up in the chapel of Sir Thomas More. He, too, had "given up things," including his head. Though Mary Stopperton, siding with Father Morris, was convinced he had now got it back, and that with the remainder of his bones it rested in the tomb before them.

There, the little pew-opener had left her, having to show the early-comers to their seats; and Joan had found an out-of-the-way pew from where she could command a view of the whole church. They were chiefly poor folk, the congregation; with here and there a sprinkling of faded gentility. They seemed in keeping with the place. The twilight faded and a snuffy old man shuffled round and lit the gas.

It was all so sweet and restful. Religion had never appealed to her before. The business-like service in the bare cold chapel where she had sat swinging her feet and yawning as a child had only repelled her. She could recall her father, aloof and awe-inspiring in his Sunday black, passing round the bag. Her mother, always veiled, sitting beside her, a thin, tall woman with passionate eyes and ever restless hands; the women mostly overdressed, and the sleek, prosperous men trying to look meek. At school and at Girton, chapel, which she had attended no oftener than she was obliged, had had about it the same atmosphere of chill compulsion. But here was poetry. She wondered if, after all, religion might not have its place in the world—in company with the other arts. It would be a pity for it to die out. There seemed nothing to take its place. All these lovely cathedrals, these dear little old churches, that for centuries had been the focus of men's thoughts and aspirations. The harbour lights, illumining the troubled waters of their lives. What could be done with them? They could hardly be maintained out of the public funds as mere mementoes of the past. Besides, there were too many of them. The tax-payer would naturally grumble. As Town Halls, Assembly Rooms? The idea was unthinkable. It would be like a performance of Barnum's Circus in the Coliseum at Rome. Yes, they would disappear. Though not, she was glad to think, in her time. In towns, the space would be required for other buildings. Here and there some gradually decaying specimen would be allowed to survive, taking its place with the feudal castles and walled cities of the Continent: the joy of the American tourist, the text-book of the antiquary. A pity! Yes, but then from the aesthetic point of view it was a pity that the groves of ancient Greece had ever been cut down and replanted with currant bushes, their altars scattered; that the stones of the temples of Isis should have come to be the shelter of the fisher of the Nile; and the corn wave in the wind above the buried shrines of Mexico. All these dead truths that from time to time had encumbered the living world. Each in its turn had had to be cleared away.

And yet was it altogether a dead truth: this passionate belief in a personal God who had ordered all things for the best: who could be appealed to for comfort, for help? Might it not be as good an explanation as any other of the mystery surrounding us? It had been so universal. She was not sure where, but somewhere she had come across an analogy that had strongly impressed her. "The fact that a man feels thirsty—though at the time he may be wandering through the Desert of Sahara—proves that somewhere in the world there is water." Might not the success of Christianity in responding to human needs be evidence in its favour? The Love of God, the Fellowship of the Holy Ghost, the Grace of Our Lord Jesus Christ. Were not all human needs provided for in that one comprehensive promise: the desperate need of man to be convinced that behind all the seeming muddle was a loving hand guiding towards good; the need of the soul in its loneliness for fellowship, for strengthening; the need of man in his weakness for the kindly grace of human sympathy, of human example.

And then, as fate would have it, the first lesson happened to be the story of Jonah and the whale. Half a dozen shocked faces turned suddenly towards her told Joan that at some point in the thrilling history she must unconsciously have laughed. Fortunately she was alone in the pew, and feeling herself scarlet, squeezed herself into its farthest corner and drew down her veil.

No, it would have to go. A religion that solemnly demanded of grown men and women in the twentieth century that they should sit and listen with reverential awe to a prehistoric edition of "Grimm's Fairy Stories," including Noah and his ark, the adventures of Samson and Delilah, the conversations between Balaam and his ass, and culminating in what if it were not so appallingly wicked an idea would be the most comical of them all: the conception of an elaborately organized Hell, into which the God of the Christians plunged his creatures for all eternity! Of what use was such a religion as that going to be to the world of the future?

She must have knelt and stood mechanically, for the service was ended. The pulpit was occupied by an elderly uninteresting-looking man with a troublesome cough. But one sentence he had let fall had gripped her attention. For a moment she could not remember it, and then it came to her: "All Roads lead to Calvary." It struck her as rather good. Perhaps he was going to be worth listening to. "To all of us, sooner or later," he was saying, "comes a choosing of two ways: either the road leading to success, the gratification of desires, the honour and approval of our fellow-men—or the path to Calvary."

And then he had wandered off into a maze of detail. The tradesman, dreaming perhaps of becoming a Whiteley, having to choose whether to go forward or remain for all time in the little shop. The statesman—should he abide by the faith that is in him and suffer loss of popularity, or renounce his God and enter the Cabinet? The artist, the writer, the mere labourer—there were too many of them. A few well-chosen examples would have sufficed. And then that irritating cough!

And yet every now and then he would be arresting. In his prime, Joan felt, he must have been a great preacher. Even now, decrepit and wheezy, he was capable of flashes of magnetism, of eloquence. The passage where he pictured the Garden of Gethsemane. The fair Jerusalem, only hidden from us by the shadows. So easy to return to. Its soft lights shining through the trees, beckoning to us; its mingled voices stealing to us through the silence, whispering to us of its well-remembered ways, its pleasant places, its open doorways, friends and loved ones waiting for us. And above, the rock-strewn Calvary: and crowning its summit, clear against the starlit sky, the cold, dark cross. "Not perhaps to us the bleeding hands and feet, but to all the bitter tears. Our Calvary may be a very little hill compared with the mountains where Prometheus suffered, but to us it is steep and lonely."

There he should have stopped. It would have been a good note on which to finish. But it seemed there was another point he wished to make. Even to the sinner Calvary calls. To Judas—even to him the gates of the life-giving Garden of Gethsemane had not been closed. "With his thirty pieces of silver he could have stolen away. In some distant crowded city of the Roman Empire have lived unknown, forgotten. Life still had its pleasures, its rewards. To him also had been given the choice. The thirty pieces of silver that had meant so much to him! He flings them at the feet of his tempters. They would not take them back. He rushes out and hangs himself. Shame and death. With his own hands he will build his own cross, none to help him. He, too—even Judas, climbs his Calvary. Enters into the fellowship of those who through all ages have trod its stony pathway."

Joan waited till the last of the congregation had disappeared, and then joined the little pew-opener who was waiting to close the doors. Joan asked her what she had thought of the sermon, but Mary Stopperton, being a little deaf, had not heard it.

"It was quite good—the matter of it," Joan told her. "All Roads lead to Calvary. The idea is that there comes a time to all of us when we have to choose. Whether, like your friend Carlyle, we will 'give up things' for our faith's sake. Or go for the carriage and pair."

Mary Stopperton laughed. "He is quite right, dear," she said. "It does seem to come, and it is so hard. You have to pray and pray and pray. And even then we cannot always do it." She touched with her little withered fingers Joan's fine white hand. "But you are so strong and brave," she continued, with another little laugh. "It won't be so difficult for you."

It was not until well on her way home that Joan, recalling the conversation, found herself smiling at Mary Stopperton's literal acceptation of the argument. At the time, she remembered, the shadow of a fear had passed over her.

Mary Stopperton did not know the name of the preacher. It was quite common for chance substitutes to officiate there, especially in the evening. Joan had insisted on her acceptance of a shilling, and had made a note of her address, feeling instinctively that the little old woman would "come in useful" from a journalistic point of view.

Shaking hands with her, she had turned eastward, intending to walk to Sloane Square and there take the bus. At the corner of Oakley Street she overtook him.

He was evidently a stranger to the neighbourhood, and was peering up through his glasses to see the name of the street; and Joan caught sight of his face beneath a gas lamp.

And suddenly it came to her that it was a face she knew. In the dim-lit church she had not seen him clearly. He was still peering upward. Joan stole another glance. Yes, she had met him somewhere. He was very changed, quite different, but she was sure of it. It was a long time ago. She must have been quite a child.

CHAPTER II

One of Joan's earliest recollections was the picture of herself standing before the high cheval glass in her mother's dressing-room. Her clothes lay scattered far and wide, falling where she had flung them; not a shred of any kind of covering was left to her. She must have been very small, for she could remember looking up and seeing high above her head the two brass knobs by which the glass was fastened to its frame. Suddenly, out of the upper portion of the glass, there looked a scared red face. It hovered there a moment, and over it in swift succession there passed the expressions, first of petrified amazement, secondly of shocked indignation, and thirdly of righteous wrath. And then it swooped down upon her, and the image in the glass became a confusion of small naked arms and legs mingled with green cotton gloves and purple bonnet strings.

"You young imp of Satan!" demanded Mrs. Munday—her feelings of outraged virtue exaggerating perhaps her real sentiments. "What are you doing?"

"Go away. I'se looking at myself," had explained Joan, struggling furiously to regain the glass.

"But where are your clothes?" was Mrs. Munday's wonder.

"I'se tooked them off," explained Joan. A piece of information that really, all things considered, seemed unnecessary.

"But can't you see yourself, you wicked child, without stripping yourself as naked as you were born?"

"No," maintained Joan stoutly. "I hate clothes." As a matter of fact she didn't, even in those early days. On the contrary, one of her favourite amusements was "dressing up." This sudden overmastering desire to arrive at the truth about herself had been a new conceit.

"I wanted to see myself. Clothes ain't me," was all she would or could vouchsafe; and Mrs. Munday had shook her head, and had freely confessed that there were things beyond her and that Joan was one of them; and had succeeded, partly by force, partly by persuasion, in restoring to Joan once more the semblance of a Christian child.

It was Mrs. Munday, poor soul, who all unconsciously had planted the seeds of disbelief in Joan's mind. Mrs. Munday's God, from Joan's point of view, was a most objectionable personage. He talked a lot—or rather Mrs. Munday talked for Him—about His love for little children. But it seemed He only loved them when they were good. Joan was under no delusions about herself. If those were His terms, well, then, so far as she could see, He wasn't going to be of much use to her. Besides, if He hated naughty children, why did He make them naughty? At a moderate estimate quite half Joan's wickedness, so it seemed to Joan, came to her unbidden. Take for example that self-examination before the cheval glass. The idea had come into her mind. It had never occurred to her that it was wicked. If, as Mrs. Munday explained, it was the Devil that had whispered it to her, then what did God mean by allowing the Devil to go about persuading little girls to do indecent things? God could do everything. Why didn't He smash the Devil? It seemed to Joan a mean trick, look at it how you would. Fancy leaving a little girl to fight the Devil all by herself. And then get angry because the Devil won! Joan came to cordially dislike Mrs. Munday's God.

Looking back it was easy enough to smile, but the agony of many nights when she had lain awake for hours battling with her childish terrors had left a burning sense of anger in Joan's heart. Poor mazed, bewildered Mrs. Munday, preaching the eternal damnation of the wicked—who had loved her, who had only thought to do her duty, the blame was not hers. But that a religion capable of inflicting such suffering upon the innocent should still be preached; maintained by the State! That its educated followers no longer believed in a physical Hell, that its more advanced clergy had entered into a conspiracy of silence on the subject was no answer. The great mass of the people were not educated. Official Christendom in every country still preached the everlasting torture of the majority of the human race as a well thought out part of the Creator's scheme. No leader had been bold enough to come forward and denounce it as an insult to his God. As one grew older, kindly mother Nature, ever seeking to ease the self-inflicted burdens of her foolish brood, gave one forgetfulness, insensibility. The condemned criminal puts the thought of the gallows away from him as long as may be: eats, and sleeps and even jokes. Man's soul grows pachydermoid. But the children! Their sensitive brains exposed to every cruel breath. No philosophic doubt permitted to them. No learned disputation on the relationship between the literal and the allegorical for the easing of their frenzied fears. How many million tiny white-faced figures scattered over Christian Europe and America, stared out each night into a vision of black horror; how many million tiny hands clutched wildly at the bedclothes. The Society for the Prevention of Cruelty to Children, if they had done their duty, would have prosecuted before now the Archbishop of Canterbury.

Of course she would go to Hell. As a special kindness some generous relative had, on Joan's seventh birthday, given her an edition of Dante's "Inferno," with illustrations by Doré. From it she was able to form some notion of what her eternity was likely to be. And God all the while up in His Heaven, surrounded by that glorious band of praise-trumpeting angels, watching her out of the corner of His eye. Her courage saved her from despair. Defiance came to her aid. Let Him send her to Hell! She was not going to pray to Him and make up to Him. He was a wicked God. Yes, He was: a cruel, wicked God. And one night she told Him so to His face.

It had been a pretty crowded day, even for so busy a sinner as little Joan. It was springtime, and they had gone into the country for her mother's health. Maybe it was the season: a stirring of the human sap, conducing to that feeling of being "too big for one's boots," as the saying is. A dangerous period of the year. Indeed, on the principle that prevention is better than cure, Mrs. Munday had made it a custom during April and May to administer to Joan a cooling mixture; but on this occasion had unfortunately come away without it. Joan, dressed for use rather than show, and without either shoes or stockings, had stolen stealthily downstairs: something seemed to be calling to her. Silently—"like a thief in the night," to adopt Mrs. Munday's metaphor—had slipped the heavy bolts; had joined the thousand creatures of the wood—had danced and leapt and shouted; had behaved, in short, more as if she had been a Pagan nymph than a happy English child. She had regained the house unnoticed, as she thought, the Devil, no doubt, assisting her; and had hidden her wet clothes in the bottom of a mighty chest. Deceitfulness in her heart, she had greeted Mrs. Munday in sleepy tones from beneath the sheets; and before breakfast, assailed by suspicious questions, had told a deliberate lie. Later in the morning, during an argument with an active young pig who was willing enough to play at Red Riding Hood so far as eating things out of a basket was concerned, but who would not wear a night-cap, she had used a wicked word. In the afternoon she "might have killed" the farmer's only son and heir. They had had a row. In one of those sad lapses from the higher Christian standards into which Satan was always egging her, she had pushed him; and he had tumbled head over heels into the horse-pond. The reason, that instead of lying there and drowning he had got up and walked back to the house howling fit to wake the Seven Sleepers, was that God, watching over little children, had arranged for the incident taking place on that side of the pond where it was shallow. Had the scrimmage occurred on the opposite bank, beneath which the water was much deeper, Joan in all probability would have had murder on her soul. It seemed to Joan that if God, all-powerful and all-foreseeing, had been so careful in selecting the site, He might with equal ease have prevented the row from ever taking place. Why couldn't the little beast have been guided back from school through the orchard, much the shorter way, instead of being brought round by the yard, so as to come upon her at a moment when she was feeling a bit short-tempered, to put it mildly? And why had God allowed him to call her "Carrots"? That Joan should have "put it" this way, instead of going down on her knees and thanking the Lord for having saved her from a crime, was proof of her inborn evil disposition. In the evening was reached the culminating point. Just before going to bed she had murdered old George the cowman. For all practical purposes she might just as well have been successful in drowning William Augustus earlier in the day. It seemed to be one of those things that had to be. Mr. Hornflower still lived, it was true, but that was not Joan's fault. Joan, standing in white nightgown beside her bed, everything around her breathing of innocence and virtue:

the spotless bedclothes, the chintz curtains, the white hyacinths upon the window-ledge, Joan's Bible, a present from Aunt Susan; her prayer-book, handsomely bound in calf, a present from Grandpapa, upon their little table; Mrs. Munday in evening black and cameo brooch (pale red with tomb and weeping willow in white relief) sacred to the memory of the departed Mr. Munday—Joan standing there erect, with pale, passionate face, defying all these aids to righteousness, had deliberately wished Mr. Hornflower dead. Old George Hornflower it was who, unseen by her, had passed her that morning in the wood. Grumpy old George it was who had overheard the wicked word with which she had cursed the pig; who had met William Augustus on his emergence from the pond. To Mr. George Hornflower, the humble instrument in the hands of Providence, helping her towards possible salvation, she ought to have been grateful. And instead of that she had flung into the agonized face of Mrs. Munday these awful words:

"I wish he was dead!"

"He who in his heart—" there was verse and chapter for it. Joan was a murderess. Just as well, so far as Joan was concerned, might she have taken a carving-knife and stabbed Deacon Hornflower to the heart.

Joan's prayers that night, to the accompaniment of Mrs. Munday's sobs, had a hopeless air of unreality about them. Mrs. Munday's kiss was cold.

How long Joan lay and tossed upon her little bed she could not tell. Somewhere about the middle of the night, or so it seemed to her, the frenzy seized her. Flinging the bedclothes away she rose to her feet. It is difficult to stand upon a spring mattress, but Joan kept her balance. Of course He was there in the room with her. God was everywhere, spying upon her. She could distinctly hear His measured breathing. Face to face with Him, she told Him what she thought of Him. She told Him He was a cruel, wicked God.

There are no Victoria Crosses for sinners, or surely little Joan that night would have earned it. It was not lack of imagination that helped her courage. God and she alone, in the darkness. He with all the forces of the Universe behind Him. He armed with His eternal pains and penalties, and eight-year-old Joan: the creature that He had made in His Own Image that He could torture and destroy. Hell yawned beneath her, but it had to be said. Somebody ought to tell Him.

"You are a wicked God," Joan told Him. "Yes, You are. A cruel, wicked God."

And then that she might not see the walls of the room open before her, hear the wild laughter of the thousand devils that were coming to bear her off, she threw herself down, her face hidden in the pillow, and clenched her hands and waited.

And suddenly there burst a song. It was like nothing Joan had ever heard before. So clear and loud and near that all the night seemed filled with harmony. It sank into a tender yearning cry throbbing with passionate desire, and then it rose again in thrilling ecstasy: a song of hope, of victory.

Joan, trembling, stole from her bed and drew aside the blind. There was nothing to be seen but the stars and the dim shape of the hills. But still that song, filling the air with its wild, triumphant melody.

CHAPTER II

Years afterwards, listening to the overture to *Tannhäuser*, there came back to her the memory of that night. Ever through the mad Satanic discords she could hear, now faint, now conquering, the Pilgrims' onward march. So through the jangled discords of the world one heard the Song of Life. Through the dim aeons of man's savage infancy; through the centuries of bloodshed and of horror; through the dark ages of tyranny and superstition; through wrong, through cruelty, through hate; heedless of doom, heedless of death, still the nightingale's song: "I love you. I love you. I love you. We will build a nest. We will rear our brood. I love you. I love you. Life shall not die."

Joan crept back into bed. A new wonder had come to her. And from that night Joan's belief in Mrs. Munday's God began to fade, circumstances helping.

Firstly there was the great event of going to school. She was glad to get away from home, a massive, stiffly furnished house in a wealthy suburb of Liverpool. Her mother, since she could remember, had been an invalid, rarely leaving her bedroom till the afternoon. Her father, the owner of large engineering works, she only saw, as a rule, at dinner-time, when she would come down to dessert. It had been different when she was very young, before her mother had been taken ill. Then she had been more with them both. She had dim recollections of her father playing with her, pretending to be a bear and growling at her from behind the sofa. And then he would seize and hug her and they would both laugh, while he tossed her into the air and caught her. He had looked so big and handsome. All through her childhood there had been the desire to recreate those days, to spring into the air and catch her arms about his neck. She could have loved him dearly if he had only let her. Once, seeking explanation, she had opened her heart a little to Mrs. Munday. It was disappointment, Mrs. Munday thought, that she had not been a boy; and with that Joan had to content herself. Maybe also her mother's illness had helped to sadden him. Or perhaps it was mere temperament, as she argued to herself later, for which they were both responsible. Those little tricks of coaxing, of tenderness, of wilfulness, by means of which other girls wriggled their way so successfully into a warm nest of cosy affection: she had never been able to employ them. Beneath her self-confidence was a shyness, an immovable reserve that had always prevented her from expressing her emotions. She had inherited it, doubtless enough, from him. Perhaps one day, between them, they would break down the barrier, the strength of which seemed to lie in its very flimsiness, its impalpability.

And then during college vacations, returning home with growing notions and views of her own, she had found herself so often in antagonism with him. His fierce puritanism, so opposed to all her enthusiasms. Arguing with him, she might almost have been listening to one of his Cromwellian ancestors risen from the dead. There had been disputes between him and his work-people, and Joan had taken the side of the men. He had not been angry with her, but coldly contemptuous. And yet, in spite of it all, if he had only made a sign! She wanted to fling herself crying into his arms and shake him—make him listen to her wisdom, sitting on his knee with her hands clasped round his neck. He was not really intolerant and stupid. That had been proved by his letting her go to a Church of England school. Her mother had expressed no wish. It was he who had selected it.

Of her mother she had always stood somewhat in fear, never knowing when the mood of passionate affection would give place to a chill aversion that seemed almost like hate. Perhaps it had been good for her, so she told herself in after years, her lonely, unguided childhood. It had forced her to think and act for herself. At school she reaped the benefit. Self-reliant, confident, original, leadership was granted to her as a natural prerogative. Nature had helped her. Nowhere does a young girl rule more supremely by reason of her beauty than among her fellows. Joan soon grew accustomed to having her boots put on and taken off for her; all her needs of service anticipated by eager slaves, contending with one another for the privilege. By giving a command, by bestowing a few moments of her conversation, it was within her power to make some small adoring girl absurdly happy for the rest of the day; while her displeasure would result in tears, in fawning pleadings for forgiveness. The homage did not spoil her. Rather it helped to develop her. She accepted it from the beginning as in the order of things. Power had been given to her. It was her duty to see to it that she did not use it capriciously, for her own gratification. No conscientious youthful queen could have been more careful in the distribution of her favours—that they should be for the encouragement of the deserving, the reward of virtue; more sparing of her frowns, reserving them for the rectification of error.

At Girton it was more by force of will, of brain, that she had to make her position. There was more competition. Joan welcomed it, as giving more zest to life. But even there her beauty was by no means a negligible quantity. Clever, brilliant young women, accustomed to sweep aside all opposition with a blaze of rhetoric, found themselves to their irritation sitting in front of her silent, not so much listening to her as looking at her. It puzzled them for a time. Because a girl's features are classical and her colouring attractive, surely that has nothing to do with the value of her political views? Until one of them discovered by chance that it has.

"Well, what does Beauty think about it?" this one had asked, laughing. She had arrived at the end of a discussion just as Joan was leaving the room. And then she gave a long low whistle, feeling that she had stumbled upon the explanation. Beauty, that mysterious force that from the date of creation has ruled the world, what does It think? Dumb, passive, as a rule, exercising its influence unconsciously. But if it should become intelligent, active! A Philosopher has dreamed of the vast influence that could be exercised by a dozen sincere men acting in unity. Suppose a dozen of the most beautiful women in the world could form themselves into a league! Joan found them late in the evening still discussing it.

Her mother died suddenly during her last term, and Joan hurried back to attend the funeral. Her father was out when she reached home. Joan changed her travel-dusty clothes, and then went into the room where her mother lay, and closed the door. She must have been a beautiful woman. Now that the fret and the restlessness had left her it had come back to her. The passionate eyes were closed. Joan kissed the marble lids, and drawing a chair to the bedside, sat down. It grieved her that she had never loved her mother—not as one ought to love one's mother, unquestioningly, unreasoningly, as a natural instinct. For a moment a strange thought came to her, and swiftly, almost guiltily, she stole across, and drawing back a corner of the blind, examined closely her own features in the glass, comparing them with the face of the dead woman, thus called upon to be a silent witness for or against the living. Joan drew a sigh of relief and let fall the blind. There could be no misreading the evidence. Death had smoothed away the lines, given back youth. It was almost uncanny, the likeness between them. It might have been her drowned sister lying there. And they had never known one another. Had this also been temperament again, keeping them apart? Why did it imprison us each one as in a moving cell, so that we never could stretch out our arms to one another, except when at rare intervals Love or Death would unlock for a while the key? Impossible that two beings should have been so alike in feature without being more or less alike in thought and feeling. Whose fault had it been? Surely her own; she was so hideously calculating. Even Mrs. Munday, because the old lady had been fond of her and had shown it, had been of more service to her, more a companion, had been nearer to her than her own mother. In self-excuse she recalled the two or three occasions when she had tried to win her mother. But fate seemed to have decreed that their moods should never correspond. Her mother's sudden fierce outbursts of love, when she would be jealous, exacting, almost cruel, had frightened her when she was a child, and later on had bored her. Other daughters would have shown patience, unselfishness, but she had always been so self-centred. Why had she never fallen in love like other girls? There had been a boy at Brighton when she was at school there—quite a nice boy, who had written her wildly extravagant love-letters. It must have cost him half his pocket-money to get them smuggled in to her. Why had she only been amused at them? They might have been beautiful if only one had read them with sympathy. One day he had caught her alone on the Downs. Evidently he had made it his business to hang about every day waiting for some such chance. He had gone down on his knees and kissed her feet, and had been so abject, so pitiful that she had given him some flowers she was wearing. And he had sworn to dedicate the rest of his life to being worthy of her condescension. Poor lad! She wondered—for the first time since that afternoon—what had become of him. There had been others; a third cousin who still wrote to her from Egypt, sending her presents that perhaps he could ill afford, and whom she answered about once a year. And promising young men she had met at Cambridge, ready, the felt instinctively, to fall down and worship her. And all the use she had had for them was to convert them to her views—a task so easy as to be quite uninteresting— with a vague idea that they might come in handy in the future, when she might need help in shaping that world of the future.

Only once had she ever thought of marriage. And that was in favour of a middle-aged, rheumatic widower with three children, a professor of chemistry, very learned and justly famous. For about a month she had thought herself in love. She pictured herself devoting her life to him, rubbing his poor left shoulder where it seemed he suffered most, and brushing his picturesque hair, inclined to grey. Fortunately his eldest daughter was a young woman of resource, or the poor gentleman, naturally carried off his feet by this adoration of youth and beauty, might have made an ass of himself. But apart from this one episode she had reached the age of twenty-three heart-whole.

She rose and replaced the chair. And suddenly a wave of pity passed over her for the dead woman, who had always seemed so lonely in the great stiffly-furnished house, and the tears came.

She was glad she had been able to cry. She had always hated herself for her lack of tears; it was so unwomanly. Even as a child she had rarely cried.

Her father had always been very tender, very patient towards her mother, but she had not expected to find him so changed. He had aged and his shoulders drooped. She had been afraid that he would want her to stay with him and take charge of the house. It had worried her considerably. It would be so difficult to refuse, and yet she would have to. But when he never broached the subject she was hurt. He had questioned her about her plans the day after the funeral, and had seemed only anxious to assist them. She proposed continuing at Cambridge till the end of the term. She had taken her degree the year before. After that, she would go to London and commence her work.

"Let me know what allowance you would like me to make you, when you have thought it out. Things are not what they were at the works, but there will always be enough to keep you in comfort," he had told her. She had fixed it there and then at two hundred a year. She would not take more, and that only until she was in a position to keep herself.

"I want to prove to myself," she explained, "that I am capable of earning my own living. I am going down into the market-place. If I'm no good, if I can't take care of even one poor woman, I'll come back and ask you to keep me." She was sitting on the arm of his chair, and laughing, she drew his head towards her and pressed it against her. "If I succeed, if I am strong enough to fight the world for myself and win, that will mean I am strong enough and clever enough to help others."

"I am only at the end of a journey when you need me," he had answered, and they had kissed. And next morning she returned to her own life.

CHAPTER III

It was at Madge Singleton's rooms that the details of Joan's entry into journalistic London were arranged. "The Coming of Beauty," was Flora Lessing's phrase for designating the event. Flora Lessing, known among her associates as "Flossie," was the girl who at Cambridge had accidentally stumbled upon the explanation of Joan's influence. In appearance she was of the Fluffy Ruffles type, with childish innocent eyes, and the "unruly curls" beloved of the *Family Herald* novelist. At the first, these latter had been the result of a habit of late rising and consequent hurried toilet operations; but on the discovery that for the purposes of her profession they possessed a market value they had been sedulously cultivated. Editors of the old order had ridiculed the idea of her being of any use to them, when two years previously she had, by combination of cheek and patience, forced herself into their sanctum; had patted her paternally upon her generally ungloved hand, and told her to go back home and get some honest, worthy young man to love and cherish her.

It was Carleton of the *Daily Dispatch* group who had first divined her possibilities. With a swift glance on his way through, he had picked her out from a line of depressed-looking men and women ranged against the wall of the dark entrance passage; and with a snap of his fingers had beckoned to her to follow him. Striding in front of her up to his room, he had pointed to a chair and had left her sitting there for three-quarters of an hour, while he held discussion with a stream of subordinates, managers and editors of departments, who entered and departed one after another, evidently in pre-arranged order. All of them spoke rapidly, without ever digressing by a single word from the point, giving her the impression of their speeches having been rehearsed beforehand.

Carleton himself never interrupted them. Indeed, one might have thought he was not listening, so engrossed he appeared to be in the pile of letters and telegrams that lay waiting for him on his desk. When they had finished he would ask them questions, still with his attention fixed apparently upon the paper in his hand. Then, looking up for the first time, he would run off curt instructions, much in the tone of a Commander-in-Chief giving orders for an immediate assault; and, finishing abruptly, return to his correspondence. When the last, as it transpired, had closed the door behind him, he swung his chair round and faced her.

"What have you been doing?" he asked her.

"Wasting my time and money hanging about newspaper offices, listening to silly talk from old fossils," she told him.

"And having learned that respectable journalism has no use for brains, you come to me," he answered her. "What do you think you can do?"

"Anything that can be done with a pen and ink," she told him.

"Interviewing?" he suggested.

"I've always been considered good at asking awkward questions," she assured him.

He glanced at the clock. "I'll give you five minutes," he said. "Interview me."

She moved to a chair beside the desk, and, opening her bag, took out a writing-block.

"What are your principles?" she asked him. "Have you got any?"

He looked at her sharply across the corner of the desk.

"I mean," she continued, "to what fundamental rule of conduct do you attribute your success?"

She leant forward, fixing her eyes on him. "Don't tell me," she persisted, "that you had none. That life is all just mere blind chance. Think of the young men who are hanging on your answer. Won't you send them a message?"

"Yes," he answered musingly. "It's your baby face that does the trick. In the ordinary way I should have known you were pulling my leg, and have shown you the door. As it was, I felt half inclined for the moment to reply with some damned silly platitude that would have set all Fleet Street laughing at me. Why do my 'principles' interest you?"

"As a matter of fact they don't," she explained. "But it's what people talk about whenever they discuss you."

"What do they say?" he demanded.

"Your friends, that you never had any. And your enemies, that they are always the latest," she informed him.

"You'll do," he answered with a laugh. "With nine men out of ten that speech would have ended your chances. You sized me up at a glance, and knew it would only interest me. And your instinct is right," he added. "What people are saying: always go straight for that."

He gave her a commission then and there for a heart to heart talk with a gentleman whom the editor of the Home News Department of the *Daily Dispatch* would have referred to as a "Leading Literary Luminary," and who had just invented a new world in two volumes. She had asked him childish questions and had listened with wide-open eyes while he, sitting over against her, and smiling benevolently, had laid bare to her all the seeming intricacies of creation, and had explained to her in simple language the necessary alterations and improvements he was hoping to bring about in human nature. He had the sensation that his hair must be standing on end the next morning after having read in cold print what he had said. Expanding oneself before the admiring gaze of innocent simplicity and addressing the easily amused ear of an unsympathetic public are not the same thing. He ought to have thought of that.

It consoled him, later, that he was not the only victim. The *Daily Dispatch* became famous for its piquant interviews; especially with elderly celebrities of the masculine gender.

"It's dirty work," Flossie confided one day to Madge Singleton. "I trade on my silly face. Don't see that I'm much different to any of these poor devils." They were walking home in the evening from a theatre. "If I hadn't been stony broke I'd never have taken it up. I shall get out of it as soon as I can afford to."

"I should make it a bit sooner than that," suggested the elder woman. "One can't always stop oneself just where one wants to when sliding down a slope. It has a knack of getting steeper and steeper as one goes on."

Madge had asked Joan to come a little earlier so that they could have a chat together before the others arrived.

"I've only asked a few," she explained, as she led Joan into the restful white-panelled sitting-room that looked out upon the gardens. Madge shared a set of chambers in Gray's Inn with her brother who was an actor. "But I have chosen them with care."

Joan murmured her thanks.

"I haven't asked any men," she added, as she fixed Joan in an easy chair before the fire. "I was afraid of its introducing the wrong element."

"Tell me," asked Joan, "am I likely to meet with much of that sort of thing?"

"Oh, about as much as there always is wherever men and women work together," answered Madge. "It's a nuisance, but it has to be faced."

"Nature appears to have only one idea in her head," she continued after a pause, "so far as we men and women are concerned. She's been kinder to the lower animals."

"Man has more interests," Joan argued, "a thousand other allurements to distract him; we must cultivate his finer instincts."

"It doesn't seem to answer," grumbled Madge. "One is always told it is the artist—the brain worker, the very men who have these fine instincts, who are the most sexual."

She made a little impatient movement with her hands that was characteristic of her. "Personally, I like men," she went on. "It is so splendid the way they enjoy life: just like a dog does, whether it's wet or fine. We are always blinking up at the clouds and worrying about our hat. It would be so nice to be able to have friendship with them.

"I don't mean that it's all their fault," she continued. "We do all we can to attract them—the way we dress. Who was it said that to every woman every man is a potential lover. We can't get it out of our minds. It's there even when we don't know it. We will never succeed in civilizing Nature."

"We won't despair of her," laughed Joan. "She's creeping up, poor lady, as Whistler said of her. We have passed the phase when everything she did was right in our childish eyes. Now we dare to criticize her. That shows we are growing up. She will learn from us, later on. She's a dear old thing, at heart."

"She's been kind enough to you," replied Madge, somewhat irrelevantly. There was a note of irritation in her tone. "I suppose you know you are supremely beautiful. You seem so indifferent to it, I wonder sometimes if you do."

"I'm not indifferent to it," answered Joan. "I'm reckoning on it to help me."

"Why not?" she continued, with a flash of defiance, though Madge had not spoken. "It is a weapon like any other—knowledge, intellect, courage. God has given me beauty. I shall use it in His service."

They formed a curious physical contrast, these two women in this moment. Joan, radiant, serene, sat upright in her chair, her head slightly thrown back, her fine hands clasping one another so strongly that the delicate muscles could be traced beneath the smooth white skin. Madge, with puckered brows, leant forward in a crouching attitude, her thin nervous hands stretched out towards the fire.

"How does one know when one is serving God?" she asked after a pause, apparently rather of herself than of Joan. "It seems so difficult."

"One feels it," explained Joan.

"Yes, but didn't they all feel it," Madge suggested. She still seemed to be arguing with herself rather than with Joan. "Nietzsche. I have been reading him. They are forming a Nietzsche Society to give lectures about him—propagate him over here. Eleanor's in it up to the neck. It seems to me awful. Every fibre in my being revolts against him. Yet they're all cocksure that he is the coming prophet. He must have convinced himself that he is serving God. If I were a fighter I should feel I was serving God trying to down Him. How do I know which of us is right? Torquemada—Calvin," she went on, without giving Joan the chance of a reply. "It's easy enough to see they were wrong now. But at the time millions of people believed in them—felt it was God's voice speaking through them. Joan of Arc! Fancy dying to put a thing like that upon a throne. It would be funny if it wasn't so tragic. You can say she drove out the English—saved France. But for what? The Bartholomew massacres. The ruin of the Palatinate by Louis XIV. The horrors of the French Revolution, ending with Napoleon and all the misery and degeneracy that he bequeathed to Europe. History might have worked itself out so much better if the poor child had left it alone and minded her sheep."

"Wouldn't that train of argument lead to nobody ever doing anything?" suggested Joan.

"I suppose it would mean stagnation," admitted Madge. "And yet I don't know. Are there not forces moving towards right that are crying to us to help them, not by violence, which only interrupts—delays them, but by quietly preparing the way for them? You know what I mean. Erasmus always said that Luther had hindered the Reformation by stirring up passion and hate." She broke off suddenly. There were tears in her eyes. "Oh, if God would only say what He wants of us," she almost cried; "call to us in trumpet tones that would ring through the world, compelling us to take sides. Why can't He speak?"

"He does," answered Joan. "I hear His voice. There are things I've got to do. Wrongs that I must fight against. Rights that I must never dare to rest till they are won." Her lips were parted. Her breasts heaving. "He does call to us. He has girded His sword upon me."

Madge looked at her in silence for quite a while. "How confident you are," she said. "How I envy you."

They talked for a time about domestic matters. Joan had established herself in furnished rooms in a quiet street of pleasant Georgian houses just behind the Abbey; a member of Parliament and his wife occupied the lower floors, the landlord, a retired butler, and his wife, an excellent cook, confining themselves to the basement and the attics. The remaining floor was tenanted by a shy young man— a poet, so the landlady thought, but was not sure. Anyhow he had long hair, lived with a pipe in his mouth, and burned his lamp long into the night. Joan had omitted to ask his name. She made a note to do so.

They discussed ways and means. Joan calculated she could get through on two hundred a year, putting aside fifty for dress. Madge was doubtful if this would be sufficient. Joan urged that she was "stock size" and would be able to pick up "models" at sales; but Madge, measuring her against herself, was sure she was too full.

"You will find yourself expensive to dress," she told her, "cheap things won't go well on you; and it would be madness, even from a business point of view, for you not to make the best of yourself."

"Men stand more in awe of a well-dressed woman than they do even of a beautiful woman," Madge was of opinion. "If you go into an office looking dowdy they'll beat you down. Tell them the price they are offering you won't keep you in gloves for a week and they'll be ashamed of themselves. There's nothing *infra dig.* in being mean to the poor; but not to sympathize with the rich stamps you as middle class." She laughed.

Joan was worried. "I told Dad I should only ask him for enough to make up two hundred a year," she explained. "He'll laugh at me for not knowing my own mind."

"I should let him," advised Madge. She grew thoughtful again. "We cranky young women, with our new-fangled, independent ways, I guess we hurt the old folks quite enough as it is."

The bell rang and Madge opened the door herself. It turned out to be Flossie. Joan had not seen her since they had been at Girton together, and was surprised at Flossie's youthful "get up." Flossie explained, and without waiting for any possible attack flew to her own defence.

"The revolution that the world is waiting for," was Flossie's opinion, "is the providing of every man and woman with a hundred and fifty a year. Then we shall all be able to afford to be noble and high-minded. As it is, nine-tenths of the contemptible things we do comes from the necessity of our having to earn our living. A hundred and fifty a year would deliver us from evil."

"Would there not still be the diamond dog-collar and the motor car left to tempt us?" suggested Madge.

"Only the really wicked," contended Flossie. "It would classify us. We should know then which were the sheep and which the goats. At present we're all jumbled together: the ungodly who sin out of mere greed and rapacity, and the just men compelled to sell their birthright of fine instincts for a mess of meat and potatoes."

"Yah, socialist," commented Madge, who was busy with the tea things.

Flossie seemed struck by an idea.

"By Jove," she exclaimed. "Why did I never think of it. With a red flag and my hair down, I'd be in all the illustrated papers. It would put up my price no end. And I'd be able to get out of this silly job of mine. I can't go on much longer. I'm getting too well known. I do believe I'll try it. The shouting's easy enough." She turned to Joan. "Are you going to take up socialism?" she demanded.

"I may," answered Joan. "Just to spank it, and put it down again. I'm rather a believer in temptation—the struggle for existence. I only want to make it a finer existence, more worth the struggle, in which the best man shall rise to the top. Your 'universal security'—that will be the last act of the human drama, the cue for ringing down the curtain."

"But do not all our Isms work towards that end?" suggested Madge.

Joan was about to reply when the maid's announcement of "Mrs. Denton" postponed the discussion.

Mrs. Denton was a short, grey-haired lady. Her large strong features must have made her, when she was young, a hard-looking woman; but time and sorrow had strangely softened them; while about the corners of the thin firm mouth lurked a suggestion of humour that possibly had not always been there. Joan, waiting to be introduced, towered head and shoulders above her; yet when she took the small proffered hand and felt those steely blue eyes surveying her, she had the sensation of being quite insignificant. Mrs. Denton seemed to be reading her, and then still retaining Joan's hand she turned to Madge with a smile.

"So this is our new recruit," she said. "She is come to bring healing to the sad, sick world—to right all the old, old wrongs."

She patted Joan's hand and spoke gravely. "That is right, dear. That is youth's *métier*; to take the banner from our failing hands, bear it still a little onward." Her small gloved hand closed on Joan's with a pressure that made Joan wince.

"And you must not despair," she continued; "because in the end it will seem to you that you have failed. It is the fallen that win the victories."

She released Joan's hand abruptly. "Come and see me to-morrow morning at my office," she said. "We will fix up something that shall be serviceable to us both."

Madge flashed Joan a look. She considered Joan's position already secured. Mrs. Denton was the doyen of women journalists. She edited a monthly review and was leader writer of one of the most important dailies, besides being the controlling spirit of various social movements. Anyone she "took up" would be assured of steady work. The pay might not be able to compete with the prices paid for more popular journalism, but it would afford a foundation, and give to Joan that opportunity for influence which was her main ambition.

Joan expressed her thanks. She would like to have had more talk with the stern old lady, but was prevented by the entrance of two new comers. The first was Miss Lavery, a handsome, loud-toned young woman. She ran a nursing paper, but her chief interest was in the woman's suffrage question, just then coming rapidly to the front. She had heard Joan speak at Cambridge and was eager to secure her adherence, being wishful to surround herself with a group of young and good-looking women who should take the movement out of the hands of the "frumps," as she termed them. Her doubt was whether Joan would prove sufficiently tractable. She intended to offer her remunerative work upon the *Nursing News* without saying anything about the real motive behind, trusting to gratitude to make her task the easier.

The second was a clumsy-looking, overdressed woman whom Miss Lavery introduced as "Mrs. Phillips, a very dear friend of mine, who is going to be helpful to us all," adding in a hurried aside to Madge, "I simply had to bring her. Will explain to you another time." An apology certainly seemed to be needed. The woman was absurdly out of her place. She stood there panting and slightly perspiring. She was short and fat, with dyed hair. As a girl she had possibly been pretty in a dimpled, giggling sort of way. Joan judged her, in spite of her complexion, to be about forty.

Joan wondered if she could be the wife of the Member of Parliament who occupied the rooms below her in Cowley Street. His name, so the landlady had told her, was Phillips. She put the suggestion in a whisper to Flossie.

"Quite likely," thought Flossie; "just the type that sort of man does marry. A barmaid, I expect."

Others continued to arrive until altogether there must have been about a dozen women present. One of them turned out to be an old schoolfellow of Joan's and two had been with her at Girton. Madge had selected those who she knew would be sympathetic, and all promised help: those who could not give it direct undertaking to provide introductions and recommendations, though some of them were frankly doubtful of journalism affording Joan anything more than the means—not always, too honest—of earning a living.

"I started out to preach the gospel: all that sort of thing," drawled a Miss Simmonds from beneath a hat that, if she had paid for it, would have cost her five guineas. "Now my chief purpose in life is to tickle silly women into spending twice as much upon their clothes as their husbands can afford, bamboozling them into buying any old thing that our Advertising Manager instructs me to boom."

"They talk about the editor's opinions," struck in a fiery little woman who was busy flinging crumbs out of the window to a crowd of noisy sparrows. "It's the Advertiser edits half the papers. Write anything that three of them object to, and your proprietor tells you to change your convictions or go. Most of us change." She jerked down the window with a slam.

"It's the syndicates that have done it," was a Mrs. Elliot's opinion. She wrote "Society Notes" for a Labour weekly. "When one man owned a paper he wanted it to express his views. A company is only out for profit. Your modern newspaper is just a shop. It's only purpose is to attract customers. Look at the *Methodist Herald*, owned by the same syndicate of Jews that runs the *Racing News*. They work it as far as possible with the same staff."

"We're a pack of hirelings," asserted the fiery little woman. "Our pens are for sale to the highest bidder. I had a letter from Jocelyn only two days ago. He was one of the original staff of the *Socialist*. He writes me that he has gone as leader writer to a Conservative paper at twice his former salary. Expected me to congratulate him."

"One of these days somebody will start a Society for the Reformation of the Press," thought Flossie. "I wonder how the papers will take it?"

"Much as Rome took Savonarola," thought Madge.

Mrs. Denton had risen.

"They are right to a great extent," she said to Joan. "But not all the temple has been given over to the hucksters. You shall place your preaching stool in some quiet corner, where the passing feet shall pause awhile to listen."

Her going was the signal for the breaking up of the party. In a short time Joan and Madge found themselves left with only Flossie.

"What on earth induced Helen to bring that poor old Dutch doll along with her?" demanded Flossie. "The woman never opened her mouth all the time. Did she tell you?"

"No," answered Madge, "but I think I can guess. She hopes—or perhaps 'fears' would be more correct—that her husband is going to join the Cabinet, and is trying to fit herself by suddenly studying political and social questions. For a month she's been clinging like a leech to Helen Lavery, who takes her to meetings and gatherings. I suppose they've struck up some sort of a bargain. It's rather pathetic."

"Good Heavens! What a tragedy for the man," commented Flossie.

"What is he like?" asked Joan.

"Not much to look at, if that's what you mean," answered Madge. "Began life as a miner, I believe. Looks like ending as Prime Minister."

"I heard him at the Albert Hall last week," said Flossie. "He's quite wonderful."

"In what way?" questioned Joan.

"Oh, you know," explained Flossie. "Like a volcano compressed into a steam engine."

They discussed Joan's plans. It looked as if things were going to be easy for her.

CHAPTER IV

Yet in the end it was Carleton who opened the door for her.

Mrs. Denton was helpful, and would have been more so, if Joan had only understood. Mrs. Denton lived alone in an old house in Gower Street, with a high stone hall that was always echoing to sounds that no one but itself could ever hear. Her son had settled, it was supposed, in one of the Colonies. No one knew what had become of him, and Mrs. Denton herself never spoke of him; while her daughter, on whom she had centred all her remaining hopes, had died years ago. To those who remembered the girl, with her weak eyes and wispy ginger coloured hair, it would have seemed comical, the idea that Joan resembled her. But Mrs. Denton's memory had lost itself in dreams; and to her the likeness had appeared quite wonderful. The gods had given her child back to her, grown strong and brave and clever. Life would have a new meaning for her. Her work would not die with her.

She thought she could harness Joan's enthusiasm to her own wisdom. She would warn her of the errors and pitfalls into which she herself had fallen: for she, too, had started as a rebel. Youth should begin where age left off. Had the old lady remembered a faded dogs-eared volume labelled "Oddments" that for many years had rested undisturbed upon its shelf in her great library, and opening it had turned to the letter E, she would have read recorded there, in her own precise thin penmanship, this very wise reflection:

"Experience is a book that all men write, but no man reads."

To which she would have found added, by way of complement, "Experience is untranslatable. We write it in the cipher of our sufferings, and the key is hidden in our memories."

And turning to the letter Y, she might have read:

"Youth comes to teach. Age remains to listen," and underneath the following:

"The ability to learn is the last lesson we acquire."

Mrs. Denton had long ago given up the practice of jotting down her thoughts, experience having taught her that so often, when one comes to use them, one finds that one has changed them. But in the case of Joan the recollection of these twin "oddments" might have saved her disappointment. Joan knew of a new road that avoided Mrs. Denton's pitfalls. She grew impatient of being perpetually pulled back.

For the *Nursing Times* she wrote a series of condensed biographies, entitled "Ladies of the Lamp," commencing with Elizabeth Fry. They formed a record of good women who had battled for the weak and suffering, winning justice for even the uninteresting. Miss Lavery was delighted with them. But when Joan proposed exposing the neglect and even cruelty too often inflicted upon the helpless patients of private Nursing Homes, Miss Lavery shook her head.

"I know," she said. "One does hear complaints about them. Unfortunately it is one of the few businesses managed entirely by women; and just now, in particular, if we were to say anything, it would be made use of by our enemies to injure the Cause."

There was a summer years ago—it came back to Joan's mind—when she had shared lodgings with a girl chum at a crowded sea-side watering-place. The rooms were shockingly dirty; and tired of dropping hints she determined one morning to clean them herself. She climbed a chair and started on a row of shelves where lay the dust of ages. It was a jerry-built house, and the result was that she brought the whole lot down about her head, together with a quarter of a hundred-weight of plaster.

"Yes, I thought you'd do some mischief," had commented the landlady, wearily.

It seemed typical. A jerry-built world, apparently. With the best intentions it seemed impossible to move in it without doing more harm than good to it, bringing things down about one that one had not intended.

She wanted to abolish steel rabbit-traps. She had heard the little beggars cry. It had struck her as such a harmless reform. But they told her there were worthy people in the neighbourhood of Wolverhampton—quite a number of them—who made their living by the manufacture of steel rabbit-traps. If, thinking only of the rabbits, you prohibited steel rabbit-traps, then you condemned all these worthy people to slow starvation. The local Mayor himself wrote in answer to her article. He drew a moving picture of the sad results that might follow such an ill-considered agitation: hundreds of grey-haired men, too old to learn new jobs, begging from door to door; shoals of little children, white-faced and pinched; sobbing women. Her editor was sorry for the rabbits. Had often spent a pleasant day with them himself. But, after all, the Human Race claimed our first sympathies.

She wanted to abolish sweating. She had climbed the rotting stairways, seen the famished creatures in their holes. But it seemed that if you interfered with the complicated system based on sweating then you dislocated the entire structure of the British export clothing trade. Not only would these poor creatures lose their admittedly wretched living—but still a living—but thousands of other innocent victims would also be involved in the common ruin. All very sad, but half a loaf—or even let us frankly say a thin slice—is better than no bread at all.

She wanted board school children's heads examined. She had examined one or two herself. It seemed to her wrong that healthy children should be compelled to sit for hours within jumping distance of the diseased. She thought it better that the dirty should be made fit company for the clean than the clean should be brought down to the level of the dirty. It seemed that in doing this you were destroying the independence of the poor. Opposition reformers, in letters scintillat-scintillating with paradox, bristling with classical allusion, denounced her attempt to impose middle-class ideals upon a too long suffering proletariat. Better far a few lively little heads than a broken-spirited people robbed of their parental rights.

Through Miss Lavery she obtained an introduction to the great Sir William. He owned a group of popular provincial newspapers, and was most encouraging. Sir William had often said to himself:

"What can I do for God who has done so much for me?" It seemed only fair.

He asked her down to his "little place in Hampshire," to talk plans over. The "little place," it turned out, ran to forty bedrooms, and was surrounded by three hundred acres of park. God had evidently done his bit quite handsomely.

It was in a secluded corner of the park that Sir William had gone down upon one knee and gallantly kissed her hand. His idea was that if she could regard herself as his "Dear Lady," and allow him the honour and privilege of being her "True Knight," that, between them, they might accomplish something really useful. There had been some difficulty about his getting up again, Sir William being an elderly gentleman subject to rheumatism, and Joan had had to expend no small amount of muscular effort in assisting him; so that the episode which should have been symbolical ended by leaving them both red and breathless.

He referred to the matter again the same evening in the library while Lady William slept peacefully in the blue drawing-room; but as it appeared necessary that the compact should be sealed by a knightly kiss Joan had failed to ratify it.

She blamed herself on her way home. The poor old gentleman could easily have been kept in his place. The suffering of an occasional harmless caress would have purchased for her power and opportunity. Had it not been somewhat selfish of her? Should she write to him—see him again?

She knew that she never would. It was something apart from her reason. It would not even listen to her. It bade or forbade as if one were a child without any right to a will of one's own. It was decidedly exasperating.

There were others. There were the editors who frankly told her that the business of a newspaper was to write what its customers wanted to read; and that the public, so far as they could judge, was just about fed up with plans for New Jerusalems at their expense. And the editors who were prepared to take up any number of reforms, insisting only that they should be new and original and promise popularity.

And then she met Greyson.

It was at a lunch given by Mrs. Denton. Greyson was a bachelor and lived with an unmarried sister, a few years older than himself. He was editor and part proprietor of an evening paper. It had ideals and was, in consequence, regarded by the general public with suspicion; but by reason of sincerity and braininess was rapidly becoming a power. He was a shy, reserved man with an aristocratic head set upon stooping shoulders. The face was that of a dreamer, but about the mouth there was suggestion of the fighter. Joan felt at her ease with him in spite of the air of detachment that seemed part of his character. Mrs. Denton had paired them off together; and, during the lunch, one of them—Joan could not remember which—had introduced the subject of reincarnation.

Greyson was unable to accept the theory because of the fact that, in old age, the mind in common with the body is subject to decay.

"Perhaps by the time I am forty—or let us say fifty," he argued, "I shall be a bright, intelligent being. If I die then, well and good. I select a likely baby and go straight on. But suppose I hang about till eighty and die a childish old gentleman with a mind all gone to seed. What am I going to do then? I shall have to begin all over again: perhaps worse off than I was before. That's not going to help us much."

Joan explained it to him: that old age might be likened to an illness. A genius lies upon a bed of sickness and babbles childish nonsense. But with returning life he regains his power, goes on increasing it. The mind, the soul, has not decayed. It is the lines of communication that old age has destroyed.

"But surely you don't believe it?" he demanded.

"Why not?" laughed Joan. "All things are possible. It was the possession of a hand that transformed monkeys into men. We used to take things up, you know, and look at them, and wonder and wonder and wonder, till at last there was born a thought and the world became visible. It is curiosity that will lead us to the next great discovery. We must take things up; and think and think and think till one day there will come knowledge, and we shall see the universe."

Joan always avoided getting excited when she thought of it.

"I love to make you excited," Flossie had once confessed to her in the old student days. "You look so ridiculously young and you are so pleased with yourself, laying down the law."

She did not know she had given way to it. He was leaning back in his chair, looking at her; and the tired look she had noticed in his eyes, when she had been introduced to him in the drawing-room, had gone out of them.

During the coffee, Mrs. Denton beckoned him to come to her; and Miss Greyson crossed over and took his vacant chair. She had been sitting opposite to them.

"I've been hearing so much about you," she said. "I can't help thinking that you ought to suit my brother's paper. He has all your ideas. Have you anything that you could send him?"

Joan considered a moment.

"Nothing very startling," she answered. "I was thinking of a series of articles on the old London Churches—touching upon the people connected with them and the things they stood for. I've just finished the first one."

"It ought to be the very thing," answered Miss Greyson. She was a thin, faded woman with a soft, plaintive voice. "It will enable him to judge your style. He's particular about that. Though I'm confident he'll like it," she hastened to add. "Address it to me, will you. I assist him as much as I can."

Joan added a few finishing touches that evening, and posted it; and a day or two later received a note asking her to call at the office.

"My sister is enthusiastic about your article on Chelsea Church and insists on my taking the whole series," Greyson informed her. "She says you have the Stevensonian touch."

Joan flushed with pleasure.

"And you," she asked, "did you think it had the Stevensonian touch?"

"No," he answered, "it seemed to me to have more of your touch."

"What's that like?" she demanded.

"They couldn't suppress you," he explained. "Sir Thomas More with his head under his arm, bloody old Bluebeard, grim Queen Bess, snarling old Swift, Pope, Addison, Carlyle—the whole grisly crowd of them! I could see you holding your own against them all, explaining things to them, getting excited." He laughed.

His sister joined them, coming in from the next room. She had a proposal to make. It was that Joan should take over the weekly letter from "Clorinda." It was supposed to give the views of a—perhaps unusually—sane and thoughtful woman upon the questions of the day. Miss Greyson had hitherto conducted it herself, but was wishful as she explained to be relieved of it; so that she might have more time for home affairs. It would necessitate Joan's frequent attendance at the office; for there would be letters from the public to be answered, and points to be discussed with her brother. She was standing behind his chair with her hands upon his head. There was something strangely motherly about her whole attitude.

Greyson was surprised, for the Letter had been her own conception, and had grown into a popular feature. But she was evidently in earnest; and Joan accepted willingly. "Clorinda" grew younger, more self-assertive; on the whole more human. But still so eminently "sane" and reasonable.

"We must not forget that she is quite a respectable lady, connected—according to her own account—with the higher political circles," Joan's editor would insist, with a laugh.

Miss Greyson, working in the adjoining room, would raise her head and listen. She loved to hear him laugh.

"It's absurd," Flossie told her one morning, as having met by chance they were walking home together along the Embankment. "You're not 'Clorinda'; you ought to be writing letters to her, not from her, waking her up, telling her to come off her perch, and find out what the earth feels like. I'll tell you what I'll do: I'll trot you round to Carleton. If you're out for stirring up strife and contention, well, that's his game, too. He'll use you for his beastly sordid ends. He'd have roped in John the Baptist if he'd been running the 'Jerusalem Star' at the time, and have given him a daily column for so long as the boom lasted. What's that matter, if he's willing to give you a start?"

Joan jibbed at first. But in the end Flossie's arguments prevailed. One afternoon, a week later, she was shown into Carleton's private room, and the door closed behind her. The light was dim, and for a moment she could see no one;

until Carleton, who had been standing near one of the windows, came forward and placed a chair for her. And they both sat down.

"I've glanced through some of your things," he said. "They're all right. They're alive. What's your idea?"

Remembering Flossie's counsel, she went straight to the point. She wanted to talk to the people. She wanted to get at them. If she had been a man, she would have taken a chair and gone to Hyde Park. As it was, she hadn't the nerve for Hyde Park. At least she was afraid she hadn't. It might have to come to that. There was a trembling in her voice that annoyed her. She was so afraid she might cry. She wasn't out for anything crazy. She wanted only those things done that could be done if the people would but lift their eyes, look into one another's faces, see the wrong and the injustice that was all around them, and swear that they would never rest till the pain and the terror had been driven from the land. She wanted soldiers—men and women who would forget their own sweet selves, not counting their own loss, thinking of the greater gain; as in times of war and revolution, when men gave even their lives gladly for a dream, for a hope—

Without warning he switched on the electric lamp that stood upon the desk, causing her to draw back with a start.

"All right," he said. "Go ahead. You shall have your tub, and a weekly audience of a million readers for as long as you can keep them interested. Up with anything you like, and down with everything you don't. Be careful not to land me in a libel suit. Call the whole Bench of Bishops hypocrites, and all the ground landlords thieves, if you will: but don't mention names. And don't get me into trouble with the police. Beyond that, I shan't interfere with you."

She was about to speak.

"One stipulation," he went on, "that every article is headed with your photograph."

He read the sudden dismay in her eyes.

"How else do you think you are going to attract their attention?" he asked her. "By your eloquence! Hundreds of men and women as eloquent as you could ever be are shouting to them every day. Who takes any notice of them? Why should they listen any the more to you—another cranky highbrow: some old maid, most likely, with a bony throat and a beaky nose. If Woman is going to come into the fight she will have to use her own weapons. If she is prepared to do that she'll make things hum with a vengeance. She's the biggest force going, if she only knew it."

He had risen and was pacing the room.

"The advertiser has found that out, and is showing the way." He snatched at an illustrated magazine, fresh from the press, that had been placed upon his desk, and opened it at the first page. "Johnson's Blacking," he read out, "advertised by a dainty little minx, showing her ankles. Who's going to stop for a moment to read about somebody's blacking? If a saucy little minx isn't there to trip him up with her ankles!"

He turned another page. "Do you suffer from gout? Classical lady preparing to take a bath and very nearly ready. The old Johnny in the train stops to look at her. Reads the advertisement because she seems to want him to. Rubber heels. Save your boot leather! Lady in evening dress—jolly pretty shoulders—waves them in front of your eyes. Otherwise you'd never think of them."

He fluttered the pages. Then flung the thing across to her.

"Look at it," he said. "Fountain pens—Corn plasters—Charitable appeals— Motor cars—Soaps—Grand pianos. It's the girl in tights and spangles outside the show that brings them trooping in."

"Let them see you," he continued. "You say you want soldiers. Throw off your veil and call for them. Your namesake of France! Do you think if she had contented herself with writing stirring appeals that Orleans would have fallen? She put on a becoming suit of armour and got upon a horse where everyone could see her. Chivalry isn't dead. You modern women are ashamed of yourselves— ashamed of your sex. You don't give it a chance. Revive it. Stir the young men's blood. Their souls will follow."

He reseated himself and leant across towards her.

"I'm not talking business," he said. "This thing's not going to mean much to me one way or the other. I want you to win. Farm labourers bringing up families on twelve and six a week. Shirt hands working half into the night for three far-things an hour. Stinking dens for men to live in. Degraded women. Half fed children. It's damnable. Tell them it's got to stop. That the Eternal Feminine has stepped out of the poster and commands it."

A dapper young man opened the door and put his head into the room.

"Railway smash in Yorkshire," he announced.

Carleton sat up. "Much of a one?" he asked.

The dapper gentleman shrugged his shoulders. "Three killed, eight injured, so far," he answered.

Carleton's interest appeared to collapse.

"Stop press column?" asked the dapper gentleman.

"Yes, I suppose so," replied Carleton. "Unless something better turns up."

The dapper young gentleman disappeared. Joan had risen.

"May I talk it over with a friend?" she asked. "Myself, I'm inclined to ac- cept."

"You will, if you're in earnest," he answered. "I'll give you twenty-four hours. Look in to-morrow afternoon, and see Finch. It will be for the *Sunday Post*—the Inset. We use surfaced paper for that and can do you justice. Finch will arrange about the photograph." He held out his hand. "Shall be seeing you again," he said.

It was but a stone's throw to the office of the *Evening Gazette*. She caught Greyson just as he was leaving and put the thing before him. His sister was with him.

He did not answer at first. He was walking to and fro; and, catching his foot in the waste paper basket, he kicked it savagely out of his way, so that the contents were scattered over the room.

"Yes, he's right," he said. "It was the Virgin above the altar that popularized Christianity. Her face has always been woman's fortune. If she's going to become a fighter, it will have to be her weapon."

He had used almost the same words that Carleton had used.

"I so want them to listen to me," she said. "After all, it's only like having a very loud voice."

He looked at her and smiled. "Yes," he said, "it's a voice men will listen to."

Mary Greyson was standing by the fire. She had not spoken hitherto.

"You won't give up 'Clorinda'?" she asked.

Joan had intended to do so, but something in Mary's voice caused her, against her will, to change her mind.

"Of course not," she answered. "I shall run them both. It will be like writing Jekyll and Hyde."

"What will you sign yourself?" he asked.

"My own name, I think," she said. "Joan Allway."

Miss Greyson suggested her coming home to dinner with them; but Joan found an excuse. She wanted to be alone.

CHAPTER V

The twilight was fading as she left the office. She turned northward, choosing a broad, ill-lighted road. It did not matter which way she took. She wanted to think; or, rather, to dream.

It would all fall out as she had intended. She would commence by becoming a power in journalism. She was reconciled now to the photograph idea—was even keen on it herself. She would be taken full face so that she would be looking straight into the eyes of her readers as she talked to them. It would compel her to be herself; just a hopeful, loving woman: a little better educated than the majority, having had greater opportunity: a little further seeing, maybe, having had more leisure for thought: but otherwise, no whit superior to any other young, eager woman of the people. This absurd journalistic pose of omniscience, of infallibility—this non-existent garment of supreme wisdom that, like the King's clothes in the fairy story, was donned to hide his nakedness by every strutting nonentity of Fleet Street! She would have no use for it. It should be a friend, a comrade, a fellow-servant of the great Master, taking counsel with them, asking their help. Government by the people for the people! It must be made real. These silent, thoughtful-looking workers, hurrying homewards through the darkening streets; these patient, shrewd-planning housewives casting their shadows on the drawn-down blinds: it was they who should be shaping the world, not the journalists to whom all life was but so much "copy." This monstrous conspiracy, once of the Sword, of the Church, now of the Press, that put all Government into the hands of a few stuffy old gentlemen, politicians, leader writers, without sympathy or understanding: it was time that it was swept away. She would raise a new standard. It should be, not "Listen to me, oh ye dumb," but, "Speak to me. Tell me your hidden hopes, your fears, your dreams. Tell me your experience, your thoughts born of knowledge, of suffering."

She would get into correspondence with them, go among them, talk to them. The difficulty, at first, would be in getting them to write to her, to open their minds to her. These voiceless masses that never spoke, but were always being spoken for by self-appointed "leaders," "representatives," who immediately they had climbed into prominence took their place among the rulers, and then from press and platform shouted to them what they were to think and feel. It was as if the Drill-Sergeant were to claim to be the "leader," the "representative" of his squad; or the sheep-dog to pose as the "delegate" of the sheep. Dealt with always as if they were mere herds, mere flocks, they had almost lost the power of individual utterance. One would have to teach them, encourage them.

She remembered a Sunday class she had once conducted; and how for a long time she had tried in vain to get the children to "come in," to take a hand. That she might get in touch with them, understand their small problems, she had urged them to ask questions. And there had fallen such long silences. Until, at last, one cheeky ragamuffin had piped out:

"Please, Miss, have you got red hair all over you? Or only on your head?"

For answer she had rolled up her sleeve, and let them examine her arm. And then, in her turn, had insisted on rolling up his sleeve, revealing the fact that his arms above the wrists had evidently not too recently been washed; and the episode had ended in laughter and a babel of shrill voices. And, at once, they were a party of chums, discussing matters together.

They were but children, these tired men and women, just released from their day's toil, hastening homeward to their play, or to their evening tasks. A little humour, a little understanding, a recognition of the wonderful likeness of us all to one another underneath our outward coverings was all that was needed to break down the barrier, establish comradeship. She stood aside a moment to watch them streaming by. Keen, strong faces were among them, high, thoughtful brows, kind eyes; they must learn to think, to speak for themselves.

She would build again the Forum. The people's business should no longer be settled for them behind lackey-guarded doors. The good of the farm labourer should be determined not exclusively by the squire and his relations. The man with the hoe, the man with the bent back and the patient ox-like eyes: he, too, should be invited to the Council board. Middle-class domestic problems should be solved not solely by fine gentlemen from Oxford; the wife of the little clerk should be allowed her say. War or peace, it should no longer be regarded as a question concerning only the aged rich. The common people—the cannon fodder, the men who would die, and the women who would weep: they should be given something more than the privilege of either cheering platform patriots or being summoned for interrupting public meetings.

From a dismal side street there darted past her a small, shapeless figure in crumpled cap and apron: evidently a member of that lazy, over-indulged class, the domestic servant. Judging from the talk of the drawing-rooms, the correspondence in the papers, a singularly unsatisfactory body. They toiled not, lived in luxury and demanded grand pianos. Someone had proposed doing something for them. They themselves—it seemed that even they had a sort of conscience—were up in arms against it. Too much kindness even they themselves perceived was bad for them. They were holding a meeting that night to explain how contented they were. Six peeresses had consented to attend, and speak for them.

Likely enough that there were good-for-nothing, cockered menials imposing upon incompetent mistresses. There were pampered slaves in Rome. But these others. These poor little helpless sluts. There were thousands such in every city, over-worked and under-fed, living lonely, pleasureless lives. They must be taught to speak in other voices than the dulcet tones of peeresses. By the light of the guttering candles, from their chill attics, they should write to her their ill-spelt vi-visions.

She had reached a quiet, tree-bordered road, surrounding a great park. Lovers, furtively holding hands, passed her by, whispering.

She would write books. She would choose for her heroine a woman of the people. How full of drama, of tragedy must be their stories: their problems the grim realities of life, not only its mere sentimental embroideries. The daily struggle for bare existence, the ever-shadowing menace of unemployment, of illness, leaving them helpless amid the grinding forces crushing them down on every side. The ceaseless need for courage, for cunning. For in the kingdom of the poor the tyrant and the oppressor still sit in the high places, the robber still rides fearless.

In a noisy, flaring street, a thin-clad woman passed her, carrying a netted bag showing two loaves. In a flash, it came to her what it must mean to the poor; this daily bread that in comfortable homes had come to be regarded as a thing like water; not to be considered, to be used without stint, wasted, thrown about. Borne by those feeble, knotted hands, Joan saw it revealed as something holy: hallowed by labour; sanctified by suffering, by sacrifice; worshipped with fear and prayer.

In quiet streets of stately houses, she caught glimpses through uncurtained windows of richly-laid dinner-tables about which servants moved noiselessly, arranging flowers and silver. She wondered idly if she would every marry. A gracious hostess, gathering around her brilliant men and women, statesmen, writers, artists, captains of industry: counselling them, even learning from them: encouraging shy genius. Perhaps, in a perfectly harmless way, allowing it the inspiration derivable from a well-regulated devotion to herself. A salon that should be the nucleus of all those forces that influence influences, over which she would rule with sweet and wise authority. The idea appealed to her.

Into the picture, slightly to the background, she unconsciously placed Greyson. His tall, thin figure with its air of distinction seemed to fit in; Greyson would be very restful. She could see his handsome, ascetic face flush with pleasure as, after the guests were gone, she would lean over the back of his chair and caress for a moment his dark, soft hair tinged here and there with grey. He would always adore her, in that distant, undemonstrative way of his that would never be tiresome or exacting. They would have children. But not too many. That would make the house noisy and distract her from her work. They would be beautiful and clever; unless all the laws of heredity were to be set aside for her especial injury. She would train them, shape them to be the heirs of her labour, bearing her message to the generations that should follow.

At a corner where the trams and buses stopped she lingered for a while, watching the fierce struggle; the weak and aged being pushed back time after time, hardly seeming to even resent it, regarding it as in the natural order of things. It was so absurd, apart from the injustice, the brutality of it! The poor, fighting among themselves! She felt as once when watching a crowd of birds to whom she had thrown a handful of crumbs in winter time. As if they had not enemies enough: cats, weasels, rats, hawks, owls, the hunger and the cold. And added to all, they must needs make the struggle yet harder for one another: pecking at each other's eyes, joining with one another to attack the fallen. These tired men, these weary women, pale-faced lads and girls, why did they not organize among themselves some system that would do away with this daily warfare of each against all. If only they could be got to grasp the fact that they were one family, bound together by suffering. Then, and not till then, would they be able to make their power felt? That would have to come first: the *Esprit de Corps* of the Poor.

In the end she would go into Parliament. It would be bound to come soon, the woman's vote. And after that the opening of all doors would follow. She would wear her college robes. It would be far more fitting than a succession of flimsy frocks that would have no meaning in them. What pity it was that the art of dressing—its relation to life—was not better understood. What beauty-hating devil had prompted the workers to discard their characteristic costumes that had been both beautiful and serviceable for these hateful slop-shop clothes that made them look like walking scarecrows. Why had the coming of Democracy coincided seemingly with the spread of ugliness: dull towns, mean streets, paper-strewn parks, corrugated iron roofs, Christian chapels that would be an insult to a heathen idol; hideous factories (Why need they be hideous!); chimney-pot hats, baggy trousers, vulgar advertisements, stupid fashions for women that spoilt every line of their figure: dinginess, drabness, monotony everywhere. It was ugliness that was strangling the soul of the people; stealing from them all dignity, all self-respect, all honour for one another; robbing them of hope, of reverence, of joy in life.

Beauty. That was the key to the riddle. All Nature: its golden sunsets and its silvery dawns; the glory of piled-up clouds, the mystery of moonlit glades; its rivers winding through the meadows; the calling of its restless seas; the tender witchery of Spring; the blazonry of autumn woods; its purple moors and the wonder of its silent mountains; its cobwebs glittering with a thousand jewels; the pageantry of starry nights. Form, colour, music! The feathered choristers of bush and brake raising their matin and their evensong, the whispering of the leaves, the singing of the waters, the voices of the winds. Beauty and grace in every living thing, but man. The leaping of the hares, the grouping of cattle, the flight of swallows, the dainty loveliness of insects' wings, the glossy skin of horses rising and falling to the play of mighty muscles. Was it not seeking to make plain to us that God's language was beauty. Man must learn beauty that he may understand God.

She saw the London of the future. Not the vision popular just then: a soaring whirl of machinery in motion, of moving pavements and flying omnibuses; of screaming gramophones and standardized "homes": a city where Electricity was King and man its soulless slave. But a city of peace, of restful spaces, of leisured men and women; a city of fine streets and pleasant houses, where each could live his own life, learning freedom, individuality; a city of noble schools; of workshops that should be worthy of labour, filled with light and air; smoke and filth driven from the land: science, no longer bound to commercialism, having discovered cleaner forces; a city of gay playgrounds where children should learn laugh-laughter; of leafy walks where the creatures of the wood and field should be as welcome guests helping to teach sympathy and kindliness: a city of music, of colour, of gladness. Beauty worshipped as religion; ugliness banished as a sin: no ugly slums, no ugly cruelty, no slatternly women and brutalized men, no ugly, sobbing children; no ugly vice flaunting in every highway its insult to humanity: a city clad in beauty as with a living garment where God should walk with man.

She had reached a neighbourhood of narrow, crowded streets. The women were mostly without hats; and swarthy men, rolling cigarettes, lounged against doorways. The place had a quaint foreign flavour. Tiny cafés, filled with smoke and noise, and clean, inviting restaurants abounded. She was feeling hungry, and, choosing one the door of which stood open, revealing white tablecloths and a pleasant air of cheerfulness, she entered. It was late and the tables were crowded. Only at one, in a far corner, could she detect a vacant place, opposite to a slight, pretty-looking girl very quietly dressed. She made her way across and the girl, anticipating her request, welcomed her with a smile. They ate for a while in silence, divided only by the narrow table, their heads, when they leant forward, almost touching. Joan noticed the short, white hands, the fragrance of some delicate scent. There was something odd about her. She seemed to be unnecessarily conscious of being alone. Suddenly she spoke.

"Nice little restaurant, this," she said. "One of the few places where you can depend upon not being annoyed."

Joan did not understand. "In what way?" she asked.

"Oh, you know, men," answered the girl. "They come and sit down opposite to you, and won't leave you alone. At most of the places, you've got to put up with it or go outside. Here, old Gustav never permits it."

Joan was troubled. She was rather looking forward to occasional restaurant dinners, where she would be able to study London's Bohemia.

"You mean," she asked, "that they force themselves upon you, even if you make it plain—"

"Oh, the plainer you make it that you don't want them, the more sport they think it," interrupted the girl with a laugh.

Joan hoped she was exaggerating. "I must try and select a table where there is some good-natured girl to keep me in countenance," she said with a smile.

"Yes, I was glad to see you," answered the girl. "It's hateful, dining by oneself. Are you living alone?"

"Yes," answered Joan. "I'm a journalist."

"I thought you were something," answered the girl. "I'm an artist. Or, rather, was," she added after a pause.

"Why did you give it up?" asked Joan.

"Oh, I haven't given it up, not entirely," the girl answered. "I can always get a couple of sovereigns for a sketch, if I want it, from one or another of the framemakers. And they can generally sell them for a fiver. I've seen them marked up. Have you been long in London?"

"No," answered Joan. "I'm a Lancashire lass."

"Curious," said the girl, "so am I. My father's a mill manager near Bolton. You weren't educated there?"

"No," Joan admitted. "I went to Rodean at Brighton when I was ten years old, and so escaped it. Nor were you," she added with a smile, "judging from your accent."

"No," answered the other, "I was at Hastings—Miss Gwyn's. Funny how we seem to have always been near to one another. Dad wanted me to be a doctor. But I'd always been mad about art."

Joan had taken a liking to the girl. It was a spiritual, vivacious face with frank eyes and a firm mouth; and the voice was low and strong.

"Tell me," she said, "what interfered with it?" Unconsciously she was leaning forward, her chin supported by her hands. Their faces were very near to one another.

The girl looked up. She did not answer for a moment. There came a hardening of the mouth before she spoke.

"A baby," she said. "Oh, it was my own fault," she continued. "I wanted it. It was all the talk at the time. You don't remember. Our right to children. No woman complete without one. Maternity, woman's kingdom. All that sort of thing. As if the storks brought them. Don't suppose it made any real difference; but it just helped me to pretend that it was something pretty and high-class. 'Overmastering passion' used to be the explanation, before that. I guess it's all much of a muchness: just natural instinct."

The restaurant had been steadily emptying. Monsieur Gustav and his ample-bosomed wife were seated at a distant table, eating their own dinner.

"Why couldn't you have married?" asked Joan.

The girl shrugged her shoulders. "Who was there for me to marry?" she answered. "The men who wanted me: clerks, young tradesmen, down at home—I wasn't taking any of that lot. And the men I might have fancied were all of them too poor. There was one student. He's got on since. Easy enough for him to talk about waiting. Meanwhile. Well, it's like somebody suggesting dinner to you the day after to-morrow. All right enough, if you're not troubled with an appetite."

The waiter came to clear the table. They were almost the last customers left. The man's tone and manner jarred upon Joan. She had not noticed it before. Joan ordered coffee and the girl, exchanging a joke with the waiter, added a liqueur.

"But why should you give up your art?" persisted Joan. It was that was sticking in her mind. "I should have thought that, if only for the sake of the child, you would have gone on with it."

"Oh, I told myself all that," answered the girl. "Was going to devote my life to it. Did for nearly two years. Till I got sick of living like a nun: never getting a bit of excitement. You see, I've got the poison in me. Or, maybe, it had always been there."

"What's become of it?" asked Joan. "The child?"

"Mother's got it," answered the girl. "Seemed best for the poor little beggar. I'm supposed to be dead, and my husband gone abroad." She gave a short, dry laugh. "Mother brings him up to see me once a year. They've got quite fond of him."

"What are you doing now?" asked Joan, in a low tone.

"Oh, you needn't look so scared," laughed the girl, "I haven't come down to that." Her voice had changed. It had a note of shrillness. In some indescribable way she had grown coarse. "I'm a kept woman," she explained. "What else is any woman?"

She reached for her jacket; and the waiter sprang forward and helped her on with it, prolonging the business needlessly. She wished him "Good evening" in a tone of distant hauteur, and led the way to the door. Outside the street was dim and silent. Joan held out her hand.

"No hope of happy endings," she said with a forced laugh. "Couldn't marry him I suppose?"

"He has asked me," answered the girl with a swagger. "Not sure that it would suit me now. They're not so nice to you when they've got you fixed up. So long."

She turned abruptly and walked rapidly away. Joan moved instinctively in the opposite direction, and after a few minutes found herself in a broad well-lighted thoroughfare. A newsboy was shouting his wares.

"'Orrible murder of a woman. Shockin' details. Speshul," repeating it over and over again in a hoarse, expressionless monotone.

He was selling the papers like hot cakes; the purchasers too eager to even wait for their change. She wondered, with a little lump in her throat, how many would have stopped to buy had he been calling instead: "Discovery of new sonnet by Shakespeare. Extra special."

Through swinging doors, she caught glimpses of foul interiors, crowded with men and women released from their toil, taking their evening pleasure. From coloured posters outside the great theatres and music halls, vulgarity and lewdness leered at her, side by side with announcements that the house was full. From every roaring corner, scintillating lights flared forth the merits of this public benefactor's whisky, of this other celebrity's beer: it seemed the only message the people cared to hear. Even among the sirens of the pavement, she noticed that the quiet and merely pretty were hardly heeded. It was everywhere the painted and the overdressed that drew the roving eyes.

She remembered a pet dog that someone had given her when she was a girl, and how one afternoon she had walked with the tears streaming down her face because, in spite of her scoldings and her pleadings, it would keep stopping to lick up filth from the roadway. A kindly passer-by had laughed and told her not to mind.

"Why, that's a sign of breeding, that is, Missie," the man had explained. "It's the classy ones that are always the worst."

It had come to her afterwards craving with its soft brown, troubled eyes for forgiveness. But she had never been able to break it of the habit.

Must man for ever be chained by his appetites to the unclean: ever be driven back, dragged down again into the dirt by his own instincts: ever be rendered useless for all finer purposes by the baseness of his own desires?

The City of her Dreams! The mingled voices of the crowd shaped itself into a mocking laugh.

It seemed to her that it was she that they were laughing at, pointing her out to one another, jeering at her, reviling her, threatening her.

She hurried onward with bent head, trying to escape them. She felt so small, so helpless. Almost she cried out in her despair.

She must have walked mechanically. Looking up she found herself in her own street. And as she reached her doorway the tears came suddenly.

She heard a quick step behind her, and turning, she saw a man with a latch key in his hand. He passed her and opened the door; and then, facing round, stood aside for her to enter. He was a sturdy, thick-set man with a strong, massive face. It would have been ugly but for the deep, flashing eyes. There was tenderness and humour in them.

"We are next floor neighbours," he said. "My name's Phillips."

Joan thanked him. As he held the door open for her their hands accidentally touched. Joan wished him good-night and went up the stairs. There was no light in her room: only the faint reflection of the street lamp outside.

She could still see him: the boyish smile. And his voice that had sent her tears back again as if at the word of command.

She hoped he had not seen them. What a little fool she was.

A little laugh escaped her.

CHAPTER VI

One day Joan, lunching at the club, met Madge Singleton.

"I've had such a funny letter from Flossie," said Joan, "begging me almost with tears in her ink to come to her on Sunday evening to meet a 'gentleman friend' of hers, as she calls him, and give her my opinion of him. What on earth is she up to?"

"It's all right," answered Madge. "She doesn't really want our opinion of him—or rather she doesn't want our real opinion of him. She only wants us to confirm hers. She's engaged to him."

"Flossie engaged!" Joan seemed surprised.

"Yes," answered Madge. "It used to be a custom. Young men used to ask young women to marry them. And if they consented it was called 'being engaged.' Still prevails, so I am told, in certain classes."

"Thanks," said Joan. "I have heard of it."

"I thought perhaps you hadn't from your tone," explained Madge.

"But if she's already engaged to him, why risk criticism of him," argued Joan, ignoring Madge's flippancy. "It's too late."

"Oh, she's going to break it off unless we all assure her that we find him brainy," Madge explained with a laugh. "It seems her father wasn't brainy and her mother was. Or else it was the other way about: I'm not quite sure. But whichever it was, it led to ructions. Myself, if he's at all possible and seems to care for her, I intend to find him brilliant."

"And suppose she repeats her mother's experience," suggested Joan.

"There were the Norton-Browns," answered Madge. "Impossible to have found a more evenly matched pair. They both write novels—very good novels, too; and got jealous of one another; and threw press-notices at one another's head all breakfast-time; until they separated. Don't know of any recipe myself for being happy ever after marriage, except not expecting it."

"Or keeping out of it altogether," added Joan.

"Ever spent a day at the Home for Destitute Gentlewomen at East Sheen?" demanded Madge.

"Not yet," admitted Joan. "May have to, later on."

"It ought to be included in every woman's education," Madge continued. "It is reserved for spinsters of over forty-five. Susan Fleming wrote an article upon it for the *Teacher's Friend*; and spent an afternoon and evening there. A month later she married a grocer with five children. The only sound suggestion for avoiding trouble that I ever came across was in a burlesque of the *Blue Bird*. You remember the scene where the spirits of the children are waiting to go down to earth and be made into babies? Someone had stuck up a notice at the entrance to the gangway: 'Don't get born. It only means worry.'"

Flossie had her dwelling-place in a second floor bed-sitting-room of a lodging house in Queen's Square, Bloomsbury; but the drawing-room floor being for the moment vacant, Flossie had persuaded her landlady to let her give her party there; it seemed as if fate approved of the idea. The room was fairly full when Joan arrived. Flossie took her out on the landing, and closed the door behind them.

"You will be honest with me, won't you?" pleaded Flossie, "because it's so important, and I don't seem able to think for myself. As they say, no man can be his own solicitor, can he? Of course I like him, and all that—very much. And I really believe he loves me. We were children together when Mummy was alive; and then he had to go abroad; and has only just come back. Of course, I've got to think of him, too, as he says. But then, on the other hand, I don't want to make a mistake. That would be so terrible, for both of us; and of course I am clever; and there was poor Mummy and Daddy. I'll tell you all about them one day. It was so awfully sad. Get him into a corner and talk to him. You'll be able to judge in a moment, you're so wonderful. He's quiet on the outside, but I think there's depth in him. We must go in now."

She had talked so rapidly Joan felt as if her hat were being blown away. She had difficulty in recognizing Flossie. All the cocksure pertness had departed. She seemed just a kid.

Joan promised faithfully; and Flossie, standing on tiptoe, suddenly kissed her and then bustled her in.

Flossie's young man was standing near the fire talking, or rather listening, to a bird-like little woman in a short white frock and blue ribbons. A sombre lady just behind her, whom Joan from the distance took to be her nurse, turned out to be her secretary, whose duty it was to be always at hand, prepared to take down any happy idea that might occur to the bird-like little woman in the course of conversation. The bird-like little woman was Miss Rose Tolley, a popular novelist. She was explaining to Flossie's young man, whose name was Sam Halliday, the reason for her having written "Running Waters," her latest novel.

"It is daring," she admitted. "I must be prepared for opposition. But it had to be stated."

"I take myself as typical," she continued. "When I was twenty I could have loved you. You were the type of man I did love."

Mr. Halliday, who had been supporting the weight of his body upon his right leg, transferred the burden to his left.

"But now I'm thirty-five; and I couldn't love you if I tried." She shook her curls at him. "It isn't your fault. It is that I have changed. Suppose I'd married you?"

"Bit of bad luck for both of us," suggested Mr. Halliday.

"A tragedy," Miss Tolley corrected him. "There are millions of such tragedies being enacted around us at this moment. Sensitive women compelled to suffer the embraces of men that they have come to loathe. What's to be done?"

Flossie, who had been hovering impatient, broke in.

"Oh, don't you believe her," she advised Mr. Halliday. "She loves you still. She's only teasing you. This is Joan."

She introduced her. Miss Tolley bowed; and allowed herself to be drawn away by a lank-haired young man who had likewise been waiting for an opening. He represented the Uplift Film Association of Chicago, and was wishful to know if Miss Tolley would consent to altering the last chapter and so providing "Running Waters" with a happy ending. He pointed out the hopelessness of it in its present form, for film purposes.

The discussion was brief. "Then I'll send your agent the contract to-morrow," Joan overheard him say a minute later.

Mr. Sam Halliday she liked at once. He was a clean-shaven, square-jawed young man, with quiet eyes and a pleasant voice.

"Try and find me brainy," he whispered to her, as soon as Flossie was out of earshot. "Talk to me about China. I'm quite intelligent on China."

They both laughed, and then shot a guilty glance in Flossie's direction.

"Do the women really crush their feet?" asked Joan.

"Yes," he answered. "All those who have no use for them. About one per cent. of the population. To listen to Miss Tolley you would think that half the women wanted a new husband every ten years. It's always the one per cent. that get themselves talked about. The other ninety-nine are too busy."

"You are young for a philosopher," said Joan.

He laughed. "I told you I'd be all right if you started me on China," he said.

"Why are you marrying. Flossie?" Joan asked him. She thought his point of view would be interesting.

"Not sure I am yet," he answered with a grin. "It depends upon how I get through this evening." He glanced round the room. "Have I got to pass all this crowd, I wonder?" he added.

Joan's eyes followed. It was certainly an odd collection. Flossie, in her hunt for brains, had issued her invitations broadcast; and her fate had been that of the Charity concert. Not all the stars upon whom she had most depended had turned up. On the other hand not a single freak had failed her. At the moment, the centre of the room was occupied by a gentleman and two ladies in classical drapery. They were holding hands in an attitude suggestive of a bas-relief. Joan remembered them, having seen them on one or two occasions wandering in the King's Road, Chelsea; still maintaining, as far as the traffic would allow, the bas-relief suggestion; and generally surrounded by a crowd of children, ever hopeful that at the next corner they would stop and do something really interesting. They belonged to a society whose object was to lure the London public by the force of example towards the adoption of the early Greek fashions and the simpler Greek attitudes. A friend of Flossie's had thrown in her lot with them, but could never be induced to abandon her umbrella. They also, as Joan told herself, were reformers. Near to them was a picturesque gentleman with a beard down to his waist whose "stunt"—as Flossie would have termed it—was hygienic clothing; it seemed to contain an undue proportion of fresh air. There were ladies in coats and stand-up collars, and gentlemen with ringlets. More than one of the guests would have been better, though perhaps not happier, for a bath.

"I fancy that's the idea," said Joan. "What will you do if you fail? Go back to China?"

"Yes," he answered. "And take her with me. Poor little girl."

Joan rather resented his tone.

"We are not all alike," she remarked. "Some of us are quite sane."

He looked straight into her eyes. "You are," he said. "I have been reading your articles. They are splendid. I'm going to help."

"How can you?" she said. "I mean, how will you?"

"Shipping is my business," he said. "I'm going to help sailor men. See that they have somewhere decent to go to, and don't get robbed. And then there are the Lascars, poor devils. Nobody ever takes their part."

"How did you come across them?" she asked. "The articles, I mean. Did Flo give them to you?"

"No," he answered. "Just chance. Caught sight of your photo."

"Tell me," she said. "If it had been the photo of a woman with a bony throat and a beaky nose would you have read them?"

He thought a moment. "Guess not," he answered. "You're just as bad," he continued. "Isn't it the pale-faced young clergyman with the wavy hair and the beautiful voice that you all flock to hear? No getting away from nature. But it wasn't only that." He hesitated.

"I want to know," she said.

"You looked so young," he answered. "I had always had the idea that it was up to the old people to put the world to rights—that all I had to do was to look after myself. It came to me suddenly while you were talking to me—I mean while I was reading you: that if you were worrying yourself about it, I'd got to come in, too—that it would be mean of me not to. It wasn't like being preached to. It was somebody calling for help."

Instinctively she held out her hand and he grasped it.

Flossie came up at the same instant. She wanted to introduce him to Miss Lavery, who had just arrived.

"Hullo!" she said. "Are you two concluding a bargain?"

"Yes," said Joan. "We are founding the League of Youth. You've got to be in it. We are going to establish branches all round the world."

Flossie's young man was whisked away. Joan, who had seated herself in a small chair, was alone for a few minutes.

Miss Tolley had chanced upon a Human Document, with the help of which she was hopeful of starting a "Press Controversy" concerning the morality, or otherwise, of "Running Waters." The secretary stood just behind her, taking notes. They had drifted quite close. Joan could not help overhearing.

"It always seemed to me immoral, the marriage ceremony," the Human Document was explaining. She was a thin, sallow woman, with an untidy head and restless eyes that seemed to be always seeking something to look at and never finding it. "How can we pledge the future? To bind oneself to live with a man when perhaps we have ceased to care for him; it's hideous."

Miss Tolley murmured agreement.

"Our love was beautiful," continued the Human Document, eager, apparently, to relate her experience for the common good; "just because it was a free gift. We were not fettered to one another. At any moment either of us could have walked out of the house. The idea never occurred to us; not for years—five, to be exact."

The secretary, at a sign from Miss Tolley, made a memorandum of it.

"And then did your feelings towards him change suddenly?" questioned Miss Tolley.

"No," explained the Human Document, in the same quick, even tones; "so far as I was concerned, I was not conscious of any alteration in my own attitude. But he felt the need of more solitude—for his development. We parted quite good friends."

"Oh," said Miss Tolley. "And were there any children?"

"Only two," answered the Human Document, "both girls."

"What has become of them?" persisted Miss Tolley.

The Human Document looked offended. "You do not think I would have permitted any power on earth to separate them from me, do you?" she answered. "I said to him, 'They are mine, mine. Where I go, they go. Where I stay, they stay.' He saw the justice of my argument."

"And they are with you now?" concluded Miss Tolley.

"You must come and see them," the Human Document insisted. "Such dear, magnetic creatures. I superintend their entire education myself. We have a cottage in Surrey. It's rather a tight fit. You see, there are seven of us now. But the three girls can easily turn in together for a night, Abner will be delighted."

"Abner is your second?" suggested Miss Tolley.

"My third," the Human Document corrected her. "After Eustace, I married Ivanoff. I say 'married' because I regard it as the holiest form of marriage. He had to return to his own country. There was a political movement on foot. He felt it his duty to go. I want you particularly to meet the boy. He will interest you."

Miss Tolley appeared to be getting muddled. "Whose boy?" she demanded.

"Ivanoff's," explained the Human Document. "He was our only child."

Flossie appeared, towing a white-haired, distinguished-looking man, a Mr. Folk. She introduced him and immediately disappeared. Joan wished she had been left alone a little longer. She would like to have heard more. Especially was she curious concerning Abner, the lady's third. Would the higher moral law compel him, likewise, to leave the poor lady saddled with another couple of children? Or would she, on this occasion, get in—or rather, get off, first? Her own fancy was to back Abner. She did catch just one sentence before Miss Tolley, having obtained more food for reflection than perhaps she wanted, signalled to her secretary that the note-book might be closed.

"Woman's right to follow the dictates of her own heart, uncontrolled by any law," the Human Document was insisting: "That is one of the first things we must fight for."

Mr. Folk was a well-known artist. He lived in Paris. "You are wonderfully like your mother," he told Joan. "In appearance, I mean," he added. "I knew her when she was Miss Caxton. I acted with her in America."

Joan made a swift effort to hide her surprise. She had never heard of her mother having been upon the stage.

"I did not know that you had been an actor," she answered.

"I wasn't really," explained Mr. Folk. "I just walked and talked naturally. It made rather a sensation at the time. Your mother was a genius. You have never thought of going on the stage yourself?"

"No," said Joan. "I don't think I've got what you call the artistic temperament. I have never felt drawn towards anything of that sort."

"I wonder," he said. "You could hardly be your mother's daughter without it."

"Tell me," said Joan. "What was my mother like? I can only remember her as more or less of an invalid."

He did not reply to her question. "Master or Mistress Eminent Artist," he said; "intends to retire from his or her particular stage, whatever it may be. That paragraph ought always to be put among the obituary notices."

"What's your line?" he asked her. "I take it you have one by your being here. Besides, I am sure you have. I am an old fighter. I can tell the young soldier. What's your regiment?"

Joan laughed. "I'm a drummer boy," she answered. "I beat my drum each week in a Sunday newspaper, hoping the lads will follow."

"You feel you must beat that drum," he suggested. "Beat it louder and louder and louder till all the world shall hear it."

"Yes," Joan agreed, "I think that does describe me."

He nodded. "I thought you were an artist," he said. "Don't let them ever take your drum away from you. You'll go to pieces and get into mischief without it."

"I know an old actress," he continued. "She's the mother of four. They are all on the stage and they've all made their mark. The youngest was born in her dressing-room, just after the curtain had fallen. She was playing the Nurse to your mother's Juliet. She is still the best Nurse that I know. 'Jack's always worrying me to chuck it and devote myself to the children,' she confided to me one evening, while she was waiting for her cue. 'But, as I tell him, I'm more helpful to them being with them half the day alive than all the day dead.' That's an anecdote worth remembering, when your time comes. If God gives woman a drum he doesn't mean man to take it away from her. She hasn't got to be playing it for twenty-four hours a day. I'd like you to have seen your mother's Cordelia."

Flossie was tacking her way towards them. Joan acted on impulse. "I wish you'd give me your address," she said "where I could write to you. Or perhaps you would not mind my coming and seeing you one day. I would like you to tell me more about my mother."

He gave her his address in Paris where he was returning almost immediately.

"Do come," he said. "It will take me back thirty-three years. I proposed to your mother on La Grande Terrasse at St. Germain. We will walk there. I'm still a bachelor." He laughed, and, kissing her hand, allowed himself to be hauled away by Flossie, in exchange for Mrs. Phillips, for whom Miss Lavery had insisted on an invitation.

Joan had met Mrs. Phillips several times; and once, on the stairs, had stopped and spoken to her; but had never been introduced to her formally till now.

"We have been meaning to call on you so often," panted Mrs. Phillips. The room was crowded and the exertion of squeezing her way through had winded the poor lady. "We take so much interest in your articles. My husband—" she paused for a second, before venturing upon the word, and the aitch came out somewhat over-aspirated—"reads them most religiously. You must come and dine with us one evening."

Joan answered that she would be very pleased.

"I will find out when Robert is free and run up and let you know," she continued. "Of course, there are so many demands upon him, especially during this period of national crisis, that I spare him all the social duties that I can. But I shall insist on his making an exception in your case."

Joan murmured her sense of favour, but hoped she would not be allowed to interfere with more pressing calls upon Mr. Phillips's time.

"It will do him good," answered Mrs. Phillips; "getting away from them all for an hour or two. I don't see much of him myself."

She glanced round and lowered her voice. "They tell me," she said, "that you're a B.A."

"Yes," answered Joan. "One goes in for it more out of vanity, I'm afraid, than for any real purpose that it serves."

"I took one or two prizes myself," said Mrs. Phillips. "But, of course, one forgets things. I was wondering if you would mind if I ran up occasionally to ask you a question. Of course, as you know, my 'usband 'as 'ad so few advantages"—the lady's mind was concerned with more important matters, and the aspirates, on this occasion, got themselves neglected—"It is wonderful what he 'as done without them. But if, now and then, I could 'elp him—"

There was something about the poor, foolish painted face, as it looked up pleadingly, that gave it a momentary touch of beauty.

"Do," said Joan, speaking earnestly. "I shall be so very pleased if you will."

"Thank you," said the woman. Miss Lavery came up in a hurry to introduce her to Miss Tolley. "I am telling all my friends to read your articles," she added, resuming the gracious patroness, as she bowed her adieus.

Joan was alone again for a while. A handsome girl, with her hair cut short and parted at the side, was discussing diseases of the spine with a curly-headed young man in a velvet suit. The gentleman was describing some of the effects in detail. Joan felt there was danger of her being taken ill if she listened any longer; and seeing Madge's brother near the door, and unoccupied, she made her way across to him.

Niel Singleton, or Keeley, as he called himself upon the stage, was quite unlike his sister. He was short and plump, with a preternaturally solemn face, contradicted by small twinkling eyes. He motioned Joan to a chair and told her to keep quiet and not disturb the meeting.

"Is he brainy?" he whispered after a minute.

"I like him," said Joan.

"I didn't ask you if you liked him," he explained to her. "I asked you if he was brainy. I'm not too sure that you like brainy men."

"Yes, I do," said Joan. "I like you, sometimes."

"Now, none of that," he said severely. "It's no good your thinking of me. I'm wedded to my art. We are talking about Mr. Halliday."

"What does Madge think of him?" asked Joan.

"Madge has fallen in love with him, and her judgment is not to be relied upon," he said. "I suppose you couldn't answer a straight question, if you tried."

"Don't be so harsh with me," pleaded Joan meekly. "I'm trying to think. Yes," she continued, "decidedly he's got brains."

"Enough for the two of them?" demanded Mr. Singleton. "Because he will want them. Now think before you speak."

Joan considered. "Yes," she answered. "I should say he's just the man to manage her."

"Then it's settled," he said. "We must save her."

"Save her from what?" demanded Joan.

"From his saying to himself: 'This is Flossie's idea of a party. This is the sort of thing that, if I marry her, I am letting myself in for.' If he hasn't broken off the engagement already, we may be in time."

He led the way to the piano. "Tell Madge I want her," he whispered. He struck a few notes; and then in a voice that drowned every other sound in the room, struck up a comic song.

The effect was magical.

He followed it up with another. This one with a chorus, consisting chiefly of "Umpty Umpty Umpty Umpty Ay," which was vociferously encored.

By the time it was done with, Madge had discovered a girl who could sing "Three Little Pigs;" and a sad, pale-faced gentleman who told stories. At the end of one of them Madge's brother spoke to Joan in a tone more of sorrow than of anger.

"Hardly the sort of anecdote that a truly noble and high-minded young woman would have received with laughter," he commented.

"Did I laugh?" said Joan.

"Your having done so unconsciously only makes the matter worse," observed Mr. Singleton. "I had hoped it emanated from politeness, not enjoyment."

"Don't tease her," said Madge. "She's having an evening off."

Joan and the Singletons were the last to go. They promised to show Mr. Halliday a short cut to his hotel in Holborn.

"Have you thanked Miss Lessing for a pleasant evening?" asked Mr. Singleton, turning to Mr. Halliday.

He laughed and put his arm round her. "Poor little woman," he said. "You're looking so tired. It was jolly at the end." He kissed her.

He had passed through the swing doors; and they were standing on the pavement waiting for Joan's bus.

"Why did we all like him?" asked Joan. "Even Miss Lavery. There's nothing extraordinary about him."

"Oh yes there is," said Madge. "Love has lent him gilded armour. From his helmet waves her crest," she quoted. "Most men look fine in that costume. Pity they can't always wear it."

The conductor seemed impatient. Joan sprang upon the step and waved her hand.

CHAPTER VII

Joan was making herself a cup of tea when there came a tap at the door. It was Mrs. Phillips.

"I heard you come in," she said. "You're not busy, are you?"

"No," answered Joan. "I hope you're not. I'm generally in about this time; and it's always nice to gossip over a dish of tea."

"Why do you say 'dish' of tea!" asked Mrs. Phillips, as she lowered herself with evident satisfaction into the easy chair Joan placed for her.

"Oh, I don't know," laughed Joan. "Dr. Johnson always talked of a 'dish' of tea. Gives it a literary flavour."

"I've heard of him," said Mrs. Phillips. "He's worth reading, isn't he?"

"Well, he talked more amusingly than he wrote," explained Joan. "Get Boswell's Life of him. Or I'll lend you mine," she added, "if you'll be careful of it. You'll find all the passages marked that are best worth remembering. At least, I think so."

"Thanks," said Mrs. Phillips. "You see, as the wife of a public man, I get so little time for study."

"Is it settled yet?" asked Joan. "Are they going to make room for him in the Cabinet?

"I'm afraid so," answered Mrs. Phillips. "Oh, of course, I want him to," she corrected herself. "And he must, of course, if the King insists upon it. But I wish it hadn't all come with such a whirl. What shall I have to do, do you think?"

Joan was pouring out the tea. "Oh, nothing," she answered, "but just be agreeable to the right people. He'll tell you who they are. And take care of him."

"I wish I'd taken more interest in politics when I was young," said Mrs. Phillips. "Of course, when I was a girl, women weren't supposed to."

"Do you know, I shouldn't worry about them, if I were you," Joan advised her. "Let him forget them when he's with you. A man can have too much of a good thing," she laughed.

"I wonder if you're right," mused Mrs. Phillips. "He does often say that he'd just as soon I didn't talk about them."

Joan shot a glance from over her cup. The poor puzzled face was staring into the fire. Joan could almost hear him saying it.

"I'm sure I am," she said. "Make home-coming a change to him. As you said yourself the other evening. It's good for him to get away from it all, now and then."

"I must try," agreed Mrs. Phillips, looking up. "What sort of things ought I to talk to him about, do you think?"

Joan gave an inward sigh. Hadn't the poor lady any friends of her own. "Oh, almost anything," she answered vaguely: "so long as it's cheerful and non-political. What used you to talk about before he became a great man?"

There came a wistful look into the worried eyes. "Oh, it was all so different then," she said. "'E just liked to—you know. We didn't seem to 'ave to talk. 'E was a rare one to tease. I didn't know 'ow clever 'e was, then."

It seemed a difficult case to advise upon. "How long have you been married?" Joan asked.

"Fifteen years," she answered. "I was a bit older than 'im. But I've never looked my age, they tell me. Lord, what a boy 'e was! Swept you off your feet, like. 'E wasn't the only one. I'd got a way with me, I suppose. Anyhow, the men seemed to think so. There was always a few 'anging about. Like flies round a 'oney-pot, Mother used to say." She giggled. "But 'e wouldn't take No for an answer. And I didn't want to give it 'im, neither. I was gone on 'im, right enough. No use saying I wasn't."

"You must be glad you didn't say No," suggested Joan.

"Yes," she answered, "'E's got on. I always think of that little poem, 'Lord Burleigh,'" she continued; "whenever I get worrying about myself. Ever read it?"

"Yes," answered Joan. "He was a landscape painter, wasn't he?"

"That's the one," said Mrs. Phillips. "I little thought I was letting myself in for being the wife of a big pot when Bob Phillips came along in 'is miner's jacket."

"You'll soon get used to it," Joan told her. "The great thing is not to be afraid of one's fate, whatever it is; but just to do one's best." It was rather like talking to a child.

"You're the right sort to put 'eart into a body. I'm glad I came up," said Mrs. Phillips. "I get a bit down in the mouth sometimes when 'e goes off into one of 'is brown studies, and I don't seem to know what 'e's thinking about. But it don't last long. I was always one of the light-'earted ones."

They discussed life on two thousand a year; the problems it would present; and Mrs. Phillips became more cheerful. Joan laid herself out to be friendly. She hoped to establish an influence over Mrs. Phillips that should be for the poor la-dy's good; and, as she felt instinctively, for poor Phillips's also. It was not an unpleasing face. Underneath the paint, it was kind and womanly. Joan was sure he would like it better clean. A few months' attention to diet would make a de-cent figure of her and improve her wind. Joan watched her spreading the butter a quarter of an inch thick upon her toast and restrained with difficulty the impulse to take it away from her. And her clothes! Joan had seen guys carried through the streets on the fifth of November that were less obtrusive.

She remembered, as she was taking her leave, what she had come for: which was to invite Joan to dinner on the following Friday.

"It's just a homely affair," she explained. She had recovered her form and was now quite the lady again. "Two other guests beside yourself: a Mr. Airlie—I am sure you will like him. He's so dilletanty—and Mr. McKean. He's the young man upstairs. Have you met him?"

Joan hadn't: except once on the stairs when, to avoid having to pass her, he had gone down again and out into the street. From the doorstep she had caught sight of his disappearing coat-tails round the corner. Yielding to impishness, she had run after him, and his expression of blank horror when, glancing over his shoulder, he found her walking abstractedly three yards behind him, had gladdened all her evening.

Joan recounted the episode—so far as the doorstep.

"He tried to be shy with me," said Mrs. Phillips, "but I wouldn't let him. I chipped him out of it. If he's going to write plays, as I told him, he will have to get over his fear of a petticoat."

She offered her cheek, and Joan kissed it, somewhat gingerly.

"You won't mind Robert not wearing evening dress," she said. "He never will if he can help it. I shall just slip on a semi-toilette myself."

Joan had difficulty in deciding on her own frock. Her four evening dresses, as she walked round them, spread out upon the bed, all looked too imposing, for what Mrs. Phillips had warned her would be a "homely affair." She had one other, a greyish-fawn, with sleeves to the elbow, that she had had made expressly for public dinners and political At Homes. But that would be going to the opposite extreme, and might seem discourteous—to her hostess. Besides, "mousey" colours didn't really suit her. They gave her a curious sense of being affected. In the end she decided to risk a black crêpe-de-chine, square cut, with a girdle of gold embroidery. There couldn't be anything quieter than black, and the gold embroidery was of the simplest. She would wear it without any jewellery whatever: except just a star in her hair. The result, as she viewed the effect in the long glass, quite satisfied her. Perhaps the jewelled star did scintillate rather. It had belonged to her mother. But her hair was so full of shadows: it wanted something to relieve it. Also she approved the curved line of her bare arms. It was certainly very beautiful, a woman's arm. She took her gloves in her hand and went down.

Mr. Phillips was not yet in the room. Mrs. Phillips, in apple-green with an ostrich feather in her hair, greeted her effusively, and introduced her to her fellow guests. Mr. Airlie was a slight, elegant gentleman of uncertain age, with sandy hair and beard cut Vandyke fashion. He asked Joan's permission to continue his cigarette.

"You have chosen the better part," he informed her, on her granting it. "When I'm not smoking, I'm talking."

Mr. McKean shook her hand vigorously without looking at her.

"And this is Hilda," concluded Mrs. Phillips. "She ought to be in bed if she hadn't a naughty Daddy who spoils her."

A lank, black-haired girl, with a pair of burning eyes looking out of a face that, but for the thin line of the lips, would have been absolutely colourless, rose suddenly from behind a bowl of artificial flowers. Joan could not suppress a slight start; she had not noticed her on entering. The girl came slowly forward, and Joan felt as if the uncanny eyes were eating her up. She made an effort and held out her hand with a smile, and the girl's long thin fingers closed on it in a pressure that hurt. She did not speak.

"She only came back yesterday for the half-term," explained Mrs. Phillips. "There's no keeping her away from her books. 'Twas her own wish to be sent to boarding-school. How would you like to go to Girton and be a B.A. like Miss Allway?" she asked, turning to the child.

Phillips's entrance saved the need of a reply. To the evident surprise of his wife he was in evening clothes.

"Hulloa. You've got 'em on," she said.

He laughed. "I shall have to get used to them sooner or later," he said.

Joan felt relieved—she hardly knew why—that he bore the test. It was a well-built, athletic frame, and he had gone to a good tailor. He looked taller in them; and the strong, clean-shaven face less rugged.

Joan sat next to him at the round dinner-table with the child the other side of him. She noticed that he ate as far as possible with his right hand—his hands were large, but smooth and well shaped—his left remaining under the cloth, beneath which the child's right hand, when free, would likewise disappear. For a while the conversation consisted chiefly of anecdotes by Mr. Airlie. There were few public men and women about whom he did not know something to their disadvantage. Joan, listening, found herself repeating the experience of a night or two previous, when, during a performance of *Hamlet*, Niel Singleton, who was playing the grave-digger, had taken her behind the scenes. Hamlet, the King of Denmark and the Ghost were sharing a bottle of champagne in the Ghost's dressing-room: it happened to be the Ghost's birthday. On her return to the front of the house, her interest in the play was gone. It was absurd that it should be so; but the fact remained.

Mr. Airlie had lunched the day before with a leonine old gentleman who every Sunday morning thundered forth Social Democracy to enthusiastic multitudes on Tower Hill. Joan had once listened to him and had almost been converted: he was so tremendously in earnest. She now learnt that he lived in Curzon Street, Mayfair, and filled, in private life, the perfectly legitimate calling of a company promoter in partnership with a Dutch Jew. His latest prospectus dwelt upon the profits to be derived from an amalgamation of the leading tanning industries: by means of which the price of leather could be enormously increased.

It was utterly illogical; but her interest in the principles of Social Democracy was gone.

A very little while ago, Mr. Airlie, in his capacity of second cousin to one of the ladies concerned, a charming girl but impulsive, had been called upon to attend a family council of a painful nature. The gentleman's name took Joan's breath away: it was the name of one of her heroes, an eminent writer: one might almost say prophet. She had hitherto read his books with grateful reverence. They pictured for her the world made perfect; and explained to her just precisely how it was to be accomplished. But, as far as his own particular corner of it was concerned, he seemed to have made a sad mess of it. Human nature of quite an old-fashioned pattern had crept in and spoilt all his own theories.

Of course it was unreasonable. The sign-post may remain embedded in weeds: it notwithstanding points the way to the fair city. She told herself this, but it left her still short-tempered. She didn't care which way it pointed. She didn't believe there was any fair city.

There was a famous preacher. He lived the simple life in a small house in Battersea, and consecrated all his energies to the service of the poor. Almost, by his unselfish zeal, he had persuaded Joan of the usefulness of the church. Mr. Airlie frequently visited him. They interested one another. What struck Mr. Airlie most was the self-sacrificing devotion with which the reverend gentleman's wife and family surrounded him. It was beautiful to see. The calls upon his moderate purse, necessitated by his wide-spread and much paragraphed activities, left but a narrow margin for domestic expenses: with the result that often the only fire in the house blazed brightly in the study where Mr. Airlie and the reverend gentleman sat talking: while mother and children warmed themselves with sense of duty in the cheerless kitchen. And often, as Mr. Airlie, who was of an inquiring turn of mind, had convinced himself, the only evening meal that resources would permit was the satisfying supper for one brought by the youngest daughter to her father where he sat alone in the small dining-room.

Mr. Airlie, picking daintily at his food, continued his stories: of philanthropists who paid starvation wages: of feminists who were a holy terror to their women folk: of socialists who travelled first-class and spent their winters in Egypt or Monaco: of stern critics of public morals who preferred the society of youthful affinities to the continued company of elderly wives: of poets who wrote divinely about babies' feet and whose children hated them.

"Do you think it's all true?" Joan whispered to her host.

He shrugged his shoulders. "No reason why it shouldn't be," he said. "I've generally found him right."

"I've never been able myself," he continued, "to understand the Lord's enthusiasm for David. I suppose it was the Psalms that did it."

Joan was about to offer comment, but was struck dumb with astonishment on hearing McKean's voice: it seemed he could talk. He was telling of an old Scotch peasant farmer. A mean, cantankerous old cuss whose curious pride it was that he had never given anything away. Not a crust, nor a sixpence, nor a rag; and never would. Many had been the attempts to make him break his boast: some for the joke of the thing and some for the need; but none had ever succeeded. It was his one claim to distinction and he guarded it.

One evening it struck him that the milk-pail, standing just inside the window, had been tampered with. Next day he marked with a scratch the inside of the pan and, returning later, found the level of the milk had sunk half an inch. So he hid himself and waited; and at twilight the next day the window was stealthily pushed open, and two small, terror-haunted eyes peered round the room. They satisfied themselves that no one was about and a tiny hand clutching a cracked jug was thrust swiftly in and dipped into the pan; and the window softly closed.

He knew the thief, the grandchild of an old bedridden dame who lived some miles away on the edge of the moor. The old man stood long, watching the small cloaked figure till it was lost in the darkness. It was not till he lay upon his dying bed that he confessed it. But each evening, from that day, he would steal into the room and see to it himself that the window was left ajar.

After the coffee, Mrs. Phillips proposed their adjourning to the "drawing-room" the other side of the folding doors, which had been left open. Phillips asked her to leave Joan and himself where they were. He wanted to talk to her. He promised not to bore her for more than ten minutes.

The others rose and moved away. Hilda came and stood before Joan with her hands behind her.

"I am going to bed now," she said. "I wanted to see you from what Papa told me. May I kiss you?"

It was spoken so gravely that Joan did not ask her, as in lighter mood she might have done, what it was that Phillips had said. She raised her face quietly, and the child bent forward and kissed her, and went out without looking back at either of them, leaving Joan more serious than there seemed any reason for. Phillips filled his pipe and lighted it.

"I wish I had your pen," he said, suddenly breaking the silence. "I'm all right at talking; but I want to get at the others: the men and women who never come, thinking it has nothing to do with them. I'm shy and awkward when I try to write. There seems a barrier in front of me. You break through it. One hears your voice. Tell me," he said, "are you getting your way? Do they answer you?"

"Yes," said Joan. "Not any great number of them, not yet. But enough to show that I really am interesting them. It grows every week."

"Tell them that," he said. "Let them hear each other. It's the same at a meeting. You wait ten minutes sometimes before one man will summon up courage to put a question; but once one or two have ventured they spring up all round you. I was wondering," he added, "if you would help me; let me use you, now and again."

"It is what I should love," she answered. "Tell me what to do." She was not conscious of the low, vibrating tone in which she spoke.

"I want to talk to them," he said, "about their stomachs. I want them to see the need of concentrating upon the food problem: insisting that it shall be solved. The other things can follow."

"There was an old Egyptian chap," he said, "a governor of one of their provinces, thousands of years before the Pharaohs were ever heard of. They dug up his tomb a little while ago. It bore this inscription: 'In my time no man went hungry.' I'd rather have that carved upon my gravestone than the boastings of all the robbers and the butchers of history. Think what it must have meant in that land of drought and famine: only a narrow strip of river bank where a grain of corn would grow; and that only when old Nile was kind. If not, your nearest supplies five hundred miles away across the desert, your only means of transport the slow-moving camel. Your convoy must be guarded against attack, provided with provisions and water for a two months' journey. Yet he never failed his people. Fat year and lean year: 'In my time no man went hungry.' And here, to-day, with our steamships and our railways, with the granaries of the world filled to overflowing, one third of our population lives on the border line of want. In India they die by the roadside. What's the good of it all: your science and your art and your religion! How can you help men's souls if their bodies are starving? A hungry man's a hungry beast.

"I spent a week at Grimsby, some years ago, organizing a fisherman's union. They used to throw the fish back into the sea, tons upon tons of it, that men had risked their lives to catch, that would have fed half London's poor. There was a 'glut' of it, they said. The 'market' didn't want it. Funny, isn't it, a 'glut' of food: and the kiddies can't learn their lessons for want of it. I was talking with a farmer down in Kent. The plums were rotting on his trees. There were too many of them: that was the trouble. The railway carriage alone would cost him more than he could get for them. They were too cheap. So nobody could have them. It's the muddle of the thing that makes me mad—the ghastly muddle-headed way the chief business of the world is managed. There's enough food could be grown in this country to feed all the people and then of the fragments each man might gather his ten basketsful. There's no miracle needed. I went into the matter once with Dalroy of the Board of Agriculture. He's the best man they've got, if they'd only listen to him. It's never been organized: that's all. It isn't the fault of the individual. It ought not to be left to the individual. The man who makes a corner in wheat in Chicago and condemns millions to privation—likely enough, he's a decent sort of fellow in himself: a kind husband and father—would be upset for the day if he saw a child crying for bread. My dog's a decent enough little chap, as dogs go, but I don't let him run my larder.

"It could be done with a little good will all round," he continued, "and nine men out of every ten would be the better off. But they won't even let you explain. Their newspapers shout you down. It's such a damned fine world for the few: never mind the many. My father was a farm labourer: and all his life he never earned more than thirteen and sixpence a week. I left when I was twelve and went into the mines. There were six of us children; and my mother brought us up healthy and decent. She fed us and clothed us and sent us to school; and when she died we buried her with the money she had put by for the purpose; and never a penny of charity had ever soiled her hands. I can see them now. Talk of your Chancellors of the Exchequer and their problems! She worked herself to death, of course. Well, that's all right. One doesn't mind that where one loves. If they would only let you. She had no opposition to contend with—no thwarting and hampering at every turn—the very people you are working for hounded on against you. The difficulty of a man like myself, who wants to do something, who could do something, is that for the best part of his life he is fighting to be allowed to do it. By the time I've lived down their lies and got my chance, my energy will be gone."

He knocked the ashes from his pipe and relit it.

"I've no quarrel with the rich," he said. "I don't care how many rich men there are, so long as there are no poor. Who does? I was riding on a bus the other day, and there was a man beside me with a bandaged head. He'd been hurt in that railway smash at Morpeth. He hadn't claimed damages from the railway company and wasn't going to. 'Oh, it's only a few scratches,' he said. 'They'll be hit hard enough as it is.' If he'd been a poor devil on eighteen shillings a week it would have been different. He was an engineer earning good wages; so he wasn't feeling sore and bitter against half the world. Suppose you tried to run an army with your men half starved while your officers had more than they could eat. It's been tried and what's been the result? See that your soldiers have their proper rations, and the General can sit down to his six-course dinner, if he will. They are not begrudging it to him.

"A nation works on its stomach. Underfeed your rank and file, and what sort of a fight are you going to put up against your rivals. I want to see England going ahead. I want to see her workers properly fed. I want to see the corn upon her unused acres, the cattle grazing on her wasted pastures. I object to the food being thrown into the sea—left to rot upon the ground while men are hungry—side-tracked in Chicago, while the children grow up stunted. I want the commissariat properly organized."

He had been staring through her rather than at her, so it had seemed to Joan. Suddenly their eyes met, and he broke into a smile.

"I'm so awfully sorry," he said. "I've been talking to you as if you were a public meeting. I'm afraid I'm more used to them than I am to women. Please forgive me."

The whole man had changed. The eyes had a timid pleading in them.

Joan laughed. "I've been feeling as if I were the King of Bavaria," she said.

"How did he feel?" he asked her, leaning forward.

"He had his own private theatre," Joan explained, "where Wagner gave his operas. And the King was the sole audience."

"I should have hated that," he said, "if I had been Wagner."

He looked at her, and a flush passed over his boyish face.

"All right," he said, "if it had been a queen."

Joan found herself tracing patterns with her spoon upon the tablecloth. "But you have won now," she said, still absorbed apparently with her drawing, "you are going to get your chance."

He gave a short laugh. "A trick," he said, "to weaken me. They think to shave my locks; show me to the people bound by their red tape. To put it another way, a rat among the terriers."

Joan laughed. "You don't somehow suggest the rat," she said: "rather another sort of beast."

"What do you advise me?" he asked. "I haven't decided yet."

They were speaking in whispered tones. Through the open doors they could see into the other room. Mrs. Phillips, under Airlie's instructions, was venturing upon a cigarette.

"To accept," she answered. "They won't influence you—the terriers, as you call them. You are too strong. It is you who will sway them. It isn't as if you were a mere agitator. Take this opportunity of showing them that you can build, plan, organize; that you were meant to be a ruler. You can't succeed without them, as things are. You've got to win them over. Prove to them that they can trust you."

He sat for a minute tattooing with his fingers on the table, before speaking.

"It's the frills and flummery part of it that frightens me," he said. "You wouldn't think that sensitiveness was my weak point. But it is. I've stood up to a Birmingham mob that was waiting to lynch me and enjoyed the experience; but I'd run ten miles rather than face a drawing-room of well-dressed people with their masked faces and ironic courtesies. It leaves me for days feeling like a lobster that has lost its shell."

"I wouldn't say it, if I didn't mean it," answered Joan; "but you haven't got to trouble yourself about that . . . You're quite passable." She smiled. It seemed to her that most women would find him more than passable.

He shook his head. "With you," he said. "There's something about you that makes one ashamed of worrying about the little things. But the others: the sneering women and the men who wink over their shoulder while they talk to you, I shall never be able to get away from them, and, of course, wherever I go—"

He stopped abruptly with a sudden tightening of the lips. Joan followed his eyes. Mrs. Phillips had swallowed the smoke and was giggling and spluttering by turns. The yellow ostrich feather had worked itself loose and was rocking to and fro as if in a fit of laughter of its own.

He pushed back his chair and rose. "Shall we join the others?" he said.

He moved so that he was between her and the other room, his back to the open doors. "You think I ought to?" he said.

"Yes," she answered firmly, as if she were giving a command. But he read pity also in her eyes.

"Well, have you two settled the affairs of the kingdom? Is it all decided?" asked Airlie.

"Yes," he answered, laughing. "We are going to say to the people, 'Eat, drink and be wise.'"

He rearranged his wife's feather and smoothed her tumbled hair. She looked up at him and smiled.

Joan set herself to make McKean talk, and after a time succeeded. They had a mutual friend, a raw-boned youth she had met at Cambridge. He was engaged to

McKean's sister. His eyes lighted up when he spoke of his sister Jenny. The Little Mother, he called her.

"She's the most beautiful body in all the world," he said. "Though merely seeing her you mightn't know it."

He saw her "home"; and went on up the stairs to his own floor.

Joan stood for a while in front of the glass before undressing; but felt less satisfied with herself. She replaced the star in its case, and took off the regal-looking dress with the golden girdle and laid it carelessly aside. She seemed to be growing smaller.

In her white night dress, with her hair in two long plaits, she looked at herself once more. She seemed to be no one of any importance at all: just a long little girl going to bed. With no one to kiss her good night.

She blew out the candle and climbed into the big bed, feeling very lonesome as she used to when a child. It had not troubled her until to-night. Suddenly she sat up again. She needn't be back in London before Tuesday evening, and to-day was only Friday. She would run down home and burst in upon her father. He would be so pleased to see her.

She would make him put his arms around her.

CHAPTER VIII

She reached home in the evening. She thought to find her father in his study. But they told her that, now, he usually sat alone in the great drawing-room. She opened the door softly. The room was dark save for a flicker of firelight; she could see nothing. Nor was there any sound.

"Dad," she cried, "are you here?"

He rose slowly from a high-backed chair beside the fire.

"It is you," he said. He seemed a little dazed.

She ran to him and, seizing his listless arms, put them round her.

"Give me a hug, Dad," she commanded. "A real hug."

He held her to him for what seemed a long while. There was strength in his arms, in spite of the bowed shoulders and white hair.

"I was afraid you had forgotten how to do it," she laughed, when at last he released her. "Do you know, you haven't hugged me, Dad, since I was five years old. That's nineteen years ago. You do love me, don't you?"

"Yes," he answered. "I have always loved you."

She would not let him light the gas. "I have dined—in the train," she explained. "Let us talk by the firelight."

She forced him gently back into his chair, and seated herself upon the floor between his knees. "What were you thinking of when I came in?" she asked. "You weren't asleep, were you?"

"No," he answered. "Not that sort of sleep." She could not see his face. But she guessed his meaning.

"Am I very like her?" she asked.

"Yes," he answered. "Marvellously like her as she used to be: except for just one thing. Perhaps that will come to you later. I thought, for the moment, as you stood there by the door . . . " He did not finish the sentence.

"Tell me about her," she said. "I never knew she had been an actress."

He did not ask her how she had learnt it. "She gave it up when we were married," he said. "The people she would have to live among would have looked askance at her if they had known. There seemed no reason why they should."

"How did it all happen?" she persisted. "Was it very beautiful, in the beginning?" She wished she had not added that last. The words had slipped from her before she knew.

"Very beautiful," he answered, "in the beginning."

"It was my fault," he went on, "that it was not beautiful all through. I ought to have let her take up her work again, as she wished to, when she found what giving it up meant to her. The world was narrower then than it is now; and I listened to the world. I thought it another voice."

"It's difficult to tell, isn't it?" she said. "I wonder how one can?"

He did not answer; and they sat for a time in silence.

"Did you ever see her act?" asked Joan.

"Every evening for about six months," he answered. A little flame shot up and showed a smile upon his face.

"I owe to her all the charity and tenderness I know. She taught it to me in those months. I might have learned more if I had let her go on teaching. It was the only way she knew."

Joan watched her as gradually she shaped herself out of the shadows: the poor, thin, fretful lady of the ever restless hands, with her bursts of jealous passion, her long moods of sullen indifference: all her music turned to waste.

"How did she come to fall in love with you?" asked Joan. "I don't mean to be uncomplimentary, Dad." She laughed, taking his hand in hers and stroking it. "You must have been ridiculously handsome, when you were young. And you must always have been strong and brave and clever. I can see such a lot of women falling in love with you. But not the artistic woman."

"It wasn't so incongruous at the time," he answered. "My father had sent me out to America to superintend a contract. It was the first time I had ever been away from home, though I was nearly thirty; and all my pent-up youth rushed out of me at once. It was a harum-scarum fellow, mad with the joy of life, that made love to her; not the man who went out, nor the man who came back. It was at San Francisco that I met her. She was touring the Western States; and I let everything go to the wind and followed her. It seemed to me that Heaven had opened up to me. I fought a duel in Colorado with a man who had insulted her. The law didn't run there in those days; and three of his hired gunmen, as they called them, held us up that night in the train and gave her the alternative of going back with them and kissing him or seeing me dead at her feet. I didn't give her time to answer, nor for them to finish. It seemed a fine death anyhow, that. And I'd have faced Hell itself for the chance of fighting for her. Though she told me afterwards that if I'd died she'd have gone back with them, and killed him."

Joan did not speak for a time. She could see him grave—a little pompous, in his Sunday black, his footsteps creaking down the stone-flagged aisle, the silver-edged collecting bag held stiffly in his hand.

"Couldn't you have saved a bit, Daddy?" she asked, "of all that wealth of youth—just enough to live on?"

"I might," he answered, "if I had known the value of it. I found a cable waiting for me in New York. My father had been dead a month; and I had to return immediately."

"And so you married her and took her drum away from her," said Joan. "Oh, the thing God gives to some of us," she explained, "to make a little noise with, and set the people marching."

The little flame died out. She could feel his body trembling.

"But you still loved her, didn't you, Dad?" she asked. "I was very little at the time, but I can just remember. You seemed so happy together. Till her illness came."

"It was more than love," he answered. "It was idolatry. God punished me for it. He was a hard God, my God."

She raised herself, putting her hands upon his shoulders so that her face was very close to his. "What has become of Him, Dad?" she said. She spoke in a cold voice, as one does of a false friend.

"I do not know," he answered her. "I don't seem to care."

"He must be somewhere," she said: "the living God of love and hope: the God that Christ believed in."

"They were His last words, too," he answered: "'My God, my God, why hast Thou forsaken me?'"

"No, not His last," said Joan: "'Lo, I am with you always, even unto the end of the world.' Love was Christ's God. He will help us to find Him."

Their arms were about one another. Joan felt that a new need had been born in her: the need of loving and of being loved. It was good to lay her head upon his breast and know that he was glad of her coming.

He asked her questions about herself. But she could see that he was tired; so she told him it was too important a matter to start upon so late. She would talk about herself to-morrow. It would be Sunday.

"Do you still go to the chapel?" she asked him a little hesitatingly.

"Yes," he answered. "One lives by habit."

"It is the only Temple I know," he continued after a moment. "Perhaps God, one day, will find me there."

He rose and lit the gas, and a letter on the mantelpiece caught his eye.

"Have you heard from Arthur?" he asked, suddenly turning to her.

"No. Not since about a month," she answered. "Why?"

"He will be pleased to find you here, waiting for him," he said with a smile, handing her the letter. "He will be here some time to-morrow."

Arthur Allway was her cousin, the son of a Nonconformist Minister. Her father had taken him into the works and for the last three years he had been in Egypt, helping in the laying of a tramway line. He was in love with her: at least so they all told her; and his letters were certainly somewhat committal. Joan replied to them—when she did not forget to do so—in a studiously sisterly vein; and always reproved him for unnecessary extravagance whenever he sent her a present. The letter announced his arrival at Southampton. He would stop at Birmingham, where his parents lived, for a couple of days, and be in Liverpool on Sunday evening, so as to be able to get straight to business on Monday morning. Joan handed back the letter. It contained nothing else.

"It only came an hour or two ago," her father explained. "If he wrote to you by the same post, you may have left before it arrived."

"So long as he doesn't think that I came down specially to see him, I don't mind," said Joan.

They both laughed. "He's a good lad," said her father.

They kissed good night, and Joan went up to her own room. She found it just as she had left it. A bunch of roses stood upon the dressing-table. Her father would never let anyone cut his roses but himself.

Young Allway arrived just as Joan and her father had sat down to supper. A place had been laid for him. He flushed with pleasure at seeing her; but was not surprised.

"I called at your diggings," he said. "I had to go through London. They told me you had started. It is good of you."

"No, it isn't," said Joan. "I came down to see Dad. I didn't know you were back." She spoke with some asperity; and his face fell.

"How are you?" she added, holding out her hand. "You've grown quite good-looking. I like your moustache." And he flushed again with pleasure.

He had a sweet, almost girlish face, with delicate skin that the Egyptian sun had deepened into ruddiness; with soft, dreamy eyes and golden hair. He looked lithe and agile rather than strong. He was shy at first, but once set going, talked freely, and was interesting.

His work had taken him into the Desert, far from the beaten tracks. He described the life of the people, very little different from what it must have been in Noah's time. For months he had been the only white man there, and had lived among them. What had struck him was how little he had missed all the paraphernalia of civilization, once he had got over the first shock. He had learnt their sports and games; wrestled and swum and hunted with them. Provided one was a little hungry and tired with toil, a stew of goat's flesh with sweet cakes and fruits, washed down with wine out of a sheep's skin, made a feast; and after, there was music and singing and dancing, or the travelling story-teller would gather round him his rapt audience. Paris had only robbed women of their grace and dignity. He preferred the young girls in their costume of the fourteenth dynasty. Progress, he thought, had tended only to complicate life and render it less enjoyable. All the essentials of happiness—love, courtship, marriage, the home, children, friendship, social intercourse, and play, were independent of it; had always been there for the asking.

Joan thought his mistake lay in regarding man's happiness as more important to him than his self-development. It was not what we got out of civilization but what we put into it that was our gain. Its luxuries and ostentations were, in themselves, perhaps bad for us. But the pursuit of them was good. It called forth thought and effort, sharpened our wits, strengthened our brains. Primitive man, content with his necessities, would never have produced genius. Art, literature, science would have been stillborn.

He hesitated before replying, glancing at her furtively while crumbling his bread. When he did, it was in the tone that one of her younger disciples might have ventured into a discussion with Hypatia. But he stuck to his guns.

How did she account for David and Solomon, Moses and the Prophets? They had sprung from a shepherd race. Yet surely there was genius, literature. Greece owed nothing to progress. She had preceded it. Her thinkers, her poets, her scientists had draws their inspiration from nature, not civilization. Her art had sprung full grown out of the soil. We had never surpassed it.

"But the Greek ideal could not have been the right one, or Greece would not so utterly have disappeared," suggested Mr. Allway. "Unless you reject the law of the survival of the fittest."

He had no qualms about arguing with his uncle.

"So did Archimedes disappear," he answered with a smile. "The nameless Roman soldier remained. That was hardly the survival of the fittest."

He thought it the tragedy of the world that Rome had conquered Greece, imposing her lower ideals upon the race. Rome should have been the servant of Greece: the hands directed by the brain. She would have made roads and harbours, conducted the traffic, reared the market place. She knew of the steam engine, employed it for pumping water in the age of the Antonines. Sooner or later, she would have placed it on rails, and in ships. Rome should have been the policeman, keeping the world in order, making it a fit habitation. Her mistake was in regarding these things as an end in themselves, dreaming of nothing beyond. From her we had inherited the fallacy that man was made for the world, not the world for man. Rome organized only for man's body. Greece would have legislated for his soul.

They went into the drawing-room. Her father asked her to sing and Arthur opened the piano for her and lit the candles. She chose some ballads and a song of Herrick's, playing her own accompaniment while Arthur turned the leaves. She had a good voice, a low contralto. The room was high and dimly lighted. It looked larger than it really was. Her father sat in his usual chair beside the fire and listened with half-closed eyes. Glancing now and then across at him, she was reminded of Orchardson's picture. She was feeling sentimental, a novel sensation to her. She rather enjoyed it.

She finished with one of Burns's lyrics; and then told Arthur that it was now his turn, and that she would play for him. He shook his head, pleading that he was out of practice.

"I wish it," she said, speaking low. And it pleased her that he made no answer but to ask her what he should sing. He had a light tenor voice. It was wobbly at first, but improved as he went on. They ended with a duet.

The next morning she went into town with them. She never seemed to have any time in London, and wanted to do some shopping. They joined her again for lunch and afterwards, at her father's suggestion, she and Arthur went for a walk. They took the tram out of the city and struck into the country. The leaves still lingered brown and red upon the trees. He carried her cloak and opened gates for her and held back brambles while she passed. She had always been indifferent to these small gallantries; but to-day she welcomed them. She wished to feel her power to attract and command. They avoided all subjects on which they could differ, even in words. They talked of people and places they had known together. They remembered their common love of animals and told of the comedies and tragedies that had befallen their pets. Joan's regret was that she had not now even a dog, thinking it cruel to keep them in London. She hated the women she met, dragging the poor little depressed beasts about at the end of a string: savage with them, if they dared to stop for a moment to exchange a passing wag of the tail with some other little lonely sufferer. It was as bad as keeping a lark in a cage. She had tried a cat: but so often she did not get home till late and that was just the time when the cat wanted to be out; so that they seldom met. He suggested a parrot. His experience of them was that they had no regular hours and would willingly sit up all night, if encouraged, and talk all the time. Joan's objection to running a parrot was that it stamped you as an old maid; and she wasn't that, at least, not yet. She wondered if she could make an owl really happy. Minerva had an owl.

He told her how one spring, walking across a common, after a fire, he had found a mother thrush burnt to death upon her nest, her charred wings spread out in a vain endeavour to protect her brood. He had buried her there among the blackened thorn and furze, and placed a little cross of stones above her.

"I hope nobody saw me," he said with a laugh. "But I couldn't bear to leave her there, unhonoured."

"It's one of the things that make me less certain than I want to be of a future existence," said Joan: "the thought that animals can have no part in it; that all their courage and love and faithfulness dies with them and is wasted."

"Are you sure it is?" he answered. "It would be so unreasonable."

They had tea at an old-fashioned inn beside a stream. It was a favourite resort in summer time, but now they had it to themselves. The wind had played pranks with her hair and he found a mirror and knelt before her, holding it.

She stood erect, looking down at him while seeming to be absorbed in the rearrangement of her hair, feeling a little ashamed of herself. She was "encouraging" him. There was no other word for it. She seemed to have developed a sudden penchant for this sort of thing. It would end in his proposing to her; and then she would have to tell him that she cared for him only in a cousinly sort of way—whatever that might mean—and that she could never marry him. She dared not ask herself why. She must manoeuvre to put it off as long as possible; and meanwhile some opening might occur to enlighten him. She would talk to him about her work; and explain to him how she had determined to devote her life to it to the exclusion of all other distractions. If, then, he chose to go on loving her—or if he couldn't help it—that would not be her fault. After all, it did him no harm. She could always be gracious and kind to him. It was not as if she had tricked him. He had always loved her. Kneeling before her, serving her: it was evident it made him supremely happy. It would be cruel of her to end it.

The landlady entered unexpectedly with the tea; but he did not rise till Joan turned away, nor did he seem disconcerted. Neither did the landlady. She was an elderly, quiet-eyed woman, and had served more than one generation of young people with their teas.

They returned home by train. Joan insisted on travelling third class, and selected a compartment containing a stout woman and two children. Arthur had to be at the works. An important contract had got behindhand and they were working overtime. She and her father dined alone. He made her fulfil her promise to talk about herself, and she told him all she thought would interest him. She passed lightly over her acquaintanceship with Phillips. He would regard it as highly undesirable, she told herself, and it would trouble him. He was reading her articles in the *Sunday Post*, as also her Letters from Clorinda: and of the two preferred the latter as being less subversive of law and order. Also he did not like seeing her photograph each week, displayed across two columns with her name beneath in one inch type. He supposed he was old-fashioned. She was getting rather tired of it herself.

"The Editor insisted upon it," she explained. "It was worth it for the opportunity it gives me. I preach every Sunday to a congregation of over a million souls. It's better than being a Bishop. Besides," she added, "the men are just as bad. You see their silly faces everywhere."

"That's like you women," he answered with a smile. "You pretend to be superior; and then you copy us."

She laughed. But the next moment she was serious.

"No, we don't," she said, "not those of us who think. We know we shall never oust man from his place. He will always be the greater. We want to help him; that's all."

"But wasn't that the Lord's idea," he said; "when He gave Eve to Adam to be his helpmeet?"

"Yes, that was all right," she answered. "He fashioned Eve for Adam and saw that Adam got her. The ideal marriage might have been the ideal solution. If the Lord had intended that, he should have kept the match-making in His own hands: not have left it to man. Somewhere in Athens there must have been the helpmeet God had made for Socrates. When they met, it was Xanthippe that she kissed."

A servant brought the coffee and went out again. Her father lighted a cigar and handed her the cigarettes.

"Will it shock you, Dad?" she asked.

"Rather late in the day for you to worry yourself about that, isn't it?" he answered with a smile.

He struck a match and held it for her. Joan sat with her elbows on the table and smoked in silence. She was thinking.

Why had he never "brought her up," never exacted obedience from her, never even tried to influence her? It could not have been mere weakness. She stole a sidelong glance at the tired, lined face with its steel-blue eyes. She had never seen them other than calm, but they must have been able to flash. Why had he always been so just and kind and patient with her? Why had he never scolded her and bullied her and teased her? Why had he let her go away, leaving him lonely in his empty, voiceless house? Why had he never made any claim upon her? The idea came to her as an inspiration. At least, it would ease her conscience. "Why don't you let Arthur live here," she said, "instead of going back to his lodgings? It would be company for you."

He did not answer for some time. She had begun to wonder if he had heard.

"What do you think of him?" he said, without looking at her.

"Oh, he's quite a nice lad," she answered.

It was some while again before he spoke. "He will be the last of the Allways," he said. "I should like to think of the name being continued; and he's a good business man, in spite of his dreaminess. Perhaps he would get on better with the men."

She seized at the chance of changing the subject.

"It was a foolish notion," she said, "that of the Manchester school: that men and women could be treated as mere figures in a sum."

To her surprise, he agreed with her. "The feudal system had a fine idea in it," he said, "if it had been honestly carried out. A master should be the friend, the helper of his men. They should be one family."

She looked at him a little incredulously, remembering the bitter periods of strikes and lock-outs.

"Did you ever try, Dad?" she asked.

"Oh, yes," he answered. "But I tried the wrong way." "The right way might be found," he added, "by the right man, and woman."

She felt that he was watching her through his half-closed eyes. "There are those cottages," he continued, "just before you come to the bridge. They might be repaired and a club house added. The idea is catching on, they tell me. Garden villages, they call them now. It gets the men and women away from the dirty streets; and gives the children a chance."

She knew the place. A sad group of dilapidated little houses forming three sides of a paved quadrangle, with a shattered fountain and withered trees in the centre. Ever since she could remember, they had stood there empty, ghostly, with creaking doors and broken windows, their gardens overgrown with weeds.

"Are they yours?" she asked. She had never connected them with the works, some half a mile away. Though had she been curious, she might have learnt that they were known as "Allway's Folly."

"Your mother's," he answered. "I built them the year I came back from America and gave them to her. I thought it would interest her. Perhaps it would, if I had left her to her own ways."

"Why didn't they want them?" she asked.

"They did, at first," he answered. "The time-servers and the hypocrites among them. I made it a condition that they should be teetotallers, and chapel goers, and everything else that I thought good for them. I thought that I could save their souls by bribing them with cheap rents and share of profits. And then the Union came, and that of course finished it."

So he, too, had thought to build Jerusalem.

"Yes," he said. "I'll sound him about giving up his lodgings."

Joan lay awake for a long while that night. The moon looked in at the window. It seemed to have got itself entangled in the tops of the tall pines. Would it not be her duty to come back—make her father happy, to say nothing of the other. He was a dear, sweet, lovable lad. Together, they might realize her father's dream: repair the blunders, plant gardens where the weeds now grew, drive out the old sad ghosts with living voices. It had been a fine thought, a "King's thought." Others had followed, profiting by his mistakes. But might it not be carried further than even they had gone, shaped into some noble venture that should serve the future.

Was not her America here? Why seek it further? What was this unknown Force, that, against all sense and reason, seemed driving her out into the wilderness to preach. Might it not be mere vanity, mere egoism. Almost she had convinced herself.

And then there flashed remembrance of her mother. She, too, had laid aside herself; had thought that love and duty could teach one to be other than one was. The Ego was the all important thing, entrusted to us as the talents of silver to the faithful servant: to be developed, not for our own purposes, but for the service of the Master.

One did no good by suppressing one's nature. In the end it proved too strong. Marriage with Arthur would be only repeating the mistake. To be worshipped, to be served. It would be very pleasant, when one was in the mood. But it would not satisfy her. There was something strong and fierce and primitive in her nature—something that had come down to her through the generations from some harness-girded ancestress—something impelling her instinctively to choose the fighter; to share with him the joy of battle, healing his wounds, giving him of her courage, exulting with him in the victory.

The moon had risen clear of the entangling pines. It rode serene and free.

Her father came to the station with her in the morning. The train was not in: and they walked up and down and talked. Suddenly she remembered: it had slipped her mind.

"Could I, as a child, have known an old clergyman?" she asked him. "At least he wouldn't have been old then. I dropped into Chelsea Church one evening and heard him preach; and on the way home I passed him again in the street. It seemed to me that I had seen his face before. But not for many years. I meant to write you about it, but forgot."

He had to turn aside for a moment to speak to an acquaintance about business.

"Oh, it's possible," he answered on rejoining her. "What was his name?"

"I do not know," she answered. "He was not the regular Incumbent. But it was someone that I seemed to know quite well—that I must have been familiar with."

"It may have been," he answered carelessly, "though the gulf was wider then than it is now. I'll try and think. Perhaps it is only your fancy."

The train drew in, and he found her a corner seat, and stood talking by the window, about common things.

"What did he preach about?" he asked her unexpectedly.

She was puzzled for the moment. "Oh, the old clergyman," she answered, recollecting. "Oh, Calvary. All roads lead to Calvary, he thought. It was rather interesting."

She looked back at the end of the platform. He had not moved.

CHAPTER IX

A pile of correspondence was awaiting her and, standing by the desk, she began to open and read it. Suddenly she paused, conscious that someone had entered the room and, turning, she saw Hilda. She must have left the door ajar, for she had heard no sound. The child closed the door noiselessly and came across, holding out a letter.

"Papa told me to give you this the moment you came in," she said. Joan had not yet taken off her things. The child must have been keeping a close watch. Save for the signature it contained but one line: "I have accepted."

Joan replaced the letter in its envelope, and laid it down upon the desk. Unconsciously a smile played about her lips.

The child was watching her. "I'm glad you persuaded him," she said.

Joan felt a flush mount to her face. She had forgotten Hilda for the instant.

She forced a laugh. "Oh, I only persuaded him to do what he had made up his mind to do," she explained. "It was all settled."

"No, it wasn't," answered the child. "Most of them were against it. And then there was Mama," she added in a lower tone.

"What do you mean," asked Joan. "Didn't she wish it?"

The child raised her eyes. There was a dull anger in them. "Oh, what's the good of pretending," she said. "He's so great. He could be the Prime Minister of England if he chose. But then he would have to visit kings and nobles, and receive them at his house, and Mama—" She broke off with a passionate gesture of the small thin hands.

Joan was puzzled what to say. She knew exactly what she ought to say: what she would have said to any ordinary child. But to say it to this uncannily knowing little creature did not promise much good.

"Who told you I persuaded him?" she asked.

"Nobody," answered the child. "I knew."

Joan seated herself, and drew the child towards her.

"It isn't as terrible as you think," she said. "Many men who have risen and taken a high place in the world were married to kind, good women unable to share their greatness. There was Shakespeare, you know, who married Anne Hathaway and had a clever daughter. She was just a nice, homely body a few years older than himself. And he seems to have been very fond of her; and was always running down to Stratford to be with her."

"Yes, but he didn't bring her up to London," answered the child. "Mama would have wanted to come; and Papa would have let her, and wouldn't have gone to see Queen Elizabeth unless she had been invited too."

Joan wished she had not mentioned Shakespeare. There had surely been others; men who had climbed up and carried their impossible wives with them. But she couldn't think of one, just then.

"We must help her," she answered somewhat lamely. "She's anxious to learn, I know."

The child shook her head. "She doesn't understand," she said. "And Papa won't tell her. He says it would only hurt her and do no good." The small hands were clenched. "I shall hate her if she spoils his life."

The atmosphere was becoming tragic. Joan felt the need of escaping from it. She sprang up.

"Oh, don't be nonsensical," she said. "Your father isn't the only man married to a woman not as clever as himself. He isn't going to let that stop him. And your mother's going to learn to be the wife of a great man and do the best she can. And if they don't like her they've got to put up with her. I shall talk to the both of them." A wave of motherliness towards the entire Phillips family passed over her. It included Hilda. She caught the child to her and gave her a hug. "You go back to school," she said, "and get on as fast as you can, so that you'll be able to be useful to him."

The child flung her arms about her. "You're so beautiful and wonderful," she said. "You can do anything. I'm so glad you came."

Joan laughed. It was surprising how easily the problem had been solved. She would take Mrs. Phillips in hand at once. At all events she should be wholesome and unobtrusive. It would be a delicate mission, but Joan felt sure of her own tact. She could see his boyish eyes turned upon her with wonder and gratitude.

"I was so afraid you would not be back before I went," said the child. "I ought to have gone this afternoon, but Papa let me stay till the evening."

"You will help?" she added, fixing on Joan her great, grave eyes.

Joan promised, and the child went out. She looked pretty when she smiled. She closed the door behind her noiselessly.

It occurred to Joan that she would like to talk matters over with Greyson. There was "Clorinda's" attitude to be decided upon; and she was interested to know what view he himself would take. Of course he would be on P---'s side. The *Evening Gazette* had always supported the "gas and water school" of socialism; and to include the people's food was surely only an extension of the principle. She rang him up and Miss Greyson answered, asking her to come round to dinner: they would be alone. And she agreed.

The Greysons lived in a small house squeezed into an angle of the Outer Circle, overlooking Regent's Park. It was charmingly furnished, chiefly with old Chippendale. The drawing-room made quite a picture. It was home-like and restful with its faded colouring, and absence of all show and overcrowding. They sat there after dinner and discussed Joan's news. Miss Greyson was repairing a piece of old embroidery she had brought back with her from Italy; and Greyson sat smoking, with his hands behind his head, and his long legs stretched out towards the fire.

"Carleton will want him to make his food policy include Tariff Reform," he said. "If he prove pliable, and is willing to throw over his free trade principles, all well and good."

"What's Carleton got to do with it?" demanded Joan with a note of indignation.

He turned his head towards her with an amused raising of the eyebrows. "Carleton owns two London dailies," he answered, "and is in treaty for a third: together with a dozen others scattered about the provinces. Most politicians find themselves, sooner or later, convinced by his arguments. Phillips may prove the exception."

"It would be rather interesting, a fight between them," said Joan. "Myself I should back Phillips."

"He might win through," mused Greyson. "He's the man to do it, if anybody could. But the odds will be against him."

"I don't see it," said Joan, with decision.

"I'm afraid you haven't yet grasped the power of the Press," he answered with a smile. "Phillips speaks occasionally to five thousand people. Carleton addresses every day a circle of five million readers."

"Yes, but when Phillips does speak, he speaks to the whole country," retorted Joan.

"Through the medium of Carleton and his like; and just so far as they allow his influence to permeate beyond the platform," answered Greyson.

"But they report his speeches. They are bound to," explained Joan.

"It doesn't read quite the same," he answered. "Phillips goes home under the impression that he has made a great success and has roused the country. He and millions of other readers learn from the next morning's headlines that it was 'A Tame Speech' that he made. What sounded to him 'Loud Cheers' have sunk to mild 'Hear, Hears.' That five minutes' hurricane of applause, during which wildly excited men and women leapt upon the benches and roared themselves hoarse, and which he felt had settled the whole question, he searches for in vain. A few silly interjections, probably pre-arranged by Carleton's young lions, become 'renewed interruptions.' The report is strictly truthful; but the impression produced is that Robert Phillips has failed to carry even his own people with him. And then follow leaders in fourteen widely-circulated Dailies, stretching from the Clyde to the Severn, foretelling how Mr. Robert Phillips could regain his waning popularity by the simple process of adopting Tariff Reform: or whatever the pet panacea of Carleton and Co. may, at the moment, happen to be."

"Don't make us out all alike," pleaded his sister with a laugh. "There are still a few old-fashioned papers that do give their opponents fair play."

"They are not increasing in numbers," he answered, "and the Carleton group is. There is no reason why in another ten years he should not control the entire popular press of the country. He's got the genius and he's got the means."

"The cleverest thing he has done," he continued, turning to Joan, "is your *Sunday Post*. Up till then, the working classes had escaped him. With the *Sunday Post*, he has solved the problem. They open their mouths; and he gives them their politics wrapped up in pictures and gossipy pars."

Miss Greyson rose and put away her embroidery. "But what's his object?" she said. "He must have more money than he can spend; and he works like a horse. I could understand it, if he had any beliefs."

"Oh, we can all persuade ourselves that we are the Heaven-ordained dictator of the human race," he answered. "Love of power is at the bottom of it. Why do our Rockefellers and our Carnegies condemn themselves to the existence of galley slaves, ruining their digestions so that they never can enjoy a square meal. It isn't the money; it's the trouble of their lives how to get rid of that. It is the notoriety, the power that they are out for. In Carleton's case, it is to feel himself the power behind the throne; to know that he can make and unmake statesmen; has the keys of peace and war in his pocket; is able to exclaim: Public opinion? It is I."

"It can be a respectable ambition," suggested Joan.

"It has been responsible for most of man's miseries," he answered. "Every world's conqueror meant to make it happy after he had finished knocking it about. We are all born with it, thanks to the devil." He shifted his position and regarded her with critical eyes. "You've got it badly," he said. "I can see it in the tilt of your chin and the quivering of your nostrils. You beware of it."

Miss Greyson left them. She had to finish an article. They debated "Clorinda's" views; and agreed that, as a practical housekeeper, she would welcome attention being given to the question of the nation's food. The *Evening Gazette* would support Phillips in principle, while reserving to itself the right of criticism when it came to details.

"What's he like in himself?" he asked her. "You've been seeing something of him, haven't you?"

"Oh, a little," she answered. "He's absolutely sincere; and he means business. He won't stop at the bottom of the ladder now he's once got his foot upon it."

"But he's quite common, isn't he?" he asked again. "I've only met him in public."

"No, that's precisely what he isn't," answered Joan. "You feel that he belongs to no class, but his own. The class of the Abraham Lincolns, and the Dantons."

"England's a different proposition," he mused. "Society counts for so much with us. I doubt if we should accept even an Abraham Lincoln: unless in some supreme crisis. His wife rather handicaps him, too, doesn't she?"

"She wasn't born to be the châtelaine of Downing Street," Joan admitted. "But it's not an official position."

"I'm not so sure that it isn't," he laughed. "It's the dinner-table that rules in England. We settle everything round a dinner-table."

She was sitting in front of the fire in a high-backed chair. She never cared to loll, and the shaded light from the electric sconces upon the mantelpiece illumined her.

"If the world were properly stage-managed, that's what you ought to be," he said, "the wife of a Prime Minister. I can see you giving such an excellent performance."

"I must talk to Mary," he added, "see if we can't get you off on some promising young Under Secretary."

"Don't give me ideas above my station," laughed Joan. "I'm a journalist."

"That's the pity of it," he said. "You're wasting the most important thing about you, your personality. You would do more good in a drawing-room, influencing the rulers, than you will ever do hiding behind a pen. It was the drawing-room that made the French Revolution."

The firelight played about her hair. "I suppose every woman dreams of reviving the old French Salon," she answered. "They must have been gloriously interesting." He was leaning forward with clasped hands. "Why shouldn't she?" he said. "The reason that our drawing-rooms have ceased to lead is that our beautiful women are generally frivolous and our clever women unfeminine. What we are waiting for is an English Madame Roland."

Joan laughed. "Perhaps I shall some day," she answered.

He insisted on seeing her as far as the bus. It was a soft, mild night; and they walked round the Circle to Gloucester Gate. He thought there would be more room in the buses at that point.

"I wish you would come oftener," he said. "Mary has taken such a liking to you. If you care to meet people, we can always whip up somebody of interest."

She promised that she would. She always felt curiously at home with the Greysons.

They were passing the long sweep of Chester Terrace. "I like this neighbourhood with its early Victorian atmosphere," she said. "It always makes me feel quiet and good. I don't know why."

"I like the houses, too," he said. "There's a character about them. You don't often find such fine drawing-rooms in London."

"Don't forget your promise," he reminded her, when they parted. "I shall tell Mary she may write to you."

She met Carleton by chance a day or two later, as she was entering the office. "I want to see you," he said; and took her up with him into his room.

"We must stir the people up about this food business," he said, plunging at once into his subject. "Phillips is quite right. It overshadows everything. We must make the country self-supporting. It can be done and must. If a war were to be sprung upon us we could be starved out in a month. Our navy, in face of these new submarines, is no longer able to secure us. France is working day and night upon them. It may be a bogey, or it may not. If it isn't, she would have us at her mercy; and it's too big a risk to run. You live in the same house with him, don't you? Do you often see him?"

"Not often," she answered.

He was reading a letter. "You were dining there on Friday night, weren't you?" he asked her, without looking up.

Joan flushed. What did he mean by cross-examining her in this way? She was not at all used to impertinence from the opposite sex.

"Your information is quite correct," she answered.

Her anger betrayed itself in her tone; and he shot a swift glance at her.

"I didn't mean to offend you," he said. "A mutual friend, a Mr. Airlie, happened to be of the party, and he mentioned you."

He threw aside the letter. "I'll tell you what I want you to do," he said. "It's nothing to object to. Tell him that you've seen me and had a talk. I understand his scheme to be that the country should grow more and more food until it eventually becomes self-supporting; and that the Government should control the distribution. Tell him that with that I'm heart and soul in sympathy; and would like to help him." He pushed aside a pile of papers and, leaning across the desk, spoke with studied deliberation. "If he can see his way to making his policy dependent upon Protection, we can work together."

"And if he can't?" suggested Joan.

He fixed his large, colourless eyes upon her. "That's where you can help him," he answered. "If he and I combine forces, we can pull this through in spite of the furious opposition that it is going to arouse. Without a good Press he is helpless; and where is he going to get his Press backing if he turns me down? From half a dozen Socialist papers whose support will do him more harm than good. If he will bring the working class over to Protection I will undertake that the Tariff Reformers and the Agricultural Interest shall accept his Socialism. It will be a victory for both of us.

"If he gain his end, what do the means matter?" he continued, as Joan did not answer. "Food may be dearer; the Unions can square that by putting up wages; while the poor devil of a farm labourer will at last get fair treatment. We can easily insist upon that. What do you think, yourself?"

"About Protection," she answered. "It's one of the few subjects I haven't made up my mind about."

He laughed. "You will find all your pet reforms depend upon it, when you come to work them out," he said. "You can't have a minimum wage without a minimum price."

They had risen.

"I'll give him your message," said Joan. "But I don't see him exchanging his principles even for your support. I admit it's important."

"Talk it over with him," he said. "And bear this in mind for your own guidance." He took a step forward, which brought his face quite close to hers: "If he fails, and all his life's work goes for nothing, I shall be sorry; but I shan't break my heart. He will."

Joan dropped a note into Phillips's letter-box on her return home, saying briefly that she wished to see him; and he sent up answer asking her if she would come to the gallery that evening, and meet him after his speech, which would be immediately following the dinner hour.

It was the first time he had risen since his appointment, and he was received with general cheers. He stood out curiously youthful against the background of grey-haired and bald-headed men behind him; and there was youth also in his clear, ringing voice that not even the vault-like atmosphere of that shadowless chamber could altogether rob of its vitality. He spoke simply and good-humouredly, without any attempt at rhetoric, relying chiefly upon a crescendo of telling facts that gradually, as he proceeded, roused the House to that tense stillness that comes to it when it begins to think.

"A distinctly dangerous man," Joan overheard a little old lady behind her comment to a friend. "If I didn't hate him, I should like him."

He met her in the corridor, and they walked up and down and talked, too absorbed to be aware of the curious eyes that were turned upon them. Joan gave him Carleton's message.

"It was clever of him to make use of you," he said. "If he'd sent it through anybody else, I'd have published it."

"You don't think it even worth considering?" suggested Joan.

"Protection?" he flashed out scornfully. "Yes, I've heard of that. I've listened, as a boy, while the old men told of it to one another, in thin, piping voices, round the fireside; how the labourers were flung eight-and-sixpence a week to die on, and the men starved in the towns; while the farmers kept their hunters, and got drunk each night on fine old crusted port. Do you know what their toast was in the big hotels on market day, with the windows open to the street: 'To a long war and a bloody one.' It would be their toast to-morrow, if they had their way. Does he think I am going to be a party to the putting of the people's neck again under their pitiless yoke?"

"But the people are more powerful now," argued Joan. "If the farmer demanded higher prices, they could demand higher wages."

"They would never overtake the farmer," he answered, with a laugh. "And the last word would always be with him. I am out to get rid of the landlords," he continued, "not to establish them as the permanent rulers of the country, as they are in Germany. The people are more powerful—just a little, because they are no longer dependent on the land. They can say to the farmer, 'All right, my son, if that's your figure, I'm going to the shop next door—to South America, to Canada, to Russia.' It isn't a satisfactory solution. I want to see England happy and healthy before I bother about the Argentine. It drives our men into the slums when they might be living fine lives in God's fresh air. In the case of war it might be disastrous. There, I agree with him. We must be able to shut our door without fear of having to open it ourselves to ask for bread. How would Protection accomplish that? Did he tell you?"

"Don't eat me," laughed Joan. "I haven't been sent to you as a missionary. I'm only a humble messenger. I suppose the argument is that, good profits assured to him, the farmer would bustle up and produce more."

"Can you see him bustling up?" he answered with a laugh; "organizing himself into a body, and working the thing out from the point of view of the public weal? I'll tell you what nine-tenths of him would do: grow just as much or little as suited his own purposes; and then go to sleep. And Protection would be his security against ever being awakened."

"I'm afraid you don't like him," Joan commented.

"He will be all right in his proper place," he answered: "as the servant of the public: told what to do, and turned out of his job if he doesn't do it. My scheme does depend upon Protection. You can tell him that. But this time, it's going to be Protection for the people."

They were at the far end of the corridor; and the few others still promenading were some distance away. She had not delivered the whole of her message. She crossed to a seat, and he followed her. She spoke with her face turned away from him.

"You have got to consider the cost of refusal," she said. "His offer wasn't help or neutrality: it was help or opposition by every means in his power. He left me in no kind of doubt as to that. He's not used to being challenged and he won't be squeamish. You will have the whole of his Press against you, and every other journalistic and political influence that he possesses. He's getting a hold upon the working classes. The *Sunday Post* has an enormous sale in the manufacturing towns; and he's talking of starting another. Are you strong enough to fight him?"

She very much wanted to look at him, but she would not. It seemed to her quite a time before he replied.

"Yes," he answered, "I'm strong enough to fight him. Shall rather enjoy doing it. And it's time that somebody did. Whether I'm strong enough to win has got to be seen."

She turned and looked at him then. She wondered why she had ever thought him ugly.

"You can face it," she said: "the possibility of all your life's work being wasted?"

"It won't be wasted," he answered. "The land is there. I've seen it from afar and it's a good land, a land where no man shall go hungry. If not I, another shall lead the people into it. I shall have prepared the way."

She liked him for that touch of exaggeration. She was so tired of the men who make out all things little, including themselves and their own work. After all, was it exaggeration? Might he not have been chosen to lead the people out of bondage to a land where there should be no more fear.

"You're not angry with me?" he asked. "I haven't been rude, have I?"

"Abominably rude," she answered, "you've defied my warnings, and treated my embassy with contempt." She turned to him and their eyes met. "I should have despised you, if you hadn't," she added.

There was a note of exultation in her voice; and, as if in answer, something leapt into his eyes that seemed to claim her. Perhaps it was well that just then the bell rang for a division; and the moment passed.

He rose and held out his hand. "We will fight him," he said. "And you can tell him this, if he asks, that I'm going straight for him. Parliament may as well close down if a few men between them are to be allowed to own the entire Press of the country, and stifle every voice that does not shout their bidding. We haven't dethroned kings to put up a newspaper Boss. He shall have all the fighting he wants."

They met more often from that day, for Joan was frankly using her two columns in the *Sunday Post* to propagate his aims. Carleton, to her surprise, made no objection. Nor did he seek to learn the result of his ultimatum. It looked, they thought, as if he had assumed acceptance; and was willing for Phillips to choose his own occasion. Meanwhile replies to her articles reached Joan in weekly increasing numbers. There seemed to be a wind arising, blowing towards Protection. Farm labourers, especially, appeared to be enthusiastic for its coming. From their ill-spelt, smeared epistles, one gathered that, after years of doubt and hesitation, they had—however reluctantly—arrived at the conclusion that without it there could be no hope for them. Factory workers, miners, engineers— more fluent, less apologetic—wrote as strong supporters of Phillips's scheme; but saw clearly how upon Protection its success depended. Shopmen, clerks—only occasionally ungrammatical—felt sure that Robert Phillips, the tried friend of the poor, would insist upon the boon of Protection being no longer held back from the people. Wives and mothers claimed it as their children's birthright. Similar views got themselves at the same time, into the correspondence columns of Carleton's other numerous papers. Evidently Democracy had been throbbing with a passion for Protection hitherto unknown, even to itself.

"He means it kindly," laughed Phillips. "He is offering me an excuse to surrender gracefully. We must have a public meeting or two after Christmas, and clear the ground." They had got into the habit of speaking in the plural.

Mrs. Phillips's conversion Joan found more difficult than she had anticipated. She had persuaded Phillips to take a small house and let her furnish it upon the hire system. Joan went with her to the widely advertised "Emporium" in the City Road, meaning to advise her. But, in the end, she gave it up out of sheer pity. Nor would her advice have served much purpose, confronted by the "rich and varied choice" provided for his patrons by Mr. Krebs, the "Furnisher for Connoisseurs."

"We've never had a home exactly," explained Mrs. Phillips, during their journey in the tram. "It's always been lodgings, up to now. Nice enough, some of them; but you know what I mean; everybody else's taste but your own. I've always fancied a little house with one's own things in it. You know, things that you can get fond of."

Oh, the things she was going to get fond of! The things that her poor, round foolish eyes gloated upon the moment that she saw them! Joan tried to enlist the shopman on her side, descending even to flirtation. Unfortunately he was a young man with a high sense of duty, convinced that his employer's interests lay in his support of Mrs. Phillips. The sight of the furniture that, between them, they selected for the dining-room gave Joan a quite distinct internal pain. They ascended to the floor above, devoted to the exhibition of "*Recherché* drawing-room suites." Mrs. Phillips's eye instinctively fastened with passionate desire upon the most atrocious. Joan grew vehement. It was impossible.

"I always was a one for cheerful colours," explained Mrs. Phillips.

Even the shopman wavered. Joan pressed her advantage; directed Mrs. Phillips's attention to something a little less awful. Mrs. Phillips yielded.

"Of course you know best, dear," she admitted. "Perhaps I am a bit too fond of bright things."

The victory was won. Mrs. Phillips had turned away. The shopman was altering the order. Joan moved towards the door, and accidentally caught sight of Mrs. Phillips's face. The flabby mouth was trembling. A tear was running down the painted cheek.

Joan slipped her hand through the other's arm.

"I'm not so sure you're not right after all," she said, fixing a critical eye upon the rival suites. "It is a bit mousey, that other."

The order was once more corrected. Joan had the consolation of witnessing the childish delight that came again into the foolish face; but felt angry with herself at her own weakness.

It was the woman's feebleness that irritated her. If only she had shown a spark of fight, Joan could have been firm. Poor feckless creature, what could have ever been her attraction for Phillips!

She followed, inwardly fuming, while Mrs. Phillips continued to pile monstrosity upon monstrosity. What would Phillips think? And what would Hilda's eyes say when they looked upon that *recherché* drawing-room suite? Hilda, who would have had no sentimental compunctions! The woman would be sure to tell them both that she, Joan, had accompanied her and helped in the choosing. The whole ghastly house would be exhibited to every visitor as the result of their joint taste. She could hear Mr. Airlie's purring voice congratulating her.

She ought to have insisted on their going to a decent shop. The mere advertisement ought to have forewarned her. It was the posters that had captured Mrs. Phillips: those dazzling apartments where bejewelled society reposed upon the "high-class but inexpensive designs" of Mr. Krebs. Artists ought to have more self-respect than to sell their talents for such purposes.

The contract was concluded in Mr. Krebs' private office: a very stout gentleman with a very thin voice, whose dream had always been to one day be of service to the renowned Mr. Robert Phillips. He was clearly under the impression that he had now accomplished it. Even as Mrs. Phillips took up the pen to sign, the wild idea occurred to Joan of snatching the paper away from her, hustling her into a cab, and in some quiet street or square making the woman see for herself that she was a useless fool; that the glowing dreams and fancies she had cherished in her silly head for fifteen years must all be given up; that she must stand aside, knowing herself of no account.

It could be done. She felt it. If only one could summon up the needful brutality. If only one could stifle that still, small voice of Pity.

Mrs. Phillips signed amid splutterings and blots. Joan added her signature as witness.

She did effect an improvement in the poor lady's dress. On Madge's advice she took her to a voluble little woman in the Earl's Court Road who was struck at once by Madame Phillips's remarkable resemblance to the Baroness von Stein. Had not Joan noticed it? Whatever suited the Baroness von Stein—allowed by common consent to be one of the best-dressed women in London—was bound to show up Madame Phillips to equal advantage. By curious coincidence a costume for the Baroness had been put in hand only the day before. It was sent for and pinned upon the delighted Madame Phillips. Perfection! As the Baroness herself would always say: "My frock must be a framework for my personality. It must never obtrude." The supremely well-dressed woman! One never notices what she has on: that is the test. It seemed it was what Mrs. Phillips had always felt herself. Joan could have kissed the voluble, emphatic little woman.

But the dyed hair and the paint put up a fight for themselves.

"I want you to do something very brave," said Joan. She had invited herself to tea with Mrs. Phillips, and they were alone in the small white-panelled room that they were soon to say good-bye to. The new house would be ready at Christmas. "It will be a little hard at first," continued Joan, "but afterwards you will be glad that you have done it. It is a duty you owe to your position as the wife of a great leader of the people."

The firelight showed to Joan a comically frightened face, with round, staring eyes and an open mouth.

"What is it you want me to do?" she faltered

"I want you to be just yourself," said Joan; "a kind, good woman of the people, who will win their respect, and set them an example." She moved across and seating herself on the arm of Mrs. Phillips's chair, touched lightly with her hand the flaxen hair and the rouged cheek. "I want you to get rid of all this," she whispered. "It isn't worthy of you. Leave it to the silly dolls and the bad women."

There was a long silence. Joan felt the tears trickling between her fingers.

"You haven't seen me," came at last in a thin, broken voice.

Joan bent down and kissed her. "Let's try it," she whispered.

A little choking sound was the only answer. But the woman rose and, Joan following, they stole upstairs into the bedroom and Mrs. Phillips turned the key.

It took a long time, and Joan, seated on the bed, remembered a night when she had taken a trapped mouse (if only he had been a quiet mouse!) into the bathroom and had waited while it drowned. It was finished at last, and Mrs Phillips stood revealed with her hair down, showing streaks of dingy brown.

Joan tried to enthuse; but the words came haltingly. She suggested to Joan a candle that some wind had suddenly blown out. The paint and powder had been obvious, but at least it had given her the mask of youth. She looked old and withered. The life seemed to have gone out of her.

"You see, dear, I began when I was young," she explained; "and he has always seen me the same. I don't think I could live like this."

The painted doll that the child fancied! the paint washed off and the golden hair all turned to drab? Could one be sure of "getting used to it," of "liking it better?" And the poor bewildered doll itself! How could one expect to make of it a statue: "The Woman of the People." One could only bruise it.

It ended in Joan's promising to introduce her to discreet theatrical friends who would tell her of cosmetics less injurious to the skin, and advise her generally in the ancient and proper art of "making up."

It was not the end she had looked for. Joan sighed as she closed her door behind her. What was the meaning of it? On the one hand that unimpeachable law, the greatest happiness of the greatest number; the sacred cause of Democracy; the moral Uplift of the people; Sanity, Wisdom, Truth, the higher Justice; all the forces on which she was relying for the regeneration of the world—all arrayed in stern demand that the flabby, useless Mrs. Phillips should be sacrificed for the general good. Only one voice had pleaded for foolish, helpless Mrs. Phillips— and had conquered. The still, small voice of Pity.

CHAPTER X

Arthur sprang himself upon her a little before Christmas. He was full of a great project. It was that she and her father should spend Christmas with his people at Birmingham. Her father thought he would like to see his brother; they had not often met of late, and Birmingham would be nearer for her than Liverpool.

Joan had no intention of being lured into the Birmingham parlour. She thought she could see in it a scheme for her gradual entanglement. Besides, she was highly displeased. She had intended asking her father to come to Brighton with her. As a matter of fact, she had forgotten all about Christmas; and the idea only came into her head while explaining to Arthur how his impulsiveness had interfered with it. Arthur, crestfallen, suggested telegrams. It would be quite easy to alter everything; and of course her father would rather be with her, wherever it was. But it seemed it was too late. She ought to have been consulted. A sudden sense of proprietorship in her father came to her assistance and added pathos to her indignation. Of course, now, she would have to spend Christmas alone. She was far too busy to think of Birmingham. She could have managed Brighton. Argument founded on the length of journey to Birmingham as compared with the journey to Brighton she refused to be drawn into. Her feelings had been too deeply wounded to permit of descent into detail.

But the sinner, confessing his fault, is entitled to forgiveness, and, having put him back into his proper place, she let him kiss her hand. She even went further and let him ask her out to dinner. As the result of her failure to reform Mrs. Phillips she was feeling dissatisfied with herself. It was an unpleasant sensation and somewhat new to her experience. An evening spent in Arthur's company might do her good. The experiment proved successful. He really was quite a dear boy. Eyeing him thoughtfully through the smoke of her cigarette, it occurred to her how like he was to Guido's painting of St. Sebastian; those soft, dreamy eyes and that beautiful, almost feminine, face! There always had been a suspicion of the saint about him even as a boy: nothing one could lay hold of: just that odd suggestion of a shadow intervening between him and the world.

It seemed a favourable opportunity to inform him of that fixed determination of hers: never—in all probability—to marry: but to devote her life to her work. She was feeling very kindly towards him; and was able to soften her decision with touches of gentle regret. He did not appear in the least upset. But 'thought' that her duty might demand, later on, that she should change her mind: that was if fate should offer her some noble marriage, giving her wider opportunity.

She was a little piqued at his unexpected attitude of aloofness. What did he mean by a "noble marriage"—to a Duke, or something of that sort?

He did not think the candidature need be confined to Dukes, though he had no objection to a worthy Duke. He meant any really great man who would help her and whom she could help.

She promised, somewhat shortly, to consider the matter, whenever the Duke, or other class of nobleman, should propose to her. At present no sign of him had appeared above the horizon. Her own idea was that, if she lived long enough, she would become a spinster. Unless someone took pity on her when she was old and decrepit and past her work.

There was a little humorous smile about his mouth. But his eyes were serious and pleading.

"When shall I know that you are old and decrepit?" he asked.

She was not quite sure. She thought it would be when her hair was grey—or rather white. She had been informed by experts that her peculiar shade of hair went white, not grey.

"I shall ask you to marry me when your hair is white," he said. "May I?"

It did not suggest any overwhelming impatience. "Yes," she answered. "In case you haven't married yourself, and forgotten all about me."

"I shall keep you to your promise," he said quite gravely.

She felt the time had come to speak seriously. "I want you to marry," she said, "and be happy. I shall be troubled if you don't."

He was looking at her with those shy, worshipping eyes of his that always made her marvel at her own wonderfulness.

"It need not do that," he answered. "It would be beautiful to be with you always so that I might serve you. But I am quite happy, loving you. Let me see you now and then: touch you and hear your voice."

Behind her drawn-down lids, she offered up a little prayer that she might always be worthy of his homage. She didn't know it would make no difference to him.

She walked with him to Euston and saw him into the train. He had given up his lodgings and was living with her father at The Pines. They were busy on a plan for securing the co-operation of the workmen, and she promised to run down and hear all about it. She would not change her mind about Birmingham, but sent everyone her love.

She wished she had gone when it came to Christmas Day. This feeling of loneliness was growing upon her. The Phillips had gone up north; and the Greysons to some relations of theirs: swell country people in Hampshire. Flossie was on a sea voyage with Sam and his mother, and even Madge had been struck homesick. It happened to be a Sunday, too, of all days in the week, and London in a drizzling rain was just about the limit. She worked till late in the afternoon, but, sitting down to her solitary cup of tea, she felt she wanted to howl. From the basement came faint sounds of laughter. Her landlord and lady were entertaining guests. If they had not been, she would have found some excuse for running down and talking to them, if only for a few minutes.

Suddenly the vision of old Chelsea Church rose up before her with its little motherly old pew-opener. She had so often been meaning to go and see her again, but something had always interfered. She hunted through her drawers and found a comparatively sober-coloured shawl, and tucked it under her cloak. The service was just commencing when she reached the church. Mary Stopperton showed her into a seat and evidently remembered her. "I want to see you afterwards," she whispered; and Mary Stopperton had smiled and nodded. The service, with its need for being continually upon the move, bored her; she was not in the mood for it. And the sermon, preached by a young curate who had not yet got over his Oxford drawl, was uninteresting. She had half hoped that the wheezy old clergyman, who had preached about Calvary on the evening she had first visited the church, would be there again. She wondered what had become of him, and if it were really a fact that she had known him when she was a child, or only her fancy. It was strange how vividly her memory of him seemed to pervade the little church. She had the feeling he was watching her from the shadows. She waited for Mary in the vestibule, and gave her the shawl, making her swear on the big key of the church door that she would wear it herself and not give it away. The little old pew-opener's pink and white face flushed with delight as she took it, and the thin, work-worn hands fingered it admiringly. "But I may lend it?" she pleaded.

They turned up Church Street. Joan confided to Mary what a rotten Christmas she had had, all by herself, without a soul to speak to except her landlady, who had brought her meals and had been in such haste to get away.

"I don't know what made me think of you," she said. "I'm so glad I did." She gave the little old lady a hug. Mary laughed. "Where are you going now, dearie?" she asked.

"Oh, I don't mind so much now," answered Joan. "Now that I've seen a friendly face, I shall go home and go to bed early."

They walked a little way in silence. Mary slipped her hand into Joan's. "You wouldn't care to come home and have a bit of supper with me, would you, dearie?" she asked.

"Oh, may I?" answered Joan.

Mary's hand gave Joan's a little squeeze. "You won't mind if anybody drops in?" she said. "They do sometimes of a Sunday evening."

"You don't mean a party?" asked Joan.

"No, dear," answered Mary. "It's only one or two who have nowhere else to go."

Joan laughed. She thought she would be a fit candidate.

"You see, it makes company for me," explained Mary.

Mary lived in a tiny house behind a strip of garden. It stood in a narrow side street between two public-houses, and was covered with ivy. It had two windows above and a window and a door below. The upstairs rooms belonged to the churchwardens and were used as a storehouse for old parish registers, deemed of little value. Mary Stopperton and her bedridden husband lived in the two rooms below. Mary unlocked the door, and Joan passed in and waited. Mary lit a candle that was standing on a bracket and turned to lead the way.

"Shall I shut the door?" suggested Joan.

Mary blushed like a child that has been found out just as it was hoping that it had not been noticed.

"It doesn't matter, dearie," she explained. "They know, if they find it open, that I'm in."

The little room looked very cosy when Mary had made up the fire and lighted the lamp. She seated Joan in the worn horsehair easy-chair; out of which one had to be careful one did not slip on to the floor; and spread her handsome shawl over the back of the dilapidated sofa.

"You won't mind my running away for a minute," she said. "I shall only be in the next room."

Through the thin partition, Joan heard a constant shrill, complaining voice. At times, it rose into an angry growl. Mary looked in at the door.

"I'm just running round to the doctor's," she whispered. "His medicine hasn't come. I shan't be long."

Joan offered to go in and sit with the invalid. But Mary feared the exertion of talking might be too much for him. "He gets so excited," she explained. She slipped out noiselessly.

It seemed, in spite of its open door, a very silent little house behind its strip of garden. Joan had the feeling that it was listening.

Suddenly she heard a light step in the passage, and the room door opened. A girl entered. She was wearing a large black hat and a black boa round her neck. Between them her face shone unnaturally white. She carried a small cloth bag. She started, on seeing Joan, and seemed about to retreat.

"Oh, please don't go," cried Joan. "Mrs. Stopperton has just gone round to the doctor's. She won't be long. I'm a friend of hers."

The girl took stock of her and, apparently reassured, closed the door behind her.

"What's he like to-night?" she asked, with a jerk of her head in the direction of the next room. She placed her bag carefully upon the sofa, and examined the new shawl as she did so.

"Well, I gather he's a little fretful," answered Joan with a smile.

"That's a bad sign," said the girl. "Means he's feeling better." She seated herself on the sofa and fingered the shawl. "Did you give it her?" she asked.

"Yes," admitted Joan. "I rather fancied her in it."

"She'll only pawn it," said the girl, "to buy him grapes and port wine."

"I felt a bit afraid of her," laughed Joan, "so I made her promise not to part with it. Is he really very ill, her husband?"

"Oh, yes, there's no make-believe this time," answered the girl. "A bad thing for her if he wasn't."

"Oh, it's only what's known all over the neighbourhood," continued the girl. "She's had a pretty rough time with him. Twice I've found her getting ready to go to sleep for the night by sitting on the bare floor with her back against the wall. Had sold every stick in the place and gone off. But she'd always some excuse for him. It was sure to be half her fault and the other half he couldn't help. Now she's got her 'reward' according to her own account. Heard he was dying in a doss-house, and must fetch him home and nurse him back to life. Seems he's getting fonder of her every day. Now that he can't do anything else."

"It doesn't seem to depress her spirits," mused Joan.

"Oh, she! She's all right," agreed the girl. "Having the time of her life: someone to look after for twenty-four hours a day that can't help themselves."

She examined Joan awhile in silence. "Are you on the stage?" she asked.

"No," answered Joan. "But my mother was. Are you?"

"Thought you looked a bit like it," said the girl. "I'm in the chorus. It's better than being in service or in a shop: that's all you can say for it."

"But you'll get out of that," suggested Joan. "You've got the actress face."

The girl flushed with pleasure. It was a striking face, with intelligent eyes and a mobile, sensitive mouth. "Oh, yes," she said, "I could act all right. I feel it. But you don't get out of the chorus. Except at a price."

Joan looked at her. "I thought that sort of thing was dying out," she said.

The girl shrugged her shoulders. "Not in my shop," she answered. "Anyhow, it was the only chance I ever had. Wish sometimes I'd taken it. It was quite a good part."

"They must have felt sure you could act," said Joan. "Next time it will be a clean offer."

The girl shook her head. "There's no next time," she said; "once you're put down as one of the stand-offs. Plenty of others to take your place."

"Oh, I don't blame them," she added. "It isn't a thing to be dismissed with a toss of your head. I thought it all out. Don't know now what decided me. Something inside me, I suppose."

Joan found herself poking the fire. "Have you known Mary Stopperton long?" she asked.

"Oh, yes," answered the girl. "Ever since I've been on my own."

"Did you talk it over with her?" asked Joan.

"No," answered the girl. "I may have just told her. She isn't the sort that gives advice."

"I'm glad you didn't do it," said Joan: "that you put up a fight for all women."

The girl gave a short laugh. "Afraid I wasn't thinking much about that," she said.

"No," said Joan. "But perhaps that's the way the best fights are fought—without thinking."

Mary peeped round the door. She had been lucky enough to find the doctor in. She disappeared again, and they talked about themselves. The girl was a Miss Ensor. She lived by herself in a room in Lawrence Street.

"I'm not good at getting on with people," she explained.

Mary joined them, and went straight to Miss Ensor's bag and opened it. She shook her head at the contents, which consisted of a small, flabby-looking meat pie in a tin dish, and two pale, flat mince tarts.

"It doesn't nourish you, dearie," complained Mary. "You could have bought yourself a nice bit of meat with the same money."

"And you would have had all the trouble of cooking it," answered the girl. "That only wants warming up."

"But I like cooking, you know, dearie," grumbled Mary. "There's no interest in warming things up."

The girl laughed. "You don't have to go far for your fun," she said. "I'll bring a sole next time; and you shall do it *au gratin*."

Mary put the indigestible-looking pasties into the oven, and almost banged the door. Miss Ensor proceeded to lay the table. "How many, do you think?" she asked. Mary was doubtful. She hoped that, it being Christmas Day, they would have somewhere better to go.

"I passed old 'Bubble and Squeak,' just now, spouting away to three men and a dog outside the World's End. I expect he'll turn up," thought Miss Ensor. She laid for four, leaving space for more if need be. "I call it the 'Cadger's Arms,'" she explained, turning to Joan. "We bring our own victuals, and Mary cooks them for us and waits on us; and the more of us the merrier. You look forward to your Sunday evening parties, don't you?" she asked of Mary.

Mary laughed. She was busy in a corner with basins and a saucepan. "Of course I do, dearie," she answered. "I've always been fond of company."

There came another opening of the door. A little hairy man entered. He wore spectacles and was dressed in black. He carried a paper parcel which he laid upon the table. He looked a little doubtful at Joan. Mary introduced them. His name was Julius Simson. He shook hands as if under protest.

"As friends of Mary Stopperton," he said, "we meet on neutral ground. But in all matters of moment I expect we are as far asunder as the poles. I stand for the People."

"We ought to be comrades," answered Joan, with a smile. "I, too, am trying to help the People."

"You and your class," said Mr. Simson, "are friends enough to the People, so long as they remember that they are the People, and keep their proper place—at the bottom. I am for putting the People at the top."

"Then they will be the Upper Classes," suggested Joan. "And I may still have to go on fighting for the rights of the lower orders."

"In this world," explained Mr. Simson, "someone has got to be Master. The only question is who."

Mary had unwrapped the paper parcel. It contained half a sheep's head. "How would you like it done?" she whispered.

Mr. Simson considered. There came a softer look into his eyes. "How did you do it last time?" he asked. "It came up brown, I remember, with thick gravy."

"Braised," suggested Mary.

"That's the word," agreed Mr. Simson. "Braised." He watched while Mary took things needful from the cupboard, and commenced to peel an onion.

"That's the sort that makes me despair of the People," said Mr. Simson. Joan could not be sure whether he was addressing her individually or imaginary thousands. "Likes working for nothing. Thinks she was born to be everybody's servant." He seated himself beside Miss Ensor on the antiquated sofa. It gave a complaining groan but held out.

"Did you have a good house?" the girl asked him. "Saw you from the distance, waving your arms about. Hadn't time to stop."

"Not many," admitted Mr. Simson. "A Christmassy lot. You know. Sort of crowd that interrupts you and tries to be funny. Dead to their own interests. It's slow work."

"Why do you do it?" asked Miss Ensor.

"Damned if I know," answered Mr. Simson, with a burst of candour. "Can't help it, I suppose. Lost me job again."

"The old story?" suggested Miss Ensor.

"The old story," sighed Mr. Simson. "One of the customers happened to be passing last Wednesday when I was speaking on the Embankment. Heard my opinion of the middle classes?"

"Well, you can't expect 'em to like it, can you?" submitted Miss Ensor.

"No," admitted Mr. Simson with generosity. "It's only natural. It's a fight to the finish between me and the Bourgeois. I cover them with ridicule and contempt and they hit back at me in the only way they know."

"Take care they don't get the best of you," Miss Ensor advised him.

"Oh, I'm not afraid," he answered. "I'll get another place all right: give me time. The only thing I'm worried about is my young woman."

"Doesn't agree with you?" inquired Miss Ensor.

"Oh, it isn't that," he answered. "But she's frightened. You know. Says life with me is going to be a bit too uncertain for her. Perhaps she's right."

"Oh, why don't you chuck it," advised Miss Ensor, "give the Bourgeois a rest."

Mr. Simson shook his head. "Somebody's got to tackle them," he said. "Tell them the truth about themselves, to their faces."

"Yes, but it needn't be you," suggested Miss Ensor.

Mary was leaning over the table. Miss Ensor's four-penny veal and ham pie was ready. Mary arranged it in front of her. "Eat it while it's hot, dearie," she counselled. "It won't be so indigestible."

Miss Ensor turned to her. "Oh, you talk to him," she urged. "Here, he's lost his job again, and is losing his girl: all because of his silly politics. Tell him he's got to have sense and stop it."

Mary seemed troubled. Evidently, as Miss Ensor had stated, advice was not her line. "Perhaps he's got to do it, dearie," she suggested.

"What do you mean by got to do it?" exclaimed Miss Ensor. "Who's making him do it, except himself?"

Mary flushed. She seemed to want to get back to her cooking. "It's something inside us, dearie," she thought: "that nobody hears but ourselves."

"That tells him to talk all that twaddle?" demanded Miss Ensor. "Have you heard him?"

"No, dearie," Mary admitted. "But I expect it's got its purpose. Or he wouldn't have to do it."

Miss Ensor gave a gesture of despair and applied herself to her pie. The hirsute face of Mr. Simson had lost the foolish aggressiveness that had irritated Joan. He seemed to be pondering matters.

Mary hoped that Joan was hungry. Joan laughed and admitted that she was. "It's the smell of all the nice things," she explained. Mary promised it should soon be ready, and went back to her corner.

A short, dark, thick-set man entered and stood looking round the room. The frame must once have been powerful, but now it was shrunken and emaciated. The shabby, threadbare clothes hung loosely from the stooping shoulders. Only the head seemed to have retained its vigour. The face, from which the long black hair was brushed straight back, was ghastly white. Out of it, deep set beneath great shaggy, overhanging brows, blazed the fierce, restless eyes of a fanatic. The huge, thin-lipped mouth seemed to have petrified itself into a savage snarl. He gave Joan the idea, as he stood there glaring round him, of a hunted beast at bay.

Miss Ensor, whose bump of reverence was undeveloped, greeted him cheerfully as Boanerges. Mr. Simson, more respectful, rose and offered his small, grimy hand. Mary took his hat and cloak away from him and closed the door behind him. She felt his hands, and put him into a chair close to the fire. And then she introduced him to Joan.

Joan started on hearing his name. It was one well known.

"The Cyril Baptiste?" she asked. She had often wondered what he might be like.

"The Cyril Baptiste," he answered, in a low, even, passionate voice, that he flung at her almost like a blow. "The atheist, the gaol bird, the pariah, the blasphemer, the anti-Christ. I've hoofs instead of feet. Shall I take off my boots and show them to you? I tuck my tail inside my coat. You can't see my horns. I've cut them off close to my head. That's why I wear my hair long: to hide the stumps."

Mary had been searching in the pockets of his cloak. She had found a paper bag. "You mustn't get excited," she said, laying her little work-worn hand upon his shoulder; "or you'll bring on the bleeding."

"Aye," he answered, "I must be careful I don't die on Christmas Day. It would make a fine text, that, for their sermons."

He lapsed into silence: his almost transparent hands stretched out towards the fire.

Mr. Simson fidgeted. The quiet of the room, broken only by Mary's ministering activities, evidently oppressed him.

"Paper going well, sir?" he asked. "I often read it myself."

"It still sells," answered the proprietor, and editor and publisher, and entire staff of *The Rationalist*.

"I like the articles you are writing on the History of Superstition. Quite illuminating," remarked Mr. Simson.

"It's many a year, I am afraid, to the final chapter," thought their author.

"They afford much food for reflection," thought Mr. Simson, "though I cannot myself go as far as you do in including Christianity under that heading."

Mary frowned at him; but Mr. Simson, eager for argument or not noticing, blundered on:—

"Whether we accept the miraculous explanation of Christ's birth," continued Mr. Simson, in his best street-corner voice, "or whether, with the great French writer whose name for the moment escapes me, we regard Him merely as a man inspired, we must, I think, admit that His teaching has been of help: especially to the poor."

The fanatic turned upon him so fiercely that Mr. Simson's arm involuntarily assumed the posture of defence.

"To the poor?" the old man almost shrieked. "To the poor that he has robbed of all power of resistance to oppression by his vile, submissive creed! that he has drugged into passive acceptance of every evil done to them by his false promises that their sufferings here shall win for them some wonderful reward when they are dead. What has been his teaching to the poor? Bow your backs to the lash, kiss the rod that scars your flesh. Be ye humble, oh, my people. Be ye poor in spirit. Let Wrong rule triumphant through the world. Raise no hand against it, lest ye suffer my eternal punishments. Learn from me to be meek and lowly. Learn to be good slaves and give no trouble to your taskmasters. Let them turn the world into a hell for you. The grave—the grave shall be your gate to happiness.

"Helpful to the poor? Helpful to their rulers, to their owners. They take good care that Christ shall be well taught. Their fat priests shall bear his message to the poor. The rod may be broken, the prison door be forced. It is Christ that shall bind the people in eternal fetters. Christ, the lackey, the jackal of the rich."

Mr. Simson was visibly shocked. Evidently he was less familiar with the opinions of *The Rationalist* than he had thought.

"I really must protest," exclaimed Mr. Simson. "To whatever wrong uses His words may have been twisted, Christ Himself I regard as divine, and entitled to be spoken of with reverence. His whole life, His sufferings—"

But the old fanatic's vigour had not yet exhausted itself.

"His sufferings!" he interrupted. "Does suffering entitle a man to be regarded as divine? If so, so also am I a God. Look at me!" He stretched out his long, thin arms with their claw-like hands, thrusting forward his great savage head that the bony, wizened throat seemed hardly strong enough to bear. "Wealth, honour, happiness: I had them once. I had wife, children and a home. Now I creep an outcast, keeping to the shadows, and the children in the street throw stones at me. Thirty years I have starved that I might preach. They shut me in their prisons, they hound me into garrets. They jibe at me and mock me, but they cannot silence me. What of my life? Am I divine?"

Miss Ensor, having finished her supper, sat smoking.

"Why must you preach?" she asked. "It doesn't seem to pay you." There was a curious smile about the girl's lips as she caught Joan's eye.

He turned to her with his last flicker of passion.

"Because to this end was I born, and for this cause came I into the world, that I should bear witness unto the truth," he answered.

He sank back a huddled heap upon the chair. There was foam about his mouth, great beads of sweat upon his forehead. Mary wiped them away with a corner of her apron, and felt again his trembling hands. "Oh, please don't talk to him any more," she pleaded, "not till he's had his supper." She fetched her fine shawl, and pinned it round him. His eyes followed her as she hovered about him. For the first time, since he had entered the room, they looked human.

They gathered round the table. Mr. Baptiste was still pinned up in Mary's bright shawl. It lent him a curious dignity. He might have been some ancient prophet stepped from the pages of the Talmud. Miss Ensor completed her supper with a cup of tea and some little cakes: "just to keep us all company," as Mary had insisted.

The old fanatic's eyes passed from face to face. There was almost the suggestion of a smile about the savage mouth.

"A strange supper-party," he said. "Cyril the Apostate; and Julius who strove against the High Priests and the Pharisees; and Inez a dancer before the people; and Joanna a daughter of the rulers, gathered together in the house of one Mary a servant of the Lord."

"Are you, too, a Christian?" he asked of Joan.

"Not yet," answered Joan. "But I hope to be, one day." She spoke without thinking, not quite knowing what she meant. But it came back to her in after years.

The talk grew lighter under the influence of Mary's cooking. Mr. Baptiste could be interesting when he got away from his fanaticism; and even the apostolic Mr. Simson had sometimes noticed humour when it had chanced his way.

A message came for Mary about ten o'clock, brought by a scared little girl, who whispered it to her at the door. Mary apologized. She had to go out. The party broke up. Mary disappeared into the next room and returned in a shawl and bonnet, carrying a small brown paper parcel. Joan walked with her as far as the King's Road.

"A little child is coming," she confided to Joan. She was quite excited about it.

Joan thought. "It's curious," she said, "one so seldom hears of anybody being born on Christmas Day."

They were passing a lamp. Joan had never seen a face look quite so happy as Mary's looked, just then.

"It always seems to me Christ's birthday," she said, "whenever a child is born."

They had reached the corner. Joan could see her bus in the distance.

She stooped and kissed the little withered face.

"Don't stop," she whispered.

Mary gave her a hug, and almost ran away. Joan watched the little child-like figure growing smaller. It glided in and out among the people.

CHAPTER XI

In the spring, Joan, at Mrs. Denton's request, undertook a mission. It was to go to Paris. Mrs. Denton had meant to go herself, but was laid up with sciatica; and the matter, she considered, would not brook of any delay.

"It's rather a delicate business," she told Joan. She was lying on a couch in her great library, and Joan was seated by her side. "I want someone who can go into private houses and mix with educated people on their own level; and especially I want you to see one or two women: they count in France. You know French pretty well, don't you?"

"Oh, sufficiently," Joan answered. The one thing her mother had done for her had been to talk French with her when she was a child; and at Girton she had chummed on with a French girl, and made herself tolerably perfect.

"You will not go as a journalist," continued Mrs. Denton; "but as a personal friend of mine, whose discretion I shall vouch for. I want you to find out what the people I am sending you among are thinking themselves, and what they consider ought to be done. If we are not very careful on both sides we shall have the newspapers whipping us into war."

The perpetual Egyptian trouble had cropped up again and the Carleton papers, in particular, were already sounding the tocsin. Carleton's argument was that we ought to fall upon France and crush her, before she could develop her supposed submarine menace. His flaming posters were at every corner. Every obscure French newspaper was being ransacked for "Insults and Pinpricks."

"A section of the Paris Press is doing all it can to help him, of course," explained Mrs. Denton. "It doesn't seem to matter to them that Germany is only waiting her opportunity, and that, if Russia comes in, it is bound to bring Austria. Europe will pay dearly one day for the luxury of a free Press."

"But you're surely not suggesting any other kind of Press, at this period of the world's history?" exclaimed Joan.

"Oh, but I am," answered the old lady with a grim tightening of the lips. "Not even Carleton would be allowed to incite to murder or arson. I would have him prosecuted for inciting a nation to war."

"Why is the Press always so eager for war?" mused Joan. "According to their own account, war doesn't pay them."

"I don't suppose it does: not directly," answered Mrs. Denton. "But it helps them to establish their position and get a tighter hold upon the public. War does pay the newspaper in the long run. The daily newspaper lives on commotion, crime, lawlessness in general. If people no longer enjoyed reading about violence and bloodshed half their occupation, and that the most profitable half would be gone. It is the interest of the newspaper to keep alive the savage in human nature; and war affords the readiest means of doing this. You can't do much to increase the number of gruesome murders and loathsome assaults, beyond giving all possible advertisement to them when they do occur. But you can preach war, and cover yourself with glory, as a patriot, at the same time."

"I wonder how many of my ideals will be left to me," sighed Joan. "I always used to regard the Press as the modern pulpit."

"The old pulpit became an evil, the moment it obtained unlimited power," answered Mrs. Denton. "It originated persecution and inflamed men's passions against one another. It, too, preached war for its own ends, taught superstition, and punished thought as a crime. The Press of to-day is stepping into the shoes of the medieval priest. It aims at establishing the worst kind of tyranny: the tyranny over men's minds. They pretend to fight among themselves, but it's rapidly becoming a close corporation. The Institute of Journalists will soon be followed by the Union of Newspaper Proprietors and the few independent journals will be squeezed out. Already we have German shareholders on English papers; and English capital is interested in the St. Petersburg Press. It will one day have its International Pope and its school of cosmopolitan cardinals."

Joan laughed. "I can see Carleton rather fancying himself in a tiara," she said. "I must tell Phillips what you say. He's out for a fight with him. Government by Parliament or Government by Press is going to be his war cry."

"Good man," said Mrs. Denton. "I'm quite serious. You tell him from me that the next revolution has got to be against the Press. And it will be the stiffest fight Democracy has ever had."

The old lady had tired herself. Joan undertook the mission. She thought she would rather enjoy it, and Mrs. Denton promised to let her have full instructions. She would write to her friends in Paris and prepare them for Joan's coming.

Joan remembered Folk, the artist she had met at Flossie's party, who had promised to walk with her on the terrace at St. Germain, and tell her more about her mother. She looked up his address on her return home, and wrote to him, giving him the name of the hotel in the Rue de Grenelle where Mrs. Denton had arranged that she should stay. She found a note from him awaiting her when she arrived there. He thought she would like to be quiet after her journey. He would call round in the morning. He had presumed on the privilege of age to send her some lilies. They had been her mother's favourite flower. "Monsieur Folk, the great artist," had brought them himself, and placed them in her dressing-room, so Madame informed her.

It was one of the half-dozen old hotels still left in Paris, and was built round a garden famous for its mighty mulberry tree. She breakfasted underneath it, and was reading there when Folk appeared before her, smiling and with his hat in his hand. He excused himself for intruding upon her so soon, thinking from what she had written him that her first morning might be his only chance. He evidently considered her remembrance of him a feather in his cap.

"We old fellows feel a little sadly, at times, how unimportant we are," he explained. "We are grateful when Youth throws us a smile."

"You told me my coming would take you back thirty-three years," Joan reminded him. "It makes us about the same age. I shall treat you as just a young man."

He laughed. "Don't be surprised," he said, "if I make a mistake occasionally and call you Lena."

Joan had no appointment till the afternoon. They drove out to St. Germain, and had *déjeuner* at a small restaurant opposite the Château; and afterwards they strolled on to the terrace.

"What was my mother doing in Paris?" asked Joan,

"She was studying for the stage," he answered. "Paris was the only school in those days. I was at Julien's studio. We acted together for some charity. I had always been fond of it. An American manager who was present offered us both an engagement, and I thought it would be a change and that I could combine the two arts."

"And it was here that you proposed to her," said Joan.

"Just by that tree that leans forward," he answered, pointing with his cane a little way ahead. "I thought that in America I'd get another chance. I might have if your father hadn't come along. I wonder if he remembers me."

"Did you ever see her again, after her marriage?" asked Joan.

"No," he answered. "We used to write to one another until she gave it up. She had got into the habit of looking upon me as a harmless sort of thing to confide in and ask advice of—which she never took."

"Forgive me," he said. "You must remember that I am still her lover." They had reached the tree that leant a little forward beyond its fellows, and he had halted and turned so that he was facing her. "Did she and your father get on together. Was she happy?"

"I don't think she was happy," answered Joan. "She was at first. As a child, I can remember her singing and laughing about the house, and she liked always to have people about her. Until her illness came. It changed her very much. But my father was gentleness itself, to the end."

They had resumed their stroll. It seemed to her that he looked at her once or twice a little oddly without speaking. "What caused your mother's illness?" he asked, abruptly.

The question troubled her. It struck her with a pang of self-reproach that she had always been indifferent to her mother's illness, regarding it as more or less imaginary. "It was mental rather than physical, I think," she answered. "I never knew what brought it about."

Again he looked at her with that odd, inquisitive expression. "She never got over it?" he asked.

"Oh, there were times," answered Joan, "when she was more like her old self again. But I don't think she ever quite got over it. Unless it was towards the end," she added. "They told me she seemed much better for a little while before she died. I was away at Cambridge at the time."

"Poor dear lady," he said, "all those years! And poor Jack Allway." He seemed to be talking to himself. Suddenly he turned to her. "How is the dear fellow?" he asked.

Again the question troubled her. She had not seen her father since that week-end, nearly six months ago, when she had ran down to see him because she wanted something from him. "He felt my mother's death very deeply," she answered. "But he's well enough in health."

"Remember me to him," he said. "And tell him I thank him for all those years of love and gentleness. I don't think he will be offended."

He drove her back to Paris, and she promised to come and see him in his studio and let him introduce her to his artist friends.

"I shall try to win you over, I warn you," he said. "Politics will never reform the world. They appeal only to men's passions and hatreds. They divide us. It is Art that is going to civilize mankind; broaden his sympathies. Art speaks to him the common language of his loves, his dreams, reveals to him the universal kinship."

Mrs. Denton's friends called upon her, and most of them invited her to their houses. A few were politicians, senators or ministers. Others were bankers, heads of business houses, literary men and women. There were also a few quiet folk with names that were historical. They all thought that war between France and England would be a world disaster, but were not very hopeful of averting it. She learnt that Carleton was in Berlin trying to secure possession of a well-known German daily that happened at the moment to be in low water. He was working for an alliance between Germany and England. In France, the Royalists had come to an understanding with the Clericals, and both were evidently making ready to throw in their lot with the war-mongers, hoping that out of the troubled waters the fish would come their way. Of course everything depended on the people. If the people only knew it! But they didn't. They stood about in puzzled flocks, like sheep, wondering which way the newspaper dog was going to hound them. They took her to the great music halls. Every allusion to war was greeted with rapturous applause. The Marseillaise was demanded and encored till the orchestra rebelled from sheer exhaustion. Joan's patience was sorely tested. She had to listen with impassive face to coarse jests and brutal gibes directed against England and everything English; to sit unmoved while the vast audience rocked with laughter at senseless caricatures of supposed English soldiers whose knees always gave way at the sight of a French uniform. Even in the eyes of her courteous hosts, Joan's quick glance would occasionally detect a curious glint. The fools! Had they never heard of Waterloo and Trafalgar? Even if their memories might be excused for forgetting Crecy and Poictiers and the campaigns of Marlborough. One evening—it had been a particularly trying one for Joan—there stepped upon the stage a wooden-looking man in a kilt with bagpipes under his arm. How he had got himself into the programme Joan could not understand. Managerial watchfulness must have gone to sleep for once. He played Scotch melodies, and the Parisians liked them, and when he had finished they called him back. Joan and her friends occupied a box close to the stage. The wooden-looking Scot glanced up at her, and their eyes met. And as the applause died down there rose the first low warning strains of the Pibroch. Joan sat up in her chair and her lips parted. The savage music quickened. It shrilled and skrealed. The blood came surging through her veins.

And suddenly something lying hidden there leaped to life within her brain. A mad desire surged hold of her to rise and shout defiance at those three thousand pairs of hostile eyes confronting her. She clutched at the arms of her chair and so kept her seat. The pibroch ended with its wild sad notes of wailing, and slowly the mist cleared from her eyes, and the stage was empty. A strange hush had fallen on the house.

She was not aware that her hostess had been watching her. She was a sweet-faced, white-haired lady. She touched Joan lightly on the hand. "That's the trouble," she whispered. "It's in our blood."

Could we ever hope to eradicate it? Was not the survival of this fighting instinct proof that war was still needful to us? In the sculpture-room of an exhibition she came upon a painted statue of Bellona. Its grotesqueness shocked her at first sight, the red streaming hair, the wild eyes filled with fury, the wide open mouth—one could almost hear it screaming—the white uplifted arms with outstretched hands! Appalling! Terrible! And yet, as she gazed at it, gradually the thing grew curiously real to her. She seemed to hear the gathering of the chariots, the neighing of the horses, the hurrying of many feet, the sound of an armouring multitude, the shouting, and the braying of the trumpets.

These cold, thin-lipped calculators, arguing that "War doesn't pay"; those lank-haired cosmopolitans, preaching their "International," as if the only business of mankind were wages! War still was the stern school where men learnt virtue, duty, forgetfulness of self, faithfulness unto death.

This particular war, of course, must be stopped: if it were not already too late. It would be a war for markets; for spheres of commercial influence; a sordid war that would degrade the people. War, the supreme test of a nation's worth, must be reserved for great ideals. Besides, she wanted to down Carleton.

One of the women on her list, and the one to whom Mrs. Denton appeared to attach chief importance, a Madame de Barante, disappointed Joan. She seemed to have so few opinions of her own. She had buried her young husband during the Franco-Prussian war. He had been a soldier. And she had remained unmarried. She was still beautiful.

"I do not think we women have the right to discuss war," she confided to Joan in her gentle, high-bred voice. "I suppose you think that out of date. I should have thought so myself forty years ago. We talk of 'giving' our sons and lovers, as if they were ours to give. It makes me a little angry when I hear pampered women speak like that. It is the men who have to suffer and die. It is for them to decide."

"But perhaps I can arrange a meeting for you with a friend," she added, "who will be better able to help you, if he is in Paris. I will let you know."

She told Joan what she remembered herself of 1870. She had turned her country house into a hospital and had seen a good deal of the fighting.

"It would not do to tell the truth, or we should have our children growing up to hate war," she concluded.

She was as good as her word, and sent Joan round a message the next morning to come and see her in the afternoon. Joan was introduced to a Monsieur de Chaumont. He was a soldierly-looking gentleman, with a grey moustache, and a deep scar across his face.

"Hanged if I can see how we are going to get out of it," he answered Joan cheerfully. "The moment there is any threat of war, it becomes a point of honour with every nation to do nothing to avoid it. I remember my old duelling days. The quarrel may have been about the silliest trifle imaginable. A single word would have explained the whole thing away. But to utter it would have stamped one as a coward. This Egyptian Tra-la-la! It isn't worth the bones of a single grenadier, as our friends across the Rhine would say. But I expect, before it's settled, there will be men's bones sufficient, bleaching on the desert, to build another Pyramid. It's so easily started: that's the devil of it. A mischievous boy can throw a lighted match into a powder magazine, and then it becomes every patriot's business to see that it isn't put out. I hate war. It accomplishes nothing, and leaves everything in a greater muddle than it was before. But if the idea ever catches fire, I shall have to do all I can to fan the conflagration. Unless I am prepared to be branded as a poltroon. Every professional soldier is supposed to welcome war. Most of us do: it's our opportunity. There's some excuse for us. But these men—Carleton and their lot: I regard them as nothing better than the Ménades of the Commune. They care nothing if the whole of Europe blazes. They cannot personally get harmed whatever happens. It's fun to them."

"But the people who can get harmed," argued Joan. "The men who will be dragged away from their work, from their business, used as 'cannon fodder.'"

He shrugged his shoulders. "Oh, they are always eager enough for it, at first," he answered. "There is the excitement. The curiosity. You must remember that life is a monotonous affair to the great mass of the people. There's the natural craving to escape from it; to court adventure. They are not so enthusiastic about it after they have tasted it. Modern warfare, they soon find, is about as dull a business as science ever invented."

There was only one hope that he could see: and that was to switch the people's mind on to some other excitement. His advices from London told him that a parliamentary crisis was pending. Could not Mrs. Denton and her party do something to hasten it? He, on his side, would consult with the Socialist leaders, who might have something to suggest.

He met Joan, radiant, a morning or two later. The English Government had resigned and preparations for a general election were already on foot.

"And God has been good to us, also," he explained.

A well-known artist had been found murdered in his bed and grave suspicion attached to his beautiful young wife.

"She deserves the Croix de Guerre, if it is proved that she did it," he thought. "She will have saved many thousands of lives—for the present."

Folk had fixed up a party at his studio to meet her. She had been there once or twice; but this was a final affair. She had finished her business in Paris and would be leaving the next morning. To her surprise, she found Phillips there. He had come over hurriedly to attend a Socialist conference, and Leblanc, the editor of *Le Nouveau Monde*, had brought him along.

"I took Smedley's place at the last moment," he whispered to her. "I've never been abroad before. You don't mind, do you?"

It didn't strike her as at all odd that a leader of a political party should ask her "if she minded" his being in Paris to attend a political conference. He was wearing a light grey suit and a blue tie. There was nothing about him, at that moment, suggesting that he was a leader of any sort. He might have been just any man, but for his eyes.

"No," she whispered. "Of course not. I don't like your tie." It seemed to depress him, that.

She felt elated at the thought that he would see her for the first time amid surroundings where she would shine. Folk came forward to meet her with that charming air of protective deference that he had adopted towards her. He might have been some favoured minister of state kissing the hand of a youthful Queen. She glanced down the long studio, ending in its fine window overlooking the park. Some of the most distinguished men in Paris were there, and the immediate stir of admiration that her entrance had created was unmistakable. Even the women turned pleased glances at her; as if willing to recognize in her their representative. A sense of power came to her that made her feel kind to all the world. There was no need for her to be clever: to make any effort to attract. Her presence, her sympathy, her approval seemed to be all that was needed of her. She had the consciousness that by the mere exercise of her will she could sway the thoughts and actions of these men: that sovereignty had been given to her. It reflected itself in her slightly heightened colour, in the increased brilliance of her eyes, in the confident case of all her movements. It added a compelling softness to her voice.

She never quite remembered what the talk was about. Men were brought up and presented to her, and hung about her words, and sought to please her. She had spoken her own thoughts, indifferent whether they expressed agreement or not; and the argument had invariably taken another plane. It seemed so important that she should be convinced. Some had succeeded, and had been strengthened.

Others had failed, and had departed sorrowful, conscious of the necessity of "thinking it out again."

Guests with other engagements were taking their leave. A piquante little woman, outrageously but effectively dressed—she looked like a drawing by Beardsley—drew her aside. "I've always wished I were a man," she said. "It seemed to me that they had all the power. From this afternoon, I shall be proud of belonging to the governing sex."

She laughed and slipped away.

Phillips was waiting for her in the vestibule. She had forgotten him; but now she felt glad of his humble request to be allowed to see her home. It would have been such a big drop from her crowded hour of triumph to the long lonely cab ride and the solitude of the hotel. She resolved to be gracious, feeling a little sorry for her neglect of him—but reflecting with satisfaction that he had probably been watching her the whole time.

"What's the matter with my tie?" he asked. "Wrong colour?"

She laughed. "Yes," she answered. "It ought to be grey to match your suit. And so ought your socks."

"I didn't know it was going to be such a swell affair, or I shouldn't have come," he said.

She touched his hand lightly.

"I want you to get used to it," she said. "It's part of your work. Put your brain into it, and don't be afraid."

"I'll try," he said.

He was sitting on the front seat, facing her. "I'm glad I went," he said with sudden vehemence. "I loved watching you, moving about among all those people. I never knew before how beautiful you are."

Something in his eyes sent a slight thrill of fear through her. It was not an unpleasant sensation—rather exhilarating. She watched the passing street till she felt that his eyes were no longer devouring her.

"You're not offended?" he asked. "At my thinking you beautiful?" he added, in case she hadn't understood.

She laughed. Her confidence had returned to her. "It doesn't generally offend a woman," she answered.

He seemed relieved. "That's what's so wonderful about you," he said. "I've met plenty of clever, brilliant women, but one could forget that they were women. You're everything."

He pleaded, standing below her on the steps of the hotel, that she would dine with him. But she shook her head. She had her packing to do. She could have managed it; but something prudent and absurd had suddenly got hold of her; and he went away with much the same look in his eyes that comes to a dog when he finds that his master cannot be persuaded into an excursion.

She went up to her room. There really was not much to do. She could quite well finish her packing in the morning. She sat down at the desk and set to work to arrange her papers. It was a warm spring evening, and the window was open.

A crowd of noisy sparrows seemed to be delighted about something. From somewhere, unseen, a blackbird was singing. She read over her report for Mrs. Denton. The blackbird seemed never to have heard of war. He sang as if the whole world were a garden of languor and love. Joan looked at her watch. The first gong would sound in a few minutes. She pictured the dreary, silent dining-room with its few scattered occupants, and her heart sank at the prospect. To her relief came remembrance of a cheerful but entirely respectable restaurant near to the Louvre to which she had been taken a few nights before. She had noticed quite a number of women dining there alone. She closed her dispatch case with a snap and gave a glance at herself in the great mirror. The blackbird was still singing.

She walked up the Rue des Sts. Pères, enjoying the delicious air. Half way across the bridge she overtook a man, strolling listlessly in front of her. There was something familiar about him. He was wearing a grey suit and had his hands in his pockets. Suddenly the truth flashed upon her. She stopped. If he strolled on, she would be able to slip back. Instead of which he abruptly turned to look down at a passing steamer, and they were face to face.

It made her mad, the look of delight that came into his eyes. She could have boxed his ears. Hadn't he anything else to do but hang about the streets.

He explained that he had been listening to the band in the gardens, returning by the Quai d'Orsay.

"Do let me come with you," he said. "I kept myself free this evening, hoping. And I'm feeling so lonesome."

Poor fellow! She had come to understand that feeling. After all, it wasn't altogether his fault that they had met. And she had been so cross to him!

He was reading every expression on her face.

"It's such a lovely evening," he said. "Couldn't we go somewhere and dine under a tree?"

It would be rather pleasant. There was a little place at Meudon, she remembered. The plane trees would just be in full leaf.

A passing cab had drawn up close to them. The chauffeur was lighting his pipe.

Even Mrs. Grundy herself couldn't object to a journalist dining with a politician!

The stars came out before they had ended dinner. She had made him talk about himself. It was marvellous what he had accomplished with his opportunities. Ten hours a day in the mines had earned for him his living, and the night had given him his leisure. An attic, lighted by a tallow candle, with a shelf of books that left him hardly enough for bread, had been his Alma Mater. History was his chief study. There was hardly an authority Joan could think of with which he was not familiar. *Julius Caesar* was his favourite play. He seemed to know it by heart. At twenty-three he had been elected a delegate, and had entered Parliament at twenty-eight. It had been a life of hardship, of privation, of constant strain; but she found herself unable to pity him. It was a tale of strength, of struggle, of victory, that he told her.

Strength! The shaded lamplight fell upon his fearless kindly face with its flashing eyes and its humorous mouth. He ought to have been drinking out of a horn, not a wine glass that his well-shaped hand could have crushed by a careless pressure. In a winged helmet and a coat of mail he would have looked so much more fitly dressed than in that soft felt hat and ridiculous blue tie.

She led him to talk on about the future. She loved to hear his clear, confident voice with its touch of boyish boastfulness. What was there to stop him? Why should he not climb from power to power till he had reached the end!

And as he talked and dreamed there grew up in her heart a fierce anger. What would her own future be? She would marry probably some man of her own class, settle down to the average woman's "life"; be allowed, like a spoilt child, to still "take an interest" in public affairs: hold "drawing-rooms" attended by cranks and political nonentities: be President, perhaps, of the local Woman's Liberal League. The alternative: to spend her days glued to a desk, penning exhortations to the people that Carleton and his like might or might not allow them to read; while youth and beauty slipped away from her, leaving her one of the ten thousand other lonely, faded women, forcing themselves unwelcome into men's jobs. There came to her a sense of having been robbed of what was hers by primitive eternal law. Greyson had been right. She did love power—power to serve and shape the world. She would have earned it and used it well. She could have helped him, inspired him. They would have worked together: he the force and she the guidance. She would have supplied the things he lacked. It was to her he came for counsel, as it was. But for her he would never have taken the first step. What right had this poor brainless lump of painted flesh to share his wounds, his triumphs? What help could she give him when the time should come that he should need it?

Suddenly he broke off. "What a fool I'm making of myself," he said. "I always was a dreamer."

She forced a laugh. "Why shouldn't it come true?" she asked.

They had the little garden to themselves. The million lights of Paris shone below them.

"Because you won't be there," he answered, "and without you I can't do it. You think I'm always like I am to-night, bragging, confident. So I am when you are with me. You give me back my strength. The plans and hopes and dreams that were slipping from me come crowding round me, laughing and holding out their hands. They are like the children. They need two to care for them. I want to talk about them to someone who understands them and loves them, as I do. I want to feel they are dear to someone else, as well as to myself: that I must work for them for her sake, as well as for my own. I want someone to help me to bring them up."

There were tears in his eyes. He brushed them angrily away. "Oh, I know I ought to be ashamed of myself," he said. "It wasn't her fault. She wasn't to know that a hot-blooded young chap of twenty hasn't all his wits about him, any more than I was. If I had never met you, it wouldn't have mattered. I'd have done my bit of good, and have stopped there, content. With you beside me"—he looked away from her to where the silent city peeped through its veil of night—"I might have left the world better than I found it."

The blood had mounted to her face. She drew back into the shadow, beyond the tiny sphere of light made by the little lamp.

"Men have accomplished great things without a woman's help," she said.

"Some men," he answered. "Artists and poets. They have the woman within them. Men like myself—the mere fighter: we are incomplete in ourselves. Male and female created He them. We are lost without our mate."

He was thinking only of himself. Had he no pity for her. So was she, also, useless without her mate. Neither was she of those, here and there, who can stand alone. Her task was that of the eternal woman: to make a home: to cleanse the world of sin and sorrow, make it a kinder dwelling-place for the children that should come. This man was her true helpmeet. He would have been her weapon, her dear servant; and she could have rewarded him as none other ever could. The lamplight fell upon his ruddy face, his strong white hands resting on the flimsy table. He belonged to an older order than her own. That suggestion about him of something primitive, of something not yet altogether tamed. She felt again that slight thrill of fear that so strangely excited her. A mist seemed to be obscuring all things. He seemed to be coming towards her. Only by keeping her eyes fixed on his moveless hands, still resting on the table, could she convince herself that his arms were not closing about her, that she was not being drawn nearer and nearer to him, powerless to resist.

Suddenly, out of the mist, she heard voices. The waiter was standing beside him with the bill. She reached out her hand and took it. The usual few mistakes had occurred. She explained them, good temperedly, and the waiter, with profuse apologies, went back to have it corrected.

He turned to her as the man went. "Try and forgive me," he said in a low voice. "It all came tumbling out before I thought what I was saying."

The blood was flowing back into her veins. "Oh, it wasn't your fault," she answered. "We must make the best we can of it."

He bent forward so that he could see into her eyes.

"Tell me," he said. There was a note of fierce exultation in his voice. "I'll promise never to speak of it again. If I had been a free man, could I have won you?"

She had risen while he was speaking. She moved to him and laid her hands upon his shoulders.

"Will you serve me and fight for me against all my enemies?" she asked.

"So long as I live," he answered.

She glanced round. There was no sign of the returning waiter. She bent over him and kissed him.

"Don't come with me," she said. "There's a cab stand in the Avenue. I shall walk to Sèvres and take the train."

She did not look back.

CHAPTER XII

She reached home in the evening. The Phillips's old rooms had been twice let since Christmas, but were now again empty. The McKean with his silent ways and his everlasting pipe had gone to America to superintend the production of one of his plays. The house gave her the feeling of being haunted. She had her dinner brought up to her and prepared for a long evening's work; but found herself unable to think—except on the one subject that she wanted to put off thinking about. To her relief the last post brought her a letter from Arthur. He had been called to Lisbon to look after a contract, and would be away for a fortnight. Her father was not as well as he had been.

It seemed to just fit in. She would run down and spend a few quiet days at Liverpool. In her old familiar room where the moon peeped in over the tops of the tall pines she would be able to reason things out. Perhaps her father would be able to help her. She had lost her childish conception of him as of someone prim and proper, with cut and dried formulas for all occasions. That glimpse he had shown her of himself had established a fellowship between them. He, too, had wrestled with life's riddles, not sure of his own answers. She found him suffering from his old heart trouble, but more cheerful than she had known him for years. Arthur seemed to be doing wonders with the men. They were coming to trust him.

"The difficulty I have always been up against," explained her father, "has been their suspicion. 'What's the cunning old rascal up to now? What's his little game?' That is always what I have felt they were thinking to themselves whenever I have wanted to do anything for them. It isn't anything he says to them. It seems to be just he, himself."

He sketched out their plans to her. It seemed to be all going in at one ear and out at the other. What was the matter with her? Perhaps she was tired without knowing it. She would get him to tell her all about it to-morrow. Also, to-morrow, she would tell him about Phillips, and ask his advice. It was really quite late. If he talked any more now, it would give her a headache. She felt it coming on.

She made her "good-night" extra affectionate, hoping to disguise her impatience. She wanted to get up to her own room.

But even that did not help her. It seemed in some mysterious way to be no longer her room, but the room of someone she had known and half forgotten: who would never come back. It gave her the same feeling she had experienced on returning to the house in London: that the place was haunted. The high cheval glass from her mother's dressing-room had been brought there for her use. The picture of an absurdly small child—the child to whom this room had once belonged—standing before it naked, rose before her eyes. She had wanted to see herself. She had thought that only her clothes stood in the way. If we could but see ourselves, as in some magic mirror? All the garments usage and education has dressed us up in laid aside. What was she underneath her artificial niceties, her prim moralities, her laboriously acquired restraints, her unconscious pretences and hypocrisies? She changed her clothes for a loose robe, and putting out the light drew back the curtains. The moon peeped in over the top of the tall pines, but it only stared at her, indifferent. It seemed to be looking for somebody else.

Suddenly, and intensely to her own surprise, she fell into a passionate fit of weeping. There was no reason for it, and it was altogether so unlike her. But for quite a while she was unable to control it. Gradually, and of their own accord, her sobs lessened, and she was able to wipe her eyes and take stock of herself in the long glass. She wondered for the moment whether it was really her own reflection that she saw there or that of some ghostly image of her mother. She had so often seen the same look in her mother's eyes. Evidently the likeness between them was more extensive than she had imagined. For the first time she became conscious of an emotional, hysterical side to her nature of which she had been unaware. Perhaps it was just as well that she had discovered it. She would have to keep a stricter watch upon herself. This question of her future relationship with Phillips: it would have to be thought out coldly, dispassionately. Nothing unexpected must be allowed to enter into it.

It was some time before she fell asleep. The high glass faced her as she lay in bed. She could not get away from the idea that it was her mother's face that every now and then she saw reflected there.

She woke late the next morning. Her father had already left for the works. She was rather glad to have no need of talking. She would take a long walk into the country, and face the thing squarely with the help of the cheerful sun and the free west wind that was blowing from the sea. She took the train up north and struck across the hills. Her spirits rose as she walked.

It was only the intellectual part of him she wanted—the spirit, not the man. She would be taking nothing away from the woman, nothing that had ever belonged to her. All the rest of him: his home life, the benefits that would come to her from his improved means, from his social position: all that the woman had ever known or cared for in him would still be hers. He would still remain to her the kind husband and father. What more was the woman capable of understanding? What more had she any right to demand?

It was not of herself she was thinking. It was for his work's sake that she wanted to be near to him always: that she might counsel him, encourage him. For this she was prepared to sacrifice herself, give up her woman's claim on life. They would be friends, comrades—nothing more. That little lurking curiosity of hers, concerning what it would be like to feel his strong arms round her, pressing her closer and closer to him: it was only a foolish fancy. She could easily laugh that out of herself. Only bad women had need to be afraid of themselves. She would keep guard for both of them. Their purity of motive, their high purpose, would save them from the danger of anything vulgar or ridiculous.

Of course they would have to be careful. There must be no breath of gossip, no food for evil tongues. About that she was determined even more for his sake than her own. It would be fatal to his career. She was quite in agreement with the popular demand, supposed to be peculiarly English, that a public man's life should be above reproach. Of what use these prophets without self-control; these social reformers who could not shake the ape out of themselves? Only the brave could give courage to others. Only through the pure could God's light shine upon men.

It was vexing his having moved round the corner, into North Street. Why couldn't the silly woman have been content where she was. Living under one roof, they could have seen one another as often as was needful without attracting attention. Now, she supposed, she would have to be more than ever the bosom friend of Mrs. Phillips—spend hours amid that hideous furniture, surrounded by those bilious wallpapers. Of course he could not come to her. She hoped he would appreciate the sacrifice she would be making for him. Fortunately Mrs. Phillips would give no trouble. She would not even understand.

What about Hilda? No hope of hiding their secret from those sharp eyes. But Hilda would approve. They could trust Hilda. The child might prove helpful.

It cast a passing shadow upon her spirits, this necessary descent into details. It brought with it the suggestion of intrigue, of deceit: robbing the thing, to a certain extent, of its fineness. Still, what was to be done? If women were coming into public life these sort of relationships with men would have to be faced and worked out. Sex must no longer be allowed to interfere with the working together of men and women for common ends. It was that had kept the world back. They would be the pioneers of the new order. Casting aside their earthly passions, humbly with pure hearts they would kneel before God's altar. He should bless their union.

A lark was singing. She stood listening. Higher and higher he rose, pouring out his song of worship; till the tiny, fragile body disappeared as if fallen from him, leaving his sweet soul still singing. The happy tears came to her eyes, and she passed on. She did not hear that little last faint sob with which he sank exhausted back to earth beside a hidden nest among the furrows.

She had forgotten the time. It was already late afternoon. Her long walk and the keen air had made her hungry. She had a couple of eggs with her tea at a village inn, and was fortunate enough to catch a train that brought her back in time for dinner. A little ashamed of her unresponsiveness the night before, she laid herself out to be sympathetic to her father's talk. She insisted on hearing again all that he and Arthur were doing, opposing him here and there with criticism just sufficient to stimulate him; careful in the end to let him convince her.

These small hypocrisies were new to her. She hoped she was not damaging her character. But it was good, watching him slyly from under drawn-down lids, to see the flash of triumph that would come into his tired eyes in answer to her half-protesting: "Yes, I see your point, I hadn't thought of that," her half reluctant admission that "perhaps" he was right, there; that "perhaps" she was wrong. It was delightful to see him young again, eager, boyishly pleased with himself. It seemed there was a joy she had not dreamed of in yielding victory as well as in gaining it. A new tenderness was growing up in her. How considerate, how patient, how self-forgetful he had always been. She wanted to mother him. To take him in her arms and croon over him, hushing away remembrance of the old sad days.

Folk's words came back to her: "And poor Jack Allway. Tell him I thank him for all those years of love and gentleness." She gave him the message.

Folk had been right. He was not offended. "Dear old chap," he said. "That was kind of him. He was always generous."

He was silent for a while, with a quiet look on his face.

"Give him our love," he said. "Tell him we came together, at the end."

It was on her tongue to ask him, as so often she had meant to do of late, what had been the cause of her mother's illness—if illness it was: what it was that had happened to change both their lives. But always something had stopped her—something ever present, ever watchful, that seemed to shape itself out of the air, bending towards her with its finger on its lips.

She stayed over the week-end; and on the Saturday, at her suggestion, they took a long excursion into the country. It was the first time she had ever asked him to take her out. He came down to breakfast in a new suit, and was quite excited. In the car his hand had sought hers shyly, and, feeling her responsive pressure, he had continued to hold it; and they had sat for a long time in silence. She decided not to tell him about Phillips, just yet. He knew of him only from the Tory newspapers and would form a wrong idea. She would bring them together and leave Phillips to make his own way. He would like Phillips when he knew him, she felt sure. He, too, was a people's man. The torch passed down to him from his old Ironside ancestors, it still glowed. More than once she had seen it leap to flame. In congenial atmosphere, it would burn clear and steadfast. It occurred to her what a delightful solution of her problem, if later on her father could be persuaded to leave Arthur in charge of the works, and come to live with her in London. There was a fine block of flats near Chelsea Church with long views up and down the river. How happy they could be there; the drawing-room in the Adams style with wine-coloured curtains! He was a father any young woman could be proud to take about. Unconsciously she gave his hand an impulsive squeeze. They lunched at an old inn upon the moors; and the landlady, judging from his shy, attentive ways, had begun by addressing her as Madame.

"You grow wonderfully like your mother," he told her that evening at dinner. "There used to be something missing. But I don't feel that, now."

She wrote to Phillips to meet her, if possible, at Euston. There were things she wanted to talk to him about. There was the question whether she should go on writing for Carleton, or break with him at once. Also one or two points that were worrying her in connection with tariff reform. He was waiting for her on the platform. It appeared he, too, had much to say. He wanted her advice concerning his next speech. He had not dined and suggested supper. They could not walk about the streets. Likely enough, it was only her imagination, but it seemed to her that people in the restaurant had recognized him, and were whispering to one another: he was bound to be well known. Likewise her own appearance, she felt, was against them as regarded their desire to avoid observation. She would have to take to those mousey colours that did not suit her, and wear a veil. She hated the idea of a veil. It came from the East and belonged there. Besides, what would be the use? Unless he wore one too. "Who is the veiled woman that Phillips goes about with?" That is what they would ask. It was going to be very awkward, the whole thing. Viewed from the distance, it had looked quite fine. "Dedicating herself to the service of Humanity" was how it had presented itself to her in the garden at Meudon, the twinkling labyrinth of Paris at her feet, its sordid by-ways hidden beneath its myriad lights. She had not bargained for the dedication involving the loss of her self-respect.

They did not talk as much as they had thought they would. He was not very helpful on the Carleton question. There was so much to be said both for and against. It might be better to wait and see how circumstances shaped themselves. She thought his speech excellent. It was difficult to discover any argument against it.

He seemed to be more interested in looking at her when he thought she was not noticing. That little faint vague fear came back to her and stayed with her, but brought no quickening of her pulse. It was a fear of something ugly. She had the feeling they were both acting, that everything depended upon their not forgetting their parts. In handing things to one another, they were both of them so careful that their hands should not meet and touch.

They walked together back to Westminster and wished each other a short good-night upon what once had been their common doorstep. With her latchkey in her hand, she turned and watched his retreating figure, and suddenly a wave of longing seized her to run after him and call him back—to see his eyes light up and feel the pressure of his hands. It was only by clinging to the railings and counting till she was sure he had entered his own house round the corner and closed the door behind him, that she restrained herself.

It was a frightened face that looked at her out of the glass, as she stood before it taking off her hat.

She decided that their future meetings should be at his own house. Mrs. Phillips's only complaint was that she knocked at the door too seldom.

"I don't know what I should do without you, I really don't," confessed the grateful lady. "If ever I become a Prime Minister's wife, it's you I shall have to thank. You've got so much courage yourself, you can put the heart into him. I never had any pluck to spare myself."

She concluded by giving Joan a hug, accompanied by a sloppy but heartfelt kiss.

She would stand behind Phillips's chair with her fat arms round his neck, nodding her approval and encouragement; while Joan, seated opposite, would strain every nerve to keep her brain fixed upon the argument, never daring to look at poor Phillips's wretched face, with its pleading, apologetic eyes, lest she should burst into hysterical laughter. She hoped she was being helpful and inspiring! Mrs. Phillips would assure her afterwards that she had been wonderful. As for herself, there were periods when she hadn't the faintest idea about what she was talking.

Sometimes Mrs. Phillips, called away by domestic duty, would leave them; returning full of excuses just as they had succeeded in forgetting her. It was evident she was under the impression that her presence was useful to them, making it easier for them to open up their minds to one another.

"Don't you be put off by his seeming a bit unresponsive," Mrs. Phillips would explain. "He's shy with women. What I'm trying to do is to make him feel you are one of the family."

"And don't you take any notice of me," further explained the good woman, "when I seem to be in opposition, like. I chip in now and then on purpose, just to keep the ball rolling. It stirs him up, a bit of contradictoriness. You have to live with a man before you understand him."

One morning Joan received a letter from Phillips, marked immediate. He informed her that his brain was becoming addled. He intended that afternoon to give it a draught of fresh air. He would be at the Robin Hood gate in Richmond Park at three o'clock. Perhaps the gods would be good to him. He would wait there for half an hour to give them a chance, anyway.

She slipped the letter unconsciously into the bosom of her dress, and sat looking out of the window. It promised to be a glorious day, and London was stifling and gritty. Surely no one but an unwholesome-minded prude could jib at a walk across a park. Mrs. Phillips would be delighted to hear that she had gone. For the matter of that, she would tell her—when next they met.

Phillips must have seen her getting off the bus, for he came forward at once from the other side of the gate, his face radiant with boyish delight. A young man and woman, entering the park at the same time, looked at them and smiled sympathetically.

Joan had no idea the park contained such pleasant by-ways. But for an occasional perambulator they might have been in the heart of the country. The fallow deer stole near to them with noiseless feet, regarding them out of their large gentle eyes with looks of comradeship. They paused and listened while a missal thrush from a branch close to them poured out his song of hope and courage. From quite a long way off they could still hear his clear voice singing, telling to the young and brave his gallant message. It seemed too beautiful a day for politics. After all, politics—one has them always with one; but the spring passes.

He saw her on to a bus at Kingston, and himself went back by train. They agreed they would not mention it to Mrs. Phillips. Not that she would have minded. The danger was that she would want to come, too; honestly thinking thereby to complete their happiness. It seemed to be tacitly understood there would be other such excursions.

The summer was propitious. Phillips knew his London well, and how to get away from it. There were winding lanes in Hertfordshire, Surrey hills and commons, deep, cool, bird-haunted woods in Buckingham. Each week there was something to look forward to, something to plan for and manoeuvre. The sense of adventure, a spice of danger, added zest. She still knocked frequently, as before, at the door of the hideously-furnished little house in North Street; but Mrs. Phillips no longer oppressed her as some old man of the sea she could never hope to shake off from her shoulders. The flabby, foolish face, robbed of its terrors, became merely pitiful. She found herself able to be quite gentle and patient with Mrs. Phillips. Even the sloppy kisses she came to bear without a shudder down her spine.

"I know you are only doing it because you sympathize with his aims and want him to win," acknowledged the good lady. "But I can't help feeling grateful to you. I don't feel how useless I am while I've got you to run to."

They still discussed their various plans for the amelioration and improvement of humanity; but there seemed less need for haste than they had thought. The world, Joan discovered, was not so sad a place as she had judged it. There were chubby, rogue-eyed children; whistling lads and smiling maidens; kindly men with ruddy faces; happy mothers crooning over gurgling babies. There was no call to be fretful and vehement. They would work together in patience and in confidence. God's sun was everywhere. It needed only that dark places should be opened up and it would enter.

Sometimes, seated on a lichened log, or on the short grass of some sloping hillside, looking down upon some quiet valley, they would find they had been holding hands while talking. It was but as two happy, thoughtless children might have done. They would look at one another with frank, clear eyes and smile.

Once, when their pathway led through a littered farm-yard, he had taken her up in his arms and carried her and she had felt a glad pride in him that he had borne her lightly as if she had been a child, looking up at her and laughing.

An old bent man paused from his work and watched them. "Lean more over him, missie," he advised her. "That's the way. Many a mile I've carried my lass like that, in flood time; and never felt her weight."

Often on returning home, not knowing why, she would look into the glass. It seemed to her that the girlhood she had somehow missed was awakening in her, taking possession of her, changing her. The lips she had always seen pressed close and firm were growing curved, leaving a little parting, as though they were not quite so satisfied with one another. The level brows were becoming slightly raised. It gave her a questioning look that was new to her. The eyes beneath were less confident. They seemed to be seeking something.

One evening, on her way home from a theatre, she met Flossie. "Can't stop now," said Flossie, who was hurrying. "But I want to see you: most particular. Was going to look you up. Will you be at home to-morrow afternoon at tea-time?"

There was a distinct challenge in Flossie's eye as she asked the question. Joan felt herself flush, and thought a moment.

"Yes," she answered. "Will you be coming alone?"

"That's the idea," answered Flossie; "a heart to heart talk between you and me, and nobody else. Half-past four. Don't forget."

Joan walked on slowly. She had the worried feeling with which, once or twice, when a schoolgirl, she had crawled up the stairs to bed after the head mistress had informed her that she would see her in her private room at eleven o'clock the next morning, leaving her to guess what about. It occurred to her, in Trafalgar Square, that she had promised to take tea with the Greysons the next afternoon, to meet some big pot from America. She would have to get out of that. She felt it wouldn't do to put off Flossie.

She went to bed wakeful. It was marvellously like being at school again. What could Flossie want to see her about that was so important? She tried to pretend to herself that she didn't know. After all, perhaps it wasn't that.

But she knew that it was the instant Flossie put up her hands in order to take off her hat. Flossie always took off her hat when she meant to be unpleasant. It was her way of pulling up her sleeves. They had their tea first. They seemed both agreed that that would be best. And then Flossie pushed back her chair and sat up.

She had just the head mistress expression. Joan wasn't quite sure she oughtn't to stand. But, controlling the instinct, leant back in her chair, and tried to look defiant without feeling it.

"How far are you going?" demanded Flossie.

Joan was not in a comprehending mood.

"If you're going the whole hog, that's something I can understand," continued Flossie. "If not, you'd better pull up."

"What do you mean by the whole hog?" requested Joan, assuming dignity.

"Oh, don't come the kid," advised Flossie. "If you don't mind being talked about yourself, you might think of him. If Carleton gets hold of it, he's done for."

"'A little bird whispers to me that Robert Phillips was seen walking across Richmond Park the other afternoon in company with Miss Joan Allway, formerly one of our contributors.' Is that going to end his political career?" retorted Joan with fine sarcasm.

Flossie fixed a relentless eye upon her. "He'll wait till the bird has got a bit more than that to whisper to him," she suggested.

"There'll be nothing more," explained Joan. "So long as my friendship is of any assistance to Robert Phillips in his work, he's going to have it. What use are we going to be in politics—what's all the fuss about, if men and women mustn't work together for their common aims and help one another?"

"Why can't you help him in his own house, instead of wandering all about the country?" Flossie wanted to know.

"So I do," Joan defended herself. "I'm in and out there till I'm sick of the hideous place. You haven't seen the inside. And his wife knows all about it, and is only too glad."

"Does she know about Richmond Park—and the other places?" asked Flossie.

"She wouldn't mind if she did," explained Joan. "And you know what she's like! How can one think what one's saying with that silly, goggle-eyed face in front of one always."

Flossie, since she had become engaged, had acquired quite a matronly train of thought. She spoke kindly, with a little grave shake of her head. "My dear," she said, "the wife is always in the way. You'd feel just the same whatever her face was like."

Joan grew angry. "If you choose to suspect evil, of course you can," she answered with hauteur. "But you might have known me better. I admire the man and sympathize with him. All the things I dream of are the things he is working for. I can do more good by helping and inspiring him"—she wished she had not let slip that word "inspire." She knew that Flossie would fasten upon it—"than I can ever accomplish by myself. And I mean to do it." She really did feel defiant, now.

"I know, dear," agreed Flossie, "you've both of you made up your minds it shall always remain a beautiful union of twin spirits. Unfortunately you've both got bodies—rather attractive bodies."

"We'll keep it off that plane, if you don't mind," answered Joan with a touch of severity.

"I'm willing enough," answered Flossie. "But what about Old Mother Nature? She's going to be in this, you know."

"Take off your glasses, and look at it straight," she went on, without giving Joan time to reply. "What is it in us that 'inspires' men? If it's only advice and sympathy he's after, what's wrong with dear old Mrs. Denton? She's a good walker, except now and then, when she's got the lumbago. Why doesn't he get her to 'inspire' him?"

"It isn't only that," explained Joan. "I give him courage. I always did have more of that than is any use to a woman. He wants to be worthy of my belief in him. What is the harm if he does admire me—if a smile from me or a touch of the hand can urge him to fresh effort? Suppose he does love me—"

Flossie interrupted. "How about being quite frank?" she suggested. "Suppose we do love one another. How about putting it that way?"

"And suppose we do?" agreed Joan, her courage rising. "Why should we shun one another, as if we were both of us incapable of decency or self-control? Why must love be always assumed to make us weak and contemptible, as if it were some subtle poison? Why shouldn't it strengthen and ennoble us?"

"Why did the apple fall?" answered Flossie. "Why, when it escapes from its bonds, doesn't it soar upward? If it wasn't for the irritating law of gravity, we could skip about on the brink of precipices without danger. Things being what they are, sensible people keep as far away from the edge as possible."

"I'm sorry," she continued; "awfully sorry, old girl. It's a bit of rotten bad luck for both of you. You were just made for one another. And Fate, knowing what was coming, bustles round and gets hold of poor, silly Mrs. Phillips so as to be able to say 'Yah.'"

"Unless it all comes right in the end," she added musingly; "and the poor old soul pegs out. I wouldn't give much for her liver."

"That's not bringing me up well," suggested Joan: "putting those ideas into my head."

"Oh, well, one can't help one's thoughts," explained Flossie. "It would be a blessing all round."

They had risen. Joan folded her hands. "Thank you for your scolding, ma'am," she said. "Shall I write out a hundred lines of Greek? Or do you think it will be sufficient if I promise never to do it again?"

"You mean it?" said Flossie. "Of course you will go on seeing him—visiting them, and all that. But you won't go gadding about, so that people can talk?"

"Only through the bars, in future," she promised. "With the gaoler between us." She put her arms round Flossie and bent her head, so that her face was hidden.

Flossie still seemed troubled. She held on to Joan.

"You are sure of yourself?" she asked. "We're only the female of the species. We get hungry and thirsty, too. You know that, kiddy, don't you?"

Joan laughed without raising her face. "Yes, ma'am, I know that," she answered. "I'll be good."

She sat in the dusk after Flossie had gone; and the laboured breathing of the tired city came to her through the open window. She had rather fancied that martyr's crown. It had not looked so very heavy, the thorns not so very alarming—as seen through the window. She would wear it bravely. It would rather become her.

Facing the mirror of the days to come, she tried it on. It was going to hurt. There was no doubt of that. She saw the fatuous, approving face of the eternal Mrs. Phillips, thrust ever between them, against the background of that hideous furniture, of those bilious wall papers—the loneliness that would ever walk with her, sit down beside her in the crowded restaurant, steal up the staircase with her, creep step by step with her from room to room—the ever unsatisfied yearning for a tender word, a kindly touch. Yes, it was going to hurt.

Poor Robert! It would be hard on him, too. She could not help feeling consolation in the thought that he also would be wearing that invisible crown.

She must write to him. The sooner it was done, the better. Half a dozen contradictory moods passed over her during the composing of that letter; but to her they seemed but the unfolding of a single thought. On one page it might have been his mother writing to him; an experienced, sagacious lady; quite aware, in spite of her affection for him, of his faults and weaknesses; solicitous that he should avoid the dangers of an embarrassing entanglement; his happiness being the only consideration of importance. On others it might have been a queen laying her immutable commands upon some loyal subject, sworn to her service. Part of it might have been written by a laughing philosopher who had learnt the folly of taking life too seriously, knowing that all things pass: that the tears of to-day will be remembered with a smile. And a part of it was the unconsidered language of a loving woman. And those were the pages that he kissed.

His letter in answer was much shorter. Of course he would obey her wishes. He had been selfish, thinking only of himself. As for his political career, he did not see how that was going to suffer by his being occasionally seen in company with one of the most brilliantly intellectual women in London, known to share his views. And he didn't care if it did. But inasmuch as she valued it, all things should be sacrificed to it. It was hers to do what she would with. It was the only thing he had to offer her.

Their meetings became confined, as before, to the little house in North Street. But it really seemed as if the gods, appeased by their submission, had decided to be kind. Hilda was home for the holidays; and her piercing eyes took in the situation at a flash. She appeared to have returned with a new-born and exacting affection for her mother, that astonished almost as much as it delighted the poor lady. Feeling sudden desire for a walk or a bus ride, or to be taken to an entertainment, no one was of any use to Hilda but her mother. Daddy had his silly politics to think and talk about. He must worry them out alone; or with the assistance of Miss Allway. That was what she was there for. Mrs. Phillips, torn between her sense of duty and fear of losing this new happiness, would yield to the child's coaxing. Often they would be left alone to discuss the nation's needs uninterrupted. Conscientiously they would apply themselves to the task. Always to find that, sooner or later, they were looking at one another, in silence.

One day Phillips burst into a curious laugh. They had been discussing the problem of the smallholder. Joan had put a question to him, and with a slight start he had asked her to repeat it. But it seemed she had forgotten it.

"I had to see our solicitor one morning," he explained, "when I was secretary to a miners' union up north. A point had arisen concerning the legality of certain payments. It was a matter of vast importance to us; but he didn't seem to be taking any interest, and suddenly he jumped up. 'I'm sorry, Phillips,' he said, 'but I've got a big trouble of my own on at home—I guess you know what—and I don't seem to care a damn about yours. You'd better see Delauny, if you're in a hurry.' And I did."

He turned and leant over his desk. "I guess they'll have to find another leader if they're in a hurry," he added. "I don't seem able to think about turnips and cows."

"Don't make me feel I've interfered with your work only to spoil it," said Joan.

"I guess I'm spoiling yours, too," he answered. "I'm not worth it. I might have done something to win you and keep you. I'm not going to do much without you."

"You mean my friendship is going to be of no use to you?" asked Joan.

He raised his eyes and fixed them on her with a pleading, dog-like look.

"For God's sake don't take even that away from me," he said. "Unless you want me to go to pieces altogether. A crust does just keep one alive. One can't help thinking what a fine, strong chap one might be if one wasn't always hungry."

She felt so sorry for him. He looked such a boy, with the angry tears in his clear blue eyes, and that little childish quivering of the kind, strong, sulky mouth.

She rose and took his head between her hands and turned his face towards her. She had meant to scold him, but changed her mind and laid his head against her breast and held it there.

He clung to her, as a troubled child might, with his arms clasped round her, and his head against her breast. And a mist rose up before her, and strange, commanding voices seemed calling to her.

He could not see her face. She watched it herself with dim half consciousness as it changed before her in the tawdry mirror above the mantelpiece, half longing that he might look up and see it, half terrified lest he should.

With an effort that seemed to turn her into stone, she regained command over herself.

"I must go now," she said in a harsh voice, and he released her.

"I'm afraid I'm an awful nuisance to you," he said. "I get these moods at times. You're not angry with me?"

"No," she answered with a smile. "But it will hurt me if you fail. Remember that."

She turned down the Embankment after leaving the house. She always found the river strong and restful. So it was not only bad women that needed to be afraid of themselves—even to the most high-class young woman, with letters after her name, and altruistic interests: even to her, also, the longing for the lover's clasp. Flossie had been right. Mother Nature was not to be flouted of her children—not even of her new daughters; to them, likewise, the family trait.

She would have run away if she could, leaving him to guess at her real reason—if he were smart enough. But that would have meant excuses and explanations all round. She was writing a daily column of notes for Greyson now, in addition to the weekly letter from Clorinda; and Mrs. Denton, having compromised with her first dreams, was delegating to Joan more and more of her work. She wrote to Mrs. Phillips that she was feeling unwell and would be unable to lunch with them on the Sunday, as had been arranged. Mrs. Phillips, much disappointed, suggested Wednesday; but it seemed on Wednesday she was no better. And so it drifted on for about a fortnight, without her finding the courage to come to any decision; and then one morning, turning the corner into Abingdon Street, she felt a slight pull at her sleeve; and Hilda was beside her. The child had shown an uncanny intuition in not knocking at the door. Joan had been fearing that, and would have sent down word that she was out. But it had to be faced.

"Are you never coming again?" asked the child.

"Of course," answered Joan, "when I'm better. I'm not very well just now. It's the weather, I suppose."

The child turned her head as they walked and looked at her. Joan felt herself smarting under that look, but persisted.

"I'm very much run down," she said. "I may have to go away."

"You promised to help him," said the child.

"I can't if I'm ill," retorted Joan. "Besides, I am helping him. There are other ways of helping people than by wasting their time talking to them."

"He wants you," said the child. "It's your being there that helps him."

Joan stopped and turned. "Did he send you?" she asked.

"No," the child answered. "Mama had a headache this morning, and I slipped out. You're not keeping your promise."

Palace Yard, save for a statuesque policeman, was empty.

"How do you know that my being with him helps him?" asked Joan.

"You know things when you love anybody," explained the child. "You feel them. You will come again, soon?"

Joan did not answer.

"You're frightened," the child continued in a passionate, low voice. "You think that people will talk about you and look down upon you. You oughtn't to think about yourself. You ought to think only about him and his work. Nothing else matters."

"I am thinking about him and his work," Joan answered. Her hand sought Hilda's and held it. "There are things you don't understand. Men and women can't help each other in the way you think. They may try to, and mean no harm in the beginning, but the harm comes, and then not only the woman but the man also suffers, and his work is spoilt and his life ruined."

The small, hot hand clasped Joan's convulsively.

"But he won't be able to do his work if you keep away and never come back to him," she persisted. "Oh, I know it. It all depends upon you. He wants you."

"And I want him, if that's any consolation to you," Joan answered with a short laugh. It wasn't much of a confession. The child was cute enough to have found that out for herself. "Only you see I can't have him. And there's an end of it."

They had reached the Abbey. Joan turned and they retraced their steps slowly.

"I shall be going away soon, for a little while," she said. The talk had helped her to decision. "When I come back I will come and see you all. And you must all come and see me, now and then. I expect I shall have a flat of my own. My father may be coming to live with me. Good-bye. Do all you can to help him."

She stooped and kissed the child, straining her to her almost fiercely. But the child's lips were cold. She did not look back.

Miss Greyson was sympathetic towards her desire for a longish holiday and wonderfully helpful; and Mrs. Denton also approved, and, to Joan's surprise, kissed her; Mrs. Denton was not given to kissing. She wired to her father, and got his reply the same evening. He would be at her rooms on the day she had fixed with his travelling bag, and at her Ladyship's orders. "With love and many thanks," he had added. She waited till the day before starting to run round and say good-bye to the Phillipses. She felt it would be unwise to try and get out of doing that. Both Phillips and Hilda, she was thankful, were out; and she and Mrs. Phillips had tea alone together. The talk was difficult, so far as Joan was concerned. If the woman had been possessed of ordinary intuition, she might have arrived at the truth. Joan almost wished she would. It would make her own future task the easier. But Mrs. Phillips, it was clear, was going to be no help to her.

For her father's sake, she made pretence of eagerness, but as the sea widened between her and the harbour lights it seemed as if a part of herself were being torn away from her.

They travelled leisurely through Holland and the Rhine land, and that helped a little: the new scenes and interests; and in Switzerland they discovered a delightful little village in an upland valley with just one small hotel, and decided to stay there for a while, so as to give themselves time to get their letters. They took long walks and climbs, returning tired and hungry, looking forward to their dinner and the evening talk with the few other guests on the veranda. The days passed restfully in that hidden valley. The great white mountains closed her in. They seemed so strong and clean.

It was on the morning they were leaving that a telegram was put into her hands. Mrs. Phillips was ill at lodgings in Folkestone. She hoped that Joan, on her way back, would come to see her.

She showed the telegram to her father. "Do you mind, Dad, if we go straight back?" she asked.

"No, dear," he answered, "if you wish it."

"I would like to go back," she said.

CHAPTER XIII

Mrs. Phillips was sitting up in an easy chair near the heavily-curtained windows when Joan arrived. It was a pleasant little house in the old part of the town, and looked out upon the harbour. She was startlingly thin by comparison with what she had been; but her face was still painted. Phillips would run down by the afternoon train whenever he could get away. She never knew when he was coming, so she explained; and she could not bear the idea of his finding her "old and ugly." She had fought against his wish that she should go into a nursing home; and Joan, who in the course of her work upon the *Nursing Times* had acquired some knowledge of them as a whole, was inclined to agree with her. She was quite comfortable where she was. The landlady, according to her account, was a dear. She had sent the nurse out for a walk on getting Joan's wire, so that they could have a cosy chat. She didn't really want much attendance. It was her heart. It got feeble now and then, and she had to keep very still; that was all. Joan told how her father had suffered for years from much the same complaint. So long as you were careful there was no danger. She must take things easily and not excite herself.

Mrs. Phillips acquiesced. "It's turning me into a lazy-bones," she said with a smile. "I can sit here by the hour, just watching the bustle. I was always one for a bit of life."

The landlady entered with Joan's tea. Joan took an instinctive dislike to her. She was a large, flashy woman, wearing a quantity of cheap jewellery. Her familiarity had about it something almost threatening. Joan waited till she heard the woman's heavy tread descending the stairs, before she expressed her opinion.

"I think she only means to be cheerful," explained Mrs. Phillips. "She's quite a good sort, when you know her." The subject seemed in some way to trouble her, and Joan dropped it.

They watched the loading of a steamer while Joan drank her tea.

"He will come this afternoon, I fancy," said Mrs. Phillips. "I seem to feel it. He will be able to see you home."

Joan started. She had been thinking about Phillips, wondering what she should say to him when they met.

"What does he think," she asked, "about your illness?"

"Oh, it worries him, of course, poor dear," Mrs. Phillips answered. "You see, I've always been such a go-ahead, as a rule. But I think he's getting more hopeful. As I tell him, I'll be all right by the autumn. It was that spell of hot weather that knocked me over."

Joan was still looking out of the window. She didn't quite know what to say. The woman's altered appearance had shocked her. Suddenly she felt a touch upon her hand.

"You'll look after him if anything does happen, won't you?" The woman's eyes were pleading with her. They seemed to have grown larger. "You know what I mean, dear, don't you?" she continued. "It will be such a comfort to me to know that it's all right."

In answer the tears sprang to Joan's eyes. She knelt down and put her arms about the woman.

"Don't be so silly," she cried. "There's nothing going to happen. You're going to get fat and well again; and live to see him Prime Minister."

"I am getting thin, ain't I?" she said. "I always wanted to be thin." They both laughed.

"But I shan't see him that, even if I do live," she went on. "He'll never be that, without you. And I'd be so proud to think that he would. I shouldn't mind going then," she added.

Joan did not answer. There seemed no words that would come.

"You will promise, won't you?" she persisted, in a whisper. "It's only 'in case'—just that I needn't worry myself."

Joan looked up. There was something in the eyes looking down upon her that seemed to be compelling her.

"If you'll promise to try and get better," she answered.

Mrs. Phillips stooped and kissed her. "Of course, dear," she said. "Perhaps I shall, now that my mind is easier."

Phillips came, as Mrs. Phillips had predicted. He was surprised at seeing Joan. He had not thought she could get back so soon. He brought an evening paper with him. It contained a paragraph to the effect that Mrs. Phillips, wife of the Rt. Hon. Robert Phillips, M.P., was progressing favourably and hoped soon to be sufficiently recovered to return to her London residence. It was the first time she had had a paragraph all to herself, headed with her name. She flushed with pleasure; and Joan noticed that, after reading it again, she folded the paper up small and slipped it into her pocket. The nurse came in from her walk a little later and took Joan downstairs with her.

"She ought not to talk to more than one person at a time," the nurse explained, with a shake of the head. She was a quiet, business-like woman. She would not express a definite opinion.

"It's her mental state that is the trouble," was all that she would say. "She ought to be getting better. But she doesn't."

"You're not a Christian Scientist, by any chance?" she asked Joan suddenly.

"No," answered Joan. "Surely you're not one?"

"I don't know," answered the woman. "I believe that would do her more good than anything else. If she would listen to it. She seems to have lost all will-power."

The nurse left her; and the landlady came in to lay the table. She understood that Joan would be dining with Mr. Phillips. There was no train till the eight-forty. She kept looking at Joan as she moved about the room. Joan was afraid she would begin to talk, but she must have felt Joan's antagonism for she remained silent. Once their eyes met, and the woman leered at her.

Phillips came down looking more cheerful. He had detected improvement in Mrs. Phillips. She was more hopeful in herself. They talked in low tones during the meal, as people do whose thoughts are elsewhere. It happened quite suddenly, Phillips explained. They had come down a few days after the rising of Parliament. There had been a spell of hot weather; but nothing remarkable. The first attack had occurred about three weeks ago. It was just after Hilda had gone back to school. He wasn't sure whether he ought to send for Hilda, or not. Her mother didn't want him to—not just yet. Of course, if she got worse, he would have to. What did Joan think?—did she think there was any real danger?

Joan could not say. So much depended upon the general state of health. There was the case of her own father. Of course she would always be subject to attacks. But this one would have warned her to be careful.

Phillips thought that living out of town might be better for her, in the future—somewhere in Surrey, where he could easily get up and down. He could sleep himself at the club on nights when he had to be late.

They talked without looking at one another. They did not speak about themselves.

Mrs. Phillips was in bed when Joan went up to say good-bye. "You'll come again soon?" she asked, and Joan promised. "You've made me so happy," she whispered. The nurse was in the room.

They discussed politics in the train. Phillips had found more support for his crusade against Carleton than he had expected. He was going to open the attack at once, thus forestalling Carleton's opposition to his land scheme.

"It isn't going to be the *Daily This* and the *Daily That* and the *Weekly the Other* all combined to down me. I'm going to tell the people that it's Carleton and only Carleton—Carleton here, Carleton there, Carleton everywhere, against them. I'm going to drag him out into the open and make him put up his own fists."

Joan undertook to sound Greyson. She was sure Greyson would support him, in his balanced, gentlemanly way, that could nevertheless be quite deadly.

They grew less and less afraid of looking at one another as they felt that darkened room further and further behind them.

They parted at Charing Cross. Joan would write. They agreed it would be better to choose separate days for their visits to Folkestone.

She ran against Madge in the morning, and invited herself to tea. Her father had returned to Liverpool, and her own rooms, for some reason, depressed her.

Flossie was there with young Halliday. They were both off the next morning to his people's place in Devonshire, from where they were going to get married, and had come to say good-bye. Flossie put Sam in the passage and drew-to the door.

"Have you seen her?" she asked. "How is she?"

"Oh, she's changed a good deal," answered Joan. "But I think she'll get over it all right, if she's careful."

"I shall hope for the best," answered Flossie. "Poor old soul, she's had a good time. Don't send me a present; and then I needn't send you one—when your time comes. It's a silly custom. Besides, I've nowhere to put it. Shall be in a ship for the next six months. Will let you know when we're back."

She gave Joan a hug and a kiss, and was gone. Joan joined Madge in the kitchen, where she was toasting buns.

"I suppose she's satisfied herself that he's brainy," she laughed.

"Oh, brains aren't everything," answered Madge. "Some of the worst rotters the world has ever been cursed with have been brainy enough—men and women. We make too much fuss about brains; just as once upon a time we did about mere brute strength, thinking that was all that was needed to make a man great. Brain is only muscle translated into civilization. That's not going to save us."

"You've been thinking," Joan accused her. "What's put all that into your head?"

Madge laughed. "Mixing with so many brainy people, perhaps," she suggested; "and wondering what's become of their souls."

"Be good, sweet child. And let who can be clever," Joan quoted. "Would that be your text?"

Madge finished buttering her buns. "Kant, wasn't it," she answered, "who marvelled chiefly at two things: the starry firmament above him and the moral law within him. And they're one and the same, if he'd only thought it out. It's rather big to be good."

They carried their tea into the sitting-room.

"Do you really think she'll get over it?" asked Madge. "Or is it one of those things one has to say?"

"I think she could," answered Joan, "if she would pull herself together. It's her lack of will-power that's the trouble."

Madge did not reply immediately. She was watching the rooks settling down for the night in the elm trees just beyond the window. There seemed to be much need of coming and going, of much cawing.

"I met her pretty often during those months that Helen Lavery was running her round," she said at length. "It always seemed to me to have a touch of the heroic, that absurd effort she was making to 'qualify' herself, so that she might be of use to him. I can see her doing something quite big, if she thought it would help him."

The cawing of the rooks grew fainter. One by one they folded their wings.

Neither spoke for a while. Later on, they talked about the coming election. If the Party got back, Phillips would go to the Board of Trade. It would afford him a better platform for the introduction of his land scheme.

"What do you gather is the general opinion?" Joan asked. "That he will succeed?"

"The general opinion seems to be that his star is in the ascendant," Madge answered with a smile; "that all things are working together for his good. It's rather a useful atmosphere to have about one, that. It breeds friendship and support!"

Joan looked at her watch. She had an article to finish. Madge stood on tiptoe and kissed her.

"Don't think me unsympathetic," she said. "No one will rejoice more than I shall if God sees fit to call you to good work. But I can't help letting fall my little tear of fellowship with the weeping."

"And mind your p's and q's," she added. "You're in a difficult position. And not all the eyes watching you are friendly."

Joan bore the germ of worry in her breast as she crossed the Gray's Inn Garden. It was a hard law, that of the world: knowing only winners and losers. Of course, the woman was to be pitied. No one could feel more sorry for her than Joan herself. But what had Madge exactly meant by those words: that she could "see her doing something really big," if she thought it would help him? There was no doubt about her affection for him. It was almost dog-like. And the child, also! There must be something quite exceptional about him to have won the devotion of two such opposite beings. Especially Hilda. It would be hard to imagine any lengths to which Hilda's blind idolatry would not lead her.

She ran down twice to Folkestone during the following week. Her visits made her mind easier. Mrs. Phillips seemed so placid, so contented. There was no suggestion of suffering, either mental or physical.

She dined with the Greysons the Sunday after, and mooted the question of the coming fight with Carleton. Greyson thought Phillips would find plenty of journalistic backing. The concentration of the Press into the hands of a few conscienceless schemers was threatening to reduce the journalist to a mere hireling, and the better-class men were becoming seriously alarmed. He found in his desk the report of a speech made by a well-known leader writer at a recent dinner of the Press Club. The man had risen to respond to the toast of his own health and had taken the opportunity to unpack his heart.

"I am paid a thousand a year," so Greyson read to them, "for keeping my own opinions out of my paper. Some of you, perhaps, earn more, and others less; but you're getting it for writing what you're told. If I were to be so foolish as to express my honest opinion, I'd be on the street, the next morning, looking for another job."

"The business of the journalist," the man had continued, "is to destroy the truth, to lie, to pervert, to vilify, to fawn at the feet of Mammon, to sell his soul for his daily bread. We are the tools and vassals of rich men behind the scenes.

We are the jumping-jacks. They pull the strings and we dance. Our talents, our possibilities, our lives are the property of other men."

"We tried to pretend it was only one of Jack's little jokes," explained Greyson as he folded up the cutting; "but it wouldn't work. It was too near the truth."

"I don't see what you are going to do," commented Mary. "So long as men are not afraid to sell their souls, there will always be a Devil's market for them."

Greyson did not so much mind there being a Devil's market, provided he could be assured of an honest market alongside, so that a man could take his choice. What he feared was the Devil's steady encroachment, that could only end by the closing of the independent market altogether. His remedy was the introduction of the American trust law, forbidding any one man being interested in more than a limited number of journals.

"But what's the difference," demanded Joan, "between a man owning one paper with a circulation of, say, six millions; or owning six with a circulation of a million apiece? By concentrating all his energies on one, a man with Carleton's organizing genius might easily establish a single journal that would cover the whole field."

"Just all the difference," answered Greyson, "between Pooh Bah as Chancellor of the Exchequer, or Lord High Admiral, or Chief Executioner, whichever he preferred to be, and Pooh Bah as all the Officers of State rolled into one. Pooh Bah may be a very able statesman, entitled to exert his legitimate influence. But, after all, his opinion is only the opinion of one old gentleman, with possible prejudices and preconceived convictions. The Mikado—or the people, according to locality—would like to hear the views of others of his ministers. He finds that the Lord Chancellor and the Lord Chief Justice and the Groom of the Bedchamber and the Attorney-General—the whole entire Cabinet, in short, are unanimously of the same opinion as Pooh Bah. He doesn't know it's only Pooh Bah speaking from different corners of the stage. The consensus of opinion convinces him. One statesman, however eminent, might err in judgment. But half a score of statesmen, all of one mind! One must accept their verdict."

Mary smiled. "But why shouldn't the good newspaper proprietor hurry up and become a multi-proprietor?" she suggested. "Why don't you persuade Lord Sutcliffe to buy up three or four papers, before they're all gone?"

"Because I don't want the Devil to get hold of him," answered Greyson.

"You've got to face this unalterable law," he continued. "That power derived from worldly sources can only be employed for worldly purposes. The power conferred by popularity, by wealth, by that ability to make use of other men that we term organization—sooner or later the man who wields that power becomes the Devil's servant. So long as Kingship was merely a force struggling against anarchy, it was a holy weapon. As it grew in power so it degenerated into an instrument of tyranny. The Church, so long as it remained a scattered body of meek, lowly men, did the Lord's work. Enthroned at Rome, it thundered its edicts against human thought. The Press is in danger of following precisely the same history. When it wrote in fear of the pillory and of the jail, it fought for

Liberty. Now it has become the Fourth Estate, it fawns—as Jack Swinton said of it—at the feet of Mammon. My Proprietor, good fellow, allows me to cultivate my plot amid the wilderness for other purposes than those of quick returns. If he were to become a competitor with the Carletons and the Bloomfields, he would have to look upon it as a business proposition. The Devil would take him up on to the high mountain, and point out to him the kingdom of huge circulations and vast profits, whispering to him: 'All this will I give thee, if thou wilt fall down and worship me.' I don't want the dear good fellow to be tempted."

"Is it impossible, then, to combine duty and success?" questioned Joan.

"The combination sometimes happens, by chance," admitted Greyson. "But it's dangerous to seek it. It is so easy to persuade ourselves that it's our duty to succeed."

"But we must succeed to be of use," urged Mary. "Must God's servants always remain powerless?"

"Powerless to rule. Powerful only to serve," he answered. "Powerful as Christ was powerful; not as Caesar was powerful—powerful as those who have suffered and have failed, leaders of forlorn hopes—powerful as those who have struggled on, despised and vilified; not as those of whom all men speak well—powerful as those who have fought lone battles and have died, not knowing their own victory. It is those that serve, not those that rule, shall conquer."

Joan had never known him quite so serious. Generally there was a touch of irony in his talk, a suggestion of aloofness that had often irritated her.

"I wish you would always be yourself, as you are now," she said, "and never pose."

"Do I pose?" he asked, raising his eyebrows.

"That shows how far it has gone," she told him, "that you don't even know it. You pretend to be a philosopher. But you're really a man."

He laughed. "It isn't always a pose," he explained. "It's some men's way of saying: Thy will be done."

"Ask Phillips to come and see me," he said. "I can be of more help, if I know exactly his views."

He walked with her to the bus. They passed a corner house that he had more than once pointed out to her. It had belonged, years ago, to a well-known artist, who had worked out a wonderful scheme of decoration in the drawing-room. A board was up, announcing that the house was for sale. A gas lamp, exactly opposite, threw a flood of light upon the huge white lettering.

Joan stopped. "Why, it's the house you are always talking about," she said. "Are you thinking of taking it?"

"I did go over it," he answered. "But it would be rather absurd for just Mary and me."

She looked up Phillips at the House, and gave him Greyson's message. He had just returned from Folkestone, and was worried.

"She was so much better last week," he explained. "But it never lasts."

"Poor old girl!" he added. "I believe she'd have been happier if I'd always remained plain Bob Phillips."

Joan had promised to go down on the Friday; but finding, on the Thursday morning, that it would be difficult, decided to run down that afternoon instead. She thought at first of sending a wire. But in Mrs. Phillips's state of health, telegrams were perhaps to be avoided. It could make no difference. The front door of the little house was standing half open. She called down the kitchen stairs to the landlady, but received no answer. The woman had probably run out on some short errand. She went up the stairs softly. The bedroom door, she knew, would be open. Mrs. Phillips had a feeling against being "shut off," as she called it. She meant to tap lightly and walk straight in, as usual. But what she saw through the opening caused her to pause. Mrs. Phillips was sitting up in bed with her box of cosmetics in front of her. She was sensitive of anyone seeing her make-up; and Joan, knowing this, drew back a step. But for some reason, she couldn't help watching. Mrs. Phillips dipped a brush into one of the compartments and then remained with it in her hand, as if hesitating. Suddenly she stuck out her tongue and passed the brush over it. At least, so it seemed to Joan. It was only a side view of Mrs. Phillips's face that she was obtaining, and she may have been mistaken. It might have been the lips. The woman gave a little gasp and sat still for a moment. Then, putting away the brush, she closed the box and slipped it under the pillow.

Joan felt her knees trembling. A cold, creeping fear was taking possession of her. Why, she could not understand. She must have been mistaken. People don't make-up their tongues. It must have been the lips. And even if not—if the woman had licked the brush! It was a silly trick people do. Perhaps she liked the taste. She pulled herself together and tapped at the door.

Mrs. Phillips gave a little start at seeing her; but was glad that she had come. Phillips had not been down for two days and she had been feeling lonesome. She persisted in talking more than Joan felt was good for her. She was feeling so much better, she explained. Joan was relieved when the nurse came back from her walk and insisted on her lying down. She dropped to sleep while Joan and the nurse were having their tea.

Joan went back by the early train. She met some people at the station that she knew and travelled up with them. That picture of Mrs. Phillips's tongue just showing beyond the line of Mrs. Phillips's cheek remained at the back of her mind; but it was not until she was alone in her own rooms that she dared let her thoughts return to it.

The suggestion that was forcing itself into her brain was monstrous—unthinkable. That, never possessed of any surplus vitality, and suffering from the added lassitude of illness, the woman should have become indifferent—willing to let a life that to her was full of fears and difficulties slip peacefully away from her, that was possible. But that she should exercise thought and ingenuity—that she should have reasoned the thing out and deliberately laid her plans, calculating at every point on their success; it was inconceivable.

Besides, what could have put the idea into her head? It was laughable, the presumption that she was a finished actress, capable of deceiving everyone about her. If she had had an inkling of the truth, Joan, with every nerve on the alert, almost hoping for it, would have detected it. She had talked with her alone the day before she had left England, and the woman had been full of hopes and projects for the future.

That picture of Mrs. Phillips, propped up against the pillows, with her make-up box upon her knees was still before her when she went to bed. All night long it haunted her: whether thinking or dreaming of it, she could not tell.

Suddenly, she sat up with a stifled cry. It seemed as if a flash of light had been turned upon her, almost blinding her.

Hilda! Why had she never thought of it? The whole thing was so obvious. "You ought not to think about yourself. You ought to think only of him and of his work. Nothing else matters." If she could say that to Joan, what might she not have said to her mother who, so clearly, she divined to be the incubus—the drag upon her father's career? She could hear the child's dry, passionate tones— could see Mrs. Phillips's flabby cheeks grow white—the frightened, staring eyes. Where her father was concerned the child had neither conscience nor compassion. She had waited her time. It was a few days after Hilda's return to school that Mrs. Phillips had been first taken ill.

She flung herself from the bed and drew the blind. A chill, grey light penetrated the room. It was a little before five. She would go round to Phillips, wake him up. He must be told.

With her hat in her hands, she paused. No. That would not do. Phillips must never know. They must keep the secret to themselves. She would go down and see the woman; reason with her, insist. She went into the other room. It was lighter there. The "A.B.C." was standing in its usual place upon her desk. There was a train to Folkestone at six-fifteen. She had plenty of time. It would be wise to have a cup of tea and something to eat. There would be no sense in arriving there with a headache. She would want her brain clear.

It was half-past five when she sat down with her tea in front of her. It was only ten minutes' walk to Charing Cross—say a quarter of an hour. She might pick up a cab. She grew calmer as she ate and drank. Her reason seemed to be returning to her. There was no such violent hurry. Hadn't she better think things over, in the clear daylight? The woman had been ill now for nearly six weeks: a few hours—a day or two—could make no difference. It might alarm the poor creature, her unexpected appearance at such an unusual hour—cause a relapse. Suppose she had been mistaken? Hadn't she better make a few inquiries first— feel her way? One did harm more often than good, acting on impulse. After all, had she the right to interfere? Oughtn't the thing to be thought over as a whole? Mightn't there be arguments, worth considering, against her interference? Her brain was too much in a whirl. Hadn't she better wait till she could collect and arrange her thoughts?

The silver clock upon her desk struck six. It had been a gift from her father when she was at Girton. It never obtruded. Its voice was a faint musical chime that she need not hear unless she cared to listen. She turned and looked at it. It seemed to be a little face looking back at her out of its two round, blinkless eyes. For the first time during all the years that it had watched beside her, she heard its quick, impatient tick.

She sat motionless, staring at it. The problem, in some way, had simplified itself into a contest between herself, demanding time to think, and the little insistent clock, shouting to her to act upon blind impulse. If she could remain motionless for another five minutes, she would have won.

The ticking of the little clock was filling the room. The thing seemed to have become alive—to be threatening to burst its heart. But the thin, delicate indicator moved on.

Suddenly its ticking ceased. It had become again a piece of lifeless mechanism. The hands pointed to six minutes past. Joan took off her hat and laid it aside.

She must think the whole thing over quietly.

CHAPTER XIV

She could help him. Without her, he would fail. The woman herself saw that, and wished it. Why should she hesitate? It was not as if she had only herself to consider. The fate—the happiness of millions was at stake. He looked to her for aid—for guidance. It must have been intended. All roads had led to it. Her going to the house. She remembered now, it was the first door at which she had knocked. Her footsteps had surely been directed. Her meeting with Mrs. Phillips in Madge's rooms; and that invitation to dinner, coinciding with that crisis in his life. It was she who had persuaded him to accept. But for her he would have doubted, wavered, let his opportunities slip by. He had confessed it to her.

And she had promised him. He needed her. The words she had spoken to Madge, not dreaming then of their swift application. They came back to her. "God has called me. He girded His sword upon me." What right had she to leave it rusting in its scabbard, turning aside from the pathway pointed out to her because of one weak, useless life, crouching in her way. It was not as if she were being asked to do evil herself that good might come. The decision had been taken out of her hands. All she had to do was to remain quiescent, not interfering, awaiting her orders. Her business was with her own part, not with another's. To be willing to sacrifice oneself: that was at the root of all service. Sometimes it was one's own duty, sometimes that of another. Must one never go forward because another steps out of one's way, voluntarily? Besides, she might have been mistaken. That picture, ever before her, of the woman pausing with the brush above her tongue—that little stilled gasp! It may have been but a phantasm, born of her own fevered imagination. She clung to that, desperately.

It was the task that had been entrusted to her. How could he hope to succeed without her. With her, he would be all powerful—accomplish the end for which he had been sent into the world. Society counts for so much in England. What public man had ever won through without its assistance. As Greyson had said: it is the dinner-table that rules. She could win it over to his side. That mission to Paris that she had undertaken for Mrs. Denton, that had brought her into contact with diplomatists, politicians, the leaders and the rulers, the bearers of names known and honoured in history. They had accepted her as one of themselves. She had influenced them, swayed them. That afternoon at Folk's studio, where all eyes had followed her, where famous men and women had waited to attract her notice, had hung upon her words. Even at school, at college, she had always commanded willing homage. As Greyson had once told her, it was herself—her personality that was her greatest asset. Was it to be utterly wasted? There were hundreds of impersonal, sexless women, equipped for nothing else, with pens as keen if not keener than hers. That was not the talent with which she had been entrusted—for which she would have to account. It was her beauty, her power to charm, to draw after her—to compel by the mere exercise of her will. Hitherto Beauty had been content to barter itself for mere coin of the realm—for ease and luxury and pleasure. She only asked to be allowed to spend it in service. As his wife, she could use it to fine ends. By herself she was helpless. One must take the world as one finds it. It gives the unmated woman no opportunity to employ the special gifts with which God has endowed her—except for evil. As the wife of a rising statesman, she could be a force for progress. She could become another Madame Roland; gather round her all that was best of English social life; give back to it its lost position in the vanguard of thought.

She could strengthen him, give him courage. Without her, he would always remain the mere fighter, doubtful of himself. The confidence, the inspiration, necessary for leadership, she alone could bring to him. Each by themselves was incomplete. Together, they would be the whole. They would build the city of their dreams.

She seemed to have become a wandering spirit rather than a living being. She had no sense of time or place. Once she had started, hearing herself laugh. She was seated at a table, and was talking. And then she had passed back into forgetfulness. Now, from somewhere, she was gazing downward. Roofs, domes and towers lay stretched before her, emerging from a sea of shadows. She held out her arms towards them and the tears came to her eyes. The poor tired people were calling to her to join with him to help them. Should she fail them—turn deaf ears to the myriad because of pity for one useless, feeble life?

She had been fashioned to be his helpmate, as surely as if she had been made of the same bone. Nature was at one with God. Spirit and body both yearned for him. It was not position—power for herself that she craved. The marriage market—if that had been her desire: it had always been open to her. She had the gold that buys these things. Wealth, ambition: they had been offered to her—spread out temptingly before her eyes. They were always within her means, if ever she chose to purchase them. It was this man alone to whom she had ever felt drawn— this man of the people, with that suggestion about him of something primitive, untamed, causing her always in his presence that faint, compelling thrill of fear, who stirred her blood as none of the polished men of her own class had ever done. His kind, strong, ugly face: it moved beside her: its fearless, tender eyes now pleading, now commanding.

He needed her. She heard his passionate, low voice, as she had heard it in the little garden above Meudon: "Because you won't be there; and without you I can do nothing." What right had this poor, worn-out shadow to stand between them, to the end? Had love and life no claims, but only weakness? She had taken all, had given nothing. It was but reparation she was making. Why stop her?

She was alone in a maze of narrow, silent streets that ended always in a high blank wall. It seemed impossible to get away from this blank wall. Whatever way she turned she was always coming back to it.

What was she to do? Drag the woman back to life against her will—lead her back to him to be a chain about his feet until the end? Then leave him to fight the battle alone?

And herself? All her world had been watching and would know. She had counted her chickens before they were dead. She had set her cap at the man, reckoning him already widowed; and his wife had come to life and snatched it from her head. She could hear the laughter—the half amused, half contemptuous pity for her "rotten bad luck." She would be their standing jest, till she was forgotten.

What would life leave to her? A lonely lodging and a pot of ink that she would come to hate the smell of. She could never marry. It would be but her body that she could give to any other man. Not even for the sake of her dreams could she bring herself to that. It might have been possible before, but not now. She could have won the victory over herself, but for hope, that had kindled the smouldering embers of her passion into flame. What cunning devil had flung open this door, showing her all her heart's desire, merely that she should be called upon to slam it to in her own face?

A fierce anger blazed up in her brain. Why should she listen? Why had reason been given to us if we were not to use it—weigh good and evil in the balance and decide for ourselves where lay the nobler gain? Were we to be led hither and thither like blind children? What was right—what wrong, but what our own God-given judgment told us? Was it wrong of the woman to perform this act of self-renunciation, yielding up all things to love? No, it was great—heroic of her. It would be her cross of victory, her crown.

If the gift were noble, so also it could not be ignoble to accept it.

To reject it would be to dishonour it.

She would accept it. The wonder of it should cast out her doubts and fears. She would seek to make herself worthy of it. Consecrate it with her steadfastness, her devotion.

She thought it ended. But yet she sat there motionless.

What was plucking at her sleeve—still holding her?

Unknowing, she had entered a small garden. It formed a passage between two streets, and was left open day and night. It was but a narrow strip of rank grass and withered shrubs with an asphalte pathway widening to a circle in the centre, where stood a gas lamp and two seats, facing one another.

And suddenly it came to her that this was her Garden of Gethsemane; and a dull laugh broke from her that she could not help. It was such a ridiculous apology for Gethsemane. There was not a corner in which one could possibly pray. Only these two iron seats, one each side of the gaunt gas lamp that glared down upon them. Even the withered shrubs were fenced off behind a railing. A ragged figure sprawled upon the bench opposite to her. It snored gently, and its breath came laden with the odour of cheap whisky.

But it was her Gethsemane: the best that Fate had been able to do for her. It was here that her choice would be made. She felt that.

And there rose before her the vision of that other Garden of Gethsemane with, below it, the soft lights of the city shining through the trees; and above, clear against the starlit sky, the cold, dark cross.

It was only a little cross, hers, by comparison. She could see that. They seemed to be standing side by side. But then she was only a woman—little more than a girl. And her courage was so small. She thought He ought to know that. For her, it was quite a big cross. She wondered if He had been listening to all her arguments. There was really a good deal of sense in some of them. Perhaps He would understand. Not all His prayer had come down to us. He, too, had put up a fight for life. He, too, was young. For Him, also, life must have seemed but just beginning. Perhaps He, too, had felt that His duty still lay among the people— teaching, guiding, healing them. To Him, too, life must have been sweet with its noble work, its loving comradeship. Even from Him the words had to be wrung: "Thy will, not Mine, be done."

She whispered them at last. Not bravely, at all. Feebly, haltingly, with a little sob: her forehead pressed against the cold iron seat, as if that could help her.

She thought that even then God might reconsider it—see her point of view. Perhaps He would send her a sign.

The ragged figure on the bench opposite opened its eyes, stared at her; then went to sleep again. A prowling cat paused to rub itself against her foot, but meeting no response, passed on. Through an open window, somewhere near, filtered the sound of a child's low whimpering.

It was daylight when she awoke. She was cold and her limbs ached. Slowly her senses came back to her. The seat opposite was vacant. The gas lamp showed but a faint blue point of flame. Her dress was torn, her boots soiled and muddy. Strands of her hair had escaped from underneath her hat.

She looked at her watch. Fortunately it was still early. She would be able to let herself in before anyone was up. It was but a little way. She wondered, while rearranging her hair, what day it was. She would find out, when she got home, from the newspaper.

In the street she paused a moment and looked back through the railings. It seemed even still more sordid in the daylight: the sooty grass and the withered shrubs and the asphalte pathway strewn with dirty paper. And again a laugh she could not help broke from her. Her Garden of Gethsemane!

She sent a brief letter round to Phillips, and a telegram to the nurse, preparing them for what she meant to do. She had just time to pack a small trunk and catch the morning train. At Folkestone, she drove first to a house where she herself had once lodged and fixed things to her satisfaction. The nurse was waiting for her in the downstairs room, and opened the door to her. She was opposed to Joan's interference. But Joan had come prepared for that. "Let me have a talk with her," she said. "I think I've found out what it is that is causing all the trouble."

The nurse shot her a swift glance. "I'm glad of that," she said dryly. She let Joan go upstairs.

Mrs. Phillips was asleep. Joan seated herself beside the bed and waited. She had not yet made herself up for the day and the dyed hair was hidden beneath a white, close-fitting cap. The pale, thin face with its closed eyes looked strangely young. Suddenly the thin hands clasped, and her lips moved, as if she were praying in her sleep. Perhaps she also was dreaming of Gethsemane. It must be quite a crowded garden, if only we could see it.

After a while, her eyes opened. Joan drew her chair nearer and slipped her arm in under her, and their eyes met.

"You're not playing the game," whispered Joan, shaking her head. "I only promised on condition that you would try to get well."

The woman made no attempt to deny. Something told her that Joan had learned her secret. She glanced towards the door. Joan had closed it.

"Don't drag me back," she whispered. "It's all finished." She raised herself up and put her arms about Joan's neck. "It was hard at first, and I hated you. And then it came to me that this was what I had been wanting to do, all my life— something to help him, that nobody else could do. Don't take it from me."

"I know," whispered Joan. "I've been there, too. I knew you were doing it, though I didn't quite know how—till the other day. I wouldn't think. I wanted to pretend that I didn't. I know all you can say. I've been listening to it. It was right of you to want to give it all up to me for his sake. But it would be wrong of me to take it. I don't quite see why. I can't explain it. But I mustn't. So you see it would be no good."

"But I'm so useless," pleaded the woman.

"I said that," answered Joan. "I wanted to do it and I talked and talked, so hard. I said everything I could think of. But that was the only answer: I mustn't do it."

They remained for a while with their arms round one another. It struck Joan as curious, even at the time, that all feeling of superiority had gone out of her. They might have been two puzzled children that had met one another on a path that neither knew. But Joan was the stronger character.

"I want you to give me up that box," she said, "and to come away with me where I can be with you and take care of you until you are well."

Mrs. Phillips made yet another effort. "Have you thought about him?" she asked.

Joan answered with a faint smile. "Oh, yes," she said. "I didn't forget that argument in case it hadn't occurred to the Lord."

"Perhaps," she added, "the helpmate theory was intended to apply only to our bodies. There was nothing said about our souls. Perhaps God doesn't have to work in pairs. Perhaps we were meant to stand alone."

Mrs. Phillips's thin hands were playing nervously with the bed clothes. There still seemed something that she had to say. As if Joan hadn't thought of everything. Her eyes were fixed upon the narrow strip of light between the window curtains.

"You don't think you could, dear," she whispered, "if I didn't do anything wicked any more. But just let things take their course."

"You see, dear," she went on, her face still turned away, "I thought it all finished. It will be hard for me to go back to him, knowing as I do now that he doesn't want me. I shall always feel that I am in his way. And Hilda," she added after a pause, "she will hate me."

Joan looked at the white patient face and was silent. What would be the use of senseless contradiction. The woman knew. It would only seem an added stab of mockery. She knelt beside the bed, and took the thin hands in hers.

"I think God must want you very badly," she said, "or He wouldn't have laid so heavy a cross upon you. You will come?"

The woman did not answer in words. The big tears were rolling down her cheeks. There was no paint to mingle with and mar them. She drew the little metal box from under the pillow and gave it into Joan's hands.

Joan crept out softly from the room.

The nurse was standing by the window. She turned sharply on Joan's entrance. Joan slipped the box into her hands.

The nurse raised the lid. "What a fool I've been," she said. "I never thought of that."

She held out a large strong hand and gave Joan a longish grip. "You're right," she said, "we must get her out of this house at once. Forgive me."

Phillips had been called up north and wired that he would not be able to get down till the Wednesday evening. Joan met him at the station.

"She won't be expecting you, just yet," she explained. "We might have a little walk."

She waited till they had reached a quiet road leading to the hills.

"You will find her changed," she said. "Mentally, I mean. Though she will try not to show it. She was dying for your sake—to set you free. Hilda seems to have had a talk with her and to have spared her no part of the truth. Her great love for you made the sacrifice possible and even welcome. It was the one gift she had in her hands. She was giving it gladly, proudly. So far as she was concerned, it would have been kinder to let her make an end of it. But during the last few days I have come to the conclusion there is a law within us that we may not argue with. She is coming back to life, knowing you no longer want her, that she is only in the way. Perhaps you may be able to think of something to say or do that will lessen her martyrdom. I can't."

They had paused where a group of trees threw a blot of shadow across the moonlit road.

"You mean she was killing herself?" he asked.

"Quite cleverly. So as to avoid all danger of after discovery: that might have hurt us," she answered.

They walked in silence, and coming to a road that led back into the town, he turned down it. She had the feeling she was following him without his knowing it. A cab was standing outside the gate of a house, having just discharged its fare. He seemed to have suddenly recollected her.

"Do you mind?" he said. "We shall get there so much quicker."

"You go," she said. "I'll stroll on quietly."

"You're sure?" he said.

"I would rather," she answered.

It struck her that he was relieved. He gave the man the address, speaking hurriedly, and jumped in.

She had gone on. She heard the closing of the door behind her, and the next moment the cab passed her.

She did not see him again that night. They met in the morning at breakfast. A curious strangeness to each other seemed to have grown up between them, as if they had known one another long ago, and had half forgotten. When they had finished she rose to leave; but he asked her to stop, and, after the table had been cleared, he walked up and down the room, while she sat sideways on the window seat from where she could watch the little ships moving to and fro across the horizon, like painted figures in a show.

"I had a long talk with Nan last night," he said. "And, trying to explain it to her, I came a little nearer to understanding it myself. My love for you would have been strong enough to ruin both of us. I see that now. It would have dominated every other thought in me. It would have swallowed up my dreams. It would have been blind, unscrupulous. Married to you, I should have aimed only at success. It would not have been your fault. You would not have known. About mere birth I should never have troubled myself. I've met daughters of a hundred earls—more or less: clever, jolly little women I could have chucked under the chin and have been chummy with. Nature creates her own ranks, and puts her ban upon misalliances. Every time I took you in my arms I should have felt that you had stepped down from your proper order to mate yourself with me and that it was up to me to make the sacrifice good to you by giving you power—position. Already within the last few weeks, when it looked as if this thing was going to be possible, I have been thinking against my will of a compromise with Carleton that would give me his support. This coming election was beginning to have terrors for me that I have never before felt. The thought of defeat—having to go back to comparative poverty, to comparative obscurity, with you as my wife, was growing into a nightmare. I should have wanted wealth, fame, victory, for your sake— to see you honoured, courted, envied, finely dressed and finely housed—grateful to me for having won for you these things. It wasn't honest, healthy love—the love that unites, that makes a man willing to take as well as to give, that I felt for you; it was worship that separates a man from a woman, that puts fear between them. It isn't good that man should worship a woman. He can't serve God and woman. Their interests are liable to clash. Nan's my helpmate—just a loving woman that the Lord brought to me and gave me when I was alone—that I still love. I didn't know it till last night. She will never stand in my way. I haven't to put her against my duty. She will leave me free to obey the voice that calls to me. And no man can hear that voice but himself."

He had been speaking in a clear, self-confident tone, as if at last he saw his road before him to the end; and felt that nothing else mattered but that he should go forward hopefully, unfalteringly. Now he paused, and his eyes wandered. But the lines about his strong mouth deepened.

"Perhaps, I am not of the stuff that conquerors are made," he went on. "Perhaps, if I were, I should be thinking differently. It comes to me sometimes that I may be one of those intended only to prepare the way—that for me there may be only the endless struggle. I may have to face unpopularity, abuse, failure. She won't mind."

"Nor would you," he added, turning to her suddenly for the first time, "I know that. But I should be afraid—for you."

She had listened to him without interrupting, and even now she did not speak for a while.

It was hard not to. She wanted to tell him that he was all wrong—at least, so far as she was concerned. It. was not the conqueror she loved in him; it was the fighter. Not in the hour of triumph but in the hour of despair she would have yearned to put her arms about him. "Unpopularity, abuse, failure," it was against the fear of such that she would have guarded him. Yes, she had dreamed of leadership, influence, command. But it was the leadership of the valiant few against the hosts of the oppressors that she claimed. Wealth, honours! Would she have given up a life of ease, shut herself off from society, if these had been her standards? "*Mésalliance*!" Had the male animal no instinct, telling it when it was loved with all a woman's being, so that any other union would be her degradation.

It was better for him he should think as he did. She rose and held out her hand.

"I will stay with her for a little while," she said. "Till I feel there is no more need. Then I must get back to work."

He looked into her eyes, holding her hand, and she felt his body trembling. She knew he was about to speak, and held up a warning hand.

"That's all, my lad," she said with a smile. "My love to you, and God speed you."

Mrs. Phillips progressed slowly but steadily. Life was returning to her, but it was not the same. Out of those days there had come to her a gentle dignity, a strengthening and refining. The face, now pale and drawn, had lost its foolishness. Under the thin, white hair, and in spite of its deep lines, it had grown younger. A great patience, a child-like thoughtfulness had come into the quiet eyes.

She was sitting by the window, her hands folded. Joan had been reading to her, and the chapter finished, she had closed the book and her thoughts had been wandering. Mrs. Phillips's voice recalled them.

"Do you remember that day, my dear," she said, "when we went furnishing together. And I would have all the wrong things. And you let me."

"Yes," answered Joan with a laugh. "They were pretty awful, some of them."

"I was just wondering," she went on. "It was a pity, wasn't it? I was silly and began to cry."

"I expect that was it," Joan confessed. "It interferes with our reason at times."

"It was only a little thing, of course, that," she answered. "But I've been thinking it must be that that's at the bottom of it all; and that is why God lets there be weak things—children and little animals and men and women in pain, that we feel sorry for, so that people like you and Robert and so many others are willing to give up all your lives to helping them. And that is what He wants."

"Perhaps God cannot help there being weak things," answered Joan. "Perhaps He, too, is sorry for them."

"It comes to the same thing, doesn't it, dear?" she answered. "They are there, anyhow. And that is how He knows those who are willing to serve Him: by their being pitiful."

They fell into a silence. Joan found herself dreaming.

Yes, it was true. It must have been the beginning of all things. Man, pitiless, deaf, blind, groping in the darkness, knowing not even himself. And to her vision, far off, out of the mist, he shaped himself before her: that dim, first standard-bearer of the Lord, the man who first felt pity. Savage, brutish, dumb—lonely there amid the desolation, staring down at some hurt creature, man or beast it mattered not, his dull eyes troubled with a strange new pain he understood not.

And suddenly, as he stooped, there must have come a great light into his eyes.

Man had heard God's voice across the deep, and had made answer.

CHAPTER XV

The years that followed—till, like some shipwrecked swimmer to whom returning light reveals the land, she felt new life and hopes come back to her—always remained in her memory vague, confused; a jumble of events, thoughts, feelings, without sequence or connection.

She had gone down to Liverpool, intending to persuade her father to leave the control of the works to Arthur, and to come and live with her in London; but had left without broaching the subject. There were nights when she would trapse the streets till she would almost fall exhausted, rather than face the solitude awaiting her in her own rooms. But so also there were moods when, like some stricken animal, her instinct was to shun all living things. At such times his presence, for all his loving patience, would have been as a knife in her wound. Besides, he would always be there, when escape from herself for a while became an absolute necessity. More and more she had come to regard him as her comforter. Not from anything he ever said or did. Rather, it seemed to her, because that with him she felt no need of words.

The works, since Arthur had shared the management, had gradually been regaining their position; and he had urged her to let him increase her allowance.

"It will give you greater freedom," he had suggested with fine assumption of propounding a mere business proposition; "enabling you to choose your work entirely for its own sake. I have always wanted to take a hand in helping things on. It will come to just the same, your doing it for me."

She had suppressed a smile, and had accepted. "Thanks, Dad," she had answered. "It will be nice, having you as my backer."

Her admiration of the independent woman had undergone some modification since she had come in contact with her. Woman was intended to be dependent upon man. It was the part appointed to him in the social scheme. Woman had hers, no less important. Earning her own living did not improve her. It was one of the drawbacks of civilization that so many had to do it of necessity. It developed her on the wrong lines—against her nature. This cry of the unsexed: that woman must always be the paid servant instead of the helper of man—paid for being mother, paid for being wife! Why not carry it to its logical conclusion, and insist that she should be paid for her embraces? That she should share in man's labour, in his hopes, that was the true comradeship. What mattered it, who held the purse-strings!

Her room was always kept ready for her. Often she would lie there, watching the moonlight creep across the floor; and a curious feeling would come to her of being something wandering, incomplete. She would see as through a mist the passionate, restless child with the rebellious eyes to whom the room had once belonged; and later the strangely self-possessed girl with that impalpable veil of mystery around her who would stand with folded hands, there by the window, seeming always to be listening. And she, too, had passed away. The tears would come into her eyes, and she would stretch out yearning arms towards their shadowy forms. But they would only turn upon her eyes that saw not, and would fade away.

In the day-time, when Arthur and her father were at the works, she would move through the high, square, stiffly-furnished rooms, or about the great formal garden, with its ordered walks and level lawns. And as with knowledge we come to love some old, stern face our childish eyes had thought forbidding, and would not have it changed, there came to her with the years a growing fondness for the old, plain brick-built house. Generations of Allways had lived and died there: men and women somewhat narrow, unsympathetic, a little hard of understanding; but at least earnest, sincere, seeking to do their duty in their solid, unimaginative way. Perhaps there were other ways besides those of speech and pen. Perhaps one did better, keeping to one's own people; the very qualities that separated us from them being intended for their need. What mattered the colours, so that one followed the flag? Somewhere, all roads would meet.

Arthur had to be in London generally once or twice a month, and it came to be accepted that he should always call upon her and "take her out." She had lost the self-sufficiency that had made roaming about London by herself a pleasurable adventure; and a newly-born fear of what people were saying and thinking about her made her shy even of the few friends she still clung to, so that his visits grew to be of the nature of childish treats to which she found herself looking forward— counting the days. Also, she came to be dependent upon him for the keeping alight within her of that little kindly fire of self-conceit at which we warm our hands in wintry days. It is not good that a young woman should remain for long a stranger to her mirror—above her frocks, indifferent to the angle of her hat. She had met the women superior to feminine vanities. Handsome enough, some of them must once have been; now sunk in slovenliness, uncleanliness, in disrespect to womanhood. It would not be fair to him. The worshipper has his rights. The goddess must remember always that she is a goddess—must pull herself together and behave as such, appearing upon her pedestal becomingly attired; seeing to it that in all things she is at her best; not allowing private grief to render her neglectful of this duty.

She had not told him of the Phillips episode. But she felt instinctively that he knew. It was always a little mysterious to her, his perception in matters pertaining to herself.

"I want your love," she said to him one day. "It helps me. I used to think it was selfish of me to take it, knowing I could never return it—not that love. But I no longer feel that now. Your love seems to me a fountain from which I can drink without hurting you."

"I should love to be with you always," he answered, "if you wished it. You won't forget your promise?"

She remembered it then. "No," she answered with a smile. "I shall keep watch. Perhaps I shall be worthy of it by that time."

She had lost her faith in journalism as a drum for the rousing of the people against wrong. Its beat had led too often to the trickster's booth, to the cheapjack's rostrum. It had lost its rallying power. The popular Press had made the newspaper a byword for falsehood. Even its supporters, while reading it because it pandered to their passions, tickled their vices, and flattered their ignorance, despised and disbelieved it. Here and there, an honest journal advocated a reform, pleaded for the sweeping away of an injustice. The public shrugged its shoulders. Another newspaper stunt! A bid for popularity, for notoriety: with its consequent financial kudos.

She still continued to write for Greyson, but felt she was labouring for the doomed. Lord Sutcliffe had died suddenly and his holding in the *Evening Gazette* had passed to his nephew, a gentleman more interested in big game shooting than in politics. Greyson's support of Phillips had brought him within the net of Carleton's operations, and negotiations for purchase had already been commenced. She knew that, sooner or later, Greyson would be offered the alternative of either changing his opinions or of going. And she knew that he would go. Her work for Mrs. Denton was less likely to be interfered with. It appealed only to the few, and aimed at informing and explaining rather than directly converting. Useful enough work in its way, no doubt; but to put heart into it seemed to require longer views than is given to the eyes of youth.

Besides, her pen was no longer able to absorb her attention, to keep her mind from wandering. The solitude of her desk gave her the feeling of a prison. Her body made perpetual claims upon her, as though it were some restless, fretful child, dragging her out into the streets without knowing where it wanted to go, discontented with everything it did: then hurrying her back to fling itself upon a chair, weary, but still dissatisfied.

If only she could do something. She was sick of thinking.

These physical activities into which women were throwing themselves! Where one used one's body as well as one's brain—hastened to appointments; gathered round noisy tables; met fellow human beings, argued with them, walked with them, laughing and talking; forced one's way through crowds; cheered, shouted; stood up on platforms before a sea of faces; roused applause, filling and emptying one's lungs; met interruptions with swift flash of wit or anger, faced opposition, danger—felt one's blood surging through one's veins, felt one's nerves quivering with excitement; felt the delirious thrill of passion; felt the mad joy of the loosened animal.

She threw herself into the suffrage movement. It satisfied her for a while. She had the rare gift of public speaking, and enjoyed her triumphs. She was temperate, reasonable; persuasive rather than aggressive; feeling her audience as she went, never losing touch with them. She had the magnetism that comes of sympathy. Medical students who came intending to tell her to go home and mind the baby, remained to wonder if man really was the undoubted sovereign of the world, born to look upon woman as his willing subject; to wonder whether under some unwritten whispered law it might not be the other way about. Perhaps she had the right—with or without the baby—to move about the kingdom, express her wishes for its care and management. Possibly his doubts may not have been brought about solely by the force and logic of her arguments. Possibly the voice of Nature is not altogether out of place in discussions upon Humanity's affairs.

She wanted votes for women. But she wanted them clean—won without dishonour. These "monkey tricks"—this apish fury and impatience! Suppose it did hasten by a few months, more or less, the coming of the inevitable. Suppose, by unlawful methods, one could succeed in dragging a reform a little prematurely from the womb of time, did not one endanger the child's health? Of what value was woman's influence on public affairs going to be, if she was to boast that she had won the right to exercise it by unscrupulousness and brutality?

They were to be found at every corner: the reformers who could not reform themselves. The believers in universal brotherhood who hated half the people. The denouncers of tyranny demanding lamp-posts for their opponents. The bloodthirsty preachers of peace. The moralists who had persuaded themselves that every wrong was justified provided one were fighting for the right. The deaf shouters for justice. The excellent intentioned men and women labouring for reforms that could only be hoped for when greed and prejudice had yielded place to reason, and who sought to bring about their ends by appeals to passion and self-interest.

And the insincere, the self-seekers, the self-advertisers! Those who were in the business for even coarser profit! The lime-light lovers who would always say and do the clever, the unexpected thing rather than the useful and the helpful thing: to whom paradox was more than principle.

Ought there not to be a school for reformers, a training college where could be inculcated self-examination, patience, temperance, subordination to duty; with lectures on the fundamental laws, within which all progress must be accomplished, outside which lay confusion and explosions; with lectures on history, showing how improvements had been brought about and how failure had been invited, thus avoiding much waste of reforming zeal; with lectures on the properties and tendencies of human nature, forbidding the attempt to treat it as a sum in rule of three?

There were the others. The men and women not in the lime-light. The lone, scattered men and women who saw no flag but Pity's ragged skirt; who heard no drum but the world's low cry of pain; who fought with feeble hands against the wrong around them; who with aching heart and troubled eyes laboured to make kinder the little space about them. The great army of the nameless reformers un-cheered, unparagraphed, unhonoured. The unknown sowers of the seed. Would the reapers of the harvest remember them?

Beyond giving up her visits to the house, she had made no attempt to avoid meeting Phillips; and at public functions and at mutual friends they sometimes found themselves near to one another. It surprised her that she could see him, talk to him, and even be alone with him without its troubling her. He seemed to belong to a part of her that lay dead and buried—something belonging to her that she had thrust away with her own hands: that she knew would never come back to her.

She was still interested in his work and keen to help him. It was going to be a stiff fight. He himself, in spite of Carleton's opposition, had been returned with an increased majority; but the Party as a whole had suffered loss, especially in the counties. The struggle centred round the agricultural labourer. If he could be won over the Government would go ahead with Phillips's scheme. Otherwise there was danger of its being shelved. The difficulty was the old problem of how to get at the men of the scattered villages, the lonely cottages. The only papers that they ever saw were those, chiefly of the Carleton group, that the farmers and the gentry took care should come within their reach; that were handed to them at the end of their day's work as a kindly gift; given to the school children to take home with them; supplied in ample numbers to all the little inns and public-houses. In all these, Phillips was held up as their arch enemy, his proposal explained as a device to lower their wages, decrease their chances of employment, and rob them of the produce of their gardens and allotments. No arguments were used. A daily stream of abuse, misrepresentation and deliberate lies, set forth under flaming headlines, served their simple purpose. The one weekly paper that had got itself established among them, that their fathers had always taken, that dimly they had come to look upon as their one friend, Carleton had at last succeeded in purchasing. When that, too, pictured Phillips's plan as a diabolical intent to take from them even the little that they had, and give it to the loafing socialist and the bloated foreigner, no room for doubt was left to them.

He had organized volunteer cycle companies of speakers from the towns, young working-men and women and students, to go out on summer evenings and hold meetings on the village greens. They were winning their way. But it was slow work. And Carleton was countering their efforts by a hired opposition that followed them from place to place, and whose interruptions were made use of to represent the whole campaign as a fiasco.

"He's clever," laughed Phillips. "I'd enjoy the fight, if I'd only myself to think of, and life wasn't so short."

The laugh died away and a shadow fell upon his face.

"If I could get a few of the big landlords to come in on my side," he continued, "it would make all the difference in the world. They're sensible men, some of them; and the whole thing could be carried out without injury to any legitimate interest. I could make them see that, if I could only get them quietly into a corner."

"But they're frightened of me," he added, with a shrug of his broad shoulders, "and I don't seem to know how to tackle them."

Those drawing-rooms? Might not something of the sort be possible? Not, perhaps, the sumptuous salon of her imagination, thronged with the fair and famous, suitably attired. Something, perhaps, more homely, more immediately attainable. Some of the women dressed, perhaps, a little dowdily; not all of them young and beautiful. The men wise, perhaps, rather than persistently witty; a few of them prosy, maybe a trifle ponderous; but solid and influential. Mrs. Denton's great empty house in Gower Street? A central situation and near to the tube. Lords and ladies had once ruffled there; trod a measure on its spacious floors; filled its echoing stone hall with their greetings and their partings. The gaping sconces, where their link-boys had extinguished their torches, still capped its grim iron railings.

Seated in the great, sombre library, Joan hazarded the suggestion. Mrs. Denton might almost have been waiting for it. It would be quite easy. A little opening of long fastened windows; a lighting of chill grates; a little mending of moth-eaten curtains, a sweeping away of long-gathered dust and cobwebs.

Mrs. Denton knew just the right people. They might be induced to bring their sons and daughters—it might be their grandchildren, youth being there to welcome them. For Joan, of course, would play her part.

The lonely woman touched her lightly on the hand. There shot a pleading look from the old stern eyes.

"You will have to imagine yourself my daughter," she said. "You are taller, but the colouring was the same. You won't mind, will you?"

The right people did come: Mrs. Denton being a personage that a landed gentry, rendered jumpy by the perpetual explosion of new ideas under their very feet, and casting about eagerly for friends, could not afford to snub. A kindly, simple folk, quite intelligent, some of them, as Phillips had surmised. Mrs. Denton made no mystery of why she had invited them. Why should all questions be left to the politicians and the journalists? Why should not the people interested take a hand; meet and talk over these little matters with quiet voices and attentive ears, amid surroundings where the unwritten law would restrain ladies and gentlemen from addressing other ladies and gentlemen as blood-suckers or anarchists, as grinders of the faces of the poor or as oily-tongued rogues; arguments not really conducive to mutual understanding and the bridging over of differences. The latest Russian dancer, the last new musical revue, the marvellous things that can happen at golf, the curious hands that one picks up at bridge, the eternal fox, the sacred bird! Excellent material for nine-tenths of our conversation. But the remaining tenth? Would it be such excruciatingly bad form for us to be intelligent, occasionally; say, on one or two Fridays during the season? Mrs. Denton wrapped it up tactfully; but that was her daring suggestion.

It took them aback at first. There were people who did this sort of thing. People of no class, who called themselves names and took up things. But for people of social standing to talk about serious subjects—except, perhaps, in bed to one's wife! It sounded so un-English.

With the elders it was sense of duty that prevailed. That, at all events, was English. The country must be saved. To their sons and daughters it was the originality, the novelty that gradually appealed. Mrs. Denton's Fridays became a new sensation. It came to be the chic and proper thing to appear at them in shades of mauve or purple. A pushing little woman in Hanover Street designed the "Denton" bodice, with hanging sleeves and square-cut neck. The younger men inclined towards a coat shaped to the waist with a roll collar.

Joan sighed. It looked as if the word had been passed round to treat the whole thing as a joke. Mrs. Denton took a different view.

"Nothing better could have happened," she was of opinion. "It means that their hearts are in it."

The stone hall was still vibrating to the voices of the last departed guests. Joan was seated on a footstool before the fire in front of Mrs. Denton's chair.

"It's the thing that gives me greatest hope," she continued. "The childishness of men and women. It means that the world is still young, still teachable."

"But they're so slow at their lessons," grumbled Joan. "One repeats it and repeats it; and then, when one feels that surely now at least one has drummed it into their heads, one finds they have forgotten all that one has ever said."

"Not always forgotten," answered Mrs. Denton; "mislaid, it may be, for the moment. An Indian student, the son of an old Rajah, called on me a little while ago. He was going back to organize a system of education among his people. 'My father heard you speak when you were over in India,' he told me. 'He has always been thinking about it.' Thirty years ago it must have been, that I undertook that mission to India. I had always looked back upon it as one of my many failures."

"But why leave it to his son," argued Joan. "Why couldn't the old man have set about it himself, instead of wasting thirty precious years?"

"I should have preferred it, myself," agreed Mrs. Denton. "I remember when I was a very little girl my mother longing for a tree upon the lawn underneath which she could sit. I found an acorn and planted it just in the right spot. I thought I would surprise her. I happened to be in the neighbourhood last summer, and I walked over. There was such a nice old lady sitting under it, knitting stockings. So you see it wasn't wasted."

"I wouldn't mind the waiting," answered Joan, "if it were not for the sorrow and the suffering that I see all round me. I want to get rid of it right away, now. I could be patient for myself, but not for others."

The little old lady straightened herself. There came a hardening of the thin, firm mouth.

"And those that have gone before?" she demanded. "Those that have won the ground from where we are fighting. Had they no need of patience? Was the cry never wrung from their lips: 'How long, oh Lord, how long?' Is it for us to lay aside the sword that they bequeath us because we cannot hope any more than they to see the far-off victory? Fifty years I have fought, and what, a few years hence, will my closing eyes still see but the banners of the foe still waving, fresh armies pouring to his standard?"

She flung back her head and the grim mouth broke into a smile.

"But I've won," she said. "I'm dying further forward. I've helped advance the line."

She put out her hands and drew Joan to her.

"Let me think of you," she said, "as taking my place, pushing the outposts a little further on."

Joan did not meet Hilda again till the child had grown into a woman— practically speaking. She had always been years older than her age. It was at a reception given in the Foreign Office. Joan's dress had been trodden on and torn. She had struggled out of the crowd into an empty room, and was examining the damage somewhat ruefully, when she heard a voice behind her, proffering help. It was a hard, cold voice, that yet sounded familiar, and she turned.

There was no forgetting those deep, burning eyes, though the face had changed. The thin red lips still remained its one touch of colour; but the un-healthy whiteness of the skin had given place to a delicate pallor; and the features that had been indistinct had shaped themselves in fine, firm lines. It was a beauti-ful, arresting face, marred only by the sullen callousness of the dark, clouded eyes.

Joan was glad of the assistance. Hilda produced pins.

"I always come prepared to these scrimmages," she explained. "I've got some Hazeline in my bag. They haven't kicked you, have they?"

"No," laughed Joan. "At least, I don't think so."

"They do sometimes," answered Hilda, "if you happen to be in the way, near the feeding troughs. If they'd only put all the refreshments into one room, one could avoid it. But they will scatter them about so that one never knows for cer-tain whether one is in the danger zone or not. I hate a mob."

"Why do you come?" asked Joan.

"Oh, I!" answered the girl. "I go everywhere where there's a chance of pick-ing up a swell husband. They've got to come to these shows, they can't help themselves. One never knows what incident may give one one's opportunity."

Joan shot a glance. The girl was evidently serious.

"You think it would prove a useful alliance?" she suggested.

"It would help, undoubtedly," the girl answered. "I don't see any other way of getting hold of them."

Joan seated herself on one of the chairs ranged round the walls, and drew the girl down beside her. Through the closed door, the mingled voices of the Foreign Secretary's guests sounded curiously like the buzzing of flies.

"It's quite easy," said Joan, "with your beauty. Especially if you're not going to be particular. But isn't there danger of your devotion to your father leading you too far? A marriage founded on a lie—no matter for what purpose!—mustn't it degrade a woman—smirch her soul for all time? We have a right to give up the things that belong to ourselves, but not the things that belong to God: our truth, our sincerity, our cleanliness of mind and body; the things that He may one day want of us. It led you into evil once before. Don't think I'm judging you. I was no better than you. I argued just as you must have done. Something stopped me just in time. That was the only difference between us."

The girl turned her dark eyes full upon Joan. "What did stop you?" she demanded.

"Does it matter what we call it?" answered Joan. "It was a voice."

"It told me to do it," answered the girl.

"Did no other voice speak to you?" asked Joan.

"Yes," answered the girl. "The voice of weakness."

There came a fierce anger into the dark eyes. "Why did you listen to it?" she demanded. "All would have been easy if you hadn't."

"You mean," answered Joan quietly, "that if I had let your mother die and had married your father, that he and I would have loved each other to the end; that I should have helped him and encouraged him in all things, so that his success would have been certain. Is that the argument?"

"Didn't you love him?" asked the girl, staring. "Wouldn't you have helped him?"

"I can't tell," answered Joan. "I should have meant to. Many men and women have loved, and have meant to help each other all their lives; and with the years have drifted asunder; coming even to be against one another. We change and our thoughts change; slight differences of temperament grow into barriers between us; unguessed antagonisms widen into gulfs. Accidents come into our lives. A friend was telling me the other day of a woman who practically proposed to and married a musical genius, purely and solely to be of use to him. She earned quite a big income, drawing fashions; and her idea was to relieve him of the necessity of doing pot-boilers for a living, so that he might devote his whole time to his real work. And a few weeks after they were married she ran the point of a lead pencil through her eye and it set up inflammation of her brain. And now all the poor fellow has to think of is how to make enough to pay for her keep at a private lunatic asylum. I don't mean to be flippant. It's the very absurdity of it all that makes the mystery of life—that renders it so hopeless for us to attempt to find our way through it by our own judgment. It is like the ants making all their clever, laborious plans, knowing nothing of chickens and the gardener's spade. That is why we have to cling to the life we can order for ourselves—the life within us. Truth, Justice, Pity. They are the strong things, the eternal things, the things we've got to sacrifice ourselves for—serve with our bodies and our souls.

"Don't think me a prig," she pleaded. "I'm talking as if I knew all about it. I don't really. I grope in the dark; and now and then—at least so it seems to me—I catch a glint of light. We are powerless in ourselves. It is only God working through us that enables us to be of any use. All we can do is to keep ourselves kind and clean and free from self, waiting for Him to come to us."

The girl rose. "I must be getting back," she said. "Dad will be wondering where I've got to."

She paused with the door in her hand, and a faint smile played round the thin red lips.

"Tell me," she said. "What is God?"

"A Labourer, together with man, according to Saint Paul," Joan answered.

The girl turned and went. Joan watched her as she descended the great staircase. She moved with a curious, gliding motion, pausing at times for the people to make way for her.

CHAPTER XVI

It was a summer's evening; Joan had dropped in at the Greysons and had found Mary alone, Francis not having yet returned from a bachelor dinner at his uncle's, who was some big pot in the Navy. They sat in the twilight, facing the open French windows, through which one caught a glimpse of the park. A great stillness seemed to be around them.

The sale and purchase of the *Evening Gazette* had been completed a few days before. Greyson had been offered the alternative of gradually and gracefully changing his opinions, or getting out; and had, of course, chosen dismissal. He was taking a holiday, as Mary explained with a short laugh.

"He had some shares in it himself, hadn't he?" Joan asked.

"Oh, just enough to be of no use," Mary answered. "Carleton was rather decent, so far as that part of it was concerned, and insisted on paying him a fair price. The market value would have been much less; and he wanted to be out of it."

Joan remained silent. It made her mad, that a man could be suddenly robbed of fifteen years' labour: the weapon that his heart and brain had made keen wrested from his hand by a legal process, and turned against the very principles for which all his life he had been fighting.

"I'm almost more sorry for myself than for him," said Mary, making a whimsical grimace. "He will start something else, so soon as he's got over his first soreness; but I'm too old to dream of another child."

He came in a little later and, seating himself between them, filled and lighted his pipe. Looking back, Joan remembered that curiously none of them had spoken. Mary had turned at the sound of his key in the door. She seemed to be watching him intently; but it was too dark to notice her expression. He pulled at his pipe till it was well alight and then removed it.

"It's war," he said.

The words made no immediate impression upon Joan. There had been rumours, threatenings and alarms, newspaper talk. But so there had been before. It would come one day: the world war that one felt was gathering in the air; that would burst like a second deluge on the nations. But it would not be in our time: it was too big. A way out would be found.

"Is there no hope?" asked Mary.

"Yes," he answered. "The hope that a miracle may happen. The Navy's got its orders."

And suddenly—as years before in a Paris music hall—there leapt to life within Joan's brain a little impish creature that took possession of her. She hoped the miracle would not happen. The little impish creature within her brain was marching up and down beating a drum. She wished he would stop a minute. Someone was trying to talk to her, telling her she ought to be tremendously shocked and grieved. He—or she, or whatever it was that was trying to talk to her, appeared concerned about Reason and Pity and Universal Brotherhood and Civilization's clock—things like that. But the little impish drummer was making such a din, she couldn't properly hear. Later on, perhaps, he would get tired; and then she would be able to listen to this humane and sensible person, whoever it might be.

Mary argued that England could and should keep out of it; but Greyson was convinced it would be impossible, not to say dishonourable: a sentiment that won the enthusiastic approval of the little drummer in Joan's brain. He played "Rule Britannia" and "God Save the King," the "Marseillaise" and the Russian National hymn, all at the same time. He would have included "Deutschland über Alles," if Joan hadn't made a supreme effort and stopped him. Evidently a sporting little devil. He took himself off into a corner after a time, where he played quietly to himself; and Joan was able to join in the conversation.

Greyson spoke with an enthusiasm that was unusual to him. So many of our wars had been mean wars—wars for the wrong; sordid wars for territory, for gold mines; wars against the weak at the bidding of our traders, our financiers. "Shouldering the white man's burden," we called it. Wars for the right of selling opium; wars to perpetuate the vile rule of the Turk because it happened to serve our commercial interests. This time, we were out to play the knight; to save the smaller peoples; to rescue our once "sweet enemy," fair France. Russia was the disturbing thought. It somewhat discounted the knight-errant idea, riding stirrup to stirrup beside that barbarian horseman. But there were possibilities about Russia. Idealism lay hid within that sleeping brain. It would be a holy war for the Kingdom of the Peoples. With Germany freed from the monster of blood and iron that was crushing out her soul, with Russia awakened to life, we would build the United States of Europe. Even his voice was changed. Joan could almost fancy it was some excited schoolboy that was talking.

Mary had been clasping and unclasping her hands, a habit of hers when troubled. Could good ever come out of evil? That was her doubt. Did war ever do anything but sow the seeds of future violence; substitute one injustice for another; change wrong for wrong. Did it ever do anything but add to the world's sum of evil, making God's task the heavier?

Suddenly, while speaking, she fell into a passionate fit of weeping. She went on through her tears:

"It will be terrible," she said. "It will last longer than you say. Every nation will be drawn into it. There will be no voice left to speak for reason. Every day we shall grow more brutalized, more pitiless. It will degrade us, crush the soul

out of us. Blood and iron! It will become our God too: the God of all the world.
You say we are going into it with clean hands, this time. How long will they keep
clean? The people who only live for making money: how long do you think they
will remain silent? What has been all the talk of the last ten years but of capturing
German trade. We shall be told that we owe it to our dead to make a profit out of
them; that otherwise they will have died in vain. Who will care for the people but
to use them for killing one another—to hound them on like dogs. In every country nothing but greed and hatred will be preached. Horrible men and women will
write to the papers crying out for more blood, more cruelty. Everything that can
make for anger and revenge will be screamed from every newspaper. Every plea
for humanity will be jeered at as 'sickly sentimentality.' Every man and woman
who remembers the ideals with which we started will be shrieked at as a traitor.
The people who are doing well out of it, they will get hold of the Press, appeal to
the passions of the mob. Nobody else will be allowed to speak. It always has
been so in war. It always will be. This will be no exception merely because it's
bigger. Every country will be given over to savagery. There will be no appeal
against it. The whole world will sink back into the beast."

She ended by rising abruptly and wishing them good-night. Her outburst had
silenced Joan's impish drummer, for the time. He appeared to be nervous and
depressed, but bucked up again on the way to the bus. Greyson walked with her
as usual. They took the long way round by the outer circle.

"Poor Mary!" he said. "I should not have talked before her if I had thought.
Her horror of war is almost physical. She will not even read about them. It has
the same effect upon her as stories of cruelty."

"But there's truth in a good deal that she says," he added. "War can bring out
all that is best in a people; but also it brings out the worst. We shall have to take
care that the ideals are not lost sight of."

"I wish this wretched business of the paper hadn't come just at this time," said
Joan: "just when your voice is most needed.

"Couldn't you get enough money together to start something quickly," she
continued, the idea suddenly coming to her. "I think I could help you. It
wouldn't matter its being something small to begin with. So long as it was entirely your own, and couldn't be taken away from you. You'd soon work it up."

"Thanks," he answered. "I may ask you to later on. But just now—" He
paused.

Of course. For war you wanted men, to fight. She had been thinking of them
in the lump: hurrying masses such as one sees on cinema screens, blurred but picturesque. Of course, when you came to think of it, they would have to be made
up of individuals—gallant-hearted, boyish sort of men who would pass through
doors, one at a time, into little rooms; give their name and address to a soldier
man seated at a big deal table. Later on, one would say good-bye to them on
crowded platforms, wave a handkerchief. Not all of them would come back.
"You can't make omelettes without breaking eggs," she told herself.

It annoyed her, that silly saying having come into her mind. She could see them lying there, with their white faces to the night. Surely she might have thought of some remark less idiotic to make to herself, at such a time.

He was explaining to her things about the air service. It seemed he had had experience in flying—some relation of his with whom he had spent a holiday last summer.

It would mean his getting out quickly. He seemed quite eager to be gone.

"Isn't it rather dangerous work?" she asked. She felt it was a footling question even as she asked it. Her brain had become stodgy.

"Nothing like as dangerous as being in the Infantry," he answered. "And that would be my only other alternative. Besides I get out of the drilling." He laughed. "I should hate being shouted at and ordered about by a husky old sergeant."

They neither spoke again till they came to the bridge, from the other side of which the busses started.

"I may not see you again before I go," he said. "Look after Mary. I shall try to persuade her to go down to her aunt in Hampshire. It's rather a bit of luck, as it turns out, the paper being finished with. I shouldn't have quite known what to do."

He had stopped at the corner. They were still beneath the shadow of the trees. Quite unconsciously she put her face up; and as if it had always been the custom at their partings, he drew her to him and kissed her; though it really was for the first time.

She walked home instead of taking the bus. She wanted to think. A day or two would decide the question. She determined that if the miracle did not happen, she would go down to Liverpool. Her father was on the committee of one of the great hospitals; and she knew one or two of the matrons. She would want to be doing something—to get out to the front, if possible. Maybe, her desire to serve was not altogether free from curiosity—from the craving for adventure. There's a spice of the man even in the best of women.

Her conscience plagued her when she thought of Mrs. Denton. For some time now, they had been very close together; and the old lady had come to depend upon her. She waited till all doubt was ended before calling to say good-bye. Mrs. Denton was seated before an old bureau that had long stood locked in a corner of the library. The drawers were open and books and papers were scattered about.

Joan told her plans. "You'll be able to get along without me for a little while?" she asked doubtfully.

Mrs. Denton laughed. "I haven't much more to do," she answered. "Just tidying up, as you see; and two or three half-finished things I shall try to complete. After that, I'll perhaps take a rest."

She took from among the litter a faded photograph and handed it to Joan. "Odd," she said. "I've just turned it out."

It represented a long, thin line of eminently respectable ladies and gentlemen in early Victorian costume. The men in peg-top trousers and silk stocks, the women in crinolines and poke bonnets. Among them, holding the hand of a be-nevolent-looking, stoutish gentleman, was a mere girl. The terminating frills of a white unmentionable garment showed beneath her skirts. She wore a porkpie hat with a feather in it.

"My first public appearance," explained Mrs. Denton. "I teased my father into taking me with him. We represented Great Britain and Ireland. I suppose I'm the only one left."

"I shouldn't have recognized you," laughed Joan. "What was the occasion?"

"The great International Peace Congress at Paris," explained Mrs. Denton; "just after the Crimean war. It made quite a stir at the time. The Emperor opened our proceedings in person, and the Pope and the Archbishop of Canterbury both sent us their blessing. We had a copy of the speeches presented to us on leaving, in every known language in Europe, bound in vellum. I'm hoping to find it. And the Press was enthusiastic. There were to be Acts of Parliament, Courts of Arbi-tration, International Laws, Diplomatic Treaties. A Sub-Committee was appointed to prepare a special set of prayers and a Palace of Peace was to be erected. There was only one thing we forgot, and that was the foundation."

"I may not be here," she continued, "when the new plans are submitted. Tell them not to forget the foundation this time. Tell them to teach the children."

Joan dined at a popular restaurant that evening. She fancied it might cheer her up. But the noisy patriotism of the over-fed crowd only irritated her. These el-derly, flabby men, these fleshy women, who would form the spectators, who would loll on their cushioned seats protected from the sun, munching contentedly from their well-provided baskets while listening to the dying groans rising up-wards from the drenched arena. She glanced from one podgy thumb to another and a feeling of nausea crept over her.

Suddenly the band struck up "God Save the King." Three commonplace enough young men, seated at a table near to her, laid down their napkins and stood up. Yes, there was something to be said for war, she felt, as she looked at their boyish faces, transfigured. Not for them Business as usual, the Capture of German Trade. Other visions those young eyes were seeing. The little imp with-in her brain had seized his drum again. "Follow me"—so he seemed to beat—"I teach men courage, duty, the laying down of self. I open the gates of honour. I make heroes out of dust. Isn't it worth my price?"

A figure was loitering the other side of the street when she reached home. She thought she somehow recognized it, and crossed over. It was McKean, smoking his everlasting pipe. Success having demanded some such change, he had mi-grated to "The Albany," and she had not seen him for some time. He had come to have a last look at the house—in case it might happen to be the last. He was off to Scotland the next morning, where he intended to "join up."

"But are you sure it's your particular duty?" suggested Joan. "I'm told you've become a household word both in Germany and France. If we really are out to end war and establish the brotherhood of nations, the work you are doing is of more importance than even the killing of Germans. It isn't as if there wouldn't be enough without you."

"To tell the truth," he answered, "that's exactly what I've been saying to myself. I shan't be any good. I don't see myself sticking a bayonet into even a German. Unless he happened to be abnormally clumsy. I tried to shoot a rabbit once. I might have done it if the little beggar, instead of running away, hadn't turned and looked at me."

"I should keep out of it if I were you," laughed Joan.

"I can't," he answered. "I'm too great a coward."

"An odd reason for enlisting," thought Joan.

"I couldn't face it," he went on; "the way people would be looking at me in trains and omnibuses; the things people would say of me, the things I should imagine they were saying; what my valet would be thinking of me. Oh, I'm ashamed enough of myself. It's the artistic temperament, I suppose. We must always be admired, praised. We're not the stuff that martyrs are made of. We must for ever be kow-towing to the cackling geese around us. We're so terrified lest they should hiss us."

The street was empty. They were pacing it slowly, up and down.

"I've always been a coward," he continued. "I fell in love with you the first day I met you on the stairs. But I dared not tell you."

"You didn't give me that impression," answered Joan.

She had always found it difficult to know when to take him seriously and when not.

"I was so afraid you would find it out," he explained.

"You thought I would take advantage of it," she suggested.

"One can never be sure of a woman," he answered. "And it would have been so difficult. There was a girl down in Scotland, one of the village girls. It wasn't anything really. We had just been children together. But they all thought I had gone away to make my fortune so as to come back and marry her—even my mother. It would have looked so mean if after getting on I had married a fine London lady. I could never have gone home again."

"But you haven't married her—or have you?" asked Joan.

"No," he answered. "She wrote me a beautiful letter that I shall always keep, begging me to forgive her, and hoping I might be happy. She had married a young farmer, and was going out to Canada. My mother will never allow her name to be mentioned in our house."

They had reached the end of the street again. Joan held out her hand with a laugh.

"Thanks for the compliment," she said. "Though I notice you wait till you're going away before telling me."

"But quite seriously," she added, "give it a little more thought—the enlisting, I mean. The world isn't too rich in kind influences. It needs men like you. Come, pull yourself together and show a little pluck." She laughed.

"I'll try," he promised, "but it won't be any use; I shall drift about the streets, seeking to put heart into myself, but all the while my footsteps will be bearing me nearer and nearer to the recruiting office; and outside the door some girl in the crowd will smile approval or some old fool will pat me on the shoulder and I shall sneak in and it will close behind me. It must be fine to have courage."

He wrote her two days later from Ayr, giving her the name of his regiment, and again some six months later from Flanders. But there would have been no sense in her replying to that last.

She lingered in the street by herself, a little time, after he had turned the corner. It had been a house of sorrow and disappointment to her; but so also she had dreamed her dreams there, seen her visions. She had never made much headway with her landlord and her landlady: a worthy couple, who had proved most excellent servants, but who prided themselves, to use their own expression, on knowing their place and keeping themselves to themselves. Joan had given them notice that morning, and had been surprised at the woman's bursting into tears.

"I felt it just the same when young Mr. McKean left us," she explained with apologies. "He had been with us five years. He was like you, miss, so unpracticable. I'd got used to looking after him."

Mary Greyson called on her in the morning, while she was still at breakfast. She had come from seeing Francis off by an early train from Euston. He had sent Joan a ring.

"He is so afraid you may not be able to wear it—that it will not fit you," said Mary, "but I told him I was sure it would."

Joan held our her hand for the letter. "I was afraid he had forgotten it," she answered, with a smile.

She placed the ring on her finger and held out her hand. "I might have been measured for it," she said. "I wonder how he knew."

"You left a glove behind you, the first day you ever came to our house," Mary explained. "And I kept it."

She was following his wishes and going down into the country. They did not meet again until after the war.

Madge dropped in on her during the week and brought Flossie with her. Flossie's husband, Sam, had departed for the Navy; and Niel Singleton, who had offered and been rejected for the Army, had joined a Red Cross unit. Madge herself was taking up canteen work. Joan rather expected Flossie to be in favour of the war, and Madge against it. Instead of which, it turned out the other way round. It seemed difficult to forecast opinion in this matter.

Madge thought that England, in particular, had been too much given up to luxury and pleasure. There had been too much idleness and empty laughter: Hitchicoo dances and women undressing themselves upon the stage. Even the working classes seemed to think of nothing else but cinemas and beer. She dreamed of a United Kingdom purified by suffering, cleansed by tears; its people drawn together by memory of common sacrifice; class antagonism buried in the grave where Duke's son and cook's son would lie side by side: of a new-born Europe rising from the ashes of the old. With Germany beaten, her lust of war burnt out, her hideous doctrine of Force proved to be false, the world would breathe a freer air. Passion and hatred would fall from man's eyes. The people would see one another and join hands.

Flossie was sceptical. "Why hasn't it done it before?" she wanted to know. "Good Lord! There's been enough of it."

"Why didn't we all kiss and be friends after the Napoleonic wars?" she demanded, "instead of getting up Peterloo massacres, and anti-Corn Law riots, and breaking the Duke of Wellington's windows?"

"All this talk of downing Militarism," she continued. "It's like trying to do away with the other sort of disorderly house. You don't stamp out a vice by chivying it round the corner. When men and women have become decent there will be no more disorderly houses. But it won't come before. Suppose we do knock Militarism out of Germany, like we did out of France, not so very long ago? It will only slip round the corner into Russia or Japan. Come and settle over here, as likely as not, especially if we have a few victories and get to fancy ourselves."

Madge was of opinion that the world would have had enough of war. Not armies but whole peoples would be involved this time. The lesson would be driven home.

"Oh, yes, we shall have had enough of it," agreed Flossie, "by the time we've paid up. There's no doubt of that. What about our children? I've just left young Frank strutting all over the house and flourishing a paper knife. And the servants have had to bar the kitchen door to prevent his bursting in every five minutes and attacking them. What's he going to say when I tell him, later on, that his father and myself have had all the war we want, and have decided there shall be no more? The old folks have had their fun. Why shouldn't I have mine? That will be his argument."

"You can't do it," she concluded, "unless you are prepared to keep half the world's literature away from the children, scrap half your music, edit your museums and your picture galleries; bowdlerize your Old Testament and rewrite your histories. And then you'll have to be careful for twenty-four hours a day that they never see a dog-fight."

Madge still held to her hope. God would make a wind of reason to pass over the earth. He would not smite again his people.

"I wish poor dear Sam could have been kept out of it," said Flossie. She wiped her eyes and finished her tea.

Joan had arranged to leave on the Monday. She ran down to see Mary Stopperton on the Saturday afternoon. Mr. Stopperton had died the year before, and Mary had been a little hurt, divining insincerity in the condolences offered to her by most of her friends.

"You didn't know him, dear," she had said to Joan. "All his faults were on the outside."

She did not want to talk about the war.

"Perhaps it's wrong of me," she said. "But it makes me so sad. And I can do nothing."

She had been busy at her machine when Joan had entered; and a pile of delicate white work lay folded on a chair beside her.

"What are you making?" asked Joan.

The little withered face lighted up. "Guess," she said, as she unfolded and displayed a tiny garment.

"I so love making them," she said. "I say to myself, 'It will all come right. God will send more and more of His Christ babies; till at last there will be thousands and thousands of them everywhere; and their love will change the world!'"

Her bright eyes had caught sight of the ring upon Joan's hand. She touched it with her little fragile fingers.

"You will let me make one for you, dearie, won't you?" she said. "I feel sure it will be a little Christ baby."

Arthur was still away when she arrived home. He had gone to Norway on business. Her father was afraid he would find it difficult to get back. Telegraphic communication had been stopped, and they had had no news of him. Her father was worried. A big Government contract had come in, while many of his best men had left to enlist.

"I've fixed you up all right at the hospital," he said. "It was good of you to think of coming home. Don't go away, for a bit." It was the first time he had asked anything of her.

Another fortnight passed before they heard from Arthur, and then he wrote them both from Hull. He would be somewhere in the North Sea, mine sweeping, when they read his letters. He had hoped to get a day or two to run across and say good-bye; but the need for men was pressing and he had not liked to plead excuses. The boat by which he had managed to leave Bergen had gone down. He and a few others had been picked up, but the sights that he had seen were haunting him. He felt sure his uncle would agree that he ought to be helping, and this was work for England he could do with all his heart. He hoped he was not leaving his uncle in the lurch; but he did not think the war would last long, and he would soon be back.

"Dear lad," said her father, "he would take the most dangerous work that he could find. But I wish he hadn't been quite so impulsive. He could have been of more use helping me with this War Office contract. I suppose he never got my letter, telling him about it."

In his letter to Joan he went further. He had received his uncle's letter, so he confided to her. Perhaps she would think him a crank, but he couldn't help it. He hated this killing business, this making of machinery for slaughtering men in bulk, like they killed pigs in Chicago. Out on the free, sweet sea, helping to keep it clean from man's abominations, he would be away from it all.

She saw the vision of him that night, as, leaning from her window, she looked out beyond the pines: the little lonely ship amid the waste of waters; his beautiful, almost womanish, face, and the gentle dreamy eyes with their haunting suggestion of a shadow.

Her little drummer played less and less frequently to her as the months passed by. It didn't seem to be the war he had looked forward to. The illustrated papers continued to picture it as a sort of glorified picnic where smiling young men lolled luxuriously in cosy dug-outs, reading their favourite paper. By curious coincidence, it generally happened to be the journal publishing the photograph. Occasionally, it appeared, they came across the enemy, who then put up both hands and shouted "Kamerad." But the weary, wounded men she talked to told another story.

She grew impatient of the fighters with their mouths; the savage old baldheads heroically prepared to sacrifice the last young man; the sleek, purring women who talked childish nonsense about killing every man, woman and child in Germany, but quite meant it; the shrieking journalists who had decided that their place was the home front; the press-spurred mobs, the spy hunters, chasing terrified old men and sobbing children through the streets. It was a relief to enter the quiet ward and close the door behind her. The camp-followers: the traders and pedlars, the balladmongers, and the mountebanks, the ghoulish sightseers! War brought out all that was worst in them. But the givers of their blood, the lads who suffered, who had made the sacrifice: war had taught them chivalry, manhood. She heard no revilings of hatred and revenge from those drawn lips. Patience, humour, forgiveness, they had learnt from war. They told her kindly stories even of Hans and Fritz.

The little drummer in her brain would creep out of his corner, play to her softly while she moved about among them.

One day she received a letter from Folk. He had come to London at the request of the French Government to consult with English artists on a matter he must not mention. He would not have the time, he told her, to run down to Liverpool. Could she get a couple of days' leave and dine with him in London.

She found him in the uniform of a French Colonel. He had quite a military bearing and seemed pleased with himself. He kissed her hand, and then held her out at arms' length.

"It's wonderful how like you are to your mother," he said, "I wish I were as young as I feel."

She had written him at the beginning of the war, telling him of her wish to get out to the front, and he thought that now he might be able to help her.

"But perhaps you've changed your mind," he said. "It isn't quite as pretty as it's painted."

"I want to," she answered. "It isn't all curiosity. I think it's time for women to insist on seeing war with their own eyes, not trust any longer to the pictures you men paint." She smiled.

"But I've got to give it up," she added. "I can't leave Dad."

They were sitting in the hall of the hotel. It was the dressing hour and the place was almost empty. He shot a swift glance at her.

"Arthur is still away," she explained, "and I feel that he wants me. I should be worrying myself, thinking of him all alone with no one to look after him. It's the mother instinct I suppose. It always has hampered woman." She laughed.

"Dear old boy," he said. He was watching her with a little smile. "I'm glad he's got some luck at last."

They dined in the great restaurant belonging to the hotel. He was still vastly pleased with himself as he marched up the crowded room with Joan upon his arm. He held himself upright and talked and laughed perhaps louder than an elderly gentleman should. "Swaggering old beggar," he must have overheard a young sub. mutter as they passed. But he did not seem to mind it.

They lingered over the meal. Folk was a brilliant talker. Most of the men whose names were filling the newspapers had sat to him at one time or another. He made them seem quite human. Joan was surprised at the time.

"Come up to my rooms, will you?" he asked. "There's something I want to say to you. And then I'll walk back with you." She was staying at a small hotel off Jermyn Street.

He sat her down by the fire and went into the next room. He had a letter in his hand when he returned. Joan noticed that the envelope was written upon across the corner, but she was not near enough to distinguish the handwriting. He placed it on the mantelpiece and sat down opposite her.

"So you have come to love the dear old chap," he said.

"I have always loved him," Joan answered. "It was he didn't love me, for a time, as I thought. But I know now that he does."

He was silent for a few moments, and then he leant across and took her hands in his.

"I am going," he said, "where there is just the possibility of an accident: one never knows. I wanted to be sure that all was well with you."

He was looking at the ring upon her hand.

"A soldier boy?" he asked.

"Yes," she answered. "If he comes back." There was a little catch in her voice.

"I know he'll come back," he said. "I won't tell you why I am so sure. Perhaps you wouldn't believe." He was still holding her hands, looking into her eyes.

"Tell me," he said, "did you see your mother before she died. Did she speak to you?"

"No," Joan answered. "I was too late. She had died the night before. I hardly recognized her when I saw her. She looked so sweet and young."

"She loved you very dearly," he said. "Better than herself. All those years of sorrow: they came to her because of that. I thought it foolish of her at the time, but now I know she was wise. I want you always to love and honour her. I wouldn't ask you if it wasn't right."

She looked at him and smiled. "It's quite easy," she answered. "I always see her as she lay there with all the sorrow gone from her. She looked so beautiful and kind."

He rose and took the letter from where he had placed it on the mantelpiece. He stooped and held it out above the fire and a little flame leaped up and seemed to take it from his hand.

They neither spoke during the short walk between the two hotels. But at the door she turned and held out her hands to him.

"Thank you," she said, "for being so kind—and wise. I shall always love and honour her."

He kissed her, promising to take care of himself.

She ran against Phillips, the next day, at one of the big stores where she was shopping. He had obtained a commission early in the war and was now a captain. He had just come back from the front on leave. The alternative had not appealed to him, of being one of those responsible for sending other men to death while remaining himself in security and comfort.

"It's a matter of temperament," he said. "Somebody's got to stop behind and do the patriotic speechifying. I'm glad I didn't. Especially after what I've seen."

He had lost interest in politics.

"There's something bigger coming," he said. "Here everything seems to be going on much the same, but over there you feel it. Something growing silently out of all this blood and mud. I find myself wondering what the men are staring at, but when I look there's nothing as far as my field-glasses will reach but waste and desolation. And it isn't only on the faces of our own men. It's in the eyes of the prisoners too. As if they saw something. A funny ending to the war, if the people began to think."

Mrs. Phillips was running a Convalescent Home in Folkestone, he told her; and had even made a speech. Hilda was doing relief work among the ruined villages of France.

"It's a new world we shall be called upon to build," he said. "We must pay more heed to the foundation this time."

She seldom discussed the war with her father. At the beginning, he had dreamed with Greyson of a short and glorious campaign that should weld all classes together, and after which we should forgive our enemies and shape with them a better world. But as the months went by, he appeared to grow indifferent; and Joan, who got about twelve hours a day of it outside, welcomed other subjects.

It surprised her when one evening after dinner he introduced it himself.

"What are you going to do when it's over?" he asked her. "You won't give up the fight, will you, whatever happens?" She had not known till then that he had been taking any interest in her work.

"No," she answered with a laugh, "no matter what happens, I shall always want to be in it."

"Good lad," he said, patting her on the shoulder. "It will be an ugly world that will come out of all this hate and anger. The Lord will want all the help that He can get."

"And you don't forget our compact, do you?" he continued, "that I am to be your backer. I want to be in it too."

She shot a glance at him. He was looking at the portrait of that old Ironside Allway who had fought and died to make a nobler England, as he had dreamed. A grim, unprepossessing gentleman, unless the artist had done him much injustice, with high, narrow forehead, and puzzled, staring eyes.

She took the cigarette from her lips and her voice trembled a little.

"I want you to be something more to me than that, sir," she said. "I want to feel that I'm an Allway, fighting for the things we've always had at heart. I'll try and be worthy of the name."

Her hand stole out to him across the table, but she kept her face away from him. Until she felt his grasp grow tight, and then she turned and their eyes met.

"You'll be the last of the name," he said. "Something tells me that. I'm glad you're a fighter. I always prayed my child might be a fighter."

Arthur had not been home since the beginning of the war. Twice he had written them to expect him, but the little fleet of mine sweepers had been hard pressed, and on both occasions his leave had been stopped at the last moment. One afternoon he turned up unexpectedly at the hospital. It was a few weeks after the Conscription Act had been passed.

Joan took him into her room at the end of the ward, from where, through the open door, she could still keep watch. They spoke in low tones.

"It's done you good," said Joan. "You look every inch the jolly Jack Tar." He was hard and tanned, and his eyes were marvellously bright.

"Yes," he said, "I love the sea. It's clean and strong."

A fear was creeping over her. "Why have you come back?" she asked.

He hesitated, keeping his eyes upon the ground.

"I don't suppose you will agree with me," he said. "Somehow I felt I had to."

A Conscientious Objector. She might have guessed it. A "Conchy," as they would call him in the Press: all the spiteful screamers who had never risked a scratch, themselves, denouncing him as a coward. The local Dogberrys of the tribunals would fire off their little stock of gibes and platitudes upon him, propound with owlish solemnity the new Christianity, abuse him and condemn him, without listening to him. Jeering mobs would follow him through the streets. More than once, of late, she had encountered such crowds made up of shrieking girls and foul-mouthed men, surging round some white-faced youngster while the well-dressed passers-by looked on and grinned.

She came to him and stood over him with her hands upon his shoulders.

"Must you, dear?" she said. "Can't you reconcile it to yourself—to go on with your work of mercy, of saving poor folks' lives?"

He raised his eyes to hers. The shadow that, to her fancy, had always rested there seemed to have departed. A light had come to them.

"There are more important things than saving men's bodies. You think that, don't you?" he asked.

"Yes," she answered. "I won't try to hold you back, dear, if you think you can do that."

He caught her hands and held them.

"I wanted to be a coward," he said, "to keep out of the fight. I thought of the shame, of the petty persecutions—that even you might despise me. But I couldn't. I was always seeing His face before me with His beautiful tender eyes, and the blood drops on His brow. It is He alone can save the world. It is perishing for want of love; and by a little suffering I might be able to help Him. And then one night—I suppose it was a piece of driftwood—there rose up out of the sea a little cross that seemed to call to me to stretch out my hand and grasp it, and gird it to my side."

He had risen. "Don't you see," he said. "It is only by suffering that one can help Him. It is the sword that He has chosen—by which one day He will conquer the world. And this is such a splendid opportunity to fight for Him. It would be like deserting Him on the eve of a great battle."

She looked into his eager, hopeful eyes. Yes, it had always been so—it always would be, to the end. Not priests and prophets, but ever that little scattered band of glad sufferers for His sake would be His army. His weapon still the cross, till the victory should be won.

She glanced through the open door to where the poor, broken fellows she always thought of as "her boys" lay so patient, and then held out her hand to him with a smile, though the tears were in her eyes.

"So you're like all the rest of them, lad," she said. "It's for King and country. Good luck to you."

After the war was over and the men, released from their long terms of solitary confinement, came back to life injured in mind and body, she was almost glad he had escaped. But at the time it filled her soul with darkness.

It was one noonday. He had been down to the tribunal and his case had been again adjourned. She was returning from a lecture, and, crossing a street in the neighbourhood of the docks, found herself suddenly faced by an oncoming crowd. It was yelping and snarling, curiously suggestive of a pack of hungry wolves. A couple of young soldiers were standing back against a wall.

"Better not go on, nurse," said one of them. "It's some poor devil of a Conchy, I expect. Must have a damned sight more pluck than I should."

It was the fear that had been haunting her. She did not know how white she had turned.

"I think it is someone I know," she said. "Won't you help me?"

The crowd gave way to them, and they had all but reached him. He was hatless and bespattered, but his tender eyes had neither fear nor anger in them. She reached out her arms and called to him. Another step and she would have been beside him, but at the moment a slim, laughing girl darted in front of him and slipped her foot between his legs and he went down.

She heard the joyous yell and the shrill laughter as she struggled wildly to force her way to him. And then for a moment there was a space and a man with bent body and clenched hands was rushing forward as if upon a football field, and there came a little sickening thud and then the crowd closed in again.

Her strength was gone and she could only wait. More soldiers had come up and were using their fists freely, and gradually the crowd retired, still snarling; and they lifted him up and brought him to her.

"There's a chemist's shop in the next street. We'd better take him there," suggested the one who had first spoken to her. And she thanked them and followed them.

They made a bed for him with their coats upon the floor, and some of them kept guard outside the shop, while one, putting aside the frightened, useless little chemist, waited upon her, bringing things needful, while she cleansed the foulness from his smooth young face, and washed the matted blood from his fair hair, and closed the lids upon his tender eyes, and, stooping, kissed the cold, quiet lips.

There had been whispered talk among the men, and when she rose the one who had first spoken to her came forward. He was nervous and stood stiffly.

"Beg pardon, nurse," he said, "but we've sent for a stretcher, as the police don't seem in any hurry. Would you like us to take him. Or would it upset him, do you think, if he knew?"

"Thank you," she answered. "He would think it kind of you, I know."

She had the feeling that he was being borne by comrades.

CHAPTER XVII

It was from a small operating hospital in a village of the Argonne that she first saw the war with her own eyes.

Her father had wished her to go. Arthur's death had stirred in him the old Puritan blood with its record of long battle for liberty of conscience. If war claimed to be master of a man's soul, then the new warfare must be against war. He remembered the saying of a Frenchwoman who had been through the Franco-Prussian war. Joan, on her return from Paris some years before, had told him of her, repeating her words: "But, of course, it would not do to tell the truth," the old lady had said, "or we should have our children growing up to hate war."

"I'll be lonely and anxious till you come back," he said. "But that will have to be my part of the fight."

She had written to Folk. No female nurses were supposed to be allowed within the battle zone; but under pressure of shortage the French staff were relaxing the rule, and Folk had pledged himself to her discretion. "I am not doing you any kindness," he had written. "You will have to share the common hardships and privations, and the danger is real. If I didn't feel instinctively that underneath your mask of sweet reasonableness you are one of the most obstinate young women God ever made, and that without me you would probably get yourself into a still worse hole, I'd have refused." And then followed a list of the things she was to be sure to take with her, including a pound or two of Keating's insect powder, and a hint that it might save her trouble, if she had her hair cut short.

There was but one other woman at the hospital. It had been a farmhouse. The man and both sons had been killed during the first year of the war, and the woman had asked to be allowed to stay on. Her name was Madame Lelanne. She was useful by reason of her great physical strength. She could take up a man as he lay and carry him on her outstretched arms. It was an expressionless face, with dull, slow-moving eyes that never changed. She and Joan shared a small *grenier* in one of the barns. Joan had brought with her a camp bedstead; but the woman, wrapping a blanket round her, would creep into a hole she had made for herself among the hay. She never took off her clothes, except the great wooden-soled boots, so far as Joan could discover.

The medical staff consisted of a Dr. Poujoulet and two assistants. The authorities were always promising to send him more help, but it never arrived. One of the assistants, a Monsieur Dubos, a little man with a remarkably big beard, was a chemist, who, at the outbreak of the war, had been on the verge, as he made sure, of an important discovery in connection with colour photography. Almost the first question he asked Joan was could she speak German. Finding that she could, he had hurried her across the yard into a small hut where patients who had borne their operation successfully awaited their turn to be moved down to one of the convalescent hospitals at the base. Among them was a German prisoner, an elderly man, belonging to the Landwehr; in private life a photographer. He also had been making experiments in the direction of colour photography. Chance had revealed to the two men their common interest, and they had been exchanging notes. The German talked a little French, but not sufficient; and on the day of Joan's arrival they had reached an impasse that was maddening to both of them. Joan found herself up against technical terms that rendered her task difficult, but fortunately had brought a dictionary with her, and was able to make them understand one another. But she had to be firm with both of them, allowing them only ten minutes together at a time. The little Frenchman would kneel by the bedside, holding the German at an angle where he could talk with least danger to his wound. It seemed that each was the very man the other had been waiting all his life to meet. They shed tears on one another's neck when they parted, making all arrangements to write to one another.

"And you will come and stay with me," persisted the little Frenchman, "when this affair is finished"—he made an impatient gesture with his hands. "My wife takes much interest. She will be delighted."

And the big German, again embracing the little Frenchman, had promised, and had sent his compliments to Madame.

The other was a young priest. He wore the regulation Red Cross uniform, but kept his cassock hanging on a peg behind his bed. He had pretty frequent occasion to take it down. These small emergency hospitals, within range of the guns, were reserved for only dangerous cases: men whose wounds would not permit of their being carried further; and there never was much more than a sporting chance of saving them. They were always glad to find there was a priest among the staff. Often it was the first question they would ask on being lifted out of the ambulance. Even those who professed to no religion seemed comforted by the idea. He went by the title of "Monsieur le Prêtre:" Joan never learned his name. It was he who had laid out the little cemetery on the opposite side of the village street. It had once been an orchard, and some of the trees were still standing. In the centre, rising out of a pile of rockwork, he had placed a crucifix that had been found upon the roadside and had surrounded it with flowers. It formed the one bright spot of colour in the village; and at night time, when all other sounds were hushed, the iron wreaths upon its little crosses, swaying against one another in the wind, would make a low, clear, tinkling music. Joan would sometimes lie awake listening to it. In some way she could not explain it always brought the thought of children to her mind.

The doctor himself was a broad-shouldered, bullet-headed man, clean shaven, with close-cropped, bristly hair. He had curiously square hands, with short, squat fingers. He had been head surgeon in one of the Paris hospitals, and had been assigned his present post because of his marvellous quickness with the knife. The hospital was the nearest to a hill of great strategical importance, and the fighting in the neighbourhood was almost continuous. Often a single ambulance would bring in three or four cases, each one demanding instant attention. Dr. Poujoulet, with his hairy arms bare to the shoulder, would polish them off one after another, with hardly a moment's rest between, not allowing time even for the washing of the table. Joan would have to summon all her nerve to keep herself from collapsing. At times the need for haste was such that it was impossible to wait for the anaesthetic to take effect. The one redeeming feature was the extraordinary heroism of the men, though occasionally there was nothing for it but to call in the orderlies to hold some poor fellow down, and to deafen one's ears.

One day, after a successful operation, she was tending a young sergeant. He was a well-built, handsome man, with skin as white as a woman's. He watched her with curious indifference in his eyes as she busied herself, trying to make him comfortable, and did nothing to help her.

"Has Mam'selle ever seen a bull fight?" he asked her.

"No," she answered. "I've seen all the horror and cruelty I want to for the rest of my life."

"Ah," he said, "you would understand if you had. When one of the horses goes down gored, his entrails lying out upon the sand, you know what they do, don't you? They put a rope round him, and drag him, groaning, into the shambles behind. And once there, kind people like you and Monsieur le Médecin tend him and wash him, and put his entrails back, and sew him up again. He thinks it so kind of them—the first time. But the second! He understands. He will be sent back into the arena to be ripped up again, and again after that. This is the third time I have been wounded, and as soon as you've all patched me up and I've got my breath again, they'll send me back into it. Mam'selle will forgive my not feeling grateful to her." He gave a short laugh that brought the blood into his mouth.

The village consisted of one long straggling street, following the course of a small stream between two lines of hills. It was on one of the great lines of communication: and troops and war material passed through it, going and coming, in almost endless procession. It served also as a camp of rest. Companies from the trenches would arrive there, generally towards the evening, weary, listless, dull-eyed, many of them staggering like over-driven cattle beneath their mass of burdens. They would fling their accoutrements from them and stand in silent groups till the sergeants and corporals returned to lead them to the barns and out-houses that had been assigned to them, the houses still habitable being mostly reserved for the officers. Like those of most French villages, they were drab, plaster-covered buildings without gardens; but some of them were covered with vines, hiding their ugliness; and the village as a whole, with its groups, here and there, of fine sycamore trees and its great stone fountain in the centre, was picturesque enough. It had twice changed hands, and a part of it was in ruins. From one or two of the more solidly built houses merely the front had fallen, leaving the rooms just as they had always been: the furniture in its accustomed place, the pictures on the walls. They suggested doll's houses standing open. One wondered when the giant child would come along and close them up. The iron spire of the little church had been hit twice. It stood above the village, twisted into the form of a note of interrogation. In the churchyard many of the graves had been ripped open. Bones and skulls lay scattered about among the shattered tombstones. But, save for a couple of holes in the roof, the body was still intact, and every afternoon a faint, timid-sounding bell called a few villagers and a sprinkling of soldiers to Mass. Most of the inhabitants had fled, but the farmers and shopkeepers had remained. At intervals, the German batteries, searching round with apparent aimlessness, would drop a score or so of shells about the neighbourhood; but the peasant, with an indifference that was almost animal, would still follow his ox-drawn plough; the old, bent crone, muttering curses, still ply the hoe. The proprietors of the tiny *épiceries* must have been rapidly making their fortunes, considering the prices that they charged the unfortunate *poilu*, dreaming of some small luxury out of his five sous a day. But as one of them, a stout, smiling lady, explained to Joan, with a gesture: "It is not often that one has a war."

Joan had gone out in September, and for a while the weather was pleasant. The men, wrapped up in their great-coats, would sleep for preference under the great sycamore trees. Through open doorways she would catch glimpses of picturesque groups of eager card-players, crowded round a flickering candle. From the darkness there would steal the sound of flute or zither, of voices singing. Occasionally it would be some strident ditty of the Paris music-halls, but more often it was sad and plaintive. But early in October the rains commenced and the stream became a roaring torrent, and a clammy mist lay like a white river between the wooded hills.

Mud! that seemed to be the one word with which to describe modern war. Mud everywhere! Mud ankle-deep upon the roads; mud into which you sank up to your knees the moment you stepped off it; tents and huts to which you waded through the mud, avoiding the slimy gangways on which you slipped and fell; mud-bespattered men, mud-bespattered horses, little donkeys, looking as if they had been sculptured out of mud, struggling up and down the light railways that every now and then would disappear and be lost beneath the mud; guns and wagons groaning through the mud; lorries and ambulances, that in the darkness had swerved from the straight course, overturned and lying abandoned in the mud, motor-cyclists ploughing swift furrows through the mud, rolling it back in liquid streams each side of them; staff cars rushing screaming through the mud, followed by a rushing fountain of mud; serried ranks of muddy men stamping through the mud with steady rhythm, moving through a rain of mud, rising upward from the ground; long lines of motor-buses filled with a mass of muddy humanity packed shoulder to shoulder, rumbling ever through the endless mud.

Men sitting by the roadside in the mud, gnawing at unsavoury food; men squatting by the ditches, examining their sores, washing their bleeding feet in the muddy water, replacing the muddy rags about their wounds.

A world without colour. No other colour to be seen beneath the sky but mud. The very buttons on the men's coats painted to make them look like mud.

Mud and dirt! Dirty faces, dirty hands, dirty clothes, dirty food, dirty beds; dirty interiors, from which there was never time to wash the mud; dirty linen hanging up to dry, beneath which dirty children played, while dirty women scolded. Filth and desolation all around. Shattered farmsteads half buried in the mud; shattered gardens trampled into mud. A weary land of foulness, breeding foulness; tangled wire the only harvest of the fields; mile after mile of gaping holes, filled with muddy water; stinking carcases of dead horses; birds of prey clinging to broken fences, flapping their great wings.

A land where man died, and vermin increased and multiplied. Vermin on your body, vermin in your head, vermin in your food, vermin waiting for you in your bed; vermin the only thing that throve, the only thing that looked at you with bright eyes; vermin the only thing to which the joy of life had still been left.

Joan had found a liking gradually growing up in her for the quick-moving, curt-tongued doctor. She had dismissed him at first as a mere butcher: his brutal haste, his indifference apparently to the suffering he was causing, his great, strong, hairy hands, with their squat fingers, his cold grey eyes. But she learnt as time went by, that his callousness was a thing that he put on at the same time that he tied his white apron round his waist, and rolled up his sleeves.

She was resting, after a morning of grim work, on a bench outside the hospital, struggling with clenched, quivering hands against a craving to fling herself upon the ground and sob. And he had found her there; and had sat down beside her.

"So you wanted to see it with your own eyes," he said. He laid his hand upon her shoulder, and she had some difficulty in not catching hold of him and clinging to him. She was feeling absurdly womanish just at that moment.

"Yes," she answered. "And I'm glad that I did it," she added, defiantly.

"So am I," he said. "Tell your children what you have seen. Tell other women."

"It's you women that make war," he continued. "Oh, I don't mean that you do it on purpose, but it's in your blood. It comes from the days when to live it was needful to kill. When a man who was swift and strong to kill was the only thing that could save a woman and her brood. Every other man that crept towards them through the grass was an enemy, and her only hope was that her man might kill him, while she watched and waited. And later came the tribe; and instead of the one man creeping through the grass, the everlasting warfare was against all other tribes. So you loved only the men ever ready and willing to fight, lest you and your children should be carried into slavery: then it was the only way. You brought up your boys to be fighters. You told them stories of their gallant sires. You sang to them the songs of battle: the glory of killing and of conquering. You have never unlearnt the lesson. Man has learnt comradeship—would have travelled further but for you. But woman is still primitive. She would still have her man the hater and the killer. To the woman the world has never changed."

"Tell the other women," he said. "Open their eyes. Tell them of their sons that you have seen dead and dying in the foolish quarrel for which there was no need. Tell them of the foulness, of the cruelty, of the senselessness of it all. Set the women against War. That is the only way to end it."

It was a morning or two later that, knocking at the door of her loft, he asked her if she would care to come with him to the trenches. He had brought an outfit for her which he handed to her with a grin. She had followed Folk's advice and had cut her hair; and when she appeared before him for inspection in trousers and overcoat, the collar turned up about her neck, and reaching to her helmet, he had laughingly pronounced the experiment safe.

A motor carried them to where the road ended, and from there, a little one-horse ambulance took them on to almost the last trees of the forest. There was no life to be seen anywhere. During the last mile, they had passed through a contin-uous double line of graves; here and there a group of tiny crosses keeping one another company; others standing singly, looking strangely lonesome amid the torn-up earth and shattered trees. But even these had ceased. Death itself seemed to have been frightened away from this terror-haunted desert.

Looking down, she could see thin wreaths of smoke, rising from the ground. From underneath her feet there came a low, faint, ceaseless murmur.

"Quick," said the doctor. He pushed her in front of him, and she almost fell down a flight of mud-covered steps that led into the earth. She found herself in a long, low gallery, lighted by a dim oil lamp, suspended from the blackened roof. A shelf ran along one side of it, covered with straw. Three men lay there. The straw was soaked with their blood. They had been brought in the night before by the stretcher-bearers. A young surgeon was rearranging their splints and bandag-es, and redressing their wounds. They would lie there for another hour or so, and then start for their twenty kilometre drive over shell-ridden roads to one or anoth-er of the great hospitals at the base. While she was there, two more cases were brought in. The doctor gave but a glance at the first one and then made a sign; and the bearers passed on with him to the further end of the gallery. He seemed to understand, for he gave a low, despairing cry and the tears sprang to his eyes. He was but a boy. The other had a foot torn off. One of the orderlies gave him two round pieces of wood to hold in his hands while the young surgeon cut away the hanging flesh and bound up the stump.

The doctor had been whispering to one of the bearers. He had the face of an old man, but his shoulders were broad and he looked sturdy. He nodded, and beckoned Joan to follow him up the slippery steps.

"It is breakfast time," he explained, as they emerged into the air. "We leave each other alone for half an hour—even the snipers. But we must be careful." She followed in his footsteps, stooping so low that her hands could have touched the ground. They had to be sure that they did not step off the narrow track marked with white stones, lest they should be drowned in the mud. They passed the head of a dead horse. It looked as if it had been cut off and laid there; the body was below it in the mud.

They spoke in whispers, and Joan at first had made an effort to disguise her voice. But her conductor had smiled. "They shall be called the brothers and the sisters of the Lord," he had said. "Mademoiselle is brave for her Brothers' sake." He was a priest. There were many priests among the stretcher-bearers.

Crouching close to the ground, behind the spreading roots of a giant oak, she raised her eyes. Before her lay a sea of smooth, soft mud nearly a mile wide. From the centre rose a solitary tree, from which all had been shot away but two bare branches like outstretched arms above the silence. Beyond, the hills rose again. There was something unearthly in the silence that seemed to brood above that sea of mud. The old priest told her of the living men, French and German, who had stood there day and night sunk in it up to their waists, screaming hour after hour, and waving their arms, sinking into it lower and lower, none able to help them: until at last only their screaming heads were left, and after a time these, too, would disappear: and the silence come again.

She saw the ditches, like long graves dug for the living, where the weary, listless men stood knee-deep in mud, hoping for wounds that would relieve them from the ghastly monotony of their existence; the holes of muddy water where the dead things lay, to which they crept out in the night to wash a little of the filth from their clammy bodies and their stinking clothes; the holes dug out of the mud in which they ate and slept and lived year after year: till brain and heart and soul seemed to have died out of them, and they remembered with an effort that they once were men.

* * * * *

After a time, the care of the convalescents passed almost entirely into Joan's hands, Madame Lelanne being told off to assist her. By dint of much persistence she had succeeded in getting the leaky roof repaired, and in place of the smoky stove that had long been her despair she had one night procured a fine calorifère by the simple process of stealing it. Madame Lelanne had heard about it from the gossips. It had been brought to a lonely house at the end of the village by a major of engineers. He had returned to the trenches the day before, and the place for the time being was empty. The thieves were never discovered. The sentry was positive that no one had passed him but two women, one of them carrying a baby. Madame Lelanne had dressed it up in a child's cloak and hood, and had carried it in her arms. As it must have weighed nearly a couple of hundred-weight suspicion had not attached to them.

Space did not allow of any separation; broken Frenchmen and broken Germans would often lie side by side. Joan would wonder, with a grim smile to herself, what the patriotic Press of the different countries would have thought had they been there to have overheard the conversations. Neither France nor Germany appeared to be the enemy, but a thing called "They," a mysterious power that worked its will upon them both from a place they always spoke of as "Back

805

there." One day the talk fell on courage. A young French soldier was holding forth when Joan entered the hut.

"It makes me laugh," he was saying, "all this newspaper talk. Every nation, properly led, fights bravely. It is the male instinct. Women go into hysterics about it, because it has not been given them. I have the Croix de Guerre with all three leaves, and I haven't half the courage of my dog, who weighs twelve kilos, and would face a regiment by himself. Why, a game cock has got more than the best of us. It's the man who doesn't think, who can't think, who has the most courage—who imagines nothing, but just goes forward with his head down, like a bull. There is, of course, a real courage. When you are by yourself, and have to do something in cold blood. But the courage required for rushing forward, shouting and yelling with a lot of other fellows—why, it would take a hundred times more pluck to turn back."

"They know that," chimed in the man lying next to him; "or they would not drug us. Why, when we stormed La Haye I knew nothing until an ugly-looking German spat a pint of blood into my face and woke me up."

A middle-aged sergeant, who had a wound in the stomach and was sitting up in his bed, looked across. "There was a line of Germans came upon us," he said, "at Bras. I thought I must be suffering from a nightmare when I saw them. They had thrown away their rifles and had all joined hands. They came dancing towards us just like a row of ballet girls. They were shrieking and laughing, and they never attempted to do anything. We just waited until they were close up and then shot them down. It was like killing a lot of kids who had come to have a game with us. The one I potted got his arms round me before he coughed himself out, calling me his 'liebe Elsa,' and wanting to kiss me. Lord! You can guess how the Boche ink-slingers spread themselves over that business: 'Sonderbar! Colossal! Unvergessliche Helden.' Poor devils!"

"They'll give us ginger before it is over," said another. He had had both his lips torn away, and appeared to be always laughing. "Stuff it into us as if we were horses at a fair. That will make us run forward, right enough."

"Oh, come," struck in a youngster who was lying perfectly flat, face downwards on his bed: it was the position in which he could breathe easiest. He raised his head a couple of inches and twisted it round so as to get his mouth free. "It isn't as bad as all that. Why, the Thirty-third swarmed into Fort Malmaison of their own accord, though 'twas like jumping into a boiling furnace, and held it for three days against pretty nearly a division. There weren't a dozen of them left when we relieved them. They had no ammunition left. They'd just been filling up the gaps with their bodies. And they wouldn't go back even then. We had to drag them away. 'They shan't pass,' 'They shan't pass!'—that's all they kept saying." His voice had sunk to a thin whisper.

A young officer was lying in a corner behind a screen. He leant forward and pushed it aside.

"Oh, give the devil his due, you fellows," he said. "War isn't a pretty game, but it does make for courage. We all know that. And things even finer than mere fighting pluck. There was a man in my company, a Jacques Decrusy. He was just a stupid peasant lad. We were crowded into one end of the trench, about a score of us. The rest of it had fallen in, and we couldn't move. And a bomb dropped into the middle of us; and the same instant that it touched the ground Decrusy threw himself flat down upon it and took the whole of it into his body. There was nothing left of him but scraps. But the rest of us got off. Nobody had drugged him to do that. There isn't one of us who was in that trench that will not be a better man to the end of his days, remembering how Jacques Decrusy gave his life for ours."

"I'll grant you all that, sir," answered the young soldier who had first spoken. He had long, delicate hands and eager, restless eyes. "War does bring out heroism. So does pestilence and famine. Read Defoe's account of the Plague of London. How men and women left their safe homes, to serve in the pest-houses, knowing that sooner or later they were doomed. Read of the mothers in India who die of slow starvation, never allowing a morsel of food to pass their lips so that they may save up their own small daily portion to add it to their children's. Why don't we pray to God not to withhold from us His precious medicine of pestilence and famine? So is shipwreck a fine school for courage. Look at the chance it gives the captain to set a fine example. And the engineers who stick to their post with the water pouring in upon them. We don't reconcile ourselves to shipwrecks as a necessary school for sailors. We do our best to lessen them. So did persecution bring out heroism. It made saints and martyrs. Why have we done away with it? If this game of killing and being killed is the fine school for virtue it is made out to be, then all our efforts towards law and order have been a mistake. We never ought to have emerged from the jungle."

He took a note-book from under his pillow and commenced to scribble.

An old-looking man spoke. He lay with his arms folded across his breast, addressing apparently the smoky rafters. He was a Russian, a teacher of languages in Paris at the outbreak of the war, and had joined the French Army.

"It is not only courage," he said, "that War brings out. It brings out vile things too. Oh, I'm not thinking merely of the Boches. That's the cant of every nation: that all the heroism is on one side and all the brutality on the other. Take men from anywhere and some of them will be devils. War gives them their opportunity, brings out the beast. Can you wonder at it? You teach a man to plunge a bayonet into the writhing flesh of a fellow human being, and twist it round and round and jamb it further in, while the blood is spurting from him like a fountain. What are you making of him but a beast? A man's got to be a beast before he can bring himself to do it. I have seen things done by our own men in cold blood, the horror of which will haunt my memory until I die. But of course, we hush it up when it happens to be our own people."

He ceased speaking. No one seemed inclined to break the silence.

They remained confused in her memory, these talks among the wounded men in the low, dimly lighted hut that had become her world. At times it was but two men speaking to one another in whispers, at others every creaking bed would be drawn into the argument.

One topic that never lost its interest was: Who made wars? Who hounded the people into them, and kept them there, tearing at one another's throats? They never settled it.

"God knows I didn't want it, speaking personally," said a German prisoner one day, with a laugh. "I had been working at a printing business sixteen hours a day for seven years. It was just beginning to pay me, and now my wife writes me that she has had to shut the place up and sell the machinery to keep them all from starving."

"But couldn't you have done anything to stop it?" demanded a Frenchman, lying next to him. "All your millions of Socialists, what were they up to? What went wrong with the Internationale, the Universal Brotherhood of Labour, and all that Tra-la-la?"

The German laughed again. "Oh, they know their business," he answered. "You have your glass of beer and go to bed, and when you wake up in the morning you find that war has been declared; and you keep your mouth shut—unless you want to be shot for a traitor. Not that it would have made much difference," he added. "I admit that. The ground had been too well prepared. England was envious of our trade. King Edward had been plotting our destruction. Our papers were full of translations from yours, talking about '*La Revanche*!' We were told that you had been lending money to Russia to enable her to build railways, and that when they were complete France and Russia would fall upon us suddenly. 'The Fatherland in danger!' It may be lies or it may not; what is one to do? What would you have done—even if you could have done anything?"

"He's right," said a dreamy-eyed looking man, laying down the book he had been reading. "We should have done just the same. 'My country, right or wrong.' After all, it is an ideal."

A dark, black-bearded man raised himself painfully upon his elbow. He was a tailor in the Rue Parnesse, and prided himself on a decided resemblance to Victor Hugo.

"It's a noble ideal," he said. "*La Patrie*! The great Mother. Right or wrong, who shall dare to harm her? Yes, if it was she who rose up in her majesty and called to us." He laughed. "What does it mean in reality: Germania, Italia, La France, Britannia? Half a score of pompous old muddlers with their fat wives egging them on: sons of the fools before them; talkers who have wormed themselves into power by making frothy speeches and fine promises. My Country!" he laughed again. "Look at them. Can't you see their swelling paunches and their flabby faces? Half a score of ambitious politicians, gouty old financiers, bald-headed old toffs, with their waxed moustaches and false teeth. That's what we mean when we talk about 'My Country': a pack of selfish, soulless, muddle-headed old men. And whether they're right or whether they're wrong, our duty is to fight at their bidding—to bleed for them, to die for them, that they may grow more sleek and prosperous." He sank back on his pillow with another laugh.

Sometimes they agreed it was the newspapers that made war—that fanned every trivial difference into a vital question of national honour—that, whenever there was any fear of peace, re-stoked the fires of hatred with their never-failing stories of atrocities. At other times they decided it was the capitalists, the traders, scenting profit for themselves. Some held it was the politicians, dreaming of going down to history as Richelieus or as Bismarcks. A popular theory was that cause for war was always discovered by the ruling classes whenever there seemed danger that the workers were getting out of hand. In war, you put the common people back in their place, revived in them the habits of submission and obedience. Napoleon the Little, it was argued, had started the war of 1870 with that idea. Russia had welcomed the present war as an answer to the Revolution that was threatening Czardom. Others contended it was the great munition industries, aided by the military party, the officers impatient for opportunities of advancement, the strategists eager to put their theories to the test. A few of the more philosophical shrugged their shoulders. It was the thing itself that sooner or later was bound to go off of its own accord. Half every country's energy, half every country's time and money was spent in piling up explosives. In every country envy and hatred of every other country was preached as a religion. They called it patriotism. Sooner or later the spark fell.

A wizened little man had been listening to it all one day. He had a curiously rat-like face, with round, red, twinkling eyes, and a long, pointed nose that twitched as he talked.

"I'll tell you who makes all the wars," he said. "It's you and me, my dears: we make the wars. We love them. That's why we open our mouths and swallow all the twaddle that the papers give us; and cheer the fine, black-coated gentlemen when they tell us it's our sacred duty to kill Germans, or Italians, or Russians, or anybody else. We are just crazy to kill something: it doesn't matter what. If it's to be Germans, we shout '*A Berlin*!'; and if it's to be Russians we cheer for Liberty. I was in Paris at the time of the Fashoda trouble. How we hissed the English in the cafés! And how they glared back at us! They were just as eager to kill us. Who makes a dog fight? Why, the dog. Anybody can do it. Who could make us fight each other, if we didn't want to? Not all the king's horses and all the King's men. No, my dears, it's we make the wars. You and me, my dears."

There came a day in early spring. All night long the guns had never ceased. It sounded like the tireless barking of ten thousand giant dogs. Behind the hills, the whole horizon, like a fiery circle, was ringed with flashing light. Shapeless forms, bent beneath burdens, passed in endless procession through the village. Masses of rushing men swept like shadowy phantoms through the fitfully-illumined darkness. Beneath that everlasting barking, Joan would hear, now the piercing wail of a child; now a clap of thunder that for the moment would drown all other sounds, followed by a faint, low, rumbling crash, like the shooting of coals into a cellar. The wounded on their beds lay with wide-open, terrified eyes, moving feverishly from side to side.

At dawn the order came that the hospital was to be evacuated. The ambulances were already waiting in the street. Joan flew up the ladder to her loft, the other side of the yard. Madame Lelanne was already there. She had thrown a few things into a bundle, and her foot was again upon the ladder, when it seemed to her that someone struck her, hurling her back upon the floor, and the house the other side of the yard rose up into the air, and then fell quite slowly, and a cloud of dust hid it from her sight.

Madame Lelanne must have carried her down the ladder. She was standing in the yard, and the dust was choking her. Across the street, beyond the ruins of the hospital, swarms of men were running about like ants when their nest has been disturbed. Some were running this way, and some that. And then they would turn and run back again, making dancing movements round one another and jostling one another. The guns had ceased; and instead, it sounded as if all the babies in the world were playing with their rattles. Suddenly Madame Lelanne reappeared out of the dust, and seizing Joan, dragged her through a dark opening and down a flight of steps, and then left her. She was in a great vaulted cellar. A faint light crept in through a grated window at the other end. There was a long table against the wall, and in front of it a bench. She staggered to it and sat down, leaning against the damp wall. The place was very silent. Suddenly she began to laugh. She tried to stop herself, but couldn't. And then she heard footsteps descending, and her memory came back to her with a rush. They were German footsteps, she felt sure by the sound: they were so slow and heavy. They should not find her in hysterics, anyhow. She fixed her teeth into the wooden table in front of her and held on to it with clenched hands. She had recovered herself before the footsteps had finished their descent. With a relief that made it difficult for her not to begin laughing again, she found it was Madame Lelanne and Monsieur Dubos. They were carrying something between them. She hardly recognized Dubos at first. His beard was gone, and a line of flaming scars had taken its place. They laid their burden on the table. It was one of the wounded men from the hut. They told her they were bringing down two more. The hut itself had not been hit, but the roof had been torn off by the force of the explosion, and the others had been killed by the falling beams. Joan wanted to return with them, but Madame Lelanne had assumed an air of authority, and told her she would be more useful where she was. From the top of the steps they threw down bundles of straw, on which they laid the wounded men, and Joan tended them, while Madame Lelanne and the little chemist went up and down continuously. Before evening the place, considering all things, was fairly habitable. Madame Lelanne brought down the great stove from the hut; and breaking a pane of glass in the barred window, they fixed it up with its chimney and lighted it. From time to time the turmoil above them would break out again: the rattling, and sometimes a dull rumbling as of rushing water. But only a faint murmur of it penetrated into the cellar. Towards night it became quiet again.

How long Joan remained there she was never quite sure. There was little difference between day and night. After it had been quiet for an hour or so, Madame

Lelanne would go out, to return a little later with a wounded man upon her back; and when one died, she would throw him across her shoulder and disappear again up the steps. Sometimes it was a Frenchman and sometimes a German she brought in. One gathered that the fight for the village still continued. There was but little they could do for them beyond dressing their wounds and easing their pain. Joan and the little chemist took it in turns to relieve one another. If Madame Lelanne ever slept, it was when she would sit in the shadow behind the stove, her hands upon her knees. Dubos had been in the house when it had fallen. Madame Lelanne had discovered him pinned against a wall underneath a great oak beam that had withstood the falling débris. His beard had been burnt off, but otherwise he had been unharmed.

She seemed to be living in a dream. She could not shake from her the feeling that it was not bodies but souls that she was tending. The men themselves gave colour to this fancy of hers. Stripped of their poor, stained, tattered uniforms, they were neither French nor Germans. Friend or foe! it was already but a memory. Often, awakening out of a sleep, they would look across at one another and smile as to a comrade. A great peace seemed to have entered there. Faint murmurs as from some distant troubled world would steal at times into the silence. It brought a pang of pity, but it did not drive away the quiet that dwelt there.

Once, someone who must have known the place and had descended the steps softly, sat there among them and talked with them. Joan could not remember seeing him enter. Perhaps unknowing, she had fallen to sleep for a few minutes. Madame Lelanne was seated by the stove, her great coarse hands upon her knees, her patient, dull, slow-moving eyes fixed upon the speaker's face. Dubos was half standing, half resting against the table, his arms folded upon his breast. The wounded men had raised themselves upon the straw and were listening. Some leant upon their elbows, some sat with their hands clasped round their knees, and one, with head bent down, remained with his face hidden in his hands.

The speaker sat a little way apart. The light from the oil lamp, suspended from the ceiling, fell upon his face. He wore a peasant's blouse. It seemed to her a face she knew. Possibly she had passed him in the village street and had looked at him without remembering. It was his eyes that for long years afterwards still haunted her. She did not notice at the time what language he was speaking. But there were none who did not understand him.

"You think of God as of a great King," he said, "a Ruler who orders all things: who could change all things in the twinkling of an eye. You see the cruelty and the wrong around you. And you say to yourselves: 'He has ordered it. If He would, He could have willed it differently.' So that in your hearts you are angry with Him. How could it be otherwise? What father, loving his children, would see them suffer wrong, when by stretching out a hand he could protect them: turn their tears to gladness? What father would see his children doing evil to one another and not check them: would see them following ways leading to their destruction, and not pluck them back? If God has ordered all things, why has He created evil, making His creatures weak and sinful? Does a father lay snares for his children: leading them into temptation: delivering them unto evil?"

"There is no God, apart from Man."

"God is a spirit. His dwelling-place is in man's heart. We are His fellow-labourers. It is through man that He shall one day rule the world."

"God is knocking at your heart, but you will not open to Him. You have filled your hearts with love of self. There is no room for Him to enter in."

"God whispers to you: 'Be pitiful. Be merciful. Be just.' But you answer Him: 'If I am pitiful, I lose my time and money. If I am merciful, I forego advantage to myself. If I am just, I lessen my own profit, and another passes me in the race.'"

"And yet in your inmost thoughts you know that you are wrong: that love of self brings you no peace. Who is happier than the lover, thinking only how to serve? Who is the more joyous: he who sits alone at the table, or he who shares his meal with a friend? It is more blessed to give than to receive. How can you doubt it? For what do you toil and strive but that you may give to your children, to your loved ones, reaping the harvest of their good?"

"Who among you is the more honoured? The miser or the giver: he who heaps up riches for himself or he who labours for others?"

"Who is the true soldier? He who has put away self. His own ease and comfort, even his own needs, his own safety: they are but as a feather in the balance when weighed against his love for his comrades, for his country. The true soldier is not afraid to love. He gives his life for his friend. Do you jeer at him? Do you say he is a fool for his pains? No, it is his honour, his glory."

"God is love. Why are you afraid to let Him in? Hate knocks also at your door and to him you open wide. Why are you afraid of love? All things are created by love. Hate can but destroy. Why choose you death instead of life? God pleads to you. He is waiting for your help."

And one answered him.

"We are but poor men," he said. "What can we do? Of what use are such as we?"

The young man looked at him and smiled.

"You can ask that," he said: "you, a soldier? Does the soldier say: 'I am of no use. I am but a poor man of no account. Who has need of such as I?' God has need of all. There is none that shall not help to win the victory. It is with his life the soldier serves. Who were they whose teaching moved the world more than it has ever yet been moved by the teaching of the wisest? They were men of little knowledge, of but little learning, poor and lowly. It was with their lives they taught."

"Cast out self, and God shall enter in, and you shall be One with God. For there is none so lowly that he may not become the Temple of God: there is none so great that he shall be greater than this."

The speaker ceased. There came a faint sound at which she turned her head; and when she looked again he was gone.

The wounded men had heard it also. Dubos had moved forward. Madame Le-lanne had risen. It came again, the thin, faint shrill of a distant bugle. Footsteps were descending the stairs. French soldiers, laughing, shouting, were crowding round them.

<h1 style="text-align: center">CHAPTER XVIII</h1>

Her father met her at Waterloo. He had business in London, and they stayed on for a few days. Reading between the lines of his later letters, she had felt that all was not well with him. His old heart trouble had come back; and she noticed that he walked to meet her very slowly. It would be all right, now that she had returned, he explained: he had been worrying himself about her.

Mrs. Denton had died. She had left Joan her library, together with her wonderful collection of note books. She had brought them all up-to-date and indexed them. They would be invaluable to Francis when he started the new paper upon which they had determined. He was still in the hospital at Breganze, near to where his machine had been shot down. She had tried to get to him; but it would have meant endless delays; and she had been anxious about her father. The Italian surgeons were very proud of him, he wrote. They had had him X-rayed before and after; and beyond a slight lameness which gave him, he thought, a touch of distinction, there was no flaw that the most careful scrutiny would be likely to detect. Any day, now, he expected to be discharged. Mary had married an old sweetheart. She had grown restless in the country with nothing to do, and, at the suggestion of some friends, had gone to Bristol to help in a children's hospital; and there they had met once more.

Neil Singleton, after serving two years in a cholera hospital at Baghdad, had died of the flu in Dover twenty-fours hours after landing. Madge was in Palestine. She had been appointed secretary to a committee for the establishment of native schools. She expected to be there for some years, she wrote. The work was interesting, and appealed to her.

Flossie 'phoned her from Paddington Station, the second day, and by luck she happened to be in. Flossie had just come up from Devonshire. Sam had "got through," and she was on her way to meet him at Hull. She had heard of Joan's arrival in London from one of Carleton's illustrated dailies. She brought the paper with her. They had used the old photograph that once had adorned each week the *Sunday Post*. Joan hardly recognized herself in the serene, self-confident young woman who seemed to be looking down upon a world at her feet. The world was strong and cruel, she had discovered; and Joans but small and weak. One had to pretend that one was not afraid of it.

Flossie had joined every society she could hear of that was working for the League of Nations. Her hope was that it would get itself established before young Frank grew up.

"Not that I really believe it will," she confessed. "A draw might have disgusted us all with fighting. As it is, half the world is dancing at Victory balls, exhibiting captured guns on every village green, and hanging father's helmet above the mantelpiece; while the other half is nursing its revenge. Young Frank only cares for life because he is looking forward to one day driving a tank. I've made up my mind to burn Sam's uniform; but I expect it will end in my wrapping it up in lavender and hiding it away in a drawer. And then there will be all the books and plays. No self-respecting heroine, for the next ten years will dream of marrying anyone but a soldier."

Joan laughed. "Difficult to get anything else, just at present," she said. "It's the soldiers I'm looking to for help. I don't think the men who have been there will want their sons to go. It's the women I'm afraid of."

Flossie caught sight of the clock and jumped up. "Who was it said that woman would be the last thing man would civilize?" she asked.

"It sounds like Meredith," suggested Joan. "I am not quite sure."

"Well, he's wrong, anyhow," retorted Flossie. "It's no good our waiting for man. He is too much afraid of us to be of any real help to us. We shall have to do it ourselves." She gave Joan a hug and was gone.

Phillips was still abroad with the Army of Occupation. He had tried to get out of it, but had not succeeded. He held it to be gaoler's work; and the sight of the starving populace was stirring in him a fierce anger.

He would not put up again for Parliament. He was thinking of going back to his old work upon the Union. "Parliament is played out," he had written her. "Kings and Aristocracies have served their purpose and have gone, and now the Ruling Classes, as they call themselves, must be content to hear the bell toll for them also. Parliament was never anything more than an instrument in their hands, and never can be. What happens? Once in every five years you wake the people up: tell them the time has come for them to exercise their Heaven-ordained privilege of putting a cross against the names of some seven hundred gentlemen who have kindly expressed their willingness to rule over them. After that, you send the people back to sleep; and for the next five years these seven hundred gentlemen, consulting no one but themselves, rule over the country as absolutely as ever a Caesar ruled over Rome. What sort of Democracy is that? Even a Labour Government—supposing that in spite of the Press it did win through—what would be its fate? Separated from its base, imprisoned within those tradition-haunted walls, it would lose touch with the people, would become in its turn a mere oligarchy. If the people are ever to govern they must keep their hand firmly upon the machine; not remain content with pulling a lever and then being shown the door."

She had sent a note by messenger to Mary Stopperton to say she was coming. Mary had looked very fragile the last time she had seen her, just before leaving for France; and she had felt a fear. Mary had answered in her neat, thin, quavering writing, asking her to come early in the morning. Sometimes she was a little tired and had to lie down again. She had been waiting for Joan. She had a present for her.

The morning promised to be fair, and she decided to walk by way of the Embankment. The great river with its deep, strong patience had always been a friend to her. It was Sunday and the city was still sleeping. The pale December sun rose above the mist as she reached the corner of Westminster Bridge, turning the river into silver and flooding the silent streets with a soft, white, tender light.

The tower of Chelsea Church brought back to her remembrance of the wheezy old clergyman who had preached there that Sunday evening, that now seemed so long ago, when her footsteps had first taken her that way by chance. Always she had intended making inquiries and discovering his name. Why had she never done so? It would surely have been easy. He was someone she had known as a child. She had become quite convinced of that. She could see his face close to hers as if he had lifted her up in his arms and was smiling at her. But pride and power had looked out of his eyes then.

It was earlier than the time she had fixed in her own mind and, pausing with her elbows resting on the granite parapet, she watched the ceaseless waters returning to the sea, bearing their burden of impurities.

"All roads lead to Calvary." It was curious how the words had dwelt with her, till gradually they had become a part of her creed. She remembered how at first they had seemed to her a threat chilling her with fear. They had grown to be a promise, a hope held out to all. The road to Calvary! It was the road to life. By the giving up of self we gained God.

And suddenly a great peace came to her. One was not alone in the fight, God was with us: the great Comrade. The evil and the cruelty all round her: she was no longer afraid of it. God was coming. Beyond the menace of the passing day, black with the war's foul aftermath of evil dreams and hatreds, she saw the breaking of the distant dawn. The devil should not always triumph. God was gathering His labourers.

God was conquering. Unceasing through the ages, God's voice had crept round man, seeking entry. Through the long darkness of that dim beginning, when man knew no law but self, unceasing God had striven: until at last one here and there, emerging from the brute, had heard—had listened to the voice of love and pity, and in that hour, unknowing, had built to God a temple in the wilderness.

Labourers together with God. The mighty host of those who through the ages had heard the voice of God and had made answer. The men and women in all lands who had made room in their hearts for God. Still nameless, scattered, unknown to one another: still powerless as yet against the world's foul law of hate, they should continue to increase and multiply, until one day they should speak with God's voice and should be heard. And a new world should be created.

God. The tireless Spirit of eternal creation, the Spirit of Love. What else was it that out of formlessness had shaped the spheres, had planned the orbits of the suns. The law of gravity we named it. What was it but another name for Love, the yearning of like for like, the calling to one another of the stars. What else but Love had made the worlds, had gathered together the waters, had fashioned the dry land. The cohesion of elements, so we explained it. The clinging of like to like. The brotherhood of the atoms.

God. The Eternal Creator. Out of matter, lifeless void, he had moulded His worlds, had ordered His endless firmament. It was finished. The greater task remained: the Universe of mind, of soul. Out of man it should be created. God in man and man in God: made in like image: fellow labourers together with one another: together they should build it. Out of the senseless strife and discord, above the chaos and the tumult should be heard the new command: "Let there be Love."

The striking of the old church clock recalled her to herself. But she had only a few minutes' walk before her. Mary had given up her Church work. It included the cleaning, and she had found it beyond her failing strength. But she still lived in the tiny cottage behind its long strip of garden. The door yielded to Joan's touch: it was seldom fast closed. And knowing Mary's ways, she entered without knocking and pushed it to behind her, leaving it still ajar.

And as she did so, it seemed to her that someone passing breathed upon her lips a little kiss: and for a while she did not move. Then, treading softly, she looked into the room.

It welcomed her, as always, with its smile of cosy neatness. The spotless curtains that were Mary's pride: the gay flowers in the window, to which she had given children's names: the few poor pieces of furniture, polished with much loving labour: the shining grate: the foolish china dogs and the little china house between them on the mantelpiece. The fire was burning brightly, and the kettle was singing on the hob.

Mary's work was finished. She sat upright in her straight-backed chair before the table, her eyes half closed. It seemed so odd to see those little work-worn hands idle upon her lap.

Joan's present lay on the table near to her, as if she had just folded it and placed it there: the little cap and the fine robe of lawn: as if for a king's child.

Joan had never thought that Death could be so beautiful. It was as if some friend had looked in at the door, and, seeing her so tired, had taken the work gently from her hands, and had folded them upon her lap. And she had yielded with a smile.

Joan heard a faint rustle and looked up. A woman had entered. It was the girl she had met there on a Christmas Day, a Miss Ensor. Joan had met her once or twice since then. She was still in the chorus. Neither of them spoke for a few minutes.

"I have been expecting every morning to find her gone," said the girl. "I think she only waited to finish this." She gently unfolded the fine lawn robe, and they saw the delicate insertion and the wonderful, embroidery.

"I asked her once," said the girl, "why she wasted so much work on them. They were mostly only for poor people. 'One never knows, dearie,' she answered, with that childish smile of hers. 'It may be for a little Christ.'"

They would not let less loving hands come near her.

* * * * *

Her father had completed his business, and both were glad to leave London. She had a sense of something sinister, foreboding, casting its shadow on the sordid, unclean streets, the neglected buildings falling into disrepair. A lurking savagery, a half-veiled enmity seemed to be stealing among the people. The town's mad lust for pleasure: its fierce, unjoyous laughter: its desire ever to be in crowds as if afraid of itself: its orgies of eating and drinking: its animal-like indifference to the misery and death that lay but a little way beyond its own horizon! She dared not remember history. Perhaps it would pass.

The long, slow journey tried her father's strength, and assuming an authority to which he yielded obedience tempered by grumbling, Joan sent him to bed, and would not let him come down till Christmas Day. The big, square house was on the outskirts of the town where it was quiet, and in the afternoon they walked in the garden sheltered behind its high brick wall.

He told her of what had been done at the works. Arthur's plan had succeeded. It might not be the last word, but at least it was on the road to the right end. The men had been brought into it and shared the management. And the disasters predicted had proved groundless.

"You won't be able to indulge in all your mad schemes," he laughed, "but there'll be enough to help on a few. And you will be among friends. Arthur told me he had explained it to you and that you had agreed."

"Yes," she answered. "It was the last time he came to see me in London. And I could not help feeling a bit jealous. He was doing things while I was writing and talking. But I was glad he was an Allway. It will be known as the Allway scheme. New ways will date from it."

She had thought it time for him to return indoors, but he pleaded for a visit to his beloved roses. He prided himself on being always able to pick roses on Christmas Day.

"This young man of yours," he asked, "what is he like?"

"Oh, just a Christian gentleman," she answered. "You will love him when you know him."

He laughed. "And this new journal of his?" he asked. "It's got to be published in London, hasn't it?"

She gave a slight start, for in their letters to one another they had been discussing this very point.

"No," she answered, "it could be circulated just as well from, say, Birmingham or Manchester."

He was choosing his roses. They held their petals wrapped tight round them, trying to keep the cold from their brave hearts. In the warmth they would open out and be gay, until the end.

"Not Liverpool?" he suggested.

"Or even Liverpool," she laughed.

They looked at one another, and then beyond the sheltering evergreens and the wide lawns to where the great square house seemed to be listening.

"It's an ugly old thing," he said.

"No, it isn't," she contradicted. "It's simple and big and kind. I always used to feel it disapproved of me. I believe it has come to love me, in its solemn old brick way."

"It was built by Kent in seventeen-forty for your great-great grandfather," he explained. He was regarding it more affectionately. "Solid respectability was the dream, then."

"I think that's why I love it," she said: "for it's dear, old-fashioned ways. We will teach it the new dreams, too. It will be so shocked, at first."

They dined in state in the great dining-room.

"I was going to buy you a present," he grumbled. "But you wouldn't let me get up."

"I want to give you something quite expensive, Dad," she said. "I've had my eye on it for years."

She slipped her hand in his. "I want you to give me that Dream of yours; that you built for my mother, and that all went wrong. They call it Allway's Folly; and it makes me so mad. I want to make it all come true. May I try?"

* * * * *

It was there that he came to her.

She stood beneath the withered trees, beside the shattered fountain. The sad-faced ghosts peeped out at her from the broken windows of the little silent houses.

She wondered later why she had not been surprised to see him. But at the time it seemed to be in the order of things that she should look up and find him there.

She went to him with outstretched arms.

"I'm so glad you've come," she said. "I was just wanting you."

They sat on the stone step of the fountain, where they were sheltered from the wind; and she buttoned his long coat about him.

"Do you think you will go on doing it?" he asked, with a laugh.

"I'm so afraid," she answered gravely. "That I shall come to love you too much: the home, the children and you. I shall have none left over."

"There is an old Hindoo proverb," he said: "That when a man and woman love they dig a fountain down to God."

"This poor, little choked-up thing," he said, "against which we are sitting; it's for want of men and women drawing water, of children dabbling their hands in it and making themselves all wet, that it has run dry."

She took his hands in hers to keep them warm. The nursing habit seemed to have taken root in her.

"I see your argument," she said. "The more I love you, the deeper will be the fountain. So that the more Love I want to come to me, the more I must love you."

"Don't you see it for yourself?" he demanded.

She broke into a little laugh.

"Perhaps you are right," she admitted. "Perhaps that is why He made us male and female: to teach us to love."

A robin broke into a song of triumph. He had seen the sad-faced ghosts steal silently away.

SKETCHES IN LAVENDER BLUE AND GREEN

La-ven-der's blue, did-dle, did-dle!
  La-ven-der's green;
When I am king, did-dle, did-dle!
  You shall be queen.
Call up your men, did-dle, did-dle!
  Set them to work;
Some to the plough, did-dle, did-dle!
  Some to the cart.
Some to make hay, did-dle, did-dle!
  Some to cut corn;
While you and I, did-dle, did-dle!
  Keep ourselves warm.

REGINALD BLAKE, FINANCIER AND CAD

The advantage of literature over life is that its characters are clearly defined, and act consistently. Nature, always inartistic, takes pleasure in creating the impossible. Reginald Blake was as typical a specimen of the well-bred cad as one could hope to find between Piccadilly Circus and Hyde Park Corner. Vicious without passion, and possessing brain without mind, existence presented to him no difficulties, while his pleasures brought him no pains. His morality was bounded by the doctor on the one side, and the magistrate on the other. Careful never to outrage the decrees of either, he was at forty-five still healthy, though stout; and had achieved the not too easy task of amassing a fortune while avoiding all risk of Holloway. He and his wife, Edith (*née* Eppington), were as ill-matched a couple as could be conceived by any dramatist seeking material for a problem play. As they stood before the altar on their wedding morn, they might have been taken as symbolising satyr and saint. More than twenty years his junior, beautiful with the beauty of a Raphael's Madonna, his every touch of her seemed a sacrilege. Yet once in his life Mr. Blake played the part of a great gentleman; Mrs. Blake, on the same occasion, contenting herself with a singularly mean *rôle*—mean even for a woman in love.

The affair, of course, had been a marriage of convenience. Blake, to do him justice, had made no pretence to anything beyond admiration and regard. Few things grow monotonous sooner than irregularity. He would tickle his jaded palate with respectability, and try for a change the companionship of a good woman. The girl's face drew him, as the moonlight holds a man who, bored by the noise, turns from a heated room to press his forehead to the window-pane. Accustomed to bid for what he wanted, he offered his price. The Eppington family was poor and numerous. The girl, bred up to the false notions of duty inculcated by a narrow conventionality, and, feminine like, half in love with martyrdom for its own sake, let her father bargain for a higher price, and then sold herself.

To a drama of this description, a lover is necessary, if the complications are to be of interest to the outside world. Harry Sennett, a pleasant-looking enough young fellow, in spite of his receding chin, was possessed, perhaps, of more good intention than sense. Under the influence of Edith's stronger character he was soon persuaded to acquiesce meekly in the proposed arrangement. Both succeeded in convincing themselves that they were acting nobly. The tone of the farewell interview, arranged for the eve of the wedding, would have been fit and proper to the occasion had Edith been a modern Joan of Arc about to sacrifice her own happiness on the altar of a great cause; as the girl was merely selling herself into ease and luxury, for no higher motive than the desire to enable a certain number of more or less worthy relatives to continue living beyond their legitimate means, the sentiment was perhaps exaggerated. Many tears were shed, and many everlasting good-byes spoken, though, seeing that Edith's new home would be only a few streets off, and that of necessity their social set would continue to be the same, more experienced persons might have counselled hope. Three months after the marriage they found themselves side by side at the same dinner-table; and after a little melodramatic fencing with what they were pleased to regard as fate, they accommodated themselves to the customary positions.

Blake was quite aware that Sennett had been Edith's lover. So had half a dozen other men, some younger, some older than himself. He felt no more embarrassment at meeting them than, standing on the pavement outside the Stock Exchange, he would have experienced greeting his brother jobbers after a settling day that had transferred a fortune from their hands into his. Sennett, in particular, he liked and encouraged. Our whole social system, always a mystery to the philosopher, owes its existence to the fact that few men and women possess sufficient intelligence to be interesting to themselves. Blake liked company, but not much company liked Blake. Young Sennett, however, could always be relied upon to break the tediousness of the domestic dialogue. A common love of sport drew the two men together. Most of us improve upon closer knowledge, and so they came to find good in one another.

"That is the man you ought to have married," said Blake one night to his wife, half laughingly, half seriously, as they sat alone, listening to Sennett's departing footsteps echoing upon the deserted pavement. "He's a good fellow—not a mere money-grubbing machine like me."

And a week later Sennett, sitting alone with Edith, suddenly broke out with:

"He's a better man than I am, with all my high-falutin' talk, and, upon my soul, he loves you. Shall I go abroad?"

"If you like," was the answer.

"What would you do?"

"Kill myself," replied the other, with a laugh, "or run away with the first man that asked me."

So Sennett stayed on.

Blake himself had made the path easy to them. There was little need for either fear or caution. Indeed, their safest course lay in recklessness, and they took it. To Sennett the house was always open. It was Blake himself who, when unable to accompany his wife, would suggest Sennett as a substitute. Club friends shrugged their shoulders. Was the man completely under his wife's thumb; or, tired of her, was he playing some devil's game of his own? To most of his acquaintances the latter explanation seemed the more plausible.

The gossip, in due course, reached the parental home. Mrs. Eppington shook the vials of her wrath over the head of her son-in-law. The father, always a cautious man, felt inclined to blame his child for her want of prudence.

"She'll ruin everything," he said. "Why the devil can't she be careful?"

"I believe the man is deliberately plotting to get rid of her," said Mrs. Eppington. "I shall tell him plainly what I think."

"You're a fool, Hannah," replied her husband, allowing himself the licence of the domestic hearth. "If you are right, you will only precipitate matters; if you are wrong, you will tell him what there is no need for him to know. Leave the matter to me. I can sound him without giving anything away, and meanwhile you talk to Edith."

So matters were arranged, but the interview between mother and daughter hardly improved the position. Mrs. Eppington was conventionally moral; Edith had been thinking for herself, and thinking in a bad atmosphere. Mrs. Eppington, grew angry at the girl's callousness.

"Have you no sense of shame?" she cried.

"I had once," was Edith's reply, "before I came to live here. Do you know what this house is for me, with its gilded mirrors, its couches, its soft carpets? Do you know what I am, and have been for two years?"

The elder woman rose, with a frightened pleading look upon her face, and the other stopped and turned away towards the window.

"We all thought it for the best," continued Mrs. Eppington meekly.

The girl spoke wearily without looking round.

"Oh! every silly thing that was ever done, was done for the best. *I* thought it would be for the best, myself. Everything would be so simple if only we were not alive. Don't let's talk any more. All you can say is quite right."

The silence continued for a while, the Dresden-china clock on the mantelpiece ticking louder and louder as if to say, "I, Time, am here. Do not make your plans forgetting me, little mortals; I change your thoughts and wills. You are but my puppets."

"Then what do you intend to do?" demanded Mrs. Eppington at length.

"Intend! Oh, the right thing of course. We all intend that. I shall send Harry away with a few well-chosen words of farewell, learn to love my husband and settle down to a life of quiet domestic bliss. Oh, it's easy enough to intend!"

The girl's face wrinkled with a laugh that aged her. In that moment it was a hard, evil face, and with a pang the elder woman thought of that other face, so like, yet so unlike—the sweet pure face of a girl that had given to a sordid home its one touch of nobility. As under the lightning's flash we see the whole arc of the horizon, so Mrs. Eppington looked and saw her child's life. The gilded, over-furnished room vanished. She and a big-eyed, fair-haired child, the only one of her children she had ever understood, were playing wonderful games in the twilight among the shadows of a tiny attic. Now she was the wolf, devouring Edith, who was Red Riding Hood, with kisses. Now Cinderella's prince, now both her wicked sisters. But in the favourite game of all, Mrs. Eppington was a beautiful princess, bewitched by a wicked dragon, so that she seemed to be an old, worn woman. But curly-headed Edith fought the dragon, represented by the three-legged rocking-horse, and slew him with much shouting and the toasting-fork. Then Mrs. Eppington became again a beautiful princess, and went away with Edith back to her own people.

In this twilight hour the misbehaviour of the "General," the importunity of the family butcher, and the airs assumed by cousin Jane, who kept two servants, were forgotten.

The games ended. The little curly head would be laid against her breast "for five minutes' love," while the restless little brain framed the endless question that children are for ever asking in all its thousand forms, "What is life, mother? I am very little, and I think, and think, until I grow frightened. Oh, mother, tell me, what is life?"

Had she dealt with these questions wisely? Might it not have been better to have treated them more seriously? Could life after all be ruled by maxims learned from copy-books? She had answered as she had been answered in her own far-back days of questioning. Might it not have been better had she thought for herself?

Suddenly Edith was kneeling on the floor beside her.

"I will try to be good, mother."

It was the old baby cry, the cry of us all, children that we are, till mother Nature kisses us and bids us go to sleep.

Their arms were round each other now, and so they sat, mother and child once more. And the twilight of the old attic, creeping westward from the east, found them again.

The masculine duet had more result, but was not conducted with the *finesse* that Mr. Eppington, who prided himself on his diplomacy, had intended. Indeed, so evidently ill at ease was that gentleman, when the moment came for talk, and so palpably were his pointless remarks mere efforts to delay an unpleasant subject, that Blake, always direct bluntly though not ill-naturedly asked him, "How much?"

Mr. Eppington was disconcerted.

"It's not that—at least that's not what I have come about," he answered confusedly.

"What have you come about?"

Inwardly Mr. Eppington cursed himself for a fool, for the which he was perhaps not altogether without excuse. He had meant to act the part of a clever counsel, acquiring information while giving none; by a blunder, he found himself in the witness-box.

"Oh, nothing, nothing," was the feeble response, "merely looked in to see how Edith was."

"Much the same as at dinner last night, when you were here," answered Blake. "Come, out with it."

It seemed the best course now, and Mr. Eppington took the plunge.

"Don't you think," he said, unconsciously glancing round the room to be sure they were alone, "that young Sennett is a little too much about the house?"

Blake stared at him.

"Of course, we know it is all right—as nice a young fellow as ever lived—and Edith—and all that. Of course, it's absurd, but—"

"But what?"

"Well, people will talk."

"What do they say?"

The other shrugged his shoulders.

Blake rose. He had an ugly look when angry, and his language was apt to be coarse.

"Tell them to mind their own business, and leave me and my wife alone." That was the sense of what he said; he expressed himself at greater length, and in stronger language.

"But, my dear Blake," urged Mr. Eppington, "for your own sake, is it wise? There was a sort of boy and girl attachment between them—nothing of any moment, but all that gives colour to gossip. Forgive me, but I am her father; I do not like to hear my child talked about."

"Then don't open your ears to the chatter of a pack of fools," replied his son-in-law roughly. But the next instant a softer expression passed over his face, and he laid his hand on the older man's arm.

"Perhaps there are many more, but there's one good woman in the world," he said, "and that's your daughter. Come and tell me that the Bank of England is getting shaky on its legs, and I'll listen to you."

But the stronger the faith, the deeper strike the roots of suspicion. Blake said no further word on the subject, and Sennett was as welcome as before. But Edith, looking up suddenly, would sometimes find her husband's eyes fixed on her with a troubled look as of some dumb creature trying to understand; and often he would slip out of the house of an evening by himself, returning home hours afterwards, tired and mud-stained.

He made attempts to show his affection. This was the most fatal thing he could have done. Ill-temper, ill-treatment even, she might have borne. His clumsy caresses, his foolish, halting words of tenderness became a horror to her. She wondered whether to laugh or to strike at his upturned face. His tactless devotion filled her life as with some sickly perfume, stifling her. If only she could be by herself for a little while to think! But he was with her night and day. There were times when, as he would cross the room towards her, he grew monstrous until he towered above her, a formless thing such as children dream of. And she would sit with her lips tight pressed, clutching the chair lest she should start up screaming.

Her only thought was to escape from him. One day she hastily packed a few necessaries in a small hand-bag and crept unperceived from the house. She drove to Charing Cross, but the Continental Express did not leave for an hour, and she had time to think.

Of what use was it? Her slender stock of money would soon be gone; how could she live? He would find her and follow her. It was all so hopeless!

Suddenly a fierce desire of life seized hold of her, the angry answer of her young blood to despair. Why should she die, never having known what it was to live? Why should she prostrate herself before this juggernaut of other people's respectability? Joy called to her; only her own cowardice stayed her from stretching forth her hand and gathering it. She returned home a different woman, for hope had come to her.

A week later the butler entered the dining room, and handed Blake a letter addressed to him in his wife's handwriting. He took it without a word, as though he had been expecting it. It simply told him that she had left him for ever.

* * * * *

The world is small, and money commands many services. Sennett had gone out for a stroll; Edith was left in the tiny *salon* of their *appartement* at Fécamp. It was the third day of their arrival in the town. The door was opened and closed, and Blake stood before her.

She rose frightened, but by a motion he reassured her. There was a quiet dignity about the man that was strange to her.

"Why have you followed me?" she asked.

"I want you to return home."

"Home!" she cried. "You must be mad. Do you not know—"

He interrupted her vehemently. "I know nothing. I wish to know nothing. Go back to London at once. I have made everything right; no one suspects. I shall not be there; you will never see me again, and you will have an opportunity of undoing your mistake—our mistake."

She listened. Hers was not a great nature, and the desire to obtain happiness without paying the price was strong upon her. As for his good name, what could that matter? he urged. People would only say that he had gone back to the evil from which he had emerged, and few would be surprised. His life would go on much as it had done, and she would only be pitied.

She quite understood his plan; it seemed mean of her to accept his proposal, and she argued feebly against it. But he overcame all her objections. For his own sake, he told her, he would prefer the scandal to be connected with his name rather than with that of his wife. As he unfolded his scheme, she began to feel that in acquiescing she was conferring a favour. It was not the first deception he had arranged for the public, and he appeared to be half in love with his own cleverness. She even found herself laughing at his mimicry of what this acquaintance and that would say. Her spirits rose; the play that might have been a painful drama seemed turning out an amusing farce.

The thing settled, he rose to go, and held out his hand. As she looked up into his face, something about the line of his lips smote upon her.

"You will be well rid of me," she said. "I have brought you nothing but trouble."

"Oh, trouble," he answered. "If that were all! A man can bear trouble."

828

"What else?" she asked.

His eyes travelled aimlessly about the room. "They taught me a lot of things when I was a boy," he said, "my mother and others—they meant well—which as I grew older I discovered to be lies; and so I came to think that nothing good was true, and that everything and everybody was evil. And then—"

His wandering eyes came round to her and he broke off abruptly. "Good-bye," he said, and the next moment he was gone.

She sat wondering for a while what he had meant. Then Sennett returned, and the words went out of her head.

* * * * *

A good deal of sympathy was felt for Mrs. Blake. The man had a charming wife; he might have kept straight; but as his friends added, "Blake always was a cad."

AN ITEM OF FASHIONABLE INTELLIGENCE

Speaking personally, I do not like the Countess of ---.   She is not the type of woman I could love. I hesitate the less giving expression to this sentiment by reason of the conviction that the Countess of --- would not be unduly depressed even were the fact to reach her ears. I cannot conceive the Countess of ---'s being troubled by the opinion concerning her of any being, human or divine, other than the Countess of ---.

But to be honest, I must admit that for the Earl of --- she makes an ideal wife. She rules him as she rules all others, relations and retainers, from the curate to the dowager, but the rod, though firmly held, is wielded with justice and kindly intent. Nor is it possible to imagine the Earl of ---'s living as contentedly as he does with any partner of a less dominating turn of mind. He is one of those weak-headed, strong-limbed, good-natured, childish men, born to be guided in all matters, from the tying of a neck-cloth to the choice of a political party, by their women folk. Such men are in clover when their proprietor happens to be a good and sensible woman, but are to be pitied when they get into the hands of the self-ish or the foolish. As very young men, they too often fall victims to bad-tempered chorus girls or to middle-aged matrons of the class from which Pope judged all womankind. They make capital husbands when well managed; treated badly, they say little, but set to work, after the manner of a dissatisfied cat, to find a kinder mistress, generally succeeding. The Earl of --- adored his wife, deeming himself the most fortunate of husbands, and better testimonial than such no wife should hope for. Till the day she snatched him away from all other competitors, and claimed him for her own, he had obeyed his mother with a dutifulness bor-dering on folly. Were the countess to die to-morrow, he would be unable to tell you his mind on any single subject until his eldest daughter and his still unmar-ried sister, ladies both of strong character, attracted towards one another by a mutual antagonism, had settled between themselves which was to be mistress of him and of his house.

However, there is little fear (bar accidents) but that my friend the countess will continue to direct the hereditary vote of the Earl of --- towards the goal of common sense and public good, guide his social policy with judgment and kind-ness, and manage his estates with prudence and economy for many years to come. She is a hearty, vigorous lady, of generous proportions, with the blood of sturdy forebears in her veins, and one who takes the same excellent good care of herself that she bestows on all others dependent upon her guidance.

"I remember," said the doctor—we were dining with the doctor in homely fashion, and our wives had adjourned to the drawing-room to discuss servants and husbands and other domestic matters with greater freedom, leaving us to the claret and the twilight—"I remember when we had the cholera in the village—it must be twenty years ago now—that woman gave up the London season to stay down here and take the whole burden of the trouble upon her own shoulders. I do not feel any call to praise her; she liked the work, and she was in her element, but it was good work for all that. She had no fear. She would carry the children in her arms if time pressed and the little ambulance was not at hand. I have known her sit all night in a room not twelve feet square, between a dying man and his dying wife. But the thing never touched her. Six years ago we had the smallpox, and she went all through that in just the same way. I don't believe she has ever had a day's illness in her life. She will be physicking this parish when my bones are rattling in my coffin, and she will be laying down the laws of literature long after your statue has become a familiar ornament of Westminster Abbey. She's a wonderful woman, but a trifle masterful."

He laughed, but I detected a touch of irritation in his voice. My host looked a man wishful to be masterful himself. I do not think he quite relished the calm way in which this grand dame took possession of all things around her, himself and his work included.

"Did you ever hear the story of the marriage?" he asked.

"No," I replied, "whose marriage? The earl's?"

"I should call it the countess's," he answered. "It was the gossip of the county when I first came here, but other curious things have happened among us to push it gradually out of memory. Most people, I really believe, have quite forgotten that the Countess of --- once served behind a baker's counter."

"You don't say so," I exclaimed. The remark, I admit, sounds weak when written down; the most natural remarks always do.

"It's a fact," said the doctor, "though she does not suggest the shop-girl, does she? But then I have known countesses, descended in a direct line from William the Conqueror, who did, so things balance one another. Mary, Countess of ---, was, thirty years ago, Mary Sewell, daughter of a Taunton linen-draper. The business, profitable enough as country businesses go, was inadequate for the needs of the Sewell family, consisting, as I believe it did, of seven boys and eight girls. Mary, the youngest, as soon as her brief schooling was over, had to shift for herself. She seems to have tried her hand at one or two things, finally taking service with a cousin, a baker and confectioner, who was doing well in Oxford Street. She must have been a remarkably attractive girl; she's a handsome woman now. I can picture that soft creamy skin when it was fresh and smooth, and the West of England girls run naturally to dimples and eyes that glisten as though they had been just washed in morning dew. The shop did a good trade in ladies' lunches—it was the glass of sherry and sweet biscuit period. I expect they dressed her in some neat-fitting grey or black dress, with short sleeves, showing her plump arms, and that she flitted around the marble-topped tables, smiling, and looking cool and sweet. There the present Earl of ---, then young Lord C---, fresh from Oxford, and new to the dangers of London bachelordom, first saw her. He had accompanied some female relatives to the photographer's, and, hotels and restaurants being deemed impossible in those days for ladies, had taken them to Sewell's to lunch. Mary Sewell waited upon the party; and now as many of that party as are above ground wait upon Mary Sewell."

"He showed good sense in marrying her," I said, "I admire him for it." The doctor's sixty-four Lafitte was excellent. I felt charitably inclined towards all men and women, even towards earls and countesses.

"I don't think he had much to do with it," laughed the doctor, "beyond being, like Barkis, 'willing.' It's a queer story; some people profess not to believe it, but those who know her ladyship best think it is just the story that must be true, because it is so characteristic of her. And besides, I happen to know that it is true."

"I should like to hear it," I said.

"I am going to tell it you," said the doctor, lighting a fresh cigar, and pushing the box towards me.

* * * * *

I will leave you to imagine the lad's suddenly developed appetite for decantered sherry at sixpence a glass, and the familiar currant bun of our youth. He lunched at Sewell's shop, he tea'd at Sewell's, occasionally he dined at Sewell's, off cutlets, followed by assorted pastry. Possibly, merely from fear lest the affair should reach his mother's ears, for he was neither worldly-wise nor vicious, he made love to Mary under an assumed name; and to do the girl justice, it must be remembered that she fell in love with and agreed to marry plain Mr. John Robinson, son of a colonial merchant, a gentleman, as she must have seen, and a young man of easy means, but of a position not so very much superior to her own. The first intimation she received that her lover was none other than Lord C---, the future Earl of ---, was vouchsafed her during a painful interview with his lordship's mother.

"I never knew it, madam," asserted Mary, standing by the window of the drawing-room above the shop, "upon my word of honour, I never knew it"

"Perhaps not," answered her ladyship coldly. "Would you have refused him if you had?"

"I cannot tell," was the girl's answer; "it would have been different from the beginning. He courted me and asked me to be his wife."

"We won't go into all that," interrupted the other; "I am not here to defend him. I do not say he acted well. The question is, how much will compensate you for your natural disappointment?"

Her ladyship prided herself upon her bluntness and practicability. As she spoke she took her cheque-book out of her reticule, and, opening it, dipped her pen into the ink. I am inclined to think that the flutter of that cheque-book was her ladyship's mistake. The girl had common sense, and must have seen the difficulties in the way of a marriage between the heir to an earldom and a linen-draper's daughter; and had the old lady been a person of discernment, the interview might have ended more to her satisfaction. She made the error of judging the world by one standard, forgetting there are individualities. Mary Sewell came from a West of England stock that, in the days of Drake and Frobisher, had given more than one able-bodied pirate to the service of the country, and that insult of the cheque-book put the fight into her. Her lips closed with a little snap, and the fear fell from her.

"I am sorry I don't see my way to obliging your ladyship," she said.

"What do you mean, girl?" asked the elder woman.

"I don't mean to be disappointed," answered the girl, but she spoke quietly and respectfully. "We have pledged our word to one another. If he is a gentleman, as I know he is, he will keep his, and I shall keep mine."

Then her ladyship began to talk reason, as people do when it is too late. She pointed out to the girl the difference of social position, and explained to her the miseries that come from marrying out of one's station. But the girl by this time had got over her surprise, and perhaps had begun to reflect that, in any case, a countess-ship was worth fighting for.   The best of women are influenced by such considerations.

* * * * *

"I am not a lady, I know," she replied quietly, "but my people have always been honest folk, well known, and I shall try to learn. I am not wishing to speak disrespectfully of my betters, but I was in service before I came here, ma'am, as lady's maid, in a place where I saw much of what is called Society. I think I can be as good a lady as some I know, if not better."

The countess began to grow angry again. "And who do you think will receive you?" she cried, "a girl who has served in a pastry-cook's shop!"

"Lady L--- came from behind the bar," Mary answered, "and that's not much better. And the Duchess of C---, I have heard, was a ballet girl, but nobody seems to remember it. I don't think the people whose opinion is worth having will object to me for very long." The girl was beginning rather to enjoy the contest.

"You profess to love my son," cried the countess fiercely, "and you are going to ruin his life. You will drag him down to your own level."

The girl must have looked rather fine at that moment, I should dearly love to have been present.

"There will be no dragging down, my lady," she replied, "on either side. I do love your son very dearly. He is one of the kindest and best of gentlemen. But I am not blind, and whatever amount of cleverness there may be between us belongs chiefly to me. I shall make it my duty to fit myself for the position of his wife, and to help him in his work. You need not fear, my lady, I shall be a good wife to him, and he shall never regret it.   You might find him a richer wife, a better educated wife, but you will never find him a wife who will be more devoted to him and to his interests."

That practically brought the scene to a close. The countess had sense enough to see that she was only losing ground by argument. She rose and replaced her cheque-book in her bag.

"I think, my good girl, you must be mad," she said; "if you will not allow me to do anything for you, there's an end to the matter. I did not come here to quarrel with you. My son knows his duty to me and to his family. You must take your own course, and I must take mine."

"Very well, my lady," said Mary Sewell, holding the door open for her ladyship to pass out, "we shall see who wins."

But however brave a front Mary Sewell may have maintained before the enemy, I expect she felt pretty limp when thinking matters calmly over after her ladyship's departure. She knew her lover well enough to guess that he would be as wax in the firm hands of his mother, while she herself would not have a chance of opposing her influence against those seeking to draw him away from her. Once again she read through the few schoolboy letters he had written her, and then looked up at the framed photograph that hung above the mantelpiece of her little bedroom. The face was that of a frank, pleasant-looking young fellow, lightened by eyes somewhat large for a man, but spoiled by a painfully weak mouth. The more Mary Sewell thought, the more sure she felt in her own mind that he loved her, and had meant honestly by her. Did the matter rest with him, she might reckon on being the future Countess of ---, but, unfortunately for her, the person to be considered was not Lord C---, but the present Countess of ---. From childhood, through boyhood, into manhood it had never once occurred to Lord C--- to dispute a single command of his mother's, and his was not the type of brain to readily receive new ideas. If she was to win in the unequal contest it would have to be by art, not by strength. She sat down and wrote a letter which under all the circumstances was a model of diplomacy. She knew that it would be read by the countess, and, writing it, she kept both mother and son in mind. She made no reproaches, and indulged in but little sentiment. It was the letter of a woman who could claim rights, but who asked only for courtesy. It stated her wish to see him alone and obtain from his own lips the assurance that he wished their engagement to cease. "Do not fear," Mary Sewell wrote, "that I shall be any annoyance to you. My own pride would not let me urge you to marry me against your desire, and I care for you too much to cause you any pain. Assure me with your own lips that you wish our engagement to be at an end, and I shall release you without another word."

The family were in town, and Mary sent her letter by a trusty hand. The countess read it with huge satisfaction, and, re-sealing it, gave it herself into her son's hands. It promised a happy solution of the problem. In imagination, she had all the night been listening to a vulgar breach of promise case. She herself had been submitted to a most annoying cross-examination by a pert barrister. Her son's assumption of the name of Robinson had been misunderstood and severely commented upon by the judge. A sympathetic jury had awarded thumping damages, and for the next six months the family title would be a peg on which music-hall singers and comic journalists would hang their ribald jokes. Lord C--- read the letter, flushed, and dutifully handed it back to his mother. She made pretence to read it as for the first time, and counselled him to accord the interview.

"I am so glad," she said, "that the girl is taking the matter sensibly. We must really do something for her in the future, when everything is settled. Let her ask for me, and then the servants will fancy she's a lady's maid or something of that sort, come after a place, and won't talk."

So that evening Mary Sewell, addressed by the butler as "young woman," was ushered into the small drawing-room that connects the library of No. --- Grosvenor Square with the other reception rooms. The countess, now all amiability, rose to meet her.

"My son will be here in a moment," she explained, "he has informed me of the purport of your letter. Believe me, my dear Miss Sewell, no one can regret his thoughtless conduct more than I do. But young men will be young men, and they do not stop to reflect that what may be a joke to them may be taken quite seriously by others."

"I don't regard the matter as a joke, my lady," replied Mary somewhat curtly.

"Of course not, my dear," added the countess, "that's what I'm saying. It was very wrong of him altogether. But with your pretty face, you will not, I am sure, have long to wait for a husband; we must see what we can do for you."

The countess certainly lacked tact; it must have handicapped her exceedingly.

"Thank you," answered the girl, "but I prefer to choose my own."

Fortunately—or the interview might have ended in another quarrel—the cause of all the trouble at this moment entered the room, and the countess, whispering a few final words of instruction to him as she passed out, left them together.

Mary took a chair in the centre of the room, at equal distance from both doors. Lord C---, finding any sort of a seat uncomfortable under the circumstances, preferred to stand with his back to the mantelpiece. Dead silence was maintained for a few seconds, and then Mary, drawing the daintiest of handkerchiefs from her pocket, began to cry. The countess must have been a poor diplomatist, or she might have thought of this; or she may have remembered her own appearance on the rare occasions when she herself, a big, raw-boned girl, had attempted the softening influence of tears, and have attached little importance to the possibility. But when these soft, dimpled women cry, and cry quietly, it is another matter. Their eyes grow brighter, and the tears, few and far between, lie like dewdrops on a rose leaf.

Lord C--- was as tender-hearted a lout as ever lived. In a moment he was on his knees with his arm round the girl's waist, pouring out such halting words of love and devotion as came to his unready brain, cursing his fate, his earldom, and his mother, and assuring Mary that his only chance of happiness lay in his making her his countess. Had Mary liked to say the word at that moment, he would have caught her to his arms, and defied the whole world—for the time being.

But Mary was a very practical young woman, and there are difficulties in the way of handling a lover, who, however ready he may be to do your bidding so long as your eyes are upon him, is liable to be turned from his purpose so soon as another influence is substituted for your own. His lordship suggested an immediate secret marriage. But you cannot run out into the street, knock up a clergyman, and get married on the spot, and Mary knew that the moment she was gone his lordship's will would revert to his mother's keeping. Then his lordship suggested flight, but flight requires money, and the countess knew enough to keep his lordship's purse in her own hands. Despair seized upon his lordship.

"It's no use," he cried, "it will end in my marrying her."

"Who's she?" exclaimed Mary somewhat quickly.

His lordship explained the position. The family estates were heavily encumbered. It was deemed advisable that his lordship should marry Money, and Money, in the person of the only daughter of rich and ambitious parvenus, had offered itself—or, to speak more correctly, had been offered.

"What's she like?" asked Mary.

"Oh, she's nice enough," was the reply, "only I don't care for her and she doesn't care for me. It won't be much fun for either of us," and his lordship laughed dismally.

"How do you know she doesn't care for you?" asked Mary. A woman may be critical of her lover's shortcomings, but at the very least he is good enough for every other woman.

"Well, she happens to care for somebody else," answered his lordship, "she told me so herself."

That would account for it.

"And is she willing to marry you?" inquired Mary.

His lordship shrugged his shoulders.

"Oh, well, you know, her people want it," he replied.

In spite of her trouble, the girl could not help a laugh. These young swells seemed to have but small wills of their own. Her ladyship, on the other side of the door, grew nervous. It was the only sound she had been able to hear.

"It's deuced awkward," explained his lordship, "when you're—well, when you are anybody, you know. You can't do as you like. Things are expected of you, and there's such a lot to be considered."

Mary rose and clasped her pretty dimpled hands, from which she had drawn her gloves, behind his neck.

"You do love me, Jack?" she said, looking up into his face.

For answer the lad hugged her to him very tightly, and there were tears in his eyes.

"Look here, Mary," he cried, "if I could only get rid of my position, and settle down with you as a country gentleman, I'd do it to-morrow. Damn the title, it's going to be the curse of my life."

Perhaps in that moment Mary also wished that the title were at the bottom of the sea, and that her lover were only the plain Mr. John Robinson she had thought him. These big, stupid men are often very loveable in spite of, or because of their weakness. They appeal to the mother side of a woman's heart, and that is the biggest side in all good women.

Suddenly however, the door opened. The countess appeared, and sentiment flew out. Lord C---, releasing Mary, sprang back, looking like a guilty school-boy.

"I thought I heard Miss Sewell go out," said her ladyship in the icy tones that had never lost their power of making her son's heart freeze within him. "I want to see you when you are free."

"I shan't be long," stammered his lordship. "Mary—Miss Sewell is just going."

Mary waited without moving until the countess had left and closed the door behind her. Then she turned to her lover and spoke in quick, low tones.

"Give me her address—the girl they want you to marry!"

"What are you going to do?" asked his lordship.

"I don't know," answered the girl, "but I'm going to see her."

She scribbled the name down, and then said, looking the boy squarely in the face:

"Tell me frankly, Jack, do you want to marry me, or do you not?"

"You know I do, Mary," he answered, and his eyes spoke stronger than his words. "If I weren't a silly ass, there would be none of this trouble. But I don't know how it is; I say to myself I'll do, a thing, but the mater talks and talks and—"

"I know," interrupted Mary with a smile. "Don't argue with her, fall in with all her views, and pretend to agree with her."

"If you could only think of some plan," said his lordship, catching at the hope of her words, "you are so clever."

"I am going to try," answered Mary, "and if I fail, you must run off with me, even if you have to do it right before your mother's eyes."

What she meant was, "I shall have to run off with you," but she thought it better to put it the other way about.

Mary found her involuntary rival a meek, gentle little lady, as much under the influence of her blustering father as was Lord C--- under that of his mother. What took place at the interview one can only surmise; but certain it is that the two girls, each for her own ends, undertook to aid and abet one another.

Much to the surprised delight of their respective parents, there came about a change in the attitude hitherto assumed towards one another by Miss Clementina Hodskiss and Lord C---. All objections to his lordship's unwilling attentions were suddenly withdrawn by the lady. Indeed, so swift to come and go are the whims of women, his calls were actually encouraged, especially when, as generally happened, they coincided with the absence from home of Mr. and Mrs. Hodskiss. Quite as remarkable was the new-born desire of Lord C--- towards Miss Clementina Hodskiss. Mary's name was never mentioned, and the suggestion of immediate marriage was listened to without remonstrance. Wiser folk would have puzzled their brains, but both her ladyship and ex-Contractor Hodskiss were accustomed to find all things yield to their wishes. The countess saw visions of a rehabilitated estate, and Clementina's father dreamed of a peerage, secured by the influence of aristocratic connections. All that the young folks stipulated for (and on that point their firmness was supernatural) was that the marriage should be quiet, almost to the verge of secrecy.

"No beastly fuss," his lordship demanded. "Let it be somewhere in the country, and no mob!" and his mother, thinking she understood his reason, patted his cheek affectionately.

"I should like to go down to Aunt Jane's and be married quietly from there," explained Miss Hodskiss to her father.

Aunt Jane resided on the outskirts of a small Hampshire village, and "sat under" a clergyman famous throughout the neighbourhood for having lost the roof to his mouth.

"You can't be married by that old fool," thundered her father—Mr. Hodskiss always thundered; he thundered even his prayers.

"He christened me," urged Miss Clementina.

"And Lord knows what he called you. Nobody can understand a word he says."

"I'd like him to marry me," reiterated Miss Clementina.

Neither her ladyship nor the contractor liked the idea.   The latter in particular had looked forward to a big function, chronicled at length in all the newspapers. But after all, the marriage was the essential thing, and perhaps, having regard to some foolish love passages that had happened between Clementina and a certain penniless naval lieutenant, ostentation might be out of place.

So in due course Clementina departed for Aunt Jane's, accompanied only by her maid.

Quite a treasure was Miss Hodskiss's new maid.

"A clean, wholesome girl," said of her Contractor Hodskiss, who cultivated affability towards the lower orders; "knows her place, and talks sense. You keep that girl, Clemmy."

"Do you think she knows enough?" hazarded the maternal Hodskiss.

"Quite sufficient for any decent woman," retorted the contractor. "When Clemmy wants painting and stuffing, it will be time enough for her to think about getting one of your '*Ach Himmels*' or '*Mon Dieus*'."

"I like the girl myself immensely," agreed Clementina's mother. "You can trust her, and she doesn't give herself airs."

Her praises reached even the countess, suffering severely at the moment from the tyranny of an elderly Fraulein.

"I must see this treasure," thought the countess to herself. "I am tired of these foreign minxes."

But no matter at what cunning hour her ladyship might call, the "treasure" always happened for some reason or other to be abroad.

"Your girl is always out when I come," laughed the countess. "One would fancy there was some reason for it."

"It does seem odd," agreed Clementina, with a slight flush.

Miss Hodskiss herself showed rather than spoke her appreciation of the girl. She seemed unable to move or think without her. Not even from the interviews with Lord C--- was the maid always absent.

The marriage, it was settled, should be by licence. Mrs. Hodskiss made up her mind at first to run down and see to the preliminaries, but really when the time arrived it hardly seemed necessary to take that trouble. The ordering of the whole affair was so very simple, and the "treasure" appeared to understand the business most thoroughly, and to be willing to take the whole burden upon her own shoulders. It was not, therefore, until the evening before the wedding that the Hodskiss family arrived in force, filling Aunt Jane's small dwelling to its utmost capacity. The swelling figure of the contractor, standing beside the tiny porch, compelled the passer-by to think of the doll's house in which the dwarf resides during fair-time, ringing his own bell out of his own first-floor window. The countess and Lord C--- were staying with her ladyship's sister, the Hon. Mrs. J---, at G--- Hall, some ten miles distant, and were to drive over in the morning. The then Earl of --- was in Norway, salmon fishing. Domestic events did not interest him.

Clementina complained of a headache after dinner, and went to bed early. The "treasure" also was indisposed. She seemed worried and excited.

"That girl is as eager about the thing," remarked Mrs. Hodskiss, "as though it was her own marriage."

In the morning Clementina was still suffering from her headache, but asserted her ability to go through the ceremony, provided everybody would keep away, and not worry her. The "treasure" was the only person she felt she could bear to have about her. Half an hour before it was time to start for church her mother looked her up again. She had grown still paler, if possible, during the interval, and also more nervous and irritable. She threatened to go to bed and stop there if she was not left quite alone. She almost turned her mother out of the room, locking the door behind her. Mrs. Hodskiss had never known her daughter to be like this before.

The others went on, leaving her to follow in the last carriage with her father. The contractor, forewarned, spoke little to her. Only once he had occasion to ask her a question, and then she answered in a strained, unnatural voice. She appeared, so far as could be seen under her heavy veil, to be crying.

"Well, this is going to be a damned cheerful wedding," said Mr. Hodskiss, and lapsed into sulkiness.

The wedding was not so quiet as had been anticipated. The village had got scent of it, and had spread itself upon the event, while half the house party from G--- Hall had insisted on driving over to take part in the proceedings. The little church was better filled than it had been for many a long year past.

The presence of the stylish crowd unnerved the ancient clergyman, long unaccustomed to the sight of a strange face, and the first sound of the ancient clergyman's voice unnerved the stylish crowd. What little articulation he possessed entirely disappeared, no one could understand a word he said. He appeared to be uttering sounds of distress.   The ancient gentleman's infliction had to be explained in low asides, and it also had to be explained why such an one had been chosen to perform the ceremony.

"It was a whim of Clementina's," whispered her mother. "Her father and myself were married from here, and he christened her. The dear child's full of sentiment. I think it so nice of her."

Everybody agreed it was charming, but wished it were over. The general effect was weird in the extreme.

Lord C--- spoke up fairly well, but the bride's responses were singularly indistinct, the usual order of things being thus reversed. The story of the naval lieutenant was remembered, and added to, and some of the more sentimental of the women began to cry in sympathy.

In the vestry things assumed a brighter tone. There was no lack of witnesses to sign the register. The verger pointed out to them the place, and they wrote their names, as people in such cases do, without stopping to read. Then it occurred to some one that the bride had not yet signed. She stood apart, with her veil still down, and appeared to have been forgotten. Encouraged, she came forward meekly, and took the pen from the hand of the verger. The countess came and stood behind her.

"Mary," wrote the bride, in a hand that looked as though it ought to have been firm, but which was not.

"Dear me," said the countess, "I never knew there was a Mary in your name. How differently you write when you write slowly."

The bride did not answer, but followed with "Susannah."

"Why, what a lot of names you must have, my dear!" exclaimed the countess. "When are you going to get to the ones we all know?"

"Ruth," continued the bride without answering.

Breeding is not always proof against strong emotion. The countess snatched the bride's veil from her face, and Mary Susannah Ruth Sewell stood before her, flushed and trembling, but looking none the less pretty because of that. At this point the crowd came in useful.

"I am sure your ladyship does not wish a scene," said Mary, speaking low. "The thing is done."

"The thing can be undone, and will be," retorted the countess in the same tone. "You, you—"

"My wife, don't forget that, mother," said Lord C--- coming between them, and slipping Mary's hand on to his arm. "We are both sorry to have had to go about the thing in this roundabout way, but we wanted to avoid a fuss. I think we had better be getting away. I'm afraid Mr. Hodskiss is going to be noisy."

* * * * *

The doctor poured himself out a glass of claret, and drank it off. His throat must have been dry.

"And what became of Clementina?" I asked. "Did the naval lieutenant, while the others were at church, dash up in a post-chaise and carry her off?"

"That's what ought to have happened, for the whole thing to be in keeping," agreed the doctor. "I believe as a matter of fact she did marry him eventually, but not till some years later, after the contractor had died."

"And did Mr. Hodskiss make a noise in the vestry?" I persisted. The doctor never will finish a story.

"I can't say for certain," answered my host, "I only saw the gentleman once. That was at a shareholders' meeting. I should incline to the opinion that he did."

"I suppose the bride and bridegroom slipped out as quietly as possible and drove straight off," I suggested.

"That would have been the sensible thing for them to do," agreed the doctor.

"But how did she manage about her travelling frock?" I continued. "She could hardly have gone back to her Aunt Jane's and changed her things." The doctor has no mind for minutiæ.

"I cannot tell you about all that," he replied. "I think I mentioned that Mary was a practical girl. Possibly she had thought of these details."

"And did the countess take the matter quietly?" I asked.

I like a tidy story, where everybody is put into his or her proper place at the end. Your modern romance leaves half his characters lying about just anyhow.

"That also I cannot tell you for certain," answered the doctor, "but I give her credit for so much sense. Lord C--- was of age, and with Mary at his elbow, quite knew his own mind. I believe they travelled for two or three years. The first time I myself set eyes on the countess (*née* Mary Sewell) was just after the late earl's death. I thought she looked a countess, every inch of her, but then I had not heard the story. I mistook the dowager for the housekeeper."

BLASÉ BILLY

It was towards the end of August. He and I appeared to be the only two men left to the Club. He was sitting by an open window, the *Times* lying on the floor beside him. I drew my chair a little closer and remarked:—"Good morning."

He suppressed a yawn, and replied "Mornin'"—dropping the "g." The custom was just coming into fashion; he was always correct.

"Going to be a very hot day, I am afraid," I continued.

"'Fraid so," was the response, after which he turned his head away and gently closed his eyes.

I opined that conversation was not to his wish, but this only made me more determined to talk, and to talk to him above all others in London. The desire took hold of me to irritate him—to break down the imperturbable calm within which he moved and had his being; and I gathered myself together, and settled down to the task.

"Interesting paper the *Times*," I observed.

"Very," he replied, taking it from the floor and handing it to me. "Won't you read it?"

I had been careful to throw into my voice an aggressive cheeriness which I had calculated would vex him, but his manner remained that of a man who is simply bored. I argued with him politely concerning the paper; but he insisted, still with the same weary air, that he had done with it. I thanked him effusively. I judged that he hated effusiveness.

"They say that to read a *Times* leader," I persisted, "is a lesson in English composition."

"So I've been told," he answered tranquilly. "Personally I don't take them."

The *Times*, I could see, was not going to be of much assistance to me. I lit a cigarette, and remarked that he was not shooting. He admitted the fact. Under the circumstances, it would have taxed him to deny it, but the necessity for confession aroused him.

"To myself," he said, "a tramp through miles of mud, in company with four gloomy men in black velveteen, a couple of depressed-looking dogs, and a heavy gun, the entire cavalcade being organised for the purpose of killing some twelve-and-sixpence worth of poultry, suggests the disproportionate."

I laughed boisterously, and cried, "Good, good—very good!"

He was the type of man that shudders inwardly at the sound of laughter. I had the will to slap him on the back, but I thought maybe that would send him away altogether.

I asked him if he hunted. He replied that fourteen hours' talk a day about horses, and only about horses tired him, and that in consequence he had abandoned hunting.

"You fish?" I said.

"I was never sufficiently imaginative," he answered.

"You travel a good deal," I suggested.

He had apparently made up his mind to abandon himself to his fate, for he turned towards me with a resigned air. An ancient nurse of mine had always described me as the most "wearing" child she had ever come across. I prefer to speak of myself as persevering.

"I should go about more," he said, "were I able to see any difference between one place and another."

"Tried Central Africa?" I inquired.

"Once or twice," he answered. "It always reminds me of Kew Gardens."

"China?" I hazarded.

"Cross between a willow-pattern plate and a New York slum," was his comment.

"The North Pole?" I tried, thinking the third time might be lucky.

"Never got quite up to it," he returned. "Reached Cape Hakluyt once."

"How did that impress you?" I asked.

"It didn't impress me," he replied.

The talk drifted to women and bogus companies, dogs, literature, and suchlike matters. I found him well informed upon and bored by all.

"They used to be amusing," he said, speaking of the first named, "until they began to take themselves seriously. Now they are merely silly."

I was forced into closer companionship with "Blasé Billy" that autumn, for by chance a month later he and I found ourselves the guests of the same delightful hostess, and I came to liking him better. He was a useful man to have about one. In matters of fashion one could always feel safe following his lead. One knew that his necktie, his collar, his socks, if not the very newest departure, were always correct; and upon social paths, as guide, philosopher, and friend, he was invaluable. He knew every one, together with his or her previous convictions. He was acquainted with every woman's past, and shrewdly surmised every man's future. He could point you out the coal-shed where the Countess of Glenleman had gambolled in her days of innocence, and would take you to breakfast at the coffee-shop off the Mile End Road where "Sam. Smith, Estd. 1820," own brother to the world-famed society novelist, Smith-Stratford, lived an uncriticised, unparagraphed, unphotographed existence upon the profits of "rashers" at three-ha'pence and "door-steps" at two a penny. He knew at what houses it was inadvisable to introduce soap, and at what tables it would be bad form to denounce political jobbery. He could tell you offhand what trade-mark went with what crest, and remembered the price paid for every baronetcy created during the last twenty-five years.

Regarding himself, he might have made claim with King Charles never to have said a foolish thing, and never to have done a wise one. He despised, or affected to despise, most of his fellow-men, and those of his fellow-men whose opinion was most worth having unaffectedly despised him.

Shortly described, one might have likened him to a Gaiety Johnny with brains. He was capital company after dinner, but in the early morning one avoided him.

So I thought of him until one day he fell in love; or to put it in the words of Teddy Tidmarsh, who brought the news to us, "got mashed on Gerty Lovell."

"The red-haired one," Teddy explained, to distinguish her from her sister, who had lately adopted the newer golden shade.

"Gerty Lovell!" exclaimed the captain, "why, I've always been told the Lovell girls hadn't a penny among them."

"The old man's stone broke, I know for a certainty," volunteered Teddy, who picked up a mysterious but, in other respects, satisfactory income in an office near Hatton Garden, and who was candour itself concerning the private affairs of everybody but himself.

"Oh, some rich pork-packing or diamond-sweating uncle has cropped up in Australia, or America, or one of those places," suggested the captain, "and Billy's got wind of it in good time. Billy knows his way about."

We agreed that some such explanation was needed, though in all other respects Gerty Lovell was just the girl that Reason (not always consulted on these occasions) might herself have chosen for "Blasé Billy's" mate.

The sunlight was not too kind to her, but at evening parties, where the lighting has been well considered, I have seen her look quite girlish. At her best she was not beautiful, but at her worst there was about her an air of breeding and distinction that always saved her from being passed over, and she dressed to perfection. In character she was the typical society woman: always charming, generally insincere. She went to Kensington for her religion and to Mayfair for her morals; accepted her literature from Mudie's and her art from the Grosvenor Gallery; and could and would gabble philanthropy, philosophy, and politics with equal fluency at every five-o'clock tea-table she visited. Her ideas could always be guaranteed as the very latest, and her opinion as that of the person to whom she was talking. Asked by a famous novelist one afternoon, at the Pioneer Club, to give him some idea of her, little Mrs. Bund, the painter's wife, had remained for a few moments with her pretty lips pursed, and had then said:

"She is a woman to whom life could bring nothing more fully satisfying than a dinner invitation from a duchess, and whose nature would be incapable of sustaining deeper suffering than that caused by an ill-fitting costume."

At the time I should have said the epigram was as true as it was cruel, but I suppose we none of us quite know each other.

I congratulated "Blasé Billy," or to drop his Club nickname and give him the full benefit of his social label, "The Hon. William Cecil Wychwood Stanley Drayton," on the occasion of our next meeting, which happened upon the steps of the Savoy Restaurant, and I thought—unless a quiver of the electric light deceived me—that he blushed.

"Charming girl," I said. "You're a lucky dog, Billy."

It was the phrase that custom demands upon such occasions, and it came of its own accord to my tongue without costing me the trouble of composition, but he seized upon it as though it had been a gem of friendly sincerity.

"You will like her even more when you know her better," he said. "She is so different from the usual woman that one meets. Come and see her to-morrow afternoon, she will be so pleased. Go about four, I will tell her to expect you."

I rang the bell at ten minutes past five. Billy was there. She greeted me with a little tremor of embarrassment, which sat oddly upon her, but which was not altogether unpleasing. She said it was kind of me to come so early. I stayed for about half an hour, but conversation flagged, and some of my cleverest remarks attracted no attention whatever.

When I rose to take my leave, Billy said that he must be off too, and that he would accompany me. Had they been ordinary lovers, I should have been careful to give them an opportunity of making their adieus in secret; but in the case of the Honourable William Drayton and the eldest Miss Lovell I concluded that such tactics were needless, so I waited till he had shaken hands, and went downstairs with him.

But in the hall Billy suddenly ejaculated, "By Jove! Half a minute," and ran back up the stairs three at a time. Apparently he found what he had gone for on the landing, for I did not hear the opening of the drawing-room door. Then the Honourable Billy redescended with a sober, nonchalent air.

"Left my gloves behind me," he explained, as he took my arm. "I am always leaving my gloves about."

I did not mention that I had seen him take them from his hat and slip them into his coat-tail pocket.

We at the Club did not see very much of Billy during the next three months, but the captain, who prided himself upon his playing of the *rôle* of smoking-room cynic—though he would have been better in the part had he occasionally displayed a little originality—was of opinion that our loss would be more than made up to us after the marriage. Once in the twilight I caught sight of a figure that reminded me of Billy's, accompanied by a figure that might have been that of the eldest Miss Lovell; but as the spot was Battersea Park, which is not a fashionable evening promenade, and the two figures were holding each other's hands, the whole picture being suggestive of the closing chapter of a *London Journal* romance, I concluded I had made an error.

But I did see them in the Adelphi stalls one evening, rapt in a sentimental melodrama. I joined them between the acts, and poked fun at the play, as one does at the Adelphi, but Miss Lovell begged me quite earnestly not to spoil her interest, and Billy wanted to enter upon a serious argument as to whether a man was justified in behaving as Will Terriss had just behaved towards the woman he loved. I left them and returned to my own party, to the satisfaction, I am inclined to think, of all concerned.

They married in due course. We were mistaken on one point. She brought Billy nothing. But they both seemed quite content on his not too extravagant fortune. They took a tiny house not far from Victoria Station, and hired a brougham for the season. They did not entertain very much, but they contrived to be seen everywhere it was right and fashionable they should be seen. The Honourable Mrs. Drayton was a much younger and brighter person than had been the eldest Miss Lovell, and as she continued to dress charmingly, her social position rose rapidly. Billy went everywhere with her, and evidently took a keen pride in her success. It was even said that he designed her dresses for her, and I have myself seen him earnestly studying the costumes in Russell and Allen's windows.

The captain's prophecy remained unfulfilled. "Blasé Billy"—if the name could still be applied to him—hardly ever visited the Club after his marriage. But I had grown to like him, and, as he had foretold, to like his wife. I found their calm indifference to the burning questions of the day a positive relief from the strenuous atmosphere of literary and artistic circles. In the drawing-room of their little house in Eaton Row, the comparative merits of George Meredith and George R. Sims were not considered worth discussion. Both were regarded as persons who afforded a certain amount of amusement in return for a certain amount of cash. And on any Wednesday afternoon, Henrick Ibsen and Arthur Roberts would have been equally welcome, as adding piquancy to the small gathering. Had I been compelled to pass my life in such a house, this Philistine attitude might have palled upon me; but, under the circumstances, it refreshed me, and I made use of my welcome, which I believe was genuine, to its full extent.

As months went by, they seemed to me to draw closer to one another, though I am given to understand that such is not the rule in fashionable circles. One evening I arrived a little before my time, and was shown up into the drawing-room by the soft-footed butler. They were sitting in the dusk with their arms round one another. It was impossible to withdraw, so I faced the situation and coughed. A pair of middle-class lovers could not have appeared more awkward or surprised.

But the incident established an understanding between us, and I came to be regarded as a friend before whom there was less necessity to act.

Studying them, I came to the conclusion that the ways and manners of love are very same-like throughout the world, as though the foolish boy, unheedful of human advance, kept but one school for minor poet and East End shop-boy, for Girton girl and little milliner; taught but the one lesson to the end-of-the-nineteenth-century Johnny that he taught to bearded Pict and Hun four thousand years ago.

Thus the summer and the winter passed pleasantly for the Honourable Billy, and then, as luck would have it, he fell ill just in the very middle of the London season, when invitations to balls and dinner parties, luncheons and "At Homes," were pouring in from every quarter; when the lawns at Hurlingham were at their smoothest, and the paddocks at their smartest.

It was unfortunate, too, that the fashions that season suited the Honourable Mrs. Billy as they had not suited her for years. In the early spring, she and Billy had been hard at work planning costumes calculated to cause a flutter through Mayfair, and the dresses and the bonnets—each one a work of art—were waiting on their stands to do their killing work. But the Honourable Mrs. Billy, for the first time in her life, had lost interest in such things.

Their friends were genuinely sorry, for society was Billy's element, and in it he was interesting and amusing. But, as Lady Gower said, there was no earthly need for his wife to constitute herself a prisoner. Her shutting herself off from the world could do him no good and it would look odd.

Accordingly the Honourable Mrs. Drayton, to whom oddness was a crime, and the voice of Lady Gower as the voice of duty, sacrificed her inclinations on the social shrine, laced the new costumes tight across her aching heart, and went down into society.

But the Honourable Mrs. Drayton achieved not the success of former seasons. Her small talk grew so very small, that even Park Lane found it unsatisfying. Her famous laugh rang mechanically. She smiled at the wisdom of dukes, and became sad at the funny stories of millionaires. Society voted her a good wife but bad company, and confined its attentions to cards of inquiry. And for this relief the Honourable Mrs. Drayton was grateful, for Billy waned weaker and weaker. In the world of shadows in which she moved, he was the one real thing. She was of very little practical use, but it comforted her to think that she was helping to nurse him.

But Billy himself it troubled.

"I do wish you would go out more," he would say. "It makes me feel that I'm such a selfish brute, keeping you tied up here in this dismal little house. Besides," he would add, "people miss you; they will hate me for keeping you away." For, where his wife was concerned, Billy's knowledge of the world availed him little. He really thought society craved for the Honourable Mrs. Drayton, and would not be comforted where she was not.

"I would rather stop with you, dear," would be the answer; "I don't care to go about by myself. You must get well quickly and take me."

And so the argument continued, until one evening, as she sat by herself, the nurse entered softly, closed the door behind her, and came over to her.

"I wish you would go out to-night, ma'am," said the nurse, "just for an hour or two. I think it would please the master; he is worrying himself because he thinks it is his fault that you do not; and just now"—the woman hesitated for a moment—"just now I want to keep him very quiet."

"Is he weaker, nurse?"

"Well, he is not stronger, ma'am, and I think—I think we must humour him."

The Honourable Mrs. Drayton rose, and, crossing to the window, stood for a while looking out.

"But where am I to go, nurse?" she said at length, turning with a smile. "I've no invitations anywhere."

"Can't you make believe to have one?" said the nurse. "It is only seven o'clock. Say you are going to a dinner-party; you can come home early then. Go and dress yourself, and come down and say good-bye to him, and then come in again about eleven, as though you had just returned."

"You think I must, nurse?"

"I think it would be better, ma'am. I wish you would try it."

The Honourable Mrs. Drayton went to the door, then paused.

"He has such sharp ears, nurse; he will listen for the opening of the door and the sound of the carriage."

"I will see to that," said the nurse. "I will tell them to have the carriage here at ten minutes to eight. Then you can drive to the end of the street, slip out, and walk back. I will let you in myself."

"And about coming home?" asked the other woman.

"You must slip out for a few minutes before eleven, and the carriage must be waiting for you at the corner again. Leave all that to me."

In half an hour the Honourable Mrs. Drayton entered the sick-room, radiant in evening dress and jewels. Fortunately the lights were low, or "Blasé-Billy" might have been doubtful as to the effect his wife was likely to produce. For her face was not the face that one takes to dinner-parties.

"Nurse tells me you are going to the Grevilles this evening. I am so glad. I've been worrying myself about you, moped up here right through the season."

He took her hands in his and held her out at arm's length from him.

"How handsome you look, dear!" he said. "How they must have all been cursing me for keeping you shut up here, like a princess in an ogre's castle! I shall never dare to face them again."

She laughed, well pleased at his words.

"I shall not be late," she said. "I shall be so anxious to get back and see how my boy has behaved. If you have not been good I shan't go again."

They kissed and parted, and at eleven she returned to the room. She told him what a delightful evening it had been, and bragged a little of her own success.

The nurse told her that he had been more cheerful that evening than for many nights.

So every day the farce was played for him. One day it was to a luncheon that she went, in a costume by Redfern; the next night to a ball, in a frock direct from Paris; again to an "At Home," or concert, or dinner-party. Loafers and passers-by would stop to stare at a haggard, red-eyed woman, dressed as for a drawing-room, slipping thief-like in and out of her own door.

I heard them talking of her one afternoon, at a house where I called, and I joined the group to listen.

"I always thought her heartless, but I gave her credit for sense," a woman was saying. "One doesn't expect a woman to be fond of her husband, but she needn't make a parade of ignoring him when he is dying."

I pleaded absence from town to inquire what was meant, and from all lips I heard the same account. One had noticed her carriage at the door two or three evenings in succession.   Another had seen her returning home. A third had seen her coming out, and so on.

I could not fit the fact in with my knowledge of her, so the next evening I called. The door was opened instantly by herself.

"I saw you from the window," she said.   "Come in here; don't speak."

I followed her, and she closed the door behind her. She was dressed in a magnificent costume, her hair sparkling with diamonds, and I looked my questions.

She laughed bitterly.

"I am supposed to be at the opera to-night," she explained. "Sit down, if you have a few minutes to spare."

I said it was for a talk that I had come; and there, in the dark room, lighted only by the street lamp without, she told me all. And at the end she dropped her head on her bare arms; and I turned away and looked out of the window for a while.

"I feel so ridiculous," she said, rising and coming towards me. "I sit here all the evening dressed like this. I'm afraid I don't act my part very well; but, fortunately, dear Billy never was much of a judge of art, and it is good enough for him. I tell him the most awful lies about what everybody has said to me, and what I've said to everybody, and how my gowns were admired. What do you think of this one?"

For answer I took the privilege of a friend.

"I'm glad you think well of me," she said. "Billy has such a high opinion of you. You will hear some funny tales. I'm glad you know."

I had to leave London again, and Billy died before I returned. I heard that she had to be fetched from a ball, and was only just in time to touch his lips before they were cold. But her friends excused her by saying that the end had come very suddenly.

I called on her a little later, and before I left I hinted to her what people were saying, and asked her if I had not better tell them the truth.

"I would rather you didn't," she answered. "It seems like making public the secret side of one's life."

"But," I urged, "they will think—"

She interrupted me.

"Does it matter very much what they think?"

Which struck me as a very remarkable sentiment, coming from the Hon. Mrs. Drayton, *née* the elder Miss Lovell.

THE CHOICE OF CYRIL HARJOHN

Between a junior resident master of twenty-one, and a backward lad of fifteen, there yawns an impassable gulf. Between a struggling journalist of one-and-thirty, and an M.D. of twenty-five, with a brilliant record behind him, and a career of exceptional promise before him, a close friendship is however permissible.

My introduction to Cyril Harjohn was through the Rev. Charles Fauerberg.

"Our young friend," said the Rev. Mr. Fauerberg, standing in the most approved tutorial attitude, with his hand upon his pupil's shoulder, "our young friend has been somewhat neglected, but I see in him possibilities warranting hope—warranting, I may say, very great hope. For the present he will be under my especial care, and you will not therefore concern yourself with his studies. He will sleep with Milling and the others in dormitory number two."

The lad formed a liking for me, and I think, and hope, I rendered his sojourn at "Alpha House" less irksome than otherwise it might have been. The Reverend Charles' method with the backward was on all fours with that adopted for the bringing on of geese; he cooped them up and crammed them. The process is profitable to the trainer, but painful to the goose.

Young Harjohn and myself left "Alpha House" at the end of the same term; he bound for Brasenose, I for Bloomsbury. He made a point of never coming up to London without calling on me, when we would dine together in one of Soho's many dingy, garlic-scented restaurants, and afterwards, over our bottle of cheap Beaune, discuss the coming of our lives; and when he entered Guy's I left John Street, and took chambers close to his in Staple Inn. Those were pleasant days. Childhood is an over-rated period, fuller of sorrow than of joy. I would not take my childhood back, were it a gift, but I would give the rest of my life to live the twenties over again.

To Cyril I was the man of the world, and he looked to me for wisdom, not seeing always, I fear, that he got it; while from him I gathered enthusiasm, and learnt the profit that comes to a man from the keeping of ideals.

Often as we have talked, I have felt as though a visible light came from him, framing his face as with the halo of some pictured saint. Nature had wasted him, putting him into this nineteenth century of ours. Her victories are accomplished. Her army of heroes, the few sung, the many forgotten, is disbanded.

The long peace won by their blood and pain is settled on the land. She had fash-ioned Cyril Harjohn for one of her soldiers. He would have been a martyr, in the days when thought led to the stake, a fighter for the truth, when to speak one's mind meant death. To lead some forlorn hope for Civilisation would have been his true work; Fate had condemned him to sentry duty in a well-ordered barrack.

But there is work to be done in the world, though the labour lies now in the vineyard, not on the battlefield. A small but sufficient fortune purchased for him freedom. To most men an assured income is the grave of ambition; to Cyril it was the foundation of desire. Relieved from the necessity of working to live, he could afford the luxury of living to work. His profession was to him a passion; he regarded it, not with the cold curiosity of the scholar, but with the imaginative devotion of the disciple. To help to push its frontiers forward, to carry its flag farther into the untravelled desert that ever lies beyond the moving boundary of human knowledge, was his dream.

One summer evening, I remember, we were sitting in his rooms, and during a silence there came to us through the open window the moaning of the city, as of a tired child. He rose and stretched his arms out towards the darkening streets, as if he would gather to him all the toiling men and women and comfort them.

"Oh, that I could help you!" he cried, "my brothers and my sisters. Take my life, oh God, and spend it for me among your people."

The speech sounds theatrical, as I read it, written down, but to the young such words are not ridiculous, as to us older men.

In the natural order of events, he fell in love, and with just the woman one would expect him to be attracted by. Elspeth Grant was of the type from which the world, by instinct rather than by convention, has drawn its Madonnas and its saints. To describe a woman in words is impossible. Her beauty was not a pos-session to be catalogued, but herself. One felt it as one feels the beauty of a summer's dawn breaking the shadows of a sleeping city, but one cannot set it down. I often met her, and, when talking to her, I knew myself—I, hack-journalist, frequenter of Fleet Street bars, retailer of smoke-room stories—a great gentleman, incapable of meanness, fit for all noble deeds.

In her presence life became a thing beautiful and gracious; a school for cour-tesy, and tenderness, and simplicity.

I have wondered since, coming to see a little more clearly into the ways of men, whether it would not have been better had she been less spiritual, had her nature possessed a greater alloy of earth, making it more fit for the uses of this work-a-day world. But at the time, these two friends of mine seemed to me to have been created for one another.

She appealed to all that was highest in Cyril's character, and he worshipped her with an unconcealed adoration that, from any man less high-minded, would have appeared affectation, and which she accepted with the sweet content that Artemis might have accorded to the homage of Endymion.

There was no formal engagement between them. Cyril seemed to shrink from the materialising of his love by any thought of marriage. To him she was an ideal of womanhood rather than a flesh-and-blood woman. His love for her was a religion; it had no taint of earthly passion in its composition.

Had I known the world better I might have anticipated the result; for the red blood ran in my friend's veins; and, alas, we dream our poems, not live them. But at the time, the idea of any other woman coming between them would have appeared to me folly. The suggestion that that other woman might be Geraldine Fawley I should have resented as an insult to my intelligence: that is the point of the story I do not understand to this day.

That he should be attracted by her, that he should love to linger near her, watching the dark flush come and go across her face, seeking to call the fire into her dark eyes was another matter, and quite comprehensible; for the girl was wonderfully handsome, with a bold, voluptuous beauty which invited while it dared. But considered in any other light than that of an animal, she repelled. At times when, for her ends, it seemed worth the exertion, she would assume a certain wayward sweetness, but her acting was always clumsy and exaggerated, capable of deceiving no one but a fool.

Cyril, at all events, was not taken in by it. One evening, at a Bohemian gathering, the *entrée* to which was notoriety rather than character, they had been talking together for some considerable time when, wishing to speak to Cyril, I strolled up to join them. As I came towards them she moved away, her dislike for me being equal to mine for her; a thing which was, perhaps, well for me.

"Miss Fawley prefers two as company to three," I observed, looking after her retreating figure.

"I am afraid she finds you what we should call an anti-sympathetic element," he replied, laughing.

"Do you like her?" I asked him, somewhat bluntly.

His eyes rested upon her as she stood in the doorway, talking to a small, black-bearded man who had just been introduced to her. After a few moments she went out upon his arm, and then Cyril turned to me.

"I think her," he replied, speaking, as was necessary, very low, "the embodiment of all that is evil in womanhood. In old days she would have been a Cleopatra, a Theodora, a Delilah. To-day, lacking opportunity, she is the 'smart woman' grubbing for an opening into society—and old Fawley's daughter. I'm tired; let us go home."

His allusion to her parentage was significant. Few people thought of connecting clever, handsome Geraldine Fawley with "Rogue Fawley," Jew renegade, ex-gaol bird, and outside broker; who, having expectations from his daughter, took care not to hamper her by ever being seen in her company.   But no one who had once met the father could ever forget the relationship while talking to the daughter. The older face, with its cruelty, its cunning, and its greed stood reproduced, feature for feature, line for line. It was as though Nature, for an artistic freak, had set herself the task of fashioning hideousness and beauty from precisely the same materials. Between the leer of the man and the smile of the girl, where lay the difference? It would have puzzled any student of anatomy to point it out. Yet the one sickened, while to gain the other most men would have given much.

Cyril's answer to my question satisfied me for the time. He met the girl often, as was natural. She was a singer of some repute, and our social circle was what is commonly called "literary and artistic." To do her justice, however, she made no attempt to fascinate him, nor even to be particularly agreeable to him. Indeed, she seemed to be at pains to show him her natural—in other words, her most objectionable side.

Coming out of the theatre one first night, we met her in the lobby. I was following Cyril at some little distance, but as he stopped to speak to her the movement of the crowd placed me just behind them.

"Will you be at Leightons' to-morrow?" I heard him ask her in a low tone.

"Yes," she answered, "and I wish you wouldn't come."

"Why not?"

"Because you're a fool, and you bore me."

Under ordinary circumstances I should have taken the speech for badinage—it was the kind of wit the woman would have indulged in. But Cyril's face clouded with anger and vexation. I said nothing. I did not wish him to know that I had overheard. I tried to believe that he was amusing himself, but my own explanation did not satisfy me.

Next evening I went to Leightons' by myself. The Grants were in town, and Cyril was dining with them. I found I did not know many people, and cared little for those I did. I was about to escape when Miss Fawley's name was announced. I was close to the door, and she had to stop and speak to me. We exchanged a few commonplaces. She either made love to a man or was rude to him. She generally talked to me without looking at me, nodding and smiling meanwhile to people around. I have met many women equally ill-mannered, and without her excuse. For a moment, however, she turned her eyes to mine.

"Where's your friend, Mr. Harjohn?" she asked. "I thought you were inseparables."

I looked at her in astonishment.

"He is dining out to-night," I replied. "I do not think he will come."

She laughed. I think it was the worst part about the woman, her laugh; it suggested so much cruelty.

"I think he will," she said.

It angered me into an indiscretion. She was moving away. I stepped in front of her and stopped her.

"What makes you think so?" I asked, and my voice, I know, betrayed the anxiety I felt as to her reply. She looked me straight in the face. There was one virtue she possessed—the virtue that animals hold above mankind—truthfulness. She knew I disliked her—hate would be, perhaps, a more exact expression, did not the word sound out of date, and she made no pretence of not knowing it and returning the compliment.

"Because I am here," she answered. "Why don't you save him? Have you no influence over him? Tell the Saint to keep him; I don't want him. You heard what I said to him last night. I shall only marry him for the sake of his position, and the money he can earn if he likes to work and not play the fool. Tell him what I have said; I shan't deny it."

She passed on to greet a decrepit old lord with a languishing smile, and I stood staring after her with, I fear, a somewhat stupid expression, until some young fool came up grinning, to ask me whether I had seen a ghost or backed a "wrong 'un."

There was no need to wait; I felt no curiosity. Something told me the woman had spoken the truth. It was mere want of motive that made me linger. I saw him come in, and watched him hanging round her, like a dog, waiting for a kind word, or failing that, a look. I knew she saw me, and I knew it added to her zest that I was there. Not till we were in the street did I speak to him. He started as I touched him. We were neither of us good actors. He must have read much in my face, and I saw that he had read it; and we walked side by side in silence, I thinking what to say, wondering whether I should do good or harm, wishing that we were anywhere but in these silent, life-packed streets, so filled with the unseen. It was not until we had nearly reached the Albert Hall that we broke the silence. Then it was he who spoke:

"Do you think I haven't told myself all that?" he said. "Do you think I don't know I'm a damned fool, a cad, a liar! What the devil's the good of talking about it?"

"But I can't understand it," I said.

"No," he replied, "because you're a fool, because you have only seen one side of me. You think me a grand gentleman, because I talk big, and am full of noble sentiment. Why, you idiot, the Devil himself could take you in. *He* has his fine moods, I suppose, talks like a saint, and says his prayers with the rest of us. Do you remember the first night at old Fauerberg's? You poked your silly head into the dormitory, and saw me kneeling by the bedside, while the other fellows stood by grinning. You closed the door softly—you thought I never saw you. I was not praying, I was trying to pray."

"It showed that you had pluck, if it showed nothing else," I answered. "Most boys would not have tried, and you kept it up."

"Ah, yes," he answered, "I promised the Mater I would, and I did. Poor old soul, she was as big a fool as you are. She believed in me. Don't you remember, finding me one Saturday afternoon all alone, stuffing myself with cake and jam?"

I laughed at the recollection, though Heaven knows I was in no laughing mood. I had found him with an array of pastry spread out before him, sufficient to make him ill for a week, and I had boxed his ears, and had thrown the whole collection into the road.

"The Mater gave me half-a-crown a week for pocket-money," he continued, "and I told the fellows I had only a shilling, so that I could gorge myself with the other eighteenpence undisturbed. Pah! I was a little beast even in those days!"

"It was only a schoolboy trick," I argued, "it was natural enough."

"Yes," he answered, "and this is only a man's trick, and is natural enough; but it is going to ruin my life, to turn me into a beast instead of a man. Good God! do you think I don't know what that woman will do for me? She will drag me down, down, down, to her own level. All my ideas, all my ambition, all my life's work will be bartered for a smug practice, among paying patients. I shall scheme and plot to make a big income that we may live like a couple of plump animals, that we may dress ourselves gaudily and parade our wealth. Nothing will satisfy her. Such women are leeches; their only cry is 'give, give, give.' So long as I can supply her with money she will tolerate me, and to get it for her I shall sell my heart, and my brain, and my soul. She will load herself with jewels, and go about from house to house, half naked, to leer at every man she comes across: that is 'life' to such women. And I shall trot behind her, the laughing stock of every fool, the contempt of every man."

His vehemence made any words I could say sound weak before they were uttered. What argument could I show stronger than that he had already put before himself? I knew his answer to everything I could urge.

My mistake had been in imagining him different from other men. I began to see that he was like the rest of us: part angel, part devil. But the new point he revealed to me was that the higher the one, the lower the other. It seems as if nature must balance her work; the nearer the leaves to heaven, the deeper the roots striking down into the darkness. I knew that his passion for this woman made no change in his truer love. The one was a spiritual, the other a mere animal passion. The memory of incidents that had puzzled me came back to enlighten me. I remembered how often on nights when I had sat up late, working, I had heard his steps pass my door, heavy and uncertain; how once in a dingy quarter of London, I had met one who had strangely resembled him. I had followed him to speak, but the man's bleared eyes had stared angrily at me, and I had turned away, calling myself a fool for my mistake. But as I looked at the face beside me now, I understood.

And then there rose up before my eyes the face I knew better, the eager noble face that to merely look upon had been good. We had reached a small, evil-smelling street, leading from Leicester Square towards Holborn. I caught him by the shoulders and turned him round with his back against some church railings. I forget what I said. We are strange mixtures. I thought of the shy, backward boy I had coached and bullied at old Fauerberg's, of the laughing handsome lad I had watched grow into manhood. The very restaurant we had most frequented in his old Oxford days—where we had poured out our souls to one another, was in this very street where we were standing. For the moment I felt towards him as perhaps his mother might have felt; I wanted to scold him and to cry with him; to shake him and to put my arms about him. I pleaded with him, and urged him, and called him every name I could put my tongue to. It must have seemed an odd conversation. A passing policeman, making a not unnatural mistake, turned his bull's-eye upon us, and advised us sternly to go home. We laughed, and with that laugh Cyril came back to his own self, and we walked on to Staple Inn more soberly. He promised me to go away by the very first train the next morning, and to travel for some four or five months, and I undertook to make all the necessary explanations for him.

We both felt better for our talk, and when I wished him good-night at his door, it was the real Cyril Harjohn whose hand I gripped—the real Cyril, because the best that is in a man is his real self. If there be any future for man beyond this world, it is the good that is in him that will live. The other side of him is of the earth; it is that he will leave behind him.

He kept his word. In the morning he was gone, and I never saw him again. I had many letters from him, hopeful at first, full of strong resolves. He told me he had written to Elspeth, not telling her everything, for that she would not understand, but so much as would explain; and from her he had had sweet womanly letters in reply. I feared she might have been cold and unsympathetic, for often good women, untouched by temptation themselves, have small tenderness for those who struggle. But her goodness was something more than a mere passive quantity; she loved him the better because he had need of her. I believe she would have saved him from himself, had not fate interfered and taken the matter out of her hands. Women are capable of big sacrifices; I think this woman would have been content to lower herself, if by so doing she could have raised him.

But it was not to be. From India he wrote to me that he was coming home. I had not met the Fawley woman for some time, and she had gone out of my mind until one day, chancing upon a theatrical paper, some weeks old, I read that "Miss Fawley had sailed for Calcutta to fulfil an engagement of long standing."

I had his last letter in my pocket. I sat down and worked out the question of date. She would arrive in Calcutta the day before he left. Whether it was chance or intention on her part I never knew; as likely as not the former, for there is a fatalism in this world shaping our ends.

I heard no more from him, I hardly expected to do so, but three months later a mutual acquaintance stopped me on the Club steps.

"Have you heard the news," he said, "about young Harjohn?"

"No," I replied. "Is he married?"

"Married," he answered, "No, poor devil, he's dead!"

"Thank God," was on my lips, but fortunately I checked myself. "How did it happen?" I asked.

"At a shooting party, up at some Rajah's place. Must have caught his gun in some brambles, I suppose. The bullet went clean through his head."

"Dear me," I said, "how very sad!" I could think of nothing else to say at the moment.

THE MATERIALISATION OF CHARLES AND MIVANWAY

The fault that most people will find with this story is that it is unconvincing. Its scheme is improbable, its atmosphere artificial. To confess that the thing real-ly happened—not as I am about to set it down, for the pen of the professional writer cannot but adorn and embroider, even to the detriment of his material—is, I am well aware, only an aggravation of my offence, for the facts of life are the impossibilities of fiction. A truer artist would have left this story alone, or at most have kept it for the irritation of his private circle. My lower instinct is to make use of it. A very old man told me the tale. He was landlord of the Crom-lech Arms, the only inn of a small, rock-sheltered village on the north-east coast of Cornwall, and had been so for nine and forty years. It is called the Cromlech Hotel now, and is under new management, and during the season some four coach-loads of tourists sit down each day to *table d'hôte* lunch in the low-ceilinged parlour.   But I am speaking of years ago, when the place was a mere fishing harbour, undiscovered by the guide books.

The old landlord talked, and I hearkened the while we both sat drinking thin ale from earthenware mugs, late one summer's evening, on the bench that runs along the wall just beneath the latticed windows. And during the many pauses, when the old landlord stopped to puff his pipe in silence, and lay in a new stock of breath, there came to us the murmuring voices of the Atlantic; and often, min-gled with the pompous roar of the big breakers farther out, we would hear the rippling laugh of some small wave that, maybe, had crept in to listen to the tale the landlord told.

The mistake that Charles Seabohn, Junior partner of the firm of Seabohn & Son, civil engineers of London and Newcastle-upon-Tyne, and Mivanway Evans, youngest daughter of the Rev. Thomas Evans, Pastor of the Presbyterian Church at Bristol, made originally, was marrying too young. Charles Seabohn could hardly have been twenty years of age, and Mivanway could have been little more than seventeen, when they first met upon the cliffs, two miles beyond the Crom-lech Arms. Young Charles Seabohn, coming across the village in the course of a walking tour, had decided to spend a day or two exploring the picturesque coast, and Mivanway's father had hired that year a neighbouring farmhouse wherein to spend his summer vacation.

Early one morning—for at twenty one is virtuous, and takes exercise before breakfast—as young Charles Seabohn lay upon the cliffs, watching the white waters coming and going upon the black rocks below, he became aware of a form rising from the waves. The figure was too far off for him to see it clearly, but judging from the costume, it was a female figure, and promptly the mind of Charles, poetically inclined, turned to thoughts of Venus—or Aphrodite, as he, being a gentleman of delicate taste would have preferred to term her. He saw the figure disappear behind a head-land, but still waited. In about ten minutes or a quarter of an hour it reappeared, clothed in the garments of the eighteen-sixties, and came towards him. Hidden from sight himself behind a group of rocks, he could watch it at his leisure, ascending the steep path from the beach, and an exceedingly sweet and dainty figure it would have appeared, even to eyes less susceptible than those of twenty. Sea-water—I stand open to correction—is not, I believe, considered anything of a substitute for curling tongs, but to the hair of the youngest Miss Evans it had given an additional and most fascinating wave. Nature's red and white had been most cunningly laid on, and the large childish eyes seemed to be searching the world for laughter, with which to feed a pair of delicious, pouting lips. Charles's upturned face, petrified into admiration, was just the sort of thing for which they were on the look-out. A startled "Oh!" came from the slightly parted lips, followed by the merriest of laughs, which in its turn was suddenly stopped by a deep blush. Then the youngest Miss Evans looked offended, as though the whole affair had been Charles's fault, which is the way of women. And Charles, feeling himself guilty under that stern gaze of indignation, rose awkwardly and apologised meekly, whether for being on the cliffs at all or for having got up too early, he would have been unable to explain.

The youngest Miss Evans graciously accepted the apology thus tendered with a bow, and passed on, and Charles stood staring after her till the valley gathered her into its spreading arms and hid her from his view.

That was the beginning of all things. I am speaking of the Universe as viewed from the standpoint of Charles and Mivanway.

Six months later they were man and wife, or perhaps it would be more correct to say boy and wifelet. Seabohn senior counselled delay, but was overruled by the impatience of his junior partner. The Reverend Mr. Evans, in common with most theologians, possessed a goodly supply of unmarried daughters, and a limited income. Personally he saw no necessity for postponement of the marriage.

The month's honeymoon was spent in the New Forest. That was a mistake to begin with. The New Forest in February is depressing, and they had chosen the loneliest spot they could find. A fortnight in Paris or Rome would have been more helpful. As yet they had nothing to talk about except love, and that they had been talking and writing about steadily all through the winter. On the tenth morning Charles yawned, and Mivanway had a quiet half-hour's cry about it in her own room. On the sixteenth evening, Mivanway, feeling irritable, and wondering why (as though fifteen damp, chilly days in the New Forest were not suffi-cient to make any woman irritable), requested Charles not to disarrange her hair; and Charles, speechless with astonishment, went out into the garden, and swore before all the stars that he would never caress Mivanway's hair again as long as he lived.

One supreme folly they had conspired to commit, even before the com-mencement of the honeymoon. Charles, after the manner of very young lovers, had earnestly requested Mivanway to impose upon him some task. He desired to do something great and noble to show his devotion. Dragons was the thing he had in mind, though he may not have been aware of it. Dragons also, no doubt, flitted through Mivanway's brain, but unfortunately for lovers the supply of dragons has lapsed. Mivanway, liking the conceit, however, thought over it, and then decided that Charles must give up smoking. She had discussed the matter with her favourite sister, and that was the only thing the girls could think of. Charles's face fell. He suggested some more Herculean labour, some sacrifice more worthy to lay at Mivanway's feet. But Mivanway had spoken. She might think of some other task, but the smoking prohibition would, in any case, re-main. She dismissed the subject with a pretty *hauteur* that would have graced Marie Antoinette.

Thus tobacco, the good angel of all men, no longer came each day to teach Charles patience and amiability, and he fell into the ways of short temper and selfishness.

They took up their residence in a suburb of Newcastle, and this was also un-fortunate for them, because there the society was scanty and middle-aged; and, in consequence, they had still to depend much upon their own resources. They knew little of life, less of each other, and nothing at all of themselves. Of course they quarrelled, and each quarrel left the wound a little more raw. No kindly, experienced friend was at hand to laugh at them. Mivanway would write down all her sorrows in a bulky diary, which made her feel worse; so that before she had written for ten minutes her pretty, unwise head would drop upon her dimpled arm, and the book—the proper place for which was behind the fire—would be-come damp with her tears; and Charles, his day's work done and the clerks gone, would linger in his dingy office and hatch trifles into troubles.

The end came one evening after dinner, when, in the heat of a silly squabble, Charles boxed Mivanway's ears. That was very ungentlemanly conduct, and he was heartily ashamed of himself the moment he had done it, which was right and proper for him to be. The only excuse to be urged on his behalf is that girls suf-ficiently pretty to have been spoilt from childhood by everyone about them can at times be intensely irritating. Mivanway rushed up to her room, and locked her-self in. Charles flew after her to apologise, but only arrived in time to have the door slammed in his face.

It had only been the merest touch. A boy's muscles move quicker than his thoughts. But to Mivanway it was a blow. This was what it had come to! This was the end of a man's love!

She spent half the night writing in the precious diary, with the result that in the morning she came down feeling more bitter than she had gone up. Charles had walked the streets of Newcastle all night, and that had not done him any good. He met her with an apology combined with an excuse, which was bad tactics. Mivanway, of course, fastened upon the excuse, and the quarrel recommenced. She mentioned that she hated him; he hinted that she had never loved him, and she retorted that he had never loved her. Had there been anybody by to knock their heads together and suggest breakfast, the thing might have blown over, but the combined effect of a sleepless night and an empty stomach upon each proved disastrous. Their words came poisoned from their brains, and each believed they meant what they said. That afternoon Charles sailed from Hull, on a ship bound for the Cape, and that evening Mivanway arrived at the paternal home in Bristol with two trunks and the curt information that she and Charles had separated for ever. The next morning both thought of a soft speech to say to the other, but the next morning was just twenty-four hours too late.

Eight days afterwards Charles's ship was run down in a fog, near the coast of Portugal, and every soul on board was supposed to have perished. Mivanway read his name among the list of lost; the child died within her, and she knew herself for a woman who had loved deeply, and will not love again.

Good luck intervening, however, Charles and one other man were rescued by a small trading vessel, and landed in Algiers. There Charles learnt of his supposed death, and the idea occurred to him to leave the report uncontradicted. For one thing, it solved a problem that had been troubling him. He could trust his father to see to it that his own small fortune, with possibly something added, was handed over to Mivanway, and she would be free if she wished to marry again. He was convinced that she did not care for him, and that she had read of his death with a sense of relief. He would make a new life for himself, and forget her.

He continued his journey to the Cape, and once there he soon gained for himself an excellent position. The colony was young, engineers were welcome, and Charles knew his business. He found the life interesting and exciting. The rough, dangerous up-country work suited him, and the time passed swiftly.

But in thinking he would forget Mivanway, he had not taken into consideration his own character, which at bottom was a very gentlemanly character. Out on the lonely veldt he found himself dreaming of her. The memory of her pretty face and merry laugh came back to him at all hours. Occasionally he would curse her roundly, but that only meant that he was sore because of the thought of her; what he was really cursing was himself and his own folly. Softened by the distance, her quick temper, her very petulance became mere added graces; and if we consider women as human beings and not as angels, it was certainly a fact that he had lost a very sweet and lovable woman. Ah! if she only were by his side now—now that he was a man capable of appreciating her, and not a foolish, selfish boy. This thought would come to him as he sat smoking at the door of his tent, and then he would regret that the stars looking down upon him were not the same stars that were watching her, it would have made him feel nearer to her.

For, though young people may not credit it, one grows more sentimental as one grows older; at least, some of us do, and they perhaps not the least wise.

One night he had a vivid dream of her. She came to him and held out her hand, and he took it, and they said good-bye to one another. They were standing on the cliff where he had first met her, and one of them was going upon a long journey, though he was not sure which.

In the towns men laugh at dreams, but away from civilisation we listen more readily to the strange tales that Nature whispers to us. Charles Seabohn recollected this dream when he awoke in the morning.

"She is dying," he said, "and she has come to wish me good-bye."

He made up his mind to return to England at once; perhaps if he made haste he would be in time to kiss her. But he could not start that day, for work was to be done; and Charles Seabohn, lover though he still was, had grown to be a man, and knew that work must not be neglected even though the heart may be calling. So for a day or two he stayed, and on the third night he dreamed of Mivanway again, and this time she lay within the little chapel at Bristol where, on Sunday mornings, he had often sat with her. He heard her father's voice reading the burial service over her, and the sister she had loved best was sitting beside him, crying softly. Then Charles knew that there was no need for him to hasten. So he remained to finish his work. That done, he would return to England. He would like again to stand upon the cliffs, above the little Cornish village, where they had first met.

Thus a few months later Charles Seabohn, or Charles Denning, as he called himself, aged and bronzed, not easily recognisable by those who had not known him well, walked into the Cromlech Arms, as six years before he had walked in with his knapsack on his back, and asked for a room, saying he would be stopping in the village for a short while.

In the evening he strolled out and made his way to the cliffs. It was twilight when he reached the place of rocks to which the fancy-loving Cornish folk had given the name of the Witches' Cauldron. It was from this spot that he had first watched Mivanway coming to him from the sea.

He took the pipe from his mouth, and leaning against a rock, whose rugged outline seemed fashioned into the face of an old friend, gazed down the narrow pathway now growing indistinct in the dim light. And as he gazed the figure of Mivanway came slowly up the pathway from the sea, and paused before him.

He felt no fear. He had half expected it. Her coming was the complement of his dreams. She looked older and graver than he remembered her, but for that the face was the sweeter.

He wondered if she would speak to him, but she only looked at him with sad eyes; and he stood there in the shadow of the rocks without moving, and she passed on into the twilight.

Had he on his return cared to discuss the subject with his landlord, had he even shown himself a ready listener—for the old man loved to gossip—he might have learnt that a young widow lady named Mrs. Charles Seabohn, accompanied by an unmarried sister, had lately come to reside in the neighbourhood, having, upon the death of a former tenant, taken the lease of a small farmhouse sheltered in the valley a mile beyond the village, and that her favourite evening's walk was to the sea and back by the steep footway leading past the Witches' Cauldron.

Had he followed the figure of Mivanway into the valley, he would have known that out of sight of the Witches' Cauldron it took to running fast till it reached a welcome door, and fell panting into the arms of another figure that had hastened out to meet it.

"My dear," said the elder woman, "you are trembling like a leaf. What has happened?"

"I have seen him," answered Mivanway.

"Seen whom?"

"Charles."

"Charles!" repeated the other, looking at Mivanway as though she thought her mad.

"His spirit, I mean," explained Mivanway, in an awed voice. "It was standing in the shadow of the rocks, in the exact spot where we first met. It looked older and more careworn; but, oh! Margaret, so sad and reproachful."

"My dear," said her sister, leading her in, "you are overwrought. I wish we had never come back to this house."

"Oh! I was not frightened," answered Mivanway, "I have been expecting it every evening. I am so glad it came. Perhaps it will come again, and I can ask it to forgive me."

So next night Mivanway, though much against her sister's wishes and advice, persisted in her usual walk, and Charles at the same twilight hour started from the inn.

Again Mivanway saw him standing in the shadow of the rocks. Charles had made up his mind that if the thing happened again he would speak, but when the silent figure of Mivanway, clothed in the fading light, stopped and gazed at him, his will failed him.

That it was the spirit of Mivanway standing before him he had not the faintest doubt. One may dismiss other people's ghosts as the phantasies of a weak brain, but one knows one's own to be realities, and Charles for the last five years had mingled with a people whose dead dwell about them. Once, drawing his courage around him, he made to speak, but as he did so the figure of Mivanway shrank from him, and only a sigh escaped his lips, and hearing that the figure of Mivanway turned and again passed down the path into the valley, leaving Charles gazing after it.

But the third night both arrived at the trysting spot with determination screwed up to the sticking point.

Charles was the first to speak. As the figure of Mivanway came towards him, with its eyes fixed sadly on him, he moved from the shadow of the rocks, and stood before it.

"Mivanway!" he said.

"Charles!" replied the figure of Mivanway. Both spoke in an awed whisper suitable to the circumstances, and each stood gazing sorrowfully upon the other.

"Are you happy?" asked Mivanway.

The question strikes one as somewhat farcical, but it must be remembered that Mivanway was the daughter of a Gospeller of the old school, and had been brought up to beliefs that were not then out of date.

"As happy as I deserve to be," was the sad reply, and the answer—the inference was not complimentary to Charles's deserts—struck a chill to Mivanway's heart.

"How could I be happy having lost you?" went on the voice of Charles.

Now this speech fell very pleasantly upon Mivanway's ears. In the first place it relieved her of her despair regarding Charles's future. No doubt his present suffering was keen, but there was hope for him. Secondly, it was a decidedly "pretty" speech for a ghost, and I am not at all sure that Mivanway was the kind of woman to be averse to a little mild flirtation with the spirit of Charles.

"Can you forgive me?" asked Mivanway.

"Forgive *you!*" replied Charles, in a tone of awed astonishment. "Can you forgive me? I was a brute—a fool—I was not worthy to love you."

A most gentlemanly spirit it seemed to be. Mivanway forgot to be afraid of it.

"We were both to blame," answered Mivanway.   But this time there was less submission in her tones.   "But I was the most at fault. I was a petulant child. I did not know how deeply I loved you."

"You loved me!" repeated the voice of Charles, and the voice lingered over the words as though it found them sweet.

"Surely you never doubted it," answered the voice of Mivanway. "I never ceased to love you. I shall love you always and ever."

The figure of Charles sprang forward as though it would clasp the ghost of Mivanway in its arms, but halted a step or two off.

"Bless me before you go," he said, and with uncovered head the figure of Charles knelt to the figure of Mivanway.

Really, ghosts could be exceedingly nice when they liked. Mivanway bent graciously towards her shadowy suppliant, and, as she did so, her eye caught sight of something on the grass beside it, and that something was a well-coloured meerschaum pipe. There was no mistaking it for anything else, even in that treacherous light; it lay glistening where Charles, in falling upon his knees had jerked it from his breast-pocket.

Charles, following Mivanway's eyes, saw it also, and the memory of the prohibition against smoking came back to him.

Without stopping to consider the futility of the action—nay, the direct confession implied thereby—he instinctively grabbed at the pipe, and rammed it back into his pocket; and then an avalanche of mingled understanding and bewilderment, fear and joy, swept Mivanway's brain before it. She felt she must do one of two things, laugh or scream and go on screaming, and she laughed. Peal after peal of laughter she sent echoing among the rocks, and Charles springing to his feet was just in time to catch her as she fell forward a dead weight into his arms.

Ten minutes later the eldest Miss Evans, hearing heavy footsteps, went to the door. She saw what she took to be the spirit of Charles Seabohn, staggering under the weight of the lifeless body of Mivanway, and the sight not unnaturally alarmed her. Charles's suggestion of brandy, however, sounded human, and the urgent need of attending to Mivanway kept her mind from dwelling upon problems tending towards insanity.

Charles carried Mivanway to her room, and laid her upon the bed.

"I'll leave her with you," he whispered to the eldest Miss Evans. "It will be better for her not to see me until she is quite recovered. She has had a shock."

Charles waited in the dark parlour for what seemed to him an exceedingly long time. But at last the eldest Miss Evans returned.

"She's all right now," were the welcome words he heard.

"I'll go and see her," he said.

"But she's in bed," exclaimed the scandalised Miss Evans.

And then as Charles only laughed, "Oh, ah—yes, I suppose—of course," she added.

And the eldest Miss Evans, left alone, sat down and wrestled with the conviction that she was dreaming.

PORTRAIT OF A LADY

My work pressed upon me, but the louder it challenged me—such is the heart of the timid fighter—the less stomach I felt for the contest. I wrestled with it in my study, only to be driven to my books. I walked out to meet it in the streets, only to seek shelter from it in music-hall or theatre. Thereupon it waxed importunate and over-bearing, till the shadow of it darkened all my doings. The thought of it sat beside me at the table, and spoilt my appetite. The memory of it followed me abroad, and stood between me and my friends, so that all talk died upon my lips, and I moved among men as one ghost-ridden.

Then the throbbing town, with its thousand distracting voices, grew maddening to me. I felt the need of converse with solitude, that master and teacher of all the arts, and I bethought me of the Yorkshire Wolds, where a man may walk all day, meeting no human creature, hearing no voice but the curlew's cry; where, lying prone upon the sweet grass, he may feel the pulsation of the earth, travelling at its eleven hundred miles a minute through the ether. So one morning I bundled many things, some needful, more needless, into a bag, hurrying lest somebody or something should happen to stay me, and that night I lay in a small northern town that stands upon the borders of smokedom at the gate of the great moors; and at seven the next morning I took my seat beside a one-eyed carrier behind an ancient piebald mare. The one-eyed carrier cracked his whip, the piebald horse jogged forward. The nineteenth century, with its turmoil, fell away behind us; the distant hills, creeping nearer, swallowed us up, and we became but a moving speck upon the face of the quiet earth.

Late in the afternoon we arrived at a village, the memory of which had been growing in my mind. It lies in the triangle formed by the sloping walls of three great fells, and not even the telegraph wire has reached it yet, to murmur to it whispers of the restless world—or had not at the time of which I write. Nought disturbs it save, once a day, the one-eyed carrier—if he and his piebald mare have not yet laid their ancient bones to rest—who, passing through, leaves a few letters and parcels to be called for by the people of the scattered hill-farms round about. It is the meeting-place of two noisy brooks. Through the sleepy days and the hushed nights, one hears them ever chattering to themselves as children playing alone some game of make-believe. Coming from their far-off homes among the hills, they mingle their waters here, and journey on in company, and then their converse is more serious, as becomes those who have joined hands and are moving onward towards life together. Later they reach sad, weary towns, black beneath a never-lifted pall of smoke, where day and night the clang of iron drowns all human voices, where the children play with ashes, where the men and women have dull, patient faces; and so on, muddy and stained, to the deep sea that ceaselessly calls to them. Here, however, their waters are fresh and clear, and their passing makes the only stir that the valley has ever known. Surely, of all peaceful places, this was the one where a tired worker might find strength.

My one-eyed friend had suggested I should seek lodgings at the house of one Mistress Cholmondley, a widow lady, who resided with her only daughter in the white-washed cottage that is the last house in the village, if you take the road that leads over Coll Fell.

"Tha' can see th' house from here, by reason o' its standing so high above t'others," said the carrier, pointing with his whip. "It's theer or nowhere, aw'm thinking, for folks don't often coom seeking lodgings in these parts."

The tiny dwelling, half smothered in June roses, looked idyllic, and after a lunch of bread and cheese at the little inn I made my way to it by the path that passes through the churchyard. I had conjured up the vision of a stout, pleasant, comfort-radiating woman, assisted by some bright, fresh girl, whose rosy cheeks and sunburnt hands would help me banish from my mind all clogging recollections of the town; and hopeful, I pushed back the half-opened door and entered.

The cottage was furnished with a taste that surprised me, but in themselves my hosts disappointed me. My bustling, comely housewife turned out a wizened, blear-eyed dame. All day long she dozed in her big chair, or crouched with shrivelled hands spread out before the fire. My dream of winsome maidenhood vanished before the reality of a weary-looking, sharp-featured woman of between forty and fifty. Perhaps there had been a time when the listless eyes had sparkled with roguish merriment, when the shrivelled, tight-drawn lips had pouted temptingly; but spinsterhood does not sweeten the juices of a woman, and strong country air, though, like old ale, it is good when taken occasionally, dulls the brain if lived upon. A narrow, uninteresting woman I found her, troubled with a shyness that sat ludicrously upon her age, and that yet failed to save her from the landlady's customary failing of loquacity concerning "better days," together with an irritating, if harmless, affectation of youthfulness.

All other details were, however, most satisfactory; and at the window commanding the road that leads through the valley towards the distant world I settled down to face my work.

But the spirit of industry, once driven forth, returns with coy steps. I wrote for perhaps an hour, and then throwing down my halting pen I looked about the room, seeking distraction. A Chippendale book-case stood against the wall and I strolled over to it. The key was in the lock, and opening its glass doors, I examined the well-filled shelves. They held a curious collection: miscellanies with quaint, glazed bindings; novels and poems; whose authors I had never heard of; old magazines long dead, their very names forgotten; "keepsakes" and annuals, redolent of an age of vastly pretty sentiments and lavender-coloured silks. On the top shelf, however, was a volume of Keats wedged between a number of the *Evangelical Rambler* and Young's *Night Thoughts*, and standing on tip-toe, I sought to draw it from its place.

The book was jambed so tightly that my efforts brought two or three others tumbling about me, covering me with a cloud of fine dust, and to my feet there fell, with a rattle of glass and metal, a small miniature painting, framed in black wood.

I picked it up, and, taking it to the window, examined it. It was the picture of a young girl, dressed in the fashion of thirty years ago—I mean thirty years ago then. I fear it must be nearer fifty, speaking as from now—when our grandmothers wore corkscrew curls, and low-cut bodices that one wonders how they kept from slipping down. The face was beautiful, not merely with the conventional beauty of tiresome regularity and impossible colouring such as one finds in all miniatures, but with soul behind the soft deep eyes. As I gazed, the sweet lips seemed to laugh at me, and yet there lurked a sadness in the smile, as though the artist, in some rare moment, had seen the coming shadow of life across the sunshine of the face. Even my small knowledge of Art told me that the work was clever, and I wondered why it should have lain so long neglected, when as a mere ornament it was valuable. It must have been placed in the book-case years ago by someone, and forgotten.

I replaced it among its dusty companions, and sat down once more to my work. But between me and the fading light came the face of the miniature, and would not be banished. Wherever I turned it looked out at me from the shadows. I am not naturally fanciful, and the work I was engaged upon—the writing of a farcical comedy—was not of the kind to excite the dreamy side of a man's nature. I grew angry with myself, and made a further effort to fix my mind upon the paper in front of me. But my thoughts refused to return from their wanderings. Once, glancing back over my shoulder, I could have sworn I saw the original of the picture sitting in the big chintz-covered chair in the far corner. It was dressed in a faded lilac frock, trimmed with some old lace, and I could not help noticing the beauty of the folded hands, though in the portrait only the head and shoulders had been drawn.

Next morning I had forgotten the incident, but with the lighting of the lamp the memory of it awoke within me, and my interest grew so strong that again I took the miniature from its hiding-place and looked at it.

And then the knowledge suddenly came to me that I knew the face. Where had I seen her, and when? I had met her and spoken to her. The picture smiled at me, as if rallying me on my forgetfulness. I put it back upon its shelf, and sat racking my brains trying to recollect. We had met somewhere—in the country— a long time ago, and had talked of common-place things. To the vision of her clung the scent of roses and the murmuring voices of haymakers. Why had I never seen her again? Why had she passed so completely out of my mind?

My landlady entered to lay my supper, and I questioned her assuming a careless tone. Reason with or laugh at myself as I would, this shadowy memory was becoming a romance to me.   It was as though I were talking of some loved, dead friend, even to speak of whom to commonplace people was a sacrilege. I did not want the woman to question me in return.

"Oh, yes," answered my landlady. Ladies had often lodged with her. Sometimes people stayed the whole summer, wandering about the woods and fells, but to her thinking the great hills were lonesome. Some of her lodgers had been young ladies, but she could not remember any of them having impressed her with their beauty. But then it was said women were never a judge of other women. They had come and gone. Few had ever returned, and fresh faces drove out the old.

"You have been letting lodgings for a long time?" I asked. "I suppose it could be fifteen—twenty years ago that strangers to you lived in this room?"

"Longer than that," she said quietly, dropping for the moment all affectation. "We came here from the farm when my father died. He had had losses, and there was but little left. That is twenty-seven years ago now."

I hastened to close the conversation, fearing long-winded recollections of "better days." I have heard such so often from one landlady and another. I had not learnt much. Who was the original of the miniature, how it came to be lying forgotten in the dusty book-case were still mysteries; and with a strange perversity I could not have explained to myself I shrank from putting a direct question.

So two days more passed by. My work took gradually a firmer grip upon my mind, and the face of the miniature visited me less often. But in the evening of the third day, which was a Sunday, a curious thing happened.

I was returning from a stroll, and dusk was falling as I reached the cottage. I had been thinking of my farce, and I was laughing to myself at a situation that seemed to me comical, when, passing the window of my room, I saw looking out the sweet fair face that had become so familiar to me. It stood close to the latticed panes, a slim, girlish figure, clad in the old-fashioned lilac-coloured frock in which I had imagined it on the first night of my arrival, the beautiful hands clasped across the breast, as then they had been folded on the lap. Her eyes were gazing down the road that passes through the village and goes south, but they seemed to be dreaming, not seeing, and the sadness in them struck upon one almost as a cry. I was close to the window, but the hedge screened me, and I remained watching, until, after a minute I suppose, though it appeared longer, the figure drew back into the darkness of the room and disappeared.

I entered, but the room was empty. I called, but no one answered. The uncomfortable suggestion took hold of me that I must be growing a little crazy. All that had gone before I could explain to myself as a mere train of thought, but this time it had come to me suddenly, uninvited, while my thoughts had been busy elsewhere. This thing had appeared not to my brain but to my senses. I am not a believer in ghosts, but I am in the hallucinations of a weak mind, and my own explanation was in consequence not very satisfactory to myself.

I tried to dismiss the incident, but it would not leave me, and later that same evening something else occurred that fixed it still clearer in my thoughts. I had taken out two or three books at random with which to amuse myself, and turning over the leaves of one of them, a volume of verses by some obscure poet, I found its sentimental passages much scored and commented upon in pencil as was common fifty years ago—as may be common now, for your Fleet Street cynic has not altered the world and its ways to quite the extent that he imagines.

One poem in particular had evidently appealed greatly to the reader's sympathies. It was the old, old story of the gallant who woos and rides away, leaving the maiden to weep. The poetry was poor, and at another time its conventionality would have excited only my ridicule. But, reading it in conjunction with the quaint, naive notes scattered about its margins, I felt no inclination to jeer. These hackneyed stories that we laugh at are deep profundities to the many who find in them some shadow of their own sorrows, and she—for it was a woman's handwriting—to whom this book belonged had loved its trite verses, because in them she had read her own heart. This, I told myself, was her story also. A common enough story in life as in literature, but novel to those who live it.

There was no reason for my connecting her with the original of the miniature, except perhaps a subtle relationship between the thin nervous handwriting and the mobile features; yet I felt instinctively they were one and the same, and that I was tracing, link by link, the history of my forgotten friend.

I felt urged to probe further, and next morning while my landlady was clearing away my breakfast things, I fenced round the subject once again.

"By the way," I said, "while I think of it, if I leave any books or papers here behind me, send them on at once. I have a knack of doing that sort of thing. I suppose," I added, "your lodgers often do leave some of their belongings behind them."

It sounded to myself a clumsy ruse. I wondered if she would suspect what was behind it.

"Not often," she answered. "Never that I can remember, except in the case of one poor lady who died here."

I glanced up quickly.

"In this room?" I asked.

My landlady seemed troubled at my tone.

"Well, not exactly in this very room. We carried her upstairs, but she died immediately. She was dying when she came here. I should not have taken her in had I known. So many people are prejudiced against a house where death has occurred, as if there were anywhere it had not. It was not quite fair to us."

I did not speak for a while, and the rattle of the plates and knives continued undisturbed.

"What did she leave here?" I asked at length.

"Oh, just a few books and photographs, and such-like small things that people bring with them to lodgings," was the reply. "Her people promised to send for them, but they never did, and I suppose I forgot them. They were not of any value."

The woman turned as she was leaving the room.

"It won't drive you away, sir, I hope, what I have told you," she said. "It all happened a long while ago.

"Of course not," I answered. "It interested me, that was all." And the woman went out, closing the door behind her.

So here was the explanation, if I chose to accept it. I sat long that morning, wondering to myself whether things I had learnt to laugh at could be after all realities. And a day or two afterwards I made a discovery that confirmed all my vague surmises.

Rummaging through this same dusty book-case, I found in one of the ill-fitting drawers, beneath a heap of torn and tumbled books, a diary belonging to the fifties, stuffed with many letters and shapeless flowers, pressed between stained pages; and there—for the writer of stories, tempted by human documents, is weak—in faded ink, brown and withered like the flowers, I read the story I already knew.

Such a very old story it was, and so conventional. He was an artist—was ever story of this type written where the hero was not an artist? They had been children together, loving each other without knowing it till one day it was revealed to them. Here is the entry:—

"May 18th.—I do not know what to say, or how to begin. Chris loves me. I have been praying to God to make me worthy of him, and dancing round the room in my bare feet for fear of waking them below. He kissed my hands and clasped them round his neck, saying they were beautiful as the hands of a goddess, and he knelt and kissed them again. I am holding them before me and kissing them myself. I am glad they are so beautiful. O God, why are you so good to me? Help me to be a true wife to him. Help me that I may never give him an instant's pain! Oh, that I had more power of loving, that I might love him better,"—and thus foolish thoughts for many pages, but foolish thoughts of the kind that has kept this worn old world, hanging for so many ages in space, from turning sour.

Later, in February, there is another entry that carries on the story:—

"Chris left this morning. He put a little packet into my hands at the last moment, saying it was the most precious thing he possessed, and that when I looked at it I was to think of him who loved it. Of course I guessed what it was, but I did not open it till I was alone in my room. It is the picture of myself that he has been so secret about, but oh, so beautiful. I wonder if I am really as beautiful as this. But I wish he had not made me look so sad. I am kissing the little lips. I love them, because he loved to kiss them. Oh, sweetheart! it will be long before you kiss them again. Of course it was right for him to go, and I am glad he has been able to manage it. He could not study properly in this quiet country place, and now he will be able to go to Paris and Rome and he will be great. Even the stupid people here see how clever he is. But, oh, it will be so long before I see him again, my love! my king!"

With each letter that comes from him, similar foolish rhapsodies are written down, but these letters of his, I gather, as I turn the pages, grow after a while colder and fewer, and a chill fear that dare not be penned creeps in among the words.

"March 12th. Six weeks and no letter from Chris, and, oh dear! I am so hungry for one, for the last I have almost kissed to pieces. I suppose he will write more often when he gets to London. He is working hard, I know, and it is selfish of me to expect him to write more often, but I would sit up all night for a week rather than miss writing to him. I suppose men are not like that. O God, help me, help me, whatever happens! How foolish I am to-night! He was always careless. I will punish him for it when he comes back, but not very much."

Truly enough a conventional story.

Letters do come from him after that, but apparently they are less and less satisfactory, for the diary grows angry and bitter, and the faded writing is blotted at times with tears. Then towards the end of another year there comes this entry, written in a hand of strange neatness and precision:—

"It is all over now. I am glad it is finished. I have written to him, giving him up. I have told him I have ceased to care for him, and that it is better we should both be free. It is best that way. He would have had to ask me to release him, and that would have given him pain. He was always gentle. Now he will be able to marry her with an easy conscience, and he need never know what I have suffered. She is more fitted for him than I am. I hope he will be happy. I think I have done the right thing."

A few lines follow, left blank, and then the writing is resumed, but in a stronger, more vehement hand.

"Why do I lie to myself? I hate her! I would kill her if I could. I hope she will make him wretched, and that he will come to hate her as I do, and that she will die! Why did I let them persuade me to send that lying letter? He will show it to her, and she will see through it and laugh at me. I could have held him to his promise; he could not have got out of it.

"What do I care about dignity, and womanliness, and right, and all the rest of the canting words! I want him. I want his kisses and his arms about me. He is mine! He loved me once! I have only given him up because I thought it a fine thing to play the saint. It is only an acted lie. I would rather be evil, and he loved me. Why do I deceive myself? I want him. I care for nothing else at the bottom of my heart—his love, his kisses!"

And towards the end. "My God, what am I saying? Have I no shame, no strength? O God, help me!"

* * * * *

And there the diary closes.

I looked among the letters lying between the pages of the book. Most of them were signed simply "Chris." or "Christopher." But one gave his name in full, and it was a name I know well as that of a famous man, whose hand I have often shaken. I thought of his hard-featured, handsome wife, and of his great chill place, half house, half exhibition, in Kensington, filled constantly with its smart, chattering set, among whom he seemed always to be the uninvited guest; of his weary face and bitter tongue. And thinking thus there rose up before me the sweet, sad face of the woman of the miniature, and, meeting her eyes as she smiled at me from out of the shadows, I looked at her my wonder.

I took the miniature from its shelf. There would be no harm now in learning her name. So I stood with it in my hand till a little later my landlady entered to lay the cloth.

"I tumbled this out of your book-case," I said, "in reaching down some books. It is someone I know, someone I have met, but I cannot think where. Do you know who it is?"

The woman took it from my hand, and a faint flush crossed her withered face. "I had lost it," she answered. "I never thought of looking there. It's a portrait of myself, painted years ago, by a friend."

I looked from her to the miniature, as she stood among the shadows, with the lamplight falling on her face, and saw her perhaps for the first time.

"How stupid of me," I answered. "Yes, I see the likeness now."

THE MAN WHO WOULD MANAGE

It has been told me by those in a position to know—and I can believe it—that at nineteen months of age he wept because his grandmother would not allow him to feed her with a spoon, and that at three and a half he was fished, in an exhausted condition, out of the water-butt, whither he had climbed for the purpose of teaching a frog to swim.

Two years later he permanently injured his left eye, showing the cat how to carry kittens without hurting them, and about the same period was dangerously stung by a bee while conveying it from a flower where, as it seemed to him, it was only wasting its time, to one more rich in honey-making properties.

His desire was always to help others. He would spend whole mornings explaining to elderly hens how to hatch eggs, and would give up an afternoon's black-berrying to sit at home and crack nuts for his pet squirrel. Before he was seven he would argue with his mother upon the management of children, and reprove his father for the way he was bringing him up.

As a child nothing could afford him greater delight than "minding" other children, or them less. He would take upon himself this harassing duty entirely of his own accord, without hope of reward or gratitude. It was immaterial to him whether the other children were older than himself or younger, stronger or weaker, whenever and wherever he found them he set to work to "mind" them. Once, during a school treat, piteous cries were heard coming from a distant part of the wood, and upon search being made, he was discovered prone upon the ground, with a cousin of his, a boy twice his own weight, sitting upon him and steadily whacking him. Having rescued him, the teacher said:

"Why don't you keep with the little boys? What are you doing along with him?"

"Please, sir," was the answer, "I was minding him."

He would have "minded" Noah if he had got hold of him.

He was a good-natured lad, and at school he was always willing for the whole class to copy from his slate—indeed he would urge them to do so. He meant it kindly, but inasmuch as his answers were invariably quite wrong—with a distinctive and inimitable wrongness peculiar to himself—the result to his followers was eminently unsatisfactory; and with the shallowness of youth that, ignoring motives, judges solely from results, they would wait for him outside and punch him.

All his energies went to the instruction of others, leaving none for his own purposes. He would take callow youths to his chambers and teach them to box.

"Now, try and hit me on the nose," he would say, standing before them in an attitude of defence. "Don't be afraid. Hit as hard as ever you can."

And they would do it. And so soon as he had recovered from his surprise, and a little lessened the bleeding, he would explain to them how they had done it all wrong, and how easily he could have stopped the blow if they had only hit him properly.

Twice at golf he lamed himself for over a week, showing a novice how to "drive"; and at cricket on one occasion I remember seeing his middle stump go down like a ninepin just as he was explaining to the bowler how to get the balls in straight. After which he had a long argument with the umpire as to whether he was in or out.

He has been known, during a stormy Channel passage, to rush excitedly upon the bridge in order to inform the captain that he had "just seen a light about two miles away to the left"; and if he is on the top of an omnibus he generally sits beside the driver, and points out to him the various obstacles likely to impede their progress.

It was upon an omnibus that my own personal acquaintanceship with him began. I was sitting behind two ladies when the conductor came up to collect fares. One of them handed him a sixpence telling him to take to Piccadilly Circus, which was twopence.

"No," said the other lady to her friend, handing the man a shilling, "I owe you sixpence, you give me fourpence and I'll pay for the two."

The conductor took the shilling, punched two twopenny tickets, and then stood trying to think it out.

"That's right," said the lady who had spoken last, "give my friend fourpence."

The conductor did so.

"Now you give that fourpence to me."

The friend handed it to her.

"And you," she concluded to the conductor, "give me eightpence, then we shall be all right."

The conductor doled out to her the eightpence—the sixpence he had taken from the first lady, with a penny and two halfpennies out of his own bag—distrustfully, and retired, muttering something about his duties not including those of a lightning calculator.

"Now," said the elder lady to the younger, "I owe you a shilling."

I deemed the incident closed, when suddenly a florid gentleman on the opposite seat called out in stentorian tones:—

"Hi, conductor! you've cheated these ladies out of fourpence."

"'Oo's cheated 'oo out 'o fourpence?" replied the indignant conductor from the top of the steps, "it was a twopenny fare."

"Two twopences don't make eightpence," retorted the florid gentleman hotly. "How much did you give the fellow, my dear?" he asked, addressing the first of the young ladies.

"I gave him sixpence," replied the lady, examining her purse. "And then I gave you fourpence, you know," she added, addressing her companion.

"That's a dear two pen'oth," chimed in a common-looking man on the seat behind.

"Oh, that's impossible, dear," returned the other, "because I owed you sixpence to begin with."

"But I did," persisted the first lady.

"You gave me a shilling," said the conductor, who had returned, pointing an accusing forefinger at the elder of the ladies.

The elder lady nodded.

"And I gave you sixpence and two pennies, didn't I?"

The lady admitted it.

"An' I give 'er"—he pointed towards the younger lady—"fourpence, didn't I?"

"Which I gave you, you know, dear," remarked the younger lady.

"Blow me if it ain't *me* as 'as been cheated out of the fourpence," cried the conductor.

"But," said the florid gentleman, "the other lady gave you sixpence."

"Which I give to 'er," replied the conductor, again pointing the finger of accusation at the elder lady. "You can search my bag if yer like. I ain't got a bloomin' sixpence on me."

By this time everybody had forgotten what they had done, and contradicted themselves and one another. The florid man took it upon himself to put everybody right, with the result that before Piccadilly Circus was reached three passengers had threatened to report the conductor for unbecoming language. The conductor had called a policeman and had taken the names and addresses of the two ladies, intending to sue them for the fourpence (which they wanted to pay, but which the florid man would not allow them to do); the younger lady had become convinced that the elder lady had meant to cheat her, and the elder lady was in tears.

The florid gentleman and myself continued to Charing Cross Station. At the booking office window it transpired that we were bound for the same suburb, and we journeyed down together. He talked about the fourpence all the way.

At my gate we shook hands, and he was good enough to express delight at the discovery that we were near neighbours. What attracted him to myself I failed to understand, for he had bored me considerably, and I had, to the best of my ability, snubbed him. Subsequently I learned that it was a peculiarity of his to be charmed with anyone who did not openly insult him.

Three days afterwards he burst into my study unannounced—he appeared to regard himself as my bosom friend—and asked me to forgive him for not having called sooner, which I did.

"I met the postman as I was coming along," he said, handing me a blue envelope, "and he gave me this, for you."

I saw it was an application for the water-rate.

"We must make a stand against this," he continued. "That's for water to the 29th September. You've no right to pay it in June."

I replied to the effect that water-rates had to be paid, and that it seemed to me immaterial whether they were paid in June or September.

"That's not it," he answered, "it's the principle of the thing. Why should you pay for water you have never had? What right have they to bully you into paying what you don't owe?"

He was a fluent talker, and I was ass enough to listen to him. By the end of half an hour he had persuaded me that the question was bound up with the inalienable rights of man, and that if I paid that fourteen and tenpence in June instead of in September, I should be unworthy of the privileges my forefathers had fought and died to bestow upon me.

He told me the company had not a leg to stand upon, and at his instigation I sat down and wrote an insulting letter to the chairman.

The secretary replied that, having regard to the attitude I had taken up, it would be incumbent upon themselves to treat it as a test case, and presumed that my solicitors would accept service on my behalf.

When I showed him this letter he was delighted.

"You leave it to me," he said, pocketing the correspondence, "and we'll teach them a lesson."

I left it to him. My only excuse is that at the time I was immersed in the writing of what in those days was termed a   comedy-drama. The little sense I possessed must, I suppose, have been absorbed by the play.

The magistrate's decision somewhat damped my ardour, but only inflamed his zeal. Magistrates, he said, were muddle-headed old fogies. This was a matter for a judge.

The judge was a kindly old gentleman, and said that bearing in mind the unsatisfactory wording of the sub-clause, he did not think he could allow the company their costs, so that, all told, I got off for something under fifty pounds, inclusive of the original fourteen and tenpence.

Afterwards our friendship waned, but living as we did in the same outlying suburb, I was bound to see a good deal of him; and to hear more.

At parties of all kinds he was particularly prominent, and on such occasions, being in his most good-natured mood, was most to be dreaded. No human being worked harder for the enjoyment of others, or produced more universal wretchedness.

One Christmas afternoon, calling upon a friend, I found some fourteen or fifteen elderly ladies and gentlemen trotting solemnly round a row of chairs in the centre of the drawing-room while Poppleton played the piano. Every now and then Poppleton would suddenly cease, and everyone would drop wearily into the nearest chair, evidently glad of a rest; all but one, who would thereupon creep quietly away, followed by the envying looks of those left behind. I stood by the door watching the weird scene. Presently an escaped player came towards me, and I enquired of him what the ceremony was supposed to signify.

"Don't ask me," he answered grumpily. "Some of Poppleton's damned tom-foolery." Then he added savagely, "We've got to play forfeits after this."

The servant was still waiting a favourable opportunity to announce me. I gave her a shilling not to, and got away unperceived.

After a satisfactory dinner, he would suggest an impromptu dance, and want you to roll up mats, or help him move the piano to the other end of the room.

He knew enough round games to have started a small purgatory of his own. Just as you were in the middle of an interesting discussion, or a delightful *tête-à-tête* with a pretty woman, he would swoop down upon you with: "Come along, we're going to play literary consequences," and dragging you to the table, and putting a piece of paper and a pencil before you, would tell you to write a description of your favourite heroine in fiction, and would see that you did it.

He never spared himself. It was always he who would volunteer to escort the old ladies to the station, and who would never leave them until he had seen them safely into the wrong train. He it was who would play "wild beasts" with the children, and frighten them into fits that would last all night.

So far as intention went, he was the kindest man alive. He never visited poor sick persons without taking with him in his pocket some little delicacy calculated to disagree with them and make them worse. He arranged yachting excursions for bad sailors, entirely at his own expense, and seemed to regard their subsequent agonies as ingratitude.

He loved to manage a wedding. Once he planned matters so that the bride arrived at the altar three-quarters of an hour before the groom, which led to unpleasantness upon a day that should have been filled only with joy, and once he forgot the clergyman. But he was always ready to admit when he made a mistake.

At funerals, also, he was to the fore, pointing out to the grief-stricken relatives how much better it was for all concerned that the corpse was dead, and expressing a pious hope that they would soon join it.

The chiefest delight of his life, however, was to be mixed up in other people's domestic quarrels. No domestic quarrel for miles round was complete without him. He generally came in as mediator, and finished as leading witness for the appellant.

As a journalist or politician his wonderful grasp of other people's business would have won for him esteem. The error he made was working it out in practice.

THE MAN WHO LIVED FOR OTHERS

The first time we met, to speak, he was sitting with his back against a pollard willow, smoking a clay pipe. He smoked it very slowly, but very conscientiously. After each whiff he removed the pipe from his mouth and fanned away the smoke with his cap.

"Feeling bad?" I asked from behind a tree, at the same time making ready for a run, big boys' answers to small boys' impertinences being usually of the nature of things best avoided.

To my surprise and relief—for at second glance I perceived I had under-estimated the length of his legs—he appeared to regard the question as a natural and proper one, replying with unaffected candour, "Not yet."

My desire became to comfort him—a sentiment I think he understood and was grateful for. Advancing into the open, I sat down over against him, and watched him for a while in silence. Presently he said:—

"Have you ever tried drinking beer?"

I admitted I had not.

"Oh, it is beastly stuff," he rejoined with an involuntary shudder.

Rendered forgetful of present trouble by bitter recollection of the past, he puffed away at his pipe carelessly and without judgment.

"Do you often drink it?" I inquired.

"Yes," he replied gloomily; "all we fellows in the fifth form drink beer and smoke pipes."

A deeper tinge of green spread itself over his face.

He rose suddenly and made towards the hedge. Before he reached it, however, he stopped and addressed me, but without turning round.

"If you follow me, young 'un, or look, I'll punch your head," he said swiftly, and disappeared with a gurgle.

He left at the end of the terms and I did not see him again until we were both young men. Then one day I ran against him in Oxford Street, and he asked me to come and spend a few days with his people in Surrey.

I found him wan-looking and depressed, and every now and then he sighed. During a walk across the common he cheered up considerably, but the moment we got back to the house door he seemed to recollect himself, and began to sigh again. He ate no dinner whatever, merely sipping a glass of wine and crumbling a piece of bread. I was troubled at noticing this, but his relatives—a maiden aunt, who kept house, two elder sisters, and a weak-eyed female cousin who had left her husband behind her in India—were evidently charmed. They glanced at each other, and nodded and smiled. Once in a fit of abstraction he swallowed a bit of crust, and immediately they all looked pained and surprised.

In the drawing-room, under cover of a sentimental song, sung by the female cousin, I questioned his aunt on the subject.

"What's the matter with him?" I said. "Is he ill?"

The old lady chuckled.

"You'll be like that one day," she whispered gleefully.

"When," I asked, not unnaturally alarmed.

"When you're in love," she answered.

"Is *he* in love?" I inquired after a pause.

"Can't you see he is?" she replied somewhat scornfully.

I was a young man, and interested in the question.

"Won't he ever eat any dinner till he's got over it?" I asked.

She looked round sharply at me, but apparently decided that I was only foolish.

"You wait till your time comes," she answered, shaking her curls at me. "You won't care much about your dinner—not if you are *really* in love."

In the night, about half-past eleven, I heard, as I thought, footsteps in the passage, and creeping to the door and opening it I saw the figure of my friend in dressing-gown and slippers, vanishing down the stairs. My idea was that, his brain weakened by trouble, he had developed sleep-walking tendencies. Partly out of curiosity, partly to watch over him, I slipped on a pair of trousers and followed him.

He placed his candle on the kitchen table and made a bee-line for the pantry door, from where he subsequently emerged with two pounds of cold beef on a plate and about a quart of beer in a jug; and I came away, leaving him fumbling for pickles.

I assisted at his wedding, where it seemed to me he endeavoured to display more ecstasy than it was possible for any human being to feel; and fifteen months later, happening to catch sight of an advertisement in the births column of *The Times*, I called on my way home from the City to congratulate him. He was pacing up and down the passage with his hat on, pausing at intervals to partake of an uninviting-looking meal, consisting of a cold mutton chop and a glass of lemonade, spread out upon a chair. Seeing that the cook and the housemaid were wandering about the house evidently bored for want of something to do, and that the dining-room, where he would have been much more out of the way, was empty and quite in order, I failed at first to understand the reason for his deliberate choice of discomfort. I, however, kept my reflections to myself, and inquired after the mother and child.

"Couldn't be better," he replied with a groan. "The doctor said he'd never had a more satisfactory case in all his experience."

"Oh, I'm glad to hear that," I answered; "I was afraid you'd been worrying yourself."

"Worried!" he exclaimed. "My dear boy, I don't know whether I'm standing on my head or my heels" (he gave one that idea). "This is the first morsel of food that's passed my lips for twenty-four hours."

At this moment the nurse appeared at the top of the stairs. He flew towards her, upsetting the lemonade in his excitement.

"What is it?" he asked hoarsely. "Is it all right?"

The old lady glanced from him to his cold chop, and smiled approvingly.

"They're doing splendidly," she answered, patting him on the shoulder in a motherly fashion. "Don't you worry."

"I can't help it, Mrs. Jobson," he replied, sitting down upon the bottom stair, and leaning his head against the banisters.

"Of course you can't," said Mrs. Jobson admiringly; "and you wouldn't be much of a man if you could." Then it was borne in upon me why he wore his hat, and dined off cold chops in the passage.

The following summer they rented a picturesque old house in Berkshire, and invited me down from a Saturday to Monday. Their place was near the river, so I slipped a suit of flannels in my bag, and on the Sunday morning I came down in them. He met me in the garden. He was dressed in a frock coat and a white waistcoat; and I noticed that he kept looking at me out of the corner of his eye, and that he seemed to have a trouble on his mind. The first breakfast bell rang, and then he said, "You haven't got any proper clothes with you, have you?"

"Proper clothes!" I exclaimed, stopping in some alarm. "Why, has anything given way?"

"No, not that," he explained. "I mean clothes to go to church in."

"Church," I said. "You're surely not going to church a fine day like this? I made sure you'd be playing tennis, or going on the river. You always used to."

"Yes," he replied, nervously flicking a rose-bush with a twig he had picked up. "You see, it isn't ourselves exactly. Maud and I would rather like to, but our cook, she's Scotch, and a little strict in her notions."

"And does she insist on your going to church every Sunday morning?" I inquired.

"Well," he answered, "she thinks it strange if we don't, and so we generally do, just in the morning—and evening. And then in the afternoon a few of the village girls drop in, and we have a little singing and that sort of thing. I never like hurting anyone's feelings if I can help it."

I did not say what I thought. Instead I said, "I've got that tweed suit I wore yesterday. I can put that on if you like."

He ceased flicking the rose-bush, and knitted his brows. He seemed to be recalling it to his imagination.

"No," he said, shaking his head, "I'm afraid it would shock her. It's my fault, I know," he added, remorsefully. "I ought to have told you."

Then an idea came to him.

"I suppose," he said, "you wouldn't care to pretend you were ill, and stop in bed just for the day?"

I explained that my conscience would not permit my being a party to such deception

"No, I thought you wouldn't," he replied. "I must explain it to her. I think I'll say you've lost your bag. I shouldn't like her to think bad of us."

Later on a fourteenth cousin died, leaving him a large fortune. He purchased an estate in Yorkshire, and became a "county family," and then his real troubles began.

From May to the middle of August, save for a little fly fishing, which generally resulted in his getting his feet wet and catching a cold, life was fairly peaceful; but from early autumn to late spring he found the work decidedly trying. He was a stout man, constitutionally nervous of fire-arms, and a six-hours' tramp with a heavy gun across ploughed fields, in company with a crowd of careless persons who kept blazing away within an inch of other people's noses, harassed and exhausted him. He had to get out of bed at four on chilly October mornings to go cub-hunting, and twice a week throughout the winter—except when a blessed frost brought him a brief respite—he had to ride to hounds. That he usually got off with nothing more serious than mere bruises and slight concussions of the spine, he probably owed to the fortunate circumstances of his being little and fat. At stiff timber he shut his eyes and rode hard; and ten yards from a river he would begin to think about bridges.

Yet he never complained.

"If you are a country gentleman," he would say, "you must behave as a country gentleman, and take the rough with the smooth."

As ill fate would have it a chance speculation doubled his fortune, and it became necessary that he should go into Parliament and start a yacht. Parliament made his head ache, and the yacht made him sick. Notwithstanding, every summer he would fill it with a lot of expensive people who bored him, and sail away for a month's misery in the Mediterranean.

During one cruise his guests built up a highly-interesting gambling scandal. He himself was confined to his cabin at the time, and knew nothing about it; but the Opposition papers, getting hold of the story, referred casually to the yacht as a "floating hell," and *The Police News* awarded his portrait the place of honour as the chief criminal of the week.

Later on he got into a cultured set, ruled by a thick-lipped undergraduate. His favourite literature had hitherto been of the Corelli and *Tit-Bits* order, but now he read Meredith and the yellow book, and tried to understand them; and instead of the Gaiety, he subscribed to the Independent Theatre, and fed "his soul," on Dutch Shakespeares. What he liked in art was a pretty girl by a cottage-door with an eligible young man in the background, or a child and a dog doing something funny. They told him these things were wrong and made him buy "Impressions" that stirred his liver to its deepest depths every time he looked at them—green cows on red hills by pink moonlight, or scarlet-haired corpses with three feet of neck.

He said meekly that such seemed to him unnatural, but they answered that nature had nothing to do with the question; that the artist saw things like that, and that whatever an artist saw—no matter in what condition he may have been when he saw it—that was art.

They took him to Wagner festivals and Burne-Jones's private views. They read him all the minor poets.   They booked seats for him at all Ibsen's plays. They introduced him into all the most soulful circles of artistic society. His days were one long feast of other people's enjoyments.

One morning I met him coming down the steps of the Arts Club. He looked weary. He was just off to a private view at the New Gallery. In the afternoon he had to attend an amateur performance of "The Cenci," given by the Shelley Society. Then followed three literary and artistic At Homes, a dinner with an Indian nabob who couldn't speak a word of English, "Tristam and Isolde" at Covent Garden Theatre, and a ball at Lord Salisbury's to wind up the day.

I laid my hand upon his shoulder.

"Come with me to Epping Forest," I said.   "There's a four-horse brake starts from Charing Cross at eleven. It's Saturday, and there's bound to be a crowd down there. I'll play you a game of skittles, and we will have a shy at the cocoa-nuts. You used to be rather smart at cocoa-nuts. We can have lunch there and be back at seven, dine at the Troc., spend the evening at the Empire, and sup at the Savoy. What do you say?"

He stood hesitating on the steps, a wistful look in his eyes.

His brougham drew up against the curb, and he started as if from a dream.

"My dear fellow," he replied, "what would people say?" And shaking me by the hand, he took his seat, and the footman slammed the door upon him.

A MAN OF HABIT

There were three of us in the smoke-room of the *Alexandra*—a very good friend of mine, myself, and, in the opposite corner, a shy-looking, unobtrusive man, the editor, as we subsequently learned, of a New York Sunday paper.

My friend and I were discussing habits, good and bad.

"After the first few months," said my friend, "it is no more effort for a man to be a saint than to be a sinner; it becomes a mere matter of habit."

"I know," I interrupted, "it is every whit as easy to spring out of bed the instant you are called as to say 'All Right,' and turn over for just another five minutes' snooze, when you have got into the way of it. It is no more trouble not to swear than to swear, if you make a custom of it. Toast and water is as delicious as champagne, when you have acquired the taste for it. Things are also just as easy the other way about. It is a mere question of making your choice and sticking to it."

He agreed with me.

"Now take these cigars of mine," he said, pushing his open case towards me.

"Thank you," I replied hurriedly, "I'm not smoking this passage."

"Don't be alarmed," he answered, "I meant merely as an argument. Now one of these would make you wretched for a week."

I admitted his premise.

"Very well," he continued. "Now I, as you know, smoke them all day long, and enjoy them. Why? Because I have got into the habit. Years ago, when I was a young man, I smoked expensive Havanas. I found that I was ruining myself. It was absolutely necessary that I should take a cheaper weed. I was living in Belgium at the time, and a friend showed me these. I don't know what they are—probably cabbage leaves soaked in guano; they tasted to me like that at first—but they were cheap. Buying them by the five hundred, they cost me three a penny. I determined to like them, and started with one a day. It was terrible work, I admit, but as I said to myself, nothing could be worse than the Havanas themselves had been in the beginning. Smoking is an acquired taste, and it must be as easy to learn to like one flavour as another. I persevered and I conquered. Before the year was over I could think of them without loathing, at the end of two I could smoke them without positive discomfort. Now I prefer them to any other brand on the market. Indeed, a good cigar disagrees with me."

I suggested it might have been less painful to have given up smoking altogether.

"I did think of it," he replied, "but a man who doesn't smoke always seems to me bad company. There is something very sociable about smoke."

He leant back and puffed great clouds into the air, filling the small den with an odour suggestive of bilge water and cemeteries.

"Then again," he resumed after a pause, "take my claret. No, you don't like it." (I had not spoken, but my face had evidently betrayed me.) "Nobody does, at least no one I have ever met. Three years ago, when I was living in Hammersmith, we caught two burglars with it. They broke open the sideboard, and swallowed five bottlefuls between them. A policeman found them afterwards, sitting on a doorstep a hundred yards off, the 'swag' beside them in a carpet bag. They were too ill to offer any resistance, and went to the station like lambs, he promising to send the doctor to them the moment they were safe in the cells. Ever since then I have left out a decanterful upon the table every night.

"Well, I like that claret, and it does me good. I come in sometimes dead beat. I drink a couple of glasses, and I'm a new man. I took to it in the first instance for the same reason that I took to the cigars—it was cheap. I have it sent over direct from Geneva, and it costs me six shillings a dozen. How they do it I don't know. I don't want to know. As you may remember, it's fairly heady and there's body in it.

"I knew one man," he continued, "who had a regular Mrs. Caudle of a wife. All day long she talked to him, or at him, or of him, and at night he fell asleep to the rising and falling rhythm of what she thought about him. At last she died, and his friends congratulated him, telling him that now he would enjoy peace. But it was the peace of the desert, and the man did not enjoy it. For two-and-twenty years her voice had filled the house, penetrated through the conservatory, and floated in faint shrilly waves of sound round the garden, and out into the road beyond. The silence now pervading everywhere frightened and disturbed him. The place was no longer home to him. He missed the breezy morning insult, the long winter evening's reproaches beside the flickering fire. At night he could not sleep. For hours he would lie tossing restlessly, his ears aching for the accustomed soothing flow of invective.

"'Ah!' he would cry bitterly to himself, 'it is the old story, we never know the value of a thing until we have lost it.'

"He grew ill. The doctors dosed him with sleeping draughts in vain. At last they told him bluntly that his life depended upon his finding another wife, able and willing to nag him to sleep.

"There were plenty of wives of the type he wanted in the neighbourhood, but the unmarried women were, of necessity, inexperienced, and his health was such that he could not afford the time to train them.

"Fortunately, just as despair was about to take possession of him, a man died in the next parish, literally talked to death, the gossip said, by his wife. He obtained an introduction, and called upon her the day after the funeral. She was a cantankerous old woman, and the wooing was a harassing affair, but his heart was in his work, and before six months were gone he had won her for his own.

"She proved, however, but a poor substitute. The spirit was willing but the flesh was weak. She had neither that command of language nor of wind that had distinguished her rival. From his favourite seat at the bottom of the garden he could not hear her at all, so he had his chair brought up into the conservatory. It was all right for him there so long as she continued to abuse him; but every now and again, just as he was getting comfortably settled down with his pipe and his newspaper, she would suddenly stop.

"He would drop his paper and sit listening, with a troubled, anxious expression.

"'Are you there, dear?' he would call out after a while.

"'Yes, I'm here. Where do you think I am you old fool?' she would gasp back in an exhausted voice.

"His face would brighten at the sound of her words. 'Go on, dear,' he would answer. 'I'm listening. I like to hear you talk.'

"But the poor woman was utterly pumped out, and had not so much as a snort left.

"Then he would shake his head sadly. 'No, she hasn't poor dear Susan's flow,' he would say. 'Ah! what a woman that was!'

"At night she would do her best, but it was a lame and halting performance by comparison. After rating him for little over three-quarters of an hour, she would sink back on the pillow, and want to go to sleep. But he would shake her gently by the shoulder.

"'Yes, dear,' he would say, 'you were speaking about Jane, and the way I kept looking at her during lunch.'

"It's extraordinary," concluded my friend, lighting a fresh cigar, "what creatures of habit we are."

"Very," I replied. "I knew a man who told tall stories till when he told a true one nobody believed it."

"Ah, that was a very sad case," said my friend.

"Speaking of habit," said the unobtrusive man in the corner, "I can tell you a true story that I'll bet my bottom dollar you won't believe."

"Haven't got a bottom dollar, but I'll bet you half a sovereign I do," replied my friend, who was of a sporting turn. "Who shall be judge?"

"I'll take your word for it," said the unobtrusive man, and started straight away.

* * * * *

"He was a Jefferson man, this man I'm going to tell you of," he begun. "He was born in the town, and for forty-seven years he never slept a night outside it. He was a most respectable man—a drysalter from nine to four, and a Presbyterian in his leisure moments. He said that a good life merely meant good habits. He rose at seven, had family prayer at seven-thirty, breakfasted at eight, got to his business at nine, had his horse brought round to the office at four, and rode for an hour, reached home at five, had a bath and a cup of tea, played with and read to the children (he was a domesticated man) till half-past six, dressed and dined at seven, went round to the club and played whist till quarter after ten, home again to evening prayer at ten-thirty, and bed at eleven. For five-and-twenty years he lived that life with never a variation. It worked into his system and became mechanical. The church clocks were set by him. He was used by the local astronomers to check the sun.

"One day a distant connection of his in London, an East Indian Merchant and an ex-Lord Mayor died, leaving him sole legatee and executor. The business was a complicated one and needed management. He determined to leave his son by his first wife, now a young man of twenty-four, in charge at Jefferson, and to establish himself with his second family in England, and look after the East Indian business.

"He set out from Jefferson City on October the fourth, and arrived in London on the seventeenth. He had been ill during the whole of the voyage, and he reached the furnished house he had hired in Bayswater somewhat of a wreck. A couple of days in bed, however, pulled him round, and on the Wednesday evening he announced his intention of going into the City the next day to see to his affairs.

"On the Thursday morning he awoke at one o'clock. His wife told him she had not disturbed him, thinking the sleep would do him good. He admitted that perhaps it had. Anyhow, he felt very well, and he got up and dressed himself. He said he did not like the idea of beginning his first day by neglecting a religious duty, and his wife agreeing with him, they assembled the servants and the children in the dining-room, and had family prayer at half-past one. After which he breakfasted and set off, reaching the City about three.

"His reputation for punctuality had preceded him, and surprise was everywhere expressed at his late arrival. He explained the circumstances, however, and made his appointments for the following day to commence from nine-thirty.

"He remained at the office until late, and then went home. For dinner, usually the chief meal of the day, he could manage to eat only a biscuit and some fruit. He attributed his loss of appetite to want of his customary ride. He was strangely unsettled all the evening. He said he supposed he missed his game of whist, and determined to look about him without loss of time for some quiet, respectable club. At eleven he retired with his wife to bed, but could not sleep. He tossed and turned, and turned and tossed, but grew only more and more wakeful and energetic. A little after midnight an overpowering desire seized him to go and wish the children good-night. He slipped on a dressing-gown and stole into the nursery. He did not intend it, but the opening of the door awoke them, and he was glad. He wrapped them up in the quilt, and, sitting on the edge of the bed, told them moral stories till one o'clock.

"Then he kissed them, bidding them be good and go to sleep; and finding himself painfully hungry, crept downstairs, where in the back kitchen he made a hearty meal off cold game pie and cucumber.

"He retired to bed feeling more peaceful, yet still could not sleep, so lay thinking about his business affairs till five, when he dropped off.

"At one o'clock to the minute he awoke. His wife told him she had made every endeavour to rouse him, but in vain. The man was vexed and irritated. If he had not been a very good man indeed, I believe he would have sworn. The same programme was repeated as on the Thursday, and again he reached the City at three.

"This state of things went on for a month. The man fought against himself, but was unable to alter himself.   Every morning, or rather every afternoon at one he awoke.   Every night at one he crept down into the kitchen and foraged for food. Every morning at five he fell asleep.

"He could not understand it, nobody could understand it. The doctor treated him for water on the brain, hypnotic irresponsibility and hereditary lunacy. Meanwhile his business suffered, and his health grew worse. He seemed to be living upside down. His days seemed to have neither beginning nor end, but to be all middle. There was no time for exercise or recreation. When he began to feel cheerful and sociable everybody else was asleep.

"One day by chance the explanation came. His eldest daughter was preparing her home studies after dinner.

"'What time is it now in New York?' she asked, looking up from her geography book.

"'New York,' said her father, glancing at his watch, 'let me see. It's just ten now, and there's a little over four and a half hours' difference. Oh, about half-past five in the afternoon.'

"'Then in Jefferson,' said the mother, 'it would be still earlier, wouldn't it?'

"'Yes,' replied the girl, examining the map, 'Jefferson is nearly two degrees further west.'

"'Two degrees,' mused the father, 'and there's forty minutes to a degree. That would make it now, at the present moment in Jefferson—'

He leaped to his feet with a cry:

"'I've got it!' he shouted, 'I see it.'

"'See what?' asked his wife, alarmed.

"'Why, it's four o'clock in Jefferson, and just time for my ride. That's what I'm wanting.'

"There could be no doubt about it. For five-and-twenty years he had lived by clockwork. But it was by Jefferson clockwork, not London clockwork. He had changed his longitude, but not himself. The habits of a quarter of a century were not to be shifted at the bidding of the sun.

"He examined the problem in all its bearings, and decided that the only solution was for him to return to the order of his old life. He saw the difficulties in his way, but they were less than those he was at present encountering.   He was too formed by habit to adapt himself to circumstances. Circumstances must adapt themselves to him.

"He fixed his office hours from three till ten, leaving himself at half-past nine. At ten he mounted his horse and went for a canter in the Row, and on very dark nights he carried a lantern. News of it got abroad, and crowds would assemble to see him ride past.

"He dined at one o'clock in the morning, and afterwards strolled down to his club. He had tried to discover a quiet, respectable club where the members were willing to play whist till four in the morning, but failing, had been compelled to join a small Soho gambling-hell, where they taught him poker. The place was occasionally raided by the police, but thanks to his respectable appearance, he generally managed to escape.

"At half-past four he returned home, and woke up the family for evening prayers. At five he went to bed and slept like a top.

"The City chaffed him, and Bayswater shook its head over him, but that he did not mind. The only thing that really troubled him was loss of spiritual communion. At five o'clock on Sunday afternoons he felt he wanted chapel, but had to do without it. At seven he ate his simple mid-day meal. At eleven he had tea and muffins, and at midnight he began to crave again for hymns and sermons. At three he had a bread-and-cheese supper, and retired early at four a.m., feeling sad and unsatisfied.

"He was essentially a man of habit."

* * * * *

The unobtrusive stranger ceased, and we sat gazing in silence at the ceiling.

At length my friend rose, and taking half-a-sovereign from his pocket, laid it upon the table, and linking his arm in mine went out with me upon the deck.

THE ABSENT-MINDED MAN

You ask him to dine with you on Thursday to meet a few people who are anxious to know him.

"Now don't make a muddle of it," you say, recollectful of former mishaps, "and come on the Wednesday."

He laughs good-naturedly as he hunts through the room for his diary.

"Shan't be able to come Wednesday," he says, "shall be at the Mansion House, sketching dresses, and on Friday I start for Scotland, so as to be at the opening of the Exhibition on Saturday. It's bound to be all right this time. Where the deuce is that diary! Never mind, I'll make a note of it on this—you can see me do it."

You stand over him while he writes the appointment down on a sheet of foolscap, and watch him pin it up over his desk. Then you come away contented.

"I do hope he'll turn up," you say to your wife on the Thursday evening, while dressing.

"Are you sure you made it clear to him?" she replies, suspiciously, and you instinctively feel that whatever happens she is going to blame you for it.

Eight o'clock arrives, and with it the other guests. At half-past eight your wife is beckoned mysteriously out of the room, where the parlour-maid informs her that the cook has expressed a determination, in case of further delay, to wash her hands, figuratively speaking, of the whole affair.

Your wife, returning, suggests that if the dinner is to be eaten at all it had better be begun. She evidently considers that in pretending to expect him you have been merely playing a part, and that it would have been manlier and more straightforward for you to have admitted at the beginning that you had forgotten to invite him.

During the soup and the fish you recount anecdotes of his unpunctuality. By the time the *entrée* arrives the empty chair has begun to cast a gloom over the dinner, and with the joint the conversation drifts into talk about dead relatives.

On Friday, at a quarter past eight, he dashes to the door and rings violently. Hearing his voice in the hall, you go to meet him.

"Sorry I'm late," he sings out cheerily. "Fool of a cabman took me to Alfred Place instead of—"

"Well, what do you want now you are come?" you interrupt, feeling anything but genially inclined towards him. He is an old friend, so you can be rude to him.

He laughs, and slaps you on the shoulder.

"Why, my dinner, my dear boy, I'm starving."

"Oh," you grunt in reply. "Well, you go and get it somewhere else, then. You're not going to have it here."

"What the devil do you mean?" he says. "You asked me to dinner."

"I did nothing of the kind," you tell him. "I asked you to dinner on Thursday, not on Friday."

He stares at you incredulously.

"How did I get Friday fixed in my mind?" inquiringly.

"Because yours is the sort of mind that would get Friday firmly fixed into it, when Thursday was the day," you explain. "I thought you had to be off to Edinburgh to-night," you add.

"Great Scott!" he cries, "so I have."

And without another word he dashes out, and you hear him rushing down the road, shouting for the cab he has just dismissed.

As you return to your study you reflect that he will have to travel all the way to Scotland in evening dress, and will have to send out the hotel porter in the morning to buy him a suit of ready-made clothes, and are glad.

Matters work out still more awkwardly when it is he who is the host. I remember being with him on his house-boat one day. It was a little after twelve, and we were sitting on the edge of the boat, dangling our feet in the river—the spot was a lonely one, half-way between Wallingford and Day's Lock. Suddenly round the bend appeared two skiffs, each one containing six elaborately-dressed persons. As soon as they caught sight of us they began waving handkerchiefs and parasols.

"Hullo!" I said, "here's some people hailing you."

"Oh, they all do that about here," he answered, without looking up. "Some beanfeast from Abingdon, I expect."

The boats draw nearer. When about two hundred yards off an elderly gentleman raised himself up in the prow of the leading one and shouted to us.

McQuae heard his voice, and gave a start that all but pitched him into the water.

"Good God!" he cried, "I'd forgotten all about it."

"About what?" I asked.

"Why, it's the Palmers and the Grahams and the Hendersons. I've asked them all over to lunch, and there's not a blessed thing on board but two mutton chops and a pound of potatoes, and I've given the boy a holiday."

Another day I was lunching with him at the Junior Hogarth, when a man named Hallyard, a mutual friend, strolled across to us.

"What are you fellows going to do this afternoon?" he asked, seating himself the opposite side of the table.

"I'm going to stop here and write letters," I answered.

"Come with me if you want something to do," said McQuae. "I'm going to drive Leena down to Richmond." ("Leena" was the young lady he recollected being engaged to. It transpired afterwards that he was engaged to three girls at the time. The other two he had forgotten all about.) "It's a roomy seat at the back."

"Oh, all right," said Hallyard, and they went away together in a hansom.

An hour and a half later Hallyard walked into the smoking-room looking depressed and worn, and flung himself into a chair.

"I thought you were going to Richmond with McQuae," I said.

"So did I," he answered.

"Had an accident?" I asked.

"Yes."

He was decidedly curt in his replies.

"Cart upset?" I continued.

"No, only me."

His grammar and his nerves seemed thoroughly shaken.

I waited for an explanation, and after a while he gave it.

"We got to Putney," he said, "with just an occasional run into a tram-car, and were going up the hill, when suddenly he turned a corner. You know his style at a corner—over the curb, across the road, and into the opposite lamp-post. Of course, as a rule one is prepared for it, but I never reckoned on his turning up there, and the first thing I recollect is finding myself sitting in the middle of the street with a dozen fools grinning at me.

"It takes a man a few minutes in such a case to think where he is and what has happened, and when I got up they were some distance away. I ran after them for a quarter of a mile, shouting at the top of my voice, and accompanied by a mob of boys, all yelling like hell on a Bank Holiday. But one might as well have tried to hail the dead, so I took the 'bus back.

"They might have guessed what had happened," he added, "by the shifting of the cart, if they'd had any sense. I'm not a light-weight."

He complained of soreness, and said he would go home. I suggested a cab, but he replied that he would rather walk.

I met McQuae in the evening at the St. James's Theatre. It was a first night, and he was taking sketches for *The Graphic*. The moment he saw me he made his way across to me.

"The very man I wanted to see," he said. "Did I take Hallyard with me in the cart to Richmond this afternoon?"

"You did," I replied.

"So Leena says," he answered, greatly bewildered, "but I'll swear he wasn't there when we got to the Queen's Hotel."

"It's all right," I said, "you dropped him at Putney."

"Dropped him at Putney!" he repeated. "I've no recollection of doing so."

"He has," I answered. "You ask him about it. He's full of it."

Everybody said he never would get married; that it was absurd to suppose he ever would remember the day, the church, and the girl, all in one morning; that if he did get as far as the altar he would forget what he had come for, and would give the bride away to his own best man. Hallyard had an idea that he was already married, but that the fact had slipped his memory. I myself felt sure that if he did marry he would forget all about it the next day.

But everybody was wrong. By some miraculous means the ceremony got itself accomplished, so that if Hallyard's idea be correct (as to which there is every possibility), there will be trouble. As for my own fears, I dismissed them the moment I saw the lady. She was a charming, cheerful little woman, but did not look the type that would let him forget all about it.

I had not seen him since his marriage, which had happened in the spring. Working my way back from Scotland by easy stages, I stopped for a few days at Scarboro'. After *table d'hôte* I put on my mackintosh, and went out for a walk. It was raining hard, but after a month in Scotland one does not notice English weather, and I wanted some air. Struggling along the dark beach with my head against the wind, I stumbled over a crouching figure, seeking to shelter itself a little from the storm under the lee of the Spa wall.

I expected it to swear at me, but it seemed too broken-spirited to mind anything.

"I beg your pardon," I said. "I did not see you."

At the sound of my voice it started to its feet.

"Is that you, old man?" it cried.

"McQuae!" I exclaimed.

"By Jove!" he said, "I was never so glad to see a man in all my life before."

And he nearly shook my hand off.

"But what in thunder!" I said, "are you doing here? Why, you're drenched to the skin."

He was dressed in flannels and a tennis-coat.

"Yes," he answered. "I never thought it would rain. It was a lovely morning."

I began to fear he had overworked himself into a brain fever.

"Why don't you go home?" I asked.

"I can't," he replied. "I don't know where I live. I've forgotten the address."

"For heaven's sake," he said, "take me somewhere, and give me something to eat. I'm literally starving."

"Haven't you any money?" I asked him, as we turned towards the hotel.

"Not a sou," he answered. "We got in here from York, the wife and I, about eleven. We left our things at the station, and started to hunt for apartments. As soon as we were fixed, I changed my clothes and came out for a walk, telling Maud I should be back at one to lunch. Like a fool, I never took the address, and never noticed the way I was going.

"It's an awful business," he continued. "I don't see how I'm ever going to find her. I hoped she might stroll down to the Spa in the evening, and I've been hanging about the gates ever since six. I hadn't the threepence to go in."

"But have you no notion of the sort of street or the kind of house it was?" I enquired.

"Not a ghost," he replied. "I left it all to Maud, and didn't trouble."

"Have you tried any of the lodging-houses?" I asked.

"Tried!" he exclaimed bitterly. "I've been knocking at doors, and asking if Mrs. McQuae lives there steadily all the afternoon, and they slam the door in my face, mostly without answering. I told a policeman—I thought perhaps he might suggest something—but the idiot only burst out laughing, and that made me so mad that I gave him a black eye, and had to cut. I expect they're on the lookout for me now."

"I went into a restaurant," he continued gloomily, "and tried to get them to trust me for a steak. But the proprietress said she'd heard that tale before, and ordered me out before all the other customers. I think I'd have drowned myself if you hadn't turned up."

After a change of clothes and some supper, he discussed the case more calmly, but it was really a serious affair. They had shut up their flat, and his wife's relatives were travelling abroad. There was no one to whom he could send a letter to be forwarded; there was no one with whom she would be likely to communicate. Their chance of meeting again in this world appeared remote.

Nor did it seem to me—fond as he was of his wife, and anxious as he undoubtedly was to recover her—that he looked forward to the actual meeting, should it ever arrive, with any too pleasurable anticipation.

"She will think it strange," he murmured reflectively, sitting on the edge of the bed, and thoughtfully pulling off his socks. "She is sure to think it strange."

The following day, which was Wednesday, we went to a solicitor, and laid the case before him, and he instituted inquiries among all the lodging-house keepers in Scarborough, with the result that on Thursday afternoon McQuae was restored (after the manner of an Adelphi hero in the last act) to his home and wife.

I asked him next time I met him what she had said.

"Oh, much what I expected," he replied.

But he never told me what he had expected.

A CHARMING WOMAN

"Not the Mr. ---, really?"

In her deep brown eyes there lurked pleased surprise, struggling with wonder. She looked from myself to the friend who introduced us with a bewitching smile of incredulity, tempered by hope.

He assured her, adding laughingly, "The only genuine and original," and left us.

"I've always thought of you as a staid, middle-aged man," she said, with a delicious little laugh, then added in low soft tones, "I'm so very pleased to meet you, really."

The words were conventional, but her voice crept round one like a warm caress.

"Come and talk to me," she said, seating herself upon a small settee, and making room for me.

I sat down awkwardly beside her, my head buzzing just a little, as with one glass too many of champagne. I was in my literary childhood. One small book and a few essays and criticisms, scattered through various obscure periodicals had been as yet my only contributions to current literature. The sudden discovery that I was the Mr. Anybody, and that charming women thought of me, and were delighted to meet me, was a brain-disturbing thought.

"And it was really you who wrote that clever book?" she continued, "and all those brilliant things, in the magazines and journals. Oh, it must be delightful to be clever."

She gave breath to a little sigh of vain regret that went to my heart. To console her I commenced a laboured compliment, but she stopped me with her fan. On after reflection I was glad she had—it would have been one of those things better expressed otherwise.

"I know what you are going to say," she laughed, "but don't. Besides, from you I should not know quite how to take it. You can be so satirical."

I tried to look as though I could be, but in her case would not.

She let her ungloved hand rest for an instant upon mine. Had she left it there for two, I should have gone down on my knees before her, or have stood on my head at her feet—have made a fool of myself in some way or another before the whole room full. She timed it to a nicety.

"I don't want *you* to pay me compliments," she said, "I want us to be friends. Of course, in years, I'm old enough to be your mother." (By the register I should say she might have been thirty-two, but looked twenty-six. I was twenty-three, and I fear foolish for my age.) "But you know the world, and you're so different to the other people one meets. Society is so hollow and artificial; don't you find it so? You don't know how I long sometimes to get away from it, to know someone to whom I could show my real self, who would understand me. You'll come and see me sometimes—I'm always at home on Wednesdays—and let me talk to you, won't you, and you must tell me all your clever thoughts."

It occurred to me that, maybe, she would like to hear a few of them there and then, but before I had got well started a hollow Society man came up and suggested supper, and she was compelled to leave me. As she disappeared, however, in the throng, she looked back over her shoulder with a glance half pathetic, half comic, that I understood. It said, "Pity me, I've got to be bored by this vapid, shallow creature," and I did.

I sought her through all the rooms before I went. I wished to assure her of my sympathy and support. I learned, however, from the butler that she had left early, in company with the hollow Society man.

A fortnight later I ran against a young literary friend in Regent Street, and we lunched together at the Monico.

"I met such a charming woman last night," he said, "a Mrs. Clifton Courtenay, a delightful woman."

"Oh, do *you* know her?" I exclaimed. "Oh, we're very old friends. She's always wanting me to go and see her. I really must."

"Oh, I didn't know *you* knew her," he answered. Somehow, the fact of my knowing her seemed to lessen her importance in his eyes. But soon he recovered his enthusiasm for her.

"A wonderfully clever woman," he continued. "I'm afraid I disappointed her a little though." He said this, however, with a laugh that contradicted his words. "She would not believe I was *the* Mr. Smith. She imagined from my book that I was quite an old man."

I could see nothing in my friend's book myself to suggest that the author was, of necessity, anything over eighteen. The mistake appeared to me to display want of acumen, but it had evidently pleased him greatly.

"I felt quite sorry for her," he went on, "chained to that bloodless, artificial society in which she lives. 'You can't tell,' she said to me, 'how I long to meet someone to whom I could show my real self—who would understand me.' I'm going to see her on Wednesday."

I went with him. My conversation with her was not as confidential as I had anticipated, owing to there being some eighty other people present in a room intended for the accommodation of eight; but after surging round for an hour in hot and aimless misery—as very young men at such gatherings do, knowing as a rule only the man who has brought them, and being unable to find him—I contrived to get a few words with her.

She greeted me with a smile, in the light of which I at once forgot my past discomfort, and let her fingers rest, with delicious pressure, for a moment upon mine.

"How good of you to keep your promise," she said. "These people have been tiring me so. Sit here, and tell me all you have been doing."

She listened for about ten seconds, and then interrupted me with—

"And that clever friend of yours that you came with. I met him at dear Lady Lennon's last week. Has *he* written anything?"

I explained to her that he had.

"Tell me about it?" she said. "I get so little time for reading, and then I only care to read the books that help me," and she gave me a grateful look more eloquent than words.

I described the work to her, and wishing to do my friend justice I even recited a few of the passages upon which, as I knew, he especially prided himself.

One sentence in particular seemed to lay hold of her. "A good woman's arms round a man's neck is a lifebelt thrown out to him from heaven."

"How beautiful!" she murmured. "Say it again."

I said it again, and she repeated it after me.

Then a noisy old lady swooped down upon her, and I drifted away into a corner, where I tried to look as if I were enjoying myself, and failed.

Later on, feeling it time to go, I sought my friend, and found him talking to her in a corner. I approached and waited. They were discussing the latest east-end murder. A drunken woman had been killed by her husband, a hard-working artizan, who had been maddened by the ruin of his home.

"Ah," she was saying, "what power a woman has to drag a man down or lift him up. I never read a case in which a woman is concerned without thinking of those beautiful lines of yours: 'A good woman's arms round a man's neck is a lifebelt thrown out to him from heaven.'"

* * * * *

Opinions differed concerning her religion and politics. Said the Low Church parson: "An earnest Christian woman, sir, of that unostentatious type that has always been the bulwark of our Church. I am proud to know that woman, and I am proud to think that poor words of mine have been the humble instrument to wean that true woman's heart from the frivolities of fashion, and to fix her thoughts upon higher things. A good Churchwoman, sir, a good Churchwoman, in the best sense of the word."

Said the pale aristocratic-looking young Abbé to the Comtesse, the light of old-world enthusiasm shining from his deep-set eyes: "I have great hopes for our dear friend. She finds it hard to sever the ties of time and love. We are all weak, but her heart turns towards our mother Church as a child, though suckled among strangers, yearns after many years for the bosom that has borne it. We have spoken, and I, even I, may be the voice in the wilderness leading the lost sheep back to the fold."

A CHARMING WOMAN

Said Sir Harry Bennett, the great Theosophist lecturer, writing to a friend: "A singularly gifted woman, and a woman evidently thirsting for the truth. A woman capable of willing her own life. A woman not afraid of thought and reason, a lover of wisdom. I have talked much with her at one time or another, and I have found her grasp my meaning with a quickness of perception quite unusual in my experience; and the arguments I have let fall, I am convinced, have borne excellent fruit. I look forward to her becoming, at no very distant date, a valued member of our little band. Indeed, without betraying confidence, I may almost say I regard her conversion as an accomplished fact."

Colonel Maxim always spoke of her as "a fair pillar of the State."

"With the enemy in our midst," said the florid old soldier, "it behoves every true man—aye, and every true woman—to rally to the defence of the country; and all honour, say I, to noble ladies such as Mrs. Clifton Courtenay, who, laying aside their natural shrinking from publicity, come forward in such a crisis as the present to combat the forces of disorder and disloyalty now rampant in the land."

"But," some listener would suggest, "I gathered from young Jocelyn that Mrs. Clifton Courtenay held somewhat advanced views on social and political questions."

"Jocelyn," the Colonel would reply with scorn; "pah! There may have been a short space of time during which the fellow's long hair and windy rhetoric impressed her. But I flatter myself I've put *my* spoke in Mr. Jocelyn's wheel. Why, damme, sir, she's consented to stand for Grand Dame of the Bermondsey Branch of the Primrose League next year. What's Jocelyn to say to that, the scoundrel!"

What Jocelyn said was:—

"I know the woman is weak. But I do not blame her; I pity her. When the time comes, as soon it will, when woman is no longer a puppet, dancing to the threads held by some brainless man—when a woman is not threatened with social ostracism for daring to follow her own conscience instead of that of her nearest male relative—then will be the time to judge her. It is not for me to betray the confidence reposed in me by a suffering woman, but you can tell that interesting old fossil, Colonel Maxim, that he and the other old women of the Bermondsey Branch of the Primrose League may elect Mrs. Clifton Courtenay for their President, and make the most of it; they have only got the outside of the woman. Her heart is beating time to the tramp of an onward-marching people; her soul's eyes are straining for the glory of a coming dawn."

But they all agreed she was a charming woman.

WHIBLEY'S SPIRIT

I never met it myself, but I knew Whibley very well indeed, so that I came to hear a goodish deal about it.

It appeared to be devoted to Whibley, and Whibley was extremely fond of it. Personally I am not interested in spirits, and no spirit has ever interested itself in me. But I have friends whom they patronise, and my mind is quite open on the subject. Of Whibley's Spirit I wish to speak with every possible respect. It was, I am willing to admit, as hard-working and conscientious a spirit as any one could wish to live with. The only thing I have to say against it is that it had no sense.

It came with a carved cabinet that Whibley had purchased in Wardour Street for old oak, but which, as a matter of fact, was chestnut wood, manufactured in Germany, and at first was harmless enough, saying nothing but "Yes!" or "No!" and that only when spoken to.

Whibley would amuse himself of an evening asking it questions, being careful to choose tolerably simple themes, such as, "Are you there?" (to which the Spirit would sometimes answer "Yes!" and sometimes "No!") "Can you hear me?" "Are you happy?"—and so on. The Spirit made the cabinet crack—three times for "Yes" and twice for "No." Now and then it would reply both "Yes!" and "No!" to the same question, which Whibley attributed to over-scrupulousness. When nobody asked it anything it would talk to itself, repeating "Yes!" "No!" "No!" "Yes!" over and over again in an aimless, lonesome sort of a way that made you feel sorry for it.

After a while Whibley bought a table, and encouraged it to launch out into more active conversation. To please Whibley, I assisted at some of the earlier séances, but during my presence it invariably maintained a reticence bordering on positive dulness. I gathered from Whibley that it disliked me, thinking that I was unsympathetic. The complaint was unjust; I was not unsympathetic, at least not at the commencement. I came to hear it talk, and I wanted to hear it talk; I would have listened to it by the hour. What tired me was its slowness in starting, and its foolishness when it had started, in using long words that it did not know how to spell. I remember on one occasion, Whibley, Jobstock (Whibley's partner), and myself, sitting for two hours, trying to understand what the thing meant by "H-e-s-t-u-r-n-e-m-y-s-f-e-a-r." It used no stops whatever. It never so much as hinted where one sentence ended and another began. It never even told us when it came to a proper name. Its idea of an evening's conversation was to plump down a hundred or so vowels and consonants in front of you and leave you to make whatever sense out of them you could.

We fancied at first it was talking about somebody named Hester (it had spelt Hester with a "u" before we allowed a margin for spelling), and we tried to work the sentence out on that basis, "Hester enemies fear," we thought it might be. Whibley had a niece named Hester, and we decided the warning had reference to her. But whether she was our enemy, and we were to fear her, or whether we had to fear her enemies (and, if so, who were they?), or whether it was our enemies who were to be frightened by Hester, or her enemies, or enemies generally, still remained doubtful. We asked the table if it meant the first suggestion, and it said "No." We asked what it did mean, and it said "Yes."

This answer annoyed me, but Whibley explained that the Spirit was angry with us for our stupidity (which seemed quaint).   He informed us that it always said first "No," and then "Yes," when it was angry, and as it was his Spirit, and we were in his house, we kept our feelings to ourselves and started afresh.

This time we abandoned the "Hestur" theory altogether. Jobstock suggested "Haste" for the first word, and, thought the Spirit might have gone on phoneti-cally.

"Haste! you are here, Miss Sfear!" was what he made of it.

Whibley asked him sarcastically if he'd kindly explain what that meant.

I think Jobstock was getting irritable. We had been sitting cramped up round a wretched little one-legged table all the evening, and this was almost the first bit of gossip we had got out of it. To further excuse him, it should also be explained that the gas had been put out by Whibley, and that the fire had gone out of its own accord. He replied that it was hard labour enough to find out what the thing said without having to make sense of it.

"It can't spell," he added, "and it's got a nasty, sulky temper. If it was my spirit I'd hire another spirit to kick it."

Whibley was one of the mildest little men I ever knew, but chaff or abuse of his Spirit roused the devil in him, and I feared we were going to have a scene. Fortunately, I was able to get his mind back to the consideration of "Hesturne-mysfear" before anything worse happened than a few muttered remarks about the laughter of fools, and want of reverence for sacred subjects being the sign of a shallow mind.

We tried "He's stern," and "His turn," and the "fear of Hesturnemy," and tried to think who "Hesturnemy" might be. Three times we went over the whole thing again from the beginning, which meant six hundred and six tiltings of the table, and then suddenly the explanation struck me—"Eastern Hemisphere."

Whibley had asked it for any information it might possess concerning his wife's uncle, from whom he had not heard for months, and that apparently was its idea of an address.

The fame of Whibley's Spirit became noised abroad, with the result that Whibley was able to command the willing service of more congenial assistants, and Jobstock and myself were dismissed. But we bore no malice.

Under these more favourable conditions the Spirit plucked up wonderfully, and talked everybody's head off. It could never have been a cheerful companion, however, for its conversation was chiefly confined to warnings and prognostications of evil. About once a fortnight Whibley would drop round on me, in a friendly way, to tell me that I was to beware of a man who lived in a street beginning with a "C," or to inform me that if I would go to a town on the coast where there were three churches I should meet someone who would do me an irreparable injury, and, that I did not rush off then and there in search of that town he regarded as flying in the face of Providence.

In its passion for poking its ghostly nose into other people's affairs it reminded me of my earthly friend Poppleton. Nothing pleased it better than being appealed to for aid and advice, and Whibley, who was a perfect slave to it, would hunt half over the parish for people in trouble and bring them to it.

It would direct ladies, eager for divorce court evidence, to go to the third house from the corner of the fifth street, past such and such a church or public-house (it never would give a plain, straightforward address), and ring the bottom bell but one twice. They would thank it effusively, and next morning would start to find the fifth street past the church, and would ring the bottom bell but one of the third house from the corner twice, and a man in his shirt sleeves would come to the door and ask them what they wanted.

They could not tell what they wanted, they did not know themselves, and the man would use bad language, and slam the door in their faces.

Then they would think that perhaps the Spirit meant the fifth street the other way, or the third house from the opposite corner, and would try again, with still more unpleasant results.

One July I met Whibley, mooning disconsolately along Princes Street, Edinburgh.

"Hullo!" I exclaimed, "what are you doing here? I thought you were busy over that School Board case."

"Yes," he answered, "I ought really to be in London, but the truth is I'm rather expecting something to happen down here."

"Oh!" I said, "and what's that?"

"Well," he replied hesitatingly, as though he would rather not talk about it, "I don't exactly know yet."

"You've come from London to Edinburgh, and don't know what you've come for!" I cried.

"Well, you see," he said, still more reluctantly, as it seemed to me, "it was Maria's idea; she wished—"

"Maria!" I interrupted, looking perhaps a little sternly at him, "who's Maria?" (His wife's name I knew was Emily Georgina Anne.)

"Oh! I forgot," he explained; "she never would tell her name before you, would she? It's the Spirit, you know."

"Oh! that," I said, "it's she that has sent you here. Didn't she tell you what for?"

"No," he answered, "that's what worries me. All she would say was, 'Go to Edinburgh—something will happen.'"

"And how long are you going to remain here?" I inquired.

"I don't know," he replied. "I've been here a week already, and Jobstock writes quite angrily. I wouldn't have come if Maria hadn't been so urgent. She repeated it three evenings running."

I hardly knew what to do. The little man was so dreadfully in earnest about the business that one could not argue much with him.

"You are sure," I said, after thinking a while, "that this Maria is a good Spirit? There are all sorts going about, I'm told. You're sure this isn't the spirit of some deceased lunatic, playing the fool with you?"

"I've thought of that," he admitted. "Of course that might be so. If nothing happens soon I shall almost begin to suspect it."

"Well, I should certainly make some inquiries into its character before I trusted it any further," I answered, and left him.

About a month later I ran against him outside the Law Courts.

"It was all right about Maria; something did happen in Edinburgh while I was there. That very morning I met you one of my oldest clients died quite suddenly at his house at Queensferry, only a few miles outside the city."

"I'm glad of that," I answered, "I mean, of course, for Maria's sake. It was lucky you went then."

"Well, not altogether," he replied, "at least, not in a worldly sense. He left his affairs in a very complicated state, and his eldest son went straight up to London to consult me about them, and, not finding me there, and time being important, went to Kebble. I was rather disappointed when I got back and heard about it."

"Umph!" I said; "she's not a smart spirit, anyway."

"No," he answered, "perhaps not. But, you see, something did really happen."

After that his affection for "Maria" increased tenfold, while her attachment to himself became a burden to his friends. She grew too big for her table, and, dispensing with all mechanical intermediaries, talked to him direct. She followed him everywhere. Mary's lamb couldn't have been a bigger nuisance. She would even go with him into the bedroom, and carry on long conversations with him in the middle of the night. His wife objected; she said it seemed hardly decent, but there was no keeping her out.

She turned up with him at picnics and Christmas parties. Nobody heard her speak to him, but it seemed necessary for him to reply to her aloud, and to see him suddenly get up from his chair and slip away to talk earnestly to nothing in a corner disturbed the festivities.

"I should really be glad," he once confessed to me, "to get a little time to myself. She means kindly, but it *is* a strain. And then the others don't like it. It makes them nervous. I can see it does."

One evening she caused quite a scene at the club. Whibley had been playing whist, with the Major for a partner. At the end of the game the Major, leaning across the table toward him, asked, in a tone of deadly calm, "May I inquire, sir, whether there was any earthly reason" (he emphasised "earthly") "for your following my lead of spades with your only trump?"

"I—I—am very sorry, Major," replied Whibley apologetically. "I—I—somehow felt I—I ought to play that queen."

"Entirely your own inspiration, or suggested?" persisted the Major, who had, of course, heard of "Maria."

Whibley admitted the play had been suggested to him. The Major rose from the table.

"Then, sir," said he, with concentrated indignation, "I decline to continue this game. A human fool I can tolerate for a partner, but if I am to be hampered by a damned spirit—"

"You've no right to say that," cried Whibley hotly.

"I apologise," returned the Major coldly; "we will say a blessed spirit. I decline to play whist with spirits of any kind; and I advise you, sir, if you intend giving many exhibitions with the lady, first to teach her the rudiments of the game."

Saying which the Major put on his hat and left the club, and I made Whibley drink a stiff glass of brandy and water, and sent him and "Maria" home in a cab.

Whibley got rid of "Maria" at last. It cost him in round figures about eight thousand pounds, but his family said it was worth it.

A Spanish Count hired a furnished house a few doors from Whibley's, and one evening he was introduced to Whibley, and came home and had a chat with him. Whibley told him about "Maria," and the Count quite fell in love with her. He said that if only he had had such a spirit to help and advise him, it might have altered his whole life.

He was the first man who had ever said a kind word about the spirit, and Whibley loved him for it. The Count seemed as though he could never see enough of Whibley after that evening, and the three of them—Whibley, the Count, and "Maria"—would sit up half the night talking together.

The precise particulars I never heard. Whibley was always very reticent on the matter. Whether "Maria" really did exist, and the Count deliberately set to work to bamboozle her (she was fool enough for anything), or whether she was a mere hallucination of Whibley's, and the man tricked Whibley by "hypnotic suggestions" (as I believe it is called), I am not prepared to say. The only thing certain is that "Maria" convinced Whibley that the Count had discovered a secret gold mine in Peru. She said she knew all about it, and counselled Whibley to beg the Count to let him put a few thousands into the working of it. "Maria," it appeared, had known the Count from his boyhood, and could answer for it that he was the most honourable man in all South America. Possibly enough he was.

The Count was astonished to find that Whibley knew all about his mine. Eight thousand pounds was needed to start the workings, but he had not mentioned it to any one, as he wanted to keep the whole thing to himself, and thought he could save the money on his estates in Portugal. However, to oblige "Maria," he would let Whibley supply the money. Whibley supplied it—in cash, and no one has ever seen the Count since.

That broke up Whibley's faith in "Maria," and a sensible doctor, getting hold of him threatened to prescribe a lunatic asylum for him if ever he found him carrying on with any spirits again. That completed the cure.

THE MAN WHO WENT WRONG

I first met Jack Burridge nearly ten years ago on a certain North-country race-course.

The saddling bell had just rung for the chief event of the day. I was sauntering along with my hands in my pockets, more interested in the crowd than in the race, when a sporting friend, crossing on his way to the paddock, seized me by the arm and whispered hoarsely in my ear:—

"Put your shirt on Mrs. Waller."

"Put my -?" I began.

"Put your shirt on Mrs. Waller," he repeated still more impressively, and disappeared in the throng.

I stared after him in blank amazement. Why should I put my shirt on Mrs. Waller? Even if it would fit a lady. And how about myself?

I was passing the grand stand, and, glancing up, I saw "Mrs. Waller, twelve to one," chalked on a bookmaker's board. Then it dawned upon me that "Mrs. Waller" was a horse, and, thinking further upon the matter, I evolved the idea that my friend's advice, expressed in more becoming language, was "Back 'Mrs. Waller' for as much as you can possibly afford."

"Thank you," I said to myself, "I have backed cast-iron certainties before. Next time I bet upon a horse I shall make the selection by shutting my eyes and putting a pin through the card."

But the seed had taken root. My friend's words surged in my brain. The birds passing overhead twittered, "Put your shirt on 'Mrs. Waller.'"

I reasoned with myself. I reminded myself of my few former ventures. But the craving to put, if not my shirt, at all events half a sovereign on "Mrs. Waller" only grew the stronger the more strongly I battled against it. I felt that if "Mrs. Waller" won and I had nothing on her, I should reproach myself to my dying day.

I was on the other side of the course. There was no time to get back to the enclosure. The horses were already forming for the start. A few yards off, under a white umbrella, an outside bookmaker was shouting his final prices in stentorian tones. He was a big, genial-looking man, with an honest red face.

"What price 'Mrs. Waller'?" I asked him.

"Fourteen to one," he answered, "and good luck to you."

I handed him half a sovereign, and he wrote me out a ticket. I crammed it into my waistcoat pocket, and hurried off to see the race. To my intense astonishment "Mrs. Waller" won. The novel sensation of having backed the winner so excited me that I forgot all about my money, and it was not until a good hour afterwards that I recollected my bet.

Then I started off to search for the man under the white umbrella. I went to where I thought I had left him, but no white umbrella could I find.

Consoling myself with the reflection that my loss served me right for having been fool enough to trust an outside "bookie," I turned on my heel and began to make my way back to my seat. Suddenly a voice hailed me:—

"Here you are, sir. It's Jack Burridge you want. Over here, sir."

I looked round, and there was Jack Burridge at my elbow.

"I saw you looking about, sir," he said, "but I could not make you hear. You was looking the wrong side of the tent."

It was pleasant to find that his honest face had not belied him.

"It is very good of you," I said; "I had given up all hopes of seeing you. Or," I added with a smile, "my seven pounds."

"Seven pun' ten," he corrected me; "you're forgetting your own thin 'un."

He handed me the money and went back to his stand.

On my way into the town I came across him again. A small crowd was collected, thoughtfully watching a tramp knocking about a miserable-looking woman.

Jack, pushing to the front, took in the scene and took off his coat in the same instant.

"Now then, my fine old English gentleman," he sang out, "come and have a try at me for a change."

The tramp was a burly ruffian, and I have seen better boxers than Jack. He got himself a black eye, and a nasty cut over the lip, before he hardly knew where he was. But in spite of that—and a good deal more—he stuck to his man and finished him.

At the end, as he helped his adversary up, I heard him say to the fellow in a kindly whisper:—

"You're too good a sort, you know, to whollop a woman. Why, you very near give me a licking. You must have forgot yourself, matey."

The fellow interested me. I waited and walked on with him. He told me about his home in London, at Mile End—about his old father and mother, his little brothers and sisters—and what he was saving up to do for them. Kindliness oozed from every pore in his skin.

Many that we met knew him, and all, when they saw his round, red face, smiled unconsciously. At the corner of the High Street a pale-faced little drudge of a girl passed us, saying as she slipped by "Good-evening, Mr. Burridge."

He made a dart and caught her by the shoulder.

"And how is father?" he asked.

"Oh, if you please, Mr. Burridge, he is out again. All the mills is closed," answered the child.

"And mother?"

"She don't get no better, sir."

"And who's keeping you all?"

"Oh, if you please, sir, Jimmy's earning something now," replied the mite.

He took a couple of sovereigns from his waistcoat pocket, and closed the child's hand upon them.

"That's all right, my lass, that's all right," he said, stopping her stammering thanks. "You write to me if things don't get better. You know where to find Jack Burridge."

Strolling about the streets in the evening, I happened to pass the inn where he was staying. The parlour window was open, and out into the misty night his deep, cheery voice, trolling forth an old-fashioned drinking song, came rolling like a wind, cleansing the corners of one's heart with its breezy humanness. He was sitting at the head of the table surrounded by a crowd of jovial cronies. I lingered for a while watching the scene. It made the world appear a less sombre dwelling-place than I had sometimes pictured it.

I determined, on my return to London, to look him up, and accordingly one evening started to find the little by-street off the Mile End Road in which he lived. As I turned the corner he drove up in his dog-cart; it was a smart turn-out. On the seat beside him sat a neat, withered little old woman, whom he introduced to me as his mother.

"I tell 'im it's a fine gell as 'e oughter 'ave up 'ere aside 'im," said the old lady, preparing to dismount, "an old woman like me takes all the paint off the show."

"Get along with yer," he replied laughingly, jumping down and handing the reins to the lad who had been waiting, "you could give some of the young uns points yet, mother. I allus promised the old lady as she should ride behind her own 'oss one day," he continued, turning to me, "didn't I, mother?"

"Ay, ay," replied the old soul, as she hobbled nimbly up the steps, "ye're a good son, Jack, ye're a good son."

He led the way into the parlour. As he entered every face lightened up with pleasure, a harmony of joyous welcome greeted him. The old hard world had been shut out with the slam of the front door. I seemed to have wandered into Dickensland. The red-faced man with the small twinkling eyes and the lungs of leather loomed before me, a large, fat household fairy. From his capacious pockets came forth tobacco for the old father; a huge bunch of hot-house grapes for a neighbour's sickly child, who was stopping with them; a book of Henty's— beloved of boys—for a noisy youngster who called him "uncle"; a bottle of port wine for a wan, elderly woman with a swollen face—his widowed sister-in-law, as I subsequently learned; sweets enough for the baby (whose baby I don't know) to make it sick for a week; and a roll of music for his youngest sister.

"We're a-going to make a lady of her," he said, drawing the child's shy face against his gaudy waistcoat, and running his coarse hand through her pretty curls; "and she shall marry a jockey when she grows up."

After supper he brewed some excellent whisky punch, and insisted upon the old lady joining us, which she eventually did with much coughing and protestation; but I noticed that she finished the tumblerful. For the children he concocted a marvellous mixture, which he called an "eye-composer," the chief ingredients being hot lemonade, ginger wine, sugar, oranges, and raspberry vinegar. It had the desired effect.

I stayed till late, listening to his inexhaustible fund of stories. Over most of them he laughed with us himself—a great gusty laugh that made the cheap glass ornaments upon the mantelpiece to tremble; but now and then a recollection came to him that spread a sudden gravity across his jovial face, bringing a curious quaver into his deep voice.

Their tongues a little loosened by the punch, the old folks would have sung his praises to the verge of tediousness had he not almost sternly interrupted them.

"Shut up, mother," he cried at last, quite gruffly, "what I does I does to please myself. I likes to see people comfortable about me. If they wasn't, it's me as would be more upset than them."

I did not see him again for nearly two years. Then one October evening, strolling about the East End, I met him coming out of a little Chapel in the Burdett Road. He was so changed that I should not have known him had not I overheard a woman as she passed him say, "Good-evening, Mr. Burridge."

A pair of bushy side-whiskers had given to his red face an aggressively respectable appearance. He was dressed in an ill-fitting suit of black, and carried an umbrella in one hand and a book in the other.

In some mysterious way he managed to look both thinner and shorter than my recollection of him. Altogether, he suggested to me the idea that he himself—the real man—had by some means or other been extracted, leaving only his shrunken husk behind. The genial juices of humanity had been squeezed out of him.

"Not Jack Burridge!" I exclaimed, confronting him in astonishment.

His little eyes wandered shiftily up and down the street. "No, sir," he replied (his tones had lost their windy boisterousness—a hard, metallic voice spoke to me), "not the one as you used to know, praise be the Lord."

"And have you given up the old business?" I asked.

"Yes, sir," he replied, "that's all over; I've been a vile sinner in my time, God forgive me for it. But, thank Heaven, I have repented in time."

"Come and have a drink," I said, slipping my arm through his, "and tell me all about it."

He disengaged himself from me, firmly but gently. "You mean well, sir," he said, "but I have given up the drink."

Evidently he would have been rid of me, but a literary man, scenting material for his stockpot, is not easily shaken off. I asked after the old folks, and if they were still stopping with him.

"Yes," he said, "for the present. Of course, a man can't be expected to keep people for ever; so many mouths to fill is hard work these times, and everybody sponges on a man just because he's good-natured."

"And how are you getting on?" I asked.

"Tolerably well, thank you, sir. The Lord provides for His servants," he replied with a smug smile. "I have got a little shop now in the Commercial Road."

"Whereabouts?" I persisted. "I would like to call and see you."

He gave me the address reluctantly, and said he would esteem it a great pleasure if I would honour him by a visit, which was a palpable lie.

The following afternoon I went. I found the place to be a pawnbroker's shop, and from all appearances he must have been doing a very brisk business. He was out himself attending a temperance committee, but his old father was behind the counter, and asked me inside. Though it was a chilly day there was no fire in the parlour, and the two old folks sat one each side of the empty hearth, silent and sad. They seemed little more pleased to see me than their son, but after a while Mrs. Burridge's natural garrulity asserted itself, and we fell into chat.

I asked what had become of his sister-in-law, the lady with the swollen face.

"I couldn't rightly tell you, sir," answered the old lady, "she ain't livin' with us now. You see, sir," she continued, "John's got different notions to what 'e used to 'ave. 'E don't cotten much to them as ain't found grace, and poor Jane never did 'ave much religion!"

"And the little one?" I inquired. "The one with the curls?"

"What, Bessie, sir?" said the old lady. "Oh, she's out at service, sir; John don't think it good for young folks to be idle."

"Your son seems to have changed a good deal, Mrs. Burridge," I remarked.

"Ay, sir," she assented, "you may well say that. It nearly broke my 'art at fust; everythin' so different to what it 'ad been. Not as I'd stand in the boy's light. If our being a bit uncomfortable like in this world is a-going to do 'im any good in the next me and father ain't the ones to begrudge it, are we, old man?"

The "old man" concurred grumpily.

"Was it a sudden conversion?" I asked. "How did it come about?"

"It was a young woman as started 'im off," explained the old lady. "She come round to our place one day a-collectin' for somethin' or other, and Jack, in 'is free-'anded way, 'e give 'er a five-pun' note. Next week she come agen for somethin' else, and stopped and talked to 'im about 'is soul in the passage. She told 'im as 'e was a-goin' straight to 'ell, and that 'e oughter give up the book-makin' and settle down to a respec'ble, God-fearin' business. At fust 'e only laughed, but she lammed in tracts at 'im full of the most awful language; and one day she fetched 'im round to one of them revivalist chaps, as fair settled 'im.

"'E ain't never been his old self since then. 'E give up the bettin' and bought this 'ere, though what's the difference blessed if I can see. It makes my 'eart ache, it do, to 'ear my Jack a-beatin' down the poor people—and it ain't like 'im. It went agen 'is grain at fust, I could see; but they told him as 'ow it was folks's own fault that they was poor, and as 'ow it was the will of God, because they was a drinkin', improvident lot.

"Then they made 'im sign the pledge. 'E'd allus been used to 'is glass, Jack 'ad, and I think as knockin' it off 'ave soured 'im a bit—seems as if all the sperit 'ad gone out of 'im—and of course me and father 'ave 'ad to give up our little drop too. Then they told 'im as 'e must give up smokin'- that was another way of goin' straight to 'ell—and that ain't made 'im any the more cheerful like, and father misses 'is little bit—don't ye, father?"

"Ay," answered the old fellow savagely; "can't say I thinks much of these 'ere folks as is going to heaven; blowed if I don't think they'll be a chirpier lot in t'other place."

An angry discussion in the shop interrupted us. Jack had returned, and was threatening an excited woman with the police. It seemed she had miscalculated the date, and had come a day too late with her interest.

Having got rid of her, he came into the parlour with the watch in his hand.

"It's providential she was late," he said, looking at it; "it's worth ten times what I lent on it."

He packed his father back into the shop, and his mother down into the kitchen to get his tea, and for a while we sat together talking.

I found his conversation a strange mixture of self-laudation, showing through a flimsy veil of self-disparagement, and of satisfaction at the conviction that he was "saved," combined with equally evident satisfaction that most other people weren't—somewhat trying, however; and, remembering an appointment, rose to go.

He made no effort to stay me, but I could see that he was bursting to tell me something. At last, taking a religious paper from his pocket, and pointing to a column, he blurted out:

"You don't take any interest in the Lord's vineyard, I suppose, sir?"

I glanced at the part of the paper indicated. It announced a new mission to the Chinese, and heading the subscription list stood the name, "Mr. John Burridge, one hundred guineas."

"You subscribe largely, Mr. Burridge," I said, handing him back the paper.

He rubbed his big hands together. "The Lord will repay a hundredfold," he answered.

"In which case it's just as well to have a note of the advance down in black and white, eh?" I added.

His little eyes looked sharply at me; but he made no reply, and, shaking hands, I left him.

THE HOBBY RIDER

Bump. Bump. Bump-bump. Bump.

I sat up in bed and listened intently. It seemed to me as if someone with a muffled hammer were trying to knock bricks out of the wall.

"Burglars," I said to myself (one assumes, as a matter of course, that everything happening in this world after 1 a.m. is due to burglars), and I reflected what a curiously literal, but at the same time slow and cumbersome, method of house-breaking they had adopted.

The bumping continued irregularly, yet uninterruptedly.

My bed was by the window. I reached out my hand and drew aside a corner of the curtain. The sunlight streamed into the room. I looked at my watch: it was ten minutes past five.

A most unbusinesslike hour for burglars, I thought. Why, it will be breakfast-time before they get in.

Suddenly there came a crash, and some substance striking against the blind fell upon the floor. I sprang out of bed and threw open the window.

A red-haired young gentleman, scantily clad in a sweater and a pair of flannel trousers, stood on the lawn below me.

"Good morning," he said cheerily. "Do you mind throwing me back my ball?"

"What ball?" I said.

"My tennis ball," he answered. "It must be somewhere in the room; it went clean through the window."

I found the ball and threw it back to him,

"What are you doing?" I asked. "Playing tennis?"

"No," he said. "I am just practising against the side of the house. It improves your game wonderfully."

"It don't improve my night's rest," I answered somewhat surlily I fear. "I came down here for peace and quiet. Can't you do it in the daytime?"

"Daytime!" he laughed. "Why it has been daytime for the last two hours. Never mind, I'll go round the other side."

He disappeared round the corner, and set to work at the back, where he woke up the dog. I heard another window smash, followed by a sound as of somebody getting up violently in a distant part of the house, and shortly afterwards I must have fallen asleep again.

I had come to spend a few weeks at a boarding establishment in Deal. He was the only other young man in the house, and I was naturally thrown a good deal upon his society. He was a pleasant, genial young fellow, but he would have been better company had he been a little less enthusiastic as regards tennis.

He played tennis ten hours a day on the average. He got up romantic parties to play it by moonlight (when half his time was generally taken up in separating his opponents), and godless parties to play it on Sundays. On wet days I have seen him practising services by himself in a mackintosh and goloshes.

He had been spending the winter with his people at Tangiers, and I asked him how he liked the place.

"Oh, a beast of a hole!" he replied.   "There is not a court anywhere in the town. We tried playing on the roof, but the *mater* thought it dangerous."

Switzerland he had been delighted with. He counselled me next time I went to stay at Zermatt.

"There is a capital court at Zermatt," he said. "You might almost fancy your-self at Wimbledon."

A mutual acquaintance whom I subsequently met told me that at the top of the Jungfrau he had said to him, his eyes fixed the while upon a small snow plateau enclosed by precipices a few hundred feet below them—

"By Jove! That wouldn't make half a bad little tennis court—that flat bit down there. Have to be careful you didn't run back too far."

When he was not playing tennis, or practising tennis, or reading about tennis, he was talking about tennis. Renshaw was the prominent figure in the tennis world at that time, and he mentioned Renshaw until there grew up within my soul a dark desire to kill Renshaw in a quiet, unostentatious way, and bury him.

One drenching afternoon he talked tennis to me for three hours on end, refer-ring to Renshaw, so far as I kept count, four thousand nine hundred and thirteen times. After tea he drew his chair to the window beside me, and commenced—

"Have you ever noticed how Renshaw—"

I said—

"Suppose someone took a gun—someone who could aim very straight—and went out and shot Renshaw till he was quite dead, would you tennis players drop him and talk about somebody else?"

"Oh, but who would shoot Renshaw?" he said indignantly.

"Never mind," I said, "supposing someone did?"

"Well, then, there would be his brother," he replied.

I had forgotten that.

"Well, we won't argue about how many of them there are," I said. "Suppose someone killed the lot, should we hear less of Renshaw?"

"Never," he replied emphatically.   "Renshaw will always be a name wherever tennis is spoken of."

I dread to think what the result might have been had his answer been other than it was.

The next year he dropped tennis completely and became an ardent amateur photographer, whereupon all his friends implored him to return to tennis, and sought to interest him in talk about services and returns and volleys, and in anecdotes concerning Renshaw. But he would not heed them.

Whatever he saw, wherever he went, he took. He took his friends, and made them his enemies. He took babies, and brought despair to fond mothers' hearts. He took young wives, and cast a shadow on the home. Once there was a young man who loved not wisely, so his friends thought, but the more they talked against her the more he clung to her. Then a happy idea occurred to the father. He got Begglely to photograph her in seven different positions.

When her lover saw the first, he said—

"What an awful looking thing! Who did it?"

When Begglely showed him the second, he said—

"But, my dear fellow, it's not a bit like her. You've made her look an ugly old woman."

At the third he said—

"Whatever have you done to her feet? They can't be that size, you know. It isn't in nature!"

At the fourth he exclaimed—

"But, heavens, man! Look at the shape you've made her. Where on earth did you get the idea from?"

At the first glimpse of the fifth he staggered.

"Great Scott!" he cried with a shudder, "what a ghastly expression you've got into it! It isn't human!"

Begglely was growing offended, but the father, who was standing by, came to his defence.

"It's nothing to do with Begglely," exclaimed the old gentleman suavely. "It can't be *his* fault. What is a photographer? Simply an instrument in the hands of science. He arranges his apparatus, and whatever is in front of it comes into it."

"No," continued the old gentleman, laying a constrained hand upon Begglely, who was about to resume the exhibition, "don't—don't show him the other two."

I was sorry for the poor girl, for I believe she really cared for the youngster; and as for her looks, they were quite up to the average. But some evil sprite seemed to have got into Begglely's camera. It seized upon defects with the unerring instinct of a born critic, and dilated upon them to the obscuration of all virtues. A man with a pimple became a pimple with a man as background. People with strongly marked features became merely adjuncts to their own noses. One man in the neighbourhood had, undetected, worn a wig for fourteen years. Begglely's camera discovered the fraud in an instant, and so completely exposed it that the man's friends wondered afterwards how the fact ever could have escaped them. The thing seemed to take a pleasure in showing humanity at its very worst. Babies usually came out with an expression of low cunning. Most young girls had to take their choice of appearing either as simpering idiots or embryo vixens. To mild old ladies it generally gave a look of aggressive cynicism. Our vicar, as excellent an old gentleman as ever breathed, Begglely presented to us as a beetle-browed savage of a peculiarly low type of intellect; while upon the lead-ing solicitor of the town he bestowed an expression of such thinly-veiled hypocrisy that few who saw the photograph cared ever again to trust him with their affairs.

As regards myself I should, perhaps, make no comment, I am possibly a prej-udiced party. All I will say, therefore, is that if I in any way resemble Begglely's photograph of me, then the critics are fully justified in everything they have at any time, anywhere, said of me—and more. Nor, I maintain—though I make no pretence of possessing the figure of Apollo—is one of my legs twice the length of the other, and neither does it curve upwards. This I can prove. Begglely al-lowed that an accident had occurred to the negative during the process of development, but this explanation does not appear on the picture, and I cannot help feeling that an injustice has been done me.

His perspective seemed to be governed by no law either human or divine. I have seen a photograph of his uncle and a windmill, judging from which I defy any unprejudiced person to say which is the bigger, the uncle or the mill.

On one occasion he created quite a scandal in the parish by exhibiting a well-known and eminently respectable maiden lady nursing a young man on her knee. The gentleman's face was indistinct, and he was dressed in a costume which, up-on a man of his size—one would have estimated him as rising 6 ft. 4 in.—appeared absurdly juvenile. He had one arm round her neck, and she was hold-ing his other hand and smirking.

I, knowing something of Begglely's machine, willingly accepted the lady's explanation, which was to the effect that the male in question was her nephew, aged eleven; but the uncharitable ridiculed this statement, and appearances were certainly against her.

It was in the early days of the photographic craze, and an inexperienced world was rather pleased with the idea of being taken on the cheap. The consequence was that nearly everyone for three miles round sat or stood or leant or laid to Begglely at one time or another, with the result that a less conceited parish than ours it would have been difficult to discover. No one who had once looked upon a photograph of himself taken by Begglely ever again felt any pride in his per-sonal appearance. The picture was invariably a revelation to him.

Later, some evil-disposed person invented Kodaks, and Begglely went every-where slung on to a thing that looked like an overgrown missionary box, and that bore a legend to the effect that if Begglely would pull the button, a shameless Company would do the rest. Life became a misery to Begglely's friends. No-body dared to do anything for fear of being taken in the act. He took an instantaneous photograph of his own father swearing at the gardener, and snapped his youngest sister and her lover at the exact moment of farewell at the garden gate. Nothing was sacred to him. He Kodaked his aunt's funeral from behind, and showed the chief mourner but one whispering a funny story into the ear of the third cousin as they stood behind their hats beside the grave.

Public indignation was at its highest when a new comer to the neighbourhood, a young fellow named Haynoth, suggested the getting together of a party for a summer's tour in Turkey. Everybody took up the idea with enthusiasm, and recommended Begglely as the "party." We had great hopes from that tour. Our idea was that Begglely would pull his button outside a harem or behind a sultana, and that a Bashi Bazouk or a Janissary would do the rest for us.

We were, however, partly doomed to disappointment—I say, "partly," because, although Begglely returned alive, he came back entirely cured of his photographic craze. He said that every English-speaking man, woman, or child whom he met abroad had its camera with it, and that after a time the sight of a black cloth or the click of a button began to madden him.

He told us that on the summit of Mount Tutra, in the Carpathians, the English and American amateur photographers waiting to take "the grand panorama" were formed by the Hungarian police in queue, two abreast, each with his or her camera under his or her arm, and that a man had to stand sometimes as long as three and a half hours before his turn came round. He also told us that the beggars in Constantinople went about with placards hung round their necks, stating their charges for being photographed. One of these price lists he brought back with him as a sample.

It ran:—

One snap shot, back or front ..   .. 2 frcs.
     ,,   with expression   ...   ... 3 ,,
     ,,   surprised in quaint attitude . 4 ,,
     ,,   while saying prayers ...   ... 5 ,,
     ,,   while fighting   ...   ... 10 ,,

He said that in some instances where a man had an exceptionally villainous cast of countenance, or was exceptionally deformed, as much as twenty francs were demanded and readily obtained.

He abandoned photography and took to golf. He showed people how, by digging a hole here and putting a brickbat or two there, they could convert a tennis-lawn into a miniature golf link,—and did it for them. He persuaded elderly ladies and gentlemen that it was the mildest exercise going, and would drag them for miles over wet gorse and heather, and bring them home dead beat, coughing, and full of evil thoughts.

The last time I saw him was in Switzerland, a few months ago. He appeared indifferent to the subject of golf, but talked much about whist. We met by chance at Grindelwald, and agreed to climb the Faulhorn together next morning. Half-way up we rested, and I strolled on a little way by myself to gain a view. Returning, I found him with a "Cavendish" in his hand and a pack of cards spread out before him on the grass, solving a problem.

THE MAN WHO DID NOT BELIEVE IN LUCK

He got in at Ipswich with seven different weekly papers under his arm. I noticed that each one insured its reader against death or injury by railway accident. He arranged his luggage upon the rack above him, took off his hat and laid it on the seat beside him, mopped his bald head with a red silk handkerchief, and then set to work steadily to write his name and address upon each of the seven papers. I sat opposite to him and read *Punch*. I always take the old humour when travelling; I find it soothing to the nerves.

Passing over the points at Manningtree the train gave a lurch, and a horse-shoe he had carefully placed in the rack above him slipped through the netting, falling with a musical ring upon his head.

He appeared neither surprised nor angry. Having staunched the wound with his handkerchief, he stooped and picked the horse-shoe up, glanced at it with, as I thought, an expression of reproach, and dropped it gently out of the window.

"Did it hurt you?" I asked.

It was a foolish question. I told myself so the moment I had uttered it. The thing must have weighed three pounds at the least; it was an exceptionally large and heavy shoe. The bump on his head was swelling visibly before my eyes. Anyone but an idiot must have seen that he was hurt. I expected an irritable reply. I should have given one myself had I been in his place. Instead, however, he seemed to regard the inquiry as a natural and kindly expression of sympathy.

"It did, a little," he replied.

"What were you doing with it?" I asked. It was an odd sort of thing for a man to be travelling with.

"It was lying in the roadway just outside the station," he explained; "I picked it up for luck."

He refolded his handkerchief so as to bring a cooler surface in contact with the swelling, while I murmured something genial about the inscrutability of Providence.

"Yes," he said, "I've had a deal of luck in my time, but it's never turned out well."

"I was born on a Wednesday," he continued, "which, as I daresay you know, is the luckiest day a man can be born on. My mother was a widow, and none of my relatives would do anything for me. They said it would be like taking coals to Newcastle, helping a boy born on a Wednesday; and my uncle, when he died, left every penny of his money to my brother Sam, as a slight compensation to him for having been born on a Friday. All I ever got was advice upon the duties and responsibilities of wealth, when it arrived, and entreaties that I would not neglect those with claims upon me when I came to be a rich man."

He paused while folding up his various insurance papers and placing them in the inside breast-pocket of his coat.

"Then there are black cats," he went on; "they're said to be lucky. Why, there never was a blacker cat than the one that followed me into my rooms in Bolsover Street the very first night I took them."

"Didn't it bring you luck?" I enquired, finding that he had stopped.

A far-away look came into his eyes.

"Well, of course it all depends," he answered dreamily. "Maybe we'd never have suited one another; you can always look at it that way. Still, I'd like to have tried."

He sat staring out of the window, and for a while I did not care to intrude upon his evidently painful memories.

"What happened then?" I asked, however, at last.

He roused himself from his reverie.

"Oh," he said. "Nothing extraordinary. She had to leave London for a time, and gave me her pet canary to take charge of while she was away."

"But it wasn't your fault," I urged.

"No, perhaps not," he agreed; "but it created a coldness which others were not slow to take advantage of."

"I offered her the cat, too," he added, but more to himself than to me.

We sat and smoked in silence. I felt that the consolations of a stranger would sound weak.

"Piebald horses are lucky, too," he observed, knocking the ashes from his pipe against the window sash. "I had one of them once."

"What did it do to you?" I enquired.

"Lost me the best crib I ever had in my life," was the simple rejoinder. "The governor stood it a good deal longer than I had any right to expect; but you can't keep a man who is *always* drunk. It gives a firm a bad name."

"It would," I agreed.

"You see," he went on, "I never had the head for it. To some men it would not have so much mattered, but the very first glass was enough to upset me. I'd never been used to it."

"But why did you take it?" I persisted. "The horse didn't make you drink, did he?"

"Well, it was this way," he explained, continuing to rub gently the lump which was now about the size of an egg. "The animal had belonged to a gentleman who travelled in the wine and spirit line, and who had been accustomed to visit in the way of business almost every public-house he came to. The result was you couldn't get that little horse past a public-house —at least I couldn't.

He sighted them a quarter of a mile off, and made straight for the door. I struggled with him at first, but it was five to ten minutes' work getting him away, and folks used to gather round and bet on us. I think, maybe, I'd have stuck to it, however, if it hadn't been for a temperance chap who stopped one day and lectured the crowd about it from the opposite side of the street. He called me Pilgrim, and said the little horse was 'Pollion,' or some such name, and kept on shouting out that I was to fight him for a heavenly crown. After that they called us "Polly and the Pilgrim, fighting for the crown." It riled me, that did, and at the very next house at which he pulled up I got down and said I'd come for two of Scotch. That was the beginning. It took me years to break myself of the habit.

"But there," he continued, "it has always been the same. I hadn't been a fortnight in my first situation before my employer gave me a goose weighing eighteen pounds as a Christmas present."

"Well, that couldn't have done you any harm," I remarked. "That was lucky enough."

"So the other clerks said at the time," he replied. "The old gentleman had never been known to give anything away before in his life. 'He's taken a fancy to you,' they said; 'you are a lucky beggar!'"

He sighed heavily. I felt there was a story attached.

"What did you do with it?" I asked.

"That was the trouble," he returned. "I didn't know what to do with it. It was ten o'clock on Christmas Eve, just as I was leaving, that he gave it to me. 'Tiddling Brothers have sent me a goose, Biggles,' he said to me as I helped him on with his great-coat. 'Very kind of 'em, but I don't want it myself; you can have it!'

"Of course I thanked him, and was very grateful. He wished me a merry Christmas and went out. I tied the thing up in brown paper, and took it under my arm. It was a fine bird, but heavy.

"Under all the circumstances, and it being Christmas time, I thought I would treat myself to a glass of beer. I went into a quiet little house at the corner of the Lane and laid the goose on the counter.

"'That's a big 'un,' said the landlord; 'you'll get a good cut off him tomorrow.'

"His words set me thinking, and for the first time it struck me that I didn't want the bird—that it was of no use to me at all. I was going down to spend the holidays with my young lady's people in Kent."

"Was this the canary young lady?" I interrupted.

"No," he replied. "This was before that one. It was this goose I'm telling you of that upset this one. Well, her folks were big farmers; it would have been absurd taking a goose down to them, and I knew no one in London to give it to, so when the landlord came round again I asked him if he would care to buy it. I told him he could have it cheap,

"'I don't want it myself,' he answered. 'I've got three in the house already. Perhaps one of these gentlemen would like to make an offer.'

"He turned to a couple of chaps who were sitting drinking gin. They didn't look to me worth the price of a chicken between them. The seediest said he'd like to look at it, however, and I undid the parcel. He mauled the thing pretty considerably, and cross-examined me as to how I come by it, ending by upsetting half a tumbler of gin and water over it. Then he offered me half a crown for it. It made me so angry that I took the brown paper and the string in one hand and the goose in the other, and walked straight out without saying a word.

"I carried it in this way for some distance, because I was excited and didn't care how I carried it; but as I cooled, I began to reflect how ridiculous I must look. One or two small boys evidently noticed the same thing. I stopped under a lamp-post and tried to tie it up again. I had a bag and an umbrella with me at the same time, and the first thing I did was to drop the goose into the gutter, which is just what I might have expected to do, attempting to handle four separate articles and three yards of string with one pair of hands. I picked up about a quart of mud with that goose, and got the greater part of it over my hands and clothes and a fair quantity over the brown paper; and then it began to rain.

"I bundled everything up into my arm and made for the nearest pub, where I thought I would ask for a piece more string and make a neat job of it.

"The bar was crowded. I pushed my way to the counter and flung the goose down in front of me. The men nearest stopped talking to look at it; and a young fellow standing next to me said—

"'Well, you've killed it.' I daresay I did seem a bit excited.

"I had intended making another effort to sell it here, but they were clearly not the right sort. I had a pint of ale—for I was feeling somewhat tired and hot— scraped as much of the mud off the bird as I could, made a fresh parcel of it, and came out.

"Crossing the road a happy idea occurred to me. I thought I would raffle it. At once I set to work to find a house where there might seem to be a likely lot. It cost me three or four whiskies—for I felt I didn't want any more beer, which is a thing that easily upsets me—but at length I found just the crowd I wanted—a quiet domestic-looking set in a homely little place off the Goswell Road.

"I explained my views to the landlord. He said he had no objection; he supposed I would stand drinks round afterwards. I said I should be delighted to do so, and showed him the bird.

"'It looks a bit poorly,' he said. He was a Devonshire man.

"'Oh, that's nothing,' I explained. 'I happened to drop it. That will all wash off.'

"'It smells a bit queer, too,' he said.

"'That's mud,' I answered; 'you know what London mud is. And a gentleman spilled some gin over it. Nobody will notice that when it's cooked.'

"'Well,' he replied. 'I don't think I'll take a hand myself, but if any other gent likes to, that's his affair.'

"Nobody seemed enthusiastic. I started it at sixpence, and took a ticket myself. The potman had a free chance for superintending the arrangements, and he succeeded in inducing five other men, much against their will, to join us. I won it myself, and paid out three and twopence for drinks. A solemn-looking individual who had been snoring in a corner suddenly woke up as I was going out, and offered me sevenpence ha'penny for it—why sevenpence ha'penny I have never been able to understand. He would have taken it away, I should never have seen it again, and my whole life might have been different. But Fate has always been against me. I replied, with perhaps unnecessary hauteur, that I wasn't a Christmas dinner fund for the destitute, and walked out.

"It was getting late, and I had a long walk home to my lodgings. I was beginning to wish I had never seen the bird. I estimated its weight by this time to be thirty-six pounds.

"The idea occurred to me to sell it to a poulterer. I looked for a shop, I found one in Myddleton Street. There wasn't a customer near it, but by the way the man was shouting you might have thought that he was doing all the trade of Clerkenwell. I took the goose out of the parcel and laid it on the shelf before him.

"'What's this?' he asked.

"'It's a goose,' I said. 'You can have it cheap.'

"He just seized the thing by the neck and flung it at me. I dodged, and it caught the side of my head. You can have no idea, if you've never been hit on the head with a goose, how if hurts. I picked it up and hit him back with it, and a policeman came up with the usual, 'Now then, what's all this about?'

"I explained the facts. The poulterer stepped to the edge of the curb and apostrophised the universe generally.

"'Look at that shop,' he said. 'It's twenty minutes to twelve, and there's seven dozen geese hanging there that I'm willing to give away, and this fool asks me if I want to buy another.'

"I perceived then that my notion had been a foolish one, and I followed the policeman's advice, and went away quietly, taking the bird with me.

"Then said I to myself, 'I will give it away. I will select some poor deserving person, and make him a present of the damned thing.' I passed a good many people, but no one looked deserving enough. It may have been the time or it may have been the neighbourhood, but those I met seemed to me to be unworthy of the bird. I offered it to a man in Judd Street, who I thought appeared hungry. He turned out to be a drunken ruffian. I could not make him understand what I meant, and he followed me down the road abusing me at the top of his voice, until, turning a corner without knowing it, he plunged down Tavistock Place, shouting after the wrong man. In the Euston Road I stopped a half-starved child and pressed it upon her. She answered 'Not me!' and ran away. I heard her calling shrilly after me, 'Who stole the goose?'

"I dropped it in a dark part of Seymour Street. A man picked it up and brought it after me. I was unequal to any more explanations or arguments. I gave him twopence and plodded on with it once more. The pubs were just closing, and I went into one for a final drink. As a matter of fact I had had enough already, being, as I am, unaccustomed to anything more than an occasional class of beer. But I felt depressed, and I thought it might cheer me. I think I had gin, which is a thing I loathe.

"I meant to fling it over into Oakley Square, but a policeman had his eye on me, and followed me twice round the railings. In Golding Road I sought to throw it down an area, but was frustrated in like manner. The whole night police of London seemed to have nothing else to do but prevent my getting rid of that goose.

"They appeared so anxious about it that I fancied they might like to have it. I went up to one in Camden Street. I called him 'Bobby,' and asked him if he wanted a goose.

"'I'll tell you what I don't want,' he replied severely, 'and that is none of your sauce.'

"He was very insulting, and I naturally answered him back. What actually passed I forget, but it ended in his announcing his intention of taking me in charge.

"I slipped out of his hands and bolted down King Street. He blew his whistle and started after me. A man sprang out from a doorway in College Street and tried to stop me. I tied him up with a butt in the stomach, and cut through the Crescent, doubling back into the Camden Road by Batt Street.

"At the Canal Bridge I looked behind me, and could see no one. I dropped the goose over the parapet, and it fell with a splash into the water.

"Heaving a sigh of relief, I turned and crossed into Randolph Street, and there a constable collared me. I was arguing with him when the first fool came up breathless. They told me I had better explain the matter to the Inspector, and I thought so too.

"The Inspector asked me why I had run away when the other constable wanted to take me in charge. I replied that it was because I did not desire to spend my Christmas holidays in the lock-up, which he evidently regarded as a singularly weak argument. He asked me what I had thrown into the canal. I told him a goose. He asked me why I had thrown a goose into the canal. I told him because I was sick and tired of the animal.

"At this stage a sergeant came in to say that they had succeeded in recovering the parcel. They opened it on the Inspector's table. It contained a dead baby.

"I pointed out to them that it wasn't my parcel, and that it wasn't my baby, but they hardly took the trouble to disguise the fact that they did not believe me.

"The Inspector said it was too grave a case for bail, which, seeing that I did not know a soul in London, was somewhat immaterial. I got them to send a telegram to my young lady to say that I was unavoidably detained in town, and passed as quiet and uneventful a Christmas Day and Boxing Day as I ever wish to spend.

"In the end the evidence against me was held to be insufficient to justify a conviction, and I got off on the minor charge of drunk and disorderly. But I lost my situation and I lost my young lady, and I don't care if I never see a goose again."

We were nearing Liverpool Street. He collected his luggage, and taking up his hat made an attempt to put it on his head. But in consequence of the swelling caused by the horseshoe it would not go anywhere near him, and he laid it sadly back upon the seat.

"No," he said quietly, "I can't say that I believe very much in luck."

DICK DUNKERMAN'S CAT

Richard Dunkerman and I had been old school-fellows, if a gentleman belonging to the Upper Sixth, and arriving each morning in a "topper" and a pair of gloves, and "a discredit to the Lower Fourth," in a Scotch cap, can by any manner of means be classed together. And though in those early days a certain amount of coldness existed between us, originating in a poem, composed and sung on occasions by myself in commemoration of an alleged painful incident connected with a certain breaking-up day, and which, if I remember rightly ran:—

> Dicky, Dicky, Dunk,
> Always in a funk,
> Drank a glass of sherry wine,
> And went home roaring drunk,

and kept alive by his brutal criticism of the same, expressed with the bony part of the knee, yet in after life we came to know and like each other better. I drifted into journalism, while he for years had been an unsuccessful barrister and dramatist; but one spring, to the astonishment of us all, he brought out the play of the season, a somewhat impossible little comedy, but full of homely sentiment and belief in human nature. It was about a couple of months after its production that he first introduced me to "Pyramids, Esquire."

I was in love at the time. Her name was, I think, Naomi, and I wanted to talk to somebody about her. Dick had a reputation for taking an intelligent interest in other men's love affairs. He would let a lover rave by the hour to him, taking brief notes the while in a bulky red-covered volume labelled "Commonplace Book." Of course everybody knew that he was using them merely as raw material for his dramas, but we did not mind that so long as he would only listen. I put on my hat and went round to his chambers.

We talked about indifferent matters for a quarter of an hour or so, and then I launched forth upon my theme. I had exhausted her beauty and goodness, and was well into my own feelings—the madness of my ever imagining I had loved before, the utter impossibility of my ever caring for any other woman, and my desire to die breathing her name—before he made a move. I thought he had risen to reach down, as usual, the "Commonplace Book," and so waited, but instead he went to the door and opened it, and in glided one of the largest and most beautiful black tom-cats I have ever seen. It sprang on Dick's knee with a soft "curroo," and sat there upright, watching me, and I went on with my tale.

After a few minutes Dick interrupted me with:—

"I thought you said her name was Naomi?"

"So it is," I replied. "Why?"

"Oh, nothing," he answered, "only just now you referred to her as Enid."

This was remarkable, as I had not seen Enid for years, and had quite forgotten her. Somehow it took the glitter out of the conversation. A dozen sentences later Dick stopped me again with:—

"Who's Julia?"

I began to get irritated. Julia, I remembered, had been cashier in a city restaurant, and had, when I was little more than a boy, almost inveigled me into an engagement. I found myself getting hot at the recollection of the spooney rhapsodies I had hoarsely poured into her powder-streaked ear while holding her flabby hand across the counter.

"Did I really say 'Julia'?" I answered somewhat sharply, "or are you joking?"

"You certainly alluded to her as Julia," he replied mildly. "But never mind, you go on as you like, I shall know whom you mean."

But the flame was dead within me. I tried to rekindle it, but every time I glanced up and met the green eyes of the black Tom it flickered out again. I recalled the thrill that had penetrated my whole being when Naomi's hand had accidently touched mine in the conservatory, and wondered whether she had done it on purpose. I thought how good and sweet she was to that irritatingly silly old frump her mother, and wondered if it really were her mother, or only hired. I pictured her crown of gold-brown hair as I had last seen it with the sunlight kissing its wanton waves, and felt I would like to be quite sure that it were all her own.

Once I clutched the flying skirts of my enthusiasm with sufficient firmness to remark that in my own private opinion a good woman was more precious than rubies; adding immediately afterwards—the words escaping me unconsciously before I was aware even of the thought—"pity it's so difficult to tell 'em."

Then I gave it up, and sat trying to remember what I had said to her the evening before, and hoping I had not committed myself.

Dick's voice roused me from my unpleasant reverie.

"No," he said, "I thought you would not be able to. None of them can."

"None of them can what?" I asked. Somehow I was feeling angry with Dick and with Dick's cat, and with myself and most other things.

"Why talk love or any other kind of sentiment before old Pyramids here?" he replied, stroking the cat's soft head as it rose and arched its back.

"What's the confounded cat got to do with it?" I snapped.

"That's just what I can't tell you," he answered, "but it's very remarkable. Old Leman dropped in here the other evening and began in his usual style about Ibsen and the destiny of the human race, and the Socialistic idea and all the rest of it—you know his way. Pyramids sat on the edge of the table there and looked at him, just as he sat looking at you a few minutes ago, and in less than a quarter of an hour Leman had come to the conclusion that society would do better without ideals and that the destiny of the human race was in all probability the dust heap. He pushed his long hair back from his eyes and looked, for the first time in his life, quite sane. 'We talk about ourselves,' he said, 'as though we were the end of creation. I get tired listening to myself sometimes. Pah!' he continued, 'for all we know the human race may die out utterly and another insect take our place, as possibly we pushed out and took the place of a former race of beings. I wonder if the ant tribe may not be the future inheritors of the earth. They understand combination, and already have an extra sense that we lack. If in the courses of evolution they grow bigger in brain and body, they may become powerful rivals, who knows?' Curious to hear old Leman talking like that, wasn't it?"

"What made you call him 'Pyramids'?" I asked of Dick.

"I don't know," he answered, "I suppose because he looked so old. The name came to me."

I leaned across and looked into the great green eyes, and the creature, never winking, never blinking, looked back into mine, until the feeling came to me that I was being drawn down into the very wells of time. It seemed as though the panorama of the ages must have passed in review before those expressionless orbs—all the loves and hopes and desires of mankind; all the everlasting truths that have been found false; all the eternal faiths discovered to save, until it was discovered they damned. The strange black creature grew and grew till it seemed to fill the room, and Dick and I to be but shadows floating in the air.

I forced from myself a laugh, that only in part, however, broke the spell, and inquired of Dick how he had acquired possession of it.

"It came to me," he answered, "one night six months ago. I was down on my luck at the time. Two of my plays, on which I had built great hopes, had failed, one on top of the other—you remember them—and it appeared absurd to think that any manager would ever look at anything of mine again. Old Walcott had just told me that he did not consider it right of me under all the circumstances to hold Lizzie any longer to her engagement, and that I ought to go away and give her a chance of forgetting me, and I had agreed with him. I was alone in the world, and heavily in debt. Altogether things seemed about as hopeless as they could be, and I don't mind confessing to you now that I had made up my mind to blow out my brains that very evening. I had loaded my revolver, and it lay before me on the desk. My hand was toying with it when I heard a faint scratching at the door. I paid no attention at first, but it grew more persistent, and at length, to stop the faint noise which excited me more than I could account for, I rose and opened the door and *it* walked in.

"It perched itself upon the corner of my desk beside the loaded pistol, and sat there bolt upright looking at me; and I, pushing back my chair, sat looking at it. And there came a letter telling me that a man of whose name I had never heard had been killed by a cow in Melbourne, and that under his will a legacy of three thousand pounds fell into the estate of a distant relative of my own who had died peacefully and utterly insolvent eighteen months previously, leaving me his sole heir and representative, and I put the revolver back into the drawer."

"Do you think Pyramids would come and stop with me for a week?" I asked, reaching over to stroke the cat as it lay softly purring on Dick's knee.

"Maybe he will some day," replied Dick in a low voice, but before the answer came—I know not why—I had regretted the jesting words.

"I came to talk to him as though he were a human creature," continued Dick, "and to discuss things with him. My last play I regard as a collaboration; indeed, it is far more his than mine."

I should have thought Dick mad had not the cat been sitting there before me with its eyes looking into mine. As it was, I only grew more interested in his tale.

"It was rather a cynical play as I first wrote it," he went on, "a truthful picture of a certain corner of society as I saw and knew it. From an artistic point of view I felt it was good; from the box-office standard it was doubtful. I drew it from my desk on the third evening after Pyramids' advent, and read it through. He sat on the arm of the chair and looked over the pages as I turned them.

"It was the best thing I had ever written. Insight into life ran through every line, I found myself reading it again with delight. Suddenly a voice beside me said:—

"'Very clever, my boy, very clever indeed. If you would just turn it topsy-turvy, change all those bitter, truthful speeches into noble sentiments; make your Under-Secretary for Foreign Affairs (who never has been a popular character) die in the last act instead of the Yorkshireman, and let your bad woman be reformed by her love for the hero and go off somewhere by herself and be good to the poor in a black frock, the piece might be worth putting on the stage.'

"I turned indignantly to see who was speaking. The opinions sounded like those of a theatrical manager. No one was in the room but I and the cat. No doubt I had been talking to myself, but the voice was strange to me.

"'Be reformed by her love for the hero!' I retorted, contemptuously, for I was unable to grasp the idea that I was arguing only with myself, 'why it's his mad passion for her that ruins his life.'

"'And will ruin the play with the great B.P.,' returned the other voice. 'The British dramatic hero has no passion, but a pure and respectful admiration for an honest, hearty English girl—pronounced "gey-url." You don't know the canons of your art.'

"'And besides,' I persisted, unheeding the interruption, 'women born and bred and soaked for thirty years in an atmosphere of sin don't reform.'

"'Well, this one's got to, that's all,' was the sneering reply, 'let her hear an organ.'

"'But as an artist -,' I protested.

"'You will be always unsuccessful,' was the rejoinder. 'My dear fellow, you and your plays, artistic or in artistic, will be forgotten in a very few years hence.

You give the world what it wants, and the world will give you what you want. Please, if you wish to live.'

"So, with Pyramids beside me day by day, I re-wrote the play, and whenever I felt a thing to be utterly impossible and false I put it down with a grin. And every character I made to talk clap-trap sentiment while Pyramids purred, and I took care that everyone of my puppets did that which was right in the eyes of the lady with the lorgnettes in the second row of the dress circle; and old Hewson says the play will run five hundred nights.

"But what is worst," concluded Dick, "is that I am not ashamed of myself, and that I seem content."

"What do you think the animal is?" I asked with a laugh, "an evil spirit"? For it had passed into the next room and so out through the open window, and its strangely still green eyes no longer drawing mine towards them, I felt my common sense returning to me.

"You have not lived with it for six months," answered Dick quietly, "and felt its eyes for ever on you as I have. And I am not the only one. You know Canon Whycherly, the great preacher?"

"My knowledge of modern church history is not extensive," I replied. "I know him by name, of course. What about him?"

"He was a curate in the East End," continued Dick, "and for ten years he laboured, poor and unknown, leading one of those noble, heroic lives that here and there men do yet live, even in this age. Now he is the prophet of the fashionable up-to-date Christianity of South Kensington, drives to his pulpit behind a pair of thorough-bred Arabs, and his waistcoat is taking to itself the curved line of prosperity. He was in here the other morning on behalf of Princess ---. They are giving a performance of one of my plays in aid of the Destitute Vicars' Fund."

"And did Pyramids discourage him?" I asked, with perhaps the suggestion of a sneer.

"No," answered Dick, "so far as I could judge, it approved the scheme. The point of the matter is that the moment Whycherly came into the room the cat walked over to him and rubbed itself affectionately against his legs. He stood and stroked it."

"'Oh, so it's come to you, has it?' he said, with a curious smile.

"There was no need for any further explanation between us. I understood what lay behind those few words."

I lost sight of Dick for some time, though I heard a good deal of him, for he was rapidly climbing into the position of the most successful dramatist of the day, and Pyramids I had forgotten all about, until one afternoon calling on an artist friend who had lately emerged from the shadows of starving struggle into the sunshine of popularity, I saw a pair of green eyes that seemed familiar to me gleaming at me from a dark corner of the studio.

"Why, surely," I exclaimed, crossing over to examine the animal more closely, "why, yes, you've got Dick Dunkerman's cat."

He raised his face from the easel and glanced across at me.

"Yes," he said, "we can't live on ideals," and I, remembering, hastened to change the conversation.

Since then I have met Pyramids in the rooms of many friends of mine. They give him different names, but I am sure it is the same cat, I know those green eyes. He always brings them luck, but they are never quite the same men again afterwards.

Sometimes I sit wondering if I hear his scratching at the door.

THE MINOR POET'S STORY

"It doesn't suit you at all," I answered.

"You're very disagreeable," said she, "I shan't ever ask your advice again."

"Nobody," I hastened to add, "would look well in it. You, of course, look less awful in it than any other woman would, but it's not your style."

"He means," exclaimed the Minor Poet, "that the thing itself not being pre-eminently beautiful, it does not suit, is not in agreement with you. The contrast between you and anything approaching the ugly or the commonplace, is too glaring to be aught else than displeasing."

"He didn't say it," replied the Woman of the World; "and besides it isn't ugly. It's the very latest fashion."

"Why is it," asked the Philosopher, "that women are such slaves to fashion? They think clothes, they talk clothes, they read clothes, yet they have never understood clothes. The purpose of dress, after the primary object of warmth has been secured, is to adorn, to beautify the particular wearer. Yet not one woman in a thousand stops to consider what colours will go best with her complexion, what cut will best hide the defects or display the advantages of her figure. If it be the fashion, she must wear it. And so we have pale-faced girls looking ghastly in shades suitable to dairy-maids, and dots waddling about in costumes fit and proper to six-footers. It is as if crows insisted on wearing cockatoo's feathers on their heads, and rabbits ran about with peacocks' tails fastened behind them."

"And are not you men every bit as foolish?" retorted the Girton Girl. "Sack coats come into fashion, and dumpy little men trot up and down in them, looking like butter-tubs on legs. You go about in July melting under frock-coats and chimney-pot hats, and because it is the stylish thing to do, you all play tennis in still shirts and stand-up collars, which is idiotic. If fashion decreed that you should play cricket in a pair of top-boots and a diver's helmet, you would play cricket in a pair of top-boots and a diver's helmet, and dub every sensible fellow who didn't a cad. It's worse in you than in us; men are supposed to think for themselves, and to be capable of it, the womanly woman isn't."

"Big women and little men look well in nothing," said the Woman of the World. "Poor Emily was five foot ten and a half, and never looked an inch under seven foot, whatever she wore. Empires came into fashion, and the poor child looked like the giant's baby in a pantomime. We thought the Greek might help her, but it only suggested a Crystal Palace statue tied up in a sheet, and tied up badly; and when puff-sleeves and shoulder-capes were in and Teddy stood up behind her at a water-party and sang 'Under the spreading chestnut-tree,' she took it as a personal insult and boxed his ears. Few men liked to be seen with her, and I'm sure George proposed to her partly with the idea of saving himself the expense of a step-ladder, she reaches down his boots for him from the top shelf."

"I," said the Minor Poet, "take up the position of not wanting to waste my brain upon the subject. Tell me what to wear, and I will wear it, and there is an end of the matter. If Society says, 'Wear blue shirts and white collars,' I wear blue shirts and white collars. If she says, 'The time has now come when hats should be broad-brimmed,' I take unto myself a broad-brimmed hat. The question does not interest me sufficiently for me to argue it. It is your fop who refuses to follow fashion. He wishes to attract attention to himself by being peculiar. A novelist whose books pass unnoticed, gains distinction by designing his own necktie; and many an artist, following the line of least resistance, learns to let his hair grow instead of learning to paint."

"The fact is," remarked the Philosopher, "we are the mere creatures of fashion. Fashion dictates to us our religion, our morality, our affections, our thoughts. In one age successful cattle-lifting is a virtue, a few hundred years later company-promoting takes its place as a respectable and legitimate business. In England and America Christianity is fashionable, in Turkey, Mohammedanism, and 'the crimes of Clapham are chaste in Martaban.' In Japan a woman dresses down to the knees, but would be considered immodest if she displayed bare arms. In Europe it is legs that no pure-minded woman is supposed to possess. In China we worship our mother-in-law and despise our wife; in England we treat our wife with respect, and regard our mother-in-law as the bulwark of comic journalism. The stone age, the iron age, the age of faith, the age of infidelism, the philosophic age, what are they but the passing fashions of the world? It is fashion, fashion, fashion wherever we turn. Fashion waits beside our cradle to lead us by the hand through life. Now literature is sentimental, now hopefully humorous, now psychological, now new-womanly. Yesterday's pictures are the laughing-stock of the up-to-date artist of to-day, and to-day's art will be sneered at to-morrow. Now it is fashionable to be democratic, to pretend that no virtue or wisdom can exist outside corduroy, and to abuse the middle classes. One season we go slumming, and the next we are all socialists. We think we are thinking; we are simply dressing ourselves up in words we do not understand for the gods to laugh at us."

"Don't be pessimistic," retorted the Minor Poet, "pessimism is going out. You call such changes fashions, I call them the footprints of progress. Each phase of thought is an advance upon the former, bringing the footsteps of the many nearer to the landmarks left by the mighty climbers of the past upon the mountain paths of truth. The crowd that was satisfied with *The Derby Day* now appreciates Millet. The public that were content to wag their heads to *The Bohemian Girl* have made Wagner popular.”

“And the play lovers, who stood for hours to listen to Shakespeare,” interrupted the Philosopher, “now crowd to music-halls.”

“The track sometimes descends for a little way, but it will wind upwards again,” returned the Poet. “The music-hall itself is improving; I consider it the duty of every intellectual man to visit such places. The mere influence of his presence helps to elevate the tone of the performance. I often go myself!”

“I was looking,” said the Woman of the World, “at some old illustrated papers of thirty years ago, showing the men dressed in those very absurd trousers, so extremely roomy about the waist, and so extremely tight about the ankles. I recollect poor papa in them; I always used to long to fill them out by pouring in sawdust at the top.”

“You mean the peg-top period,” I said. “I remember them distinctly myself, but it cannot be more than three-and-twenty years ago at the outside.”

“That is very nice of you,” replied the Woman of the World, “and shows more tact than I should have given you credit for. It could, as you say, have been only twenty-three years ago. I know I was a very little girl at the time. I think there must be some subtle connection between clothes and thought. I cannot imagine men in those trousers and Dundreary whiskers talking as you fellows are talking now, any more than I could conceive of a woman in a crinoline and a poke bonnet smoking a cigarette. I think it must be so, because dear mother used to be the most easy-going woman in the world in her ordinary clothes, and would let papa smoke all over the house. But about once every three weeks she would put on a hideous old-fashioned black silk dress, that looked as if Queen Elizabeth must have slept in it during one of those seasons when she used to go about sleeping anywhere, and then we all had to sit up. ‘Look out, ma’s got her black silk dress on,’ came to be a regular formula. We could always make papa take us out for a walk or a drive by whispering it to him.”

“I can never bear to look at those pictures of by-gone fashions,” said the Old Maid, “I see the by-gone people in them, and it makes me feel as though the faces that we love are only passing fashions with the rest. We wear them for a little while upon our hearts, and think so much of them, and then there comes a time when we lay them by, and forget them, and newer faces take their place, and we are satisfied. It seems so sad.”

“I wrote a story some years ago,” remarked the Minor Poet, “about a young Swiss guide, who was betrothed to a laughing little French peasant girl.”

“Named Suzette,” interrupted the Girton Girl. “I know her. Go on.”

“Named Jeanne,” corrected the Poet, “the majority of laughing French girls, in fiction, are named Suzette, I am well aware. But this girl’s mother’s family was English. She was christened Jeanne after an aunt Jane, who lived in Birmingham, and from whom she had expectations.”

“I beg your pardon,” apologised the Girton Girl, “I was not aware of that fact. What happened to her?”

"One morning, a few days before the date fixed for the wedding," said the Minor Poet, "she started off to pay a visit to a relative living in the village, the other side of the mountain. It was a dangerous track, climbing half-way up the mountain before it descended again, and skirting more than one treacherous slope, but the girl was mountain born and bred, sure-footed as a goat, and no one dreamed of harm."

"She went over, of course," said the Philosopher, "those sure-footed girls always do."

"What happened," replied the Minor Poet, "was never known. The girl was never seen again."

"And what became of her lover?" asked the Girton Girl. "Was he, when next year's snow melted, and the young men of the village went forth to gather Edelweiss, wherewith to deck their sweethearts, found by them dead, beside her, at the bottom of the crevasse?"

"No," said the Poet; "you do not know this story, you had better let me tell it. Her lover returned the morning before the wedding day, to be met with the news. He gave way to no sign of grief, he repelled all consolation. Taking his rope and axe he went up into the mountain by himself. All through the winter he haunted the track by which she must have travelled, indifferent to the danger that he ran, impervious apparently to cold, or hunger, or fatigue, undeterred by storm, or mist, or avalanche. At the beginning of the spring he returned to the village, purchased building utensils, and day after day carried them back with him up into the mountain. He hired no labour, he rejected the proffered assistance of his brother guides. Choosing an almost inaccessible spot, at the edge of the great glacier, far from all paths, he built himself a hut, with his own hands; and there for eighteen years he lived alone.

"In the 'season' he earned good fees, being known far and wide as one of the bravest and hardiest of all the guides, but few of his clients liked him, for he was a silent, gloomy man, speaking little, and with never a laugh or jest on the journey. Each fall, having provisioned himself, he would retire to his solitary hut, and bar the door, and no human soul would set eyes on him again until the snows melted.

"One year, however, as the spring days wore on, and he did not appear among the guides, as was his wont, the elder men, who remembered his story and pitied him, grew uneasy; and, after much deliberation, it was determined that a party of them should force their way up to his eyrie. They cut their path across the ice where no foot among them had trodden before, and finding at length the lonely snow-encompassed hut, knocked loudly with their axe-staves on the door; but only the whirling echoes from the glacier's thousand walls replied, so the foremost put his strong shoulder to the worn timber and the door flew open with a crash.

"They found him dead, as they had more than half expected, lying stiff and frozen on the rough couch at the farther end of the hut; and, beside him, looking down upon him with a placid face, as a mother might watch beside her sleeping child, stood Jeanne. She wore the flowers pinned to her dress that she had gathered when their eyes had last seen her. The girl's face that had laughed back to their good-bye in the village, nineteen years ago.

"A strange steely light clung round her, half illuminating, half obscuring her, and the men drew back in fear, thinking they saw a vision, till one, bolder than the rest, stretched out his hand and touched the ice that formed her coffin.

"For eighteen years the man had lived there with this face that he had loved. A faint flush still lingered on the fair cheeks, the laughing lips were still red. Only at one spot, above her temple, the wavy hair lay matted underneath a clot of blood."

The Minor Poet ceased.

"What a very unpleasant way of preserving one's love!" said the Girton Girl.

"When did the story appear?" I asked. "I don't remember reading it."

"I never published it," explained the Minor Poet. "Within the same week two friends of mine, one of whom had just returned from Norway and the other from Switzerland, confided to me their intention of writing stories about girls who had fallen into glaciers, and who had been found by their friends long afterwards, looking as good as new; and a few days later I chanced upon a book, the heroine of which had been dug out of a glacier alive three hundred years after she had fallen in. There seemed to be a run on ice maidens, and I decided not to add to their number."

"It is curious," said the Philosopher, "how there seems to be a fashion even in thought. An idea has often occurred to me that has seemed to me quite new, and taking up a newspaper I have found that some man in Russia or San Francisco has just been saying the very same thing in almost the very same words. We say a thing is 'in the air'; it is more true than we are aware of. Thought does not grow in us. It is a thing apart, we simply gather it. All truths, all discoveries, all inventions, they have not come to us from any one man. The time grows ripe for them, and from this corner of the earth and from that, hands, guided by some instinct, grope for and grasp them. Buddha and Christ seize hold of the morality needful to civilisation, and promulgate it, unknown to one another, the one on the shores of the Ganges, the other by the Jordan. A dozen forgotten explorers, *feeling* America, prepared the way for Columbus to discover it. A deluge of blood is required to sweep away old follies, and Rousseau and Voltaire, and a myriad others are set to work to fashion the storm clouds. The steam-engine, the spinning loom is 'in the air.' A thousand brains are busy with them, a few go further than the rest. It is idle to talk of human thought; there is no such thing. Our minds are fed as our bodies with the food God has provided for us. Thought hangs by the wayside, and we pick it and cook it, and eat it, and cry out what clever 'thinkers' we are!"

"I cannot agree with you," replied the Minor Poet, "if we were simply automata, as your argument would suggest, what was the purpose of creating us?"

"The intelligent portion of mankind has been asking itself that question for many ages," returned the Philosopher.

"I hate people who always think as I do," said the Girton Girl; "there was a girl in our corridor who never would disagree with me. Every opinion I expressed turned out to be her opinion also. It always irritated me."

"That might have been weak-mindedness," said the Old Maid, which sounded ambiguous.

"It is not so unpleasant as having a person always disagreeing with you," said the Woman of the World. "My cousin Susan never would agree with any one. If I came down in red she would say, 'Why don't you try green, dear? every one says you look so well in green'; and when I wore green she would say, 'Why have you given up red dear? I thought you rather fancied yourself in red.' When I told her of my engagement to Tom, she burst into tears and said she couldn't help it. She had always felt that George and I were intended for one another; and when Tom never wrote for two whole months, and behaved disgracefully in—in other ways, and I told her I was engaged to George, she reminded me of every word I had ever said about my affection for Tom, and of how I had ridiculed poor George. Papa used to say, 'If any man ever tells Susan that he loves her, she will argue him out of it, and will never accept him until he has jilted her, and will refuse to marry him every time he asks her to fix the day.'"

"Is she married?" asked the Philosopher.

"Oh, yes," answered the Woman of the World, "and is devoted to her children. She lets them do everything they don't want to."

THE DEGENERATION OF THOMAS HENRY

The most respectable cat I have ever known was Thomas Henry. His original name was Thomas, but it seemed absurd to call him that. The family at Hawarden would as soon think of addressing Mr. Gladstone as "Bill." He came to us from the Reform Club, *viâ* the butcher, and the moment I saw him I felt that of all the clubs in London that was the club he must have come from. Its atmosphere of solid dignity and petrified conservatism seemed to cling to him. Why he left the club I am unable, at this distance of time, to remember positively, but I am inclined to think that it came about owing to a difference with the new *chef*, an overbearing personage who wanted all the fire to himself. The butcher, hearing of the quarrel, and knowing us as a catless family, suggested a way out of the *impasse* that was welcomed both by cat and cook. The parting between them, I believe, was purely formal, and Thomas arrived prejudiced in our favour.

My wife, the moment she saw him, suggested Henry as a more suitable name. It struck me that the combination of the two would be still more appropriate, and accordingly, in the privacy of the domestic circle, Thomas Henry he was called. When speaking of him to friends, we generally alluded to him as Thomas Henry, Esquire.

He approved of us in his quiet, undemonstrative way. He chose my own particular easy chair for himself, and stuck to it. An ordinary cat I should have shot out, but Thomas Henry was not the cat one chivvies. Had I made it clear to him that I objected to his presence in my chair, I feel convinced he would have regarded me much as I should expect to be regarded by Queen Victoria, were that gracious Lady to call upon me in a friendly way, and were I to inform her that I was busy, and request her to look in again some other afternoon. He would have risen, and have walked away, but he never would have spoken to me again so long as we lived under the same roof.

We had a lady staying with us at the time—she still resides with us, but she is now older, and possessed of more judgment—who was no respecter of cats. Her argument was that seeing the tail stuck up, and came conveniently to one's hand, that was the natural appendage by which to raise a cat. She also laboured under the error that the way to feed a cat was to ram things into its head, and that its pleasure was to be taken out for a ride in a doll's perambulator. I dreaded the first meeting of Thomas Henry with this lady. I feared lest she should give him a false impression of us as a family, and that we should suffer in his eyes.

But I might have saved myself all anxiety. There was a something about Thomas Henry that checked forwardness and damped familiarity. His attitude towards her was friendly but firm. Hesitatingly, and with a new-born respect for cats, she put out her hand timidly towards its tail. He gently put it on the other side, and looked at her. It was not an angry look nor an offended look. It was the expression with which Solomon might have received the advances of the Queen of Sheba. It expressed condescension, combined with distance.

He was really a most gentlemanly cat. A friend of mine, who believes in the doctrine of the transmigration of souls, was convinced that he was Lord Chesterfield. He never clamoured for food, as other cats do. He would sit beside me at meals, and wait till he was served. He would eat only the knuckle-end of a leg of mutton, and would never look at over-done beef. A visitor of ours once offered him a piece of gristle; he said nothing, but quietly left the room, and we did not see him again until our friend had departed.

But every one has his price, and Thomas Henry's price was roast duck. Thomas Henry's attitude in the presence of roast duck came to me as a psychological revelation. It showed me at once the lower and more animal side of his nature. In the presence of roast duck Thomas Henry became simply and merely a cat, swayed by all the savage instincts of his race. His dignity fell from him as a cloak. He clawed for roast duck, he grovelled for it. I believe he would have sold himself to the devil for roast duck.

We accordingly avoided that particular dish: it was painful to see a cat's character so completely demoralised. Besides, his manners, when roast duck was on the table, afforded a bad example to the children.

He was a shining light among all the eats of our neighbourhood. One might have set one's watch by his movements. After dinner he invariably took half an hour's constitutional in the square; at ten o'clock each night, precisely, he returned to the area door, and at eleven o'clock he was asleep in my easy chair. He made no friends among the other cats. He took no pleasure in fighting, and I doubt his ever having loved, even in youth; his was too cold and self-contained a nature, female society he regarded with utter indifference.

So he lived with us a blameless existence during the whole winter. In the summer we took him down with us into the country. We thought the change of air would do him good; he was getting decidedly stout. Alas, poor Thomas Henry! the country was his ruin. What brought about the change I cannot say: maybe the air was too bracing. He slid down the moral incline with frightful rapidity. The first night he stopped out till eleven, the second night he never came home at all, the third night he came home at six o'clock in the morning, minus half the fur on the top of his head. Of course, there was a lady in the case, indeed, judging by the riot that went on all night, I am inclined to think there must have been a dozen. He was certainly a fine cat, and they took to calling for him in the day time. Then gentleman cats who had been wronged took to calling also, and demanding explanations, which Thomas Henry, to do him justice, was always ready to accord.

The village boys used to loiter round all day to watch the fights, and angry housewives would be constantly charging into our kitchen to fling dead cats upon the table, and appeal to Heaven and myself for justice. Our kitchen became a veritable cat's morgue, and I had to purchase a new kitchen table. The cook said it would make her work simpler if she could keep a table entirely to herself. She said it quite confused her, having so many dead cats lying round among her joints and vegetables: she was afraid of making a mistake. Accordingly, the old table was placed under the window, and devoted to the cats; and, after that, she would never allow anyone to bring a cat, however dead, to her table.

"What do you want me to do with it," I heard her asking an excited lady on one occasion; "cook it?"

"It's my cat," said the lady; "that's what that is."

"Well, I'm not making cat pie to-day," answered our cook. "You take it to its proper table. This is my table."

At first, "Justice" was generally satisfied with half a crown, but as time went on cats rose. I had hitherto regarded cats as a cheap commodity, and I became surprised at the value attached to them. I began to think seriously of breeding cats as an industry. At the prices current in that village, I could have made an income of thousands.

"Look what your beast has done," said one irate female, to whom I had been called out in the middle of dinner.

I looked. Thomas Henry appeared to have "done" a mangy, emaciated animal, that must have been far happier dead than alive. Had the poor creature been mine I should have thanked him; but some people never know when they are well off.

"I wouldn't ha' taken a five-pun' note for that cat," said the lady.

"It's a matter of opinion," I replied, "but personally I think you would have been unwise to refuse it. Taking the animal as it stands, I don't feel inclined to give you more than a shilling for it. If you think you can do better by taking it elsewhere, you do so."

"He was more like a Christian than a cat," said the lady.

"I'm not taking dead Christians," I answered firmly, "and even if I were I wouldn't give more than a shilling for a specimen like that. You can consider him as a Christian, or you can consider him as a cat; but he's not worth more than a shilling in either case."

We settled eventually for eighteenpence.

The number of cats that Thomas Henry contrived to dispose of also surprised me. Quite a massacre of cats seemed to be in progress.

One evening, going into the kitchen, for I made it a practice now to visit the kitchen each evening, to inspect the daily consignment of dead cats, I found, among others, a curiously marked tortoiseshell cat, lying on the table.

"That cat's worth half a sovereign," said the owner, who was standing by, drinking beer.

I took up the animal, and examined it.

"Your cat killed him yesterday," continued the man. "It's a burning shame."

"My cat has killed him three times," I replied. "He was killed on Saturday as Mrs. Hedger's cat; on Monday he was killed for Mrs. Myers. I was not quite positive on Monday; but I had my suspicions, and I made notes. Now I recognise him. You take my advice, and bury him before he breeds a fever. I don't care how many lives a cat has got; I only pay for one."

We gave Thomas Henry every chance to reform; but he only went from bad to worse, and added poaching and chicken-stalking to his other crimes, and I grew tired of paying for his vices.

I consulted the gardener, and the gardener said he had known cats taken that way before.

"Do you know of any cure for it?" I asked.

"Well, sir," replied the gardener, "I have heard as how a dose of brickbat and pond is a good thing in a general way."

"We'll try him with a dose just before bed time," I answered. The gardener administered it, and we had no further trouble with him.

Poor Thomas Henry! It shows to one how a reputation for respectability may lie in the mere absence of temptation. Born and bred in the atmosphere of the Reform Club, what gentleman could go wrong? I was sorry for Thomas Henry, and I have never believed in the moral influence of the country since.

THE CITY OF THE SEA

They say, the chroniclers who have written the history of that low-lying, wind-swept coast, that years ago the foam fringe of the ocean lay further to the east; so that where now the North Sea creeps among the treacherous sand-reefs, it was once dry land. In those days, between the Abbey and the sea, there stood a town of seven towers and four rich churches, surrounded by a wall of twelve stones' thickness, making it, as men reckoned then, a place of strength and much import; and the monks, glancing their eyes downward from the Abbey garden on the hill, saw beneath their feet its narrow streets, gay with the ever passing of rich merchandise, saw its many wharves and water-ways, ever noisy with the babel of strange tongues, saw its many painted masts, wagging their grave heads above the dormer roofs and quaintly-carved oak gables.

Thus the town prospered till there came a night when it did evil in the sight of God and man. Those were troublous times to Saxon dwellers by the sea, for the Danish water-rats swarmed round each river mouth, scenting treasure from afar; and by none was the white flash of their sharp, strong teeth more often seen than by the men of Eastern Anglia, and by none in Eastern Anglia more often than by the watchers on the walls of the town of seven towers that once stood upon the dry land, but which now lies twenty fathom deep below the waters. Many a bloody fight raged now without and now within its wall of twelve stones' thickness. Many a groan of dying man, many a shriek of murdered woman, many a wail of mangled child, knocked at the Abbey door upon its way to Heaven, calling the trembling-monks from their beds, to pray for the souls that were passing by.

But at length peace came to the long-troubled land: Dane and Saxon agreeing to dwell in friendship side by side, East Anglia being wide, and there being room for both. And all men rejoiced greatly, for all were weary of a strife in which little had been gained on either side beyond hard blows, and their thoughts were of the ingle-nook. So the long-bearded Danes, their thirsty axes harmless on their backs, passed to and fro in straggling bands, seeking where undisturbed and undisturbing they might build their homes; and thus it came about that Haafager and his company, as the sun was going down, drew near to the town of seven towers, that in those days stood on dry land between the Abbey and the sea.

And the men of the town, seeing the Danes, opened wide their gates saying:—

"We have fought, but now there is peace. Enter, and make merry with us, and to-morrow go your way."

But Haafager made answer:—

"I am an old man, I pray you do not take my words amiss. There is peace between us, as you say, and we thank you for your courtesy, but the stains are still fresh upon our swords. Let us camp here without your walls, and a little later, when the grass has grown upon the fields where we have striven, and our young men have had time to forget, we will make merry together, as men should who dwell side by side in the same land."

But the men of the town still urged Haafager, calling his people neighbours; and the Abbot, who had hastened down, fearing there might be strife, added his words to theirs, saying:—

"Pass in, my children. Let there indeed be peace between you, that the blessing of God may be upon the land, and upon both Dane and Saxon"; for the Abbot saw that the townsmen were well disposed towards the Danes, and knew that men, when they have feasted and drunk together, think kinder of one another.

Then answered Haafager, who knew the Abbot for a holy man:—

"Hold up your staff, my father, that the shadow of the cross your people worship may fall upon our path, so we will pass into the town and there shall be peace between us, for though your gods are not our gods, faith between man and man is of all altars."

And the Abbot held his staff aloft between Haafager's people and the sun, it being fashioned in the form of a cross, and under its shadow the Danes passed by into the town of seven towers, there being of them, with the women and the children, nearly two thousand souls, and the gates were made fast behind them.

So they who had fought face to face, feasted side by side, pledging one another in the wine cup, as was the custom; and Haafager's men, knowing themselves amongst friends, cast aside their arms, and when the feast was done, being weary, they lay down to sleep.

Then an evil voice arose in the town, and said: "Who are these that have come among us to share our land? Are not the stones of our streets red with the blood of wife and child that they have slain? Do men let the wolf go free when they have trapped him with meat? Let us fall upon them now that they are heavy with food and wine, so that not one of them shall escape. Thus no further harm shall come to us from them nor from their children."

And the voice of evil prevailed, and the men of the town of seven towers fell upon the Danes with whom they had broken meat, even to the women and the little children; and the blood of the people of Haafager cried with a loud voice at the Abbey door, through the long night it cried, saying:—

"I trusted in your spoken word. I broke meat with you. I put my faith in you and in your God. I passed beneath the shadow of your cross to enter your doors. Let your God make answer!"

Nor was there silence till the dawn.

Then the Abbot rose from where he knelt and called to God, saying:—

"Thou hast heard, O God. Make answer."

And there came a great sound from the sea as though a tongue had been given to the deep, so that the monks fell upon their knees in fear; but the Abbot answered:—

"It is the voice of God speaking through the waters. He hath made answer."

And that winter a mighty storm arose, the like of which no man had known before; for the sea was piled upon the dry land until the highest tower of the town of seven towers was not more high; and the waters moved forward over the dry land. And the men of the town of seven towers fled from the oncoming of the waters, but the waters overtook them so that not one of them escaped. And the town of the seven towers and of the four churches, and of the many streets and quays, was buried underneath the waters, and the feet of the waters still moved till they came to the hill whereon the Abbey stood. Then the Abbot prayed to God that the waters might be stayed, and God heard, and the sea came no farther.

And that this tale is true, and not a fable made by the weavers of words, he who doubts may know from the fisher-folk, who to-day ply their calling amongst the reefs and sandbanks of that lonely coast. For there are those among them who, peering from the bows of their small craft, have seen far down beneath their keels a city of strange streets and many quays. But as to this, I, who repeat these things to you, cannot speak of my own knowledge, for this city of the sea is only visible when a rare wind, blowing from the north, sweeps the shadows from the waves; and though on many a sunny day I have drifted where its seven towers should once have stood, yet for me that wind has never blown, pushing back the curtains of the sea, and, therefore, I have strained my eyes in vain.

But this I do know, that the rumbling stones of that ancient Abbey, between which and the foam fringe of the ocean the town of seven towers once lay, now stand upon a wave-washed cliff, and that he who looks forth from its shattered mullions to-day sees only the marshland and the wrinkled waters, hears only the plaint of the circling gulls and the weary crying of the sea.

And that God's anger is not everlasting, and that the evil that there is in men shall be blotted out, he who doubts may also learn from the wisdom of the simple fisher-folk, who dwell about the borders of the marsh-land; for they will tell him that on stormy nights there speaks a deep voice from the sea, calling the dead monks to rise from their forgotten graves, and chant a mass for the souls of the men of the town of seven towers.   Clothed in long glittering white, they move with slowly pacing feet around the Abbey's grass-grown aisles, and the music of their prayers is heard above the screaming of the storm. And to this I also can bear witness, for I have seen the passing of their shrouded forms behind the blackness of the shattered shafts; I have heard their sweet, sad singing above the wailing of the wind.

Thus for many ages have the dead monks prayed that the men of the town of seven towers may be forgiven. Thus, for many ages yet shall they so pray, till the day come when of their once fair Abbey not a single stone shall stand upon its fellow; and in that day it shall be known that the anger of God against the men of the town of seven towers has passed away; and in that day the feet of the waters shall move back, and the town of seven towers shall stand again upon the dry land.

There be some, I know, who say that this is but a legend; who will tell you that the shadowy shapes that you may see with your own eyes on stormy nights, waving their gleaming arms behind the ruined buttresses are but of phosphorescent foam, tossed by the raging waves above the cliffs; and that the sweet, sad harmony cleaving the trouble of the night is but the æolian music of the wind.

But such are of the blind, who see only with their eyes. For myself I see the white-robed monks, and hear the chanting of their mass for the souls of the sinful men of the town of seven towers. For it has been said that when an evil deed is done, a prayer is born to follow it through time into eternity, and plead for it. Thus is the whole world clasped around with folded hands both of the dead and of the living, as with a shield, lest the shafts of God's anger should consume it.

Therefore, I know that the good monks of this nameless Abbey are still praying that the sin of those they love may be forgiven.

God grant good men may say a mass for us.

DRIFTWOOD

CHARACTERS

MR. TRAVERS.
MRS. TRAVERS.
MARION [their daughter].
DAN [a gentleman of no position].

* * * * *

SCENE: A room opening upon a garden. The shadows creep from their corners, driving before them the fading twilight.

MRS. TRAVERS sits in a wickerwork easy chair. MR. TRAVERS, smoking a cigar, sits the other side of the room.   MARION stands by the open French window, looking out.

MR. TRAVERS. Nice little place Harry's got down here.

MRS. TRAVERS. Yes; I should keep this on if I were you, Marion. You'll find it very handy. One can entertain so cheaply up the river; one is not expected to make much of a show. [She turns to her husband.] Your poor cousin Emily used to work off quite half her list that way—relations and Americans, and those sort of people, you know—at that little place of theirs at Goring. You remember it—a poky hole I always thought it, but it had a lot of green stuff over the door—looked very pretty from the other side of the river. She always used to have cold meat and pickles for lunch—called it a picnic. People said it was so homely and simple.

MR. TRAVERS. They didn't stop long, I remember.

MRS. TRAVERS. And there was a special champagne she always kept for the river—only twenty-five shillings a dozen, I think she told me she paid for it, and very good it was too, for the price. That old Indian major—what was his name?—said it suited him better than anything else he had ever tried. He always used to drink a tumblerful before breakfast; such a funny thing to do. I've often wondered where she got it.

MR. TRAVERS. So did most people who tasted it.   Marion wants to forget those lessons, not learn them. She is going to marry a rich man who will be able to entertain his guests decently.

MRS. TRAVERS. Oh, well, James, I don't know. None of us can afford to live up to the income we want people to think we've got. One must economise somewhere. A pretty figure we should cut in the county if I didn't know how to make fivepence look like a shilling. And, besides, there are certain people that one has to be civil to, that, at the same time, one doesn't want to introduce into one's regular circle. If you take my advice, Marion, you won't encourage those sisters of Harry's more than you can help. They're dear sweet girls, and you can be very nice to them; but don't have them too much about. Their manners are terribly old-fashioned, and they've no notion how to dress, and those sort of people let down the tone of a house.

MARION. I'm not likely to have many "dear sweet girls" on my visiting list. [With a laugh.] There will hardly be enough in common to make the company desired, on either side.

MRS. TRAVERS. Well, I only want you to be careful, my dear. So much depends on how you begin, and with prudence there's really no reason why you shouldn't do very well. I suppose there's no doubt about Harry's income. He won't object to a few inquiries?

MARION. I think you may trust me to see to that, mamma. It would be a bad bargain for me, if even the cash were not certain.

MR. TRAVERS [jumping up]. Oh, I do wish you women wouldn't discuss the matter in that horribly business-like way. One would think the girl was selling herself.

MRS. TRAVERS. Oh, don't be foolish, James.   One must look at the practical side of these things.   Marriage is a matter of sentiment to a man—very proper that it should be. A woman has to remember that she's fixing her position for life.

MARION. You see, papa dear, it's her one venture. If she doesn't sell herself to advantage then, she doesn't get another opportunity—very easily.

MR. TRAVERS. Umph! When I was a young man, girls talked more about love and less about income.

MARION. Perhaps they had not our educational advantages.

[DAN enters from the garden. He is a man of a little over forty, his linen somewhat frayed about the edges.]

MRS. TRAVERS. Ah! We were just wondering where all you people had got to.

DAN. We've been out sailing. I've been sent up to fetch you. It's delightful on the river. The moon is just rising.

MRS. TRAVERS. But it's so cold.

MR. TRAVERS. Oh, never mind the cold. It's many a long year since you and I looked at the moon together. It will do us good.

MRS. TRAVERS. Ah, dear. Boys will be boys. Give me my wrap then.

[DAN places it about her. They move towards the window, where they stand talking. MARION has slipped out and returns with her father's cap. He takes her face between his hands and looks at her.]

MR. TRAVERS. Do you really care for Harry, Marion?

MARION. As much as one can care for a man with five thousand a year. Perhaps he will make it ten one day—then I shall care for him twice as much. [Laughs.]

MR. TRAVERS. And are you content with this marriage?

MARION. Quite.

[He shakes his head gravely at her.]

MRS. TRAVERS. Aren't you coming, Marion?

MARION. No. I'm feeling tired.

[MR. and MRS. TRAVERS go out.]

DAN. Are you going to leave Harry alone with two pairs of lovers?

MARION [with a laugh]. Yes—let him see how ridiculous they look. I hate the night—it follows you and asks questions. Shut it out. Come and talk to me. Amuse me.

DAN. What shall I talk to you about?

MARION. Oh, tell me all the news. What is the world doing? Who has run away with whose wife? Who has been swindling whom? Which philanthropist has been robbing the poor? What saint has been discovered sinning? What is the latest scandal? Who has been found out? and what is it they have been do- ing? and what is everybody saying about it?

DAN. Would it amuse you?

MARION [she sits by the piano, softly touching the keys, idly recalling many memories]. What should it do? Make me weep? Should not one be glad to know one's friends better?

DAN. I wish you wouldn't be clever. Everyone one meets is clever nowa- days. It came in when the sun-flower went out. I preferred the sun-flower; it was more amusing.

MARION. And stupid people, I suppose, will come in when the clever people go out. I prefer the clever. They have better manners. You're exceedingly dis- agreeable. [She leaves the piano, and, throwing herself upon the couch, takes up a book.]

DAN. I know I am. The night has been with me also. It follows one and asks questions.

MARION. What questions has it been asking you?

DAN. Many—and so many of them have no answer. Why am I a useless, drifting log upon the world's tide? Why have all the young men passed me? Why am I, at thirty-nine, let us say, with brain, with power, with strength— nobody thinks I am worth anything, but I am—I know it. I might have been an able editor, devoting every morning from ten till three to arranging the affairs of the Universe, or a popular politician, trying to understand what I was talking about, and to believe it. And what am I? A newspaper reporter, at three-ha'pence a line—I beg their pardon, its occasionally twopence.

MARION. Does it matter?

DAN. Does it matter! Does it matter whether a Union Jack or a Tricolor floats over the turrets of Badajoz? yet we pour our blood into its ditches to decide the argument.   Does it matter whether one star more or less is marked upon our charts? yet we grow blind peering into their depths. Does it matter that one keel should slip through the grip of the Polar ice? yet nearer, nearer to it, we pile our whitening bones. And it's worth playing, the game of life. And there's a meaning in it. It's worth playing, if only that it strengthens the muscles of our souls. I'd like to have taken a hand in it.

MARION. Why didn't you?

DAN. No partner. Dull playing by oneself. No object.

MARION [after a silence]. What was she like?

DAN. So like you that there are times when I almost wish I had never met you. You set me thinking about myself, and that is a subject I find it pleasanter to forget.

MARION. And this woman that was like me—she could have made a man's life?

DAN. Ay!

MARION. Won't you tell me about her? Had she many faults?

DAN. Enough to love her by.

MARION. But she must have been good.

DAN. Good enough to be a woman.

MARION. That might mean so much or so little.

DAN. It should mean much to my thinking. There are few women.

MARION. Few! I thought the economists held that there were too many of us.

DAN. Not enough—not enough to go round. That is why a true woman has many lovers.

[There is a silence between them. Then MARION rises, but their eyes do not meet.]

MARION. How serious we have grown!

DAN. They say a dialogue between a man and woman always does.

MARION [she moves away, then, hesitating, half returns]. May I ask you a question?

DAN. That is an easy favour to grant.

MARION. If—if at any time you felt regard again for a woman, would you, for her sake, if she wished it, seek to gain, even now, that position in the world which is your right—which would make her proud of your friendship—would make her feel that even her life had not been altogether without purpose?

DAN. Too late! The old hack can only look over the hedge, and watch the field race by. The old ambition stirs within me at times—especially after a glass of good wine—and Harry's wine—God bless him—is excellent—but to-morrow morning—[with a shrug of his shoulders he finishes his meaning].

MARION. Then she could do nothing?

DAN. Nothing for his fortunes—much for himself. My dear young lady, never waste pity on a man in love—nor upon a child crying for the moon. The moon is a good thing to cry for.

MARION. I am glad I am like her. I am glad that I have met you.

[She gives him her hand, and for a moment he holds it. Then she goes out.]

[A flower has fallen from her breast, whether by chance or meaning, he knows not. He picks it up and kisses it; stands twirling it, undecided for a second, then lets it fall again upon the floor.]

**Make Way for Lucia - The Complete Mapp & Lucia -
Queen Lucia, Miss Mapp including 'The Male Imper-
sonator', Lucia in London, Mapp and Lucia, Lucia's
Progress (also known as The Worshipful Lucia), &
Trouble for Lucia
E F Benson**
Benediction Classics, 2012
1052 pages
ISBN: 978-1-78139-148-8

Available from www.amazon.com, www.amazon.co.uk

Make way for Lucia is a series of novels written by E.F Benson. They feature
hilarious incidents in the lives of upper-middle class people in the 1920s and
'30s. The characters vie for social standing in an extremely snobby world. In
the series the two main characters - sophisticated Lucia and frumpy Miss
Mapp compete with each other and have to extricate themselves from a series of social disasters in comical style. The novels are: Queen Lucia (1920)
Miss Mapp (1922) The Male Impersonator (a short story) Lucia in London
(1927) Mapp and Lucia (1931) Lucia's Progress (1935) (published in the U.S.
as The Worshipful Lucia) Trouble for Lucia (1939)

**Jeeves and Psmith Collection - Mike, Psmith in the City,
Psmith, Journalist, The Man with Two Left Feet, My
Man Jeeves and Right Ho, Jeeves
P G Wodehouse**
Oxford City Press, 2012
990 pages
ISBN: 978-1-78139-291-1

Available from www.amazon.com, www.amazon.co.uk

Sir Pelham Grenville Wodehouse was an English hu-
mourist and master of prose. He is widely admired by writers of every generation. He is best known for his Jeeves, Blandish Castle and Psmith Novels
which feature foppish upper class eccentric characters. This collection features a selection of these works: Mike (1909), Psmith in the City (1910),
Psmith, Journalist (1915), The Man with Two Left Feet (1917) - A collection
of thirteen short stories, My Man Jeeves (1919) - Eight short stories, Right
Ho, Jeeves (1934). This collection is a must-have for those who love Wodehouse's writings.

**Collected Works of E F Benson, Across the Stream,
The Blotting Book, Collected Short Stories, Paying
Guests, Mrs Ames, Spook Stories.**
E F Benson
Benediction Classics, 2012
994 pages
ISBN: 978-1-78139-290-4

Available from www.amazon.com, www.amazon.co.uk

E F Benson was a prolific writer, producing over a
hundred books. He is perhaps most well-known for his mysteries and tales of
the supernatural as well as the comic Mapp and Lucia series. This collection
includes a variety of fiction stories - Across the Stream (spiritualism), The
Blotting Book (mystery), Collected Short Stories (variety), Paying Guests
(precursor to Mapp and Lucia), Mrs Ames (similar to Mapp and Lucia) and a
collection of Spook Stories.

The Pat Hobby Stories
F. Scott Fitzgerald
Benediction Classics, 2011
120 pages
ISBN: 978-1-84902-367-2

Available from www.amazon.com, www.amazon.co.uk

The Pat Hobby Stories are a collection of 17 comedic
short stories written by F. Scott Fitzgerald. They first
appeared in Esquire magazine between January 1940
and May 1941, but in 1962 they were collected into a
single book and published posthumously. Pat Hobby is a once successful
screenwriter in Hollywood, but now an alcoholic and broke, who spends his
time hanging around the studio, hoping for work. The stories generally re-
volve around him hatching a plan to earn money or glory in some way, but
they usually end in further humiliation. The introduction to the book states,
"while it would be unfair to judge this book as a novel, it would be less than
fair to consider it as anything but a full-length portrait. It was as such that
Fitzgerald worked on it, and would have wanted it presented in book form,
after its original magazine publication. He thought of it as a comedy."

Also from Benediction Books …
Wandering Between Two Worlds: Essays on Faith and Art
Anita Mathias
Benediction Books, 2007
152 pages
ISBN: 0955373700

Available from www.amazon.com, www.amazon.co.uk

In these wide-ranging lyrical essays, Anita Mathias writes, in lush, lovely prose, of her naughty Catholic childhood in Jamshedpur, India; her large, eccentric family in Mangalore, a sea-coast town converted by the Portuguese in the sixteenth century; her rebellion and atheism as a teenager in her Himalayan boarding school, run by German missionary nuns, St. Mary's Convent, Nainital; and her abrupt religious conversion after which she entered Mother Teresa's convent in Calcutta as a novice. Later rich, elegant essays explore the dualities of her life as a writer, mother, and Christian in the United States-- Domesticity and Art, Writing and Prayer, and the experience of being "an alien and stranger" as an immigrant in America, sensing the need for roots.

About the Author

Anita Mathias is the author of *Wandering Between Two Worlds: Essays on Faith and Art.* She has a B.A. and M.A. in English from Somerville College, Oxford University, and an M.A. in Creative Writing from the Ohio State University, USA. Anita won a National Endowment of the Arts fellowship in Creative Non-fiction in 1997. She lives in Oxford, England with her husband, Roy, and her daughters, Zoe and Irene.

Anita's website:
    http://www.anitamathias.com, and
Anita's blog Dreaming Beneath the Spires:
    http://dreamingbeneaththespires.blogspot.com

The Church That Had Too Much
Anita Mathias
Benediction Books, 2010
52 pages
ISBN: 9781849026567

Available from www.amazon.com, www.amazon.co.uk

The Church That Had Too Much was very well-intentioned. She wanted to love
God, she wanted to love people, but she was both hampered by her muchness and
the abundance of her possessions, and beset by ambition, power struggles and .
snobbery. Read about the surprising way The Church That Had Too Much began
to resolve her problems in this deceptively simple and enchanting fable.

About the Author

Anita Mathias is the author of *Wandering Between Two Worlds: Essays on Faith
and Art*. She has a B.A. and M.A. in English from Somerville College, Oxford
University, and an M.A. in Creative Writing from the Ohio State University,
USA. Anita won a National Endowment of the Arts fellowship in Creative Non-
fiction in 1997. She lives in Oxford, England with her husband, Roy, and her
daughters, Zoe and Irene.

Anita's website:
    http://www.anitamathias.com, and
Anita's blog Dreaming Beneath the Spires:
    http://dreamingbeneaththespires.blogspot.com